W9-DIS-048

JULES VERNE

LIBRARY OF ESSENTIAL WRITERS

JULES VERNE

◆

SEVEN NOVELS

◆

COMPLETE AND UNABRIDGED

Five Weeks in a Balloon • A Journey to the
Center of the Earth • From the Earth to the Moon •
Round the Moon • Twenty Thousand Leagues
Under the Sea • Around the World in Eighty Days •
The Mysterious Island

BARNES & NOBLE
NEW YORK

2006 Barnes & Noble Publishing

ISBN-13: 978-0-7607-8123-4
ISBN-10: 0-7607-8123-0

Printed and bound in China

3 5 7 9 10 8 6 4 2

CONTENTS

Introduction   VII

Five Weeks in a Balloon   1

A Journey to the Center of the Earth   181

From the Earth to the Moon   323

Round the Moon   403

Twenty Thousand Leagues Under the Sea   503

Around the World in Eighty Days   703

The Mysterious Island   825

INTRODUCTION

J ULES VERNE WAS ONE OF THE MOST POPULAR AND WIDELY READ AUTHORS OF THE SEC-
ond half of the nineteenth century. Today, more than a century after his death, his
books are as alive for us now as they were for readers who were still to discover the potential of the motor car, the telephone, and the aeroplane. We remember Verne quite
rightly as the grandfather of science fiction, though we go a little too far if we believe that
he was the first to predict space travel, the submarine, the helicopter, and all manner of
other scientific marvels. He was, however, perhaps the first great popularizer of science at
a time when science and technology were only just starting to take a hold on people's lives.

Verne was born in Nantes on the River Loire in northwest France on February 8,
1828. His father, Pierre, was a lawyer; his mother, Sophie, came from a Breton seafaring
family of Scottish descent. Nantes was a major seaport, and young Jules was intoxicated
by the sea and ships from an early age. He yearned to travel, though it was not until he was
twelve that he was able to take a boat trip beyond the estuary of the Loire into open sea.
His favorite childhood reading was *The Swiss Family Robinson* by Johann Wyss, a book
that not only instilled in him the thrill of travel and adventure but also served as a model
for many of his later books.

Verne moved to Paris in 1847 to train as a lawyer, but his heart was not in it and by his
early twenties he had become a stockbroker, another profession he failed at. His passion
was for the theatre and his imagination ran far beyond the confines of the courts or the
stock exchange. He had been a voracious reader, and despite his later claims that he could
not read English in his youth, he almost certainly did, as he devoured the works of Edgar
Allan Poe.

Verne also delighted in the works of Alexandre Dumas, Victor Hugo, and E. T. A.
Hoffmann, all of which influenced his writing. It was under Hugo's influence that Verne
first thought he might make a success in the theatre. His earliest surviving work is the
manuscript of a play, *Alexander VI*, dating from May 1847, soon after he had arrived in
Paris. His first play to be performed, the one-act comedy *Les pailles rompues (Broken
Straws)*, ran for twelve nights during June 1850 at the Théâtre Historique, under the di-
rection of Alexandre Dumas *père*. A small edition of five hundred copies was printed by
Madame Beck for the theatre and thus was technically Verne's first book.

Verne continued to write plays throughout his career, later adapting some of his novels for the stage. He also wrote the libretti for several comic operettas, some of which were
performed with moderate success, but at that time his creativity began to move in a new
direction. Two of his short stories were selected by another of his mentors, Pitre-
Chevalier, who edited the family magazine *Musée des familles*. The first, "Les premiers
navires de la marine mexicaine," appeared in the issue for July 1851 and was followed in
the next issue by "Un voyage en ballon." This second story, usually reprinted as "Drama

in the Air," is significant in several respects. Not only was it the first of Verne's balloon stories, but it was the first where he sought to make the tale scientifically accurate—the editor even introduced it as a piece of popular science. It would also become the first of Verne's stories to appear in English when the Philadelphia publisher John Sartain ran a translation as "A Voyage in a Balloon" in the May 1852 issue of *Sartain's Union Magazine.*

Though Verne sold a few more stories to *Musée des familles,* his main work was still for the theatre. In 1857 he married Honorine de Viane, the daughter of an army officer. She was a young widow with two daughters. It was a happy marriage, and in addition to the two girls they had a son, Michel.

A holiday in Scotland in 1859 led Verne to write his first full-length book, *Voyage en Angleterre et en Ecosse,* but it was rejected by the Parisian publisher Jules Hetzel and was not published in France until 1989. Undaunted, Verne tried again. Friendship with the eccentric adventurer and photographer Félix Tournachon (who had adopted the alias Nadar) revived interest in the idea of a balloon voyage and Verne set to working out how it might be possible to design a navigable balloon to explore Africa. The result was *Cinq semaines en ballon (Five Weeks in a Balloon)* which Verne succeeded in selling to Hetzel. It was published in January 1863 with much success.

Verne's contact with Hetzel was propitious. Hetzel had been planning a magazine for the young, which emerged as *Magasin d'education et de recreation* in March 1864, and he contracted with Verne to provide three adventure novels each year for serialization in the magazine. It started a partnership that would last for the rest of their lives. The novels Verne wrote came to be known collectively as the *Voyages extraordinaires* and were beautifully illustrated by such artists as Leon Benett, Alphonse de Neuville, Jules-Descartes Ferat, and in particular Edouard Riou. Verne's first work to appear in the magazine was *Les Anglais au Pole Nord (The English at the North Pole).* It ran for a year, but before it finished, Hetzel rushed Verne's third novel into print directly in book form. This was *Voyage au centre de la terre (Journey to the Center of the Earth,* 1864), the first of Verne's more imaginative stories because it went beyond the earth's surface to a world totally of his own creation.

Verne's first few books, despite their popularity in France, did not catch the attention of the British or Americans because no instant translated copies appeared. It was not until February 1869 that *Five Weeks in a Balloon* became his first English-language book edition when it was published in New York by Appleton—and this was only after the success of Verne's fifth novel, *De la terre a la lune (From the Earth to the Moon).* Published in France in 1865, this work had been serialized by the *New York Weekly Magazine* during 1867. The serialization coincided with Verne's visit to New York with his brother, Paul, in March that year. Verne was a great admirer of the Americans and the English and was also proud of his Scottish ancestry. Because he saw American society as more likely to embrace new technology and encourage scientific experimentation, American or English characters frequently take a lead role in his stories.

From the Earth to the Moon was the first novel to attempt a scientific basis for a lunar voyage. Verne did not do the calculations himself, and they have since proved to be in error. What's more, and somewhat surprisingly, Verne chose to have his intrepid travelers shot into space inside a hollow bullet fired by a giant cannon. As a consequence of using this method Verne could not have his adventurers land on the moon, or return to earth. So, in the sequel, *Autour de la lune* (*Round the Moon*, 1869), he has them orbit the moon and return to earth.

Some of Verne's books suffered in translation, either because of hasty work or because of severe editing to adapt the book for a young adult readership. Some translators took considerable liberties, such as with the first British edition of *A Journey to the Center of the Earth* in 1871, in which they not only changed the name of the main characters but rewrote much of the text. The versions included in this collection, however, use the best of the early translations, with the text further corrected and improved. The original translator of the version of *A Journey to the Center of the Earth* used here not only remained faithful to Verne's text, but also corrected some of Verne's inadvertent errors.

Verne's next two novels were *Les Forceurs de blocus* (*The Blockade Runners*, 1865) and the seemingly endless *Les Enfants du Capitaine Grant* (*The Children of Captain Grant*, 1865-1867; better known as *In Search of the Castaways*), the first of his reworkings of *Swiss Family Robinson*. Then came a pause as Verne slaved over arguably his greatest work, *Vingt mille lieues sous les mers* (*Twenty Thousand Leagues Under the Sea*). Serialized in France from March 1869 to June 1870, the first English-language version appeared in England at Christmas 1872 bearing the title correctly translated as *Twenty Thousand Leagues under the Seas* (plural). It was the cover of the near simultaneous U.S. edition from James R. Osgood in Boston that changed the title to "under the Sea," by which it is best known today.

This novel contains one of Verne's most memorable characters, Captain Nemo, as well as one of his most memorable creations, the submarine *Nautilus*. What Verne showed so dramatically in *Twenty Thousand Leagues* was the full potential of the submarine, both for good and for evil. He was the first author to depict a scientific genius turned criminal mastermind. In fact in an earlier draft Verne had depicted Nemo as so vengeful that Hetzel refused to publish it unless Verne toned down the characterization.

After several lesser works, Verne completed the book that established his reputation once and for all, *Le Tour du monde en quarter-vingts jours* (*Around the World in Eighty Days*). It was serialized daily in *Le Temps* between November 6 and December 22, 1872, and was so popular that it had people queuing for each issue to see how Phileas Fogg would win his wager. Not since the serialization of Charles Dickens's early works had there been such an intense demand for each new episode of a novel. With this work, Verne justifiably became an international star.

Following this novel, there was an upsurge in translations of Verne's earlier material leading to new British and American editions flooding the market. Thereafter, the English-language editions appeared almost simultaneously with the French ones. His next novel, *L'île mystérieuse* (*The Mysterious Island*), yet another variant on *Swiss Family Robinson* and also a sequel to *Twenty Thousand Leagues Under the Sea*, was serialized between 1874 and 1875 in France, and in the United States, where it actually ran to completion first.

Verne loved to travel. The year after his return from the United States he bought a boat, the *Saint-Michel*, on which he sailed throughout Europe, voyaging as far as Norway and around the Scottish islands. The 1870s were probably his happiest period, although he had lost his father in 1871 and there were increasing problems with his wayward son.

Whether it was the distraction of traveling or the creative spark dimmed, it is fair to say that after *The Mysterious Island* Verne's creativity went into decline. He was writing too much, struggling to meet Hetzel's demand for three novels a year (later reduced to two). He had occasional moments of brilliance, as with *Robur the Conqueror* (1886) and *The Castle of the Carpathians* (1892), but generally his works became repetitive. Verne wrote more than sixty novels in a career of forty years, but we really remember a half-dozen or so, primarily those included in this volume.

The real decline began in March 1886 after Verne was shot in the leg by his nephew, Gaston, who was mentally confused and became annoyed when his uncle would not lend him any money. It was a period of sadness for Verne. A week after he was shot, his publisher Jules Hetzel died. Verne and Hetzel had been great friends and his passing left a void in Verne's life. Within a year Verne's mother had also died. His injury made it painful to walk, and his ability to travel was seriously reduced. He had already been forced to sell his yacht, and he sadly missed those golden days. He became a local councillor, and much of his time was spent with public and administrative affairs. He continued to write, though now hampered by failing eyesight, and these later books lack the verve and hope of his early works.

Verne died in Amiens, which had been his home for more than thirty years, from complications arising from diabetes, on March 24, 1905, at age seventy-seven. He lies buried in the Madeleine cemetery in Amiens with a wonderful tombstone that depicts him arising again. The sculpture is called (though not inscribed) *Vers l'immortalite et l'eternelle jeunesse* ("Toward Immortality and Eternal Youth"), a fitting tribute.

Verne left behind many unpublished works after his death. Some are lesser works, and others were revised (in some cases completely rewritten) by his son Michel, who was no author. The past twenty years has seen a significant re-evaluation of Verne's work with efforts to make available more authentic texts so we can better appreciate his literary and scientific genius.

Verne may not have been the great prophet that everyone remembers but his writings inspired millions. He may not have predicted the future but through his work he certainly helped others create it.

MIKE ASHLEY

Mike Ashley is one of the world's foremost scholars of science fiction. His more than sixty books include the definitive biography *Starlight Man: The Extraordinary Life of Algernon Blackwood*, the four-volume *History of the Science Fiction Magazine*, and *The Gernsback Days: The Evolution of Modern Science Fiction from 1911-1937*. He has also compiled more than twenty-five anthologies of fiction, including *The Mammoth Book of New Jules Verne Adventures*.

FIVE WEEKS IN A BALLOON
OR, JOURNEYS AND DISCOVERIES
IN AFRICA BY THREE ENGLISHMEN

Compiled in French
By Jules Verne,

From the Original Notes of Dr. Ferguson.
And Done into English by
"William Lackland."

CONTENTS

CHAPTER

I   The End of a much-applauded Speech—The Presentation of Dr.
    Samuel Ferguson—Excelsior—Full-length Portrait of the Doctor—
    A Fatalist convinced—A Dinner at the Travellers' Club—Several
    Toasts for the Occasion   11

II The Article in the *Daily Telegraph*—War between the Scientific
    Journals—Mr. Petermann backs his Friend Dr. Ferguson—Reply of
    the Savant Koner—Bets made—Sundry Propositions offered to the
    Doctor   15

III The Doctor's Friend—The Origin of their Friendship—Dick
    Kennedy at London—An unexpected but not very consoling
    Proposal—A Proverb by no means cheering—A few Names from
    the African Martyrology—The Advantages of a Balloon—Dr.
    Ferguson's Secret   17

IV African Explorations—Barth, Richardson, Overweg, Werne, Brun-
    Roliet, Penney, Andrea, Debono, Miani, Guillaume Lejean, Bruce,
    Krapf and Rebmann, Maizan, Roscher, Burton and Speke   21

V   Kennedy's Dreams—Articles and Pronouns in the Plural—Dick's
    Insinuations—A Promenade over the Map of Africa—What is
    contained between two Points of the Compass—Expeditions now
    on foot—Speke and Grant—Krapf, De Decken, and De Heuglin 24

VI A Servant—match him!—He can see the Satellites of Jupiter—
    Dick and Joe hard at it—Doubt and Faith—The Weighing
    Ceremony—Joe and Wellington—He gets a Half-crown   28

VII Geometrical Details—Calculation of the Capacity of the Balloon—
    The Double Receptacle—The Covering—The Car—The
    Mysterious Apparatus—The Provisions and Stores—The Final
    Summing up   31

VIII   Joe's Importance—The Commander of the *Resolute*—Kennedy's
       Arsenal—Mutual Amenities—The Farewell Dinner—Departure on
       the 21st of February—The Doctor's Scientific Sessions—Duveyrier—
       Livingstone—Details of the Aerial Voyage—Kennedy silenced   34

  IX   They double the Cape—The Forecastle—A Course of Cosmography
       by Professor Joe—Concerning the Method of guiding Balloons—
       How to seek out Atmospheric Currents—Eureka   37

   X   Former Experiments—The Doctor's Five Receptacles—The Gas
       Cylinder—The Calorifere—The System of Maneuvring—Success
       certain   40

  XI   The Arrival at Zanzibar—The English Consul—Ill-will of the
       Inhabitants—The Island of Koumbeni—The Rain-Makers—
       Inflation of the Balloon—Departure on the 18th of April—The last
       Good-by—The *Victoria*   43

 XII   Crossing the Strait—The Mrima—Dick's Remark and Joe's
       Proposition—A Recipe for Coffee-making—The Uzaramo—The
       Unfortunate Maizan—Mount Duthumi—The Doctor's Cards—
       Night under a Nopal   46

XIII   Change of Weather—Kennedy has the Fever—The Doctor's
       Medicine—Travels on Land—The Basin of Imengé—Mount
       Rubeho—Six Thousand Feet Elevation—A Halt in the Daytime 51

XIV   The Forest of Gum-Trees—The Blue Antelope—The Rallying-
       Signal—An Unexpected Attack—The Kanyemé—A Night in the
       Open Air—The Mabunguru—Jihoue-la-Mkoa—A Supply of
       Water—Arrival at Kazeh   55

 XV   Kazeh—The Noisy Market-place—The Appearance of the
       Balloon—The Wangaga—The Sons of the Moon—The Doctor's
       Walk—The Population of the Place—The Royal Tembé—The
       Sultan's Wives—A Royal Drunken-Bout—Joe an Object of
       Worship—How they Dance in the Moon—A Reaction—Two
       Moons in one Sky—The Instability of Divine Honours   60

XVI   Symptoms of a Storm—The Country of the Moon—The Future of
       the African Continent—The Last Machine of all—A View of the
       Country at Sunset—Flora and Fauna—The Tempest—The Zone
       of Fire—The Starry Heavens   66

XVII   The Mountains of the Moon—An Ocean of Verdure—They cast Anchor—The Towing Elephant—A Running Fire—Death of the Monster—The Field-Oven—A Meal on the Grass—A Night on the Ground   71

XVIII   The Karagwah—Lake Ukéréoué—A Night on an Island—The Equator—Crossing the Lake—The Cascades—A View of the Country—The Sources of the Nile—The Island of Benga—The Signature of Andrea Debono—The Flag with the Arms of England   76

XIX   The Nile—The Trembling Mountain—A Remembrance of the Country—The Narratives of the Arabs—The Nyam-Nyams—Joe's Shrewd Cogitations—The Balloon runs the Gantlet—Aerostatic Ascensions—Madame Blanchard   82

XX   The Celestial Bottle—The Fig-Palms—The Mammoth Trees—The Tree of War—The Winged Team—Two Native Tribes in Battle—A Massacre—An Intervention from above   85

XXI   Strange Sounds—A Night Attack—Kennedy and Joe in the Tree— Two Shots—"Help! help!"—Reply in French—The Morning—The Missionary—The Plan of Rescue   88

XXII   The Jet of Light—The Missionary—The Rescue in a Ray of Electricity—A Lazarist Priest—But little Hope—The Doctor's Care—A Life of Self-Denial—Passing a Volcano   93

XXIII   Joe in a Fit of Rage—The Death of a Good Man—The Night of watching by the Body—Barrenness and Drought—The Burial— The Quartz Rocks—Joe's Hallucinations—A Precious Ballast—A Survey of the Gold-bearing Mountains—The Beginning of Joe's Despair   98

XXIV   The Wind dies away—The Vicinity of the Desert—The Mistake in the Water-Supply—The Nights of the Equator—Dr. Ferguson's Anxieties—The Situation flatly stated—Energetic Replies of Kennedy and Joe—One Night more   103

XXV   A Little Philosophy—A Cloud on the Horizon—In the Midst of a Fog—The Strange Balloon—An Exact View of the *Victoria*—The Palm-Trees—Traces of a Caravan—The Well in the Midst of the Desert   107

XXVI   One Hundred and Thirteen Degrees—The Doctor's Reflections—
        A Desperate Search—The Cylinder goes out—One Hundred and
        Twenty-two Degrees—Contemplation of the Desert—A Night
        Walk—Solitude—Debility—Joe's Prospects—He gives himself
        One Day more   111

XXVII   Terrific Heat—Hallucinations—The Last Drops of Water—Nights
        of Despair—An Attempt at Suicide—The Simoom—The Oasis—
        The Lion and Lioness   115

XXVIII An Evening of Delight—Joe's Culinary Performances—A Dissertation
        on Raw Meat—The Narrative of James Bruce—Camping out—Joe's
        Dreams—The Barometer begins to fall—The Barometer rises again—
        Preparations for Departure—The Tempest   118

XXIX   Signs of Vegetation—The Fantastic Notion of a French Author—A
        Magnificent Country—The Kingdom of Adamova—The
        Explorations of Speke and Burton connected with those of Dr.
        Barth—The Atlantika Mountains—The River Benoué—The City
        of Yola—The Bagélé—Mount Mendif   122

XXX   Mosfeia—The Sheik—Denham, Clapperton, and Oudney—
        Vogel—The Capital of Loggoum—Toole—Becalmed above
        Kernak—The Governor and his Court—The Attack—The
        Incendiary Pigeons   126

XXXI   Departure in the Night-time—All Three—Kennedy's Instincts—
        Precautions—The Course of the Shari River—Lake Tchad—The
        Water of the Lake—The Hippopotamus—One Bullet thrown
        away   130

XXXII   The Capital of Bornou—The Islands of the Biddiomahs—The
        Condors—The Doctor's Anxieties—His Precautions—An Attack
        in Mid-air—The Balloon Covering torn—The Fall—Sublime Self-
        Sacrifice—The Northern Coast of the Lake   133

XXXIII Conjectures—Re-establishment of the *Victoria's* Equilibrium—Dr.
        Ferguson's New Calculations—Kennedy's Hunt—A Complete
        Exploration of Lake Tchad—Tangalia—The Return—Lari   137

XXXIV   The Hurricane—A Forced Departure—Loss of an Anchor—
        Melancholy Reflections—The Resolution adopted—The Sand-

Storm—The Buried Caravan—A Contrary yet Favourable Wind—
The Return southward—Kennedy at his Post   141

XXXV   What happened to Joe—The Island of the Biddiomahs—The
Adoration shown him—The Island that sank—The Shores of the
Lake—The Tree of the Serpents—The Foot-Tramp—Terrible
Suffering—Mosquitoes and Ants—Hunger—The *Victoria* seen—
She disappears—The Swamp—One Last Despairing Cry   144

XXXVI   A Throng of People on the Horizon—A Troop of Arabs—The
Pursuit—It is He—Fall from Horseback—The Strangled Arab—A
Ball from Kennedy—Adroit Maneuvres—Caught up flying—Joe
saved at last   149

XXXVII   The Western Route—Joe wakes up—His Obstinacy—End of Joe's
Narrative—Tagelei—Kennedy's Anxieties—The Route to the
North—A Night near Aghades   153

XXXVIII   A Rapid Passage—Prudent Resolves—Caravans in Sight—
Incessant Rains—Goa—The Niger—Golberry, Geoffroy, and
Gray—Mungo Park—Laing—René Caillié—Clapperton—John
and Richard Lander   156

XXXIX   The Country in the Elbow of the Niger—A Fantastic View of the
Hombori Mountains—Kabra—Timbuctoo—The Chart of Dr.
Barth—A Decaying City—Whither Heaven wills   161

XL   Dr. Ferguson's Anxieties—Persistent Movement southward—A
Cloud of Grasshoppers—A View of Jenné—A View of Sego—
Change of the Wind—Joe's Regrets   164

XLI   The Approaches to Senegal—The Balloon sinks lower and lower—
They keep throwing out, throwing out—The Marabout Al-Hadji—
Messrs. Pascal, Vincent, and Lambert—A Rival of Mohammed—
The Difficult Mountains—Kennedy's Weapons—One of Joe's
Maneuvres—A Halt over a Forest   166

XLII   A Struggle of Generosity—The Last Sacrifice—The Dilating
Apparatus—Joe's Adroitness—Midnight—The Doctor's Watch—
Kennedy's Watch—The Latter falls asleep at his Post—The Fire—
The Howlings of the Natives—Out of Range   171

XLIII   The Talabas—The Pursuit—A Devastated Country—The Wind
         begins to fall—The *Victoria* sinks—The last of the Provisions—The
         Leaps of the Balloon—A Defence with Fire-arms—The Wind
         freshens—The Senegal River—The Cataracts of Gouina—The Hot
         Air—The Passage of the River   174

XLIV   Conclusion—The Certificate—The French Settlements—The Post
         of Medina—The *Basilic*—Saint Louis—The English Frigate—The
         Return to London   179

Chapter I

THE END OF A MUCH-APPLAUDED SPEECH—THE PRESENTATION OF
DR. SAMUEL FERGUSON—EXCELSIOR—FULL-LENGTH PORTRAIT OF
THE DOCTOR—A FATALIST CONVINCED—A DINNER AT THE
TRAVELLERS' CLUB—SEVERAL TOASTS FOR THE OCCASION

THERE WAS A LARGE AUDIENCE ASSEMBLED ON THE 14TH OF JANUARY, 1862, AT THE session of the Royal Geographical Society, No. 3 Waterloo Place, London. The president, Sir Francis M——, made an important communication to his colleagues, in an address that was frequently interrupted by applause.

This rare specimen of eloquence terminated with the following sonorous phrases bubbling over with patriotism:

"England has always marched at the head of nations" (for, the reader will observe, the nations always march at the head of each other), "by the intrepidity of her explorers in the line of geographical discovery." (General assent). "Dr. Samuel Ferguson, one of her most glorious sons, will not reflect discredit on his origin." ("No, indeed!" from all parts of the hall.)

"This attempt, should it succeed" ("It will succeed!"), "will complete and link together the notions, as yet disjointed, which the world entertains of African cartology" (vehement applause); "and, should it fail, it will, at least, remain on record as one of the most daring conceptions of human genius!" (Tremendous cheering.)

"Huzza! huzza!" shouted the immense audience, completely electrified by these inspiring words.

"Huzza for the intrepid Ferguson!" cried one of the most excitable of the enthusiastic crowd.

The wildest cheering resounded on all sides; the name of Ferguson was in every mouth, and we may safely believe that it lost nothing in passing through English throats. Indeed, the hall fairly shook with it.

And there were present, also, those fearless travellers and explorers whose energetic temperaments had borne them through every quarter of the globe, many of them grown old and worn out in the service of science. All had, in some degree, physically or morally, undergone the sorest trials. They had escaped shipwreck; conflagration; Indian tomahawks and war-clubs; the fagot and the stake; nay, even the cannibal maws of the South Sea Islanders. But still their hearts beat high during Sir Francis M——'s address, which certainly was the finest oratorical success that the Royal Geographical Society of London had yet achieved.

But, in England, enthusiasm does not stop short with mere words. It strikes off money faster than the dies of the Royal Mint itself. So a subscription to encourage Dr. Ferguson was voted there and then, and it at once attained the handsome amount of two thousand five hundred pounds. The sum was made commensurate with the importance of the enterprise.

A member of the Society then enquired of the president whether Dr. Ferguson was not to be officially introduced.

"The doctor is at the disposition of the meeting," replied Sir Francis.

"Let him come in, then! Bring him in!" shouted the audience. "We'd like to see a man of such extraordinary daring, face to face!"

"Perhaps this incredible proposition of his is only intended to mystify us," growled an apoplectic old admiral.

"Suppose that there should turn out to be no such person as Dr. Ferguson?" exclaimed another voice, with a malicious twang.

"Why, then, we'd have to invent one!" replied a facetious member of this grave Society.

"Ask Dr. Ferguson to come in," was the quiet remark of Sir Francis M——.

And come in the doctor did, and stood there, quite unmoved by the thunders of applause that greeted his appearance.

He was a man of about forty years of age, of medium height and physique. His sanguine temperament was disclosed in the deep colour of his cheeks. His countenance was coldly expressive, with regular features, and a large nose—one of those noses that resemble the prow of a ship, and stamp the faces of men predestined to accomplish great discoveries. His eyes, which were gentle and intelligent, rather than bold, lent a peculiar charm to his physiognomy. His arms were long, and his feet were planted with that solidity which indicates a great pedestrian.

A calm gravity seemed to surround the doctor's entire person, and no one would dream that he could become the agent of any mystification, however harmless.

Hence, the applause that greeted him at the outset continued until he, with a friendly gesture, claimed silence on his own behalf. He stepped towards the seat that had been prepared for him on his presentation, and then, standing erect and motionless, he, with a determined glance, pointed his right forefinger upward, and pronounced aloud the single word—

"Excelsior!"

Never had one of Bright's or Cobden's sudden onslaughts, never had one of Palmerston's abrupt demands for funds to plate the rocks of the English coast with iron, made such a sensation. Sir Francis M——'s address was completely overshadowed. The doctor had shown himself moderate, sublime, and self-contained, in one; he had uttered the word of the situation—

"Excelsior!"

The gouty old admiral who had been finding fault, was completely won over by the singular man before him, and immediately moved the insertion of Dr. Ferguson's speech in "The Proceedings of the Royal Geographical Society of London."

Who, then, was this person, and what was the enterprise that he proposed?

Ferguson's father, a brave and worthy captain in the English Navy, had associated his son with him, from the young man's earliest years, in the perils and adventures of his profession. The fine little fellow, who seemed to have never known the meaning of fear, early revealed a keen and active mind, an investigating intelligence, and a remarkable turn for scientific study; moreover, he disclosed uncommon address in extricating himself from difficulty; he was never perplexed, not even in handling his fork for the first time—an exercise in which children generally have so little success.

His fancy kindled early at the recitals he read of daring enterprise and maritime adventure, and he followed with enthusiasm the discoveries that signalised the first part of the nineteenth century. He mused over the glory of the Mungo Parks, the Bruces, the Caillies, the Levaillants, and to some extent, I verily believe, of Selkirk (Robinson Crusoe), whom he considered in no wise inferior to the rest. How many a well-employed hour he passed with that hero on his isle of Juan Fernandez! Often he criticised the ideas of the shipwrecked sailor, and sometimes discussed his plans and projects. He would have done differently, in such and such a case, or quite as well at least—of that he felt assured. But of one thing he was satisfied, that he never should have left that pleasant island, where he was as happy as a king without subjects—no, not if the inducement held out had been promotion to the first lordship in the admiralty!

It may readily be conjectured whether these tendencies were developed during a youth of adventure, spent in every nook and corner of the Globe. Moreover, his father, who was a man of thorough instruction, omitted no opportunity to consolidate this keen intelligence by serious studies in hydrography, physics, and mechanics, along with a slight tincture of botany, medicine, and astronomy.

Upon the death of the estimable captain, Samuel Ferguson, then twenty-two years of age, had already made his voyage around the world. He had enlisted in the Bengalese Corps of Engineers, and distinguished himself in several affairs; but this soldier's life had not exactly suited him; caring but little for command, he had not been fond of obeying. He, therefore, sent in his resignation, and half botanizing, half playing the hunter, he made his way towards the north of the Indian Peninsula, and crossed it from Calcutta to Surat—a mere amateur trip for him.

From Surat we see him going over to Australia, and in 1845 participating in Captain Sturt's expedition, which had been sent out to explore the new Caspian Sea, supposed to exist in the centre of New Holland.

Samuel Ferguson returned to England about 1850, and, more than ever possessed by the demon of discovery, he spent the intervening time, until 1853, in accompanying Captain McClure on the expedition that went around the American Continent from Behring's Straits to Cape Farewell.

Notwithstanding fatigues of every description, and in all climates, Ferguson's constitution continued marvellously sound. He felt at ease in the midst of the most complete privations; in fine, he was the very type of the thoroughly accomplished explorer whose stomach expands or contracts at will; whose limbs grow longer or shorter according to the resting-place that each stage of a journey may bring; who can fall asleep at any hour of the day or awake at any hour of the night.

Nothing, then, was less surprising, after that, than to find our traveller, in the period from 1855 to 1857, visiting the whole region west of the Thibet, in company with the brothers Schlagintweit, and bringing back some curious ethnographic observations from that expedition.

During these different journeys, Ferguson had been the most active and interesting correspondent of the *Daily Telegraph*, the penny newspaper whose circulation amounts to 140,000 copies, and yet scarcely suffices for its many legions of readers. Thus, the doctor had become well known to the public, although he could not claim membership in either of the Royal Geographical Societies of London, Paris, Berlin, Vienna, or St. Petersburg, or yet with the Travellers' Club, or even the Royal Polytechnic Institute, where his friend the statistician Cockburn ruled in state.

The latter savant had, one day, gone so far as to propose to him the following problem: Given the number of miles travelled by the doctor in making the circuit of the Globe, how many more had his head described than his feet, by reason of the different lengths of the radii?—or, the number of miles traversed by the doctor's head and feet respectively being given, required the exact height of that gentleman?

This was done with the idea of complimenting him, but the doctor had held himself aloof from all the learned bodies—belonging, as he did, to the church militant and not to the church polemical. He found his time better employed in seeking than in discussing, in discovering rather than discoursing.

There is a story told of an Englishman who came one day to Geneva, intending to visit the lake. He was placed in one of those odd vehicles in which the passengers sit side by side, as they do in an omnibus. Well, it so happened that the Englishman got a seat that left him with his back turned towards the lake. The vehicle completed its circular trip without his thinking to turn around once, and he went back to London delighted with the Lake of Geneva.

Doctor Ferguson, however, had turned around to look about him on his journeyings, and turned to such good purpose that he had seen a great deal. In doing so, he had simply obeyed the laws of his nature, and we have good reason to believe that he was, to some extent, a fatalist, but of an orthodox school of fatalism withal, that led him to rely upon himself and even upon Providence. He claimed that he was impelled, rather than drawn by his own volition, to journey as he did, and that he traversed the world like the locomotive, which does not direct itself, but is guided and directed by the track it runs on.

"I do not follow my route"; he often said, "it is my route that follows me."

The reader will not be surprised, then, at the calmness with which the doctor received the applause that welcomed him in the Royal Society. He was above all such trifles, having no pride, and less vanity. He looked upon the proposition addressed to him by Sir Francis M——— as the simplest thing in the world, and scarcely noticed the immense effect that it produced.

When the session closed, the doctor was escorted to the rooms of the Travellers' Club, in Pall Mall. A superb entertainment had been prepared there in his honour. The dimensions of the dishes served were made to correspond with the importance of the personage entertained, and the boiled sturgeon that figured at this magnificent repast was not an inch shorter than Dr. Ferguson himself.

Numerous toasts were offered and quaffed, in the wines of France, to the celebrated travellers who had made their names illustrious by their explorations of African territory. The guests drank to their health or to their memory, in alphabetical order, a good old English way of doing the thing. Among those remembered thus, were: Abbadie, Adams, Adamson, Anderson, Arnaud, Baikie, Baldwin, Barth, Batouda, Beke, Beltram, Du Berba, Bimbachi, Bolognesi, Bolwik, Belzoni, Bonnemain, Brisson, Browne, Bruce, Brun-Roliet, Burchell, Burckhardt, Burton, Caillaud, Caillie, Campbell, Chapman, Clapperton, Clot-Bey, Colomieu, Courval, Cumming, Cuny, Debono, Decken, Denham, Desavanchers, Dicksen, Dickson, Dochard, Du Chaillu, Duncan, Durand, Duroule, Duveyrier, D'Escayrac, De Lauture, Erhardt, Ferret, Fresnel, Galinier, Galton, Geoffroy, Golberry, Hahn, Halm, Harnier, Hecquart, Heuglin, Hornemann, Houghton, Imbert, Kauffmann, Knoblecher, Krapf, Kummer, Lafargue, Laing, Lafaille, Lambert, Lamiral, Lamprière,

John Lander, Richard Lander, Lefebvre, Lejean, Levaillant, Livingstone, MacCarthy, Maggiar, Maizan, Malzac, Moffat, Mollien, Monteiro, Morrison, Mungo Park, Neimans, Overwey, Panet, Partarrieau, Pascal, Pearse, Peddie, Peney, Petherick, Poncet, Prax, Raffenel, Rabh, Rebmann, Richardson, Riley, Ritchey, Rochet d'Hericourt, Rongäwi, Roscher, Ruppel, Saugnier, Speke, Steidner, Thibaud, Thompson, Thornton, Toole, Tousny, Trotter, Tuckey, Tyrwhitt, Vaudey, Veyssière, Vincent, Vinco, Vogel, Wahlberg, Warrington, Washington, Werne, Wild, and last, but not least, Dr. Ferguson, who, by his incredible attempt, was to link together the achievements of all these explorers, and complete the series of African discovery.

Chapter II

THE ARTICLE IN THE DAILY TELEGRAPH—WAR BETWEEN THE SCIENTIFIC JOURNALS—MR. PETERMANN BACKS HIS FRIEND DR. FERGUSON—REPLY OF THE SAVANT KONER—BETS MADE—SUNDRY PROPOSITIONS OFFERED TO THE DOCTOR

ON THE NEXT DAY, IN ITS NUMBER OF JANUARY 15TH, THE *DAILY TELEGRAPH* PUBLISHED an article couched in the following terms:

"Africa is, at length, about to surrender the secret of her vast solitudes; a modern Œdipus is to give us the key to that enigma which the learned men of sixty centuries have not been able to decipher. In other days, to seek the sources of the Nile—*fontes Nili quoerere*—was regarded as a mad endeavour, a chimera that could not be realised.

"Dr. Barth, in following out to Soudan the track traced by Denham and Clapperton; Dr. Livingstone, in multiplying his fearless explorations from the Cape of Good Hope to the basin of the Zambesi; Captains Burton and Speke, in the discovery of the great interior lakes, have opened three highways to modern civilisation. *Their point of intersection,* which no traveller has yet been able to reach, is the very heart of Africa, and it is thither that all efforts should now be directed.

"The labours of these hardy pioneers of science are now about to be knit together by the daring project of Dr. Samuel Ferguson, whose fine explorations our readers have frequently had the opportunity of appreciating.

"This intrepid discoverer proposes to traverse all Africa from east to west *in a balloon.* If we are well informed, the point of departure for this surprising journey is to be the island of Zanzibar, upon the eastern coast. As for the point of arrival, it is reserved for Providence alone to designate.

"The proposal for this scientific undertaking was officially made, yesterday, at the rooms of the Royal Geographical Society, and the sum of twenty-five hundred pounds was voted to defray the expenses of the enterprise.

"We shall keep our readers informed as to the progress of this enterprise, which has no precedent in the annals of exploration."

As may be supposed, the foregoing article had an enormous echo among scientific people. At first, it stirred up a storm of incredulity; Dr. Ferguson passed for a purely chimerical personage of the Barnum stamp, who, after having gone through the United States, proposed to "do" the British Isles.

A humorous reply appeared in the February number of the *Bulletins de la Société Geographique* of Geneva, which very wittily showed up the Royal Society of London and their phenomenal sturgeon.

But Herr Petermann, in his *Mittheilungen,* published at Gotha, reduced the Geneva journal to the most absolute silence. Herr Petermann knew Dr. Ferguson personally, and guaranteed the intrepidity of his dauntless friend.

Besides, all manner of doubt was quickly put out of the question: preparations for the trip were set on foot at London; the factories of Lyons received a heavy order for the silk required for the body of the balloon; and, finally, the British Government placed the transport-ship *Resolute,* Captain Bennett, at the disposal of the expedition.

At once, upon word of all this, a thousand encouragements were offered, and felicitations came pouring in from all quarters. The details of the undertaking were published in full in the bulletins of the Geographical Society of Paris; a remarkable article appeared in the *Nouvelles Annales des Voyages, de la Géographie, de l'Histoire, et de l'Archaeologie de M. V. A. Malte-Brun* ("New Annals of Travels, Geography, History, and Archaeology, by M. V. A. Malte-Brun"); and a searching essay in the *Zeitschrift für Allgemeine Erdkunde,* by Dr. W. Koner, triumphantly demonstrated the feasibility of the journey, its chances of success, the nature of the obstacles existing, the immense advantages of the aerial mode of locomotion, and found fault with nothing but the selected point of departure, which it contended should be Massowah, a small port in Abyssinia, whence James Bruce, in 1768, started upon his explorations in search of the sources of the Nile. Apart from that, it mentioned, in terms of unreserved admiration, the energetic character of Dr. Ferguson, and the heart, thrice panoplied in bronze, that could conceive and undertake such an enterprise.

The *North American Review* could not, without some displeasure, contemplate so much glory monopolized by England. It therefore rather ridiculed the doctor's scheme, and urged him, by all means, to push his explorations as far as America, while he was about it.

In a word, without going over all the journals in the world, there was not a scientific publication, from the *Journal of Evangelical Missions* to the *Revue Algérienne et Coloniale,* from the *Annales de la Propagation de la Foi* to the *Church Missionary Intelligencer,* that had not something to say about the affair in all its phases.

Many large bets were made at London and throughout England generally, first, as to the real or supposititious existence of Dr. Ferguson; secondly, as to the trip itself, which, some contended, would not be undertaken at all, and which was really contemplated, according to others; thirdly, upon the success or failure of the enterprise; and fourthly, upon the probabilities of Dr. Ferguson's return. The betting-books were covered with entries of immense sums, as though the Epsom races were at stake.

Thus, believers and unbelievers, the learned and the ignorant, alike had their eyes fixed on the doctor, and he became the lion of the day, without knowing that he carried such a mane. On his part, he willingly gave the most accurate information touching his project. He was very easily approached, being naturally the most affable man in the world. More than one bold adventurer presented himself, offering to share the dangers as well as the glory of the undertaking; but he refused them all, without giving his reasons for rejecting them.

Numerous inventors of mechanism applicable to the guidance of balloons came to propose their systems, but he would accept none; and, when he was asked whether he had discovered something of his own for that purpose, he constantly refused to give any explanation, and merely busied himself more actively than ever with the preparations for his journey.

Chapter III

THE DOCTOR'S FRIEND—THE ORIGIN OF THEIR FRIENDSHIP— DICK KENNEDY AT LONDON—AN UNEXPECTED BUT NOT VERY CONSOLING PROPOSAL—A PROVERB BY NO MEANS CHEERING— A FEW NAMES FROM THE AFRICAN MARTYROLOGY—THE ADVANTAGES OF A BALLOON—DR. FERGUSON'S SECRET

DR. FERGUSON HAD A FRIEND—NOT ANOTHER SELF, INDEED, AN *ALTER EGO*, FOR friendship could not exist between two beings exactly alike.

But, if they possessed different qualities, aptitudes, and temperaments, Dick Kennedy and Samuel Ferguson lived with one and the same heart, and that gave them no great trouble. In fact, quite the reverse.

Dick Kennedy was a Scotchman, in the full acceptation of the word—open, resolute, and headstrong. He lived in the town of Leith, which is near Edinburgh, and, in truth, is a mere suburb of *Auld Reekie*. Sometimes he was a fisherman, but he was always and everywhere a determined hunter, and that was nothing remarkable for a son of Caledonia, who had known some little climbing among the Highland mountains. He was cited as a wonderful shot with the rifle, since not only could he split a bullet on a knife-blade, but he could divide it into two such equal parts that, upon weighing them, scarcely any difference would be perceptible.

Kennedy's countenance strikingly recalled that of Herbert Glendinning, as Sir Walter Scott has depicted it in "The Monastery"; his stature was above six feet; full of grace and easy movement, he yet seemed gifted with herculean strength; a face embrowned by the sun; eyes keen and black; a natural air of daring courage; in fine, something sound, solid, and reliable in his entire person, spoke, at first glance, in favour of the bonny Scot.

The acquaintanceship of these two friends had been formed in India, when they belonged to the same regiment. While Dick would be out in pursuit of the tiger and the elephant, Samuel would be in search of plants and insects. Each could call himself expert in his own province, and more than one rare botanical specimen, that to science was as great a victory won as the conquest of a pair of ivory tusks, became the doctor's booty.

These two young men, moreover, never had occasion to save each other's lives, or to render any reciprocal service. Hence, an unalterable friendship. Destiny sometimes bore them apart, but sympathy always united them again.

Since their return to England they had been frequently separated by the doctor's distant expeditions; but, on his return, the latter never failed to go, not to *ask* for hospitality, but to bestow some weeks of his presence at the home of his crony Dick.

The Scot talked of the past; the doctor busily prepared for the future. The one looked back, the other forward. Hence, a restless spirit personified in Ferguson; perfect calmness typified in Kennedy—such was the contrast.

After his journey to the Thibet, the doctor had remained nearly two years without hinting at new explorations; and Dick, supposing that his friend's instinct for travel and thirst for adventure had at length died out, was perfectly enchanted. They would have ended badly, someday or other, he thought to himself; no matter what experience one has with men, one does not travel always with impunity among cannibals and wild beasts. So, Kennedy besought the doctor to tie up his bark for life, having done enough for science, and too much for the gratitude of men.

The doctor contented himself with making no reply to this. He remained absorbed in his own reflections, giving himself up to secret calculations, passing his nights among heaps of figures, and making experiments with the strangest-looking machinery, inexplicable to everybody but himself. It could readily be guessed, though, that some great thought was fermenting in his brain.

"What can he have been planning?" wondered Kennedy, when, in the month of January, his friend quitted him to return to London.

He found out one morning when he looked into the *Daily Telegraph*.

"Merciful Heaven!" he exclaimed, "the lunatic! the madman! Cross Africa in a balloon! Nothing but that was wanted to cap the climax! That's what he's been bothering his wits about these two years past!"

Now, reader, substitute for all these exclamation points, as many ringing thumps with a brawny fist upon the table, and you have some idea of the manual exercise that Dick went through while he thus spoke.

When his confidential maid-of-all-work, the aged Elspeth, tried to insinuate that the whole thing might be a hoax—

"Not a bit of it!" said he. "Don't I know my man? Isn't it just like him? Travel through the air! There, now, he's jealous of the eagles, next! No! I warrant you, he'll not do it! I'll find a way to stop him! He! why if they'd let him alone, he'd start someday for the moon!"

On that very evening Kennedy, half alarmed, and half exasperated, took the train for London, where he arrived next morning.

Three-quarters of an hour later a cab deposited him at the door of the doctor's modest dwelling, in Soho Square, Greek Street. Forthwith he bounded up the steps and announced his arrival with five good, hearty, sounding raps at the door.

Ferguson opened, in person.

"Dick! you here?" he exclaimed, but with no great expression of surprise, after all.

"Dick himself!" was the response.

"What, my dear boy, you at London, and this the mid-season of the winter shooting?"

"Yes! here I am, at London!"

"And what have you come to town for?"

"To prevent the greatest piece of folly that ever was conceived."

"Folly!" said the doctor.

"Is what this paper says, the truth?" rejoined Kennedy, holding out the copy of the *Daily Telegraph*, mentioned above.

"Ah! that's what you mean, is it? These newspapers are great tattlers! But, sit down, my dear Dick."

"No, I won't sit down!—Then, you really intend to attempt this journey?"

"Most certainly! all my preparations are getting along finely, and I—"

"Where are your traps? Let me have a chance at them! I'll make them fly! I'll put your preparations in fine order." And so saying, the gallant Scot gave way to a genuine explosion of wrath.

"Come, be calm, my dear Dick!" resumed the doctor. "You're angry at me because I did not acquaint you with my new project."

"He calls this his new project!"

"I have been very busy," the doctor went on, without heeding the interruption; "I have had so much to look after! But rest assured that I should not have started without writing to you."

"Oh, indeed! I'm highly honoured."

"Because it is my intention to take you with me."

Upon this, the Scotchman gave a leap that a wild goat would not have been ashamed of among his native crags.

"Ah! really, then, you want them to send us both to Bedlam!"

"I have counted positively upon you, my dear Dick, and I have picked you out from all the rest."

Kennedy stood speechless with amazement.

"After listening to me for ten minutes," said the doctor, "you will thank me!"

"Are you speaking seriously?"

"Very seriously."

"And suppose that I refuse to go with you?"

"But you won't refuse."

"But, suppose that I were to refuse?"

"Well, I'd go alone."

"Let us sit down," said Kennedy, "and talk without excitement. The moment you give up jesting about it, we can discuss the thing."

"Let us discuss it, then, at breakfast, if you have no objections, my dear Dick."

The two friends took their seats opposite to each other, at a little table with a plate of toast and a huge tea-urn before them.

"My dear Samuel," said the sportsman, "your project is insane! it is impossible! it has no resemblance to anything reasonable or practicable!"

"That's for us to find out when we shall have tried it!"

"But trying it is exactly what you ought not to attempt."

"Why so, if you please?"

"Well, the risks, the difficulty of the thing."

"As for difficulties," replied Ferguson, in a serious tone, "they were made to be overcome; as for risks and dangers, who can flatter himself that he is to escape them? Everything in life involves danger; it may even be dangerous to sit down at one's own table, or to put one's hat on one's own head. Moreover, we must look upon what is to occur as having already occurred, and see nothing but the present in the future, for the future is but the present a little farther on."

"There it is!" exclaimed Kennedy, with a shrug. "As great a fatalist as ever!"

"Yes! but in the good sense of the word. Let us not trouble ourselves, then, about what fate has in store for us, and let us not forget our good old English proverb: 'The man who was born to be hung will never be drowned!' "

There was no reply to make, but that did not prevent Kennedy from resuming a series of arguments which may be readily conjectured, but which were too long for us to repeat.

"Well, then," he said, after an hour's discussion, "if you are absolutely determined to make this trip across the African continent—if it is necessary for your happiness, why not pursue the ordinary routes?"

"Why?" ejaculated the doctor, growing animated. "Because, all attempts to do so, up to this time, have utterly failed. Because, from Mungo Park, assassinated on the Niger, to Vogel, who disappeared in the Wadai country; from Oudney, who died at Murmur, and Clapperton, lost at Sackatou, to the Frenchman Maizan, who was cut to pieces; from Major Laing, killed by the Touaregs, to Roscher, from Hamburg, massacred in the beginning of 1860, the names of victim after victim have been inscribed on the lists of African martyrdom! Because, to contend successfully against the elements; against hunger, and thirst, and fever; against savage beasts, and still more savage men, is impossible! Because, what cannot be done in one way, should be tried in another. In fine, because what one cannot pass through directly in the middle, must be passed by going to one side or overhead!"

"If passing over it were the only question!" interposed Kennedy; "but passing high up in the air, doctor, there's the rub!"

"Come, then," said the doctor, "what have I to fear? You will admit that I have taken my precautions in such manner as to be certain that my balloon will not fall; but, should it disappoint me, I should find myself on the ground in the normal conditions imposed upon other explorers. But, my balloon will not deceive me, and we need make no such calculations."

"Yes, but you must take them into view."

"No, Dick. I intend not to be separated from the balloon until I reach the western coast of Africa. With it, everything is possible; without it, I fall back into the dangers and difficulties as well as the natural obstacles that ordinarily attend such an expedition: with it, neither heat, nor torrents, nor tempests, nor the simoom, nor unhealthy climates, nor wild animals, nor savage men, are to be feared! If I feel too hot, I can ascend; if too cold, I can come down. Should there be a mountain, I can pass over it; a precipice, I can sweep across it; a river, I can sail beyond it; a storm, I can rise away above it; a torrent, I can skim it like a bird! I can advance without fatigue, I can halt without need of repose! I can soar above the nascent cities! I can speed onward with the rapidity of a tornado, sometimes at the loftiest heights, sometimes only a hundred feet above the soil, while the map of Africa unrolls itself beneath my gaze in the great atlas of the world."

Even the stubborn Kennedy began to feel moved, and yet the spectacle thus conjured up before him gave him the vertigo. He riveted his eyes upon the doctor with wonder and admiration, and yet with fear, for he already felt himself swinging aloft in space.

"Come, come," said he, at last. "Let us see, Samuel. Then you have discovered the means of guiding a balloon?"

"Not by any means. That is a Utopian idea."

"Then, you will go—"

"Whithersoever Providence wills; but, at all events, from east to west."

"Why so?"

"Because I expect to avail myself of the trade-winds, the direction of which is always the same."

"Ah! yes, indeed!" said Kennedy, reflecting; "the trade-winds—yes—truly—one might—there's something in that!"

"Something in it—yes, my excellent friend—there's *everything* in it. The English Government has placed a transport at my disposal, and three or four vessels are to cruise off the western coast of Africa, about the presumed period of my arrival. In three months, at most, I shall be at Zanzibar, where I will inflate my balloon, and from that point we shall launch ourselves."

"We!" said Dick.

"Have you still a shadow of an objection to offer? Speak, friend Kennedy."

"An objection! I have a thousand; but among other things, tell me, if you expect to see the country. If you expect to mount and descend at pleasure, you cannot do so, without losing your gas. Up to this time no other means have been devised, and it is this that has always prevented long journeys in the air."

"My dear Dick, I have only one word to answer—I shall not lose one particle of gas."

"And yet you can descend when you please?"

"I shall descend when I please."

"And how will you do that?"

"Ah, ha! therein lies my secret, friend Dick. Have faith, and let my device be yours—'Excelsior!'"

"'Excelsior' be it then," said the sportsman, who did not understand a word of Latin.

But he made up his mind to oppose his friend's departure by all means in his power, and so pretended to give in, at the same time keeping on the watch. As for the doctor, he went on diligently with his preparations.

Chapter IV

African Explorations—Barth, Richardson, Overweg, Werne, Brun-Roliet, Penney, Andrea, Debono, Miani, Guillaume Lejean, Bruce, Krapf and Rebmann, Maizan, Roscher, Burton and Speke

THE AERIAL LINE WHICH DR. FERGUSON COUNTED UPON FOLLOWING HAD NOT BEEN chosen at random; his point of departure had been carefully studied, and it was not without good cause that he had resolved to ascend at the island of Zanzibar. This island, lying near to the eastern coast of Africa, is in the sixth degree of south latitude, that is to say, four hundred and thirty geographical miles below the equator.

From this island the latest expedition, sent by way of the great lakes to explore the sources of the Nile, had just set out.

But it would be well to indicate what explorations Dr. Ferguson hoped to link together. The two principal ones were those of Dr. Barth in 1849, and of Lieutenants Burton and Speke in 1858.

Dr. Barth is a Hamburger, who obtained permission for himself and for his countryman Overweg to join the expedition of the Englishman Richardson. The latter was charged with a mission in the Soudan.

This vast region is situated between the fifteenth and tenth degrees of north latitude; that is to say, that, in order to approach it, the explorer must penetrate fifteen hundred miles into the interior of Africa.

Until then, the country in question had been known only through the journeys of Denham, of Clapperton, and of Oudney, made from 1822 to 1824. Richardson, Barth, and Overweg, jealously anxious to push their investigations farther, arrived at Tunis and Tripoli, like their predecessors, and got as far as Mourzouk, the capital of Fezzan.

They then abandoned the perpendicular line, and made a sharp turn westward towards Ghât, guided, with difficulty, by the Touaregs. After a thousand scenes of pillage, of vexation, and attacks by armed forces, their caravan arrived, in October, at the vast oasis of Asben. Dr. Barth separated from his companions, made an excursion to the town of Aghades, and rejoined the expedition, which resumed its march on the 12th of December. At length it reached the province of Damerghou; there the three travellers parted, and Barth took the road to Kano, where he arrived by dint of perseverance, and after paying considerable tribute.

In spite of an intense fever, he quitted that place on the 7th of March, accompanied by a single servant. The principal aim of his journey was to reconnoitre Lake Tchad, from which he was still three hundred and fifty miles distant. He therefore advanced towards the east, and reached the town of Zouricolo, in the Bornou country, which is the core of the great central empire of Africa. There he heard of the death of Richardson, who had succumbed to fatigue and privation. He next arrived at Kouka, the capital of Bornou, on the borders of the lake. Finally, at the end of three weeks, on the 14th of April, twelve months after having quitted Tripoli, he reached the town of Ngornou.

We find him again setting forth on the 29th of March, 1851, with Overweg, to visit the kingdom of Adamaoua, to the south of the lake, and from there he pushed on as far as the town of Yola, a little below nine degrees north latitude. This was the extreme southern limit reached by that daring traveller.

He returned in the month of August to Kouka; from there he successively traversed the Mandara, Barghimi, and Klanem countries, and reached his extreme limit in the east, the town of Masena, situated at seventeen degrees twenty minutes west longitude.

On the 25th of November, 1852, after the death of Overweg, his last companion, he plunged into the west, visited Sockoto, crossed the Niger, and finally reached Timbuctoo, where he had to languish, during eight long months, under vexations inflicted upon him by the sheik, and all kinds of ill-treatment and wretchedness. But the presence of a Christian in the city could not long be tolerated, and the Foullans threatened to besiege it. The doctor, therefore, left it on the 17th of March, 1854, and fled to the frontier, where he remained for thirty-three days in the most abject destitution. He then managed to get back to Kano in November, thence to Kouka, where he resumed Denham's route after four months' delay. He regained Tripoli towards the close of August, 1855, and arrived in London on the 6th of September, the only survivor of his party.

Such was the venturesome journey of Dr. Barth.

Dr. Ferguson carefully noted the fact, that he had stopped at four degrees north latitude and seventeen degrees west longitude.

Now let us see what Lieutenants Burton and Speke accomplished in Eastern Africa.

The various expeditions that had ascended the Nile could never manage to reach the mysterious source of that river. According to the narrative of the German doctor, Ferdinand Werne, the expedition attempted in 1840, under the auspices of Mehemet Ali, stopped at Gondokoro, between the fourth and fifth parallels of north latitude.

In 1855, Brun-Roliet, a native of Savoy, appointed consul for Sardinia in Eastern Soudan, to take the place of Vaudey, who had just died, set out from Karthoum, and, under the name of Yacoub the merchant, trading in gums and ivory, got as far as Belenia, beyond the fourth degree, but had to return in ill-health to Karthoum, where he died in 1857.

Neither Dr. Penney—the head of the Egyptian medical service, who, in a small steamer, penetrated one degree beyond Gondokoro, and then came back to die of exhaustion at Karthoum—nor Miani, the Venetian, who, turning the cataracts below Gondokoro, reached the second parallel—nor the Maltese trader, Andrea Debono, who pushed his journey up the Nile still farther—could work their way beyond the apparently impassable limit.

In 1859, M. Guillaume Lejean, entrusted with a mission by the French Government, reached Karthoum by way of the Red Sea, and embarked upon the Nile with a retinue of twenty-one hired men and twenty soldiers, but he could not get past Gondokoro, and ran extreme risk of his life among the negro tribes, who were in full revolt. The expedition directed by M. d'Escayrac de Lauture made an equally unsuccessful attempt to reach the famous sources of the Nile.

This fatal limit invariably brought every traveller to a halt. In ancient times, the ambassadors of Nero reached the ninth degree of latitude, but in eighteen centuries only from five to six degrees, or from three hundred to three hundred and sixty geographical miles, were gained.

Many travellers endeavoured to reach the sources of the Nile by taking their point of departure on the eastern coast of Africa.

Between 1768 and 1772 the Scotch traveller, Bruce, set out from Massowah, a port of Abyssinia, traversed the Tigré, visited the ruins of Axum, saw the sources of the Nile where they did not exist, and obtained no serious result.

In 1844, Dr. Krapf, an Anglican missionary, founded an establishment at Monbaz, on the coast of Zanguebar, and, in company with the Rev. Dr. Rebmann, discovered two mountain-ranges three hundred miles from the coast. These were the mountains of Kilimandjaro and Kenia, which Messrs. de Heuglin and Thornton have partly scaled so recently.

In 1845, Maizan, the French explorer, disembarked alone, at Bagamayo, directly opposite to Zanzibar, and got as far as Deje-la-Mhora, where the chief caused him to be put to death in the most cruel torment.

In 1859, in the month of August, the young traveller, Roscher, from Hamburg, set out with a caravan of Arab merchants, reached Lake Nyassa, and was there assassinated while he slept.

Finally, in 1857, Lieutenants Burton and Speke, both officers in the Bengal army, were sent by the London Geographical Society to explore the great African lakes, and on the 17th of June they quitted Zanzibar, and plunged directly into the west.

After four months of incredible suffering, their baggage having been pillaged, and their attendants beaten and slain, they arrived at Kazeh, a sort of central rendezvous for traders and caravans. They were in the midst of the country of the Moon, and there they collected some precious documents concerning the manners, government, religion, fauna, and flora of the region. They next made for the first of the great lakes, the one named Tanganayika, situated between the third and eighth degrees of south latitude. They reached it on the 14th of February, 1858, and visited the various tribes residing on its banks, the most of whom are cannibals.

They departed again on the 26th of May, and re-entered Kazeh on the 20th of June. There Burton, who was completely worn out, lay ill for several months, during which time Speke made a push to the northward of more than three hundred miles, going as far as Lake Ukéréoué, which he came in sight of on the 3d of August; but he could descry only the opening of it at latitude two degrees thirty minutes.

He reached Kazeh, on his return, on the 25th of August, and, in company with Burton, again took up the route to Zanzibar, where they arrived in the month of March in the following year. These two daring explorers then re-embarked for England; and the Geographical Society of Paris decreed them its annual prize medal.

Dr. Ferguson carefully remarked that they had not gone beyond the second degree of south latitude, nor the twenty-ninth of east longitude.

The problem, therefore, was how to link the explorations of Burton and Speke with those of Dr. Barth, since to do so was to undertake to traverse an extent of more than twelve degrees of territory.

Chapter V

KENNEDY'S DREAMS—ARTICLES AND PRONOUNS IN THE PLURAL—
DICK'S INSINUATIONS—A PROMENADE OVER THE MAP OF
AFRICA—WHAT IS CONTAINED BETWEEN TWO POINTS OF THE
COMPASS—EXPEDITIONS NOW ON FOOT—SPEKE AND GRANT—
KRAPF, DE DECKEN, AND DE HEUGLIN

DR. FERGUSON ENERGETICALLY PUSHED THE PREPARATIONS FOR HIS DEPARTURE, AND in person superintended the construction of his balloon, with certain modifications; in regard to which he observed the most absolute silence. For a long time past he had been applying himself to the study of the Arab language and the various Mandingoe idioms, and, thanks to his talents as a polyglot, he had made rapid progress.

In the meanwhile his friend, the sportsman, never let him out of his sight—afraid, no doubt, that the doctor might take his departure, without saying a word to anybody. On this subject, he regaled him with the most persuasive arguments, which, however, did *not* persuade Samuel Ferguson, and wasted his breath in pathetic entreaties, by which the latter seemed to be but slightly moved. In fine, Dick felt that the doctor was slipping through his fingers.

The poor Scot was really to be pitied. He could not look upon the azure vault without a sombre terror: when asleep, he felt oscillations that made his head reel; and every night he had visions of being swung aloft at immeasurable heights.

We must add that, during these fearful nightmares, he once or twice fell out of bed. His first care then was to show Ferguson a severe contusion that he had received on the cranium. "And yet," he would add, with warmth, "that was at the height of only three feet—not an inch more—and such a bump as this! Only think, then!"

This insinuation, full of sad meaning as it was, did not seem to touch the doctor's heart.

"We'll not fall," was his invariable reply.

"But, still, suppose that we *were* to fall!"

"We will *not* fall!"

This was decisive, and Kennedy had nothing more to say.

What particularly exasperated Dick was, that the doctor seemed completely to lose sight of his personality—of his—Kennedy's—and to look upon him as irrevocably destined to become his aerial companion. Not even the shadow of a doubt was ever suggested; and Samuel made an intolerable misuse of the first person plural:

" 'We' are getting along; 'we' shall be ready on the ——; 'we' shall start on the ——," etc., etc.

And then there was the singular possessive adjective:

" 'Our' balloon; 'our' car; 'our' expedition."

And the same in the plural, too:

" 'Our' preparations; 'our' discoveries; 'our' ascensions."

Dick shuddered at them, although he was determined not to go; but he did not want to annoy his friend. Let us also disclose the fact that, without knowing exactly why himself, he had sent to Edinburgh for a certain selection of heavy clothing, and his best hunting-gear and fire-arms.

One day, after having admitted that, with an overwhelming run of good-luck, there *might* be one chance of success in a thousand, he pretended to yield entirely to the doctor's wishes; but, in order to still put off the journey, he opened the most varied series of subterfuges. He threw himself back upon questioning the utility of the expedition—its opportuneness, etc. This discovery of the sources of the Nile, was it likely to be of any use?—Would one have really laboured for the welfare of humanity?—When, after all, the African tribes should have been civilised, would they be any happier?—Were folks certain that civilisation had not its chosen abode there rather than in Europe?—Perhaps!—And then, couldn't one wait a little longer?—The trip across Africa would certainly be accomplished someday, and in a less hazardous manner.—In another month, or in six months before the year was over, some explorer would undoubtedly come in—etc., etc.

These hints produced an effect exactly opposite to what was desired or intended, and the doctor trembled with impatience.

"Are you willing, then, wretched Dick—are you willing, false friend—that this glory should belong to another? Must I then be untrue to my past history; recoil before obstacles that are not serious; requite with cowardly hesitation what both the English Government and the Royal Society of London have done for me?"

"But," resumed Kennedy, who made great use of that conjunction.

"But," said the doctor, "are you not aware that my journey is to compete with the success of the expeditions now on foot? Don't you know that fresh explorers are advancing towards the centre of Africa?"

"Still—"

"Listen to me, Dick, and cast your eyes over that map."

Dick glanced over it, with resignation.

"Now, ascend the course of the Nile."

"I have ascended it," replied the Scotchman, with docility.

"Stop at Gondokoro."

"I am there."

And Kennedy thought to himself how easy such a trip was—on the map!

"Now, take one of the points of these dividers and let it rest upon that place beyond which the most daring explorers have scarcely gone."

"I have done so."

"And now look along the coast for the island of Zanzibar, in latitude six degrees south."

"I have it."

"Now, follow the same parallel and arrive at Kazeh."

"I have done so."

"Run up again along the thirty-third degree of longitude to the opening of Lake Ukéréoué, at the point where Lieutenant Speke had to halt."

"I am there; a little more, and I should have tumbled into the lake."

"Very good! Now, do you know what we have the right to suppose, according to the information given by the tribes that live along its shores?"

"I haven't the least idea."

"Why, that this lake, the lower extremity of which is in two degrees and thirty minutes, must extend also two degrees and a half above the equator."

"Really!"

"Well from this northern extremity there flows a stream which must necessarily join the Nile, if it be not the Nile itself."

"That is, indeed, curious."

"Then, let the other point of your dividers rest upon that extremity of Lake Ukéréoué."

"It is done, friend Ferguson."

"Now, how many degrees can you count between the two points?"

"Scarcely two."

"And do you know what that means, Dick?"

"Not the least in the world."

"Why, that makes scarcely one hundred and twenty miles—in other words, a nothing."

"Almost nothing, Samuel."

"Well, do you know what is taking place at this moment?"

"No, upon my honour, I do not."

"Very well, then, I'll tell you. The Geographical Society regards as very important the exploration of this lake of which Speke caught a glimpse. Under their auspices, Lieutenant (now Captain) Speke has associated with him Captain Grant, of the army in India; they have put themselves at the head of a numerous and well-equipped expedition; their mission is to ascend the lake and return to Gondokoro; they have received a subsidy of more than five thousand pounds, and the Governor of the Cape of Good Hope has placed Hottentot soldiers at their disposal; they set out from Zanzibar at the close of October, 1860. In the meanwhile John Petherick, the English consul at the city of Karthoum, has received about seven hundred pounds from the foreign office; he is to equip a steamer at Karthoum, stock it with sufficient provisions, and make his way to Gondokoro; there, he will await Captain Speke's caravan, and be able to replenish its supplies to some extent."

"Well planned," said Kennedy.

"You can easily see, then, that time presses if we are to take part in these exploring labours. And that is not all, since, while some are thus advancing with sure steps to the discovery of the sources of the Nile, others are penetrating to the very heart of Africa."

"On foot?" said Kennedy.

"Yes, on foot," rejoined the doctor, without noticing the insinuation. "Doctor Krapf proposes to push forward, in the west, by way of the Djob, a river lying under the equator. Baron de Decken has already set out from Monbaz, has reconnoitered the mountains of Kenaia and Kilimandjaro, and is now plunging in towards the centre."

"But all this time on foot?"

"On foot or on mules."

"Exactly the same, so far as I am concerned," ejaculated Kennedy.

"Lastly," resumed the doctor, "M. de Heuglin, the Austrian vice-consul at Karthoum, has just organised a very important expedition, the first aim of which is to search for the traveller Vogel, who, in 1853, was sent into the Soudan to associate himself with the labours of Dr. Barth. In 1856, he quitted Bornou, and determined to explore the unknown country that lies between Lake Tchad and Darfur. Nothing has been seen of him since that time. Letters that were received in Alexandria, in 1860, said that he was killed at the order of the King of Wadai; but other letters, addressed by Dr. Hartmann to the traveller's father, relate that, according to the recital of a fellatah of Bornou, Vogel was merely held as a prisoner at Wara. All hope is not then lost. Hence, a committee has been organised under the presidency of the Regent of Saxe-Cogurg-Gotha; my friend Petermann is its secretary; a national subscription has provided for the expense of the expedition, whose strength has been increased by the voluntary accession of several learned men, and M. de Heuglin set out from Massowah, in the month of June. While engaged in looking for Vogel, he is also to explore all the country between the Nile and Lake Tchad, that is to say, to knit together the operations of Captain Speke and those of Dr. Barth, and then Africa will have been traversed from east to west."*

---

*After the departure of Dr. Ferguson, it was ascertained that M. de Heuglin, owing to some disagreement, took a route different from the one assigned to his expedition, the command of the latter having been transferred to Mr. Muntzinger.

"Well," said the canny Scot, "since everything is getting on so well, what's the use of our going down there?"

Dr. Ferguson made no reply, but contented himself with a significant shrug of the shoulders.

Chapter VI

A Servant—match him!—He can see the Satellites of Jupiter—Dick and Joe hard at it—Doubt and Faith— The Weighing Ceremony—Joe and Wellington— He gets a Half-crown

DR. FERGUSON HAD A SERVANT WHO ANSWERED WITH ALACRITY TO THE NAME OF JOE. He was an excellent fellow, who testified the most absolute confidence in his master, and the most unlimited devotion to his interests, even anticipating his wishes and orders, which were always intelligently executed. In fine, he was a Caleb without the growling, and a perfect pattern of constant good-humour. Had he been made on purpose for the place, it could not have been better done. Ferguson put himself entirely in his hands, so far as the ordinary details of existence were concerned, and he did well. Incomparable, whole-souled Joe! a servant who orders your dinner; who likes what you like; who packs your trunk, without forgetting your socks or your linen; who has charge of your keys and your secrets, and takes no advantage of all this!

But then, what a man the doctor was in the eyes of this worthy Joe! With what respect and what confidence the latter received all his decisions! When Ferguson had spoken, he would be a fool who should attempt to question the matter. Everything he thought was exactly right; everything he said, the perfection of wisdom; everything he ordered to be done, quite feasible; all that he undertook, practicable; all that he accomplished, admirable. You might have cut Joe to pieces—not an agreeable operation, to be sure—and yet he would not have altered his opinion of his master.

So, when the doctor conceived the project of crossing Africa through the air, for Joe the thing was already done; obstacles no longer existed; from the moment when the doctor had made up his mind to start, he had arrived—along with his faithful attendant, too, for the noble fellow knew, without a word uttered about it, that he would be one of the party.

Moreover, he was just the man to render the greatest service by his intelligence and his wonderful agility. Had the occasion arisen to name a professor of gymnastics for the monkeys in the Zoological Garden (who are smart enough, by the way!), Joe would certainly have received the appointment. Leaping, climbing, almost flying—these were all sport to him.

If Ferguson was the head and Kennedy the arm, Joe was to be the right hand of the expedition. He had, already, accompanied his master on several journeys, and had a smat-

tering of science appropriate to his condition and style of mind, but he was especially remarkable for a sort of mild philosophy, a charming turn of optimism. In his sight everything was easy, logical, natural, and, consequently, he could see no use in complaining or
grumbling.

Among other gifts, he possessed a strength and range of vision that were perfectly
surprising. He enjoyed, in common with Moestlin, Kepler's professor, the rare faculty of
distinguishing the satellites of Jupiter with the naked eye, and of counting fourteen of the
stars in the group of Pleiades, the remotest of them being only of the ninth magnitude. He
presumed none the more for that; on the contrary, he made his bow to you, at a distance,
and when occasion arose he bravely knew how to use his eyes.

With such profound faith as Joe felt in the doctor, it is not to be wondered at that incessant discussions sprang up between him and Kennedy, without any lack of respect to
the latter, however.

One doubted, the other believed; one had a prudent foresight, the other blind confidence. The doctor, however, vibrated between doubt and confidence; that is to say, he
troubled his head with neither one nor the other.

"Well, Mr. Kennedy," Joe would say.

"Well, my boy?"

"The moment's at hand. It seems that we are to sail for the moon."

"You mean the Mountains of the Moon, which are not quite so far off. But, never
mind, one trip is just as dangerous as the other!"

"Dangerous! What! with a man like Dr. Ferguson?"

"I don't want to spoil your illusions, my good Joe; but this undertaking of his is nothing more nor less than the act of a madman. He won't go, though!"

"He won't go, eh? Then you haven't seen his balloon at Mitchell's factory in the
Borough?"

"I'll take precious good care to keep away from it!"

"Well, you'll lose a fine sight, sir. What a splendid thing it is! What a pretty shape!
What a nice car! How snug we'll feel in it!"

"Then you really think of going with your master?"

"I?" answered Joe, with an accent of profound conviction. "Why, I'd go with him
wherever he pleases! Who ever heard of such a thing? Leave him to go off alone, after
we've been all over the world together! Who would help him, when he was tired? Who
would give him a hand in climbing over the rocks? Who would attend him when he was
sick? No, Mr. Kennedy, Joe will always stick to the doctor!"

"You're a fine fellow, Joe!"

"But, then, you're coming with us!"

"Oh! certainly," said Kennedy; "that is to say, I will go with you up to the last moment,
to prevent Samuel even then from being guilty of such an act of folly! I will follow him as
far as Zanzibar, so as to stop him there, if possible."

"You'll stop nothing at all, Mr. Kennedy, with all respect to you, sir. My master is no
hare-brained person; he takes a long time to think over what he means to do, and then,
when he once gets started, the Evil One himself couldn't make him give it up."

"Well, we'll see about that."

"Don't flatter yourself, sir—but then, the main thing is, to have you with us. For a hunter like you, sir, Africa's a great country. So, either way, you won't be sorry for the trip."

"No, that's a fact, I shan't be sorry for it, if I can get this crazy man to give up his scheme."

"By the way," said Joe, "you know that the weighing comes off to-day."

"The weighing—what weighing?"

"Why, my master, and you, and I, are all to be weighed to-day!"

"What! like horse-jockeys?"

"Yes, like jockeys. Only, never fear, you won't be expected to make yourself lean, if you're found to be heavy. You'll go as you are."

"Well, I can tell you, I am not going to let myself be weighed," said Kennedy, firmly.

"But, sir, it seems that the doctor's machine requires it."

"Well, his machine will have to do without it."

"Humph! and suppose that it couldn't go up, then?"

"Egad! that's all I want!"

"Come! come Mr. Kennedy! My master will be sending for us directly."

"I shan't go."

"Oh! now, you won't vex the doctor in that way!"

"Aye! that I will."

"Well!" said Joe with a laugh, "you say that because he's not here; but when he says to your face, 'Dick!' (with all respect to you, sir,) 'Dick, I want to know exactly how much you weigh,' you'll go, I warrant it."

"No, I will *not* go!"

At this moment the doctor entered his study, where this discussion had been taking place; and, as he came in, cast a glance at Kennedy, who did not feel altogether at his ease.

"Dick," said the doctor, "come with Joe; I want to know how much you both weigh."

"But—"

"You may keep your hat on. Come!" And Kennedy went.

They repaired in company to the workshop of the Messrs. Mitchell, where one of those so-called "Roman" scales was in readiness. It was necessary, by the way, for the doctor to know the weight of his companions, so as to fix the equilibrium of his balloon; so he made Dick get upon the platform of the scales. The latter, without making any resistance, said, in an undertone:

"Oh! well, that doesn't bind me to anything."

"One hundred and fifty-three pounds," said the doctor, noting it down on his tablets.

"Am I too heavy?"

"Why, no, Mr. Kennedy!" said Joe; "and then, you know, I am light to make up for it."

So saying, Joe, with enthusiasm, took his place on the scales, and very nearly upset them in his ready haste. He struck the attitude of Wellington where he is made to ape Achilles, at Hyde-Park entrance, and was superb in it, without the shield.

"One hundred and twenty pounds," wrote the doctor.

"Ah! ha!" said Joe, with a smile of satisfaction And why did he smile? He never could tell himself.

"It's my turn now," said Ferguson—and he put down one hundred and thirty-five pounds to his own account.

"All three of us," said he, "do not weigh much more than four hundred pounds."

"But, sir," said Joe, "if it was necessary for your expedition, I could make myself thinner by twenty pounds, by not eating so much."

"Useless, my boy!" replied the doctor. "You may eat as much as you like, and here's half-a-crown to buy you the ballast."

Chapter VII

GEOMETRICAL DETAILS—CALCULATION OF THE CAPACITY OF THE BALLOON—THE DOUBLE RECEPTACLE— THE COVERING—THE CAR—THE MYSTERIOUS APPARATUS— THE PROVISIONS AND STORES—THE FINAL SUMMING UP

DR. FERGUSON HAD LONG BEEN ENGAGED UPON THE DETAILS OF HIS EXPEDITION. IT IS easy to comprehend that the balloon—that marvellous vehicle which was to convey him through the air—was the constant object of his solicitude.

At the outset, in order not to give the balloon too ponderous dimensions, he had decided to fill it with hydrogen gas, which is fourteen and a half times lighter than common air. The production of this gas is easy, and it has given the greatest satisfaction hitherto in aerostatic experiments.

The doctor, according to very accurate calculations, found that, including the articles indispensable to his journey and his apparatus, he should have to carry a weight of 4,000 pounds; therefore he had to find out what would be the ascensional force of a balloon capable of raising such a weight, and, consequently, what would be its capacity.

A weight of four thousand pounds is represented by a displacement of the air amounting to forty-four thousand eight hundred and forty-seven cubic feet; or, in other words, forty-four thousand eight hundred and forty-seven cubic feet of air weigh about four thousand pounds.

By giving the balloon these cubic dimensions, and filling it with hydrogen gas, instead of common air—the former being fourteen and a half times lighter and weighing therefore only two hundred and seventy-six pounds—a difference of three thousand seven hundred and twenty-four pounds in equilibrium is produced; and it is this difference between the weight of the gas contained in the balloon and the weight of the surrounding atmosphere that constitutes the ascensional force of the former.

However, were the forty-four thousand eight hundred and forty-seven cubic feet of gas of which we speak, all introduced into the balloon, it would be entirely filled; but that would not do, because, as the balloon continued to mount into the more rarefied layers of the atmosphere, the gas within would dilate, and soon burst the cover containing it. Balloons, then, are usually only two-thirds filled.

But the doctor, in carrying out a project known only to himself, resolved to fill his balloon only one-half; and, since he had to carry forty-four thousand eight hundred and forty-seven cubic feet of gas, to give his balloon nearly double capacity he arranged it in that elongated, oval shape which has come to be preferred. The horizontal diameter was fifty feet, and the vertical diameter seventy-five feet. He thus obtained a spheroid, the capacity of which amounted, in round numbers, to ninety thousand cubic feet.

Could Dr. Ferguson have used two balloons, his chances of success would have been increased; for, should one burst in the air, he could, by throwing out ballast, keep himself up with the other. But the management of two balloons would, necessarily, be very difficult, in view of the problem how to keep them both at an equal ascensional force.

After having pondered the matter carefully, Dr. Ferguson, by an ingenious arrangement, combined the advantages of two balloons, without incurring their inconveniences. He constructed two of different sizes, and enclosed the smaller in the larger one. His external balloon, which had the dimensions given above, contained a less one of the same shape, which was only forty-five feet in horizontal, and sixty-eight feet in vertical diameter. The capacity of this interior balloon was only sixty-seven thousand cubic feet: it was to float in the fluid surrounding it. A valve opened from one balloon into the other, and thus enabled the aeronaut to communicate with both.

This arrangement offered the advantage, that if gas had to be let off, so as to descend, that which was in the outer balloon would go first; and, were it completely emptied, the smaller one would still remain intact. The outer envelope might then be cast off as a useless encumbrance; and the second balloon, left free to itself, would not offer the same hold to the currents of air as a half-inflated one must needs present.

Moreover, in case of an accident happening to the outside balloon, such as getting torn, for instance, the other would remain intact.

The balloons were made of a strong but light Lyons silk, coated with gutta percha. This gummy, resinous substance is absolutely water-proof, and also resists acids and gas perfectly. The silk was doubled, at the upper extremity of the oval, where most of the strain would come.

Such an envelope as this could retain the inflating fluid for any length of time. It weighed half-a-pound per nine square feet. Hence the surface of the outside balloon being about eleven thousand six hundred square feet, its envelope weighed six hundred and fifty pounds. The envelope of the second or inner balloon, having nine thousand two hundred square feet of surface, weighed only about five hundred and ten pounds, or say eleven hundred and sixty pounds for both.

The network that supported the car was made of very strong hempen cord, and the two valves were the object of the most minute and careful attention, as the rudder of a ship would be.

The car, which was of a circular form and fifteen feet in diameter, was made of wicker-work, strengthened with a slight covering of iron, and protected below by a system of elastic springs, to deaden the shock of collision. Its weight, along with that of the network, did not exceed two hundred and fifty pounds.

In addition to the above, the doctor caused to be constructed two sheet-iron chests two lines in thickness. These were connected by means of pipes furnished with stopcocks. He joined to these a spiral, two inches in diameter, which terminated in two branch pieces of unequal length, the longer of which, however, was twenty-five feet in height and the shorter only fifteen feet.

These sheet-iron chests were embedded in the car in such a way as to take up the least possible amount of space. The spiral, which was not to be adjusted until some future moment, was packed up, separately, along with a very strong Buntzen electric battery. This apparatus had been so ingeniously combined that it did not weigh more than seven hundred pounds, even including twenty-five gallons of water in another receptacle.

The instruments provided for the journey consisted of two barometers, two thermometers, two compasses, a sextant, two chronometers, an artificial horizon, and an altazimuth, to throw out the height of distant and inaccessible objects.

The Greenwich Observatory had placed itself at the doctor's disposal. The latter, however, did not intend to make experiments in physics; he merely wanted to be able to know in what direction he was passing, and to determine the position of the principal rivers, mountains, and towns.

He also provided himself with three thoroughly tested iron anchors, and a light but strong silk ladder fifty feet in length.

He at the same time carefully weighed his stores of provision, which consisted of tea, coffee, biscuit, salted meat, and *pemmican*, a preparation which comprises many nutritive elements in a small space. Besides a sufficient stock of pure brandy, he arranged two water-tanks, each of which contained twenty-two gallons.

The consumption of these articles would necessarily, little by little, diminish the weight to be sustained, for it must be remembered that the equilibrium of a balloon floating in the atmosphere is extremely sensitive. The loss of an almost insignificant weight suffices to produce a very noticeable displacement.

Nor did the doctor forget an awning to shelter the car, nor the coverings and blankets that were to be the bedding of the journey, nor some fowling pieces and rifles, with their requisite supply of powder and ball.

Here is the summing up of his various items, and their weight, as he computed it:

Ferguson	135 pounds
Kennedy	153 "
Joe	120 "
Weight of the outside balloon	650 "
Weight of the second balloon	510 "
Car and network	280 "
Anchors, instruments, awnings, and sundry utensils, guns,	
coverings, etc.	190 "
Meat, *pemmican*, biscuits, tea, coffee, brandy.	386 "
Water.	400 "
Apparatus	700 "
Weight of the hydrogen	276 "
Ballast	200 "
	4,000 pounds

Such were the items of the four thousand pounds that Dr. Ferguson proposed to carry up with him. He took only two hundred pounds of ballast for "unforeseen emergencies," as he remarked, since otherwise he did not expect to use any, thanks to the peculiarity of his apparatus.

Chapter VIII

JOE'S IMPORTANCE—THE COMMANDER OF THE RESOLUTE—
KENNEDY'S ARSENAL—MUTUAL AMENITIES—THE FAREWELL
DINNER—DEPARTURE ON THE 21ST OF FEBRUARY—THE DOCTOR'S
SCIENTIFIC SESSIONS—DUVEYRIER—LIVINGSTONE—DETAILS OF
THE AERIAL VOYAGE—KENNEDY SILENCED

ABOUT THE 10TH OF FEBRUARY, THE PREPARATIONS WERE PRETTY WELL COMPLETED; and the balloons, firmly secured, one within the other, were altogether finished. They had been subjected to a powerful pneumatic pressure in all parts, and the test gave excellent evidence of their solidity and of the care applied in their construction.

Joe hardly knew what he was about, with delight. He trotted incessantly to and fro between his home in Greek Street, and the Mitchell establishment, always full of business, but always in the highest spirits, giving details of the affair to people who did not even ask him, so proud was he, above all things, of being permitted to accompany his master. I have even a shrewd suspicion that what with showing the balloon, explaining the plans and views of the doctor, giving folks a glimpse of the latter, through a half-opened window, or pointing him out as he passed along the streets, the clever scamp earned a few half-crowns, but we must not find fault with him for that. He had as much right as anybody else to speculate upon the admiration and curiosity of his contemporaries.

On the 16th of February, the *Resolute* cast anchor near Greenwich. She was a screw propeller of eight hundred tons, a fast sailer, and the very vessel that had been sent out to the polar regions, to revictual the last expedition of Sir James Ross. Her commander, Captain Bennet, had the name of being a very amiable person, and he took a particular interest in the doctor's expedition, having been one of that gentleman's admirers for a long time. Bennet was rather a man of science than a man of war, which did not, however, prevent his vessel from carrying four carronades, that had never hurt anybody, to be sure, but had performed the most pacific duty in the world.

The hold of the *Resolute* was so arranged as to find a stowing-place for the balloon. The latter was shipped with the greatest precaution on the 18th of February, and was then carefully deposited at the bottom of the vessel in such a way as to prevent accident. The car and its accessories, the anchors, the cords, the supplies, the water-tanks, which were to be filled on arriving, all were embarked and put away under Ferguson's own eyes.

Ten tons of sulphuric acid and ten tons of iron filings, were put on board for the future production of the hydrogen gas. The quantity was more than enough, but it was well to be provided against accident. The apparatus to be employed in manufacturing the gas, including some thirty empty casks, was also stowed away in the hold.

These various preparations were terminated on the 18th of February, in the evening. Two state-rooms, comfortably fitted up, were ready for the reception of Dr. Ferguson and his friend Kennedy. The latter, all the while swearing that he would not go, went on board with a regular arsenal of hunting weapons, among which were two double-barrelled breech-loading fowling-pieces, and a rifle that had withstood every test, of the make of Purdey, Moore & Dickson, at Edinburgh. With such a weapon a marksman would find no difficulty in lodging a bullet in the eye of a chamois at the distance of two thousand paces. Along with these implements, he had two of Colt's six-shooters, for unforeseen emergencies. His powder-case, his cartridge-pouch, his lead, and his bullets, did not exceed a certain weight prescribed by the doctor.

The three travellers got themselves to rights on board during the working-hours of February 19th. They were received with much distinction by the captain and his officers, the doctor continuing as reserved as ever, and thinking of nothing but his expedition. Dick seemed a good deal moved, but was unwilling to betray it; while Joe was fairly dancing and breaking out in laughable remarks. The worthy fellow soon became the jester and merry-andrew of the boatswain's mess, where a berth had been kept for him.

On the 20th, a grand farewell dinner was given to Dr. Ferguson and Kennedy by the Royal Geographical Society. Commander Bennet and his officers were present at the entertainment, which was signalised by copious libations and numerous toasts. Healths were drunk, in sufficient abundance to guarantee all the guests a lifetime of centuries. Sir Francis M——— presided, with restrained but dignified feeling.

To his own supreme confusion, Dick Kennedy came in for a large share in the jovial felicitations of the night. After having drunk to the "intrepid Ferguson, the glory of England," they had to drink to "the no less courageous Kennedy, his daring companion."

Dick blushed a good deal, and that passed for modesty; whereupon the applause redoubled, and Dick blushed again.

A message from the Queen arrived while they were at dessert. Her Majesty offered her compliments to the two travellers, and expressed her wishes for their safe and successful journey. This, of course, rendered imperative fresh toasts to "Her most gracious Majesty."

At midnight, after touching farewells and warm shaking of hands, the guests separated.

The boats of the *Resolute* were in waiting at the stairs of Westminster Bridge. The captain leaped in, accompanied by his officers and passengers, and the rapid current of the Thames, aiding the strong arms of the rowers, bore them swiftly to Greenwich. In an hour's time all were asleep on board.

The next morning, February 21st, at three o'clock, the furnaces began to roar; at five, the anchors were weighed, and the *Resolute*, powerfully driven by her screw, began to plough the water towards the mouth of the Thames.

It is needless to say that the topic of conversation with everyone on board was Dr. Ferguson's enterprise. Seeing and hearing the doctor soon inspired everybody with such confidence that, in a very short time, there was no one, excepting the incredulous Scotchman, on the steamer who had the least doubt of the perfect feasibility and success of the expedition.

During the long, unoccupied hours of the voyage, the doctor held regular sittings, with lectures on geographical science, in the officers' mess-room. These young men felt an intense interest in the discoveries made during the last forty years in Africa; and the doctor related to them the explorations of Barth, Burton, Speke, and Grant, and depicted the wonders of this vast, mysterious country, now thrown open on all sides to the investigations of science. On the north, the young Duveyrier was exploring Sahara, and bringing the chiefs of the Touaregs to Paris. Under the inspiration of the French Government, two expeditions were preparing, which, descending from the north, and coming from the west, would cross each other at Timbuctoo. In the south, the indefatigable Livingstone was still advancing towards the equator; and, since March, 1862, he had, in company with Mackenzie, ascended the river Rovoonia. The nineteenth century would, assuredly, not pass, contended the doctor, without Africa having been compelled to surrender the secrets she has kept locked up in her bosom for six thousand years.

But the interest of Dr. Ferguson's hearers was excited to the highest pitch when he made known to them, in detail, the preparations for his own journey. They took pleasure in verifying his calculations; they discussed them; and the doctor frankly took part in the discussion.

As a general thing, they were surprised at the limited quantity of provision that he took with him; and one day one of the officers questioned him on that subject.

"That peculiar point astonishes you, does it?" said Ferguson.

"It does, indeed."

"But how long do you think my trip is going to last? Whole months? If so, you are greatly mistaken. Were it to be a long one, we should be lost; we should never get back. But you must know that the distance from Zanzibar to the coast of Senegal is only thirty-five hundred—say four thousand miles. Well, at the rate of two hundred and forty miles every twelve hours, which does not come near the rapidity of our railroad trains, by travelling day and night, it would take only seven days to cross Africa!"

"But then you could see nothing, make no geographical observations, or reconnoitre the face of the country."

"Ah!" replied the doctor, "if I am master of my balloon—if I can ascend and descend at will, I shall stop when I please, especially when too violent currents of air threaten to carry me out of my way with them."

"And you will encounter such," said Captain Bennet. "There are tornadoes that sweep at the rate of more than two hundred and forty miles per hour."

"You see, then, that with such speed as that, we could cross Africa in twelve hours. One would rise at Zanzibar, and go to bed at St. Louis!"

"But," rejoined the officer, "could any balloon withstand the wear and tear of such velocity?"

"It has happened before," replied Ferguson.

"And the balloon withstood it?"

"Perfectly well. It was at the time of the coronation of Napoleon, in 1804. The aeronaut, Gernerin, sent up a balloon at Paris, about eleven o'clock in the evening. It bore the following inscription, in letters of gold: 'Paris, 25 Frimaire; year XIII; Coronation of the Emperor Napoleon by his Holiness, Pius VII.' On the next morning, the inhabitants of Rome saw the same balloon soaring above the Vatican, whence it crossed the Campagna, and finally fluttered down into the lake of Bracciano. So you see, gentlemen, that a balloon can resist such velocities."

"A balloon—that might be; but a man?" insinuated Kennedy.

"Yes, a man, too!—for the balloon is always motionless with reference to the air that surrounds it. What moves is the mass of the atmosphere itself: for instance, one may light a taper in the car, and the flame will not even waver. An aeronaut in Garnerin's balloon would not have suffered in the least from the speed. But then I have no occasion to attempt such velocity; and if I can anchor to some tree, or some favourable inequality of the ground, at night, I shall not fail to do so. Besides, we take provision for two months with us, after all; and there is nothing to prevent our skilful huntsman here from furnishing game in abundance when we come to alight."

"Ah! Mr. Kennedy," said a young midshipman, with envious eyes, "what splendid shots you'll have!"

"Without counting," said another, "that you'll have the glory as well as the sport!"

"Gentlemen," replied the hunter, stammering with confusion, "I greatly—appreciate—your compliments—but they—don't—belong to me."

"You!" exclaimed everybody, "don't you intend to go?"

"I am not going!"

"You won't accompany Dr. Ferguson?"

"Not only shall I not accompany him, but I am here so as to be present at the last moment to prevent his going."

Every eye was now turned to the doctor.

"Never mind him!" said the latter, calmly. "This is a matter that we can't argue with him. At heart he knows perfectly well that he *is* going."

"By Saint Andrew!" said Kennedy, "I swear—"

"Swear to nothing, friend Dick; you have been gauged and weighed—you and your powder, your guns, and your bullets; so don't let us say anything more about it."

And, in fact, from that day until the arrival at Zanzibar, Dick never opened his mouth. He talked neither about that nor about anything else. He kept absolutely silent.

Chapter IX

THEY DOUBLE THE CAPE—THE FORECASTLE—A COURSE OF COSMOGRAPHY BY PROFESSOR JOE—CONCERNING THE METHOD OF GUIDING BALLOONS—HOW TO SEEK OUT ATMOSPHERIC CURRENTS—EUREKA

THE *RESOLUTE* PLUNGED ALONG RAPIDLY TOWARDS THE CAPE OF GOOD HOPE, THE weather continuing fine, although the sea ran heavier.

On the 30th of March, twenty-seven days after the departure from London, the Table Mountain loomed upon the horizon. Cape City lying at the foot of an amphitheatre of hills, could be distinguished through the ship's glasses, and soon the *Resolute* cast anchor in the port. But the captain touched there only to replenish his coal bunkers, and that was but a day's job. On the morrow, he steered away to the south'ard, so as to double the southernmost point of Africa, and enter the Mozambique Channel.

This was not Joe's first sea-voyage, and so, for his part, he soon found himself at home on board; everybody liked him for his frankness and good-humour. A considerable share of his master's renown was reflected upon him. He was listened to as an oracle, and he made no more mistakes than the next one.

So, while the doctor was pursuing his descriptive course of lecturing in the officers' mess, Joe reigned supreme on the forecastle, holding forth in his own peculiar manner, and making history to suit himself—a style of procedure pursued, by the way, by the greatest historians of all ages and nations.

The topic of discourse was, naturally, the aerial voyage. Joe had experienced some trouble in getting the rebellious spirits to believe in it; but, once accepted by them, nothing connected with it was any longer an impossibility to the imaginations of the seamen stimulated by Joe's harangues.

Our dazzling narrator persuaded his hearers that, after this trip, many others still more wonderful would be undertaken. In fact, it was to be but the first of a long series of superhuman expeditions.

"You see, my friends, when a man has had a taste of that kind of travelling, he can't get along afterward with any other; so, on our next expedition, instead of going off to one side, we'll go right ahead, going up, too, all the time."

"Humph! then you'll go to the moon!" said one of the crowd, with a stare of amazement.

"To the moon!" exclaimed Joe, "To the moon! pooh! that's too common. Everybody might go to the moon, that way. Besides, there's no water there, and you have to carry such a lot of it along with you. Then you have to take air along in bottles, so as to breathe."

"Ay! ay! that's all right! But can a man get a drop of the real stuff there?" said a sailor who liked his toddy.

"Not a drop!" was Joe's answer. "No! old fellow, not in the moon. But we're going to skip round among those little twinklers up there—the stars—and the splendid planets that my old man so often talks about. For instance, we'll commence with Saturn—"

"That one with the ring?" asked the boatswain.

"Yes! the wedding-ring—only no one knows what's become of his wife!"

"What? will you go so high up as that?" said one of the ship-boys, gaping with wonder. "Why, your master must be Old Nick himself."

"Oh! no, he's too good for that."

"But, after Saturn—what then?" was the next enquiry of his impatient audience.

"After Saturn? Well, we'll visit Jupiter. A funny place that is, too, where the days are only nine hours and a half long—a good thing for the lazy fellows—and the years, would you believe it—last twelve of ours, which is fine for folks who have only six months to live. They get off a little longer by that."

"Twelve years!" ejaculated the boy.

"Yes, my youngster; so that in that country you'd be toddling after your mammy yet, and that old chap yonder, who looks about fifty, would only be a little shaver of four and a half."

"Blazes! that's a good 'un!" shouted the whole forecastle together.

"Solemn truth!" said Joe, stoutly.

"But what can you expect? When people will stay in this world, they learn nothing and keep as ignorant as bears. But just come along to Jupiter and you'll see. But they have to look out up there, for he's got satellites that are not just the easiest things to pass."

All the men laughed, but they more than half believed him. Then he went on to talk about Neptune, where seafaring men get a jovial reception, and Mars, where the military get the best of the sidewalk to such an extent that folks can hardly stand it. Finally, he drew them a heavenly picture of the delights of Venus.

"And when we get back from that expedition," said the indefatigable narrator, "they'll decorate us with the Southern Cross that shines up there in the Creator's button-hole."

"Ay, and you'd have well earned it!" said the sailors.

Thus passed the long evenings on the forecastle in merry chat, and during the same time the doctor went on with his instructive discourses.

One day the conversation turned upon the means of directing balloons, and the doctor was asked his opinion about it.

"I don't think," said he, "that we shall succeed in finding out a system of directing them. I am familiar with all the plans attempted and proposed, and not one has succeeded, not one is practicable. You may readily understand that I have occupied my mind with this subject, which was, necessarily, so interesting to me, but I have not been able to solve the problem with the appliances now known to mechanical science. We would have to discover a motive power of extraordinary force, and almost impossible lightness of machinery. And, even then, we could not resist atmospheric currents of any considerable strength. Until now, the effort has been rather to direct the car than the balloon, and that has been one great error."

"Still there are many points of resemblance between a balloon and a ship which is directed at will."

"Not at all," retorted the doctor, "there is little or no similarity between the two cases. Air is infinitely less dense than water, in which the ship is only half submerged, while the whole bulk of a balloon is plunged in the atmosphere, and remains motionless with reference to the element that surrounds it."

"You think, then, that aerostatic science has said its last word?"

"Not at all! not at all! But we must look for another point in the case, and if we cannot manage to guide our balloon, we must, at least, try to keep it in favourable aerial currents. In proportion as we ascend, the latter become much more uniform and flow more constantly in one direction. They are no longer disturbed by the mountains and valleys that traverse the surface of the globe, and these, you know, are the chief cause of the variations of the wind and the inequality of their force. Therefore, these zones having been once determined, the balloon will merely have to be placed in the currents best adapted to its destination."

"But then," continued Captain Bennet, "in order to reach them, you must keep constantly ascending or descending. That is the real difficulty, doctor."

"And why, my dear captain?"

"Let us understand one another. It would be a difficulty and an obstacle only for long journeys, and not for short aerial excursions."

"And why so, if you please?"

"Because you can ascend only by throwing out ballast; you can descend only after letting off gas, and by these processes your ballast and your gas are soon exhausted."

"My dear sir, that's the whole question. There is the only difficulty that science need now seek to overcome. The problem is not how to guide the balloon, but how to take it up and down without expending the gas which is its strength, its life-blood, its soul, if I may use the expression."

"You are right, my dear doctor; but this problem is not yet solved; this means has not yet been discovered."

"I beg your pardon, it *has* been discovered."

"By whom?"

"By me!"

"By you?"

"You may readily believe that otherwise I should not have risked this expedition across Africa in a balloon. In twenty-four hours I should have been without gas!"

"But you said nothing about that in England?"

"No! I did not want to have myself overhauled in public. I saw no use in that. I made my preparatory experiments in secret and was satisfied. I have no occasion, then, to learn anything more from them."

"Well! doctor, would it be proper to ask what is your secret?"

"Here it is, gentlemen—the simplest thing in the world!"

The attention of his auditory was now directed to the doctor in the utmost degree as he quietly proceeded with his explanation.

Chapter X

FORMER EXPERIMENTS—THE DOCTOR'S FIVE RECEPTACLES— THE GAS CYLINDER—THE CALORIFERE—THE SYSTEM OF MANEUVRING—SUCCESS CERTAIN

THE ATTEMPT HAS OFTEN BEEN MADE, GENTLEMEN," SAID THE DOCTOR, "TO RISE AND descend at will, without losing ballast or gas from the balloon. A French aeronaut, M. Meunier, tried to accomplish this by compressing air in an inner receptacle. A Belgian, Dr. Van Hecke, by means of wings and paddles, obtained a vertical power that would have sufficed in most cases, but the practical results secured from these experiments have been insignificant.

"I therefore resolved to go about the thing more directly; so, at the start, I dispensed with ballast altogether, excepting as a provision for cases of special emergency, such as the breakage of my apparatus, or the necessity of ascending very suddenly, so as to avoid unforeseen obstacles.

"My means of ascent and descent consist simply in dilating or contracting the gas that is in the balloon by the application of different temperatures, and here is the method of obtaining that result.

"You saw me bring on board with the car several cases or receptacles, the use of which you may not have understood. They are five in number.

"The first contains about twenty-five gallons of water, to which I add a few drops of sulphuric acid, so as to augment its capacity as a conductor of electricity, and then I decompose it by means of a powerful Buntzen battery. Water, as you know, consists of two parts of hydrogen to one of oxygen gas.

"The latter, through the action of the battery, passes at its positive pole into the second receptacle. A third receptacle, placed above the second one, and of double its capacity, receives the hydrogen passing into it by the negative pole.

"Stopcocks, of which one has an orifice twice the size of the other, communicate between these receptacles and a fourth one, which is called the *mixture reservoir*, since in it the two gases obtained by the decomposition of the water do really commingle. The capacity of this fourth tank is about forty-one cubic feet.

"On the upper part of this tank is a platinum tube provided with a stopcock.

"You will now readily understand, gentlemen, the apparatus that I have described to you is really a gas cylinder and blow-pipe for oxygen and hydrogen, the heat of which exceeds that of a forge fire.

"This much established, I proceed to the second part of my apparatus. From the lowest part of my balloon, which is hermetically closed, issue two tubes a little distance apart. The one starts among the upper layers of the hydrogen gas, the other amid the lower layers.

"These two pipes are provided at intervals with strong jointings of india-rubber, which enable them to move in harmony with the oscillations of the balloon.

"Both of them run down as far as the car, and lose themselves in an iron receptacle of cylindrical form, which is called the heat-tank. The latter is closed at its two ends by two strong plates of the same metal.

"The pipe running from the lower part of the balloon runs into this cylindrical receptacle through the lower plate; it penetrates the latter and then takes the form of a helicoidal or screw-shaped spiral, the rings of which, rising one over the other, occupy nearly the whole of the height of the tank. Before again issuing from it, this spiral runs into a small cone with a concave base, that is turned downward in the shape of a spherical cap.

"It is from the top of this cone that the second pipe issues, and it runs, as I have said, into the upper beds of the balloon.

"The spherical cap of the small cone is of platinum, so as not to melt by the action of the cylinder and blow-pipe, for the latter are placed upon the bottom of the iron tank in the midst of the helicoidal spiral, and the extremity of their flame will slightly touch the cap in question.

"You all know, gentlemen, what a calorifere, to heat apartments, is. You know how it acts. The air of the apartments is forced to pass through its pipes, and is then released with a heightened temperature. Well, what I have just described to you is nothing more nor less than a calorifere.

"In fact, what is it that takes place? The cylinder once lighted, the hydrogen in the spiral and in the concave cone becomes heated, and rapidly ascends through the pipe that leads to the upper part of the balloon. A vacuum is created below, and it attracts the gas in the lower parts; this becomes heated in its turn, and is continually replaced; thus, an extremely rapid current of gas is established in the pipes and in the spiral, which issues from the balloon and then returns to it, and is heated over again, incessantly.

"Now, the gases increase $\frac{1}{480}$ of their volume for each degree of heat applied. If, then, I force the temperature 18 degrees, the hydrogen of the balloon will dilate $\frac{18}{480}$ or 1614 cubic feet, and will, therefore, displace 1614 more cubic feet of air, which will increase its ascensional power by 160 pounds. This is equivalent to throwing out that weight of ballast. If I augment the temperature by 180 degrees, the gas will dilate $\frac{180}{480}$ and will displace 16,740 cubic feet more, and its ascensional force will be augmented by 1,600 pounds.

"Thus, you see, gentlemen, that I can easily effect very considerable changes of equilibrium. The volume of the balloon has been calculated in such manner that, when half inflated, it displaces a weight of air exactly equal to that of the envelope containing the hydrogen gas, and of the car occupied by the passengers, and all its apparatus and accessories. At this point of inflation, it is in exact equilibrium with the air, and neither mounts nor descends.

"In order, then, to effect an ascent, I give the gas a temperature superior to the temperature of the surrounding air by means of my cylinder. By this excess of heat it obtains a larger distention, and inflates the balloon more. The latter, then, ascends in proportion as I heat the hydrogen.

"The descent, of course, is effected by lowering the heat of the cylinder, and letting the temperature abate. The ascent would be, usually, more rapid than the descent; but that is a fortunate circumstance, since it is of no importance to me to descend rapidly, while, on the other hand, it is by a very rapid ascent that I avoid obstacles. The real danger lurks below, and not above.

"Besides, as I have said, I have a certain quantity of ballast, which will enable me to ascend more rapidly still, when necessary. My valve, at the top of the balloon, is nothing more nor less than a safety-valve. The balloon always retains the same quantity of hydrogen, and the variations of temperature that I produce in the midst of this shut-up gas are, of themselves, sufficient to provide for all these ascending and descending movements.

"Now, gentlemen, as a practical detail, let me add this:

"The combustion of the hydrogen and of the oxygen at the point of the cylinder produces solely the vapour or steam of water. I have, therefore, provided the lower part of the cylindrical iron box with a scape-pipe, with a valve operating by means of a pressure of two atmospheres; consequently, so soon as this amount of pressure is attained, the steam escapes of itself.

"Here are the exact figures: 25 gallons of water, separated into its constituent elements, yield 200 pounds of oxygen and 25 pounds of hydrogen. This represents, at atmospheric tension, 1,890 cubic feet of the former and 3,780 cubic feet of the latter, or 5,670 cubic feet, in all, of the mixture. Hence, the stopcock of my cylinder, when fully open, expends 27 cubic feet per hour, with a flame at least six times as strong as that of the large lamps used for lighting streets. On an average, then, and in order to keep myself at a very moderate elevation, I should not burn more than nine cubic feet per hour, so that my twenty-five gallons of water represent six hundred and thirty-six hours of aerial navigation, or a little more than twenty-six days.

"Well, as I can descend when I please, to replenish my stock of water on the way, my trip might be indefinitely prolonged.

"Such, gentlemen, is my secret. It is simple, and, like most simple things, it cannot fail to succeed. The dilation and contraction of the gas in the balloon is my means of locomotion, which calls for neither cumbersome wings, nor any other mechanical motor. A calorifere to produce the changes of temperature, and a cylinder to generate the heat, are neither inconvenient nor heavy. I think, therefore, that I have combined all the elements of success."

Dr. Ferguson here terminated his discourse, and was most heartily applauded. There was not an objection to make to it; all had been foreseen and decided.

"However," said the captain, "the thing may prove dangerous."

"What matters that," replied the doctor, "provided that it be practicable?"

Chapter XI

THE ARRIVAL AT ZANZIBAR—THE ENGLISH CONSUL—ILL-WILL OF
THE INHABITANTS—THE ISLAND OF KOUMBENI—THE RAIN-
MAKERS—INFLATION OF THE BALLOON—DEPARTURE ON THE
18TH OF APRIL—THE LAST GOOD-BY—THE VICTORIA

AN INVARIABLY FAVOURABLE WIND HAD ACCELERATED THE PROGRESS OF THE *RESOLUTE* towards the place of her destination. The navigation of the Mozambique Channel was especially calm and pleasant. The agreeable character of the trip by sea was regarded as a good omen of the probable issue of the trip through the air. Everyone looked forward to the hour of arrival, and sought to give the last touch to the doctor's preparations.

At length the vessel hove in sight of the town of Zanzibar, upon the island of the same name, and, on the 15th of April, at 11 o'clock in the morning, she anchored in the port.

The island of Zanzibar belongs to the Imaum of Muscat, an ally of France and England, and is, undoubtedly, his finest settlement. The port is frequented by a great many vessels from the neighbouring countries.

The island is separated from the African coast only by a channel, the greatest width of which is but thirty miles.

It has a large trade in gums, ivory, and, above all, in "ebony," for Zanzibar is the great slave-market. Thither converges all the booty captured in the battles which the chiefs of the interior are continually fighting. This traffic extends along the whole eastern coast, and as far as the Nile latitudes. Mr. G. Lejean even reports that he has seen it carried on, openly, under the French flag.

Upon the arrival of the *Resolute,* the English consul at Zanzibar came on board to offer his services to the doctor, of whose projects the European newspapers had made him aware for a month past. But, up to that moment, he had remained with the numerous phalanx of the incredulous.

"I doubted," said he, holding out his hand to Dr. Ferguson, "but now I doubt no longer."

He invited the doctor, Kennedy, and the faithful Joe, of course, to his own dwelling. Through his courtesy, the doctor was enabled to have knowledge of the various letters that he had received from Captain Speke. The captain and his companions had suffered dreadfully from hunger and bad weather before reaching the Ugogo country. They could advance only with extreme difficulty, and did not expect to be able to communicate again for a long time.

"Those are perils and privations which we shall manage to avoid," said the doctor.

The baggage of the three travellers was conveyed to the consul's residence. Arrangements were made for disembarking the balloon upon the beach at Zanzibar. There was a convenient spot, near the signal-mast, close by an immense building, that would serve to shelter it from the east winds. This huge tower, resembling a tun standing on one end, beside which the famous Heidelberg tun would have seemed but a very ordinary barrel, served as a fortification, and on its platform were stationed Belootchees, armed with lances. These Belootchees are a kind of brawling, good-for-nothing Janizaries.

But, when about to land the balloon, the consul was informed that the population of the island would oppose their doing so by force. Nothing is so blind as fanatical passion. The news of the arrival of a Christian, who was to ascend into the air, was received with rage. The negroes, more exasperated than the Arabs, saw in this project an attack upon their religion. They took it into their heads that some mischief was meant to the sun and the moon. Now, these two luminaries are objects of veneration to the African tribes, and they determined to oppose so sacrilegious an enterprise.

The consul, informed of their intentions, conferred with Dr. Ferguson and Captain Bennet on the subject. The latter was unwilling to yield to threats, but his friend dissuaded him from any idea of violent retaliation.

"We shall certainly come out winners," he said. "Even the imaum's soldiers will lend us a hand, if we need it. But, my dear captain, an accident may happen in a moment, and it would require but one unlucky blow to do the balloon an irreparable injury, so that the trip would be totally defeated; therefore we must act with the greatest caution."

"But what are we to do? If we land on the coast of Africa, we shall encounter the same difficulties. What are we to do?"

"Nothing is more simple," replied the consul. "You observe those small islands outside of the port; land your balloon on one of them; surround it with a guard of sailors, and you will have no risk to run."

"Just the thing!" said the doctor, "and we shall be entirely at our ease in completing our preparations."

The captain yielded to these suggestions, and the *Resolute* was headed for the island of Koumbeni. During the morning of the 16th April, the balloon was placed in safety in the middle of a clearing in the great woods, with which the soil is studded.

Two masts, eighty feet in height, were raised at the same distance from each other. Blocks and tackle, placed at their extremities, afforded the means of elevating the balloon, by the aid of a transverse rope. It was then entirely uninflated. The interior balloon was fastened to the exterior one, in such manner as to be lifted up in the same way. To the lower end of each balloon were fixed the pipes that served to introduce the hydrogen gas.

The whole day, on the 17th, was spent in arranging the apparatus destined to produce the gas; it consisted of some thirty casks, in which the decomposition of water was effected by means of iron-filings and sulphuric acid placed together in a large quantity of the first-named fluid. The hydrogen passed into a huge central cask, after having been washed on the way, and thence into each balloon by the conduit-pipes. In this manner each of them received a certain accurately-ascertained quantity of gas. For this purpose, there had to be employed eighteen hundred and sixty-six pounds of sulphuric acid, sixteen thousand and fifty pounds of iron, and nine thousand one hundred and sixty-six gallons of water. This operation commenced on the following night, about three A.M., and lasted nearly eight hours. The next day, the balloon, covered with its network, undulated gracefully above its car, which was held to the ground by numerous sacks of earth. The inflating apparatus was put together with extreme care, and the pipes issuing from the balloon were securely fitted to the cylindrical case.

The anchors, the cordage, the instruments, the travelling-wraps, the awning, the provisions, and the arms, were put in the place assigned to them in the car. The supply of water was procured at Zanzibar. The two hundred pounds of ballast were distributed in fifty bags placed at the bottom of the car, but within arm's-reach.

These preparations were concluded about five o'clock in the evening, while sentinels kept close watch around the island, and the boats of the *Resolute* patrolled the channel.

The blacks continued to show their displeasure by grimaces and contortions. Their *obi-men*, or wizards, went up and down among the angry throngs, pouring fuel on the flame of their fanaticism; and some of the excited wretches, more furious and daring than the rest, attempted to get to the island by swimming, but they were easily driven off.

Thereupon the sorceries and incantations commenced; the "rain-makers," who pretend to have control over the clouds, invoked the storms and the "stone-showers," as the blacks call hail, to their aid. To compel them to do so, they plucked leaves of all the different trees that grow in that country, and boiled them over a slow fire, while, at the same time, a sheep was killed by thrusting a long needle into its heart. But, in spite of all their ceremonies, the sky remained clear and beautiful, and they profited nothing by their slaughtered sheep and their ugly grimaces.

The blacks then abandoned themselves to the most furious orgies, and got fearfully drunk on "tembo," a kind of ardent spirits drawn from the cocoa-nut-tree, and an extremely heady sort of beer called "togwa." Their chants, which were destitute of all melody, but were sung in excellent time, continued until far into the night.

About six o'clock in the evening, the captain assembled the travellers and the officers of the ship at a farewell repast in his cabin. Kennedy, whom nobody ventured to question now, sat with his eyes riveted on Dr. Ferguson, murmuring indistinguishable words. In other respects, the dinner was a gloomy one. The approach of the final moment filled everybody with the most serious reflections. What had fate in store for these daring adventurers? Should they ever again find themselves in the midst of their friends, or seated at the domestic hearth? Were their travelling apparatus to fail, what would become of them, among those ferocious savage tribes, in regions that had never been explored, and in the midst of boundless deserts?

Such thoughts as these, which had been dim and vague until then, or but slightly regarded when they came up, returned upon their excited fancies with intense force at this parting moment. Dr. Ferguson, still cold and impassible, talked of this, that, and the other; but he strove in vain to overcome this infectious gloominess. He utterly failed.

As some demonstration against the personal safety of the doctor and his companions was feared, all three slept that night on board the *Resolute*. At six o'clock in the morning they left their cabin, and landed on the island of Koumbeni.

The balloon was swaying gently to and fro in the morning breeze; the sand-bags that had held it down were now replaced by some twenty strong-armed sailors, and Captain Bennet and his officers were present to witness the solemn departure of their friends.

At this moment Kennedy went right up to the doctor, grasped his hand, and said:

"Samuel, have you absolutely determined to go?"

"Solemnly determined, my dear Dick."

"I have done everything that I could to prevent this expedition, have I not?"

"Everything!"

"Well, then, my conscience is clear on that score, and I will go with you."

"I was sure you would!" said the doctor, betraying in his features swift traces of emotion.

At last the moment of final leave-taking arrived. The captain and his officers embraced their dauntless friends with great feeling, not excepting even Joe, who, worthy fellow, was as proud and happy as a prince. Everyone in the party insisted upon having a final shake of the doctor's hand.

At nine o'clock the three travellers got into their car. The doctor lit the combustible in his cylinder and turned the flame so as to produce a rapid heat, and the balloon, which had rested on the ground in perfect equipoise, began to rise in a few minutes, so that the seamen had to slacken the ropes they held it by. The car then rose about twenty feet above their heads.

"My friends!" exclaimed the doctor, standing up between his two companions, and taking off his hat, "let us give our aerial ship a name that will bring her good-luck! let us christen her *Victoria!*"

This speech was answered with stentorian cheers of "Huzza for the Queen! Huzza for Old England!"

At this moment the ascensional force of the balloon increased prodigiously, and Ferguson, Kennedy, and Joe, waved a last good-by to their friends.

"Let go all!" shouted the doctor, and at the word the *Victoria* shot rapidly up into the sky, while the four carronades on board the *Resolute* thundered forth a parting salute in her honour.

Chapter XII

CROSSING THE STRAIT—THE MRIMA—DICK'S REMARK AND JOE'S PROPOSITION—A RECIPE FOR COFFEE-MAKING—THE UZARAMO— THE UNFORTUNATE MAIZAN—MOUNT DUTHUMI— THE DOCTOR'S CARDS—NIGHT UNDER A NOPAL

THE AIR WAS PURE, THE WIND MODERATE, AND THE BALLOON ASCENDED ALMOST PERpendicularly to a height of fifteen hundred feet, as indicated by a depression of two inches in the barometric column.

At this height a more decided current carried the balloon towards the south-west.

What a magnificent spectacle was then outspread beneath the gaze of the travellers! The island of Zanzibar could be seen in its entire extent, marked out by its deeper colour upon a vast planisphere; the fields had the appearance of patterns of different colours, and thick clumps of green indicated the groves and thickets.

The inhabitants of the island looked no larger than insects. The huzzaing and shouting were little by little lost in the distance, and only the discharge of the ship's guns could be heard in the concavity beneath the balloon, as the latter sped on its flight.

"How fine that is!" said Joe, breaking silence for the first time.

He got no reply. The doctor was busy observing the variations of the barometer and noting down the details of his ascent.

Kennedy looked on, and had not eyes enough to take in all that he saw.

The rays of the sun coming to the aid of the heating cylinder, the tension of the gas increased, and the *Victoria* attained the height of twenty-five hundred feet.

The *Resolute* looked like a mere cockle-shell, and the African coast could be distinctly seen in the west marked out by a fringe of foam.

"You don't talk?" said Joe, again.

"We are looking!" said the doctor, directing his spy-glass towards the mainland.

"For my part, I must talk!"

"As much as you please, Joe; talk as much as you like!"

And Joe went on alone with a tremendous volley of exclamations. The "ohs!" and the "ahs!" exploded one after the other, incessantly, from his lips.

During his passage over the sea the doctor deemed it best to keep at his present elevation. He could thus reconnoitre a greater stretch of the coast. The thermometer and the barometer, hanging up inside of the half-opened awning, were always within sight, and a second barometer suspended outside was to serve during the night watches.

At the end of about two hours the *Victoria*, driven along at a speed of a little more than eight miles, very visibly neared the coast of the mainland. The doctor, thereupon, determined to descend a little nearer to the ground. So he moderated the flame of his cylinder, and the balloon, in a few moments, had descended to an altitude only three hundred feet above the soil.

It was then found to be passing just over the Mrima country, the name of this part of the eastern coast of Africa. Dense borders of mango-trees protected its margin, and the ebb-tide disclosed to view their thick roots, chafed and gnawed by the teeth of the Indian Ocean. The sands which, at an earlier period, formed the coast-line, rounded away along the distant horizon, and Mount Nguru reared aloft its sharp summit in the north-west.

The *Victoria* passed near to a village which the doctor found marked upon his chart as Kaole. Its entire population had assembled in crowds, and were yelling with anger and fear, at the same time vainly directing their arrows against this monster of the air that swept along so majestically away above all their powerless fury.

The wind was setting to the southward, but the doctor felt no concern on that score, since it enabled him the better to follow the route traced by Captains Burton and Speke.

Kennedy had, at length, become as talkative as Joe, and the two kept up a continual interchange of admiring interjections and exclamations.

"Out upon stage-coaches!" said one.

"Steamers indeed!" said the other.

"Railroads! eh? rubbish!" put in Kennedy, "that you travel on, without seeing the country!"

"Balloons! they're the sort for me!" Joe would add. "Why, you don't feel yourself going, and Nature takes the trouble to spread herself out before one's eyes!"

"What a splendid sight! What a spectacle! What a delight! a dream in a hammock!"

"Suppose we take our breakfast?" was Joe's unpoetical change of tune, at last, for the keen, open air had mightily sharpened his appetite.

"Good idea, my boy!"

"Oh! it won't take us long to do the cooking—biscuit and potted meat?"

"And as much coffee as you like," said the doctor. "I give you leave to borrow a little heat from my cylinder. There's enough and to spare, for that matter, and so we shall avoid the risk of a conflagration."

"That would be a dreadful misfortune!" ejaculated Kennedy. "It's the same as a powder-magazine suspended over our heads."

"Not precisely," said Ferguson, "but still if the gas were to take fire it would burn up gradually, and we should settle down on the ground, which would be disagreeable; but never fear—our balloon is hermetically sealed."

"Let us eat a bite, then," replied Kennedy.

"Now, gentlemen," put in Joe, "while doing the same as you, I'm going to get you up a cup of coffee that I think you'll have something to say about."

"The fact is," added the doctor, "that Joe, along with a thousand other virtues, has a remarkable talent for the preparation of that delicious beverage: he compounds it of a mixture of various origin, but he never would reveal to me the ingredients."

"Well, master, since we are so far above-ground, I can tell you the secret. It is just to mix equal quantities of Mocha, of Bourbon coffee, and of Rio Nunez."

A few moments later, three steaming cups of coffee were served, and topped off a substantial breakfast, which was additionally seasoned by the jokes and repartees of the guests. Each one then resumed his post of observation.

The country over which they were passing was remarkable for its fertility. Narrow, winding paths plunged in beneath the overarching verdure. They swept along above cultivated fields of tobacco, maize, and barley, at full maturity, and here and there immense rice-fields, full of straight stalks and purple blossoms. They could distinguish sheep and goats too, confined in large cages, set upon piles to keep them out of reach of the leopards' fangs. Luxuriant vegetation spread in wild profuseness over this prodigal soil.

Village after village rang with yells of terror and astonishment at the sight of the *Victoria*, and Dr. Ferguson prudently kept her above the reach of the barbarian arrows. The savages below, thus baffled, ran together from their huddle of huts and followed the travellers with their vain imprecations while they remained in sight.

At noon, the doctor, upon consulting his map, calculated that they were passing over the Uzaramo* country. The soil was thickly studded with cocoa-nut, papaw, and cotton-wood-trees, above which the balloon seemed to disport itself like a bird. Joe found this splendid vegetation a matter of course, seeing that they were in Africa. Kennedy descried some hares and quails that asked nothing better than to get a good shot from his

*U and Ou signify *country* in the language of that region.

fowling-piece, but it would have been powder wasted, since there was no time to pick up the game.

The aeronauts swept on with the speed of twelve miles per hour, and soon were passing in thirty-eight degrees twenty minutes east longitude, over the village of Tounda.

"It was there," said the doctor, "that Burton and Speke were seized with violent fevers, and for a moment thought their expedition ruined. And yet they were only a short distance from the coast, but fatigue and privation were beginning to tell upon them severely."

In fact, there is a perpetual malaria reigning throughout the country in question. Even the doctor could hope to escape its effects only by rising above the range of the miasma that exhales from this damp region whence the blazing rays of the sun pump up its poisonous vapours. Once in a while they could descry a caravan resting in a *"kraal,"* awaiting the freshness and cool of the evening to resume its route. These kraals are wide patches of cleared land, surrounded by hedges and jungles, where traders take shelter against not only the wild beasts, but also the robber tribes of the country. They could see the natives running and scattering in all directions at the sight of the *Victoria.* Kennedy was keen to get a closer look at them, but the doctor invariably held out against the idea.

"The chiefs are armed with muskets," he said, "and our balloon would be too conspicuous a mark for their bullets."

"Would a bullet-hole bring us down?" asked Joe.

"Not immediately; but such a hole would soon become a large torn orifice through which our gas would escape."

"Then, let us keep at a respectful distance from yon miscreants. What must they think as they see us sailing in the air? I'm sure they must feel like worshipping us!"

"Let them worship away, then," replied the doctor, "but at a distance. There is no harm done in getting as far away from them as possible. See! the country is already changing its aspect: the villages are fewer and farther between; the mango-trees have disappeared, for their growth ceases at this latitude. The soil is becoming hilly and portends mountains not far off."

"Yes," said Kennedy, "it seems to me that I can see some high land on this side."

"In the west—those are the nearest ranges of the Ourizara—Mount Duthumi, no doubt, behind which I hope to find shelter for the night. I'll stir up the heat in the cylinder a little, for we must keep at an elevation of five or six hundred feet."

"That was a grand idea of yours, sir," said Joe. "It's mighty easy to manage it; you turn a cock, and the thing's done."

"Ah! here we are more at our ease," said the sportsman, as the balloon ascended; "the reflection of the sun on those red sands was getting to be insupportable."

"What splendid trees!" cried Joe. "They're quite natural, but they are very fine! Why a dozen of them would make a forest!"

"Those are baobabs," replied Dr. Ferguson. "See, there's one with a trunk fully one hundred feet in circumference. It was, perhaps, at the foot of that very tree that Maizan, the French traveller, expired in 1845, for we are over the village of Deje-la-Mhora, to which he pushed on alone. He was seized by the chief of this region, fastened to the foot of a baobab, and the ferocious black then severed all his joints while the war-song of his tribe was chanted; he then made a gash in the prisoner's neck, stopped to sharpen his knife, and fairly tore away the poor wretch's head before it had been cut from the body. The unfortunate Frenchman was but twenty-six years of age."

"And France has never avenged so hideous a crime?" said Kennedy.

"France did demand satisfaction, and the Said of Zanzibar did all in his power to capture the murderer, but in vain."

"I move that we don't stop here!" urged Joe; "let us go up, master, let us go up higher by all means."

"All the more willingly, Joe, that there is Mount Duthumi right ahead of us. If my calculations be right we shall have passed it before seven o'clock in the evening."

"Shall we not travel at night?" asked the Scotchman.

"No, as little as possible. With care and vigilance we might do so safely, but it is not enough to sweep across Africa. We want to see it."

"Up to this time we have nothing to complain of, master. The best cultivated and most fertile country in the world instead of a desert! Believe the geographers after that!"

"Let us wait, Joe! we shall see by and by."

About half-past six in the evening the *Victoria* was directly opposite Mount Duthumi; in order to pass, it had to ascend to a height of more than three thousand feet, and to accomplish that the doctor had only to raise the temperature of his gas eighteen degrees. It might have been correctly said that he held his balloon in his hand. Kennedy had only to indicate to him the obstacles to be surmounted, and the *Victoria* sped through the air, skimming the summits of the range.

At eight o'clock it descended the farther slope, the acclivity of which was much less abrupt. The anchors were thrown out from the car and one of them, coming in contact with the branches of an enormous nopal, caught on it firmly. Joe at once let himself slide down the rope and secured it. The silk ladder was then lowered to him and he remounted to the car with agility. The balloon now remained perfectly at rest sheltered from the eastern winds.

The evening meal was got ready, and the aeronauts, excited by their day's journey, made a heavy onslaught upon the provisions.

"What distance have we traversed to-day?" asked Kennedy, disposing of some alarming mouthfuls.

The doctor took his bearings, by means of lunar observations, and consulted the excellent map that he had with him for his guidance. It belonged to the Atlas of *Der Neuester Endeckungen in Afrika (The Latest Discoveries in Africa)*, published at Gotha by his learned friend Dr. Petermann, and by that *savant* sent to him. This Atlas was to serve the doctor on his whole journey; for it contained the itinerary of Burton and Speke to the great lakes; the Soudan, according to Dr. Barth; the Lower Senegal, according to Guillaume Lejean; and the Delta of the Niger, by Dr. Blaikie.

Ferguson had also provided himself with a work which combined in one compilation all the notions already acquired concerning the Nile. It was entitled *The Sources of the Nile; being a General Survey of the Basin of that River and of its Head-Stream, with the History of the Nilotic Discovery, by Charles Beke, D.D.*

He also had the excellent charts published in the *Bulletins of the Geographical Society of London*; and not a single point of the countries already discovered could, therefore, escape his notice.

Upon tracing on his maps, he found that his latitudinal route had been two degrees, or one hundred and twenty miles, to the westward.

Kennedy remarked that the route tended towards the south; but this direction was satisfactory to the doctor, who desired to reconnoitre the tracks of his predecessors as much as possible. It was agreed that the night should be divided into three watches, so that each of the party should take his turn in watching over the safety of the rest. The doctor took the watch commencing at nine o'clock; Kennedy, the one commencing at midnight; and Joe, the three o'clock morning watch.

So Kennedy and Joe, well wrapped in their blankets, stretched themselves at full length under the awning, and slept quietly; while Dr. Ferguson kept on the look-out.

Chapter XIII

CHANGE OF WEATHER—KENNEDY HAS THE FEVER—THE DOCTOR'S MEDICINE—TRAVELS ON LAND—THE BASIN OF IMENGÉ—MOUNT RUBEHO—SIX THOUSAND FEET ELEVATION— A HALT IN THE DAYTIME

THE NIGHT WAS CALM. HOWEVER, ON SATURDAY MORNING, KENNEDY, AS HE AWOKE, complained of lassitude and feverish chills. The weather was changing. The sky, covered with clouds, seemed to be laying in supplies for a fresh deluge. A gloomy region is that Zungomoro country, where it rains continually, excepting, perhaps, for a couple of weeks in the month of January.

A violent shower was not long in drenching our travellers. Below them, the roads, intersected by "nullahs," a sort of instantaneous torrent, were soon rendered impracticable, entangled as they were, besides, with thorny thickets and gigantic lianas, or creeping vines. The sulphuretted hydrogen emanations, which Captain Burton mentions, could be distinctly smelled.

"According to his statement, and I think he's right," said the doctor, "one could readily believe that there is a corpse hidden behind every thicket."

"An ugly country this!" sighed Joe; "and it seems to me that Mr. Kennedy is none the better for having passed the night in it."

"To tell the truth, I have quite a high fever," said the sportsman.

"There's nothing remarkable about that, my dear Dick, for we are in one of the most unhealthy regions in Africa; but we shall not remain here long; so let's be off."

Thanks to a skilful maneuvre achieved by Joe, the anchor was disengaged, and Joe reascended to the car by means of the ladder. The doctor vigorously dilated the gas, and the *Victoria* resumed her flight, driven along by a spanking breeze.

Only a few scattered huts could be seen through the pestilential mists; but the appearance of the country soon changed, for it often happens in Africa that some of the unhealthiest districts lie close beside others that are perfectly salubrious.

Kennedy was visibly suffering, and the fever was mastering his vigourous constitution.

"It won't do to fall ill, though," he grumbled; and so saying, he wrapped himself in a blanket, and lay down under the awning.

"A little patience, Dick, and you'll soon get over this," said the doctor.

"Get over it! Egad, Samuel, if you've any drug in your travelling-chest that will set me on my feet again, bring it without delay. I'll swallow it with my eyes shut!"

"Oh, I can do better than that, friend Dick; for I can give you a febrifuge that won't cost anything."

"And how will you do that?"

"Very easily. I am simply going to take you up above these clouds that are now deluging us, and remove you from this pestilential atmosphere. I ask for only ten minutes, in order to dilate the hydrogen."

The ten minutes had scarcely elapsed ere the travellers were beyond the rainy belt of country.

"Wait a little, now, Dick, and you'll begin to feel the effect of pure air and sunshine."

"There's a cure for you!" said Joe; "why, it's wonderful!"

"No, it's merely natural."

"Oh! natural; yes, no doubt of that!"

"I bring Dick into good air, as the doctors do, everyday, in Europe, or, as I would send a patient at Martinique to the Pitons, a lofty mountain on that island, to get clear of the yellow fever."

"Ah! by Jove, this balloon is a paradise!" exclaimed Kennedy, feeling much better already.

"It leads to it, anyhow!" replied Joe, quite gravely.

It was a curious spectacle—that mass of clouds piled up, at the moment, away below them! The vapours rolled over each other, and mingled together in confused masses of superb brilliance, as they reflected the rays of the sun. The *Victoria* had attained an altitude of four thousand feet, and the thermometer indicated a certain diminution of temperature. The land below could no longer be seen. Fifty miles away to the westward, Mount Rubeho raised its sparkling crest, marking the limit of the Ugogo country in east longitude thirty-six degrees twenty minutes. The wind was blowing at the rate of twenty miles an hour, but the aeronauts felt nothing of this increased speed. They observed no jar, and had scarcely any sense of motion at all.

Three hours later, the doctor's prediction was fully verified. Kennedy no longer felt a single shiver of the fever, but partook of some breakfast with an excellent appetite.

"That beats sulphate of quinine!" said the energetic Scot, with hearty emphasis and much satisfaction.

"Positively," said Joe, "this is where I'll have to retire to when I get old!"

About ten o'clock in the morning the atmosphere cleared up, the clouds parted, and the country beneath could again be seen, the *Victoria* meanwhile rapidly descending. Dr. Ferguson was in search of a current that would carry him more to the north-east, and he found it about six hundred feet from the ground. The country was becoming more broken, and even mountainous. The Zungomoro district was fading out of sight in the east with the last cocoa-nut-trees of that latitude.

Ere long, the crests of a mountain-range assumed a more decided prominence. A few peaks rose here and there, and it became necessary to keep a sharp look-out for the pointed cones that seemed to spring up every moment.

"We're right among the breakers!" said Kennedy.

"Keep cool, Dick. We shan't touch them," was the doctor's quiet answer.

"It's a jolly way to travel, anyhow!" said Joe, with his usual flow of spirits.

In fact, the doctor managed his balloon with wondrous dexterity.

"Now, if we had been compelled to go afoot over that drenched soil," said he, "we should still be dragging along in a pestilential mire. Since our departure from Zanzibar, half our beasts of burden would have died with fatigue. We should be looking like ghosts ourselves, and despair would be seizing on our hearts. We should be in continual squabbles with our guides and porters, and completely exposed to their unbridled brutality. During the daytime, a damp, penetrating, unendurable humidity! At night, a cold frequently intolerable, and the stings of a kind of fly whose bite pierces the thickest cloth, and drives the victim crazy! All this, too, without saying anything about wild beasts and ferocious native tribes!"

"I move that we don't try it!" said Joe, in his droll way.

"I exaggerate nothing," continued Ferguson, "for, upon reading the narratives of such travellers as have had the hardihood to venture into these regions, your eyes would fill with tears."

About eleven o'clock they were passing over the basin of Imengé, and the tribes scattered over the adjacent hills were impotently menacing the *Victoria* with their weapons. Finally, she sped along as far as the last undulations of the country which precede Rubeho. These form the last and loftiest chain of the mountains of Usagara.

The aeronauts took careful and complete note of the orographic conformation of the country. The three ramifications mentioned, of which the Duthumi forms the first link, are separated by immense longitudinal plains. These elevated summits consist of rounded cones, between which the soil is bestrewn with erratic blocks of stone and gravelly bowlders. The most abrupt declivity of these mountains confronts the Zanzibar coast, but the western slopes are merely inclined planes. The depressions in the soil are covered with a black, rich loam, on which there is a vigourous vegetation. Various water-courses filter through, towards the east, and work their way onward to flow into the Kingani, in the midst of gigantic clumps of sycamore, tamarind, calabash, and palmyra trees.

"Attention!" said Dr. Ferguson. "We are approaching Rubeho, the name of which signifies, in the language of the country, the 'Passage of the Winds,' and we would do well to double its jagged pinnacles at a certain height. If my chart be exact, we are going to ascend to an elevation of five thousand feet."

"Shall we often have occasion to reach those far upper belts of the atmosphere?"

"Very seldom: the height of the African mountains appears to be quite moderate compared with that of the European and Asiatic ranges; but, in any case, our good *Victoria* will find no difficulty in passing over them."

In a very little while, the gas expanded under the action of the heat, and the balloon took a very decided ascensional movement. Besides, the dilation of the hydrogen involved no danger, and only three-fourths of the vast capacity of the balloon was filled when the barometer, by a depression of eight inches, announced an elevation of six thousand feet.

"Shall we go this high very long?" asked Joe.

"The atmosphere of the earth has a height of six thousand fathoms," said the doctor;

"and, with a very large balloon, one might go far. That is what Messrs. Brioschi and Gay-Lussac did; but then the blood burst from their mouths and ears. Respirable air was wanting. Some years ago, two fearless Frenchmen, Messrs. Barral and Bixio, also ventured into the very lofty regions; but their balloon burst—"

"And they fell?" asked Kennedy, abruptly.

"Certainly they did; but as learned men should always fall—namely, without hurting themselves."

"Well, gentlemen," said Joe, "you may try their fall over again, if you like; but, as for me, who am but a dolt, I prefer keeping at the medium height—neither too far up, nor too low down. It won't do to be too ambitious."

At the height of six thousand feet, the density of the atmosphere has already greatly diminished; sound is conveyed with difficulty, and the voice is not so easily heard. The view of objects becomes confused; the gaze no longer takes in any but large, quite ill-distinguishable masses; men and animals on the surface become absolutely invisible; the roads and rivers get to look like threads, and the lakes dwindle to ponds.

The doctor and his friends felt themselves in a very anomalous condition; an atmospheric current of extreme velocity was bearing them away beyond arid mountains upon whose summits vast fields of snow surprised the gaze; while their convulsed appearance told of Titanic travail in the earliest epoch of the world's existence.

The sun shone at the zenith, and his rays fell perpendicularly upon those lonely summits. The doctor took an accurate design of these mountains, which form four distinct ridges almost in a straight line, the northernmost being the longest.

The *Victoria* soon descended the slope opposite to the Rubeho, skirting an acclivity covered with woods, and dotted with trees of very deep-green foliage. Then came crests and ravines, in a sort of desert which preceded the Ugogo country; and lower down were yellow plains, parched and fissured by the intense heat, and, here and there, bestrewn with saline plants and brambly thickets.

Some underbrush, which, farther on, became forests, embellished the horizon. The doctor went nearer to the ground; the anchors were thrown out, and one of them soon caught in the boughs of a huge sycamore.

Joe, slipping nimbly down the tree, carefully attached the anchor, and the doctor left his cylinder at work to a certain degree in order to retain sufficient ascensional force in the balloon to keep it in the air. Meanwhile the wind had suddenly died away.

"Now," said Ferguson, "take two guns, friend Dick—one for yourself and one for Joe—and both of you try to bring back some nice cuts of antelope-meat; they will make us a good dinner."

"Off to the hunt!" exclaimed Kennedy, joyously.

He climbed briskly out of the car and descended. Joe had swung himself down from branch to branch, and was waiting for him below, stretching his limbs in the meantime.

"Don't fly away without us, doctor!" shouted Joe.

"Never fear, my boy!—I am securely lashed. I'll spend the time getting my notes into shape. A good hunt to you! but be careful. Besides, from my post here, I can observe the face of the country, and, at the least suspicious thing I notice, I'll fire a signal-shot, and with that you must rally home."

"Agreed!" said Kennedy; and off they went.

Chapter XIV

THE FOREST OF GUM-TREES—THE BLUE ANTELOPE—THE
RALLYING-SIGNAL—AN UNEXPECTED ATTACK—THE KANYEMÉ—
A NIGHT IN THE OPEN AIR—THE MABUNGURU—
JIHOUE-LA-MKOA—A SUPPLY OF WATER—ARRIVAL AT KAZEH

THE COUNTRY, DRY AND PARCHED AS IT WAS, CONSISTING OF A CLAYEY SOIL THAT cracked open with the heat, seemed, indeed, a desert: here and there were a few traces of caravans; the bones of men and animals, that had been half-gnawed away, mouldering together in the same dust.

After half-an-hour's walking, Dick and Joe plunged into a forest of gum-trees, their eyes alert on all sides, and their fingers on the trigger. There was no foreseeing what they might encounter. Without being a rifleman, Joe could handle fire-arms with no trifling dexterity.

"A walk does one good, Mr. Kennedy, but this isn't the easiest ground in the world," he said, kicking aside some fragments of quartz with which the soil was bestrewn.

Kennedy motioned to his companion to be silent and to halt. The present case compelled them to dispense with hunting-dogs, and, no matter what Joe's agility might be, he could not be expected to have the scent of a setter or a greyhound.

A herd of a dozen antelopes were quenching their thirst in the bed of a torrent where some pools of water had lodged. The graceful creatures, snuffing danger in the breeze, seemed to be disturbed and uneasy. Their beautiful heads could be seen between every draught, raised in the air with quick and sudden motion as they sniffed the wind in the direction of our two hunters, with their flexible nostrils.

Kennedy stole around behind some clumps of shrubbery, while Joe remained motionless where he was. The former, at length, got within gunshot and fired.

The herd disappeared in the twinkling of an eye; one male antelope only, that was hit just behind the shoulder-joint, fell headlong to the ground, and Kennedy leaped towards his booty.

It was a *blauwbok*, a superb animal of a pale-bluish colour shading upon the grey, but with the belly and the inside of the legs as white as the driven snow.

"A splendid shot!" exclaimed the hunter. "It's a very rare species of the antelope, and I hope to be able to prepare his skin in such a way as to keep it."

"Indeed!" said Joe, "do you think of doing that, Mr. Kennedy?"

"Why, certainly I do! Just see what a fine hide it is!"

"But Dr. Ferguson will never allow us to take such an extra weight!"

"You're right, Joe. Still it is a pity to have to leave such a noble animal."

"The whole of it? Oh, we won't do that, sir; we'll take all the good eatable parts of it, and, if you'll let me, I'll cut him up just as well as the chairman of the honourable corporation of butchers of the city of London could do."

"As you please, my boy! But you know that in my hunter's way I can just as easily skin and cut up a piece of game as kill it."

"I'm sure of that, Mr. Kennedy. Well, then, you can build a fireplace with a few stones; there's plenty of dry dead-wood, and I can make the hot coals tell in a few minutes."

"Oh! that won't take long," said Kennedy, going to work on the fireplace, where he had a brisk flame crackling and sparkling in a minute or two.

Joe had cut some of the nicest steaks and the best parts of the tenderloin from the carcass of the antelope, and these were quickly transformed to the most savory of broils.

"There, those will tickle the doctor!" said Kennedy.

"Do you know what I was thinking about?" said Joe.

"Why, about the steaks you're broiling, to be sure!" replied Dick.

"Not the least in the world. I was thinking what a figure we'd cut if we couldn't find the balloon again."

"By George, what an idea! Why, do you think the doctor would desert us?"

"No; but suppose his anchor were to slip!"

"Impossible! and, besides, the doctor would find no difficulty in coming down again with his balloon; he handles it at his ease."

"But suppose the wind were to sweep it off, so that he couldn't come back towards us?"

"Come, come, Joe! a truce to your suppositions; they're anything but pleasant."

"Ah! sir, everything that happens in this world is natural, of course; but, then, anything may happen, and we ought to look out beforehand."

At this moment the report of a gun rang out upon the air.

"What's that?" exclaimed Joe.

"It's my rifle, I know the ring of her!" said Kennedy.

"A signal!"

"Yes; danger for us!"

"For him, too, perhaps."

"Let's be off!"

And the hunters, having gathered up the product of their expedition, rapidly made their way back along the path that they had marked by breaking boughs and bushes when they came. The density of the underbrush prevented their seeing the balloon, although they could not be far from it.

A second shot was heard.

"We must hurry!" said Joe.

"There! a third report!"

"Why, it sounds to me as if he was defending himself against something."

"Let us make haste!"

They now began to run at the top of their speed. When they reached the outskirts of the forest, they, at first glance, saw the balloon in its place and the doctor in the car.

"What's the matter?" shouted Kennedy.

"Good God!" suddenly exclaimed Joe.

"What do you see?"

"Down there! look! a crowd of blacks surrounding the balloon!"

And, in fact, there, two miles from where they were, they saw some thirty wild natives close together, yelling, gesticulating, and cutting all kinds of antics at the foot of the sycamore. Some, climbing into the tree itself, were making their way to the topmost branches. The danger seemed pressing.

"My master is lost!" cried Joe.

"Come! a little more coolness, Joe, and let us see how we stand. We hold the lives of four of those villains in our hands. Forward, then!"

They had made a mile with headlong speed, when another report was heard from the car. The shot had, evidently, told upon a huge black demon, who had been hoisting himself up by the anchor-rope. A lifeless body fell from bough to bough, and hung about twenty feet from the ground, its arms and legs swaying to and fro in the air.

"Ha!" said Joe, halting, "what does that fellow hold by?"

"No matter what!" said Kennedy; "let us run! let us run!"

"Ah! Mr. Kennedy," said Joe, again, in a roar of laughter, "by his tail! by his tail! it's an ape! They're all apes!"

"Well, they're worse than men!" said Kennedy, as he dashed into the midst of the howling crowd.

It was, indeed, a troop of very formidable baboons of the dog-faced species. These creatures are brutal, ferocious, and horrible to look upon, with their dog-like muzzles and savage expression. However, a few shots scattered them, and the chattering horde scampered off, leaving several of their number on the ground.

In a moment Kennedy was on the ladder, and Joe, clambering up the branches, detached the anchor; the car then dipped to where he was, and he got into it without difficulty. A few minutes later, the *Victoria* slowly ascended and soared away to the eastward, wafted by a moderate wind.

"That was an attack for you!" said Joe.

"We thought you were surrounded by natives."

"Well, fortunately, they were only apes," said the doctor.

"At a distance there's no great difference," remarked Kennedy.

"Nor close at hand, either," added Joe.

"Well, however that may be," resumed Ferguson, "this attack of apes might have had the most serious consequences. Had the anchor yielded to their repeated efforts, who knows whither the wind would have carried me?"

"What did I tell you, Mr. Kennedy?"

"You were right, Joe; but, even right as you may have been, you were, at that moment, preparing some antelope-steaks, the very sight of which gave me a monstrous appetite."

"I believe you!" said the doctor; "the flesh of the antelope is exquisite."

"You may judge of that yourself, now, sir, for supper's ready."

"Upon my word as a sportsman, those venison-steaks have a gamy flavor that's not to be sneezed at, I tell you."

"Good!" said Joe, with his mouth full, "I could live on antelope all the days of my life; and all the better with a glass of grog to wash it down."

So saying, the good fellow went to work to prepare a jorum of that fragrant beverage, and all hands tasted it with satisfaction.

"Everything has gone well thus far," said he.

"Very well indeed!" assented Kennedy.

"Come, now, Mr. Kennedy, are you sorry that you came with us?"

"I'd like to see anybody prevent my coming!"

It was now four o'clock in the afternoon. The *Victoria* had struck a more rapid current. The face of the country was gradually rising, and, ere long, the barometer indicated a height of fifteen hundred feet above the level of the sea. The doctor was, therefore, obliged to keep his balloon up by a quite considerable dilation of gas, and the cylinder was hard at work all the time.

Towards seven o'clock, the balloon was sailing over the basin of Kanyemé. The doctor immediately recognised that immense clearing, ten miles in extent, with its villages buried in the midst of baobab and calabash trees. It is the residence of one of the sultans of the Ugogo country, where civilization is, perhaps, the least backward. The natives there are less addicted to selling members of their own families, but still, men and animals all live together in round huts, without frames, that look like haystacks.

Beyond Kanyemé the soil becomes arid and stony, but in an hour's journey, in a fertile dip of the soil, vegetation had resumed all its vigour at some distance from Mdaburu. The wind fell with the close of the day, and the atmosphere seemed to sleep. The doctor vainly sought for a current of air at different heights, and, at last, seeing this calm of all nature, he resolved to pass the night afloat, and, for greater safety, rose to the height of one thousand feet, where the balloon remained motionless. The night was magnificent, the heavens glittering with stars, and profoundly silent in the upper air.

Dick and Joe stretched themselves on their peaceful couch, and were soon sound asleep, the doctor keeping the first watch. At twelve o'clock the latter was relieved by Kennedy.

"Should the slightest accident happen, waken me," said Ferguson, "and, above all things, don't lose sight of the barometer. To us it is the compass!"

The night was cold. There were twenty-seven degrees of difference between its temperature and that of the daytime. With nightfall had begun the nocturnal concert of animals driven from their hiding-places by hunger and thirst. The frogs struck in their guttural soprano, redoubled by the yelping of the jackals, while the imposing bass of the African lion sustained the accords of this living orchestra.

Upon resuming his post, in the morning, the doctor consulted his compass, and found that the wind had changed during the night. The balloon had been bearing about thirty miles to the north-west during the last two hours. It was then passing over Mabunguru, a stony country, strewn with blocks of syenite of a fine polish, and knobbed with huge bowlders and angular ridges of rock; conic masses, like the rocks of Karnak, studded the soil like so many Druidic dolmens; the bones of buffaloes and elephants whitened it here and there; but few trees could be seen, excepting in the east, where there were dense woods, among which a few villages lay half concealed.

Towards seven o'clock they saw a huge round rock nearly two miles in extent, like an immense tortoise.

"We are on the right track," said Dr. Ferguson. "There's Jihoue-la-Mkoa, where we must halt for a few minutes. I am going to renew the supply of water necessary for my cylinder, and so let us try to anchor somewhere."

"There are very few trees," replied the hunger.

"Never mind, let us try. Joe, throw out the anchors!"

The balloon, gradually losing its ascensional force, approached the ground; the anchors ran along until, at last, one of them caught in the fissure of a rock, and the balloon remained motionless.

It must not be supposed that the doctor could entirely extinguish his cylinder, during these halts. The equilibrium of the balloon had been calculated at the level of the sea; and, as the country was continually ascending, and had reached an elevation of from six to seven hundred feet, the balloon would have had a tendency to go lower than the surface of the soil itself. It was, therefore, necessary to sustain it by a certain dilation of the gas. But, in case the doctor, in the absence of all wind, had let the car rest upon the ground, the balloon, thus relieved of a considerable weight, would have kept up of itself, without the aid of the cylinder.

The maps indicated extensive ponds on the western slope of the Jihoue-la-Mkoa. Joe went thither alone with a cask that would hold about ten gallons. He found the place pointed out to him, without difficulty, near to a deserted village; got his stock of water, and returned in less than three-quarters of an hour. He had seen nothing particular excepting some immense elephant-pits. In fact, he came very near falling into one of them, at the bottom of which lay a half-eaten carcass.

He brought back with him a sort of clover which the apes eat with avidity. The doctor recognised the fruit of the "mbenbu"-tree which grows in profusion, on the western part of Jihoue-la-Mkoa. Ferguson waited for Joe with a certain feeling of impatience, for even a short halt in this inhospitable region always inspires a degree of fear.

The water was got aboard without trouble, as the car was nearly resting on the ground. Joe then found it easy to loosen the anchor and leaped lightly to his place beside the doctor. The latter then replenished the flame in the cylinder, and the balloon majestically soared into the air.

It was then about one hundred miles from Kazeh, an important establishment in the interior of Africa, where, thanks to a south-southeasterly current, the travellers might hope to arrive on that same day. They were moving at the rate of fourteen miles per hour, and the guidance of the balloon was becoming difficult, as they dared not rise very high without extreme dilation of the gas, the country itself being at an average height of three thousand feet. Hence, the doctor preferred not to force the dilation, and so adroitly followed the sinuosities of a pretty sharply-inclined plane, and swept very close to the villages of Thembo and Tura-Wels. The latter forms part of the Unyamwezy, a magnificent country, where the trees attain enormous dimensions; among them the cactus, which grows to gigantic size.

About two o'clock, in magnificent weather, but under a fiery sun that devoured the least breath of air, the balloon was floating over the town of Kazeh, situated about three hundred and fifty miles from the coast.

"We left Zanzibar at nine o'clock in the morning," said the doctor, consulting his notes, "and, after two days' passage, we have, including our deviations, travelled nearly five hundred geographical miles. Captains Burton and Speke took four months and a half to make the same distance!"

Chapter XV

KAZEH—THE NOISY MARKET-PLACE—THE APPEARANCE OF THE
BALLOON—THE WANGAGA—THE SONS OF THE MOON—
THE DOCTOR'S WALK—THE POPULATION OF THE PLACE—
THE ROYAL TEMBÉ—THE SULTAN'S WIVES—A ROYAL DRUNKEN-
BOUT—JOE AN OBJECT OF WORSHIP—HOW THEY DANCE IN THE
MOON—A REACTION—TWO MOONS IN ONE SKY—
THE INSTABILITY OF DIVINE HONOURS

KAZEH, AN IMPORTANT POINT IN CENTRAL AFRICA, IS NOT A CITY; IN TRUTH, THERE ARE
no cities in the interior. Kazeh is but a collection of six extensive excavations. There
are enclosed a few houses and slave-huts, with little court-yards and small gardens, carefully cultivated with onions, potatoes, cucumbers, pumpkins, and mushrooms, of perfect
flavor, growing most luxuriantly.

The Unyamwezy is the country of the Moon—above all the rest, the fertile and magnificent garden-spot of Africa. In its centre is the district of Unyanembé—a delicious region,
where some families of Omani, who are of very pure Arabic origin, live in luxurious idleness.

They have, for a long period, held the commerce between the interior of Africa and
Arabia: they trade in gums, ivory, fine muslin, and slaves. Their caravans traverse these
equatorial regions on all sides; and they even make their way to the coast in search of those
articles of luxury and enjoyment which the wealthy merchants covet; while the latter, surrounded by their wives and their attendants, lead in this charming country the least disturbed and most horizontal of lives—always stretched at full length, laughing, smoking,
or sleeping.

Around these excavations are numerous native dwellings; wide, open spaces for the
markets; fields of *cannabis* and *datura*; superb trees and depths of freshest shade—such is
Kazeh!

There, too, is held the general rendezvous of the caravans—those of the south, with
their slaves and their freightage of ivory; and those of the west, which export cotton,
glassware, and trinkets, to the tribes of the great lakes.

So in the market-place there reigns perpetual excitement, a nameless hubbub, made up
of the cries of mixed-breed porters and carriers, the beating of drums, and the twanging
of horns, the neighing of mules, the braying of donkeys, the singing of women, the
squalling of children, and the banging of the huge rattan, wielded by the jemadar or leader
of the caravans, who beats time to this pastoral symphony.

There, spread forth, without regard to order—indeed, we may say, in charming
disorder—are the showy stuffs, the glass beads, the ivory tusks, the rhinoceros'-teeth, the
shark's-teeth, the honey, the tobacco, and the cotton of these regions, to be purchased at
the strangest of bargains by customers in whose eyes each article has a price only in proportion to the desire it excites to possess it.

All at once this agitation, movement and noise stopped as though by magic. The balloon had just come in sight, far aloft in the sky, where it hovered majestically for a few moments, and then descended slowly, without deviating from its perpendicular. Men, women, children, merchants and slaves, Arabs and negroes, as suddenly disappeared within the "tembés" and the huts.

"My dear doctor," said Kennedy, "if we continue to produce such a sensation as this, we shall find some difficulty in establishing commercial relations with the people hereabouts."

"There's one kind of trade that we might carry on, though, easily enough," said Joe; "and that would be to go down there quietly, and walk off with the best of the goods, without troubling our heads about the merchants; we'd get rich that way!"

"Ah!" said the doctor, "these natives are a little scared at first; but they won't be long in coming back, either through suspicion or through curiosity."

"Do you really think so, doctor?"

"Well, we'll see pretty soon. But it wouldn't be prudent to go too near to them, for the balloon is not iron-clad, and is, therefore, not proof against either an arrow or a bullet."

"Then you expect to hold a parley with these blacks?"

"If we can do so safely, why should we not? There must be some Arab merchants here at Kazeh, who are better informed than the rest, and not so barbarous. I remember that Burton and Speke had nothing but praises to utter concerning the hospitality of these people; so we might, at least, make the venture."

The balloon having, meanwhile, gradually approached the ground, one of the anchors lodged in the top of a tree near the market-place.

By this time the whole population had emerged from their hiding-places stealthily, thrusting their heads out first. Several "waganga," recognizable by their badges of conical shellwork, came boldly forward. They were the sorcerers of the place. They bore in their girdles small gourds, coated with tallow, and several other articles of witchcraft, all of them, by the way, most professionally filthy.

Little by little the crowd gathered beside them, the women and children grouped around them, the drums renewed their deafening uproar, hands were violently clapped together, and then raised towards the sky.

"That's their style of praying," said the doctor; "and, if I'm not mistaken, we're going to be called upon to play a great part."

"Well, sir, play it!"

"You, too, my good Joe—perhaps you're to be a god!"

"Well, master, that won't trouble me much. I like a little flattery!"

At this moment, one of the sorcerers, a "myanga," made a sign, and all the clamor died away into the profoundest silence. He then addressed a few words to the strangers, but in an unknown tongue.

Dr. Ferguson, not having understood them, shouted some sentences in Arabic, at a venture, and was immediately answered in that language.

The speaker below then delivered himself of a very copious harangue, which was also very flowery and very gravely listened to by his audience. From it the doctor was not slow in learning that the balloon was mistaken for nothing less than the moon in person, and that the amiable goddess in question had condescended to approach the town with her three sons—an honour that would never be forgotten in this land so greatly loved by the god of day.

The doctor responded, with much dignity, that the moon made her provincial tour every thousand years, feeling the necessity of showing herself nearer at hand to her worshippers. He, therefore, begged them not to be disturbed by her presence, but to take advantage of it to make known all their wants and longings.

The sorcerer, in his turn, replied that the sultan, the "mwani," who had been sick for many years, implored the aid of heaven, and he invited the son of the moon to visit him.

The doctor acquainted his companions with the invitation.

"And you are going to call upon this negro king?" asked Kennedy.

"Undoubtedly so; these people appear well disposed; the air is calm; there is not a breath of wind, and we have nothing to fear for the balloon?"

"But, what will you do?"

"Be quiet on that score, my dear Dick. With a little medicine, I shall work my way through the affair!"

Then, addressing the crowd, he said:

"The moon, taking compassion on the sovereign who is so dear to the children of Unyamwezy, has charged us to restore him to health. Let him prepare to receive us!"

The clamor, the songs and demonstrations of all kinds increased twofold, and the whole immense ants' nest of black heads was again in motion.

"Now, my friends," said Dr. Ferguson, "we must look out for everything beforehand; we may be forced to leave this at any moment, unexpectedly, and be off with extra speed. Dick had better remain, therefore, in the car, and keep the cylinder warm so as to secure a sufficient ascensional force for the balloon. The anchor is solidly fastened, and there is nothing to fear in that respect. I shall descend, and Joe will go with me, only that he must remain at the foot of the ladder."

"What! are you going alone into that blackamoor's den?"

"How! doctor, am I not to go with you?"

"No! I shall go alone; these good folks imagine that the goddess of the moon has come to see them, and their superstition protects me; so have no fear, and each one remain at the post that I have assigned to him."

"Well, since you wish it," sighed Kennedy.

"Look closely to the dilation of the gas."

"Agreed!"

By this time the shouts of the natives had swelled to double volume as they vehemently implored the aid of the heavenly powers.

"There, there," said Joe, "they're rather rough in their orders to their good moon and her divine sons."

The doctor, equipped with his travelling medicine-chest, descended to the ground, preceded by Joe, who kept a straight countenance and looked as grave and knowing as the circumstances of the case required. He then seated himself at the foot of the ladder in the Arab fashion, with his legs crossed under him, and a portion of the crowd collected around him in a circle, at respectful distances.

In the meanwhile the doctor, escorted to the sound of savage instruments, and with wild religious dances, slowly proceeded towards the royal "tembé," situated a considerable distance outside of the town. It was about three o'clock, and the sun was shining brilliantly. In fact, what less could it do upon so grand an occasion!

The doctor stepped along with great dignity, the waganga surrounding him and keeping off the crowd. He was soon joined by the natural son of the sultan, a handsomely-built young fellow, who, according to the custom of the country, was the sole heir of the paternal goods, to the exclusion of the old man's legitimate children. He prostrated himself before the son of the moon, but the latter graciously raised him to his feet.

Three-quarters of an hour later, through shady paths, surrounded by all the luxuriance of tropical vegetation, this enthusiastic procession arrived at the sultan's palace, a sort of square edifice called *ititénya*, and situated on the slope of a hill.

A kind of veranda, formed by the thatched roof, adorned the outside, supported upon wooden pillars, which had some pretensions to being carved. Long lines of dark-red clay decorated the walls in characters that strove to reproduce the forms of men and serpents, the latter better imitated, of course, than the former. The roofing of this abode did not rest directly upon the walls, and the air could, therefore, circulate freely, but windows there were none, and the door hardly deserved the name.

Dr. Ferguson was received with all the honours by the guards and favourites of the sultan; these were men of a fine race, the Wanyamwezi so-called, a pure type of the central African populations, strong, robust, well made, and in splendid condition. Their hair, divided into a great number of small tresses, fell over their shoulders, and by means of black-and-blue incisions they had tattooed their cheeks from the temples to the mouth. Their ears, frightfully distended, held dangling to them disks of wood and plates of gum copal. They were clad in brilliantly-painted cloths, and the soldiers were armed with the saw-toothed war-club, the bow and arrows barbed and poisoned with the juice of the euphorbium, the cutlass, the "sima," a long sabre (also with saw-like teeth), and some small battle-axes.

The doctor advanced into the palace, and there, notwithstanding the sultan's illness, the din, which was terrific before, redoubled the instant that he arrived. He noticed, at the lintels of the door, some rabbits' tails and zebras' manes, suspended as talismans. He was received by the whole troop of his majesty's wives, to the harmonious accords of the "upatu," a sort of cymbal made of the bottom of a copper kettle, and to the uproar of the "kilindo," a drum five feet high, hollowed out from the trunk of a tree, and hammered by the ponderous, horny fists of two jet-black *virtuosi*.

Most of the women were rather good-looking, and they laughed and chattered merrily as they smoked their tobacco and "thang" in huge black pipes. They seemed to be well made, too, under the long robes that they wore gracefully flung about their persons, and carried a sort of "kilt" woven from the fibres of calabash fastened around their girdles.

Six of them were not the least merry of the party, although put aside from the rest, and reserved for a cruel fate. On the death of the sultan, they were to be buried alive with him, so as to occupy and divert his mind during the period of eternal solitude.

Dr. Ferguson, taking in the whole scene at a rapid glance, approached the wooden couch on which the sultan lay reclining. There he saw a man of about forty, completely brutalized by orgies of every description, and in a condition that left little or nothing to be done. The sickness that had afflicted him for so many years was simply perpetual drunkenness. The royal sot had nearly lost all consciousness, and all the ammonia in the world would not have set him on his feet again.

His favourites and the women kept on bended knees during this solemn visit. By means of a few drops of powerful cordial, the doctor for a moment reanimated the imbruted carcass that lay before him. The sultan stirred, and, for a dead body that had given no sign whatever of life for several hours previously, this symptom was received with a tremendous repetition of shouts and cries in the doctor's honour.

The latter, who had seen enough of it by this time, by a rapid motion put aside his too demonstrative admirers and went out of the palace, directing his steps immediately towards the balloon, for it was now six o'clock in the evening.

Joe, during his absence, had been quietly waiting at the foot of the ladder, where the crowd paid him their most humble respects. Like a genuine son of the moon, he let them keep on. For a divinity, he had the air of a very clever sort of fellow, by no means proud, nay, even pleasingly familiar with the young negresses, who seemed never to tire of looking at him. Besides, he went so far as to chat agreeably with them.

"Worship me, ladies! worship me!" he said to them. "I'm a clever sort of devil, if I am the son of a goddess."

They brought him propitiatory gifts, such as are usually deposited in the *fetich* huts or *mʒimu*. These gifts consisted of stalks of barley and of "pombé." Joe considered himself in duty bound to taste the latter species of strong beer, but his palate, although accustomed to gin and whisky, could not withstand the strength of the new beverage, and he had to make a horrible grimace, which his dusky friends took to be a benevolent smile.

Thereupon, the young damsels, conjoining their voices in a drawling chant, began to dance around him with the utmost gravity.

"Ah! you're dancing, are you?" said he. "Well, I won't be behind you in politeness, and so I'll give you one of my country reels."

So at it he went, in one of the wildest jigs that ever was seen, twisting, turning, and jerking himself in all directions; dancing with his hands, dancing with his body, dancing with his knees, dancing with his feet; describing the most fearful contortions and extravagant evolutions; throwing himself into incredible attitudes; grimacing beyond all belief, and, in fine, giving his savage admirers a strange idea of the style of ballet adopted by the deities in the moon.

Then, the whole collection of blacks, naturally as imitative as monkeys, at once reproduced all his airs and graces, his leaps and shakes and contortions; they did not lose a single gesticulation; they did not forget an attitude; and the result was, such a pandemonium of movement, noise, and excitement, as it would be out of the question even feebly to describe. But, in the very midst of the fun, Joe saw the doctor approaching.

The latter was coming at full speed, surrounded by a yelling and disorderly throng. The chiefs and sorcerers seemed to be highly excited. They were close upon the doctor's heels, crowding and threatening him.

Singular reaction! What had happened? Had the sultan unluckily perished in the hands of his celestial physician?

Kennedy, from his post of observation, saw the danger without knowing what had caused it, and the balloon, powerfully urged by the dilation of the gas, strained and tugged at the ropes that held it as though impatient to soar away.

The doctor had got as far as the foot of the ladder. A superstitious fear still held the crowd aloof and hindered them from committing any violence on his person. He rapidly scaled the ladder, and Joe followed him with his usual agility.

"Not a moment to lose!" said the doctor. "Don't attempt to let go the anchor! We'll cut the cord! Follow me!"

"But what's the matter?" asked Joe, clambering into the car.

"What's happened?" questioned Kennedy, rifle in hand.

"Look!" replied the doctor, pointing to the horizon.

"Well?" ejaculated the Scot.

"Well! the moon!"

And, in fact, there was the moon rising red and magnificent, a globe of fire in a field of blue! It was she, indeed—she and the balloon!—both in one sky!

Either there were two moons, then, or these strangers were imposters, designing scamps, false deities!

Such were the very natural reflections of the crowd, and hence the reaction in their feelings.

Joe could not, for the life of him, keep in a roar of laughter; and the population of Kazeh, comprehending that their prey was slipping through their clutches, set up prolonged howlings, aiming, the while, their bows and muskets at the balloon.

But one of the sorcerers made a sign, and all the weapons were lowered. He then began to climb into the tree, intending to seize the rope and bring the machine to the ground.

Joe leaned out with a hatchet ready. "Shall I cut away?" said he.

"No; wait a moment," replied the doctor.

"But this black?"

"We may, perhaps, save our anchor—and I hold a great deal by that. There'll always be time enough to cut loose."

The sorcerer, having climbed to the right place, worked so vigourously that he succeeded in detaching the anchor, and the latter, violently jerked, at that moment, by the start of the balloon, caught the rascal between the limbs, and carried him off astride of it through the air.

The stupefaction of the crowd was indescribable as they saw one of their waganga thus whirled away into space.

"Huzza!" roared Joe, as the balloon—thanks to its ascensional force—shot up higher into the sky, with increased rapidity.

"He holds on well," said Kennedy; "a little trip will do him good."

"Shall we let this darky drop all at once?" enquired Joe.

"Oh no," replied the doctor, "we'll let him down easily; and I warrant me that, after such an adventure, the power of the wizard will be enormously enhanced in the sight of his comrades."

"Why, I wouldn't put it past them to make a god of him!" said Joe, with a laugh.

The *Victoria*, by this time, had risen to the height of one thousand feet, and the black hung to the rope with desperate energy. He had become completely silent, and his eyes were fixed, for his terror was blended with amazement. A light west wind was sweeping the balloon right over the town, and far beyond it.

Half-an-hour later, the doctor, seeing the country deserted, moderated the flame of his cylinder, and descended towards the ground. At twenty feet above the turf, the affrighted sorcerer made up his mind in a twinkling: he let himself drop, fell on his feet, and scampered off at a furious pace towards Kazeh; while the balloon, suddenly relieved of his weight, again shot up on her course.

Chapter XVI

SYMPTOMS OF A STORM—THE COUNTRY OF THE MOON—
THE FUTURE OF THE AFRICAN CONTINENT—THE LAST MACHINE
OF ALL—A VIEW OF THE COUNTRY AT SUNSET—
FLORA AND FAUNA—THE TEMPEST—THE ZONE OF FIRE—
THE STARRY HEAVENS

SEE," SAID JOE, "WHAT COMES OF PLAYING THE SONS OF THE MOON WITHOUT HER LEAVE! She came near serving us an ugly trick. But say, master, did you damage your credit as a physician?"

"Yes, indeed," chimed in the sportsman. "What kind of a dignitary was this Sultan of Kazeh?"

"An old half-dead sot," replied the doctor, "whose loss will not be very severely felt. But the moral of all this is that honours are fleeting, and we must not take too great a fancy to them."

"So much the worse!" rejoined Joe. "I liked the thing—to be worshipped!—Play the god as you like! Why, what would anyone ask more than that? By the way, the moon did come up, too, and all red, as if she was in a rage."

While the three friends went on chatting of this and other things, and Joe examined the luminary of night from an entirely novel point of view, the heavens became covered with heavy clouds to the northward, and the lowering masses assumed a most sinister and threatening look. Quite a smart breeze, found about three hundred feet from the earth, drove the balloon towards the north-northeast; and above it the blue vault was clear; but the atmosphere felt close and dull.

The aeronauts found themselves, at about eight in the evening, in thirty-two degrees forty minutes east longitude, and four degrees seventeen minutes latitude. The atmospheric currents, under the influence of a tempest not far off, were driving them at the rate of from thirty to thirty-five miles an hour; the undulating and fertile plains of Mfuto were passing swiftly beneath them. The spectacle was one worthy of admiration—and admire it they did.

"We are now right in the country of the Moon," said Dr. Ferguson; "for it has retained the name that antiquity gave it, undoubtedly, because the moon has been worshipped there in all ages. It is, really, a superb country."

"It would be hard to find more splendid vegetation."

"If we found the like of it around London it would not be natural, but it would be very pleasant," put in Joe. "Why is it that such savage countries get all these fine things?"

"And who knows," said the doctor, "that this country may not, one day, become the centre of civilisation? The races of the future may repair hither, when Europe shall have become exhausted in the effort to feed her inhabitants."

"Do you think so, really?" asked Kennedy.

"Undoubtedly, my dear Dick. Just note the progress of events: consider the migrations of races, and you will arrive at the same conclusion assuredly. Asia was the first nurse of the world, was she not? For about four thousand years she travailed, she grew pregnant, she produced, and then, when stones began to cover the soil where the golden harvests sung by Homer had flourished, her children abandoned her exhausted and barren bosom. You next see them precipitating themselves upon young and vigourous Europe, which has nourished them for the last two thousand years. But already her fertility is beginning to die out; her productive powers are diminishing everyday. Those new diseases that annually attack the products of the soil, those defective crops, those insufficient resources, are all signs of a vitality that is rapidly wearing out and of an approaching exhaustion. Thus, we already see the millions rushing to the luxuriant bosom of America, as a source of help, not inexhaustible indeed, but not yet exhausted. In its turn, that new continent will grow old; its virgin forests will fall before the axe of industry, and its soil will become weak through having too fully produced what had been demanded of it. Where two harvests bloomed every year, hardly one will be gathered from a soil completely drained of its strength. Then, Africa will be there to offer to new races the treasures that for centuries have been accumulating in her breast. Those climates now so fatal to strangers will be purified by cultivation and by drainage of the soil, and those scattered water supplies will be gathered into one common bed to form an artery of navigation. Then this country over which we are now passing, more fertile, richer, and fuller of vitality than the rest, will become some grand realm where more astonishing discoveries than steam and electricity will be brought to light."

"Ah! sir," said Joe, "I'd like to see all that."

"You got up too early in the morning, my boy!"

"Besides," said Kennedy, "that may prove to be a very dull period when industry will swallow up everything for its own profit. By dint of inventing machinery, men will end in being eaten up by it! I have always fancied that the end of the earth will be when some enormous boiler, heated to three thousand millions of atmospheric pressure, shall explode and blow up our Globe!"

"And I add that the Americans," said Joe, "will not have been the last to work at the machine!"

"In fact," assented the doctor, "they are great boiler-makers! But, without allowing ourselves to be carried away by such speculations, let us rest content with enjoying the beauties of this country of the Moon, since we have been permitted to see it."

The sun, darting his last rays beneath the masses of heaped-up cloud, adorned with a crest of gold the slightest inequalities of the ground below; gigantic trees, arborescent bushes, mosses on the even surface—all had their share of this luminous effulgence. The soil, slightly undulating, here and there rose into little conical hills; there were no mountains visible on the horizon; immense brambly palisades, impenetrable hedges of thorny jungle, separated the clearings dotted with numerous villages, and immense euphorbiae surrounded them with natural fortifications, interlacing their trunks with the coral-shaped branches of the shrubbery and undergrowth.

Ere long, the Malagazeri, the chief tributary of Lake Tanganayika, was seen winding between heavy thickets of verdure, offering an asylum to many water-courses that spring from the torrents formed in the season of freshets, or from ponds hollowed in the clayey soil. To observers looking from a height, it was a chain of waterfalls thrown across the whole western face of the country.

Animals with huge humps were feeding in the luxuriant prairies, and were half hidden, sometimes, in the tall grass; spreading forests in bloom redolent of spicy perfumes presented themselves to the gaze like immense bouquets; but, in these bouquets, lions, leopards, hyenas, and tigers, were then crouching for shelter from the last hot rays of the setting sun. From time to time, an elephant made the tall tops of the undergrowth sway to and fro, and you could hear the crackling of huge branches as his ponderous ivory tusks broke them in his way.

"What a sporting country!" exclaimed Dick, unable longer to restrain his enthusiasm; "why, a single ball fired at random into those forests would bring down game worthy of it. Suppose we try it once!"

"No, my dear Dick; the night is close at hand—a threatening night with a tempest in the background—and the storms are awful in this country, where the heated soil is like one vast electric battery."

"You are right, sir," said Joe, "the heat has got to be enough to choke one, and the breeze has died away. One can feel that something's coming."

"The atmosphere is saturated with electricity," replied the doctor; "every living creature is sensible that this state of the air portends a struggle of the elements, and I confess that I never before was so full of the fluid myself."

"Well, then," suggested Dick, "would it not be advisable to alight?"

"On the contrary, Dick, I'd rather go up, only that I am afraid of being carried out of my course by these counter-currents contending in the atmosphere."

"Have you any idea, then, of abandoning the route that we have followed since we left the coast?"

"If I can manage to do so," replied the doctor, "I will turn more directly northward, by from seven to eight degrees; I shall then endeavour to ascend towards the presumed latitudes of the sources of the Nile; perhaps we may discover some traces of Captain Speke's expedition or of M. de Heuglin's caravan. Unless I am mistaken, we are at thirty-two degrees forty minutes east longitude, and I should like to ascend directly north of the equator."

"Look there!" exclaimed Kennedy, suddenly, "see those hippopotami sliding out of the pools—those masses of blood-coloured flesh—and those crocodiles snuffing the air aloud!"

"They're choking!" ejaculated Joe. "Ah! what a fine way to travel this is; and how one can snap his fingers at all that vermin!—Doctor! Mr. Kennedy! see those packs of wild animals hurrying along close together. There are fully two hundred. Those are wolves."

"No! Joe, not wolves, but wild dogs; a famous breed that does not hesitate to attack the lion himself. They are the worst customers a traveller could meet, for they would instantly tear him to pieces."

"Well, it isn't Joe that'll undertake to muzzle them!" responded that amiable youth. "After all, though, if that's the nature of the beast, we mustn't be too hard on them for it!"

Silence gradually settled down under the influence of the impending storm: the thickened air actually seemed no longer adapted to the transmission of sound; the atmosphere appeared *muffled*, and, like a room hung with tapestry, lost all its sonorous reverberation. The "rover bird" so-called, the coroneted crane, the red and blue jays, the mocking-bird, the flycatcher, disappeared among the foliage of the immense trees, and all nature revealed symptoms of some approaching catastrophe.

At nine o'clock the *Victoria* hung motionless over Mséné, an extensive group of villages scarcely distinguishable in the gloom. Once in a while, the reflection of a wandering ray of light in the dull water disclosed a succession of ditches regularly arranged, and, by one last gleam, the eye could make out the calm and sombre forms of palm-trees, sycamores, and gigantic euphorbiae.

"I am stifling!" said the Scot, inhaling, with all the power of his lungs, as much as possible of the rarefied air. "We are not moving an inch! Let us descend!"

"But the tempest!" said the doctor, with much uneasiness.

"If you are afraid of being carried away by the wind, it seems to me that there is no other course to pursue."

"Perhaps the storm won't burst to-night," said Joe; "the clouds are very high."

"That is just the thing that makes me hesitate about going beyond them; we should have to rise still higher, lose sight of the earth, and not know all night whether we were moving forward or not, or in what direction we were going."

"Make up your mind, dear doctor, for time presses!"

"It's a pity that the wind has fallen," said Joe, again; "it would have carried us clear of the storm."

"It is, indeed, a pity, my friends," rejoined the doctor. "The clouds are dangerous for us; they contain opposing currents which might catch us in their eddies, and lightnings that might set on fire. Again, those perils avoided, the force of the tempest might hurl us to the ground, were we to cast our anchor in the tree-tops."

"Then what shall we do?"

"Well, we must try to get the balloon into a medium zone of the atmosphere, and there keep her suspended between the perils of the heavens and those of the earth. We have enough water for the cylinder, and our two hundred pounds of ballast are untouched. In case of emergency I can use them."

"We will keep watch with you," said the hunter.

"No, my friends, put the provisions under shelter, and lie down; I will rouse you, if it becomes necessary."

"But, master, wouldn't you do well to take some rest yourself, as there's no danger close on us just now?" insisted poor Joe.

"No, thank you, my good fellow, I prefer to keep awake. We are not moving, and should circumstances not change, we'll find ourselves to-morrow in exactly the same place."

"Good-night, then, sir!"

"Good-night, if you can only find it so!"

Kennedy and Joe stretched themselves out under their blankets, and the doctor remained alone in the immensity of space.

However, the huge dome of clouds visibly descended, and the darkness became profound. The black vault closed in upon the earth as if to crush it in its embrace.

All at once a violent, rapid, incisive flash of lightning pierced the gloom, and the rent it made had not closed ere a frightful clap of thunder shook the celestial depths.

"Up! up! turn out!" shouted Ferguson.

The two sleepers, aroused by the terrible concussion, were at the doctor's orders in a moment.

"Shall we descend?" said Kennedy.

"No! the balloon could not stand it. Let us go up before those clouds dissolve in water, and the wind is let loose!" and, so saying, the doctor actively stirred up the flame of the cylinder, and turned it on the spirals of the serpentine siphon.

The tempests of the tropics develop with a rapidity equalled only by their violence. A second flash of lightning rent the darkness, and was followed by a score of others in quick succession. The sky was crossed and dotted, like the zebra's hide, with electric sparks, which danced and flickered beneath the great drops of rain.

"We have delayed too long," exclaimed the doctor; "we must now pass through a zone of fire, with our balloon filled as it is with inflammable gas!"

"But let us descend, then! let us descend!" urged Kennedy.

"The risk of being struck would be just about even, and we should soon be torn to pieces by the branches of the trees!"

"We are going up, doctor!"

"Quicker, quicker still!"

In this part of Africa, during the equatorial storms, it is not rare to count from thirty to thirty-five flashes of lightning per minute. The sky is literally on fire, and the crashes of thunder are continuous.

The wind burst forth with frightful violence in this burning atmosphere; it twisted the blazing clouds; one might have compared it to the breath of some gigantic bellows, fanning all this conflagration.

Dr. Ferguson kept his cylinder at full heat, and the balloon dilated and went up, while Kennedy, on his knees, held together the curtains of the awning. The balloon whirled round wildly enough to make their heads turn, and the aeronauts got some very alarming jolts, indeed, as their machine swung and swayed in all directions. Huge cavities would form in the silk of the balloon as the wind fiercely bent it in, and the stuff fairly cracked like a pistol as it flew back from the pressure. A sort of hail, preceded by a rumbling noise, hissed through the air and rattled on the covering of the *Victoria*. The latter, however, continued to ascend, while the lightning described tangents to the convexity of her circumference; but she bore on, right through the midst of the fire.

"God protect us!" said Dr. Ferguson, solemnly, "we are in His hands; He alone can save us—but let us be ready for every event, even for fire—our fall could not be very rapid."

The doctor's voice could scarcely be heard by his companions; but they could see his countenance calm as ever even amid the flashing of the lightnings; he was watching the phenomena of phosphorescence produced by the fires of St. Elmo, that were now skipping to and fro along the network of the balloon.

The latter whirled and swung, but steadily ascended, and, ere the hour was over, it had passed the stormy belt. The electric display was going on below it like a vast crown of artificial fireworks suspended from the car.

Then they enjoyed one of the grandest spectacles that Nature can offer to the gaze of man. Below them, the tempest; above them, the starry firmament, tranquil, mute, impassible, with the moon projecting her peaceful rays over these angry clouds.

Dr. Ferguson consulted the barometer; it announced twelve thousand feet of elevation. It was then eleven o'clock at night.

"Thank Heaven, all danger is past; all we have to do now, is, to keep ourselves at this height," said the doctor.

"It was frightful!" remarked Kennedy.

"Oh!" said Joe, "it gives a little variety to the trip, and I'm not sorry to have seen a storm from a trifling distance up in the air. It's a fine sight!"

Chapter XVII

THE MOUNTAINS OF THE MOON—AN OCEAN OF VERDURE—
THEY CAST ANCHOR—THE TOWING ELEPHANT—A RUNNING
FIRE—DEATH OF THE MONSTER—THE FIELD-OVEN—
A MEAL ON THE GRASS—A NIGHT ON THE GROUND

ABOUT FOUR IN THE MORNING, MONDAY, THE SUN REAPPEARED IN THE HORIZON; THE clouds had dispersed, and a cheery breeze refreshed the morning dawn.

The earth, all redolent with fragrant exhalations, reappeared to the gaze of our travellers. The balloon, whirled about by opposing currents, had hardly budged from its place, and the doctor, letting the gas contract, descended so as to get a more northerly direction. For a long while his quest was fruitless; the wind carried him towards the west until he came in sight of the famous Mountains of the Moon, which grouped themselves in a semicircle around the extremity of Lake Tanganayika; their ridges, but slightly indented, stood out against the bluish horizon, so that they might have been mistaken for a natural fortification, not to be passed by the explorers of the centre of Africa. Among them were a few isolated cones, revealing the mark of the eternal snows.

"Here we are at last," said the doctor, "in an unexplored country! Captain Burton pushed very far to the westward, but he could not reach those celebrated mountains; he even denied their existence, strongly as it was affirmed by Speke, his companion. He pretended that they were born in the latter's fancy; but for us, my friends, there is no further doubt possible."

"Shall we cross them?" asked Kennedy.

"Not, if it please God. I am looking for a wind that will take me back towards the equator. I will even wait for one, if necessary, and will make the balloon like a ship that casts anchor, until favourable breezes come up."

But the foresight of the doctor was not long in bringing its reward; for, after having tried different heights, the *Victoria* at length began to sail off to the north-eastward with medium speed.

"We are in the right track," said the doctor, consulting his compass, "and scarcely two hundred feet from the surface; lucky circumstances for us, enabling us, as they do, to reconnoitre these new regions. When Captain Speke set out to discover Lake Ukéréoué, he ascended more to the eastward in a straight line above Kazeh."

"Shall we keep on long in this way?" enquired the Scot.

"Perhaps. Our object is to push a point in the direction of the sources of the Nile; and we have more than six hundred miles to make before we get to the extreme limit reached by the explorers who came from the north."

"And we shan't set foot on the solid ground?" murmured Joe; "it's enough to cramp a fellow's legs!"

"Oh, yes, indeed, my good Joe," said the doctor, reassuring him; "we have to economise our provisions, you know; and on the way, Dick, you must get us some fresh meat."

"Whenever you like, doctor."

"We shall also have to replenish our stock of water. Who knows but we may be carried to some of the dried-up regions? So we cannot take too many precautions."

At noon the *Victoria* was at twenty-nine degrees fifteen minutes east longitude, and three degrees fifteen minutes south latitude. She passed the village of Uyofu, the last northern limit of the Unyamwezi, opposite to the Lake Ukéréoué, which could still be seen.

The tribes living near to the equator seem to be a little more civilised, and are governed by absolute monarchs, whose control is an unlimited despotism. Their most compact union of power constitutes the province of Karagwah.

It was decided by the aeronauts that they would alight at the first favourable place. They found that they should have to make a prolonged halt, and take a careful inspection of the balloon: so the flame of the cylinder was moderated, and the anchors, flung out from the car, ere long began to sweep the grass of an immense prairie, that, from a certain height, looked like a shaven lawn, but the growth of which, in reality, was from seven to eight feet in height.

The balloon skimmed this tall grass without bending it, like a gigantic butterfly: not an obstacle was in sight; it was an ocean of verdure without a single breaker.

"We might proceed a long time in this style," remarked Kennedy; "I don't see one tree that we could approach, and I'm afraid that our hunt's over."

"Wait, Dick; you could not hunt anyhow in this grass, that grows higher than your head. We'll find a favourable place presently."

In truth, it was a charming excursion that they were making now—a veritable navigation on this green, almost transparent sea, gently undulating in the breath of the wind. The little car seemed to cleave the waves of verdure, and, from time to time, coveys of birds of magnificent plumage would rise fluttering from the tall herbage, and speed away with joyous cries. The anchors plunged into this lake of flowers, and traced a furrow that closed behind them, like the wake of a ship.

All at once a sharp shock was felt—the anchor had caught in the fissure of some rock hidden in the high grass.

"We are fast!" exclaimed Joe.

These words had scarcely been uttered when a shrill cry rang through the air, and the following phrases, mingled with exclamations, escaped from the lips of our travellers:

"What's that?"

"A strange cry!"

"Look! Why, we're moving!"

"The anchor has slipped!"

"No; it holds, and holds fast too!" said Joe, who was tugging at the rope.

"It's the rock, then, that's moving!"

An immense rustling was noticed in the grass, and soon an elongated, winding shape was seen rising above it.

"A serpent!" shouted Joe.

"A serpent!" repeated Kennedy, handling his rifle.

"No," said the doctor, "it's an elephant's trunk!"

"An elephant, Samuel?"

And, as Kennedy said this, he drew his rifle to his shoulder.

"Wait, Dick; wait!"

"That's a fact! The animal's towing us!"

"And in the right direction, Joe—in the right direction."

The elephant was now making some headway, and soon reached a clearing where his whole body could be seen. By his gigantic size, the doctor recognised a male of a superb species. He had two whitish tusks, beautifully curved, and about eight feet in length; and in these the shanks of the anchor had firmly caught. The animal was vainly trying with his trunk to disengage himself from the rope that attached him to the car.

"Get up—go ahead, old fellow!" shouted Joe, with delight, doing his best to urge this rather novel team. "Here is a new style of travelling!—no more horses for me. An elephant, if you please!"

"But where is he taking us to?" said Kennedy, whose rifle itched in his grasp.

"He's taking us exactly to where we want to go, my dear Dick. A little patience!"

" 'Wig-a-more! wig-a-more!' as the Scotch country folks say," shouted Joe, in high glee. "Gee-up! gee-up there!"

The huge animal now broke into a very rapid gallop. He flung his trunk from side to side, and his monstrous bounds gave the car several rather heavy thumps. Meanwhile the doctor stood ready, hatchet in hand, to cut the rope, should need arise.

"But," said he, "we shall not give up our anchor until the last moment."

This drive, with an elephant for the team, lasted about an hour and a half; yet the animal did not seem in the least fatigued. These immense creatures can go over a great deal of ground, and, from one day to another, are found at enormous distances from where they were last seen, like the whales, whose mass and speed they rival.

"In fact," said Joe, "it's a whale that we have harpooned; and we're only doing just what whalemen do when out fishing."

But a change in the nature of the ground compelled the doctor to vary his style of locomotion. A dense grove of *calmadores* was descried on the horizon, about three miles away, on the north of the prairie. So it became necessary to detach the balloon from its draught-animal at last.

Kennedy was entrusted with the job of bringing the elephant to a halt. He drew his rifle to his shoulder, but his position was not favourable to a successful shot; so that the first ball fired flattened itself on the animal's skull, as it would have done against an iron plate. The creature did not seem in the least troubled by it; but, at the sound of the discharge, he had increased his speed, and now was going as fast as a horse at full gallop.

"The deuce!" ejaculated Kennedy.

"What a solid head!" commented Joe.

"We'll try some conical balls behind the shoulder-joint," said Kennedy, reloading his rifle with care. In another moment he fired.

The animal gave a terrible cry, but went on faster than ever.

"Come!" said Joe, taking aim with another gun, "I must help you, or we'll never end it." And now two balls penetrated the creature's side.

The elephant halted, lifted his trunk, and resumed his run towards the wood with all his speed; he shook his huge head, and the blood began to gush from his wounds.

"Let us keep up our fire, Mr. Kennedy."

"And a continuous fire, too," urged the doctor, "for we are close on the woods."

Ten shots more were discharged. The elephant made a fearful bound; the car and balloon cracked as though everything were going to pieces, and the shock made the doctor drop his hatchet on the ground.

The situation was thus rendered really very alarming; the anchor-rope, which had securely caught, could not be disengaged, nor could it yet be cut by the knives of our aeronauts, and the balloon was rushing headlong towards the wood, when the animal received a ball in the eye just as he lifted his head. On this he halted, faltered, his knees bent under him, and he uncovered his whole flank to the assaults of his enemies in the balloon.

"A bullet in his heart!" said Kennedy, discharging one last rifle-shot.

The elephant uttered a long bellow of terror and agony, then raised himself up for a moment, twirling his trunk in the air, and finally fell with all his weight upon one of his tusks, which he broke off short. He was dead.

"His tusk's broken!" exclaimed Kennedy—"ivory too that in England would bring thirty-five guineas per hundred pounds."

"As much as that?" said Joe, scrambling down to the ground by the anchor-rope.

"What's the use of sighing over it, Dick?" said the doctor. "Are we ivory merchants? Did we come hither to make money?"

Joe examined the anchor and found it solidly attached to the unbroken tusk. The doctor and Dick leaped out on the ground, while the balloon, now half emptied, hovered over the body of the huge animal.

"What a splendid beast!" said Kennedy, "what a mass of flesh! I never saw an elephant of that size in India!"

"There's nothing surprising about that, my dear Dick; the elephants of Central Africa are the finest in the world. The Andersons and the Cummings have hunted so incessantly in the neighbourhood of the Cape, that these animals have migrated to the equator, where they are often met with in large herds."

"In the meanwhile, I hope," added Joe, "that we'll taste a morsel of this fellow. I'll undertake to get you a good dinner at his expense. Mr. Kennedy will go off and hunt for an hour or two; the doctor will make an inspection of the balloon, and, while they're busy in that way, I'll do the cooking."

"A good arrangement!" said the doctor; "so do as you like, Joe."

"As for me," said the hunter, "I shall avail myself of the two hours' recess that Joe has condescended to let me have."

"Go, my friend, but no imprudence! Don't wander too far away."

"Never fear, doctor!" and, so saying, Dick, shouldering his gun, plunged into the woods.

Forthwith Joe went to work at his vocation. At first he made a hole in the ground two feet deep; this he filled with the dry wood that was so abundantly scattered about, where it had been strewn by the elephants, whose tracks could be seen where they had made their way through the forest. This hole filled, he heaped a pile of fagots on it a foot in height, and set fire to it.

Then he went back to the carcass of the elephant, which had fallen only about a hundred feet from the edge of the forest; he next proceeded adroitly to cut off the trunk, which might have been two feet in diameter at the base; of this he selected the most delicate portion, and then took with it one of the animal's spongy feet. In fact, these are the finest morsels, like the hump of the bison, the paws of the bear, and the head of the wild boar.

When the pile of fagots had been thoroughly consumed, inside and outside, the hole, cleared of the cinders and hot coals, retained a very high temperature. The pieces of elephant-meat, surrounded with aromatic leaves, were placed in this extempore oven and covered with hot coals. Then Joe piled up a second heap of sticks over all, and when it had burned out the meat was cooked to a turn.

Then Joe took the viands from the oven, spread the savory mess upon green leaves, and arranged his dinner upon a magnificent patch of greensward. He finally brought out some biscuit, some coffee, and some cognac, and got a can of pure, fresh water from a neighbouring streamlet.

The repast thus prepared was a pleasant sight to behold, and Joe, without being too proud, thought that it would also be pleasant to eat.

"A journey without danger or fatigue," he soliloquized; "your meals when you please; a swinging hammock all the time! What more could a man ask? And there was Kennedy, who didn't want to come!"

On his part, Dr. Ferguson was engrossed in a serious and thorough examination of the balloon. The latter did not appear to have suffered from the storm; the silk and the gutta percha had resisted wonderfully, and, upon estimating the exact height of the ground and the ascensional force of the balloon, our aeronaut saw, with satisfaction, that the hydrogen was in exactly the same quantity as before. The covering had remained completely water-proof.

It was now only five days since our travellers had quitted Zanzibar; their *pemmican* had not yet been touched; their stock of biscuit and potted meat was enough for a long trip, and there was nothing to be replenished but the water.

The pipes and spiral seemed to be in perfect condition, since, thanks to their india-rubber jointings, they had yielded to all the oscillations of the balloon. His examination ended, the doctor betook himself to setting his notes in order. He made a very accurate sketch of the surrounding landscape, with its long prairie stretching away out of sight, the forest of *calmadores*, and the balloon resting motionless over the body of the dead elephant.

At the end of his two hours, Kennedy returned with a string of fat partridges and the haunch of an *oryx*, a sort of *gemsbok* belonging to the most agile species of antelopes. Joe took upon himself to prepare this surplus stock of provisions for a later repast.

"But, dinner's ready!" he shouted in his most musical voice.

And the three travellers had only to sit down on the green turf. The trunk and feet of the elephant were declared to be exquisite. Old England was toasted, as usual, and delicious Havanas perfumed this charming country for the first time.

Kennedy ate, drank, and chatted, like four; he was perfectly delighted with his new life, and seriously proposed to the doctor to settle in this forest, to construct a cabin of boughs and foliage, and, there and then, to lay the foundation of a Robinson Crusoe dynasty in Africa.

The proposition went no further, although Joe had, at once, selected the part of Man Friday for himself.

The country seemed so quiet, so deserted, that the doctor resolved to pass the night on the ground, and Joe arranged a circle of watch-fires as an indispensable barrier against wild animals, for the hyenas, cougars, and jackals, attracted by the smell of the dead elephant, were prowling about in the neighbourhood. Kennedy had to fire his rifle several times at these unceremonious visitors, but the night passed without any untoward occurrence.

Chapter XVIII

THE KARAGWAH—LAKE UKÉRÉOUÉ—A NIGHT ON AN ISLAND—
THE EQUATOR—CROSSING THE LAKE—THE CASCADES—
A VIEW OF THE COUNTRY—THE SOURCES OF THE NILE—
THE ISLAND OF BENGA—THE SIGNATURE OF ANDREA DEBONO—
THE FLAG WITH THE ARMS OF ENGLAND

AT FIVE O'CLOCK IN THE MORNING, PREPARATIONS FOR DEPARTURE COMMENCED. JOE, with the hatchet which he had fortunately recovered, broke the elephant's tusks. The balloon, restored to liberty, sped away to the north-west with our travellers, at the rate of eighteen miles per hour.

The doctor had carefully taken his position by the altitude of the stars, during the preceding night. He knew that he was in latitude two degrees forty minutes below the equator, or at a distance of one hundred and sixty geographical miles. He swept along over many villages without heeding the cries that the appearance of the balloon excited; he took note of the conformation of places with quick sights; he passed the slopes of the Rubemhe, which are nearly as abrupt as the summits of the Ousagara, and, farther on, at Tenga, encountered the first projections of the Karagwah chains, which, in his opinion, are direct spurs of the Mountains of the Moon. So, the ancient legend which made these mountains the cradle of the Nile, came near to the truth, since they really border upon Lake Ukéréoué, the conjectured reservoir of the waters of the great river.

From Kafuro, the main district of the merchants of that country, he descried, at length, on the horizon, the lake so much desired and so long sought for, of which Captain Speke caught a glimpse on the 3d of August, 1858.

Samuel Ferguson felt real emotion: he was almost in contact with one of the principal points of his expedition, and, with his spy-glass constantly raised, he kept every nook and corner of the mysterious region in sight. His gaze wandered over details that might have been thus described:

"Beneath him extended a country generally destitute of cultivation; only here and there some ravines seemed under tillage; the surface, dotted with peaks of medium height, grew flat as it approached the lake; barley-fields took the place of rice-plantations, and there, too, could be seen growing the species of plantain from which the wine of the country is drawn, and *mwani*, the wild plant which supplies a substitute for coffee. A collection of some fifty or more circular huts, covered with a flowering thatch, constituted the capital of the Karagwah country."

He could easily distinguish the astonished countenances of a rather fine-looking race of natives of yellowish-brown complexion. Women of incredible corpulence were dawdling about through the cultivated grounds, and the doctor greatly surprised his companions by informing them that this rotundity, which is highly esteemed in that region, was obtained by an obligatory diet of curdled milk.

At noon, the *Victoria* was in one degree forty-five minutes south latitude, and at one o'clock the wind was driving her directly towards the lake.

This sheet of water was christened *Uyanza Victoria*, or Victoria Lake, by Captain Speke. At the place now mentioned it might measure about ninety miles in breadth, and at its southern extremity the captain found a group of islets, which he named the Archipelago of Bengal. He pushed his survey as far as Muanza, on the eastern coast, where he was received by the sultan. He made a triangulation of this part of the lake, but he could not procure a boat, either to cross it or to visit the great island of Ukéréoué, which is very populous, is governed by three sultans, and appears to be only a promontory at low tide.

The balloon approached the lake more to the northward, to the doctor's great regret, for it had been his wish to determine its lower outlines. Its shores seemed to be thickly set with brambles and thorny plants, growing together in wild confusion, and were literally hidden, sometimes, from the gaze, by myriads of mosquitoes of a light-brown hue. The country was evidently habitable and inhabited. Troops of hippopotami could be seen disporting themselves in the forests of reeds, or plunging beneath the whitish waters of the lake.

The latter, seen from above, presented, towards the west, so broad an horizon that it might have been called a sea; the distance between the two shores is so great that communication cannot be established, and storms are frequent and violent, for the winds sweep with fury over this elevated and unsheltered basin.

The doctor experienced some difficulty in guiding his course; he was afraid of being carried towards the east, but, fortunately, a current bore him directly towards the north, and at six o'clock in the evening the balloon alighted on a small desert island in thirty minutes south latitude, and thirty-two degrees fifty-two minutes east longitude, about twenty miles from the shore.

The travellers succeeded in making fast to a tree, and, the wind having fallen calm towards evening, they remained quietly at anchor. They dared not dream of taking the ground, since here, as on the shores of the Uyanza, legions of mosquitoes covered the soil in dense clouds. Joe even came back, from securing the anchor in the tree, speckled with bites, but he kept his temper, because he found it quite the natural thing for mosquitoes to treat him as they had done.

Nevertheless, the doctor, who was less of an optimist, let out as much rope as he could, so as to escape these pitiless insects, that began to rise towards him with a threatening hum.

The doctor ascertained the height of the lake above the level of the sea, as it had been determined by Captain Speke, say three thousand seven hundred and fifty feet.

"Here we are, then, on an island!" said Joe, scratching as though he'd tear his nails out.

"We could make the tour of it in a jiffy," added Kennedy, "and, excepting these confounded mosquitoes, there's not a living being to be seen on it."

"The islands with which the lake is dotted," replied the doctor, "are nothing, after all, but the tops of submerged hills; but we are lucky to have found a retreat among them, for the shores of the lake are inhabited by ferocious tribes. Take your sleep, then, since Providence has granted us a tranquil night."

"Won't you do the same, doctor?"

"No, I could not close my eyes. My thoughts would banish sleep. To-morrow, my friends, should the wind prove favourable, we shall go due north, and we shall, perhaps, discover the sources of the Nile, that grand secret which has so long remained impenetrable. Near as we are to the sources of the renowned river, I could not sleep."

Kennedy and Joe, whom scientific speculations failed to disturb to that extent, were not long in falling into sound slumber, while the doctor held his post.

On Wednesday, April 23d, the balloon started at four o'clock in the morning, with a greyish sky overhead; night was slow in quitting the surface of the lake, which was enveloped in a dense fog, but presently a violent breeze scattered all the mists, and, after the balloon had been swung to and fro for a moment, in opposite directions, it at length veered in a straight line towards the north.

Dr. Ferguson fairly clapped his hands for joy.

"We are on the right track!" he exclaimed. "To-day or never we shall see the Nile! Look, my friends, we are crossing the equator! We are entering our own hemisphere!"

"Ah!" said Joe, "do you think, doctor, that the equator passes here?"

"Just here, my boy!"

"Well, then, with all respect to you, sir, it seems to me that this is the very time to moisten it."

"Good!" said the doctor, laughing. "Let us have a glass of punch. You have a way of comprehending cosmography that is anything but dull."

And thus was the passage of the *Victoria* over the equator duly celebrated.

The balloon made rapid headway. In the west could be seen a low and but slightly-diversified coast, and, farther away in the background, the elevated plains of the Uganda and the Usoga. At length, the rapidity of the wind became excessive, approaching thirty miles per hour.

The waters of the Nyanza, violently agitated, were foaming like the billows of a sea. By the appearance of certain long swells that followed the sinking of the waves, the doctor was enabled to conclude that the lake must have great depth of water. Only one or two rude boats were seen during this rapid passage.

"This lake is evidently, from its elevated position, the natural reservoir of the rivers in the eastern part of Africa, and the sky gives back to it in rain what it takes in vapour from the streams that flow out of it. I am certain that the Nile must here take its rise."

"Well, we shall see!" said Kennedy.

About nine o'clock they drew nearer to the western coast. It seemed deserted, and covered with woods; the wind freshened a little towards the east, and the other shore of the lake could be seen. It bent around in such a curve as to end in a wide angle towards two degrees forty minutes north latitude. Lofty mountains uplifted their arid peaks at this extremity of Nyanza; but, between them, a deep and winding gorge gave exit to a turbulent and foaming river.

While busy managing the balloon, Dr. Ferguson never ceased reconnoitring the country with eager eyes.

"Look!" he exclaimed, "look, my friends! the statements of the Arabs were correct! They spoke of a river by which Lake Ukéréoué discharged its waters towards the north, and this river exists, and we are descending it, and it flows with a speed analogous to our own! And this drop of water now gliding away beneath our feet is, beyond all question, rushing on, to mingle with the Mediterranean! It is the Nile!"

"It is the Nile!" re-echoed Kennedy, carried away by the enthusiasm of his friend.

"Hurrah for the Nile!" shouted Joe, glad, and always ready to cheer for something.

Enormous rocks, here and there, embarrassed the course of this mysterious river. The water foamed as it fell in rapids and cataracts, which confirmed the doctor in his preconceived ideas on the subject. From the environing mountains numerous torrents came plunging and seething down, and the eye could take them in by hundreds. There could be seen, starting from the soil, delicate jets of water scattering in all directions, crossing and recrossing each other, mingling, contending in the swiftness of their progress, and all rushing towards that nascent stream which became a river after having drunk them in.

"Here is, indeed, the Nile!" reiterated the doctor, with the tone of profound conviction. "The origin of its name, like the origin of its waters, has fired the imagination of the learned; they have sought to trace it from the Greek, the Coptic, the Sanscrit; but all that matters little now, since we have made it surrender the secret of its source!"

"But," said the Scotchman, "how are you to make sure of the identity of this river with the one recognised by the travellers from the north?"

"We shall have certain, irrefutable, convincing, and infallible proof," replied Ferguson, "should the wind hold another hour in our favour!"

The mountains drew farther apart, revealing in their place numerous villages, and fields of white Indian corn, doura, and sugar-cane. The tribes inhabiting the region seemed excited and hostile; they manifested more anger than adoration, and evidently saw in the aeronauts only obtrusive strangers, and not condescending deities. It appeared as though, in approaching the sources of the Nile, these men came to rob them of something, and so the *Victoria* had to keep out of range of their muskets.

"To land here would be a ticklish matter!" said the Scot.

"Well!" said Joe, "so much the worse for these natives. They'll have to do without the pleasure of our conversation."

"Nevertheless, descend I must," said the doctor, "were it only for a quarter of an hour. Without doing so I cannot verify the results of our expedition."

"It is indispensable, then, doctor?"

"Indispensable; and we will descend, even if we have to do so with a volley of musketry."

"The thing suits me," said Kennedy, toying with his pet rifle.

"And I'm ready, master, whenever you say the word!" added Joe, preparing for the fight.

"It would not be the first time," remarked the doctor, "that science has been followed up, sword in hand. The same thing happened to a French *savant* among the mountains of Spain, when he was measuring the terrestrial meridian."

"Be easy on that score, doctor, and trust to your two body-guards."

"Are we there, master?"

"Not yet. In fact, I shall go up a little, first, in order to get an exact idea of the configuration of the country."

The hydrogen expanded, and in less than ten minutes the balloon was soaring at a height of twenty-five hundred feet above the ground.

From that elevation could be distinguished an inextricable network of smaller streams which the river received into its bosom; others came from the west, from between numerous hills, in the midst of fertile plains.

"We are not ninety miles from Gondokoro," said the doctor, measuring off the distance on his map, "and less than five miles from the point reached by the explorers from the north. Let us descend with great care."

And, upon this, the balloon was lowered about two thousand feet.

"Now, my friends, let us be ready, come what may."

"Ready it is!" said Dick and Joe, with one voice.

"Good!"

In a few moments the balloon was advancing along the bed of the river, and scarcely one hundred feet above the ground. The Nile measured but fifty fathoms in width at this point, and the natives were in great excitement, rushing to and fro, tumultuously, in the villages that lined the banks of the stream. At the second degree it forms a perpendicular cascade of ten feet in height, and consequently impassable by boats.

"Here, then, is the cascade mentioned by Debono!" exclaimed the doctor.

The basin of the river spread out, dotted with numerous islands, which Dr. Ferguson devoured with his eyes. He seemed to be seeking for a point of reference which he had not yet found.

By this time, some blacks, having ventured in a boat just under the balloon, Kennedy saluted them with a shot from his rifle, that made them regain the bank at their utmost speed.

"A good journey to you," bawled Joe, "and if I were in your place, I wouldn't try coming back again. I should be mightily afraid of a monster that can hurl thunderbolts when he pleases."

But, all at once, the doctor snatched up his spy-glass, and directed it towards an island reposing in the middle of the river.

"Four trees!" he exclaimed; "look, down there!" Sure enough, there were four trees standing alone at one end of it.

"It is Bengal Island! It is the very same," repeated the doctor, exultingly.

"And what of that?" asked Dick.

"It is there that we shall alight, if God permits."

"But, it seems to be inhabited, doctor."

"Joe is right; and, unless I'm mistaken, there is a group of about a score of natives on it now."

"We'll make them scatter; there'll be no great trouble in that," responded Ferguson.

"So be it," chimed in the hunter.

The sun was at the zenith as the balloon approached the island.

The blacks, who were members of the Makado tribe, were howling lustily, and one of them waved his bark hat in the air. Kennedy took aim at him, fired, and his hat flew about him in pieces. Thereupon there was a general scamper. The natives plunged headlong into the river, and swam to the opposite bank. Immediately, there came a shower of balls from both banks, along with a perfect cloud of arrows, but without doing the balloon any damage, where it rested with its anchor snugly secured in the fissure of a rock. Joe lost no time in sliding to the ground.

"The ladder!" cried the doctor. "Follow me, Kennedy."

"What do you wish, sir?"

"Let us alight. I want a witness."

"Here I am!"

"Mind your post, Joe, and keep a good look-out."

"Never fear, doctor; I'll answer for all that."

"Come, Dick," said the doctor, as he touched the ground.

So saying, he drew his companion along towards a group of rocks that rose upon one point of the island; there, after searching for some time, he began to rummage among the brambles, and, in so doing, scratched his hands until they bled.

Suddenly he grasped Kennedy's arm, exclaiming: "Look! look!"

"Letters!"

Yes; there, indeed, could be descried, with perfect precision of outline, some letters carved on the rock. It was quite easy to make them out:

A. D.

"A.D.!" repeated Dr. Ferguson. "Andrea Debono—the very signature of the traveller who farthest ascended the current of the Nile."

"No doubt of that, friend Samuel," assented Kennedy.

"Are you now convinced?"

"It is the Nile! We cannot entertain a doubt on that score now," was the reply.

The doctor, for the last time, examined those precious initials, the exact form and size of which he carefully noted.

"And now," said he—"now for the balloon!"

"Quickly, then, for I see some of the natives getting ready to recross the river."

"That matters little to us now. Let the wind but send us northward for a few hours, and we shall reach Gondokoro, and press the hands of some of our countrymen."

Ten minutes more, and the balloon was majestically ascending, while Dr. Ferguson, in token of success, waved the English flag triumphantly from his car.

Chapter XIX

THE NILE—THE TREMBLING MOUNTAIN—A REMEMBRANCE
OF THE COUNTRY—THE NARRATIVES OF THE ARABS—
THE NYAM-NYAMS—JOE'S SHREWD COGITATIONS—
THE BALLOON RUNS THE GANTLET—AEROSTATIC ASCENSIONS—
MADAME BLANCHARD

WHICH WAY DO WE HEAD?" ASKED KENNEDY, AS HE SAW HIS FRIEND CONSULTING THE compass.

"North-northeast."

"The deuce! but that's not the north?"

"No, Dick; and I'm afraid that we shall have some trouble in getting to Gondokoro. I am sorry for it; but, at last, we have succeeded in connecting the explorations from the east with those from the north; and we must not complain."

The balloon was now receding gradually from the Nile.

"One last look," said the doctor, "at this impassable latitude, beyond which the most intrepid travellers could not make their way. There are those intractable tribes, of whom Petherick, Arnaud, Miuni, and the young traveller Lejean, to whom we are indebted for the best work on the Upper Nile, have spoken."

"Thus, then," added Kennedy, enquiringly, "our discoveries agree with the speculations of science."

"Absolutely so. The sources of the White Nile, of the Bahr-el-Abiad, are immersed in a lake as large as a sea; it is there that it takes its rise. Poesy, undoubtedly, loses something thereby. People were fond of ascribing a celestial origin to this king of rivers. The ancients gave it the name of an ocean, and were not far from believing that it flowed directly from the sun; but we must come down from these flights from time to time, and accept what science teaches us. There will not always be scientific men, perhaps; but there always will be poets."

"We can still see cataracts," said Joe.

"Those are the cataracts of Makedo, in the third degree of latitude. Nothing could be more accurate. Oh, if we could only have followed the course of the Nile for a few hours!"

"And down yonder, below us, I see the top of a mountain," said the hunter.

"That is Mount Longwek, the *Trembling Mountain* of the Arabs. This whole country was visited by Debono, who went through it under the name of Latif-Effendi. The tribes living near the Nile are hostile to each other, and are continually waging a war of extermination. You may form some idea, then, of the difficulties he had to encounter."

The wind was carrying the balloon towards the north-west, and, in order to avoid Mount Longwek, it was necessary to seek a more slanting current.

"My friends," said the doctor, "here is where *our* passage of the African Continent really commences; up to this time we have been following the traces of our predecessors. Henceforth we are to launch ourselves upon the unknown. We shall not lack the courage, shall we?"

"Never!" said Dick and Joe together, almost in a shout.

"Onward, then, and may we have the help of Heaven!"

At ten o'clock at night, after passing over ravines, forests, and scattered villages, the aeronauts reached the side of the Trembling Mountain, along whose gentle slopes they went quietly gliding. In that memorable day, the 23d of April, they had, in fifteen hours, impelled by a rapid breeze, traversed a distance of more than three hundred and fifteen miles.

But this latter part of the journey had left them in dull spirits, and complete silence reigned in the car. Was Dr. Ferguson absorbed in the thought of his discoveries? Were his two companions thinking of their trip through those unknown regions? There were, no doubt, mingled with these reflections, the keenest reminiscences of home and distant friends. Joe alone continued to manifest the same careless philosophy, finding it *quite natural* that home should not be there, from the moment that he left it; but he respected the silent mood of his friends, the doctor and Kennedy.

About ten the balloon anchored on the side of the Trembling Mountain, so called, because, in Arab tradition, it is said to tremble the instant that a Mussulman sets foot upon it. The travellers then partook of a substantial meal, and all quietly passed the night as usual, keeping the regular watches.

On awaking the next morning, they all had pleasanter feelings. The weather was fine, and the wind was blowing from the right quarter; so that a good breakfast, seasoned with Joe's merry pranks, put them in high good-humour.

The region they were now crossing is very extensive. It borders on the Mountains of the Moon on one side, and those of Darfour on the other—a space about as broad as Europe.

"We are, no doubt, crossing what is supposed to be the kingdom of Usoga. Geographers have pretended that there existed, in the centre of Africa, a vast depression, an immense central lake. We shall see whether there is any truth in that idea," said the doctor.

"But how did they come to think so?" asked Kennedy.

"From the recitals of the Arabs. Those fellows are great narrators—too much so, probably. Some travellers, who had got as far as Kazeh, or the great lakes, saw slaves that had been brought from this region; interrogated them concerning it, and, from their different narratives, made up a jumble of notions, and deduced systems from them. Down at the bottom of it all there is some appearance of truth; and you see that they were right about the sources of the Nile."

"Nothing could be more correct," said Kennedy. "It was by the aid of these documents that some attempts at maps were made, and so I am going to try to follow our route by one of them, rectifying it when need be."

"Is all this region inhabited?" asked Joe.

"Undoubtedly; and disagreeably inhabited, too."

"I thought so."

"These scattered tribes come, one and all, under the title of Nyam-Nyams, and this compound word is only a sort of nickname. It imitates the sound of chewing."

"That's it! Excellent!" said Joe, champing his teeth as though he were eating; "Nyam-Nyam."

"My good Joe, if you were the immediate object of this chewing, you wouldn't find it so excellent."

"Why, what's the reason, sir?"

"These tribes are considered man-eaters."

"Is that really the case?"

"Not a doubt of it! It has also been asserted that these natives had tails, like mere quadrupeds; but it was soon discovered that these appendages belonged to the skins of animals that they wore for clothing."

"More's the pity! a tail's a nice thing to chase away mosquitoes."

"That may be, Joe; but we must consign the story to the domain of fable, like the dogs' heads which the traveller, Brun-Roliet, attributed to other tribes."

"Dogs' heads, eh? Quite convenient for barking, and even for man-eating!"

"But one thing that has been, unfortunately, proven true, is, the ferocity of these tribes, who are really very fond of human flesh, and devour it with avidity."

"I only hope that they won't take such a particular fancy to mine!" said Joe, with comic solemnity.

"See that!" said Kennedy.

"Yes, indeed, sir; if I have to be eaten, in a moment of famine, I want it to be for your benefit and my master's; but the idea of feeding those black fellows—gracious! I'd die of shame!"

"Well, then, Joe," said Kennedy, "that's understood; we count upon you in case of need!"

"At your service, gentlemen!"

"Joe talks in this way so as to make us take good care of him, and fatten him up."

"Maybe so!" said Joe. "Every man for himself."

In the afternoon, the sky became covered with a warm mist, that oozed from the soil; the brownish vapour scarcely allowed the beholder to distinguish objects, and so, fearing collision with some unexpected mountain-peak, the doctor, about five o'clock, gave the signal to halt.

The night passed without accident, but in such profound obscurity, that it was necessary to use redoubled vigilance.

The monsoon blew with extreme violence during all the next morning. The wind buried itself in the lower cavities of the balloon and shook the appendage by which the dilating-pipes entered the main apparatus. They had, at last, to be tied up with cords, Joe acquitting himself very skilfully in performing that operation.

He had occasion to observe, at the same time, that the orifice of the balloon still remained hermetically sealed.

"That is a matter of double importance for us," said the doctor; "in the first place, we avoid the escape of precious gas, and then, again, we do not leave behind us an inflammable train, which we should at last inevitably set fire to, and so be consumed."

"That would be a disagreeable travelling incident!" said Joe.

"Should we be hurled to the ground?" asked Kennedy.

"Hurled! No, not quite that. The gas would burn quietly, and we should descend little by little. A similar accident happened to a French aeronaut, Madame Blanchard. She ignited her balloon while sending off fireworks, but she did not fall, and she would not have been killed, probably, had not her car dashed against a chimney and precipitated her to the ground."

"Let us hope that nothing of the kind may happen to us," said the hunter. "Up to this time our trip has not seemed to me very dangerous, and I can see nothing to prevent us reaching our destination."

"Nor can I either, my dear Dick; accidents are generally caused by the imprudence of the aeronauts, or the defective construction of their apparatus. However, in thousands of aerial ascensions, there have not been twenty fatal accidents. Usually, the danger is in the moment of leaving the ground, or of alighting, and therefore at those junctures we should never omit the utmost precaution."

"It's breakfast-time," said Joe; "we'll have to put up with preserved meat and coffee until Mr. Kennedy has had another chance to get us a good slice of venison."

Chapter XX

The Celestial Bottle—The Fig-Palms—The Mammoth Trees—The Tree of War—The Winged Team— Two Native Tribes in Battle—A Massacre— An Intervention from above

THE WIND HAD BECOME VIOLENT AND IRREGULAR; THE BALLOON WAS RUNNING THE gantlet through the air. Tossed at one moment towards the north, at another towards the south, it could not find one steady current.

"We are moving very swiftly without advancing much," said Kennedy, remarking the frequent oscillations of the needle of the compass.

"The balloon is rushing at the rate of at least thirty miles an hour. Lean over, and see how the country is gliding away beneath us!" said the doctor.

"See! that forest looks as though it were precipitating itself upon us!"

"The forest has become a clearing!" added the other.

"And the clearing a village!" continued Joe, a moment or two later. "Look at the faces of those astonished darkys!"

"Oh! it's natural enough that they should be astonished," said the doctor. "The French peasants, when they first saw a balloon, fired at it, thinking that it was an aerial monster. A Soudan negro may be excused, then, for opening his eyes *very* wide!"

"Faith!" said Joe, as the *Victoria* skimmed closely along the ground, at scarcely the elevation of one hundred feet, and immediately over a village, "I'll throw them an empty bottle, with your leave, doctor, and if it reaches them safe and sound, they'll worship it; if it breaks, they'll make talismans of the pieces."

So saying, he flung out a bottle, which, of course, was broken into a thousand fragments, while the negroes scampered into their round huts, uttering shrill cries.

A little farther on, Kennedy called out: "Look at that strange tree! The upper part is of one kind and the lower part of another!"

"Well!" said Joe, "here's a country where the trees grow on top of each other."

"It's simply the trunk of a fig-tree," replied the doctor, "on which there is a little vegetating earth. Some fine day, the wind left the seed of a palm on it, and the seed has taken root and grown as though it were on the plain ground."

"A fine new style of gardening," said Joe, "and I'll import the idea to England. It would be just the thing in the London parks; without counting that it would be another way to increase the number of fruit-trees. We could have gardens up in the air; and the small house-owners would like that!"

At this moment, they had to raise the balloon so as to pass over a forest of trees that were more than three hundred feet in height—a kind of ancient banyan.

"What magnificent trees!" exclaimed Kennedy. "I never saw anything so fine as the appearance of these venerable forests. Look, doctor!"

"The height of these banyans is really remarkable, my dear Dick; and yet, they would be nothing astonishing in the New World."

"Why, are there still loftier trees in existence?"

"Undoubtedly; among the 'mammoth trees' of California, there is a cedar four hundred and eighty feet in height. It would overtop the Houses of Parliament, and even the Great Pyramid of Egypt. The trunk at the surface of the ground was one hundred and twenty feet in circumference, and the concentric layers of the wood disclosed an age of more than four thousand years."

"But then, sir, there was nothing wonderful in it! When one has lived four thousand years, one ought to be pretty tall!" was Joe's remark.

Meanwhile, during the doctor's recital and Joe's response, the forest had given place to a large collection of huts surrounding an open space. In the middle of this grew a solitary tree, and Joe exclaimed, as he caught sight of it:

"Well! if that tree has produced such flowers as those, for the last four thousand years, I have to offer it my compliments, anyhow," and he pointed to a gigantic sycamore, whose whole trunk was covered with human bones. The flowers of which Joe spoke were heads freshly severed from the bodies, and suspended by daggers thrust into the bark of the tree.

"The war-tree of these cannibals!" said the doctor; "the Indians merely carry off the scalp, but these negroes take the whole head."

"A mere matter of fashion!" said Joe. But, already, the village and the bleeding heads were disappearing on the horizon. Another place offered a still more revolting spectacle—half-devoured corpses; skeletons mouldering to dust; human limbs scattered here and there, and left to feed the jackals and hyenas."

"No doubt, these are the bodies of criminals; according to the custom in Abyssinia, these people have left them a prey to the wild beasts, who kill them with their terrible teeth and claws, and then devour them at their leisure."

"Not a whit more cruel than hanging!" said the Scot; "filthier, that's all!"

"In the southern regions of Africa, they content themselves," resumed the doctor, "with shutting up the criminal in his own hut with his cattle, and sometimes with his family. They then set fire to the hut, and the whole party are burned together. I call that cruel; but, like friend Kennedy, I think that the gallows is quite as cruel, quite as barbarous."

Joe, by the aid of his keen sight, which he did not fail to use continually, noticed some flocks of birds of prey flitting about the horizon.

"They are eagles!" exclaimed Kennedy, after reconnoitring them through the glass, "magnificent birds, whose flight is as rapid as ours."

"Heaven preserve us from their attacks!" said the doctor, "they are more to be feared by us than wild beasts or savage tribes."

"Bah!" said the hunter, "we can drive them off with a few rifle-shots."

"Nevertheless, I would prefer, dear Dick, not having to rely upon your skill, this time, for the silk of our balloon could not resist their sharp beaks; fortunately, the huge birds will, I believe, be more frightened than attracted by our machine."

"Yes! but a new idea, and I have dozens of them," said Joe; "if we could only manage to capture a team of live eagles, we could hitch them to the balloon, and they'd haul us through the air!"

"The thing has been seriously proposed," replied the doctor, "but I think it hardly practicable with creatures naturally so restive."

"Oh! we'd tame them," said Joe. "Instead of driving them with bits, we'd do it with eye-blinkers that would cover their eyes. Half blinded in that way, they'd go to the right or to the left, as we desired; when blinded completely, they would stop."

"Allow me, Joe, to prefer a favourable wind to your team of eagles. It costs less for fodder, and is more reliable."

"Well, you may have your choice, master, but I stick to my idea."

It now was noon. The *Victoria* had been going at a more moderate speed for some time; the country merely passed below it; it no longer flew.

Suddenly, shouts and whistlings were heard by our aeronauts, and, leaning over the edge of the car, they saw on the open plain below them an exciting spectacle.

Two hostile tribes were fighting furiously, and the air was dotted with volleys of arrows. The combatants were so intent upon their murderous work that they did not notice the arrival of the balloon; there were about three hundred mingled confusedly in the deadly struggle: most of them, red with the blood of the wounded, in which they fairly wallowed, were horrible to behold.

As they at last caught sight of the balloon, there was a momentary pause; but their yells redoubled, and some arrows were shot at the *Victoria,* one of them coming close enough for Joe to catch it with his hand.

"Let us rise out of range," exclaimed the doctor; "there must be no rashness! We are forbidden any risk."

Meanwhile, the massacre continued on both sides, with battle-axes and war-clubs; as quickly as one of the combatants fell, a hostile warrior ran up to cut off his head, while the women, mingling in the fray, gathered up these bloody trophies, and piled them together at either extremity of the battle-field. Often, too, they even fought for these hideous spoils.

"What a frightful scene!" said Kennedy, with profound disgust.

"They're ugly acquaintances!" added Joe; "but then, if they had uniforms they'd be just like the fighters of all the rest of the world!"

"I have a keen hankering to take a hand in at that fight," said the hunter, brandishing his rifle.

"No! no!" objected the doctor, vehemently; "no, let us not meddle with what don't concern us. Do you know which is right or which is wrong, that you would assume the part of the Almighty? Let us, rather, hurry away from this revolting spectacle. Could the great captains of the world float thus above the scenes of their exploits, they would at last, perhaps, conceive a disgust for blood and conquest."

The chieftain of one of the contending parties was remarkable for his athletic proportions, his great height, and herculean strength. With one hand he plunged his spear into the compact ranks of his enemies, and with the other mowed large spaces in them with his battle-axe. Suddenly he flung away his war-club, red with blood, rushed upon a wounded warrior, and, chopping off his arm at a single stroke, carried the dissevered member to his mouth, and bit it again and again.

"Ah!" ejaculated Kennedy, "the horrible brute! I can hold back no longer," and, as he spoke, the huge savage, struck full in the forehead with a rifle-ball, fell headlong to the ground.

Upon this sudden mishap of their leader, his warriors seemed struck dumb with amazement; his supernatural death awed them, while it reanimated the courage and ardour of their adversaries, and, in a twinkling, the field was abandoned by half the combatants.

"Come, let us look higher up for a current to bear us away. I am sick of this spectacle," said the doctor.

But they could not get away so rapidly as to avoid the sight of the victorious tribe rushing upon the dead and the wounded, scrambling and disputing for the still warm and reeking flesh, and eagerly devouring it.

"Faugh!" uttered Joe, "it's sickening."

The balloon rose as it expanded; the howlings of the brutal horde, in the delirium of their orgy, pursued them for a few minutes; but, at length, borne away towards the south, they were carried out of sight and hearing of this horrible spectacle of cannibalism.

The surface of the country was now greatly varied, with numerous streams of water, bearing towards the east. The latter, undoubtedly, ran into those affluents of Lake Nu, or of the River of the Gazelles, concerning which M. Guillaume Lejean has given such curious details.

At nightfall, the balloon cast anchor in twenty-seven degrees east longitude, and four degrees twenty minutes north latitude, after a day's trip of one hundred and fifty miles.

Chapter XXI

STRANGE SOUNDS—A NIGHT ATTACK—KENNEDY AND JOE IN
THE TREE—TWO SHOTS—"HELP! HELP!"—REPLY IN FRENCH—
THE MORNING—THE MISSIONARY—THE PLAN OF RESCUE

THE NIGHT CAME ON VERY DARK. THE DOCTOR HAD NOT BEEN ABLE TO RECONNOITRE the country. He had made fast to a very tall tree, from which he could distinguish only a confused mass through the gloom.

As usual, he took the nine o'clock watch, and at midnight Dick relieved him.

"Keep a sharp look-out, Dick!" was the doctor's good-night injunction.

"Is there anything new on the carpet?"

"No; but I thought that I heard vague sounds below us, and, as I don't exactly know where the wind has carried us to, even an excess of caution would do no harm."

"You've probably heard the cries of wild beasts."

"No! the sounds seemed to me something altogether different from that; at all events, on the least alarm don't fail to waken us."

"I'll do so, doctor; rest easy."

After listening attentively for a moment or two longer, the doctor, hearing nothing more, threw himself on his blankets and went asleep.

The sky was covered with dense clouds, but not a breath of air was stirring; and the balloon, kept in its place by only a single anchor, experienced not the slightest oscillation.

Kennedy, leaning his elbow on the edge of the car, so as to keep an eye on the cylinder, which was actively at work, gazed out upon the calm obscurity; he eagerly scanned the horizon, and, as often happens to minds that are uneasy or possessed with preconceived notions, he fancied that he sometimes detected vague gleams of light in the distance.

At one moment he even thought that he saw them only two hundred paces away, quite distinctly, but it was a mere flash that was gone as quickly as it came, and he noticed nothing more. It was, no doubt, one of those luminous illusions that sometimes impress the eye in the midst of very profound darkness.

Kennedy was getting over his nervousness and falling into his wandering meditations again, when a sharp whistle pierced his ear.

Was that the cry of an animal or of a night-bird, or did it come from human lips?

Kennedy, perfectly comprehending the gravity of the situation, was on the point of waking his companions, but he reflected that, in any case, men or animals, the creatures that he had heard must be out of reach. So he merely saw that his weapons were all right, and then, with his night-glass, again plunged his gaze into space.

It was not long before he thought he could perceive below him vague forms that seemed to be gliding towards the tree, and then, by the aid of a ray of moonlight that shot like an electric flash between two masses of cloud, he distinctly made out a group of human figures moving in the shadow.

The adventure with the dog-faced baboons returned to his memory, and he placed his hand on the doctor's shoulder.

The latter was awake in a moment.

"Silence!" said Dick. "Let us speak below our breath."

"Has anything happened?"

"Yes, let us waken Joe."

The instant that Joe was aroused, Kennedy told him what he had seen.

"Those confounded monkeys again!" said Joe.

"Possibly, but we must be on our guard."

"Joe and I," said Kennedy, "will climb down the tree by the ladder."

"And, in the meanwhile," added the doctor, "I will take my measures so that we can ascend rapidly at a moment's warning."

"Agreed!"

"Let us go down, then!" said Joe.

"Don't use your weapons, excepting at the last extremity! It would be a useless risk to make the natives aware of our presence in such a place as this."

Dick and Joe replied with signs of assent, and then letting themselves slide noiselessly towards the tree, took their position in a fork among the strong branches where the anchor had caught.

For some moments they listened minutely and motionlessly among the foliage, and ere long Joe seized Kennedy's hand as he heard a sort of rubbing sound against the bark of the tree.

"Don't you hear that?" he whispered.

"Yes, and it's coming nearer."

"Suppose it should be a serpent? That hissing or whistling that you heard before—"

"No! there was something human in it."

"I'd prefer the savages, for I have a horror of those snakes."

"The noise is increasing," said Kennedy, again, after a lapse of a few moments.

"Yes! something's coming up towards us—climbing."

"Keep watch on this side, and I'll take care of the other."

"Very good!"

There they were, isolated, at the top of one of the larger branches shooting out in the midst of one of those miniature forests called baobab-trees. The darkness, heightened by the density of the foliage, was profound; however, Joe, leaning over to Kennedy's ear and pointing down the tree, whispered:

"The blacks! They're climbing towards us."

The two friends could even catch the sound of a few words uttered in the lowest possible tones.

Joe gently brought his rifle to his shoulder as he spoke.

"Wait!" said Kennedy.

Some of the natives had really climbed the baobab, and now they were seen rising on all sides, winding along the boughs like reptiles, and advancing slowly but surely, all the time plainly enough discernible, not merely to the eye but to the nostrils, by the horrible odors of the rancid grease with which they bedaub their bodies.

Ere long, two heads appeared to the gaze of Kennedy and Joe, on a level with the very branch to which they were clinging.

"Attention!" said Kennedy. "Fire!"

The double concussion resounded like a thunderbolt and died away into cries of rage and pain, and in a moment the whole horde had disappeared.

But, in the midst of these yells and howls, a strange, unexpected—nay what seemed an impossible—cry had been heard! A human voice had, distinctly, called aloud in the French language—

"Help! help!"

Kennedy and Joe, dumb with amazement, had regained the car immediately.

"Did you hear that?" the doctor asked them.

"Undoubtedly, that supernatural cry, '*À moi! à moi!*' comes from a Frenchman in the hands of these barbarians!"

"A traveller."

"A missionary, perhaps."

"Poor wretch!" said Kennedy, "they're assassinating him—making a martyr of him!"

The doctor then spoke, and it was impossible for him to conceal his emotions.

"There can be no doubt of it," he said; "some unfortunate Frenchman has fallen into the hands of these savages. We must not leave this place without doing all in our power to save him. When he heard the sound of our guns, he recognised an unhoped-for assistance, a providential interposition. We shall not disappoint his last hope. Are such your views?"

"They are, doctor, and we are ready to obey you."

"Let us, then, lay our heads together to devise some plan, and in the morning we'll try to rescue him."

"But how shall we drive off those abominable blacks?" asked Kennedy.

"It's quite clear to me, from the way in which they made off, that they are unacquainted with fire-arms. We must, therefore, profit by their fears; but we shall await daylight before acting, and then we can form our plans of rescue according to circumstances."

"The poor captive cannot be far off," said Joe, "because—"

"Help! help!" repeated the voice, but much more feebly this time.

"The savage wretches!" exclaimed Joe, trembling with indignation. "Suppose they should kill him to-night!"

"Do you hear, doctor," resumed Kennedy, seizing the doctor's hand. "Suppose they should kill him to-night!"

"It is not at all likely, my friends. These savage tribes kill their captives in broad daylight; they must have the sunshine."

"Now, if I were to take advantage of the darkness to slip down to the poor fellow?" said Kennedy.

"And I'll go with you," said Joe, warmly.

"Pause, my friends—pause! The suggestion does honour to your hearts and to your courage; but you would expose us all to great peril, and do still greater harm to the unfortunate man whom you wish to aid."

"Why so?" asked Kennedy. "These savages are frightened and dispersed: they will not return."

"Dick, I implore you, heed what I say. I am acting for the common good; and if by any accident you should be taken by surprise, all would be lost."

"But, think of that poor wretch, hoping for aid, waiting there, praying, calling aloud. Is no one to go to his assistance? He must think that his senses deceived him; that he heard nothing!"

"We can reassure him, on that score," said Dr. Ferguson—and, standing erect, making a speaking-trumpet of his hands, he shouted at the top of his voice, in French: "Whoever you are, be of good cheer! Three friends are watching over you."

A terrific howl from the savages responded to these words—no doubt drowning the prisoner's reply.

"They are murdering him! they are murdering him!" exclaimed Kennedy. "Our interference will have served no other purpose than to hasten the hour of his doom. We must act!"

"But how, Dick? What do you expect to do in the midst of this darkness?"

"Oh, if it was only daylight!" sighed Joe.

"Well, and suppose it were daylight?" said the doctor, in a singular tone.

"Nothing more simple, doctor," said Kennedy. "I'd go down and scatter all these savage villains with powder and ball!"

"And you, Joe, what would you do?"

"I, master? why, I'd act more prudently, maybe, by telling the prisoner to make his escape in a certain direction that we'd agree upon."

"And how would you get him to know that?"

"By means of this arrow that I caught flying the other day. I'd tie a note to it, or I'd just call out to him in a loud voice what you want him to do, because these black fellows don't understand the language that you'd speak in!"

"Your plans are impracticable, my dear friends. The greatest difficulty would be for this poor fellow to escape at all—even admitting that he should manage to elude the vigilance of his captors. As for you, my dear Dick, with determined daring, and profiting by their alarm at our fire-arms, your project might possibly succeed; but, were it to fail, you would be lost, and we should have two persons to save instead of one. No! we must put *all* the chances on *our* side, and go to work differently."

"But let us act at once!" said the hunter.

"Perhaps we may," said the doctor, throwing considerable stress upon the words.

"Why, doctor, can you light up such darkness as this?"

"Who knows, Joe?"

"Ah! if you can do that, you're the greatest learned man in the world!"

The doctor kept silent for a few moments; he was thinking. His two companions looked at him with much emotion, for they were greatly excited by the strangeness of the situation. Ferguson at last resumed:

"Here is my plan: We have two hundred pounds of ballast left, since the bags we brought with us are still untouched. I'll suppose that this prisoner, who is evidently exhausted by suffering, weighs as much as one of us; there will still remain sixty pounds of ballast to throw out, in case we should want to ascend suddenly."

"How do you expect to manage the balloon?" asked Kennedy.

"This is the idea, Dick: you will admit that if I can get to the prisoner, and throw out a quantity of ballast, equal to his weight, I shall have in nowise altered the equilibrium of the balloon. But, then, if I want to get a rapid ascension, so as to escape these savages, I must employ means more energetic than the cylinder. Well, then, in throwing out this overplus of ballast at a given moment, I am certain to rise with great rapidity."

"That's plain enough."

"Yes; but there is one drawback: it consists in the fact that, in order to descend after that, I should have to part with a quantity of gas proportionate to the surplus ballast that I had thrown out. Now, the gas is precious; but we must not haggle over it when the life of a fellow-creature is at stake."

"You are right, sir; we must do everything in our power to save him."

"Let us work, then, and get these bags all arranged on the rim of the car, so that they may be thrown overboard at one movement."

"But this darkness?"

"It hides our preparations, and will be dispersed only when they are finished. Take care to have all our weapons close at hand. Perhaps we may have to fire; so we have one shot in the rifle; four for the two muskets; twelve in the two revolvers; or seventeen in all, which might be fired in a quarter of a minute. But perhaps we shall not have to resort to all this noisy work. Are you ready?"

"We're ready," responded Joe.

The sacks were placed as requested, and the arms were put in good order.

"Very good!" said the doctor. "Have an eye to everything. Joe will see to throwing out the ballast, and Dick will carry off the prisoner; but let nothing be done until I give the word. Joe will first detach the anchor, and then quickly make his way back to the car."

Joe let himself slide down by the rope; and, in a few moments, reappeared at his post; while the balloon, thus liberated, hung almost motionless in the air.

In the meantime the doctor assured himself of the presence of a sufficient quantity of gas in the mixing-tank to feed the cylinder, if necessary, without there being any need of resorting for some time to the Buntzen battery. He then took out the two perfectly-isolated conducting-wires, which served for the decomposition of the water, and, searching in his travelling-sack, brought forth two pieces of charcoal, cut down to a sharp point, and fixed one at the end of each wire.

His two friends looked on, without knowing what he was about, but they kept perfectly silent. When the doctor had finished, he stood up erect in the car, and, taking the two pieces of charcoal, one in each hand, drew their points nearly together.

In a twinkling, an intense and dazzling light was produced, with an insupportable glow between the two pointed ends of charcoal, and a huge jet of electric radiance literally broke the darkness of the night.

"Oh!" ejaculated the astonished friends.

"Not a word!" cautioned the doctor.

Chapter XXII

THE JET OF LIGHT—THE MISSIONARY—THE RESCUE IN A RAY OF ELECTRICITY—A LAZARIST PRIEST—BUT LITTLE HOPE— THE DOCTOR'S CARE—A LIFE OF SELF-DENIAL— PASSING A VOLCANO

DR. FERGUSON DARTED HIS POWERFUL ELECTRIC JET TOWARDS VARIOUS POINTS OF space, and caused it to rest on a spot from which shouts of terror were heard. His companions fixed their gaze eagerly on the place.

The baobab, over which the balloon was hanging almost motionless, stood in the centre of a clearing, where, between fields of Indian-corn and sugar-cane, were seen some fifty low, conical huts, around which swarmed a numerous tribe.

A hundred feet below the balloon stood a large post, or stake, and at its foot lay a human being—a young man of thirty years or more, with long black hair, half naked, wasted and wan, bleeding, covered with wounds, his head bowed over upon his breast, as Christ's was, when He hung upon the cross.

The hair, cut shorter on the top of his skull, still indicated the place of a half-effaced tonsure.

"A missionary! a priest!" exclaimed Joe.

"Poor, unfortunate man!" said Kennedy.

"We must save him, Dick!" responded the doctor; "we must save him!"

The crowd of blacks, when they saw the balloon over their heads, like a huge comet with a train of dazzling light, were seized with a terror that may be readily imagined. Upon hearing their cries, the prisoner raised his head. His eyes gleamed with sudden hope, and, without too thoroughly comprehending what was taking place, he stretched out his hands to his unexpected deliverers.

"He is alive!" exclaimed Ferguson. "God be praised! The savages have got a fine scare, and we shall save him! Are you ready, friends?"

"Ready, doctor, at the word."

"Joe, shut off the cylinder!"

The doctor's order was executed. An almost imperceptible breath of air impelled the balloon directly over the prisoner, at the same time that it gently lowered with the contraction of the gas. For about ten minutes it remained floating in the midst of luminous waves, for Ferguson continued to flash right down upon the throng his glowing sheaf of rays, which, here and there, marked out swift and vivid sheets of light. The tribe, under the influence of an indescribable terror, disappeared little by little in the huts, and there was complete solitude around the stake. The doctor had, therefore, been right in counting upon the fantastic appearance of the balloon throwing out rays, as vivid as the sun's, through this intense gloom.

The car was approaching the ground; but a few of the savages, more audacious than the rest, guessing that their victim was about to escape from their clutches, came back with loud yells, and Kennedy seized his rifle. The doctor, however, besought him not to fire.

The priest, on his knees, for he had not the strength to stand erect, was not even fastened to the stake, his weakness rendering that precaution superfluous. At the instant when the car was close to the ground, the brawny Scot, laying aside his rifle, and seizing the priest around the waist, lifted him into the car, while, at the same moment, Joe tossed over the two hundred pounds of ballast.

The doctor had expected to ascend rapidly, but, contrary to his calculations, the balloon, after going up some three or four feet, remained there perfectly motionless.

"What holds us?" he asked, with an accent of terror.

Some of the savages were running towards them, uttering ferocious cries.

"Ah, ha!" said Joe, "one of those cursed blacks is hanging to the car!"

"Dick! Dick!" cried the doctor, "the water-tank!"

Kennedy caught his friend's idea on the instant, and, snatching up with desperate strength one of the water-tanks weighing about one hundred pounds, he tossed it overboard. The balloon, thus suddenly lightened, made a leap of three hundred feet into the air, amid the howlings of the tribe whose prisoner thus escaped them in a blaze of dazzling light.

"Hurrah!" shouted the doctor's comrades.

Suddenly, the balloon took a fresh leap, which carried it up to an elevation of a thousand feet.

"What's that?" said Kennedy, who had nearly lost his balance.

"Oh! nothing; only that black villain leaving us!" replied the doctor, tranquilly, and Joe, leaning over, saw the savage that had clung to the car whirling over and over, with his arms outstretched in the air, and presently dashed to pieces on the ground. The doctor then separated his electric wires, and everything was again buried in profound obscurity. It was now one o'clock in the morning.

The Frenchman, who had swooned away, at length opened his eyes.

"You are saved!" were the doctor's first words.

"Saved!" he with a sad smile replied in English, "saved from a cruel death! My brethren, I thank you, but my days are numbered, nay, even my hours, and I have but little longer to live."

With this, the missionary, again yielding to exhaustion, relapsed into his fainting-fit.

"He is dying!" said Kennedy.

"No," replied the doctor, bending over him, "but he is very weak; so let us lay him under the awning."

And they did gently deposit on their blankets that poor, wasted body, covered with scars and wounds, still bleeding where fire and steel had, in twenty places, left their agonizing marks. The doctor, taking an old handkerchief, quickly prepared a little lint, which he spread over the wounds, after having washed them. These rapid attentions were bestowed with the celerity and skill of a practised surgeon, and, when they were complete, the doctor, taking a cordial from his medicine-chest, poured a few drops upon his patient's lips.

The latter feebly pressed his kind hands, and scarcely had the strength to say, "Thank you! thank you!"

The doctor comprehended that he must be left perfectly quiet; so he closed the folds of the awning and resumed the guidance of the balloon.

The latter, after taking into account the weight of the new passenger, had been lightened of one hundred and eighty pounds, and therefore kept aloft without the aid of the cylinder. At the first dawn of day, a current drove it gently towards the west-northwest. The doctor went in under the awning for a moment or two, to look at his still sleeping patient.

"May Heaven spare the life of our new companion! Have you any hope?" said the Scot.

"Yes, Dick, with care, in this pure, fresh atmosphere."

"How that man has suffered!" said Joe, with feeling. "He did bolder things than we've done, in venturing all alone among those savage tribes!"

"That cannot be questioned," assented the hunter.

During the entire day the doctor would not allow the sleep of his patient to be disturbed. It was really a long stupor, broken only by an occasional murmur of pain that continued to disquiet and agitate the doctor greatly.

Towards evening the balloon remained stationary in the midst of the gloom, and during the night, while Kennedy and Joe relieved each other in carefully tending the sick man, Ferguson kept watch over the safety of all.

By the morning of the next day, the balloon had moved, but very slightly, to the westward. The dawn came up pure and magnificent. The sick man was able to call his friends with a stronger voice. They raised the curtains of the awning, and he inhaled with delight the keen morning air.

"How do you feel to-day?" asked the doctor.

"Better, perhaps," he replied. "But you, my friends, I have not seen you yet, excepting in a dream! I can, indeed, scarcely recall what has occurred. Who are you—that your names may not be forgotten in my dying prayers?"

"We are English travellers," replied Ferguson. "We are trying to cross Africa in a balloon, and, on our way, we have had the good fortune to rescue you."

"Science has its heroes," said the missionary.

"But religion its martyrs!" rejoined the Scot.

"Are you a missionary?" asked the doctor.

"I am a priest of the Lazarist mission. Heaven sent you to me—Heaven be praised! The sacrifice of my life had been accomplished! But you come from Europe; tell me about Europe, about France! I have been without news for the last five years!"

"Five years! alone! and among these savages!" exclaimed Kennedy with amazement.

"They are souls to redeem! ignorant and barbarous brethren, whom religion alone can instruct and civilise."

Dr. Ferguson, yielding to the priest's request, talked to him long and fully about France. He listened eagerly, and his eyes filled with tears. He seized Kennedy's and Joe's hands by turns in his own, which were burning with fever. The doctor prepared him some tea, and he drank it with satisfaction. After that, he had strength enough to raise himself up a little, and smiled with pleasure at seeing himself borne along through so pure a sky.

"You are daring travellers!" he said, "and you will succeed in your bold enterprise. You will again behold your relatives, your friends, your country—you—"

At this moment, the weakness of the young missionary became so extreme that they had to lay him again on the bed, where a prostration, lasting for several hours, held him like a dead man under the eye of Dr. Ferguson. The latter could not suppress his emotion, for he felt that this life now in his charge was ebbing away. Were they then so soon to lose him whom they had snatched from an agonizing death? The doctor again washed and dressed the young martyr's frightful wounds, and had to sacrifice nearly his whole stock of water to refresh his burning limbs. He surrounded him with the tenderest and most intelligent care, until, at length, the sick man revived, little by little, in his arms, and recovered his consciousness if not his strength.

The doctor was able to gather something of his history from his broken murmurs.

"Speak in your native language," he said to the sufferer; "I understand it, and it will fatigue you less."

The missionary was a poor young man from the village of Aradon, in Brittany, in the Morbihan country. His earliest instincts had drawn him towards an ecclesiastical career, but to this life of self-sacrifice he was also desirous of joining a life of danger, by entering the mission of the order of priesthood of which St. Vincent de Paul was the founder, and, at twenty, he quitted his country for the inhospitable shores of Africa. From the sea-coast, overcoming obstacles, little by little, braving all privations, pushing onward, afoot, and praying, he had advanced to the very centre of those tribes that dwell among the tributary streams of the Upper Nile. For two years his faith was spurned, his zeal denied recognition, his charities taken in ill part, and he remained a prisoner to one of the cruelest tribes of the Nyambarra, the object of every species of maltreatment. But still he went on teaching, instructing, and praying. The tribe having been dispersed and he left for dead, in one of those combats which are so frequent between the tribes, instead of retracing his steps, he persisted in his evangelical mission. His most tranquil time was when he was taken for a madman. Meanwhile, he had made himself familiar with the idioms of the country, and he catechised in them. At length, during two more long years, he traversed these barbarous regions, impelled by that superhuman energy that comes from God. For a year past he had been residing with that tribe of the Nyam-Nyams known as the *Barafri*, one of the wildest and most ferocious of them all. The chief having died a few days before our travellers appeared, his sudden death was attributed to the missionary, and the tribe resolved to immolate him. His sufferings had already continued for the space of forty hours, and, as the doctor had supposed, he was to have perished in the blaze of the noonday sun. When he heard the sound of fire-arms, nature got the best of him, and he had cried out, "Help! help!" He then thought that he must have been dreaming, when a voice, that seemed to come from the sky, had uttered words of consolation.

"I have no regrets," he said, "for the life that is passing away from me; my life belongs to God!"

"Hope still!" said the doctor; "we are near you, and we will save you now, as we saved you from the tortures of the stake."

"I do not ask so much of Heaven," said the priest, with resignation. "Blessed be God for having vouchsafed to me the joy before I die of having pressed your friendly hands, and having heard, once more, the language of my country!"

The missionary here grew weak again, and the whole day went by between hope and fear, Kennedy deeply moved, and Joe drawing his hand over his eyes more than once when he thought that no one saw him.

The balloon made little progress, and the wind seemed as though unwilling to jostle its precious burden.

Towards evening, Joe discovered a great light in the west. Under more elevated latitudes, it might have been mistaken for an immense aurora borealis, for the sky appeared on fire. The doctor very attentively examined the phenomenon.

"It is, perhaps, only a volcano in full activity," said he.

"But the wind is carrying us directly over it," replied Kennedy.

"Very well, we shall cross it then at a safe height!" said the doctor.

Three hours later, the *Victoria* was right among the mountains. Her exact position was twenty-four degrees fifteen minutes east longitude, and four degrees forty-two minutes north latitude. In front of her a volcanic crater was pouring forth torrents of melted lava, and hurling masses of rock to an enormous height. There were jets, too, of liquid fire that fell back in dazzling cascades—a superb but dangerous spectacle, for the wind with unswerving certainty was carrying the balloon directly towards this blazing atmosphere.

This obstacle, which could not be turned, had to be crossed, so the cylinder was put to its utmost power, and the balloon rose to the height of six thousand feet, leaving between it and the volcano a space of more than three hundred fathoms.

From his bed of suffering, the dying missionary could contemplate that fiery crater from which a thousand jets of dazzling flame were that moment escaping.

"How grand it is!" said he, "and how infinite is the power of God even in its most terrible manifestations!"

This overflow of blazing lava wrapped the sides of the mountain with a veritable drapery of flame; the lower half of the balloon glowed redly in the upper night; a torrid heat ascended to the car, and Dr. Ferguson made all possible haste to escape from this perilous situation.

By ten o'clock the volcano could be seen only as a red point on the horizon, and the balloon tranquilly pursued her course in a less elevated zone of the atmosphere.

Chapter XXIII

JOE IN A FIT OF RAGE—THE DEATH OF A GOOD MAN—
THE NIGHT OF WATCHING BY THE BODY—BARRENNESS AND
DROUGHT—THE BURIAL—THE QUARTZ ROCKS—
JOE'S HALLUCINATIONS—A PRECIOUS BALLAST—
A SURVEY OF THE GOLD-BEARING MOUNTAINS—
THE BEGINNING OF JOE'S DESPAIR

A MAGNIFICENT NIGHT OVERSPREAD THE EARTH, AND THE MISSIONARY LAY QUIETLY asleep in utter exhaustion.

"He'll not get over it!" sighed Joe. "Poor young fellow—scarcely thirty years of age!"

"He'll die in our arms. His breathing, which was so feeble before, is growing weaker still, and I can do nothing to save him," said the doctor, despairingly.

"The infamous scoundrels!" exclaimed Joe, grinding his teeth, in one of those fits of rage that came over him at long intervals; "and to think that, in spite of all, this good man could find words only to pity them, to excuse, to pardon them!"

"Heaven has given him a lovely night, Joe—his last on earth, perhaps! He will suffer but little more after this, and his dying will be only a peaceful falling asleep."

The dying man uttered some broken words, and the doctor at once went to him. His breathing became difficult, and he asked for air. The curtains were drawn entirely back, and he inhaled with rapture the light breezes of that clear, beautiful night. The stars sent him their trembling rays, and the moon wrapped him in the white winding-sheet of its effulgence.

"My friends," said he, in an enfeebled voice, "I am going. May God requite you, and bring you to your safe harbor! May he pay for me the debt of gratitude that I owe to you!"

"You must still hope," replied Kennedy. "This is but a passing fit of weakness. You will not die. How could anyone die on this beautiful summer night?"

"Death is at hand," replied the missionary, "I know it! Let me look it in the face! Death, the commencement of things eternal, is but the end of earthly cares. Place me upon my knees, my brethren, I beseech you!"

Kennedy lifted him up, and it was distressing to see his weakened limbs bend under him.

"My God! my God!" exclaimed the dying apostle, "have pity on me!"

His countenance shone. Far above that earth on which he had known no joys; in the midst of that night which sent to him its softest radiance; on the way to that heaven towards which he uplifted his spirit, as though in a miraculous assumption, he seemed already to live and breathe in the new existence.

His last gesture was a supreme blessing on his new friends of only one day. Then he fell back into the arms of Kennedy, whose countenance was bathed in hot tears.

"Dead!" said the doctor, bending over him, "dead!" And with one common accord, the three friends knelt together in silent prayer.

"To-morrow," resumed the doctor, "we shall bury him in the African soil which he has besprinkled with his blood."

During the rest of the night the body was watched, turn by turn, by the three travellers, and not a word disturbed the solemn silence. Each of them was weeping.

The next day the wind came from the south, and the balloon moved slowly over a vast plateau of mountains: there, were extinct craters; here, barren ravines; not a drop of water on those parched crests; piles of broken rocks; huge stony masses scattered hither and thither, and, interspersed with whitish marl, all indicated the most complete sterility.

Towards noon, the doctor, for the purpose of burying the body, decided to descend into a ravine, in the midst of some plutonic rocks of primitive formation. The surrounding mountains would shelter him, and enable him to bring his car to the ground, for there was no tree in sight to which he could make it fast.

But, as he had explained to Kennedy, it was now impossible for him to descend, except by releasing a quantity of gas proportionate to his loss of ballast at the time when he had rescued the missionary. He therefore opened the valve of the outside balloon. The hydrogen escaped, and the *Victoria* quietly descended into the ravine.

As soon as the car touched the ground, the doctor shut the valve. Joe leaped out, holding on the while to the rim of the car with one hand, and with the other gathering up a quantity of stones equal to his own weight. He could then use both hands, and had soon heaped into the car more than five hundred pounds of stones, which enabled both the doctor and Kennedy, in their turn, to get out. Thus the *Victoria* found herself balanced, and her ascensional force insufficient to raise her.

Moreover, it was not necessary to gather many of these stones, for the blocks were extremely heavy, so much so, indeed, that the doctor's attention was attracted by the circumstance. The soil, in fact, was bestrewn with quartz and porphyritic rocks.

"This is a singular discovery!" said the doctor, mentally.

In the meanwhile, Kennedy and Joe had strolled away a few paces, looking up a proper spot for the grave. The heat was extreme in this ravine, shut in as it was like a sort of furnace. The noonday sun poured down its rays perpendicularly into it.

The first thing to be done was to clear the surface of the fragments of rock that encumbered it, and then a quite deep grave had to be dug, so that the wild animals should not be able to disinter the corpse.

The body of the martyred missionary was then solemnly placed in it. The earth was thrown in over his remains, and above it masses of rock were deposited, in rude resemblance to a tomb.

The doctor, however, remained motionless, and lost in his reflections. He did not even heed the call of his companions, nor did he return with them to seek a shelter from the heat of the day.

"What are you thinking about, doctor?" asked Kennedy.

"About a singular freak of Nature, a curious effect of chance. Do you know, now, in what kind of soil that man of self-denial, that poor one in spirit, has just been buried?"

"No! what do you mean, doctor?"

"That priest, who took the oath of perpetual poverty, now reposes in a gold-mine!"

"A gold-mine!" exclaimed Kennedy and Joe in one breath.

"Yes, a gold-mine," said the doctor, quietly. "Those blocks which you are trampling under foot, like worthless stones, contain gold-ore of great purity."

"Impossible! impossible!" repeated Joe.

"You would not have to look long among those fissures of slaty schist without finding pepites of considerable value."

Joe at once rushed like a crazy man among the scattered fragments, and Kennedy was not long in following his example.

"Keep cool, Joe," said his master.

"Why, doctor, you speak of the thing quite at your ease."

"What! a philosopher of your mettle—"

"Ah, master, no philosophy holds good in this case!"

"Come! come! Let us reflect a little. What good would all this wealth do you? We cannot carry any of it away with us."

"We can't take any of it with us, indeed?"

"It's rather too heavy for our car! I even hesitated to tell you anything about it, for fear of exciting your regret!"

"What!" said Joe, again, "abandon these treasures—a fortune for us!—really for us—our own—leave it behind!"

"Take care, my friend! Would you yield to the thirst for gold? Has not this dead man whom you have just helped to bury, taught you the vanity of human affairs?"

"All that is true," replied Joe, "but gold! Mr. Kennedy, won't you help to gather up a trifle of all these millions?"

"What could we do with them, Joe?" said the hunter, unable to repress a smile. "We did not come hither in search of fortune, and we cannot take one home with us."

"The millions are rather heavy, you know," resumed the doctor, "and cannot very easily be put into one's pocket."

"But, at least," said Joe, driven to his last defences, "couldn't we take some of that ore for ballast, instead of sand?"

"Very good! I consent," said the doctor, "but you must not make too many wry faces when we come to throw some thousands of crowns' worth overboard."

"Thousands of crowns!" echoed Joe; "is it possible that there is so much gold in them, and that all this is the same?"

"Yes, my friend, this is a reservoir in which Nature has been heaping up her wealth for centuries! There is enough here to enrich whole nations! An Australia and a California both together in the midst of the wilderness!"

"And the whole of it is to remain useless!"

"Perhaps! but at all events, here's what I'll do to console you."

"That would be rather difficult to do!" said Joe, with a contrite air.

"Listen! I will take the exact bearings of this spot, and give them to you, so that, upon your return to England, you can tell our countrymen about it, and let them have a share, if you think that so much gold would make them happy."

"Ah! master, I give up; I see that you are right, and that there is nothing else to be done. Let us fill our car with the precious mineral, and what remains at the end of the trip will be so much made."

And Joe went to work. He did so, too, with all his might, and soon had collected more than a thousand pieces of quartz, which contained gold enclosed as though in an extremely hard crystal casket.

The doctor watched him with a smile; and, while Joe went on, he took the bearings, and found that the missionary's grave lay in twenty-two degrees twenty-three minutes east longitude, and four degrees fifty-five minutes north latitude.

Then, casting one glance at the swelling of the soil, beneath which the body of the poor Frenchman reposed, he went back to his car.

He would have erected a plain, rude cross over the tomb, left solitary thus in the midst of the African deserts, but not a tree was to be seen in the environs.

"God will recognise it!" said Kennedy.

An anxiety of another sort now began to steal over the doctor's mind. He would have given much of the gold before him for a little water—for he had to replace what had been thrown overboard when the negro was carried up into the air. But it was impossible to find it in these arid regions; and this reflection gave him great uneasiness. He had to feed his cylinder continually; and he even began to find that he had not enough to quench the thirst of his party. Therefore he determined to lose no opportunity of replenishing his supply.

Upon getting back to the car, he found it burdened with the quartz-blocks that Joe's greed had heaped in it. He got in, however, without saying anything. Kennedy took his customary place, and Joe followed, but not without casting a covetous glance at the treasures in the ravine.

The doctor rekindled the light in the cylinder; the spiral became heated; the current of hydrogen came in a few minutes, and the gas dilated; but the balloon did not stir an inch.

Joe looked on uneasily, but kept silent.

"Joe!" said the doctor.

Joe made no reply.

"Joe! Don't you hear me?"

Joe made a sign that he heard; but he would not understand.

"Do me the kindness to throw out some of that quartz!"

"But, doctor, you gave me leave—"

"I gave you leave to replace the ballast; that was all!"

"But—"

"Do you want to stay forever in this desert?"

Joe cast a despairing look at Kennedy; but the hunter put on the air of a man who could do nothing in the matter.

"Well, Joe?"

"Then your cylinder don't work," said the obstinate fellow.

"My cylinder? It is lit, as you perceive. But the balloon will not rise until you have thrown off a little ballast."

Joe scratched his ear, picked up a piece of quartz, the smallest in the lot, weighed and reweighed it, and tossed it up and down in his hand. It was a fragment of about three or four pounds. At last he threw it out.

But the balloon did not budge.

"Humph!" said he; "we're not going up yet."

"Not yet," said the doctor. "Keep on throwing."

Kennedy laughed. Joe now threw out some ten pounds, but the balloon stood still.

Joe got very pale.

"Poor fellow!" said the doctor. "Mr. Kennedy, you and I weigh, unless I am mistaken, about four hundred pounds—so that you'll have to get rid of at least that weight, since it was put in here to make up for us."

"Throw away four hundred pounds!" said Joe, piteously.

"And some more with it, or we can't rise. Come, courage, Joe!"

The brave fellow, heaving deep sighs, began at last to lighten the balloon; but, from time to time, he would stop, and ask:

"Are you going up?"

"No, not yet," was the invariable response.

"It moves!" said he, at last.

"Keep on!" replied the doctor.

"It's going up; I'm sure."

"Keep on yet," said Kennedy.

And Joe, picking up one more block, desperately tossed it out of the car. The balloon rose a hundred feet or so, and, aided by the cylinder, soon passed above the surrounding summits.

"Now, Joe," resumed the doctor, "there still remains a handsome fortune for you; and, if we can only keep the rest of this with us until the end of our trip, there you are—rich for the balance of your days!"

Joe made no answer, but stretched himself out luxuriously on his heap of quartz.

"See, my dear Dick!" the doctor went on. "Just see the power of this metal over the cleverest lad in the world! What passions, what greed, what crimes, the knowledge of such a mine as that would cause! It is sad to think of it!"

By evening the balloon had made ninety miles to the westward, and was, in a direct line, fourteen hundred miles from Zanzibar.

Chapter XXIV

THE WIND DIES AWAY—THE VICINITY OF THE DESERT—
THE MISTAKE IN THE WATER-SUPPLY—THE NIGHTS OF THE
EQUATOR—DR. FERGUSON'S ANXIETIES—THE SITUATION FLATLY
STATED—ENERGETIC REPLIES OF KENNEDY AND JOE—
ONE NIGHT MORE

THE BALLOON, HAVING BEEN MADE FAST TO A SOLITARY TREE, ALMOST COMPLETELY dried up by the aridity of the region in which it stood, passed the night in perfect quietness; and the travellers were enabled to enjoy a little of the repose which they so greatly needed. The emotions of the day had left sad impressions on their minds.

Towards morning, the sky had resumed its brilliant purity and its heat. The balloon ascended, and, after several ineffectual attempts, fell into a current that, although not rapid, bore them towards the north-west.

"We are not making progress," said the doctor. "If I am not mistaken, we have accomplished nearly half of our journey in ten days; but, at the rate at which we are going, it would take months to end it; and that is all the more vexatious, that we are threatened with a lack of water."

"But we'll find some," said Joe. "It is not to be thought of that we shouldn't discover some river, some stream, or pond, in all this vast extent of country."

"I hope so."

"Now don't you think that it's Joe's cargo of stone that is keeping us back?"

Kennedy asked this question only to tease Joe; and he did so the more willingly because he had, for a moment, shared the poor lad's hallucinations; but, not finding anything in them, he had fallen back into the attitude of a strong-minded looker-on, and turned the affair off with a laugh.

Joe cast a mournful glance at him; but the doctor made no reply. He was thinking, not without secret terror, probably, of the vast solitudes of Sahara—for there whole weeks sometimes pass without the caravans meeting with a single spring of water. Occupied with these thoughts, he scrutinised every depression of the soil with the closest attention.

These anxieties, and the incidents recently occurring, had not been without their effect upon the spirits of our three travellers. They conversed less, and were more wrapped in their own thoughts.

Joe, clever lad as he was, seemed no longer the same person since his gaze had plunged into that ocean of gold. He kept entirely silent, and gazed incessantly upon the stony fragments heaped up in the car—worthless to-day, but of inestimable value to-morrow.

The appearance of this part of Africa was, moreover, quite calculated to inspire alarm: the desert was gradually expanding around them; not another village was to be seen—not even a collection of a few huts; and vegetation also was disappearing. Barely a few dwarf plants could now be noticed, like those on the wild heaths of Scotland; then came the first tract of greyish sand and flint, with here and there a lentisk tree and brambles. In the midst of this sterility, the rudimental carcass of the Globe appeared in ridges of sharply-jutting rock. These symptoms of a totally dry and barren region greatly disquieted Dr. Ferguson.

It seemed as though no caravan had ever braved this desert expanse, or it would have left visible traces of its encampments, or the whitened bones of men and animals. But nothing of the kind was to be seen, and the aeronauts felt that, ere long, an immensity of sand would cover the whole of this desolate region.

However, there was no going back; they must go forward; and, indeed, the doctor asked for nothing better; he would even have welcomed a tempest to carry him beyond this country. But, there was not a cloud in the sky. At the close of the day, the balloon had not made thirty miles.

If there had been no lack of water! But, there remained only three gallons in all! The doctor put aside one gallon, destined to quench the burning thirst that a heat of ninety degrees rendered intolerable. Two gallons only then remained to supply the cylinder. Hence, they could produce no more than four hundred and eighty cubic feet of gas; yet the cylinder consumed about nine cubic feet per hour. Consequently, they could not keep on longer than fifty-four hours—and all this was a mathematical calculation!

"Fifty-four hours!" said the doctor to his companions. "Therefore, as I am determined not to travel by night, for fear of passing some stream or pool, we have but three days and a half of journeying during which we must find water, at all hazards. I have thought it my duty to make you aware of the real state of the case, as I have retained only one gallon for drinking, and we shall have to put ourselves on the shortest allowance."

"Put us on short allowance, then, doctor," responded Kennedy, "but we must not despair. We have three days left, you say?"

"Yes, my dear Dick!"

"Well, as grieving over the matter won't help us, in three days there will be time enough to decide upon what is to be done; in the meanwhile, let us redouble our vigilance!"

At their evening meal, the water was strictly measured out, and the brandy was increased in quantity in the punch they drank. But they had to be careful with the spirits, the latter being more likely to produce than to quench thirst.

The car rested, during the night, upon an immense plateau, in which there was a deep hollow; its height was scarcely eight hundred feet above the level of the sea. This circumstance gave the doctor some hope, since it recalled to his mind the conjectures of geographers concerning the existence of a vast stretch of water in the centre of Africa. But, if such a lake really existed, the point was to reach it, and not a sign of change was visible in the motionless sky.

To the tranquil night and its starry magnificence succeeded the unchanging daylight and the blazing rays of the sun; and, from the earliest dawn, the temperature became scorching. At five o'clock in the morning, the doctor gave the signal for departure, and, for a considerable time, the balloon remained immovable in the leaden atmosphere.

The doctor might have escaped this intense heat by rising into a higher range, but, in order to do so, he would have had to consume a large quantity of water, a thing that had now become impossible. He contented himself, therefore, with keeping the balloon at one hundred feet from the ground, and, at that elevation, a feeble current drove it towards the western horizon.

The breakfast consisted of a little dried meat and *pemmican*. By noon, the *Victoria* had advanced only a few miles.

"We cannot go any faster," said the doctor; "we no longer command—we have to obey."

"Ah! doctor, here is one of those occasions when a propeller would not be a thing to be despised."

"Undoubtedly so, Dick, provided it would not require an expenditure of water to put it in motion, for, in that case, the situation would be precisely the same; moreover, up to this time, nothing practical of the sort has been invented. Balloons are still at that point where ships were before the invention of steam. It took six thousand years to invent propellers and screws; so we have time enough yet."

"Confounded heat!" said Joe, wiping away the perspiration that was streaming from his forehead.

"If we had water, this heat would be of service to us, for it dilates the hydrogen in the balloon, and diminishes the amount required in the spiral, although it is true that, if we were not short of the useful liquid, we should not have to economise it. Ah! that rascally savage who cost us the tank!"*

"You don't regret, though, what you did, doctor?"

"No, Dick, since it was in our power to save that unfortunate missionary from a horrible death. But, the hundred pounds of water that we threw overboard would be very useful to us now; it would be thirteen or fourteen days more of progress secured, or quite enough to carry us over this desert."

"We've made at least half the journey, haven't we?" asked Joe.

"In distance, yes; but in duration, no, should the wind leave us; and it, even now, has a tendency to die away altogether."

"Come, sir," said Joe, again, "we must not complain; we've got along pretty well, thus far, and whatever happens to me, I can't get desperate. We'll find water; mind, I tell you so."

The soil, however, ran lower from mile to mile; the undulations of the gold-bearing mountains they had left died away into the plain, like the last throes of exhausted Nature. Scanty grass took the place of the fine trees of the east; only a few belts of half-scorched herbage still contended against the invasion of the sand, and the huge rocks, that had rolled down from the distant summits, crushed in their fall, had scattered in sharp-edged pebbles which soon again became coarse sand, and finally impalpable dust.

"Here, at last, is Africa, such as you pictured it to yourself, Joe! Was I not right in saying, 'Wait a little?' eh?"

"Well, master, it's all natural, at least—heat and dust. It would be foolish to look for anything else in such a country. Do you see," he added, laughing, "I had no confidence, for my part, in your forests and your prairies; they were out of reason. What was the use of coming so far to find scenery just like England? Here's the first time that I believe in Africa, and I'm not sorry to get a taste of it."

Towards evening, the doctor calculated that the balloon had not made twenty miles during that whole burning day, and a heated gloom closed in upon it, as soon as the sun

---

*The water-tank had been thrown overboard when the native clung to the car.

had disappeared behind the horizon, which was traced against the sky with all the precision of a straight line.

The next day was Thursday, the 1st of May, but the days followed each other with desperate monotony. Each morning was like the one that had preceded it; noon poured down the same exhaustless rays, and night condensed in its shadow the scattered heat which the ensuing day would again bequeath to the succeeding night. The wind, now scarcely observable, was rather a gasp than a breath, and the morning could almost be foreseen when even that gasp would cease.

The doctor reacted against the gloominess of the situation and retained all the coolness and self-possession of a disciplined heart. With his glass he scrutinised every quarter of the horizon; he saw the last rising ground gradually melting to the dead level, and the last vegetation disappearing, while, before him, stretched the immensity of the desert.

The responsibility resting upon him pressed sorely, but he did not allow his disquiet to appear. Those two men, Dick and Joe, friends of his, both of them, he had induced to come with him almost by the force alone of friendship and of duty. Had he done well in that? Was it not like attempting to tread forbidden paths? Was he not, in this trip, trying to pass the borders of the impossible? Had not the Almighty reserved for later ages the knowledge of this inhospitable continent?

All these thoughts, of the kind that arise in hours of discouragement, succeeded each other and multiplied in his mind, and, by an irresistible association of ideas, the doctor allowed himself to be carried beyond the bounds of logic and of reason. After having established in his own mind what he should *not* have done, the next question was, what he should do, then. Would it be impossible to retrace his steps? Were there not currents higher up that would waft him to less arid regions? Well informed with regard to the countries over which he had passed, he was utterly ignorant of those to come, and thus his conscience speaking aloud to him, he resolved, in his turn, to speak frankly to his two companions. He thereupon laid the whole state of the case plainly before them; he showed them what had been done, and what there was yet to do; at the worst, they could return, or attempt it, at least.—What did they think about it?

"I have no other opinion than that of my excellent master," said Joe; "what he may have to suffer, I can suffer, and that better than he can, perhaps. Where he goes, there I'll go!"

"And you, Kennedy?"

"I, doctor, I'm not the man to despair; no one was less ignorant than I of the perils of the enterprise, but I did not want to see them, from the moment that you determined to brave them. Under present circumstances, my opinion is, that we should persevere—go clear to the end. Besides, to return looks to me quite as perilous as the other course. So onward, then! you may count upon us!"

"Thanks, my gallant friends!" replied the doctor, with much real feeling, "I expected such devotion as this; but I needed these encouraging words. Yet, once again, thank you, from the bottom of my heart!"

And, with this, the three friends warmly grasped each other by the hand.

"Now, hear me!" said the doctor. "According to my solar observations, we are not more than three hundred miles from the Gulf of Guinea; the desert, therefore, cannot extend indefinitely, since the coast is inhabited, and the country has been explored for some distance back into the interior. If needs be, we can direct our course to that quarter, and it seems out of the question that we should not come across some oasis, or some well, where we could replenish our stock of water. But, what we want now, is the wind, for without it we are held here suspended in the air at a dead calm."

"Let us wait with resignation," said the hunter.

But, each of the party, in his turn, vainly scanned the space around him during that long wearisome day. Nothing could be seen to form the basis of a hope. The very last inequalities of the soil disappeared with the setting sun, whose horizontal rays stretched in long lines of fire over the flat immensity. It was the Desert!

Our aeronauts had scarcely gone a distance of fifteen miles, having expended, as on the preceding day, one hundred and thirty-five cubic feet of gas to feed the cylinder, and two pints of water out of the remaining eight had been sacrificed to the demands of intense thirst.

The night passed quietly—too quietly, indeed, but the doctor did not sleep!

Chapter XXV

A Little Philosophy—A Cloud on the Horizon—In the Midst of a Fog—The Strange Balloon—An Exact View of the VICTORIA—The Palm-Trees—Traces of a Caravan— The Well in the Midst of the Desert

ON THE MORROW, THERE WAS THE SAME PURITY OF SKY, THE SAME STILLNESS OF THE atmosphere. The balloon rose to an elevation of five hundred feet, but it had scarcely changed its position to the westward in any perceptible degree.

"We are right in the open desert," said the doctor. "Look at that vast reach of sand! What a strange spectacle! What a singular arrangement of nature! Why should there be, in one place, such extreme luxuriance of vegetation yonder, and here, this extreme aridity, and that in the same latitude, and under the same rays of the sun?"

"The why concerns me but little," answered Kennedy, "the reason interests me less than the fact. The thing is so; that's the important part of it!"

"Oh, it is well to philosophise a little, Dick; it does no harm."

"Let us philosophise, then, if you will; we have time enough before us; we are hardly moving; the wind is afraid to blow; it sleeps."

"That will not last forever," put in Joe; "I think I see some banks of clouds in the east."

"Joe's right!" said the doctor, after he had taken a look.

"Good!" said Kennedy; "now for our clouds, with a fine rain, and a fresh wind to dash it into our faces!"

"Well, we'll see, Dick, we'll see!"

"But this is Friday, master, and I'm afraid of Fridays!"

"Well, I hope that this very day you'll get over those notions."

"I hope so, master, too. Whew!" he added, mopping his face, "heat's a good thing, especially in winter, but in summer it don't do to take too much of it."

"Don't you fear the effect of the sun's heat on our balloon?" asked Kennedy, addressing the doctor.

"No! the gutta-percha coating resists much higher temperatures than even this. With my spiral I have subjected it inside to as much as one hundred and fifty-eight degrees sometimes, and the covering does not appear to have suffered."

"A cloud! a real cloud!" shouted Joe at this moment, for that piercing eyesight of his beat all the glasses.

And, in fact, a thick bank of vapour, now quite distinct, could be seen slowly emerging above the horizon. It appeared to be very deep, and, as it were, puffed out. It was, in reality, a conglomeration of smaller clouds. The latter invariably retained their original formation, and from this circumstance the doctor concluded that there was no current of air in their collected mass.

This compact body of vapour had appeared about eight o'clock in the morning, and, by eleven, it had already reached the height of the sun's disk. The latter then disappeared entirely behind the murky veil, and the lower belt of cloud, at the same moment, lifted above the line of the horizon, which was again disclosed in a full blaze of daylight.

"It's only an isolated cloud," remarked the doctor. "It won't do to count much upon that."

"Look, Dick, its shape is just the same as when we saw it this morning!"

"Then, doctor, there's to be neither rain nor wind, at least for us!"

"I fear so; the cloud keeps at a great height."

"Well, doctor, suppose we were to go in pursuit of this cloud, since it refuses to burst upon us?"

"I fancy that to do so wouldn't help us much; it would be a consumption of gas, and, consequently, of water, to little purpose; but, in our situation, we must not leave anything untried; therefore, let us ascend!"

And with this, the doctor put on a full head of flame from the cylinder, and the dilation of the hydrogen, occasioned by such sudden and intense heat, sent the balloon rapidly aloft.

About fifteen hundred feet from the ground, it encountered an opaque mass of cloud, and entered a dense fog, suspended at that elevation; but it did not meet with the least breath of wind. This fog seemed even destitute of humidity, and the articles brought in contact with it were scarcely dampened in the slightest degree. The balloon, completely enveloped in the vapour, gained a little increase of speed, perhaps, and that was all.

The doctor gloomily recognised what trifling success he had obtained from his maneuvre, and was relapsing into deep meditation, when he heard Joe exclaim, in tones of most intense astonishment:

"Ah! by all that's beautiful!"

"What's the matter, Joe?"

"Doctor! Mr. Kennedy! Here's something curious!"

"What is it, then?"

"We are not alone, up here! There are rogues about! They've stolen our invention!"

"Has he gone crazy?" asked Kennedy.

Joe stood there, perfectly motionless, the very picture of amazement.

"Can the hot sun have really affected the poor fellow's brain?" said the doctor, turning towards him.

"Will you tell me?—"

"Look!" said Joe, pointing to a certain quarter of the sky.

"By St. James!" exclaimed Kennedy, in turn, "why, who would have believed it? Look, look! doctor!"

"I see it!" said the doctor, very quietly.

"Another balloon! and other passengers, like ourselves!"

And, sure enough, there was another balloon about two hundred paces from them, floating in the air with its car and its aeronauts. It was following exactly the same route as the *Victoria*.

"Well," said the doctor, "nothing remains for us but to make signals; take the flag, Kennedy, and show them our colours."

It seemed that the travellers by the other balloon had just the same idea, at the same moment, for the same kind of flag repeated precisely the same salute with a hand that moved in just the same manner.

"What does that mean?" asked Kennedy.

"They are apes," said Joe, "imitating us."

"It means," said the doctor, laughing, "that it is you, Dick, yourself, making that signal to yourself; or, in other words, that we see ourselves in the second balloon, which is no other than the *Victoria*."

"As to that, master, with all respect to you," said Joe, "you'll never make me believe it."

"Climb up on the edge of the car, Joe; wave your arms, and then you'll see."

Joe obeyed, and all his gestures were instantaneously and exactly repeated.

"It is merely the effect of the *mirage*," said the doctor, "and nothing else—a simple optical phenomenon due to the unequal refraction of light by different layers of the atmosphere, and that is all."

"It's wonderful," said Joe, who could not make up his mind to surrender, but went on repeating his gesticulations.

"What a curious sight! Do you know," said Kennedy, "that it's a real pleasure to have a view of our noble balloon in that style? She's a beauty, isn't she?—and how stately her movements as she sweeps along!"

"You may explain the matter as you like," continued Joe, "it's a strange thing, anyhow!"

But ere long this picture began to fade away; the clouds rose higher, leaving the balloon, which made no further attempt to follow them, and in about an hour they disappeared in the open sky.

The wind, which had been scarcely perceptible, seemed still to diminish, and the doctor in perfect desperation descended towards the ground, and all three of the travellers, whom the incident just recorded had, for a few moments, diverted from their anxieties, relapsed into gloomy meditation, sweltering the while beneath the scorching heat.

About four o'clock, Joe descried some object standing out against the vast background of sand, and soon was able to declare positively that there were two palm-trees at no great distance.

"Palm-trees!" exclaimed Ferguson; "why then there's a spring—a well!"

He took up his glass and satisfied himself that Joe's eyes had not been mistaken.

"At length!" he said, over and over again, "water! water! and we are saved; for if we do move slowly, still we move, and we shall arrive at last!"

"Good, master! but suppose we were to drink a mouthful in the meantime, for this air is stifling?"

"Let us drink then, my boy!"

No one waited to be coaxed. A whole pint was swallowed then and there, reducing the total remaining supply to three pints and a half.

"Ah! that does one good!" said Joe; "wasn't it fine? Barclay and Perkins never turned out ale equal to that!"

"See the advantage of being put on short allowance!" moralised the doctor.

"It is not great, after all," retorted Kennedy; "and if I were never again to have the pleasure of drinking water, I should agree on condition that I should never be deprived of it."

At six o'clock the balloon was floating over the palm-trees.

They were two shrivelled, stunted, dried-up specimens of trees—two ghosts of palms—without foliage, and more dead than alive. Ferguson examined them with terror.

At their feet could be seen the half-worn stones of a spring, but these stones, pulverised by the baking heat of the sun, seemed to be nothing now but impalpable dust. There was not the slightest sign of moisture. The doctor's heart shrank within him, and he was about to communicate his thoughts to his companions, when their exclamations attracted his attention. As far as the eye could reach to the eastward, extended a long line of whitened bones; pieces of skeletons surrounded the fountain; a caravan had evidently made its way to that point, marking its progress by its bleaching remains; the weaker had fallen one by one upon the sand; the stronger, having at length reached this spring for which they panted, had there found a horrible death.

Our travellers looked at each other and turned pale.

"Let us not alight!" said Kennedy, "let us fly from this hideous spectacle! There's not a drop of water here!"

"No, Dick, as well pass the night here as elsewhere; let us have a clear conscience in the matter. We'll dig down to the very bottom of the well. There has been a spring here, and perhaps there's something left in it!"

The *Victoria* touched the ground; Joe and Kennedy put into the car a quantity of sand equal to their weight, and leaped out. They then hastened to the well, and penetrated to the interior by a flight of steps that was now nothing but dust. The spring appeared to have been dry for years. They dug down into a parched and powdery sand—the very driest of all sand, indeed—there was not one trace of moisture!

The doctor saw them come up to the surface of the desert, saturated with perspiration, worn out, covered with fine dust, exhausted, discouraged and despairing.

He then comprehended that their search had been fruitless. He had expected as much, and he kept silent, for he felt that, from this moment forth, he must have courage and energy enough for three.

Joe brought up with him some pieces of a leathern bottle that had grown hard and horn-like with age, and angrily flung them away among the bleaching bones of the caravan.

At supper, not a word was spoken by our travellers, and they even ate without appetite. Yet they had not, up to this moment, endured the real agonies of thirst, and were in no desponding mood, excepting for the future.

Chapter XXVI

One Hundred and Thirteen Degrees—The Doctor's Reflections—A Desperate Search—The Cylinder goes out—One Hundred and Twenty-two Degrees—Contemplation of the Desert—A Night Walk—Solitude—Debility—Joe's Prospects—He gives himself One Day more

THE DISTANCE MADE BY THE BALLOON DURING THE PRECEDING DAY DID NOT EXCEED ten miles, and, to keep it afloat, one hundred and sixty-two cubic feet of gas had been consumed.

On Saturday morning the doctor again gave the signal for departure.

"The cylinder can work only six hours longer; and, if in that time we shall not have found either a well or a spring of water, God alone knows what will become of us!"

"Not much wind this morning, master," said Joe; "but it will come up, perhaps," he added, suddenly remarking the doctor's ill-concealed depression.

Vain hope! The atmosphere was in a dead calm—one of those calms which hold vessels captive in tropical seas. The heat had become intolerable; and the thermometer, in the shade under the awning, indicated one hundred and thirteen degrees.

Joe and Kennedy, reclining at full length near each other, tried, if not in slumber, at least in torpor, to forget their situation, for their forced inactivity gave them periods of leisure far from pleasant. That man is to be pitied the most who cannot wean himself from gloomy reflections by actual work, or some practical pursuit. But here there was nothing to look after, nothing to undertake, and they had to submit to the situation, without having it in their power to ameliorate it.

The pangs of thirst began to be severely felt; brandy, far from appeasing this imperious necessity, augmented it, and richly merited the name of "tiger's milk" applied to it by the African natives. Scarcely two pints of water remained, and that was heated. Each of the party devoured the few precious drops with his gaze, yet neither of them dared to moisten his lips with them. Two pints of water in the midst of the desert!

Then it was that Dr. Ferguson, buried in meditation, asked himself whether he had acted with prudence. Would he not have done better to have kept the water that he had decomposed in pure loss, in order to sustain him in the air? He had gained a little distance, to be sure; but was he any nearer to his journey's end? What difference did sixty miles to the rear make in this region, when there was no water to be had where they were? The wind, should it rise, would blow there as it did here, only less strongly at this point, if it came from the east. But hope urged him onward. And yet those two gallons of water, expended in vain, would have sufficed for nine days' halt in the desert. And what changes might not have occurred in nine days! Perhaps, too, while retaining the water, he might have ascended by throwing out ballast, at the cost merely of discharging some gas, when he had again to descend. But the gas in his balloon was his blood, his very life!

A thousand and one such reflections whirled in succession through his brain; and, resting his head between his hands, he sat there for hours without raising it.

"We must make one final effort," he said, at last, about ten o'clock in the morning. "We must endeavour, just once more, to find an atmospheric current to bear us away from here, and, to that end, must risk our last resources."

Therefore, while his companions slept, the doctor raised the hydrogen in the balloon to an elevated temperature, and the huge globe, filling out by the dilation of the gas, rose straight up in the perpendicular rays of the sun. The doctor searched vainly for a breath of wind, from the height of one hundred feet to that of five miles; his starting-point remained fatally right below him, and absolute calm seemed to reign, up to the extreme limits of the breathing atmosphere.

At length the feeding-supply of water gave out; the cylinder was extinguished for lack of gas; the Buntzen battery ceased to work, and the balloon, shrinking together, gently descended to the sand, in the very place that the car had hollowed out there.

It was noon; and solar observations gave nineteen degrees thirty-five minutes east longitude, and six degrees fifty-one minutes north latitude, or nearly five hundred miles from Lake Tchad, and more than four hundred miles from the western coast of Africa.

On the balloon taking ground, Kennedy and Joe awoke from their stupor.

"We have halted," said the Scot.

"We had to do so," replied the doctor, gravely.

His companions understood him. The level of the soil at that point corresponded with the level of the sea, and, consequently, the balloon remained in perfect equilibrium, and absolutely motionless.

The weight of the three travellers was replaced with an equivalent quantity of sand, and they got out of the car. Each was absorbed in his own thoughts; and for many hours neither of them spoke. Joe prepared their evening meal, which consisted of biscuit and *pemmican*, and was hardly tasted by either of the party. A mouthful of scalding water from their little store completed this gloomy repast.

During the night none of them kept awake; yet none could be precisely said to have slept. On the morrow there remained only half-a-pint of water, and this the doctor put away, all three having resolved not to touch it until the last extremity.

It was not long, however, before Joe exclaimed:

"I'm choking, and the heat is getting worse! I'm not surprised at that, though," he added, consulting the thermometer; "one hundred and forty degrees!"

"The sand scorches me," said the hunter, "as though it had just come out of a furnace; and not a cloud in this sky of fire. It's enough to drive one mad!"

"Let us not despair," responded the doctor. "In this latitude these intense heats are invariably followed by storms, and the latter come with the suddenness of lightning.

Notwithstanding this disheartening clearness of the sky, great atmospheric changes may take place in less than an hour."

"But," asked Kennedy, "is there any sign whatever of that?"

"Well," replied the doctor, "I think that there is some slight symptom of a fall in the barometer."

"May Heaven hearken to you, Samuel! for here we are pinned to the ground, like a bird with broken wings."

"With this difference, however, my dear Dick, that our wings are unhurt, and I hope that we shall be able to use them again."

"Ah! wind! wind!" exclaimed Joe; "enough to carry us to a stream or a well, and we'll be all right. We have provisions enough, and, with water, we could wait a month without suffering; but thirst is a cruel thing!"

It was not thirst alone, but the unchanging sight of the desert, that fatigued the mind. There was not a variation in the surface of the soil, not a hillock of sand, not a pebble, to relieve the gaze. This unbroken level discouraged the beholder, and gave him that kind of malady called the "desert-sickness." The impassible monotony of the arid blue sky, and the vast yellow expanse of the desert-sand, at length produced a sensation of terror. In this inflamed atmosphere the heat appeared to vibrate as it does above a blazing hearth, while the mind grew desperate in contemplating the limitless calm, and could see no reason why the thing should ever end, since immensity is a species of eternity.

Thus, at last, our hapless travellers, deprived of water in this torrid heat, began to feel symptoms of mental disorder. Their eyes swelled in their sockets, and their gaze became confused.

When night came on, the doctor determined to combat this alarming tendency by rapid walking. His idea was to pace the sandy plain for a few hours, not in search of anything, but simply for exercise.

"Come along!" he said to his companions; "believe me, it will do you good."

"Out of the question!" said Kennedy; "I could not walk a step."

"And I," said Joe, "would rather sleep!"

"But sleep, or even rest, would be dangerous to you, my friends; you must react against this tendency to stupor. Come with me!"

But the doctor could do nothing with them, and, therefore, set off alone, amid the starry clearness of the night. The first few steps he took were painful, for they were the steps of an enfeebled man quite out of practise in walking. However, he quickly saw that the exercise would be beneficial to him, and pushed on several miles to the westward. Once in rapid motion, he felt his spirits greatly cheered, when, suddenly, a vertigo came over him; he seemed to be poised on the edge of an abyss; his knees bent under him; the vast solitude struck terror to his heart; he found himself the minute mathematical point, the centre of an infinite circumference, that is to say—a nothing! The balloon had disappeared entirely in the deepening gloom. The doctor, cool, impassible, reckless explorer that he was, felt himself at last seized with a nameless dread. He strove to retrace his steps, but in vain. He called aloud. Not even an echo replied, and his voice died out in the empty vastness of surrounding space, like a pebble cast into a bottomless gulf; then, down he sank, fainting, on the sand, alone, amid the eternal silence of the desert.

At midnight he came to, in the arms of his faithful follower, Joe. The latter, uneasy at his master's prolonged absence, had set out after him, easily tracing him by the clear imprint of his feet in the sand, and had found him lying in a swoon.

"What has been the matter, sir?" was the first enquiry.

"Nothing, Joe, nothing! Only a touch of weakness, that's all. It's over now."

"Oh! it won't amount to anything, sir, I'm sure of that; but get up on your feet, if you can. There! lean upon me, and let us get back to the balloon."

And the doctor, leaning on Joe's arm, returned along the track by which he had come.

"You were too bold, sir; it won't do to run such risks. You might have been robbed," he added, laughing. "But, sir, come now, let us talk seriously."

"Speak! I am listening to you."

"We must positively make up our minds to do something. Our present situation cannot last more than a few days longer, and if we get no wind, we are lost."

The doctor made no reply.

"Well, then, one of us must sacrifice himself for the good of all, and it is most natural that it should fall to me to do so."

"What have you to propose? What is your plan?"

"A very simple one! It is to take provisions enough, and to walk right on until I come to some place, as I must do, sooner or later. In the meantime, if Heaven sends you a good wind, you need not wait, but can start again. For my part, if I come to a village, I'll work my way through with a few Arabic words that you can write for me on a slip of paper, and I'll bring you help or lose my hide. What do you think of my plan?"

"It is absolute folly, Joe, but worthy of your noble heart. The thing is impossible. You will not leave us."

"But, sir, we must do something, and this plan can't do you any harm, for, I say again, you need not wait; and then, after all, I may succeed."

"No, Joe, no! We will not separate. That would only be adding sorrow to trouble. It was written that matters should be as they are; and it is very probably written that it shall be quite otherwise by and by. Let us wait, then, with resignation."

"So be it, master; but take notice of one thing: I give you a day longer, and I'll not wait after that. To-day is Sunday; we might say Monday, as it is one o'clock in the morning, and if we don't get off by Tuesday, I'll run the risk. I've made up my mind to that!"

The doctor made no answer, and in a few minutes they got back to the car, where he took his place beside Kennedy, who lay there plunged in silence so complete that it could not be considered sleep.

Chapter XXVII

TERRIFIC HEAT—HALLUCINATIONS—THE LAST DROPS OF WATER—NIGHTS OF DESPAIR—AN ATTEMPT AT SUICIDE— THE SIMOOM—THE OASIS—THE LION AND LIONESS

THE DOCTOR'S FIRST CARE, ON THE MORROW, WAS TO CONSULT THE BAROMETER. HE found that the mercury had scarcely undergone any perceptible depression.

"Nothing!" he murmured, "nothing!"

He got out of the car and scrutinised the weather; there was only the same heat, the same cloudless sky, the same merciless drought.

"Must we, then, give up to despair?" he exclaimed, in agony.

Joe did not open his lips. He was buried in his own thoughts, and planning the expedition he had proposed.

Kennedy got up, feeling very ill, and a prey to nervous agitation. He was suffering horribly with thirst, and his swollen tongue and lips could hardly articulate a syllable.

There still remained a few drops of water. Each of them knew this, and each was thinking of it, and felt himself drawn towards them; but neither of the three dared to take a step.

Those three men, friends and companions as they were, fixed their haggard eyes upon each other with an instinct of ferocious longing, which was most plainly revealed in the hardy Scot, whose vigourous constitution yielded the soonest to these unnatural privations.

Throughout the day he was delirious, pacing up and down, uttering hoarse cries, gnawing his clinched fists, and ready to open his veins and drink his own hot blood.

"Ah!" he cried, "land of thirst! Well might you be called the land of despair!"

At length he sank down in utter prostration, and his friends heard no other sound from him than the hissing of his breath between his parched and swollen lips.

Towards evening, Joe had his turn of delirium. The vast expanse of sand appeared to him an immense pond, full of clear and limpid water; and, more than once, he dashed himself upon the scorching waste to drink long draughts, and rose again with his mouth clogged with hot dust.

"Curses on it!" he yelled, in his madness, "it's nothing but salt water!"

Then, while Ferguson and Kennedy lay there motionless, the resistless longing came over him to drain the last few drops of water that had been kept in reserve. The natural instinct proved too strong. He dragged himself towards the car, on his knees; he glared at the bottle containing the precious fluid; he gave one wild, eager glance, seized the treasured store, and bore it to his lips.

At that instant he heard a heart-rending cry close beside him—"Water! water!"

It was Kennedy, who had crawled up close to him, and was begging there, upon his knees, and weeping piteously.

Joe, himself in tears, gave the poor wretch the bottle, and Kennedy drained the last drop with savage haste.

"Thanks!" he murmured hoarsely, but Joe did not hear him, for both alike had dropped fainting on the sand.

What took place during that fearful night neither of them knew, but, on Tuesday morning, under those showers of heat which the sun poured down upon them, the unfortunate men felt their limbs gradually drying up, and when Joe attempted to rise he found it impossible.

He looked around him. In the car, the doctor, completely overwhelmed, sat with his arms folded on his breast, gazing with idiotic fixedness upon some imaginary point in space. Kennedy was frightful to behold. He was rolling his head from right to left like a wild beast in a cage.

All at once, his eyes rested on the butt of his rifle, which jutted above the rim of the car.

"Ah!" he screamed, raising himself with a superhuman effort.

Desperate, mad, he snatched at the weapon, and turned the barrel towards his mouth.

"Kennedy!" shouted Joe, throwing himself upon his friend.

"Let go! hands off!" moaned the Scot, in a hoarse, grating voice—and then the two struggled desperately for the rifle.

"Let go, or I'll kill you!" repeated Kennedy. But Joe clung to him only the more fiercely, and they had been contending thus without the doctor seeing them for many seconds, when, suddenly the rifle went off. At the sound of its discharge, the doctor rose up erect, like a spectre, and glared around him.

But all at once his glance grew more animated; he extended his hand towards the horizon, and in a voice no longer human shrieked:

"There! there—off there!"

There was such fearful force in the cry that Kennedy and Joe released each other, and both looked where the doctor pointed.

The plain was agitated like the sea shaken by the fury of a tempest; billows of sand went tossing over each other amid blinding clouds of dust; an immense pillar was seen whirling towards them through the air from the south-east, with terrific velocity; the sun was disappearing behind an opaque veil of cloud whose enormous barrier extended clear to the horizon, while the grains of fine sand went gliding together with all the supple ease of liquid particles, and the rising dust-tide gained more and more with every second.

Ferguson's eyes gleamed with a ray of energetic hope.

"The simoom!" he exclaimed.

"The simoom!" repeated Joe, without exactly knowing what it meant.

"So much the better!" said Kennedy, with the bitterness of despair. "So much the better—we shall die!"

"So much the better!" echoed the doctor, "for we shall live!" and, so saying, he began rapidly to throw out the sand that encumbered the car.

At length his companions understood him, and took their places at his side.

"And now, Joe," said the doctor, "throw out some fifty pounds of your ore, there!"

Joe no longer hesitated, although he still felt a fleeting pang of regret. The balloon at once began to ascend.

"It was high time!" said the doctor.

The simoom, in fact, came rushing on like a thunderbolt, and a moment later the balloon would have been crushed, torn to atoms, annihilated. The awful whirlwind was almost upon it, and it was already pelted with showers of sand driven like hail by the storm.

"Out with more ballast!" shouted the doctor.

"There!" responded Joe, tossing over a huge fragment of quartz.

With this, the *Victoria* rose swiftly above the range of the whirling column, but, caught in the vast displacement of the atmosphere thereby occasioned, it was borne along with incalculable rapidity away above this foaming sea.

The three travellers did not speak. They gazed, and hoped, and even felt refreshed by the breath of the tempest.

About three o'clock, the whirlwind ceased; the sand, falling again upon the desert, formed numberless little hillocks, and the sky resumed its former tranquillity.

The balloon, which had again lost its momentum, was floating in sight of an oasis, a sort of islet studded with green trees, thrown up upon the surface of this sandy ocean.

"Water! we'll find water there!" said the doctor.

And, instantly, opening the upper valve, he let some hydrogen escape, and slowly descended, taking the ground at about two hundred feet from the edge of the oasis.

In four hours the travellers had swept over a distance of two hundred and forty miles!

The car was at once ballasted, and Kennedy, closely followed by Joe, leaped out.

"Take your guns with you!" said the doctor; "take your guns, and be careful!"

Dick grasped his rifle, and Joe took one of the fowling-pieces. They then rapidly made for the trees, and disappeared under the fresh verdure, which announced the presence of abundant springs. As they hurried on, they had not taken notice of certain large footprints and fresh tracks of some living creature marked here and there in the damp soil.

Suddenly, a dull roar was heard not twenty paces from them.

"The roar of a lion!" said Joe.

"Good for that!" said the excited hunter; "we'll fight him. A man feels strong when only a fight's in question."

"But be careful, Mr. Kennedy; be careful! The lives of all depend upon the life of one."

But Kennedy no longer heard him; he was pushing on, his eye blazing; his rifle cocked; fearful to behold in his daring rashness. There, under a palm-tree, stood an enormous black-maned lion, crouching for a spring on his antagonist. Scarcely had he caught a glimpse of the hunter, when he bounded through the air; but he had not touched the ground ere a bullet pierced his heart, and he fell to the earth dead.

"Hurrah! hurrah!" shouted Joe, with wild exultation.

Kennedy rushed towards the well, slid down the dampened steps, and flung himself at full length by the side of a fresh spring, in which he plunged his parched lips. Joe followed suit, and for some minutes nothing was heard but the sound they made with their mouths, drinking more like maddened beasts than men.

"Take care, Mr. Kennedy," said Joe at last; "let us not overdo the thing!" and he panted for breath.

But Kennedy, without a word, drank on. He even plunged his hands, and then his head, into the delicious tide—he fairly revelled in its coolness.

"But the doctor?" said Joe; "our friend, Dr. Ferguson?"

That one word recalled Kennedy to himself, and, hastily filling a flask that he had brought with him, he started on a run up the steps of the well.

But what was his amazement when he saw an opaque body of enormous dimensions blocking up the passage! Joe, who was close upon Kennedy's heels, recoiled with him.

"We are blocked in—entrapped!"

"Impossible! What does that mean?——"

Dick had no time to finish; a terrific roar made him only too quickly aware what foe confronted him.

"Another lion!" exclaimed Joe.

"A lioness, rather," said Kennedy. "Ah! ferocious brute!" he added, "I'll settle you in a moment more!" and swiftly reloaded his rifle.

In another instant he fired, but the animal had disappeared.

"Onward!" shouted Kennedy.

"No!" interposed the other, "that shot did not kill her; her body would have rolled down the steps; she's up there, ready to spring upon the first of us who appears, and he would be a lost man!"

"But what are we to do? We must get out of this, and the doctor is expecting us."

"Let us decoy the animal. Take my piece, and give me your rifle."

"What is your plan?"

"You'll see."

And Joe, taking off his linen jacket, hung it on the end of the rifle, and thrust it above the top of the steps. The lioness flung herself furiously upon it. Kennedy was on the alert for her, and his bullet broke her shoulder. The lioness, with a frightful howl of agony, rolled down the steps, overturning Joe in her fall. The poor fellow imagined that he could already feel the enormous paws of the savage beast in his flesh, when a second detonation resounded in the narrow passage, and Dr. Ferguson appeared at the opening above with his gun in hand, and still smoking from the discharge.

Joe leaped to his feet, clambered over the body of the dead lioness, and handed up the flask full of sparkling water to his master.

To carry it to his lips, and to half empty it at a draught, was the work of an instant, and the three travellers offered up thanks from the depths of their hearts to that Providence who had so miraculously saved them.

Chapter XXVIII

AN EVENING OF DELIGHT—JOE'S CULINARY PERFORMANCES—
A DISSERTATION ON RAW MEAT—THE NARRATIVE OF JAMES
BRUCE—CAMPING OUT—JOE'S DREAMS—THE BAROMETER BEGINS
TO FALL—THE BAROMETER RISES AGAIN—PREPARATIONS FOR
DEPARTURE—THE TEMPEST

THE EVENING WAS LOVELY, AND OUR THREE FRIENDS ENJOYED IT IN THE COOL SHADE of the mimosas, after a substantial repast, at which the tea and the punch were dealt out with no niggardly hand.

Kennedy had traversed the little domain in all directions. He had ransacked every thicket and satisfied himself that the balloon party were the only living creatures in this terrestrial paradise; so they stretched themselves upon their blankets and passed a peaceful night that brought them forgetfulness of their past sufferings.

On the morrow, May 7th, the sun shone with all his splendour, but his rays could not penetrate the dense screen of the palm-tree foliage, and as there was no lack of provisions, the doctor resolved to remain where he was while waiting for a favourable wind.

Joe had conveyed his portable kitchen to the oasis, and proceeded to indulge in any number of culinary combinations, using water all the time with the most profuse extravagance.

"What a strange succession of annoyances and enjoyments!" moralized Kennedy. "Such abundance as this after such privations; such luxury after such want! Ah! I nearly went mad!"

"My dear Dick," replied the doctor, "had it not been for Joe, you would not be sitting here, to-day, discoursing on the instability of human affairs."

"Whole-hearted friend!" said Kennedy, extending his hand to Joe.

"There's no occasion for all that," responded the latter; "but you can take your revenge some time, Mr. Kennedy, always hoping though that you may never have occasion to do the same for me!"

"It's a poor constitution this of ours to succumb to so little," philosophised Dr. Ferguson.

"So little water, you mean, doctor," interposed Joe; "that element must be very necessary to life."

"Undoubtedly, and persons deprived of food hold out longer than those deprived of water."

"I believe it. Besides, when needs must, one can eat anything he comes across, even his fellow-creatures, although that must be a kind of food that's pretty hard to digest."

"The savages don't boggle much about it!" said Kennedy.

"Yes; but then they are savages, and accustomed to devouring raw meat; it's something that I'd find very disgusting, for my part."

"It is disgusting enough," said the doctor, "that's a fact; and so much so, indeed, that nobody believed the narratives of the earliest travellers in Africa who brought back word that many tribes on that continent subsisted upon raw meat, and people generally refused to credit the statement. It was under such circumstances that a very singular adventure befell James Bruce."

"Tell it to us, doctor; we've time enough to hear it," said Joe, stretching himself voluptuously on the cool greensward.

"By all means.—James Bruce was a Scotchman, of Stirlingshire, who, between 1768 and 1772, traversed all Abyssinia, as far as Lake Tyana, in search of the sources of the Nile. He afterward returned to England, but did not publish an account of his journeys until 1790. His statements were received with extreme incredulity, and such may be the reception accorded to our own. The manners and customs of the Abyssinians seemed so different from those of the English, that no one would credit the description of them. Among other details, Bruce had put forward the assertion that the tribes of Eastern Africa fed upon raw flesh, and this set everybody against him. He might say so as much as he pleased; there was no one likely to go and see! One day, in a parlor at Edinburgh, a Scotch gentleman took up the subject in his presence, as it had become the topic of daily pleasantry, and, in reference to the eating of raw flesh, said that the thing was neither possible nor true. Bruce made no reply, but went out and returned a few minutes later with a raw steak, seasoned with pepper and salt, in the African style.

" 'Sir,' said he to the Scotchman, 'in doubting my statements, you have grossly affronted me; in believing the thing to be impossible, you have been egregiously mistaken; and, in proof thereof, you will now eat this beef-steak raw, or you will give me instant satisfaction!' The Scotchman had a wholesome dread of the brawny traveller, and *did* eat the steak, although not without a good many wry faces. Thereupon, with the utmost coolness, James Bruce added: 'Even admitting, sir, that the thing were untrue, you will, at least, no longer maintain that it is impossible.' "

"Well put in!" said Joe, "and if the Scotchman found it lie heavy on his stomach, he got no more than he deserved. If, on our return to England, they dare to doubt what we say about our travels—"

"Well, Joe, what would you do?"

"Why, I'll make the doubters swallow the pieces of the balloon, without either salt or pepper!"

All burst out laughing at Joe's queer notions, and thus the day slipped by in pleasant chat. With returning strength, hope had revived, and with hope came the courage to do and to dare. The past was obliterated in the presence of the future with providential rapidity.

Joe would have been willing to remain forever in this enchanting asylum; it was the realm he had pictured in his dreams; he felt himself at home; his master had to give him his exact location, and it was with the gravest air imaginable that he wrote down on his tablets fifteen degrees forty-three minutes east longitude, and eight degrees thirty-two minutes north latitude.

Kennedy had but one regret, to wit, that he could not hunt in that miniature forest, because, according to his ideas, there was a slight deficiency of ferocious wild beasts in it.

"But, my dear Dick," said the doctor, "haven't you rather a short memory? How about the lion and the lioness?"

"Oh, that!" he ejaculated with the contempt of a thorough-bred sportsman for game already killed. "But the fact is, that finding them here would lead one to suppose that we can't be far from a more fertile country."

"It don't prove much, Dick, for those animals, when goaded by hunger or thirst, will travel long distances, and I think that, to-night, we had better keep a more vigilant look-out, and light fires, besides."

"What, in such heat as this?" said Joe. "Well, if it's necessary, we'll have to do it, but I do think it a real pity to burn this pretty grove that has been such a comfort to us!"

"Oh! above all things, we must take the utmost care not to set it on fire," replied the doctor, "so that others in the same strait as ourselves may someday find shelter here in the middle of the desert."

"I'll be very careful, indeed, doctor; but do you think that this oasis is known?"

"Undoubtedly; it is a halting-place for the caravans that frequent the centre of Africa, and a visit from one of them might be anything but pleasant to you, Joe."

"Why, are there any more of those rascally Nyam-Nyams around here?"

"Certainly; that is the general name of all the neighbouring tribes, and, under the same climates, the same races are likely to have similar manners and customs."

"Pah!" said Joe, "but, after all, it's natural enough. If savages had the ways of gentlemen, where would be the difference? By George, these fine fellows wouldn't have to be coaxed long to eat the Scotchman's raw steak, nor the Scotchman either, into the bargain!"

With this very sensible observation, Joe began to get ready his firewood for the night, making just as little of it as possible. Fortunately, these precautions were superfluous; and each of the party, in his turn, dropped off into the soundest slumber.

On the next day the weather still showed no sign of change, but kept provokingly and obstinately fair. The balloon remained motionless, without any oscillation to betray a breath of wind.

The doctor began to get uneasy again. If their stay in the desert were to be prolonged like this, their provisions would give out. After nearly perishing for want of water, they would, at last, have to starve to death!

But he took fresh courage as he saw the mercury fall considerably in the barometer, and noticed evident signs of an early change in the atmosphere. He therefore resolved to make all his preparations for a start, so as to avail himself of the first opportunity. The feeding-tank and the water-tank were both completely filled.

Then he had to re-establish the equilibrium of the balloon, and Joe was obliged to part with another considerable portion of his precious quartz. With restored health, his ambitious notions had come back to him, and he made more than one wry face before obeying his master; but the latter convinced him that he could not carry so considerable a weight with him through the air, and gave him his choice between the water and the gold. Joe hesitated no longer, but flung out the requisite quantity of his much-prized ore upon the sand.

"The next people who come this way," he remarked, "will be rather surprised to find a fortune in such a place."

"And suppose some learned traveller should come across these specimens, eh?" suggested Kennedy.

"You may be certain, Dick, that they would take him by surprise, and that he would publish his astonishment in several folios; so that someday we shall hear of a wonderful deposit of gold-bearing quartz in the midst of the African sands!"

"And Joe there, will be the cause of it all!"

This idea of mystifying some learned sage tickled Joe hugely, and made him laugh.

During the rest of the day the doctor vainly kept on the watch for a change of weather. The temperature rose, and, had it not been for the shade of the oasis, would have been insupportable. The thermometer marked a hundred and forty-nine degrees in the sun, and a veritable rain of fire filled the air. This was the most intense heat that they had yet noted.

Joe arranged their bivouac for that evening, as he had done for the previous night; and during the watches kept by the doctor and Kennedy there was no fresh incident.

But, towards three o'clock in the morning, while Joe was on guard, the temperature suddenly fell; the sky became overcast with clouds, and the darkness increased.

"Turn out!" cried Joe, arousing his companions. "Turn out! Here's the wind!"

"At last!" exclaimed the doctor, eying the heavens. "But it is a storm! The balloon! Let us hasten to the balloon!"

It was high time for them to reach it. The *Victoria* was bending to the force of the hurricane, and dragging along the car, the latter grazing the sand. Had any portion of the ballast been accidentally thrown out, the balloon would have been swept away, and all hope of recovering it have been forever lost.

But fleet-footed Joe put forth his utmost speed, and checked the car, while the balloon beat upon the sand, at the risk of being torn to pieces. The doctor, followed by Kennedy, leaped in, and lit his cylinder, while his companions threw out the superfluous ballast.

The travellers took one last look at the trees of the oasis bowing to the force of the hurricane, and soon, catching the wind at two hundred feet above the ground, disappeared in the gloom.

Chapter XXIX

Signs of Vegetation—The Fantastic Notion of a French Author—A Magnificent Country—The Kingdom of Adamova—The Explorations of Speke and Burton connected with those of Dr. Barth—The Atlantika Mountains—The River Benoué—The City of Yola— The Bagélé—Mount Mendif

FROM THE MOMENT OF THEIR DEPARTURE, THE TRAVELLERS MOVED WITH GREAT VELOCITY. They longed to leave behind them the desert, which had so nearly been fatal to them.

About a quarter-past nine in the morning, they caught a glimpse of some signs of vegetation: herbage floating on that sea of sand, and announcing, as the weeds upon the ocean did to Christopher Columbus, the nearness of the shore—green shoots peeping up timidly between pebbles that were, in their turn, to be the rocks of that vast expanse.

Hills, but of trifling height, were seen in wavy lines upon the horizon. Their profile, muffled by the heavy mist, was defined but vaguely. The monotony, however, was beginning to disappear.

The doctor hailed with joy the new country thus disclosed, and, like a seaman on look-out at the mast-head, he was ready to shout aloud:

"Land, ho! land!"

An hour later the continent spread broadly before their gaze, still wild in aspect, but less flat, less dénuded, and with a few trees standing out against the grey sky.

"We are in a civilised country at last!" said the hunter.

"Civilised? Well, that's one way of speaking; but there are no people to be seen yet."

"It will not be long before we see them," said Ferguson, "at our present rate of travel."

"Are we still in the negro country, doctor?"

"Yes, and on our way to the country of the Arabs."

"What! real Arabs, sir, with their camels?"

"No, not many camels; they are scarce, if not altogether unknown, in these regions. We must go a few degrees farther north to see them."

"What a pity!"

"And why, Joe?"

"Because, if the wind fell contrary, they might be of use to us."

"How so?"

"Well, sir, it's just a notion that's got into my head: we might hitch them to the car, and make them tow us along. What do you say to that, doctor?"

"Poor Joe! Another person had that idea in advance of you. It was used by a very gifted French author—M. Méry—in a romance, it is true. He has his travellers drawn along in a balloon by a team of camels; then a lion comes up, devours the camels, swallows the tow-rope, and hauls the balloon in their stead; and so on through the story. You see that the whole thing is the top-flower of fancy, but has nothing in common with our style of locomotion."

Joe, a little cut down at learning that his idea had been used already, cudgelled his wits to imagine what animal could have devoured the lion; but he could not guess it, and so quietly went on scanning the appearance of the country.

A lake of medium extent stretched away before him, surrounded by an amphitheatre of hills, which yet could not be dignified with the name of mountains. There were winding valleys, numerous and fertile, with their tangled thickets of the most various trees. The African oil-tree rose above the mass, with leaves fifteen feet in length upon its stalk, the latter studded with sharp thorns; the bombax, or silk-cotton-tree, filled the wind, as it swept by, with the fine down of its seeds; the pungent odors of the *pendanus*, the "kenda" of the Arabs, perfumed the air up to the height where the *Victoria* was sailing; the papaw-tree, with its palm-shaped leaves; the *sterculier*, which produces the Soudan-nut; the baobab, and the banana-tree, completed the luxuriant flora of these inter-tropical regions.

"The country is superb!" said the doctor.

"Here are some animals," added Joe. "Men are not far away."

"Oh, what magnificent elephants!" exclaimed Kennedy. "Is there no way to get a little shooting?"

"How could we manage to halt in a current as strong as this? No, Dick; you must taste a little of the torture of Tantalus just now. You shall make up for it afterward."

And, in truth, there was enough to excite the fancy of a sportsman. Dick's heart fairly leaped in his breast as he grasped the butt of his Purdy.

The *fauna* of the region were as striking as its flora. The wild-ox revelled in dense herbage that often concealed his whole body; grey, black, and yellow elephants of the most gigantic size burst headlong, like a living hurricane, through the forests, breaking, rending, tearing down, devastating everything in their path; upon the woody slopes of the hills trickled cascades and springs flowing northward; there, too, the hippopotami bathed their huge forms, splashing and snorting as they frolicked in the water, and lamantines, twelve feet long, with bodies like seals, stretched themselves along the banks, turning up towards the sun their rounded teats swollen with milk.

It was a whole menagerie of rare and curious beasts in a wondrous hot-house, where numberless birds with plumage of a thousand hues gleamed and fluttered in the sunshine.

By this prodigality of Nature, the doctor recognised the splendid kingdom of Adamova.

"We are now beginning to trench upon the realm of modern discovery. I have taken up the lost scent of preceding travellers. It is a happy chance, my friends, for we shall be enabled to link the toils of Captains Burton and Speke with the explorations of Dr. Barth. We have left the Englishmen behind us, and now have caught up with the Hamburger. It will not be long, either, before we arrive at the extreme point attained by that daring explorer."

"It seems to me that there is a vast extent of country between the two explored routes," remarked Kennedy; "at least, if I am to judge by the distance that we have made."

"It is easy to determine: take the map and see what is the longitude of the southern point of Lake Ukéréoué, reached by Speke."

"It is near the thirty-seventh degree."

"And the city of Yola, which we shall sight this evening, and to which Barth penetrated, what is its position?"

"It is about in the twelfth degree of east longitude."

"Then there are twenty-five degrees, or, counting sixty miles to each, about fifteen hundred miles in all."

"A nice little walk," said Joe, "for people who have to go on foot."

"It will be accomplished, however. Livingstone and Moffat are pushing on up this line towards the interior. Nyassa, which they have discovered, is not far from Lake Tanganayika, seen by Burton. Ere the close of the century these regions will, undoubtedly, be explored. But," added the doctor, consulting his compass, "I regret that the wind is carrying us so far to the westward. I wanted to get to the north."

After twelve hours of progress, the *Victoria* found herself on the confines of Nigritia. The first inhabitants of this region, the Chouas Arabs, were feeding their wandering flocks. The immense summits of the Atlantika Mountains seen above the horizon—mountains that no European foot had yet scaled, and whose height is computed to be ten thousand feet! Their western slope determines the flow of all the waters in this region of Africa towards the ocean. They are the Mountains of the Moon to this part of the continent.

At length a real river greeted the gaze of our travellers, and, by the enormous ant-hills seen in its vicinity, the doctor recognised the Benoué, one of the great tributaries of the Niger, the one which the natives have called "The Fountain of the Waters."

"This river," said the doctor to his companions, "will, one day, be the natural channel of communication with the interior of Nigritia. Under the command of one of our brave captains, the steamer *Pleiad* has already ascended as far as the town of Yola. You see that we are not in an unknown country."

Numerous slaves were engaged in the labours of the field, cultivating sorgho, a kind of millet which forms the chief basis of their diet; and the most stupid expressions of astonishment ensued as the *Victoria* sped past like a meteor. That evening the balloon halted about forty miles from Yola, and ahead of it, but in the distance, rose the two sharp cones of Mount Mendif.

The doctor threw out his anchors and made fast to the top of a high tree; but a very violent wind beat upon the balloon with such force as to throw it over on its side, thus rendering the position of the car sometimes extremely dangerous. Ferguson did not close his eyes all night, and he was repeatedly on the point of cutting the anchor-rope and scudding away before the gale. At length, however, the storm abated, and the oscillations of the balloon ceased to be alarming.

On the morrow the wind was more moderate, but it carried our travellers away from the city of Yola, which recently rebuilt by the Fouillans, excited Ferguson's curiosity. However, he had to make up his mind to being borne farther to the northward and even a little to the east.

Kennedy proposed to halt in this fine hunting-country, and Joe declared that the need of fresh meat was beginning to be felt; but the savage customs of the country, the attitude of the population, and some shots fired at the *Victoria*, admonished the doctor to continue his journey. They were then crossing a region that was the scene of massacres and burnings, and where warlike conflicts between the barbarian sultans, contending for their power amid the most atrocious carnage, never cease.

Numerous and populous villages of long low huts stretched away between broad pasture-fields whose dense herbage was besprinkled with violet-coloured blossoms. The huts, looking like huge beehives, were sheltered behind bristling palisades. The wild hillsides and hollows frequently reminded the beholder of the glens in the Highlands of Scotland, as Kennedy more than once remarked.

In spite of all he could do, the doctor bore directly to the north-east, towards Mount Mendif, which was lost in the midst of environing clouds. The lofty summits of these mountains separate the valley of the Niger from the basin of Lake Tchad.

Soon afterward was seen the Bagélé, with its eighteen villages clinging to its flanks like a whole brood of children to their mother's bosom—a magnificent spectacle for the beholder whose gaze commanded and took in the entire picture at one view. Even the ravines were seen to be covered with fields of rice and of arachides.

By three o'clock the *Victoria* was directly in front of Mount Mendif. It had been impossible to avoid it; the only thing to be done was to cross it. The doctor, by means of a temperature increased to one hundred and eighty degrees, gave the balloon a fresh ascensional force of nearly sixteen hundred pounds, and it went up to an elevation of more than eight thousand feet, the greatest height attained during the journey. The temperature of the atmosphere was so much cooler at that point that the aeronauts had to resort to their blankets and thick coverings.

Ferguson was in haste to descend; the covering of the balloon gave indications of bursting, but in the meanwhile he had time to satisfy himself of the volcanic origin of the mountain, whose extinct craters are now but deep abysses. Immense accumulations of bird-guano gave the sides of Mount Mendif the appearance of calcareous rocks, and there was enough of the deposit there to manure all the lands in the United Kingdom.

At five o'clock the *Victoria*, sheltered from the south winds, went gently gliding along the slopes of the mountain, and stopped in a wide clearing remote from any habitation. The instant it touched the soil, all needful precautions were taken to hold it there firmly; and Kennedy, fowling-piece in hand, sallied out upon the sloping plain. Ere long, he returned with half-a-dozen wild ducks and a kind of snipe, which Joe served up in his best style. The meal was heartily relished, and the night was passed in undisturbed and refreshing slumber.

Chapter XXX

MOSFEIA—THE SHEIK—DENHAM, CLAPPERTON, AND OUDNEY—
VOGEL—THE CAPITAL OF LOGGOUM—TOOLE—BECALMED ABOVE
KERNAK—THE GOVERNOR AND HIS COURT—THE ATTACK—
THE INCENDIARY PIGEONS

ON THE NEXT DAY, MAY 11TH, THE *VICTORIA* RESUMED HER ADVENTUROUS JOURNEY. Her passengers had the same confidence in her that a good seaman has in his ship.

In terrific hurricanes, in tropical heats, when making dangerous departures, and descents still more dangerous, it had, at all times and in all places, come out safely. It might almost have been said that Ferguson managed it with a wave of the hand; and hence, without knowing in advance, where the point of arrival would be, the doctor had no fears concerning the successful issue of his journey. However, in this country of barbarians and fanatics, prudence obliged him to take the strictest precautions. He therefore counselled his companions to have their eyes wide open for everything and at all hours.

The wind drifted a little more to the northward, and, towards nine o'clock, they sighted the larger city of Mosfeia, built upon an eminence which was itself enclosed between two lofty mountains. Its position was impregnable, a narrow road running between a marsh and a thick wood being the only channel of approach to it.

At the moment of which we write, a sheik, accompanied by a mounted escort, and clad in a garb of brilliant colours, preceded by couriers and trumpeters, who put aside the boughs of the trees as he rode up, was making his grand entry into the place.

The doctor lowered the balloon in order to get a better look at this cavalcade of natives; but, as the balloon grew larger to their eyes, they began to show symptoms of intense affright, and at length made off in different directions as fast as their legs and those of their horses could carry them.

The sheik alone did not budge an inch. He merely grasped his long musket, cocked it, and proudly waited in silence. The doctor came on to within a hundred and fifty feet of him, and then, with his roundest and fullest voice, saluted him courteously in the Arabic tongue.

But, upon hearing these words falling, as it seemed, from the sky, the sheik dismounted and prostrated himself in the dust of the highway, where the doctor had to leave him, finding it impossible to divert him from his adoration.

"Unquestionably," Ferguson remarked, "those people take us for supernatural beings. When Europeans came among them for the first time, they were mistaken for creatures of a higher race. When this sheik comes to speak of to-day's meeting, he will not fail to embellish the circumstance with all the resources of an Arab imagination. You may, therefore, judge what an account their legends will give of us someday."

"Not such a desirable thing, after all," said the Scot, "in the point of view that affects civilization; it would be better to pass for mere men. That would give these negro races a superior idea of European power."

"Very good, my dear Dick; but what can we do about it? You might sit all day explaining the mechanism of a balloon to the *savants* of this country, and yet they would not comprehend you, but would persist in ascribing it to supernatural aid."

"Doctor, you spoke of the first time Europeans visited these regions. Who were the visitors?" enquired Joe.

"My dear fellow, we are now upon the very track of Major Denham. It was at this very city of Mosfeia that he was received by the Sultan of Mandara; he had quitted the Bornou country; he accompanied the sheik in an expedition against the Fellatahs; he assisted in the attack on the city, which, with its arrows alone, bravely resisted the bullets of the Arabs, and put the sheik's troops to flight. All this was but a pretext for murders, raids, and pillage. The major was completely plundered and stripped, and had it not been for his horse, under whose stomach he clung with the skill of an Indian rider, and was borne with a headlong gallop from his barbarous pursuers, he never could have made his way back to Kouka, the capital of Bornou."

"Who was this Major Denham?"

"A fearless Englishman, who, between 1822 and 1824, commanded an expedition into the Bornou country, in company with Captain Clapperton and Dr. Oudney. They set out from Tripoli in the month of March, reached Mourzouk, the capital of Fez, and, following the route which at a later period Dr. Barth was to pursue on his way back to Europe, they arrived, on the 16th of February, 1823, at Kouka, near Lake Tchad. Denham made several explorations in Bornou, in Mandara, and to the eastern shores of the lake. In the meantime, on the 15th of December, 1823, Captain Clapperton and Dr. Oudney had pushed their way through the Soudan country as far as Sackatoo, and Oudney died of fatigue and exhaustion in the town of Murmur."

"This part of Africa has, therefore, paid a heavy tribute of victims to the cause of science," said Kennedy.

"Yes, this country is fatal to travellers. We are moving directly towards the kingdom of Baghirmi, which Vogel traversed in 1856, so as to reach the Wadai country, where he disappeared. This young man, at the age of twenty-three, had been sent to cooperate with Dr. Barth. They met on the 1st of December, 1854, and thereupon commenced his explorations of the country. Towards 1856, he announced, in the last letters received from him, his intention to reconnoitre the kingdom of Wadai, which no European had yet penetrated. It appears that he got as far as Wara, the capital, where, according to some accounts, he was made prisoner, and, according to others, was put to death for having attempted to ascend a sacred mountain in the environs. But, we must not too lightly admit the death of travellers, since that does away with the necessity of going in search of them. For instance, how often was the death of Dr. Barth reported, to his own great annoyance! It is, therefore, very possible that Vogel may still be held as a prisoner by the Sultan of Wadai, in the hope of obtaining a good ransom for him.

"Baron de Neimans was about starting for the Wadai country when he died at Cairo, in 1855; and we now know that De Heuglin has set out on Vogel's track with the expedition sent from Leipsic, so that we shall soon be accurately informed as to the fate of that young and interesting explorer."*

---

*Since the doctor's departure, letters written from El'Obeid by Mr. Muntzinger, the newly-appointed head of the expedition, unfortunately place the death of Vogel beyond a doubt.

Mosfeia had disappeared from the horizon long ere this, and the Mandara country was developing to the gaze of our aeronauts its astonishing fertility, with its forests of acacias, its locust-trees covered with red flowers, and the herbaceous plants of its fields of cotton and indigo trees. The river Shari, which eighty miles farther on rolled its impetuous waters into Lake Tchad, was quite distinctly seen.

The doctor got his companions to trace its course upon the maps drawn by Dr. Barth.

"You perceive," said he, "that the labours of this *savant* have been conducted with great precision; we are moving directly towards the Loggoum region, and perhaps towards Kernak, its capital. It was there that poor Toole died, at the age of scarcely twenty-two. He was a young Englishman, an ensign in the 80th regiment, who, a few weeks before, had joined Major Denham in Africa, and it was not long ere he there met his death. Ah! this vast country might well be called the graveyard of European travellers."

Some boats, fifty feet long, were descending the current of the Shari. The *Victoria*, then one thousand feet above the soil, hardly attracted the attention of the natives; but the wind, which until then had been blowing with a certain degree of strength, was falling off.

"Is it possible that we are to be caught in another dead calm?" sighed the doctor.

"Well, we've no lack of water, nor the desert to fear, anyhow, master," said Joe.

"No; but there are races here still more to be dreaded."

"Why!" said Joe, again, "there's something like a town."

"That is Kernak. The last puffs of the breeze are wafting us to it, and, if we choose, we can take an exact plan of the place."

"Shall we not go nearer to it?" asked Kennedy.

"Nothing easier, Dick! We are right over it. Allow me to turn the stopcock of the cylinder, and we'll not be long in descending."

Half-an-hour later the balloon hung motionless about two hundred feet from the ground.

"Here we are!" said the doctor, "nearer to Kernak than a man would be to London, if he were perched in the cupola of St. Paul's. So we can take a survey at our ease."

"What is that tick-tacking sound that we hear on all sides?"

Joe looked attentively, and at length discovered that the noise they heard was produced by a number of weavers beating cloth stretched in the open air, on large trunks of trees.

The capital of Loggoum could then be seen in its entire extent, like an unrolled chart. It is really a city with straight rows of houses and quite wide streets. In the midst of a large open space there was a slave-market, attended by a great crowd of customers, for the Mandara women, who have extremely small hands and feet, are in excellent request, and can be sold at lucrative rates.

At the sight of the *Victoria*, the scene so often produced occurred again. At first there were outcries, and then followed general stupefaction; business was abandoned; work was flung aside, and all noise ceased. The aeronauts remained as they were, completely motionless, and lost not a detail of the populous city. They even went down to within sixty feet of the ground.

Hereupon the Governor of Loggoum came out from his residence, displaying his green standard, and accompanied by his musicians, who blew on hoarse buffalo-horns, as though they would split their cheeks or anything else, excepting their own lungs. The crowd at once gathered around him. In the meanwhile Dr. Ferguson tried to make himself heard, but in vain.

This population looked like proud and intelligent people, with their high foreheads, their almost aquiline noses, and their curling hair; but the presence of the *Victoria* troubled them greatly. Horsemen could be seen galloping in all directions, and it soon became evident that the governor's troops were assembling to oppose so extraordinary a foe. Joe wore himself out waving handkerchiefs of every colour and shape to them; but his exertions were all to no purpose.

However, the sheik, surrounded by his court, proclaimed silence, and pronounced a discourse, of which the doctor could not understand a word. It was Arabic, mixed with Baghirmi. He could make out enough, however, by the universal language of gestures, to be aware that he was receiving a very polite invitation to depart. Indeed, he would have asked for nothing better, but for lack of wind, the thing had become impossible. His non-compliance, therefore, exasperated the governor, whose courtiers and attendants set up a furious howl to enforce immediate obedience on the part of the aerial monster.

They were odd-looking fellows those courtiers, with their five or six shirts swathed around their bodies! They had enormous stomachs, some of which actually seemed to be artificial. The doctor surprised his companions by informing them that this was the way to pay court to the sultan. The rotundity of the stomach indicated the ambition of its possessor. These corpulent gentry gesticulated and bawled at the top of their voices—one of them particularly distinguishing himself above the rest—to such an extent, indeed, that he must have been a prime minister—at least, if the disturbance he made was any criterion of his rank. The common rabble of dusky denizens united their howlings with the uproar of the court, repeating their gesticulations like so many monkeys, and thereby producing a single and instantaneous movement of ten thousand arms at one time.

To these means of intimidation, which were presently deemed insufficient, were added others still more formidable. Soldiers, armed with bows and arrows, were drawn up in line of battle; but by this time the balloon was expanding, and rising quietly beyond their reach. Upon this the governor seized a musket and aimed it at the balloon; but, Kennedy, who was watching him, shattered the uplifted weapon in the sheik's grasp.

At this unexpected blow there was a general rout. Every mother's son of them scampered for his dwelling with the utmost celerity, and stayed there, so that the streets of the town were absolutely deserted for the remainder of that day.

Night came, and not a breath of wind was stirring. The aeronauts had to make up their minds to remain motionless at the distance of but three hundred feet above the ground. Not a fire or light shone in the deep gloom, and around reigned the silence of death; but the doctor only redoubled his vigilance, as this apparent quiet might conceal some snare.

And he had reason to be watchful. About midnight, the whole city seemed to be in a blaze. Hundreds of streaks of flame crossed each other, and shot to and fro in the air like rockets, forming a regular network of fire.

"That's really curious!" said the doctor, somewhat puzzled to make out what it meant.

"By all that's glorious!" shouted Kennedy, "it looks as if the fire were ascending and coming up towards us!"

And, sure enough, with an accompaniment of musket-shots, yelling, and din of every description, the mass of fire was, indeed, mounting towards the *Victoria*. Joe got ready to throw out ballast, and Ferguson was not long at guessing the truth. Thousands of pigeons, their tails garnished with combustibles, had been set loose and driven towards the *Victoria*; and now, in their terror, they were flying high up, zigzagging the atmosphere with lines of fire. Kennedy was preparing to discharge all his batteries into the middle of the ascending multitude, but what could he have done against such a numberless army? The pigeons were already whisking around the car; they were even surrounding the balloon, the sides of which, reflecting their illumination, looked as though enveloped with a network of fire.

The doctor dared hesitate no longer; and, throwing out a fragment of quartz, he kept himself beyond the reach of these dangerous assailants; and, for two hours afterward, he could see them wandering hither and thither through the darkness of the night, until, little by little, their light diminished, and they, one by one, died out.

"Now we may sleep in quiet," said the doctor.

"Not badly got up for barbarians," mused friend Joe, speaking his thoughts aloud.

"Oh, they employ these pigeons frequently, to set fire to the thatch of hostile villages; but this time the village mounted higher than they could go."

"Why, positively, a balloon need fear no enemies!"

"Yes, indeed, it may!" objected Ferguson.

"What are they, then, doctor?"

"They are the careless people in the car! So, my friends, let us have vigilance in all places and at all times."

Chapter XXXI

DEPARTURE IN THE NIGHT-TIME—ALL THREE—KENNEDY'S INSTINCTS—PRECAUTIONS—THE COURSE OF THE SHARI RIVER— LAKE TCHAD—THE WATER OF THE LAKE—THE HIPPOPOTAMUS— ONE BULLET THROWN AWAY

ABOUT THREE O'CLOCK IN THE MORNING, JOE, WHO WAS THEN ON WATCH, AT LENGTH saw the city move away from beneath his feet. The *Victoria* was once again in motion, and both the doctor and Kennedy awoke.

The former consulted his compass, and saw, with satisfaction, that the wind was carrying them towards the north-northeast.

"We are in luck!" said he; "everything works in our favour: we shall discover Lake Tchad this very day."

"Is it a broad sheet of water?" asked Kennedy.

"Somewhat, Dick. At its greatest length and breadth, it measures about one hundred and twenty miles."

"It will spice our trip with a little variety to sail over a spacious sheet of water."

"After all, though, I don't see that we have much to complain of on that score. Our trip has been very much varied, indeed; and, moreover, we are getting on under the best possible conditions."

"Unquestionably so; excepting those privations on the desert, we have encountered no serious danger."

"It is not to be denied that our noble balloon has behaved wonderfully well. To-day is May 12th, and we started on the 18th of April. That makes twenty-five days of journeying. In ten days more we shall have reached our destination."

"Where is that?"

"I do not know. But what does that signify?"

"You are right again, Samuel! Let us entrust to Providence the care of guiding us and of keeping us in good health as we are now. We don't look much as though we had been crossing the most pestilential country in the world!"

"We had an opportunity of getting up in life, and that's what we have done!"

"Hurrah for trips in the air!" cried Joe. "Here we are at the end of twenty-five days in good condition, well fed, and well rested. We've had too much rest in fact, for my legs begin to feel rusty, and I wouldn't be vexed a bit to stretch them with a run of thirty miles or so!"

"You can do that, Joe, in the streets of London, but in fine we set out three together, like Denham, Clapperton, and Overweg; like Barth, Richardson, and Vogel, and, more fortunate than our predecessors here, we are three in number still. But it is most important for us not to separate. If, while one of us was on the ground, the *Victoria* should have to ascend in order to escape some sudden danger, who knows whether we should ever see each other again? Therefore it is that I say again to Kennedy frankly that I do not like his going off alone to hunt."

"But still, Samuel, you will permit me to indulge that fancy a little. There is no harm in renewing our stock of provisions. Besides, before our departure, you held out to me the prospect of some superb hunting, and thus far I have done but little in the line of the Andersons and Cummings."

"But, my dear Dick, your memory fails you, or your modesty makes you forget your own exploits. It really seems to me that, without mentioning small game, you have already an antelope, an elephant, and two lions on your conscience."

"But what's all that to an African sportsman who sees all the animals in creation strutting along under the muzzle of his rifle? There! there! look at that troop of giraffes!"

"Those giraffes," roared Joe; "why, they're not as big as my fist."

"Because we are a thousand feet above them; but close to them you would discover that they are three times as tall as you are!"

"And what do you say to yon herd of gazelles, and those ostriches, that run with the speed of the wind?" resumed Kennedy.

"Those ostriches?" remonstrated Joe, again; "those are chickens, and the greatest kind of chickens!"

"Come, doctor, can't we get down nearer to them?" pleaded Kennedy.

"We can get closer to them, Dick, but we must not land. And what good will it do you to strike down those poor animals when they can be of no use to you? Now, if the question were to destroy a lion, a tiger, a cat, a hyena, I could understand it; but to deprive an antelope or a gazelle of life, to no other purpose than the gratification of your instincts as a sportsman, seems hardly worth the trouble. But, after all, my friend, we are going to keep at about one hundred feet only from the soil, and, should you see any ferocious wild beast, oblige us by sending a ball through its heart!"

The *Victoria* descended gradually, but still keeping at a safe height, for, in a barbarous, yet very populous country, it was necessary to keep on the watch for unexpected perils.

The travellers were then directly following the course of the Shari. The charming banks of this river were hidden beneath the foliage of trees of various dyes; lianas and climbing plants wound in and out on all sides and formed the most curious combinations of colour. Crocodiles were seen basking in the broad blaze of the sun or plunging beneath the waters with the agility of lizards, and in their gambols they sported about among the many green islands that intercept the current of the stream.

It was thus, in the midst of rich and verdant landscapes that our travellers passed over the district of Maffatay, and about nine o'clock in the morning reached the southern shore of Lake Tchad.

There it was at last, outstretched before them, that Caspian Sea of Africa, the existence of which was so long consigned to the realms of fable—that interior expanse of water to which only Denham's and Barth's expeditions had been able to force their way.

The doctor strove in vain to fix its precise configuration upon paper. It had already changed greatly since 1847. In fact, the chart of Lake Tchad is very difficult to trace with exactitude, for it is surrounded by muddy and almost impassable morasses, in which Barth thought that he was doomed to perish. From year to year these marshes, covered with reeds and papyrus fifteen feet high, become the lake itself. Frequently, too, the villages on its shores are half submerged, as was the case with Ngornou in 1856, and now the hippopotamus and the alligator frisk and dive where the dwellings of Bornou once stood.

The sun shot his dazzling rays over this placid sheet of water, and towards the north the two elements merged into one and the same horizon.

The doctor was desirous of determining the character of the water, which was long believed to be salt. There was no danger in descending close to the lake, and the car was soon skimming its surface like a bird at the distance of only five feet.

Joe plunged a bottle into the lake and drew it up half filled. The water was then tasted and found to be but little fit for drinking, with a certain carbonate-of-soda flavor.

While the doctor was jotting down the result of this experiment, the loud report of a gun was heard close beside him. Kennedy had not been able to resist the temptation of firing at a huge hippopotamus. The latter, who had been basking quietly, disappeared at the sound of the explosion, but did not seem to be otherwise incommoded by Kennedy's conical bullet.

"You'd have done better if you had harpooned him," said Joe.

"But how?"

"With one of our anchors. It would have been a hook just big enough for such a rousing beast as that!"

"Humph!" ejaculated Kennedy, "Joe really has an idea this time—"

"Which I beg of you not to put into execution," interposed the doctor. "The animal would very quickly have dragged us where we could not have done much to help ourselves, and where we have no business to be."

"Especially now since we've settled the question as to what kind of water there is in Lake Tchad. Is that sort of fish good to eat, Dr. Ferguson?"

"That fish, as you call it, Joe, is really a mammiferous animal of the pachydermal species. Its flesh is said to be excellent and is an article of important trade between the tribes living along the borders of the lake."

"Then I'm sorry that Mr. Kennedy's shot didn't do more damage."

"The animal is vulnerable only in the stomach and between the thighs. Dick's ball hasn't even marked him; but should the ground strike me as favourable, we shall halt at the northern end of the lake, where Kennedy will find himself in the midst of a whole menagerie, and can make up for lost time."

"Well," said Joe, "I hope then that Mr. Kennedy will hunt the hippopotamus a little; I'd like to taste the meat of that queer-looking beast. It doesn't look exactly natural to get away into the centre of Africa, to feed on snipe and partridge, just as if we were in England."

Chapter XXXII

THE CAPITAL OF BORNOU—THE ISLANDS OF THE BIDDIOMAHS— THE CONDORS—THE DOCTOR'S ANXIETIES—HIS PRECAUTIONS— AN ATTACK IN MID-AIR—THE BALLOON COVERING TORN— THE FALL—SUBLIME SELF-SACRIFICE—THE NORTHERN COAST OF THE LAKE

SINCE ITS ARRIVAL AT LAKE TCHAD, THE BALLOON HAD STRUCK A CURRENT THAT EDGED it farther to the westward. A few clouds tempered the heat of the day, and, besides, a little air could be felt over this vast expanse of water; but about one o'clock, the *Victoria*, having slanted across this part of the lake, again advanced over the land for a space of seven or eight miles.

The doctor, who was somewhat vexed at first at this turn of his course, no longer thought of complaining when he caught sight of the city of Kouka, the capital of Bornou. He saw it for a moment, encircled by its walls of white clay, and a few rudely-constructed mosques rising clumsily above that conglomeration of houses that look like playing-dice, which form most Arab towns. In the court-yards of the private dwellings, and on the public squares, grew palms and caoutchouc-trees topped with a dome of foliage more than one hundred feet in breadth. Joe called attention to the fact that these immense parasols were in proper accordance with the intense heat of the sun, and made thereon some pious reflections which it were needless to repeat.

Kouka really consists of two distinct towns, separated by the "Dendal," a large boulevard three hundred yards wide, at that hour crowded with horsemen and foot passengers. On one side, the rich quarter stands squarely with its airy and lofty houses, laid out in regular order; on the other, is huddled together the poor quarter, a miserable collection of low hovels of a conical shape, in which a poverty-stricken multitude vegetate rather than live, since Kouka is neither a trading nor a commercial city.

Kennedy thought it looked something like Edinburgh, were that city extended on a plain, with its two distinct boroughs.

But our travellers had scarcely the time to catch even this glimpse of it, for, with the fickleness that characterizes the air-currents of this region, a contrary wind suddenly swept them some forty miles over the surface of Lake Tchad.

Then then were regaled with a new spectacle. They could count the numerous islets of the lake, inhabited by the Biddiomahs, a race of bloodthirsty and formidable pirates, who are as greatly feared when neighbours as are the Touregs of Sahara.

These estimable people were in readiness to receive the *Victoria* bravely with stones and arrows, but the balloon quickly passed their islands, fluttering over them, from one to the other with butterfly motion, like a gigantic beetle.

At this moment, Joe, who was scanning the horizon, said to Kennedy:

"There, sir, as you are always thinking of good sport, yonder is just the thing for you!"

"What is it, Joe?"

"This time, the doctor will not disapprove of your shooting."

"But what is it?"

"Don't you see that flock of big birds making for us?"

"Birds?" exclaimed the doctor, snatching his spy-glass.

"I see them," replied Kennedy; "there are at least a dozen of them."

"Fourteen, exactly!" said Joe.

"Heaven grant that they may be of a kind sufficiently noxious for the doctor to let me peg away at them!"

"I should not object, but I would much rather see those birds at a distance from us!"

"Why, are you afraid of those fowls?"

"They are condors, and of the largest size. Should they attack us—"

"Well, if they do, we'll defend ourselves. We have a whole arsenal at our disposal. I don't think those birds are so very formidable."

"Who can tell?" was the doctor's only remark.

Ten minutes later, the flock had come within gunshot, and were making the air ring with their hoarse cries. They came right towards the *Victoria*, more irritated than frightened by her presence.

"How they scream! What a noise!" said Joe.

"Perhaps they don't like to see anybody poaching in their country up in the air, or daring to fly like themselves!"

"Well, now, to tell the truth, when I take a good look at them, they are an ugly, ferocious set, and I should think them dangerous enough if they were armed with Purdy-Moore rifles," admitted Kennedy.

"They have no need of such weapons," said Ferguson, looking very grave.

The condors flew around them in wide circles, their flight growing gradually closer and closer to the balloon. They swept through the air in rapid, fantastic curves, occasionally precipitating themselves headlong with the speed of a bullet, and then breaking their line of projection by an abrupt and daring angle.

The doctor, much disquieted, resolved to ascend so as to escape this dangerous proximity. He therefore dilated the hydrogen in his balloon, and it rapidly rose.

But the condors mounted with him, apparently determined not to part company.

"They seem to mean mischief!" said the hunter, cocking his rifle.

And, in fact, they were swooping nearer, and more than one came within fifty feet of them, as if defying the fire-arms.

"By George, I'm itching to let them have it!" exclaimed Kennedy.

"No, Dick; not now! Don't exasperate them needlessly. That would only be exciting them to attack us!"

"But I could soon settle those fellows!"

"You may think so, Dick. But you are wrong!"

"Why, we have a bullet for each of them!"

"And suppose that they were to attack the upper part of the balloon, what would you do? How would you get at them? Just imagine yourself in the presence of a troop of lions on the plain, or a school of sharks in the open ocean! For travellers in the air, this situation is just as dangerous."

"Are you speaking seriously, doctor?"

"Very seriously, Dick."

"Let us wait, then!"

"Wait! Hold yourself in readiness in case of an attack, but do not fire without my orders."

The birds then collected at a short distance, yet so near that their naked necks, entirely bare of feathers, could be plainly seen, as they stretched them out with the effort of their cries, while their gristly crests, garnished with a comb and gills of deep violet, stood erect with rage. They were of the very largest size, their bodies being more than three feet in length, and the lower surface of their white wings glittering in the sunlight. They might well have been considered winged sharks, so striking was their resemblance to those ferocious rangers of the deep.

"They are following us!" said the doctor, as he saw them ascending with him, "and, mount as we may, they can fly still higher!"

"Well, what are we to do?" asked Kennedy.

The doctor made no answer.

"Listen, Samuel!" said the sportsman. "There are fourteen of those birds; we have seventeen shots at our disposal if we discharge all our weapons. Have we not the means, then, to destroy them or disperse them? I will give a good account of some of them!"

"I have no doubt of your skill, Dick; I look upon all as dead that may come within range of your rifle, but I repeat that, if they attack the upper part of the balloon, you could not get a sight at them. They would tear the silk covering that sustains us, and we are three thousand feet up in the air!"

At this moment, one of the ferocious birds darted right at the balloon, with out-stretched beak and claws, ready to rend it with either or both.

"Fire! fire at once!" cried the doctor.

He had scarcely ceased, ere the huge creature, stricken dead, dropped headlong, turning over and over in space as he fell.

Kennedy had already grasped one of the two-barrelled fowling-pieces and Joe was taking aim with another.

Frightened by the report, the condors drew back for a moment, but they almost instantly returned to the charge with extreme fury. Kennedy severed the head of one from its body with his first shot, and Joe broke the wing of another.

"Only eleven left," said he.

Thereupon the birds changed their tactics, and by common consent soared above the balloon. Kennedy glanced at Ferguson. The latter, in spite of his imperturbability, grew pale. Then ensued a moment of terrifying silence. In the next they heard a harsh tearing noise, as of something rending the silk, and the car seemed to sink from beneath the feet of our three aeronauts.

"We are lost!" exclaimed Ferguson, glancing at the barometer, which was now swiftly rising.

"Over with the ballast!" he shouted, "over with it!"

And in a few seconds the last lumps of quartz had disappeared.

"We are still falling! Empty the water-tanks! Do you hear me, Joe? We are pitching into the lake!"

Joe obeyed. The doctor leaned over and looked out. The lake seemed to come up towards him like a rising tide. Every object around grew rapidly in size while they were looking at it. The car was not two hundred feet from the surface of Lake Tchad.

"The provisions! the provisions!" cried the doctor.

And the box containing them was launched into space.

Their descent became less rapid, but the luckless aeronauts were still falling, and into the lake.

"Throw out something—something more!" cried the doctor.

"There is nothing more to throw!" was Kennedy's despairing response.

"Yes, there is!" called Joe, and with a wave of the hand he disappeared like a flash, over the edge of the car.

"Joe! Joe!" exclaimed the doctor, horror-stricken.

The *Victoria* thus relieved resumed her ascending motion, mounted a thousand feet into the air, and the wind, burying itself in the disinflated covering, bore them away towards the northern part of the lake.

"Lost!" exclaimed the sportsman, with a gesture of despair.

"Lost to save us!" responded Ferguson.

And these men, intrepid as they were, felt the large tears streaming down their cheeks. They leaned over with the vain hope of seeing some trace of their heroic companion, but they were already far away from him.

"What course shall we pursue?" asked Kennedy.

"Alight as soon as possible, Dick, and then wait."

After a sweep of some sixty miles the *Victoria* halted on a desert shore, on the north of the lake. The anchors caught in a low tree and the sportsman fastened it securely. Night came, but neither Ferguson nor Kennedy could find one moment's sleep.

Chapter XXXIII

CONJECTURES—RE-ESTABLISHMENT OF THE VICTORIA'S
EQUILIBRIUM—DR. FERGUSON'S NEW CALCULATIONS—KENNEDY'S
HUNT—A COMPLETE EXPLORATION OF LAKE TCHAD—
TANGALIA—THE RETURN—LARI

ON THE MORROW, THE 13TH OF MAY, OUR TRAVELLERS, FOR THE FIRST TIME, RECONnoitred the part of the coast on which they had landed. It was a sort of island of solid ground in the midst of an immense marsh. Around this fragment of *terra firma* grew reeds as lofty as trees are in Europe, and stretching away out of sight.

These impenetrable swamps gave security to the position of the balloon. It was necessary to watch only the borders of the lake. The vast stretch of water broadened away from the spot, especially towards the east, and nothing could be seen on the horizon, neither mainland nor islands.

The two friends had not yet ventured to speak of their recent companion. Kennedy first imparted his conjectures to the doctor.

"Perhaps Joe is not lost after all," he said. "He was a skilful lad, and had few equals as a swimmer. He would find no difficulty in swimming across the Firth of Forth at Edinburgh. We shall see him again—but how and where I know not. Let us omit nothing on our part to give him the chance of rejoining us."

"May God grant it as you say, Dick!" replied the doctor, with much emotion. "We shall do everything in the world to find our lost friend again. Let us, in the first place, see where we are. But, above all things, let us rid the *Victoria* of this outside covering, which is of no further use. That will relieve us of six hundred and fifty pounds, a weight not to be despised—and the end is worth the trouble!"

The doctor and Kennedy went to work at once, but they encountered great difficulty. They had to tear the strong silk away piece by piece, and then cut it in narrow strips so as to extricate it from the meshes of the network. The tear made by the beaks of the condors was found to be several feet in length.

This operation took at least four hours, but at length the inner balloon once completely extricated did not appear to have suffered in the least degree. The *Victoria* was thus diminished in size by one fifth, and this difference was sufficiently noticeable to excite Kennedy's surprise.

"Will it be large enough?" he asked.

"Have no fears on that score, I will re-establish the equilibrium, and should our poor Joe return we shall find a way to start off with him again on our old route."

"At the moment of our fall, unless I am mistaken, we were not far from an island."

"Yes, I recollect it," said the doctor, "but that island, like all the islands on Lake Tchad, is, no doubt, inhabited by a gang of pirates and murderers. They certainly witnessed our misfortune, and should Joe fall into their hands, what will become of him unless protected by their superstitions?"

"Oh, he's just the lad to get safely out of the scrape, I repeat. I have great confidence in his shrewdness and skill."

"I hope so. Now, Dick, you may go and hunt in the neighbourhood, but don't get far away whatever you do. It has become a pressing necessity for us to renew our stock of provisions, since we had to sacrifice nearly all the old lot."

"Very good, doctor, I shall not be long absent."

Hereupon, Kennedy took a double-barrelled fowling-piece, and strode through the long grass towards a thicket not far off, where the frequent sound of shooting soon let the doctor know that the sportsman was making a good use of his time.

Meanwhile Ferguson was engaged in calculating the relative weight of the articles still left in the car, and in establishing the equipoise of the second balloon. He found that there were still left some thirty pounds of *pemmican*, a supply of tea and coffee, about a gallon and a half of brandy, and one empty water-tank. All the dried meat had disappeared.

The doctor was aware that, by the loss of the hydrogen in the first balloon, the ascensional force at his disposal was now reduced to about nine hundred pounds. He therefore had to count upon this difference in order to rearrange his equilibrium. The new balloon measured sixty-seven thousand cubic feet, and contained thirty-three thousand four hundred and eighty feet of gas. The dilating apparatus appeared to be in good condition, and neither the battery nor the spiral had been injured.

The ascensional force of the new balloon was then about three thousand pounds, and, in adding together the weight of the apparatus, of the passengers, of the stock of water, of the car and its accessories, and putting aboard fifty gallons of water, and one hundred pounds of fresh meat, the doctor got a total weight of twenty-eight hundred and thirty pounds. He could then take with him one hundred and seventy pounds of ballast, for unforeseen emergencies, and the balloon would be in exact balance with the surrounding atmosphere.

His arrangements were completed accordingly, and he made up for Joe's weight with a surplus of ballast. He spent the whole day in these preparations, and the latter were finished when Kennedy returned. The hunter had been successful, and brought back a regular cargo of geese, wild-duck, snipe, teal, and plover. He went to work at once to draw and smoke the game. Each piece, suspended on a small, thin skewer, was hung over a fire of green wood. When they seemed in good order, Kennedy, who was perfectly at home in the business, packed them away in the car.

On the morrow, the hunter was to complete his supplies.

Evening surprised our travellers in the midst of this work. Their supper consisted of *pemmican*, biscuit, and tea; and fatigue, after having given them appetite, brought them sleep. Each of them strained eyes and ears into the gloom during his watch, sometimes fancying that they heard the voice of poor Joe; but, alas! the voice that they so longed to hear, was far away.

"At the first streak of day, the doctor aroused Kennedy.

"I have been long and carefully considering what should be done," said he, "to find our companion."

"Whatever your plan may be, doctor, it will suit me. Speak!"

"Above all things, it is important that Joe should hear from us in some way."

"Undoubtedly. Suppose the brave fellow should take it into his head that we have abandoned him?"

"He! He knows us too well for that. Such a thought would never come into his mind. But he must be informed as to where we are."

"How can that be managed?"

"We shall get into our car and be off again through the air."

"But, should the wind bear us away?"

"Happily, it will not. See, Dick! it is carrying us back to the lake; and this circumstance, which would have been vexatious yesterday, is fortunate now. Our efforts, then, will be limited to keeping ourselves above that vast sheet of water throughout the day. Joe cannot fail to see us, and his eyes will be constantly on the look-out in that direction. Perhaps he will even manage to let us know the place of his retreat."

"If he be alone and at liberty, he certainly will."

"And if a prisoner," resumed the doctor, "it not being the practise of the natives to confine their captives, he will see us, and comprehend the object of our researches."

"But, at last," put in Kennedy—"for we must anticipate everything—should we find no trace—if he should have left no mark to follow him by, what are we to do?"

"We shall endeavour to regain the northern part of the lake, keeping ourselves as much in sight as possible. There we'll wait; we'll explore the banks; we'll search the water's edge, for Joe will assuredly try to reach the shore; and we will not leave the country without having done everything to find him."

"Let us set out, then!" said the hunter.

The doctor hereupon took the exact bearings of the patch of solid land they were about to leave, and arrived at the conclusion that it lay on the north shore of Lake Tchad, between the village of Lari and the village of Ingemini, both visited by Major Denham. During this time Kennedy was completing his stock of fresh meat. Although the neighbouring marshes showed traces of the rhinoceros, the lamantine (or *manatee*), and the hippopotamus, he had no opportunity to see a single specimen of those animals.

At seven in the morning, but not without great difficulty—which to Joe would have been nothing—the balloon's anchor was detached from its hold, the gas dilated, and the new *Victoria* rose two hundred feet into the air. It seemed to hesitate at first, and went spinning around, like a top; but at last a brisk current caught it, and it advanced over the lake, and was soon borne away at a speed of twenty miles per hour.

The doctor continued to keep at a height of from two hundred to five hundred feet. Kennedy frequently discharged his rifle; and, when passing over islands, the aeronauts approached them even imprudently, scrutinizing the thickets, the bushes, the underbrush—in fine, every spot where a mass of shade or jutting rock could have afforded a retreat to their companion. They swooped down close to the long pirogues that navigated the lake; and the wild fishermen, terrified at the sight of the balloon, would plunge into the water and regain their islands with every symptom of undisguised affright.

"We can see nothing," said Kennedy, after two hours of search.

"Let us wait a little longer, Dick, and not lose heart. We cannot be far away from the scene of our accident."

By eleven o'clock the balloon had gone ninety miles. It then fell in with a new current, which, blowing almost at right angles to the other, drove them eastward about sixty miles. It next floated over a very large and populous island, which the doctor took to be Farram, on which the capital of the Biddiomahs is situated. Ferguson expected at every moment to see Joe spring up out of some thicket, flying for his life, and calling for help. Were he free, they could pick him up without trouble; were he a prisoner, they could rescue him by repeating the maneuvre they had practised to save the missionary, and he would soon be with his friends again; but nothing was seen, not a sound was heard. The case seemed desperate.

About half-past two o'clock, the *Victoria* hove in sight of Tangalia, a village situated on the eastern shore of Lake Tchad, where it marks the extreme point attained by Denham at the period of his exploration.

The doctor became uneasy at this persistent setting of the wind in that direction, for he felt that he was being thrown back to the eastward, towards the centre of Africa, and the interminable deserts of that region.

"We must absolutely come to a halt," said he, "and even alight. For Joe's sake, particularly, we ought to go back to the lake; but, to begin with, let us endeavour to find an opposite current."

During more than an hour he searched at different altitudes: the balloon always came back towards the mainland. But at length, at the height of a thousand feet, a very violent breeze swept to the north-westward.

It was out of the question that Joe should have been detained on one of the islands of the lake; for, in such case, he would certainly have found means to make his presence there known. Perhaps he had been dragged to the mainland. The doctor was reasoning thus to himself, when he again came in sight of the northern shore of Lake Tchad.

As for supposing that Joe had been drowned, that was not to be believed for a moment. One horrible thought glanced across the minds of both Kennedy and the doctor: caymans swarm in these waters! But neither one nor the other had the courage to distinctly communicate this impression. However, it came up to them so forcibly at last that the doctor said, without further preface:

"Crocodiles are found only on the shores of the islands or of the lake, and Joe will have skill enough to avoid them. Besides, they are not very dangerous; and the Africans bathe with impunity, and quite fearless of their attacks."

Kennedy made no reply. He preferred keeping quiet to discussing this terrible possibility.

The doctor made out the town of Lari about five o'clock in the evening. The inhabitants were at work gathering in their cotton-crop in front of their huts, constructed of woven reeds, and standing in the midst of clean and neatly-kept enclosures. This collection of about fifty habitations occupied a slight depression of the soil, in a valley extending between two low mountains. The force of the wind carried the doctor farther onward than he wanted to go; but it changed a second time, and bore him back exactly to his starting-point, on the sort of enclosed island where he had passed the preceding night. The anchor, instead of catching the branches of the tree, took hold in the masses of reeds mixed with the thick mud of the marshes, which offered considerable resistance.

The doctor had much difficulty in restraining the balloon; but at length the wind died away with the setting in of nightfall; and the two friends kept watch together in an almost desperate state of mind.

Chapter XXXIV

THE HURRICANE—A FORCED DEPARTURE—LOSS OF AN
ANCHOR—MELANCHOLY REFLECTIONS—THE RESOLUTION
ADOPTED—THE SAND-STORM—THE BURIED CARAVAN—
A CONTRARY YET FAVOURABLE WIND—THE RETURN
SOUTHWARD—KENNEDY AT HIS POST

AT THREE O'CLOCK IN THE MORNING THE WIND WAS RAGING. IT BEAT DOWN WITH SUCH violence that the *Victoria* could not stay near the ground without danger. It was thrown almost flat over upon its side, and the reeds chafed the silk so roughly that it seemed as though they would tear it.

"We must be off, Dick," said the doctor; "we cannot remain in this situation."

"But, doctor, what of Joe?"

"I am not likely to abandon him. No, indeed! and should the hurricane carry me a thousand miles to the northward, I will return! But here we are endangering the safety of all."

"Must we go without him?" asked the Scot, with an accent of profound grief.

"And do you think, then," rejoined Ferguson, "that my heart does not bleed like your own? Am I not merely obeying an imperious necessity?"

"I am entirely at your orders," replied the hunter; "let us start!"

But their departure was surrounded with unusual difficulty. The anchor, which had caught very deeply, resisted all their efforts to disengage it; while the balloon, drawing in the opposite direction, increased its tension. Kennedy could not get it free. Besides, in his present position, the maneuvre had become a very perilous one, for the *Victoria* threatened to break away before he should be able to get into the car again.

The doctor, unwilling to run such a risk, made his friend get into his place, and resigned himself to the alternative of cutting the anchor-rope. The *Victoria* made one bound of three hundred feet into the air, and took her route directly northward.

Ferguson had no other choice than to scud before the storm. He folded his arms, and soon became absorbed in his own melancholy reflections.

After a few moments of profound silence, he turned to Kennedy, who sat there no less taciturn.

"We have, perhaps, been tempting Providence," said he; "it does not belong to man to undertake such a journey!"—and a sigh of grief escaped him as he spoke.

"It is but a few days," replied the sportsman, "since we were congratulating ourselves upon having escaped so many dangers! All three of us were shaking hands!"

"Poor Joe! kindly and excellent disposition! brave and candid heart! Dazzled for a moment by his sudden discovery of wealth, he willingly sacrificed his treasures! And now, he is far from us; and the wind is carrying us still farther away with resistless speed!"

"Come, doctor, admitting that he may have found refuge among the lake tribes, can he not do as the travellers who visited them before us, did;—like Denham, like Barth? Both of those men got back to their own country."

"Ah! my dear Dick! Joe doesn't know one word of the language; he is alone, and without resources. The travellers of whom you speak did not attempt to go forward without sending many presents in advance of them to the chiefs, and surrounded by an escort armed and trained for these expeditions. Yet, they could not avoid sufferings of the worst description! What, then, can you expect the fate of our companion to be? It is horrible to think of, and this is one of the worst calamities that it has ever been my lot to endure!"

"But, we'll come back again, doctor!"

"Come back, Dick? Yes, if we have to abandon the balloon! if we should be forced to return to Lake Tchad on foot, and put ourselves in communication with the Sultan of Bornou! The Arabs cannot have retained a disagreeable remembrance of the first Europeans."

"I will follow you, doctor," replied the hunter, with emphasis. "You may count upon me! We would rather give up the idea of prosecuting this journey than not return. Joe forgot himself for our sake; we will sacrifice ourselves for his!"

This resolve revived some hope in the hearts of these two men; they felt strong in the same inspiration. Ferguson forthwith set everything at work to get into a contrary current, that might bring him back again to Lake Tchad; but this was impracticable at that moment, and even to alight was out of the question on ground completely bare of trees, and with such a hurricane blowing.

The *Victoria* thus passed over the country of the Tibbous, crossed the Belad el Djerid, a desert of briers that forms the border of the Soudan, and advanced into the desert of sand streaked with the long tracks of the many caravans that pass and repass there. The last line of vegetation was speedily lost in the dim southern horizon, not far from the principal oasis in this part of Africa, whose fifty wells are shaded by magnificent trees; but it was impossible to stop. An Arab encampment, tents of striped stuff, some camels, stretching out their viper-like heads and necks along the sand, gave life to this solitude, but the *Victoria* sped by like a shooting-star, and in this way traversed a distance of sixty miles in three hours, without Ferguson being able to check or guide her course.

"We cannot halt, we cannot alight!" said the doctor; "not a tree, not an inequality of the ground! Are we then to be driven clear across Sahara? Surely, Heaven is indeed against us!"

He was uttering these words with a sort of despairing rage, when suddenly he saw the desert sands rising aloft in the midst of a dense cloud of dust, and go whirling through the air, impelled by opposing currents.

Amid this tornado, an entire caravan, disorganised, broken, and overthrown, was disappearing beneath an avalanche of sand. The camels, flung pell-mell together, were uttering dull and pitiful groans; cries and howls of despair were heard issuing from that dusty and stifling cloud, and, from time to time, a parti-coloured garment cut the chaos of the scene with its vivid hues, and the moaning and shrieking sounded over all, a terrible accompaniment to this spectacle of destruction.

Ere long the sand had accumulated in compact masses; and there, where so recently stretched a level plain as far as the eye could see, rose now a ridgy line of hillocks, still moving from beneath—the vast tomb of an entire caravan!

The doctor and Kennedy, pallid with emotion, sat transfixed by this fearful spectacle. They could no longer manage their balloon, which went whirling round and round in contending currents, and refused to obey the different dilations of the gas. Caught in these eddies of the atmosphere, it spun about with a rapidity that made their heads reel, while the car oscillated and swung to and fro violently at the same time. The instruments suspended under the awning clattered together as though they would be dashed to pieces; the pipes of the spiral bent to and fro, threatening to break at every instant; and the water-tanks jostled and jarred with tremendous din. Although but two feet apart, our aeronauts could not hear each other speak, but with firmly-clinched hands they clung convulsively to the cordage, and endeavoured to steady themselves against the fury of the tempest.

Kennedy, with his hair blown wildly about his face, looked on without speaking; but the doctor had regained all his daring in the midst of this deadly peril, and not a sign of his emotion was betrayed in his countenance, even when, after a last violent twirl, the *Victoria* stopped suddenly in the midst of a most unlooked-for calm; the north wind had abruptly got the upper hand, and now drove her back with equal rapidity over the route she had traversed in the morning.

"Whither are we going now?" cried Kennedy.

"Let us leave that to Providence, my dear Dick; I was wrong in doubting it. It knows better than we, and here we are, returning to places that we had expected never to see again!"

The surface of the country, which had looked so flat and level when they were coming, now seemed tossed and uneven, like the ocean-billows after a storm; a long succession of hillocks, that had scarcely settled to their places yet, indented the desert; the wind blew furiously, and the balloon fairly flew through the atmosphere.

The direction taken by our aeronauts differed somewhat from that of the morning, and thus about nine o'clock, instead of finding themselves again near the borders of Lake Tchad, they saw the desert still stretching away before them.

Kennedy remarked the circumstance.

"It matters little," replied the doctor, "the important point is to return southward; we shall come across the towns of Bornou, Wouddie, or Kouka, and I should not hesitate to halt there."

"If you are satisfied, I am content," replied the Scot, "but Heaven grant that we may not be reduced to cross the desert, as those unfortunate Arabs had to do! What we saw was frightful!"

"It often happens, Dick; these trips across the desert are far more perilous than those across the ocean. The desert has all the dangers of the sea, including the risk of being swallowed up, and added thereto are unendurable fatigues and privations."

"I think the wind shows some symptoms of moderating; the sand-dust is less dense; the undulations of the surface are diminishing, and the sky is growing clearer."

"So much the better! We must now reconnoitre attentively with our glasses, and take care not to omit a single point."

"I will look out for that, doctor, and not a tree shall be seen without my informing you of it."

And, suiting the action to the word, Kennedy took his station, spy-glass in hand, at the forward part of the car.

Chapter XXXV

WHAT HAPPENED TO JOE—THE ISLAND OF THE BIDDIOMAHS—THE
ADORATION SHOWN HIM—THE ISLAND THAT SANK—THE SHORES
OF THE LAKE—THE TREE OF THE SERPENTS—THE FOOT-TRAMP—
TERRIBLE SUFFERING—MOSQUITOES AND ANTS—HUNGER—
THE VICTORIA SEEN—SHE DISAPPEARS—THE SWAMP—
ONE LAST DESPAIRING CRY

WHAT HAD BECOME OF JOE, WHILE HIS MASTER WAS THUS VAINLY SEEKING FOR HIM? When he had dashed headlong into the lake, his first movement on coming to the surface was to raise his eyes and look upward. He saw the *Victoria* already risen far above the water, still rapidly ascending and growing smaller and smaller. It was soon caught in a rapid current and disappeared to the northward. His master—both his friends were saved!

"How lucky it was," thought he, "that I had that idea to throw myself out into the lake! Mr. Kennedy would soon have jumped at it, and he would not have hesitated to do as I did, for nothing's more natural than for one man to give himself up to save two others. That's mathematics!"

Satisfied on this point, Joe began to think of himself. He was in the middle of a vast lake, surrounded by tribes unknown to him, and probably ferocious. All the greater reason why he should get out of the scrape by depending only on himself. And so he gave himself no farther concern about it.

Before the attack by the birds of prey, which, according to him, had behaved like real condors, he had noticed an island on the horizon, and determining to reach it, if possible, he put forth all his knowledge and skill in the art of swimming, after having relieved himself of the most troublesome part of his clothing. The idea of a stretch of five or six miles by no means disconcerted him; and therefore, so long as he was in the open lake, he thought only of striking out straight ahead and manfully.

In about an hour and a half the distance between him and the island had greatly diminished.

But as he approached the land, a thought, at first fleeting and then tenacious, arose in his mind. He knew that the shores of the lake were frequented by huge alligators, and was well aware of the voracity of those monsters.

Now, no matter how much he was inclined to find everything in this world quite natural, the worthy fellow was no little disturbed by this reflection. He feared greatly lest white flesh like his might be particularly acceptable to the dreaded brutes, and advanced only with extreme precaution, his eyes on the alert on both sides and all around him. At length, he was not more than one hundred yards from a bank, covered with green trees, when a puff of air strongly impregnated with a musky odor reached him.

"There!" said he to himself, "just what I expected. The crocodile isn't far off!"

With this he dived swiftly, but not sufficiently so to avoid coming into contact with an enormous body, the scaly surface of which scratched him as he passed. He thought himself lost and swam with desperate energy. Then he rose again to the top of the water, took breath and dived once more. Thus passed a few minutes of unspeakable anguish, which all his philosophy could not overcome, for he thought, all the while, that he heard behind him the sound of those huge jaws ready to snap him up forever. In this state of mind he was striking out under the water as noiselessly as possible when he felt himself seized by the arm and then by the waist.

Poor Joe! he gave one last thought to his master; and began to struggle with all the energy of despair, feeling himself the while drawn along, but not towards the bottom of the lake, as is the habit of the crocodile when about to devour its prey, but towards the surface.

So soon as he could get breath and look around him, he saw that he was between two natives as black as ebony, who held him, with a firm gripe, and uttered strange cries.

"Ha!" said Joe, "blacks instead of crocodiles! Well, I prefer it as it is; but how in the mischief dare these fellows go in bathing in such places?"

Joe was not aware that the inhabitants of the islands of Lake Tchad, like many other negro tribes, plunge with impunity into sheets of water infested with crocodiles and caymans, and without troubling their heads about them. The amphibious denizens of this lake enjoy the well-deserved reputation of being quite inoffensive.

But had not Joe escaped one peril only to fall into another? That was a question which he left events to decide; and, since he could not do otherwise, he allowed himself to be conducted to the shore without manifesting any alarm.

"Evidently," thought he, "these chaps saw the *Victoria* skimming the waters of the lake, like a monster of the air. They were the distant witnesses of my tumble, and they can't fail to have some respect for a man that fell from the sky! Let them have their own way, then."

Joe was at this stage of his meditations, when he was landed amid a yelling crowd of both sexes, and all ages and sizes, but not of all colours. In fine, he was surrounded by a tribe of Biddiomahs as black as jet. Nor had he to blush for the scantiness of his costume, for he saw that he was in "undress" in the highest style of that country.

But before he had time to form an exact idea of the situation, there was no mistaking the agitation of which he instantly became the object, and this soon enabled him to pluck up courage, although the adventure of Kazah did come back rather vividly to his memory.

"I foresee that they are going to make a god of me again," thought he, "some son of the Moon most likely. Well, one trade's as good as another when a man has no choice. The main thing is to gain time. Should the *Victoria* pass this way again, I'll take advantage of my new position to treat my worshippers here to a miracle when I go sailing up into the sky!"

While Joe's thoughts were running thus, the throng pressed around him. They prostrated themselves before him; they howled; they felt him; they became even annoyingly familiar; but at the same time they had the consideration to offer him a superb banquet consisting of sour milk and rice pounded in honey. The worthy fellow, making the best of everything, took one of the heartiest luncheons he ever ate in his life, and gave his new adorers an exalted idea of how the gods tuck away their food upon grand occasions.

When evening came, the sorcerers of the island took him respectfully by the hand, and conducted him to a sort of house surrounded with talismans; but, as he was entering it, Joe cast an uneasy look at the heaps of human bones that lay scattered around this sanctuary. But he had still more time to think about them when he found himself at last shut up in the cabin.

During the evening and through a part of the night, he heard festive chantings, the reverberations of a kind of drum, and a clatter of old iron, which were very sweet, no doubt, to African ears. Then there were howling choruses, accompanied by endless dances by gangs of natives who circled round and round the sacred hut with contortions and grimaces.

Joe could catch the sound of this deafening orchestra, through the mud and reeds of which his cabin was built; and perhaps under other circumstances he might have been amused by these strange ceremonies; but his mind was soon disturbed by quite different and less agreeable reflections. Even looking at the bright side of things, he found it both stupid and sad to be left alone in the midst of this savage country and among these wild tribes. Few travellers who had penetrated to these regions had ever again seen their native land. Moreover, could he trust to the worship of which he saw himself the object? He had good reason to believe in the vanity of human greatness; and he asked himself whether, in this country, adoration did not sometimes go to the length of eating the object adored!

But, notwithstanding this rather perplexing prospect, after some hours of meditation, fatigue got the better of his gloomy thoughts, and Joe fell into a profound slumber, which would have lasted no doubt until sunrise, had not a very unexpected sensation of dampness awakened the sleeper. Ere long this dampness became water, and that water gained so rapidly that it had soon mounted to Joe's waist.

"What can this be?" said he; "a flood! a water-spout! or a new torture invented by these blacks? Faith, though, I'm not going to wait here till it's up to my neck!"

And, so saying, he burst through the frail wall with a jog of his powerful shoulder, and found himself—where?—in the open lake! Island there was none. It had sunk during the night. In its place, the watery immensity of Lake Tchad!

"A poor country for the land-owners!" said Joe, once more vigourously resorting to his skill in the art of natation.

One of those phenomena, which are by no means unusual on Lake Tchad, had liberated our brave Joe. More than one island, that previously seemed to have the solidity of rock, has been submerged in this way; and the people living along the shores of the mainland have had to pick up the unfortunate survivors of these terrible catastrophes.

Joe knew nothing about this peculiarity of the region, but he was none the less ready to profit by it. He caught sight of a boat drifting about, without occupants, and was soon aboard of it. He found it to be but the trunk of a tree rudely hollowed out; but there were a couple of paddles in it, and Joe, availing himself of a rapid current, allowed his craft to float along.

"But let us see where we are," he said. "The polar-star there, that does its work honourably in pointing out the direction due north to everybody else, will, most likely, do me that service."

He discovered, with satisfaction, that the current was taking him towards the northern shore of the lake, and he allowed himself to glide with it. About two o'clock in the morning he disembarked upon a promontory covered with prickly reeds, that proved very provoking and inconvenient even to a philosopher like him; but a tree grew there expressly to offer him a bed among its branches, and Joe climbed up into it for greater security, and there, without sleeping much, however, awaited the dawn of day.

When morning had come with that suddenness which is peculiar to the equatorial regions, Joe cast a glance at the tree which had sheltered him during the last few hours, and beheld a sight that chilled the marrow in his bones. The branches of the tree were literally covered with snakes and chameleons! The foliage actually was hidden beneath their coils, so that the beholder might have fancied that he saw before him a new kind of tree that bore reptiles for its leaves and fruit. And all this horrible living mass writhed and twisted in the first rays of the morning sun! Joe experienced a keen sensation or terror mingled with disgust, as he looked at it, and he leaped precipitately from the tree amid the hissings of these new and unwelcome bedfellows.

"Now, there's something that I would never have believed!" said he.

He was not aware that Dr. Vogel's last letters had made known this singular feature of the shores of Lake Tchad, where reptiles are more numerous than in any other part of the world. But after what he had just seen, Joe determined to be more circumspect for the future; and, taking his bearings by the sun, he set off afoot towards the north-east, avoiding with the utmost care cabins, huts, hovels, and dens of every description, that might serve in any manner as a shelter for human beings.

How often his gaze was turned upward to the sky! He hoped to catch a glimpse, each time, of the *Victoria*; and, although he looked vainly during all that long, fatiguing day of sore foot-travel, his confident reliance on his master remained undiminished. Great energy of character was needed to enable him thus to sustain the situation with philosophy. Hunger conspired with fatigue to crush him, for a man's system is not greatly restored and fortified by a diet of roots, the pith of plants, such as the *mélé*, or the fruit of the *doum* palm-tree; and yet, according to his own calculations, Joe was enabled to push on about twenty miles to the westward.

His body bore in scores of places the marks of the thorns with which the lake-reeds, the acacias, the mimosas, and other wild shrubbery through which he had to force his way, are thickly studded; and his torn and bleeding feet rendered walking both painful and difficult. But at length he managed to react against all these sufferings; and when evening came again, he resolved to pass the night on the shores of Lake Tchad.

There he had to endure the bites of myriads of insects—gnats, mosquitoes, ants half-an-inch long, literally covered the ground; and, in less than two hours, Joe had not a rag remaining of the garments that had covered him, the insects having devoured them! It was a terrible night, that did not yield our exhausted traveller an hour of sleep. During all this time the wild-boars and native buffaloes, re-enforced by the *ajoub*—a very dangerous species of *lamantine*—carried on their ferocious revels in the bushes and under the waters of the lake, filling the night with a hideous concert. Joe dared scarcely breathe. Even his courage and coolness had hard work to bear up against so terrible a situation.

At length, day came again, and Joe sprang to his feet precipitately; but judge of the loathing he felt when he saw what species of creature had shared his couch—a toad!—but a toad five inches in length, a monstrous, repulsive specimen of vermin that sat there staring at him with huge round eyes. Joe felt his stomach revolt at the sight, and, regaining a little strength from the intensity of his repugnance, he rushed at the top of his speed and plunged into the lake. This sudden bath somewhat allayed the pangs of the itching that tortured his whole body; and, chewing a few leaves, he set forth resolutely, again feeling an obstinate resolution in the act, for which he could hardly account even to his own mind. He no longer seemed to have entire control of his own acts, and, nevertheless, he felt within him a strength superior to despair.

However, he began now to suffer terribly from hunger. His stomach, less resigned than he was, rebelled, and he was obliged to fasten a tendril of wild-vine tightly about his waist. Fortunately, he could quench his thirst at any moment, and, in recalling the sufferings he had undergone in the desert, he experienced comparative relief in his exemption from that other distressing want.

"What can have become of the *Victoria?*" he wondered. "The wind blows from the north, and she should be carried back by it towards the lake. No doubt the doctor has gone to work to right her balance, but yesterday would have given him time enough for that, so that may be to-day—but I must act just as if I was never to see him again. After all, if I only get to one of the large towns on the lake, I'll find myself no worse off than the travellers my master used to talk about. Why shouldn't I work my way out of the scrape as well as they did? Some of them got back home again. Come, then! the deuce! Cheer up, my boy!"

Thus talking to himself and walking on rapidly, Joe came right upon a horde of natives in the very depths of the forest, but he halted in time and was not seen by them. The negroes were busy poisoning arrows with the juice of the *euphorbium*—a piece of work deemed a great affair among these savage tribes, and carried on with a sort of ceremonial solemnity.

Joe, entirely motionless and even holding his breath, was keeping himself concealed in a thicket, when, happening to raise his eyes, he saw through an opening in the foliage the welcome apparition of the balloon—the *Victoria* herself—moving towards the lake, at a height of only about one hundred feet above him. But he could not make himself heard; he dared not, could not make his friends even see him!

Tears came to his eyes, not of grief but of thankfulness; his master was then seeking him; his master had not left him to perish! He would have to wait for the departure of the blacks; then he could quit his hiding-place and run towards the borders of Lake Tchad!

But by this time the *Victoria* was disappearing in the distant sky. Joe still determined to wait for her; she would come back again, undoubtedly. She did, indeed, return, but farther to the eastward. Joe ran, gesticulated, shouted—but all in vain! A strong breeze was sweeping the balloon away with a speed that deprived him of all hope.

For the first time, energy and confidence abandoned the heart of the unfortunate man. He saw that he was lost. He thought his master gone beyond all prospect of return. He dared no longer think; he would no longer reflect!

Like a crazy man, his feet bleeding, his body cut and torn, he walked on during all that day and a part of the next night. He even dragged himself along, sometimes on his knees, sometimes with his hands. He saw the moment nigh when all his strength would fail, and nothing would be left to him but to sink upon the ground and die.

Thus working his way along, he at length found himself close to a marsh, or what he knew would soon become a marsh, for night had set in some hours before, and he fell by a sudden misstep into a thick, clinging mire. In spite of all his efforts, in spite of his desperate struggles, he felt himself sinking gradually in the swampy ooze, and in a few minutes he was buried to his waist.

"Here, then, at last, is death!" he thought, in agony, "and what a death!"

He now began to struggle again, like a madman; but his efforts only served to bury him deeper in the tomb that the poor doomed lad was hollowing for himself; not a log of wood or a branch to buoy him up; not a reed to which he might cling! He felt that all was over! His eyes convulsively closed!

"Master! master!—Help!" were his last words; but his voice, despairing, unaided, half stifled already by the rising mire, died away feebly on the night.

Chapter XXXVI

A Throng of People on the Horizon—A Troop of Arabs—
The Pursuit—It is He—Fall from Horseback—The
Strangled Arab—A Ball from Kennedy—Adroit
Maneuvres—Caught up flying—Joe saved at last

FROM THE MOMENT WHEN KENNEDY RESUMED HIS POST OF OBSERVATION IN THE FRONT of the car, he had not ceased to watch the horizon with his utmost attention.

After the lapse of some time he turned towards the doctor and said:

"If I am not greatly mistaken I can see, off yonder in the distance, a throng of men or animals moving. It is impossible to make them out yet, but I observe that they are in violent motion, for they are raising a great cloud of dust."

"May it not be another contrary breeze?" said the doctor, "another whirlwind coming to drive us back northward again?" and while speaking he stood up to examine the horizon.

"I think not, Samuel; it is a troop of gazelles or of wild oxen."

"Perhaps so, Dick; but yon throng is some nine or ten miles from us at least, and on my part, even with the glass, I can make nothing of it!"

"At all events I shall not lose sight of it. There is something remarkable about it that excites my curiosity. Sometimes it looks like a body of cavalry maneuvring. Ah! I was not mistaken. It is, indeed, a squadron of horsemen. Look—look there!"

The doctor eyed the group with great attention, and, after a moment's pause, remarked:

"I believe that you are right. It is a detachment of Arabs or Tibbous, and they are galloping in the same direction with us, as though in flight, but we are going faster than they, and we are rapidly gaining on them. In half-an-hour we shall be near enough to see them and know what they are."

Kennedy had again lifted his glass and was attentively scrutinising them. Meanwhile the crowd of horsemen was becoming more distinctly visible, and a few were seen to detach themselves from the main body.

"It is some hunting maneuvre, evidently," said Kennedy. "Those fellows seem to be in pursuit of something. I would like to know what they are about."

"Patience, Dick! In a little while we shall overtake them, if they continue on the same route. We are going at the rate of twenty miles per hour, and no horse can keep up with that."

Kennedy again raised his glass, and a few minutes later he exclaimed:

"They are Arabs, galloping at the top of their speed; I can make them out distinctly. They are about fifty in number. I can see their *bournouses* puffed out by the wind. It is some cavalry exercise that they are going through. Their chief is a hundred paces ahead of them and they are rushing after him at headlong speed."

"Whoever they may be, Dick, they are not to be feared, and then, if necessary, we can go higher."

"Wait, doctor—wait a little!"

"It's curious," said Kennedy again, after a brief pause, "but there's something going on that I can't exactly explain. By the efforts they make, and the irregularity of their line, I should fancy that those Arabs are pursuing someone, instead of following."

"Are you certain of that, Dick?"

"Oh! yes, it's clear enough now. I am right! It is a pursuit—a hunt—but a man-hunt! That is not their chief riding ahead of them, but a fugitive."

"A fugitive!" exclaimed the doctor, growing more and more interested.

"Yes!"

"Don't lose sight of him, and let us wait!"

Three or four miles more were quickly gained upon these horsemen, who nevertheless were dashing onward with incredible speed.

"Doctor! doctor!" shouted Kennedy in an agitated voice.

"What is the matter, Dick?"

"Is it an illusion? Can it be possible?"

"What do you mean?"

"Wait!" and so saying, the Scot wiped the sights of his spy-glass carefully, and looked through it again intently.

"Well?" questioned the doctor.

"It is he, doctor!"

"He!" exclaimed Ferguson with emotion.

"It is he! no other!" and it was needless to pronounce the name.

"Yes! it is he! on horseback, and only a hundred paces in advance of his enemies! He is pursued!"

"It is Joe—Joe himself!" cried the doctor, turning pale.

"He cannot see us in his flight!"

"He will see us, though!" said the doctor, lowering the flame of his blow-pipe.

"But how?"

"In five minutes we shall be within fifty feet of the ground, and in fifteen we shall be right over him!"

"We must let him know it by firing a gun!"

"No! he can't turn back to come this way. He's headed off!"

"What shall we do, then?"

"We must wait."

"Wait?—and these Arabs!"

"We shall overtake them. We'll pass them. We are not more than two miles from them, and provided that Joe's horse holds out!"

"Great God!" exclaimed Kennedy, suddenly.

"What is the matter?"

Kennedy had uttered a cry of despair as he saw Joe fling himself to the ground. His horse, evidently exhausted, had just fallen headlong.

"He sees us!" cried the doctor, "and he motions to us, as he gets upon his feet!"

"But the Arabs will overtake him! What is he waiting for? Ah! the brave lad! Huzza!" shouted the sportsman, who could no longer restrain his feelings.

Joe, who had immediately sprung up after his fall, just as one of the swiftest horsemen rushed upon him, bounded like a panther, avoided his assailant by leaping to one side, jumped up behind him on the crupper, seized the Arab by the throat, and, strangling him with his sinewy hands and fingers of steel, flung him on the sand, and continued his headlong flight.

A tremendous howl was heard from the Arabs, but, completely engrossed by the pursuit, they had not taken notice of the balloon, which was now but five hundred paces behind them, and only about thirty feet from the ground. On their part, they were not twenty lengths of their horses from the fugitive.

One of them was very perceptibly gaining on Joe, and was about to pierce him with his lance, when Kennedy, with fixed eye and steady hand, stopped him short with a ball, that hurled him to the earth.

Joe did not even turn his head at the report. Some of the horsemen reined in their barbs, and fell on their faces in the dust as they caught sight of the *Victoria;* the rest continued their pursuit.

"But what is Joe about?" said Kennedy; "he don't stop!"

"He's doing better than that, Dick! I understand him! He's keeping on in the same direction as the balloon. He relies upon our intelligence. Ah! the noble fellow! We'll carry him off in the very teeth of those Arab rascals! We are not more than two hundred paces from him!"

"What are we to do?" asked Kennedy.

"Lay aside your rifle, Dick."

And the Scot obeyed the request at once.

"Do you think that you can hold one hundred and fifty pounds of ballast in your arms?"

"Ay, more than that!"

"No! That will be enough!"

And the doctor proceeded to pile up bags of sand in Kennedy's arms.

"Hold yourself in readiness in the back part of the car, and be prepared to throw out that ballast at a single effort. But, for your life, don't do so until I give the word!"

"Be easy on that point."

"Otherwise, we should miss Joe, and he would be lost."

"Count upon me!"

The *Victoria* at that moment almost commanded the troop of horsemen who were still desperately urging their steeds at Joe's heels. The doctor, standing in the front of the car, held the ladder clear, ready to throw it at any moment. Meanwhile, Joe had still maintained the distance between himself and his pursuers—say about fifty feet. The *Victoria* was now ahead of the party.

"Attention!" exclaimed the doctor to Kennedy.

"I'm ready!"

"Joe, look out for yourself!" shouted the doctor in his sonorous, ringing voice, as he flung out the ladder, the lowest ratlines of which tossed up the dust of the road.

As the doctor shouted, Joe had turned his head, but without checking his horse. The ladder dropped close to him, and at the instant he grasped it the doctor again shouted to Kennedy:

"Throw ballast!"

"It's done!"

And the *Victoria,* lightened by a weight greater than Joe's, shot up one hundred and fifty feet into the air.

Joe clung with all his strength to the ladder during the wide oscillations that it had to describe, and then making an indescribable gesture to the Arabs, and climbing with the agility of a monkey, he sprang up to his companions, who received him with open arms.

The Arabs uttered a scream of astonishment and rage. The fugitive had been snatched from them on the wing, and the *Victoria* was rapidly speeding far beyond their reach.

"Master! Kennedy!" ejaculated Joe, and overwhelmed, at last, with fatigue and emotion, the poor fellow fainted away, while Kennedy, almost beside himself, kept exclaiming:

"Saved—saved!"

"Saved indeed!" murmured the doctor, who had recovered all his phlegmatic coolness.

Joe was almost naked. His bleeding arms, his body covered with cuts and bruises, told what his sufferings had been. The doctor quietly dressed his wounds, and laid him comfortably under the awning.

Joe soon returned to consciousness, and asked for a glass of brandy, which the doctor did not see fit to refuse, as the faithful fellow had to be indulged.

After he had swallowed the stimulant, Joe grasped the hands of his two friends and announced that he was ready to relate what had happened to him.

But they would not allow him to talk at that time, and he sank back into a profound sleep, of which he seemed to have the greatest possible need.

The *Victoria* was then taking an oblique line to the westward. Driven by a tempestuous wind, it again approached the borders of the thorny desert, which the travellers descried over the tops of palm-trees, bent and broken by the storm; and, after having made a run of two hundred miles since rescuing Joe, it passed the tenth degree of east longitude about nightfall.

Chapter XXXVII

THE WESTERN ROUTE—JOE WAKES UP—HIS OBSTINACY—END OF JOE'S NARRATIVE—TAGELEI—KENNEDY'S ANXIETIES— THE ROUTE TO THE NORTH—A NIGHT NEAR AGHADES

DURING THE NIGHT THE WIND LULLED AS THOUGH REPOSING AFTER THE BOISTEROUSness of the day, and the *Victoria* remained quietly at the top of the tall sycamore. The doctor and Kennedy kept watch by turns, and Joe availed himself of the chance to sleep most sturdily for twenty-four hours at a stretch.

"That's the remedy he needs," said Dr. Ferguson. "Nature will take charge of his care."

With the dawn the wind sprang up again in quite strong, and moreover capricious gusts. It shifted abruptly from south to north, but finally the *Victoria* was carried away by it towards the west.

The doctor, map in hand, recognised the kingdom of Damerghou, an undulating region of great fertility, in which the huts that compose the villages are constructed of long reeds interwoven with branches of the *asclepia*. The grain-mills were seen raised in the cultivated fields, upon small scaffoldings or platforms, to keep them out of the reach of the mice and the huge ants of that country.

They soon passed the town of Zinder, recognised by its spacious place of execution, in the centre of which stands the "tree of death." At its foot the executioner stands waiting, and whoever passes beneath its shadow is immediately hung!

Upon consulting his compass, Kennedy could not refrain from saying:

"Look! we are again moving northward."

"No matter; if it only takes us to Timbuctoo, we shall not complain. Never was a finer voyage accomplished under better circumstances!"

"Nor in better health," said Joe, at that instant thrusting his jolly countenance from between the curtains of the awning.

"There he is! there's our gallant friend—our preserver!" exclaimed Kennedy, cordially.— "How goes it, Joe?"

"Oh! why, naturally enough, Mr. Kennedy, very naturally! I never felt better in my life! Nothing sets a man up like a little pleasure-trip with a bath in Lake Tchad to start on— eh, doctor?"

"Brave fellow!" said Ferguson, pressing Joe's hand, "what terrible anxiety you caused us!"

"Humph! and you, sir? Do you think that I felt easy in my mind about you, gentlemen? You gave me a fine fright, let me tell you!"

"We shall never agree in the world, Joe, if you take things in that style."

"I see that his tumble hasn't changed him a bit," added Kennedy.

"Your devotion and self-forgetfulness were sublime, my brave lad, and they saved us, for the *Victoria* was falling into the lake, and, once there, nobody could have extricated her."

"But, if my devotion, as you are pleased to call my summerset, saved you, did it not save me too, for here we are, all three of us, in first-rate health? Consequently we have nothing to squabble about in the whole affair."

"Oh! we can never come to a settlement with that youth," said the sportsman.

"The best way to settle it," replied Joe, "is to say nothing more about the matter. What's done is done. Good or bad, we can't take it back."

"You obstinate fellow!" said the doctor, laughing; "you can't refuse, though, to tell us your adventures, at all events."

"Not if you think it worthwhile. But, in the first place, I'm going to cook this fat goose to a turn, for I see that Mr. Kennedy has not wasted his time."

"All right, Joe!"

"Well, let us see then how this African game will sit on a European stomach!"

The goose was soon roasted by the flame of the blow-pipe, and not long afterward was comfortably stowed away. Joe took his own good share, like a man who had eaten nothing for several days. After the tea and the punch, he acquainted his friends with his recent adventures. He spoke with some emotion, even while looking at things with his usual philosophy. The doctor could not refrain from frequently pressing his hand when he saw his worthy servant more considerate of his master's safety than of his own, and, in relation to the sinking of the island of the Biddiomahs, he explained to him the frequency of this phenomenon upon Lake Tchad.

At length Joe, continuing his recital, arrived at the point where, sinking in the swamp, he had uttered a last cry of despair.

"I thought I was gone," said he, "and as you came right into my mind, I made a hard fight for it. How, I couldn't tell you—but I'd made up my mind that I wouldn't go under without knowing why. Just then, I saw—two or three feet from me—what do you think? the end of a rope that had been fresh cut; so I took leave to make another jerk, and, by hook or by crook, I got to the rope. Then I pulled, it didn't give; so I pulled again and hauled away and there I was on dry ground! At the end of the rope, I found an anchor! Ah, master, I've a right to call that the anchor of safety, anyhow, if you have no objection. I knew it again! It was the anchor of the *Victoria!* You had grounded there! So I followed the direction of the rope and that gave me your direction, and, after trying hard a few times more, I got out of the swamp. I had got my strength back with my spunk, and I walked on part of the night away from the lake, until I got to the edge of a very big wood. There I saw a fenced-in place, where some horses were grazing, without thinking of any harm. Now, there are times when everybody knows how to ride a horse, are there not, doctor? So I didn't spend much time thinking about it, but jumped right on the back of one of those innocent animals and away we went galloping north as fast as our legs could carry us. I needn't tell you about the towns that I didn't see nor the villages that I took good care to go around. No! I crossed the ploughed fields; I leaped the hedges; I scrambled over the fences; I dug my heels into my nag; I thrashed him; I fairly lifted the poor fellow off his feet! At last I got to the end of the tilled land. Good! There was the desert. 'That suits me!' said I, 'for I can see better ahead of me and farther too.' I was hoping all the time to see the balloon tacking about and waiting for me. But not a bit of it; and so, in about three hours, I go plump, like a fool, into a camp of Arabs! Whew! what a hunt that was! You see, Mr. Kennedy, a hunter don't know what a real hunt is until he's been hunted himself! Still I advise him not to try it if he can keep out of it! My horse was so tired, he was ready to drop off his legs; they were close on me; I threw myself to the ground; then I jumped up again behind an Arab! I didn't mean the fellow any harm, and I hope he has no grudge against me for choking him, but I saw you—and you know the rest. The *Victoria* came on at my heels, and you caught me up flying, as a circus-rider does a ring. Wasn't I right in counting on you? Now, doctor, you see how simple all that was! Nothing more natural in the world! I'm ready to begin over again, if it would be of any service to you. And besides, master, as I said a while ago, it's not worth mentioning."

"My noble, gallant Joe!" said the doctor, with great feeling. "Heart of gold! we were not astray in trusting to your intelligence and skill."

"Poh! doctor, one has only just to follow things along as they happen, and he can always work his way out of a scrape! The safest plan, you see, is to take matters as they come."

While Joe was telling his experience, the balloon had rapidly passed over a long reach of country, and Kennedy soon pointed out on the horizon a collection of structures that looked like a town. The doctor glanced at his map and recognised the place as the large village of Tagelei, in the Damerghou country.

"Here," said he, "we come upon Dr. Barth's route. It was at this place that he parted from his companions, Richardson and Overweg; the first was to follow the Zinder route, and the second that of Maradi; and you may remember that, of these three travellers, Barth was the only one who ever returned to Europe."

"Then," said Kennedy, following out on the map the direction of the *Victoria*, "we are going due north."

"Due north, Dick."

"And don't that give you a little uneasiness?"

"Why should it?"

"Because that line leads to Tripoli, and over the Great Desert."

"Oh, we shall not go so far as that, my friend—at least, I hope not."

"But where do you expect to halt?"

"Come, Dick, don't you feel some curiosity to see Timbuctoo?"

"Timbuctoo?"

"Certainly," said Joe; "nobody nowadays can think of making the trip to Africa without going to see Timbuctoo."

"You will be only the fifth or sixth European who has ever set eyes on that mysterious city."

"Ho, then, for Timbuctoo!"

"Well, then, let us try to get as far as between the seventeenth and eighteenth degrees of north latitude, and there we will seek a favourable wind to carry us westward."

"Good!" said the hunter. "But have we still far to go to the northward?"

"One hundred and fifty miles at least."

"In that case," said Kennedy, "I'll turn in and sleep a bit."

"Sleep, sir; sleep!" urged Joe. "And you, doctor, do the same yourself: you must have need of rest, for I made you keep watch a little out of time."

The sportsman stretched himself under the awning; but Ferguson, who was not easily conquered by fatigue, remained at his post.

In about three hours the *Victoria* was crossing with extreme rapidity an expanse of stony country, with ranges of lofty, naked mountains of granitic formation at the base. A few isolated peaks attained the height of even four thousand feet. Giraffes, antelopes, and ostriches were seen running and bounding with marvellous agility in the midst of forests of acacias, mimosas, souahs, and date-trees. After the barrenness of the desert, vegetation was now resuming its empire. This was the country of the Kailouas, who veil their faces with a bandage of cotton, like their dangerous neighbours, the Touaregs.

At ten o'clock in the evening, after a splendid trip of two hundred and fifty miles, the *Victoria* halted over an important town. The moonlight revealed glimpses of one district half in ruins; and some pinnacles of mosques and minarets shot up here and there, glistening in the silvery rays. The doctor took a stellar observation, and discovered that he was in the latitude of Aghades.

This city, once the seat of an immense trade, was already falling into ruin when Dr. Barth visited it.

The *Victoria*, not being seen in the obscurity of night, descended about two miles above Aghades, in a field of millet. The night was calm, and began to break into dawn about three o'clock A.M.; while a light wind coaxed the balloon westward, and even a little towards the south.

Dr. Ferguson hastened to avail himself of such good fortune, and rapidly ascending resumed his aerial journey amid a long wake of golden morning sunshine.

Chapter XXXVIII

A RAPID PASSAGE—PRUDENT RESOLVES—CARAVANS IN SIGHT—
INCESSANT RAINS—GOA—THE NIGER—GOLBERRY, GEOFFROY,
AND GRAY—MUNGO PARK—LAING—RENÉ CAILLIÉ—
CLAPPERTON—JOHN AND RICHARD LANDER

THE 17TH OF MAY PASSED TRANQUILLY, WITHOUT ANY REMARKABLE INCIDENT; THE desert gained upon them once more; a moderate wind bore the *Victoria* towards the south-west, and she never swerved to the right or to the left, but her shadow traced a perfectly straight line on the sand.

Before starting, the doctor had prudently renewed his stock of water, having feared that he should not be able to touch ground in these regions, infested as they are by the Aouelim-Minian Touaregs. The plateau, at an elevation of eighteen hundred feet above the level of the sea, sloped down towards the south. Our travellers, having crossed the Aghades route at Murzouk—a route often pressed by the feet of camels—arrived that evening, in the sixteenth degree of north latitude, and four degrees fifty-five minutes east longitude, after having passed over one hundred and eighty miles of a long and monotonous day's journey.

During the day Joe dressed the last pieces of game, which had been only hastily prepared, and he served up for supper a mess of snipe, that were greatly relished. The wind continuing good, the doctor resolved to keep on during the night, the moon, still nearly at the full, illumining it with her radiance. The *Victoria* ascended to a height of five hundred feet, and, during her nocturnal trip of about sixty miles, the gentle slumbers of an infant would not have been disturbed by her motion.

On Sunday morning, the direction of the wind again changed, and it bore to the north-westward. A few crows were seen sweeping through the air, and, off on the horizon, a flock of vultures which, fortunately, however, kept at a distance.

The sight of these birds led Joe to compliment his master on the idea of having two balloons.

"Where would we be," said he, "with only one balloon? The second balloon is like the life-boat to a ship; in case of wreck we could always take to it and escape."

"You are right, friend Joe," said the doctor, "only that my life-boat gives me some uneasiness. It is not so good as the main craft."

"What do you mean by that, doctor?" asked Kennedy.

"I mean to say that the new *Victoria* is not so good as the old one. Whether it be that the stuff it is made of is too much worn, or that the heat of the spiral has melted the gutta percha, I can observe a certain loss of gas. It don't amount to much thus far, but still it is noticeable. We have a tendency to sink, and, in order to keep our elevation, I am compelled to give greater dilation to the hydrogen."

"The deuce!" exclaimed Kennedy with concern; "I see no remedy for that."

"There is none, Dick, and that is why we must hasten our progress, and even avoid night halts."

"Are we still far from the coast?" asked Joe.

"Which coast, my boy? How are we to know whither chance will carry us? All that I can say is, that Timbuctoo is still about four hundred miles to the westward."

"And how long will it take us to get there?"

"Should the wind not carry us too far out of the way, I hope to reach that city by Tuesday evening."

"Then," remarked Joe, pointing to a long file of animals and men winding across the open desert, "we shall arrive there sooner than that caravan."

Ferguson and Kennedy leaned over and saw an immense cavalcade. There were at least one hundred and fifty camels of the kind that, for twelve *mutkals* of gold, or about twenty-five dollars, go from Timbuctoo to Tafilet with a load of five hundred pounds upon their backs. Each animal had dangling to its tail a bag to receive its excrement, the only fuel on which the caravans can depend when crossing the desert.

These Touareg camels are of the very best race. They can go from three to seven days without drinking, and for two without eating. Their speed surpasses that of the horse, and they obey with intelligence the voice of the *khabir*, or guide of the caravan. They are known in the country under the name of *mehari*.

Such were the details given by the doctor while his companions continued to gaze upon that multitude of men, women, and children, advancing on foot and with difficulty over a waste of sand half in motion, and scarcely kept in its place by scanty nettles, withered grass, and stunted bushes that grew upon it. The wind obliterated the marks of their feet almost instantly.

Joe enquired how the Arabs managed to guide themselves across the desert, and come to the few wells scattered far between throughout this vast solitude.

"The Arabs," replied Dr. Ferguson, "are endowed by nature with a wonderful instinct in finding their way. Where a European would be at a loss, they never hesitate for a moment. An insignificant fragment of rock, a pebble, a tuft of grass, a different shade of colour in the sand, suffice to guide them with accuracy. During the night they go by the polar star. They never travel more than two miles per hour, and always rest during the noonday heat. You may judge from that how long it takes them to cross Sahara, a desert more than nine hundred miles in breadth."

But the *Victoria* had already disappeared from the astonished gaze of the Arabs, who must have envied her rapidity. That evening she passed two degrees twenty minutes east longitude, and during the night left another degree behind her.

On Monday the weather changed completely. Rain began to fall with extreme violence, and not only had the balloon to resist the power of this deluge, but also the increase of weight which it caused by wetting the whole machine, car and all. This continuous shower accounted for the swamps and marshes that formed the sole surface of the country. Vegetation reappeared, however, along with the mimosas, the baobabs, and the tamarind-trees.

Such was the Sonray country, with its villages topped with roofs turned over like Armenian caps. There were few mountains, and only such hills as were enough to form the ravines and pools where the *pintadoes* and snipes went sailing and diving through. Here and there, an impetuous torrent cut the roads, and had to be crossed by the natives on long vines stretched from tree to tree. The forests gave place to jungles, which alligators, hippopotami, and the rhinoceros, made their haunts.

"It will not be long before we see the Niger," said the doctor. "The face of the country always changes in the vicinity of large rivers. These moving highways, as they are sometimes correctly called, have first brought vegetation with them, as they will at last bring civilisation. Thus, in its course of twenty-five hundred miles, the Niger has scattered along its banks the most important cities of Africa."

"By the way," put in Joe, "that reminds me of what was said by an admirer of the goodness of Providence, who praised the foresight with which it had generally caused rivers to flow close to large cities!"

At noon the *Victoria* was passing over a petty town, a mere assemblage of miserable huts, which once was Goa, a great capital.

"It was there," said the doctor, "that Barth crossed the Niger, on his return from Timbuctoo. This is the river so famous in antiquity, the rival of the Nile, to which pagan superstition ascribed a celestial origin. Like the Nile, it has engaged the attention of geographers in all ages; and like it, also, its exploration has cost the lives of many victims; yes, even more of them than perished on account of the other."

The Niger flowed broadly between its banks, and its waters rolled southward with some violence of current; but our travellers, borne swiftly by as they were, could scarcely catch a glimpse of its curious outline.

"I wanted to talk to you about this river," said Dr. Ferguson, "and it is already far from us. Under the names of Dhiouleba, Mayo, Egghirreou, Quorra, and other titles besides, it traverses an immense extent of country, and almost competes in length with the Nile. These appellations signify simply 'the River,' according to the dialects of the countries through which it passes."

"Did Dr. Barth follow this route?" asked Kennedy.

"No, Dick: in quitting Lake Tchad, he passed through the different towns of Bornou, and intersected the Niger at Say, four degrees below Goa; then he penetrated to the bosom of those unexplored countries which the Niger embraces in its elbow; and, after eight months of fresh fatigues, he arrived at Timbuctoo; all of which we may do in about three days with as swift a wind as this."

"Have the sources of the Niger been discovered?" asked Joe.

"Long since," replied the doctor. "The exploration of the Niger and its tributaries was the object of several expeditions, the principal of which I shall mention: Between 1749 and 1758, Adamson made a reconnaissance of the river, and visited Gorea; from 1785 to 1788, Golberry and Geoffroy travelled across the deserts of Senegambia, and ascended as far as the country of the Moors, who assassinated Saugnier, Brisson, Adam, Riley, Cochelet, and so many other unfortunate men. Then came the illustrious Mungo Park, the friend of Sir Walter Scott, and, like him, a Scotchman by birth. Sent out in 1795 by the African Society of London, he got as far as Bambarra, saw the Niger, travelled five hundred miles with a slave-merchant, reconnoitred the Gambia River, and returned to England in 1797. He again set out, on the 30th of January, 1805, with his brother-in-law Anderson, Scott, the designer, and a gang of workmen; he reached Gorea, there added a detachment of thirty-five soldiers to his party, and saw the Niger again on the 19th of August. But, by that time, in consequence of fatigue, privations, ill-usage, the inclemencies of the weather, and the unhealthiness of the country, only eleven persons remained alive of the forty Europeans in the party. On the 16th of November, the last letters from Mungo Park reached his wife; and, a year later a trader from that country gave information that, having got as far as Boussa, on the Niger, on the 23d of December, the unfortunate traveller's boat was upset by the cataracts in that part of the river, and he was murdered by the natives."

"And his dreadful fate did not check the efforts of others to explore that river?"

"On the contrary, Dick. Since then, there were two objects in view: namely, to recover the lost man's papers, as well as to pursue the exploration. In 1816, an expedition was organised, in which Major Grey took part. It arrived in Senegal, penetrated to the Fonta-Jallon, visited the Foullah and Mandingo populations, and returned to England without further results. In 1822, Major Laing explored all the western part of Africa near to the British possessions; and he it was who got so far as the sources of the Niger; and, according to his documents, the spring in which that immense river takes its rise is not two feet broad."

"Easy to jump over," said Joe.

"How's that? Easy you think, eh?" retorted the doctor. "If we are to believe tradition, whoever attempts to pass that spring, by leaping over it, is immediately swallowed up; and whoever tries to draw water from it, feels himself repulsed by an invisible hand."

"I suppose a man has a right not to believe a word of that!" persisted Joe.

"Oh, by all means!—Five years later, it was Major Laing's destiny to force his way across the desert of Sahara, penetrate to Timbuctoo, and perish a few miles above it, by strangling, at the hands of the Ouelad-shiman, who wanted to compel him to turn Mussulman."

"Still another victim!" said the sportsman.

"It was then that a brave young man, with his own feeble resources, undertook and accomplished the most astonishing of modern journeys—I mean the Frenchman René Caillié, who, after sundry attempts in 1819 and 1824, set out again on the 19th of April, 1827, from Rio Nunez. On the 3d of August he arrived at Timé, so thoroughly exhausted and ill that he could not resume his journey until six months later, in January, 1828. He then joined a caravan, and, protected by his Oriental dress, reached the Niger on the 10th of March, penetrated to the city of Jenné, embarked on the river, and descended it, as far as Timbuctoo, where he arrived on the 30th of April. In 1760, another Frenchman, Imbert by name, and, in 1810, an Englishman, Robert Adams, had seen this curious place; but René Caillié was to be the first European who could bring back any authentic data concerning it. On the 4th of May he quitted this 'Queen of the desert'; on the 9th, he surveyed the very spot where Major Laing had been murdered; on the 19th, he arrived at El-Arouan, and left that commercial town to brave a thousand dangers in crossing the vast solitudes comprised between the Soudan and the northern regions of Africa. At length he entered Tangiers, and on the 28th of September sailed for Toulon. In nineteen months, notwithstanding one hundred and eighty days' sickness, he had traversed Africa from west to north. Ah! had Caillié been born in England, he would have been honoured as the most intrepid traveller of modern times, as was the case with Mungo Park. But in France he was not appreciated according to his worth."

"He was a sturdy fellow!" said Kennedy, "but what became of him?"

"He died at the age of thirty-nine, from the consequences of his long fatigues. They thought they had done enough in decreeing him the prize of the Geographical Society in 1828; the highest honours would have been paid to him in England.

"While he was accomplishing this remarkable journey, an Englishman had conceived a similar enterprise and was trying to push it through with equal courage, if not with equal good fortune. This was Captain Clapperton, the companion of Denham. In 1829 he re-entered Africa by the western coast of the Gulf of Benin; he then followed in the track of Mungo Park and of Laing, recovered at Boussa the documents relative to the death of the former, and arrived on the 20th of August at Sackatoo, where he was seized and held as a prisoner, until he expired in the arms of his faithful attendant Richard Lander."

"And what became of this Lander?" asked Joe, deeply interested.

"He succeeded in regaining the coast and returned to London, bringing with him the captain's papers, and an exact narrative of his own journey. He then offered his services to the government to complete the reconnaissance of the Niger. He took with him his brother John, the second child of a poor couple in Cornwall, and, together, these men, between 1829 and 1831, redescended the river from Boussa to its mouth, describing it village by village, mile by mile."

"So both the brothers escaped the common fate?" queried Kennedy.

"Yes, on this expedition, at least; but in 1833 Richard undertook a third trip to the Niger, and perished by a bullet, near the mouth of the river. You see, then, my friends, that the country over which we are now passing has witnessed some noble instances of self-sacrifice which, unfortunately, have only too often had death for their reward."

Chapter XXXIX

THE COUNTRY IN THE ELBOW OF THE NIGER—A FANTASTIC VIEW OF THE HOMBORI MOUNTAINS—KABRA—TIMBUCTOO— THE CHART OF DR. BARTH—A DECAYING CITY— WHITHER HEAVEN WILLS

DURING THIS DULL MONDAY, DR. FERGUSON DIVERTED HIS THOUGHTS BY GIVING HIS companions a thousand details concerning the country they were crossing. The surface, which was quite flat, offered no impediment to their progress. The doctor's sole anxiety arose from the obstinate north-east wind which continued to blow furiously, and bore them away from the latitude of Timbuctoo.

The Niger, after running northward as far as that city, sweeps around, like an immense water-jet from some fountain, and falls into the Atlantic in a broad sheaf. In the elbow thus formed the country is of varied character, sometimes luxuriantly fertile, and sometimes extremely bare; fields of maize succeeded by wide spaces covered with broom-corn and uncultivated plains. All kinds of aquatic birds—pelicans, wild-duck, kingfishers, and the rest—were seen in numerous flocks hovering about the borders of the pools and torrents.

From time to time there appeared an encampment of Touaregs, the men sheltered under their leather tents, while their women were busied with the domestic toil outside, milking their camels and smoking their huge-bowled pipes.

By eight o'clock in the evening the *Victoria* had advanced more than two hundred miles to the westward, and our aeronauts became the spectators of a magnificent scene.

A mass of moonbeams forcing their way through an opening in the clouds, and gliding between the long lines of falling rain, descended in a golden shower on the ridges of the Hombori Mountains. Nothing could be more weird than the appearance of these seemingly basaltic summits; they stood out in fantastic profile against the sombre sky, and the beholder might have fancied them to be the legendary ruins of some vast city of the middle ages, such as the icebergs of the polar seas sometimes mimic them in nights of gloom.

"An admirable landscape for the *Mysteries of Udolpho!*" exclaimed the doctor. "Ann Radcliffe could not have depicted yon mountains in a more appalling aspect."

"Faith!" said Joe, "I wouldn't like to be strolling alone in the evening through this country of ghosts. Do you see now, master, if it wasn't so heavy, I'd like to carry that whole landscape home to Scotland! It would do for the borders of Loch Lomond, and tourists would rush there in crowds."

"Our balloon is hardly large enough to admit of that little experiment—but I think our direction is changing. Bravo!—the elves and fairies of the place are quite obliging. See, they've sent us a nice little south-east breeze, that will put us on the right track again."

In fact, the *Victoria* was resuming a more northerly route, and on the morning of the 20th she was passing over an inextricable network of channels, torrents, and streams, in fine, the whole complicated tangle of the Niger's tributaries. Many of these channels, covered with a thick growth of herbage, resembled luxuriant meadow-lands. There the doctor recognised the route followed by the explorer Barth when he launched upon the river to descend to Timbuctoo. Eight hundred fathoms broad at this point, the Niger flowed between banks richly grown with cruciferous plants and tamarind-trees. Herds of agile gazelles were seen skipping about, their curling horns mingling with the tall herbage, within which the alligator, half concealed, lay silently in wait for them with watchful eyes.

Long files of camels and asses laden with merchandise from Jenné were winding in under the noble trees. Ere long, an amphitheatre of low-built houses was discovered at a turn of the river, their roofs and terraces heaped up with hay and straw gathered from the neighbouring districts.

"There's Kabra!" exclaimed the doctor, joyously; "there is the harbor of Timbuctoo, and the city is not five miles from here!"

"Then, sir, you are satisfied?" half queried Joe.

"Delighted, my boy!"

"Very good; then everything's for the best!"

In fact, about two o'clock, the Queen of the Desert, mysterious Timbuctoo, which once, like Athens and Rome, had her schools of learned men, and her professorships of philosophy, stretched away before the gaze of our travellers.

Ferguson followed the most minute details upon the chart traced by Barth himself, and was enabled to recognise its perfect accuracy.

The city forms an immense triangle marked out upon a vast plain of white sand, its acute angle directed towards the north and piercing a corner of the desert. In the environs there was almost nothing, hardly even a few grasses, with some dwarf mimosas and stunted bushes.

As for the appearance of Timbuctoo, the reader has but to imagine a collection of billiard-balls and thimbles—such is the bird's-eye view! The streets, which are quite narrow, are lined with houses only one story in height, built of bricks dried in the sun, and huts of straw and reeds, the former square, the latter conical. Upon the terraces were seen some of the male inhabitants, carelessly lounging at full length in flowing apparel of bright colours, and lance or musket in hand; but no women were visible at that hour of the day.

"Yet they are said to be handsome," remarked the doctor. "You see the three towers of the three mosques that are the only ones left standing of a great number—the city has indeed fallen from its ancient splendour! At the top of the triangle rises the Mosque of Sankore, with its ranges of galleries resting on arcades of sufficiently pure design. Farther on, and near to the Sane-Gungu quarter, is the Mosque of Sidi-Yahia and some two-story houses. But do not look for either palaces or monuments: the sheik is a mere son of traffic, and his royal palace is a counting-house."

"It seems to me that I can see half-ruined ramparts," said Kennedy.

"They were destroyed by the Fouillanes in 1826; the city was one-third larger then, for Timbuctoo, an object generally coveted by all the tribes, since the eleventh century, has belonged in succession to the Touaregs, the Sonrayans, the Morocco men, and the Fouillanes; and this great centre of civilization, where a sage like Ahmed-Baba owned, in the sixteenth century, a library of sixteen hundred manuscripts, is now nothing but a mere half-way house for the trade of Central Africa."

The city, indeed, seemed abandoned to supreme neglect; it betrayed that indifference which seems epidemic to cities that are passing away. Huge heaps of rubbish encumbered the suburbs, and, with the hill on which the market-place stood, formed the only inequalities of the ground.

When the *Victoria* passed, there was some slight show of movement; drums were beaten; but the last learned man still lingering in the place had hardly time to notice the new phenomenon, for our travellers, driven onward by the wind of the desert, resumed the winding course of the river, and, ere long, Timbuctoo was nothing more than one of the fleeting reminiscences of their journey.

"And now," said the doctor, "Heaven may waft us whither it pleases!"

"Provided only that we go westward," added Kennedy.

"Bah!" said Joe; "I wouldn't be afraid if it was to go back to Zanzibar by the same road, or to cross the ocean to America."

"We would first have to be able to do that, Joe!"

"And what's wanting, doctor?"

"Gas, my boy; the ascending force of the balloon is evidently growing weaker, and we shall need all our management to make it carry us to the sea-coast. I shall even have to throw over some ballast. We are too heavy."

"That's what comes of doing nothing, doctor; when a man lies stretched out all day long in his hammock, he gets fat and heavy. It's a lazybones trip, this of ours, master, and when we get back everybody will find us big and stout."

"Just like Joe," said Kennedy; "just the ideas for him: but wait a bit! Can you tell what we may have to go through yet? We are still far from the end of our trip. Where do you expect to strike the African coast, doctor?"

"I should find it hard to answer you, Kennedy. We are at the mercy of very variable winds; but I should think myself fortunate were we to strike it between Sierra Leone and Portendick. There is a stretch of country in that quarter where we should meet with friends."

"And it would be a pleasure to press their hands; but, are we going in the desirable direction?"

"Not any too well, Dick; not any too well! Look at the needle of the compass; we are bearing southward, and ascending the Niger towards its sources."

"A fine chance to discover them," said Joe, "if they were not known already. Now, couldn't we just find others for it, on a pinch?"

"Not exactly, Joe; but don't be alarmed: I hardly expect to go so far as that."

At nightfall the doctor threw out the last bags of sand. The *Victoria* rose higher, and the blow-pipe, although working at full blast, could scarcely keep her up. At that time she was sixty miles to the southward of Timbuctoo, and in the morning the aeronauts awoke over the banks of the Niger, not far from Lake Debo.

Chapter XL

Dr. Ferguson's Anxieties—Persistent Movement southward—A Cloud of Grasshoppers—A View of Jenné— A View of Sego—Change of the Wind—Joe's Regrets

THE FLOW OF THE RIVER WAS, AT THAT POINT, DIVIDED BY LARGE ISLANDS INTO NAR-
row branches, with a very rapid current. Upon one among them stood some shepherds' huts, but it had become impossible to take an exact observation of them, because the
speed of the balloon was constantly increasing. Unfortunately, it turned still more towards
the south, and in a few moments crossed Lake Debo.

Dr. Ferguson, forcing the dilation of his aerial craft to the utmost, sought for other currents of air at different heights, but in vain; and he soon gave up the attempt, which was
only augmenting the waste of gas by pressing it against the well-worn tissue of the balloon.

He made no remark, but he began to feel very anxious. This persistence of the
wind to head him off towards the southern part of Africa was defeating his calculations,
and he no longer knew upon whom or upon what to depend. Should he not reach the
English or French territories, what was to become of him in the midst of the barbarous
tribes that infest the coasts of Guinea? How should he there get to a ship to take him
back to England? And the actual direction of the wind was driving him along to the
kingdom of Dahomey, among the most savage races, and into the power of a ruler who
was in the habit of sacrificing thousands of human victims at his public orgies. There
he would be lost!

On the other hand, the balloon was visibly wearing out, and the doctor felt it failing
him. However, as the weather was clearing up a little, he hoped that the cessation of the
rain would bring about a change in the atmospheric currents.

It was therefore a disagreeable reminder of the actual situation when Joe said aloud:

"There! the rain's going to pour down harder than ever; and this time it will be the
deluge itself, if we're to judge by yon cloud that's coming up!"

"What! another cloud?" asked Ferguson.

"Yes, and a famous one," replied Kennedy.

"I never saw the like of it," added Joe.

"I breathe freely again!" said the doctor, laying down his spy-glass. "That's not a
cloud!"

"Not a cloud?" queried Joe, with surprise.

"No; it is a swarm."

"Eh?"

"A swarm of grasshoppers!"

"That? Grasshoppers!"

"Myriads of grasshoppers, that are going to sweep over this country like a water-
spout; and woe to it! for, should these insects alight, it will be laid waste."

"That would be a sight worth beholding!"

"Wait a little, Joe. In ten minutes that cloud will have arrived where we are, and you can then judge by the aid of your own eyes."

The doctor was right. The cloud, thick, opaque, and several miles in extent, came on with a deafening noise, casting its immense shadow over the fields. It was composed of numberless legions of that species of grasshopper called crickets. About a hundred paces from the balloon, they settled down upon a tract full of foliage and verdure. Fifteen minutes later, the mass resumed its flight, and our travellers could, even at a distance, see the trees and the bushes entirely stripped, and the fields as bare as though they had been swept with the scythe. One would have thought that a sudden winter had just descended upon the earth and struck the region with the most complete sterility.

"Well, Joe, what do you think of that?"

"Well, doctor, it's very curious, but quite natural. What one grasshopper does on a small scale, thousands do on a grand scale."

"It's a terrible shower," said the hunter; "more so than hail itself in the devastation it causes."

"It is impossible to prevent it," replied Ferguson. "Sometimes the inhabitants have had the idea to burn the forests, and even the standing crops, in order to arrest the progress of these insects; but the first ranks plunging into the flames would extinguish them beneath their mass, and the rest of the swarm would then pass irresistibly onward. Fortunately, in these regions, there is some sort of compensation for their ravages, since the natives gather these insects in great numbers and greedily eat them."

"They are the prawns of the air," said Joe, who added that he was sorry that he had never had the chance to taste them—just for information's sake!

The country became more marshy towards evening; the forests dwindled to isolated clumps of trees; and on the borders of the river could be seen plantations of tobacco, and swampy meadow-lands fat with forage. At last the city of Jenné, on a large island, came in sight, with the two towers of its clay-built mosque, and the putrid odor of the millions of swallows' nests accumulated in its walls. The tops of some baobabs, mimosas, and date-trees peeped up between the houses; and, even at night, the activity of the place seemed very great. Jenné is, in fact, quite a commercial city: it supplies all the wants of Timbuctoo. Its boats on the river, and its caravans along the shaded roads, bear thither the various products of its industry.

"Were it not that to do so would prolong our journey," said the doctor, "I should like to alight at this place. There must be more than one Arab there who has travelled in England and France, and to whom our style of locomotion is not altogether new. But it would not be prudent."

"Let us put off the visit until our next trip," said Joe, laughing.

"Besides, my friends, unless I am mistaken, the wind has a slight tendency to veer a little more to the eastward, and we must not lose such an opportunity."

The doctor threw overboard some articles that were no longer of use—some empty bottles, and a case that had contained preserved-meat—and thereby managed to keep the balloon in a belt of the atmosphere more favourable to his plans. At four o'clock in the morning the first rays of the sun lighted up Sego, the capital of Bambarra, which could be recognised at once by the four towns that compose it, by its Saracenic mosques, and by the incessant going and coming of the flat-bottomed boats that convey its inhabitants from one quarter to the other. But the travellers were not more seen than they saw. They sped rapidly and directly to the north-west, and the doctor's anxiety gradually subsided.

"Two more days in this direction, and at this rate of speed, and we'll reach the Senegal River."

"And we'll be in a friendly country?" asked the hunter.

"Not altogether; but, if the worst came to the worst, and the balloon were to fail us, we might make our way to the French settlements. But, let it hold out only for a few hundred miles, and we shall arrive without fatigue, alarm, or danger, at the western coast."

"And the thing will be over!" added Joe. "Heigh-ho! so much the worse. If it wasn't for the pleasure of telling about it, I would never want to set foot on the ground again! Do you think anybody will believe our story, doctor?"

"Who can tell, Joe? One thing, however, will be undeniable: a thousand witnesses saw us start on one side of the African Continent, and a thousand more will see us arrive on the other."

"And, in that case, it seems to me that it would be hard to say that we had not crossed it," added Kennedy.

"Ah, doctor!" said Joe again, with a deep sigh, "I'll think more than once of my lumps of solid gold-ore! There was something that would have given *weight* to our narrative! At a grain of gold per head, I could have got together a nice crowd to listen to me, and even to admire me!"

Chapter XLI

THE APPROACHES TO SENEGAL—THE BALLOON SINKS LOWER AND
LOWER—THEY KEEP THROWING OUT, THROWING OUT—THE
MARABOUT AL-HADJI—MESSRS. PASCAL, VINCENT, AND
LAMBERT—A RIVAL OF MOHAMMED—THE DIFFICULT
MOUNTAINS—KENNEDY'S WEAPONS—ONE OF JOE'S
MANEUVRES—A HALT OVER A FOREST

ON THE 27TH OF MAY, AT NINE O'CLOCK IN THE MORNING, THE COUNTRY PRESENTED AN entirely different aspect. The slopes, extending far away, changed to hills that gave evidence of mountains soon to follow. They would have to cross the chain which separates the basin of the Niger from the basin of the Senegal, and determines the course of the water-shed, whether to the Gulf of Guinea on the one hand, or to the bay of Cape Verde on the other.

As far as Senegal, this part of Africa is marked down as dangerous. Dr. Ferguson knew it through the recitals of his predecessors. They had suffered a thousand privations and been exposed to a thousand dangers in the midst of these barbarous negro tribes. It was this fatal climate that had devoured most of the companions of Mungo Park. Ferguson, therefore, was more than ever decided not to set foot in this inhospitable region.

But he had not enjoyed one moment of repose. The *Victoria* was descending very perceptibly, so much so that he had to throw overboard a number more of useless articles, especially when there was a mountain-top to pass. Things went on thus for more than one hundred and twenty miles; they were worn out with ascending and falling again; the balloon, like another rock of Sisyphus, kept continually sinking back towards the ground. The rotundity of the covering, which was now but little inflated, was collapsing already. It assumed an elongated shape, and the wind hollowed large cavities in the silken surface.

Kennedy could not help observing this.

"Is there a crack or a tear in the balloon?" he asked.

"No, but the gutta percha has evidently softened or melted in the heat, and the hydrogen is escaping through the silk."

"How can we prevent that?"

"It is impossible. Let us lighten her. That is the only help. So let us throw out everything we can spare."

"But what shall it be?" said the hunter, looking at the car, which was already quite bare.

"Well, let us get rid of the awning, for its weight is quite considerable."

Joe, who was interested in this order, climbed upon the circle which kept together the cordage of the network, and from that place easily managed to detach the heavy curtains of the awning and throw them overboard.

"There's something that will gladden the hearts of a whole tribe of blacks," said he; "there's enough to dress a thousand of them, for they're not very extravagant with cloth."

The balloon had risen a little, but it soon became evident that it was again approaching the ground.

"Let us alight," suggested Kennedy, "and see what can be done with the covering of the balloon."

"I tell you, again, Dick, that we have no means of repairing it."

"Then what shall we do?"

"We'll have to sacrifice everything not absolutely indispensable; I am anxious, at all hazards, to avoid a detention in these regions. The forests over the tops of which we are skimming are anything but safe."

"What! are there lions in them, or hyenas?" asked Joe, with an expression of sovereign contempt.

"Worse than that, my boy! There are men, and some of the most cruel, too, in all Africa."

"How is that known?"

"By the statements of travellers who have been here before us. Then the French settlers, who occupy the colony of Senegal, necessarily have relations with the surrounding tribes. Under the administration of Colonel Faidherbe, reconnaissances have been pushed far up into the country. Officers such as Messrs. Pascal, Vincent, and Lambert, have brought back precious documents from their expeditions. They have explored these countries formed by the elbow of the Senegal in places where war and pillage have left nothing but ruins."

"What, then, took place?"

"I will tell you. In 1854 a Marabout of the Senegalese Fouta, Al-Hadji by name, declaring himself to be inspired like Mohammed, stirred up all the tribes to war against the infidels—that is to say, against the Europeans. He carried destruction and desolation over the regions between the Senegal River and its tributary, the Fatémé. Three hordes of fanatics led on by him scoured the country, sparing neither a village nor a hut in their pillaging, massacring career. He advanced in person on the town of Ségo, which was a long time threatened. In 1857 he worked up farther to the northward, and invested the fortification of Medina, built by the French on the bank of the river. This stronghold was defended by Paul Holl, who, for several months, without provisions or ammunition, held out until Colonel Faidherbe came to his relief. Al-Hadji and his bands then repassed the Senegal, and reappeared in the Kaarta, continuing their rapine and murder.—Well, here below us is the very country in which he has found refuge with his hordes of banditti; and I assure you that it would not be a good thing to fall into his hands."

"We shall not," said Joe, "even if we have to throw overboard our clothes to save the *Victoria*."

"We are not far from the river," said the doctor, "but I foresee that our balloon will not be able to carry us beyond it."

"Let us reach its banks, at all events," said the Scot, "and that will be so much gained."

"That is what we are trying to do," rejoined Ferguson, "only that one thing makes me feel anxious."

"What is that?"

"We shall have mountains to pass, and that will be difficult to do, since I cannot augment the ascensional force of the balloon, even with the greatest possible heat that I can produce."

"Well, wait a bit," said Kennedy, "and we shall see!"

"The poor *Victoria!*" sighed Joe; "I had got fond of her as the sailor does of his ship, and I'll not give her up so easily. She may not be what she was at the start—granted; but we shouldn't say a word against her. She has done us good service, and it would break my heart to desert her."

"Be at your ease, Joe; if we leave her, it will be in spite of ourselves. She'll serve us until she's completely worn out, and I ask of her only twenty-four hours more!"

"Ah, she's getting used up! She grows thinner and thinner," said Joe, dolefully, while he eyed her. "Poor balloon!"

"Unless I am deceived," said Kennedy, "there on the horizon are the mountains of which you were speaking, doctor."

"Yes, there they are, indeed!" exclaimed the doctor, after having examined them through his spy-glass, "and they look very high. We shall have some trouble in crossing them."

"Can we not avoid them?"

"I am afraid not, Dick. See what an immense space they occupy—nearly one-half of the horizon!"

"They even seem to shut us in," added Joe. "They are gaining on both our right and our left."

"We must then pass over them."

These obstacles, which threatened such imminent peril, seemed to approach with extreme rapidity, or, to speak more accurately, the wind, which was very fresh, was hurrying the balloon towards the sharp peaks. So rise it must, or be dashed to pieces.

"Let us empty our tank of water," said the doctor, "and keep only enough for one day."

"There it goes," shouted Joe.

"Does the balloon rise at all?" asked Kennedy.

"A little—some fifty feet," replied the doctor, who kept his eyes fixed on the barometer. "But that is not enough."

In truth the lofty peaks were starting up so swiftly before the travellers that they seemed to be rushing down upon them. The balloon was far from rising above them. She lacked an elevation of more than five hundred feet more.

The stock of water for the cylinder was also thrown overboard and only a few pints were retained, but still all this was not enough.

"We must pass them though!" urged the doctor.

"Let us throw out the tanks—we have emptied them." said Kennedy.

"Over with them!"

"There they go!" panted Joe. "But it's hard to see ourselves dropping off this way by piecemeal."

"Now, for your part, Joe, make no attempt to sacrifice yourself as you did the other day! Whatever happens, swear to me that you will not leave us!"

"Have no fears, my master, we shall not be separated."

The *Victoria* had ascended some hundred and twenty feet, but the crest of the mountain still towered above it. It was an almost perpendicular ridge that ended in a regular wall rising abruptly in a straight line. It still rose more than two hundred feet over the aeronauts.

"In ten minutes," said the doctor to himself, "our car will be dashed against those rocks unless we succeed in passing them!"

"Well, doctor?" queried Joe.

"Keep nothing but our *pemmican,* and throw out all the heavy meat."

Thereupon the balloon was again lightened by some fifty pounds, and it rose very perceptibly, but that was of little consequence, unless it got above the line of the mountaintops. The situation was terrifying. The *Victoria* was rushing on with great rapidity. They could feel that she would be dashed to pieces—that the shock would be fearful.

The doctor glanced around him in the car. It was nearly empty.

"If needs be, Dick, hold yourself in readiness to throw over your fire-arms!"

"Sacrifice my fire-arms?" repeated the sportsman, with intense feeling.

"My friend, I ask it; it will be absolutely necessary!"

"Samuel! Doctor!"

"Your guns, and your stock of powder and ball might cost us our lives."

"We are close to it!" cried Joe.

Sixty feet! The mountain still overtopped the balloon by sixty feet.

Joe took the blankets and other coverings and tossed them out; then, without a word to Kennedy, he threw over several bags of bullets and lead.

The balloon went up still higher; it surmounted the dangerous ridge, and the rays of the sun shone upon its uppermost extremity; but the car was still below the level of certain broken masses of rock, against which it would inevitably be dashed.

"Kennedy! Kennedy! throw out your fire-arms, or we are lost!" shouted the doctor.

"Wait, sir; wait one moment!" they heard Joe exclaim, and, looking around, they saw Joe disappear over the edge of the balloon.

"Joe! Joe!" cried Kennedy.

"Wretched man!" was the doctor's agonised expression.

The flat top of the mountain may have had about twenty feet in breadth at this point, and, on the other side, the slope presented a less declivity. The car just touched the level of this plane, which happened to be quite even, and it glided over a soil composed of sharp pebbles that grated as it passed.

"We're over it! we're over it! we're clear!" cried out an exulting voice that made Ferguson's heart leap to his throat.

The daring fellow was there, grasping the lower rim of the car, and running afoot over the top of the mountain, thus lightening the balloon of his whole weight. He had to hold on with all his strength, too, for it was likely to escape his grasp at any moment.

When he had reached the opposite declivity, and the abyss was before him, Joe, by a vigourous effort, hoisted himself from the ground, and, clambering up by the cordage, rejoined his friends.

"That was all!" he coolly ejaculated.

"My brave Joe! my friend!" said the doctor, with deep emotion.

"Oh! what I did," laughed the other, "was not for you; it was to save Mr. Kennedy's rifle. I owed him that good turn for the affair with the Arab! I like to pay my debts, and now we are even," added he, handing to the sportsman his favourite weapon. "I'd feel very badly to see you deprived of it."

Kennedy heartily shook the brave fellow's hand, without being able to utter a word.

The *Victoria* had nothing to do now but to descend. That was easy enough, so that she was soon at a height of only two hundred feet from the ground, and was then in equilibrium. The surface seemed very much broken, as though by a convulsion of nature. It presented numerous inequalities, which would have been very difficult to avoid during the night with a balloon that could no longer be controlled. Evening was coming on rapidly, and, notwithstanding his repugnance, the doctor had to make up his mind to halt until morning.

"We'll now look for a favourable stopping-place," said he.

"Ah!" replied Kennedy, "you have made up your mind, then, at last?"

"Yes, I have for a long time been thinking over a plan which we'll try to put into execution; it is only six o'clock in the evening, and we shall have time enough. Throw out your anchors, Joe!"

Joe immediately obeyed, and the two anchors dangled below the balloon.

"I see large forests ahead of us," said the doctor; "we are going to sweep along their tops, and we shall grapple to some tree, for nothing would make me think of passing the night below, on the ground."

"But can we not descend?" asked Kennedy.

"To what purpose? I repeat that it would be dangerous for us to separate, and, besides, I claim your help for a difficult piece of work."

The *Victoria,* which was skimming along the tops of immense forests, soon came to a sharp halt. Her anchors had caught, and, the wind falling as dusk came on, she remained motionlessly suspended above a vast field of verdure, formed by the tops of a forest of sycamores.

Chapter XLII

A STRUGGLE OF GENEROSITY—THE LAST SACRIFICE—
THE DILATING APPARATUS—JOE'S ADROITNESS—MIDNIGHT—
THE DOCTOR'S WATCH—KENNEDY'S WATCH—THE LATTER
FALLS ASLEEP AT HIS POST—THE FIRE—THE HOWLINGS OF
THE NATIVES—OUT OF RANGE

DOCTOR FERGUSON'S FIRST CARE WAS TO TAKE HIS BEARINGS BY STELLAR OBSERVATION, and he discovered that he was scarcely twenty-five miles from Senegal.

"All that we can manage to do, my friends," said he, after having pointed his map, "is to cross the river; but, as there is neither bridge nor boat, we must, at all hazards, cross it with the balloon, and, in order to do that, we must still lighten up."

"But I don't exactly see how we can do that?" replied Kennedy, anxious about his firearms, "unless one of us makes up his mind to sacrifice himself for the rest—that is, to stay behind, and, in my turn, I claim that honour."

"You, indeed!" remonstrated Joe; "ain't I used to—"

"The question now is, not to throw ourselves out of the car, but simply to reach the coast of Africa on foot. I am a first-rate walker, a good sportsman, and—"

"I'll never consent to it!" insisted Joe.

"Your generous rivalry is useless, my brave friends," said Ferguson; "I trust that we shall not come to any such extremity: besides, if we did, instead of separating, we should keep together, so as to make our way across the country in company."

"That's the talk," said Joe; "a little tramp won't do us any harm."

"But before we try that," resumed the doctor, "we must employ a last means of lightening the balloon."

"What will that be? I should like to see it," said Kennedy, incredulously.

"We must get rid of the cylinder-chests, the spiral, and the Buntzen battery. Nine hundred pounds make a rather heavy load to carry through the air."

"But then, Samuel, how will you dilate your gas?"

"I shall not do so at all. We'll have to get along without it."

"But—"

"Listen, my friends: I have calculated very exactly the amount of ascensional force left to us, and it is sufficient to carry us every one with the few objects that remain. We shall make in all a weight of hardly five hundred pounds, including the two anchors which I desire to keep."

"Dear doctor, you know more about the matter than we do; you are the sole judge of the situation. Tell us what we ought to do, and we will do it."

"I am at your orders, master," added Joe.

"I repeat, my friends, that however serious the decision may appear, we must sacrifice our apparatus."

"Let it go, then!" said Kennedy, promptly.

"To work!" said Joe.

It was no easy job. The apparatus had to be taken down piece by piece. First, they took out the mixing reservoir, then the one belonging to the cylinder, and lastly the tank in which the decomposition of the water was effected. The united strength of all three travellers was required to detach these reservoirs from the bottom of the car in which they had been so firmly secured; but Kennedy was so strong, Joe so adroit, and the doctor so ingenious, that they finally succeeded. The different pieces were thrown out, one after the other, and they disappeared below, making huge gaps in the foliage of the sycamores.

"The black fellows will be mightily astonished," said Joe, "at finding things like those in the woods; they'll make idols of them!"

The next thing to be looked after was the displacement of the pipes that were fastened in the balloon and connected with the spiral. Joe succeeded in cutting the caoutchouc jointings above the car, but when he came to the pipes he found it more difficult to disengage them, because they were held by their upper extremity and fastened by wires to the very circlet of the valve.

Then it was that Joe showed wonderful adroitness. In his naked feet, so as not to scratch the covering, he succeeded by the aid of the network, and in spite of the oscillations of the balloon, in climbing to the upper extremity, and after a thousand difficulties, in holding on with one hand to that slippery surface, while he detached the outside screws that secured the pipes in their place. These were then easily taken out, and drawn away by the lower end, which was hermetically sealed by means of a strong ligature.

The *Victoria*, relieved of this considerable weight, rose upright in the air and tugged strongly at the anchor-rope.

About midnight this work ended without accident, but at the cost of most severe exertion, and the trio partook of a luncheon of *pemmican* and cold punch, as the doctor had no more fire to place at Joe's disposal.

Besides, the latter and Kennedy were dropping off their feet with fatigue.

"Lie down, my friends, and get some rest," said the doctor. "I'll take the first watch; at two o'clock I'll waken Kennedy; at four, Kennedy will waken Joe, and at six we'll start; and may Heaven have us in its keeping for this last day of the trip!"

Without waiting to be coaxed, the doctor's two companions stretched themselves at the bottom of the car and dropped into profound slumber on the instant.

The night was calm. A few clouds broke against the last quarter of the moon, whose uncertain rays scarcely pierced the darkness. Ferguson, resting his elbows on the rim of the car, gazed attentively around him. He watched with close attention the dark screen of foliage that spread beneath him, hiding the ground from his view. The least noise aroused his suspicions, and he questioned even the slightest rustling of the leaves.

He was in that mood which solitude makes more keenly felt, and during which vague terrors mount to the brain. At the close of such a journey, after having surmounted so many obstacles, and at the moment of touching the goal, one's fears are more vivid, one's emotions keener. The point of arrival seems to fly farther from our gaze.

Moreover, the present situation had nothing very consolatory about it. They were in the midst of a barbarous country, and dependent upon a vehicle that might fail them at any moment. The doctor no longer counted implicitly on his balloon; the time had gone by when he maneuvred it boldly because he felt sure of it.

Under the influence of these impressions, the doctor, from time to time, thought that he heard vague sounds in the vast forests around him; he even fancied that he saw a swift gleam of fire shining between the trees. He looked sharply and turned his night-glass towards the spot; but there was nothing to be seen, and the profoundest silence appeared to return.

He had, no doubt, been under the dominion of a mere hallucination. He continued to listen, but without hearing the slightest noise. When his watch had expired, he woke Kennedy, and, enjoining upon him to observe the extremest vigilance, took his place beside Joe, and fell sound asleep.

Kennedy, while still rubbing his eyes, which he could scarcely keep open, calmly lit his pipe. He then ensconced himself in a corner, and began to smoke vigourously by way of keeping awake.

The most absolute silence reigned around him; a light wind shook the tree-tops and gently rocked the car, inviting the hunter to taste the sleep that stole over him in spite of himself. He strove hard to resist it, and repeatedly opened his eyes to plunge into the outer darkness one of those looks that see nothing; but at last, yielding to fatigue, he sank back and slumbered.

How long he had been buried in this stupor he knew not, but he was suddenly aroused from it by a strange, unexpected crackling sound.

He rubbed his eyes and sprang to his feet. An intense glare half-blinded him and heated his cheek—the forest was in flames!

"Fire! fire!" he shouted, scarcely comprehending what had happened.

His two companions started up in alarm.

"What's the matter?" was the doctor's immediate exclamation.

"Fire!" said Joe. "But who could—"

At this moment loud yells were heard under the foliage, which was now illuminated as brightly as the day.

"Ah! the savages!" cried Joe again; "they have set fire to the forest so as to be the more certain of burning us up."

"The Talabas! Al-Hadji's marabouts, no doubt," said the doctor.

A circle of fire hemmed the *Victoria* in; the crackling of the dry wood mingled with the hissing and sputtering of the green branches; the clambering vines, the foliage, all the living part of this vegetation, writhed in the destructive element. The eye took in nothing but one vast ocean of flame; the large trees stood forth in black relief in this huge furnace, their branches covered with glowing coals, while the whole blazing mass, the entire conflagration, was reflected on the clouds, and the travellers could fancy themselves enveloped in a hollow globe of fire.

"Let us escape to the ground!" shouted Kennedy, "it is our only chance of safety!"

But Ferguson checked him with a firm grasp, and, dashing at the anchor-rope, severed it with one well-directed blow of his hatchet. Meanwhile, the flames, leaping up at the balloon, already quivered on its illuminated sides; but the *Victoria*, released from her fastenings, spun upward a thousand feet into the air.

Frightful yells resounded through the forest, along with the report of fire-arms, while the balloon, caught in a current of air that rose with the dawn of day, was borne to the westward.

It was now four o'clock in the morning.

Chapter XLIII

THE TALABAS—THE PURSUIT—A DEVASTATED COUNTRY—
THE WIND BEGINS TO FALL—THE VICTORIA SINKS—
THE LAST OF THE PROVISIONS—THE LEAPS OF THE BALLOON—
A DEFENCE WITH FIRE-ARMS—THE WIND FRESHENS—
THE SENEGAL RIVER—THE CATARACTS OF GOUINA—
THE HOT AIR—THE PASSAGE OF THE RIVER

HAD WE NOT TAKEN THE PRECAUTION TO LIGHTEN THE BALLOON YESTERDAY EVENING, we should have been lost beyond redemption," said the doctor, after a long silence.

"See what's gained by doing things at the right time!" replied Joe. "One gets out of scrapes then, and nothing is more natural."

"We are not out of danger yet," said the doctor.

"What do you still apprehend?" queried Kennedy. "The balloon can't descend without your permission, and even were it to do so—"

"Were it to do so, Dick? Look!"

They had just passed the borders of the forest, and the three friends could see some thirty mounted men clad in broad pantaloons and the floating bournouse. They were armed, some with lances, and others with long muskets, and they were following, on their quick, fiery little steeds, the direction of the balloon, which was moving at only moderate speed.

When they caught sight of the aeronauts, they uttered savage cries, and brandished their weapons. Anger and menace could be read upon their swarthy faces, made more ferocious by thin but bristling beards. Meanwhile they galloped along without difficulty over the low levels and gentle declivities that lead down to the Senegal.

"It is, indeed, they!" said the doctor; "the cruel Talabas! the ferocious marabouts of Al-Hadji! I would rather find myself in the middle of the forest encircled by wild beasts than fall into the hands of these banditti."

"They haven't a very obliging look!" assented Kennedy; "and they are rough, stalwart fellows."

"Happily those brutes can't fly," remarked Joe; "and that's something."

"See," said Ferguson, "those villages in ruins, those huts burned down—that is their work! Where vast stretches of cultivated land were once seen, they have brought barrenness and devastation."

"At all events, however," interposed Kennedy, "they can't overtake us; and, if we succeed in putting the river between us and them, we are safe."

"Perfectly, Dick," replied Ferguson; "but we must not fall to the ground!" and, as he said this, he glanced at the barometer.

"In any case, Joe," added Kennedy, "it would do us no harm to look to our fire-arms."

"No harm in the world, Mr. Dick! We are lucky that we didn't scatter them along the road."

"My rifle!" said the sportsman. "I hope that I shall never be separated from it!"

And so saying, Kennedy loaded the pet piece with the greatest care, for he had plenty of powder and ball remaining.

"At what height are we?" he asked the doctor.

"About seven hundred and fifty feet; but we no longer have the power of seeking favourable currents, either going up or coming down. We are at the mercy of the balloon!"

"That is vexatious!" rejoined Kennedy. "The wind is poor; but if we had come across a hurricane like some of those we met before, these vile brigands would have been out of sight long ago."

"The rascals follow us at their leisure," said Joe. "They're only at a short gallop. Quite a nice little ride!"

"If we were within range," sighed the sportsman, "I should amuse myself with dismounting a few of them."

"Exactly," said the doctor; "but then they would have you within range also, and our balloon would offer only too plain a target to the bullets from their long guns; and, if they were to make a hole in it, I leave you to judge what our situation would be!"

The pursuit of the Talabas continued all morning; and by eleven o'clock the aeronauts had made scarcely fifteen miles to the westward.

The doctor was anxiously watching for the least cloud on the horizon. He feared, above all things, a change in the atmosphere. Should he be thrown back towards the Niger, what would become of him? Besides, he remarked that the balloon tended to fall considerably. Since the start, he had already lost more than three hundred feet, and the Senegal must be about a dozen miles distant. At his present rate of speed, he could count upon travelling only three hours longer.

At this moment his attention was attracted by fresh cries. The Talabas appeared to be much excited, and were spurring their horses.

The doctor consulted his barometer, and at once discovered the cause of these symptoms.

"Are we descending?" asked Kennedy.

"Yes!" replied the doctor.

"The mischief!" thought Joe

In the lapse of fifteen minutes the *Victoria* was only one hundred and fifty feet above the ground; but the wind was much stronger than before.

The Talabas checked their horses, and soon a volley of musketry pealed out on the air.

"Too far, you fools!" bawled Joe. "I think it would be well to keep those scamps at a distance."

And, as he spoke, he aimed at one of the horsemen who was farthest to the front, and fired. The Talaba fell headlong, and, his companions halting for a moment, the balloon gained upon them.

"They are prudent!" said Kennedy.

"Because they think that they are certain to take us," replied the doctor; "and, they will succeed if we descend much farther. We must, absolutely, get higher into the air."

"What can we throw out?" asked Joe.

"All that remains of our stock of *pemmican*; that will be thirty pounds less weight to carry."

"Out it goes, sir!" said Joe, obeying orders.

The car, which was now almost touching the ground, rose again, amid the cries of the Talabas; but, half-an-hour later, the balloon was again falling rapidly, because the gas was escaping through the pores of the covering.

Ere long the car was once more grazing the soil, and Al-Hadji's black riders rushed towards it; but, as frequently happens in like cases, the balloon had scarcely touched the surface ere it rebounded, and only came down again a mile away.

"So we shall not escape!" said Kennedy, between his teeth.

"Throw out our reserved store of brandy, Joe," cried the doctor; "our instruments, and everything that has any weight, even to our last anchor, because go they must!"

Joe flung out the barometers and thermometers, but all that amounted to little; and the balloon, which had risen for an instant, fell again towards the ground.

The Talabas flew towards it, and at length were not more than two hundred paces away.

"Throw out the two fowling-pieces!" shouted Ferguson.

"Not without discharging them, at least," responded the sportsman; and four shots in quick succession struck the thick of the advancing group of horsemen. Four Talabas fell, amid the frantic howls and imprecations of their comrades.

The *Victoria* ascended once more, and made some enormous leaps, like a huge gum-elastic ball, bounding and rebounding through the air. A strange sight it was to see these unfortunate men endeavouring to escape by those huge aerial strides, and seeming, like the giant Antæus, to receive fresh strength every time they touched the earth. But this situation had to terminate. It was now nearly noon; the *Victoria* was getting empty and exhausted, and assuming a more and more elongated form every instant. Its outer covering was becoming flaccid, and floated loosely in the air, and the folds of the silk rustled and grated on each other.

"Heaven abandons us!" said Kennedy; "we have to fall!"

Joe made no answer. He kept looking intently at his master.

"No!" said the latter; "we have more than one hundred and fifty pounds yet to throw out."

"What can it be, then?" said Kennedy, thinking that the doctor must be going mad.

"The car!" was his reply; "we can cling to the network. There we can hang on in the meshes until we reach the river. Quick! quick!"

And these daring men did not hesitate a moment to avail themselves of this last desperate means of escape. They clutched the network, as the doctor directed, and Joe, holding on by one hand, with the other cut the cords that suspended the car; and the latter dropped to the ground just as the balloon was sinking for the last time.

"Hurrah! hurrah!" shouted the brave fellow exultingly, as the *Victoria*, once more relieved, shot up again to a height of three hundred feet.

The Talabas spurred their horses, which now came tearing on at a furious gallop; but the balloon, falling in with a much more favourable wind, shot ahead of them, and was rapidly carried towards a hill that stretched across the horizon to the westward. This was a circumstance favourable to the aeronauts, because they could rise over the hill, while Al-Hadji's horde had to diverge to the northward in order to pass this obstacle.

The three friends still clung to the network. They had been able to fasten it under their feet, where it had formed a sort of swinging pocket.

Suddenly, after they had crossed the hill, the doctor exclaimed: "The river! the river! the Senegal, my friends!"

And about two miles ahead of them, there was indeed the river rolling along its broad mass of water, while the farther bank, which was low and fertile, offered a sure refuge, and a place favourable for a descent.

"Another quarter of an hour," said Ferguson, "and we are saved!"

But it was not to happen thus; the empty balloon descended slowly upon a tract almost entirely bare of vegetation. It was made up of long slopes and stony plains, a few bushes and some coarse grass, scorched by the sun.

The *Victoria* touched the ground several times, and rose again, but her rebound was diminishing in height and length. At the last one, it caught by the upper part of the network in the lofty branches of a baobab, the only tree that stood there, solitary and alone, in the midst of the waste.

"It's all over," said Kennedy.

"And at a hundred paces only from the river!" groaned Joe.

The three hapless aeronauts descended to the ground, and the doctor drew his companions towards the Senegal.

At this point the river sent forth a prolonged roaring; and when Ferguson reached its bank, he recognised the falls of Gouina. But not a boat, not a living creature was to be seen. With a breadth of two thousand feet, the Senegal precipitates itself for a height of one hundred and fifty, with a thundering reverberation. It ran, where they saw it, from east to west, and the line of rocks that barred its course extended from north to south. In the midst of the falls, rocks of strange forms started up like huge ante-diluvian animals, petrified there amid the waters.

The impossibility of crossing this gulf was self-evident, and Kennedy could not restrain a gesture of despair.

But Dr. Ferguson, with an energetic accent of undaunted daring, exclaimed—

"All is not over!"

"I knew it," said Joe, with that confidence in his master which nothing could ever shake.

The sight of the dried-up grass had inspired the doctor with a bold idea. It was the last chance of escape. He led his friends quickly back to where they had left the covering of the balloon.

"We have at least an hour's start of those banditti," said he; "let us lose no time, my friends; gather a quantity of this dried grass; I want a hundred pounds of it, at least."

"For what purpose?" asked Kennedy, surprised.

"I have no more gas; well, I'll cross the river with hot air!"

"Ah, doctor," exclaimed Kennedy, "you are, indeed, a great man!"

Joe and Kennedy at once went to work, and soon had an immense pile of dried grass heaped up near the baobab.

In the meantime, the doctor had enlarged the orifice of the balloon by cutting it open at the lower end. He then was very careful to expel the last remnant of hydrogen through the valve, after which he heaped up a quantity of grass under the balloon, and set fire to it.

It takes but a little while to inflate a balloon with hot air. A heat of one hundred and eighty degrees is sufficient to diminish the weight of the air it contains to the extent of one-half, by rarefying it. Thus, the *Victoria* quickly began to assume a more rounded form. There was no lack of grass; the fire was kept in full blast by the doctor's assiduous efforts, and the balloon grew fuller every instant.

It was then a quarter to four o'clock.

At this moment the band of Talabas reappeared about two miles to the northward, and the three friends could hear their cries, and the clatter of their horses galloping at full speed.

"In twenty minutes they will be here!" said Kennedy.

"More grass! more grass, Joe! In ten minutes we shall have her full of hot air."

"Here it is, doctor!"

The *Victoria* was now two-thirds inflated.

"Come, my friends, let us take hold of the network, as we did before."

"All right!" they answered together.

In about ten minutes a few jerking motions by the balloon indicated that it was disposed to start again. The Talabas were approaching. They were hardly five hundred paces away.

"Hold on fast!" cried Ferguson.

"Have no fear, master—have no fear!"

And the doctor, with his foot pushed another heap of grass upon the fire.

With this the balloon, now completely inflated by the increased temperature, moved away, sweeping the branches of the baobab in her flight.

"We're off!" shouted Joe.

A volley of musketry responded to his exclamation. A bullet even ploughed his shoulder; but Kennedy, leaning over, and discharging his rifle with one hand, brought another of the enemy to the ground.

Cries of fury exceeding all description hailed the departure of the balloon, which had at once ascended nearly eight hundred feet. A swift current caught and swept it along with the most alarming oscillations, while the intrepid doctor and his friends saw the gulf of the cataracts yawning below them.

Ten minutes later, and without having exchanged a word, they descended gradually towards the other bank of the river.

There, astonished, speechless, terrified, stood a group of men clad in the French uniform. Judge of their amazement when they saw the balloon rise from the right bank of the river. They had well-nigh taken it for some celestial phenomenon, but their officers, a lieutenant of marines and a naval ensign, having seen mention made of Dr. Ferguson's daring expedition, in the European papers, quickly explained the real state of the case.

The balloon, losing its inflation little by little, settled with the daring travellers still clinging to its network; but it was doubtful whether it would reach the land. At once some of the brave Frenchmen rushed into the water and caught the three aeronauts in their arms just as the *Victoria* fell at the distance of a few fathoms from the left bank of the Senegal.

"Dr. Ferguson!" exclaimed the lieutenant.

"The same, sir," replied the doctor, quietly, "and his two friends."

The Frenchmen escorted our travellers from the river, while the balloon, half-empty, and borne away by a swift current, sped on, to plunge, like a huge bubble, headlong with the waters of the Senegal, into the cataracts of Gouina.

"The poor *Victoria!*" was Joe's farewell remark.

The doctor could not restrain a tear, and extending his hands his two friends wrung them silently with that deep emotion which requires no spoken words.

Chapter XLIV

CONCLUSION—THE CERTIFICATE—THE FRENCH SETTLEMENTS—
THE POST OF MEDINA—THE BASILIC—SAINT LOUIS—THE
ENGLISH FRIGATE—THE RETURN TO LONDON

THE EXPEDITION UPON THE BANK OF THE RIVER HAD BEEN SENT BY THE GOVERNOR OF Senegal. It consisted of two officers, Messrs. Dufraisse, lieutenant of marines, and Rodamel, naval ensign, and with these were a sergeant and seven soldiers. For two days they had been engaged in reconnoitring the most favourable situation for a post at Gouina, when they became witnesses of Dr. Ferguson's arrival.

The warm greetings and felicitations of which our travellers were the recipients may be imagined. The Frenchmen, and they alone, having had ocular proof of the accomplishment of the daring project, naturally became Dr. Ferguson's witnesses. Hence the doctor at once asked them to give their official testimony of his arrival at the cataracts of Gouina.

"You would have no objection to signing a certificate of the fact, would you?" he enquired of Lieutenant Dufraisse.

"At your orders!" the latter instantly replied.

The Englishmen were escorted to a provisional post established on the bank of the river, where they found the most assiduous attention, and everything to supply their wants. And there the following certificate was drawn up in the terms in which it appears to-day, in the archives of the Royal Geographical Society of London:

We, the undersigned, do hereby declare that, on the day herein mentioned, we witnessed the arrival of Dr. Ferguson and his two companions, Richard Kennedy and Joseph Wilson, clinging to the cordage and network of a balloon, and that the said balloon fell at a distance of a few paces from us into the river, and being swept away by the current was lost in the cataracts of Gouina. In testimony whereof, we have hereunto set our hands and seals beside those of the persons hereinabove named, for the information of all whom it may concern.

Done at the Cataracts of Gouina, on the 24th of May, 1862.

(Signed),   SAMUEL FERGUSON,
              RICHARD KENNEDY,
              JOSEPH WILSON,
              DUFRAISSE, *Lieutenant of Marines,*
              RODAMEL, *Naval Ensign,*
              DUFAYS, *Sergeant,*
              FLIPPEAU, MAYOR, ⎫
              PELISSIER, LOROIS, ⎬ *Privates.*
              RASCAGNET, GUIL- ⎭
              LON, LEBEL

Here ended the astonishing journey of Dr. Ferguson and his brave companions, as vouched for by undeniable testimony; and they found themselves among friends in the midst of most hospitable tribes, whose relations with the French settlements are frequent and amicable.

They had arrived at Senegal on Saturday, the 24th of May, and on the 27th of the same month they reached the post of Medina, situated a little farther to the north, but on the river.

There the French officers received them with open arms, and lavished upon them all the resources of their hospitality. Thus aided, the doctor and his friends were enabled to embark almost immediately on the small steamer called the *Basilic*, which ran down to the mouth of the river.

Two weeks later, on the 10th of June, they arrived at Saint Louis, where the governor gave them a magnificent reception, and they recovered completely from their excitement and fatigue.

Besides, Joe said to everyone who chose to listen:

"That was a stupid trip of ours, after all, and I wouldn't advise anybody who is greedy for excitement to undertake it. It gets very tiresome at the last, and if it hadn't been for the adventures on Lake Tchad and at the Senegal River, I do believe that we'd have died of yawning."

An English frigate was just about to sail, and the three travellers procured passage on board of her. On the 25th of June they arrived at Portsmouth, and on the next day at London.

We will not describe the reception they got from the Royal Geographical Society, nor the intense curiosity and consideration of which they became the objects. Kennedy set off, at once, for Edinburgh, with his famous rifle, for he was in haste to relieve the anxiety of his faithful old housekeeper.

The doctor and his devoted Joe remained the same men that we have known them, excepting that one change took place at their own suggestion.

They ceased to be master and servant, in order to become bosom friends.

The journals of all Europe were untiring in their praises of the bold explorers, and the *Daily Telegraph* struck off an edition of three hundred and seventy-seven thousand copies on the day when it published a sketch of the trip.

Doctor Ferguson, at a public meeting of the Royal Geographical Society, gave a recital of his journey through the air, and obtained for himself and his companions the golden medal set apart to reward the most remarkable exploring expedition of the year 1862.

The first result of Dr. Ferguson's expedition was to establish, in the most precise manner, the facts and geographical surveys reported by Messrs. Barth, Burton, Speke, and others. Thanks to the still more recent expeditions of Messrs. Speke and Grant, De Heuglin and Munzinger, who have been ascending to the sources of the Nile, and penetrating to the centre of Africa, we shall be enabled ere long to verify, in turn, the discoveries of Dr. Ferguson in that vast region comprised between the fourteenth and thirty-third degrees of east longitude.

A JOURNEY TO THE CENTER
OF THE EARTH

CONTENTS

CHAPTER

I	The Professor and His Family	185
II	A Mystery to Be Solved at any Price	187
III	The Runic Writing Exercises the Professor	190
IV	The Enemy to be Starved into Submission	194
V	Famine, Then Victory, Followed by Dismay	196
VI	Exciting Discussions about an Unparalleled Enterprise	200
VII	A Woman's Courage	204
VIII	Serious Preparations for Vertical Descent	208
IX	Iceland! But What Next?	212
X	Interesting Conversations with Icelandic Savants	215
XI	A Guide Found to the Center of the Earth	219
XII	A Barren Land	222
XIII	Hospitality under the Arctic Circle	225
XIV	But Arctics Can Be Inhospitable, Too	228
XV	Snæfell at Last	232
XVI	Boldly Down the Crater	235
XVII	Vertical Descent	238
XVIII	The Wonders of Terrestrial Depths	241
XIX	Geological Studies *in Situ*	244
XX	The First Signs of Distress	247
XXI	Compassion Fuses the Professor's Heart	249
XXII	Total Failure of Water	252
XXIII	Water Discovered	254
XXIV	Well Said, Old Mole! Canst Thou Work i' the Ground so Fast?	257
XXV	*De Profundis*	259
XXVI	The Worst Peril of All	262
XXVII	Lost in the Bowels of the Earth	263
XXVIII	The Rescue in the Whispering Gallery	265
XXIX	Thalatta! Thalatta!	269
XXX	A New *Mare Internum*	271
XXXI	Preparations for a Voyage of Discovery	275

XXXII	Wonders of the Deep	278
XXXIII	A Battle of Monsters	281
XXXIV	The Great Geyser	285
XXXV	An Electric Storm	288
XXXVI	Calm Philosophic Discussions	291
XXXVII	The Liedenbrock Museum of Geology	295
XXXVIII	The Professor in His Chair Again	297
XXXIX	Forest Scenery Illuminated by Electricity	301
XL	Preparations for Blasting a Passage to the Center of the Earth	304
XLI	The Great Explosion and the Rush Down Below	307
XLII	Headlong Speed Upward Through the Horrors of Darkness	310
XLIII	Shot Out of a Volcano at Last!	313
XLIV	Sunny Lands in the Blue Mediterranean	317
XLV	All's Well That Ends Well	320

Chapter I

The Professor and his Family

O N THE 24TH OF MAY, 1863, MY UNCLE, PROFESSOR LIEDENBROCK, RUSHED INTO HIS little house, No. 19 Königstrasse, one of the oldest streets in the oldest portion of the city of Hamburg.

Martha must have concluded that she was very much behindhand, for the dinner had only just been put into the oven.

"Well, now," said I to myself, "if that most impatient of men is hungry, what a disturbance he will make!"

"M. Liedenbrock so soon!" cried poor Martha in great alarm, half opening the dining-room door.

"Yes, Martha; but very likely the dinner is not half cooked, for it is not two yet. Saint Michael's clock has only just struck half-past one."

"Then why has the master come home so soon?"

"Perhaps he will tell us that himself."

"Here he is, Monsieur Axel; I will run and hide myself while you argue with him."

And Martha retreated in safety into her own dominions.

I was left alone. But how was it possible for a man of my undecided turn of mind to argue successfully with so irascible a person as the Professor? With this persuasion I was hurrying away to my own little retreat upstairs, when the street door creaked upon its hinges; heavy feet made the whole flight of stairs to shake; and the master of the house, passing rapidly through the dining-room, threw himself in haste into his own sanctum.

But on his rapid way he had found time to fling his hazel stick into a corner, his rough broadbrim upon the table, and these few emphatic words at his nephew:

"Axel, follow me!"

I had scarcely had time to move when the Professor was again shouting after me:

"What! not come yet?"

And I rushed into my redoubtable master's study.

Otto Liedenbrock had no mischief in him, I willingly allow that; but unless he very considerably changes as he grows older, at the end he will be a most original character.

He was professor at the Johannæum, and was delivering a series of lectures on mineralogy, in the course of every one of which he broke into a passion once or twice at least. Not at all that he was overanxious about the improvement of his class, or about the degree of attention with which they listened to him, or the success which might eventually crown his labours. Such little matters of detail never troubled him much. His teaching was as the German philosophy calls it, "subjective"; it was to benefit himself, not others. He was a learned egotist. He was a well of science, and the pulleys worked uneasily when you wanted to draw anything out of it. In a word, he was a learned miser.

Germany has not a few professors of this sort.

To his misfortune, my uncle was not gifted with a sufficiently rapid utterance; not, to be sure, when he was talking at home, but certainly in his public delivery; this is a want much to be deplored in a speaker. The fact is, that during the course of his lectures at the Johannæum, the Professor often came to a complete standstill; he fought with wilful words that refused to pass his struggling lips, such words as resist and distend the cheeks, and at last break out into the unasked-for shape of a round and most unscientific oath: then his fury would gradually abate.

Now in mineralogy there are many half-Greek and half-Latin terms, very hard to articulate, and which would be most trying to a poet's measures. I don't wish to say a word against so respectable a science, far be that from me. True, in the august presence of rhombohedral crystals, retinasphaltic resins, gehlenites, Fassaites, molybdenites, tungstates of manganese, and titanite of zirconium, why, the most facile of tongues may make a slip now and then.

It therefore happened that this venial fault of my uncle's came to be pretty well understood in time, and an unfair advantage was taken of it; the students laid wait for him in dangerous places, and when he began to stumble, loud was the laughter, which is not in good taste, not even in Germans. And if there was always a full audience to honour the Liedenbrock courses, I should be sorry to conjecture how many came to make merry at my uncle's expense.

Nevertheless my good uncle was a man of deep learning—a fact I am most anxious to assert and reassert. Sometimes he might irretrievably injure a specimen by his too great ardour in handling it; but still he united the genius of a true geologist with the keen eye of the mineralogist. Armed with his hammer, his steel pointer, his magnetic needles, his blow-pipe, and his bottle of nitric acid, he was a powerful man of science. He would refer any mineral to its proper place among the six hundred* elementary substances now enumerated, by its fracture, its appearance, its hardness, its fusibility, its sonorousness, its smell, and its taste.

The name of Liedenbrock was honourably mentioned in colleges and learned societies. Humphry Davy,† Humboldt, Captain Sir John Franklin, General Sabine, never failed to call upon him on their way through Hamburg. Becquerel, Ebelman, Brewster, Dumas, Milne-Edwards, Saint-Claire-Deville frequently consulted him upon the most difficult problems in chemistry, a science which was indebted to him for considerable discoveries, for in 1853 there had appeared at Leipzig an imposing folio by Otto Liedenbrock, entitled, *A Treatise upon Transcendental Chemistry,* with plates; a work, however, which failed to cover its expenses.

To all these titles to honour let me add that my uncle was the curator of the museum of mineralogy formed by M. Struve, the Russian ambassador; a most valuable collection, the fame of which is European.

Such was the gentleman who addressed me in that impetuous manner. Fancy a tall, spare man, of an iron constitution, and with a fair complexion which took off a good ten years from the fifty he must own to. His restless eyes were in incessant motion behind his full-sized spectacles. His long, thin nose was like a knife blade. Boys have been heard to remark that that organ was magnetised and attracted iron filings. But this was merely a

---

*Sixty-three. (Tr.)

†As Sir Humphry Davy died in 1829, the translator must be pardoned for pointing out here an anachronism, unless we are to assume that the learned Professor's celebrity dawned in his earliest years. (Tr.)

mischievous report; it had no attraction except for snuff, which it seemed to draw to itself in great quantities.

When I have added, to complete my portrait, that my uncle walked by mathematical strides of a yard and a half, and that in walking he kept his fists firmly closed, a sure sign of an irritable temperament, I think I shall have said enough to disenchant anyone who should by mistake have coveted much of his company.

He lived in his own little house in Königstrasse, a structure half brick and half wood, with a gable cut into steps; it looked upon one of those winding canals which intersect each other in the middle of the ancient quarter of Hamburg, and which the great fire of 1842 had fortunately spared.

It is true that the old house stood slightly off the perpendicular, and bulged out a little towards the street; its roof sloped a little to one side, like the cap over the left ear of a Tugendbund student; its lines wanted accuracy; but after all, it stood firm, thanks to an old elm which buttressed it in front, and which often in spring sent its young sprays through the window panes.

My uncle was tolerably well off for a German professor. The house was his own, and everything in it. The living contents were his god-daughter Gräuben, a young Virlandaise of seventeen, Martha, and myself. As his nephew and an orphan, I became his laboratory assistant.

I freely confess that I was exceedingly fond of geology and all its kindred sciences; the blood of a mineralogist was in my veins, and in the midst of my specimens I was always happy.

In a word, a man might live happily enough in the little old house in the Königstrasse, in spite of the restless impatience of its master, for although he was a little too excitable—he was very fond of me. But the man had no notion how to wait; nature herself was too slow for him. In April, after he had planted in the terra-cotta pots outside his window seedling plants of mignonette and convolvulus, he would go every evening and give them a little pull by their leaves to make them grow faster. In dealing with such a strange individual there was nothing for it but prompt obedience. I therefore rushed after him.

Chapter II

A Mystery to Be Solved at Any Price

That study of his was a museum, and nothing else. Specimens of everything known in mineralogy lay there in their places in perfect order, and correctly named, divided into inflammable, metallic, and lithoid minerals.

How well I knew all these bits of science! Many a time, instead of enjoying the company of lads of my own age, I had preferred dusting these graphites, anthracites, coals, lignites, and peats! And there were bitumens, resins, organic salts, to be protected from the least grain of dust; and metals, from iron to gold; metals whose current value altogether disappeared in the presence of the republican equality of scientific specimens; and stones too, enough to rebuild entirely the house in Königstrasse, even with a handsome additional room, which would have suited me admirably.

But on entering this study now I thought of none of all these wonders; my uncle alone filled my thoughts. He had thrown himself into a velvet easy-chair, and was grasping between his hands a book over which he bent, pondering with intense admiration.

"Here's a remarkable book! What a wonderful book!" he was exclaiming.

These ejaculations brought to my mind the fact that my uncle was liable to occasional fits of bibliomania; but no old book had any value in his eyes unless it had the virtue of being nowhere else to be found, or, at any rate, of being illegible.

"Well, now; don't you see it yet? Why I have got a priceless treasure, that I found his morning, in rummaging in old Hevelius's shop, the Jew."

"Magnificent!" I replied, with a good imitation of enthusiasm.

What was the good of all this fuss about an old quarto, bound in rough calf, a yellow, faded volume, with a ragged seal depending from it?

But for all that there was no lull yet in the admiring exclamations of the Professor.

"See," he went on, both asking the questions and supplying the answers. "Isn't it a beauty? Yes; splendid! Did you ever see such a binding? Doesn't the book open easily? Yes; it stops open anywhere. But does it shut equally well? Yes; for the binding and the leaves are flush, all in a straight line, and no gaps or openings anywhere. And look at its back, after seven hundred years. Why, Bozerian, Closs, or Purgold might have been proud of such a binding!"

While rapidly making these comments my uncle kept opening and shutting the old tome. I really could do no less than ask a question about its contents, although I did not feel the slightest interest.

"And what is the title of this marvellous work?" I asked with an affected eagerness which he must have been very blind not to see through.

"This work," replied my uncle, firing up with renewed enthusiasm, "this work is the Heims Kringla of Snorre Turlleson, the most famous Icelandic author of the twelfth century! It is the chronicle of the Norwegian princes who ruled in Iceland."

"Indeed"; I cried, keeping up wonderfully, "of course it is a German translation?"

"What!" sharply replied the Professor, "a translation! What should I do with a translation? This is the Icelandic original, in the magnificent idiomatic vernacular, which is both rich and simple, and admits of an infinite variety of grammatical combinations and verbal modifications."

"Like German," I happily ventured.

"Yes," replied my uncle, shrugging his shoulders; "but, in addition to all this, the Icelandic has three numbers like the Greek, and irregular declensions of nouns proper like the Latin."

"Ah!" said I, a little moved out of my indifference; "and is the type good?"

"Type! What do you mean by talking of type, wretched Axel? Type! Do you take it for a printed book, you ignorant fool? It is a manuscript, a Runic manuscript."

"Runic?"

"Yes. Do you want me to explain what that is?"

"Of course not," I replied in the tone of an injured man. But my uncle persevered, and told me, against my will, of many things I cared nothing about.

"Runic characters were in use in Iceland in former ages. They were invented, it is said, by Odin himself. Look there, and wonder, impious young man, and admire these letters, the invention of the Scandinavian god!"

Well, well! not knowing what to say, I was going to prostrate myself before this wonderful book, a way of answering equally pleasing to gods and kings, and which has the advantage of never giving them any embarrassment, when a little incident happened to divert conversation into another channel.

This was the appearance of a dirty slip of parchment, which slipped out of the volume and fell upon the floor.

My uncle pounced upon this shred with incredible avidity. An old document, enclosed an immemorial time within the folds of this old book, had for him an immeasurable value.

"What's this?" he cried.

And he laid out upon the table a piece of parchment, five inches by three, and along which were traced certain mysterious characters.

Here is the exact facsimile. I think it important to let these strange signs be publicly known, for they were the means of drawing on Professor Liedenbrock and his nephew to undertake the most wonderful expedition of the nineteenth century.

The Professor mused a few moments over this series of characters; then raising his spectacles he pronounced:

"These are Runic letters; they are exactly like those of the manuscript of Snorre Turlleson. But, what on earth is their meaning?"

Runic letters appearing to my mind to be an invention of the learned to mystify this poor world, I was not sorry to see my uncle suffering the pangs of mystification. At least, so it seemed to me, judging from his fingers, which were beginning to work with terrible energy.

"It is certainly old Icelandic," he muttered between his teeth.

And Professor Liedenbrock must have known, for he was acknowledged to be quite a polyglot. Not that he could speak fluently in the two thousand languages and twelve thousand dialects which are spoken on the earth, but he knew at least his share of them.

So he was going, in the presence of this difficulty, to give way to all the impetuosity of his character, and I was preparing for a violent outbreak, when two o'clock struck by the little timepiece over the fireplace.

At that moment our good housekeeper Martha opened the study door, saying:

"Dinner is ready!"

I am afraid he sent that soup to where it would boil away to nothing, and Martha took to her heels for safety. I followed her, and hardly knowing how I got there I found myself seated in my usual place.

I waited a few minutes. No Professor came. Never within my remembrance had he missed the important ceremonial of dinner. And yet what a good dinner it was! There was parsley soup, an omelette of ham garnished with spiced sorrel, a fillet of veal with *compôte* of prunes; for dessert, crystallised fruit; the whole washed down with sweet Moselle.

All this my uncle was going to sacrifice to a bit of old parchment. As an affectionate and attentive nephew I considered it my duty to eat for him as well as for myself, which I did conscientiously.

"I have never known such a thing," said Martha. "M. Liedenbrock is not at table!"

"Who could have believed it?" I said, with my mouth full.

"Something serious is going to happen," said the old servant, shaking her head.

My opinion was, that nothing more serious would happen than an awful scene when my uncle should have discovered that his dinner was devoured. I had come to the last of the fruit when a very loud voice tore me away from the pleasures of my dessert. With one spring I bounded out of the dining-room into the study.

Chapter III

THE RUNIC WRITING EXERCISES THE PROFESSOR

UNDOUBTEDLY IT IS RUNIC," SAID THE PROFESSOR, BENDING HIS BROWS; "BUT THERE IS a secret in it, and I mean to discover the key."

A violent gesture finished the sentence.

"Sit there," he added, holding out his fist towards the table. "Sit there, and write."

I was seated in a trice.

"Now I will dictate to you every letter of our alphabet which corresponds with each of these Icelandic characters. We will see what that will give us. But, by St. Michael, if you should dare to deceive me—"

The dictation commenced. I did my best. Every letter was given me one after the other, with the following remarkable result:

m̅.rnlls	esrevel	seecIde
sgtssmf	vnteief	niedrke
kt,samn	atrateS	saodrrn
emtnaeI	nvaect	rrilSa
Atsaar	.nvcrc	ieaabs
ccdrmi	eevtVl	frAntv
dt,iac	oseibo	KediiI

When this work was ended my uncle tore the paper from me and examined it attentively for a long time.

"What does it all mean?" he kept repeating mechanically.

Upon my honour I could not have enlightened him. Besides he did not ask me, and he went on talking to himself.

"This is what is called a cryptogram, or cipher," he said, "in which letters are purposely thrown in confusion, which if properly arranged would reveal their sense. Only think that under this jargon there may lie concealed the clue to some great discovery!"

As for me, I was of opinion that there was nothing at all in it; though, of course, I took care not to say so.

Then the Professor took the book and the parchment, and diligently compared them together.

"These two writings are not by the same hand," he said; "the cipher is of later date than the book, an undoubted proof of which I see in a moment. The first letter is a double m, a letter which is not to be found in Turlleson's book, and which was only added to the alphabet in the fourteenth century. Therefore there are two hundred years between the manuscript and the document."

I admitted that this was a strictly logical conclusion.

"I am therefore led to imagine," continued my uncle, "that some possessor of this book wrote these mysterious letters. But who was that possessor? Is his name nowhere to be found in the manuscript?"

My uncle raised his spectacles, took up a strong lens, and carefully examined the blank pages of the book. On the front of the second, the title-page, he noticed a sort of stain which looked like an ink blot. But in looking at it very closely he thought he could distinguish some half-effaced letters. My uncle at once fastened upon this as the center of interest, and he laboured at that blot, until by the help of his microscope he ended by making out the following Runic characters which he read without difficulty.

"Arne Saknussemm!" he cried in triumph. "Why that is the name of another Icelander, a savant of the sixteenth century, a celebrated alchemist!"

I gazed at my uncle with satisfactory admiration.

"Those alchemists," he resumed, "Avicenna, Bacon, Lully, Paracelsus, were the real and only savants of their time. They made discoveries at which we are astonished. Has not this Saknussemm concealed under his cryptogram some surprising invention? It is so; it must be so!"

The Professor's imagination took fire at this hypothesis.

"No doubt," I ventured to reply; "but what interest would he have in thus hiding so marvellous a discovery?"

"Why? Why? How can I tell? Did not Galileo do the same by Saturn? We shall see. I will get at the secret of this document, and I will neither sleep nor eat until I have found it out."

My comment on this was a half-suppressed "Oh!"

"Nor you either, Axel," he added.

"The deuce!" said I to myself; "then it is lucky I have eaten two dinners to-day!"

"First of all we must find out the key to this cipher; that cannot be difficult."

At these words I quickly raised my head; but my uncle went on soliloquising.

"There's nothing easier. In this document there are a hundred and thirty-two letters, viz., seventy-seven consonants and fifty-five vowels. This is the proportion found in southern languages, whilst northern tongues are much richer in consonants; therefore this is in a southern language."

These were very fair conclusions, I thought.

"But what language is it?"

Here I looked for a display of learning, but I met instead with profound analysis.

"This Saknussemm," he went on, "was a very well-informed man; now since he was not writing in his own mother tongue, he would naturally select that which was currently adopted by the choice spirits of the sixteenth century; I mean Latin. If I am mistaken, I can but try Spanish, French, Italian, Greek, or Hebrew. But the savants of the sixteenth century generally wrote in Latin. I am therefore entitled to pronounce this, *à priori*, to be Latin. It is Latin."

I jumped up in my chair. My Latin memories rose in revolt against the notion that these barbarous words could belong to the sweet language of Virgil.

"Yes, it is Latin," my uncle went on; "but it is Latin confused and in disorder; '*perturbata seu inordinata,*' as Euclid has it."

"Very well," thought I, "if you can bring order out of that confusion, my dear uncle, you are a clever man."

"Let us examine carefully," said he again, taking up the leaf upon which I had written. "Here is a series of one hundred and thirty-two letters in apparent disorder. There are words consisting of consonants only, as *m̄.rnlls*; others, on the other hand, in which vowels predominate, as for instance the fifth, *vnteief*, or the last but one, *oseibo*. Now this arrangement has evidently not been premeditated; it has arisen mathematically in obedience to the unknown law which has ruled in the succession of these letters. It appears to me a certainty that the original sentence was written in a proper manner, and afterwards distorted by a law which we have yet to discover. Whoever possesses the key of this cipher will read it with fluency. What is that key? Axel, have you got it?"

I answered not a word, and for a very good reason. My eyes had fallen upon a charming picture, suspended against the wall, the portrait of Gräuben. My uncle's ward was at that time at Altona, staying with a relation, and in her absence I was very downhearted; for I may confess it to you now, the pretty Virlandaise and the professor's nephew loved each other with a patience and a calmness entirely German. We had become engaged unknown to my uncle, who was too much taken up with geology to be able to enter into such feelings as ours. Gräuben was a lovely blue-eyed blonde, rather given to gravity and seriousness; but that did not prevent her from loving me very sincerely. As for me, I *adored* her, if there is such a word in the German language. Thus it happened that the picture of my pretty Virlandaise threw me in a moment out of the world of realities into that of memory and fancy.

There looked down upon me the faithful companion of my labours and my recreations. Everyday she helped me to arrange my uncle's precious specimens; she and I labelled them together. Mademoiselle Gräuben was an accomplished mineralogist; she could have taught a few things to a savant. She was fond of investigating abstruse scientific questions. What pleasant hours we have spent in study; and how often I envied the very stones which she handled with her charming fingers.

Then, when our leisure hours came, we used to go out together and turn into the shady avenues by the Alster, and went happily side by side up to the old windmill, which forms such an improvement to the landscape at the head of the lake. On the road we chatted hand in hand; I told her amusing tales at which she laughed heartily. Then we reached the banks of the Elbe, and after having bid good-by to the swan, sailing gracefully amidst the white water lilies, we returned to the quay by the steamer.

That is just where I was in my dream, when my uncle with a vehement thump on the table dragged me back to the realities of life.

"Come," said he, "the very first idea which would come into anyone's head to confuse the letters of a sentence would be to write the words vertically instead of horizontally."

"Indeed!" said I.

"Now we must see what would be the effect of that, Axel; put down upon this paper any sentence you like; only instead of arranging the letters in the usual way, one after the other, place them in succession in vertical columns, so as to group them together in five or six vertical lines."

I caught his meaning, and immediately produced the following literary wonder:

I	y	l	o	a	u
l	o	l	w	r	b
o	u	,	n	G	e
v	w	m	d	r	n
e	e	y	e	a	!

"Good," said the professor, without reading them, "now set down those words in a horizontal line."

I obeyed, and with this result:

Iyloau lolwrb ou,nGe vwmdrn
eeyea!

"Excellent!" said my uncle, taking the paper hastily out of my hands. "This begins to look just like an ancient document; the vowels and the consonants are grouped together in equal disorder; there are even capitals in the middle of words, and commas too, just as in Saknussemm's parchment."

I considered these remarks very clever.

"Now," said my uncle, looking straight at me, "to read the sentence which you have just written, and with which I am wholly unacquainted, I shall only have to take the first letter of each word, then the second, the third, and so forth."

And my uncle, to his great astonishment, and my much greater, read:

"I love you well, my own dear Gräuben!"

"Hallo!" cried the Professor.

Yes, indeed, without knowing what I was about, like an awkward and unlucky lover, I had compromised myself by writing this unfortunate sentence.

"Aha! you are in love with Gräuben?" he said, with the right look for a guardian.

"Yes; no!" I stammered.

"You love Gräuben," he went on once or twice dreamily. "Well, let us apply the process I have suggested to the document in question."

My uncle, falling back into his absorbing contemplations, had already forgotten my imprudent words. I merely say imprudent, for the great mind of so learned a man of course had no place for love affairs, and happily the grand business of the document gained me the victory.

Just as the moment of the supreme experiment arrived, the Professor's eyes flashed right through his spectacles. There was a quivering in his fingers as he grasped the old parchment. He was deeply moved. At last he gave a preliminary cough, and with profound gravity, naming in succession the first, then the second letter of each word, he dictated me the following:

messvnkaSenrA.icefdoK.segnittamvrtn
ecertserrette,rotaisadva,ednecsedsadne
lacartniiilvIsiratracSarbmvtabiledmek
meretarcsilvcoIsleffenSnI.

I confess I felt considerably excited in coming to the end; these letters named, one at a time, had carried no sense to my mind; I therefore waited for the Professor with great pomp to unfold the magnificent but hidden Latin of this mysterious phrase.

But who could have foretold the result? A violent thump made the furniture rattle, and spilt some ink, and my pen dropped from between my fingers.

"That's not it," cried my uncle, "there's no sense in it."

Then darting out like a shot, bowling downstairs like an avalanche, he rushed into the Königstrasse and fled.

Chapter IV

THE ENEMY TO BE STARVED INTO SUBMISSION

HE IS GONE!" CRIED MARTHA, RUNNING OUT OF HER KITCHEN AT THE NOISE OF THE VI-olent slamming of doors.

"Yes," I replied, "completely gone."

"Well; and how about his dinner?" said the old servant.

"He won't have any."

"And his supper?"

"He won't have any."

"What?" cried Martha, with clasped hands.

"No, my dear Martha, he will eat no more. No one in the house is to eat anything at all. Uncle Liedenbrock is going to make us all fast until he has succeeded in deciphering an undecipherable scrawl."

"Oh, my dear! must we then all die of hunger?"

I hardly dared to confess that, with so absolute a ruler as my uncle, this fate was inevitable.

The old servant, visibly moved, returned to the kitchen, moaning piteously.

When I was alone, I thought I would go and tell Gräuben all about it. But how should I be able to escape from the house? The Professor might return at any moment. And suppose he called me? And suppose he tackled me again with this logomachy, which might vainly have been set before ancient Œdipus. And if I did not obey his call, who could answer for what might happen?

The wisest course was to remain where I was. A mineralogist at Besançon had just sent us a collection of siliceous nodules, which I had to classify: so I set to work; I sorted, labelled, and arranged in their own glass case all these hollow specimens, in the cavity of each of which was a nest of little crystals.

But this work did not succeed in absorbing all my attention. That old document kept working in my brain. My head throbbed with excitement, and I felt an undefined uneasiness. I was possessed with a presentiment of coming evil.

In an hour my nodules were all arranged upon successive shelves. Then I dropped down into the old velvet arm-chair, my head thrown back and my hands joined over it. I lighted my long crooked pipe, with a painting on it of an idle-looking naiad; then I amused myself watching the process of the conversion of the tobacco into carbon, which was by slow degrees making my naiad into a negress. Now and then I listened to hear whether a well-known step was on the stairs. No. Where could my uncle be at that moment? I fancied him running under the noble trees which line the road to Altona, gesticulating, making shots with his cane, thrashing the long grass, cutting the heads off the thistles, and disturbing the contemplative storks in their peaceful solitude.

Would he return in triumph or in discouragement? Which would get the upper hand, he or the secret? I was thus asking myself questions, and mechanically taking between my fingers the sheet of paper mysteriously disfigured with the incomprehensible succession of letters I had written down; and I repeated to myself: "What does it all mean?"

I sought to group the letters so as to form words. Quite impossible! When I put them together by twos, threes, fives or sixes, nothing came of it but nonsense. To be sure the fourteenth, fifteenth and sixteenth letters made the English word "ice"; the eighty-third and two following made "sir"; and in the midst of the document, in the second and third lines, I observed the words, "rota," "mutabile," "ira," "nec," "atra."

"Come now," I thought, "these words seem to justify my uncle's view about the language of the document. In the fourth line appeared the word "luco," which means a sacred wood. It is true that in the third line was the word "tabiled," which looked like Hebrew, and in the last the purely French words "mer," "arc," "mère."

All this was enough to drive a poor fellow crazy. Four different languages in this ridiculous sentence! What connection could there possibly be between such words as ice, sir, anger, cruel, sacred wood, changeable, mother, bow, and sea? The first and the last might have something to do with each other; it was not at all surprising that in a document written in Iceland there should be mention of a sea of ice; but it was quite another thing to get to the end of this cryptogram with so small a clue. So I was struggling with an insurmountable difficulty; my brain got heated, my eyes watered over that sheet of paper; its hundred and thirty-two letters seemed to flutter and fly around me like those motes of mingled light and darkness which float in the air around the head when the blood is rushing upwards with undue violence. I was a prey to a kind of hallucination; I was stifling; I wanted air. Unconsciously I fanned myself with the bit of paper, the back and front of which successively came before my eyes. What was my surprise when, in one of those rapid revolutions, at the moment when the back was turned to me I thought I caught sight of the Latin words "craterem," "terrestre," and others.

A sudden light burst in upon me; these hints alone gave me the first glimpse of the truth; I had discovered the key to the cipher. To read the document, it would not even be necessary to read it through the paper. Such as it was, just such as it had been dictated to me, so it might be spelt out with ease. All those ingenious professorial combinations were coming right. He was right as to the arrangement of the letters; he was right as to the language. He had been within a hair's breadth of reading this Latin document from end to end; but that hair's breadth, chance had given it to me!

You may be sure I felt stirred up. My eyes were dim, I could scarcely see. I had laid the paper upon the table. At a glance I could tell the whole secret.

At last I became more calm. I made a wise resolve to walk twice round the room quietly and settle my nerves, and then I returned into the deep gulf of the huge arm-chair.

"Now I'll read it," I cried, after having well distended my lungs with air.

I leaned over the table; I laid my finger successively upon every letter; and without a pause, without one moment's hesitation, I read off the whole sentence aloud.

Stupefaction! terror! I sat overwhelmed as if with a sudden deadly blow. What! that which I read had actually, really been done! A mortal man had had the audacity to penetrate! . . .

"Ah!" I cried, springing up. "But no! no! My uncle shall never know it. He would insist upon doing it too. He would want to know all about it. Ropes could not hold him, such a determined geologist as he is! He would start, he would, in spite of everything and everybody, and he would take me with him, and we should never get back. No, never! never!"

My overexcitement was beyond all description.

"No! no! it shall not be," I declared energetically; "and as it is in my power to prevent the knowledge of it coming into the mind of my tyrant, I will do it. By dint of turning this document round and round, he too might discover the key. I will destroy it."

There was a little fire left on the hearth. I seized not only the paper but Saknussemm's parchment; with a feverish hand I was about to fling it all upon the coals and utterly destroy and abolish this dangerous secret, when the study door opened, and my uncle appeared.

Chapter V

FAMINE, THEN VICTORY, FOLLOWED BY DISMAY

I HAD ONLY JUST TIME TO REPLACE THE UNFORTUNATE DOCUMENT UPON THE TABLE. Professor Liedenbrock seemed to be greatly abstracted.

The ruling thought gave him no rest. Evidently he had gone deeply into the matter, analytically and with profound scrutiny. He had brought all the resources of his mind to bear upon it during his walk, and he had come back to apply some new combination.

He sat in his arm-chair, and pen in hand he began what looked very much like algebraic formulae. I followed with my eyes his trembling hands, I took count of every movement. Might not some unhoped-for result come of it? I trembled, too, very unnecessarily, since the true key was in my hands, and no other would open the secret.

For three long hours my uncle worked on without a word, without lifting his head; rubbing out, beginning again, then rubbing out again, and so on a hundred times.

I knew very well that if he succeeded in setting down these letters in every possible relative position, the sentence would come out. But I knew also that twenty letters alone could form two quintillions, four hundred and thirty-two quadrillions, nine hundred and two trillions, eight billions, a hundred and seventy-six millions, six hundred and forty thousand combinations. Now, here were a hundred and thirty-two letters in this sentence, and these hundred and thirty-two letters would give a number of different sentences, each made up of at least a hundred and thirty-three figures, a number which passed far beyond all calculation or conception.

So I felt reassured as far as regarded this heroic method of solving the difficulty.

But time was passing away; night came on; the street noises ceased; my uncle, bending over his task, noticed nothing, not even Martha half opening the door; he heard not a sound, not even that excellent woman saying:

"Will not monsieur take any supper to-night?"

And poor Martha had to go away unanswered. As for me, after long resistance, I was overcome by sleep, and fell off at the end of the sofa, while uncle Liedenbrock went on calculating and rubbing out his calculations.

When I awoke next morning that indefatigable worker was still at his post. His red eyes, his pale complexion, his hair tangled between his feverish fingers, the red spots on his cheeks, revealed his desperate struggle with impossibilities, and the weariness of spirit, the mental wrestlings he must have undergone all through that unhappy night.

To tell the plain truth, I pitied him. In spite of the reproaches which I considered I had a right to lay upon him, a certain feeling of compassion was beginning to gain upon me. The poor man was so entirely taken up with his one idea that he had even forgotten how to get angry. All the strength of his feelings was concentrated upon one point alone; and as their usual vent was closed, it was to be feared lest extreme tension should give rise to an explosion sooner or later.

I might with a word have loosened the screw of the steel vice that was crushing his brain; but that word I would not speak.

Yet I was not an ill-natured fellow. Why was I dumb at such a crisis? Why so insensible to my uncle's interests?

"No, no," I repeated, "I shall not speak. He would insist upon going; nothing on earth could stop him. His imagination is a volcano, and to do that which other geologists have never done he would risk his life. I will preserve silence. I will keep the secret which mere chance has revealed to me. To discover it, would be to kill Professor Liedenbrock! Let him find it out himself if he can. I will never have it laid to my door that I led him to his destruction."

Having formed this resolution, I folded my arms and waited. But I had not reckoned upon one little incident which turned up a few hours after.

When our good Martha wanted to go to Market, she found the door locked. The big key was gone. Who could have taken it out? Assuredly, it was my uncle, when he returned the night before from his hurried walk.

Was this done on purpose? Or was it a mistake? Did he want to reduce us by famine? This seemed like going rather too far! What! should Martha and I be victims of a position of things in which we had not the smallest interest? It was a fact that a few years before this, whilst my uncle was working at his great classification of minerals, he was forty-eight hours without eating, and all his household were obliged to share in this scientific fast. As for me, what I remember is, that I got severe cramps in my stomach, which hardly suited the constitution of a hungry, growing lad.

Now it appeared to me as if breakfast was going to be wanting, just as supper had been the night before. Yet I resolved to be a hero, and not to be conquered by the pangs of hunger. Martha took it very seriously, and, poor woman, was very much distressed. As for me, the impossibility of leaving the house distressed me a good deal more, and for a very good reason. A caged lover's feelings may easily be imagined.

My uncle went on working, his imagination went off rambling into the ideal world of combinations; he was far away from earth, and really far away from earthly wants.

About noon hunger began to stimulate me severely. Martha had, without thinking any harm, cleared out the larder the night before, so that now there was nothing left in the house. Still I held out; I made it a point of honour.

Two o'clock struck. This was becoming ridiculous; worse than that, unbearable. I began to say to myself that I was exaggerating the importance of the document; that my uncle would surely not believe in it, that he would set it down as a mere puzzle; that if it came to the worst, we should lay violent hands on him and keep him at home if he thought on venturing on the expedition that, after all, he might himself discover the key of the cipher, and that then I should be clear at the mere expense of my involuntary abstinence.

These reasons seemed excellent to me, though on the night before I should have rejected them with indignation; I even went so far as to condemn myself for my absurdity in having waited so long, and I finally resolved to let it all out.

I was therefore meditating a proper introduction to the matter, so as not to seem too abrupt, when the Professor jumped up, clapped on his hat, and prepared to go out.

Surely he was not going out, to shut us in again! no, never!

"Uncle!" I cried.

He seemed not to hear me.

"Uncle Liedenbrock!" I cried, lifting up my voice.

"Ay," he answered like a man suddenly waking.

"Uncle, that key!"

"What key? The door key?"

"No, no!" I cried. "The key of the document."

The Professor stared at me over his spectacles; no doubt he saw something unusual in the expression of my countenance; for he laid hold of my arm, and speechlessly questioned me with his eyes. Yes, never was a question more forcibly put.

I nodded my head up and down.

He shook his pityingly, as if he was dealing with a lunatic. I gave a more affirmative gesture.

His eyes glistened and sparkled with live fire, his hand was shaken threateningly.

This mute conversation at such a momentous crisis would have riveted the attention of the most indifferent. And the fact really was that I dared not speak now, so intense was the excitement for fear lest my uncle should smother me in his first joyful embraces. But he became so urgent that I was at last compelled to answer.

"Yes, that key, chance—"

"What is that you are saying?" he shouted with indescribable emotion.

"There, read that!" I said, presenting a sheet of paper on which I had written.

"But there is nothing in this," he answered, crumpling up the paper.

"No, nothing until you proceed to read from the end to the beginning."

I had not finished my sentence when the Professor broke out into a cry, nay, a roar. A new revelation burst in upon him. He was transformed!

"Aha, clever Saknussemm!" he cried. "You had first written out your sentence the wrong way."

And darting upon the paper, with eyes bedimmed, and voice choked with emotion, he read the whole document from the last letter to the first.

It was conceived in the following terms:

In Sneffels Joculis craterem quem delibat
Umbra Scartaris Julii intra calendas descende,
Audax viator, et terrestre centrum attinges.
Quod feci, Arne Saknussemm.*

Which bad Latin may be translated thus:

"Descend, bold traveller, into the crater of the jokul of Sneffels, which the shadow of Scartaris touches before the kalends of July, and you will attain the center of the earth; which I have done, Arne Saknussemm."

In reading this, my uncle gave a spring as if he had touched a Leyden jar. His audacity, his joy, and his convictions were magnificent to behold. He came and he went; he seized his head between both his hands; he pushed the chairs out of their places, he piled up his books; incredible as it may seem, he rattled his precious nodules of flints together; he sent a kick here, a thump there. At last his nerves calmed down, and like a man exhausted by too lavish an expenditure of vital power, he sank back exhausted into his arm-chair.

"What o'clock is it?" he asked after a few moments of silence.

"Three o'clock," I replied.

"Is it really? The dinner hour is past, and I did not know it. I am half dead with hunger. Come on, and after dinner—"

"Well?"

"After dinner, pack up my trunk."

"What?" I cried.

"And yours!" replied the indefatigable Professor, entering the dining-room.

---

*In the cipher, *audax* is written *avdas*, and *quod* and *quem*, *hod* and *kem*. (Tr.)

Chapter VI

EXCITING DISCUSSIONS ABOUT AN UNPARALLELLED ENTERPRISE

AT THESE WORDS A COLD SHIVER RAN THROUGH ME. YET I CONTROLLED MYSELF; I EVEN resolved to put a good face upon it. Scientific arguments alone could have any weight with Professor Liedenbrock. Now there were good ones against the practicability of such a journey. Penetrate to the center of the earth! What nonsense! But I kept my dialectic battery in reserve for a suitable opportunity, and I interested myself in the prospect of my dinner, which was not yet forthcoming.

It is no use to tell of the rage and imprecations of my uncle before the empty table. Explanations were given, Martha was set at liberty, ran off to the market, and did her part so well that in an hour afterwards my hunger was appeased, and I was able to return to the contemplation of the gravity of the situation.

During all dinner-time my uncle was almost merry; he indulged in some of those learned jokes which never do anybody any harm. Dessert over, he beckoned me into his study.

I obeyed; he sat at one end of his table, I at the other.

"Axel," said he very mildly; "you are a very ingenious young man, you have done me a splendid service, at a moment when, wearied out with the struggle, I was going to abandon the contest. Where should I have lost myself? None can tell. Never, my lad, shall I forget it; and you shall have your share in the glory to which your discovery will lead."

"Oh, come!" thought I, "he is in a good way. Now is the time for discussing that same glory."

"Before all things," my uncle resumed, "I enjoin you to preserve the most inviolable secrecy: you understand? There are not a few in the scientific world who envy my success, and many would be ready to undertake this enterprise, to whom our return should be the very first news of it."

"Do you really think there are many people bold enough?" said I.

"Certainly; who would hesitate to acquire such renown? If that document were divulged, a whole army of geologists would be ready to rush into the footsteps of Arne Saknussemm."

"I don't feel so very sure of that, uncle," I replied; "for we have no proof of the authenticity of this document."

"What! not of the book, inside which we have discovered it?"

"Granted. I admit that Saknussemm may have written these lines. But does it follow that he has really accomplished such a journey? And may it not be that this old parchment is intended to mislead?"

I almost regretted having uttered this last word, which dropped from me in an unguarded moment. The Professor bent his shaggy brows, and I feared I had seriously compromised my own safety. Happily no great harm came of it. A smile flitted across the lip of my severe companion, and he answered:

"That is what we shall see."

"Ah!" said I, rather put out. "But do let me exhaust all the possible objections against this document."

"Speak, my boy, don't be afraid. You are quite at liberty to express your opinions. You are no longer my nephew only, but my colleague. Pray go on."

"Well, in the first place, I wish to ask what are this Jokul, this Sneffels, and this Scartaris, names which I have never heard before?"

"Nothing easier. I received not long ago a map from my friend, Augustus Petermann, at Liepzig. Nothing could be more apropos. Take down the third atlas in the second shelf in the large bookcase, series Z, plate 4."

I rose, and with the help of such precise instructions could not fail to find the required atlas. My uncle opened it and said:

"Here is one of the best maps of Iceland, that of Handersen, and I believe this will solve the worst of our difficulties."

I bent over the map.

"You see this volcanic island," said the Professor; "observe that all the volcanoes are called jokuls, a word which means glacier in Icelandic, and under the high latitude of Iceland nearly all the active volcanoes discharge through beds of ice. Hence this term of jokul is applied to all the irruptive mountains in Iceland."

"Very good," said I; "but what of Sneffels?"

I was hoping that this question would be unanswerable; but I was mistaken. My uncle replied:

"Follow my finger along the west coast of Iceland. Do you see Rejkiavik, the capital? You do. Well; ascend the innumerable fiords that indent those sea-beaten shores, and stop at the sixty-fifth degree of latitude. What do you see there?"

"I see a peninsula looking like a thigh bone with the knee bone at the end of it."

"A very fair comparison, my lad. Now do you see anything upon that knee bone?"

"Yes; a mountain rising out of the sea."

"Right. That is Snæfell."

"That Snæfell?"

"It is. It is a mountain five thousand feet high, one of the most remarkable in the island, and undoubtedly the most remarkable in the world, if its crater leads down to the center of the earth."

"But that is impossible," I said shrugging my shoulders, and disgusted at such a ridiculous supposition.

"Impossible?" said the Professor severely; "and why, pray?"

"Because this crater is evidently filled with lava and burning rocks, and therefore—"

"But suppose it is an extinct volcano?"

"Extinct?"

"Yes; the number of active volcanoes on the surface of the globe is at the present time only about three hundred. But there is a very much larger number of extinct ones. Now, Snæfell is one of these. Since historic times there has been but one irruption of this mountain, that of 1219; from that time it has quieted down more and more, and now it is no longer reckoned among active volcanoes."

To such positive statements I could make no reply. I therefore took refuge in other dark passages of the document.

"What is the meaning of this word Scartaris, and what have the kalends of July to do with it?"

My uncle took a few minutes to consider. For one short moment I felt a ray of hope, speedily to be extinguished. For he soon answered thus:

"What is darkness to you is light to me. This proves the ingenious care with which Saknussemm guarded and defined his discovery. Sneffels, or Snæfell, has several craters. It was therefore necessary to point out which of these leads to the center of the globe. What did the Icelandic sage do? He observed that at the approach of the kalends of July, that is to say in the last days of June, one of the peaks, called Scartaris, flung its shadow down the mouth of that particular crater, and he committed that fact to his document. Could there possibly have been a more exact guide? As soon as we have arrived at the summit of Snæfell we shall have no hesitation as to the proper road to take."

Decidedly, my uncle had answered every one of my objections. I saw that his position on the old parchment was impregnable. I therefore ceased to press him upon that part of the subject, and as above all things he must be convinced, I passed on to scientific objections, which in my opinion were far more serious.

"Well, then," I said, "I am forced to admit that Saknussemm's sentence is clear, and leaves no room for doubt. I will even allow that the document bears every mark and evidence of authenticity. That learned philosopher did get to the bottom of Sneffels, he has seen the shadow of Scartaris touch the edge of the crater before the kalends of July; he may even have heard the legendary stories told in his day about that crater reaching to the center of the world; but as for reaching it himself, as for performing the journey, and returning, if he ever went, I say no—he never, never did that."

"Now for your reason?" said my uncle ironically.

"All the theories of science demonstrate such a feat to be impracticable."

"The theories say that, do they?" replied the Professor in the tone of a meek disciple. "Oh! unpleasant theories! How the theories will hinder us, won't they?"

I saw that he was only laughing at me; but I went on all the same.

"Yes; it is perfectly well known that the internal temperature rises one degree for every 70 feet in depth; now, admitting this proportion to be constant, and the radius of the earth being fifteen hundred leagues, there must be a temperature of 360,032 degrees at the center of the earth. Therefore, all the substances that compose the body of this earth must exist there in a state of incandescent gas; for the metals that most resist the action of heat, gold, and platinum, and the hardest rocks, can never be either solid or liquid under such a temperature. I have therefore good reason for asking if it is possible to penetrate through such a medium."

"So, Axel, it is the heat that troubles you?"

"Of course it is. Were we to reach a depth of thirty miles we should have arrived at the limit of the terrestrial crust, for there the temperature will be more than 2372 degrees."

"Are you afraid of being put into a state of fusion?"

"I will leave you to decide that question," I answered rather sullenly.

"This is my decision," replied Professor Liedenbrock, putting on one of his grandest airs. "Neither you nor anybody else knows with any certainty what is going on in the interior of this globe, since not the twelve thousandth part of its radius is known; science is eminently perfectible; and every new theory is soon routed by a newer. Was it not always believed until Fourier that the temperature of the interplanetary spaces decreased perpetually? and is it not known at the present time that the greatest cold of the ethereal regions is never lower than 40 degrees below zero Fahr.? Why should it not be the same with the internal heat? Why should it not, at a certain depth, attain an impassable limit, instead of rising to such a point as to fuse the most infusible metals?"

As my uncle was now taking his stand upon hypotheses, of course, there was nothing to be said.

"Well, I will tell you that true savants, amongst them Poisson, have demonstrated that if a heat of 360,000 degrees* existed in the interior of the globe, the fiery gases arising from the fused matter would acquire an elastic force which the crust of the earth would be unable to resist, and that it would explode like the plates of a bursting boiler."

"That is Poisson's opinion, my uncle, nothing more."

"Granted. But it is likewise the creed adopted by other distinguished geologists, that the interior of the globe is neither gas nor water, nor any of the heaviest minerals known, for in none of these cases would the earth weigh what it does."

"Oh, with figures you may prove anything!"

"But is it the same with facts! Is it not known that the number of volcanoes has diminished since the first days of creation? and if there is central heat may we not thence conclude that it is in process of diminution?"

"My good uncle, if you will enter into the region of speculation, I can discuss the matter no longer."

"But I have to tell you that the highest names have come to the support of my views. Do you remember a visit paid to me by the celebrated chemist, Humphry Davy, in 1825?"

"Not at all, for I was not born until nineteen years afterwards."

"Well, Humphry Davy did call upon me on his way through Hamburg. We were long engaged in discussing, amongst other problems, the hypothesis of the liquid structure of the terrestrial nucleus. We were agreed that it could not be in a liquid state, for a reason which science has never been able to confute."

"What is that reason?" I said, rather astonished.

"Because this liquid mass would be subject, like the ocean, to the lunar attraction, and therefore twice everyday there would be internal tides, which, upheaving the terrestrial crust, would cause periodical earthquakes!"

"Yet it is evident that the surface of the globe has been subject to the action of fire," I replied, "and it is quite reasonable to suppose that the external crust cooled down first, whilst the heat took refuge down to the center."

"Quite a mistake," my uncle answered. "The earth has been heated by combustion on its surface, that is all. Its surface was composed of a great number of metals, such as potassium and sodium, which have the peculiar property of igniting at the mere contact with air and water; these metals kindled when the atmospheric vapours fell in rain upon the soil; and by and by, when the waters penetrated into the fissures of the crust of the earth, they broke out into fresh combustion with explosions and irruptions. Such was the cause of the numerous volcanoes at the origin of the earth."

---

*The degrees of temperature are given by Jules Verne according to the centigrade system, for which we will in each case substitute the Fahrenheit measurement. (Tr.)

"Upon my word, this is a very clever hypothesis," I exclaimed, in spite rather of myself.

"And which Humphry Davy demonstrated to me by a simple experiment. He formed a small ball of the metals which I have named, and which was a very fair representation of our globe; whenever he caused a fine dew of rain to fall upon its surface, it heaved up into little monticules, it became oxydised and formed miniature mountains; a crater broke open at one of its summits; the irruption took place, and communicated to the whole of the ball such a heat that it could not be held in the hand."

In truth, I was beginning to be shaken by the Professor's arguments, besides which he gave additional weight to them by his usual ardour and fervent enthusiasm.

"You see, Axel," he added, "the condition of the terrestrial nucleus has given rise to various hypotheses among geologists; there is no proof at all for this internal heat; my opinion is that there is no such thing; it cannot be; besides we shall see for ourselves, and, like Arne Saknussemm, we shall know exactly what to hold as truth concerning this grand question."

"Very well, we *shall* see," I replied, feeling myself carried off by his contagious enthusiasm. "Yes, we shall see; that is, if it is possible to see anything there."

"And why not? May we not depend upon electric phenomena to give us light? May we not even expect light from the atmosphere, the pressure of which may render it luminous as we approach the center?"

"Yes, yes," said I; "that is possible, too."

"It is certain," exclaimed my uncle in a tone of triumph. "But silence, do you hear me? silence upon the whole subject; and let no one get before us in this design of discovering the center of the earth."

Chapter VII

A WOMAN'S COURAGE

THUS ENDED THIS MEMORABLE SEANCE. THAT CONVERSATION THREW ME INTO A FEVER. I came out of my uncle's study as if I had been stunned, and as if there was not air enough in all the streets of Hamburg to put me right again. I therefore made for the banks of the Elbe, where the steamer lands her passengers which forms the communication between the city and the Hamburg railway.

Was I convinced of the truth of what I had heard? Had I not bent under the iron rule of the Professor Liedenbrock? Was I to believe him in earnest in his intention to penetrate to the center of this massive globe? Had I been listening to the mad speculations of a lunatic, or to the scientific conclusions of a lofty genius? Where did truth stop? Where did error begin?

I was all adrift amongst a thousand contradictory hypotheses, but I could not lay hold of one.

Yet I remembered that I had been convinced, although now my enthusiasm was beginning to cool down; but I felt a desire to start at once, and not to lose time and courage by calm reflection. I had at that moment quite courage enough to strap my knapsack to my shoulders and start.

But I must confess that in another hour this unnatural excitement abated, my nerves became unstrung, and from the depths of the abysses of this earth I ascended to its surface again.

"It is quite absurd!" I cried, "there is no sense about it. No sensible young man should for a moment entertain such a proposal. The whole thing is non-existent. I have had a bad night, I have been dreaming of horrors."

But I had followed the banks of the Elbe and passed the town. After passing the port too, I had reached the Altona road. I was led by a presentiment, soon to be realised; for shortly I espied my little Gräuben bravely returning with her light step to Hamburg.

"Gräuben!" I cried from afar off.

The young girl stopped, rather frightened perhaps to hear her name called after her on the high road. Ten yards more, and I had joined her.

"Axel!" she cried surprised. "What! have you come to meet me? Is this why you are here, sir?"

But when she had looked upon me, Gräuben could not fail to see the uneasiness and distress of my mind.

"What is the matter?" she said, holding out her hand.

"What is the matter, Gräuben?" I cried.

In a couple of minutes my pretty Virlandaise was fully informed of the position of affairs. For a time she was silent. Did her heart palpitate as mine did? I don't know about that, but I know that her hand did not tremble in mine. We went on a hundred yards without speaking.

At last she said, "Axel!"

"My dear Gräuben."

"That will be a splendid journey!"

I gave a bound at these words.

"Yes, Axel, a journey worthy of the nephew of a savant; it is a good thing for a man to be distinguished by some great enterprise."

"What, Gräuben, won't you dissuade me from such an undertaking?"

"No, my dear Axel, and I would willingly go with you, but that a poor girl would only be in your way."

"Is that quite true?"

"It is true."

Ah! women and young girls, how incomprehensible are your feminine hearts! When you are not the timidest, you are the bravest of creatures. Reason has nothing to do with your actions. What! did this child encourage me in such an expedition! Would she not be afraid to join it herself? And she was driving me to it, one whom she loved!

I was disconcerted, and, if I must tell the whole truth, I was ashamed.

"Gräuben, we will see whether you will say the same thing to-morrow."

"To-morrow, dear Axel, I will say what I say to-day."

Gräuben and I, hand in hand, but in silence, pursued our way. The emotions of that day were breaking my heart.

After all, I thought, the kalends of July are a long way off, and between this and then many things may take place which will cure my uncle of his desire to travel underground.

It was night when we arrived at the house in Königstrasse. I expected to find all quiet there, my uncle in bed as was his custom, and Martha giving her last touches with the feather brush.

But I had not taken into account the Professor's impatience. I found him shouting and working himself up amidst a crowd of porters and messengers who were all depositing various loads in the passage. Our old servant was at her wits' end.

"Come, Axel, come, you miserable wretch," my uncle cried from as far off as he could see me. "Your boxes are not packed, and my papers are not arranged; where's the key of my carpet bag? and what have you done with my gaiters?"

I stood thunderstruck. My voice failed. Scarcely could my lips utter the words:

"Are we really going?"

"Of course, you unhappy boy! Could I have dreamed that you would have gone out for a walk instead of hurrying your preparations forward?"

"Are we to go?" I asked again, with sinking hopes.

"Yes; the day after to-morrow, early."

I could hear no more. I fled for refuge into my own little room.

All hope was now at an end. My uncle had been all the morning making purchases of a part of the tools and apparatus required for this desperate undertaking. The passage was encumbered with rope ladders, knotted cords, torches, flasks, grappling irons, alpenstocks, pickaxes, iron shod sticks, enough to load ten men.

I spent an awful night. Next morning I was called early. I had quite decided I would not open the door. But how was I to resist the sweet voice which was always music to my ears, saying, "My dear Axel"?

I came out of my room. I thought my pale countenance and my red and sleepless eyes would work upon Gräuben's sympathies and change her mind.

"Ah! my dear Axel," she said, "I see you are better. A night's rest has done you good."

"Done me good!" I exclaimed.

I rushed to the glass. Well, in fact I did look better than I had expected. I could hardly believe my own eyes.

"Axel," she said, "I have had a long talk with my guardian. He is a bold philosopher, a man of immense courage, and you must remember that his blood flows in your veins. He has confided to me his plans, his hopes, and why and how he hopes to attain his object. He will no doubt succeed. My dear Axel, it is a grand thing to devote yourself to science! What honour will fall upon Herr Liedenbrock, and so be reflected upon his companion! When you return, Axel, you will be a man, his equal, free to speak and to act independently, and free to—"

The dear girl only finished this sentence by blushing. Her words revived me. Yet I refused to believe we should start. I drew Gräuben into the Professor's study.

"Uncle, is it true that we are to go?"

"Why do you doubt?"

"Well, I don't doubt," I said, not to vex him; "but, I ask, what need is there to hurry?"

"Time, time, flying with irreparable rapidity."

"But it is only the 16th May, and until the end of June—"

"What, you monument of ignorance! do you think you can get to Iceland in a couple of days? If you had not deserted me like a fool I should have taken you to the Copenhagen office, to Liffender & Co., and you would have learned then that there is only one trip every month from Copenhagen to Rejkiavik, on the 22d."

"Well?"

"Well, if we waited for the 22d June we should be too late to see the shadow of Scartaris touch the crater of Sneffels. Therefore we must get to Copenhagen as fast as we can to secure our passage. Go and pack up."

There was no reply to this. I went up to my room. Gräuben followed me. She undertook to pack up all things necessary for my voyage. She was no more moved than if I had been starting for a little trip to Lübeck or Heligoland. Her little hands moved without haste. She talked quietly. She supplied me with sensible reasons for our expedition. She delighted me, and yet I was angry with her. Now and then I felt I ought to break out into a passion, but she took no notice and went on her way as methodically as ever.

Finally the last strap was buckled; I came downstairs. All that day the philosophical instrument makers and the electricians kept coming and going. Martha was distracted.

"Is master mad?" she asked.

I nodded my head.

"And is he going to take you with him?"

I nodded again.

"Where to?"

I pointed with my finger downward.

"Down into the cellar?" cried the old servant.

"No," I said. "Lower down than that."

Night came. But I knew nothing about the lapse of time.

"To-morrow morning at six precisely," my uncle decreed, "we start."

At ten o'clock I fell upon my bed, a dead lump of inert matter. All through the night terror had hold of me. I spent it dreaming of abysses. I was a prey to delirium. I felt myself grasped by the Professor's sinewy hand, dragged along, hurled down, shattered into little bits. I dropped down unfathomable precipices with the accelerating velocity of bodies falling through space. My life had become an endless fall. I awoke at five with shattered nerves, trembling and weary. I came downstairs. My uncle was at table, devouring his breakfast. I stared at him with horror and disgust. But dear Gräuben was there; so I said nothing, and could eat nothing.

At half-past five there was a rattle of wheels outside. A large carriage was there to take us to the Altona railway station. It was soon piled up with my uncle's multifarious preparations.

"Where's your box?" he cried.

"It is ready," I replied, with faltering voice.

"Then make haste down, or we shall lose the train."

It was now manifestly impossible to maintain the struggle against destiny. I went up again to my room, and rolling my portmanteaus downstairs I darted after him.

At that moment my uncle was solemnly investing Gräuben with the reins of government. My pretty Virlandaise was as calm and collected as was her wont. She kissed her guardian; but could not restrain a tear in touching my cheek with her gentle lips.

"Gräuben!" I murmured.

"Go, my dear Axel, go! I am now your betrothed; and when you come back I will be your wife."

I pressed her in my arms and took my place in the carriage. Martha and the young girl, standing at the door, waved their last farewell. Then the horses, roused by the driver's whistling, darted off at a gallop on the road to Altona.

Chapter VIII

SERIOUS PREPARATIONS FOR VERTICAL DESCENT

ALTONA, WHICH IS BUT A SUBURB OF HAMBURG, IS THE TERMINUS OF THE KIEL RAILWAY, which was to carry us to the Belts. In twenty minutes we were in Holstein.

At half-past six the carriage stopped at the station; my uncle's numerous packages, his voluminous *impedimenta*, were unloaded, removed, labelled, weighed, put into the luggage vans, and at seven we were seated face to face in our compartment. The whistle sounded, the engine started, we were off.

Was I resigned? No, not yet. Yet the cool morning air and the scenes on the road, rapidly changed by the swiftness of the train, drew me away somewhat from my sad reflections.

As for the Professor's reflections, they went far in advance of the swiftest express. We were alone in the carriage, but we sat in silence. My uncle examined all his pockets and his travelling bag with the minutest care. I saw that he had not forgotten the smallest matter of detail.

Amongst other documents, a sheet of paper, carefully folded, bore the heading of the Danish consulate with the signature of W. Christiensen, consul at Hamburg and the Professor's friend. With this we possessed the proper introductions to the Governor of Iceland.

I also observed the famous document most carefully laid up in a secret pocket in his portfolio. I bestowed a malediction upon it, and then proceeded to examine the country.

It was a very long succession of uninteresting loamy and fertile flats, a very easy country for the construction of railways, and propitious for the laying-down of these direct level lines so dear to railway companies.

I had no time to get tired of the monotony; for in three hours we stopped at Kiel, close to the sea.

The luggage being labelled for Copenhagen, we had no occasion to look after it. Yet the Professor watched every article with jealous vigilance, until all were safe on board. There they disappeared in the hold.

My uncle, notwithstanding his hurry, had so well calculated the relations between the train and the steamer that we had a whole day to spare. The steamer *Ellenora* did not start until night. Thence sprang a feverish state of excitement in which the impatient irascible traveller devoted to perdition the railway directors and the steamboat companies and the governments which allowed such intolerable slowness. I was obliged to act chorus to him when he attacked the captain of the *Ellenora* upon this subject. The captain disposed of us summarily.

At Kiel, as elsewhere, we must do something to while away the time. What with walking on the verdant shores of the bay within which nestles the little town, exploring the thick woods which make it look like a nest embowered amongst thick foliage, admiring the villas, each provided with a little bathing house, and moving about and grumbling, at last ten o'clock came.

The heavy coils of smoke from the *Ellenora*'s funnel unrolled in the sky, the bridge shook with the quivering of the struggling steam; we were on board, and owners for the time of two berths, one over the other, in the only saloon cabin on board.

At a quarter past the moorings were loosed and the throbbing steamer pursued her way over the dark waters of the Great Belt.

The night was dark; there was a sharp breeze and a rough sea, a few lights appeared on shore through the thick darkness; later on, I cannot tell when, a dazzling light from some lighthouse threw a bright stream of fire along the waves; and this is all I can remember of this first portion of our sail.

At seven in the morning we landed at Korsör, a small town on the west coast of Zealand. There we were transferred from the boat to another line of railway, which took us by just as flat a country as the plain of Holstein.

Three hours' travelling brought us to the capital of Denmark. My uncle had not shut his eyes all night. In his impatience I believe he was trying to accelerate the train with his feet.

At last he discerned a stretch of sea.

"The Sound!" he cried.

At our left was a huge building that looked like a hospital.

"That's a lunatic asylum," said one of our travelling companions.

Very good! thought I, just the place we want to end our days in; and great as it is, that asylum is not big enough to contain all Professor Liedenbrock's madness!

At ten in the morning, at last, we set our feet in Copenhagen; the luggage was put upon a carriage and taken with ourselves to the Phœnix Hotel in Breda Gate. This took half-an-hour, for the station is out of the town. Then my uncle, after a hasty toilet, dragged me after him. The porter at the hotel could speak German and English; but the Professor, as a polyglot, questioned him in good Danish, and it was in the same language that that personage directed him to the Museum of Northern Antiquities.

The curator of this curious establishment, in which wonders are gathered together out of which the ancient history of the country might be reconstructed by means of its stone weapons, its cups and its jewels, was a learned savant, the friend of the Danish consul at Hamburg, Professor Thomsen.

My uncle had a cordial letter of introduction to him. As a general rule one savant greets another with coolness. But here the case was different. M. Thomsen, like a good friend, gave the Professor Liedenbrock a cordial greeting, and he even vouchsafed the same kindness to his nephew. It is hardly necessary to say the secret was sacredly kept from the excellent curator; we were simply disinterested travellers visiting Iceland out of harmless curiosity.

M. Thomsen placed his services at our disposal, and we visited the quays with the object of finding out the next vessel to sail.

I was yet in hopes that there would be no means of getting to Iceland. But there was no such luck. A small Danish schooner, the *Valkyria,* was to set sail for Rejkiavik on the 2d of June. The captain, M. Bjarne, was on board. His intending passenger was so joyful that he almost squeezed his hands till they ached. That good man was rather surprised at his energy. To him it seemed a very simple thing to go to Iceland, as that was his business; but to my uncle it was sublime. The worthy captain took advantage of his enthusiasm to charge double fares; but we did not trouble ourselves about mere trifles.

"You must be on board on Tuesday, at seven in the morning," said Captain Bjarne, after having pocketed more dollars than were his due.

Then we thanked M. Thomsen for his kindness, and we returned to the Phœnix Hotel.

"It's all right, it's all right," my uncle repeated. "How fortunate we are to have found this boat ready for sailing. Now let us have some breakfast and go about the town."

We went first to Kongens-nye-Torw, an irregular square in which are two innocent-looking guns, which need not alarm anyone. Close by, at No. 5, there was a French "restaurant," kept by a cook of the name of Vincent, where we had an ample breakfast for four marks each (2s. 4d.).

Then I took a childish pleasure in exploring the city; my uncle let me take him with me, but he took notice of nothing, neither the insignificant king's palace, nor the pretty seventeenth century bridge, which spans the canal before the museum, nor that immense cenotaph of Thorwaldsen's, adorned with horrible mural painting, and containing within it a collection of the sculptor's works, nor in a fine park the toylike chateau of Rosenberg, nor the beautiful renaissance edifice of the Exchange, nor its spire composed of the twisted tails of four bronze dragons, nor the great windmill on the ramparts, whose huge arms dilated in the sea-breeze like the sails of a ship.

What delicious walks we should have had together, my pretty Virlandaise and I, along the harbour where the two-deckers and the frigate slept peaceably by the red roofing of the warehouse, by the green banks of the strait, through the deep shades of the trees amongst which the fort is half concealed, where the guns are thrusting out their black throats between branches of alder and willow.

But, alas! Gräuben was far away; and I never hoped to see her again.

But if my uncle felt no attraction towards these romantic scenes he was very much struck with the aspect of a certain church spire situated in the island of Amak, which forms the south-west quarter of Copenhagen.

I was ordered to direct my feet that way; I embarked on a small steamer which plies on the canals, and in a few minutes she touched the quay of the dockyard.

After crossing a few narrow streets where some convicts, in trousers half yellow and half grey, were at work under the orders of the gangers, we arrived at the Vor Frelsers Kirk. There was nothing remarkable about the church; but there was a reason why its tall spire had attracted the Professor's attention. Starting from the top of the tower, an external staircase wound around the spire, the spirals circling up into the sky.

"Let us get to the top," said my uncle.

"I shall be dizzy," I said.

"The more reason why we should go up; we must get used to it."

"But—"

"Come, I tell you; don't waste our time."

I had to obey. A keeper who lived at the other end of the street handed us the key, and the ascent began.

My uncle went ahead with a light step. I followed him not without alarm, for my head was very apt to feel dizzy; I possessed neither the equilibrium of an eagle nor his fearless nature.

As long as we were protected on the inside of the winding staircase up the tower, all was well enough; but after toiling up a hundred and fifty steps the fresh air came to salute my face, and we were on the leads of the tower. There the aerial staircase began its gyrations, only guarded by a thin iron rail, and the narrowing steps seemed to ascend into infinite space!

"Never shall I be able to do it," I said.

"Don't be a coward; come up, sir"; said my uncle with the coldest cruelty.

I had to follow, clutching at every step. The keen air made me giddy; I felt the spire rocking with every gust of wind; my knees began to fail; soon I was crawling on my knees, then creeping on my stomach; I closed my eyes; I seemed to be lost in space.

At last I reached the apex, with the assistance of my uncle dragging me up by the collar.

"Look down!" he cried. "Look down well! You must take a lesson in abysses."

I opened my eyes. I saw houses squashed flat as if they had all fallen down from the skies; a smoke fog seemed to drown them. Over my head ragged clouds were drifting past, and by an optical inversion they seemed stationary, while the steeple, the ball and I were all spinning along with fantastic speed. Far away on one side was the green country, on the other the sea sparkled, bathed in sunlight. The Sound stretched away to Elsinore, dotted with a few white sails, like sea-gulls' wings; and in the misty east and away to the northeast lay outstretched the faintly-shadowed shores of Sweden. All this immensity of space whirled and wavered, fluctuating beneath my eyes.

But I was compelled to rise, to stand up, to look. My first lesson in dizziness lasted an hour. When I got permission to come down and feel the solid street pavements I was afflicted with severe lumbago.

"To-morrow we will do it again," said the Professor.

And it was so; for five days in succession, I was obliged to undergo this anti-vertiginous exercise; and whether I would or not, I made some improvement in the art of "lofty contemplations."

Chapter IX

ICELAND! BUT WHAT NEXT?

THE DAY FOR OUR DEPARTURE ARRIVED. THE DAY BEFORE IT OUR KIND FRIEND M. Thomsen brought us letters of introduction to Count Trampe, the Governor of Iceland, M. Picturssen, the bishop's suffragan, and M. Finsen, mayor of Rejkiavik. My uncle expressed his gratitude by tremendous compressions of both his hands.

On the 2d, at six in the evening, all our precious baggage being safely on board the *Valkyria,* the captain took us into a very narrow cabin.

"Is the wind favourable?" my uncle asked.

"Excellent," replied Captain Bjarne; "a sou'-easter. We shall pass down the Sound full speed, with all sails set."

In a few minutes the schooner, under her mizen, brigantine, topsail, and topgallant sail, loosed from her moorings and made full sail through the straits. In an hour the capital of Denmark seemed to sink below the distant waves, and the *Valkyria* was skirting the coast by Elsinore. In my nervous frame of mind I expected to see the ghost of Hamlet wandering on the legendary castle terrace.

"Sublime madman!" I said, "no doubt you would approve of our expedition. Perhaps you would keep us company to the center of the globe, to find the solution of your eternal doubts."

But there was no ghostly shape upon the ancient walls. Indeed, the castle is much younger than the heroic prince of Denmark. It now answers the purpose of a sumptuous lodge for the doorkeeper of the straits of the Sound, before which every year there pass fifteen thousand ships of all nations.

The castle of Kronsberg soon disappeared in the mist, as well as the tower of Helsingborg, built on the Swedish coast, and the schooner passed lightly on her way urged by the breezes of the Cattegat.

The *Valkyria* was a splendid sailer, but on a sailing vessel you can place no dependence. She was taking to Rejkiavik coal, household goods, earthenware, woollen clothing, and a cargo of wheat. The crew consisted of five men, all Danes.

"How long will the passage take?" my uncle asked.

"Ten days," the captain replied, "if we don't meet a nor'-wester in passing the Faroes."

"But are you not subject to considerable delays?"

"No, M. Liedenbrock, don't be uneasy, we shall get there in very good time."

At evening the schooner doubled the Skaw at the northern point of Denmark, in the night passed the Skager Rack, skirted Norway by Cape Lindness, and entered the North Sea.

In two days more we sighted the coast of Scotland near Peterhead, and the *Valkyria* turned her head towards the Faroe Islands, passing between the Orkneys and Shetlands.

Soon the schooner encountered the great Atlantic swell; she had to tack against the north wind, and reached the Faroes only with some difficulty. On the 8th the captain made out Myganness, the southernmost of these islands, and from that moment took a straight course for Cape Portland, the most southerly point of Iceland.

The passage was marked by nothing unusual. I bore the troubles of the sea pretty well; my uncle, to his own intense disgust and his greater shame, was ill all through the voyage.

He therefore was unable to converse with the captain about Snæfell, the way to get to it, the facilities for transport; he was obliged to put off these enquiries until his arrival, and spent all his time at full length in his cabin, of which the timbers creaked and shook with every pitch she took. It must be confessed he was not undeserving of his punishment.

On the 11th we reached Cape Portland. The clear open weather gave us a good view of Myrdals jokul, which overhangs it. The cape is merely a low hill with steep sides, standing lonely by the beach.

The *Valkyria* kept at some distance from the coast, taking a westerly course amidst great shoals of whales and sharks. Soon we came in sight of an enormous perforated rock, through which the sea dashed furiously. The Westman islets seemed to rise out of the ocean like a group of rocks in a liquid plain. From that time the schooner took a wide berth and swept at a great distance round Cape Rejkianess, which forms the western point of Iceland.

The rough sea prevented my uncle from coming on deck to admire these shattered and surf-beaten coasts.

Forty-eight hours after, coming out of a storm which forced the schooner to scud under bare poles, we sighted east of us the beacon on Cape Skagen, where dangerous rocks extend far away seaward. An Icelandic pilot came on board, and in three hours the *Valkyria* dropped her anchor before Rejkiavik, in Faxa Bay.

The Professor at last emerged from his cabin, rather pale and wretched-looking, but still full of enthusiasm, and with ardent satisfaction shining in his eyes.

The population of the town, wonderfully interested in the arrival of a vessel from which everyone expected something, formed in groups upon the quay.

My uncle left in haste his floating prison, or rather hospital. But before quitting the deck of the schooner he dragged me forward, and pointing with outstretched finger north of the bay at a distant mountain terminating in a double peak, a pair of cones covered with perpetual snow, he cried:

"Snæfell! Snæfell!"

Then recommending me, by an impressive gesture, to keep silence, he went into the boat which awaited him. I followed, and presently we were treading the soil of Iceland.

The first man we saw was a good-looking fellow enough, in a general's uniform. Yet he was not a general but a magistrate, the Governor of the island, M. le Baron Trampe himself. The Professor was soon aware of the presence he was in. He delivered him his letters from Copenhagen, and then followed a short conversation in the Danish language, the purport of which I was quite ignorant of, and for a very good reason. But the result of this first conversation was, that Baron Trampe placed himself entirely at the service of Professor Liedenbrock.

My uncle was just as courteously received by the mayor, M. Finsen, whose appearance was as military, and disposition and office as pacific, as the Governor's.

As for the bishop's suffragan, M. Picturssen, he was at that moment engaged on an episcopal visitation in the north. For the time we must be resigned to wait for the honour of being presented to him. But M. Fridrikssen, professor of natural sciences at the school of Rejkiavik, was a delightful man, and his friendship became very precious to me. This modest philosopher spoke only Danish and Latin. He came to proffer me his good offices in the language of Horace, and I felt that we were made to understand each other. In fact he was the only person in Iceland with whom I could converse at all.

This good-natured gentleman made over to us two of the three rooms which his house contained, and we were soon installed in it with all our luggage, the abundance of which rather astonished the good people of Rejkiavik.

"Well, Axel," said my uncle, "we are getting on, and now the worst is over."

"The worst!" I said, astonished.

"To be sure, now we have nothing to do but go down."

"Oh, if that is all, you are quite right; but after all, when we have gone down, we shall have to get up again, I suppose?"

"Oh I don't trouble myself about that. Come, there's no time to lose; I am going to the library. Perhaps there is some manuscript of Saknussemm's there, and I should be glad to consult it."

"Well, while you are there I will go into the town. Won't you?"

"Oh, that is very uninteresting to me. It is not what is upon this island, but what is underneath, that interests me."

I went out, and wandered wherever chance took me.

It would not be easy to lose your way in Rejkiavik. I was therefore under no necessity to enquire the road, which exposes one to mistakes when the only medium of intercourse is gesture.

The town extends along a low and marshy level, between two hills. An immense bed of lava bounds it on one side, and falls gently towards the sea. On the other extends the vast bay of Faxa, shut in at the north by the enormous glacier of the Snæfell, and of which the *Valkyria* was for the time the only occupant. Usually the English and French conservators of fisheries moor in this bay, but just then they were cruising about the western coasts of the island.

The longest of the only two streets that Rejkiavik possesses was parallel with the beach. Here live the merchants and traders, in wooden cabins made of red planks set horizontally; the other street, running west, ends at the little lake between the house of the bishop and other non-commercial people.

I had soon explored these melancholy ways; here and there I got a glimpse of faded turf, looking like a worn-out bit of carpet, or some appearance of a kitchen garden, the sparse vegetables of which (potatoes, cabbages, and lettuces), would have figured appropriately upon a Lilliputian table. A few sickly wallflowers were trying to enjoy the air and sunshine.

About the middle of the un-commercial street I found the public cemetery, enclosed with a mud wall, and where there seemed plenty of room.

Then a few steps brought me to the Governor's house, a hut compared with the town hall of Hamburg, a palace in comparison with the cabins of the Icelandic population.

Between the little lake and the town the church is built in the Protestant style, of calcined stones extracted out of the volcanoes by *their* own labour and at *their* own expense;

in high westerly winds it was manifest that the red tiles of the roof would be scattered in the air, to the great danger of the faithful worshippers.

On a neighbouring hill I perceived the national school, where, as I was informed later by our host, were taught Hebrew, English, French, and Danish, four languages of which, with shame I confess it, I don't know a single word; after an examination I should have had to stand last of the forty scholars educated at this little college, and I should have been held unworthy to sleep along with them in one of those little double closets, where more delicate youths would have died of suffocation the very first night.

In three hours I had seen not only the town but its environs. The general aspect was wonderfully dull. No trees, and scarcely any vegetation. Everywhere bare rocks, signs of volcanic action. The Icelandic huts are made of earth and turf, and the walls slope inward; they rather resemble roofs placed on the ground. But then these roofs are meadows of comparative fertility. Thanks to the internal heat, the grass grows on them to some degree of perfection. It is carefully mown in the hay season; if it were not, the horses would come to pasture on these green abodes.

In my excursion I met but few people. On returning to the main street I found the greater part of the population busied in drying, salting, and putting on board codfish, their chief export. The men looked like robust but heavy, blond Germans with pensive eyes, conscious of being far removed from their fellow creatures, poor exiles relegated to this land of ice, poor creatures who should have been Esquimaux, since nature had condemned them to live only just outside the arctic circle! In vain did I try to detect a smile upon their lips; sometimes by a spasmodic and involuntary contraction of the muscles they seemed to laugh, but they never smiled.

Their costume consisted of a coarse jacket of black woollen cloth called in Scandinavian lands a "vadmel," a hat with a very broad brim, trousers with a narrow edge of red, and a bit of leather rolled round the foot for shoes.

The women looked as sad and as resigned as the men; their faces were agreeable but expressionless, and they wore gowns and petticoats of dark "vadmel"; as maidens, they wore over their braided hair a little knitted brown cap; when married, they put around their heads a coloured handkerchief, crowned with a peak of white linen.

After a good walk I returned to M. Fridrikssen's house, where I found my uncle already in his host's company.

Chapter X

Interesting Conversations with Icelandic Savants

DINNER WAS READY. PROFESSOR LIEDENBROCK DEVOURED HIS PORTION VORACIOUSLY, for his compulsory fast on board had converted his stomach into a vast unfathomable gulf. There was nothing remarkable in the meal itself; but the hospitality of our host, more Danish than Icelandic, reminded me of the heroes of old. It was evident that we were more at home than he was himself.

The conversation was carried on in the vernacular tongue, which my uncle mixed with German and M. Fridrikssen with Latin for my benefit. It turned upon scientific questions as befits philosophers; but Professor Liedenbrock was excessively reserved, and at every sentence spoke to me with his eyes, enjoining the most absolute silence upon our plans.

In the first place M. Fridrikssen wanted to know what success my uncle had had at the library.

"Your library! why there is nothing but a few tattered books upon almost deserted shelves."

"Indeed!" replied M. Fridrikssen, "why we possess eight thousand volumes, many of them valuable and scarce, works in the old Scandinavian language, and we have all the novelties that Copenhagen sends us every year."

"Where do you keep your eight thousand volumes? For my part—"

"Oh, M. Liedenbrock, they are all over the country. In this icy region we are fond of study. There is not a farmer nor a fisherman that cannot read and does not read. Our principle is, that books, instead of growing mouldy behind an iron grating, should be worn out under the eyes of many readers. Therefore, these volumes are passed from one to another, read over and over, referred to again and again; and it often happens that they find their way back to their shelves only after an absence of a year or two."

"And in the meantime," said my uncle rather spitefully, "strangers—"

"Well, what would you have? Foreigners have their libraries at home, and the first essential for labouring people is that they should be educated. I repeat to you the love of reading runs in Icelandic blood. In 1816 we founded a prosperous literary society; learned strangers think themselves honoured in becoming members of it. It publishes books which educate our fellow-countrymen, and do the country great service. If you will consent to be a corresponding member, Herr Liedenbrock, you will be giving us great pleasure."

My uncle, who had already joined about a hundred learned societies, accepted with a grace which evidently touched M. Fridrikssen.

"Now," said he, "will you be kind enough to tell me what books you hoped to find in our library, and I may perhaps enable you to consult them?"

My uncle's eyes and mine met. He hesitated. This direct question went to the root of the matter. But after a moment's reflection he decided on speaking.

"Monsieur Fridrikssen, I wished to know if amongst your ancient books you possessed any of the works of Arne Saknussemm?"

"Arne Saknussemm!" replied the Rejkiavik professor. "You mean that learned sixteenth century savant, a naturalist, a chemist, and a traveller?"

"Just so!"

"One of the glories of Icelandic literature and science?"

"That's the man."

"An illustrious man anywhere!"

"Quite so."

"And whose courage was equal to his genius!"

"I see that you know him well."

My uncle was bathed in delight at hearing his hero thus described. He feasted his eyes upon M. Fridrikssen's face.

"Well," he cried, "where are his works?"

"His works, we have them not."

"What—not in Iceland?"

"They are neither in Iceland nor anywhere else."

"Why is that?"

"Because Arne Saknussemm was persecuted for heresy, and in 1573 his books were burned by the hands of the common hangman."

"Very good! Excellent!" cried my uncle, to the great scandal of the professor of natural history.

"What!" he cried.

"Yes, yes; now it is all clear, now it is all unravelled; and I see why Saknussemm, put into the Index Expurgatorius, and compelled to hide the discoveries made by his genius, was obliged to bury in an incomprehensible cryptogram the secret—"

"What secret?" asked M. Fridrikssen, starting.

"Oh, just a secret which—" my uncle stammered.

"Have you some private document in your possession?" asked our host.

"No; I was only supposing a case."

"Oh, very well," answered M. Fridrikssen, who was kind enough not to pursue the subject when he had noticed the embarrassment of his friend. "I hope you will not leave our island until you have seen some of its mineralogical wealth."

"Certainly," replied my uncle; "but I am rather late; or have not others been here before me?"

"Yes, Herr Liedenbrock; the labours of MM. Olafsen and Povelsen, pursued by order of the king, the researches of Troïl, the scientific mission of MM. Gaimard and Robert on the French corvette *La Recherche*,* and lately the observations of scientific men who came in the *Reine Hortense*, have added materially to our knowledge of Iceland. But I assure you there is plenty left."

"Do you think so?" said my uncle, pretending to look very modest, and trying to hide the curiosity that was flashing out of his eyes.

"Oh, yes; how many mountains, glaciers, and volcanoes there are to study, which are as yet but imperfectly known! Then, without going any further, see that mountain in the horizon. That is Snæfell."

"Ah!" said my uncle, as coolly as he was able, "is that Snæfell?"

"Yes; one of the most curious volcanoes, and the crater of which has scarcely ever been visited."

"Is it extinct?"

"Oh, yes; more than five hundred years."

"Well," replied my uncle, who was frantically locking his legs together to keep himself from jumping up in the air, "that is where I mean to begin my geological studies, there on that Seffel—Fessel—what do you call it?"

"Snæfell," replied the excellent M. Fridrikssen.

This part of the conversation was in Latin; I had understood every word of it, and I

---

*The *Recherche* was sent out in 1835 by Admiral Duperré to learn the fate of the lost expedition of M. de Blosseville in the *Lilloise* which has never been heard of.

could hardly conceal my amusement at seeing my uncle trying to keep down the excitement and satisfaction which were brimming over in every limb and every feature. He tried hard to put on an innocent little expression of simplicity; but it looked like a diabolical grin.

"Yes," said he, "your words decide me. We will try to scale that Snæfell; perhaps even we may pursue our studies in its crater!"

"I am very sorry," said M. Fridrikssen, "that my engagements will not allow me to absent myself, or I would have accompanied you myself with both pleasure and profit."

"Oh, no; no!" replied my uncle with great animation, "we would not disturb anyone for the world, M. Fridrikssen. Still, I thank you with all my heart: the company of such a talented man would have been very serviceable, but the duties of your profession—"

I am glad to think that our host, in the innocence of his Icelandic soul, was blind to the transparent artifices of my uncle.

"I very much approve of your beginning with that volcano, M. Liedenbrock. You will gather a harvest of interesting observations. But, tell me, how do you expect to get to the peninsula of Snæfell?"

"By sea, crossing the bay. That's the most direct way."

"No doubt; but it is impossible."

"Why?"

"Because we don't possess a single boat at Rejkiavik."

"You don't mean to say so?"

"You will have to go by land, following the shore. It will be longer, but more interesting."

"Very well, then; and now I shall have to see about a guide."

"I have one to offer you."

"A safe, intelligent man."

"Yes; an inhabitant of that peninsula. He is an eiderdown hunter, and very clever. He speaks Danish perfectly."

"When can I see him?"

"To-morrow, if you like."

"Why not to-day?"

"Because he won't be here till to-morrow."

"To-morrow, then," added my uncle with a sigh.

This momentous conversation ended in a few minutes with warm acknowledgments paid by the German to the Icelandic Professor. At this dinner my uncle had just elicited important facts, amongst others, the history of Saknussemm, the reason of the mysterious document, that his host would not accompany him in his expedition, and that the very next day a guide would be waiting upon him.

Chapter XI

A GUIDE FOUND TO THE CENTER OF THE EARTH

IN THE EVENING I TOOK A SHORT WALK ON THE BEACH AND RETURNED AT NIGHT TO MY plank-bed, where I slept soundly all night.

When I awoke I heard my uncle talking at a great rate in the next room. I immediately dressed and joined him.

He was conversing in the Danish language with a tall man, of robust build. This fine fellow must have been possessed of great strength. His eyes, set in a large and ingenuous face, seemed to me very intelligent; they were of a dreamy sea-blue. Long hair, which would have been called red even in England, fell in long meshes upon his broad shoulders. The movements of this native were lithe and supple; but he made little use of his arms in speaking, like a man who knew nothing or cared nothing about the language of gestures. His whole appearance bespoke perfect calmness and self-possession, not indolence but tranquility. It was felt at once that he would be beholden to nobody, that he worked for his own convenience, and that nothing in this world could astonish or disturb his philosophic calmness.

I caught the shades of this Icelander's character by the way in which he listened to the impassioned flow of words which fell from the Professor. He stood with arms crossed, perfectly unmoved by my uncle's incessant gesticulations. A negative was expressed by a slow movement of the head from left to right, an affirmative by a slight bend, so slight that his long hair scarcely moved. He carried economy of motion even to parsimony.

Certainly I should never have dreamed in looking at this man that he was a hunter; he did not look likely to frighten his game, nor did he seem as if he would even get near it. But the mystery was explained when M. Fridrikssen informed me that this tranquil personage was only a hunter of the eider duck, whose under plumage constitutes the chief wealth of the island. This is the celebrated eider down, and it requires no great rapidity of movement to get it.

Early in summer the female, a very pretty bird, goes to build her nest among the rocks of the fiords with which the coast is fringed. After building the nest she feathers it with down plucked from her own breast. Immediately the hunter, or rather the trader, comes and robs the nest, and the female recommences her work. This goes on as long as she has any down left. When she has stripped herself bare the male takes his turn to pluck himself. But as the coarse and hard plumage of the male has no commercial value, the hunter does not take the trouble to rob the nest of this; the female therefore lays her eggs in the spoils of her mate, the young are hatched, and next year the harvest begins again.

Now, as the eider duck does not select steep cliffs for her nest, but rather the smooth terraced rocks which slope to the sea, the Icelandic hunter might exercise his calling without any inconvenient exertion. He was a farmer who was not obliged either to sow or reap his harvest, but merely to gather it in.

This grave, phlegmatic, and silent individual was called Hans Bjelke; and he came recommended by M. Fridrikssen. He was our future guide. His manners were a singular contrast with my uncle's.

Nevertheless, they soon came to understand each other. Neither looked at the amount of the payment: the one was ready to accept whatever was offered; the other was ready to give whatever was demanded. Never was bargain more readily concluded.

The result of the treaty was, that Hans engaged on his part to conduct us to the village of Stapi, on the south shore of the Snæfell peninsula, at the very foot of the volcano. By land this would be about twenty-two miles, to be done, said my uncle, in two days.

But when he learned that the Danish mile was 24,000 feet long, he was obliged to modify his calculations and allow seven or eight days for the march.

Four horses were to be placed at our disposal—two to carry him and me, two for the baggage. Hams, as was his custom, would go on foot. He knew all that part of the coast perfectly, and promised to take us the shortest way.

His engagement was not to terminate with our arrival at Stapi; he was to continue in my uncle's service for the whole period of his scientific researches, for the remuneration of three rixdales a week (about twelve shillings), but it was an express article of the covenant that his wages should be counted out to him every Saturday at six o'clock in the evening, which, according to him, was one indispensable part of the engagement.

The start was fixed for the 16th of June. My uncle wanted to pay the hunter a portion in advance, but he refused with one word:

"*Efter,*" said he.

"After," said the Professor for my edification.

The treaty concluded, Hans silently withdrew.

"A famous fellow," cried my uncle; "but he little thinks of the marvellous part he has to play in the future."

"So he is to go with us as far as—"

"As far as the center of the earth, Axel."

Forty-eight hours were left before our departure; to my great regret I had to employ them in preparations; for all our ingenuity was required to pack every article to the best advantage; instruments here, arms there, tools in this package, provisions in that: four sets of packages in all.

The instruments were:

1. An Eigel's centigrade thermometer, graduated up to 150 degrees (302 degrees Fahr.), which seemed to me too much or too little. Too much if the internal heat was to rise so high, for in this case we should be baked, not enough to measure the temperature of springs or any matter in a state of fusion.

2. An aneroid barometer, to indicate extreme pressures of the atmosphere. An ordinary barometer would not have answered the purpose, as the pressure would increase during our descent to a point which the mercurial barometer* would not register.

3. A chronometer, made by Boissonnas, jun., of Geneva, accurately set to the meridan of Hamburg.

*In M. Verne's book a "manometer" is the instrument used, of which very little is known. In a complete list of philosophical instruments the translator cannot find the name. As he is assured by a first-rate instrument maker, Chadburn, of Liverpool, that an aneroid *can* be constructed to measure any depth, he has thought it best to furnish the adventurous professor with this more familiar instrument. The "manometer" is generally known as a pressure gauge.—TRANS.

4. Two compasses, viz., a common compass and a dipping needle.

5. A night-glass.

6. Two of Ruhmkorff's apparatus, which, by means of an electric current, supplied a safe and handy portable light.*

The arms consisted of two of Purdy's rifles and two brace of pistols. But what did we want arms for? We had neither savages nor wild beasts to fear, I supposed. But my uncle seemed to believe in his arsenal as in his instruments, and more especially in a considerable quantity of gun-cotton, which is unaffected by moisture, and the explosive force of which exceeds that of gunpowder.

The tools comprised two pickaxes, two spades, a silk rope-ladder, three iron-tipped sticks, a hatchet, a hammer, a dozen wedges and iron spikes, and a long knotted rope. Now this was a large load, for the ladder was 300 feet long.

And there were provisions too: this was not a large parcel, but it was comforting to know that of essence of beef and biscuits there were six months' consumption. Spirits were the only liquid, and of water we took none; but we had flasks, and my uncle depended on springs from which to fill them. Whatever objections I hazarded as to their quality, temperature, and even absence, remained ineffectual.

To complete the exact inventory of all our travelling accompaniments, I must not forget a pocket medicine chest, containing blunt scissors, splints for broken limbs, a piece of tape of unbleached linen, bandages and compresses, lint, a lancet for bleeding, all dreadful articles to take with one. Then there was a row of phials containing dextrine, alcoholic ether, liquid acetate of lead, vinegar, and ammonia, drugs which afforded me no comfort. Finally, all the articles needful to supply Ruhmkorff's apparatus.

My uncle did not forget a supply of tobacco, coarse grained powder, and amadou, nor a leathern belt in which he carried a sufficient quantity of gold, silver, and paper money. Six pairs of boots and shoes, made waterproof with a composition of India rubber and naphtha, were packed amongst the tools.

"Clothed, shod, and equipped like this," said my uncle, "there is no telling how far we may go."

The 14th was wholly spent in arranging all our different articles. In the evening we dined with Baron Trampe; the mayor of Rejkiavik, and Dr. Hyaltalin, the first medical man of the place, being of the party. M. Fridrikssen was not there. I learned afterwards that he and the Governor disagreed upon some question of administration, and did not

---

*Ruhmkorff's apparatus consists of a Bunsen pile worked with bichromate of potash, which makes no smell; an induction coil carries the electricity generated by the pile into communication with a lantern of peculiar construction; in this lantern there is a spiral glass tube from which the air has been excluded, and in which remains only a residuum of carbonic acid gas or of nitrogen. When the apparatus is put in action this gas becomes luminous, producing a white steady light. The pile and coil are placed in a leathern bag which the traveller carries over his shoulders; the lantern outside of the bag throws sufficient light into deep darkness; it enables one to venture without fear of explosions into the midst of the most inflammable gases, and is not extinguished even in the deepest waters. M. Ruhmkorff is a learned and most ingenious man of science; his great discovery is his induction coil, which produces a powerful stream of electricity. He obtained in 1864 the quinquennial prize of 50,000 francs reserved by the French government for the most ingenious application of electricity.

speak to each other. I therefore knew not a single word of all that was said at this semi-official dinner; but I could not help noticing that my uncle talked the whole time.

On the 15th our preparations were all made. Our host gave the Professor very great pleasure by presenting him with a map of Iceland far more complete than that of Hendersen. It was the map of M. Olaf Nikolas Olsen, in the proportion of 1 to 480,000 of the actual size of the island, and published by the Icelandic Literary Society. It was a precious document for a mineralogist.

Our last evening was spent in intimate conversation with M. Fridrikssen, with whom I felt the liveliest sympathy; then, after the talk, succeeded, for me, at any rate, a disturbed and restless night.

At five in the morning I was awoke by the neighing and pawing of four horses under my window. I dressed hastily and came down into the street. Hans was finishing our packing, almost as it were without moving a limb; and yet he did his work cleverly. My uncle made more noise than execution, and the guide seemed to pay very little attention to his energetic directions.

At six o'clock our preparations were over. M. Fridrikssen shook hands with us. My uncle thanked him heartily for his extreme kindness. I constructed a few fine Latin sentences to express my cordial farewell. Then we bestrode our steeds, and with his last adieu M. Fridrikssen treated me to a line of Virgil eminently applicable to such uncertain wanderers as we were likely to be:

Et quacumque viam dedent fortuna sequamur.

Wherever fortune clears a way,
Thither our ready footsteps stray.

Chapter XII

A Barren Land

WE HAD STARTED UNDER A SKY OVERCAST BUT CALM. THERE WAS NO FEAR OF HEAT, none of disastrous rain. It was just the weather for tourists.

The pleasure of riding on horseback over an unknown country made me easy to be pleased at our first start. I threw myself wholly into the pleasure of the trip, and enjoyed the feeling of freedom and satisfied desire. I was beginning to take a real share in the enterprise.

"Besides," I said to myself, "where's the risk? Here we are travelling all through a most interesting country! We are about to climb a very remarkable mountain; at the worst we are going to scramble down an extinct crater. It is evident that Saknussemm did nothing more than this. As for a passage leading to the center of the globe, it is mere rubbish! perfectly impossible! Very well, then; let us get all the good we can out of this expedition, and don't let us haggle about the chances."

This reasoning having settled my mind, we got out of Rejkiavik.

Hans moved steadily on, keeping ahead of us at an even, smooth, and rapid pace. The two baggage horses followed him without giving any trouble. Then came my uncle and myself, looking not so very ill-mounted on our small but hardy animals.

Iceland is one of the largest islands in Europe. Its surface is 14,000 square miles, and it contains but 16,000 inhabitants. Geographers have divided it into four quarters, and we were crossing diagonally the south-west quarter, called the "Sudvester Fjordungr."

On leaving Rejkiavik Hans took us by the seashore. We passed lean pastures which were trying very hard, but in vain, to look green; yellow came out best. The rugged peaks of the trachyte rocks presented faint outlines on the eastern horizon; at times a few patches of snow, concentrating the vague light, glittered upon the slopes of the distant mountains; certain peaks, boldly uprising, passed through the grey clouds, and reappeared above the moving mists, like breakers emerging in the heavens.

Often these chains of barren rocks made a dip towards the sea, and encroached upon the scanty pasturage; but there was always enough room to pass. Besides, our horses instinctively chose the easiest places without ever slackening their pace. My uncle was refused even the satisfaction of stirring up his beast with whip or voice. He had no excuse for being impatient. I could not help smiling to see so tall a man on so small a pony, and as his long legs nearly touched the ground he looked like a six-legged centaur.

"Good horse! good horse!" he kept saying. "You will see, Axel, that there is no more sagacious animal than the Icelandic horse. He is stopped by neither snow, nor storm, nor impassable roads, nor rocks, glaciers, or anything. He is courageous, sober, and surefooted. He never makes a false step, never shies. If there is a river or fiord to cross (and we shall meet with many) you will see him plunge in at once, just as if he were amphibious, and gain the opposite bank. But we must not hurry him; we must let him have his way, and we shall get on at the rate of thirty miles a day."

"*We* may; but how about our guide?"

"Oh, never mind him. People like him get over the ground without a thought. There is so little action in this man that he will never get tired; and besides, if he wants it, he shall have my horse. I shall get cramped if I don't have a little action. The arms are all right, but the legs want exercise."

We were advancing at a rapid pace. The country was already almost a desert. Here and there was a lonely farm, called a boër, built either of wood, or of sods, or of pieces of lava, looking like a poor beggar by the wayside. These ruinous huts seemed to solicit charity from passers-by; and on very small provocation we should have given alms for the relief of the poor inmates. In this country there were no roads and paths, and the poor vegetation, however slow, would soon efface the rare travellers' footsteps.

Yet this part of the province, at a very small distance from the capital, is reckoned among the inhabited and cultivated portions of Iceland. What, then, must other tracts be, more desert than this desert? In the first half mile we had not seen one farmer standing before his cabin door, nor one shepherd tending a flock less wild than himself, nothing but a few cows and sheep left to themselves. What then would be those convulsed regions upon which we were advancing, regions subject to the dire phenomena of irruptions, the offspring of volcanic explosions and subterranean convulsions?

We were to know them before long; but on consulting Olsen's map, I saw that they would be avoided by winding along the seashore. In fact, the great plutonic action is confined to the central portion of the island; there, rocks of the trappean and volcanic class, including trachyte, basalt, and tuffs and agglomerates associated with streams of lava, have made this a land of supernatural horrors. I had no idea of the spectacle which was awaiting us in the peninsula of Snæfell, where these ruins of a fiery nature have formed a frightful chaos.

In two hours from Rejkiavik we arrived at the burgh of Gufunes, called Aolkirkja, or principal church. There was nothing remarkable here but a few houses, scarcely enough for a German hamlet.

Hans stopped here half-an-hour. He shared with us our frugal breakfast; answering my uncle's questions about the road and our resting-place that night with merely yes or no, except when he said "Gardär."

I consulted the map to see where Gardär was. I saw there was a small town of that name on the banks of the Hvalfiord, four miles from Rejkiavik. I showed it to my uncle.

"Four miles only!" he exclaimed; "four miles out of twenty-eight. What a nice little walk!"

He was about to make an observation to the guide, who without answering resumed his place at the head, and went on his way.

Three hours later, still treading on the colourless grass of the pasture land, we had to work round the Kolla fiord, a longer way but an easier one than across that inlet. We soon entered into a "pingstaoer" or parish called Ejulberg, from whose steeple twelve o'clock would have struck, if Icelandic churches were rich enough to possess clocks. But they are like the parishioners who have no watches and do without.

There our horses were baited; then taking the narrow path left between a chain of hills and the sea, they carried us to our next stage, the aolkirkja of Brantär, and one mile farther on, to Saurboër "Annexia," a chapel of ease built on the south shore of the Hvalfiord.

It was now four o'clock, and we had gone four Icelandic miles, or twenty-four English miles.

In that place the fiord was at least three English miles wide; the waves rolled with a rushing din upon the sharp-pointed rocks; this inlet was confined between walls of rock, precipices crowned by sharp peaks 2,000 feet high, and remarkable for the brown strata which separated the beds of reddish tuff. However much I might respect the intelligence of our quadrupeds, I hardly cared to put it to the test by trusting myself to it on horseback across an arm of the sea.

If they are as intelligent as they are said to be, I thought, they won't try it. In any case, I will tax my intelligence to direct theirs.

But my uncle would not wait. He spurred on to the edge. His steed lowered his head to examine the nearest waves and stopped. My uncle, who had an instinct of his own, too, applied pressure, and was again refused by the animal significantly shaking his head. Then followed strong language, and the whip; but the brute answered these arguments with kicks and endeavours to throw his rider. At last the clever little pony, with a bend of his knees, started from under the Professor's legs, and left him standing upon two boulders on the shore just like the colossus of Rhodes.

"Confounded brute!" cried the unhorsed horseman, suddenly degraded into a pedestrian, just as ashamed as a cavalry officer degraded to a foot soldier.

"*Färja,*" said the guide, touching his shoulder.

"What! a boat?"

"*Der,*" replied Hans, pointing to one.

"Yes," I cried; "there is a boat."

"Why did not you say so then? Well, let us go on."

"*Tidvatten,*" said the guide.

"What is he saying?"

"He says tide," said my uncle, translating the Danish word.

"No doubt we must wait for the tide."

"*Förbida,*" said my uncle.

"*Ja,*" replied Hans.

My uncle stamped with his foot, while the horses went on to the boat.

I perfectly understood the necessity of abiding a particular moment of the tide to undertake the crossing of the fiord, when, the sea having reached its greatest height, it should be slack water. Then the ebb and flow have no sensible effect, and the boat does not risk being carried either to the bottom or out to sea.

That favourable moment arrived only with six o'clock; when my uncle, myself, the guide, two other passengers and the four horses, trusted ourselves to a somewhat fragile raft. Accustomed as I was to the swift and sure steamers on the Elbe, I found the oars of the rowers rather a slow means of propulsion. It took us more than an hour to cross the fiord; but the passage was effected without any mishap.

In another half-hour we had reached the aolkirkja of Gardär

Chapter XIII

Hospitality under the Artic Circle

IT OUGHT TO HAVE BEEN NIGHT-TIME, BUT UNDER THE 65TH PARALLEL THERE WAS NOTHing surprising in the nocturnal polar light. In Iceland during the months of June and July the sun does not set.

But the temperature was much lower. I was cold and more hungry than cold. Welcome was the sight of the boër which was hospitably opened to receive us.

It was a peasant's house, but in point of hospitality it was equal to a king's. On our arrival the master came with outstretched hands, and without more ceremony he beckoned us to follow him.

To accompany him down the long, narrow, dark passage, would have been impossible. Therefore, we followed, as he bid us. The building was constructed of roughly squared timbers, with rooms on both sides, four in number, all opening out into the one passage: these were the kitchen, the weaving shop, the badstofa, or family sleeping-room, and the visitors' room, which was the best of all. My uncle, whose height had not been thought of in building the house, of course hit his head several times against the beams that projected from the ceilings.

We were introduced into our apartment, a large room with a floor of earth stamped hard down, and lighted by a window, the panes of which were formed of sheep's bladder, not admitting too much light. The sleeping accommodation consisted of dry litter, thrown into two wooden frames painted red, and ornamented with Icelandic sentences. I was hardly expecting so much comfort; the only discomfort proceeded from the strong odour of dried fish, hung meat, and sour milk, of which my nose made bitter complaints.

When we had laid aside our travelling wraps the voice of the host was heard inviting us to the kitchen, the only room where a fire was lighted even in the severest cold.

My uncle lost no time in obeying the friendly call, nor was I slack in following.

The kitchen chimney was constructed on the ancient pattern; in the middle of the room was a stone for a hearth, over it in the roof a hole to let the smoke escape. The kitchen was also a dining-room.

At our entrance the host, as if he had never seen us, greeted us with the word *"Sæl-lvertu,"* which means "be happy," and came and kissed us on the cheek.

After him his wife pronounced the same words, accompanied with the same ceremonial; then the two placing their hands upon their hearts, inclined profoundly before us.

I hasten to inform the reader that this Icelandic lady was the mother of nineteen children, all, big and little, swarming in the midst of the dense wreaths of smoke with which the fire on the hearth filled the chamber. Every moment I noticed a fair-haired and rather melancholy face peeping out of the rolling volumes of smoke—they were a perfect cluster of unwashed angels.

My uncle and I treated this little tribe with kindness; and in a very short time we each had three or four of these brats on our shoulders, as many on our laps, and the rest between our knees. Those who could speak kept repeating *"Sællvertu"* in every conceivable tone; those that could not speak made up for that want by shrill cries.

This concert was brought to a close by the announcement of dinner. At that moment our hunter returned, who had been seeing his horses provided for; that is to say, he had economically let them loose in the fields, where the poor beasts had to content themselves with the scanty moss they could pull off the rocks and a few meagre sea-weeds, and the next day they would not fail to come of themselves and resume the labours of the previous day.

"Sællvertu," said Hans.

Then calmly, automatically, and dispassionately he kissed the host, the hostess, and their nineteen children.

This ceremony over, we sat at table, twenty-four in number, and therefore one upon another. The luckiest had only two urchins upon their knees.

But silence reigned in all this little world at the arrival of the soup, and the national taciturnity resumed its empire even over the children. The host served out to us a soup made of lichen and by no means unpleasant, then an immense piece of dried fish floating in butter rancid with twenty years' keeping, and, therefore, according to Icelandic gastronomy, much preferable to fresh butter. Along with this, we had "skye," a sort of clotted milk, with biscuits, and a liquid prepared from juniper berries; for beverage we had a thin milk mixed with water, called in this country "blanda." It is not for me to decide whether this diet is wholesome or not; all I can say is, that I was desperately hungry, and that at dessert I swallowed to the very last gulp of a thick broth made from buckwheat.

As soon as the meal was over the children disappeared, and their elders gathered round the peat fire, which also burned such miscellaneous fuel as briars, cow-dung, and fishbones. After this little pinch of warmth the different groups retired to their respective rooms. Our hostess hospitably offered us her assistance in undressing, according to Icelandic usage; but on our gracefully declining, she insisted no longer, and I was able at last to curl myself up in my mossy bed.

At five next morning we bade our host farewell, my uncle with difficulty persuading him to accept a proper remuneration; and Hans signalled the start.

At a hundred yards from Gardär the soil began to change its aspect; it became boggy and less favourable to progress. On our right the chain of mountains was indefinitely prolonged like an immense system of natural fortifications, of which we were following the counter-scarp or lesser steep; often we were met by streams, which we had to ford with great care, not to wet our packages.

The desert became wider and more hideous; yet from time to time we seemed to descry a human figure that fled at our approach, sometimes a sharp turn would bring us suddenly within a short distance of one of these spectres, and I was filled with loathing at the sight of a huge deformed head, the skin shining and hairless, and repulsive sores visible through the gaps in the poor creature's wretched rags.

The unhappy being forbore to approach us and offer his mis-shapen hand. He fled away, but not before Hans had saluted him with the customary *"Sællvertu."*

"Spetelsk," said he.

"A leper!" my uncle repeated.

This word produced a repulsive effect. The horrible disease of leprosy is too common in Iceland; it is not contagious, but hereditary, and lepers are forbidden to marry.

These apparitions were not cheerful, and did not throw any charm over the less and less attractive landscapes. The last tufts of grass had disappeared from beneath our feet. Not a tree was to be seen, unless we except a few dwarf birches as low as brushwood. Not an animal but a few wandering ponies that their owners would not feed. Sometimes we could see a hawk balancing himself on his wings under the grey cloud, and then darting away south with rapid flight. I felt melancholy under this savage aspect of nature, and my thoughts went away to the cheerful scenes I had left in the far south.

We had to cross a few narrow fiords, and at last quite a wide gulf; the tide, then high, allowed us to pass over without delay, and to reach the hamlet of Alftanes, one mile beyond.

That evening, after having forded two rivers full of trout and pike, called Alfa and Heta, we were obliged to spend the night in a deserted building worthy to be haunted by all the elfins of Scandinavia. The ice king certainly held court here, and gave us all night long samples of what he could do.

No particular event marked the next day. Bogs, dead levels, melancholy desert tracks, wherever we travelled. By nightfall we had accomplished half our journey, and we lay at Krösolbt.

On the 19th of June, for about a mile, that is an Icelandic mile, we walked upon hardened lava; this ground is called in the country "hraun"; the writhen surface presented the appearance of distorted, twisted cables, sometimes stretched in length, sometimes contorted together; an immense torrent, once liquid, now solid, ran from the nearest mountains, now extinct volcanoes, but the ruins around revealed the violence of the past irruptions. Yet here and there were a few jets of steam from hot springs.

We had no time to watch these phenomena; we had to proceed on our way. Soon at the foot of the mountains the boggy land reappeared, intersected by little lakes. Our route now lay westward; we had turned the great bay of Faxa, and the twin peaks of Snæfell rose white into the cloudy sky at the distance of at least five miles.

The horses did their duty well, no difficulties stopped them in their steady career. I was getting tired; but my uncle was as firm and straight as he was at our first start. I could not help admiring his persistency, as well as the hunter's, who treated our expedition like a mere promenade.

June 20. At six P.M. we reached Büdir, a village on the seashore; and the guide there claiming his due, my uncle settled with him. It was Hans' own family, that is, his uncles and cousins, who gave us hospitality; we were kindly received, and without taxing too much the goodness of these folks, I would willingly have tarried here to recruit after my fatigues. But my uncle, who wanted no recruiting, would not hear of it, and the next morning we had to bestride our beasts again.

The soil told of the neighbourhood of the mountain, whose granite foundations rose from the earth like the knotted roots of some huge oak. We were rounding the immense base of the volcano. The Professor hardly took his eyes off it. He tossed up his arms and seemed to defy it, and to declare, "There stands the giant that I shall conquer." After about four hours' walking the horses stopped of their own accord at the door of the priest's house at Stapi.

Chapter XIV

But Arctics Can Be Inhospitable, Too

STAPI IS A VILLAGE CONSISTING OF ABOUT THIRTY HUTS, BUILT OF LAVA, AT THE SOUTH side of the base of the volcano. It extends along the inner edge of a small fiord, enclosed between basaltic walls of the strangest construction.

Basalt is a brownish rock of igneous origin. It assumes regular forms, the arrangement of which is often very surprising. Here nature had done her work geometrically, with square and compass and plummet. Everywhere else her art consists alone in throwing down huge masses together in disorder. You see cones imperfectly formed, irregular pyramids, with a fantastic disarrangement of lines; but here, as if to exhibit an example of regularity, though in advance of the very earliest architects, she has created a severely simple order of architecture, never surpassed either by the splendours of Babylon or the wonders of Greece.

I had heard of the Giant's Causeway in Ireland, and Fingal's Cave in Staffa, one of the Hebrides; but I had never yet seen a basaltic formation.

At Stapi I beheld this phenomenon in all its beauty.

The wall that confined the fiord, like all the coast of the peninsula, was composed of a series of vertical columns thirty feet high. These straight shafts, of fair proportions, supported an architrave of horizontal slabs, the overhanging portion of which formed a semiarch over the sea. At intervals, under this natural shelter, there spread out vaulted entrances in beautiful curves, into which the waves came dashing with foam and spray. A few shafts of basalt, torn from their hold by the fury of tempests, lay along the soil like remains of an ancient temple, in ruins forever fresh, and over which centuries passed without leaving a trace of age upon them.

This was our last stage upon the earth. Hans had exhibited great intelligence, and it gave me some little comfort to think then that he was not going to leave us.

On arriving at the door of the rector's house, which was not different from the others, I saw a man shoeing a horse, hammer in hand, and with a leathern apron on.

"*Sællvertu,*" said the hunter.

"*God dag,*" said the blacksmith in good Danish.

"*Kyrkoherde,*" said Hans, turning round to my uncle.

"The rector," repeated the Professor. "It seems, Axel, that this good man is the rector."

Our guide in the meanwhile was making the "kyrkoherde" aware of the position of things; when the latter, suspending his labours for a moment, uttered a sound no doubt understood between horses and farriers, and immediately a tall and ugly hag appeared from the hut. She must have been six feet at the least. I was in great alarm lest she should treat me to the Icelandic kiss; but there was no occasion to fear, nor did she do the honours at all too gracefully.

The visitors' room seemed to me the worst in the whole cabin. It was close, dirty, and evil smelling. But we had to be content. The rector did not seem to go in for antique hospitality. Very far from it. Before the day was over I saw that we had to do with a blacksmith, a fisherman, a hunter, a joiner, but not at all with a minister of the Gospel. To be sure, it was a week-day; perhaps on a Sunday he made amends.

I don't mean to say anything against these poor priests, who after all are very wretched. They receive from the Danish Government a ridiculously small pittance, and they get from the parish the fourth part of the tithe, which does not come to sixty marks a year (about £4). Hence the necessity to work for their livelihood; but after fishing, hunting, and shoeing horses for any length of time, one soon gets into the ways and manners of fishermen, hunters, and farriers, and other rather rude and uncultivated people; and that evening I found out that temperance was not among the virtues that distinguished my host.

My uncle soon discovered what sort of a man he had to do with; instead of a good and learned man he found a rude and coarse peasant. He therefore resolved to commence the grand expedition at once, and to leave this inhospitable parsonage. He cared nothing about fatigue, and resolved to spend some days upon the mountain.

The preparations for our departure were therefore made the very day after our arrival at Stapi. Hans hired the services of three Icelanders to do the duty of the horses in the transport of the burdens; but as soon as we had arrived at the crater these natives were to turn back and leave us to our own devices. This was to be clearly understood.

My uncle now took the opportunity to explain to Hans that it was his intention to explore the interior of the volcano to its farthest limits.

Hans merely nodded. There or elsewhere, down in the bowels of the earth, or any-where on the surface, all was alike to him. For my own part the incidents of the journey had hitherto kept me amused, and made me forgetful of coming evils; but now my fears again were beginning to get the better of me. But what could I do? The place to resist the Professor would have been Hamburg, not the foot of Snæfell.

One thought, above all others, harassed and alarmed me; it was one calculated to shake firmer nerves than mine.

Now, thought I, here we are, about to climb Snæfell. Very good. We will explore the crater. Very good, too; others have done as much without dying for it. But that is not all. If there *is* a way to penetrate into the very bowels of the island, if that ill-advised Saknussemm has told a true tale, we shall lose our way amidst the deep subterranean pas-sages of this volcano. Now, there is no proof that Snæfell is extinct. Who can assure us that an irruption is not brewing at this very moment? Does it follow that because the monster has slept since 1229 he must therefore never awake again? And if he wakes up presently, where shall we be?

It was worthwhile debating this question, and I did debate it. I could not sleep for dreaming about irruptions. Now, the part of ejected scoriae and ashes seemed to my mind a very rough one to act.

So, at last, when I could hold out no longer, I resolved to lay the case before my uncle, as prudently and as cautiously as possible, just under the form of an almost impossible hypothesis.

I went to him. I communicated my fears to him, and drew back a step to give him room for the explosion which I knew must follow. But I was mistaken.

"I was thinking of that," he replied with great simplicity.

What could those words mean? Was he actually going to listen to reason? Was he con-templating the abandonment of his plans? This was too good to be true.

After a few moments' silence, during which I dared not question him, he resumed:

"I was thinking of that. Ever since we arrived at Stapi I have been occupied with the important question you have just opened, for we must not be guilty of imprudence."

"No, indeed!" I replied with forcible emphasis.

"For six hundred years Snæfell has been dumb; but he may speak again. Now, irrup-tions are always preceded by certain well-known phenomena. I have therefore examined the natives, I have studied external appearances, and I can assure you, Axel, that there will be no irruption."

At this positive affirmation I stood amazed and speechless.

"You don't doubt my word?" said my uncle. "Well, follow me."

I obeyed like an automaton. Coming out from the priest's house, the Professor took a straight road, which, through an opening in the basaltic wall, led away from the sea. We were soon in the open country, if one may give that name to a vast extent of mounds of volcanic products. This tract seemed crushed under a rain of enormous ejected rocks of trap, basalt, granite, and all kinds of igneous rocks.

Here and there I could see puffs and jets of steam curling up into the air, called in Ice-landic "reykir," issuing from thermal springs, and indicating by their violent motion the volcanic energy underneath. This seemed to justify my fears. But I fell from the height of my new-born hopes when my uncle said:

"You see all these volumes of steam, Axel; well, they demonstrate that we have nothing to fear from the fury of a volcanic irruption."

"Am I to believe that?" I cried.

"Understand this clearly," added the Professor. "At the approach of an irruption these jets would redouble their activity, but disappear altogether during the period of the irruption. For the elastic fluids, being no longer under pressure, go off by way of the crater instead of escaping by their usual passages through the fissures in the soil. Therefore, if these vapours remain in their usual condition, if they display no augmentation of force, and if you add to this the observation that the wind and rain are not ceasing and being replaced by a still and heavy atmosphere, then you may affirm that no irruption is preparing."

"But—"

"No more; that is sufficient. When science has uttered her voice, let babblers hold their peace."

I returned to the parsonage, very crestfallen. My uncle had beaten me with the weapons of science. Still I had one hope left, and this was, that when we had reached the bottom of the crater it would be impossible, for want of a passage, to go deeper, in spite of all the Saknussemm's in Iceland.

I spent that whole night in one constant nightmare; in the heart of a volcano, and from the deepest depths of the earth I saw myself tossed up amongst the interplanetary spaces under the form of an irruptive rock.

The next day, June 23, Hans was awaiting us with his companions carrying provisions, tools, and instruments; two iron-pointed sticks, two rifles, and two shot belts were for my uncle and myself. Hans, as a cautious man, had added to our luggage a leathern bottle full of water, which, with that in our flasks, would ensure us a supply of water for eight days.

It was nine in the morning. The priest and his tall Megæra were awaiting us at the door. We supposed they were standing there to bid us a kind farewell. But the farewell was put in the unexpected form of a heavy bill, in which everything was charged, even to the very air we breathed in the pastoral house, infected as it was. This worthy couple were fleecing us just as a Swiss innkeeper might have done, and estimated their imperfect hospitality at the highest price.

My uncle paid without a remark: a man who is starting for the center of the earth need not be particular about a few rix dollars.

This point being settled, Hans gave the signal, and we soon left Stapi behind us.

Chapter XV

SNÆFELL AT LAST

S NÆFELL IS 5,000 FEET HIGH. ITS DOUBLE CONE FORMS THE LIMIT OF A TRACHYTIC BELT which stands out distinctly in the mountain system of the island. From our starting point we could see the two peaks boldly projected against the dark grey sky; I could see an enormous cap of snow coming low down upon the giant's brow.

We walked in single file, headed by the hunter, who ascended by narrow tracks, where two could not have gone abreast. There was therefore no room for conversation.

After we had passed the basaltic wall of the fiord of Stapi we passed over a vegetable fibrous peat bog, left from the ancient vegetation of this peninsula. The vast quantity of this unworked fuel would be sufficient to warm the whole population of Iceland for a century; this vast turbary measured in certain ravines had in many places a depth of seventy feet, and presented layers of carbonised remains of vegetation alternating with thinner layers of tufaceous pumice.

As a true nephew of the Professor Liedenbrock, and in spite of my dismal prospects, I could not help observing with interest the mineralogical curiosities which lay about me as in a vast museum, and I constructed for myself a complete geological account of Iceland.

This most curious island has evidently been projected from the bottom of the sea at a comparatively recent date. Possibly, it may still be subject to gradual elevation. If this is the case, its origin may well be attributed to subterranean fires. Therefore, in this case, the theory of Sir Humphry Davy, Saknussemm's document, and my uncle's theories would all go off in smoke. This hypothesis led me to examine with more attention the appearance of the surface, and I soon arrived at a conclusion as to the nature of the forces which presided at its birth.

Iceland, which is entirely devoid of alluvial soil, is wholly composed of volcanic tufa, that is to say, an agglomeration of porous rocks and stones. Before the volcanoes broke out it consisted of trap rocks slowly upraised to the level of the sea by the action of central forces. The internal fires had not yet forced their way through.

But at a later period a wide chasm formed diagonally from south-west to north-east, through which was gradually forced out the trachyte which was to form a mountain chain. No violence accompanied this change; the matter thrown out was in vast quantities, and the liquid material oozing out from the abysses of the earth slowly spread in extensive plains or in hillocky masses. To this period belong the felspar, syenites, and porphyries.

But with the help of this outflow the thickness of the crust of the island increased materially, and therefore also its powers of resistance. It may easily be conceived what vast quantities of elastic gases, what masses of molten matter accumulated beneath its solid surface, whilst no exit was practicable after the cooling of the trachytic crust. Therefore a time would come when the elastic and explosive forces of the imprisoned gases would upheave this ponderous cover and drive out for themselves openings through tall chimneys. Hence then the volcano would distend and lift up the crust, and then burst through a crater suddenly formed at the summit or thinnest part of the volcano.

To the irruption succeeded other volcanic phenomena. Through the outlets now made first escaped the ejected basalt of which the plain we had just left presented such marvellous specimens. We were moving over grey rocks of dense and massive formation, which in cooling had formed into hexagonal prisms. Everywhere around us we saw truncated cones, formerly so many fiery mouths.

After the exhaustion of the basalt, the volcano, the power of which grew by the extinction of the lesser craters, supplied an egress to lava, ashes, and scoriae, of which I could see lengthened screes streaming down the sides of the mountain like flowing hair.

Such was the succession of phenomena which produced Iceland, all arising from the action of internal fire; and to suppose that the mass within did not still exist in a state of liquid incandescence was absurd; and nothing could surpass the absurdity of fancying that it was possible to reach the earth's center.

So I felt a little comforted as we advanced to the assault of Snæfell.

The way was growing more and more arduous, the ascent steeper and steeper; the loose fragments of rock trembled beneath us, and the utmost care was needed to avoid dangerous falls.

Hans went on as quietly as if he were on level ground; sometimes he disappeared altogether behind the huge blocks, then a shrill whistle would direct us on our way to him. Sometimes he would halt, pick up a few bits of stone, build them up into a recognisable form, and thus made landmarks to guide us in our way back. A very wise precaution in itself, but, as things turned out, quite useless.

Three hours' fatiguing march had only brought us to the base of the mountain. There Hans bid us come to a halt, and a hasty breakfast was served out. My uncle swallowed two mouthfuls at a time to get on faster. But, whether he liked it or not, this was a rest as well as a breakfast hour, and he had to wait till it pleased our guide to move on, which came to pass in an hour. The three Icelanders, just as taciturn as their comrade the hunter, never spoke, and ate their breakfasts in silence.

We were now beginning to scale the steep sides of Snæfell. Its snowy summit, by an optical illusion not unfrequent in mountains, seemed close to us, and yet how many weary hours it took to reach it! The stones, adhering by no soil or fibrous roots of vegetation, rolled away from under our feet, and rushed down the precipice below with the swiftness of an avalanche.

At some places the flanks of the mountain formed an angle with the horizon of at least 36 degrees; it was impossible to climb them, and these stony cliffs had to be tacked round, not without great difficulty. Then we helped each other with our sticks.

I must admit that my uncle kept as close to me as he could; he never lost sight of me, and in many straits his arm furnished me with a powerful support. He himself seemed to possess an instinct for equilibrium, for he never stumbled. The Icelanders, though burdened with our loads, climbed with the agility of mountaineers.

To judge by the distant appearance of the summit of Snæfell, it would have seemed too steep to ascend on our side. Fortunately, after an hour of fatigue and athletic exercises, in the midst of the vast surface of snow presented by the hollow between the two peaks, a kind of staircase appeared unexpectedly which greatly facilitated our ascent. It was formed by one of those torrents of stones flung up by the irruptions, called "stina" by the Icelanders. If this torrent had not been arrested in its fall by the formation of the sides of the mountain, it would have gone on to the sea and formed more islands.

Such as it was, it did us good service. The steepness increased, but these stone steps allowed us to rise with facility, and even with such rapidity that, having rested for a moment while my companions continued their ascent, I perceived them already reduced by distance to microscopic dimensions.

At seven we had ascended the two thousand steps of this grand staircase, and we had attained a bulge in the mountain, a kind of bed on which rested the cone proper of the crater.

Three thousand two hundred feet below us stretched the sea. We had passed the limit of perpetual snow, which, on account of the moisture of the climate, is at a greater elevation in Iceland than the high latitude would give reason to suppose. The cold was excessively keen. The wind was blowing violently. I was exhausted. The Professor saw that my limbs were refusing to perform their office, and in spite of his impatience he decided on stopping. He therefore spoke to the hunter, who shook his head, saying:

"*Ofvanför.*"

"It seems we must go higher," said my uncle.

Then he asked Hans for his reason.

"*Mistour,*" replied the guide.

"*Ja Mistour,*" said one of the Icelanders in a tone of alarm.

"What does that word mean?" I asked uneasily.

"Look!" said my uncle.

I looked down upon the plain. An immense column of pulverised pumice, sand and dust was rising with a whirling circular motion like a water-spout; the wind was lashing it on to that side of Snæfell where we were holding on; this dense veil, hung across the sun, threw a deep shadow over the mountain. If that huge revolving pillar sloped down, it would involve us in its whirling eddies. This phenomenon, which is not unfrequent when the wind blows from the glaciers, is called in Icelandic "mistour."

"*Hastigt! hastigt!*" cried our guide.

Without knowing Danish I understood at once that we must follow Hans at the top of our speed. He began to circle round the cone of the crater, but in a diagonal direction so as to facilitate our progress. Presently the dust storm fell upon the mountain, which quivered under the shock; the loose stones, caught with the irresistible blasts of wind, flew about in a perfect hail as in an irruption. Happily we were on the opposite side, and sheltered from all harm. But for the precaution of our guide, our mangled bodies, torn and pounded into fragments, would have been carried afar like the ruins hurled along by some unknown meteor.

Yet Hans did not think it prudent to spend the night upon the sides of the cone. We continued our zigzag climb. The fifteen hundred remaining feet took us five hours to clear; the circuitous route, the diagonal and the counter marches, must have measured at least three leagues. I could stand it no longer. I was yielding to the effects of hunger and cold. The rarefied air scarcely gave play to the action of my lungs.

At last, at eleven in the sunlight night, the summit of Snæfell was reached, and before going in for shelter into the crater I had time to observe the midnight sun, at his lowest point, gilding with his pale rays the island that slept at my feet.

Chapter XVI

Boldly Down the Crater

Supper was rapidly devoured, and the little company housed themselves as best they could. The bed was hard, the shelter not very substantial, and our position an anxious one, at five thousand feet above the sea level. Yet I slept particularly well; it was one of the best nights I had ever had, and I did not even dream.

Next morning we awoke half frozen by the sharp keen air, but with the light of a splendid sun. I rose from my granite bed and went out to enjoy the magnificent spectacle that lay unrolled before me.

I stood on the very summit of the southernmost of Snæfell's peaks. The range of the eye extended over the whole island. By an optical law which obtains at all great heights, the shores seemed raised and the center depressed. It seemed as if one of Helbesmer's raised maps lay at my feet. I could see deep valleys intersecting each other in every direction, precipices like low walls, lakes reduced to ponds, rivers abbreviated into streams. On my right were numberless glaciers and innumerable peaks, some plumed with feathery clouds of smoke. The undulating surface of these endless mountains, crested with sheets of snow, reminded one of a stormy sea. If I looked westward, there the ocean lay spread out in all its magnificence, like a mere continuation of those flock-like summits. The eye could hardly tell where the snowy ridges ended and the foaming waves began.

I was thus steeped in the marvellous ecstasy which all high summits develop in the mind; and now without giddiness, for I was beginning to be accustomed to these sublime aspects of nature. My dazzled eyes were bathed in the bright flood of the solar rays. I was forgetting where and who I was, to live the life of elves and sylphs, the fanciful creation of Scandinavian superstitions. I felt intoxicated with the sublime pleasure of lofty elevations without thinking of the profound abysses into which I was shortly to be plunged. But I was brought back to the realities of things by the arrival of Hans and the Professor, who joined me on the summit.

My uncle pointed out to me in the far west a light steam or mist, a semblance of land, which bounded the distant horizon of waters.

"Greenland!" said he.

"Greenland?" I cried.

"Yes; we are only thirty-five leagues from it; and during thaws the white bears, borne by the ice fields from the north, are carried even into Iceland. But never mind that. Here we are at the top of Snæfell and here are two peaks, one north and one south. Hans will tell us the name of that on which we are now standing."

The question being put, Hans replied:

"Scartaris."

My uncle shot a triumphant glance at me.

"Now for the crater!" he cried.

The crater of Snæfell resembled an inverted cone, the opening of which might be half a league in diameter. Its depth appeared to be about two thousand feet. Imagine the aspect of such a reservoir, brim full and running over with liquid fire amid the rolling thunder. The bottom of the funnel was about 250 feet in circuit, so that the gentle slope allowed its lower brim to be reached without much difficulty. Involuntarily I compared the whole crater to an enormous erected mortar, and the comparison put me in a terrible fright.

"What madness," I thought, "to go down into a mortar, perhaps a loaded mortar, to be shot up into the air at a moment's notice!"

But I did not try to back out of it. Hans with perfect coolness resumed the lead, and I followed him without a word.

In order to facilitate the descent, Hans wound his way down the cone by a spiral path. Our route lay amidst irruptive rocks, some of which, shaken out of their loosened beds, rushed bounding down the abyss, and in their fall awoke echoes remarkable for their loud and well-defined sharpness.

In certain parts of the cone there were glaciers. Here Hans advanced only with extreme precaution, sounding his way with his iron-pointed pole, to discover any crevasses in it. At particularly dubious passages we were obliged to connect ourselves with each other by a long cord, in order that any man who missed his footing might be held up by his companions. This solid formation was prudent, but did not remove all danger.

Yet, notwithstanding the difficulties of the descent, down steeps unknown to the guide, the journey was accomplished without accidents, except the loss of a coil of rope, which escaped from the hands of an Icelander, and took the shortest way to the bottom of the abyss.

At midday we arrived. I raised my head and saw straight above me the upper aperture of the cone, framing a bit of sky of very small circumference, but almost perfectly round. Just upon the edge appeared the snowy peak of Scartaris, standing out sharp and clear against endless space.

At the bottom of the crater were three chimneys, through which, in its irruptions, Snæfell had driven forth fire and lava from its central furnace. Each of these chimneys was a hundred feet in diameter. They gaped before us right in our path. I had not the courage to look down either of them. But Professor Liedenbrock had hastily surveyed all three; he was panting, running from one to the other, gesticulating, and uttering incoherent expressions. Hans and his comrades, seated upon loose lava rocks, looked at him with as much wonder as they knew how to express, and perhaps taking him for an escaped lunatic.

Suddenly my uncle uttered a cry. I thought his foot must have slipped and that he had fallen down one of the holes. But, no; I saw him, with arms outstretched, and legs straddling wide apart, erect before a granite rock that stood in the center of the crater, just like a pedestal made ready to receive a statue of Pluto. He stood like a man stupefied, but the stupefaction soon gave way to delirious rapture.

"Axel, Axel," he cried. "Come, come!"

I ran. Hans and the Icelanders never stirred.

"Look!" cried the Professor.

And, sharing his astonishment, but I think not his joy, I read on the western face of the block, in Runic characters, half mouldered away with lapse of ages, this thrice-accursed name:

ᛏᛂᚾᛁ ᛋᛁᚴᛐᚾᛋᛋᛁᚵ

"Arne Saknussemm!" replied my uncle. "Do you yet doubt?"

I made no answer; and I returned in silence to my lava seat in a state of utter speechless consternation. Here was crushing evidence.

How long I remained plunged in agonizing reflections I cannot tell; all that I know is, that on raising my head again, I saw only my uncle and Hans at the bottom of the crater. The Icelanders had been dismissed, and they were now descending the outer slopes of Snæfell to return to Stapi.

Hans slept peaceably at the foot of a rock, in a lava bed, where he had found a suitable couch for himself; but my uncle was pacing around the bottom of the crater like a wild beast in a cage. I had neither the wish nor the strength to rise, and following the guide's example I went off into an unhappy slumber, fancying I could hear ominous noises or feel tremblings within the recesses of the mountain.

Thus the first night in the crater passed away.

The next morning, a grey, heavy, cloudy sky seemed to droop over the summit of the cone. I did not know this first from the appearances of nature, but I found it out by my uncle's impetuous wrath.

I soon found out the cause, and hope dawned again in my heart. For this reason.

Of the three ways open before us, one had been taken by Saknussemm. The indications of the learned Icelander hinted at in the cryptogram, pointed to this fact that the shadow of Scartaris came to touch that particular way during the latter days of the month of June.

That sharp peak might hence be considered as the gnomon of a vast sun dial, the shadow projected from which on a certain day would point out the road to the center of the earth.

Now, no sun no shadow, and therefore no guide. Here was June 25. If the sun was clouded for six days we must postpone our visit till next year.

My limited powers of description would fail, were I to attempt a picture of the Professor's angry impatience. The day wore on, and no shadow came to lay itself along the bottom of the crater. Hans did not move from the spot he had selected; yet he must be asking himself what were we waiting for, if he asked himself anything at all. My uncle spoke not a word to me. His gaze, ever directed upwards, was lost in the grey and misty space beyond.

On the 26th nothing yet. Rain mingled with snow was falling all day long. Hans built a hut of pieces of lava. I felt a malicious pleasure in watching the thousand rills and cascades that came tumbling down the sides of the cone, and the deafening continuous din awaked by every stone against which they bounded.

My uncle's rage knew no bounds. It was enough to irritate a meeker man than he; for it was foundering almost within the port.

But Heaven never sends unmixed grief, and for Professor Liedenbrock there was a satisfaction in store proportioned to his desperate anxieties.

The next day the sky was again overcast; but on the 29th of June, the last day but one of the month, with the change of the moon came a change of weather. The sun poured a flood of light down the crater. Every hillock, every rock and stone, every projecting surface, had its share of the beaming torrent, and threw its shadow on the ground. Amongst them all, Scartaris laid down his sharp-pointed angular shadow which began to move slowly in the opposite direction to that of the radiant orb.

My uncle turned too, and followed it.

At noon, being at its least extent, it came and softly fell upon the edge of the middle chimney.

"There it is! there it is!" shouted the Professor. "Now for the center of the globe!" he added in Danish.

I looked at Hans, to hear what he would say.

"Forüt!" was his tranquil answer.

"Forward!" replied my uncle.

It was thirteen minutes past one.

Chapter XVII

VERTICAL DESCENT

NOW BEGAN OUR REAL JOURNEY. HITHERTO OUR TOIL HAD OVERCOME ALL DIFFICUL-ties, now difficulties would spring up at every step.

I had not yet ventured to look down the bottomless pit into which I was about to take a plunge. The supreme hour had come. I might now either share in the enterprise or refuse to move forward. But I was ashamed to recoil in the presence of the hunter. Hans accepted the enterprise with such calmness, such indifference, such perfect disregard of any possible danger, that I blushed at the idea of being less brave than he. If I had been alone I might have once more tried the effect of argument; but in the presence of the guide I held my peace; my heart flew back to my sweet Virlandaise, and I approached the central chimney.

I have already mentioned that it was a hundred feet in diameter, and three hundred feet round. I bent over a projecting rock and gazed down. My hair stood on end with terror. The bewildering feeling of vacuity laid hold upon me. I felt my center of gravity shifting its place, and giddiness mounting into my brain like drunkenness. There is nothing more treacherous than this attraction down deep abysses. I was just about to drop down, when a hand laid hold of me. It was that of Hans. I suppose I had not taken as many lessons on gulf exploration as I ought to have done in the Frelsers Kirk at Copenhagen.

But, however short was my examination of this well, I had taken some account of its conformation. Its almost perpendicular walls were bristling with innumerable projections which would facilitate the descent. But if there was no want of steps, still there was no rail. A rope fastened to the edge of the aperture might have helped us down. But how were we to unfasten it, when arrived at the other end?

My uncle employed a very simple expedient to obviate this difficulty. He uncoiled a cord of the thickness of a finger, and four hundred feet long; first he dropped half of it down, then he passed it round a lava block that projected conveniently, and threw the other half down the chimney. Each of us could then descend by holding with the hand both halves of the rope, which would not be able to unroll itself from its hold; when two hundred feet down, it would be easy to get possession of the whole of the rope by letting one end go and pulling down by the other. Then the exercise would go on again *ad infinitum*.

"Now," said my uncle, after having completed these preparations, "now let us look to our loads. I will divide them into three lots; each of us will strap one upon his back. I mean only fragile articles."

Of course, we were not included under that head.

"Hans," said he, "will take charge of the tools and a portion of the provisions; you, Axel, will take another third of the provisions, and the arms; and I will take the rest of the provisions and the delicate instruments."

"But," said I, "the clothes, and that mass of ladders and ropes, what is to become of them?"

"They will go down by themselves."

"How so?" I asked.

"You will see presently."

My uncle was always willing to employ magnificent resources. Obeying orders, Hans tied all the non-fragile articles in one bundle, corded them firmly, and sent them bodily down the gulf before us.

I listened to the dull thuds of the descending bale. My uncle, leaning over the abyss, followed the descent of the luggage with a satisfied nod, and only rose erect when he had quite lost sight of it.

"Very well, now it is our turn."

Now I ask any sensible man if it was possible to hear those words without a shudder.

The Professor fastened his package of instruments upon his shoulders; Hans took the tools; I took the arms: and the descent commenced in the following order; Hans, my uncle, and myself. It was effected in profound silence, broken only by the descent of loosened stones down the dark gulf.

I dropped as it were, frantically clutching the double cord with one hand and buttressing myself from the wall with the other by means of my stick. One idea overpowered me almost, fear lest the rock should give way from which I was hanging. This cord seemed a fragile thing for three persons to be suspended from. I made as little use of it as possible, performing wonderful feats of equilibrium upon the lava projections which my foot seemed to catch hold of like a hand.

When one of these slippery steps shook under the heavier form of Hans, he said in his tranquil voice:

"*Gif akt!*"

"Attention!" repeated my uncle.

In half-an-hour we were standing upon the surface of a rock jammed in across the chimney from one side to the other.

Hans pulled the rope by one of its ends, the other rose in the air; after passing the higher rock it came down again, bringing with it a rather dangerous shower of bits of stone and lava.

Leaning over the edge of our narrow standing ground, I observed that the bottom of the hole was still invisible.

The same maneuvre was repeated with the cord, and half-an-hour after we had descended another two hundred feet.

I don't suppose the maddest geologist under such circumstances would have studied the nature of the rocks that we were passing. I am sure I did trouble my head about them.

Pliocene, miocene, eocene, cretaceous, jurassic, triassic, permian, carboniferous, devonian, silurian, or primitive was all one to me. But the Professor, no doubt, was pursuing his observations or taking notes, for in one of our halts he said to me:

"The farther I go the more confidence I feel. The order of these volcanic formations affords the strongest confirmation to the theories of Davy. We are now among the primitive rocks, upon which the chemical operations took place which are produced by the contact of elementary bases of metals with water. I repudiate the notion of central heat altogether. We shall see further proof of that very soon."

No variation, always the same conclusion. Of course, I was not inclined to argue. My silence was taken for consent and the descent went on.

Another three hours, and I saw no bottom to the chimney yet. When I lifted my head I perceived the gradual contraction of its aperture. Its walls, by a gentle incline, were drawing closer to each other, and it was beginning to grow darker.

Still we kept descending. It seemed to me that the falling stones were meeting with an earlier resistance, and that the concussion gave a more abrupt and deadened sound.

As I had taken care to keep an exact account of our maneuvres with the rope, which I knew that we had repeated fourteen times, each descent occupying half-an-hour, the conclusion was easy that we had been seven hours, plus fourteen quarters of rest, making ten hours and a half. We had started at one, it must therefore now be eleven o'clock; and the depth to which we had descended was fourteen times 200 feet, or 2,800 feet.

At this moment I heard the voice of Hans.

"Halt!" he cried.

I stopped short just as I was going to place my feet upon my uncle's head.

"We are there," he cried.

"Where?" said I, stepping near to him.

"At the bottom of the perpendicular chimney," he answered.

"Is there no way farther?"

"Yes; there is a sort of passage which inclines to the right. We will see about that to-morrow. Let us have our supper, and go to sleep."

The darkness was not yet complete. The provision case was opened; we refreshed ourselves, and went to sleep as well as we could upon a bed of stones and lava fragments.

When lying on my back, I opened my eyes and saw a bright sparkling point of light at the extremity of the gigantic tube 3,000 feet long, now a vast telescope.

It was a star which, seen from this depth, had lost all scintillation, and which by my computation should be 3 *Ursa minor*. Then I fell fast asleep.

Chapter XVIII

THE WONDERS OF TERRESTRIAL DEPTHS

AT EIGHT IN THE MORNING A RAY OF DAYLIGHT CAME TO WAKE US UP. THE THOUSAND shining surfaces of lava on the walls received it on its passage, and scattered it like a shower of sparks.

There was light enough to distinguish surrounding objects.

"Well, Axel, what do you say to it?" cried my uncle, rubbing his hands. "Did you ever spend a quieter night in our little house at Königsberg? No noise of cart wheels, no cries of basket women, no boatmen shouting!"

"No doubt it is very quiet at the bottom of this well, but there is something alarming in the quietness itself."

"Now come!" my uncle cried; "if you are frightened already, what will you be by and by? We have not gone a single inch yet into the bowels of the earth."

"What do you mean?"

"I mean that we have only reached the level of the island. This long vertical tube, which terminates at the mouth of the crater, has its lower end only at the level of the sea."

"Are you sure of that?"

"Quite sure. Consult the barometer."

In fact, the mercury, which had risen in the instrument as fast as we descended, had stopped at twenty-nine inches.

"You see," said the Professor, "we have now only the pressure of our atmosphere, and I shall be glad when the aneroid takes the place of the barometer."

And in truth this instrument would become useless as soon as the weight of the atmosphere should exceed the pressure ascertained at the level of the sea.

"But," I said, "is there not reason to fear that this ever-increasing pressure will become at last very painful to bear?"

"No; we shall descend at a slow rate, and our lungs will become inured to a denser atmosphere. Aeronauts find the want of air as they rise to high elevations, but we shall perhaps have too much: of the two, this is what I should prefer. Don't let us lose a moment. Where is the bundle we sent down before us?"

I then remembered that we had searched for it in vain the evening before. My uncle questioned Hans, who, after having examined attentively with the eye of a huntsman, replied:

"*Der huppe!*"

"Up there."

And so it was. The bundle had been caught by a projection a hundred feet above us. Immediately the Icelander climbed up like a cat, and in a few minutes the package was in our possession.

"Now," said my uncle, "let us breakfast; but we must lay in a good stock, for we don't know how long we may have to go on."

The biscuit and extract of meat were washed down with a draught of water mingled with a little gin.

Breakfast over, my uncle drew from his pocket a small note-book, intended for scientific observations. He consulted his instruments, and recorded:

Monday, July 1.
Chronometer, 8:17 A.M.; barometer, 29.7 in.; thermometer, 6° (43° F.). Direction, E.S.E.

This last observation applied to the dark gallery, and was indicated by the compass.

"Now, Axel," cried the Professor with enthusiasm, "now we are really going into the interior of the earth. At this precise moment the journey commences."

So saying, my uncle took in one hand Ruhmkorff's apparatus, which was hanging from his neck; and with the other he formed an electric communication with the coil in the lantern, and a sufficiently bright light dispersed the darkness of the passage.

Hans carried the other apparatus, which was also put into action. This ingenious application of electricity would enable us to go on for a long time by creating an artificial light even in the midst of the most inflammable gases.

"Now, march!" cried my uncle.

Each shouldered his package. Hans drove before him the load of cords and clothes; and, myself walking last, we entered the gallery.

At the moment of becoming engulfed in this dark gallery, I raised my head, and saw for the last time through the length of that vast tube the sky of Iceland, which I was never to behold again.

The lava, in the last irruption of 1229, had forced a passage through this tunnel. It still lined the walls with a thick and glistening coat. The electric light was here intensified a hundredfold by reflection.

The only difficulty in proceeding lay in not sliding too fast down an incline of about forty-five degrees; happily certain asperities and a few blisterings here and there formed steps, and we descended, letting our baggage slip before us from the end of a long rope.

But that which formed steps under our feet became stalactites overhead. The lava, which was porous in many places, had formed a surface covered with small rounded blisters; crystals of opaque quartz, set with limpid tears of glass, and hanging like clustered chandeliers from the vaulted roof, seemed as it were to kindle and form a sudden illumination as we passed on our way. It seemed as if the genii of the depths were lighting up their palace to receive their terrestrial guests.

"It is magnificent!" I cried spontaneously. "My uncle, what a sight! Don't you admire those blending hues of lava, passing from reddish brown to bright yellow by imperceptible shades? And these crystals are just like globes of light."

"Ah, you think so, do you, Axel, my boy? Well, you will see greater splendours than these, I hope. Now let us march: march!"

He had better have said slide, for we did nothing but drop down the steep inclines. It was the *facilis descensus Averni* of Virgil. The compass, which I consulted frequently, gave our direction as south-east with inflexible steadiness. This lava stream deviated neither to the right nor to the left.

Yet there was no sensible increase of temperature. This justified Davy's theory, and more than once I consulted the thermometer with surprise. Two hours after our departure it only marked 10° (50° Fahr.), an increase of only 4°. This gave reason for believing that our descent was more horizontal than vertical. As for the exact depth reached, it was very easy to ascertain that; the Professor measured accurately the angles of deviation and inclination on the road, but he kept the results to himself.

About eight in the evening he signalled to stop. Hans sat down at once. The lamps were hung upon a projection in the lava; we were in a sort of cavern where there was plenty of air. Certain puffs of air reached us. What atmospheric disturbance was the cause of them? I could not answer that question at the moment. Hunger and fatigue made me incapable of reasoning. A descent of seven hours consecutively is not made without considerable expenditure of strength. I was exhausted. The order to "halt" therefore gave me pleasure. Hans laid our provisions upon a block of lava, and we ate with a good appetite. But one thing troubled me, our supply of water was half consumed. My uncle reckoned upon a fresh supply from subterranean sources, but hitherto we had met with none. I could not help drawing his attention to this circumstance.

"Are you surprised at this want of springs?" he said.

"More than that, I am anxious about it; we have only water enough for five days."

"Don't be uneasy, Axel, we shall find more than we want."

"When?"

"When we have left this bed of lava behind us. How could springs break through such walls as these?"

"But perhaps this passage runs to a very great depth. It seems to me that we have made no great progress vertically."

"Why do you suppose that?"

"Because if we had gone deep into the crust of the earth, we should have encountered greater heat."

"According to your system," said my uncle. "But what does the thermometer say?"

"Hardly fifteen degrees (59° Fahr.), nine degrees only since our departure."

"Well, what is your conclusion?"

"This is my conclusion. According to exact observations, the increase of temperature in the interior of the globe advances at the rate of one degree (1⅘° Fahr.) for every hundred feet. But certain local conditions may modify this rate. Thus at Yakoutsk in Siberia the increase of a degree is ascertained to be reached every 36 feet. This difference depends upon the heat-conducting power of the rocks. Moreover, in the neighbourhood of an extinct volcano, through gneiss, it has been observed that the increase of a degree is only attained at every 125 feet. Let us therefore assume this last hypothesis as the most suitable to our situation, and calculate."

"Well, do calculate, my boy."

"Nothing is easier," said I, putting down figures in my note-book. "Nine times a hundred and twenty-five feet gives a depth of eleven hundred and twenty-five feet."

"Very accurate indeed."

"Well?"

"By my observation we are at 10,000 feet below the level of the sea."

"Is that possible?"

"Yes, or figures are of no use."

The Professor's calculations were quite correct. We had already attained a depth of six thousand feet beyond that hitherto reached by the foot of man, such as the mines of Kitz Bahl in Tyrol, and those of Wuttembourg in Bohemia.

The temperature, which ought to have been 81° (178° Fahr.) was scarcely 15° (59° Fahr.). Here was cause for reflection.

Chapter XIX

GEOLOGICAL STUDIES IN SITU

NEXT DAY, TUESDAY, JUNE 30, AT 6 A.M., THE DESCENT BEGAN AGAIN.
We were still following the gallery of lava, a real natural staircase, and as gently sloping as those inclined planes which in some old houses are still found instead of flights of steps. And so we went on until 12:17, the precise moment when we overtook Hans, who had stopped.

"Ah! here we are," exclaimed my uncle, "at the very end of the chimney."

I looked around me. We were standing at the intersection of two roads, both dark and narrow. Which were we to take? This was a difficulty.

Still my uncle refused to admit an appearance of hesitation, either before me or the guide; he pointed out the Eastern tunnel, and we were soon all three in it.

Besides there would have been interminable hesitation before this choice of roads; for since there was no indication whatever to guide our choice, we were obliged to trust to chance.

The slope of this gallery was scarcely perceptible, and its sections very unequal. Sometimes we passed a series of arches succeeding each other like the majestic arcades of a gothic cathedral. Here the architects of the middle ages might have found studies for every form of the sacred art which sprang from the development of the pointed arch. A mile farther we had to bow or heads under corniced elliptic arches in the romanesque style; and massive pillars standing out from the wall bent under the spring of the vault that rested heavily upon them. In other places this magnificence gave way to narrow channels between low structures which looked like beaver's huts, and we had to creep along through extremely narrow passages.

The heat was perfectly bearable. Involuntarily I began to think of its heat when the lava thrown out by Snæfell was boiling and working through this now silent road. I imagined the torrents of fire hurled back at every angle in the gallery, and the accumulation of intensely heated vapours in the midst of this confined channel.

I only hope, thought I, that this so-called extinct volcano won't take a fancy in his old age to begin his sports again!

I abstained from communicating these fears to Professor Liedenbrock. He would never have understood them at all. He had but one idea—forward! He walked, he slid, he scrambled, he tumbled, with a persistency which one could not but admire.

By six in the evening, after a not very fatiguing walk, we had gone two leagues south, but scarcely a quarter of a mile down.

My uncle said it was time to go to sleep. We ate without talking, and went to sleep without reflection.

Our arrangements for the night were very simple; a railway rug each, into which we rolled ourselves, was our sole covering. We had neither cold nor intrusive visits to fear. Travellers who penetrate into the wilds of central Africa, and into the pathless forests of the New World, are obliged to watch over each other by night. But we enjoyed absolute safety and utter seclusion; no savages or wild beasts infested these silent depths.

Next morning, we awoke fresh and in good spirits. The road was resumed. As the day before, we followed the path of the lava. It was impossible to tell what rocks we were passing: the tunnel, instead of tending lower, approached more and more nearly to a horizontal direction, I even fancied a slight rise. But about ten this upward tendency became so evident, and therefore so fatiguing, that I was obliged to slacken my pace.

"Well, Axel?" demanded the Professor impatiently.

"Well, I cannot stand it any longer," I replied.

"What! after three hours' walk over such easy ground."

"It may be easy, but it is tiring all the same."

"What, when we have nothing to do but keep going down!"

"Going up, if you please."

"Going up!" said my uncle, with a shrug.

"No doubt, for the last half-hour the inclines have gone the other way, and at this rate we shall soon arrive upon the level soil of Iceland."

The Professor nodded slowly and uneasily like a man that declines to be convinced. I tried to resume the conversation. He answered not a word, and gave the signal for a start. I saw that his silence was nothing but ill-humour.

Still I had courageously shouldered my burden again, and was rapidly following Hans, whom my uncle preceded. I was anxious not to be left behind. My greatest care was not to lose sight of my companions. I shuddered at the thought of being lost in the mazes of this vast subterranean labyrinth.

Besides, if the ascending road did become steeper, I was comforted with the thought that it was bringing us nearer to the surface. There was hope in this. Every step confirmed me in it, and I was rejoicing at the thought of meeting my little Gräuben again.

By midday there was a change in the appearance of this wall of the gallery. I noticed it by a diminution of the amount of light reflected from the sides; solid rock was appearing in the place of the lava coating. The mass was composed of inclined and sometimes vertical strata. We were passing through rocks of the transition or silurian* system.

"It is evident," I cried, "the marine deposits formed in the second period, these shales, limestones, and sandstones. We are turning away from the primary granite. We are just as if we were people of Hamburg going to Lubeck by way of Hanover!"

I had better have kept my observations to myself. But my geological instinct was stronger than my prudence, and uncle Liedenbrock heard my exclamation.

"What's that you are saying?" he asked.

---

*The name given by Sir Roderick Murchison to a vast series of fossiliferous strata, which lies between the non-fossiliferous slaty schists below and the old red sandstone above. The system is well developed in the region of Shropshire, etc., once inhabited by the Silures under Caractacus, or Caradoc. (Tr.)

"See," I said, pointing to the varied series of sandstones and limestones, and the first indication of slate.

"Well?"

"We are at the period when the first plants and animals appeared."

"Do you think so?"

"Look close, and examine."

I obliged the Professor to move his lamp over the walls of the gallery. I expected some signs of astonishment; but he spoke not a word, and went on.

Had he understood me or not? Did he refuse to admit, out of self-love as an uncle and a philosopher, that he had mistaken his way when he chose the eastern tunnel? or was he determined to examine this passage to its farthest extremity? It was evident that we had left the lava path, and that this road could not possibly lead to the extinct furnace of Snæfell.

Yet I asked myself if I was not depending too much on this change in the rock. Might I not myself be mistaken? Were we really crossing the layers of rock which overlie the granite foundation?

If I am right, I thought, I must soon find some fossil remains of primitive life; and then we must yield to evidence. I will look.

I had not gone a hundred paces before incontestable proofs presented themselves. It could not be otherwise, for in the silurian age the seas contained at least fifteen hundred vegetable and animal species. My feet, which had become accustomed to the indurated lava floor, suddenly rested upon a dust composed of the debris of plants and shells. In the walls were distinct impressions of fucoids and lycopodites.

Professor Liedenbrock could not be mistaken, I thought, and yet he pushed on, with, I suppose, his eyes resolutely shut.

This was only invincible obstinacy. I could hold out no longer. I picked up a perfectly formed shell, which had belonged to an animal not unlike the woodlouse: then, joining my uncle, I said:

"Look at this!"

"Very well," said he quietly, "it is the shell of a crustacean, of an extinct species called a trilobite. Nothing more."

"But don't you conclude—?"

"Just what you conclude yourself. Yes; I do, perfectly. We have left the granite and the lava. It is possible that I may be mistaken. But I cannot be sure of that until I have reached the very end of this gallery."

"You are right in doing this, my uncle, and I should quite approve of your determination, if there were not a danger threatening us nearer and nearer."

"What danger?"

"The want of water."

"Well, Axel, we will put ourselves upon rations."

Chapter XX

THE FIRST SIGNS OF DISTRESS

IN FACT, WE HAD TO RATION OURSELVES. OUR PROVISION OF WATER COULD NOT LAST more than three days. I found that out for certain when supper-time came. And, to our sorrow, we had little reason to expect to find a spring in these transition beds.

The whole of the next day the gallery opened before us its endless arcades. We moved on almost without a word. Hans' silence seemed to be infecting us.

The road was now not ascending, at least not perceptibly. Sometimes, even, it seemed to have a slight fall. But this tendency, which was very trifling, could not do anything to reassure the Professor; for there was no change in the beds, and the transitional characteristics became more and more decided.

The electric light was reflected in sparkling splendour from the schist, limestone, and old red sandstone of the walls. It might have been thought that we were passing through a section of Wales, of which an ancient people gave its name to this system. Specimens of magnificent marbles clothed the walls, some of a greyish agate fantastically veined with white, others of rich crimson or yellow dashed with splotches of red; then came dark cherry-coloured marbles relieved by the lighter tints of limestone.

The greater part of these bore impressions of primitive organisms. Creation had evidently advanced since the day before. Instead of rudimentary trilobites, I noticed remains of a more perfect order of beings, amongst others ganoid fishes and some of those sauroids in which palaeontologists have discovered the earliest reptile forms. The Devonian seas were peopled by animals of these species, and deposited them by thousands in the rocks of the newer formation.

It was evident that we were ascending that scale of animal life in which man fills the highest place. But Professor Liedenbrock seemed not to notice it.

He was awaiting one of two events, either the appearance of a vertical well opening before his feet, down which our descent might be resumed, or that of some obstacle which should effectually turn us back on our own footsteps. But evening came and neither wish was gratified.

On Friday, after a night during which I felt the first pangs of thirst, our little troop again plunged into the winding passages of the gallery.

After ten hours' walking I observed a singular deadening of the reflection of our lamps from the side walls. The marble, the schist, the limestone, and the sandstone were giving way to a dark and lustreless lining. At one moment, the tunnel becoming very narrow, I leaned against the wall.

When I removed my hand it was black. I looked nearer, and found we were in a coal formation.

"A coal mine!" I cried.

"A mine without miners," my uncle replied.

"Who knows?" I asked.

"I know," the Professor pronounced decidedly; "I am certain that this gallery driven through beds of coal was never pierced by the hand of man. But whether it be the hand of nature or not does not matter. Suppertime is come; let us sup."

Hans prepared some food. I scarcely ate, and I swallowed down the few drops of water rationed out to me. One flask half full was all we had left to slake the thirst of three men.

After their meal my two companions laid themselves down upon their rugs, and found in sleep a solace for their fatigue. But I could not sleep, and I counted every hour until morning.

On Saturday, at six, we started afresh. In twenty minutes we reached a vast open space; I then knew that the hand of man had not hollowed out this mine; the vaults would have been shored up, and, as it was, they seemed to be held up by a miracle of equilibrium.

This cavern was about a hundred feet wide and a hundred and fifty in height. A large mass had been rent asunder by a subterranean disturbance. Yielding to some vast power from below it had broken asunder, leaving this great hollow into which human beings were now penetrating for the first time.

The whole history of the carboniferous period was written upon these gloomy walls, and a geologist might with ease trace all its diverse phases. The beds of coal were separated by strata of sandstone or compact clays, and appeared crushed under the weight of overlying strata.

At the age of the world which preceded the secondary period, the earth was clothed with immense vegetable forms, the product of the double influence of tropical heat and constant moisture; a vapoury atmosphere surrounded the earth, still veiling the direct rays of the sun.

Thence arises the conclusion that the high temperature then existing was due to some other source than the heat of the sun. Perhaps even the orb of day may not have been ready yet to play the splendid part he now acts. There were no "climates" as yet, and a torrid heat, equal from pole to equator, was spread over the whole surface of the globe. Whence this heat? Was it from the interior of the earth?

Notwithstanding the theories of Professor Liedenbrock, a violent heat did at that time brood within the body of the spheroid. Its action was felt to the very last coats of the terrestrial crust; the plants, unacquainted with the beneficent influences of the sun, yielded neither flowers nor scent. But their roots drew vigorous life from the burning soil of the early days of this planet.

There were but few trees. Herbaceous plants alone existed. There were tall grasses, ferns, lycopods, besides sigillaria, asterophyllites, now scarce plants, but then the species might be counted by thousands.

The coal measures owe their origin to this period of profuse vegetation. The yet elastic and yielding crust of the earth obeyed the fluid forces beneath. Thence innumerable fissures and depressions. The plants, sunk underneath the waters, formed by degrees into vast accumulated masses.

Then came the chemical action of nature; in the depths of the seas the vegetable accumulations first became peat; then, acted upon by generated gases and the heat of fermentation, they underwent a process of complete mineralization.

Thus were formed those immense coalfields, which nevertheless, are not inexhaustible, and which three centuries at the present accelerated rate of consumption will exhaust unless the industrial world will devise a remedy.

These reflections came into my mind whilst I was contemplating the mineral wealth stored up in this portion of the globe. These no doubt, I thought, will never be discovered; the working of such deep mines would involve too large an outlay, and where would be the use as long as coal is yet spread far and wide near the surface? Such as my eyes behold these virgin stores, such they will be when this world comes to an end.

But still we marched on, and I alone was forgetting the length of the way by losing myself in the midst of geological contemplations. The temperature remained what it had been during our passage through the lava and schists. Only my sense of smell was forcibly affected by an odour of protocarburet of hydrogen. I immediately recognised in this gallery the presence of a considerable quantity of the dangerous gas called by miners firedamp, the explosion of which has often occasioned such dreadful catastrophes.

Happily, our light was from Ruhmkorff's ingenious apparatus. If unfortunately we had explored this gallery with torches, a terrible explosion would have put an end to travelling and travellers at one stroke.

This excursion through the coal mine lasted till night. My uncle scarcely could restrain his impatience at the horizontal road. The darkness, always deep twenty yards before us, prevented us from estimating the length of the gallery; and I was beginning to think it must be endless, when suddenly at six o'clock a wall very unexpectedly stood before us. Right or left, top or bottom, there was no road farther; we were at the end of a blind alley.

"Very well, it's all right!" cried my uncle, "now, at any rate, we shall know what we are about. We are not in Saknussemm's road, and all we have to do is to go back. Let us take a night's rest, and in three days we shall get to the fork in the road."

"Yes," said I, "if we have any strength left."

"Why not?"

"Because to-morrow we shall have no water."

"Nor courage either?" asked my uncle severely.

I dared make no answer.

Chapter XXI

COMPASSION FUSES THE PROFESSOR'S HEART

NEXT DAY WE STARTED EARLY. WE HAD TO HASTEN FORWARD. IT WAS A THREE DAYS' march to the cross roads.

I will not speak of the sufferings we endured in our return. My uncle bore them with the angry impatience of a man obliged to own his weakness; Hans with the resignation of his passive nature; I, I confess, with complaints and expressions of despair. I had no spirit to oppose this ill fortune.

As I had foretold, the water failed entirely by the end of the first day's retrograde march. Our fluid aliment was now nothing but gin; but this infernal fluid burned my throat, and I could not even endure the sight of it. I found the temperature and the air stifling. Fatigue paralysed my limbs. More than once I dropped down motionless. Then there was a halt; and my uncle and the Icelander did their best to restore me. But I saw that the former was struggling painfully against excessive fatigue and the tortures of thirst.

At last, on Tuesday, July 8, we arrived on our hands and knees, and half dead, at the junction of the two roads. There I dropped like a lifeless lump, extended on the lava soil. It was ten in the morning.

Hans and my uncle, clinging to the wall, tried to nibble a few bits of biscuit. Long moans escaped from my swollen lips.

After some time my uncle approached me and raised me in his arms.

"Poor boy!" said he, in genuine tones of compassion.

I was touched with these words, not being accustomed to see the excitable Professor in a softened mood. I grasped his trembling hands in mine. He let me hold them and looked at me. His eyes were moistened.

Then I saw him take the flask that was hanging at his side. To my amazement he placed it on my lips.

"Drink!" said he.

Had I heard him? Was my uncle beside himself? I stared at him stupidly, and felt as if I could not understand him.

"Drink!" he said again.

And raising his flask he emptied it every drop between my lips.

Oh! infinite pleasure! a slender sip of water came to moisten my burning mouth. It was but one sip but it was enough to recall my ebbing life.

I thanked my uncle with clasped hands.

"Yes," he said, "a draught of water; but it is the very last—you hear!—the last. I had kept it as a precious treasure at the bottom of my flask. Twenty times, nay, a hundred times, have I fought against a frightful impulse to drink it off. But no, Axel, I kept it for you."

"My dear uncle," I said, whilst hot tears trickled down my face.

"Yes, my poor boy, I knew that as soon as you arrived at these cross roads you would drop half dead, and I kept my last drop of water to reanimate you."

"Thank you, thank you," I said. Although my thirst was only partially quenched, yet some strength had returned. The muscles of my throat, until then contracted, now relaxed again; and the inflammation of my lips abated somewhat; and I was now able to speak.

"Let us see," I said, "we have now but one thing to do. We have no water; we must go back."

While I spoke my uncle avoided looking at me; he hung his head down; his eyes avoided mine.

"We must return," I exclaimed vehemently; "we must go back on our way to Snæfell. May God give us strength to climb up the crater again!"

"Return!" said my uncle, as if he was rather answering himself than me.

"Yes, return, without the loss of a minute."

A long silence followed.

"So then, Axel," replied the Professor ironically, "you have found no courage or energy in these few drops of water?"

"Courage?"

"I see you just as feeble-minded as you were before, and still expressing only despair!"

What sort of a man was this I had to do with, and what schemes was he now revolving in his fearless mind?

"What! you won't go back?"

"Should I renounce this expedition just when we have the fairest chance of success! Never!"

"Then must we resign ourselves to destruction?"

"No, Axel, no; go back. Hans will go with you. Leave me to myself!"

"Leave you here!"

"Leave me, I tell you. I have undertaken this expedition. I will carry it out to the end, and I will not return. Go, Axel, go!"

My uncle was in high state of excitement. His voice, which had for a moment been tender and gentle, had now become hard and threatening. He was struggling with gloomy resolutions against impossibilities. I would not leave him in this bottomless abyss, and on the other hand the instinct of self-preservation prompted me to fly.

The guide watched this scene with his usual phlegmatic unconcern. Yet he understood perfectly well what was going on between his two companions. The gestures themselves were sufficient to show that we were each bent on taking a different road; but Hans seemed to take no part in a question upon which depended his life. He was ready to start at a given signal, or to stay, if his master so willed it.

How I wished at this moment I could have made him understand me. My words, my complaints, my sorrow would have had some influence over that frigid nature. Those dangers which our guide could not understand I could have demonstrated and proved to him. Together we might have over-ruled the obstinate Professor; if it were needed, we might perhaps have compelled him to regain the heights of Snæfell.

I drew near to Hans. I placed my hand upon his. He made no movement. My parted lips sufficiently revealed my sufferings. The Icelander slowly moved his head, and calmly pointing to my uncle said: "Master."

"Master!" I shouted; "you madman! no, he is not the master of our life; we must fly, we must drag him. Do you hear me? Do you understand?"

I had seized Hans by the arm. I wished to oblige him to rise. I strove with him. My uncle interposed.

"Be calm, Axel! you will get nothing from that immovable servant. Therefore, listen to my proposal."

I crossed my arms, and confronted my uncle boldly.

"The want of water," he said, "is the only obstacle in our way. In this eastern gallery made up of lavas, schists, and coal, we have not met with a single particle of moisture. Perhaps we shall be more fortunate if we follow the western tunnel."

I shook my head incredulously.

"Hear me to the end," the Professor went on with a firm voice. "Whilst you were lying there motionless, I went to examine the conformation of that gallery. It penetrates directly downward, and in a few hours it will bring us to the granite rocks. There we must meet with abundant springs. The nature of the rock assures me of this, and instinct agrees with logic to support my conviction. Now, this is my proposal. When Columbus asked of his ships' crews for three days more to discover a new world, those crews, disheartened and sick as they were, recognised the justice of the claim, and he discovered America. I am the Columbus of this nether world, and I only ask for one more day. If in a single day I have not met with the water that we want, I swear to you we will return to the surface of the earth."

In spite of my irritation I was moved with these words, as well as with the violence my uncle was doing to his own wishes in making so hazardous a proposal.

"Well," I said, "do as you will, and God reward your superhuman energy. You have now but a few hours to tempt fortune. Let us start!"

Chapter XXII

TOTAL FAILURE OF WATER

THIS TIME THE DESCENT COMMENCED BY THE NEW GALLERY. HANS WALKED FIRST AS was his custom.

We had not gone a hundred yards when the Professor, moving his lantern along the walls, cried:

"Here are primitive rocks. Now we are in the right way. Forward!"

When in its early stages the earth was slowly cooling, its contraction gave rise in its crust to disruptions, distortions, fissures, and chasms. The passage through which we were moving was such a fissure, through which at one time granite poured out in a molten state. Its thousands of windings formed an inextricable labyrinth through the primeval mass.

As fast as we descended, the succession of beds forming the primitive foundation came out with increasing distinctness. Geologists consider this primitive matter to be the base of the mineral crust of the earth, and have ascertained it to be composed of three different formations, schist, gneiss, and mica schist, resting upon that unchangeable foundation, the granite.

Never had mineralogists found themselves in so marvellous a situation to study nature *in situ.* What the boring machine, an insensible, inert instrument, was unable to bring to the surface of the inner structure of the globe, we were able to peruse with our own eyes and handle with our own hands.

Through the beds of schist, coloured with delicate shades of green, ran in winding course threads of copper and manganese, with traces of platinum and gold. I thought, what riches are here buried at an unapproachable depth in the earth, hidden forever from the covetous eyes of the human race! These treasures have been buried at such a profound depth by the convulsions of primeval times that they run no chance of ever being molested by the pickaxe or the spade.

To the schists succeeded gneiss, partially stratified, remarkable for the parallelism and regularity of its lamina, then mica schists, laid in large plates or flakes, revealing their lamellated structure by the sparkle of the white shining mica.

The light from our apparatus, reflected from the small facets of quartz, shot sparkling rays at every angle, and I seemed to be moving through a diamond, within which the quickly darting rays broke across each other in a thousand flashing coruscations.

About six o'clock this brilliant fête of illuminations underwent a sensible abatement of splendour, then almost ceased. The walls assumed a crystallised though sombre appearance; mica was more closely mingled with the feldspar and quartz to form the proper rocky foundations of the earth, which bears without distortion or crushing the weight of the four terrestrial systems. We were immured within prison walls of granite.

It was eight in the evening. No signs of water had yet appeared. I was suffering horribly. My uncle strode on. He refused to stop. He was listening anxiously for the murmur of distant springs. But, no, there was dead silence.

And now my limbs were failing beneath me. I resisted pain and torture, that I might not stop my uncle, which would have driven him to despair, for the day was drawing near to its end, and it was his last.

At last I failed utterly; I uttered a cry and fell.

"Come to me, I am dying."

My uncle retraced his steps. He gazed upon me with his arms crossed; then these muttered words passed his lips:

"It's all over!"

The last thing I saw was a fearful gesture of rage, and my eyes closed.

When I reopened them I saw my two companions motionless and rolled up in their coverings. Were they asleep? As for me, I could not get one moment's sleep. I was suffering too keenly, and what embittered my thoughts was that there was no remedy. My uncle's last words echoed painfully in my ears: "it's all over!" For in such a fearful state of debility it was madness to think of ever reaching the upper world again.

We had above us a league and a half of terrestrial crust. The weight of it seemed to be crushing down upon my shoulders. I felt weighed down, and I exhausted myself with imaginary violent exertions to turn round upon my granite couch.

A few hours passed away. A deep silence reigned around us, the silence of the grave. No sound could reach us through walls, the thinnest of which were five miles thick.

Yet in the midst of my stupefaction I seemed to be aware of a noise. It was dark down the tunnel, but I seemed to see the Icelander vanishing from our sight with the lamp in his hand.

Why was he leaving us? Was Hans going to forsake us? My uncle was fast asleep. I wanted to shout, but my voice died upon my parched and swollen lips. The darkness became deeper, and the last sound died away in the far distance.

"Hans has abandoned us," I cried. "Hans! Hans!"

But these words were only spoken within me. They went no farther. Yet after the first moment of terror I felt ashamed of suspecting a man of such extraordinary faithfulness. Instead of ascending he was descending the gallery. An evil design would have taken him up not down. This reflection restored me to calmness, and I turned to other thoughts. None but some weighty motive could have induced so quiet a man to forfeit his sleep. Was he on a journey of discovery? Had he during the silence of the night caught a sound, a murmuring of something in the distance, which had failed to affect my hearing?

Chapter XXIII

WATER DISCOVERED

FOR A WHOLE HOUR I WAS TRYING TO WORK OUT IN MY DELIRIOUS BRAIN THE REASONS which might have influenced this seemingly tranquil huntsman. The absurdest notions ran in utter confusion through my mind. I thought madness was coming on!

But at last a noise of footsteps was heard in the dark abyss. Hans was approaching. A flickering light was beginning to glimmer on the wall of our darksome prison; then it came out full at the mouth of the gallery. Hans appeared.

He drew close to my uncle, laid his hand upon his shoulder, and gently woke him. My uncle rose up.

"What is the matter?" he asked.

"*Watten!*" replied the huntsman.

No doubt under the inspiration of intense pain everybody becomes endowed with the gift of divers tongues. I did not know a word of Danish, yet instinctively I understood the word he had uttered.

"Water! water!" I cried, clapping my hands and gesticulating like a madman.

"Water!" repeated my uncle. "*Hvar?*" he asked, in Icelandic.

"*Nedat,*" replied Hans.

"Where? Down below!" I understood it all. I seized the hunter's hands, and pressed them while he looked on me without moving a muscle of his countenance.

The preparations for our departure were not long in making, and we were soon on our way down a passage inclining two feet in seven. In an hour we had gone a mile and a quarter, and descended two thousand feet.

Then I began to hear distinctly quite a new sound of something running within the thickness of the granite wall, a kind of dull, dead rumbling, like distant thunder. During the first part of our walk, not meeting with the promised spring, I felt my agony returning; but then my uncle acquainted me with the cause of the strange noise.

"Hans was not mistaken," he said. "What you hear is the rushing of a torrent."

"A torrent?" I exclaimed.

"There can be no doubt; a subterranean river is flowing around us."

We hurried forward in the greatest excitement. I was no longer sensible of my fatigue. This murmuring of waters close at hand was already refreshing me. It was audibly increasing. The torrent, after having for some time flowed over our heads, was now running within the left wall, roaring and rushing. Frequently I touched the wall, hoping to feel some indications of moisture. But there was no hope here.

Yet another half-hour, another half league was passed.

Then it became clear that the hunter had gone no farther. Guided by an instinct peculiar to mountaineers he had as it were felt this torrent through the rock; but he had certainly seen none of the precious liquid; he had drunk nothing himself.

Soon it became evident that if we continued our walk we should widen the distance between ourselves and the stream, the noise of which was becoming fainter.

We returned. Hans stopped where the torrent seemed closest. I sat near the wall, while the waters were flowing past me at a distance of two feet with extreme violence. But there was a thick granite wall between us and the object of our desires.

Without reflection, without asking if there were any means of procuring the water, I gave way to a movement of despair.

Hans glanced at me with, I thought, a smile of compassion.

He rose and took the lamp. I followed him. He moved towards the wall. I looked on. He applied his ear against the dry stone, and moved it slowly to and fro, listening intently. I perceived at once that he was examining to find the exact place where the torrent could be heard the loudest. He met with that point on the left side of the tunnel, at three feet from the ground.

I was stirred up with excitement. I hardly dared guess what the hunter was about to do. But I could not but understand, and applaud and cheer him on, when I saw him lay hold of the pickaxe to make an attack upon the rock.

"We are saved!" I cried.

"Yes," cried my uncle, almost frantic with excitement. "Hans is right. Capital fellow! Who but he would have thought of it?"

Yes; who but he? Such an expedient, however simple, would never have entered into our minds. True, it seemed most hazardous to strike a blow of the hammer in this part of the earth's structure. Suppose some displacement should occur and crush us all! Suppose the torrent, bursting through, should drown us in a sudden flood! There was nothing vain in these fancies. But still no fears of falling rocks or rushing floods could stay us now; and our thirst was so intense that, to satisfy it, we would have dared the waves of the north Atlantic.

Hans set about the task which my uncle and I together could not have accomplished. If our impatience had armed our hands with power, we should have shattered the rock into a thousand fragments. Not so Hans. Full of self-possession, he calmly wore his way through the rock with a steady succession of light and skilful strokes, working through an aperture six inches wide at the outside. I could hear a louder noise of flowing waters, and I fancied I could feel the delicious fluid refreshing my parched lips.

The pick had soon penetrated two feet into the granite partition, and our man had worked for above an hour. I was in an agony of impatience. My uncle wanted to employ stronger measures, and I had some difficulty in dissuading him; still he had just taken a pickaxe in his hand, when a sudden hissing was heard, and a jet of water spurted out with violence against the opposite wall.

Hans, almost thrown off his feet by the violence of the shock, uttered a cry of grief and disappointment, of which I soon understood the cause, when plunging my hands into the spouting torrent, I withdrew them in haste, for the water was scalding hot.

"The water is at the boiling point," I cried.

"Well, never mind, let it cool," my uncle replied.

The tunnel was filling with steam, whilst a stream was forming, which by degrees wandered away into subterranean windings, and soon we had the satisfaction of swallowing our first draught.

Could anything be more delicious than the sensation that our burning intolerable thirst was passing away, and leaving us to enjoy comfort and pleasure? But where was this water from? No matter. It was water; and though still warm, it brought life back to the dying. I kept drinking without stopping, and almost without tasting.

At last, after a most delightful time of reviving energy, I cried, "Why, this is a chalybeate spring!"

"Nothing could be better for the digestion," said my uncle. "It is highly impregnated with iron. It will be as good for us as going to the Spa, or to Töplitz."

"Well, it is delicious!"

"Of course it is, water should be, found six miles underground. It has an inky flavour, which is not at all unpleasant. What a capital source of strength Hans has found for us here. We will call it after his name."

"Agreed," I cried.

And Hansbach it was from that moment.

Hans was none the prouder. After a moderate draught, he went quietly into a corner to rest.

"Now," I said, "we must not lose this water."

"What is the use of troubling ourselves?" my uncle replied. "I fancy it will never fail."

"Never mind, we cannot be sure; let us fill the water bottle and our flasks, and then stop up the opening."

My advice was followed so far as getting in a supply; but the stopping up of the hole was not so easy to accomplish. It was in vain that we took up fragments of granite, and stuffed them in with tow, we only scalded our hands without succeeding. The pressure was too great, and our efforts were fruitless.

"It is quite plain," said I, "that the higher body of this water is at a considerable elevation. The force of the jet shows that."

"No doubt," answered my uncle. "If this column of water is 32,000 feet high—that is, from the surface of the earth, it is equal to the weight of a thousand atmospheres. But I have got an idea."

"Well?"

"Why should we trouble ourselves to stop the stream from coming out at all?"

"Because—" Well, I could not assign a reason.

"When our flasks are empty, where shall we fill them again? Can we tell that?"

No; there was no certainty.

"Well, let us allow the water to run on. It will flow down, and will both guide and refresh us."

"That is well planned," I cried. "With this stream for our guide, there is no reason why we should not succeed in our undertaking."

"Ah, my boy! you agree with me now," cried the Professor, laughing.

"I agree with you most heartily."

"Well, let us rest a while; and then we will start again."

I was forgetting that it was night. The chronometer soon informed me of that fact; and in a very short time, refreshed and thankful, we all three fell into a sound sleep.

Chapter XXIV

Well Said, Old Mole!
Canst Thou Work i' the Ground so Fast?

B Y THE NEXT DAY WE HAD FORGOTTEN ALL OUR SUFFERINGS. AT FIRST, I WAS WONDER-ing that I was no longer thirsty, and I was for asking for the reason. The answer came in the murmuring of the stream at my feet.

We breakfasted, and drank of this excellent chalybeate water. I felt wonderfully stronger, and quite decided upon pushing on. Why should not so firmly convinced a man as my uncle, furnished with so industrious a guide as Hans, and accompanied by so deter-mined a nephew as myself, go on to final success? Such were the magnificent plans which struggled for mastery within me. If it had been proposed to me to return to the summit of Snæfell, I should have indignantly declined.

Most fortunately, all we had to do was to descend.

"Let us start!" I cried, awakening by my shouts the echoes of the vaulted hollows of the earth.

On Thursday, at 8 a.m., we started afresh. The granite tunnel winding from side to side, carried us past unexpected turns, and seemed almost to form a labyrinth; but, on the whole, its direction seemed to be south-easterly. My uncle never ceased to consult his com-pass, to keep account of the ground gone over.

The gallery dipped down a very little way from the horizontal, scarcely more than two inches in a fathom, and the stream ran gently murmuring at our feet. I compared it to a friendly genius guiding us underground, and caressed with my hand the soft naiad, whose comforting voice accompanied our steps. With my reviving spirits these mythological no-tions seemed to come unbidden.

As for my uncle, he was beginning to storm against the horizontal road. He loved nothing better than a vertical path; but this way seemed indefinitely prolonged, and instead of sliding along the hypothenuse as we were now doing, he would willingly have dropped down the terrestrial radius. But there was no help for it, and as long as we were approach-ing the center at all we felt that we must not complain.

From time to time, a steeper path appeared; our naiad then began to tumble before us with a hoarser murmur, and we went down with her to a greater depth.

On the whole, that day and the next we made considerable way horizontally, very lit-tle vertically.

On Friday evening, the 10th of July, according to our calculations, we were thirty leagues south-east of Rejkiavik, and at a depth of two leagues and a half.

At our feet there now opened a frightful abyss. My uncle, however, was not to be daunted, and he clapped his hands at the steepness of the descent.

"This will take us a long way," he cried, "and without much difficulty; for the pro-jections in the rock form quite a staircase."

The ropes were so fastened by Hans as to guard against accident, and the descent commenced. I can hardly call it perilous, for I was beginning to be familiar with this kind of exercise.

This well, or abyss, was a narrow cleft in the mass of the granite, called by geologists a "fault," and caused by the unequal cooling of the globe of the earth. If it had at one time been a passage for irruptive matter thrown out by Snæfell, I still could not understand why no trace was left of its passage. We kept going down a kind of winding staircase, which seemed almost to have been made by the hand of man.

Every quarter of an hour we were obliged to halt, to take a little necessary repose and restore the action of our limbs. We then sat down upon a fragment of rock, and we talked as we ate and drank from the stream.

Of course, down this fault the Hansbach fell in a cascade, and lost some of its volume; but there was enough and to spare to slake our thirst. Besides, when the incline became more gentle, it would of course resume its peaceable course. At this moment it reminded me of my worthy uncle, in his frequent fits of impatience and anger, while below it ran with the calmness of the Icelandic hunter.

On the 6th and 7th of July we kept following the spiral curves of this singular well, penetrating in actual distance no more than two leagues; but being carried to a depth of five leagues below the level of the sea. But on the 8th, about noon, the fault took, towards the south-east, a much gentler slope, one of about forty-five degrees.

Then the road became monotonously easy. It could not be otherwise, for there was no landscape to vary the stages of our journey.

On Wednesday, the 15th, we were seven leagues underground, and had travelled fifty leagues away from Snæfell. Although we were tired, our health was perfect, and the medicine chest had not yet had occasion to be opened.

My uncle noted every hour the indications of the compass, the chronometer, the aneroid, and the thermometer the very same which he has published in his scientific report of our journey. It was therefore not difficult to know exactly our whereabouts. When he told me that we had gone fifty leagues horizontally, I could not repress an exclamation of astonishment, at the thought that we had now long left Iceland behind us.

"What is the matter?" he cried.

"I was reflecting that if your calculations are correct we are no longer under Iceland."

"Do you think so?"

"I am not mistaken," I said, and examining the map, I added, "We have passed Cape Portland, and those fifty leagues bring us under the wide expanse of ocean."

"Under the sea," my uncle repeated, rubbing his hands with delight.

"Can it be?" I said. "Is the ocean spread above our heads?"

"Of course, Axel. What can be more natural? At Newcastle are there not coal mines extending far under the sea?"

It was all very well for the Professor to call this so simple, but I could not feel quite easy at the thought that the boundless ocean was rolling over my head. And yet it really mattered very little whether it was the plains and mountains that covered our heads, or the Atlantic waves, as long as we were arched over by solid granite. And, besides, I was getting used to this idea; for the tunnel, now running straight, now winding as capriciously in its inclines as in its turnings, but constantly preserving its south-easterly direction, and always running deeper, was gradually carrying us to very great depths indeed.

Four days later, Saturday, the 18th of July, in the evening, we arrived at a kind of vast grotto; and here my uncle paid Hans his weekly wages, and it was settled that the next day, Sunday, should be a day of rest.

Chapter XXV

De Profundis

I THEREFORE AWOKE NEXT DAY RELIEVED FROM THE PREOCCUPATION OF AN IMMEDIATE start. Although we were in the very deepest of known depths, there was something not unpleasant about it. And, besides, we were beginning to get accustomed to this troglodyte* life. I no longer thought of sun, moon, and stars, trees, houses, and towns, nor of any of those terrestrial superfluities which are necessaries of men who live upon the earth's surface. Being fossils, we looked upon all those things as mere jokes.

The grotto was an immense apartment. Along its granite floor ran our faithful stream. At this distance from its spring the water was scarcely tepid, and we drank of it with pleasure.

After breakfast the Professor gave a few hours to the arrangement of his daily notes.

"First," said he, "I will make a calculation to ascertain our exact position. I hope, after our return, to draw a map of our journey, which will be in reality a vertical section of the globe, containing the track of our expedition."

"That will be curious, uncle; but are your observations sufficiently accurate to enable you to do this correctly?"

"Yes; I have everywhere observed the angles and the inclines. I am sure there is no error. Let us see where we are now. Take your compass, and note the direction."

I looked, and replied carefully:

"South-east by east."

"Well," answered the Professor, after a rapid calculation, "I infer that we have gone eighty-five leagues since we started."

"Therefore we are under mid-Atlantic?"

"To be sure we are."

"And perhaps at this very moment there is a storm above, and ships over our heads are being rudely tossed by the tempest."

"Quite probable."

"And whales are lashing the roof of our prison with their tails?"

"It may be, Axel, but they won't shake us here. But let us go back to our calculation. Here we are eighty-five leagues south-east of Snæfell, and I reckon that we are at a depth of sixteen leagues."

---

* τρώγλη, a hole; δύω, to creep into. The name of an Ethiopian tribe who lived in caves and holes.

"Sixteen leagues?" I cried.

"No doubt."

"Why, this is the very limit assigned by science to the thickness of the crust of the earth."

"I don't deny it."

"And here, according to the law of increasing temperature, there ought to be a heat of 2,732° Fahr.!"

"So there should, my lad."

"And all this solid granite ought to be running in fusion."

"You see that it is not so, and that, as so often happens, facts come to overthrow theories."

"I am obliged to agree; but, after all, it is surprising."

"What does the thermometer say?"

"Twenty-seven, six tenths (82° Fahr.)."

"Therefore the savants are wrong by 2,705°, and the proportional increase is a mistake. Therefore Humphry Davy was right, and I am not wrong in following him. What do you say now?"

"Nothing."

In truth, I had a good deal to say. I gave way in no respect to Davy's theory. I still held to the central heat, although I did not feel its effects. I preferred to admit in truth, that this chimney of an extinct volcano, lined with lavas, which are non-conductors of heat, did not suffer the heat to pass through its walls.

But without stopping to look up new arguments I simply took up our situation such as it was.

"Well, admitting all your calculations to be quite correct, you must allow me to draw one rigid result therefrom."

"What is it. Speak freely."

"At the latitude of Iceland, where we now are, the radius of the earth, the distance from the center to the surface is about 1,583 leagues; let us say in round numbers 1,600 leagues, or 4,800 miles. Out of 1,600 leagues we have gone twelve!"

"So you say."

"And these twelve at a cost of 85 leagues diagonally?"

"Exactly so."

"In twenty days?"

"Yes."

"Now, sixteen leagues are the hundredth part of the earth's radius. At this rate we shall be two thousand days, or nearly five years and a half, in getting to the center."

No answer was vouchsafed to this rational conclusion. "Without reckoning, too, that if a vertical depth of sixteen leagues can be attained only by a diagonal descent of eighty-four, it follows that we must go eight thousand miles in a south-easterly direction; so that we shall emerge from some point in the earth's circumference instead of getting to the center!"

"Confusion to all your figures, and all your hypotheses besides," shouted my uncle in a sudden rage. "What is the basis of them all? How do you know that this passage does not run straight to our destination? Besides, there is a precedent. What one man has done, another may do."

"I hope so; but, still, I may be permitted—"

"You shall have my leave to hold your tongue, Axel, but not to talk in that irrational way."

I could see the awful Professor bursting through my uncle's skin, and I took timely warning.

"Now look at your aneroid. What does that say?"

"It says we are under considerable pressure."

"Very good; so you see that by going gradually down, and getting accustomed to the density of the atmosphere, we don't suffer at all."

"Nothing, except a little pain in the ears."

"That's nothing, and you may get rid of even that by quick breathing whenever you feel the pain."

"Exactly so," I said, determined not to say a word that might cross my uncle's prejudices. "There is even positive pleasure in living in this dense atmosphere. Have you observed how intense sound is down here?"

"No doubt it is. A deaf man would soon learn to hear perfectly."

"But won't this density augment?"

"Yes; according to a rather obscure law. It is well known that the weight of bodies diminishes as fast as we descend. You know that it is at the surface of the globe that weight is most sensibly felt, and that at the center there is no weight at all."

"I am aware of that; but, tell me, will not air at last acquire the density of water?"

"Of course, under a pressure of seven hundred and ten atmospheres."

"And how, lower down still?"

"Lower down the density will still increase."

"But how shall we go down then."

"Why, we must fill our pockets with stones."

"Well, indeed, my worthy uncle, you are never at a loss for an answer."

I dared venture no farther into the region of probabilities, for I might presently have stumbled upon an impossibility, which would have brought the Professor on the scene when he was not wanted.

Still, it was evident that the air, under a pressure which might reach that of thousands of atmospheres, would at last reach the solid state, and then, even if our bodies could resist the strain, we should be stopped, and no reasonings would be able to get us on any farther.

But I did not advance this argument. My uncle would have met it with his inevitable Saknussemm, a precedent which possessed no weight with me; for even if the journey of the learned Icelander were really attested, there was one very simple answer, that in the sixteenth century there was neither barometer or aneroid, and therefore Saknussemm could not tell how far he had gone.

But I kept this objection to myself, and waited the course of events.

The rest of the day was passed in calculations and in conversations. I remained a steadfast adherent of the opinions of Professor Liedenbrock, and I envied the stolid indifference of Hans, who, without going into causes and effects, went on with his eyes shut wherever his destiny guided him.

Chapter XXVI

THE WORST PERIL OF ALL

IT MUST BE CONFESSED THAT HITHERTO THINGS HAD NOT GONE ON SO BADLY, AND THAT I had small reason to complain. If our difficulties became no worse, we might hope to reach our end. And to what a height of scientific glory we should then attain! I had become quite a Liedenbrock in my reasonings; seriously I had. But would this state of things last in the strange place we had come to? Perhaps it might.

For several days steeper inclines, some even frightfully near to the perpendicular, brought us deeper and deeper into the mass of the interior of the earth. Some days we advanced nearer to the center by a league and a half, or nearly two leagues. These were perilous descents, in which the skill and marvellous coolness of Hans were invaluable to us. That unimpassioned Icelander devoted himself with incomprehensible deliberation; and, thanks to him, we crossed many a dangerous spot which we should never have cleared alone.

But his habit of silence gained upon him day by day, and was infecting us. External objects produce decided effects upon the brain. A man shut up between four walls soon loses the power to associate words and ideas together. How many prisoners in solitary confinement become idiots, if not mad, for want of exercise for the thinking faculty!

During the fortnight following our last conversation, no incident occurred worthy of being recorded. But I have good reason for remembering one very serious event which took place at this time, and of which I could scarcely now forget the smallest details.

By the 7th of August our successive descents had brought us to a depth of thirty leagues; that is, that for a space of thirty leagues there were over our heads solid beds of rock, ocean, continents, and towns. We must have been two hundred leagues from Iceland.

On that day the tunnel went down a gentle slope. I was ahead of the others. My uncle was carrying one of Ruhmkorff's lamps and I the other. I was examining the beds of granite.

Suddenly turning round I observed that I was alone.

Well, well, I thought; I have been going too fast, or Hans and my uncle have stopped on the way. Come, this won't do; I must join them. Fortunately there is not much of an ascent.

I retraced my steps. I walked for a quarter of an hour. I gazed into the darkness. I shouted. No reply: my voice was lost in the midst of the cavernous echoes which alone replied to my call.

I began to feel uneasy. A shudder ran through me.

"Calmly!" I said aloud to myself, "I am sure to find my companions again. There are not two roads. I was too far ahead. I will return!"

For half-an-hour I climbed up. I listened for a call, and in that dense atmosphere a voice could reach very far. But there was a dreary silence in all that long gallery. I stopped. I could not believe that I was lost. I was only bewildered for a time, not lost. I was sure I should find my way again.

"Come," I repeated, "since there is but one road, and they are on it, I *must* find them again. I have but to ascend still. Unless, indeed, missing me, and supposing me to be behind, they too should have gone back. But even in this case I have only to make the greater haste. I shall find them, I am sure."

I repeated these words in the fainter tones of a half-convinced man. Besides, to associate even such simple ideas with words, and reason with them, was a work of time.

A doubt then seized upon me. Was I indeed in advance when we became separated? Yes, to be sure I was. Hans was after me, preceding my uncle. He had even stopped for a while to strap his baggage better over his shoulders. I could remember this little incident. It was at that very moment that I must have gone on.

Besides, I thought, have not I a guarantee that I shall not lose my way, a clue in the labyrinth, that cannot be broken, my faithful stream? I have but to trace it back, and I must come upon them.

This conclusion revived my spirits, and I resolved to resume my march without loss of time.

How I then blessed my uncle's foresight in preventing the hunter from stopping up the hole in the granite. This beneficent spring, after having satisfied our thirst on the road, would now be my guide among the windings of the terrestrial crust.

Before starting afresh I thought a wash would do me good. I stooped to bathe my face in the Hansbach.

To my stupefaction and utter dismay my feet trod only the rough dry granite. The stream was no longer at my feet.

Chapter XXVII

LOST IN THE BOWELS OF THE EARTH

To DESCRIBE MY DESPAIR WOULD BE IMPOSSIBLE. NO WORDS COULD TELL IT. I WAS buried alive, with the prospect before me of dying of hunger and thirst.

Mechanically I swept the ground with my hands. How dry and hard the rock seemed to me!

But how had I left the course of the stream? For it was a terrible fact that it no longer ran at my side. Then I understood the reason of that fearful silence, when for the last time I listened to hear if any sound from my companions could reach my ears. At the moment when I left the right road I had not noticed the absence of the stream. It is evident that at that moment a deviation had presented itself before me, whilst the Hansbach, following the caprice of another incline, had gone with my companions away into unknown depths.

How was I to return? There was not a trace of their footsteps or of my own, for the foot left no mark upon the granite floor. I racked my brain for a solution of this impracticable problem. One word described my position. Lost!

Lost at an immeasurable depth! Thirty leagues of rock seemed to weigh upon my shoulders with a dreadful pressure. I felt crushed.

I tried to carry back my ideas to things on the surface of the earth. I could scarcely succeed. Hamburg, the house in the Königstrasse, my poor Gräuben, all that busy world underneath which I was wandering about, was passing in rapid confusion before my terrified memory. I could revive with vivid reality all the incidents of our voyage, Iceland, M. Fridriksson, Snæfell. I said to myself that if, in such a position as I was now in, I was fool enough to cling to one glimpse of hope, it would be madness, and that the best thing I could do was to despair.

What human power could restore me to the light of the sun by rending asunder the huge arches of rock which united over my head, buttressing each other with impregnable strength? Who could place my feet on the right path, and bring me back to my company?

"Oh, my uncle!" burst from my lips in the tone of despair.

It was my only word of reproach, for I knew how much he must be suffering in seeking me, wherever he might be.

When I saw myself thus far removed from all earthly help I had recourse to heavenly succour. The remembrance of my childhood, the recollection of my mother, whom I had only known in my tender early years, came back to me, and I knelt in prayer imploring for the Divine help of which I was so little worthy.

This return of trust in God's providence allayed the turbulence of my fears, and I was enabled to concentrate upon my situation all the force of my intelligence.

I had three days' provisions with me and my flask was full. But I could not remain alone for long. Should I go up or down?

Up, of course; up continually.

I must thus arrive at the point where I had left the stream, that fatal turn in the road. With the stream at my feet, I might hope to regain the summit of Snæfell.

Why had I not thought of that sooner? Here was evidently a chance of safety. The most pressing duty was to find out again the course of the Hansbach. I rose, and leaning upon my iron-pointed stick I ascended the gallery. The slope was rather steep. I walked on without hope but without indecision, like a man who has made up his mind.

For half-an-hour I met with no obstacle. I tried to recognise my way by the form of the tunnel, by the projections of certain rocks, by the disposition of the fractures. But no particular sign appeared, and I soon saw that this gallery could not bring me back to the turning point. It came to an abrupt end. I struck against an impenetrable wall, and fell down upon the rock.

Unspeakable despair then seized upon me. I lay overwhelmed, aghast! My last hope was shattered against this granite wall.

Lost in this labyrinth, whose windings crossed each other in all directions, it was no use to think of flight any longer. Here I must die the most dreadful of deaths. And, strange to say, the thought came across me that when someday my petrified remains should be found thirty leagues below the surface in the bowels of the earth, the discovery might lead to grave scientific discussions.

I tried to speak aloud, but hoarse sounds alone passed my dry lips. I panted for breath.

In the midst of my agony a new terror laid hold of me. In falling my lamp had got wrong. I could not set it right, and its light was paling and would soon disappear altogether.

I gazed painfully upon the luminous current growing weaker and weaker in the wire coil. A dim procession of moving shadows seemed slowly unfolding down the darkening walls. I scarcely dared to shut my eyes for one moment, for fear of losing the least glimmer of this precious light. Every instant it seemed about to vanish, and the dense blackness to come rolling in palpably upon me.

One last trembling glimmer shot feebly up. I watched it in trembling and anxiety; I drank it in as if I could preserve it, concentrating upon it the full power of my eyes, as upon the very last sensation of light which they were ever to experience, and the next moment I lay in the heavy gloom of deep, thick, unfathomable darkness.

A terrible cry of anguish burst from me. Upon earth, in the midst of the darkest night, light never abdicates its functions altogether. It is still subtle and diffusive, but whatever little there may be, the eye still catches that little. Here there was not an atom; the total darkness made me totally blind.

Then I began to lose my head. I arose with my arms stretched out before me, attempting painfully to feel my way. I began to run wildly, hurrying through the inextricable maze, still descending, still running through the substance of the earth's thick crust, a struggling denizen of geological "faults," crying, shouting, yelling, soon bruised by contact with the jagged rock, falling and rising again bleeding, trying to drink the blood which covered my face, and even waiting for some rock to shatter my skull against.

I shall never know whither my mad career took me. After the lapse of some hours, no doubt exhausted, I fell like a lifeless lump at the foot of the wall, and lost all consciousness.

Chapter XXVIII

THE RESCUE IN THE WHISPERING GALLERY

WHEN I RETURNED TO PARTIAL LIFE MY FACE WAS WET WITH TEARS. HOW LONG THAT state of insensibility had lasted I cannot say. I had no means now of taking account of time. Never was solitude equal to this, never had any living being been so utterly forsaken.

After my fall I had lost a good deal of blood. I felt it flowing over me. Ah! how happy I should have been could I have died, and if death were not yet to be gone through. I would think no longer. I drove away every idea, and, conquered by my grief, I rolled myself to the foot of the opposite wall.

Already I was feeling the approach of another faint, and was hoping for complete annihilation, when a loud noise reached me. It was like the distant rumble of continuous thunder, and I could hear its sounding undulations rolling far away into the remote recesses of the abyss.

Whence could this noise proceed? It must be from some phenomenon proceeding in the great depths amidst which I lay helpless. Was it an explosion of gas? Was it the fall of some mighty pillar of the globe?

I listened still. I wanted to know if the noise would be repeated. A quarter of an hour passed away. Silence reigned in this gallery. I could not hear even the beating of my heart.

Suddenly my ear, resting by chance against the wall, caught, or seemed to catch, certain vague, indescribable, distant, articulate sounds, as of words.

"This is a delusion," I thought.

But it was not. Listening more attentively, I heard in reality a murmuring of voices. But my weakness prevented me from understanding what the voices said. Yet it was language, I was sure of it.

For a moment I feared the words might be my own, brought back by the echo. Perhaps I had been crying out unknown to myself. I closed my lips firmly, and laid my ear against the wall again.

"Yes, truly, someone is speaking; those are words!"

Even a few feet from the wall I could hear distinctly. I succeeded in catching uncertain, strange, undistinguishable words. They came as if pronounced in low murmured whispers. The word *"forlorad"* was several times repeated in a tone of sympathy and sorrow.

"Help!" I cried with all my might. "Help!"

I listened, I watched in the darkness for an answer, a cry, a mere breath of sound, but nothing came. Some minutes passed. A whole world of ideas had opened in my mind. I thought that my weakened voice could never penetrate to my companions.

"It is they," I repeated. "What other men can be thirty leagues underground?"

I again began to listen. Passing my ear over the wall from one place to another, I found the point where the voices seemed to be best heard. The word *"forlorad"* again returned; then the rolling of thunder which had roused me from my lethargy.

"No," I said, "no; it is not through such a mass that a voice can be heard. I am surrounded by granite walls, and the loudest explosion could never be heard here! This noise comes along the gallery. There must be here some remarkable exercise of acoustic laws!"

I listened again, and this time, yes this time, I did distinctly hear my name pronounced across the wide interval.

It was my uncle's own voice! He was talking to the guide. And *"forlorad"* is a Danish word.

Then I understood it all. To make myself heard, I must speak along this wall, which would conduct the sound of my voice just as wire conducts electricity.

But there was no time to lose. If my companions moved but a few steps away, the acoustic phenomenon would cease. I therefore approached the wall, and pronounced these words as clearly as possible:

"Uncle Liedenbrock!"

I waited with the deepest anxiety. Sound does not travel with great velocity. Even increased density of air has no effect upon its rate of travelling; it merely augments its intensity. Seconds, which seemed ages, passed away, and at last these words reached me:

"Axel! Axel! is it you?"

. . . .

"Yes, yes," I replied.

. . . .

"My boy, where are you?"

. . . .

"Lost, in the deepest darkness."

. . . .

"Where is your lamp?"

. . . .

"It is out."

. . . .

"And the stream?"

. . . .

"Disappeared."

. . . .

"Axel, Axel, take courage!"

. . . .

"Wait! I am exhausted! I can't answer. Speak to me!"

. . . .

"Courage," resumed my uncle. "Don't speak. Listen to me. We have looked for you up the gallery and down the gallery. Could not find you. I wept for you, my poor boy. At last, supposing you were still on the Hansbach, we fired our guns. Our voices are audible to each other, but our hands cannot touch. But don't despair, Axel! It is a great thing that we can hear each other."

. . . .

During this time I had been reflecting. A vague hope was returning to my heart. There was one thing I must know to begin with. I placed my lips close to the wall, saying:

"My uncle!"

. . . .

"My boy!" came to me after a few seconds.

. . . .

"We must know how far we are apart."

. . . .

"That is easy."

. . . .

"You have your chronometer?"

. . . .

"Yes."

. . . .

"Well, take it. Pronounce my name, noting exactly the second when you speak. I will repeat it as soon as it shall come to me, and you will observe the exact moment when you get my answer."

. . . .

"Yes; and half the time between my call and your answer will exactly indicate that which my voice will take in coming to you."

. . . .

"Just so, my uncle."

. . . .

"Are you ready?"

. . . .

"Yes."

. . . .

"Now, attention. I am going to call your name."

. . . .

I put my ear to the wall, and as soon as the name "Axel" came, I immediately replied "Axel," then waited.

. . .

"Forty seconds," said my uncle. "Forty seconds between the two words; so the sound takes twenty seconds in coming. Now, at the rate of 1,120 feet in a second, this is 22,400 feet, or four miles and a quarter, nearly."

. . . .

"Four miles and a quarter!" I murmured.

. . . .

"It will soon be over, Axel."

. . . .

"Must I go up or down?"

. . . .

"Down—for this reason: We are in a vast chamber, with endless galleries. Yours must lead into it, for it seems as if all the clefts and fractures of the globe radiated round this vast cavern. So get up, and begin walking. Walk on, drag yourself along, if necessary slide down the steep places, and at the end you will find us ready to receive you. Now begin moving."

. . . .

These words cheered me up.

"Good-by, uncle." I cried. "I am going. There will be no more voices heard when once I have started. So good-by!"

. . . .

"Good-by, Axel, *au revoir!*"

. . . .

These were the last words I heard.

This wonderful underground conversation, carried on with a distance of four miles and a quarter between us, concluded with these words of hope. I thanked God from my heart, for it was He who had conducted me through those vast solitudes to the point where, alone of all others perhaps, the voices of my companions could have reached me.

This acoustic effect is easily explained on scientific grounds. It arose from the concave form of the gallery and the conducting power of the rock. There are many examples of this propagation of sounds which remain unheard in the intermediate space. I remember that a similar phenomenon has been observed in many places; amongst others on the internal surface of the gallery of the dome of St. Paul's in London, and especially in the midst of the curious caverns among the quarries near Syracuse, the most wonderful of which is called Dionysius' Ear.

These remembrances came into my mind, and I clearly saw that since my uncle's voice really reached me, there could be no obstacle between us. Following the direction by which the sound came, of course I should arrive in his presence, if my strength did not fail me.

I therefore rose; I rather dragged myself than walked. The slope was rapid, and I slid down.

Soon the swiftness of the descent increased horribly, and threatened to become a fall. I had no longer the strength to stop myself.

Suddenly there was no ground under me. I felt myself revolving in air, striking and rebounding against the craggy projections of a vertical gallery, quite a well; my head struck against a sharp corner of the rock, and I became unconscious.

Chapter XXIX

Thalatta! Thalatta!

WHEN I CAME TO MYSELF, I WAS STRETCHED IN HALF DARKNESS, COVERED WITH THICK coats and blankets. My uncle was watching over me, to discover the least sign of life. At my first sigh he took my hand; when I opened my eyes he uttered a cry of joy.

"He lives! he lives!" he cried.

"Yes, I am still alive," I answered feebly.

"My dear nephew," said my uncle, pressing me to his breast, "you are saved."

I was deeply touched with the tenderness of his manner as he uttered these words, and still more with the care with which he watched over me. But such trials were wanted to bring out the Professor's tenderer qualities.

At this moment Hans came, he saw my hand in my uncle's, and I may safely say that there was joy in his countenance.

"*God dag,*" said he.

"How do you do, Hans? How are you? And now, uncle, tell me where we are at the present moment?"

"To-morrow, Axel, to-morrow. Now you are too faint and weak. I have bandaged your head with compresses which must not be disturbed. Sleep now, and to-morrow I will tell you all."

"But do tell me what time it is, and what day."

"It is Sunday, the 8th of August, and it is ten at night. You must ask me no more questions until the 10th."

In truth I was very weak, and my eyes involuntarily closed. I wanted a good night's rest; and I therefore went off to sleep, with the knowledge that I had been four long days alone in the heart of the earth.

Next morning, on awakening, I looked round me. My couch, made up of all our travelling gear, was in a charming grotto, adorned with splendid stalactites, and the soil of which was a fine sand. It was half light. There was no torch, no lamp, yet certain mysterious glimpses of light came from without through a narrow opening in the grotto. I heard too a vague and indistinct noise, something like the murmuring of waves breaking upon a shingly shore, and at times I seemed to hear the whistling of wind.

I wondered whether I was awake, whether I dreaming, whether my brain, crazed by my fall, was not affected by imaginary noises. Yet neither eyes, nor ears could be so utterly deceived.

It is a ray of daylight, I thought, sliding in through this cleft in the rock! That is indeed the murmuring of waves! That is the rustling noise of wind. Am I quite mistaken, or have we returned to the surface of the earth? Has my uncle given up the expedition, or is it happily terminated?

I was asking myself these unanswerable questions when the Professor entered.

"Good morning, Axel," he cried cheerily. "I feel sure you are better."

"Yes, I am indeed," said I, sitting up on my couch.

"You can hardly fail to be better, for you have slept quietly. Hans and I watched you by turns, and we have noticed you were evidently recovering."

"Indeed, I do feel a great deal better, and I will give you a proof of that presently if you will let me have my breakfast."

"You shall eat, lad. The fever has left you. Hans rubbed your wounds with some ointment or other of which the Icelanders keep the secret, and they have healed marvellously. Our hunter is a splendid fellow!"

Whilst he went on talking, my uncle prepared a few provisions, which I devoured eagerly, notwithstanding his advice to the contrary. All the while I was overwhelming him with questions which he answered readily.

I then learned that my providential fall had brought me exactly to the extremity of an almost perpendicular shaft; and as I had landed in the midst of an accompanying torrent of stones, the least of which would have been enough to crush me, the conclusion was that a loose portion of the rock had come down with me. This frightful conveyance had thus carried me into the arms of my uncle, where I fell bruised, bleeding, and insensible.

"Truly it is wonderful that you have not been killed a hundred times over. But, for the love of God, don't let us ever separate again, or we many never see each other more."

"Not separate! Is the journey not over, then?" I opened a pair of astonished eyes, which immediately called for the question:

"What is the matter, Axel?"

"I have a question to ask you. You say that I am safe and sound?"

"No doubt you are."

"And all my limbs unbroken?"

"Certainly."

"And my head?"

"Your head, except for a few bruises, is all right; and it is on your shoulders, where it ought to be."

"Well, I am afraid my brain is affected."

"Your mind affected!"

"Yes, I fear so. Are we again on the surface of the globe?"

"No, certainly not."

"Then I must be mad; for don't I see the light of day, and don't I hear the wind blowing, and the sea breaking on the shore?"

"Ah! is that all?"

"Do tell me all about it."

"I can't explain the inexplicable, but you will soon see and understand that geology has not yet learned all it has to learn."

"Then let us go," I answered quickly.

"No, Axel; the open air might be bad for you."

"Open air?"

"Yes; the wind is rather strong. You must not expose yourself."

"But I assure you I am perfectly well."

"A little patience, my nephew. A relapse might get us into trouble, and we have no time to lose, for the voyage may be a long one."

"The voyage!"

"Yes, rest to-day, and to-morrow we will set sail."

"Set sail!"—and I almost leaped up.

What did it all mean? Had we a river, a lake, a sea to depend upon? Was there a ship at our disposal in some underground harbour?

My curiosity was highly excited, my uncle vainly tried to restrain me. When he saw that my impatience was doing me harm, he yielded.

I dressed in haste. For greater safety I wrapped myself in a blanket, and came out of the grotto.

Chapter XXX

A NEW MARE INTERNUM

AT FIRST I COULD HARDLY SEE ANYTHING. MY EYES, UNACCUSTOMED TO THE LIGHT, quickly closed. When I was able to reopen them, I stood more stupefied even than surprised.

"The sea!" I cried.

"Yes," my uncle replied, "the Liedenbrock Sea; and I don't suppose any other discoverer will ever dispute my claim to name it after myself as its first discoverer."

A vast sheet of water, the commencement of a lake or an ocean, spread far away beyond the range of the eye, reminding me forcibly of that open sea which drew from Xenophon's ten thousand Greeks, after their long retreat, the simultaneous cry, "Thalatta! thalatta!" the sea! the sea! The deeply indented shore was lined with a breadth of fine shining sand, softly lapped by the waves, and strewn with the small shells which had been inhabited by the first of created beings. The waves broke on this shore with the hollow echoing murmur peculiar to vast enclosed spaces. A light foam flew over the waves before the breath of a moderate breeze, and some of the spray fell upon my face. On this slightly inclining shore, about a hundred fathoms from the limit of the waves, came down the foot of a huge wall of vast cliffs, which rose majestically to an enormous height. Some of these, dividing the beach with their sharp spurs, formed capes and promontories, worn away by the ceaseless action of the surf. Farther on the eye discerned their massive outline sharply defined against the hazy distant horizon.

It was quite an ocean, with the irregular shores of earth, but desert and frightfully wild in appearance.

If my eyes were able to range afar over this great sea, it was because a peculiar light brought to view every detail of it. It was not the light of the sun, with his dazzling shafts of brightness and the splendour of his rays; nor was it the pale and uncertain shimmer of the moonbeams, the dim reflection of a nobler body of light. No; the illuminating power of this light, its trembling diffusiveness, its bright, clear whiteness, and its low temperature, showed that it must be of electric origin. It was like an aurora borealis, a continuous cosmical phenomenon, filling a cavern of sufficient extent to contain an ocean.

The vault that spanned the space above, the sky, if it could be called so, seemed composed of vast plains of cloud, shifting and variable vapours, which by their condensation must at certain times fall in torrents of rain. I should have thought that under so powerful a pressure of the atmosphere there could be no evaporation; and yet, under a law unknown to me, there were broad tracts of vapour suspended in the air. But then "the weather was fine." The play of the electric light produced singular effects upon the upper strata of cloud. Deep shadows reposed upon their lower wreaths; and often, between two separated fields of cloud, there glided down a ray of unspeakable lustre. But it was not solar light, and there was no heat. The general effect was sad, supremely melancholy. Instead of the shining firmament, spangled with its innumerable stars, shining singly or in clusters, I felt that all these subdued and shaded lights were ribbed in by vast walls of granite, which seemed to overpower me with their weight, and that all this space, great as it was, would not be enough for the march of the humblest of satellites.

Then I remembered the theory of an English captain, who likened the earth to a vast hollow sphere, in the interior of which the air became luminous because of the vast pressure that weighed upon it; while two stars, Pluto and Proserpine, rolled within upon the circuit of their mysterious orbits.

We were in reality shut up inside an immeasurable excavation. Its width could not be estimated, since the shore ran widening as far as eye could reach, nor could its length, for the dim horizon bounded the view. As for its height, it must have been several leagues. Where this vault rested upon its granite base no eye could tell; but there was a cloud hanging far above, the height of which we estimated at 12,000 feet, a greater height than that of any terrestrial vapour, and no doubt due to the great density of the air.

The word cavern does not convey any idea of this immense space; words of human tongue are inadequate to describe the discoveries of him who ventures into the deep abysses of earth.

Besides I could not tell upon what geological theory to account for the existence of such an excavation. Had the cooling of the globe produced it? I knew of celebrated caverns from the descriptions of travellers, but had never heard of any of such dimensions as this.

If the grotto of Guachara, in Colombia, visited by Humboldt, had not given up the whole of the secret of its depth to the philosopher, who investigated it to the depth of 2,500 feet, it probably did not extend much farther. The immense mammoth cave in Kentucky is of gigantic proportions, since its vaulted roof rises five hundred feet* above the level of an unfathomable lake, and travellers have explored its ramifications to the extent of forty miles. But what were these cavities compared to that in which I stood with wonder and admiration, with its sky of luminous vapours, its bursts of electric light, and a vast sea filling its bed? My imagination fell powerless before such immensity.

*One hundred and twenty. (Trans.)

I gazed upon these wonders in silence. Words failed me to express my feelings. I felt as if I was in some distant planet—Uranus or Neptune—and in the presence of phenomena of which my terrestrial experience gave me no cognisance. For such novel sensations, new words were wanted; and my imagination failed to supply them. I gazed, I thought, I admired, with a stupefaction mingled with a certain amount of fear.

The unforeseen nature of this spectacle brought back the colour to my cheeks. I was under a new course of treatment with the aid of astonishment, and my convalescence was promoted by this novel system of therapeutics; besides, the dense and breezy air invigorated me, supplying more oxygen to my lungs.

It will be easily conceived that after an imprisonment of forty-seven days in a narrow gallery it was the height of physical enjoyment to breathe a moist air impregnated with saline particles.

I was delighted to leave my dark grotto. My uncle, already familiar with these wonders, had ceased to feel surprise.

"You feel strong enough to walk a little way now?" he asked.

"Yes, certainly; and nothing could be more delightful."

"Well, take my arm, Axel, and let us follow the windings of the shore."

I eagerly accepted, and we began to coast along this new sea. On the left huge pyramids of rock, piled one upon another, produced a prodigious titanic effect. Down their sides flowed numberless waterfalls, which went on their way in brawling but pellucid streams. A few light vapours, leaping from rock to rock, denoted the place of hot springs; and streams flowed softly down to the common basin, gliding down the gentle slopes with a softer murmur.

Amongst these streams I recognised our faithful travelling companion, the Hansbach, coming to lose its little volume quietly in the mighty sea, just as if it had done nothing else since the beginning of the world.

"We shall see it no more," I said, with a sigh.

"What matters," replied the philosopher, "whether this or another serves to guide us?"

I thought him rather ungrateful.

But at that moment my attention was drawn to an unexpected sight. At a distance of five hundred paces, at the turn of a high promontory, appeared a high, tufted, dense forest. It was composed of trees of moderate height, formed like umbrellas, with exact geometrical outlines. The currents of wind seemed to have had no effect upon their shape, and in the midst of the windy blasts they stood unmoved and firm, just like a clump of petrified cedars.

I hastened forward. I could not give any name to these singular creations. Were they some of the two hundred thousand species of vegetables known hitherto, and did they claim a place of their own in the lacustrine flora? No; when we arrived under their shade my surprise turned into admiration. There stood before me productions of earth, but of gigantic stature, which my uncle immediately named.

"It is only a forest of mushrooms," said he.

And he was right. Imagine the large development attained by these plants, which prefer a warm, moist climate. I knew that the *Lycopodon giganteum* attains, according to Bulliard, a circumference of eight or nine feet; but here were pale mushrooms, thirty to forty feet high, and crowned with a cap of equal diameter. There they stood in thousands. No light could penetrate between their huge cones, and complete darkness reigned beneath those giants; they formed settlements of domes placed in close array like the round, thatched roofs of a central African city.

Yet I wanted to penetrate farther underneath, though a chill fell upon me as soon as I came under those cellular vaults. For half-an-hour we wandered from side to side in the damp shades, and it was a comfortable and pleasant change to arrive once more upon the seashore.

But the subterranean vegetation was not confined to these fungi. Farther on rose groups of tall trees of colourless foliage and easy to recognise. They were lowly shrubs of earth, here attaining gigantic size; lycopodiums, a hundred feet high; the huge sigillaria, found in our coal mines; tree ferns, as tall as our fir-trees in northern latitudes; lepidodendra, with cylindrical forked stems, terminated by long leaves, and bristling with rough hairs like those of the cactus.

"Wonderful, magnificent, splendid!" cried my uncle. "Here is the entire flora of the second period of the world—the transition period. These, humble garden plants with us, were tall trees in the early ages. Look, Axel, and admire it all. Never had botanist such a feast as this!"

"You are right, my uncle. Providence seems to have preserved in this immense conservatory the antediluvian plants which the wisdom of philosophers has so sagaciously put together again."

"It is a conservatory, Axel; but is it not also a menagerie?"

"Surely not a menagerie!"

"Yes; no doubt of it. Look at that dust under your feet; see the bones scattered on the ground."

"So there are!" I cried; "bones of extinct animals."

I had rushed upon these remains, formed of indestructible phosphates of lime, and without hesitation I named these monstrous bones, which lay scattered about like decayed trunks of trees.

"Here is the lower jaw of a mastodon,"* I said. "These are the molar teeth of the deinotherium; this femur must have belonged to the greatest of those beasts, the megatherium. It certainly is a menagerie, for these remains were not brought here by a deluge. The animals to which they belonged roamed on the shores of this subterranean sea, under the shade of those arborescent trees. Here are entire skeletons. And yet I cannot understand the appearance of these quadrupeds in a granite cavern."

"Why?"

"Because animal life existed upon the earth only in the secondary period, when a sediment of soil had been deposited by the rivers, and taken the place of the incandescent rocks of the primitive period."

"Well, Axel, there is a very simple answer to your objection—that this soil is alluvial."

"What! at such a depth below the surface of the earth?"

"No doubt; and there is a geological explanation of the fact. At a certain period the earth consisted only of an elastic crust or bark, alternately acted on by forces from above

---

*These animals belonged to a late geological period, the Pliocene, just before the glacial epoch, and therefore could have no connection with the carboniferous vegetation. (Trans.)

or below, according to the laws of attraction and gravitation. Probably there were subsidences of the outer crust, when a portion of the sedimentary deposits was carried down sudden openings."

"That may be," I replied; "but if there have been creatures now extinct in these underground regions, why may not some of those monsters be now roaming through these gloomy forests, or hidden behind the steep crags?"

And as this unpleasant notion got hold of me, I surveyed with anxious scrutiny the open spaces before me; but no living creature appeared upon the barren strand.

I felt rather tired, and went to sit down at the end of a promontory, at the foot of which the waves came and beat themselves into spray. Thence my eye could sweep every part of the bay; within its extremity a little harbour was formed between the pyramidal cliffs, where the still waters slept untouched by the boisterous winds. A brig and two or three schooners might have moored within it in safety. I almost fancied I should presently see some ship issue from it, full sail, and take to the open sea under the southern breeze.

But this illusion lasted a very short time. We were the only living creatures in this subterranean world. When the wind lulled, a deeper silence than that of the deserts fell upon the arid, naked rocks, and weighed upon the surface of the ocean. I then desired to pierce the distant haze, and to rend asunder the mysterious curtain that hung across the horizon. Anxious queries arose to my lips. Where did that sea terminate? Where did it lead to? Should we ever know anything about its opposite shores?

My uncle made no doubt about it at all; I both desired and feared.

After spending an hour in the contemplation of this marvellous spectacle, we returned to the shore to regain the grotto, and I fell asleep in the midst of the strangest thoughts.

Chapter XXXI

PREPARATIONS FOR A VOYAGE OF DISCOVERY

THE NEXT MORNING I AWOKE FEELING PERFECTLY WELL. I THOUGHT A BATHE WOULD do me good, and I went to plunge for a few minutes into the waters of this mediterranean sea, for assuredly it better deserved this name than any other sea.

I came back to breakfast with a good appetite. Hans was a good caterer for our little household; he had water and fire at his disposal, so that he was able to vary our bill of fare now and then. For dessert he gave us a few cups of coffee, and never was coffee so delicious.

"Now," said my uncle, "now is the time for high tide, and we must not lose the opportunity to study this phenomenon."

"What! the tide!" I cried. "Can the influence of the sun and moon be felt down here?"

"Why not? Are not all bodies subject throughout their mass to the power of universal attraction? This mass of water cannot escape the general law. And in spite of the heavy atmospheric pressure on the surface, you will see it rise like the Atlantic itself."

At the same moment we reached the sand on the shore, and the waves were by slow degrees encroaching on the shore.

"Here is the tide rising," I cried.

"Yes, Axel; and judging by these ridges of foam, you may observe that the sea will rise about twelve feet."

"This is wonderful," I said.

"No; it is quite natural."

"You may say so, uncle; but to me it is most extraordinary, and I can hardly believe my eyes. Who would ever have imagined, under this terrestrial crust, an ocean with ebbing and flowing tides, with winds and storms?"

"Well," replied my uncle, "is there any scientific reason against it?"

"No; I see none, as soon as the theory of central heat is given up."

"So then, thus far," he answered, "the theory of Sir Humphry Davy is confirmed."

"Evidently it is; and now there is no reason why there should not be seas and continents in the interior of the earth."

"No doubt," said my uncle; "and inhabited too."

"To be sure," said I; "and why should not these waters yield to us fishes of unknown species?"

"At any rate," he replied, "we have not seen any yet."

"Well, let us make some lines, and see if the bait will draw here as it does in sublunary regions."

"We will try, Axel, for we must penetrate all secrets of these newly discovered regions."

"But where are we, uncle? for I have not yet asked you that question, and your instruments must be able to furnish the answer."

"Horizontally, three hundred and fifty leagues from Iceland."

"So much as that?"

"I am sure of not being a mile out of my reckoning."

"And does the compass still show south-east?"

"Yes; with a westerly deviation of nineteen degrees forty-five minutes, just as above ground. As for its dip, a curious fact is coming to light, which I have observed carefully: that the needle, instead of dipping towards the pole as in the northern hemisphere, on the contrary, rises from it."

"Would you then conclude," I said, "that the magnetic pole is somewhere between the surface of the globe and the point where we are?"

"Exactly so; and it is likely enough that if we were to reach the spot beneath the polar regions, about that seventy-first degree where Sir James Ross has discovered the magnetic pole to be situated, we should see the needle point straight up. Therefore that mysterious center of attraction is at no great depth."

I remarked: " It is so; and here is a fact which science has scarcely suspected."

"Science, my lad, has been built upon many errors; but they are errors which it was good to fall into, for they led to the truth."

"What depth have we now reached?"

"We are thirty-five leagues below the surface."

"So," I said, examining the map, "the Highlands of Scotland are over our heads, and the Grampians are raising their rugged summits above us."

"Yes," answered the Professor laughing. "It is rather a heavy weight to bear, but a solid arch spans over our heads. The great Architect has built it of the best materials; and never could man have given it so wide a stretch. What are the finest arches of bridges and the arcades of cathedrals, compared with this far-reaching vault, with a radius of three leagues, beneath which a wide and tempest-tossed ocean may flow at its ease?"

"Oh, I am not afraid that it will fall down upon my head. But now what are your plans? Are you not thinking of returning to the surface now?"

"Return! no, indeed! We will continue our journey, everything having gone on well so far."

"But how are we to get down below this liquid surface?"

"Oh, I am not going to dive head foremost. But if all oceans are properly speaking but lakes, since they are encompassed by land, of course this internal sea will be surrounded by a coast of granite, and on the opposite shores we shall find fresh passages opening."

"How long do you suppose this sea to be?"

"Thirty or forty leagues; so that we have no time to lose, and we shall set sail to-morrow."

I looked about for a ship.

"Set sail, shall we? But I should like to see my boat first."

"It will not be a boat at all, but a good, well-made raft."

"Why," I said, "a raft would be just as hard to make as a boat, and I don't see—"

"I know you don't see; but you might hear if you would listen. Don't you hear the hammer at work? Hans is already busy at it."

"What, has he already felled the trees?"

"Oh, the trees were already down. Come, and you will see for yourself."

After half-an-hour's walking, on the other side of the promontory which formed the little natural harbour, I perceived Hans at work. In a few more steps I was at his side. To my great surprise a half-finished raft was already lying on the sand, made of a peculiar kind of wood, and a great number of planks, straight and bent, and of frames, were covering the ground, enough almost for a little fleet.

"Uncle, what wood is this?" I cried.

"It is fir, pine, or birch, and other northern coniferae, mineralised by the action of the sea. It is called surturbrand, a variety of brown coal or lignite, found chiefly in Iceland."

"But surely, then, like other fossil wood, it must be as hard as stone, and cannot float?"

"Sometimes that may happen; some of these woods become true anthracites; but others, such as this, have only gone through the first stage of fossil transformation. Just look," added my uncle, throwing into the sea one of those precious waifs.

The bit of wood, after disappearing, returned to the surface and oscillated to and fro with the waves.

"Are you convinced?" said my uncle.

"I am quite convinced, although it is incredible!"

By next evening, thanks to the industry and skill of our guide, the raft was made. It was ten feet by five; the planks of surturbrand, braced strongly together with cords, presented an even surface, and when launched this improvised vessel floated easily upon the waves of the Liedenbrock Sea.

Chapter XXXII

WONDERS OF THE DEEP

O N THE 13TH OF AUGUST WE AWOKE EARLY. WE WERE NOW TO BEGIN TO ADOPT A MODE of travelling both more expeditious and less fatiguing than hitherto.

A mast was made of two poles spliced together, a yard was made of a third, a blanket borrowed from our coverings made a tolerable sail. There was no want of cordage for the rigging, and everything was well and firmly made.

The provisions, the baggage, the instruments, the guns, and a good quantity of fresh water from the rocks around, all found their proper places on board; and at six the Professor gave the signal to embark. Hans had fitted up a rudder to steer his vessel. He took the tiller, and unmoored; the sail was set, and we were soon afloat. At the moment of leaving the harbour, my uncle, who was tenaciously fond of naming his new discoveries, wanted to give it a name, and proposed mine amongst others.

"But I have a better to propose," I said: "Grauben. Let it be called Port Gräuben; it will look very well upon the map."

"Port Gräuben let it be then."

And so the cherished remembrance of my Virlandaise became associated with our adventurous expedition.

The wind was from the north-west. We went with it at a high rate of speed. The dense atmosphere acted with great force and impelled us swiftly on.

In an hour my uncle had been able to estimate our progress. At this rate, he said, we shall make thirty leagues in twenty-four hours, and we shall soon come in sight of the opposite shore.

I made no answer, but went and sat forward. The northern shore was already beginning to dip under the horizon. The eastern and western strands spread wide as if to bid us farewell. Before our eyes lay far and wide a vast sea; shadows of great clouds swept heavily over its silver-grey surface; the glistening bluish rays of electric light, here and there reflected by the dancing drops of spray, shot out little sheaves of light from the track we left in our rear. Soon we entirely lost sight of land; no object was left for the eye to judge by, and but for the frothy track of the raft, I might have thought we were standing still.

About twelve, immense shoals of sea-weeds came in sight. I was aware of the great powers of vegetation that characterise these plants, which grow at a depth of twelve thousand feet, reproduce themselves under a pressure of four hundred atmospheres, and sometimes form barriers strong enough to impede the course of a ship. But never, I think, were such sea-weeds as those which we saw floating in immense waving lines upon the sea of Liedenbrock.

Our raft skirted the whole length of the fuci, three or four thousand feet long, undulating like vast serpents beyond the reach of sight; I found some amusement in tracing these endless waves, always thinking I should come to the end of them, and for hours my patience was vying with my surprise.

What natural force could have produced such plants, and what must have been the appearance of the earth in the first ages of its formation, when, under the action of heat and moisture, the vegetable kingdom alone was developing on its surface?

Evening came, and, as on the previous day, I perceived no change in the luminous condition of the air. It was a constant condition, the permanency of which might be relied upon.

After supper I laid myself down at the foot of the mast, and fell asleep in the midst of fantastic reveries.

Hans, keeping fast by the helm, let the raft run on, which, after all, needed no steering, the wind blowing directly aft.

Since our departure from Port Gräuben, Professor Liedenbrock had entrusted the log to my care; I was to register every observation, make entries of interesting phenomena, the direction of the wind, the rate of sailing, the way we made—in a word, every particular of our singular voyage.

I shall therefore reproduce here these daily notes, written, so to speak, as the course of events directed, in order to furnish an exact narrative of our passage.

Friday, August 14.—Wind steady, N.W. The raft makes rapid way in a direct line. Coast thirty leagues to leeward. Nothing in sight before us. Intensity of light the same. Weather fine; that is to say, that the clouds are flying high, are light, and bathed in a white atmosphere resembling silver in a state of fusion. Therm. 89° Fahr.

At noon Hans prepared a hook at the end of a line. He baited it with a small piece of meat and flung it into the sea. For two hours nothing was caught. Are these waters, then, bare of inhabitants? No, there's a pull at the line. Hans draws it in and brings out a struggling fish.

"A sturgeon," I cried; "a small sturgeon."

The Professor eyes the creature attentively, and his opinion differs from mine.

The head of this fish was flat, but rounded in front, and the anterior part of its body was plated with bony, angular scales; it had no teeth, its pectoral fins were large, and of tail there was none. The animal belonged to the same order as the sturgeon, but differed from that fish in many essential particulars. After a short examination my uncle pronounced his opinion.

"This fish belongs to an extinct family, of which only fossil traces are found in the devonian formations."

"What!" I cried. "Have we taken alive an inhabitant of the seas of primitive ages?"

"Yes; and you will observe that these fossil fishes have no identity with any living species. To have in one's possession a living specimen is a happy event for a naturalist."

"But to what family does it belong?"

"It is of the order of ganoids, of the family of the cephalaspidae and a species of pterichthys. But this one displays a peculiarity confined to all fishes that inhabit subterranean waters. It is blind, and not only blind, but actually has no eyes at all."

I looked: nothing could be more certain. But supposing it might be a solitary case, we baited afresh, and threw out our line. Surely this ocean is well peopled with fish, for in another couple of hours we took a large quantity of pterichthydes, as well as of others belonging to the extinct family of the dipterides, but of which my uncle could not tell the species; none had organs of sight. This unhoped-for catch recruited our stock of provisions.

Thus it is evident that this sea contains none but species known to us in their fossil state, in which fishes as well as reptiles are the less perfectly and completely organised the farther back their date of creation.

Perhaps we may yet meet with some of those saurians which science has reconstructed out of a bit of bone or cartilage. I took up the telescope and scanned the whole horizon, and found it everywhere a desert sea. We are far away removed from the shores.

I gaze upward in the air. Why should not some of the strange birds restored by the immortal Cuvier again flap their "sail-broad vans" in this dense and heavy atmosphere? There are sufficient fish for their support. I survey the whole space that stretches overhead; it is as desert as the shore was.

Still my imagination carried me away amongst the wonderful speculations of palaeontology. Though awake I fell into a dream. I thought I could see floating on the surface of the waters enormous chelonia, preadamite tortoises, resembling floating islands. Over the dimly lighted strand there trod the huge mammals of the first ages of the world, the leptotherium (slender beast), found in the caverns of Brazil; the merycotherium (ruminating beast), found in the "drift" of iceclad Siberia. Farther on, the pachydermatous lophiodon (crested toothed), a gigantic tapir, hides behind the rocks to dispute its prey with the anoplotherium (unarmed beast), a strange creature, which seemed a compound of horse, rhinoceros, camel, and hippopotamus. The colossal mastodon (nipple-toothed) twists and untwists his trunk, and brays and pounds with his huge tusks the fragments of rock that cover the shore; whilst the megatherium (huge beast), buttressed upon his enormous hinder paws, grubs in the soil, awaking the sonorous echoes of the granite rocks with his tremendous roarings. Higher up, the protopitheca—the first monkey that appeared on the globe—is climbing up the steep ascents. Higher yet, the pterodactyle (wing-fingered) darts in irregular zigzags to and fro in the heavy air. In the uppermost regions of the air immense birds, more powerful than the cassowary, and larger than the ostrich, spread their vast breadth of wings and strike with their heads the granite vault that bounds the sky.

All this fossil world rises to life again in my vivid imagination. I return to the scriptural periods or ages of the world, conventionally called "days," long before the appearance of man, when the unfinished world was as yet unfitted for his support. Then my dream backed even farther still into the ages before the creation of living beings. The mammals disappear, then the birds vanish, then the reptiles of the secondary period, and finally the fish, the crustaceans, molluscs, and articulated beings. Then the zoophytes of the transition period also return to nothing. I am the only living thing in the world: all life is concentrated in my beating heart alone. There are no more seasons; climates are no more; the heat of the globe continually increases and neutralises that of the sun. Vegetation becomes accelerated. I glide like a shade amongst arborescent ferns, treading with unsteady feet the coloured marls and the particoloured clays; I lean for support against the trunks of immense conifers; I lie in the shade of sphenophylla (wedge-leaved), asterophylla (star-leaved), and lycopods, a hundred feet high.

Ages seem no more than days! I am passed, against my will, in retrograde order, through the long series of terrestrial changes. Plants disappear; granite rocks soften; intense heat converts solid bodies into thick fluids; the waters again cover the face of the earth; they boil, they rise in whirling eddies of steam; white and ghastly mists wrap round the shifting forms of the earth, which by imperceptible degrees dissolves into a gaseous mass, glowing fiery red and white, as large and as shining as the sun.

And I myself am floating with wild caprice in the midst of this nebulous mass of fourteen hundred thousand times the volume of the earth into which it will one day be condensed, and carried forward amongst the planetary bodies. My body is no longer firm and terrestrial; it is resolved into its constituent atoms, subtilised, volatilised. Sublimed into imponderable vapour, I mingle and am lost in the endless foods of those vast globular volumes of vaporous mists, which roll upon their flaming orbits through infinite space.

But is it not a dream? Whither is it carrying me? My feverish hand has vainly attempted to describe upon paper its strange and wonderful details. I have forgotten everything that surrounds me. The Professor, the guide, the raft—are all gone out of my ken. An illusion has laid hold upon me.

"What is the matter?" my uncle breaks in.

My staring eyes are fixed vacantly upon him.

"Take care, Axel, or you will fall overboard."

At that moment I felt the sinewy hand of Hans seizing me vigorously. But for him, carried away by my dream, I should have thrown myself into the sea.

"Is he mad?" cried the Professor.

"What is it all about?" at last I cried, returning to myself.

"Do you feel ill?" my uncle asked.

"No; but I have had a strange hallucination; it is over now. Is all going on right?"

"Yes, it is a fair wind and a fine sea; we are sailing rapidly along, and if I am not out in my reckoning, we shall soon land."

At these words I rose and gazed round upon the horizon, still everywhere bounded by clouds alone.

Chapter XXXIII

A Battle of Monsters

Saturday, August 15.—The sea unbroken all round. No land in sight. The horizon seems extremely distant.

My head is still stupefied with the vivid reality of my dream.

My uncle has had no dreams, but he is out of temper. He examines the horizon all round with his glass, and folds his arms with the air of an injured man.

I remark that Professor Liedenbrock has a tendency to relapse into an impatient mood, and I make a note of it in my log. All my danger and sufferings were needed to strike a spark of human feeling out of him; but now that I am well his nature has resumed its sway. And yet, what cause was there for anger? Is not the voyage prospering as favourably as possible under the circumstances? Is not the raft spinning along with marvellous speed?

"You seem anxious, my uncle," I said, seeing him continually with his glass to his eye.

"Anxious! No, not at all."

"Impatient, then?"

"One might be, with less reason than now."

"Yet we are going very fast."

"What does that signify? I am not complaining that the rate is slow, but that the sea is so wide."

I then remembered that the Professor, before starting, had estimated the length of this underground sea at thirty leagues. Now we had made three times the distance, yet still the southern coast was not in sight.

"We are not descending as we ought to be," the Professor declares. "We are losing time, and the fact is, I have not come all this way to take a little sail upon a pond on a raft."

He called this sea a pond, and our long voyage, taking a little sail!

"But," I remarked, "since we have followed the road that Saknussemm has shown us—"

"That is just the question. Have we followed that road? Did Saknussemm meet this sheet of water? Did he cross it? Has not the stream that we followed led us altogether astray?"

"At any rate we cannot feel sorry to have come so far. This prospect is magnificent, and—"

"But I don't care for prospects. I came with an object, and I mean to attain it. Therefore don't talk to me about views and prospects."

I take this as my answer, and I leave the Professor to bite his lips with impatience. At six in the evening Hans asks for his wages, and his three rix dollars are counted out to him.

Sunday, August 16.—Nothing new. Weather unchanged. The wind freshens. On awaking, my first thought was to observe the intensity of the light. I was possessed with an apprehension lest the electric light should grow dim, or fail altogether. But there seemed no reason to fear. The shadow of the raft was clearly outlined upon the surface of the waves.

Truly this sea is of infinite width. It must be as wide as the Mediterranean or the Atlantic—and why not?

My uncle took soundings several times. He tied the heaviest of our pickaxes to a long rope which he let down two hundred fathoms. No bottom yet; and we had some difficulty in hauling up our plummet.

But when the pick was shipped again, Hans pointed out on its surface deep prints as if it had been violently compressed between two hard bodies.

I looked at the hunter.

"*Tänder,* " said he.

I could not understand him, and turned to my uncle who was entirely absorbed in his calculations. I had rather not disturb him while he is quiet. I return to the Icelander. He by a snapping motion of his jaws conveys his ideas to me.

"Teeth!" I cried, considering the iron bar with more attention.

Yes, indeed, those are the marks of teeth imprinted upon the metal! The jaws which they arm must be possessed of amazing strength. Is there some monster beneath us belonging to the extinct races, more voracious than the shark, more fearful in vastness than the whale? I could not take my eyes off this indented iron bar. Surely will my last night's dream be realised?

These thoughts agitated me all day, and my imagination scarcely calmed down after several hours' sleep.

Monday, August 17.—I am trying to recall the peculiar instincts of the monsters of the preadamite world, who, coming next in succession after the molluscs, the crustaceans and the fishes, preceded the animals of mammalian race upon the earth. The world then belonged to reptiles. Those monsters held the mastery in the seas of the secondary period. They possessed a perfect organisation, gigantic proportions, prodigious strength. The saurians of our day, the alligators and the crocodiles, are but feeble reproductions of their forefathers of primitive ages.

I shudder as I recall these monsters to my remembrance. No human eye has ever beheld them living. They burdened this earth a thousand ages before man appeared, but their fossil remains, found in the argillaceous limestone called by the English the lias, have enabled their colossal structure to be perfectly built up again and anatomically ascertained.

I saw at the Hamburg museum the skeleton of one of these creatures thirty feet in length. Am I then fated—I, a denizen of earth—to be placed face to face with these representatives of long extinct families? No; surely it cannot be! Yet the deep marks of conical teeth upon the iron pick are certainly those of the crocodile.

My eyes are fearfully bent upon the sea. I dread to see one of these monsters darting forth from its submarine caverns. I suppose Professor Liedenbrock was of my opinion too, and even shared my fears, for after having examined the pick, his eyes traversed the ocean from side to side. What a very bad notion that was of his, I thought to myself, to take soundings just here! He has disturbed some monstrous beast in its remote den, and if we are not attacked on our voyage—

I look at our guns and see that they are all right. My uncle notices it, and looks on approvingly.

Already widely disturbed regions on the surface of the water indicate some commotion below. The danger is approaching. We must be on the look-out.

Tuesday, August 18.—Evening came, or rather the time came when sleep weighs down the weary eyelids, for there is no night here, and the ceaseless light wearies the eyes with its persistency just as if we were sailing under an arctic sun. Hans was at the helm. During his watch I slept.

Two hours afterwards a terrible shock awoke me. The raft was heaved up on a watery mountain and pitched down again, at a distance of twenty fathoms.

"What is the matter?" shouted my uncle. "Have we struck land?"

Hans pointed with his finger at a dark mass six hundred yards away, rising and falling alternately with heavy plunges. I looked and cried:

"It is an enormous porpoise."

"Yes," replied my uncle, "and there is a sea lizard of vast size."

"And farther on a monstrous crocodile. Look at its vast jaws and its rows of teeth! It is diving down!"

"There's a whale, a whale!" cried the Professor. "I can see its great fins. See how he is throwing out air and water through his blowers."

And in fact two liquid columns were rising to a considerable height above the sea. We stood amazed, thunderstruck, at the presence of such a herd of marine monsters. They were of supernatural dimensions; the smallest of them would have crunched our raft, crew and all, at one snap of its huge jaws.

Hans wants to tack to get away from this dangerous neighbourhood; but he sees on the other hand enemies not less terrible; a tortoise forty feet long, and a serpent of thirty, lifting its fearful head and gleaming eyes above the flood.

Flight was out of the question now. The reptiles rose; they wheeled around our little raft with a rapidity greater than that of express trains. They described around us gradually narrowing circles. I took up my rifle. But what could a ball do against the scaly armour with which these enormous beasts were clad?

We stood dumb with fear. They approach us close: on one side the crocodile, on the other the serpent. The remainder of the sea monsters have disappeared. I prepare to fire. Hans stops me by a gesture. The two monsters pass within a hundred and fifty yards of the raft, and hurl themselves the one upon the other, with a fury which prevents them from seeing us.

At three hundred yards from us the battle was fought. We could distinctly observe the two monsters engaged in deadly conflict. But it now seems to me as if the other animals were taking part in the fray—the porpoise, the whale, the lizard, the tortoise. Every moment I seem to see one or other of them. I point them to the Icelander. He shakes his head negatively.

"*Tva,*" says he.

"What two? Does he mean that there are only two animals?"

"He is right," said my uncle, whose glass has never left his eye.

"Surely you must be mistaken," I cried.

"No: the first of those monsters has a porpoise's snout, a lizard's head, a crocodile's teeth; and hence our mistake. It is the ichthyosaurus (the fish lizard), the most terrible of the ancient monsters of the deep."

"And the other?"

"The other is a plesiosaurus (almost lizard), a serpent, armoured with the carapace and the paddles of a turtle; he is the dreadful enemy of the other."

Hans had spoken truly. Two monsters only were creating all this commotion; and before my eyes are two reptiles of the primitive world. I can distinguish the eye of the ichthyosaurus glowing like a red-hot coal, and as large as a man's head. Nature has endowed it with an optical apparatus of extreme power, and capable of resisting the pressure of the great volume of water in the depths it inhabits. It has been appropriately called the saurian whale, for it has both the swiftness and the rapid movements of this monster of our own day. This one is not less than a hundred feet long, and I can judge of its size when it sweeps over the waters the vertical coils of its tail. Its jaw is enormous, and according to naturalists it is armed with no less than one hundred and eighty-two teeth.

The plesiosaurus, a serpent with a cylindrical body and a short tail, has four flappers or paddles to act like oars. Its body is entirely covered with a thick armour of scales, and its neck, as flexible as a swan's, rises thirty feet above the waves.

Those huge creatures attacked each other with the greatest animosity. They heaved around them liquid mountains, which rolled even to our raft and rocked it perilously. Twenty times we were near capsizing. Hissings of prodigious force are heard. The two beasts are fast locked together; I cannot distinguish the one from the other. The probable rage of the conqueror inspires us with intense fear.

One hour, two hours, pass away. The struggle continues with unabated ferocity. The combatants alternately approach and recede from our raft. We remain motionless, ready to fire. Suddenly the ichthyosaurus and the plesiosaurus disappear below, leaving a whirlpool eddying in the water. Several minutes pass by while the fight goes on under water.

All at once an enormous head is darted up, the head of the plesiosaurus. The monster is wounded to death. I no longer see his scaly armour. Only his long neck shoots up, drops again, coils and uncoils, droops, lashes the waters like a gigantic whip, and writhes like a worm that you tread on. The water is splashed for a long way around. The spray almost blinds us. But soon the reptile's agony draws to an end; its movements become fainter, its contortions cease to be so violent, and the long serpentine form lies a lifeless log on the labouring deep.

As for the ichthyosaurus—has he returned to his submarine cavern? or will he reappear on the surface of the sea?

Chapter XXXIV

The Great Geyser

Wednesday, August 19.—Fortunately the wind blows violently, and has enabled us to flee from the scene of the late terrible struggle. Hans keeps at his post at the helm. My uncle, whom the absorbing incidents of the combat had drawn away from his contemplations, began again to look impatiently around him.

The voyage resumes its uniform tenour, which I don't care to break with a repetition of such events as yesterday's.

Thursday, Aug. 20.—Wind N.N.E., unsteady and fitful. Temperature high. Rate three and a half leagues an hour.

About noon a distant noise is heard. I note the fact without being able to explain it. It is a continuous roar.

"In the distance," says the Professor, "there is a rock or islet, against which the sea is breaking."

Hans climbs up the mast, but sees no breakers. The ocean is smooth and unbroken to its farthest limit.

Three hours pass away. The roarings seem to proceed from a very distant waterfall.

I remark upon this to my uncle, who replies doubtfully: "Yes, I am convinced that I am right." Are we, then, speeding forward to some cataract which will cast us down an abyss? This method of getting on may please the Professor, because it is vertical; but for my part I prefer the more ordinary modes of horizontal progression.

At any rate, some leagues to the windward there must be some noisy phenomenon, for now the roarings are heard with increasing loudness. Do they proceed from the sky or the ocean?

I look up to the atmospheric vapours, and try to fathom their depths. The sky is calm and motionless. The clouds have reached the utmost limit of the lofty vault, and there lie still bathed in the bright glare of the electric light. It is not there that we must seek for the cause of this phenomenon. Then I examine the horizon, which is unbroken and clear of all mist. There is no change in its aspect. But if this noise arises from a fall, a cataract, if all this ocean flows away headlong into a lower basin yet, if that deafening roar is produced by a mass of falling water, the current must needs accelerate, and its increasing speed will give me the measure of the peril that threatens us. I consult the current: there is none. I throw an empty bottle into the sea: it lies still.

About four Hans rises, lays hold of the mast, and climbs to its top. Thence his eye sweeps a large area of sea, and it is fixed, upon a point. His countenance exhibits no surprise, but his eye is immovably steady.

"He sees something," says my uncle.

"I believe he does."

Hans comes down, then stretches his arm to the south, saying:

"*Dere nere!*"

"Down there?" repeated my uncle.

Then, seizing his glass, he gazes attentively for a minute, which seems to me an age.

"Yes, yes!" he cried. "I see a vast inverted cone rising from the surface."

"Is it another sea beast?"

"Perhaps it is."

"Then let us steer farther westward, for we know something of the danger of coming across monsters of that sort."

"Let us go straight on," replied my uncle.

I appealed to Hans. He maintained his course inflexibly.

Yet, if at our present distance from the animal, a distance of twelve leagues at the least, the column of water driven through its blowers may be distinctly seen, it must needs be of vast size. The commonest prudence would counsel immediate flight; but we did not come so far to be prudent.

Imprudently, therefore, we pursue our way. The nearer we approach, the higher mounts the jet of water. What monster can possibly fill itself with such a quantity of water, and spurt it up so continuously?

At eight in the evening we are not two leagues distant from it. Its body—dusky, enormous, hillocky—lies spread upon the sea like an islet. Is it illusion or fear? Its length seems to me a couple of thousand yards. What can be this cetacean, which neither Cuvier nor Blumenbach knew anything about? It lies motionless, as if asleep; the sea seems unable to move it in the least; it is the waves that undulate upon its sides. The column of water thrown up to a height of five hundred feet falls in rain with a deafening uproar. And here are we scudding like lunatics before the wind, to get near to a monster that a hundred whales a day would not satisfy!

Terror seizes upon me. I refuse to go further. I will cut the halliards if necessary! I am in open mutiny against the Professor, who vouchsafes no answer.

Suddenly Hans rises, and pointing with his finger at the menacing object, he says: *"Holm."*

"An island!" cries my uncle.

"That's not an island!" I cried skeptically.

"It's nothing else," shouted the Professor, with a loud laugh.

"But that column of water?"

"Geyser," said Hans.

"No doubt it is a geyser, like those in Iceland."

At first I protest against being so widely mistaken as to have taken an island for a marine monster. But the evidence is against me, and I have to confess my error. It is nothing worse than a natural phenomenon.

As we approach nearer the dimensions of the liquid column become magnificent. The islet resembles, with a most deceiving likeness, an enormous cetacean, whose head dominates the waves at a height of twenty yards. The geyser, a word meaning "fury," rises majestically from its extremity. Deep and heavy explosions are heard from time to time, when the enormous jet, possessed with more furious violence, shakes its plumy crest, and springs with a bound till it reaches the lowest stratum of the clouds. It stands alone. No steam vents, no hot springs surround it, and all the volcanic power of the region is concentrated here. Sparks of electric fire mingle with the dazzling sheaf of lighted fluid, every drop of which refracts the prismatic colours.

"Let us land," said the Professor.

"But we must carefully avoid this waterspout, which would sink our raft in a moment."

Hans, steering with his usual skill, brought us to the other extremity of the islet.

I leaped up on the rock; my uncle lightly followed, while our hunter remained at his post, like a man far too wise ever to be astonished.

We walked upon granite mingled with siliceous tufa. The soil shivers and shakes under our feet, like the sides of an overheated boiler filled with steam struggling to get loose. We come in sight of a small central basin, out of which the geyser springs. I plunge a register thermometer into the boiling water. It marks an intense heat of 325°, which is far above the boiling point; therefore this water issues from an ardent furnace, which is not at all in harmony with Professor Liedenbrock's theories. I cannot help making the remark.

"Well," he replied, "how does that make against my doctrine?"

"Oh, nothing at all," I said, seeing that I was going in opposition to immovable obstinacy.

Still I am constrained to confess that hitherto we have been wonderfully favoured, and that for some reason unknown to myself we have accomplished our journey under singularly favourable conditions of temperature. But it seems manifest to me that someday we shall reach a region where the central heat attains its highest limits, and goes beyond a point that can be registered by our thermometers.

"That is what we shall see." So says the Professor, who, having named this volcanic islet after his nephew, gives the signal to embark again.

For some minutes I am still contemplating the geyser. I notice that it throws up its column of water with variable force: sometimes sending it to a great height, then again to a lower, which I attribute to the variable pressure of the steam accumulated in its reservoir.

At last we leave the island, rounding away past the low rocks on its southern shore. Hans has taken advantage of the halt to refit his rudder.

But before going any farther I make a few observations, to calculate the distance we have gone over, and note them in my journal. We have crossed two hundred and seventy leagues of sea since leaving Port Gräuben; and we are six hundred and twenty leagues from Iceland, under England.*

Chapter XXXV

An Electric Storm

Friday, August 21.—On the morrow the magnificent geyser has disappeared. The wind has risen, and has rapidly carried us away from Axel Island. The roarings become lost in the distance.

The weather—if we may use that term—will change before long. The atmosphere is charged with vapours, pervaded with the electricity generated by the evaporation of saline waters. The clouds are sinking lower, and assume an olive hue. The electric light can scarcely penetrate through the dense curtain which has dropped over the theatre on which the battle of the elements is about to be waged.

I feel peculiar sensations, like many creatures on earth at the approach of violent atmospheric changes. The heavily voluted cumulus clouds lower gloomily and threateningly; they wear that implacable look which I have sometimes noticed at the outbreak of a great storm. The air is heavy; the sea is calm.

In the distance the clouds resemble great bales of cotton, piled up in picturesque disorder. By degrees they dilate, and gain in huge size what they lose in number. Such is their ponderous weight that they cannot rise from the horizon; but, obeying an impulse from higher currents, their dense consistency slowly yields. The gloom upon them deepens; and they soon present to our view a ponderous mass of almost level surface. From time to time a fleecy tuft of mist, with yet some gleaming light left upon it, drops down upon the dense floor of grey, and loses itself in the opaque and impenetrable mass.

The atmosphere is evidently charged and surcharged with electricity. My whole body is saturated; my hair bristles just as when you stand upon an insulated stool under the action of an electrical machine. It seems to me as if my companions, the moment they touched me, would receive a severe shock like that from an electric eel.

At ten in the morning the symptoms of storm become aggravated. The wind never lulls but to acquire increased strength; the vast bank of heavy clouds is a huge reservoir of fearful windy gusts and rushing storms.

I am loth to believe these atmospheric menaces, and yet I cannot help muttering:

"Here's some very bad weather coming on."

*This distance carries the travellers as far as under the Pyrenees, if the league measures three miles. (Trans.)

The Professor made no answer. His temper is awful, to judge from the working of his features, as he sees this vast length of ocean unrolling before him to an indefinite extent. He can only spare time to shrug his shoulders viciously.

"There's a heavy storm coming on," I cried, pointing towards the horizon. "Those clouds seem as if they were going to crush the sea."

A deep silence falls on all around. The lately roaring winds are hushed into a dead calm; nature seems to breathe no more, and to be sinking into the stillness of death. On the mast already I see the light play of a lambent St. Elmo's fire; the outstretched sail catches not a breath of wind, and hangs like a sheet of lead. The rudder stands motionless in a sluggish, waveless sea. But if we have now ceased to advance why do we yet leave that sail loose, which at the first shock of the tempest may capsize us in a moment?

"Let us reef the sail and cut the mast down!" I cried. "That will be safest."

"No, no! Never!" shouted my impetuous uncle. "Never! Let the wind catch us if it will! What I want is to get the least glimpse of rock or shore, even if our raft should be smashed into shivers!"

The words were hardly out of his mouth when a sudden change took place in the southern sky. The piled-up vapours condense into water; and the air, put into violent action to supply the vacuum left by the condensation of the mists, rouses itself into a whirlwind. It rushes on from the farthest recesses of the vast cavern. The darkness deepens; scarcely can I jot down a few hurried notes. The helm makes a bound. My uncle falls full length; I creep close to him. He has laid a firm hold upon a rope, and appears to watch with grim satisfaction this awful display of elemental strife.

Hans stirs not. His long hair blown by the pelting storm, and laid flat across his immovable countenance, makes him a strange figure; for the end of each lock of loose flowing hair is tipped with little luminous radiations. This frightful mask of electric sparks suggests to me, even in this dizzy excitement, a comparison with preadamite man, the contemporary of the ichthyosaurus and the megatherium.*

The mast yet holds firm. The sail stretches tight like a bubble ready to burst. The raft flies at a rate that I cannot reckon, but not so fast as the foaming clouds of spray which it dashes from side to side in its headlong speed.

"The sail! the sail!" I cry, motioning to lower it.

"No!" replies my uncle.

"*Nej!*" repeats Hans, leisurely shaking his head.

But now the rain forms a rushing cataract in front of that horizon towards which we are running with such maddening speed. But before it has reached us the rain cloud parts asunder, the sea boils, and the electric fires are brought into violent action by a mighty chemical power that descends from the higher regions. The most vivid flashes of lightning are mingled with the violent crash of continuous thunder. Ceaseless fiery arrows dart in and out amongst the flying thunderclouds; the vapourous mass soon glows with incandescent heat; hailstones rattle fiercely down, and as they dash upon our iron tools they too emit gleams and flashes of lurid light. The heaving waves resemble fiery volcanic hills, each belching forth its own interior flames, and every crest is plumed with dancing fire. My eyes fail under the dazzling light, my ears are stunned with the incessant

*Rather of the mammoth and the mastodon. (Trans.)

crash of thunder. I must be bound to the mast, which bows like a reed before the mighty strength of the storm.

(Here my notes become vague and indistinct. I have only been able to find a few which I seem to have jotted down almost unconsciously. But their very brevity and their obscurity reveal the intensity of the excitement which dominated me, and describe the actual position even better than my memory could do.)

Sunday, August 23.—Where are we? Driven forward with a swiftness that cannot be measured.

The night was fearful; no abatement of the storm. The din and uproar are incessant; our ears are bleeding; to exchange a word is impossible.

The lightning flashes with intense brilliancy, and never seems to cease for a moment. Zigzag streams of bluish white fire dash down upon the sea and rebound, and then take an upward flight till they strike the granite vault that overarches our heads. Suppose that solid roof should crumble down upon our heads! Other flashes with incessant play cross their vivid fires, while others again roll themselves into balls of living fire which explode like bombshells, but the music of which scarcely adds to the din of the battle strife that almost deprives us of our senses of hearing and sight; the limit of intense loudness has been passed within which the human ear can distinguish one sound from another. If all the powder magazines in the world were to explode at once, we should hear no more than we do now.

From the undersurface of the clouds there are continual emissions of lurid light; electric matter is in continual evolution from their component molecules; the gaseous elements of the air need to be slaked with moisture; for innumerable columns of water rush upwards into the air and fall back again in white foam.

Whither are we flying? My uncle lies full length across the raft.

The heat increases. I refer to the thermometer; it indicates . . . (the figure is obliterated).

Monday, August 24.—Will there be an end to it? Is the atmospheric condition, having once reached this density, to become final?

We are prostrated and worn out with fatigue. But Hans is as usual. The raft bears on still to the south-east. We have made two hundred leagues since we left Axel Island.

At noon the violence of the storm redoubles. We are obliged to secure as fast as possible every article that belongs to our cargo. Each of us is lashed to some part of the raft. The waves rise above our heads.

For three days we have never been able to make each other hear a word. Our mouths open, our lips move, but not a word can be heard. We cannot even make ourselves heard by approaching our mouth close to the ear.

My uncle has drawn nearer to me. He has uttered a few words. They seem to be: "We are lost"; but I am not sure.

At last I write down the words: "Let us lower the sail."

He nods his consent.

Scarcely has he lifted his head again before a ball of fire has bounded over the waves and lighted on board our raft. Mast and sail flew up in an instant together, and I saw them carried up to prodigious height, resembling in appearance a pterodactyle, one of those strong birds of the infant world.

We lay there, our blood running cold with unspeakable terror. The fireball, half of it white, half azure blue, and the size of a ten-inch shell, moved slowly about the raft, but revolving on its own axis with astonishing velocity, as if whipped round by the force of the whirlwind. Here it comes, there it glides, now it is up the ragged stump of the mast, thence it lightly leaps on the provision bag, descends with a light bound, and just skims the powder magazine. Horrible! we shall be blown up; but no, the dazzling disk of mysterious light nimbly leaps aside; it approaches Hans, who fixes his blue eye upon it steadily; it threatens the head of my uncle, who falls upon his knees with his head down to avoid it. And now my turn comes; pale and trembling under the blinding splendour and the melting heat, it drops at my feet, spinning silently round upon the deck; I try to move my foot away, but cannot.

A suffocating smell of nitrogen fills the air, it enters the throat, it fills the lungs. We suffer stifling pains.

Why am I unable to move my foot? Is it riveted to the planks? Alas! the fall upon our fated raft of this electric globe has magnetised every iron article on board. The instruments, the tools, our guns, are clashing and clanking violently in their collisions with each other; the nails of my boots cling tenaciously to a plate of iron let into the timbers, and I cannot draw my foot away from the spot. At last by a violent effort I release myself at the instant when the ball in its gyrations was about to seize upon it, and carry me off my feet. . . .

Ah! what a flood of intense and dazzling light! the globe has burst, and we are deluged with tongues of fire!

Then all the light disappears. I could just see my uncle at full length on the raft, and Hans still at his helm and spitting fire under the action of the electricity which has saturated him.

But where are we going to? Where?

. . . .

Tuesday, August 25.—I recover from a long swoon. The storm continues to roar and rage; the lightnings dash hither and thither, like broods of fiery serpents filling all the air. Are we still under the sea? Yes, we are borne at incalculable speed. We have been carried under England, under the channel, under France, perhaps under the whole of Europe.

. . . .

A fresh noise is heard! Surely it is the sea breaking upon the rocks! But then . . .

. . . .

Chapter XXXVI

CALM PHILOSOPHIC DISCUSSIONS

HERE I END WHAT I MAY CALL MY LOG, HAPPILY SAVED FROM THE WRECK, AND I RESUME my narrative as before.

What happened when the raft was dashed upon the rocks is more than I can tell. I felt myself hurled into the waves; and if I escaped from death, and if my body was not torn over the sharp edges of the rocks, it was because the powerful arm of Hans came to my rescue.

The brave Icelander carried me out of the reach of the waves, over a burning sand where I found myself by the side of my uncle.

Then he returned to the rocks, against which the furious waves were beating, to save what he could. I was unable to speak. I was shattered with fatigue and excitement; I wanted a whole hour to recover even a little.

But a deluge of rain was still falling, though with that violence which generally denotes the near cessation of a storm. A few overhanging rocks afforded us some shelter from the storm. Hans prepared some food, which I could not touch; and each of us, exhausted with three sleepless nights, fell into a broken and painful sleep.

The next day the weather was splendid. The sky and the sea had sunk into sudden repose. Every trace of the awful storm had disappeared. The exhilarating voice of the Professor fell upon my ears as I awoke; he was ominously cheerful.

"Well, my boy," he cried, "have you slept well?"

Would not anyone have thought that we were still in our cheerful little house on the Königstrasse and that I was only just coming down to breakfast, and that I was to be married to Gräuben that day?

Alas! if the tempest had but sent the raft a little more east, we should have passed under Germany, under my beloved town of Hamburg, under the very street where dwelt all that I loved most in the world. Then only forty leagues would have separated us! But they were forty leagues perpendicular of solid granite wall, and in reality we were a thousand leagues asunder!

All these painful reflections rapidly crossed my mind before I could answer my uncle's question.

"Well, now," he repeated, "won't you tell me how you have slept?"

"Oh, very well," I said. "I am only a little knocked up, but I shall soon be better."

"Oh," says my uncle, "that's nothing to signify. You are only a little bit tired."

"But you, uncle, you seem in very good spirits this morning."

"Delighted, my boy, delighted. We have got there."

"To our journey's end?"

"No; but we have got to the end of that endless sea. Now we shall go by land, and really begin to go down! down! down!"

"But, my dear uncle, do let me ask you one question."

"Of course, Axel."

"How about returning?"

"Returning? Why, you are talking about the return before the arrival."

"No, I only want to know how that is to be managed."

"In the simplest way possible. When we have reached the center of the globe, either we shall find some new way to get back, or we shall come back like decent folks the way we came. I feel pleased at the thought that it is sure not to be shut against us."

"But then we shall have to refit the raft."

"Of course."

"Then, as to provisions, have we enough to last?"

"Yes; to be sure we have. Hans is a clever fellow, and I am sure he must have saved a large part of our cargo. But still let us go and make sure."

We left this grotto which lay open to every wind. At the same time I cherished a trembling hope, which was a fear as well. It seemed to me impossible that the terrible wreck of the raft should not have destroyed everything on board. On my arrival on the shore, I found Hans surrounded by an assemblage of articles all arranged in good order. My uncle shook hands with him with a lively gratitude. This man, with almost superhuman devotion, had been at work all the while that we were asleep, and had saved the most precious of the articles at the risk of his life.

Not that we had suffered no losses. For instance, our fire-arms; but we might do without them. Our stock of powder had remained uninjured after having risked blowing up during the storm.

"Well," cried the Professor, "as we have no guns we cannot hunt, that's all."

"Yes, but how about the instruments?"

"Here is the aneroid, the most useful of all, and for which I would have given all the others. By means of it I can calculate the depth and know when we have reached the center; without it we might very likely go beyond, and come out at the antipodes!"

Such high spirits as these were rather too strong.

"But where is the compass? I asked.

"Here it is, upon this rock, in perfect condition, as well as the thermometers and the chronometer. The hunter is a splendid fellow."

There was no denying it. We had all our instruments. As for tools and appliances, there they all lay on the ground—ladders, ropes, picks, spades, etc.

Still there was the question of provisions to be settled, and I asked—"How are we off for provisions?"

The boxes containing these were in a line upon the shore, in a perfect state of preservation; for the most part the sea had spared them, and what with biscuits, salt meat, spirits, and salt fish, we might reckon on four months' supply.

"Four months!" cried the Professor. "We have time to go and to return; and with what is left I will give a grand dinner to my friends at the Johannæum."

I ought by this time to have been quite accustomed to my uncle's ways; yet there was always something fresh about him to astonish me.

"Now," said he, "we will replenish our supply of water with the rain which the storm has left in all these granite basins; therefore we shall have no reason to fear anything from thirst. As for the raft, I will recommend Hans to do his best to repair it, although I don't expect it will be of any further use to us."

"How so?" I cried.

"An idea of my own, my lad. I don't think we shall come out by the way that we went in."

I stared at the Professor with a good deal of mistrust. I asked, was he not touched in the brain? And yet there was method in his madness.

"And now let us go to breakfast," said he.

I followed him to a headland, after he had given his instructions to the hunter. There preserved meat, biscuit, and tea made us an excellent meal, one of the best I ever remember. Hunger, the fresh air, the calm quiet weather, after the commotions we had gone through, all contributed to give me a good appetite.

Whilst breakfasting I took the opportunity to put to my uncle the question where we were now.

"That seems to me," I said, "rather difficult to make out."

"Yes, it is difficult," he said, "to calculate exactly; perhaps even impossible, since during these three stormy days I have been unable to keep any account of the rate or direction of the raft; but still we may get an approximation.".

"The last observation," I remarked, "was made on the island, when the geyser was—"

"You mean Axel Island. Don't decline the honour of having given your name to the first island ever discovered in the central parts of the globe."

"Well," said I, "let it be Axel Island. Then we had cleared two hundred and seventy leagues of sea, and we were six hundred leagues from Iceland."

"Very well," answered my uncle; "let us start from that point and count four days' storm, during which our rate cannot have been less than eighty leagues in the twenty-four hours."

"That is right; and this would make three hundred leagues more."

"Yes, and the Liedenbrock sea would be six hundred leagues from shore to shore. Surely, Axel, it may vie in size with the Mediterranean itself."

"Especially," I replied, "if it happens that we have only crossed it in its narrowest part. And it is a curious circumstance," I added, "that if my computations are right, and we are nine hundred leagues from Rejkiavik, we have now the Mediterranean above our head."

"That is a good long way, my friend. But whether we are under Turkey or the Atlantic depends very much upon the question in what direction we have been moving. Perhaps we have deviated."

"No, I think not. Our course has been the same all along, and I believe this shore is south-east of Port Gräuben."

"Well," replied my uncle, "we may easily ascertain this by consulting the compass. Let us go and see what it says."

The Professor moved towards the rock upon which Hans had laid down the instruments. He was gay and full of spirits; he rubbed his hands, he studied his attitudes. I followed him, curious to know if I was right in my estimate. As soon as we had arrived at the rock my uncle took the compass, laid it horizontally, and questioned the needle, which, after a few oscillations, presently assumed a fixed position. My uncle looked, and looked, and looked again. He rubbed his eyes, and then turned to me thunderstruck with some unexpected discovery.

"What is the matter?" I asked.

He motioned to me to look. An exclamation of astonishment burst from me. The north pole of the needle was turned to what we supposed to be the south. It pointed to the shore instead of to the open sea! I shook the box, examined it again, it was in perfect condition. In whatever position I placed the box the needle pertinaciously returned to this unexpected quarter. Therefore there seemed no reason to doubt that during the storm there had been a sudden change of wind unperceived by us, which had brought our raft back to the shore which we thought we had left so long a distance behind us.

Chapter XXXVII

THE LIEDENBROCK MUSEUM OF GEOLOGY

HOW SHALL I DESCRIBE THE STRANGE SERIES OF PASSIONS WHICH IN SUCCESSION SHOOK the breast of Professor Liedenbrock? First stupefaction, then incredulity, lastly a downright burst of rage. Never had I seen the man so put out of countenance and so disturbed. The fatigues of our passage across, the dangers met, had all to be begun over again. We had gone backwards instead of forwards!

But my uncle rapidly recovered himself.

"Aha! will fate play tricks upon me? Will the elements lay plots against me? Shall fire, air, and water make a combined attack against me? Well, they shall know what a determined man can do. I will not yield. I will not stir a single foot backwards, and it will be seen whether man or nature is to have the upper hand!"

Erect upon the rock, angry and threatening, Otto Liedenbrock was a rather grotesque parody upon the fierce Achilles defying the lightning. But I thought it my duty to interpose and attempt to lay some restraint upon this unmeasured fanaticism.

"Just listen to me," I said firmly. "Ambition must have a limit somewhere; we cannot perform impossibilities; we are not at all fit for another sea voyage; who would dream of undertaking a voyage of five hundred leagues upon a heap of rotten planks, with a blanket in rags for a sail, a stick for a mast, and fierce winds in our teeth? We cannot steer; we shall be buffeted by the tempests, and we should be fools and madmen to attempt to cross a second time."

I was able to develop this series of unanswerable reasons for ten minutes without interruption; not that the Professor was paying any respectful attention to his nephew's arguments, but because he was deaf to all my eloquence.

"To the raft!" he shouted.

Such was his only reply. It was no use for me to entreat, supplicate, get angry, or do anything else in the way of opposition; it would only have been opposing a will harder than the granite rock.

Hans was finishing the repairs of the raft. One would have thought that this strange being was guessing at my uncle's intentions. With a few more pieces of surturbrand he had refitted our vessel. A sail already hung from the new mast, and the wind was playing in its waving folds.

The Professor said a few words to the guide, and immediately he put everything on board and arranged every necessary for our departure. The air was clear—and the northwest wind blew steadily.

What could I do? Could I stand against the two? It was impossible? If Hans had but taken my side! But no, it was not to be. The Icelander seemed to have renounced all will of his own and made a vow to forget and deny himself. I could get nothing out of a servant so feudalised, as it were, to his master. My only course was to proceed.

I was therefore going with as much resignation as I could find to resume my accustomed place on the raft, when my uncle laid his hand upon my shoulder.

"We shall not sail until to-morrow," he said.

I made a movement intended to express resignation.

"I must neglect nothing," he said; "and since my fate has driven me on this part of the coast, I will not leave it until I have examined it."

To understand what followed, it must be borne in mind that, through circumstances hereafter to be explained, we were not really where the Professor supposed we were. In fact we were *not* upon the north shore of the sea.

"Now let us start upon fresh discoveries," I said.

And leaving Hans to his work we started off together. The space between the water and the foot of the cliffs was considerable. It took half-an-hour to bring us to the wall of rock. We trampled under our feet numberless shells of all the forms and sizes which existed in the earliest ages of the world. I also saw immense carapaces more than fifteen feet in diameter. They had been the coverings of those gigantic glyptodons or armadilloes of the pleiocene period, of which the modern tortoise is but a miniature representative.* The soil was besides this scattered with stony fragments, boulders rounded by water action, and ridged up in successive lines. I was therefore led to the conclusion that at one time the sea must have covered the ground on which we were treading. On the loose and scattered rocks, now out of the reach of the highest tides, the waves had left manifest traces of their power to wear their way in the hardest stone.

This might up to a certain point explain the existence of an ocean forty leagues beneath the surface of the globe. But in my opinion this liquid mass would be lost by degrees farther and farther within the interior of the earth, and it certainly had its origin in the waters of the ocean overhead, which had made their way hither through some fissure. Yet it must be believed that that fissure is now closed, and that all this cavern or immense reservoir was filled in a very short time. Perhaps even this water, subjected to the fierce action of central heat, had partly been resolved into vapour. This would explain the existence of those clouds suspended over our heads and the development of that electricity which raised such tempests within the bowels of the earth.

This theory of the phenomena we had witnessed seemed satisfactory to me; for however great and stupendous the phenomena of nature, fixed physical laws will or may always explain them.

We were therefore walking upon sedimentary soil, the deposits of the waters of former ages. The Professor was carefully examining every little fissure in the rocks. Wherever he saw a hole he always wanted to know the depth of it. To him this was important.

We had traversed the shores of the Liedenbrock sea for a mile when we observed a sudden change in the appearance of the soil. It seemed upset, contorted, and convulsed by a violent upheaval of the lower strata. In many places depressions or elevations gave witness to some tremendous power effecting the dislocation of strata.

We moved with difficulty across these granite fissures and chasms mingled with silex, crystals of quartz, and alluvial deposits, when a field, nay, more than a field, a vast plain, of bleached bones lay spread before us. It seemed like an immense cemetery, where the remains of twenty ages mingled their dust together. Huge mounds of bony fragments rose

---

*The glyptodon and armadillo are mammalian; the tortoise is a chelonian, a reptile, distinct classes of the animal kingdom; therefore the latter cannot be a representative of the former. (Trans.)

stage after stage in the distance. They undulated away to the limits of the horizon, and melted in the distance in a faint haze. There within three square miles were accumulated the materials for a complete history of the animal life of ages, a history scarcely outlined in the too recent strata of the inhabited world.

But an impatient curiosity impelled our steps; crackling and rattling, our feet were trampling on the remains of prehistoric animals and interesting fossils, the possession of which is a matter of rivalry and contention between the museums of great cities. A thousand Cuviers could never have reconstructed the organic remains deposited in this magnificent and unparalleled collection.

I stood amazed. My uncle had uplifted his long arms to the vault which was our sky; his mouth gaping wide, his eyes flashing behind his shining spectacles, his head balancing with an up-and-down motion, his whole attitude denoted unlimited astonishment. Here he stood facing an immense collection of scattered leptotheria, mericotheria, lophiodia, anoplotheria, megatheria, mastodons, protopithecae, pterodactyles, and all sorts of extinct monsters here assembled together for his special satisfaction. Fancy an enthusiastic bibliomaniac suddenly brought into the midst of the famous Alexandrian library burned by Omar and restored by a miracle from its ashes! just such a crazed enthusiast was my uncle, Professor Liedenbrock.

But more was to come, when, with a rush through clouds of bone dust, he laid his hand upon a bare skull, and cried with a voice trembling with excitement:

"Axel! Axel! a human head!"

"A human skull?" I cried, no less astonished.

"Yes, nephew. Aha! M. Milne-Edwards! Ah! M. de Quatrefages, how I wish you were standing here at the side of Otto Liedenbrock!"

Chapter XXXVIII

THE PROFESSOR IN HIS CHAIR AGAIN

To UNDERSTAND THIS APOSTROPHE OF MY UNCLE'S, MADE TO ABSENT FRENCH SAVANTS, it will be necessary to allude to an event of high importance in a palaeontological point of view, which had occurred a little while before our departure.

On the 28th of March, 1863, some excavators working under the direction of M. Boucher de Perthes, in the stone quarries of Moulin Quignon, near Abbeville, in the department of Somme, found a human jawbone fourteen feet beneath the surface. It was the first fossil of this nature that had ever been brought to light. Not far distant were found stone hatchets and flint arrow-heads stained and encased by lapse of time with a uniform coat of rust.

The noise of this discovery was very great, not in France alone, but in England and in Germany. Several savants of the French Institute, and amongst them MM. Milne-Edwards and de Quatrefages, saw at once the importance of this discovery, proved to demonstration the genuineness of the bone in question, and became the most ardent defendants in what the English called this "trial of a jawbone."

To the geologists of the United Kingdom, who believed in the certainty of the fact—Messrs. Falconer, Busk, Carpenter, and others—scientific Germans were soon joined, and amongst them the forwardest, the most fiery, and the most enthusiastic, was my uncle Liedenbrock.

Therefore the genuineness of a fossil human relic of the quaternary period seemed to be incontestably proved and admitted.

It is true that this theory met with a most obstinate opponent in M. Elie de Beaumont. This high authority maintained that the soil of Moulin Quignon was not diluvial at all, but was of much more recent formation; and, agreeing in that with Cuvier, he refused to admit that the human species could be contemporary with the animals of the quaternary period. My uncle Liedenbrock, along with the great body of the geologists, had maintained his ground, disputed, and argued, until M. Elie de Beaumont stood almost alone in his opinion.

We knew all these details, but we were not aware that since our departure the question had advanced to farther stages. Other similar maxillaries, though belonging to individuals of various types and different nations, were found in the loose grey soil of certain grottoes in France, Switzerland, and Belgium, as well as weapons, tools, earthen utensils, bones of children and adults. The existence therefore of man in the quaternary period seemed to become daily more certain.

Nor was this all. Fresh discoveries of remains in the pleiocene formation had emboldened other geologists to refer back the human species to a higher antiquity still. It is true that these remains were not human bones, but objects bearing the traces of his handiwork, such as fossil leg-bones of animals, sculptured and carved evidently by the hand of man.

Thus, at one bound, the record of the existence of man receded far back into the history of the ages past; he was a predecessor of the mastodon; he was a contemporary of the southern elephant; he lived a hundred thousand years ago, when, according to geologists, the pleiocene formation was in progress.

Such then was the state of palaeontological science, and what we knew of it was sufficient to explain our behaviour in the presence of this stupendous Golgotha. Anyone may now understand the frenzied excitement of my uncle, when, twenty yards farther on, he found himself face to face with a primitive man!

It was a perfectly recognisable human body. Had some particular soil, like that of the cemetery St. Michel, at Bordeaux, preserved it thus for so many ages? It might be so. But this dried corpse, with its parchment-like skin drawn tightly over the bony frame, the limbs still preserving their shape, sound teeth, abundant hair, and finger and toe nails of frightful length, this desiccated mummy startled us by appearing just as it had lived countless ages ago. I stood mute before this apparition of remote antiquity. My uncle, usually so garrulous, was struck dumb likewise. We raised the body. We stood it up against a rock. It seemed to stare at us out of its empty orbits. We sounded with our knuckles his hollow frame.

After some moments' silence the Professor was himself again. Otto Liedenbrock, yielding to his nature, forgot all the circumstances of our eventful journey, forgot where we were standing, forgot the vaulted cavern which contained us. No doubt he was in mind back again in his Johannæum, holding forth to his pupils, for he assumed his learned air; and addressing himself to an imaginary audience, he proceeded thus:

"Gentlemen, I have the honour to introduce to you a man of the quaternary or post-tertiary system. Eminent geologists have denied his existence, others no less eminent have affirmed it. The St. Thomases of palaeontology, if they were here, might now touch him with their fingers, and would be obliged to acknowledge their error. I am quite aware that science has to be on its guard with discoveries of this kind. I know what capital enterprising individuals like Barnum have made out of fossil men. I have heard the tale of the kneepan of Ajax, the pretended body of Orestes claimed to have been found by the Spartans, and of the body of Asterius, ten cubits long, of which Pausanias speaks. I have read the reports of the skeleton of Trapani, found in the fourteenth century, and which was at the time identified as that of Polyphemus; and the history of the giant unearthed in the sixteenth century near Palermo. You know as well as I do, gentlemen, the analysis made at Lucerne in 1577 of those huge bones which the celebrated Dr. Felix Plater affirmed to be those of a giant nineteen feet high. I have gone through the treatises of Cassanion, and all those memoirs, pamphlets, answers, and rejoinders published respecting the skeleton of Teutobochus, the invader of Gaul, dug out of a sandpit in the Dauphiné, in 1613. In the eighteenth century I would have stood up for Scheuchzer's pre-adamite man against Peter Campet. I have perused a writing, entitled Gigan—"

Here my uncle's unfortunate infirmity met him—that of being unable in public to pronounce hard words.

"The pamphlet entitled Gigan—"

He could get no further.

"Giganteo—"

It was not to be done. The unlucky word would not come out. At the Johannæum there would have been a laugh.

"Gigantostéologie," at last the Professor burst out, between two words which I shall not record here.

Then rushing on with renewed vigour, and with great animation:

"Yes, gentlemen, I know all these things, and more. I know that Cuvier and Blumenbach have recognised in these bones nothing more remarkable than the bones of the mammoth and other mammals of the post-tertiary period. But in the presence of this specimen to doubt would be to insult science. There stands the body! You may see it, touch it. It is not a mere skeleton; it is an entire body, preserved for a purely anthropological end and purpose."

I was good enough not to contradict this startling assertion.

"If I could only wash it in a solution of sulphuric acid," pursued my uncle, "I should be able to clear it from all the earthy particles and the shells which are incrusted about it. But I do not possess that valuable solvent. Yet, such as it is, the body shall tell us its own wonderful story."

Here the Professor laid hold of the fossil skeleton, and handled it with the skill of a dexterous showman.

"You see," he said, "that it is not six feet long, and that we are still separated by a long interval from the pretended race of giants. As for the family to which it belongs, it is evidently Caucasian. It is the white race, our own. The skull of this fossil is a regular oval, or rather ovoid. It exhibits no prominent cheekbones, no projecting jaws. It presents no appearance of that prognathism which diminishes the facial angle.* Measure that angle. It is nearly ninety degrees. But I will go further in my deductions, and I will affirm that this specimen of the human family is of the Japhetic race, which has since spread from the Indies to the Atlantic. Don't smile, gentlemen."

Nobody was smiling; but the learned Professor was frequently disturbed by the broad smiles provoked by his learned eccentricities.

"Yes," he pursued with animation, "this is a fossil man, the contemporary of the mastodons whose remains fill this amphitheatre. But if you ask me how he came there, how those strata on which he lay slipped down into this enormous hollow in the globe, I confess I cannot answer that question. No doubt in the post-tertiary period considerable commotions were still disturbing the crust of the earth. The long-continued cooling of the globe produced chasms, fissures, clefts, and faults, into which, very probably, portions of the upper earth may have fallen. I make no rash assertions; but there is the man surrounded by his own works, by hatchets, by flint arrow-heads, which are the characteristics of the stone age. And unless he came here, like myself, as a tourist on a visit and as a pioneer of science, I can entertain no doubt of the authenticity of his remote origin."

The Professor ceased to speak, and the audience broke out into loud and unanimous applause. For of course my uncle was right, and wiser men than his nephew would have had some trouble to refute his statements.

Another remarkable thing. This fossil body was not the only one in this immense catacomb. We came upon other bodies at every step amongst this mortal dust, and my uncle might select the most curious of these specimens to demolish the incredulity of skeptics.

In fact it was a wonderful spectacle, that of these generations of men and animals commingled in a common cemetery. Then one very serious question arose presently which we scarcely dared to suggest. Had all those creatures slided through a great fissure in the crust of the earth, down to the shores of the Liedenbrock sea, when they were dead and turning to dust, or had they lived and grown and died here in this subterranean world under a false sky, just like inhabitants of the upper earth? Until the present time we had seen alive only marine monsters and fishes. Might not some living man, some native of the abyss, be yet a wanderer below on this desert strand?

*The facial angle is formed by two lines; one touching the brow and the front teeth, the other from the orifice of the ear to the lower line of the nostrils. The greater this angle, the higher intelligence denoted by the formation of the skull. Prognathism is that projection of the jaw-bones which sharpens or lessons this angle, and which is illustrated in the negro countenance and in the lowest savages.

Chapter XXXIX

FOREST SCENERY ILLUMINATED BY ELECTRICITY

FOR ANOTHER HALF-HOUR WE TROD UPON A PAVEMENT OF BONES. WE PUSHED ON, IMpelled by our burning curiosity. What other marvels did this cavern contain? What new treasures lay here for science to unfold? I was prepared for any surprise, my imagination was ready for any astonishment however astounding.

We had long lost sight of the seashore behind the hills of bones. The rash Professor, careless of losing his way, hurried me forward. We advanced in silence, bathed in luminous electric fluid. By some phenomenon which I am unable to explain, it lighted up all sides of every object equally. Such was its diffusiveness, there being no central point from which the light emanated, that shadows no longer existed. You might have thought yourself under the rays of a vertical sun in a tropical region at noonday and the height of summer. No vapour was visible. The rocks, the distant mountains, a few isolated clumps of forest trees in the distance, presented a weird and wonderful aspect under these totally new conditions of a universal diffusion of light. We were like Hoffmann's shadowless man.

After walking a mile we reached the outskirts of a vast forest, but not one of those forests of fungi which bordered Port Gräuben.

Here was the vegetation of the tertiary period in its fullest blaze of magnificence. Tall palms, belonging to species no longer living, splendid palmacites, firs, yews, cypress-trees, thujas, representatives of the coniferae, were linked together by a tangled network of long climbing plants. A soft carpet of moss and hepaticas luxuriously clothed the soil. A few sparkling streams ran almost in silence under what would have been the shade of the trees, but that there was no shadow. On their banks grew tree-ferns similar to those we grow in hot-houses. But a remarkable feature was the total absence of colour in all those trees, shrubs, and plants, growing without the life-giving heat and light of the sun. Everything seemed mixed-up and confounded in one uniform silver grey or light brown tint like that of fading and faded leaves. Not a green leaf anywhere, and the flowers—which were abundant enough in the tertiary period, which first gave birth to flowers—looked like brown-paper flowers, without colour or scent.

My uncle Liedenbrock ventured to penetrate under this colossal grove. I followed him, not without fear. Since nature had here provided vegetable nourishment, why should not the terrible mammals be there too? I perceived in the broad clearings left by fallen trees, decayed with age, leguminose plants, acerineae, rubiaceae, and many other eatable shrubs, dear to ruminant animals at every period. Then I observed, mingled together in confusion, trees of countries far apart on the surface of the globe. The oak and the palm were growing side by side, the Australian eucalyptus leaned against the Norwegian pine, the birch-tree of the north mingled its foliage with New Zealand kauris. It was enough to distract the most ingenious classifier of terrestrial botany.

Suddenly I halted. I drew back my uncle.

The diffused light revealed the smallest object in the dense and distant thickets. I had thought I saw—no! I did see, with my own eyes, vast colossal forms moving amongst the trees. They were gigantic animals; it was a herd of mastodons—not fossil remains, but living and resembling those the bones of which were found in the marshes of Ohio in 1801. I saw those huge elephants whose long, flexible trunks were grouting and turning up the soil under the trees like a legion of serpents. I could hear the crashing noise of their long ivory tusks boring into the old decaying trunks. The boughs cracked, and the leaves torn away by cartloads went down the cavernous throats of the vast brutes.

So, then, the dream in which I had had a vision of the prehistoric world, of the tertiary and post-tertiary periods, was now realised. And there we were alone, in the bowels of the earth, at the mercy of its wild inhabitants!

My uncle was gazing with intense and eager interest.

"Come on!" said he, seizing my arm. "Forward! forward!"

"No, I will not!" I cried. "We have no fire-arms. What could we do in the midst of a herd of these four-footed giants? Come away, uncle—come! No human being may with safety dare the anger of these monstrous beasts."

"No human creature?" replied my uncle in a lower voice. "You are wrong, Axel. Look, look down there! I fancy I see a living creature similar to ourselves; it is a man!"

I looked, shaking my head incredulously. But though at first I was unbelieving I had to yield to the evidence of my senses.

In fact, at a distance of a quarter of a mile, leaning against the trunk of a gigantic kauri, stood a human being, the Proteus of those subterranean regions, a new son of Neptune, watching this countless herd of mastodons.

Immanis pecoris custos, immanior ipse. *

Yes, truly, huger still himself. It was no longer a fossil being like him whose dried remains we had easily lifted up in the field of bones; it was a giant, able to control those monsters. In stature he was at least twelve feet high. His head, huge and unshapely as a buffalo's, was half hidden in the thick and tangled growth of his unkempt hair. It most resembled the mane of the primitive elephant. In his hand he wielded with ease an enormous bough, a staff worthy of this shepherd of the geologic period.

We stood petrified and speechless with amazement. But he might see us! We must fly!

"Come, do come!" I said to my uncle, who for once allowed himself to be persuaded.

In another quarter of an hour our nimble heels had carried us beyond the reach of this horrible monster.

And yet, now that I can reflect quietly, now that my spirit has grown calm again, now that months have slipped by since this strange and supernatural meeting, what am I to think? what am I to believe? I must conclude that it was impossible that our senses had been deceived, that our eyes did not see what we supposed they saw. No human being lives in this subterranean world; no generation of men dwells in those inferior caverns of the globe, unknown to and unconnected with the inhabitants of its surface. It is absurd to believe it!

I had rather admit that it may have been some animal whose structure resembled the human, some ape or baboon of the early geological ages, some protopitheca, or some

*"The shepherd of gigantic herds, and huger still himself."

mesopitheca, some early or middle ape like that discovered by Mr. Lartet in the bone cave of Sansau. But this creature surpassed in stature all the measurements known in modern palaeontology. But that a man, a living man, and therefore whole generations doubtless besides, should be buried there in the bowels of the earth, is impossible.

However, we had left behind us the luminous forest, dumb with astonishment, overwhelmed and struck down with a terror which amounted to stupefaction. We kept running on for fear the horrible monster might be on our track. It was a flight, a fall, like that fearful pulling and dragging which is peculiar to nightmare. Instinctively we got back to the Liedenbrock sea, and I cannot say into what vagaries my mind would not have carried me but for a circumstance which brought me back to practical matters.

Although I was certain that we were now treading upon a soil not hitherto touched by our feet, I often perceived groups of rocks which reminded me of those about Port Gräuben. Besides, this seemed to confirm the indications of the needle, and to show that we had against our will returned to the north of the Liedenbrock sea. Occasionally we felt quite convinced. Brooks and waterfalls were tumbling everywhere from the projections in the rocks. I thought I recognised the bed of surturbrand, our faithful Hansbach, and the grotto in which I had recovered life and consciousness. Then, a few paces farther on, the arrangement of the cliffs, the appearance of an unrecognised stream, or the strange outline of a rock, came to throw me again into doubt.

I communicated my doubts to my uncle. Like myself, he hesitated; he could recognise nothing again amidst this monotonous scene.

"Evidently," said I, "we have not landed again at our original starting point, but the storm has carried us a little higher, and if we follow the shore we shall find Port Gräuben."

"If that is the case it will be useless to continue our exploration, and we had better return to our raft. But, Axel, are you not mistaken?"

"It is difficult to speak decidedly, uncle, for all these rocks are so very much alike. Yet I think I recognise the promontory at the foot of which Hans constructed our launch. We must be very near the little port, if indeed this is not it," I added, examining a creek which I thought I recognised.

"No, Axel, we should at least find our own traces and I see nothing—"

"But I do see," I cried, darting upon an object lying on the sand.

And I showed my uncle a rusty dagger which I had just picked up.

"Come," said he, "had you this weapon with you?"

"I! No, certainly! But you, perhaps—"

"Not that I am aware," said the Professor. "I have never had this object in my possession."

"Well, this is strange!"

"No, Axel, it is very simple. The Icelanders often wear arms of this kind. This must have belonged to Hans, and he has lost it."

I shook my head. Hans had never had an object like this in his possession.

"Did it not belong to some pre-adamite warrior?" I cried, "to some living man, contemporary with the huge cattle-driver? But no. This is not a relic of the stone age. It is not even of the iron age. This blade is steel—"

My uncle stopped me abruptly on my way to a dissertation which would have taken me a long way, and said coolly:

"Be calm, Axel, and reasonable. This dagger belongs to the sixteenth century; it is a poniard, such as gentlemen carried in their belts to give the *coup de grace*. Its origin is Spanish. It was never either yours, or mine, or the hunter's, nor did it belong to any of those human beings who may or may not inhabit this inner world. See, it was never jagged like this by cutting men's throats; its blade is coated with a rust neither a day, nor a year, nor a hundred years old."

The Professor was getting excited according to his wont, and was allowing his imagination to run away with him.

"Axel, we are on the way towards the grand discovery. This blade has been left on the strand for from one to three hundred years, and has blunted its edge upon the rocks that fringe this subterranean sea!"

"But it has not come alone. It has not twisted itself out of shape; someone has been here before us!

"Yes—a man has."

"And who was that man?"

"A man who has engraved his name somewhere with that dagger. That man wanted once more to mark the way to the center of the earth. Let us look about: look about!"

And, wonderfully interested, we peered all along the high wall, peeping into every fissure which might open out into a gallery.

And so we arrived at a place where the shore was much narrowed. Here the sea came to lap the foot of the steep cliff, leaving a passage no wider than a couple of yards. Between two boldly projecting rocks appeared the mouth of a dark tunnel.

There, upon a granite slab, appeared two mysterious graven letters, half eaten away by time. They were the initials of the bold and daring traveller:—

$$\cdot \; \mathbf{\mathcal{1}} \cdot \mathbf{\mathcal{4}} \cdot$$

"A. S.," shouted my uncle. "Arne Saknussemm! Arne Saknussemm everywhere!"

Chapter XL

PREPARATIONS FOR BLASTING A PASSAGE TO THE CENTER OF THE EARTH

SINCE THE START UPON THIS MARVELLOUS PILGRIMAGE I HAD BEEN THROUGH SO MANY astonishments that I might well be excused for thinking myself well hardened against any further surprise. Yet at the sight of these two letters, engraved on this spot three hundred years ago, I stood aghast in dumb amazement. Not only were the initials of the learned alchemist visible upon the living rock, but there lay the iron point with which the letters had been engraved. I could no longer doubt of the existence of that wonderful traveller and of the fact of his unparalleled journey, without the most glaring incredulity.

Whilst these reflections were occupying me, Professor Liedenbrock had launched into a somewhat rhapsodical eulogium, of which Arne Saknussemm was, of course, the hero.

"Thou marvellous genius!" he cried, "thou hast not forgotten one indication which might serve to lay open to mortals the road through the terrestrial crust; and thy fellow-creatures may even now, after the lapse of three centuries, again trace thy footsteps through these deep and darksome ways. You reserved the contemplation of these wonders for other eyes besides your own. Your name, graven from stage to stage, leads the bold follower of your footsteps to the very center of our planet's core, and there again we shall find your own name written with your own hand. I too will inscribe my name upon this dark granite page. But forever henceforth let this cape that advances into the sea discovered by yourself be known by your own illustrious name—Cape Saknussemm."

Such were the glowing words of panegyric which fell upon my attentive ear, and I could not resist the sentiment of enthusiasm with which I too was infected. The fire of zeal kindled afresh in me. I forgot everything. I dismissed from my mind the past perils of the journey, the future danger of our return. That which another had done I supposed we might also do, and nothing that was not superhuman appeared impossible to me.

"Forward! forward!" I cried.

I was already darting down the gloomy tunnel when the Professor stopped me; he, the man of impulse, counselled patience and coolness.

"Let us first return to Hans," he said, "and bring the raft to this spot."

I obeyed, not without dissatisfaction, and passed out rapidly among the rocks on the shore.

I said: "Uncle, do you know it seems to me that circumstances have wonderfully befriended us hitherto?"

"You think so, Axel?"

"No doubt; even the tempest has put us on the right way. Blessings on that storm! It has brought us back to this coast from which fine weather would have carried us far away. Suppose we had touched with our prow (the prow of a rudder!) the southern shore of the Liedenbrock sea, what would have become of us? We should never have seen the name of Saknussemm, and we should at this moment be imprisoned on a rockbound, impassable coast."

"Yes, Axel, it is providential that whilst supposing we were steering south we should have just got back north at Cape Saknussemm. I must say that this is astonishing, and that I feel I have no way to explain it."

"What does that signify, uncle? Our business is not to explain facts, but to use them!"

"Certainly; but—"

"Well, uncle, we are going to resume the northern route, and to pass under the north countries of Europe—under Sweden, Russia, Siberia: who knows where?—instead of burrowing under the deserts of Africa, or perhaps the waves of the Atlantic; and that is all I want to know."

"Yes, Axel, you are right. It is all for the best, since we have left that weary, horizontal sea, which led us nowhere. Now we shall go down, down, down! Do you know that it is now only 1,500 leagues to the center of the globe?"

"Is that all?" I cried. "Why, that's nothing. Let us start: march!"

All this crazy talk was going on still when we met the hunter. Everything was made ready for our instant departure. Every bit of cordage was put on board. We took our places, and with our sail set, Hans steered us along the coast to Cape Saknussemm.

The wind was unfavourable to a species of launch not calculated for shallow water. In many places we were obliged to push ourselves along with iron-pointed sticks. Often the sunken rocks just beneath the surface obliged us to deviate from our straight course. At last, after three hours' sailing, about six in the evening we reached a place suitable for our landing. I jumped ashore, followed by my uncle and the Icelander. This short passage had not served to cool my ardour. On the contrary, I even proposed to burn "our ship," to prevent the possibility of return; but my uncle would not consent to that. I thought him singularly lukewarm.

"At least," I said, "don't let us lose a minute."

"Yes, yes, lad," he replied; "but first let us examine this new gallery, to see if we shall require our ladders."

My uncle put his Ruhmkorff's apparatus in action; the raft moored to the shore was left alone; the mouth of the tunnel was not twenty yards from us; and our party, with myself at the head, made for it without a moment's delay.

The aperture, which was almost round, was about five feet in diameter; the dark passage was cut out in the live rock and lined with a coat of the irruptive matter which formerly issued from it; the interior was level with the ground outside, so that we were able to enter without difficulty. We were following a horizontal plane, when, only six paces in, our progress was interrupted by an enormous block just across our way.

"Accursed rock!" I cried in a passion, finding myself suddenly confronted by an impassable obstacle.

Right and left we searched in vain for a way, up and down, side to side; there was no getting any farther. I felt fearfully disappointed, and I would not admit that the obstacle was final. I stopped, I looked underneath the block: no opening. Above: granite still. Hans passed his lamp over every portion of the barrier in vain. We must give up all hope of passing it.

I sat down in despair. My uncle strode from side to side in the narrow passage.

"But how was it with Saknussemm?" I cried.

"Yes," said my uncle, "was he stopped by this stone barrier?"

"No, no," I replied with animation. "This fragment of rock has been shaken down by some shock or convulsion, or by one of those magnetic storms which agitate these regions, and has blocked up the passage which lay open to him. Many years have elapsed since the return of Saknussemm to the surface and the fall of this huge fragment. Is it not evident that this gallery was once the way open to the course of the lava, and that at that time there must have been a free passage? See here are recent fissures grooving and channelling the granite roof. This roof itself is formed of fragments of rock carried down, of enormous stones, as if by some giant's hand; but at one time the expulsive force was greater than usual, and this block, like the falling keystone of a ruined arch, has slipped down to the ground and blocked up the way. It is only an accidental obstruction, not met by Saknussemm, and if we don't destroy it we shall be unworthy to reach the center of the earth."

Such was my sentence! The soul of the Professor had passed into me. The genius of discovery possessed me wholly. I forgot the past, I scorned the future. I gave not a thought to the things of the surface of this globe into which I had dived; its cities and its sunny plains, Hamburg and the Königstrasse, even poor Gräuben, who must have given us up for lost, all were for the time dismissed from the pages of my memory.

"Well," cried my uncle, "let us make a way with our pickaxes."

"Too hard for the pickaxe."

"Well, then, the spade."

"That would take us too long."

"What, then?"

"Why gunpowder, to be sure! Let us mine the obstacle and blow it up."

"Oh, yes, it is only a bit of rock to blast!"

"Hans, to work!" cried my uncle.

The Icelander returned to the raft and soon came back with an iron bar which he made use of to bore a hole for the charge. This was no easy work. A hole was to be made large enough to hold fifty pounds of guncotton, whose expansive force is four times that of gunpowder.

I was terribly excited. Whilst Hans was at work I was actively helping my uncle to prepare a slow match of wetted powder encased in linen.

"This will do it," I said.

"It will," replied my uncle.

By midnight our mining preparations were over; the charge was rammed into the hole, and the slow match uncoiled along the gallery showed its end outside the opening.

A spark would now develop the whole of our preparations into activity.

"To-morrow," said the Professor.

I had to be resigned, and to wait six long hours.

Chapter XLI

The Great Explosion and the Rush Down Below

THE NEXT DAY, THURSDAY, AUGUST 27, IS A WELL-REMEMBERED DATE IN OUR SUBTERranean journey. It never returns to my memory without sending through me a shudder of horror and a palpitation of the heart. From that hour we had no further occasion for the exercise of reason, or judgment, or skill, or contrivance. We were henceforth to be hurled along, the playthings of the fierce elements of the deep.

At six we were afoot. The moment drew near to clear a way by blasting through the opposing mass of granite.

I begged for the honour of lighting the fuse. This duty done, I was to join my companions on the raft, which had not yet been unloaded; we should then push off as far as we could and avoid the dangers arising from the explosion, the effects of which were not likely to be confined to the rock itself.

The fuse was calculated to burn ten minutes before setting fire to the mine. I therefore had sufficient time to get away to the raft.

I prepared to fulfil my task with some anxiety.

After a hasty meal, my uncle and the hunter embarked whilst I remained on shore. I was supplied with a lighted lantern to set fire to the fuse.

"Now go," said my uncle, "and return immediately to us."

"Don't be uneasy," I replied. "I will not play by the way."

I immediately proceeded to the mouth of the tunnel. I opened my lantern. I laid hold of the end of the match.

The Professor stood, chronometer in hand.

"Ready?" he cried.

"Ay."

"Fire!"

I instantly plunged the end of the fuse into the lantern. It spluttered and flamed, and I ran at the top of my speed to the raft.

"Come on board quickly, and let us push off."

Hans, with a vigorous thrust, sent us from the shore. The raft shot twenty fathoms out to sea.

It was a moment of intense excitement. The Professor was watching the hand of the chronometer.

"Five minutes more!" he said. "Four! Three!"

My pulse beat half-seconds.

"Two! One! Down, granite rocks; down with you."

What took place at that moment? I believe I did not hear the dull roar of the explosion. But the rocks suddenly assumed a new arrangement: they rent asunder like a curtain. I saw a bottomless pit open on the shore. The sea, lashed into sudden fury, rose up in an enormous billow, on the ridge of which the unhappy raft was uplifted bodily in the air with all its crew and cargo.

We all three fell down flat. In less than a second we were in deep, unfathomable darkness. Then I felt as if not only myself but the raft also had no support beneath. I thought it was sinking; but it was not so. I wanted to speak to my uncle, but the roaring of the waves prevented him from hearing even the sound of my voice.

In spite of darkness, noise, astonishment, and terror, I then understood what had taken place.

On the other side of the blown-up rock was an abyss. The explosion had caused a kind of earthquake in this fissured and abysmal region; a great gulf had opened; and the sea, now changed into a torrent, was hurrying us along into it.

I gave myself up for lost.

An hour passed away—two hours, perhaps—I cannot tell. We clutched each other fast, to save ourselves from being thrown off the raft. We felt violent shocks whenever we were borne heavily against the craggy projections. Yet these shocks were not very frequent, from which I concluded that the gully was widening. It was no doubt the same road that Saknussemm had taken; but instead of walking peaceably down it, as he had done, we were carrying a whole sea along with us.

These ideas, it will be understood, presented themselves to my mind in a vague and undetermined form. I had difficulty in associating any ideas together during this headlong race, which seemed like a vertical descent. To judge by the air which was whistling past me and made a whizzing in my ears, we were moving faster than the fastest express trains. To light a torch under these conditions would have been impossible; and our last electric apparatus had been shattered by the force of the explosion.

I was therefore much surprised to see a clear light shining near me. It lighted up the calm and unmoved countenance of Hans. The skilful huntsman had succeeded in lighting the lantern; and although it flickered so much as to threaten to go out, it threw a fitful light across the awful darkness.

I was right in my supposition. It was a wide gallery. The dim light could not show us both its walls at once. The fall of the waters which were carrying us away exceeded that of the swiftest rapids in American rivers. Its surface seemed composed of a sheaf of arrows hurled with inconceivable force; I cannot convey my impressions by a better comparison. The raft, occasionally seized by an eddy, spun round as it still flew along. When it approached the walls of the gallery I threw on them the light of the lantern, and I could judge somewhat of the velocity of our speed by noticing how the jagged projections of the rocks spun into endless ribbons and bands, so that we seemed confined within a network of shifting lines. I supposed we were running at the rate of thirty leagues an hour.

My uncle and I gazed on each other with haggard eyes, clinging to the stump of the mast, which had snapped asunder at the first shock of our great catastrophe. We kept our backs to the wind, not to be stifled by the rapidity of a movement which no human power could check.

Hours passed away. No change in our situation; but a discovery came to complicate matters and make them worse.

In seeking to put our cargo into somewhat better order, I found that the greater part of the articles embarked had disappeared at the moment of the explosion, when the sea broke in upon us with such violence. I wanted to know exactly what we had saved, and with the lantern in my hand I began my examination. Of our instruments none were saved but the compass and the chronometer; our stock of ropes and ladders was reduced to the bit of cord rolled round the stump of the mast! Not a spade, not a pickaxe, not a hammer was left us; and, irreparable disaster! we had only one day's provisions left.

I searched every nook and corner, every crack and cranny in the raft. There was nothing. Our provisions were reduced to one bit of salt meat and a few biscuits.

I stared at our failing supplies stupidly. I refused to take in the gravity of our loss. And yet what was the use of troubling myself. If we had had provisions enough for months, how could we get out of the abyss into which we were being hurled by an irresistible torrent? Why should we fear the horrors of famine, when death was swooping down upon us in a multitude of other forms? Would there be time left to die of starvation?

Yet by an inexplicable play of the imagination I forgot my present dangers, to contemplate the threatening future. Was there any chance of escaping from the fury of this impetuous torrent, and of returning to the surface of the globe? I could not form the slightest conjecture how or when. But one chance in a thousand, or ten thousand, is still a chance; whilst death from starvation would leave us not the smallest hope in the world.

The thought came into my mind to declare the whole truth to my uncle, to show him the dreadful straits to which we were reduced, and to calculate how long we might yet expect to live. But I had the courage to preserve silence. I wished to leave him cool and self-possessed.

At that moment the light from our lantern began to sink by little and little, and then went out entirely. The wick had burned itself out. Black night reigned again; and there was no hope left of being able to dissipate the palpable darkness. We had yet a torch left, but we could not have kept it alight. Then, like a child, I closed my eyes firmly, not to see the darkness.

After a considerable lapse of time our speed redoubled. I could perceive it by the sharpness of the currents that blew past my face. The descent became steeper. I believe we were no longer sliding, but falling down. I had an impression that we were dropping vertically. My uncle's hand, and the vigorous arm of Hans, held me fast.

Suddenly, after a space of time that I could not measure, I felt a shock. The raft had not struck against any hard resistance, but had suddenly been checked in its fall. A waterspout, an immense liquid column, was beating upon the surface of the waters. I was suffocating! I was drowning!

But this sudden flood was not of long duration. In a few seconds I found myself in the air again, which I inhaled with all the force of my lungs. My uncle and Hans were still holding me fast by the arms; and the raft was still carrying us.

Chapter XLII

HEADLONG SPEED UPWARD THROUGH
THE HORRORS OF DARKNESS

IT MIGHT HAVE BEEN, AS I GUESSED, ABOUT TEN AT NIGHT. THE FIRST OF MY SENSES WHICH came into play after this last bout was that of hearing. All at once I could hear; and it was a real exercise of the sense of hearing. I could hear the silence in the gallery after the din which for hours had stunned me. At last these words of my uncle's came to me like a vague murmuring:

"We are going up."

"What do you mean?" I cried.

"Yes, we are going up—up!"

I stretched out my arm. I touched the wall, and drew back my hand bleeding. We were ascending with extreme rapidity.

"The torch! The torch!" cried the Professor.

Not without difficulty Hans succeeded in lighting the torch; and the flame, preserving its upward tendency, threw enough light to show us what kind of a place we were in.

"Just as I thought," said the Professor. "We are in a tunnel not four-and-twenty feet in diameter. The water had reached the bottom of the gulf. It is now rising to its level, and carrying us with it."

"Where to?"

"I cannot tell; but we must be ready for anything. We are mounting at a speed which seems to me of fourteen feet in a second, or ten miles an hour. At this rate we shall get on."

"Yes, if nothing stops us; if this well has an aperture. But suppose it to be stopped. If the air is condensed by the pressure of this column of water we shall be crushed."

"Axel," replied the Professor with perfect coolness, "our situation is almost desperate; but there are some chances of deliverance, and it is these that I am considering. If at every instant we may perish, so at every instant we may be saved. Let us then be prepared to seize upon the smallest advantage."

"But what shall we do now?"

"Recruit our strength by eating."

At these words I fixed a haggard eye upon my uncle. That which I had been so unwilling to confess at last had to be told.

"Eat, did you say?"

"Yes, at once."

The Professor added a few words in Danish, but Hans shook his head mournfully.

"What!" cried my uncle. "Have we lost our provisions?"

"Yes; here is all we have left; one bit of salt meat for the three."

My uncle stared at me as if he could not understand.

"Well," said I, "do you think we have any chance of being saved?"

My question was unanswered.

An hour passed away. I began to feel the pangs of a violent hunger. My companions were suffering too; and not one of us dared touch this wretched remnant of our goodly store.

But now we were mounting up with excessive speed. Sometimes the air would cut our breath short, as is experienced by aeronauts ascending too rapidly. But whilst they suffer from cold in proportion to their rise, we were beginning to feel a contrary effect. The heat was increasing in a manner to cause us the most fearful anxiety, and certainly the temperature was at this moment at the height of 100° Fahr.

What could be the meaning of such a change? Up to this time facts had supported the theories of Davy and of Liedenbrock; until now particular conditions of non-conducting rocks, electricity and magnetism, had tempered the laws of nature, giving us only a moderately warm climate, for the theory of a central fire remained in my estimation the only one that was true and explicable. Were we then turning back to where the phenomena of central heat ruled in all their rigour and would reduce the most refractory rocks to the state of a molten liquid? I feared this, and said to the Professor:

"If we are neither drowned, nor shattered to pieces, nor starved to death, there is still the chance that we may be burned alive and reduced to ashes."

At this he shrugged his shoulders and returned to his thoughts.

Another hour passed, and, except some slight increase in the temperature, nothing new had happened.

"Come," said he, "we must determine upon something."

"Determine on what?" said I.

"Yes, we must recruit our strength by carefully rationing ourselves, and so prolong our existence by a few hours. But we shall be reduced to very great weakness at last."

"And our last hour is not far off."

"Well, if there is a chance of safety, if a moment for active exertion presents itself, where should we find the required strength if we allowed ourselves to be enfeebled by hunger?"

"Well, uncle, when this bit of meat has been devoured what shall we have left?"

"Nothing, Axel, nothing at all. But will it do you any more good to devour it with your eyes than with your teeth? Your reasoning has in it neither sense nor energy."

"Then don't you despair?" I cried irritably.

"No, certainly not," was the Professor's firm reply.

"What! do you think there is any chance of safety left?"

"Yes, I do; as long as the heart beats, as long as body and soul keep together, I cannot admit that any creature endowed with a will has need to despair of life."

Resolute words these! The man who could speak so, under such circumstances, was of no ordinary type.

"Finally, what do you mean to do?" I asked.

"Eat what is left to the last crumb, and recruit our fading strength. This meal will be our last, perhaps: so let it be! But at any rate we shall once more be men, and not exhausted, empty bags."

"Well, let us consume it then," I cried.

My uncle took the piece of meat and the few biscuits which had escaped from the general destruction. He divided them into three equal portions and gave one to each. This made about a pound of nourishment for each. The Professor ate his greedily, with a kind of feverish rage. I ate without pleasure, almost with disgust; Hans quietly, moderately, masticating his small mouthfuls without any noise, and relishing them with the calmness of a man above all anxiety about the future. By diligent search he had found a flask of Hollands; he offered it to us each in turn, and this generous beverage cheered us up slightly.

"Forträfflig," said Hans, drinking in his turn.

"Excellent," replied my uncle.

A glimpse of hope had returned, although without cause. But our last meal was over, and it was now five in the morning.

Man is so constituted that health is a purely negative state. Hunger once satisfied, it is difficult for a man to imagine the horrors of starvation; they cannot be understood without being felt. Therefore it was that after our long fast these few mouthfuls of meat and biscuit made us triumph over our past agonies.

But as soon as the meal was done, we each of us fell deep into thought. What was Hans thinking of—that man of the far West, but who seemed ruled by the fatalist doctrines of the East?

As for me, my thoughts were made up of remembrances, and they carried me up to the surface of the globe of which I ought never to have taken leave. The house in the Königstrasse, my poor dear Gräuben, that kind soul Martha, flitted like visions before my eyes, and in the dismal moanings which from time to time reached my ears I thought I could distinguish the roar of the traffic of the great cities upon earth.

My uncle still had his eye upon his work. Torch in hand, he tried to gather some idea of our situation from the observation of the strata. This calculation could, at best, be but a vague approximation; but a learned man is always a philosopher when he succeeds in remaining cool, and assuredly Professor Liedenbrock possessed this quality to a surprising degree.

I could hear him murmuring geological terms. I could understand them, and in spite of myself I felt interested in this last geological study.

"Irruptive granite," he was saying. "We are still in the primitive period. But we are going up, up, higher still. Who can tell?"

Ah! who can tell? With his hand he was examining the perpendicular wall, and in a few more minutes he continued:

"This is gneiss! here is mica schist! Ah! presently we shall come to the transition period, and then—"

What did the Professor mean? Could he be trying to measure the thickness of the crust of the earth that lay between us and the world above? Had he any means of making this calculation? No, he had not the aneroid, and no guessing could supply its place.

Still the temperature kept rising, and I felt myself steeped in a broiling atmosphere. I could only compare it to the heat of a furnace at the moment when the molten metal is running into the mould. Gradually we had been obliged to throw aside our coats and waistcoats, the lightest covering became uncomfortable and even painful.

"Are we rising into a fiery furnace?" I cried at one moment when the heat was redoubling.

"No," replied my uncle, "that is impossible—quite impossible!"

"Yet," I answered, feeling the wall, "this well is burning hot."

At the same moment, touching the water, I had to withdraw my hand in haste.

"The water is scalding," I cried.

This time the Professor's only answer was an angry gesture.

Then an unconquerable terror seized upon me, from which I could no longer get free. I felt that a catastrophe was approaching before which the boldest spirit must quail. A dim, vague notion laid hold of my mind, but which was fast hardening into certainty. I tried to repel it, but it would return. I dared not express it in plain terms. Yet a few involuntary observations confirmed me in my view. By the flickering light of the torch I could distinguish contortions in the granite beds; a phenomenon was unfolding in which electricity would play the principal part; then this unbearable heat, this boiling water! I consulted the compass.

The compass had lost its properties! it had ceased to act properly!

Chapter XLIII

Shot Out of a Volcano at Last!

Yes: our compass was no longer a guide; the needle flew from pole to pole with a kind of frenzied impulse; it ran round the dial, and spun hither and thither as if it were giddy or intoxicated.

I knew quite well that according to the best received theories the mineral covering of the globe is never at absolute rest; the changes brought about by the chemical decomposition of its component parts, the agitation caused by great liquid torrents, and the magnetic currents, are continually tending to disturb it—even when living beings upon its surface may fancy that all is quiet below. A phenomenon of this kind would not have greatly alarmed me, or at any rate it would not have given rise to dreadful apprehensions.

But other facts, other circumstances, of a peculiar nature, came to reveal to me by degrees the true state of the case. There came incessant and continuous explosions. I could only compare them to the loud rattle of a long train of chariots driven at full speed over the stones, or a roar of unintermitting thunder.

Then the disordered compass, thrown out of gear by the electric currents, confirmed me in a growing conviction. The mineral crust of the globe threatened to burst up, the granite foundations to come together with a crash, the fissure through which we were helplessly driven would be filled up, the void would be full of crushed fragments of rock, and we poor wretched mortals were to be buried and annihilated in this dreadful consummation.

"My uncle," I cried, "we are lost now, utterly lost!"

"What are you in a fright about now?" was the calm rejoinder. "What is the matter with you?"

"The matter? Look at those quaking walls! look at those shivering rocks. Don't you feel the burning heat? Don't you see how the water boils and bubbles? Are you blind to the dense vapours and steam growing thicker and denser every minute? See this agitated compass needle. It is an earthquake that is threatening us."

My undaunted uncle calmly shook his head.

"Do you think," said he, "an earthquake is coming?"

"I do."

"Well, I think you are mistaken."

"What! don't you recognise the symptoms?"

"Of an earthquake? no! I am looking out for something better."

"What can you mean? Explain?"

"It is an irruption, Axel."

"An irruption! Do you mean to affirm that we are running up the shaft of a volcano?"

"I believe we are," said the indomitable Professor with an air of perfect self-possession; "and it is the best thing that could possibly happen to us under our circumstances."

The best thing! Was my uncle stark mad? What did the man mean? and what was the use of saying facetious things at a time like this?

"What!" I shouted. "Are we being taken up in an irruption? Our fate has flung us here among burning lavas, molten rocks, boiling waters, and all kind of volcanic matter; we are going to be pitched out, expelled, tossed up, vomited, spit out high into the air, along with fragments of rock, showers of ashes and scoriae, in the midst of a towering rush of smoke and flames; and it is the best thing that could happen to us!"

"Yes," replied the Professor, eyeing me over his spectacles, "I don't see any other way of reaching the surface of the earth."

I pass rapidly over the thousand ideas which passed through my mind. My uncle was right, undoubtedly right; and never had he seemed to me more daring and more confirmed in his notions than at this moment, when he was calmly contemplating the chances of being shot out of a volcano!

In the meantime up we went; the night passed away in continual ascent; the din and uproar around us became more and more intensified; I was stifled and stunned; I thought my last hour was approaching; and yet imagination is such a strong thing that even in this supreme hour I was occupied with strange and almost childish speculations. But I was the victim, not the master, of my own thoughts.

It was very evident that we were being hurried upward upon the crest of a wave of irruption; beneath our raft were boiling waters, and under these the more sluggish lava was working its way up in a heated mass, together with shoals of fragments of rock which, when they arrived at the crater, would be dispersed in all directions high and low. We were imprisoned in the shaft or chimney of some volcano. There was no room to doubt of that.

But this time, instead of Snæfell, an extinct volcano, we were inside one in full activity. I wondered, therefore, where could this mountain be, and in what part of the world we were to be shot out.

I made no doubt but that it would be in some northern region. Before its disorders set in, the needle had never deviated from that direction. From Cape Saknussemm we had been carried due north for hundreds of leagues. Were we under Iceland again? Were we destined to be thrown up out of Hecla, or by which of the seven other fiery craters in that island? Within a radius of five hundred leagues to the west I remembered under this parallel of latitude only the imperfectly known volcanoes of the north-east coast of America. To the east there was only one in the 80th degree of north latitude, the Esk in Jan Mayen Island, not far from Spitzbergen! Certainly there was no lack of craters, and there were some capacious enough to throw out a whole army! But I wanted to know which of them was to serve us for an exit from the inner world.

Towards morning the ascending movement became accelerated. If the heat increased, instead of diminishing, as we approached nearer to the surface of the globe, this effect was due to local causes alone, and those volcanic. The manner of our locomotion left no doubt in my mind. An enormous force, a force of hundreds of atmospheres, generated by the extreme pressure of confined vapours, was driving us irresistibly forward. But to what numberless dangers it exposed us!

Soon lurid lights began to penetrate the vertical gallery which widened as we went up. Right and left I could see deep channels, like huge tunnels, out of which escaped dense volumes of smoke; tongues of fire lapped the walls, which crackled and sputtered under the intense heat.

"See, see, my uncle!" I cried.

"Well, those are only sulphureous flames and vapours, which one must expect to see in an irruption. They are quite natural."

"But suppose they should wrap us round."

"But they won't wrap us round."

"But we shall be stifled."

"We shall not be stifled at all. The gallery is widening, and if it becomes necessary, we shall abandon the raft, and creep into a crevice."

"But the water—the rising water?"

"There is no more water, Axel; only a lava paste, which is bearing us up on its surface to the top of the crater."

The liquid column had indeed disappeared, to give place to dense and still boiling irruptive matter of all kinds. The temperature was becoming unbearable. A thermometer exposed to this atmosphere would have marked 150°. The perspiration streamed from my body. But for the rapidity of our ascent we should have been suffocated.

But the Professor gave up his idea of abandoning the raft, and it was well he did. However roughly joined together, those planks afforded us a firmer support than we could have found anywhere else.

About eight in the morning a new incident occurred. The upward movement ceased. The raft lay motionless.

"What is this?" I asked, shaken by this sudden stoppage as if by a shock.

"It is a halt," replied my uncle.

"Is the irruption checked?" I asked.

"I hope not."

I rose, and tried to look around me. Perhaps the raft itself, stopped in its course by a projection, was staying the volcanic torrent. If this were the case we should have to release it as soon as possible.

But it was not so. The blast of ashes, scoriae, and rubbish had ceased to rise.

"Has the irruption stopped?" I cried.

"Ah!" said my uncle between his clenched teeth, "you are afraid. But don't alarm yourself—this lull cannot last long. It has lasted now five minutes, and in a short time we shall resume our journey to the mouth of the crater."

As he spoke, the Professor continued to consult his chronometer, and he was again right in his prognostications. The raft was soon hurried and driven forward with a rapid but irregular movement, which lasted about ten minutes, and then stopped again.

"Very good," said my uncle; "in ten minutes more we shall be off again, for our present business lies with an intermittent volcano. It gives us time now and then to take breath."

This was perfectly true. When the ten minutes were over we started off again with renewed and increased speed. We were obliged to lay fast hold of the planks of the raft, not to be thrown off. Then again the paroxysm was over.

I have since reflected upon this singular phenomenon without being able to explain it. At any rate it was clear that we were not in the main shaft of the volcano, but in a lateral gallery where there were felt recurrent times of reaction.

How often this operation was repeated I cannot say. All I know is, that at each fresh impulse we were hurled forward with a greatly increased force, and we seemed as if we were mere projectiles. During the short halts we were stifled with the heat; whilst we were being projected forward the hot air almost stopped my breath. I thought for a moment how delightful it would be to find myself carried suddenly into the arctic regions, with a cold 30° below the freezing point. My overheated brain conjured up visions of white plains of cool snow, where I might roll and allay my feverish heat. Little by little my brain, weakened by so many constantly repeated shocks, seemed to be giving way altogether. But for the strong arm of Hans I should more than once have had my head broken against the granite roof of our burning dungeon.

I have therefore no exact recollection of what took place during the following hours. I have a confused impression left of continuous explosions, loud detonations, a general shaking of the rocks all around us, and of a spinning movement with which our raft was once whirled helplessly round. It rocked upon the lava torrent, amidst a dense fall of ashes. Snorting flames darted their fiery tongues at us. There were wild, fierce puffs of stormy wind from below, resembling the blasts of vast iron furnaces blowing all at one time; and I caught a glimpse of the figure of Hans lighted up by the fire; and all the feeling I had left was just what I imagine must be the feeling of an unhappy criminal doomed to be blown away alive from the mouth of a cannon, just before the trigger is pulled, and the flying limbs and rags of flesh and skin fill the quivering air and spatter the blood-stained ground.

Chapter XLIV

SUNNY LANDS IN THE BLUE MEDITERRANEAN

W HEN I OPENED MY EYES AGAIN I FELT MYSELF GRASPED BY THE BELT WITH THE STRONG hand of our guide. With the other arm he supported my uncle. I was not seriously hurt, but I was shaken and bruised and battered all over. I found myself lying on the sloping side of a mountain only two yards from a gaping gulf, which would have swallowed me up had I leaned at all that way. Hans had saved me from death whilst I lay rolling on the edge of the crater.

"Where are we?" asked my uncle irascibly, as if he felt much injured by being landed upon the earth again.

The hunter shook his head in token of complete ignorance.

"Is it Iceland?" I asked.

"*Nej,*" replied Hans.

"What! Not Iceland?" cried the Professor.

"Hans must be mistaken," I said, raising myself up.

This was our final surprise after all the astonishing events of our wonderful journey. I expected to see a white cone covered with the eternal snow of ages rising from the midst of the barren deserts of the icy north, faintly lighted with the pale rays of the arctic sun, far away in the highest latitudes known; but contrary to all our expectations, my uncle, the Icelander, and myself were sitting half-way down a mountain baked under the burning rays of a southern sun, which was blistering us with the heat, and blinding us with the fierce light of his nearly vertical rays.

I could not believe my own eyes; but the heated air and the sensation of burning left me no room for doubt. We had come out of the crater half naked, and the radiant orb to which we had been strangers for two months was lavishing upon us out of his blazing splendours more of his light and heat than we were able to receive with comfort.

When my eyes had become accustomed to the bright light to which they had been so long strangers, I began to use them to set my imagination right. At least I would have it to be Spitzbergen, and I was in no humour to give up this notion.

The Professor was the first to speak, and said:

"Well, this is not much like Iceland."

"But is it Jan Mayen?" I asked.

"Nor that either," he answered. "This is no northern mountain; here are no granite peaks capped with snow. Look, Axel, look!"

Above our heads, at a height of five hundred feet or more, we saw the crater of a volcano, through which, at intervals of fifteen minutes or so, there issued with loud explosions lofty columns of fire, mingled with pumice stones, ashes, and flowing lava. I could feel the heaving of the mountain, which seemed to breathe like a huge whale, and puff out fire and wind from its vast blow-holes. Beneath, down a pretty steep declivity, ran streams of lava for eight or nine hundred feet, giving the mountain a height of about 1,300 or 1,400 feet. But the base of the mountain was hidden in a perfect bower of rich verdure, amongst which I was able to distinguish the olive, the fig, and vines, covered with their luscious purple bunches.

I was forced to confess that there was nothing arctic here.

When the eye passed beyond these green surroundings it rested on a wide, blue expanse of sea or lake, which appeared to enclose this enchanting island, within a compass of only a few leagues. Eastward lay a pretty little white seaport town or village, with a few houses scattered around it, and in the harbour of which a few vessels of peculiar rig were gently swayed by the softly swelling waves. Beyond it, groups of islets rose from the smooth, blue waters, but in such numbers that they seemed to dot the sea like a shoal. To the west distant coasts lined the dim horizon, on some rose blue mountains of smooth, undulating forms; on a more distant coast arose a prodigious cone crowned on its summit with a snowy plume of white cloud. To the northward lay spread a vast sheet of water, sparkling and dancing under the hot, bright rays, the uniformity broken here and there by the topmast of a gallant ship appearing above the horizon, or a swelling sail moving slowly before the wind.

This unforeseen spectacle was most charming to eyes long used to underground darkness.

"Where are we? Where are we?" I asked faintly.

Hans closed his eyes with lazy indifference. What did it matter to him? My uncle looked round with dumb surprise.

"Well, whatever mountain this may be," he said at last, "it is very hot here. The explosions are going on still, and I don't think it would look well to have come out by an irruption, and then to get our heads broken by bits of falling rock. Let us get down. Then we shall know better what we are about. Besides, I am starving, and parching with thirst."

Decidedly the Professor was not given to contemplation. For my part, I could for another hour or two have forgotten my hunger and my fatigue to enjoy the lovely scene before me; but I had to follow my companions.

The slope of the volcano was in many places of great steepness. We slid down screes of ashes, carefully avoiding the lava streams which glided sluggishly by us like fiery serpents. As we went I chattered and asked all sorts of questions as to our whereabouts, for I was too much excited not to talk a great deal.

"We are in Asia," I cried, "on the coasts of India, in the Malay Islands, or in Oceania. We have passed through half the globe, and come out nearly at the antipodes."

"But the compass?" said my uncle.

"Ay, the compass!" I said, greatly puzzled. "According to the compass we have gone northward."

"Has it lied?"

"Surely not. Could it lie?"

"Unless, indeed, this is the North Pole!"

"Oh, no, it is not the Pole; but——"

Well, here was something that baffled us completely. I could not tell what to say.

But now we were coming into that delightful greenery, and I was suffering greatly from hunger and thirst. Happily, after two hours' walking, a charming country lay open before us, covered with olive-trees, pomegranate-trees, and delicious vines, all of which seemed to belong to anybody who pleased to claim them. Besides, in our state of destitution and famine we were not likely to be particular. Oh, the inexpressible pleasure of pressing those cool, sweet fruits to our lips, and eating grapes by mouthfuls off the rich, full bunches! Not far off, in the grass, under the delicious shade of the trees, I discovered a spring of fresh, cool water, in which we luxuriously bathed our faces, hands, and feet.

Whilst we were thus enjoying the sweets of repose a child appeared out of a grove of olive-trees.

"Ah!" I cried, "here is an inhabitant of this happy land!"

It was but a poor boy, miserably ill-clad, a sufferer from poverty, and our aspect seemed to alarm him a great deal; in fact, only half clothed, with ragged hair and beards, we were a suspicious-looking party; and if the people of the country knew anything about thieves, we were very likely to frighten them.

Just as the poor little wretch was going to take to his heels, Hans caught hold of him, and brought him to us, kicking and struggling.

My uncle began to encourage him as well as he could, and said to him in good German:

"*Was heiszt diesen Berg, mein Knablein? Sage mir geschwind!*" ("What is this mountain called, my little friend?")

The child made no answer.

"Very well," said my uncle. "I infer that we are not in Germany."

He put the same question in English.

We got no forwarder. I was a good deal puzzled.

"Is the child dumb?" cried the Professor, who, proud of his knowledge of many languages, now tried French: "*Comment appelle-t-on cette montagne, mon enfant?*"

Silence still.

"Now let us try Italian," said my uncle; and he said: "*Dove noi siamo?*"

"Yes, where are we?" I impatiently repeated.

But there was no answer still.

"Will you speak when you are told?" exclaimed my uncle, shaking the urchin by the ears. "*Come si noma questa isola?*"

"STROMBOLI," replied the little herdboy, slipping out of Hans' hands, and scudding into the plain across the olive-trees.

We were hardly thinking of that. Stromboli! What an effect this unexpected name produced upon my mind! We were in the midst of the Mediterranean Sea, on an island of the Æolian archipelago, in the ancient Strongyle, where Æolus kept the winds and the storms chained up, to be let loose at his will. And those distant blue mountains in the east were the mountains of Calabria. And that threatening volcano far away in the south was the fierce Etna.

"Stromboli, Stromboli!" I repeated.

My uncle kept time to my exclamations with hands and feet, as well as with words. We seemed to be chanting in chorus!

What a journey we had accomplished! How marvellous! Having entered by one volcano, we had issued out of another more than two thousand miles from Snæfell and from that barren, far-away Iceland! The strange chances of our expedition had carried us into the heart of the fairest region in the world. We had exchanged the bleak regions of perpetual snow and of impenetrable barriers of ice for those of brightness and "the rich hues of all glorious things." We had left over our heads the murky sky and cold fogs of the frigid zone to revel under the azure sky of Italy!

After our delicious repast of fruits and cold, clear water we set off again to reach the port of Stromboli. It would not have been wise to tell how we came there. The superstitious Italians would have set us down for fire-devils vomited out of hell; so we presented ourselves in the humble guise of shipwrecked mariners. It was not so glorious, but it was safer.

On my way I could hear my uncle murmuring: "But the compass! that compass! It pointed due north. How are we to explain that fact?"

"My opinion is," I replied disdainfully, "that it is best not to explain it. That is the easiest way to shelve the difficulty."

"Indeed, sir! The occupant of a professorial chair at the Johannæum unable to explain the reason of a cosmical phenomenon! Why, it would be simply disgraceful!"

And as he spoke, my uncle, half undressed, in rags, a perfect scarecrow, with his leathern belt around him, settling his spectacles upon his nose and looking learned and imposing, was himself again, the terrible German professor of mineralogy.

One hour after we had left the grove of olives, we arrived at the little port of San Vicenzo, where Hans claimed his thirteen week's wages, which was counted out to him with a hearty shaking of hands all round.

At that moment, if he did not share our natural emotion, at least his countenance expanded in a manner very unusual with him, and while with the ends of his fingers he lightly pressed our hands, I believe he smiled.

Chapter XLV

ALL'S WELL THAT ENDS WELL

SUCH IS THE CONCLUSION OF A HISTORY WHICH I CANNOT EXPECT EVERYBODY TO BElieve, for some people will believe nothing against the testimony of their own experience. However, I am indifferent to their incredulity, and they may believe as much or as little as they please.

The Stromboliotes received us kindly as shipwrecked mariners. They gave us food and clothing. After waiting forty-eight hours, on the 31st of August, a small craft took us to Messina, where a few days' rest completely removed the effect of our fatigues.

On Friday, September the 4th, we embarked on the steamer *Volturno*, employed by the French Messageries Impériales, and in three days more we were at Marseilles, having no care on our minds except that abominable deceitful compass, which we had mislaid somewhere and could not now examine; but its inexplicable behaviour exercised my mind fearfully. On the 9th of September, in the evening, we arrived at Hamburg.

I cannot describe to you the astonishment of Martha or the joy of Gräuben.

"Now you are a hero, Axel," said to me my blushing *fiancée*, my betrothed, "you will not leave me again!"

I looked tenderly upon her, and she smiled through her tears.

How can I describe the extraordinary sensation produced by the return of Professor Liedenbrock? Thanks to Martha's ineradicable tattling, the news that the Professor had gone to discover a way to the center of the earth had spread over the whole civilised world. People refused to believe it, and when they saw him they would not believe him any the more. Still, the appearance of Hans, and sundry pieces of intelligence derived from Iceland, tended to shake the confidence of the unbelievers.

Then my uncle became a great man, and I was now the nephew of a great man— which is not a privilege to be despised.

Hamburg gave a grand fête in our honour. A public audience was given to the Professor at the Johannæum, at which he told all about our expedition, with only one omission, the unexplained and inexplicable behaviour of our compass. On the same day, with much state, he deposited in the archives of the city the now famous document of Saknussemm, and expressed his regret that circumstances over which he had no control had prevented him from following to the very center of the earth the track of the learned Icelander. He was modest notwithstanding his glory, and he was all the more famous for his humility.

So much honour could not but excite envy. There were those who envied him his fame; and as his theories, resting upon known facts, were in opposition to the systems of science upon the question of the central fire, he sustained with his pen and by his voice remarkable discussions with the learned of every country.

For my part I cannot agree with his theory of gradual cooling: in spite of what I have seen and felt, I believe, and always shall believe, in the central heat. But I admit that certain circumstances not yet sufficiently understood may tend to modify in places the action of natural phenomena.

While these questions were being debated with great animation, my uncle met with a real sorrow. Our faithful Hans, in spite of our entreaties, had left Hamburg; the man to whom we owed all our success and our lives too would not suffer us to reward him as we could have wished. He was seized with the *mal de pays*, a complaint for which we have not even a name in English.

"*Farval,*" said he one day; and with that simple word he left us and sailed for Rejkiavik, which he reached in safety.

We were strongly attached to our brave eider-down hunter; though far away in the remotest north, he will never be forgotten by those whose lives he protected, and certainly I shall not fail to endeavour to see him once more before I die.

To conclude, I have to add that this "Journey to the Center of the Earth" created a wonderful sensation in the world. It was translated into all civilised languages. The leading newspapers extracted the most interesting passages, which were commented upon, picked to pieces, discussed, attacked, and defended with equal enthusiasm and determination, both by believers and skeptics. Rare privilege! my uncle enjoyed during his lifetime the glory he had deservedly won; and he may even boast the distinguished honour of an offer from Mr. Barnum, to exhibit him on most advantageous terms in all the principal cities in the United States!

But there was one "dead fly" amidst all this glory and honour; one fact, one incident, of the journey remained a mystery. Now to a man eminent for his learning, an unexplained phenomenon is an unbearable hardship. Well! it was yet reserved for my uncle to be completely happy.

One day, while arranging a collection of minerals in his cabinet, I noticed in a corner this unhappy compass, which we had long lost sight of; I opened it, and began to watch it.

It had been in that corner for six months, little mindful of the trouble it was giving.

Suddenly, to my intense astonishment, I noticed a strange fact, and I uttered a cry of surprise.

"What is the matter?" my uncle asked.

"That compass!"

"Well?"

"See, its poles are reversed!"

"Reversed?"

"Yes, they point the wrong way."

My uncle looked, he compared, and the house shook with his triumphant leap of exultation.

A light broke in upon his spirit and mine.

"See there," he cried, as soon as he was able to speak. "After our arrival at Cape Saknussemm the north pole of the needle of this confounded compass began to point south instead of north."

"Evidently!"

"Here, then, is the explanation of our mistake. But what phenomenon could have caused this reversal of the poles?"

"The reason is evident, uncle."

"Tell me, then, Axel."

"During the electric storm on the Liedenbrock sea, that ball of fire, which magnetised all the iron on board, reversed the poles of our magnet!"

"Aha! aha!" shouted the Professor with a loud laugh. "So it was just an electric joke!"

From that day forth the Professor was the most glorious of savants, and I was the happiest of men; for my pretty Virlandaise, resigning her place as ward, took her position in the old house on the Königstrasse in the double capacity of niece to my uncle and wife to a certain happy youth. What is the need of adding that the illustrious Otto Liedenbrock, corresponding member of all the scientific, geographical, and mineralogical societies of all the civilised world, was now her uncle and mine?

FROM THE EARTH TO THE MOON

Contents

CHAPTER

I	The Gun Club	327
II	President Barbicane's Communication	330
III	Effect of the President's Communication	334
IV	Reply From the Observatory of Cambridge	336
V	The Romance of the Moon	339
VI	The Permissive Limits of Ignorance and Belief in the United States	341
VII	The Hymn of the Cannon-Ball	344
VIII	History of the Cannon	347
IX	The Question of the Powders	349
X	One Enemy *v.* Twenty-Five Millions of Friends	352
XI	Florida and Texas	355
XII	*Urbi et Orbi*	358
XIII	Stones Hill	361
XIV	Pickaxe and Trowel	364
XV	The *Fête* of the Casting	366
XVI	The *Columbiad*	369
XVII	A Telegraphic Despatch	371
XVIII	The Passenger of the *Atlanta*	372
XIX	A Monster Meeting	375
XX	Attack and *Riposte*	378
XXI	How a Frenchman Manages an Affair	383
XXII	The New Citizen of the United States	388
XXIII	The Projectile-Vehicle	390
XXIV	The Telescope of the Rocky Mountains	392
XXV	Final Details	394
XXVI	Fire!	397
XXVII	Foul Weather	399
XXVIII	A New Star	400

Chapter I

The Gun Club

D URING THE WAR OF THE REBELLION, A NEW AND INFLUENTIAL CLUB WAS ESTAB-
lished in the city of Baltimore in the State of Maryland. It is well known with
what energy the taste for military matters became developed among that nation
of ship-owners, shopkeepers, and mechanics. Simple tradesmen jumped their counters to
become extemporised captains, colonels, and generals, without having ever passed the
School of Instruction at West Point; nevertheless; they quickly rivaled their compeers of
the old continent, and, like them, carried off victories by dint of lavish expenditure in ammunition, money, and men.

But the point in which the Americans singularly distanced the Europeans was in the
science of gunnery. Not, indeed, that their weapons retained a higher degree of perfection
than theirs, but that they exhibited unheard-of dimensions, and consequently attained
hitherto unheard-of ranges. In point of grazing, plunging, oblique, or enfilading, or point-
blank firing, the English, French, and Prussians have nothing to learn; but their cannon,
howitzers, and mortars are mere pocket-pistols compared with the formidable engines of
the American artillery.

This fact need surprise no one. The Yankees, the first mechanicians in the world, are
engineers—just as the Italians are musicians and the Germans, metaphysicians—by right
of birth. Nothing is more natural, therefore, than to perceive them applying their audacious ingenuity to the science of gunnery. Witness the marvels of Parrott, Dahlgren, and
Rodman. The Armstrong, Palliser, and Beaulieu guns were compelled to bow before their
transatlantic rivals.

Now when an American has an idea, he directly seeks a second American to share it.
If there be three, they elect a president and two secretaries. Given four, they name a keeper
of records, and the office is ready for work; five, they convene a general meeting, and the
club is fully constituted. So things were managed in Baltimore. The inventor of a new cannon associated himself with the caster and the borer. Thus was formed the nucleus of the
"Gun Club." In a single month after its formation it numbered 1,833 effective members
and 30,565 corresponding members.

One condition was imposed as a *sine qua non* upon every candidate for admission into the
association, and that was the condition of having designed, or (more or less) perfected a cannon; or, in default of a cannon, at least a fire-arm of some description. It may, however, be
mentioned that mere inventors of revolvers, fire-shooting carbines, and similar small arms,
met with but little consideration. Artillerists always commanded the chief place of favour.

The estimation in which these gentlemen were held, according to one of the most scientific exponents of the Gun Club, was "proportional to the masses of their guns, and in
the direct ratio of the square of the distances attained by their projectiles."

The Gun Club once founded, it is easy to conceive the result of the inventive genius
of the Americans. Their military weapons attained colossal proportions, and their projectiles, exceeding the prescribed limits, unfortunately occasionally cut in two some unof-

fending pedestrians. These inventions, in fact, left far in the rear the timid instruments of European artillery.

It is but fair to add that these Yankees, brave as they have ever proved themselves to be, did not confine themselves to theories and formulae, but that they paid heavily, *in propria persona,* for their inventions. Among them were to be counted officers of all ranks, from lieutenants to generals; military men of every age, from those who were just making their *début* in the profession of arms up to those who had grown old on the gun-carriage. Many had found their rest on the field of battle whose names figured in the "Book of Honour" of the Gun Club; and of those who made good their return the greater proportion bore the marks of their indisputable valor. Crutches, wooden legs, artificial arms, steel hooks, caoutchouc jaws, silver craniums, platinum noses, were all to be found in the collection; and it was calculated by the great statistician Pitcairn that throughout the Gun Club there was not quite one arm between four persons, and exactly two legs between six.

Nevertheless, these valiant artillerists took no particular account of these little facts, and felt justly proud when the despatches of a battle returned the number of victims at tenfold the quantity of projectiles expended.

One day, however—sad and melancholy day!—peace was signed between the survivors of the war; the thunder of the guns gradually ceased, the mortars were silent, the howitzers were muzzled for an indefinite period, the cannon, with muzzles depressed, were returned into the arsenal, the shot were repiled, all bloody reminiscences were effaced; the cotton-plants grew luxuriantly in the well-manured fields, all mourning garments were laid aside, together with grief; and the Gun Club was relegated to profound inactivity.

Some few of the more advanced and inveterate theorists set themselves again to work upon calculations regarding the laws of projectiles. They reverted invariably to gigantic shells and howitzers of unparalleled calibre. Still in default of practical experience what was the value of mere theories? Consequently, the clubrooms became deserted, the servants dozed in the antechambres, the newspapers grew mouldy on the tables, sounds of snoring came from dark corners, and the members of the Gun Club, erstwhile so noisy in their seances, were reduced to silence by this disastrous peace and gave themselves up wholly to dreams of a Platonic kind of artillery.

"This is horrible!" said Tom Hunter one evening, while rapidly carbonising his wooden legs in the fireplace of the smoking-room; "nothing to do! nothing to look forward to! what a loathsome existence! When again shall the guns arouse us in the morning with their delightful reports?"

"Those days are gone by," said jolly Bilsby, trying to extend his missing arms. "It was delightful once upon a time! One invented a gun, and hardly was it cast, when one hastened to try it in the face of the enemy! Then one returned to camp with a word of encouragement from Sherman or a friendly shake of the hand from McClellan. But now the generals are gone back to their counters; and in place of projectiles, they despatch bales of cotton. By Jove, the future of gunnery in America is lost!"

"Ay! and no war in prospect!" continued the famous James T. Maston, scratching with his steel hook his gutta percha cranium. "Not a cloud on the horizon! and that too at such a critical period in the progress of the science of artillery! Yes, gentlemen! I who address you have myself this very morning perfected a model (plan, section, elevation, etc.) of a mortar destined to change all the conditions of warfare!"

"No! is it possible?" replied Tom Hunter, his thoughts reverting involuntarily to a former invention of the Hon. J. T. Maston, by which, at its first trial, he had succeeded in killing three hundred and thirty-seven people.

"Fact!" replied he. "Still, what is the use of so many studies worked out, so many difficulties vanquished? It's mere waste of time! The New World seems to have made up its mind to live in peace; and our bellicose *Tribune* predicts some approaching catastrophes arising out of this scandalous increase of population."

"Nevertheless," replied Colonel Blomsberry, "they are always struggling in Europe to maintain the principle of nationalities."

"Well?"

"Well, there might be some field for enterprise down there; and if they would accept our services—"

"What are you dreaming of?" screamed Bilsby; "work at gunnery for the benefit of foreigners?"

"That would be better than doing nothing here," returned the colonel.

"Quite so," said J. T. Matson; "but still we need not dream of that expedient."

"And why not?" demanded the colonel.

"Because their ideas of progress in the Old World are contrary to our American habits of thought. Those fellows believe that one can't become a general without having served first as an ensign; which is as much as to say that one can't point a gun without having first cast it oneself!"

"Ridiculous!" replied Tom Hunter, whittling with his bowie-knife the arms of his easy-chair; "but if that be the case there, all that is left for us is to plant tobacco and distill whale-oil."

"What!" roared J. T. Maston, "shall we not employ these remaining years of our life in perfecting fire-arms? Shall there never be a fresh opportunity of trying the ranges of projectiles? Shall the air never again be lighted with the glare of our guns? No international difficulty ever arise to enable us to declare war against some transatlantic power? Shall not the French sink one of our steamers, or the English, in defiance of the rights of nations, hang a few of our countrymen?"

"No such luck," replied Colonel Blomsberry; "nothing of the kind is likely to happen; and even if it did, we should not profit by it. American susceptibility is fast declining, and we are all going to the dogs."

"It is too true," replied J. T. Maston, with fresh violence; "there are a thousand grounds for fighting, and yet we don't fight. We save up our arms and legs for the benefit of nations who don't know what to do with them! But stop—without going out of one's way to find a cause for war—did not North America once belong to the English?"

"Undoubtedly," replied Tom Hunter, stamping his crutch with fury.

"Well, then," replied J. T. Maston, "why should not England in her turn belong to the Americans?"

"It would be but just and fair," returned Colonel Blomsberry.

"Go and propose it to the President of the United States," cried J. T. Maston, "and see how he will receive you."

"Bah!" growled Bilsby between the four teeth which the war had left him; "that will never do!"

"By Jove!" cried J. T. Maston, "he mustn't count on my vote at the next election!"

"Nor on ours," replied unanimously all the bellicose invalids.

"Meanwhile," replied J. T. Maston, "allow me to say that, if I cannot get an opportunity to try my new mortars on a real field of battle, I shall say good-by to the members of the Gun Club, and go and bury myself in the prairies of Arkansas!"

"In that case we will accompany you," cried the others.

Matters were in this unfortunate condition, and the club was threatened with approaching dissolution, when an unexpected circumstance occurred to prevent so deplorable a catastrophe.

On the morrow after this conversation every member of the association received a sealed circular couched in the following terms:

> BALTIMORE, *October 3.*
>
> The president of the Gun Club has the honour to inform his colleagues that, at the meeting of the 5th instant, he will bring before them a communication of an extremely interesting nature. He requests, therefore, that they will make it convenient to attend in accordance with the present invitation.
>
> Very cordially,
> IMPEY BARBICANE, P.G.C.

Chapter II

PRESIDENT BARBICANE'S COMMUNICATION

ON THE 5TH OF OCTOBER, AT EIGHT P.M., A DENSE CROWD PRESSED TOWARDS THE SAloons of the Gun Club at No. 21 Union Square. All the members of the association resident in Baltimore attended the invitation of their president. As regards the corresponding members, notices were delivered by hundreds throughout the streets of the city, and, large as was the great hall, it was quite inadequate to accommodate the crowd of savants. They overflowed into the adjoining rooms, down the narrow passages, into the outer court-yards. There they ran against the vulgar herd who pressed up to the doors, each struggling to reach the front ranks, all eager to learn the nature of the important communication of President Barbicane; all pushing, squeezing, crushing with that perfect freedom of action which is so peculiar to the masses when educated in ideas of "self-government."

On that evening a stranger who might have chanced to be in Baltimore could not have gained admission for love or money into the great hall. That was reserved exclusively for resident or corresponding members; no one else could possibly have obtained a place; and the city magnates, municipal councilors, and "select men" were compelled to mingle with the mere townspeople in order to catch stray bits of news from the interior.

Nevertheless the vast hall presented a curious spectacle. Its immense area was singularly adapted to the purpose. Lofty pillars formed of cannon, superposed upon huge mortars as a base, supported the fine iron-work of the arches, a perfect piece of cast-iron lace-work. Trophies of blunderbuses, matchlocks, arquebuses, carbines, all kinds of fire-arms, ancient and modern, were picturesquely interlaced against the walls. The gas lit up in full glare myriads of revolvers grouped in the form of lustres, while groups of pistols, and candelabra formed of muskets bound together, completed this magnificent display of brilliance. Models of cannon, bronze castings, sights covered with dents, plates battered by the shots of the Gun Club, assortments of rammers and sponges, chaplets of shells, wreaths of projectiles, garlands of howitzers—in short, all the apparatus of the artillerist, enchanted the eye by this wonderful arrangement and induced a kind of belief that their real purpose was ornamental rather than deadly.

At the further end of the saloon the president, assisted by four secretaries, occupied a large platform. His chair, supported by a carved gun-carriage, was modelled upon the ponderous proportions of a 32-inch mortar. It was pointed at an angle of ninety degrees, and suspended upon trundions, so that the president could balance himself upon it as upon a rocking-chair, a very agreeable fact in the very hot weather. Upon the table (a huge iron plate supported upon six carronades) stood an inkstand of exquisite elegance, made of a beautifully chased Spanish piece, and a sonnette, which, when required, could give forth a report equal to that of a revolver. During violent debates this novel kind of bell scarcely sufficed to drown the clamor of these excitable artillerists.

In front of the table benches arranged in zigzag form, like the circumvallations of a retrenchment, formed a succession of bastions and curtains set apart for the use of the members of the club; and on this especial evening one might say, "All the world was on the ramparts." The president was sufficiently well known, however, for all to be assured that he would not put his colleagues to discomfort without some very strong motive.

Impey Barbicane was a man of forty years of age, calm, cold, austere; of a singularly serious and self-contained demeanor, punctual as a chronometer, of imperturbable temper and immovable character; by no means chivalrous, yet adventurous withal, and always bringing practical ideas to bear upon the very rashest enterprises; an essentially New Englander, a Northern colonist, a descendant of the old anti-Stuart Roundheads, and the implacable enemy of the gentlemen of the South, those ancient cavaliers of the mother country. In a word, he was a Yankee to the backbone.

Barbicane had made a large fortune as a timber merchant. Being nominated director of artillery during the war, he proved himself fertile in invention. Bold in his conceptions, he contributed powerfully to the progress of that arm and gave an immense impetus to experimental researches.

He was personage of the middle height, having, by a rare exception in the Gun Club, all his limbs complete. His strongly marked features seemed drawn by square and rule; and if it be true that, in order to judge a man's character one must look at his profile, Barbicane, so examined, exhibited the most certain indications of energy, audacity, and *sang-froid*.

At this moment he was sitting in his arm-chair, silent, absorbed, lost in reflection, sheltered under his high-crowned hat—a kind of black cylinder which always seems firmly screwed upon the head of an American.

Just when the deep-toned clock in the great hall struck eight, Barbicane, as if he had been set in motion by a spring, raised himself up. A profound silence ensued, and the speaker, in a somewhat emphatic tone of voice, commenced as follows:

"My brave colleagues, too long already a paralyzing peace has plunged the members of the Gun Club in deplorable inactivity. After a period of years full of incidents we have been compelled to abandon our labours, and to stop short on the road of progress. I do not hesitate to state, baldly, that any war which would recall us to arms would be welcome!" (Tremendous applause!) "But war, gentlemen, is impossible under existing circumstances; and, however we may desire it, many years may elapse before our cannon shall again thunder in the field of battle. We must make up our minds, then, to seek in another train of ideas some field for the activity which we all pine for."

The meeting felt that the president was now approaching the critical point, and redoubled their attention accordingly.

"For some months past, my brave colleagues," continued Barbicane, "I have been asking myself whether, while confining ourselves to our own particular objects, we could not enter upon some grand experiment worthy of the nineteenth century; and whether the progress of artillery science would not enable us to carry it out to a successful issue. I have been considering, working, calculating; and the result of my studies is the conviction that we are safe to succeed in an enterprise which to any other country would appear wholly impracticable. This project, the result of long elaboration, is the object of my present communication. It is worthy of yourselves, worthy of the antecedents of the Gun Club; and it cannot fail to make some noise in the world."

A thrill of excitement ran through the meeting.

Barbicane, having by a rapid movement firmly fixed his hat upon his head, calmly continued his harangue:

"There is no one among you, my brave colleagues, who has not seen the Moon, or, at least, heard speak of it. Don't be surprised if I am about to discourse to you regarding the Queen of the Night. It is perhaps reserved for us to become the Columbuses of this unknown world. Only enter into my plans, and second me with all your power, and I will lead you to its conquest, and its name shall be added to those of the thirty-six States which compose this Great Union."

"Three cheers for the Moon!" roared the Gun Club, with one voice.

"The moon, gentlemen, has been carefully studied," continued Barbicane; "her mass, density, and weight; her constitution, motions, distance, as well as her place in the solar system, have all been exactly determined. Selenographic charts have been constructed with a perfection which equals, if it does not even surpass, that of our terrestrial maps. Photography has given us proofs of the incomparable beauty of our satellite; all is known regarding the moon which mathematical science, astronomy, geology, and optics can learn about her. But up to the present moment no direct communication has been established with her."

A violent movement of interest and surprise here greeted this remark of the speaker.

"Permit me," he continued, "to recount to you briefly how certain ardent spirits, starting on imaginary journeys, have penetrated the secrets of our satellite. In the seventeenth century a certain David Fabricius boasted of having seen with his own eyes the inhabitants of the moon. In 1649 a Frenchman, one Jean Baudoin, published a 'Journey performed from the Earth to the Moon by Domingo Gonzalez,' a Spanish adventurer. At the same period Cyrano de Bergerac published that celebrated 'Journeys in the Moon' which met with such success in France. Somewhat later another Frenchman, named Fontenelle, wrote 'The

Plurality of Worlds,' a *chef-d'oeuvre* of its time. About 1835 a small treatise, translated from the New York *American,* related how Sir John Herschel, having been despatched to the Cape of Good Hope for the purpose of making there some astronomical calculations, had, by means of a telescope brought to perfection by means of internal lighting, reduced the apparent distance of the moon to eighty yards! He then distinctly perceived caverns frequented by hippopotami, green mountains bordered by golden lace-work, sheep with horns of ivory, a white species of deer and inhabitants with membranous wings, like bats. This *brochure,* the work of an American named Locke, had a great sale. But, to bring this rapid sketch to a close, I will only add that a certain Hans Pfaal, of Rotterdam, launching himself in a balloon filled with a gas extracted from nitrogen, thirty-seven times lighter than hydrogen, reached the moon after a passage of nineteen hours. This journey, like all previous ones, was purely imaginary; still, it was the work of a popular American author—I mean Edgar Poe!"

"Cheers for Edgar Poe!" roared the assemblage, electrified by their president's words.

"I have now enumerated," said Barbicane, "the experiments which I call purely paper ones, and wholly insufficient to establish serious relations with the Queen of the Night. Nevertheless, I am bound to add that some practical geniuses have attempted to establish actual communication with her. Thus, a few days ago, a German geometrician proposed to send a scientific expedition to the steppes of Siberia. There, on those vast plains, they were to describe enormous geometric figures, drawn in characters of reflecting luminosity, among which was the proposition regarding the 'square of the hypothenuse,' commonly called the 'Ass's Bridge' by the French. 'Every intelligent being,' said the geometrician, 'must understand the scientific meaning of that figure. The Selenites, do they exist, will respond by a similar figure; and, a communication being thus once established, it will be easy to form an alphabet which shall enable us to converse with the inhabitants of the moon.' So spoke the German geometrician; but his project was never put into practice, and up to the present day there is no bond in existence between the Earth and her satellite. It is reserved for the practical genius of Americans to establish a communication with the sidereal world. The means of arriving thither are simple, easy, certain, infallible—and that is the purpose of my present proposal."

A storm of acclamations greeted these words. There was not a single person in the whole audience who was not overcome, carried away, lifted out of himself by the speaker's words!

Long-continued applause resounded from all sides.

As soon as the excitement had partially subsided, Barbicane resumed his speech in a somewhat graver voice.

"You know," said he, "what progress artillery science has made during the last few years, and what a degree of perfection fire-arms of every kind have reached. Moreover, you are well aware that, in general terms, the resisting power of cannon and the expansive force of gunpowder are practically unlimited. Well! starting from this principle, I ask myself whether, supposing sufficient apparatus could be obtained constructed upon the conditions of ascertained resistance, it might not be possible to project a shot up to the moon?"

At these words a murmur of amazement escaped from a thousand panting chests; then succeeded a moment of perfect silence, resembling that profound stillness which precedes the bursting of a thunderstorm. In point of fact, a thunderstorm did peal forth, but it was the thunder of applause, of cries, and of uproar which made the very hall tremble. The president attempted to speak, but could not. It was fully ten minutes before he could make himself heard.

"Suffer me to finish," he calmly continued. "I have looked at the question in all its bearings, I have resolutely attacked it, and by incontrovertible calculations I find that a projectile endowed with an initial velocity of 12,000 yards per second, and aimed at the moon, must necessarily reach it. I have the honour, my brave colleagues, to propose a trial of this little experiment."

Chapter III

EFFECT OF THE PRESIDENT'S COMMUNICATION

IT IS IMPOSSIBLE TO DESCRIBE THE EFFECT PRODUCED BY THE LAST WORDS OF THE HONourable president—the cries, the shouts, the succession of roars, hurrahs, and all the varied vociferations which the American language is capable of supplying. It was a scene of indescribable confusion and uproar. They shouted, they clapped, they stamped on the floor of the hall. All the weapons in the museum discharged at once could not have more violently set in motion the waves of sound. One need not be surprised at this. There are some cannoneers nearly as noisy as their own guns.

Barbicane remained calm in the midst of this enthusiastic clamor; perhaps he was desirous of addressing a few more words to his colleagues, for by his gestures he demanded silence, and his powerful alarum was worn out by its violent reports. No attention, however, was paid to his request. He was presently torn from his seat and passed from the hands of his faithful colleagues into the arms of a no less excited crowd.

Nothing can astound an American. It has often been asserted that the word "impossible" is not a French one. People have evidently been deceived by the dictionary. In America, all is easy, all is simple; and as for mechanical difficulties, they are overcome before they arise. Between Barbicane's proposition and its realisation no true Yankee would have allowed even the semblance of a difficulty to be possible. A thing with them is no sooner said than done.

The triumphal progress of the president continued throughout the evening. It was a regular torchlight procession. Irish, Germans, French, Scotch, all the heterogeneous units which make up the population of Maryland shouted in their respective vernaculars; and the "vivas," "hurrahs," and "bravos" were intermingled in inexpressible enthusiasm.

Just at this crisis, as though she comprehended all this agitation regarding herself, the moon shone forth with serene splendour, eclipsing by her intense illumination all the surrounding lights. The Yankees all turned their gaze towards her resplendent orb, kissed their hands, called her by all kinds of endearing names. Between eight o'clock and midnight one optician in Jones'-Fall Street made his fortune by the sale of opera-glasses.

Midnight arrived, and the enthusiasm showed no signs of diminution. It spread equally among all classes of citizens—men of science, shopkeepers, merchants, porters,

chair-men, as well as "greenhorns," were stirred in their innermost fibres. A national enterprise was at stake. The whole city, high and low, the quays bordering the Patapsco, the
ships lying in the basins, disgorged a crowd drunk with joy, gin, and whisky. Everyone
chattered, argued, discussed, disputed, applauded, from the gentleman lounging upon the
bar-room settee with his tumbler of sherry-cobbler before him down to the waterman who
got drunk upon his "knock-me-down" in the dingy taverns of Fell Point.

About two A.M., however, the excitement began to subside. President Barbicane
reached his house, bruised, crushed, and squeezed almost to a mummy. Hercules could not
have resisted a similar outbreak of enthusiasm. The crowd gradually deserted the squares
and streets. The four railways from Philadelphia and Washington, Harrisburg and Wheel-
ing, which converge at Baltimore, whirled away the heterogeneous population to the four
corners of the United States, and the city subsided into comparative tranquillity.

On the following day, thanks to the telegraphic wires, five hundred newspapers and
journals, daily, weekly, monthly, or bi-monthly, all took up the question. They examined it
under all its different aspects, physical, meteorological, economical, or moral, up to its bearings on politics or civilisation. They debated whether the moon was a finished world, or
whether it was destined to undergo any further transformation. Did it resemble the earth at
the period when the latter was destitute as yet of an atmosphere? What kind of spectacle
would its hidden hemisphere present to our terrestrial spheroid? Granting that the question
at present was simply that of sending a projectile up to the moon, everyone must see that
that involved the commencement of a series of experiments. All must hope that someday
America would penetrate the deepest secrets of that mysterious orb; and some even seemed
to fear lest its conquest should not sensibly derange the equilibrium of Europe.

The project once under discussion, not a single paragraph suggested a doubt of its realisation. All the papers, pamphlets, reports—all the journals published by the scientific,
literary, and religious societies enlarged upon its advantages; and the Society of Natural
History of Boston, the Society of Science and Art of Albany, the Geographical and Statistical Society of New York, the Philosophical Society of Philadelphia, and the Smithsonian of Washington sent innumerable letters of congratulation to the Gun Club,
together with offers of immediate assistance and money.

From that day forward Impey Barbicane became one of the greatest citizens of the
United States, a kind of Washington of science. A single trait of feeling, taken from many
others, will serve to show the point which this homage of a whole people to a single individual attained.

Some few days after this memorable meeting of the Gun Club, the manager of an English company announced, at the Baltimore theatre, the production of *Much ado about
Nothing*. But the populace, seeing in that title an allusion damaging to Barbicane's project,
broke into the auditorium, smashed the benches, and compelled the unlucky director to
alter his playbill. Being a sensible man, he bowed to the public will and replaced the of-
fending comedy by *As you like it;* and for many weeks he realised fabulous profits.

Chapter IV

REPLY FROM THE OBSERVATORY OF CAMBRIDGE

B ARBICANE, HOWEVER, LOST NOT ONE MOMENT AMID ALL THE ENTHUSIASM OF WHICH he had become the object. His first care was to reassemble his colleagues in the board-room of the Gun Club. There, after some discussion, it was agreed to consult the as-tronomers regarding the astronomical part of the enterprise. Their reply once ascertained, they could then discuss the mechanical means, and nothing should be wanting to ensure the success of this great experiment.

A note couched in precise terms, containing special interrogatories, was then drawn up and addressed to the Observatory of Cambridge in Massachusetts. This city, where the first university of the United States was founded, is justly celebrated for its astronomical staff. There are to be found assembled all the most eminent men of science. Here is to be seen at work that powerful telescope which enabled Bond to resolve the nebula of An-dromeda, and Clarke to discover the satellite of Sirius. This celebrated institution fully justified on all points the confidence reposed in it by the Gun Club. So, after two days, the reply so impatiently awaited was placed in the hands of President Barbicane.

It was couched in the following terms:

> *The Director of the Cambridge Observatory to the*
> *President of the Gun Club at Baltimore.*
>
> CAMBRIDGE, *October 7.*

On the receipt of your favour of the 6th instant, addressed to the Observatory of Cam-bridge in the name of the members of the Baltimore Gun Club, our staff was immediately called together, and it was judged expedient to reply as follows:

The questions which have been proposed to it are these—

1. Is it possible to transmit a projectile up to the moon?

2. What is the exact distance which separates the earth from its satellite?

3. What will be the period of transit of the projectile when endowed with sufficient initial velocity? and, consequently, at what moment ought it to be discharged in order that it may touch the moon at a particular point?

4. At what precise moment will the moon present herself in the most favourable posi-tion to be reached by the projectile?

5. What point in the heavens ought the cannon to be aimed at which is intended to dis-charge the projectile?

6. What place will the moon occupy in the heavens at the moment of the projectile's departure?"

Regarding the *first* question, "Is it possible to transmit a projectile up to the moon?"

Answer.—Yes; provided it possess an initial velocity of 1,200 yards per second; calcu-lations prove that to be sufficient. In proportion as we recede from the earth the action of gravitation diminishes in the inverse ratio of the square of the distance; that is to say, *at three times a given distance the action is nine times less.* Consequently, the weight of a shot will decrease, and will become reduced to *zero* at the instant that the attraction of the moon exactly counterpoises that of the earth; that is to say at ⁴⁷⁄₅₂ of its passage. At that instant the projectile will have no weight whatever; and, if it passes that point, it will fall into the moon by the sole effect of the lunar attraction. The *theoretical possibility* of the experiment is therefore absolutely demonstrated; its *success* must depend upon the power of the engine employed.

As to the *second* question, "What is the exact distance which separates the earth from its satellite?"

Answer.—The moon does not describe a *circle* round the earth, but rather an *ellipse*, of which our earth occupies one of the *foci*; the consequence, therefore, is, that at certain times it approaches nearer to, and at others it recedes farther from, the earth; in astronomical language, it is at one time in *apogee*, at another in *perigee*. Now the difference between its greatest and its least distance is too considerable to be left out of consideration. In point of fact, in its apogee the moon is 247,552 miles, and in its perigee, 218,657 miles only distant; a fact which makes a difference of 28,895 miles, or more than one-ninth of the entire distance. The perigee distance, therefore, is that which ought to serve as the basis of all calculations.

To the *third* question:

Answer.—If the shot should preserve continuously its initial velocity of 12,000 yards per second, it would require little more than nine hours to reach its destination; but, inasmuch as that initial velocity will be continually decreasing, it will occupy 300,000 seconds, that is 83hrs. 20m. in reaching the point where the attraction of the earth and moon will be *in equilibrio*. From this point it will fall into the moon in 50,000 seconds, or 13hrs. 53m. 20sec. It will be desirable, therefore, to discharge it 97hrs. 13m. 20sec. before the arrival of the moon at the point aimed at.

Regarding question *four*, "At what precise moment will the moon present herself in the most favourable position, etc.?"

Answer.—After what has been said above, it will be necessary, first of all, to choose the period when the moon will be in perigee, and *also* the moment when she will be crossing the zenith, which latter event will further diminish the entire distance by a length equal to the radius of the earth, *i. e.* 3,919 miles; the result of which will be that the final passage remaining to be accomplished will be 214,976 miles. But although the moon passes her perigee every month, she does not reach the zenith always *at exactly the same moment*. She does not appear under these two conditions simultaneously, except at long intervals of time. It will be necessary, therefore, to wait for the moment when her passage in perigee shall coincide with that in the zenith. Now, by a fortunate circumstance, on the 4th of December in the ensuing year the moon *will* present these two conditions. At midnight she will be in perigee, that is, at her shortest distance from the earth, and at the same moment she will be crossing the zenith.

On the *fifth* question, "At what point in the heavens ought the cannon to be aimed?"

Answer.—The preceding remarks being admitted, the cannon ought to be pointed to the zenith of the place. Its fire, therefore, will be perpendicular to the plane of the horizon; and the projectile will soonest pass beyond the range of the terrestrial attraction. But, in order that the moon should reach the zenith of a given place, it is necessary that the place should not exceed in latitude the declination of the luminary; in other words, it must be comprised within the degrees 0° and 28° of lat. N. or S. In every other spot the fire must necessarily be oblique, which would seriously militate against the success of the experiment.

As to the *sixth* question, "What place will the moon occupy in the heavens at the moment of the projectile's departure?"

Answer. —At the moment when the projectile shall be discharged into space, the moon, which travels daily forward 13° 10' 35", will be distant from the zenith point by four times that quantity, *i. e.* by 52° 42' 20," a space which corresponds to the path which she will describe during the entire journey of the projectile. But, inasmuch as it is equally necessary to take into account the deviation which the rotary motion of the earth will impart to the shot, and as the shot cannot reach the moon until after a deviation equal to 16 radii of the earth, which, calculated upon the moon's orbit, are equal to about eleven degrees, it becomes necessary to add these eleven degrees to those which express the retardation of the moon just mentioned: that is to say, in round numbers, about sixty-four degrees. Consequently, at the moment of firing the visual radius applied to the moon will describe, with the vertical line of the place, an angle of sixty-four degrees.

These are our answers to the questions proposed to the Observatory of Cambridge by the members of the Gun Club:

To sum up—

1st. The cannon ought to be planted in a country situated between 0° and 28° of N. or S. lat.

2d. It ought to be pointed directly towards the zenith of the place.

3d. The projectile ought to be propelled with an initial velocity of 12,000 yards per second.

4th. It ought to be discharged at 10hrs. 46m. 40sec. of the 1st of December of the ensuing year.

5th. It will meet the moon four days after its discharge, precisely at midnight on the 4th of December, at the moment of its transit across the zenith.

The members of the Gun Club ought, therefore, without delay, to commence the works necessary for such an experiment, and to be prepared to set to work at the moment determined upon; for, if they should suffer this 4th of December to go by, they will not find the moon again under the same conditions of perigee and of zenith until eighteen years and eleven days afterward.

The staff of the Cambridge Observatory place themselves entirely at their disposal in respect of all questions of theoretical astronomy; and herewith add their congratulations to those of all the rest of America.

For the Astronomical Staff,

J. M. BELFAST,
DIRECTOR OF THE OBSERVATORY OF CAMBRIDGE

Chapter V

The Romance of the Moon

AN OBSERVER ENDUED WITH AN INFINITE RANGE OF VISION, AND PLACED IN THAT UN-known centre around which the entire world revolves, might have beheld myriads of atoms filling all space during the chaotic epoch of the universe. Little by little, as ages went on, a change took place; a general law of attraction manifested itself, to which the hitherto errant atoms became obedient: these atoms combined together chemically according to their affinities, formed themselves into molecules, and composed those nebulous masses with which the depths of the heavens are strewed.

These masses became immediately endued with a rotary motion around their own central point. This centre, formed of indefinite molecules, began to revolve around its own axis during its gradual condensation; then, following the immutable laws of mechanics, in proportion as its bulk diminished by condensation, its rotary motion became accelerated, and these two effects continuing, the result was the formation of one principal star, the centre of the nebulous mass.

By attentively watching, the observer would then have perceived the other molecules of the mass, following the example of this central star, become likewise condensed by gradually accelerated rotation, and gravitating round it in the shape of innumerable stars. Thus was formed the *Nebulæ*, of which astronomers have reckoned up nearly 5,000.

Among these 5,000 nebulae there is one which has received the name of the Milky Way, and which contains eighteen millions of stars, each of which has become the centre of a solar world.

If the observer had then specially directed his attention to one of the more humble and less brilliant of these stellar bodies, a star of the fourth class, that which is arrogantly called the Sun, all the phenomena to which the formation of the Universe is to be ascribed would have been successively fulfilled before his eyes. In fact, he would have perceived this sun, as yet in the gaseous state, and composed of moving molecules, revolving round its axis in order to accomplish its work of concentration. This motion, faithful to the laws of mechanics, would have been accelerated with the diminution of its volume; and a moment would have arrived when the centrifugal force would have overpowered the centripetal, which causes the molecules all to tend towards the centre.

Another phenomenon would now have passed before the observer's eye, and the molecules situated on the plane of the equator escaping, like a stone from a sling of which the cord had suddenly snapped, would have formed around the sun sundry concentric rings resembling that of Saturn. In their turn, again, these rings of cosmical matter, excited by a rotary motion about the central mass, would have been broken up and decomposed into secondary nebulosities, that is to say, into planets. Similarly he would have observed these planets throw off one or more rings each, which became the origin of the secondary bodies which we call satellites.

Thus, then, advancing from atom to molecule, from molecule to nebulous mass, from that to principal star, from star to sun, from sun to planet, and hence to satellite, we have the whole series of transformations undergone by the heavenly bodies during the first days of the world.

Now, of those attendant bodies which the sun maintains in their elliptical orbits by the great law of gravitation, some few in turn possess satellites. Uranus has eight, Saturn eight, Jupiter four, Neptune possibly three, and the Earth one. This last, one of the least important of the entire solar system, we call the Moon; and it is she whom the daring genius of the Americans professed their intention of conquering.

The moon, by her comparative proximity, and the constantly varying appearances produced by her several phases, has always occupied a considerable share of the attention of the inhabitants of the earth.

From the time of Thales of Miletus, in the fifth century B.C., down to that of Copernicus in the fifteenth and Tycho Brahé in the sixteenth century A.D., observations have been from time to time carried on with more or less correctness, until in the present day the altitudes of the lunar mountains have been determined with exactitude. Galileo explained the phenomena of the lunar light produced during certain of her phases by the existence of mountains, to which he assigned a mean altitude of 27,000 feet. After him Hévelius, an astronomer of Dantzic, reduced the highest elevations to 15,000 feet; but the calculations of Riccioli brought them up again to 21,000 feet.

At the close of the eighteenth century Herschel, armed with a powerful telescope, considerably reduced the preceding measurements. He assigned a height of 11,400 feet to the maximum elevations, and reduced the mean of the different altitudes to little more than 2,400 feet. But Herschel's calculations were in their turn corrected by the observations of Halley, Nasmyth, Bianchini, Gruithuysen, and others; but it was reserved for the labours of Bœer and Moëdler finally to solve the question. They succeeded in measuring 1,905 different elevations, of which six exceed 15,000 feet, and twenty-two exceed 14,400 feet. The highest summit of all towers to a height of 22,606 feet above the surface of the lunar disc. At the same period the examination of the moon was completed. She appeared completely riddled with craters, and her essentially volcanic character was apparent at each observation. By the absence of refraction in the rays of the planets occulted by her we conclude that she is absolutely devoid of an atmosphere. The absence of air entails the absence of water. It became, therefore, manifest that the Selenites, to support life under such conditions, must possess a special organisation of their own, must differ remarkably from the inhabitants of the earth.

At length, thanks to modern art, instruments of still higher perfection searched the moon without intermission, not leaving a single point of her surface unexplored; and notwithstanding that her diameter measures 2,150 miles, her surface equals the one-fifteenth part of that of our globe, and her bulk the one-forty-ninth part of that of the terrestrial spheroid—not one of her secrets was able to escape the eyes of the astronomers; and these skillful men of science carried to an even greater degree their prodigious observations.

Thus they remarked that, during full moon, the disc appeared scored in certain parts with white lines; and, during the phases, with black. On prosecuting the study of these with still greater precision, they succeeded in obtaining an exact account of the nature of these lines. They were long and narrow furrows sunk between parallel ridges, bordering generally upon the edges of the craters. Their length varied between ten and 100 miles, and their width was about 1,600 yards. Astronomers called them chasms, but they could not get any further. Whether these chasms were the dried-up beds of ancient rivers or not they were unable thoroughly to ascertain.

The Americans, among others, hoped one day or other to determine this geological question. They also undertook to examine the true nature of that system of parallel ramparts discovered on the moon's surface by Gruithuysen, a learned professor of Munich, who considered them to be "a system of fortifications thrown up by the Selenitic engineers." These two points, yet obscure, as well as others, no doubt, could not be definitely settled except by direct communication with the moon.

Regarding the degree of intensity of its light, there was nothing more to learn on this point. It was known that it is 300,000 times weaker than that of the sun, and that its heat has no appreciable effect upon the thermometer. As to the phenomenon known as the "ashy light," it is explained naturally by the effect of the transmission of the solar rays from the earth to the moon, which give the appearance of completeness to the lunar disc, while it presents itself under the crescent form during its first and last phases.

Such was the state of knowledge acquired regarding the earth's satellite, which the Gun Club undertook to perfect in all its aspects, cosmographic, geological, political, and moral.

Chapter VI

THE PERMISSIVE LIMITS OF IGNORANCE AND BELIEF IN THE UNITED STATES

THE IMMEDIATE RESULT OF BARBICANE'S PROPOSITION WAS TO PLACE UPON THE ORDERS of the day all the astronomical facts relative to the Queen of the Night. Everybody set to work to study assiduously. One would have thought that the moon had just appeared for the first time, and that no one had ever before caught a glimpse of her in the heavens. The papers revived all the old anecdotes in which the "sun of the wolves" played a part; they recalled the influences which the ignorance of past ages ascribed to her; in short, all America was seized with selenomania, or had become moon-mad.

The scientific journals, for their part, dealt more especially with the questions which touched upon the enterprise of the Gun Club. The letter of the Observatory of Cambridge was published by them, and commented upon with unreserved approval.

Until that time most people had been ignorant of the mode in which the distance which separates the moon from the earth is calculated. They took advantage of this fact to explain to them that this distance was obtained by measuring the parallax of the moon. The term parallax proving "caviare to the general," they further explained that it meant the angle formed by the inclination of two straight lines drawn from either extremity of the earth's radius to the moon. On doubts being expressed as to the correctness of this method, they immediately proved that not only was the mean distance 234,347 miles, but that astronomers could not possibly be in error in their estimate by more than seventy miles either way.

To those who were not familiar with the motions of the moon, they demonstrated that she possesses two distinct motions, the first being that of rotation upon her axis, the second being that of revolution round the earth, accomplishing both together in an equal period of time, that is to say, in twenty-seven and one-third days.

The motion of rotation is that which produces day and night on the surface of the moon; save that there is only one day and one night in the lunar month, each lasting three hundred and fifty-four and one-third hours. But, happily for her, the face turned towards the terrestrial globe is illuminated by it with an intensity equal to that of fourteen moons. As to the other face, always invisible to us, it has of necessity three hundred and fifty-four hours of absolute night, tempered only by that "pale glimmer which falls upon it from the stars."

Some well-intentioned, but rather obstinate persons, could not at first comprehend how, if the moon displays invariably the same face to the earth during her revolution, she can describe one turn round herself. To such they answered, "Go into your dining-room, and walk round the table in such a way as to always keep your face turned towards the centre; by the time you will have achieved one complete round you will have completed one turn around yourself, since your eye will have traversed successively every point of the room. Well, then, the room is the heavens, the table is the earth, and the moon is yourself." And they would go away delighted.

So, then, the moon displays invariably the same face to the earth; nevertheless, to be quite exact, it is necessary to add that, in consequence of certain fluctuations of north and south, and of west and east, termed her libration, she permits rather more than half, that is to say, five-sevenths, to be seen.

As soon as the ignoramuses came to understand as much as the director of the observatory himself knew, they began to worry themselves regarding her revolution round the earth, whereupon twenty scientific reviews immediately came to the rescue. They pointed out to them that the firmament, with its infinitude of stars, may be considered as one vast dial-plate, upon which the moon travels, indicating the true time to all the inhabitants of the earth; that it is during this movement that the Queen of Night exhibits her different phases; that the moon is *full* when she is in *opposition* with the sun, that is, when the three bodies are on the same straight line, the earth occupying the centre; that she is *new* when she is in *conjunction* with the sun, that is, when she is between it and the earth; and, lastly that she is in her *first* or *last* quarter, when she makes with the sun and the earth an angle of which she herself occupies the apex.

Regarding the altitude which the moon attains above the horizon, the letter of the Cambridge Observatory had said all that was to be said in this respect. Everyone knew that this altitude varies according to the latitude of the observer. But the only zones of the globe in which the moon passes the zenith, that is, the point directly over the head of the spectator, are of necessity comprised between the twenty-eighth parallels and the equator. Hence the importance of the advice to try the experiment upon some point of that part of the globe, in order that the projectile might be discharged perpendicularly, and so the soonest escape the action of gravitation. This was an essential condition to the success of the enterprise, and continued actively to engage the public attention.

Regarding the path described by the moon in her revolution round the earth, the Cambridge Observatory had demonstrated that this path is a re-entering curve, not a perfect circle, but an ellipse, of which the earth occupies one of the *foci*. It was also well understood that it is farthest removed from the earth during its *apogee*, and approaches most nearly to it at its *perigee*.

Such was then the extent of knowledge possessed by every American on the subject, and of which no one could decently profess ignorance. Still, while these principles were being rapidly disseminated many errors and illusory fears proved less easy to eradicate.

For instance, some worthy persons maintained that the moon was an ancient comet which, in describing its elongated orbit round the sun, happened to pass near the earth, and became confined within her circle of attraction. These drawing-room astronomers professed to explain the charred aspect of the moon—a disaster which they attributed to the intensity of the solar heat; only, on being reminded that comets have an atmosphere, and that the moon has little or none, they were fairly at a loss for a reply.

Others again, belonging to the doubting class, expressed certain fears as to the position of the moon. They had heard it said that, according to observations made in the time of the Caliphs, her revolution had become accelerated in a certain degree. Hence they concluded, logically enough, that an acceleration of motion ought to be accompanied by a corresponding diminution in the distance separating the two bodies; and that, supposing the double effect to be continued to infinity, the moon would end by one day falling into the earth. However, they became reassured as to the fate of future generations on being apprised that, according to the calculations of Laplace, this acceleration of motion is confined within very restricted limits, and that a proportional diminution of speed will be certain to succeed it. So, then, the stability of the solar system would not be deranged in ages to come.

There remains but the third class, the superstitious. These worthies were not content merely to rest in ignorance; they must know all about things which had no existence whatever, and as to the moon, they had long known all about her. One set regarded her disc as a polished mirror, by means of which people could see each other from different points of the earth and interchange their thoughts. Another set pretended that out of one thousand new moons that had been observed, nine hundred and fifty had been attended with remarkable disturbances, such as cataclysms, revolutions, earthquakes, the deluge, etc. Then they believed in some mysterious influence exercised by her over human destinies—that every Selenite was attached to some inhabitant of the earth by a tie of sympathy; they maintained that the entire vital system is subject to her control, etc. But in time the majority renounced these vulgar errors, and espoused the true side of the question. As for the Yankees, they had no other ambition than to take possession of this new continent of the sky, and to plant upon the summit of its highest elevation the star-spangled banner of the United States of America.

Chapter VII

THE HYMN OF THE CANNON-BALL

THE OBSERVATORY OF CAMBRIDGE IN ITS MEMORABLE LETTER HAD TREATED THE QUES-tion from a purely astronomical point of view. The mechanical part still remained.

President Barbicane had, without loss of time, nominated a working committee of the Gun Club. The duty of this committee was to resolve the three grand questions of the cannon, the projectile, and the powder. It was composed of four members of great technical knowledge, Barbicane (with a casting vote in case of equality), General Morgan, Major Elphinstone, and J. T. Maston, to whom were confided the functions of secretary. On the 8th of October the committee met at the house of President Barbicane, 3 Republican Street. The meeting was opened by the president himself.

"Gentlemen," said he, "we have to resolve one of the most important problems in the whole of the noble science of gunnery. It might appear, perhaps, the most logical course to devote our first meeting to the discussion of the engine to be employed. Nevertheless, after mature consideration, it has appeared to me that the question of the projectile must take precedence of that of the cannon, and that the dimensions of the latter must necessarily depend on those of the former."

"Suffer me to say a word," here broke in J. T. Maston. Permission having been granted, "Gentlemen," said he, with an inspired accent, "our president is right in placing the question of the projectile above all others. The ball we are about to discharge at the moon is our ambassador to her, and I wish to consider it from a moral point of view. The cannon-ball, gentlemen, to my mind, is the most magnificent manifestation of human power. If Providence has created the stars and the planets, man has called the cannon-ball into existence. Let Providence claim the swiftness of electricity and of light, of the stars, the comets, and the planets, of wind and sound—we claim to have invented the swiftness of the cannon-ball, a hundred times superior to that of the swiftest horses or railway train. How glorious will be the moment when, infinitely exceeding all hitherto attained velocities, we shall launch our new projectile with the rapidity of seven miles a second! Shall it not, gentlemen—shall it not be received up there with the honours due to a terrestrial ambassador?"

Overcome with emotion the orator sat down and applied himself to a huge plate of sandwiches before him.

"And now," said Barbicane, "let us quit the domain of poetry and come direct to the question."

"By all means," replied the members, each with his mouth full of sandwich.

"The problem before us," continued the president, "is how to communicate to a projectile a velocity of 12,000 yards per second. Let us at present examine the velocities hitherto attained. General Morgan will be able to enlighten us on this point."

"And the more easily," replied the general, "that during the war I was a member of the committee of experiments. I may say, then, that the 100-pounder Dahlgrens, which carried a distance of 5,000 yards, impressed upon their projectile an initial velocity of 500 yards a second. The Rodman *Columbiad* threw a shot weighing half a ton a distance of six miles, with a velocity of 800 yards per second—a result which Armstrong and Palisser have never obtained in England."

"This," replied Barbicane, "is, I believe, the maximum velocity ever attained?"

"It is so," replied the general.

"Ah!" groaned J. T. Maston, "if my mortar had not burst—"

"Yes," quietly replied Barbicane, "but it did burst. We must take, then, for our starting point, this velocity of 800 yards. We must increase it twenty-fold. Now, reserving for another discussion the means of producing this velocity, I will call your attention to the dimensions which it will be proper to assign to the shot. You understand that we have nothing to do here with projectiles weighing at most but half a ton."

"Why not?" demanded the major.

"Because the shot," quickly replied J. T. Maston, "must be big enough to attract the attention of the inhabitants of the moon, if there are any?"

"Yes," replied Barbicane, "and for another reason more important still."

"What mean you?" asked the major.

"I mean that it is not enough to discharge a projectile, and then take no further notice of it; we must follow it throughout its course, up to the moment when it shall reach its goal."

"What?" shouted the general and the major in great surprise.

"Undoubtedly," replied Barbicane composedly, "or our experiment would produce no result."

"But then," replied the major, "you will have to give this projectile enormous dimensions."

"No! Be so good as to listen. You know that optical instruments have acquired great perfection; with certain instruments we have succeeded in obtaining enlargements of 6,000 times and reducing the moon to within forty miles' distance. Now, at this distance, any objects sixty feet square would be perfectly visible.

"If, then, the penetrative power of telescopes has not been further increased, it is because that power detracts from their light; and the moon, which is but a reflecting mirror, does not give back sufficient light to enable us to perceive objects of lesser magnitude."

"Well, then, what do you propose to do?" asked the general. "Would you give your projectile a diameter of sixty feet?"

"Not so."

"Do you intend, then, to increase the luminous power of the moon?"

"Exactly so. If I can succeed in diminishing the density of the atmosphere through which the moon's light has to travel I shall have rendered her light more intense. To effect that object it will be enough to establish a telescope on some elevated mountain. That is what we will do."

"I give it up," answered the major. "You have such a way of simplifying things. And what enlargement do you expect to obtain in this way?"

"One of 48,000 times, which should bring the moon within an apparent distance of five miles; and, in order to be visible, objects need not have a diameter of more than nine feet."

"So, then," cried J. T. Maston, "our projectile need not be more than nine feet in diameter."

"Let me observe, however," interrupted Major Elphinstone, "this will involve a weight such as—"

"My dear major," replied Barbicane, "before discussing its weight permit me to enumerate some of the marvels which our ancestors have achieved in this respect. I don't mean to pretend that the science of gunnery has not advanced, but it is as well to bear in mind that during the middle ages they obtained results more surprising, I will venture to say, than ours. For instance, during the siege of Constantinople by Mahomet II, in 1453, stone shot of 1,900 pounds weight were employed. At Malta, in the time of the knights, there was a gun of the fortress of St. Elmo which threw a projectile weighing 2,500 pounds. And, now, what is the extent of what we have seen ourselves? Armstrong guns discharging shot of 500 pounds, and the Rodman guns projectiles of half a ton! It seems, then, that if projectiles have gained in range, they have lost far more in weight. Now, if we turn our efforts in that direction, we ought to arrive, with the progress on science, at ten times the weight of the shot of Mahomet II and the Knights of Malta."

"Clearly," replied the major; "but what metal do you calculate upon employing?"

"Simply cast-iron," said General Morgan.

"But," interrupted the major, "since the weight of a shot is proportionate to its volume, an iron ball of nine feet in diameter would be of tremendous weight."

"Yes, if it were solid, not if it were hollow."

"Hollow? then it would be a shell?"

"Yes, a shell," replied Barbicane; "decidedly it must be. A solid shot of 108 inches would weigh more than 200,000 pounds, a weight evidently far too great. Still, as we must reserve a certain stability for our projectile, I propose to give it a weight of 20,000 pounds."

"What, then, will be the thickness of the sides?" asked the major.

"If we follow the usual proportion," replied Morgan, "a diameter of 108 inches would require sides of two feet thickness, or less."

"That would be too much," replied Barbicane; "for you will observe that the question is not that of a shot intended to pierce an iron plate: it will suffice to give it sides strong enough to resist the pressure of the gas. The problem, therefore, is this—What thickness ought a cast-iron shell to have in order not to weigh more than 20,000 pounds? Our clever secretary will soon enlighten us upon this point."

"Nothing easier." replied the worthy secretary of the committee; and, rapidly tracing a few algebraical formulae upon paper, among which n^2 and x^2 frequently appeared, he presently said:

"The sides will require a thickness of less than two inches."

"Will that be enough?" asked the major doubtfully.

"Clearly not!" replied the president.

"What is to be done, then?" said Elphinstone, with a puzzled air.

"Employ another metal instead of iron."

"Copper?" said Morgan.

"No; that would be too heavy. I have better than that to offer."

"What then?" asked the major.

"Aluminum!" replied Barbicane.

"Aluminum?" cried his three colleagues in chorus.

"Unquestionably, my friends. This valuable metal possesses the whiteness of silver, the indestructibility of gold, the tenacity of iron, the fusibility of copper, the lightness of glass. It is easily wrought, is very widely distributed, forming the base of most of the rocks, is three times lighter than iron, and seems to have been created for the express purpose of furnishing us with the material for our projectile."

"But, my dear president," said the major, "is not the cost price of aluminum extremely high?"

"It was so at its first discovery, but it has fallen now to nine dollars the pound."

"But still, nine dollars the pound!" replied the major, who was not willing readily to give in; "even that is an enormous price."

"Undoubtedly, my dear major; but not beyond our reach."

"What will the projectile weigh then?" asked Morgan.

"Here is the result of my calculations," replied Barbicane. "A shot of 108 inches in diameter, and twelve inches in thickness, would weigh, in cast-iron, 67,440 pounds; cast in aluminum, its weight will be reduced to 19,250 pounds."

"Capital!" cried the major; "but do you know that, at nine dollars a pound, this projectile will cost—"

"One hundred and seventy-three thousand and fifty dollars ($173,050). I know it quite well. But fear not, my friends; the money will not be wanting for our enterprise, I will answer for it. Now what say you to aluminum, gentlemen?"

"Adopted!" replied the three members of the committee. So ended the first meeting. The question of the projectile was definitively settled.

Chapter VIII

HISTORY OF THE CANNON

THE RESOLUTIONS PASSED AT THE LAST MEETING PRODUCED A GREAT EFFECT OUT OF doors. Timid people took fright at the idea of a shot weighing 20,000 pounds being launched into space; they asked what cannon could ever transmit a sufficient velocity to such a mighty mass. The minutes of the second meeting were destined triumphantly to answer such questions. The following evening the discussion was renewed.

"My dear colleagues," said Barbicane, without further preamble, "the subject now before us is the construction of the engine, its length, its composition, and its weight. It is probable that we shall end by giving it gigantic dimensions; but however great may be the difficulties in the way, our mechanical genius will readily surmount them. Be good enough, then, to give me your attention, and do not hesitate to make objections at the close. I have no fear of them. The problem before us is how to communicate an initial force of 12,000 yards per second to a shell of 108 inches in diameter, weighing 20,000 pounds. Now when a projectile is launched into space, what happens to it? It is acted upon by three independent forces: the resistance of the air, the attraction of the earth, and the force of impulsion with which it is endowed. Let us examine these three forces. The resistance of the air is of little importance. The atmosphere of the earth does not exceed forty miles. Now, with the given rapidity, the projectile will have traversed this in five seconds, and the period is too brief for the resistance of the medium to be regarded otherwise than as insignificant. Proceding, then, to the attraction of the earth, that is, the weight of the shell, we know that this weight will diminish in the inverse ratio of the square of the distance. When a body left to itself falls to the surface of the earth, it falls five feet in the first second; and if the same body were removed 257,542 miles further off, in other words, to the distance of the moon, its fall would be reduced to about half a line in the first second. That is almost equivalent to a state of perfect rest. Our business, then, is to overcome progressively this action of gravitation. The mode of accomplishing that is by the force of impulsion."

"There's the difficulty," broke in the major.

"True," replied the president; "but we will overcome that, for the force of impulsion will depend on the length of the engine and the powder employed, the latter being limited only by the resisting power of the former. Our business, then, to-day is with the dimensions of the cannon."

"Now, up to the present time," said Barbicane, "our longest guns have not exceeded twenty-five feet in length. We shall therefore astonish the world by the dimensions we shall be obliged to adopt. It must evidently be, then, a gun of great range, since the length of the piece will increase the detention of the gas accumulated behind the projectile; but there is no advantage in passing certain limits."

"Quite so," said the major. "What is the rule in such a case?"

"Ordinarily the length of a gun is twenty to twenty-five times the diameter of the shot, and its weight two hundred and thirty-five to two hundred and forty times that of the shot."

"That is not enough," cried J. T. Maston impetuously.

"I agree with you, my good friend; and, in fact, following this proportion for a projectile nine feet in diameter, weighing 30,000 pounds, the gun would only have a length of two hundred and twenty-five feet, and a weight of 7,200,000 pounds."

"Ridiculous!" rejoined Maston. "As well take a pistol."

"I think so too," replied Barbicane; "that is why I propose to quadruple that length, and to construct a gun of nine hundred feet."

The general and the major offered some objections; nevertheless, the proposition, actively supported by the secretary, was definitely adopted.

"But," said Elphinstone, "what thickness must we give it?"

"A thickness of six feet," replied Barbicane.

"You surely don't think of mounting a mass like that upon a carriage?" asked the major.

"It would be a superb idea, though," said Maston.

"But impracticable," replied Barbicane. "No; I think of sinking this engine in the earth alone, binding it with hoops of wrought iron, and finally surrounding it with a thick mass of masonry of stone and cement. The piece once cast, it must be bored with great precision, so as to preclude any possible windage. So there will be no loss whatever of gas, and all the expansive force of the powder will be employed in the propulsion."

"One simple question," said Elphinstone: "is our gun to be rifled?"

"No, certainly not," replied Barbicane; "we require an enormous initial velocity; and you are well aware that a shot quits a rifled gun less rapidly than it does a smooth-bore."

"True," rejoined the major.

The committee here adjourned for a few minutes to tea and sandwiches.

On the discussion being renewed, "Gentlemen," said Barbicane, "we must now take into consideration the metal to be employed. Our cannon must be possessed of great tenacity, great hardness, be infusible by heat, indissoluble, and inoxidable by the corrosive action of acids."

"There is no doubt about that," replied the major; "and as we shall have to employ an immense quantity of metal, we shall not be at a loss for choice."

"Well, then," said Morgan, "I propose the best alloy hitherto known, which consists of one hundred parts of copper, twelve of tin, and six of brass."

"I admit," replied the president, "that this composition has yielded excellent results, but in the present case it would be too expensive, and very difficult to work. I think, then, that we ought to adopt a material excellent in its way and of low price, such as cast-iron. What is your advice, major?"

"I quite agree with you," replied Elphinstone.

"In fact," continued Barbicane, "cast-iron costs ten times less than bronze; it is easy to cast, it runs readily from the moulds of sand, it is easy of manipulation, it is at once economical of money and of time. In addition, it is excellent as a material, and I well remember that during the war, at the siege of Atlanta, some iron guns fired one thousand rounds at intervals of twenty minutes without injury."

"Cast-iron is very brittle, though," replied Morgan.

"Yes, but it possesses great resistance. I will now ask our worthy secretary to calculate the weight of a cast-iron gun with a bore of nine feet and a thickness of six feet of metal."

"In a moment," replied Maston. Then, dashing off some algebraical formulae with marvellous facility, in a minute or two he declared the following result:

"The cannon will weigh 68,040 tons. And, at two cents a pound, it will cost—"

"Two million five hundred and ten thousand seven hundred and one dollars."

Maston, the major, and the general regarded Barbicane with uneasy looks.

"Well, gentlemen," replied the president, "I repeat what I said yesterday. Make yourselves easy; the millions will not be wanting."

With this assurance of their president the committee separated, after having fixed their third meeting for the following evening.

Chapter IX

The Question of the Powders

THERE REMAINED FOR CONSIDERATION MERELY THE QUESTION OF POWDERS. THE PUBlic awaited with interest its final decision. The size of the projectile, the length of the cannon being settled, what would be the quantity of powder necessary to produce impulsion?

It is generally asserted that gunpowder was invented in the fourteenth century by the monk Schwartz, who paid for his grand discovery with his life. It is, however, pretty well proved that this story ought to be ranked among the legends of the middle ages. Gunpowder was not invented by anyone; it was the lineal successor of the Greek fire, which, like itself, was composed of sulphur and saltpeter. Few persons are acquainted with the mechanical power of gunpowder. Now this is precisely what is necessary to be understood in order to comprehend the importance of the question submitted to the committee.

A litre of gunpowder weighs about two pounds; during combustion it produces 400 litres of gas. This gas, on being liberated and acted upon by temperature raised to 2,400 degrees, occupies a space of 4,000 litres: consequently the volume of powder is to the volume of gas produced by its combustion as 1 to 4,000. One may judge, therefore, of the tremendous pressure on this gas when compressed within a space 4,000 times too confined. All this was, of course, well known to the members of the committee when they met on the following evening.

The first speaker on this occasion was Major Elphinstone, who had been the director of the gunpowder factories during the war.

"Gentlemen," said this distinguished chemist, "I begin with some figures which will serve as the basis of our calculation. The old 24-pounder shot required for its discharge sixteen pounds of powder."

"You are certain of this amount?" broke in Barbicane.

"Quite certain," replied the major. "The Armstrong cannon employs only seventy-five pounds of powder for a projectile of eight hundred pounds, and the Rodman *Columbiad* uses only one hundred and sixty pounds of powder to send its half-ton shot a distance of six miles. These facts cannot be called in question, for I myself raised the point during the depositions taken before the committee of artillery."

"Quite true," said the general.

"Well," replied the major, "these figures go to prove that the quantity of powder is not increased with the weight of the shot; that is to say, if a 24-pounder shot requires sixteen pounds of powder;—in other words, if in ordinary guns we employ a quantity of powder equal to two-thirds of the weight of the projectile, this proportion is not constant. Calculate, and you will see that in place of three hundred and thirty-three pounds of powder, the quantity is reduced to no more than one hundred and sixty pounds."

"What are you aiming at?" asked the president.

"If you push your theory to extremes, my dear major," said J. T. Maston, "you will get to this, that as soon as your shot becomes sufficiently heavy you will not require any powder at all."

"Our friend Maston is always at his jokes, even in serious matters," cried the major; "but let him make his mind easy, I am going presently to propose gunpowder enough to satisfy his artillerist's propensities. I only keep to statistical facts when I say that, during the war, and for the very largest guns, the weight of the powder was reduced, as the result of experience, to a tenth part of the weight of the shot."

"Perfectly correct," said Morgan; "but before deciding the quantity of powder necessary to give the impulse, I think it would be as well—"

"We shall have to employ a large-grained powder," continued the major; "its combustion is more rapid than that of the small."

"No doubt about that," replied Morgan; "but it is very destructive, and ends by enlarging the bore of the pieces."

"Granted; but that which is injurious to a gun destined to perform long service is not so to our *Columbiad*. We shall run no danger of an explosion; and it is necessary that our powder should take fire instantaneously in order that its mechanical effect may be complete."

"We must have," said Maston, "several touch-holes, so as to fire it at different points at the same time."

"Certainly," replied Elphinstone; "but that will render the working of the piece more difficult. I return then to my large-grained powder, which removes those difficulties. In his *Columbiad* charges Rodman employed a powder as large as chestnuts, made of willow charcoal, simply dried in cast-iron pans. This powder was hard and glittering, left no trace upon the hand, contained hydrogen and oxygen in large proportion, took fire instantaneously, and, though very destructive, did not sensibly injure the mouth-piece."

Up to this point Barbicane had kept aloof from the discussion; he left the others to speak while he himself listened; he had evidently got an idea. He now simply said, "Well, my friends, what quantity of powder do you propose?"

The three members looked at one another.

"Two hundred thousand pounds." at last said Morgan.

"Five hundred thousand," added the major.

"Eight hundred thousand," screamed Maston.

A moment of silence followed this triple proposal; it was at last broken by the president.

"Gentlemen," he quietly said, "I start from this principle, that the resistance of a gun, constructed under the given conditions, is unlimited. I shall surprise our friend Maston, then, by stigmatising his calculations as timid; and I propose to double his 800,000 pounds of powder."

"Sixteen hundred thousand pounds?" shouted Maston, leaping from his seat.

"Just so."

"We shall have to come then to my ideal of a cannon half-a-mile long; for you see 1,600,000 pounds will occupy a space of about 20,000 cubic feet; and since the contents of your cannon do not exceed 54,000 cubic feet, it would be half full; and the bore will not be more than long enough for the gas to communicate to the projectile sufficient impulse."

"Nevertheless," said the president, "I hold to that quantity of powder. Now, 1,600,000 pounds of powder will create 6,000,000,000 litres of gas. Six thousand millions! You quite understand?"

"What is to be done then?" said the general.

"The thing is very simple; we must reduce this enormous quantity of powder, while preserving to it its mechanical power."

"Good; but by what means?"

"I am going to tell you," replied Barbicane quietly.

"Nothing is more easy than to reduce this mass to one quarter of its bulk. You know that curious cellular matter which constitutes the elementary tissues of vegetable? This substance is found quite pure in many bodies, especially in cotton, which is nothing more than the down of the seeds of the cotton plant. Now cotton, combined with cold nitric acid, become transformed into a substance eminently insoluble, combustible, and explosive. It was first discovered in 1832, by Braconnot, a French chemist, who called it xyloidine. In 1838 another Frenchman, Pelouze, investigated its different properties, and finally, in 1846, Schonbein, professor of chemistry at Bâle, proposed its employment for purposes of war. This powder, now called pyroxyle, or fulminating cotton, is prepared with great facility by simply plunging cotton for fifteen minutes in nitric acid, then washing it in water, then drying it, and it is ready for use."

"Nothing could be more simple," said Morgan.

"Moreover, pyroxyle is unaltered by moisture—a valuable property to us, inasmuch as it would take several days to charge the cannon. It ignites at 170 degrees in place of 240, and its combustion is so rapid that one may set light to it on the top of the ordinary powder, without the latter having time to ignite."

"Perfect!" exclaimed the major.

"Only it is more expensive."

"What matter?" cried J. T. Maston.

"Finally, it imparts to projectiles a velocity four times superior to that of gunpowder. I will even add, that if we mix it with one-eighth of its own weight of nitrate of potassium, its expansive force is again considerably augmented."

"Will that be necessary?" asked the major.

"I think not," replied Barbicane. "So, then, in place of 1,600,000 pounds of powder, we shall have but 400,000 pounds of fulminating cotton; and since we can, without danger, compress 500 pounds of cotton into twenty-seven cubic feet, the whole quantity will not occupy a height of more than 180 feet within the bore of the *Columbiad*. In this way the shot will have more than 700 feet of bore to traverse under a force of 6,000,000,000 litres of gas before taking its flight towards the moon."

At this juncture J. T. Maston could not repress his emotion; he flung himself into the arms of his friend with the violence of a projectile, and Barbicane would have been stove in if he had not been boomproof.

This incident terminated the third meeting of the committee.

Barbicane and his bold colleagues, to whom nothing seemed impossible, had succeeding in solving the complex problems of projectile, cannon, and powder. Their plan was drawn up, and it only remained to put it into execution.

"A mere matter of detail, a bagatelle," said J. T. Maston.

Chapter X

ONE ENEMY V. TWENTY-FIVE MILLIONS OF FRIENDS

THE AMERICAN PUBLIC TOOK A LIVELY INTEREST IN THE SMALLEST DETAILS OF THE ENterprise of the Gun Club. It followed day by day the discussion of the committee. The most simple preparations for the great experiment, the questions of figures which it involved, the mechanical difficulties to be resolved—in one word, the entire plan of work—roused the popular excitement to the highest pitch.

The purely scientific attraction was suddenly intensified by the following incident:

We have seen what legions of admirers and friends Barbicane's project had rallied round its author. There was, however, one single individual alone in all the States of the Union who protested against the attempt of the Gun Club. He attacked it furiously on every opportunity, and human nature is such that Barbicane felt more keenly the opposition of that one man than he did the applause of all the others. He was well aware of the motive of this antipathy, the origin of this solitary enmity, the cause of its personality and old standing, and in what rivalry of self-love it had its rise.

This persevering enemy the president of the Gun Club had never seen. Fortunate that it was so, for a meeting between the two men would certainly have been attended with serious consequences. This rival was a man of science, like Barbicane himself, of a fiery, daring, and violent disposition; a pure Yankee. His name was Captain Nicholl; he lived at Philadelphia.

Most people are aware of the curious struggle which arose during the Federal war between the guns and armour of iron-plated ships. The result was the entire reconstruction of the navy of both the continents; as the one grew heavier, the other became thicker in proportion. The *Merrimac,* the *Monitor,* the *Tennessee,* the *Weehawken* discharged enormous projectiles themselves, after having been armour-clad against the projectiles of others. In fact they did to others that which they would not they should do to them—that grand principle of immortality upon which rests the whole art of war.

Now if Barbicane was a great founder of shot, Nicholl was a great forger of plates; the one cast night and day at Baltimore, the other forged day and night at Philadelphia. As soon as ever Barbicane invented a new shot, Nicholl invented a new plate; each followed a current of ideas essentially opposed to the other. Happily for these citizens, so useful to their country, a distance of from fifty to sixty miles separated them from one another, and they had never yet met. Which of these two inventors had the advantage over the other it was difficult to decide from the results obtained. By last accounts, however, it would seem that the armour-plate would in the end have to give way to the shot; nevertheless, there were competent judges who had their doubts on the point.

At the last experiment the cylindro-conical projectiles of Barbicane stuck like so many pins in the Nicholl plates. On that day the Philadelphia iron-forger then believed himself victorious, and could not evince contempt enough for his rival; but when the other afterward substituted for conical shot simple 600-pound shells, at very moderate velocity, the captain was obliged to give in. In fact, these projectiles knocked his best metal plate to shivers.

Matters were at this stage, and victory seemed to rest with the shot, when the war came to an end on the very day when Nicholl had completed a new armour-plate of wrought steel. It was a masterpiece of its kind, and bid defiance to all the projectiles of the world. The captain had it conveyed to the Polygon at Washington, challenging the president of the Gun Club to break it. Barbicane, peace having been declared, declined to try the experiment.

Nicholl, now furious, offered to expose his plate to the shock of any shot, solid, hollow, round, or conical. Refused by the president, who did not choose to compromise his last success.

Nicholl, disgusted by this obstinacy, tried to tempt Barbicane by offering him every chance. He proposed to fix the plate within two hundred yards of the gun. Barbicane still obstinate in refusal. A hundred yards? Not even seventy-five!

"At fifty then!" roared the captain through the newspapers. "At twenty-five yards! and I'll stand behind!"

Barbicane returned for answer that, even if Captain Nicholl would be so good as to stand in front, he would not fire any more.

Nicholl could not contain himself at this reply; threw out hints of cowardice; that a man who refused to fire a cannon-shot was pretty near being afraid of it; that artillerists who fight at six miles' distance are substituting mathematical formulae for individual courage.

To these insinuations Barbicane returned no answer; perhaps he never heard of them, so absorbed was he in the calculations for his great enterprise.

When his famous communication was made to the Gun Club, the captain's wrath passed all bounds; with his intense jealousy was mingled a feeling of absolute impotence. How was he to invent anything to beat this 900-feet *Columbiad*? What armour-plate could ever resist a projectile of 30,000 pounds weight? Overwhelmed at first under this violent shock, he by and by recovered himself, and resolved to crush the proposal by weight of his arguments.

He then violently attacked the labours of the Gun Club, published a number of letters in the newspapers, endeavoured to prove Barbicane ignorant of the first principles of gunnery. He maintained that it was absolutely impossible to impress upon any body whatever a velocity of 12,000 yards per second; that even with such a velocity a projectile of such a weight could not transcend the limits of the earth's atmosphere. Further still, even regarding the velocity to be acquired, and granting it to be sufficient, the shell could not resist the pressure of the gas developed by the ignition of 1,600,000 pounds of powder; and supposing it to resist that pressure, it would be less able to support that temperature; it would melt on quitting the *Columbiad*, and fall back in a red-hot shower upon the heads of the imprudent spectators.

Barbicane continued his work without regarding these attacks.

Nicholl then took up the question in its other aspects. Without touching upon its uselessness in all points of view, he regarded the experiment as fraught with extreme danger, both to the citizens, who might sanction by their presence so reprehensible a spectacle, and also to the towns in the neighbourhood of this deplorable cannon. He also observed that if the projectile did not succeed in reaching its destination (a result absolutely impossible), it must inevitably fall back upon the earth, and that the shock of such a mass, multiplied by the square of its velocity, would seriously endanger every point of the globe. Under the circumstances, therefore, and without interfering with the rights of free citizens, it was a case for the intervention of Government, which ought not to endanger the safety of all for the pleasure of one individual.

Spite of all his arguments, however, Captain Nicholl remained alone in his opinion. Nobody listened to him, and he did not succeed in alienating a single admirer from the president of the Gun Club. The latter did not even take the pains to refute the arguments of his rival.

Nicholl, driven into his last entrenchments, and not able to fight personally in the cause, resolved to fight with money. He published, therefore, in the Richmond *Inquirer* a series of wagers, conceived in these terms, and on an increasing scale:

No. 1 ($1,000).—That the necessary funds for the experiment of the Gun Club will not be forthcoming.

No. 2 ($2,000).—That the operation of casting a cannon of 900 feet is impracticable, and cannot possibly succeed.

No. 3 ($3,000).—That it is impossible to load the *Columbiad*, and that the pyroxyle will take fire spontaneously under the pressure of the projectile.

No. 4 ($4,000).—That the *Columbiad* will burst at the first fire.

No. 5 ($5,000).—That the shot will not travel farther than six miles, and that it will fall back again a few seconds after its discharge.

It was an important sum, therefore, which the captain risked in his invincible obstinacy. He had no less than $15,000 at stake.

Notwithstanding the importance of the challenge, on the 19th of May he received a sealed packet containing the following superbly laconic reply:

Baltimore, October 19.
Done.

Barbicane

Chapter XI

Florida and Texas

ONE QUESTION REMAINED YET TO BE DECIDED; IT WAS NECESSARY TO CHOOSE A favourable spot for the experiment. According to the advice of the Observatory of Cambridge, the gun must be fired perpendicularly to the plane of the horizon, that is to say, towards the zenith. Now the moon does not traverse the zenith, except in places situated between 0° and 28° of latitude. It became, then, necessary to determine exactly that spot on the globe where the immense *Columbiad* should be cast.

On the 20th of October, at a general meeting of the Gun Club, Barbicane produced a magnificent map of the United States. "Gentlemen," said he, in opening the discussion, "I presume that we are all agreed that this experiment cannot and ought not to be tried anywhere but within the limits of the soil of the Union. Now, by good fortune, certain frontiers of the United States extend downward as far as the 28th parallel of the north latitude. If you will cast your eye over this map, you will see that we have at our disposal the whole of the southern portion of Texas and Florida."

It was finally agreed, then, that the *Columbiad* must be cast on the soil of either Texas or Florida. The result, however, of this decision was to create a rivalry entirely without precedent between the different towns of these two States.

The 28th parallel, on reaching the American coast, traverses the peninsula of Florida, dividing it into two nearly equal portions. Then, plunging into the Gulf of Mexico, it subtends the arc formed by the coast of Alabama, Mississippi, and Louisiana; then skirting Texas, off which it cuts an angle, it continues its course over Mexico, crosses the Sonora, Old California, and loses itself in the Pacific Ocean. It was, therefore, only those portions of Texas and Florida which were situated below this parallel which came within the prescribed conditions of latitude.

Florida, in its southern part, reckons no cities of importance; it is simply studded with forts raised against the roving Indians. One solitary town, Tampa Town, was able to put in a claim in favour of its situation.

In Texas, on the contrary, the towns are much more numerous and important. Corpus Christi, in the county of Nueces, and all the cities situated on the Rio Bravo, Laredo, Comalites, San Ignacio on the Web, Rio Grande City on the Starr, Edinburgh in the Hidalgo, Santa Rita, Elpanda, Brownsville in the Cameron, formed an imposing league against the pretensions of Florida. So, scarcely was the decision known, when the Texan and Floridan deputies arrived at Baltimore in an incredibly short space of time. From that very moment President Barbicane and the influential members of the Gun Club were besieged day and night by formidable claims. If seven cities of Greece contended for the honour of having given birth to a Homer, here were two entire States threatening to come to blows about the question of a cannon.

The rival parties promenaded the streets with arms in their hands; and at every occasion of their meeting a collision was to be apprehended which might have been attended with disastrous results. Happily the prudence and address of President Barbicane averted the danger. These personal demonstrations found a division in the newspapers of the different States. The New York *Herald* and the *Tribune* supported Texas, while the *Times* and the *American Review* espoused the cause of the Floridan deputies. The members of the Gun Club could not decide to which to give the preference.

Texas produced its array of twenty-six counties; Florida replied that twelve counties were better than twenty-six in a country only one-sixth part of the size.

Texas plumed itself upon its 330,000 natives; Florida, with a far smaller territory, boasted of being much more densely populated with 56,000.

The Texans, through the columns of the *Herald,* claimed that some regard should be had to a State which grew the best cotton in all America, produced the best green oak for the service of the navy, and contained the finest oil, besides iron mines, in which the yield was fifty per cent of pure metal.

To this the *American Review* replied that the soil of Florida, although not equally rich, afforded the best conditions for the moulding and casting of the *Columbiad,* consisting as it did of sand and argillaceous earth.

"That may be all very well," replied the Texans; "but you must first get to this country. Now the communications with Florida are difficult, while the coast of Texas offers the bay of Galveston, which possesses a circumference of fourteen leagues, and is capable of containing the navies of the entire world!"

"A pretty notion truly," replied the papers in the interest of Florida, "that of Galveston bay *below the 29th parallel!* Have we not got the bay of Espiritu Santo, opening precisely upon *the 28th degree,* and by which ships can reach Tampa Town by direct route?"

"A fine bay! half choked with sand!"

"Choked yourselves!" returned the others.

Thus the war went on for several days, when Florida endeavoured to draw her adversary away on to fresh ground; and one morning the *Times* hinted that, the enterprise being essentially American, it ought not to be attempted upon other than purely American territory.

To these words Texas retorted, "American! are we not as much so as you? Were not Texas and Florida both incorporated into the Union in 1845?"

"Undoubtedly," replied the *Times*; "but we have belonged to the Americans ever since 1820."

"Yes!" returned the *Tribune*; "after having been Spaniards or English for two hundred years, you were sold to the United States for five million dollars!"

"Well! and why need we blush for that? Was not Louisiana bought from Napoleon in 1803 at the price of sixteen million dollars?"

"Scandalous!" roared the Texas deputies. "A wretched little strip of country like Florida to dare to compare itself to Texas, who, in place of selling herself, asserted her own independence, drove out the Mexicans in March 2, 1846, and declared herself a federal republic after the victory gained by Samuel Houston, on the banks of the San Jacinto, over the troops of Santa Anna!—a country, in fine, which voluntarily annexed itself to the United States of America!"

"Yes; because it was afraid of the Mexicans!" replied Florida.

"Afraid!" From this moment the state of things became intolerable. A sanguinary encounter seemed daily imminent between the two parties in the streets of Baltimore. It became necessary to keep an eye upon the deputies.

President Barbicane knew not which way to look. Notes, documents, letters full of menaces showered down upon his house. Which side ought he to take? As regarded the appropriation of the soil, the facility of communication, the rapidity of transport, the claims of both States were evenly balanced. As for political prepossessions, they had nothing to do with the question.

This dead block had existed for some little time, when Barbicane resolved to get rid of it all at once. He called a meeting of his colleagues, and laid before them a proposition which, it will be seen, was profoundly sagacious.

"On carefully considering," he said, "what is going on now between Florida and Texas, it is clear that the same difficulties will recur with all the towns of the favoured State. The rivalry will descend from State to city, and so on downward. Now Texas possesses eleven towns within the prescribed conditions, which will further dispute the honour and create us new enemies, while Florida has only one. I go in, therefore, for Florida and Tampa Town."

This decision, on being made known, utterly crushed the Texan deputies. Seized with an indescribable fury, they addressed threatening letters to the different members of the Gun Club by name. The magistrates had but one course to take, and they took it. They chartered a special train, forced the Texans into it whether they would or no; and they quitted the city with a speed of thirty miles an hour.

Quickly, however, as they were despatched, they found time to hurl one last and bitter sarcasm at their adversaries.

Alluding to the extent of Florida, a mere peninsula confined between two seas, they pretended that it could never sustain the shock of the discharge, and that it would "bust up" at the very first shot.

"Very well, let it bust up!" replied the Floridans, with a brevity of the days of ancient Sparta.

Chapter XII

URBI ET ORBI

THE ASTRONOMICAL, MECHANICAL, AND TOPOGRAPHICAL DIFFICULTIES RESOLVED, FI-
nally came the question of finance. The sum required was far too great for any individual, or even any single State, to provide the requisite millions.

President Barbicane undertook, despite of the matter being a purely American affair,
to render it one of universal interest, and to request the financial co-operation of all peo-
ples. It was, he maintained, the right and duty of the whole earth to interfere in the affairs
of its satellite. The subscription opened at Baltimore extended properly to the whole
world—*Urbi et orbi.*

This subscription was successful beyond all expectation; notwithstanding that it was a
question not of lending but of giving the money. It was a purely disinterested operation in
the strictest sense of the term, and offered not the slightest chance of profit.

The effect, however, of Barbicane's communication was not confined to the frontiers
of the United States; it crossed the Atlantic and Pacific, invading simultaneously Asia and
Europe, Africa and Oceanica. The observatories of the Union placed themselves in immediate communication with those of foreign countries. Some, such as those of Paris, Petersburg, Berlin, Stockholm, Hamburg, Malta, Lisbon, Benares, Madras, and others,
transmitted their good wishes; the rest maintained a prudent silence, quietly awaiting the
result. As for the observatory at Greenwich, seconded as it was by the twenty-two astronomical establishments of Great Britain, it spoke plainly enough. It boldly denied the possibility of success, and pronounced in favour of the theories of Captain Nicholl. But this
was nothing more than mere English jealousy.

On the 8th of October President Barbicane published a manifesto full of enthusiasm,
in which he made an appeal to "all persons of good-will upon the face of the earth." This
document, translated into all languages, met with immense success.

Subscription lists were opened in all the principal cities of the Union, with a central
office at the Baltimore Bank, 9 Baltimore Street.

In addition, subscriptions were received at the following banks in the different states
of the two continents:

At Vienna, with S. M. de Rothschild.
At Petersburg, Stieglitz and Co.
At Paris, The Crédit Mobilier.
At Stockholm, Tottie and Arfuredson.
At London, N. M. Rothschild and Son.
At Turin, Ardouin and Co.
At Berlin, Mendelssohn.
At Geneva, Lombard, Odier and Co.
At Constantinople, The Ottoman Bank.
At Brussels, J. Lambert.

At Madrid, Daniel Weisweller.
At Amsterdam, Netherlands Credit Co.
At Rome, Torlonia and Co.
At Lisbon, Lecesne.
At Copenhagen, Private Bank.
At Rio Janeiro, Private Bank.
At Montevideo, Private Bank.
At Valparaiso and Lima, Thos. la Chambre and Co.
At Mexico, Martin Daran and Co.

Three days after the manifesto of President Barbicane $4,000,000 were paid into the different towns of the Union. With such a balance the Gun Club might begin operations at once. But some days later advices were received to the effect that foreign subscriptions were being eagerly taken up. Certain countries distinguished themselves by their liberality; others untied their purse-strings with less facility—matter of temperament. Figures are, however, more eloquent than words, and here is the official statement of the sums which were paid in to the credit of the Gun Club at the close of the subscription.

Russia paid in as her contingent the enormous sum of 368,733 roubles. No one need be surprised at this, who bears in mind the scientific taste of the Russians, and the impetus which they have given to astronomical studies—thanks to their numerous observatories.

France began by deriding the pretensions of the Americans. The moon served as a pretext for a thousand stale puns and a score of ballads, in which bad taste contested the palm with ignorance. But as formerly the French paid before singing, so now they paid after having had their laugh, and they subscribed for a sum of 1,253,930 francs. At that price they had a right to enjoy themselves a little.

Austria showed herself generous in the midst of her financial crisis. Her public contributions amounted to the sum of 216,000 florins—a perfect godsend.

Fifty-two thousand rix-dollars were the remittance of Sweden and Norway; the amount is large for the country, but it would undoubtedly have been considerably increased had the subscription been opened in Christiana simultaneously with that at Stockholm. For some reason or other the Norwegians do not like to send their money to Sweden.

Prussia, by a remittance of 250,000 thalers, testified her high approval of the enterprise.

Turkey behaved generously; but she had a personal interest in the matter. The moon, in fact, regulates the cycle of her years and her fast of Ramadan. She could not do less than give 1,372,640 piastres; and she gave them with an eagerness which denoted, however, some pressure on the part of the government.

Belgium distinguished herself among the second-rate states by a grant of 513,000 francs—about two centimes per head of her population.

Holland and her colonies interested themselves to the extent of 110,000 florins, only demanding an allowance of five per cent discount for paying ready money.

Denmark, a little contracted in territory, gave nevertheless 9,000 ducats, proving her love for scientific experiments.

The Germanic Confederation pledged itself to 34,285 florins. It was impossible to ask for more; besides, they would not have given it.

Though very much crippled, Italy found 200,000 lire in the pockets of her people. If she had had Venetia she would have done better; but she had not.

The States of the Church thought that they could not send less than 7,040 Roman crowns; and Portugal carried her devotion to science as far as 30,000 cruzados. It was the widow's mite—eighty-six piastres; but self-constituted empires are always rather short of money.

Two hundred and fifty-seven francs, this was the modest contribution of Switzerland to the American work. One must freely admit that she did not see the practical side of the matter. It did not seem to her that the mere despatch of a shot to the moon could possibly establish any relation of affairs with her; and it did not seem prudent to her to embark her capital in so hazardous an enterprise. After all, perhaps she was right.

As to Spain, she could not scrape together more than 110 reals. She gave as an excuse that she had her railways to finish. The truth is, that science is not favourably regarded in that country, it is still in a backward state; and, moreover, certain Spaniards, not by any means the least educated, did not form a correct estimate of the bulk of the projectile compared with that of the moon. They feared that it would disturb the established order of things. In that case it were better to keep aloof; which they did to the tune of some reals.

There remained but England; and we know the contemptuous antipathy with which she received Barbicane's proposition. The English have but one soul for the whole twenty-six millions of inhabitants which Great Britain contains. They hinted that the enterprise of the Gun Club was contrary to the "principle of non-intervention." And they did not subscribe a single farthing.

At this intimation the Gun Club merely shrugged its shoulders and returned to its great work. When South America, that is to say, Peru, Chili, Brazil, the provinces of La Plata and Columbia, had poured forth their quota into their hands, the sum of $300,000, it found itself in possession of a considerable capital, of which the following is a statement:

United States subscriptions, ... $4,000,000
Foreign subscriptions, ... $1,446,675
Total, ... $5,446,675

Such was the sum which the public poured into the treasury of the Gun Club.

Let no one be surprised at the vastness of the amount. The work of casting, boring, masonry, the transport of workmen, their establishment in an almost uninhabited country, the construction of furnaces and workshops, the plant, the powder, the projectile, and incipient expenses, would, according to the estimates, absorb nearly the whole. Certain cannon-shots in the Federal war cost one thousand dollars apiece. This one of President Barbicane, unique in the annals of gunnery, might well cost five thousand times more.

On the 20th of October a contract was entered into with the manufactory at Coldspring, near New York, which during the war had furnished the largest Parrott, cast-iron guns. It was stipulated between the contracting parties that the manufactory of Coldspring should engage to transport to Tampa Town, in southern Florida, the necessary materials for casting the *Columbiad*. The work was bound to be completed at latest by the 15th of October following, and the cannon delivered in good condition under penalty of a forfeit of one hundred dollars a day to the moment when the moon should again present herself under the same conditions—that is to say, in eighteen years and eleven days.

The engagement of the workmen, their pay, and all the necessary details of the work, devolved upon the Coldspring Company.

This contract, executed in duplicate, was signed by Barbicane, president of the Gun Club, of the one part, and T. Murchison, director of the Coldspring manufactory, of the other, who thus executed the deed on behalf of their respective principals.

Chapter XIII

STONES HILL

WHEN THE DECISION WAS ARRIVED AT BY THE GUN CLUB, TO THE DISPARAGEMENT OF Texas, everyone in America, where reading is a universal acquirement, set to work to study the geography of Florida. Never before had there been such a sale for works like *Bertram's Travels in Florida, Roman's Natural History of East and West Florida, William's Territory of Florida,* and *Cleland on the Cultivation of the Sugar-Cane in Florida.* It became necessary to issue fresh editions of these works.

Barbicane had something better to do than to read. He desired to see things with his own eyes, and to mark the exact position of the proposed gun. So, without a moment's loss of time, he placed at the disposal of the Cambridge Observatory the funds necessary for the construction of a telescope, and entered into negotiations with the house of Breadwill and Co., of Albany, for the construction of an aluminum projectile of the required size. He then quitted Baltimore, accompanied by J. T. Maston, Major Elphinstone, and the manager of the Coldspring factory.

On the following day, the four fellow-travellers arrived at New Orleans. There they immediately embarked on board the *Tampico,* a despatch-boat belonging to the Federal navy, which the government had placed at their disposal; and, getting up steam, the banks of Louisiana speedily disappeared from sight.

The passage was not long. Two days after starting, the *Tampico,* having made four hundred and eighty miles, came in sight of the coast of Florida. On a nearer approach Barbicane found himself in view of a low, flat country of somewhat barren aspect. After coasting along a series of creeks abounding in lobsters and oysters, the *Tampico* entered the bay of Espiritu Santo, where she finally anchored in a small natural harbor, formed by the *embouchure* of the River Hillisborough, at seven P.M., on the 22d of October.

Our four passengers disembarked at once. "Gentlemen," said Barbicane, "we have no time to lose; to-morrow we must obtain horses, and proceed to reconnoitre the country."

Barbicane had scarcely set his foot on shore when three thousand of the inhabitants of Tampa Town came forth to meet him, an honour due to the president who had signalised their country by his choice.

Declining, however, every kind of ovation, Barbicane ensconced himself in a room of the Franklin Hotel.

On the morrow some of the small horses of the Spanish breed, full of vigour and of fire, stood snorting under his windows; but instead of four steeds, here were fifty, together with their riders. Barbicane descended with his three fellow-travellers; and much astonished were they all to find themselves in the midst of such a cavalcade. He remarked that every horseman carried a carbine slung across his shoulders and pistols in his holsters.

On expressing his surprise at these preparations, he was speedily enlightened by a young Floridan, who quietly said:

"Sir, there are Seminoles there."

"What do you mean by Seminoles?"

"Savages who scour the prairies. We thought it best, therefore, to escort you on your road."

"Pooh!" cried J. T. Maston, mounting his steed.

"All right," said the Floridan; "but it is true enough, nevertheless."

"Gentlemen," answered Barbicane, "I thank you for your kind attention; but it is time to be off."

It was five A.M. when Barbicane and his party, quitting Tampa Town, made their way along the coast in the direction of Alifia Creek. This little river falls into Hillsborough Bay twelve miles above Tampa Town. Barbicane and his escort coasted along its right bank to the eastward. Soon the waves of the bay disappeared behind a bend of rising ground, and the Floridan "champagne" alone offered itself to view.

Florida, discovered on Palm Sunday, in 1512, by Juan Ponce de Leon, was originally named *Pascha Florida*. It little deserved that designation, with its dry and parched coasts. But after some few miles of tract the nature of the soil gradually changes and the country shows itself worthy of the name. Cultivated plains soon appear, where are united all the productions of the northern and tropical floras, terminating in prairies abounding with pineapples and yams, tobacco, rice, cotton-plants, and sugar-canes, which extend beyond reach of sight, flinging their riches broadcast with careless prodigality.

Barbicane appeared highly pleased on observing the progressive elevation of the land; and in answer to a question of J. T. Maston, replied:

"My worthy friend, we cannot do better than sink our *Columbiad* in these high grounds."

"To get nearer the moon, perhaps?" said the secretary of the Gun Club.

"Not exactly," replied Barbicane, smiling; "do you not see that among these elevated plateaus we shall have a much easier work of it? No struggles with the water-springs, which will save us long expensive tubings; and we shall be working in daylight instead of down a deep and narrow well. Our business, then, is to open our trenches upon ground some hundreds of yards above the level of the sea."

"You are right, sir," struck in Murchison, the engineer; "and, if I mistake not, we shall ere long find a suitable spot for our purpose."

"I wish we were at the first stroke of the pickaxe," said the president.

"And I wish we were at the *last*," cried J. T. Maston.

About ten A.M. the little band had crossed a dozen miles. To fertile plains succeeded a region of forests. There perfumes of the most varied kinds mingled together in tropical profusion. These almost impenetrable forests were composed of pomegranates, orange-trees, citrons, figs, olives, apricots, bananas, huge vines, whose blossoms and fruits rivalled each other in colour and perfume. Beneath the odorous shade of these magnificent trees fluttered and warbled a little world of brilliantly plumaged birds.

J. T. Maston and the major could not repress their admiration on finding themselves in the presence of the glorious beauties of this wealth of nature. President Barbicane, however, less sensitive to these wonders, was in haste to press forward; the very luxuriance of the country was displeasing to him. They hastened onward, therefore, and were compelled to ford several rivers, not without danger, for they were infested with huge alligators from fifteen to eighteen feet long. Maston courageously menaced them with his steel hook, but he only succeeded in frightening some pelicans and teal, while tall flamingos stared stupidly at the party.

At length these denizens of the swamps disappeared in their turn; smaller trees became thinly scattered among less dense thickets—a few isolated groups detached in the midst of endless plains over which ranged herds of startled deer.

"At last," cried Barbicane, rising in his stirrups, "here we are at the region of pines!"

"Yes! and of savages too," replied the major.

In fact, some Seminoles had just come in sight upon the horizon; they rode violently backward and forward on their fleet horses, brandishing their spears or discharging their guns with a dull report. These hostile demonstrations, however, had no effect upon Barbicane and his companions.

They were then occupying the centre of a rocky plain, which the sun scorched with its parching rays. This was formed by a considerable elevation of the soil, which seemed to offer to the members of the Gun Club all the conditions requisite for the construction of their *Columbiad*.

"Halt!" said Barbicane, reining up. "Has this place any local appellation?"

"It is called Stones Hill," replied one of the Floridans.

Barbicane, without saying a word, dismounted, seized his instruments, and began to note his position with extreme exactness. The little band, drawn up in the rear, watched his proceedings in profound silence.

At this moment the sun passed the meridian. Barbicane, after a few moments, rapidly wrote down the result of his observations, and said:

"This spot is situated eighteen hundred feet above the level of the sea, in 27° 7' N. lat. and 5° 7' W. long. of the meridian of Washington. It appears to me by its rocky and barren character to offer all the conditions requisite for our experiment. On that plain will be raised our magazines, workshops, furnaces, and workmen's huts; and here, from this very spot," said he, stamping his foot on the summit of Stones Hill, "hence shall our projectile take its flight into the regions of the Solar World."

Chapter XIV

PICKAXE AND TROWEL

THE SAME EVENING BARBICANE AND HIS COMPANIONS RETURNED TO TAMPA TOWN; AND Murchison, the engineer, re-embarked on board the *Tampico* for New Orleans. His object was to enlist an army of workmen, and to collect together the greater part of the materials. The members of the Gun Club remained at Tampa Town, for the purpose of setting on foot the preliminary works by the aid of the people of the country.

Eight days after its departure, the *Tampico* returned into the bay of Espiritu Santo, with a whole flotilla of steamboats. Murchison had succeeded in assembling together fifteen hundred artisans. Attracted by the high pay and considerable bounties offered by the Gun Club, he had enlisted a choice legion of stokers, iron-founders, lime-burners, miners, brick-makers, and artisans of every trade, without distinction of colour. As many of these people brought their families with them, their departure resembled a perfect emigration.

On the 31st of October, at ten o'clock in the morning, the troop disembarked on the quays of Tampa Town; and one may imagine the activity which pervaded that little town, whose population was thus doubled in a single day.

During the first few days they were busy discharging the cargo brought by the flotilla, the machines, and the rations, as well as a large number of huts constructed of iron plates, separately pieced and numbered. At the same period Barbicane laid the first sleepers of a railway fifteen miles in length, intended to unite Stones Hill with Tampa Town. On the first of November Barbicane quitted Tampa Town with a detachment of workmen; and on the following day the whole town of huts was erected round Stones Hill. This they enclosed with palisades; and in respect of energy and activity, it might have been mistaken for one of the great cities of the Union. Everything was placed under a complete system of discipline, and the works were commenced in most perfect order.

The nature of the soil having been carefully examined, by means of repeated borings, the work of excavation was fixed for the 4th of November.

On that day Barbicane called together his foremen and addressed them as follows: "You are well aware, my friends, of the object with which I have assembled you together in this wild part of Florida. Our business is to construct a cannon measuring nine feet in its interior diameter, six feet thick, and with a stone revetment of nineteen and a half feet in thickness. We have, therefore, a well of sixty feet in diameter to dig down to a depth of nine hundred feet. This great work must be completed within eight months, so that you have 2,543,400 cubic feet of earth to excavate in 255 days; that is to say, in round numbers, 2,000 cubic feet per day. That which would present no difficulty to a thousand navvies working in open country will be of course more troublesome in a comparatively confined space. However, the thing must be done, and I reckon for its accomplishment upon your courage as much as upon your skill."

At eight o'clock the next morning the first stroke of the pickaxe was struck upon the soil of Florida; and from that moment that prince of tools was never inactive for one moment in the hands of the excavators. The gangs relieved each other every three hours.

On the 4th of November fifty workmen commenced digging, in the very centre of the enclosed space on the summit of Stones Hill, a circular hole sixty feet in diameter. The pickaxe first struck upon a kind of black earth, six inches in thickness, which was speedily disposed of. To this earth succeeded two feet of fine sand, which was carefully laid aside as being valuable for serving the casting of the inner mould. After the sand appeared some compact white clay, resembling the chalk of Great Britain, which extended down to a depth of four feet. Then the iron of the picks struck upon the hard bed of the soil; a kind of rock formed of petrified shells, very dry, very solid, and which the picks could with difficulty penetrate. At this point the excavation exhibited a depth of six and a half feet and the work of the masonry was begun.

At the bottom of the excavation they constructed a wheel of oak, a kind of circle strongly bolted together, and of immense strength. The centre of this wooden disc was hollowed out to a diameter equal to the exterior diameter of the *Columbiad*. Upon this wheel rested the first layers of the masonry, the stones of which were bound together by hydraulic cement, with irresistible tenacity. The workmen, after laying the stones from the circumference to the centre, were thus enclosed within a kind of well twenty-one feet in diameter. When this work was accomplished, the miners resumed their picks and cut away the rock from underneath the wheel itself, taking care to support it as they advanced upon blocks of great thickness. At every two feet which the hole gained in depth they successively withdrew the blocks. The wheel then sank little by little, and with it the massive ring of masonry, on the upper bed of which the masons laboured incessantly, always reserving some vent holes to permit the escape of gas during the operation of the casting.

This kind of work required on the part of the workmen extreme nicety and minute attention. More than one, in digging underneath the wheel, was dangerously injured by the splinters of stone. But their ardour never relaxed, night or day. By day they worked under the rays of the scorching sun; by night, under the gleam of the electric light. The sounds of the picks against the rock, the bursting of mines, the grinding of the machines, the wreaths of smoke scattered through the air, traced around Stones Hill a circle of terror which the herds of buffaloes and the war parties of the Seminoles never ventured to pass. Nevertheless, the works advanced regularly, as the steam-cranes actively removed the rubbish. Of unexpected obstacles there was little account; and with regard to foreseen difficulties, they were speedily disposed of.

At the expiration of the first month the well had attained the depth assigned for that lapse of time, namely, 112 feet. This depth was doubled in December, and trebled in January.

During the month of February the workmen had to contend with a sheet of water which made its way right across the outer soil. It became necessary to employ very powerful pumps and compressed-air engines to drain it off, so as to close up the orifice from whence it issued; just as one stops a leak on board ship. They at last succeeded in getting the upper hand of these untoward streams; only, in consequence of the loosening of the soil, the wheel partly gave way, and a slight partial settlement ensued. This accident cost the life of several workmen.

No fresh occurrence thenceforward arrested the progress of the operation; and on the 10th of June, twenty days before the expiration of the period fixed by Barbicane, the well, lined throughout with its facing of stone, had attained the depth of 900 feet. At the bottom the masonry rested upon a massive block measuring thirty feet in thickness, while on the upper portion it was level with the surrounding soil.

President Barbicane and the members of the Gun Club warmly congratulated their engineer Murchison: the cyclopean work had been accomplished with extraordinary rapidity.

During these eight months Barbicane never quitted Stones Hill for a single instant. Keeping ever close by the work of excavation, he busied himself incessantly with the welfare and health of his workpeople, and was singularly fortunate in warding off the epidemics common to large communities of men, and so disastrous in those regions of the globe which are exposed to the influences of tropical climates.

Many workmen, it is true, paid with their lives for the rashness inherent in these dangerous labours; but these mishaps are impossible to be avoided, and they are classed among the details with which the Americans trouble themselves but little. They have in fact more regard for human nature in general than for the individual in particular.

Nevertheless, Barbicane professed opposite principles to these, and put them in force at every opportunity. So, thanks to his care, his intelligence, his useful intervention in all difficulties, his prodigious and humane sagacity, the average of accidents did not exceed that of transatlantic countries, noted for their excessive precautions—France, for instance, among others, where they reckon about one accident for every two hundred thousand francs of work.

Chapter XV

The Fête of the Casting

DURING THE EIGHT MONTHS WHICH WERE EMPLOYED IN THE WORK OF EXCAVATION THE preparatory works of the casting had been carried on simultaneously with extreme rapidity. A stranger arriving at Stones Hill would have been surprised at the spectacle offered to his view.

At 600 yards from the well, and circularly arranged around it as a central point, rose 1,200 reverberating ovens, each six feet in diameter, and separated from each other by an interval of three feet. The circumference occupied by these 1,200 ovens presented a length of two miles. Being all constructed on the same plan, each with its high quadrangular chimney, they produced a most singular effect.

It will be remembered that on their third meeting the committee had decided to use cast-iron for the *Columbiad*, and in particular the white description. This metal, in fact, is the most tenacious, the most ductile, and the most malleable, and consequently suitable for all moulding operations; and when smelted with pit coal, is of superior quality for all engineering works requiring great resisting power, such as cannon, steam boilers, hydraulic presses, and the like.

Cast-iron, however, if subjected to only one single fusion, is rarely sufficiently homogeneous; and it requires a second fusion completely to refine it by dispossessing it of its last earthly deposits. So long before being forwarded to Tampa Town, the iron ore, molten in the great furnaces of Coldspring, and brought into contact with coal and silicium heated to a high temperature, was carburised and transformed into cast-iron. After this first operation, the metal was sent on to Stones Hill. They had, however, to deal with 136,000,000 pounds of iron, a quantity far too costly to send by railway. The cost of transport would have been double that of material. It appeared preferable to freight vessels at New York, and to load them with the iron in bars. This, however, required not less than sixty-eight vessels of 1,000 tons, a veritable fleet, which, quitting New York on the 3d of May, on the 10th of the same month ascended the Bay of Espiritu Santo, and discharged their cargoes, without dues, in the port at Tampa Town. Thence the iron was transported by rail to Stones Hill, and about the middle of January this enormous mass of metal was delivered at its destination.

It will easily be understood that 1,200 furnaces were not too many to melt simultaneously these 60,000 tons of iron. Each of these furnaces contained nearly 140,000 pounds weight of metal. They were all built after the model of those which served for the casting of the Rodman gun; they were trapezoidal in shape, with a high elliptical arch. These furnaces, constructed of fireproof brick, were especially adapted for burning pit coal, with a flat bottom upon which the iron bars were laid. This bottom, inclined at an angle of 25 degrees, allowed the metal to flow into the receiving troughs; and the 1,200 converging trenches carried the molten metal down to the central well.

The day following that on which the works of the masonry and boring had been completed, Barbicane set to work upon the central mould. His object now was to raise within the centre of the well, and with a coincident axis, a cylinder 900 feet high, and nine feet in diameter, which should exactly fill up the space reserved for the bore of the *Columbiad*. This cylinder was composed of a mixture of clay and sand, with the addition of a little hay and straw. The space left between the mould and the masonry was intended to be filled up by the molten metal, which would thus form the walls six feet in thickness. This cylinder, in order to maintain its equilibrium, had to be bound by iron bands, and firmly fixed at certain intervals by cross-clamps fastened into the stone lining; after the castings these would be buried in the block of metal, leaving no external projection.

This operation was completed on the 8th of July, and the run of the metal was fixed for the following day.

"This *fête* of the casting will be a grand ceremony," said J. T. Maston to his friend Barbicane.

"Undoubtedly," said Barbicane; "but it will not be a public *fête*."

"What! will you not open the gates of the enclosure to all comers?"

"I must be very careful, Maston. The casting of the *Columbiad* is an extremely delicate, not to say a dangerous operation, and I should prefer its being done privately. At the discharge of the projectile, a *fête* if you like—till then, no!"

The president was right. The operation involved unforeseen dangers, which a great influx of spectators would have hindered him from averting. It was necessary to preserve complete freedom of movement. No one was admitted within the enclosure except a delegation of members of the Gun Club, who had made the voyage to Tampa Town. Among these was the brisk Bilsby, Tom Hunter, Colonel Blomsberry, Major Elphinstone, General Morgan, and the rest of the lot to whom the casting of the *Columbiad* was a matter of personal interest. J. T. Maston became their cicerone. He omitted no point of detail; he conducted them throughout the magazines, workshops, through the midst of the engines, and compelled them to visit the whole 1,200 furnaces one after the other. At the end of the twelve-hundredth visit they were pretty well knocked up.

The casting was to take place at twelve o'clock precisely. The previous evening each furnace had been charged with 114,000 pounds weight of metal in bars disposed crossways to each other, so as to allow the hot air to circulate freely between them. At daybreak the 1,200 chimneys vomited their torrents of flame into the air, and the ground was agitated with dull tremblings. As many pounds of metal as there were to cast, so many pounds of coal were there to burn. Thus there were 68,000 tons of coal which projected in the face of the sun a thick curtain of smoke. The heat soon became insupportable within the circle of furnaces, the rumbling of which resembled the rolling of thunder. The powerful ventilators added their continuous blasts and saturated with oxygen the glowing plates. The operation, to be successful, required to be conducted with great rapidity. On a signal given by a cannon-shot each furnace was to give vent to the molten iron and completely to empty itself. These arrangements made, foremen and workmen waited the preconcerted moment with an impatience mingled with a certain amount of emotion. Not a soul remained within the enclosure. Each superintendent took his post by the aperture of the run.

Barbicane and his colleagues, perched on a neighbouring eminence, assisted at the operation. In front of them was a piece of artillery ready to give fire on the signal from the engineer. Some minutes before midday the first driblets of metal began to flow; the reservoirs filled little by little; and, by the time that the whole melting was completely accomplished, it was kept in abeyance for a few minutes in order to facilitate the separation of foreign substances.

Twelve o'clock struck! A gunshot suddenly pealed forth and shot its flame into the air. Twelve hundred melting-troughs were simultaneously opened and twelve hundred fiery serpents crept towards the central well, unrolling their incandescent curves. There, down they plunged with a terrific noise into a depth of 900 feet. It was an exciting and a magnificent spectacle. The ground trembled, while these molten waves, launching into the sky their wreaths of smoke, evaporated the moisture of the mould and hurled it upward through the vent-holes of the stone lining in the form of dense vapour-clouds. These artificial clouds unrolled their thick spirals to a height of 1,000 yards into the air. A savage, wandering somewhere beyond the limits of the horizon, might have believed that some new crater was forming in the bosom of Florida, although there was neither any irruption, nor typhoon, nor storm, nor struggle of the elements, nor any of those terrible phenomena which nature is capable of producing. No, it was man alone who had produced these reddish vapours, these gigantic flames worthy of a volcano itself, these tremendous vibrations resembling the shock of an earthquake, these reverberations rivaling those of hurricanes and storms; and it was his hand which precipitated into an abyss, dug by himself, a whole Niagara of molten metal!

Chapter XVI

The COLUMBIAD

HAD THE CASTING SUCCEEDED? THEY WERE REDUCED TO MERE CONJECTURE. THERE was indeed every reason to expect success, since the mould has absorbed the entire mass of the molten metal; still some considerable time must elapse before they could arrive at any certainty upon the matter.

The patience of the members of the Gun Club was sorely tried during this period of time. But they could do nothing. J. T. Maston escaped roasting by a miracle. Fifteen days after the casting an immense column of smoke was still rising in the open sky and the ground burned the soles of the feet within a radius of two hundred feet round the summit of Stones Hill. It was impossible to approach nearer. All they could do was to wait with what patience they might.

"Here we are at the 10th of August," exclaimed J. T. Maston one morning, "only four months to the 1st of December! We shall never be ready in time!" Barbicane said nothing, but his silence covered serious irritation.

However, daily observations revealed a certain change going on in the state of the ground. About the 15th of August the vapours ejected had sensibly diminished in intensity and thickness. Some days afterward the earth exhaled only a slight puff of smoke, the last breath of the monster enclosed within its circle of stone. Little by little the belt of heat contracted, until on the 22d of August, Barbicane, his colleagues, and the engineer were enabled to set foot on the iron sheet which lay level upon the summit of Stones Hill.

"At last!" exclaimed the president of the Gun Club, with an immense sigh of relief.

The work was resumed the same day. They proceeded at once to extract the interior mould, for the purpose of clearing out the boring of the piece. Pickaxes and boring irons were set to work without intermission. The clayey and sandy soils had acquired extreme hardness under the action of the heat; but, by the aid of the machines, the rubbish on being dug out was rapidly carted away on railway wagons; and such was the ardour of the work, so persuasive the arguments of Barbicane's dollars, that by the 3d of September all traces of the mould had entirely disappeared.

Immediately the operation of boring was commenced; and by the aid of powerful machines, a few weeks later, the inner surface of the immense tube had been rendered perfectly cylindrical, and the bore of the piece had acquired a thorough polish.

At length, on the 22d of September, less than a twelvemonth after Barbicane's original proposition, the enormous weapon, accurately bored, and exactly vertically pointed, was ready for work. There was only the moon now to wait for; and they were pretty sure that she would not fail in the rendezvous.

The ecstasy of J. T. Maston knew no bounds, and he narrowly escaped a frightful fall while staring down the tube. But for the strong hand of Colonel Blomsberry, the worthy secretary, like a modern Erostratus, would have found his death in the depths of the *Columbiad*.

The cannon was then finished; there was no possible doubt as to its perfect completion. So, on the 6th of October, Captain Nicholl opened an account between himself and President Barbicane, in which he debited himself to the latter in the sum of two thousand dollars. One may believe that the captain's wrath was increased to its highest point, and must have made him seriously ill. However, he had still three bets of three, four, and five thousand dollars, respectively; and if he gained two out of these, his position would not be very bad. But the money question did not enter into his calculations; it was the success of his rival in casting a cannon against which iron plates sixty feet thick would have been ineffectual, that dealt him a terrible blow.

After the 23d of September the enclosure of Stones Hill was thrown open to the public; and it will be easily imagined what was the concourse of visitors to this spot! There was an incessant flow of people to and from Tampa Town and the place, which resembled a procession, or rather, in fact, a pilgrimage.

It was already clear to be seen that, on the day of the experiment itself, the aggregate of spectators would be counted by millions; for they were already arriving from all parts of the earth upon this narrow strip of promontory. Europe was emigrating to America.

Up to that time, however, it must be confessed, the curiosity of the numerous comers was but scantily gratified. Most had counted upon witnessing the spectacle of the casting, and they were treated to nothing but smoke. This was sorry food for hungry eyes; but Barbicane would admit no one to that operation. Then ensued grumbling, discontent, murmurs; they blamed the president, taxed him with dictatorial conduct. His proceedings were declared "un-American." There was very nearly a riot round Stones Hill; but Barbicane remained inflexible. When, however, the *Columbiad* was entirely finished, this state of closed doors could no longer be maintained; besides it would have been bad taste, and even imprudence, to affront the public feeling. Barbicane, therefore, opened the enclosure to all comers; but, true to his practical disposition, he determined to coin money out of the public curiosity.

It was something, indeed, to be enabled to contemplate this immense *Columbiad;* but to descend into its depths, this seemed to the Americans the *ne plus ultra* of earthly felicity. Consequently, there was not one curious spectator who was not willing to give himself the treat of visiting the interior of this great metallic abyss. Baskets suspended from steam-cranes permitted them to satisfy their curiosity. There was a perfect mania. Women, children, old men, all made it a point of duty to penetrate the mysteries of the colossal gun. The fare for the descent was fixed at five dollars per head; and despite this high charge, during the two months which preceded the experiment, the influx of visitors enabled the Gun Club to pocket nearly five hundred thousand dollars!

It is needless to say that the first visitors of the *Columbiad* were the members of the Gun Club. This privilege was justly reserved for that illustrious body. The ceremony took place on the 25th of September. A basket of honour took down the president, J. T. Maston, Major Elphinstone, General Morgan, Colonel Blomsberry, and other members of the club, to the number of ten in all. How hot it was at the bottom of that long tube of metal! They were half suffocated. But what delight! What ecstasy! A table had been laid with six covers on the massive stone which formed the bottom of the *Columbiad*, and lighted by a jet of electric light resembling that of day itself. Numerous exquisite dishes, which seemed to descend from heaven, were placed successively before the guests, and the richest wines of France flowed in profusion during this splendid repast, served nine hundred feet beneath the surface of the earth!

The festival was animated, not to say somewhat noisy. Toasts flew backward and forward. They drank to the earth and to her satellite, to the Gun Club, the Union, the Moon, Diana, Phœbe, Selene, the "peaceful courier of the night!" All the hurrahs, carried upward upon the sonorous waves of the immense acoustic tube, arrived with the sound of thunder at its mouth; and the multitude ranged round Stones Hill heartily united their shouts with those of the ten revelers hidden from view at the bottom of the gigantic *Columbiad*.

J. T. Maston was no longer master of himself. Whether he shouted or gesticulated, ate or drank most, would be a difficult matter to determine. At all events, he would not have given his place up for an empire, "not even if the cannon—loaded, primed, and fired at that very moment—were to blow him in pieces into the planetary world."

Chapter XVII

A Telegraphic Despatch

THE GREAT WORKS UNDERTAKEN BY THE GUN CLUB HAD NOW VIRTUALLY COME TO AN end; and two months still remained before the day for the discharge of the shot to the moon. To the general impatience these two months appeared as long as years! Hitherto the smallest details of the operation had been daily chronicled by the journals, which the public devoured with eager eyes.

Just at this moment a circumstance, the most unexpected, the most extraordinary and incredible, occurred to rouse afresh their panting spirits, and to throw every mind into a state of the most violent excitement.

One day, the 30th of September, at 3:47 P.M., a telegram, transmitted by cable from Valentia (Ireland) to Newfoundland and the American Mainland, arrived at the address of President Barbicane.

The president tore open the envelope, read the despatch, and, despite his remarkable powers of self-control, his lips turned pale and his eyes grew dim, on reading the twenty words of this telegram.

Here is the text of the despatch, which figures now in the archives of the Gun Club:

> FRANCE, PARIS,
> *30 September, 4 A.M.*

Barbicane, Tampa Town, Florida, United States.

Substitute for your spherical shell a cylindro-conical projectile. I shall go inside. Shall arrive by steamer *Atlanta*.

> MICHEL ARDAN

Chapter XVIII

THE PASSENGER OF THE ATLANTA

I F THIS ASTOUNDING NEWS, INSTEAD OF FLYING THROUGH THE ELECTRIC WIRES, HAD SIM-
ply arrived by post in the ordinary sealed envelope, Barbicane would not have hesitated
a moment. He would have held his tongue about it, both as a measure of prudence, and in
order not to have to reconsider his plans. This telegram might be a cover for some jest, especially as it came from a Frenchman. What human being would ever have conceived the
idea of such a journey? and, if such a person really existed, he must be an idiot, whom one
would shut up in a lunatic ward, rather than within the walls of the projectile.

The contents of the despatch, however, speedily became known; for the telegraphic
officials possessed but little discretion, and Michel Ardan's proposition ran at once
throughout the several States of the Union. Barbicane, had, therefore, no further motives
for keeping silence. Consequently, he called together such of his colleagues as were at the
moment in Tampa Town, and without any expression of his own opinions simply read to
them the laconic text itself. It was received with every possible variety of expressions of
doubt, incredulity, and derision from everyone, with the exception of J. T. Maston, who
exclaimed, "It is a grand idea, however!"

When Barbicane originally proposed to send a shot to the moon everyone looked
upon the enterprise as simple and practicable enough—a mere question of gunnery; but
when a person, professing to be a reasonable being, offered to take passage within the projectile, the whole thing became a farce, or, in plainer language a humbug.

One question, however, remained. Did such a being exist? This telegram flashed
across the depths of the Atlantic, the designation of the vessel on board which he was to
take his passage, the date assigned for his speedy arrival, all combined to impart a certain
character of reality to the proposal. They must get some clearer notion of the matter.
Scattered groups of enquirers at length condensed themselves into a compact crowd,
which made straight for the residence of President Barbicane. That worthy individual
was keeping quiet with the intention of watching events as they arose. But he had forgotten to take into account the public impatience; and it was with no pleasant countenance
that he watched the population of Tampa Town gathering under his windows. The murmurs and vociferations below presently obliged him to appear. He came forward, therefore, and on silence being procured, a citizen put point-blank to him the following
question: "Is the person mentioned in the telegram, under the name of Michel Ardan, on
his way here? Yes or no."

"Gentlemen," replied Barbicane, "I know no more than you do."

"We must know," roared the impatient voices.

"Time will show," calmly replied the president.

"Time has no business to keep a whole country in suspense," replied the orator.
"Have you altered the plans of the projectile according to the request of the telegram?"

"Not yet, gentlemen; but you are right! we must have better information to go by. The
telegraph must complete its information."

"To the telegraph!" roared the crowd.

Barbicane descended; and heading the immense assemblage, led the way to the telegraph office. A few minutes later a telegram was despatched to the secretary of the underwriters at Liverpool, requesting answers to the following queries:

"About the ship *Atlanta*—when did she leave Europe? Had she on board a Frenchman named Michel Ardan?"

Two hours afterward Barbicane received information too exact to leave room for the smallest remaining doubt.

"The steamer *Atlanta* from Liverpool put to sea on the 2d of October, bound for Tampa Town, having on board a Frenchman borne on the list of passengers by the name of Michel Ardan."

That very evening he wrote to the house of Breadwill and Co., requesting them to suspend the casting of the projectile until the receipt of further orders. On the 20th of October, at nine A.M., the semaphores of the Bahama Canal signalled a thick smoke on the horizon. Two hours later a large steamer exchanged signals with them. The name of the *Atlanta* flew at once over Tampa Town. At four o'clock the English vessel entered the Bay of Espiritu Santo. At five it crossed the passage of Hillisborough Bay at full steam. At six she cast anchor at Port Tampa. The anchor had scarcely caught the sandy bottom when five hundred boats surrounded the *Atlanta*, and the steamer was taken by assault. Barbicane was the first to set foot on deck, and in a voice of which he vainly tried to conceal the emotion, called "Michel Ardan."

"Here!" replied an individual perched on the poop.

Barbicane, with arms crossed, looked fixedly at the passenger of the *Atlanta*.

He was a man of about forty-two years of age, of large build, but slightly round-shouldered. His massive head momentarily shook a shock of reddish hair, which resembled a lion's mane. His face was short with a broad forehead, and furnished with a moustache as bristly as a cat's, and little patches of yellowish whiskers upon full cheeks. Round, wildish eyes, slightly near-sighted, completed a physiognomy essentially feline. His nose was firmly shaped, his mouth particularly sweet in expression, high forehead, intelligent and furrowed with wrinkles like a newly-plowed field. The body was powerfully developed and firmly fixed upon long legs. Muscular arms, and a general air of decision gave him the appearance of a hardy, jolly companion. He was dressed in a suit of ample dimensions, loose neckerchief, open shirt-collar, disclosing a robust neck; his cuffs were invariably unbuttoned, through which appeared a pair of red hands.

On the bridge of the steamer, in the midst of the crowd, he bustled to and fro, never still for a moment, "dragging his anchors," as the sailors say, gesticulating, making free with everybody, biting his nails with nervous avidity. He was one of those originals which nature sometimes invents in the freak of a moment, and of which she then breaks the mould.

Among other peculiarities, this curiosity gave himself out for a sublime ignoramus, "like Shakespeare," and professed supreme contempt for all scientific men. Those "fellows," as he called them, "are only fit to mark the points, while we play the game." He was, in fact, a thorough Bohemian, adventurous, but not an adventurer; a hair-brained fellow, a kind of Icarus, only possessing relays of wings. For the rest, he was ever in scrapes, ending invariably by falling on his feet, like those little figures which they sell for children's toys. In a few words, his motto was "I have my opinions," and the love of the impossible constituted his ruling passion.

Such was the passenger of the *Atlanta*, always excitable, as if boiling under the action of some internal fire by the character of his physical organisation. If ever two individuals offered a striking contrast to each other, these were certainly Michel Ardan and the Yankee Barbicane; both, moreover, being equally enterprising and daring, each in his own way.

The scrutiny which the president of the Gun Club had instituted regarding this new rival was quickly interrupted by the shouts and hurrahs of the crowd. The cries became at last so uproarious, and the popular enthusiasm assumed so personal a form, that Michel Ardan, after having shaken hands some thousands of times, at the imminent risk of leaving his fingers behind him, was fain at last to make a bolt for his cabin.

Barbicane followed him without uttering a word.

"You are Barbicane, I suppose?" said Michel Ardan, in a tone of voice in which he would have addressed a friend of twenty years' standing.

"Yes," replied the president of the Gun Club.

"All right! how d'ye do, Barbicane? how are you getting on—pretty well? that's right."

"So," said Barbicane without further preliminary, "you are quite determined to go."

"Quite decided."

"Nothing will stop you?"

"Nothing. Have you modified your projectile according to my telegram."

"I waited for your arrival. But," asked Barbicane again, "have you carefully reflected?"

"Reflected? have I any time to spare? I find an opportunity of making a tour in the moon, and I mean to profit by it. There is the whole gist of the matter."

Barbicane looked hard at this man who spoke so lightly of his project with such complete absence of anxiety. "But, at least," said he, "you have some plans, some means of carrying your project into execution?"

"Excellent, my dear Barbicane; only permit me to offer one remark: My wish is to tell my story once for all, to everybody, and then have done with it; then there will be no need for recapitulation. So, if you have no objection, assemble your friends, colleagues, the whole town, all Florida, all America if you like, and to-morrow I shall be ready to explain my plans and answer any objections whatever that may be advanced. You may rest assured I shall wait without stirring. Will that suit you?"

"All right," replied Barbicane.

So saying, the president left the cabin and informed the crowd of the proposal of Michel Ardan. His words were received with clappings of hands and shouts of joy. They had removed all difficulties. To-morrow everyone would contemplate at his ease this European hero. However, some of the spectators, more infatuated than the rest, would not leave the deck of the *Atlanta*. They passed the night on board. Among others J. T. Maston got his hook fixed in the combing of the poop, and it pretty nearly required the capstan to get it out again.

"He is a hero! a hero!" he cried, a theme of which he was never tired of ringing the changes; "and we are only like weak, silly women, compared with this European!"

As to the president, after having suggested to the visitors it was time to retire, he reentered the passenger's cabin, and remained there till the bell of the steamer made it midnight.

But then the two rivals in popularity shook hands heartily and parted on terms of intimate friendship.

Chapter XIX

A Monster Meeting

O N THE FOLLOWING DAY BARBICANE, FEARING THAT INDISCREET QUESTIONS MIGHT BE put to Michel Ardan, was desirous of reducing the number of the audience to a few of the initiated, his own colleagues for instance. He might as well have tried to check the Falls of Niagara! He was compelled, therefore, to give up the idea, and let his new friend run the chances of a public conference. The place chosen for this monster meeting was a vast plain situated in the rear of the town. In a few hours, thanks to the help of the shipping in port, an immense roofing of canvas was stretched over the parched prairie, and protected it from the burning rays of the sun. There three hundred thousand people braved for many hours the stifling heat while awaiting the arrival of the Frenchman. Of this crowd of spectators a first set could both see and hear; a second set saw badly and heard nothing at all; and as for the third, it could neither see nor hear anything at all. At three o'clock Michel Ardan made his appearance, accompanied by the principal members of the Gun Club. He was supported on his right by President Barbicane, and on his left by J. T. Maston, more radiant than the midday sun, and nearly as ruddy. Ardan mounted a platform, from the top of which his view extended over a sea of black hats.

He exhibited not the slightest embarrassment; he was just as gay, familiar, and pleasant as if he were at home. To the hurrahs which greeted him he replied by a graceful bow; then, waving his hands to request silence, he spoke in perfectly correct English as follows:

"Gentlemen, despite the very hot weather I request your patience for a short time while I offer some explanations regarding the projects which seem to have so interested you. I am neither an orator nor a man of science, and I had no idea of addressing you in public; but my friend Barbicane has told me that you would like to hear me, and I am quite at your service. Listen to me, therefore, with your six hundred thousand ears, and please to excuse the faults of the speaker. Now pray do not forget that you see before you a perfect ignoramus whose ignorance goes so far that he cannot even understand the difficulties! It seemed to him that it was a matter quite simple, natural, and easy to take one's place in a projectile and start for the moon! That journey must be undertaken sooner or later; and, as for the mode of locomotion adopted, it follows simply the law of progress. Man began by walking on all-fours; then, one fine day, on two feet; then in a carriage; then in a stage-coach; and lastly by railway. Well, the projectile is the vehicle of the future, and the planets themselves are nothing else! Now some of you, gentlemen, may imagine that the velocity we propose to impart to it is extravagant. It is nothing of the kind. All the stars exceed it in rapidity, and the earth herself is at this moment carrying us round the sun at three times as rapid a rate, and yet she is a mere lounger on the way compared with many others of the planets! And her velocity is constantly decreasing. Is it not evident, then, I ask you, that there will someday appear velocities far greater than these, of which light or electricity will probably be the mechanical agent?

"Yes, gentlemen," continued the orator, "in spite of the opinions of certain narrow-minded people, who would shut up the human race upon this globe, as within some magic circle which it must never outstep, we shall one day travel to the moon, the planets, and the stars, with the same facility, rapidity, and certainty as we now make the voyage from Liverpool to New York! Distance is but a relative expression, and must end by being reduced to zero."

The assembly, strongly predisposed as they were in favour of the French hero, were slightly staggered at this bold theory. Michel Ardan perceived the fact.

"Gentlemen," he continued with a pleasant smile, "you do not seem quite convinced. Very good! Let us reason the matter out. Do you know how long it would take for an express train to reach the moon? Three hundred days; no more! And what is that? The distance is no more than nine times the circumference of the earth; and there are no sailors or travellers, of even moderate activity, who have not made longer journeys than that in their lifetime. And now consider that I shall be only ninety-seven hours on my journey. Ah! I see you are reckoning that the moon is a long way off from the earth, and that one must think twice before making the experiment. What would you say, then, if we were talking of going to Neptune, which revolves at a distance of more than two thousand seven hundred and twenty millions of miles from the sun! And yet what is that compared with the distance of the fixed stars, some of which, such as Arcturus, are billions of miles distant from us? And then you talk of the distance which separates the planets from the sun! And there are people who affirm that such a thing as distance exists. Absurdity, folly, idiotic nonsense! Would you know what I think of our own solar universe? Shall I tell you my theory? It is very simple! In my opinion the solar system is a solid homogeneous body; the planets which compose it are in actual contact with each other; and whatever space exists between them is nothing more than the space which separates the molecules of the densest metal, such as silver, iron, or platinum! I have the right, therefore, to affirm, and I repeat, with the conviction which must penetrate all your minds, 'Distance is but an empty name; distance does not really exist!'"

"Hurrah!" cried one voice (need it be said it was that of J. T. Maston). "Distance does not exist!" And overcome by the energy of his movements, he nearly fell from the platform to the ground. He just escaped a severe fall, which would have proved to him that distance was by no means an empty name.

"Gentlemen," resumed the orator, "I repeat that the distance between the earth and her satellite is a mere trifle, and undeserving of serious consideration. I am convinced that before twenty years are over one-half of our earth will have paid a visit to the moon. Now, my worthy friends, if you have any question to put to me, you will, I fear, sadly embarrass a poor man like myself; still I will do my best to answer you."

Up to this point the president of the Gun Club had been satisfied with the turn which the discussion had assumed. It became now, however, desirable to divert Ardan from questions of a practical nature, with which he was doubtless far less conversant. Barbicane, therefore, hastened to get in a word, and began by asking his new friend whether he thought that the moon and the planets were inhabited.

"You put before me a great problem, my worthy president," replied the orator, smiling. "Still, men of great intelligence, such as Plutarch, Swedenborg, Bernardin de St. Pierre, and others have, if I mistake not, pronounced in the affirmative. Looking at the question from the natural philosopher's point of view, I should say that nothing useless existed in the world; and, replying to your question by another, I should venture to assert, that if these worlds are habitable, they either are, have been, or will be inhabited."

"No one could answer more logically or fairly," replied the president. "The question then reverts to this: Are these worlds habitable? For my own part I believe they are."

"For myself, I feel certain of it," said Michel Ardan.

"Nevertheless," retorted one of the audience, "there are many arguments against the habitability of the worlds. The conditions of life must evidently be greatly modified upon the majority of them. To mention only the planets, we should be either broiled alive in some, or frozen to death in others, according as they are more or less removed from the sun."

"I regret," replied Michel Ardan, "that I have not the honour of personally knowing my contradictor, for I would have attempted to answer him. His objection has its merits, I admit; but I think we may successfully combat it, as well as all others which affect the habitability of other worlds. If I were a natural philosopher, I would tell him that if less of caloric were set in motion upon the planets which are nearest to the sun, and more, on the contrary, upon those which are farthest removed from it, this simple fact would alone suffice to equalise the heat, and to render the temperature of those worlds supportable by beings organised like ourselves. If I were a naturalist, I would tell him that, according to some illustrious men of science, nature has furnished us with instances upon the earth of animals existing under very varying conditions of life; that fish respire in a medium fatal to other animals; that amphibious creatures possess a double existence very difficult of explanation; that certain denizens of the seas maintain life at enormous depths, and there support a pressure equal to that of fifty or sixty atmospheres without being crushed; that several aquatic insects, insensible to temperature, are met with equally among boiling springs and in the frozen plains of the Polar Sea; in fine, that we cannot help recognising in nature a diversity of means of operation oftentimes incomprehensible, but not the less real. If I were a chemist, I would tell him that the aerolites, bodies evidently formed exteriorly of our terrestrial globe, have, upon analysis, revealed indisputable traces of carbon, a substance which owes its origin solely to organised beings, and which, according to the experiments of Reichenbach, must necessarily itself have been endued with animation. And lastly, were I a theologian, I would tell him that the scheme of the Divine Redemption, according to St. Paul, seems to be applicable, not merely to the earth, but to all the celestial worlds. But, unfortunately, I am neither theologian, nor chemist, nor naturalist, nor philosopher; therefore, in my absolute ignorance of the great laws which govern the universe, I confine myself to saying in reply, 'I do not know whether the worlds are inhabited or not: and since I do not know, I am going to see!' "

Whether Michel Ardan's antagonist hazarded any further arguments or not it is impossible to say, for the uproarious shouts of the crowd would not allow any expression of opinion to gain a hearing. On silence being restored, the triumphant orator contented himself with adding the following remarks:

"Gentlemen, you will observe that I have but slightly touched upon this great question. There is another altogether different line of argument in favour of the habitability of the stars, which I omit for the present. I only desire to call attention to one point. To those who maintain that the planets are *not* inhabited one may reply: You might be perfectly in the right, if you could only show that the earth is the best possible world, in spite of what Voltaire has said. She has but *one* satellite, while Jupiter, Uranus, Saturn, Neptune have each several, an advantage by no means to be despised. But that which renders our own globe so uncomfortable is the inclination of its axis to the plane of its orbit. Hence the inequality of days and nights; hence the disagreeable diversity of the seasons. On the surface of our unhappy spheroid we are always either too hot or too cold; we are frozen in winter, broiled in summer; it is the planet of rheumatism, coughs, bronchitis; while on the surface of Jupiter, for example, where the axis is but slightly inclined, the inhabitants may enjoy uniform temperatures. It possesses zones of perpetual springs, summers, autumns, and winters; every Jovian may choose for himself what climate he likes, and there spend the whole of his life in security from all variations of temperature. You will, I am sure, readily admit this superiority of Jupiter over our own planet, to say nothing of his years, which each equal twelve of ours! Under such auspices and such marvellous conditions of existence, it appears to me that the inhabitants of so fortunate a world must be in every respect superior to ourselves. All we require, in order to attain such perfection, is the mere trifle of having an axis of rotation less inclined to the plane of its orbit!"

"Hurrah!" roared an energetic voice, "let us unite our efforts, invent the necessary machines, and rectify the earth's axis!"

A thunder of applause followed this proposal, the author of which was, of course, no other than J. T. Maston. And, in all probability, if the truth must be told, if the Yankees could only have found a point of application for it, they would have constructed a lever capable of raising the earth and rectifying its axis. It was just this deficiency which baffled these daring mechanicians.

Chapter XX

ATTACK AND RIPOSTE

AS SOON AS THE EXCITEMENT HAD SUBSIDED, THE FOLLOWING WORDS WERE HEARD UTtered in a strong and determined voice:

"Now that the speaker has favoured us with so much imagination, would he be so good as to return to his subject, and give us a little practical view of the question?"

All eyes were directed towards the person who spoke. He was a little dried-up man, of an active figure, with an American "goatee" beard. Profiting by the different movements in the crowd, he had managed by degrees to gain the front row of spectators. There, with arms crossed and stern gaze, he watched the hero of the meeting. After having put his question he remained silent, and appeared to take no notice of the thousands of looks directed towards himself, nor of the murmur of disapprobation excited by his words. Meeting at first with no reply, he repeated his question with marked emphasis, adding, "We are here to talk about the *moon* and not about the *earth*."

"You are right, sir," replied Michel Ardan; "the discussion has become irregular. We will return to the moon."

"Sir," said the unknown, "you pretend that our satellite is inhabited. Very good; but if Selenites do exist, that race of beings assuredly must live without breathing, for—I warn you for your own sake—there is not the smallest particle of air on the surface of the moon."

At this remark Ardan pushed up his shock of red hair; he saw that he was on the point of being involved in a struggle with this person upon the very gist of the whole question. He looked sternly at him in his turn and said:

"Oh! so there is no air in the moon? And pray, if you are so good, who ventures to affirm that?

"The men of science."

"Really?"

"Really."

"Sir," replied Michel, "pleasantry apart, I have a profound respect for men of science who do possess science, but a profound contempt for men of science who do not."

"Do you know any who belong to the latter category?"

"Decidedly. In France there are some who maintain that, mathematically, a bird cannot possibly fly; and others who demonstrate theoretically that fishes were never made to live in water."

"I have nothing to do with persons of that description, and I can quote, in support of my statement, names which you cannot refuse deference to."

"Then, sir, you will sadly embarrass a poor ignorant, who, besides, asks nothing better than to learn."

"Why, then, do you introduce scientific questions if you have never studied them?" asked the unknown somewhat coarsely.

"For the reason that 'he is always brave who never suspects danger.' I know nothing, it is true; but it is precisely my very weakness which constitutes my strength."

"Your weakness amounts to folly," retorted the unknown in a passion.

"All the better," replied our Frenchman, "if it carries me up to the moon."

Barbicane and his colleagues devoured with their eyes the intruder who had so boldly placed himself in antagonism to their enterprise. Nobody knew him, and the president, uneasy as to the result of so free a discussion, watched his new friend with some anxiety. The meeting began to be somewhat fidgety also, for the contest directed their attention to the dangers, if not the actual impossibilities, of the proposed expedition.

"Sir," replied Ardan's antagonist, "there are many and incontrovertible reasons which prove the absence of an atmosphere in the moon. I might say that, *a priori*, if one ever did exist, it must have been absorbed by the earth; but I prefer to bring forward indisputable facts."

"Bring them forward then, sir, as many as you please."

"You know," said the stranger, "that when any luminous rays cross a medium such as the air, they are deflected out of the straight line; in other words, they undergo refraction. Well! When stars are occulted by the moon, their rays, on grazing the edge of her disc, exhibit not the least deviation, nor offer the slightest indication of refraction. It follows, therefore, that the moon cannot be surrounded by an atmosphere."

"In point of fact," replied Ardan, "this is your chief, if not your *only* argument; and a really scientific man might be puzzled to answer it. For myself, I will simply say that it is defective, because it assumes that the angular diameter of the moon has been completely determined, which is not the case. But let us proceed. Tell me, my dear sir, do you admit the existence of volcanoes on the moon's surface?"

"Extinct, yes! In activity, no!"

"These volcanoes, however, were at one time in a state of activity?"

"True, but, as they furnish themselves the oxygen necessary for combustion, the mere fact of their irruption does not prove the presence of an atmosphere."

"Proceed again, then; and let us set aside this class of arguments in order to come to direct observations. In 1715 the astronomers Louville and Halley, watching the eclipse of the 3d of May, remarked some very extraordinary scintillations. These jets of light, rapid in nature, and of frequent recurrence, they attributed to thunderstorms generated in the lunar atmosphere."

"In 1715," replied the unknown, "the astronomers Louville and Halley mistook for lunar phenomena some which were purely terrestrial, such as meteoric or other bodies which are generated in our own atmosphere. This was the scientific explanation at the time of the facts; and that is my answer now."

"On again, then," replied Ardan; "Herschel, in 1787, observed a great number of luminous points on the moon's surface, did he not?"

"Yes! but without offering any solution of them. Herschel himself never inferred from them the necessity of a lunar atmosphere. And I may add that Baeer and Maedler, the two great authorities upon the moon, are quite agreed as to the entire absence of air on its surface."

A movement was here manifest among the assemblage, who appeared to be growing excited by the arguments of this singular personage.

"Let us proceed," replied Ardan, with perfect coolness, "and come to one important fact. A skillful French astronomer, M. Laussedat, in watching the eclipse of July 18, 1860, proved that the horns of the lunar crescent were rounded and truncated. Now, this appearance could only have been produced by a deviation of the solar rays in traversing the atmosphere of the moon. There is no other possible explanation of the facts."

"But is this established as a fact?"

"Absolutely certain!"

A counter-movement here took place in favour of the hero of the meeting, whose opponent was now reduced to silence. Ardan resumed the conversation; and without exhibiting any exultation at the advantage he had gained, simply said:

"You see, then, my dear sir, we must not pronounce with absolute positiveness against the existence of an atmosphere in the moon. That atmosphere is, probably, of extreme rarity; nevertheless at the present day science generally admits that it exists."

"Not in the mountains, at all events," returned the unknown, unwilling to give in.

"No! but at the bottom of the valleys, and not exceeding a few hundred feet in height."

"In any case you will do well to take every precaution, for the air will be terribly rarified."

"My good sir, there will always be enough for a solitary individual; besides, once arrived up there, I shall do my best to economise, and not to breathe except on grand occasions!"

A tremendous roar of laughter rang in the ears of the mysterious interlocutor, who glared fiercely round upon the assembly.

"Then," continued Ardan, with a careless air, "since we are in accord regarding the presence of a certain atmosphere, we are forced to admit the presence of a certain quantity of water. This is a happy consequence for me. Moreover, my amiable contradictor, permit me to submit to you one further observation. We only know *one* side of the moon's disc; and if there is but little air on the face presented to us, it is possible that there is plenty on the one turned away from us."

"And for what reason?"

"Because the moon, under the action of the earth's attraction, has assumed the form of an egg, which we look at from the smaller end. Hence it follows, by Hausen's calculations, that its centre of gravity is situated in the other hemisphere. Hence it results that the great mass of air and water must have been drawn away to the other face of our satellite during the first days of its creation."

"Pure fancies!" cried the unknown.

"No! Pure theories! which are based upon the laws of mechanics, and it seems difficult to me to refute them. I appeal then to this meeting, and I put it to them whether life, such as exists upon the earth, is possible on the surface of the moon?"

Three hundred thousand auditors at once applauded the proposition. Ardan's opponent tried to get in another word, but he could not obtain a hearing. Cries and menaces fell upon him like hail.

"Enough! enough!" cried some.

"Drive the intruder off!" shouted others.

"Turn him out!" roared the exasperated crowd.

But he, holding firmly on to the platform, did not budge an inch, and let the storm pass on, which would soon have assumed formidable proportions, if Michel Ardan had not quieted it by a gesture. He was too chivalrous to abandon his opponent in an apparent extremity.

"You wished to say a few more words?" he asked, in a pleasant voice.

"Yes, a thousand; or rather, no, only one! If you persevere in your enterprise, you must be a—"

"Very rash person! How can you treat me as such? me, who have demanded a cylindro-conical projectile, in order to prevent turning round and round on my way like a squirrel?"

"But, unhappy man, the dreadful recoil will smash you to pieces at your starting."

"My dear contradictor, you have just put your finger upon the true and only difficulty; nevertheless, I have too good an opinion of the industrial genius of the Americans not to believe that they will succeed in overcoming it."

"But the heat developed by the rapidity of the projectile in crossing the strata of air?"

"Oh! the walls are thick, and I shall soon have crossed the atmosphere."

"But victuals and water?"

"I have calculated for a twelvemonth's supply, and I shall be only four days on the journey."

"But for air to breathe on the road?"

"I shall make it by a chemical process."

"But your fall on the moon, supposing you ever reach it?"

"It will be six times less dangerous than a sudden fall upon the earth, because the weight will be only one-sixth as great on the surface of the moon."

"Still it will be enough to smash you like glass!"

"What is to prevent my retarding the shock by means of rockets conveniently placed, and lighted at the right moment?"

"But after all, supposing all difficulties surmounted, all obstacles removed, supposing everything combined to favour you, and granting that you may arrive safe and sound in the moon, how will you come back?"

"I am not coming back!"

At this reply, almost sublime in its very simplicity, the assembly became silent. But its silence was more eloquent than could have been its cries of enthusiasm. The unknown profited by the opportunity and once more protested:

"You will inevitably kill yourself!" he cried; "and your death will be that of a madman, useless even to science!"

"Go on, my dear unknown, for truly your prophecies are most agreeable!"

"It really is too much!" cried Michel Ardan's adversary. "I do not know why I should continue so frivolous a discussion! Please yourself about this insane expedition! We need not trouble ourselves about you!"

"Pray don't stand upon ceremony!"

"No! another person is responsible for your act."

"Who, may I ask?" demanded Michel Ardan in an imperious tone.

"The ignoramus who organised this equally absurd and impossible experiment!"

The attack was direct. Barbicane, ever since the interference of the unknown, had been making fearful efforts of self-control; now, however, seeing himself directly attacked, he could restrain himself no longer. He rose suddenly, and was rushing upon the enemy who thus braved him to the face, when all at once he found himself separated from him.

The platform was lifted by a hundred strong arms, and the president of the Gun Club shared with Michel Ardan triumphal honours. The shield was heavy, but the bearers came in continuous relays, disputing, struggling, even fighting among themselves in their eagerness to lend their shoulders to this demonstration.

However, the unknown had not profited by the tumult to quit his post. Besides he could not have done it in the midst of that compact crowd. There he held on in the front row with crossed arms, glaring at President Barbicane.

The shouts of the immense crowd continued at their highest pitch throughout this triumphant march. Michel Ardan took it all with evident pleasure. His face gleamed with delight. Several times the platform seemed seized with pitching and rolling like a weatherbeaten ship. But the two heroes of the meeting had good sea-legs. They never stumbled; and their vessel arrived without dues at the port of Tampa Town.

Michel Ardan managed fortunately to escape from the last embraces of his vigourous admirers. He made for the Hotel Franklin, quickly gained his chamber, and slid under the bedclothes, while an army of a hundred thousand men kept watch under his windows.

During this time a scene, short, grave, and decisive, took place between the mysterious personage and the president of the Gun Club.

Barbicane, free at last, had gone straight at his adversary.

"Come!" he said shortly.

The other followed him on the quay; and the two presently found themselves alone at the entrance of an open wharf on Jones' Fall.

The two enemies, still mutually unknown, gazed at each other.

"Who are you?" asked Barbicane.

"Captain Nicholl!"

"So I suspected. Hitherto chance has never thrown you in my way."

"I am come for that purpose."

"You have insulted me."

"Publicly!"

"And you will answer to me for this insult?"

"At this very moment."

"No! I desire that all that passes between us shall be secret. Their is a wood situated three miles from Tampa, the wood of Skersnaw. Do you know it?"

"I know it."

"Will you be so good as to enter it to-morrow morning at five o'clock, on one side?"

"Yes! if you will enter at the other side at the same hour."

"And you will not forget your rifle?" said Barbicane.

"No more than you will forget yours?" replied Nicholl.

These words having been coldly spoken, the president of the Gun Club and the captain parted. Barbicane returned to his lodging; but instead of snatching a few hours of repose, he passed the night in endeavouring to discover a means of evading the recoil of the projectile, and resolving the difficult problem proposed by Michel Ardan during the discussion at the meeting.

Chapter XXI

How a Frenchman Manages an Affair

WHILE THE CONTRACT OF THIS DUEL WAS BEING DISCUSSED BY THE PRESIDENT AND the captain—this dreadful, savage duel, in which each adversary became a manhunter—Michel Ardan was resting from the fatigues of his triumph. Resting is hardly an appropriate expression, for American beds rival marble or granite tables for hardness.

Ardan was sleeping, then, badly enough, tossing about between the cloths which served him for sheets, and he was dreaming of making a more comfortable couch in his projectile when a frightful noise disturbed his dreams. Thundering blows shook his door. They seemed to be caused by some iron instrument. A great deal of loud talking was distinguishable in this racket, which was rather too early in the morning. "Open the door," someone shrieked, "for heaven's sake!" Ardan saw no reason for complying with a demand so roughly expressed. However, he got up and opened the door just as it was giving way before the blows of this determined visitor. The secretary of the Gun Club burst into the room. A bomb could not have made more noise or have entered the room with less ceremony.

"Last night," cried J. T. Maston, *ex abrupto,* "our president was publicly insulted during the meeting. He provoked his adversary, who is none other than Captain Nicholl! They are fighting this morning in the wood of Skersnaw. I heard all the particulars from the mouth of Barbicane himself. If he is killed, then our scheme is at an end. We must prevent this duel; and one man alone has enough influence over Barbicane to stop him, and that man is Michel Ardan."

While J. T. Maston was speaking, Michel Ardan, without interrupting him, had hastily put on his clothes; and, in less than two minutes, the two friends were making for the suburbs of Tampa Town with rapid strides.

It was during this walk that Maston told Ardan the state of the case. He told him the real causes of the hostility between Barbicane and Nicholl; how it was of old date, and why, thanks to unknown friends, the president and the captain had, as yet, never met face to face. He added that it arose simply from a rivalry between iron plates and shot, and, finally, that the scene at the meeting was only the long-wished-for opportunity for Nicholl to pay off an old grudge.

Nothing is more dreadful than private duels in America. The two adversaries attack each other like wild beasts. Then it is that they might well covet those wonderful properties of the Indians of the prairies—their quick intelligence, their ingenious cunning, their scent of the enemy. A single mistake, a moment's hesitation, a single false step may cause death. On these occasions Yankees are often accompanied by their dogs, and keep up the struggle for hours.

"What demons you are!" cried Michel Ardan, when his companion had depicted this scene to him with much energy.

"Yes, we are," replied J. T. modestly; "but we had better make haste."

Though Michel Ardan and he had crossed the plains still wet with dew, and had taken the shortest route over creeks and ricefields, they could not reach Skersnaw in under five hours and a half.

Barbicane must have passed the border half-an-hour ago.

There was an old bushman working there, occupied in selling fagots from trees that had been leveled by his axe.

Maston ran towards him, saying, "Have you seen a man go into the wood, armed with a rifle? Barbicane, the president, my best friend?"

The worthy secretary of the Gun Club thought that his president must be known by all the world. But the bushman did not seem to understand him.

"A hunter?" said Ardan.

"A hunter? Yes," replied the bushman.

"Long ago?"

"About an hour."

"Too late!" cried Maston.

"Have you heard any gunshots?" asked Ardan.

"No!"

"Not one?"

"Not one! that hunter did not look as if he knew how to hunt!"

"What is to be done?" said Maston.

"We must go into the wood, at the risk of getting a ball which is not intended for us."

"Ah!" cried Maston, in a tone which could not be mistaken, "I would rather have twenty balls in my own head than one in Barbicane's."

"Forward, then," said Ardan, pressing his companion's hand.

A few moments later the two friends had disappeared in the copse. It was a dense thicket, in which rose huge cypresses, sycamores, tulip-trees, olives, tamarinds, oaks, and magnolias. These different trees had interwoven their branches into an inextricable maze, through which the eye could not penetrate. Michel Ardan and Maston walked side by side in silence through the tall grass, cutting themselves a path through the strong creepers, casting curious glances on the bushes, and momentarily expecting to hear the sound of rifles. As for the traces which Barbicane ought to have left of his passage through the wood, there was not a vestige of them visible: so they followed the barely perceptible paths along which Indians had tracked some enemy, and which the dense foliage darkly overshadowed.

After an hour spent in vain pursuit the two stopped, in intensified anxiety.

"It must be all over," said Maston, discouraged. "A man like Barbicane would not dodge with his enemy, or ensnare him, would not even maneuvre! He is too open, too brave. He has gone straight ahead, right into the danger, and doubtless far enough from the bushman for the wind to prevent his hearing the report of the rifles."

"But surely," replied Michel Ardan, "since we entered the wood we should have heard!"

"And what if we came too late?" cried Maston in tones of despair.

For once Ardan had no reply to make, he and Maston resuming their walk in silence. From time to time, indeed, they raised great shouts, calling alternately Barbicane and Nicholl, neither of whom, however, answered their cries. Only the birds, awakened by the sound, flew past them and disappeared among the branches, while some frightened deer fled precipitately before them.

For another hour their search was continued. The greater part of the wood had been explored. There was nothing to reveal the presence of the combatants. The information of the bushman was after all doubtful, and Ardan was about to propose their abandoning this useless pursuit, when all at once Maston stopped.

"Hush!" said he, "there is someone down there!"

"Someone?" repeated Michel Ardan.

"Yes; a man! He seems motionless. His rifle is not in his hands. What can he be doing?"

"But can you recognise him?" asked Ardan, whose short sight was of little use to him in such circumstances.

"Yes! yes! He is turning towards us," answered Maston.

"And it is?"

"Captain Nicholl!"

"Nicholl?" cried Michel Ardan, feeling a terrible pang of grief.

"Nicholl unarmed! He has, then, no longer any fear of his adversary!"

"Let us go to him," said Michel Ardan, "and find out the truth."

But he and his companion had barely taken fifty steps, when they paused to examine the captain more attentively. They expected to find a bloodthirsty man, happy in his revenge.

On seeing him, they remained stupefied.

A net, composed of very fine meshes, hung between two enormous tulip-trees, and in the midst of this snare, with its wings entangled, was a poor little bird, uttering pitiful cries, while it vainly struggled to escape. The bird-catcher who had laid this snare was no human being, but a venomous spider, peculiar to that country, as large as a pigeon's egg, and armed with enormous claws. The hideous creature, instead of rushing on its prey, had beaten a sudden retreat and taken refuge in the upper branches of the tulip-tree, for a formidable enemy menaced its stronghold.

Here, then, was Nicholl, his gun on the ground, forgetful of danger, trying if possible to save the victim from its cobweb prison. At last it was accomplished, and the little bird flew joyfully away and disappeared.

Nicholl lovingly watched its flight, when he heard these words pronounced by a voice full of emotion:

"You are indeed a brave man!"

He turned. Michel Ardan was before him, repeating in a different tone:

"And a kindhearted one!"

"Michel Ardan!" cried the captain. "Why are you here?"

"To press your hand, Nicholl, and to prevent you from either killing Barbicane or being killed by him."

"Barbicane!" returned the captain. "I have been looking for him for the last two hours in vain. Where is he hiding?"

"Nicholl!" said Michel Ardan, "this is not courteous! we ought always to treat an adversary with respect; rest assured if Barbicane is still alive we shall find him all the more easily; because if he has not, like you, been amusing himself with freeing oppressed birds, he must be looking for *you*. When we have found him, Michel Ardan tells you this, there will be no duel between you."

"Between President Barbicane and myself," gravely replied Nicholl, "there is a rivalry which the death of one of us—"

"Pooh, pooh!" said Ardan. "Brave fellows like you indeed! you shall not fight!"

"I will fight, sir!"

"No!"

"Captain," said J. T. Maston, with much feeling, "I am a friend of the president's, his *alter ego*, his second self; if you really must kill someone, *shoot me!* it will do just as well!"

"Sir," Nicholl replied, seizing his rifle convulsively, "these jokes—"

"Our friend Maston is not joking," replied Ardan. "I fully understand his idea of being killed himself in order to save his friend. But neither he nor Barbicane will fall before the balls of Captain Nicholl. Indeed I have so attractive a proposal to make to the two rivals, that both will be eager to accept it."

"What is it?" asked Nicholl with manifest incredulity.

"Patience!" exclaimed Ardan. "I can only reveal it in the presence of Barbicane."

"Let us go in search of him then!" cried the captain.

The three men started off at once; the captain having discharged his rifle threw it over his shoulder, and advanced in silence. Another half-hour passed, and the pursuit was still fruitless. Maston was oppressed by sinister forebodings. He looked fiercely at Nicholl, asking himself whether the captain's vengeance had already been satisfied, and the unfortunate Barbicane, shot, was perhaps lying dead on some bloody track. The same thought seemed to occur to Ardan; and both were casting enquiring glances on Nicholl, when suddenly Maston paused.

The motionless figure of a man leaning against a gigantic catalpa twenty feet off appeared, half-veiled by the foliage.

"It is he!" said Maston.

Barbicane never moved. Ardan looked at the captain, but he did not wince. Ardan went forward crying:

"Barbicane! Barbicane!"

No answer! Ardan rushed towards his friend; but in the act of seizing his arms, he stopped short and uttered a cry of surprise.

Barbicane, pencil in hand, was tracing geometrical figures in a memorandum book, while his unloaded rifle lay beside him on the ground.

Absorbed in his studies, Barbicane, in his turn forgetful of the duel, had seen and heard nothing.

When Ardan took his hand, he looked up and stared at his visitor in astonishment.

"Ah, it is you!" he cried at last. "I have found it, my friend, I have found it!"

"What?"

"My plan!"

"What plan?"

"The plan for countering the effect of the shock at the departure of the projectile!"

"Indeed?" said Michel Ardan, looking at the captain out of the corner of his eye.

"Yes! water! simply water, which will act as a spring—ah! Maston," cried Barbicane, "you here also?"

"Himself," replied Ardan; "and permit me to introduce to you at the same time the worthy Captain Nicholl!"

"Nicholl!" cried Barbicane, who jumped up at once. "Pardon me, captain, I had quite forgotten—I am ready!"

Michel Ardan interfered, without giving the two enemies time to say anything more.

"Thank heaven!" said he. "It is a happy thing that brave men like you two did not meet sooner! we should now have been mourning for one or other of you. But, thanks to Providence, which has interfered, there is now no further cause for alarm. When one forgets one's anger in mechanics or in cobwebs, it is a sign that the anger is not dangerous."

Michel Ardan then told the president how the captain had been found occupied.

"I put it to you now," said he in conclusion, "are two such good fellows as you are made on purpose to smash each other's skulls with shot?"

There was in "the situation" somewhat of the ridiculous, something quite unexpected; Michel Ardan saw this, and determined to effect a reconciliation.

"My good friends," said he, with his most bewitching smile, "this is nothing but a misunderstanding. Nothing more! well! to prove that it is all over between you, accept frankly the proposal I am going to make to you."

"Make it," said Nicholl.

"Our friend Barbicane believes that his projectile will go straight to the moon?"

"Yes, certainly," replied the president.

"And our friend Nicholl is persuaded it will fall back upon the earth?"

"I am certain of it," cried the captain.

"Good!" said Ardan. "I cannot pretend to make you agree; but I suggest this: Go with me, and so see whether we are stopped on our journey."

"What?" exclaimed J. T. Maston, stupefied.

The two rivals, on this sudden proposal, looked steadily at each other. Barbicane waited for the captain's answer. Nicholl watched for the decision of the president.

"Well?" said Michel. "There is now no fear of the shock!"

"Done!" cried Barbicane.

But quickly as he pronounced the word, he was not before Nicholl.

"Hurrah! bravo! hip! hip! hurrah!" cried Michel, giving a hand to each of the late adversaries. "Now that it is all settled, my friends, allow me to treat you after French fashion. Let us be off to breakfast!"

Chapter XXII

THE NEW CITIZEN OF THE UNITED STATES

THAT SAME DAY ALL AMERICA HEARD OF THE AFFAIR OF CAPTAIN NICHOLL AND PRESIdent Barbicane, as well as its singular *denouement*. From that day forth, Michel Ardan had not one moment's rest. Deputations from all corners of the Union harassed him without cessation or intermission. He was compelled to receive them all, whether he would or no. How many hands he shook, how many people he was "hail-fellow-well-met" with, it is impossible to guess! Such a triumphal result would have intoxicated any other man; but he managed to keep himself in a state of delightful *semi*tipsiness.

Among the deputations of all kinds which assailed him, that of "The Lunatics" were careful not to forget what they owed to the future conqueror of the moon. One day, certain of these poor people, so numerous in America, came to call upon him, and requested permission to return with him to their native country.

"Singular hallucination!" said he to Barbicane, after having dismissed the deputation with promises to convey numbers of messages to friends in the moon. "Do you believe in the influence of the moon upon distempers?"

"Scarcely!"

"No more do I, despite some remarkable recorded facts of history. For instance, during an epidemic in 1693, a large number of persons died at the very moment of an eclipse. The celebrated Bacon always fainted during an eclipse. Charles VI relapsed six times into madness during the year 1399, sometimes during the new, sometimes during the full moon. Gall observed that insane persons underwent an accession of their disorder twice in every month, at the epochs of new and full moon. In fact, numerous observations made upon fevers, somnambulisms, and other human maladies, seem to prove that the moon does exercise some mysterious influence upon man."

"But the how and the wherefore?" asked Barbicane.

"Well, I can only give you the answer which Arago borrowed from Plutarch, which is nineteen centuries old. 'Perhaps the stories are not true!' "

In the height of his triumph, Michel Ardan had to encounter all the annoyances incidental to a man of celebrity. Managers of entertainments wanted to exhibit him. Barnum offered him a million dollars to make a tour of the United States in his show. As for his photographs, they were sold of all size, and his portrait taken in every imaginable posture. More than half a million copies were disposed of in an incredibly short space of time.

But it was not only the men who paid him homage, but the women as well. He might have married well a hundred times over, if he had been willing to settle in life. The old maids, in particular, of forty years and upward, and dry in proportion, devoured his photographs day and night. They would have married him by hundreds, even if he had imposed upon them the condition of accompanying him into space. He had, however, no intention of transplanting a race of Franco-Americans upon the surface of the moon.

He therefore declined all offers.

As soon as he could withdraw from these somewhat embarrassing demonstrations, he went, accompanied by his friends, to pay a visit to the *Columbiad*. He was highly gratified by his inspection, and made the descent to the bottom of the tube of this gigantic machine which was presently to launch him to the regions of the moon.

It is necessary here to mention a proposal of J. T. Maston's. When the secretary of the Gun Club found that Barbicane and Nicholl accepted the proposal of Michel Ardan, he determined to join them, and make one of a smug party of four. So one day he determined to be admitted as one of the travellers. Barbicane, pained at having to refuse him, gave him clearly to understand that the projectile could not possibly contain so many passengers. Maston, in despair, went in search of Michel Ardan, who counselled him to resign himself to the situation, adding one or two arguments *ad hominem*.

"You see, old fellow," he said, "you must not take what I say in bad part; but really, between ourselves, you are in too incomplete a condition to appear in the moon!"

"Incomplete?" shrieked the valiant invalid.

"Yes, my dear fellow! imagine our meeting some of the inhabitants up there! Would you like to give them such a melancholy notion of what goes on down here? to teach them what war is, to inform them that we employ our time chiefly in devouring each other, in smashing arms and legs, and that too on a globe which is capable of supporting a hundred billions of inhabitants, and which actually does contain nearly two hundred millions? Why, my worthy friend, we should have to turn you out of doors!"

"But still, if you arrive there in pieces, you will be as incomplete as I am."

"Unquestionably," replied Michel Ardan; "but we shall not."

In fact, a preparatory experiment, tried on the 18th of October, had yielded the best results and caused the most well-grounded hopes of success. Barbicane, desirous of obtaining some notion of the effect of the shock at the moment of the projectile's departure, had procured a 38-inch mortar from the arsenal of Pensacola. He had this placed on the bank of Hillisborough Roads, in order that the shell might fall back into the sea, and the shock be thereby destroyed. His object was to ascertain the extent of the shock of departure, and not that of the return.

A hollow projectile had been prepared for this curious experiment. A thick padding fastened upon a kind of elastic network, made of the best steel, lined the inside of the walls. It was a veritable *nest* most carefully wadded.

"What a pity I can't find room in there," said J. T. Maston, regretting that his height did not allow of his trying the adventure.

Within this shell were shut up a large cat, and a squirrel belonging to J. T. Maston, and of which he was particularly fond. They were desirous, however, of ascertaining how this little animal, least of all others subject to giddiness, would endure this experimental voyage.

The mortar was charged with 160 pounds of powder, and the shell placed in the chamber. On being fired, the projectile rose with great velocity, described a majestic parabola, attained a height of about a thousand feet, and with a graceful curve descended in the midst of the vessels that lay there at anchor.

Without a moment's loss of time a small boat put off in the direction of its fall; some active divers plunged into the water and attached ropes to the handles of the shell, which was quickly dragged on board. Five minutes did not elapse between the moment of enclosing the animals and that of unscrewing the coverlid of their prison.

Ardan, Barbicane, Maston, and Nicholl were present on board the boat, and assisted at the operation with an interest which may readily be comprehended. Hardly had the shell been opened when the cat leaped out, slightly bruised, but full of life, and exhibiting no signs whatever of having made an aerial expedition. No trace, however, of the squirrel could be discovered. The truth at last became apparent—the cat had eaten its fellow-traveller!

J. T. Maston grieved much for the loss of his poor squirrel, and proposed to add its case to that of other martyrs to science.

After this experiment all hesitation, all fear disappeared. Besides, Barbicane's plans would ensure greater perfection for his projectile, and go far to annihilate altogether the effects of the shock. Nothing now remained but to go!

Two days later Michel Ardan received a message from the President of the United States, an honour of which he showed himself especially sensible.

After the example of his illustrious fellow-countryman, the Marquis de la Fayette, the government had decreed to him the title of "Citizen of the United States of America."

Chapter XXIII

THE PROJECTILE-VEHICLE

ON THE COMPLETION OF THE COLUMBIAD THE PUBLIC INTEREST CENTERED IN THE PROjectile itself, the vehicle which was destined to carry the three hardy adventurers into space.

The new plans had been sent to Breadwill and Co., of Albany, with the request for their speedy execution. The projectile was consequently cast on the 2d of November, and immediately forwarded by the Eastern Railway to Stones Hill, which it reached without accident on the 10th of that month, where Michel Ardan, Barbicane, and Nicholl were waiting impatiently for it.

The projectile had now to be filled to the depth of three feet with a bed of water, intended to support a water-tight wooden disc, which worked easily within the walls of the projectile. It was upon this kind of raft that the travellers were to take their place. This body of water was divided by horizontal partitions, which the shock of the departure would have to break in succession. Then each sheet of the water, from the lowest to the highest, running off into escape tubes towards the top of the projectile, constituted a kind of spring; and the wooden disc, supplied with extremely powerful plugs, could not strike the lowest plate except after breaking successively the different partitions. Undoubtedly the travellers would still have to encounter a violent recoil after the complete escapement of the water; but the first shock would be almost entirely destroyed by this powerful spring. The upper parts of the walls were lined with a thick padding of leather, fastened upon springs of the best steel, behind which the escape tubes were completely concealed; thus all imaginable precautions had been taken for averting the first shock; and if they did get crushed, they must, as Michel Ardan said, be made of very bad materials.

The entrance into this metallic tower was by a narrow aperture contrived in the wall of the cone. This was hermetically closed by a plate of aluminum, fastened internally by powerful screw-pressure. The travellers could therefore quit their prison at pleasure, as soon as they should reach the moon.

Light and view were given by means of four thick lenticular glass scuttles, two pierced in the circular wall itself, the third in the bottom, the fourth in the top. These scuttles then were protected against the shock of departure by plates let into solid grooves, which could easily be opened outward by unscrewing them from the inside. Reservoirs firmly fixed contained water and the necessary provisions; and fire and light were procurable by means of gas, contained in a special reservoir under a pressure of several atmospheres. They had only to turn a tap, and for six hours the gas would light and warm this comfortable vehicle.

There now remained only the question of air; for allowing for the consumption of air by Barbicane, his two companions, and two dogs which he proposed taking with him, it was necessary to renew the air of the projectile. Now air consists principally of twenty-one parts of oxygen and seventy-nine of nitrogen. The lungs absorb the oxygen, which is indispensable for the support of life, and reject the nitrogen. The air expired loses nearly five per cent of the former and contains nearly an equal volume of carbonic acid, produced by the combustion of the elements of the blood. In an air-tight enclosure, then, after a certain time, all the oxygen of the air will be replaced by the carbonic acid—a gas fatal to life. There were two things to be done then—first, to replace the absorbed oxygen; secondly, to destroy the expired carbonic acid; both easy enough to do, by means of chlorate of potassium and caustic potash. The former is a salt which appears under the form of white crystals; when raised to a temperature of 400 degrees it is transformed into chlorure of potassium, and the oxygen which it contains is entirely liberated. Now twenty-eight pounds of chlorate of potassium produces seven pounds of oxygen, or 2,400 litres—the quantity necessary for the travellers during twenty-four hours.

Caustic potash has a great affinity for carbonic acid; and it is sufficient to shake it in order for it to seize upon the acid and form bicarbonate of potassium. By these two means they would be enabled to restore to the vitiated air its life-supporting properties.

It is necessary, however, to add that the experiments had hitherto been made *in anima vili*. Whatever its scientific accuracy was, they were at present ignorant how it would answer with human beings. The honour of putting it to the proof was energetically claimed by J. T. Maston.

"Since I am not to go," said the brave artillerist, "I may at least live for a week in the projectile."

It would have been hard to refuse him; so they consented to his wish. A sufficient quantity of chlorate of potassium and of caustic potash was placed at his disposal, together with provisions for eight days. And having shaken hands with his friends, on the 12th of November, at six o'clock A.M., after strictly informing them not to open his prison before the 20th, at six o'clock P.M., he slid down the projectile, the plate of which was at once hermetically sealed. What did he do with himself during that week? They could get no information. The thickness of the walls of the projectile prevented any sound reaching from the inside to the outside. On the 20th of November, at six P.M. exactly, the plate was opened. The friends of J. T. Maston had been all along in a state of much anxiety; but they were promptly reassured on hearing a jolly voice shouting a boisterous hurrah.

Presently afterward the secretary of the Gun Club appeared at the top of the cone in a triumphant attitude. He had grown fat!

Chapter XXIV

THE TELESCOPE OF THE ROCKY MOUNTAINS

ON THE 20TH OF OCTOBER IN THE PRECEDING YEAR, AFTER THE CLOSE OF THE SUB-scription, the president of the Gun Club had credited the Observatory of Cambridge with the necessary sums for the construction of a gigantic optical instrument. This instrument was designed for the purpose of rendering visible on the surface of the moon any object exceeding nine feet in diameter.

At the period when the Gun Club essayed their great experiment, such instruments had reached a high degree of perfection, and produced some magnificent results. Two telescopes in particular, at this time, were possessed of remarkable power and of gigantic dimensions. The first, constructed by Herschel, was thirty-six feet in length, and had an object-glass of four feet six inches; it possessed a magnifying power of 6,000. The second was raised in Ireland, in Parsonstown Park, and belongs to Lord Rosse. The length of this tube is forty-eight feet, and the diameter of its object-glass six feet; it magnifies 6,400 times, and required an immense erection of brick work and masonry for the purpose of working it, its weight being twelve and a half tons.

Still, despite these colossal dimensions, the actual enlargements scarcely exceeded 6,000 times in round numbers; consequently, the moon was brought within no nearer an apparent distance than thirty-nine miles; and objects of less than sixty feet in diameter, unless they were of very considerable length, were still imperceptible.

In the present case, dealing with a projectile nine feet in diameter and fifteen feet long, it became necessary to bring the moon within an apparent distance of five miles at most; and, for that purpose, to establish a magnifying power of 48,000 times.

Such was the question proposed to the Observatory of Cambridge. There was no lack of funds; the difficulty was purely one of construction.

After considerable discussion as to the best form and principle of the proposed instrument the work was finally commenced. According to the calculations of the Observatory of Cambridge, the tube of the new reflector would require to be 280 feet in length, and the object-glass sixteen feet in diameter. Colossal as these dimensions may appear, they were diminutive in comparison with the 10,000 foot telescope proposed by the astronomer Hooke only a few years ago!

Regarding the choice of locality, that matter was promptly determined. The object was to select some lofty mountain, and there are not many of these in the United States. In fact there are but two chains of moderate elevation, between which runs the magnificent Mississippi, the "king of rivers," as these Republican Yankees delight to call it.

Eastwards rise the Appalachians, the very highest point of which, in New Hampshire, does not exceed the very moderate altitude of 5,600 feet.

On the west, however, rise the Rocky Mountains, that immense range which, commencing at the Straights of Magellan, follows the western coast of Southern America under the name of the Andes or the Cordilleras, until it crosses the Isthmus of Panama, and runs up the whole of North America to the very borders of the Polar Sea. The highest elevation of this range still does not exceed 10,700 feet. With this elevation, nevertheless, the Gun Club were compelled to be content, inasmuch as they had determined that both telescope and *Columbiad* should be erected within the limits of the Union. All the necessary apparatus was consequently sent on to the summit of Long's Peak, in the territory of Missouri.

Neither pen nor language can describe the difficulties of all kinds which the American engineers had to surmount, of the prodigies of daring and skill which they accomplished. They had to raise enormous stones, massive pieces of wrought iron, heavy corner-clamps and huge portions of cylinder, with an object-glass weighing nearly 30,000 pounds, above the line of perpetual snow for more than 10,000 feet in height, after crossing desert prairies, impenetrable forests, fearful rapids, far from all centres of population, and in the midst of savage regions, in which every detail of life becomes an almost insoluble problem. And yet, notwithstanding these innumerable obstacles, American genius triumphed. In less than a year after the commencement of the works, towards the close of September, the gigantic reflector rose into the air to a height of 280 feet. It was raised by means of an enormous iron crane; an ingenious mechanism allowed it to be easily worked towards all the points of the heavens, and to follow the stars from the one horizon to the other during their journey through the heavens.

It had cost $400,000. The first time it was directed towards the moon the observers evinced both curiosity and anxiety. What were they about to discover in the field of this telescope which magnified objects 48,000 times? Would they perceive peoples, herds of lunar animals, towns, lakes, seas? No! there was nothing which science had not already discovered! and on all the points of its disc the volcanic nature of the moon became determinable with the utmost precision.

But the telescope of the Rocky Mountains, before doing its duty to the Gun Club, rendered immense services to astronomy. Thanks to its penetrative power, the depths of the heavens were sounded to the utmost extent; the apparent diameter of a great number of stars was accurately measured; and Mr. Clark, of the Cambridge staff, resolved the Crab nebula in Taurus, which the reflector of Lord Rosse had never been able to decompose.

Chapter XXV

FINAL DETAILS

IT WAS THE 22D OF NOVEMBER; THE DEPARTURE WAS TO TAKE PLACE IN TEN DAYS. ONE OPeration alone remained to be accomplished to bring all to a happy termination; an operation delicate and perilous, requiring infinite precautions, and against the success of which Captain Nicholl had laid his third bet. It was, in fact, nothing less than the loading of the *Columbiad*, and the introduction into it of 400,000 pounds of gun-cotton. Nicholl had thought, not perhaps without reason, that the handling of such formidable quantities of pyroxyle would, in all probability, involve a grave catastrophe; and at any rate, that this immense mass of eminently inflammable matter would inevitably ignite when submitted to the pressure of the projectile.

There were indeed dangers accruing as before from the carelessness of the Americans, but Barbicane had set his heart on success, and took all possible precautions. In the first place, he was very careful as to the transportation of the gun-cotton to Stones Hill. He had it conveyed in small quantities, carefully packed in sealed cases. These were brought by rail from Tampa Town to the camp, and from thence were taken to the *Columbiad* by barefooted workmen, who deposited them in their places by means of cranes placed at the orifice of the cannon. No steam-engine was permitted to work, and every fire was extinguished within two miles of the works.

Even in November they feared to work by day, lest the sun's rays acting on the gun-cotton might lead to unhappy results. This led to their working at night, by light produced in a vacuum by means of Ruhmkorff's apparatus, which threw an artificial brightness into the depths of the *Columbiad*. There the cartridges were arranged with the utmost regularity, connected by a metallic thread, destined to communicate to them all simultaneously the electric spark, by which means this mass of gun-cotton was eventually to be ignited.

By the 28th of November eight hundred cartridges had been placed in the bottom of the *Columbiad*. So far the operation had been successful! But what confusion, what anxieties, what struggles were undergone by President Barbicane! In vain had he refused admission to Stones Hill; everyday the inquisitive neighbours scaled the palisades, some even carrying their imprudence to the point of smoking while surrounded by bales of gun-cotton. Barbicane was in a perpetual state of alarm. J. T. Maston seconded him to the best of his ability, by giving vigourous chase to the intruders, and carefully picking up the still lighted cigar ends which the Yankees threw about. A somewhat difficult task! seeing that more than 300,000 persons were gathered round the enclosure. Michel Ardan had volunteered to superintend the transport of the cartridges to the mouth of the *Columbiad*; but the president, having surprised him with an enormous cigar in his mouth, while he was hunting out the rash spectators to whom he himself offered so dangerous an example, saw that he could not trust this fearless smoker, and was therefore obliged to mount a special guard over him.

At last, Providence being propitious, this wonderful loading came to a happy termination, Captain Nicholl's third bet being thus lost. It remained now to introduce the projectile into the *Columbiad*, and to place it on its soft bed of gun-cotton.

But before doing this, all those things necessary for the journey had to be carefully arranged in the projectile vehicle. These necessaries were numerous; and had Ardan been allowed to follow his own wishes, there would have been no space remaining for the travellers. It is impossible to conceive of half the things this charming Frenchman wished to convey to the moon. A veritable stock of useless trifles! But Barbicane interfered and refused admission to anything not absolutely needed. Several thermometers, barometers, and telescopes were packed in the instrument case.

The travellers being desirous of examing the moon carefully during their voyage, in order to facilitate their studies, they took with them Bœer and Mœdler's excellent *Mappa Selenographica*, a masterpiece of patience and observation, which they hoped would enable them to identify those physical features in the moon, with which they were acquainted. This map reproduced with scrupulous fidelity the smallest details of the lunar surface which faces the earth; the mountains, valleys, craters, peaks, and ridges were all represented, with their exact dimensions, relative positions, and names; from the mountains Doërfel and Leibnitz on the eastern side of the disc, to the *Mare frigoris* of the North Pole.

They took also three rifles and three fowling-pieces, and a large quantity of balls, shot, and powder.

"We cannot tell whom we shall have to deal with," said Michel Ardan. "Men or beasts may possibly object to our visit. It is only wise to take all precautions."

These defensive weapons were accompanied by pickaxes, crowbars, saws, and other useful implements, not to mention clothing adapted to every temperature, from that of polar regions to that of the torrid zone.

Ardan wished to convey a number of animals of different sorts, not indeed a pair of every known species, as he could not see the necessity of acclimatising serpents, tigers, alligators, or any other noxious beasts in the moon. "Nevertheless," he said to Barbicane, "some valuable and useful beasts, bullocks, cows, horses, and donkeys, would bear the journey very well, and would also be very useful to us."

"I daresay, my dear Ardan," replied the president, "but our projectile-vehicle is no Noah's ark, from which it differs both in dimensions and object. Let us confine ourselves to possibilities."

After a prolonged discussion, it was agreed that the travellers should restrict themselves to a sporting-dog belonging to Nicholl, and to a large Newfoundland. Several packets of seeds were also included among the necessaries. Michel Ardan, indeed, was anxious to add some sacks full of earth to sow them in; as it was, he took a dozen shrubs carefully wrapped up in straw to plant in the moon.

The important question of provisions still remained; it being necessary to provide against the possibility of their finding the moon absolutely barren. Barbicane managed so successfully, that he supplied them with sufficient rations for a year. These consisted of preserved meats and vegetables, reduced by strong hydraulic pressure to the smallest possible dimensions. They were also supplied with brandy, and took water enough for two months, being confident, from astronomical observations, that there was no lack of water on the moon's surface. As to provisions, doubtless the inhabitants of the *earth* would find nourishment somewhere in the *moon*. Ardan never questioned this; indeed, had he done so, he would never have undertaken the journey.

"Besides," he said one day to his friends, "we shall not be completely abandoned by our terrestrial friends; they will take care not to forget us."

"No, indeed!" replied J. T. Maston.

"Nothing would be simpler," replied Ardan; "the *Columbiad* will be always there. Well! whenever the moon is in a favourable condition as to the zenith, if not to the perigee, that is to say about once a year, could you not send us a shell packed with provisions, which we might expect on some appointed day?"

"Hurrah! hurrah!" cried J. T. Matson; "what an ingenious fellow! what a splendid idea! Indeed, my good friends, we shall not forget you!"

"I shall reckon upon you! Then, you see, we shall receive news regularly from the earth, and we shall indeed be stupid if we hit upon no plan for communicating with our good friends here!"

These words inspired such confidence, that Michel Ardan carried all the Gun Club with him in his enthusiasm. What he said seemed so simple and so easy, so sure of success, that none could be so sordidly attached to this earth as to hesitate to follow the three travellers on their lunar expedition.

All being ready at last, it remained to place the projectile in the *Columbiad*, an operation abundantly accompanied by dangers and difficulties.

The enormous shell was conveyed to the summit of Stones Hill. There, powerful cranes raised it, and held it suspended over the mouth of the cylinder.

It was a fearful moment! What if the chains should break under its enormous weight? The sudden fall of such a body would inevitably cause the gun-cotton to explode!

Fortunately this did not happen; and some hours later the projectile-vehicle descended gently into the heart of the cannon and rested on its couch of pyroxyle, a veritable bed of explosive eider-down. Its pressure had no result, other than the more effectual ramming down of the charge in the *Columbiad*.

"I have lost," said the captain, who forthwith paid President Barbicane the sum of three thousand dollars.

Barbicane did not wish to accept the money from one of his fellow-travellers, but gave way at last before the determination of Nicholl, who wished before leaving the earth to fulfill all his engagements.

"Now," said Michel Ardan, "I have only one thing more to wish for you, my brave captain."

"What is that?" asked Nicholl.

"It is that you may lose your two other bets! Then we shall be sure not to be stopped on our journey!"

Chapter XXVI

FIRE!

THE FIRST OF DECEMBER HAD ARRIVED! THE FATAL DAY! FOR, IF THE PROJECTILE WERE not discharged that very night at 10h. 48m. 40s. P.M., more than eighteen years must roll by before the moon would again present herself under the same conditions of zenith and perigee.

The weather was magnificent. Despite the approach of winter, the sun shone brightly, and bathed in its radiant light that earth which three of its denizens were about to abandon for a new world.

How many persons lost their rest on the night which preceded this long-expected day! All hearts beat with disquietude, save only the heart of Michel Ardan. That imperturbable personage came and went with his habitual business-like air, while nothing whatever denoted that any unusual matter preoccupied his mind.

After dawn, an innumerable multitude covered the prairie which extends, as far as the eye can reach, round Stones Hill. Every quarter of an hour the railway brought fresh accessions of sightseers; and, according to the statement of the Tampa Town *Observer*, not less than five millions of spectators thronged the soil of Florida.

For a whole month previously, the mass of these persons had bivouacked round the enclosure, and laid the foundations for a town which was afterward called "Ardan's Town." The whole plain was covered with huts, cottages, and tents. Every nation under the sun was represented there; and every language might be heard spoken at the same time. It was a perfect Babel re-enacted. All the various classes of American society were mingled together in terms of absolute equality. Bankers, farmers, sailors, cotton-planters, brokers, merchants, watermen, magistrates, elbowed each other in the most free-and-easy way. Louisiana Creoles fraternised with farmers from Indiana; Kentucky and Tennessee gentlemen and haughty Virginians conversed with trappers and the half-savages of the lakes and butchers from Cincinnati. Broad-brimmed white hats and Panamas, blue cotton trowsers, light-coloured stockings, cambric frills, were all here displayed; while upon shirt-fronts, wristbands, and neckties, upon every finger, even upon the very ears, they wore an assortment of rings, shirt-pins, brooches, and trinkets, of which the value only equalled the execrable taste. Women, children, and servants, in equally expensive dress, surrounded their husbands, fathers, or masters, who resembled the patriarchs of tribes in the midst of their immense households.

At mealtimes all fell to work upon the dishes peculiar to the Southern States, and consumed with an appetite that threatened speedy exhaustion of the victualing powers of Florida, fricasseed frogs, stuffed monkey, fish chowder, underdone 'possum, and raccoon steaks. And as for the liquors which accompanied this indigestible repast! The shouts, the vociferations that resounded through the bars and taverns decorated with glasses, tankards, and bottles of marvellous shape, mortars for pounding sugar, and bundles of straws! "Mint-julep" roars one of the barmen; "Claret sangaree!" shouts another; "Cocktail!" "Brandy-smash!" "Real mint-julep in the new style!" All these cries intermingled produced a bewildering and deafening hubbub.

But on this day, 1st of December, such sounds were rare. No one thought of eating or drinking, and at four P.M. there were vast numbers of spectators who had not even taken their customary lunch! And, a still more significant fact, even the national passion for play seemed quelled for the time under the general excitement of the hour.

Up till nightfall, a dull, noiseless agitation, such as precedes great catastrophes, ran through the anxious multitude. An indescribable uneasiness pervaded all minds, an indefinable sensation which oppressed the heart. Everyone wished it was over.

However, about seven o'clock, the heavy silence was dissipated. The moon rose above the horizon. Millions of hurrahs hailed her appearance. She was punctual to the rendezvous, and shouts of welcome greeted her on all sides, as her pale beams shone gracefully in the clear heavens. At this moment the three intrepid travellers appeared. This was the signal for renewed cries of still greater intensity. Instantly the vast assemblage, as with one accord, struck up the national hymn of the United States, and "Yankee Doodle," sung by five million of hearty throats, rose like a roaring tempest to the farthest limits of the atmosphere. Then a profound silence reigned throughout the crowd.

The Frenchman and the two Americans had by this time entered the enclosure reserved in the centre of the multitude. They were accompanied by the members of the Gun Club, and by deputations sent from all the European Observatories. Barbicane, cool and collected, was giving his final directions. Nicholl, with compressed lips, his arms crossed behind his back, walked with a firm and measured step. Michel Ardan, always easy, dressed in thorough traveller's costume, leathern gaiters on his legs, pouch by his side, in loose velvet suit, cigar in mouth, was full of inexhaustible gayety, laughing, joking, playing pranks with J. T. Maston. In one word, he was the thorough "Frenchman" (and worse, a "Parisian") to the last moment.

Ten o'clock struck! The moment had arrived for taking their places in the projectile! The necessary operations for the descent, and the subsequent removal of the cranes and scaffolding that inclined over the mouth of the *Columbiad*, required a certain period of time.

Barbicane had regulated his chronometer to the tenth part of a second by that of Murchison the engineer, who was charged with the duty of firing the gun by means of an electric spark. Thus the travellers enclosed within the projectile were enabled to follow with their eyes the impassive needle which marked the precise moment of their departure.

The moment had arrived for saying "good-by!" The scene was a touching one. Despite his feverish gayety, even Michel Ardan was touched. J. T. Maston had found in his own dry eyes one ancient tear, which he had doubtless reserved for the occasion. He dropped it on the forehead of his dear president.

"Can I not go?" he said, "there is still time!"

"Impossible, old fellow!" replied Barbicane. A few moments later, the three fellow-travellers had ensconced themselves in the projectile, and screwed down the plate which covered the entrance-aperture. The mouth of the *Columbiad*, now completely disencumbered, was open entirely to the sky.

The moon advanced upward in a heaven of the purest clearness, outshining in her passage the twinkling light of the stars. She passed over the constellation of the Twins, and was now nearing the half-way point between the horizon and the zenith. A terrible silence weighed upon the entire scene! Not a breath of wind upon the earth! not a sound of breathing from the countless chests of the spectators! Their hearts seemed afraid to beat! All eyes were fixed upon the yawning mouth of the *Columbiad*.

Murchison followed with his eye the hand of his chronometer. It wanted scarce forty seconds to the moment of departure, but each second seemed to last an age! At the twentieth there was a general shudder, as it occurred to the minds of that vast assemblage that the bold travellers shut up within the projectile were also counting those terrible seconds. Some few cries here and there escaped the crowd.

"Thirty-five!—thirty-six!—thirty-seven!—thirty-eight!—thirty-nine!—forty! FIRE!!!"

Instantly Murchison pressed with his finger the key of the electric battery, restored the current of the fluid, and discharged the spark into the breech of the *Columbiad*.

An appalling unearthly report followed instantly, such as can be compared to nothing whatever known, not even to the roar of thunder, or the blast of volcanic explosions! No words can convey the slightest idea of the terrific sound! An immense spout of fire shot up from the bowels of the earth as from a crater. The earth heaved up, and with great difficulty some few spectators obtained a momentary glimpse of the projectile victoriously cleaving the air in the midst of the fiery vapours!

Chapter XXVII

Foul Weather

AT THE MOMENT WHEN THAT PYRAMID OF FIRE ROSE TO A PRODIGIOUS HEIGHT INTO the air, the glare of flame lit up the whole of Florida; and for a moment day superseded night over a considerable extent of the country. This immense canopy of fire was perceived at a distance of one hundred miles out at sea, and more than one ship's captain entered in his log the appearance of this gigantic meteor.

The discharge of the *Columbiad* was accompanied by a perfect earthquake. Florida was shaken to its very depths. The gases of the powder, expanded by heat, forced back the atmospheric strata with tremendous violence, and this artificial hurricane rushed like a water-spout through the air.

Not a single spectator remained on his feet! Men, women children, all lay prostrate like ears of corn under a tempest. There ensued a terrible tumult; a large number of persons were seriously injured. J. T. Maston, who, despite all dictates of prudence, had kept in advance of the mass, was pitched back 120 feet, shooting like a projectile over the heads of his fellow-citizens. Three hundred thousand persons remained deaf for a time, and as though struck stupefied.

As soon as the first effects were over, the injured, the deaf, and lastly, the crowd in general, woke up with frenzied cries. "Hurrah for Ardan! Hurrah for Barbicane! Hurrah for Nicholl!" rose to the skies. Thousands of persons, noses in air, armed with telescopes and race-glasses, were questioning space, forgetting all contusions and emotions in the one idea of watching for the projectile. They looked in vain! It was no longer to be seen, and they were obliged to wait for telegrams from Long's Peak. The director of the Cambridge Observatory was at his post on the Rocky Mountains; and to him, as a skilful and persevering astronomer, all observations had been confided.

But an unforeseen phenomenon came in to subject the public impatience to a severe trial.

The weather, hitherto so fine, suddenly changed; the sky became heavy with clouds. It could not have been otherwise after the terrible derangement of the atmospheric strata, and the dispersion of the enormous quantity of vapour arising from the combustion of 200,000 pounds of pyroxyle!

On the morrow the horizon was covered with clouds—a thick and impenetrable curtain between earth and sky, which unhappily extended as far as the Rocky Mountains. It was a fatality! But since man had chosen so to disturb the atmosphere, he was bound to accept the consequences of his experiment.

Supposing, now, that the experiment had succeeded, the travellers having started on the 1st of December, at 10h. 46m. 40s. P.M., were due on the 4th at 0h. P.M. at their destination. So that up to that time it would have been very difficult after all to have observed, under such conditions, a body so small as the shell. Therefore they waited with what patience they might.

From the 4th to the 6th of December inclusive, the weather remaining much the same in America, the great European instruments of Herschel, Rosse, and Foucault, were constantly directed towards the moon, for the weather was then magnificent; but the comparative weakness of their glasses prevented any trustworthy observations being made.

On the 7th the sky seemed to lighten. They were in hopes now, but their hope was of but short duration, and at night again thick clouds hid the starry vault from all eyes.

Matters were now becoming serious, when on the 9th the sun reappeared for an instant, as if for the purpose of teasing the Americans. It was received with hisses; and wounded, no doubt, by such a reception, showed itself very sparing of its rays.

On the 10th, no change! J. T. Maston went nearly mad, and great fears were entertained regarding the brain of this worthy individual, which had hitherto been so well preserved within his gutta percha cranium.

But on the 11th one of those inexplicable tempests peculiar to those intertropical regions was let loose in the atmosphere. A terrific east wind swept away the groups of clouds which had been so long gathering, and at night the semidisc of the orb of night rode majestically amid the soft constellations of the sky.

Chapter XXVIII

A NEW STAR

THAT VERY NIGHT, THE STARTLING NEWS SO IMPATIENTLY AWAITED, BURST LIKE A THUNderbolt over the United States of the Union, and thence, darting across the ocean, ran through all the telegraphic wires of the globe. The projectile had been detected, thanks to the gigantic reflector of Long's Peak! Here is the note received by the director of the Observatory of Cambridge. It contains the scientific conclusion regarding this great experiment of the Gun Club.

Long's Peak, December 12.

To the Officers of the Observatory of Cambridge.

The projectile discharged by the *Columbiad* at Stones Hill has been detected by Messrs. Belfast and J. T. Maston, 12th of December, at 8:47 P.M., the moon having entered her last quarter. This projectile has not arrived at its destination. It has passed by the side; but sufficiently near to be retained by the lunar attraction.

The rectilinear movement has thus become changed into a circular motion of extreme velocity, and it is now pursuing an elliptical orbit round the moon, of which it has become a true satellite.

The elements of this new star we have as yet been unable to determine; we do not yet know the velocity of its passage. The distance which separates it from the surface of the moon may be estimated at about 2,833 miles.

However, two hypotheses come here into our consideration.

1. Either the attraction of the moon will end by drawing them into itself, and the travellers will attain their destination; or,

2. The projectile, following an immutable law, will continue to gravitate round the moon till the end of time.

At some future time, our observations will be able to determine this point, but till then the experiment of the Gun Club can have no other result than to have provided our solar system with a new star.

J. Belfast

To how many questions did this unexpected *denouement* give rise? What mysterious results was the future reserving for the investigation of science? At all events, the names of Nicholl, Barbicane, and Michel Ardan were certain to be immortalised in the annals of astronomy!

When the despatch from Long's Peak had once become known, there was but one universal feeling of surprise and alarm. Was it possible to go to the aid of these bold travellers? No! for they had placed themselves beyond the pale of humanity, by crossing the limits imposed by the Creator on his earthly creatures. They had air enough for *two* months; they had victuals enough for *twelve;—but after that?* There was only one man who would not admit that the situation was desperate—he alone had confidence; and that was their devoted friend J. T. Maston.

Besides, he never let them get out of sight. His home was henceforth the post at Long's Peak; his horizon, the mirror of that immense reflector. As soon as the moon rose above the horizon, he immediately caught her in the field of the telescope; he never let her go for an instant out of his sight, and followed her assiduously in her course through the stellar spaces. He watched with untiring patience the passage of the projectile across her silvery disc, and really the worthy man remained in perpetual communication with his three friends, whom he did not despair of seeing again someday.

"Those three men," said he, "have carried into space all the resources of art, science, and industry. With that, one can do anything; and you will see that, someday, they will come out all right."

ROUND THE MOON

CONTENTS

CHAPTER

Preliminary Chapter—Recapitulating the First Part of This Work,
and Serving as a Preface to the Second   407

I   From Twenty Minutes Past Ten to Forty-Seven Minutes
Past Ten P.M.   409

II   The First Half-Hour   413

III   Their Place of Shelter   419

IV   A Little Algebra   424

V   The Cold of Space   428

VI   Question and Answer   433

VII   A Moment of Intoxication   437

VIII   At Seventy-Eight Thousand Five Hundred and Fourteen Leagues   442

IX   The Consequences of a Deviation   447

X   The Observers of the Moon   451

XI   Fancy and Reality   453

XII   Orographic Details   454

XIII   Lunar Landscapes   458

XIV   The Night of Three Hundred and Fifty-Four Hours and a Half   462

XV   Hyperbola or Parabola   467

XVI   The Southern Hemisphere   472

XVII   Tycho   474

XVIII   Grave Questions   478

XIX   A Struggle Against the Impossible   482

XX   The Soundings of the *Susquehanna*   487

XXI   J. T. Maston Recalled   491

XXII   Recovered from the Sea   495

XXIII   The End   499

Preliminary Chapter

RECAPITULATING THE FIRST PART OF THIS WORK, AND SERVING AS A PREFACE TO THE SECOND

URING THE YEAR 186–, THE WHOLE WORLD WAS GREATLY EXCITED BY A SCIENTIFIC experiment unprecedented in the annals of science. The members of the Gun Club, a circle of artillerymen formed at Baltimore after the American war, conceived the idea of putting themselves in communication with the moon!—yes, with the moon—by sending to her a projectile. Their president, Barbicane, the promoter of the enterprise, having consulted the astronomers of the Cambridge Observatory upon the subject, took all necessary means to ensure the success of this extraordinary enterprise, which had been declared practicable by the majority of competent judges. After setting on foot a public subscription, which realised nearly £1,200,000, they began the gigantic work.

According to the advice forwarded from the members of the Observatory, the gun destined to launch the projectile had to be fixed in a country situated between the 0 and 28th degrees of north or south latitude, in order to aim at the moon when at the zenith; and its initiatory velocity was fixed at twelve thousand yards to the second. Launched on the 1st of December, at 10hrs. 46m. 40s. P.M., it ought to reach the moon four days after its departure, that is on the 5th of December, at midnight precisely, at the moment of her attaining her perigee, that is her nearest distance from the earth, which is exactly 86,410 leagues (French), or 238,833 miles mean distance (English).

The principal members of the Gun Club, President Barbicane, Major Elphinstone, the secretary Joseph T. Maston, and other learned men, held several meetings, at which the shape and composition of the projectile were discussed, also the position and nature of the gun, and the quality and quantity of powder to be used. It was decided: First, that the projectile should be a shell made of aluminum with a diameter of 108 inches and a thickness of twelve inches to its walls; and should weigh 19,250 pounds. Second, that the gun should be a *Columbiad* cast in iron, 900 feet long, and run perpendicularly into the earth. Third, that the charge should contain 400,000 pounds of gun-cotton, which, giving out six billions of litres of gas in rear of the projectile, would easily carry it towards the orb of night.

These questions determined President Barbicane, assisted by Murchison the engineer, to choose a spot situated in Florida, in 27° 7' North latitude, and 77° 3' West (Greenwich) longitude. It was on this spot, after stupendous labor, that the *Columbiad* was cast with full success. Things stood thus, when an incident took place which increased the interest attached to this great enterprise a hundredfold.

A Frenchman, an enthusiastic Parisian, as witty as he was bold, asked to be enclosed in the projectile, in order that he might reach the moon, and reconnoitre this terrestrial satellite. The name of this intrepid adventurer was Michel Ardan. He landed in America, was received with enthusiasm, held meetings, saw himself carried in triumph, reconciled President Barbicane to his mortal enemy, Captain Nicholl, and, as a token of reconciliation, persuaded them both to start with him in the projectile. The proposition being accepted, the shape of the projectile was slightly altered. It was made of a cylindro-conical form. This species of aerial car was lined with strong springs and partitions to deaden the shock of departure. It was provided with food for a year, water for some months, and gas for some days. A self-acting apparatus supplied the three travellers with air to breathe. At the same time, on one of the highest points of the Rocky Mountains, the Gun Club had a gigantic telescope erected, in order that they might be able to follow the course of the projectile through space. All was then ready.

On the 30th of November, at the hour fixed upon, from the midst of an extraordinary crowd of spectators, the departure took place, and for the first time, three human beings quitted the terrestrial globe, and launched into interplanetary space with almost a certainty of reaching their destination. These bold travellers, Michel Ardan, President Barbicane, and Captain Nicholl, ought to make the passage in ninety-seven hours, thirteen minutes, and twenty seconds. Consequently, their arrival on the lunar disc could not take place until the 5th of December at twelve at night, at the exact moment when the moon should be full, and not on the 4th, as some badly informed journalists had announced.

But an unforeseen circumstance, viz., the detonation produced by the *Columbiad*, had the immediate effect of troubling the terrestrial atmosphere, by accumulating a large quantity of vapour, a phenomenon which excited universal indignation, for the moon was hidden from the eyes of the watchers for several nights.

The worthy Joseph T. Maston, the staunchest friend of the three travellers, started for the Rocky Mountains, accompanied by the Hon. J. Belfast, director of the Cambridge Observatory, and reached the station of Long's Peak, where the telescope was erected which brought the moon within an apparent distance of two leagues. The honourable secretary of the Gun Club wished himself to observe the vehicle of his daring friends.

The accumulation of the clouds in the atmosphere prevented all observation on the 5th, 6th, 7th, 8th, 9th, and 10th of December. Indeed it was thought that all observations would have to be put off to the 3d of January in the following year; for the moon entering its last quarter on the 11th, would then only present an ever-decreasing portion of her disc, insufficient to allow of their following the course of the projectile.

At length, to the general satisfaction, a heavy storm cleared the atmosphere on the night of the 11th and 12th of December, and the moon, with half-illuminated disc, was plainly to be seen upon the black sky.

That very night a telegram was sent from the station of Long's Peak by Joseph T. Maston and Belfast to the gentlemen of the Cambridge Observatory, announcing that on the 11th of December at 8h. 47m. P.M., the projectile launched by the *Columbiad* of Stones Hill had been detected by Messrs. Belfast and Maston—that it had deviated from its course from some unknown cause, and had not reached its destination; but that it had passed near enough to be retained by the lunar attraction; that its rectilinear movement had been changed to a circular one, and that following an elliptical orbit round the star of night it had become its satellite. The telegram added that the elements of this new star had not yet been calculated; and indeed three observations made upon a star in three different positions are necessary to determine these elements. Then it showed that the distance separating the projectile from the lunar surface "might" be reckoned at about 2,833 miles.

It ended with the double hypothesis: either the attraction of the moon would draw it to herself, and the travellers thus attain their end; or that the projectile, held in one immutable orbit, would gravitate around the lunar disc to all eternity.

With such alternatives, what would be the fate of the travellers? Certainly they had food for some time. But supposing they did succeed in their rash enterprise, how would they return? Could they ever return? Should they hear from them? These questions, debated by the most learned pens of the day, strongly engrossed the public attention.

It is advisable here to make a remark which ought to be well considered by hasty observers. When a purely speculative discovery is announced to the public, it cannot be done with too much prudence. No one is obliged to discover either a planet, a comet, or a satellite; and whoever makes a mistake in such a case exposes himself justly to the derision of the mass. Far better is it to wait; and that is what the impatient Joseph T. Maston should have done before sending this telegram forth to the world, which, according to his idea, told the whole result of the enterprise. Indeed this telegram contained two sorts of errors, as was proved eventually. First, errors of observation, concerning the distance of the projectile from the surface of the moon, for on the 11th of December it was impossible to see it; and what Joseph T. Maston had seen, or thought he saw, could not have been the projectile of the *Columbiad*. Second, errors of theory on the fate in store for the said projectile; for in making it a satellite of the moon, it was putting it in direct contradiction of all mechanical laws.

One single hypothesis of the observers of Long's Peak could ever be realised, that which foresaw the case of the travellers (if still alive) uniting their efforts with the lunar attraction to attain the surface of the disc.

Now these men, as clever as they were daring, had survived the terrible shock consequent on their departure, and it is their journey in the projectile car which is here related in its most dramatic as well as in its most singular details. This recital will destroy many illusions and surmises; but it will give a true idea of the singular changes in store for such an enterprise; it will bring out the scientific instincts of Barbicane, the industrious resources of Nicholl, and the audacious humour of Michel Ardan. Besides this, it will prove that their worthy friend, Joseph T. Maston, was wasting his time, while leaning over the gigantic telescope he watched the course of the moon through the starry space.

Chapter I

FROM TWENTY MINUTES PAST TEN TO FORTY-SEVEN MINUTES PAST TEN P.M.

AS TEN O'CLOCK STRUCK, MICHEL ARDAN, BARBICANE, AND NICHOLL, TOOK LEAVE OF the numerous friends they were leaving on the earth. The two dogs, destined to propagate the canine race on the lunar continents, were already shut up in the projectile.

The three travellers approached the orifice of the enormous cast-iron tube, and a crane let them down to the conical top of the projectile. There, an opening made for the purpose gave them access to the aluminum car. The tackle belonging to the crane being hauled from outside, the mouth of the *Columbiad* was instantly disencumbered of its last supports.

Nicholl, once introduced with his companions inside the projectile, began to close the opening by means of a strong plate, held in position by powerful screws. Other plates, closely fitted, covered the lenticular glasses, and the travellers, hermetically enclosed in their metal prison, were plunged in profound darkness.

"And now, my dear companions," said Michel Ardan, "let us make ourselves at home; I am a domesticated man and strong in housekeeping. We are bound to make the best of our new lodgings, and make ourselves comfortable. And first let us try and see a little. Gas was not invented for moles."

So saying, the thoughtless fellow lit a match by striking it on the sole of his boot; and approached the burner fixed to the receptacle, in which the carbonised hydrogen, stored at high pressure, sufficed for the lighting and warming of the projectile for a hundred and forty-four hours, or six days and six nights. The gas caught fire, and thus lighted the projectile looked like a comfortable room with thickly padded walls, furnished with a circular divan, and a roof rounded in the shape of a dome.

Michel Ardan examined everything, and declared himself satisfied with his installation.

"It is a prison," said he, "but a travelling prison; and, with the right of putting my nose to the window, I could well stand a lease of a hundred years. You smile, Barbicane. Have you any *arrière-pensée?* Do you say to yourself, 'This prison may be our tomb?' Tomb, perhaps; still I would not change it for Mahomet's, which floats in space but never advances an inch!"

While Michel Ardan was speaking, Barbicane and Nicholl were making their last preparations.

Nicholl's chronometer marked twenty minutes past ten P.M. when the three travellers were finally enclosed in their projectile. This chronometer was set within the tenth of a second by that of Murchison the engineer. Barbicane consulted it.

"My friends," said he, "it is twenty minutes past ten. At forty-seven minutes past ten Murchison will launch the electric spark on the wire which communicates with the charge of the *Columbiad*. At that precise moment we shall leave our spheroid. Thus we still have twenty-seven minutes to remain on the earth."

"Twenty-six minutes thirteen seconds," replied the methodical Nicholl.

"Well!" exclaimed Michel Ardan, in a good-humored tone, "much may be done in twenty-six minutes. The gravest questions of morals and politics may be discussed, and even solved. Twenty-six minutes well employed are worth more than twenty-six years in which nothing is done. Some seconds of a Pascal or a Newton are more precious than the whole existence of a crowd of raw simpletons—"

"And you conclude, then, you everlasting talker?" asked Barbicane.

"I conclude that we have twenty-six minutes left," replied Ardan.

"Twenty-four only," said Nicholl.

"Well, twenty-four, if you like, my noble captain," said Ardan; "twenty-four minutes in which to investigate—"

"Michel," said Barbicane, "during the passage we shall have plenty of time to investigate the most difficult questions. For the present we must occupy ourselves with our departure."

"Are we not ready?"

"Doubtless; but there are still some precautions to be taken, to deaden as much as possible the first shock."

"Have we not the water-cushions placed between the partition-breaks, whose elasticity will sufficiently protect us?"

"I hope so, Michel," replied Barbicane gently, "but I am not sure."

"Ah, the joker!" exclaimed Michel Ardan. "He hopes!—He is not sure!—and he waits for the moment when we are encased to make this deplorable admission! I beg to be allowed to get out!"

"And how?" asked Barbicane.

"Humph!" said Michel Ardan, "it is not easy; we are in the train, and the guard's whistle will sound before twenty-four minutes are over."

"Twenty," said Nicholl.

For some moments the three travellers looked at each other. Then they began to examine the objects imprisoned with them.

"Everything is in its place," said Barbicane. "We have now to decide how we can best place ourselves to resist the shock. Position cannot be an indifferent matter; and we must, as much as possible, prevent the rush of blood to the head."

"Just so," said Nicholl.

"Then," replied Michel Ardan, ready to suit the action to the word, "let us put our heads down and our feet in the air, like the clowns in the grand circus."

"No," said Barbicane, "let us stretch ourselves on our sides; we shall resist the shock better that way. Remember that, when the projectile starts, it matters little whether we are in it or before it; it amounts to much the same thing."

"If it is only 'much the same thing,' I may cheer up," said Michel Ardan.

"Do you approve of my idea, Nicholl?" asked Barbicane.

"Entirely," replied the captain. "We've still thirteen minutes and a half."

"That Nicholl is not a man," exclaimed Michel; "he is a chronometer with seconds, an escape, and eight holes."

But his companions were not listening; they were taking up their last positions with the most perfect coolness. They were like two methodical travellers in a car, seeking to place themselves as comfortably as possible.

We might well ask ourselves of what materials are the hearts of these Americans made, to whom the approach of the most frightful danger added no pulsation.

Three thick and solidly-made couches had been placed in the projectile. Nicholl and Barbicane placed them in the centre of the disc forming the floor. There the three travellers were to stretch themselves some moments before their departure.

During this time, Ardan, not being able to keep still, turned in his narrow prison like a wild beast in a cage, chatting with his friends, speaking to the dogs Diana and Satellite, to whom, as may be seen, he had given significant names.

"Ah, Diana! Ah, Satellite!" he exclaimed, teasing them; "so you are going to show the moon-dogs the good habits of the dogs of the earth! That will do honour to the canine race! If ever we do come down again, I will bring a cross type of 'moon-dogs,' which will make a stir!"

"If there *are* dogs in the moon," said Barbicane.

"There are," said Michel Ardan, "just as there are horses, cows, donkeys, and chickens. I bet that we shall find chickens."

"A hundred dollars we shall find none!" said Nicholl.

"Done, my captain!" replied Ardan, clasping Nicholl's hand. "But, by the by, you have already lost three bets with our president, as the necessary funds for the enterprise have been found, as the operation of casting has been successful, and lastly, as the *Columbiad* has been loaded without accident, six thousand dollars."

"Yes," replied Nicholl. "Thirty-seven minutes six seconds past ten."

"It is understood, captain. Well, before another quarter of an hour you will have to count nine thousand dollars to the president; four thousand because the *Columbiad* will not burst, and five thousand because the projectile will rise more than six miles in the air."

"I have the dollars," replied Nicholl, slapping the pocket of this coat. "I only ask to be allowed to pay."

"Come, Nicholl. I see that you are a man of method, which I could never be; but indeed you have made a series of bets of very little advantage to yourself, allow me to tell you."

"And why?" asked Nicholl.

"Because, if you gain the first, the *Columbiad* will have burst, and the projectile with it; and Barbicane will no longer be there to reimburse your dollars."

"My stake is deposited at the bank in Baltimore," replied Barbicane simply; "and if Nicholl is not there, it will go to his heirs."

"Ah, you practical men!" exclaimed Michel Ardan; "I admire you the more for not being able to understand you."

"Forty-two minutes past ten!" said Nicholl.

"Only five minutes more!" answered Barbicane.

"Yes, five little minutes!" replied Michel Ardan; "and we are enclosed in a projectile, at the bottom of a gun 900 feet long! And under this projectile are rammed 400,000 pounds of gun-cotton, which is equal to 1,600,000 pounds of ordinary powder! And friend Murchison, with his chronometer in hand, his eye fixed on the needle, his finger on the electric apparatus, is counting the seconds preparatory to launching us into interplanetary space."

"Enough, Michel, enough!" said Barbicane, in a serious voice; "let us prepare. A few instants alone separate us from an eventful moment. One clasp of the hand, my friends."

"Yes," exclaimed Michel Ardan, more moved than he wished to appear; and the three bold companions were united in a last embrace.

"God preserve us!" said the religious Barbicane.

Michel Ardan and Nicholl stretched themselves on the couches placed in the centre of the disc.

"Forty-seven minutes past ten!" murmured the captain.

"Twenty seconds more!" Barbicane quickly put out the gas and lay down by his companions, and the profound silence was only broken by the ticking of the chronometer marking the seconds.

Suddenly a dreadful shock was felt, and the projectile, under the force of six billions of litres of gas, developed by the combustion of pyroxyle, mounted into space.

Chapter II

THE FIRST HALF-HOUR

WHAT HAD HAPPENED? WHAT EFFECT HAD THIS FRIGHTFUL SHOCK PRODUCED? HAD the ingenuity of the constructors of the projectile obtained any happy result? Had the shock been deadened, thanks to the springs, the four plugs, the water-cushions, and the partition-breaks? Had they been able to subdue the frightful pressure of the initiatory speed of more than 11,000 yards, which was enough to traverse Paris or New York in a second? This was evidently the question suggested to the thousand spectators of this moving scene. They forgot the aim of the journey, and thought only of the travellers. And if one of them—Joseph T. Maston for example—could have cast one glimpse into the projectile, what would he have seen?

Nothing then. The darkness was profound. But its cylindro-conical partitions had resisted wonderfully. Not a rent or a dent anywhere! The wonderful projectile was not even heated under the intense deflagration of the powder, nor liquefied, as they seemed to fear, in a shower of aluminum.

The interior showed but little disorder; indeed, only a few objects had been violently thrown towards the roof; but the most important seemed not to have suffered from the shock at all; their fixtures were intact.

On the movable disc, sunk down to the bottom by the smashing of the partition-breaks and the escape of the water, three bodies lay apparently lifeless. Barbicane, Nicholl, and Michel Ardan—did they still breathe? or was the projectile nothing now but a metal coffin, bearing three corpses into space?

Some minutes after the departure of the projectile, one of the bodies moved, shook its arms, lifted its head, and finally succeeded in getting on its knees. It was Michel Ardan. He felt himself all over, gave a sonorous "Hem!" and then said:

"Michel Ardan is whole. How about the others?"

The courageous Frenchman tried to rise, but could not stand. His head swam, from the rush of blood; he was blind; he was a drunken man.

"Bur-r!" said he. "It produces the same effect as two bottles of Corton, though perhaps less agreeable to swallow." Then, passing his hand several times across his forehead and rubbing his temples, he called in a firm voice:

"Nicholl! Barbicane!"

He waited anxiously. No answer; not even a sigh to show that the hearts of his companions were still beating. He called again. The same silence.

"The devil!" he exclaimed. "They look as if they had fallen from a fifth story on their heads. Bah!" he added, with that imperturbable confidence which nothing could check, "if a Frenchman can get on his knees, two Americans ought to be able to get on their feet. But first let us light up."

Ardan felt the tide of life return by degrees. His blood became calm, and returned to its accustomed circulation. Another effort restored his equilibrium. He succeeded in rising, drew a match from his pocket, and approaching the burner lighted it. The receiver had not suffered at all. The gas had not escaped. Besides, the smell would have betrayed it; and in that case Michel Ardan could not have carried a lighted match with impunity through the space filled with hydrogen. The gas mixing with the air would have produced a detonating mixture, and the explosion would have finished what the shock had perhaps begun. When the burner was lit, Ardan leaned over the bodies of his companions: they were lying one on the other, an inert mass, Nicholl above, Barbicane underneath.

Ardan lifted the captain, propped him up against the divan, and began to rub vigourously. This means, used with judgment, restored Nicholl, who opened his eyes, and instantly recovering his presence of mind, seized Ardan's hand and looked around him.

"And Barbicane?" said he.

"Each in turn," replied Michel Ardan. "I began with you, Nicholl, because you were on the top. Now let us look to Barbicane." Saying which, Ardan and Nicholl raised the president of the Gun Club and laid him on the divan. He seemed to have suffered more than either of his companions; he was bleeding, but Nicholl was reassured by finding that the hemorrhage came from a slight wound on the shoulder, a mere graze, which he bound up carefully.

Still, Barbicane was a long time coming to himself, which frightened his friends, who did not spare friction.

"He breathes though," said Nicholl, putting his ear to the chest of the wounded man.

"Yes," replied Ardan, "he breathes like a man who has some notion of that daily operation. Rub, Nicholl; let us rub harder." And the two improvised practitioners worked so hard and so well that Barbicane recovered his senses. He opened his eyes, sat up, took his two friends by the hands, and his first words were—

"Nicholl, are we moving?"

Nicholl and Ardan looked at each other; they had not yet troubled themselves about the projectile; their first thought had been for the traveller, not for the car.

"Well, are we really moving?" repeated Michel Ardan.

"Or quietly resting on the soil of Florida?" asked Nicholl.

"Or at the bottom of the Gulf of Mexico?" added Michel Ardan.

"What an idea!" exclaimed the president.

And this double hypothesis suggested by his companions had the effect of recalling him to his senses. In any case they could not decide on the position of the projectile. Its apparent immovability, and the want of communication with the outside, prevented them from solving the question. Perhaps the projectile was unwinding its course through space. Perhaps after a short rise it had fallen upon the earth, or even in the Gulf of Mexico—a fall which the narrowness of the peninsula of Florida would render not impossible.

The case was serious, the problem interesting, and one that must be solved as soon as possible. Thus, highly excited, Barbicane's moral energy triumphed over physical weakness, and he rose to his feet. He listened. Outside was perfect silence; but the thick padding was enough to intercept all sounds coming from the earth. But one circumstance struck Barbicane, viz., that the temperature inside the projectile was singularly high. The president drew a thermometer from its case and consulted it. The instrument showed 81° Fahr.

"Yes," he exclaimed, "yes, we are moving! This stifling heat, penetrating through the partitions of the projectile, is produced by its friction on the atmospheric strata. It will soon diminish, because we are already floating in space, and after having nearly stifled, we shall have to suffer intense cold."

"What!" said Michel Ardan. "According to your showing, Barbicane, we are already beyond the limits of the terrestrial atmosphere?"

"Without a doubt, Michel. Listen to me. It is fifty-five minutes past ten; we have been gone about eight minutes; and if our initiatory speed has not been checked by the friction, six seconds would be enough for us to pass through the forty miles of atmosphere which surrounds the globe."

"Just so," replied Nicholl; "but in what proportion do you estimate the diminution of speed by friction?"

"In the proportion of one-third, Nicholl. This diminution is considerable, but according to my calculations it is nothing less. If, then, we had an initiatory speed of 12,000 yards, on leaving the atmosphere this speed would be reduced to 9,165 yards. In any case we have already passed through this interval, and—"

"And then," said Michel Ardan, "friend Nicholl has lost his two bets: four thousand dollars because the *Columbiad* did not burst; five thousand dollars because the projectile has risen more than six miles. Now, Nicholl, pay up."

"Let us prove it first," said the captain, "and we will pay afterward. It is quite possible that Barbicane's reasoning is correct, and that I have lost my nine thousand dollars. But a new hypothesis presents itself to my mind, and it annuls the wager."

"What is that?" asked Barbicane quickly.

"The hypothesis that, for some reason or other, fire was never set to the powder, and we have not started at all."

"My goodness, captain," exclaimed Michel Ardan, "that hypothesis is not worthy of my brain! It cannot be a serious one. For have we not been half annihilated by the shock? Did I not recall you to life? Is not the president's shoulder still bleeding from the blow it has received?"

"Granted," replied Nicholl; "but one question."

"Well, captain?"

"Did you hear the detonation, which certainly ought to be loud?"

"No," replied Ardan, much surprised; "certainly I did not hear the detonation."

"And you, Barbicane?"

"Nor I, either."

"Very well," said Nicholl.

"Well now," murmured the president "why did we not hear the detonation?"

The three friends looked at each other with a disconcerted air. It was quite an inexplicable phenomenon. The projectile had started, and consequently there must have been a detonation.

"Let us first find out where we are," said Barbicane, "and let down this panel."

This very simple operation was soon accomplished.

The nuts which held the bolts to the outer plates of the right-hand scuttle gave way under the pressure of the English wrench. These bolts were pushed outside, and the buffers covered with India-rubber stopped up the holes which let them through. Immediately the outer plate fell back upon its hinges like a porthole, and the lenticular glass which closed the scuttle appeared. A similar one was let into the thick partition on the opposite side of the projectile, another in the top of the dome, and finally, a fourth in the middle of the base. They could, therefore, make observations in four different directions: the firmament by the side and most direct windows, the earth or the moon by the upper and under openings in the projectile.

Barbicane and his two companions immediately rushed to the uncovered window. But it was lit by no ray of light. Profound darkness surrounded them, which, however, did not prevent the president from exclaiming:

"No, my friends, we have not fallen back upon the earth; no, nor are we submerged in the Gulf of Mexico. Yes! we are mounting into space. See those stars shining in the night, and that impenetrable darkness heaped up between the earth and us!"

"Hurrah! hurrah!" exclaimed Michel Ardan and Nicholl in one voice.

Indeed, this thick darkness proved that the projectile had left the earth, for the soil, brilliantly lit by the moon-beams would have been visible to the travellers, if they had been lying on its surface. This darkness also showed that the projectile had passed the atmospheric strata, for the diffused light spread in the air would have been reflected on the metal walls, which reflection was wanting. This light would have lit the window, and the window was dark. Doubt was no longer possible; the travellers had left the earth.

"I have lost," said Nicholl.

"I congratulate you," replied Ardan.

"Here are the nine thousand dollars," said the captain, drawing a roll of paper dollars from his pocket.

"Will you have a receipt for it?" asked Barbicane, taking the sum.

"If you do not mind," answered Nicholl; "it is more business-like."

And coolly and seriously, as if he had been at his strong-box, the president drew forth his note-book, tore out a blank leaf, wrote a proper receipt in pencil, dated and signed it with the usual flourish,* and gave it to the captain, who carefully placed it in his pocket-book. Michel Ardan, taking off his hat, bowed to his two companions without speaking. So much formality under such circumstances left him speechless. He had never before seen anything so "American."

This affair settled, Barbicane and Nicholl had returned to the window, and were watching the constellations. The stars looked like bright points on the black sky. But from that side they could not see the orb of night, which, travelling from east to west, would rise by degrees towards the zenith. Its absence drew the following remark from Ardan:

"And the moon; will she perchance fail at our rendezvous?"

"Do not alarm yourself," said Barbicane; "our future globe is at its post, but we cannot see her from this side; let us open the other."

As Barbicane was about leaving the window to open the opposite scuttle, his attention was attracted by the approach of a brilliant object. It was an enormous disc, whose colossal dimension could not be estimated. Its face, which was turned to the earth, was very bright. One might have thought it a small moon reflecting the light of the large one. She advanced with great speed, and seemed to describe an orbit round the earth, which would

---

*This is a purely French habit.

intersect the passage of the projectile. This body revolved upon its axis, and exhibited the phenomena of all celestial bodies abandoned in space.

"Ah!" exclaimed Michel Ardan, "What is that? another projectile?"

Barbicane did not answer. The appearance of this enormous body surprised and troubled him. A collision was possible, and might be attended with deplorable results; either the projectile would deviate from its path, or a shock, breaking its impetus, might precipitate it to earth; or, lastly, it might be irresistibly drawn away by the powerful asteroid. The president caught at a glance the consequences of these three hypotheses, either of which would, one way or the other, bring their experiment to an unsuccessful and fatal termination. His companions stood silently looking into space. The object grew rapidly as it approached them, and by an optical illusion the projectile seemed to be throwing itself before it.

"By Jove!" exclaimed Michel Ardan, "we shall run into one another!"

Instinctively the travellers drew back. Their dread was great, but it did not last many seconds. The asteroid passed several hundred yards from the projectile and disappeared, not so much from the rapidity of its course, as that its face being opposite the moon, it was suddenly merged into the perfect darkness of space.

"A happy journey to you," exclaimed Michel Ardan, with a sigh of relief. "Surely infinity of space is large enough for a poor little projectile to walk through without fear. Now, what is this portentous globe which nearly struck us?"

"I know," replied Barbicane.

"Oh, indeed! you know everything."

"It is," said Barbicane, "a simple meteorite, but an enormous one, which the attraction of the earth has retained as a satellite."

"Is it possible!" exclaimed Michel Ardan; "the earth then has two moons like Neptune?"

"Yes, my friends, two moons, though it passes generally for having only one; but this second moon is so small, and its speed so great, that the inhabitants of the earth cannot see it. It was by noticing disturbances that a French astronomer, M. Petit, was able to determine the existence of this second satellite and calculate its elements. According to his observations, this meteorite will accomplish its revolution around the earth in three hours and twenty minutes, which implies a wonderful rate of speed."

"Do all astronomers admit the existence of this satellite?" asked Nicholl.

"No," replied Barbicane; "but if, like us, they had met it, they could no longer doubt it. Indeed, I think that this meteorite, which, had it struck the projectile, would have much embarrassed us, will give us the means of deciding what our position in space is."

"How?" said Ardan.

"Because its distance is known, and when we met it, we were exactly four thousand six hundred and fifty miles from the surface of the terrestrial globe."

"More than two thousand French leagues," exclaimed Michel Ardan. "That beats the express trains of the pitiful globe called the earth."

"I should think so," replied Nicholl, consulting his chronometer; "it is eleven o'clock, and it is only thirteen minutes since we left the American continent."

"Only thirteen minutes?" said Barbicane.

"Yes," said Nicholl; "and if our initiatory speed of twelve thousand yards has been kept up, we shall have made about twenty thousand miles in the hour."

"That is all very well, my friends," said the president, "but the insoluble question still remains. Why did we not hear the detonation of the *Columbiad*?"

For want of an answer the conversation dropped, and Barbicane began thoughtfully to let down the shutter of the second side. He succeeded; and through the uncovered glass the moon filled the projectile with a brilliant light. Nicholl, as an economical man, put out the gas, now useless, and whose brilliancy prevented any observation of the interplanetary space.

The lunar disc shone with wonderful purity. Her rays, no longer filtered through the vapoury atmosphere of the terrestrial globe, shone through the glass, filling the air in the interior of the projectile with silvery reflections. The black curtain of the firmament in reality heightened the moon's brilliancy, which in this void of ether unfavorable to diffusion did not eclipse the neighbouring stars. The heavens, thus seen, presented quite a new aspect, and one which the human eye could never dream of. One may conceive the interest with which these bold men watched the orb of night, the great aim of their journey.

In its motion the earth's satellite was insensibly nearing the zenith, the mathematical point which it ought to attain ninety-six hours later. Her mountains, her plains, every projection was as clearly discernible to their eyes as if they were observing it from some spot upon the earth; but its light was developed through space with wonderful intensity. The disc shone like a platinum mirror. Of the earth flying from under their feet, the travellers had lost all recollection.

It was Captain Nicholl who first recalled their attention to the vanishing globe.

"Yes," said Michel Ardan, "do not let us be ungrateful to it. Since we are leaving our country, let our last looks be directed to it. I wish to see the earth once more before it is quite hidden from my eyes."

To satisfy his companions, Barbicane began to uncover the window at the bottom of the projectile, which would allow them to observe the earth direct. The disc, which the force of the projection had beaten down to the base, was removed, not without difficulty. Its fragments, placed carefully against a wall, might serve again upon occasion. Then a circular gap appeared, nineteen inches in diameter, hollowed out of the lower part of the projectile. A glass cover, six inches thick and strengthened with upper fastenings, closed it tightly. Beneath was fixed an aluminum plate, held in place by bolts. The screws being undone, and the bolts let go, the plate fell down, and visible communication was established between the interior and the exterior.

Michel Ardan knelt by the glass. It was cloudy, seemingly opaque.

"Well!" he exclaimed, "and the earth?"

"The earth?" said Barbicane. "There it is."

"What! that little thread; that silver crescent?"

"Doubtless, Michel. In four days, when the moon will be full, at the very time we shall reach it, the earth will be new, and will only appear to us as a slender crescent which will soon disappear, and for some days will be enveloped in utter darkness."

"That the earth?" repeated Michel Ardan, looking with all his eyes at the thin slip of his native planet.

The explanation given by President Barbicane was correct. The earth, with respect to the projectile, was entering its last phase. It was in its octant, and showed a crescent finely traced on the dark background of the sky. Its light, rendered bluish by the thick strata of the atmosphere was less intense than that of the crescent moon, but it was of considerable dimensions, and looked like an enormous arch stretched across the firmament. Some parts brilliantly lighted, especially on its concave part, showed the presence of high mountains, often disappearing behind thick spots, which are never seen on the lunar disc. They were rings of clouds placed concentrically round the terrestrial globe.

While the travellers were trying to pierce the profound darkness, a brilliant cluster of shooting-stars burst upon their eyes. Hundreds of meteorites, ignited by the friction of the atmosphere, irradiated the shadow of the luminous train, and lined the cloudy parts of the disc with their fire. At this period the earth was in its perihelium, and the month of December is so propitious to these shooting-stars, that astronomers have counted as many as twenty-four thousand in an hour. But Michel Ardan, disdaining scientific reasonings, preferred thinking that the earth was thus saluting the departure of her three children with her most brilliant fireworks.

Indeed this was all they saw of the globe lost in the solar world, rising and setting to the great planets like a simple morning or evening star! This globe, where they had left all their affections, was nothing more than a fugitive crescent!

Long did the three friends look without speaking, though united in heart, while the projectile sped onward with an ever-decreasing speed. Then an irresistible drowsiness crept over their brain. Was it weariness of body and mind? No doubt; for after the over-excitement of those last hours passed upon earth, reaction was inevitable.

"Well," said Nicholl, "since we must sleep, let us sleep."

And stretching themselves on their couches, they were all three soon in a profound slumber.

But they had not forgotten themselves more than a quarter of an hour, when Barbicane sat up suddenly, and rousing his companions with a loud voice, exclaimed—

"I have found it!"

"What have you found?" asked Michel Ardan, jumping from his bed.

"The reason why we did not hear the detonation of the *Columbiad*."

"And it is—?" said Nicholl.

"Because our projectile travelled faster than the sound!"

Chapter III

THEIR PLACE OF SHELTER

THIS CURIOUS BUT CERTAINLY CORRECT EXPLANATION ONCE GIVEN, THE THREE FRIENDS returned to their slumbers. Could they have found a calmer or more peaceful spot to sleep in? On the earth, houses, towns, cottages, and country feel every shock given to the exterior of the globe. On sea, the vessels rocked by the waves are still in motion; in the air, the balloon oscillates incessantly on the fluid strata of divers densities. This projectile alone, floating in perfect space, in the midst of perfect silence, offered perfect repose.

Thus the sleep of our adventurous travellers might have been indefinitely prolonged, if an unexpected noise had not awakened them at about seven o'clock in the morning of the 2d of December, eight hours after their departure.

This noise was a very natural barking.

"The dogs! it is the dogs!" exclaimed Michel Ardan, rising at once.

"They are hungry," said Nicholl.

"By Jove!" replied Michel, "we have forgotten them."

"Where are they?" asked Barbicane.

They looked and found one of the animals crouched under the divan. Terrified and shaken by the initiatory shock, it had remained in the corner till its voice returned with the pangs of hunger. It was the amiable Diana, still very confused, who crept out of her retreat, though not without much persuasion, Michel Ardan encouraging her with most gracious words.

"Come, Diana," said he; "come, my girl! thou whose destiny will be marked in the cynegetic annals; thou whom the pagans would have given as companion to the god Anubis, and Christians as friend to St. Roch; thou who art rushing into interplanetary space, and wilt perhaps be the Eve of all Selenite dogs! come, Diana, come here."

Diana, flattered or not, advanced by degrees, uttering plaintive cries.

"Good," said Barbicane: "I see Eve, but where is Adam?"

"Adam?" replied Michel; "Adam cannot be far off; he is there somewhere; we must call him. Satellite! here, Satellite!"

But Satellite did not appear. Diana would not leave off howling. They found, however, that she was not bruised, and they gave her a pie, which silenced her complaints. As to Satellite, he seemed quite lost. They had to hunt a long time before finding him in one of the upper compartments of the projectile, whither some unaccountable shock must have violently hurled him. The poor beast, much hurt, was in a piteous state.

"The devil!" said Michel.

They brought the unfortunate dog down with great care. Its skull had been broken against the roof, and it seemed unlikely that he could recover from such a shock. Meanwhile, he was stretched comfortably on a cushion. Once there, he heaved a sigh.

"We will take care of you," said Michel; "we are responsible for your existence. I would rather lose an arm than a paw of my poor Satellite."

Saying which, he offered some water to the wounded dog, who swallowed it with avidity.

This attention paid, the travellers watched the earth and the moon attentively. The earth was now only discernible by a cloudy disc ending in a crescent, rather more contracted than that of the previous evening; but its expanse was still enormous, compared with that of the moon, which was approaching nearer and nearer to a perfect circle.

"By Jove!" said Michel Ardan, "I am really sorry that we did not start when the earth was full, that is to say, when our globe was in opposition to the sun."

"Why?" said Nicholl.

"Because we should have seen our continents and seas in a new light—the first resplendent under the solar rays, the latter cloudy as represented on some maps of the world. I should like to have seen those poles of the earth on which the eye of man has never yet rested."

"I daresay," replied Barbicane; "but if the earth had been *full*, the moon would have been *new*; that is to say, invisible, because of the rays of the sun. It is better for us to see the destination we wish to reach, than the point of departure."

"You are right, Barbicane," replied Captain Nicholl; "and, besides, when we have reached the moon, we shall have time during the long lunar nights to consider at our leisure the globe on which our likenesses swarm."

"Our likenesses!" exclaimed Michel Ardan; "they are no more our likenesses than the Selenites are! We inhabit a new world, peopled by ourselves—the projectile! I am Barbicane's likeness, and Barbicane is Nicholl's. Beyond us, around us, human nature is at an end, and we are the only population of this microcosm until we become pure Selenites."

"In about eighty-eight hours," replied the captain.

"Which means to say?" asked Michel Ardan.

"That it is half-past eight," replied Nicholl.

"Very well," retorted Michel; "then it is impossible for me to find even the shadow of a reason why we should not go to breakfast."

Indeed the inhabitants of the new star could not live without eating, and their stomachs were suffering from the imperious laws of hunger. Michel Ardan, as a Frenchman, was declared chief cook, an important function, which raised no rival. The gas gave sufficient heat for the culinary apparatus, and the provision-box furnished the elements of this first feast.

The breakfast began with three bowls of excellent soup, thanks to the liquefaction in hot water of those precious cakes of Liebig, prepared from the best parts of the ruminants of the Pampas. To the soup succeeded some beefsteaks, compressed by an hydraulic press, as tender and succulent as if brought straight from the kitchen of an English eating-house. Michel, who was imaginative, maintained that they were even "red."

Preserved vegetables ("fresher than nature," said the amiable Michel) succeeded the dish of meat; and was followed by some cups of tea with bread and butter, after the American fashion.

The beverage was declared exquisite, and was due to the infusion of the choicest leaves, of which the emperor of Russia had given some chests for the benefit of the travellers.

And lastly, to crown the repast, Ardan had brought out a fine bottle of Nuits, which was found "by chance" in the provision-box. The three friends drank to the union of the earth and her satellite.

And, as if he had not already done enough for the generous wine which he had distilled on the slopes of Burgundy, the sun chose to be part of the party. At this moment the projectile emerged from the conical shadow cast by the terrestrial globe, and the rays of the radiant orb struck the lower disc of the projectile direct, occasioned by the angle which the moon's orbit makes with that of the earth.

"The sun!" exclaimed Michel Ardan.

"No doubt," replied Barbicane; "I expected it."

"But," said Michel, "the conical shadow which the earth leaves in space extends beyond the moon?"

"Far beyond it, if the atmospheric refraction is not taken into consideration," said Barbicane. "But when the moon is enveloped in this shadow, it is because the centres of the three stars, the sun, the earth, and the moon, are all in one and the same straight line. Then the *nodes* coincide with the *phases* of the moon, and there is an eclipse. If we had started when there was an eclipse of the moon, all our passage would have been in the shadow, which would have been a pity."

"Why?"

"Because, though we are floating in space, our projectile, bathed in the solar rays, will receive light and heat. It economises the gas, which is in every respect a good economy."

Indeed, under these rays which no atmosphere can temper, either in temperature or brilliancy, the projectile grew warm and bright, as if it had passed suddenly from winter to summer. The moon above, the sun beneath, were inundating it with their fire.

"It is pleasant here," said Nicholl.

"I should think so," said Michel Ardan. "With a little earth spread on our aluminum planet we should have green peas in twenty-four hours. I have but one fear, which is that the walls of the projectile might melt."

"Calm yourself, my worthy friend," replied Barbicane; "the projectile withstood a very much higher temperature than this as it slid through the strata of the atmosphere. I should not be surprised if it did not look like a meteor on fire to the eyes of the spectators in Florida."

"But then Joseph T. Maston will think we are roasted!"

"What astonishes me," said Barbicane, "is that we have not been. That was a danger we had not provided for."

"I feared it," said Nicholl simply.

"And you never mentioned it, my sublime captain," exclaimed Michel Ardan, clasping his friend's hand.

Barbicane now began to settle himself in the projectile as if he was never to leave it. One must remember that this aerial car had a base with a *superficies* of fifty-four square feet. Its height to the roof was twelve feet. Carefully laid out in the inside, and little encumbered by instruments and travelling utensils, which each had their particular place, it left the three travellers a certain freedom of movement. The thick window inserted in the bottom could bear any amount of weight, and Barbicane and his companions walked upon it as if it were solid plank; but the sun striking it directly with its rays lit the interior of the projectile from beneath, thus producing singular effects of light.

They began by investigating the state of their store of water and provisions, neither of which had suffered, thanks to the care taken to deaden the shock. Their provisions were abundant, and plentiful enough to last the three travellers for more than a year. Barbicane wished to be cautious, in case the projectile should land on a part of the moon which was utterly barren. As to water and the reserve of brandy, which consisted of fifty gallons, there was only enough for two months; but according to the last observations of astronomers, the moon had a low, dense, and thick atmosphere, at least in the deep valleys, and there springs and streams could not fail. Thus, during their passage, and for the first year of their settlement on the lunar continent, these adventurous explorers would suffer neither hunger nor thirst.

Now about the air in the projectile. There, too, they were secure. Reiset and Regnaut's apparatus, intended for the production of oxygen, was supplied with chlorate of potassium for two months. They necessarily consumed a certain quantity of gas, for they were obliged to keep the producing substance at a temperature of above 400°. But there again they were all safe. The apparatus only wanted a little care. But it was not enough to renew the oxygen; they must absorb the carbonic acid produced by expiration. During the last twelve hours the atmosphere of the projectile had become charged with this deleterious gas. Nicholl discovered the state of the air by observing Diana panting painfully. The carbonic acid, by a phenomenon similar to that produced in the famous Grotto del Cane, had collected at the bottom of the projectile owing to its weight. Poor Diana, with her head low, would suffer before her masters from the presence of this gas. But Captain Nicholl hastened to remedy this state of things, by placing on the floor several receivers containing caustic potash, which he shook about for a time, and this substance, greedy of carbonic acid, soon completely absorbed it, thus purifying the air.

An inventory of instruments was then begun. The thermometers and barometers had resisted, all but one minimum thermometer, the glass of which was broken. An excellent aneroid was drawn from the wadded box which contained it and hung on the wall. Of course it was only affected by and marked the pressure of the air inside the projectile, but it also showed the quantity of moisture which it contained. At that moment its needle oscillated between 25.24 and 25.08.

It was fine weather.

Barbicane had also brought several compasses, which he found intact. One must understand that under present conditions their needles were acting *wildly,* that is without any *constant* direction. Indeed, at the distance they were from the earth, the magnetic pole could have no perceptible action upon the apparatus; but the box placed on the lunar disc might perhaps exhibit some strange phenomena. In any case it would be interesting to see whether the earth's satellite submitted like herself to its magnetic influence.

A hypsometer to measure the height of the lunar mountains, a sextant to take the height of the sun, glasses which would be useful as they neared the moon, all these instruments were carefully looked over, and pronounced good in spite of the violent shock.

As to the pickaxes and different tools which were Nicholl's especial choice; as to the sacks of different kinds of grain and shrubs which Michel Ardan hoped to transplant into Selenite ground, they were stowed away in the upper part of the projectile. There was a sort of granary there, loaded with things which the extravagant Frenchman had heaped up. What they were no one knew, and the good-tempered fellow did not explain. Now and then he climbed up by cramp-irons riveted to the walls, but kept the inspection to himself. He arranged and rearranged, he plunged his hand rapidly into certain mysterious boxes, singing in one of the falsest of voices an old French refrain to enliven the situation.

Barbicane observed with some interest that his guns and other arms had not been damaged. These were important, because, heavily loaded, they were to help lessen the fall of the projectile, when drawn by the lunar attraction (after having passed the point of neutral attraction) on to the moon's surface; a fall which ought to be six times less rapid than it would have been on the earth's surface, thanks to the difference of bulk. The inspection ended with general satisfaction, when each returned to watch space through the side windows and the lower glass coverlid.

There was the same view. The whole extent of the celestial sphere swarmed with stars and constellations of wonderful purity, enough to drive an astronomer out of his mind! On one side the sun, like the mouth of a lighted oven, a dazzling disc without a halo, standing out on the dark background of the sky! On the other, the moon returning its fire by reflection, and apparently motionless in the midst of the starry world. Then, a large spot seemingly nailed to the firmament, bordered by a silvery cord: it was the earth! Here and there nebulous masses like large flakes of starry snow; and from the zenith to the nadir, an immense ring formed by an impalpable dust of stars, the "Milky Way," in the midst of which the sun ranks only as a star of the fourth magnitude. The observers could not take their eyes from this novel spectacle, of which no description could give an adequate idea. What reflections it suggested! What emotions hitherto unknown awoke in their souls! Barbicane wished to begin the relation of his journey while under its first impressions, and hour after hour took notes of all facts happening in the beginning of the enterprise. He wrote quietly, with his large square writing, in a business-like style.

During this time Nicholl, the calculator, looked over the minutes of their passage, and worked out figures with unparallelled dexterity. Michel Ardan chatted first with Barbicane, who did not answer him, and then with Nicholl, who did not hear him, with Diana, who understood none of his theories, and lastly with himself, questioning and answering, going and coming, busy with a thousand details; at one time bent over the lower glass, at another roosting in the heights of the projectile, and always singing. In this microcosm he represented French loquacity and excitability, and we beg you to believe that they were well represented. The day, or rather (for the expression is not correct) the lapse of twelve hours, which forms a day upon the earth, closed with a plentiful supper carefully prepared. No accident of any nature had yet happened to shake the travellers' confidence; so, full of hope, already sure of success, they slept peacefully, while the projectile under a uniformly decreasing speed was crossing the sky.

Chapter IV

A LITTLE ALGEBRA

THE NIGHT PASSED WITHOUT INCIDENT. THE WORD "NIGHT," HOWEVER, IS SCARCELY applicable.

The position of the projectile with regard to the sun did not change. Astronomically, it was daylight on the lower part, and night on the upper; so when during this narrative these words are used, they represent the lapse of time between rising and setting of the sun upon the earth.

The travellers' sleep was rendered more peaceful by the projectile's excessive speed, for it seemed absolutely motionless. Not a motion betrayed its onward course through space. The rate of progress, however rapid it might be, cannot produce any sensible effect on the human frame when it takes place in a vacuum, or when the mass of air circulates with the body which is carried with it. What inhabitant of the earth perceives its speed, which, however, is at the rate of 68,000 miles per hour? Motion under such conditions is "felt" no more than repose; and when a body is in repose it will remain so as long as no strange force displaces it; if moving, it will not stop unless an obstacle comes in its way. This indifference to motion or repose is called inertia.

Barbicane and his companions might have believed themselves perfectly stationary, being shut up in the projectile; indeed, the effect would have been the same if they had been on the outside of it. Had it not been for the moon, which was increasing above them, they might have sworn that they were floating in complete stagnation.

That morning, the 3d of December, the travellers were awakened by a joyous but unexpected noise; it was the crowing of a cock which sounded through the car. Michel Ardan, who was the first on his feet, climbed to the top of the projectile, and shutting a box, the lid of which was partly open, said in a low voice, "Will you hold your tongue? That creature will spoil my design!"

But Nicholl and Barbicane were awake.

"A cock!" said Nicholl.

"Why no, my friends," Michel answered quickly; "it was I who wished to awake you by this rural sound." So saying, he gave vent to a splendid cock-a-doodledoo, which would have done honour to the proudest of poultry-yards.

The two Americans could not help laughing.

"Fine talent that," said Nicholl, looking suspiciously at his companion.

"Yes," said Michel; "a joke in my country. It is very Gallic; they play the cock so in the best society."

Then turning the conversation:

"Barbicane, do you know what I have been thinking of all night?"

"No," answered the president.

"Of our Cambridge friends. You have already remarked that I am an ignoramus in mathematical subjects; and it is impossible for me to find out how the savants of the observatory were able to calculate what initiatory speed the projectile ought to have on leaving the *Columbiad* in order to attain the moon."

"You mean to say," replied Barbicane, "to attain that neutral point where the terrestrial and lunar attractions are equal; for, starting from that point, situated about nine-tenths of the distance travelled over, the projectile would simply fall upon the moon, on account of its weight."

"So be it," said Michel; "but, once more; how could they calculate the initiatory speed?"

"Nothing can be easier," replied Barbicane.

"And you knew how to make that calculation?" asked Michel Ardan.

"Perfectly. Nicholl and I would have made it, if the observatory had not saved us the trouble."

"Very well, old Barbicane," replied Michel; "they might have cut off my head, beginning at my feet, before they could have made me solve that problem."

"Because you do not know algebra," answered Barbicane quietly.

"Ah, there you are, you eaters of x^1; you think you have said all when you have said 'Algebra.'"

"Michel," said Barbicane, "can you use a forge without a hammer, or a plow without a plowshare?"

"Hardly."

"Well, algebra is a tool, like the plow or the hammer, and a good tool to those who know how to use it."

"Seriously?"

"Quite seriously."

"And can you use that tool in my presence?"

"If it will interest you."

"And show me how they calculated the initiatory speed of our car?"

"Yes, my worthy friend; taking into consideration all the elements of the problem, the distance from the centre of the earth to the centre of the moon, of the radius of the earth, of its bulk, and of the bulk of the moon, I can tell exactly what ought to be the initiatory speed of the projectile, and that by a simple formula."

"Let us see."

"You shall see it; only I shall not give you the real course drawn by the projectile between the moon and the earth in considering their motion round the sun. No, I shall consider these two orbs as perfectly motionless, which will answer all our purpose."

"And why?"

"Because it will be trying to solve the problem called 'the problem of the three bodies,' for which the integral calculus is not yet far enough advanced."

"Then," said Michel Ardan, in his sly tone, "mathematics have not said their last word?"

"Certainly not," replied Barbicane.

"Well, perhaps the Selenites have carried the integral calculus farther than you have; and, by the by, what is this 'integral calculus?'"

"It is a calculation the converse of the differential," replied Barbicane seriously.

"Much obliged; it is all very clear, no doubt."

"And now," continued Barbicane, "a slip of paper and a bit of pencil, and before a half-hour is over I will have found the required formula."

Half-an-hour had not elapsed before Barbicane, raising his head, showed Michel Ardan a page covered with algebraical signs, in which the general formula for the solution was contained.

"Well, and does Nicholl understand what that means?"

"Of course, Michel," replied the captain. "All these signs, which seem cabalistic to you, form the plainest, the clearest, and the most logical language to those who know how to read it."

"And you pretend, Nicholl," asked Michel, "that by means of these hieroglyphics, more incomprehensible than the Egyptian Ibis, you can find what initiatory speed it was necessary to give the projectile?"

"Incontestably," replied Nicholl; "and even by this same formula I can always tell you its speed at any point of its transit."

"On your word?"

"On my word."

"Then you are as cunning as our president."

"No, Michel; the difficult part is what Barbicane has done; that is, to get an equation which shall satisfy all the conditions of the problem. The remainder is only a question of arithmetic, requiring merely the knowledge of the four rules."

"That is something!" replied Michel Ardan, who for his life could not do addition right, and who defined the rule as a Chinese puzzle, which allowed one to obtain all sorts of totals.

"The expression ν zero, which you see in that equation, is the speed which the projectile will have on leaving the atmosphere."

"Just so," said Nicholl; "it is from that point that we must calculate the velocity, since we know already that the velocity at departure was exactly one and a half times more than on leaving the atmosphere."

"I understand no more," said Michel.

"It is a very simple calculation," said Barbicane.

"Not as simple as I am," retorted Michel.

"That means, that when our projectile reached the limits of the terrestrial atmosphere it had already lost one-third of its initiatory speed."

"As much as that?"

"Yes, my friend; merely by friction against the atmospheric strata. You understand that the faster it goes the more resistance it meets with from the air."

"That I admit," answered Michel; "and I understand it, although your x's and zero's, and algebraic formula, are rattling in my head like nails in a bag."

"First effects of algebra," replied Barbicane; "and now, to finish, we are going to prove the given number of these different expressions, that is, work out their value."

"Finish me!" replied Michel.

Barbicane took the paper, and began to make his calculations with great rapidity. Nicholl looked over and greedily read the work as it proceeded.

"That's it! that's it!" at last he cried.

"Is it clear?" asked Barbicane.

"It is written in letters of fire," said Nicholl.

"Wonderful fellows!" muttered Ardan.

"Do you understand it at last?" asked Barbicane.

"Do I understand it?" cried Ardan; "my head is splitting with it."

"And now," said Nicholl, "to find out the speed of the projectile when it left the atmosphere, we have only to calculate that."

The captain, as a practical man equal to all difficulties, began to write with frightful rapidity. Divisions and multiplications grew under his fingers; the figures were like hail on the white page. Barbicane watched him, while Michel Ardan nursed a growing headache with both hands.

"Very well?" asked Barbicane, after some minutes' silence.

"Well!" replied Nicholl; "every calculation made, ν zero, that is to say, the speed necessary for the projectile on leaving the atmosphere, to enable it to reach the equal point of attraction, ought to be—"

"Yes?" said Barbicane.

"Twelve thousand yards."

"What!" exclaimed Barbicane, starting; "you say—"

"Twelve thousand yards."

"The devil!" cried the president, making a gesture of despair.

"What is the matter?" asked Michel Ardan, much surprised.

"What is the matter! why, if at this moment our speed had already diminished one-third by friction, the initiatory speed ought to have been—"

"Seventeen thousand yards."

"And the Cambridge Observatory declared that twelve thousand yards was enough at starting; and our projectile, which only started with that speed—"

"Well?" asked Nicholl.

"Well, it will not be enough."

"Good."

"We shall not be able to reach the neutral point."

"The deuce!"

"We shall not even get half-way."

"In the name of the projectile!" exclaimed Michel Ardan, jumping as if it was already on the point of striking the terrestrial globe.

"And we shall fall back upon the earth!"

Chapter V

THE COLD OF SPACE

THIS REVELATION CAME LIKE A THUNDERBOLT. WHO COULD HAVE EXPECTED SUCH AN error in calculation? Barbicane would not believe it. Nicholl revised his figures: they were exact. As to the formula which had determined them, they could not suspect its truth; it was evident that an initiatory velocity of seventeen thousand yards in the first second was necessary to enable them to reach the neutral point.

The three friends looked at each other silently. There was no thought of breakfast. Barbicane, with clenched teeth, knitted brows, and hands clasped convulsively, was watching through the window. Nicholl had crossed his arms, and was examining his calculations. Michel Ardan was muttering:

"That is just like these scientific men: they never do anything else. I would give twenty pistoles if we could fall upon the Cambridge Observatory and crush it, together with the whole lot of dabblers in figures which it contains."

Suddenly a thought struck the captain, which he at once communicated to Barbicane.

"Ah!" said he; "it is seven o'clock in the morning; we have already been gone thirty-two hours; more than half our passage is over, and we are not falling that I am aware of."

Barbicane did not answer, but after a rapid glance at the captain, took a pair of compasses wherewith to measure the angular distance of the terrestrial globe; then from the lower window he took an exact observation, and noticed that the projectile was apparently stationary. Then rising and wiping his forehead, on which large drops of perspiration were standing, he put some figures on paper. Nicholl understood that the president was deducting from the terrestrial diameter the projectile's distance from the earth. He watched him anxiously.

"No," exclaimed Barbicane, after some moments, "no, we are not falling! no, we are already more than 50,000 leagues from the earth. We have passed the point at which the projectile would have stopped if its speed had only been 12,000 yards at starting. We are still going up."

"That is evident," replied Nicholl; "and we must conclude that our initial speed, under the power of the 400,000 pounds of gun-cotton, must have exceeded the required 12,000 yards. Now I can understand how, after thirteen minutes only, we met the second satellite, which gravitates round the earth at more than 2,000 leagues' distance."

"And this explanation is the more probable," added Barbicane, "because, in throwing off the water enclosed between its partition-breaks, the projectile found itself lightened of a considerable weight."

"Just so," said Nicholl.

"Ah, my brave Nicholl, we are saved!"

"Very well then," said Michel Ardan quietly; "as we are safe, let us have breakfast."

Nicholl was not mistaken. The initial speed had been, very fortunately, much above that estimated by the Cambridge Observatory; but the Cambridge Observatory had nevertheless made a mistake.

The travellers, recovered from this false alarm, breakfasted merrily. If they ate a good deal, they talked more. Their confidence was greater after than before "the incident of the algebra."

"Why should we not succeed?" said Michel Ardan; "why should we not arrive safely? We are launched; we have no obstacle before us, no stones in the way; the road is open, more so than that of a ship battling with the sea; more open than that of a balloon battling with the wind; and if a ship can reach its destination, a balloon go where it pleases, why cannot our projectile attain its end and aim?"

"It *will* attain it," said Barbicane.

"If only to do honour to the Americans," added Michel Ardan, "the only people who could bring such an enterprise to a happy termination, and the only one which could produce a President Barbicane. Ah, now we are no longer uneasy, I begin to think, What will become of us? We shall get right royally weary."

Barbicane and Nicholl made a gesture of denial.

"But I have provided for the contingency, my friends," replied Michel; "you have only to speak, and I have chess, draughts, cards, and dominoes at your disposal; nothing is wanting but a billiard-table."

"What!" exclaimed Barbicane; "you brought away such trifles?"

"Certainly," replied Michel, "and not only to distract ourselves, but also with the laudable intention of endowing the Selenite smoking divans with them."

"My friend," said Barbicane, "if the moon is inhabited, its inhabitants must have appeared some thousands of years before those of the earth, for we cannot doubt that their star is much older than ours. If then these Selenites have existed their hundreds of thousands of years, and if their brain is of the same organisation of the human brain, they have already invented all that we have invented, and even what we may invent in future ages. They have nothing to learn from *us*, and we have everything to learn from *them*."

"What!" said Michel; "you believe that they have artists like Phidias, Michael Angelo, or Raphael?"

"Yes."

"Poets like Homer, Virgil, Milton, Lamartine, and Hugo?"

"I am sure of it."

"Philosophers like Plato, Aristotle, Descartes, Kant?"

"I have no doubt of it."

"Scientific men like Archimedes, Euclid, Pascal, Newton?"

"I could swear it."

"Comic writers like Arnal, and photographers like—like Nadar?"

"Certain."

"Then, friend Barbicane, if they are as strong as we are, and even stronger—these Selenites—why have they not tried to communicate with the earth? why have they not launched a lunar projectile to our terrestrial regions?"

"Who told you that they have never done so?" said Barbicane seriously.

"Indeed," added Nicholl, "it would be easier for them than for us, for two reasons; first, because the attraction on the moon's surface is six times less than on that of the earth, which would allow a projectile to rise more easily; secondly, because it would be enough to send such a projectile only at 8,000 leagues instead of 80,000, which would require the force of projection to be ten times less strong."

"Then," continued Michel, "I repeat it, why have they not done it?"

"And I repeat," said Barbicane; "who told you that they have not done it?"

"When?"

"Thousands of years before man appeared on earth."

"And the projectile—where is the projectile? I demand to see the projectile."

"My friend," replied Barbicane, "the sea covers five-sixths of our globe. From that we may draw five good reasons for supposing that the lunar projectile, if ever launched, is now at the bottom of the Atlantic or the Pacific, unless it sped into some crevasse at that period when the crust of the earth was not yet hardened."

"Old Barbicane," said Michel, "you have an answer for everything, and I bow before your wisdom. But there is one hypothesis that would suit me better than all the others, which is, the Selenites, being older than we, are wiser, and have not invented gunpowder."

At this moment Diana joined in the conversation by a sonorous barking. She was asking for her breakfast.

"Ah!" said Michel Ardan, "in our discussion we have forgotten Diana and Satellite."

Immediately a good-sized pie was given to the dog, which devoured it hungrily.

"Do you see, Barbicane," said Michel, "we should have made a second Noah's ark of this projectile, and borne with us to the moon a couple of every kind of domestic animal."

"I daresay; but room would have failed us."

"Oh!" said Michel, "we might have squeezed a little."

"The fact is," replied Nicholl, "that cows, bulls, and horses, and all ruminants, would have been very useful on the lunar continent, but unfortunately the car could neither have been made a stable nor a shed."

"Well, we might have at least brought a donkey, only a little donkey; that courageous beast which old Silenus loved to mount. I love those old donkeys; they are the least favoured animals in creation; they are not only beaten while alive, but even after they are dead."

"How do you make that out?" asked Barbicane.

"Why," said Michel, "they make their skins into drums."

Barbicane and Nicholl could not help laughing at this ridiculous remark. But a cry from their merry companion stopped them. The latter was leaning over the spot where Satellite lay. He rose, saying:

"My good Satellite is no longer ill."

"Ah!" said Nicholl.

"No," answered Michel, "he is dead! There," added he, in a piteous tone, "that is embarrassing. I much fear, my poor Diana, that you will leave no progeny in the lunar regions!"

Indeed the unfortunate Satellite had not survived its wound. It was quite dead. Michel Ardan looked at his friends with a rueful countenance.

"One question presents itself," said Barbicane. "We cannot keep the dead body of this dog with us for the next forty-eight hours."

"No! certainly not," replied Nicholl; "but our scuttles are fixed on hinges; they can be let down. We will open one, and throw the body out into space."

The president thought for some moments, and then said:

"Yes, we must do so, but at the same time taking very great precautions."

"Why?" asked Michel.

"For two reasons which you will understand," answered Barbicane. "The first relates to the air shut up in the projectile, and of which we must lose as little as possible."

"But we manufacture the air?"

"Only in part. We make only the oxygen, my worthy Michel; and with regard to that, we must watch that the apparatus does not furnish the oxygen in too great a quantity; for an excess would bring us very serious physiological troubles. But if we make the oxygen, we do not make the azote, that medium which the lungs do not absorb, and which ought to remain intact; and that azote will escape rapidly through the open scuttles."

"Oh! the time for throwing out poor Satellite?" said Michel.

"Agreed; but we must act quickly."

"And the second reason?" asked Michel.

"The second reason is that we must not let the outer cold, which is excessive, penetrate the projectile or we shall be frozen to death."

"But the sun?"

"The sun warms our projectile, which absorbs its rays; but it does not warm the vacuum in which we are floating at this moment. Where there is no air, there is no more heat than diffused light; and the same with darkness; it is cold where the sun's rays do not strike direct. This temperature is only the temperature produced by the radiation of the stars; that is to say, what the terrestrial globe would undergo if the sun disappeared one day."

"Which is not to be feared," replied Nicholl.

"Who knows?" said Michel Ardan. "But, in admitting that the sun does not go out, might it not happen that the earth might move away from it?"

"There!" said Barbicane, "there is Michel with his ideas."

"And," continued Michel, "do we not know that in 1861 the earth passed through the tail of a comet? Or let us suppose a comet whose power of attraction is greater than that of the sun. The terrestrial orbit will bend towards the wandering star, and the earth, becoming its satellite, will be drawn such a distance that the rays of the sun will have no action on its surface."

"That *might* happen, indeed," replied Barbicane, "but the consequences of such a displacement need not be so formidable as you suppose."

"And why not?"

"Because the heat and cold would be equalised on our globe. It has been calculated that, had our earth been carried along in its course by the comet of 1861, at its perihelion, that is, its nearest approach to the sun, it would have undergone a heat 28,000 times greater than that of summer. But this heat, which is sufficient to evaporate the waters, would have formed a thick ring of cloud, which would have modified that excessive temperature; hence the compensation between the cold of the aphelion and the heat of the perihelion."

"At how many degrees," asked Nicholl, "is the temperature of the planetary spaces estimated?"

"Formerly," replied Barbicane, "it was greatly exagerated; but now, after the calculations of Fourier, of the French Academy of Science, it is not supposed to exceed 60° Centigrade below zero."

"Pooh!" said Michel, "that's nothing!"

"It is very much," replied Barbicane; "the temperature which was observed in the polar regions, at Melville Island and Fort Reliance, that is 76° Fahrenheit below zero."

"If I mistake not," said Nicholl, "M. Pouillet, another savant, estimates the temperature of space at 250° Fahrenheit below zero. We shall, however, be able to verify these calculations for ourselves."

"Not at present; because the solar rays, beating directly upon our thermometer, would give, on the contrary, a very high temperature. But, when we arrive in the moon, during its fifteen days of night at either face, we shall have leisure to make the experiment, for our satellite lies in a vacuum."

"What do you mean by a vacuum?" asked Michel. "Is it perfectly such?"

"It is absolutely void of air."

"And is the air replaced by nothing whatever?"

"By the ether only," replied Barbicane.

"And pray what is the ether?"

"The ether, my friend, is an agglomeration of imponderable atoms, which, relatively to their dimensions, are as far removed from each other as the celestial bodies are in space. It is these atoms which, by their vibratory motion, produce both light and heat in the universe."

They now proceeded to the burial of Satellite. They had merely to drop him into space, in the same way that sailors drop a body into the sea; but, as President Barbicane suggested, they must act quickly, so as to lose as little as possible of that air whose elasticity would rapidly have spread it into space. The bolts of the right scuttle, the opening of which measured about twelve inches across, were carefully drawn, while Michel, quite grieved, prepared to launch his dog into space. The glass, raised by a powerful lever, which enabled it to overcome the pressure of the inside air on the walls of the projectile, turned rapidly on its hinges, and Satellite was thrown out. Scarcely a particle of air could have escaped, and the operation was so successful that later on Barbicane did not fear to dispose of the rubbish which encumbered the car.

Chapter VI

QUESTION AND ANSWER

O N THE 4TH OF DECEMBER, WHEN THE TRAVELLERS AWOKE AFTER FIFTY-FOUR HOURS' journey, the chronometer marked five o'clock of the terrestrial morning. In time it was just over five hours and forty minutes, half of that assigned to their sojourn in the projectile; but they had already accomplished nearly seven-tenths of the way. This peculiarity was due to their regularly decreasing speed.

Now when they observed the earth through the lower window, it looked like nothing more than a dark spot, drowned in the solar rays. No more crescent, no more cloudy light! The next day, at midnight, the earth would be *new*, at the very moment when the moon would be full. Above, the orb of night was nearing the line followed by the projectile, so as to meet it at the given hour. All around the black vault was studded with brilliant points, which seemed to move slowly; but, at the great distance they were from them, their relative size did not seem to change. The sun and stars appeared exactly as they do to us upon earth. As to the moon, she was considerably larger; but the travellers' glasses, not very powerful, did not allow them as yet to make any useful observations upon her surface, or reconnoitre her topographically or geologically.

Thus the time passed in never-ending conversations all about the moon. Each one brought forward his own contingent of particular facts; Barbicane and Nicholl always serious, Michel Ardan always enthusiastic. The projectile, its situation, its direction, incidents which might happen, the precautions necessitated by their fall on to the moon, were inexhaustible matters of conjecture.

As they were breakfasting, a question of Michel's, relating to the projectile, provoked rather a curious answer from Barbicane, which is worth repeating. Michel, supposing it to be roughly stopped, while still under its formidable initial speed, wished to know what the consequences of the stoppage would have been.

"But," said Barbicane, "I do not see how it could have been stopped."

"But let us suppose so," said Michel.

"It is an impossible supposition," said the practical Barbicane; "unless that impulsive force had failed; but even then its speed would diminish by degrees, and it would not have stopped suddenly."

"Admit that it had struck a body in space."

"What body?"

"Why that enormous meteor which we met."

"Then," said Nicholl, "the projectile would have been broken into a thousand pieces, and we with it."

"More than that," replied Barbicane; "we should have been burned to death."

"Burned?" exclaimed Michel, "by Jove! I am sorry it did not happen, 'just to see.' "

"And you would have seen," replied Barbicane. "It is known now that heat is only a modification of motion. When water is warmed—that is to say, when heat is added to it—its particles are set in motion."

"Well," said Michel, "that is an ingenious theory!"

"And a true one, my worthy friend; for it explains every phenomenon of caloric. Heat is but the motion of atoms, a simple oscillation of the particles of a body. When they apply the brake to a train, the train comes to a stop; but what becomes of the motion which it had previously possessed? It is transformed into heat, and the brake becomes hot. Why do they grease the axles of the wheels? To prevent their heating, because this heat would be generated by the motion which is thus lost by transformation."

"Yes, I understand," replied Michel, "perfectly. For example, when I have run a long time, when I am swimming, when I am perspiring in large drops, why am I obliged to stop? Simply because my motion is changed into heat."

Barbicane could not help smiling at Michel's reply; then, returning to his theory, said:

"Thus, in case of a shock, it would have been with our projectile as with a ball which falls in a burning state after having struck the metal plate; it is its motion which is turned into heat. Consequently I affirm that, if our projectile had struck the meteor, its speed thus suddenly checked would have raised a heat great enough to turn it into vapour instantaneously."

"Then," asked Nicholl, "what would happen if the earth's motion were to stop suddenly?"

"Her temperature would be raised to such a pitch," said Barbicane, "that she would be at once reduced to vapor."

"Well," said Michel, "that is a way of ending the earth which will greatly simplify things."

"And if the earth fell upon the sun?" asked Nicholl.

"According to calculation," replied Barbicane, "the fall would develop a heat equal to that produced by 16,000 globes of coal, each equal in bulk to our terrestrial globe."

"Good additional heat for the sun," replied Michel Ardan, "of which the inhabitants of Uranus or Neptune would doubtless not complain; they must be perished with cold on their planets."

"Thus, my friends," said Barbicane, "all motion suddenly stopped produces heat. And this theory allows us to infer that the heat of the solar disc is fed by a hail of meteors falling incessantly on its surface. They have even calculated—"

"Oh, dear!" murmured Michel, "the figures are coming."

"They have even calculated," continued the imperturbable Barbicane, "that the shock of each meteor on the sun ought to produce a heat equal to that of 4,000 masses of coal of an equal bulk."

"And what is the solar heat?" asked Michel.

"It is equal to that produced by the combustion of a stratum of coal surrounding the sun to a depth of forty-seven miles."

"And that heat—"

"Would be able to boil two billions nine hundred millions of cubic myriameters* of water."

"And it does not roast us!" exclaimed Michel.

"No," replied Barbicane, "because the terrestrial atmosphere absorbs four-tenths of

*The myriameter is equal to rather more than 10,936 cubic yards English.

the solar heat; besides, the quantity of heat intercepted by the earth is but a billionth part of the entire radiation."

"I see that all is for the best," said Michel, "and that this atmosphere is a useful invention; for it not only allows us to breathe, but it prevents us from roasting."

"Yes!" said Nicholl, "unfortunately, it will not be the same in the moon."

"Bah!" said Michel, always hopeful. "If there are inhabitants, they must breathe. If there are no longer any, they must have left enough oxygen for three people, if only at the bottom of ravines, where its own weight will cause it to accumulate, and we will not climb the mountains; that is all." And Michel, rising, went to look at the lunar disc, which shone with intolerable brilliancy.

"By Jove!" said he, "it must be hot up there!"

"Without considering," replied Nicholl, "that the day lasts 360 hours!"

"And to compensate that," said Barbicane, "the nights have the same length; and as heat is restored by radiation, their temperature can only be that of the planetary space."

"A pretty country, that!" exclaimed Michel. "Never mind! I wish I was there! Ah! my dear comrades, it will be rather curious to have the earth for our moon, to see it rise on the horizon, to recognise the shape of its continents, and to say to oneself, 'There is America, there is Europe'; then to follow it when it is about to lose itself in the sun's rays! By the by, Barbicane, have the Selenites eclipses?"

"Yes, eclipses of the sun," replied Barbicane, "when the centres of the three orbs are on a line, the earth being in the middle. But they are only partial, during which the earth, cast like a screen upon the solar disc, allows the greater portion to be seen."

"And why," asked Nicholl, "is there no total eclipse? Does not the cone of the shadow cast by the earth extend beyond the moon?"

"Yes, if we do not take into consideration the refraction produced by the terrestrial atmosphere. No, if we take that refraction into consideration. Thus let δ be the horizontal parallel, and p the apparent semidiameter—"

"Oh!" said Michel. "Do speak plainly, you man of algebra!"

"Very well," replied Barbicane; "in popular language the mean distance from the moon to the earth being sixty terrestrial radii, the length of the cone of the shadow, on account of refraction, is reduced to less than forty-two radii. The result is that when there are eclipses, the moon finds itself beyond the cone of pure shadow, and that the sun sends her its rays, not only from its edges, but also from its centre."

"Then," said Michel, in a merry tone, "why are there eclipses, when there ought not to be any?"

"Simply because the solar rays are weakened by this refraction, and the atmosphere through which they pass extinguished the greater part of them!"

"That reason satisfies me," replied Michel. "Besides we shall see when we get there. Now, tell me, Barbicane, do you believe that the moon is an old comet?"

"There's an idea!"

"Yes," replied Michel, with an amiable swagger, "I have a few ideas of that sort."

"But that idea does not spring from Michel," answered Nicholl.

"Well, then, I am a plagiarist."

"No doubt about it. According to the ancients, the Arcadians pretend that their ancestors inhabited the earth before the moon became her satellite. Starting from this fact, some scientific men have seen in the moon a comet whose orbit will one day bring it so near to the earth that it will be held there by its attraction."

"Is there any truth in this hypothesis?" asked Michel.

"None whatever," said Barbicane, "and the proof is, that the moon has preserved no trace of the gaseous envelope which always accompanies comets."

"But," continued Nicholl, "before becoming the earth's satellite, could not the moon, when in her perihelion, pass so near the sun as by evaporation to get rid of all those gaseous substances?"

"It is possible, friend Nicholl, but not probable."

"Why not?"

"Because—Faith I do not know."

"Ah!" exclaimed Michel, "what hundred of volumes we might make of all that we do not know!"

"Ah! indeed. What time is it?" asked Barbicane.

"Three o'clock," answered Nicholl.

"How time goes," said Michel, "in the conversation of scientific men such as we are! Certainly, I feel I know too much! I feel that I am becoming a well!"

Saying which, Michel hoisted himself to the roof of the projectile, "to observe the moon better," he pretended. During this time his companions were watching through the lower glass. Nothing new to note!

When Michel Ardan came down, he went to the side scuttle; and suddenly they heard an exclamation of surprise!

"What is it?" asked Barbicane.

The president approached the window, and saw a sort of flattened sack floating some yards from the projectile. This object seemed as motionless as the projectile, and was consequently animated with the same ascending movement.

"What is that machine?" continued Michel Ardan. "Is it one of the bodies which our projectile keeps within its attraction, and which will accompany it to the moon?"

"What astonishes me," said Nicholl, "is that the specific weight of the body, which is certainly less than that of the projectile, allows it to keep so perfectly on a level with it."

"Nicholl," replied Barbicane, after a moment's reflection, "I do not know what the object is, but I do know why it maintains our level."

"And why?"

"Because we are floating in space, my dear captain, and in space bodies fall or move (which is the same thing) with equal speed whatever be their weight or form; it is the air, which by its resistance creates these differences in weight. When you create a vacuum in a tube, the objects you send through it, grains of dust or grains of lead, fall with the same rapidity. Here in space is the same cause and the same effect."

"Just so," said Nicholl, "and everything we throw out of the projectile will accompany it until it reaches the moon."

"Ah! fools that we are!" exclaimed Michel.

"Why that expletive?" asked Barbicane.

"Because we might have filled the projectile with useful objects, books, instruments, tools, etc. We could have thrown them all out, and all would have followed in our train. But happy thought! Why cannot we walk outside like the meteor? Why cannot we launch into space through the scuttle? What enjoyment it would be to feel oneself thus suspended in ether, more favoured than the birds who must use their wings to keep themselves up!"

"Granted," said Barbicane, "but how to breathe?"

"Hang the air, to fail so inopportunely!"

"But if it did not fail, Michel, your density being less than that of the projectile, you would soon be left behind."

"Then we must remain in our car?"

"We must!"

"Ah!" exclaimed Michel, in a loud voice.

"What is the matter," asked Nicholl.

"I know, I guess, what this pretended meteor is! It is no asteroid which is accompanying us! It is not a piece of a planet."

"What is it then?" asked Barbicane.

"It is our unfortunate dog! It is Diana's husband!"

Indeed, this deformed, unrecognizable object, reduced to nothing, was the body of Satellite, flattened like a bagpipe without wind, and ever mounting, mounting!

Chapter VII

A Moment of Intoxication

THUS A PHENOMENON, CURIOUS BUT EXPLICABLE, WAS HAPPENING UNDER THESE strange conditions.

Every object thrown from the projectile would follow the same course and never stop until it did. There was a subject for conversation which the whole evening could not exhaust.

Besides, the excitement of the three travellers increased as they drew near the end of their journey. They expected unforseen incidents, and new phenomena; and nothing would have astonished them in the frame of mind they then were in. Their overexcited imagination went faster than the projectile, whose speed was evidently diminishing, though insensibly to themselves. But the moon grew larger to their eyes, and they fancied if they stretched out their hands they could seize it.

The next day, the 5th of December, at five in the morning, all three were on foot. That day was to be the last of their journey, if all calculations were true. That very night, at twelve o'clock, in eighteen hours, exactly at the full moon, they would reach its brilliant disc. The next midnight would see that journey ended, the most extraordinary of ancient or modern times. Thus from the first of the morning, through the scuttles silvered by its rays, they saluted the orb of night with a confident and joyous hurrah.

The moon was advancing majestically along the starry firmament. A few more degrees, and she would reach the exact point where her meeting with the projectile was to take place.

According to his own observations, Barbicane reckoned that they would land on her northern hemisphere, where stretch immense plains, and where mountains are rare. A favourable circumstance if, as they thought, the lunar atmosphere was stored only in its depths.

"Besides," observed Michel Ardan, "a plain is easier to disembark upon than a mountain. A Selenite, deposited in Europe on the summit of Mont Blanc, or in Asia on the top of the Himalayas, would not be quite in the right place."

"And," added Captain Nicholl, "on a flat ground, the projectile will remain motionless when it has once touched; whereas on a declivity it would roll like an avalanche, and not being squirrels we should not come out safe and sound. So it is all for the best."

Indeed, the success of the audacious attempt no longer appeared doubtful. But Barbicane was preoccupied with one thought; but not wishing to make his companions uneasy, he kept silence on this subject.

The direction the projectile was taking towards the moon's northern hemisphere, showed that her course had been slightly altered. The discharge, mathematically calculated, would carry the projectile to the very centre of the lunar disc. If it did not land there, there must have been some deviation. What had caused it? Barbicane could neither imagine nor determine the importance of the deviation, for there were no points to go by.

He hoped, however, that it would have no other result than that of bringing them nearer the upper border of the moon, a region more suitable for landing.

Without imparting his uneasiness to his companions, Barbicane contented himself with constantly observing the moon, in order to see whether the course of the projectile would not be altered; for the situation would have been terrible if it failed in its aim, and being carried beyond the disc should be launched into interplanetary space. At that moment, the moon, instead of appearing flat like a disc, showed its convexity. If the sun's rays had struck it obliquely, the shadow thrown would have brought out the high mountains, which would have been clearly detached. The eye might have gazed into the crater's gaping abysses, and followed the capricious fissures which wound through the immense plains. But all relief was as yet levelled in intense brilliancy. They could scarcely distinguish those large spots which give the moon the appearance of a human face.

"Face, indeed!" said Michel Ardan; "but I am sorry for the amiable sister of Apollo. A very pitted face!"

But the travellers, now so near the end, were incessantly observing this new world. They imagined themselves walking through its unknown countries, climbing its highest peaks, descending into its lowest depths. Here and there they fancied they saw vast seas, scarcely kept together under so rarefied an atmosphere, and water-courses emptying the mountain tributaries. Leaning over the abyss, they hoped to catch some sounds from that orb forever mute in the solitude of space. That last day left them.

They took down the most trifling details. A vague uneasiness took possession of them as they neared the end. This uneasiness would have been doubled had they felt how their speed had decreased. It would have seemed to them quite insufficient to carry them to the end. It was because the projectile then "weighed" almost nothing. Its weight was ever decreasing, and would be entirely annihilated on that line where the lunar and terrestrial attractions would neutralise each other.

But in spite of his preoccupation, Michel Ardan did not forget to prepare the morning repast with his accustomed punctuality. They ate with a good appetite. Nothing was so excellent as the soup liquefied by the heat of the gas; nothing better than the preserved meat. Some glasses of good French wine crowned the repast, causing Michel Ardan to remark that the lunar vines, warmed by that ardent sun, ought to distill even more generous wines; that is, if they existed. In any case, the far-seeing Frenchman had taken care not to forget in his collection some precious cuttings of the Médoc and Côte d'Or, upon which he founded his hopes.

Reiset and Regnault's apparatus worked with great regularity. Not an atom of carbonic acid resisted the potash; and as to the oxygen, Captain Nicholl said "it was of the first quality." The little watery vapour enclosed in the projectile mixing with the air tempered the dryness; and many apartments in London, Paris, or New York, and many theatres, were certainly not in such a healthy condition.

But that it might act with regularity, the apparatus must be kept in perfect order; so each morning Michel visited the escape regulators, tried the taps, and regulated the heat of the gas by the pyrometer. Everything had gone well up to that time, and the travellers, imitating the worthy Joseph T. Maston, began to acquire a degree of embonpoint which would have rendered them unrecognizable if their imprisonment had been prolonged to some months. In a word, they behaved like chickens in a coop; they were getting fat.

In looking through the scuttle Barbicane saw the specter of the dog, and other divers objects which had been thrown from the projectile, obstinately following them. Diana howled lugubriously on seeing the remains of Satellite, which seemed as motionless as if they reposed on solid earth.

"Do you know, my friends," said Michel Ardan, "that if one of us had succumbed to the shock consequent on departure, we should have had a great deal of trouble to bury him? What am I saying? to *etherise* him, as here ether takes the place of earth. You see the accusing body would have followed us into space like a remorse."

"That would have been sad," said Nicholl.

"Ah!" continued Michel, "what I regret is not being able to take a walk outside. What voluptuousness to float amid this radiant ether, to bathe oneself in it, to wrap oneself in the sun's pure rays. If Barbicane had only thought of furnishing us with a diving apparatus and an air-pump, I could have ventured out and assumed fanciful attitudes of feigned monsters on the top of the projectile."

"Well, old Michel," replied Barbicane, "you would not have made a feigned monster long, for in spite of your diver's dress, swollen by the expansion of air within you, you would have burst like a shell, or rather like a balloon which has risen too high. So do not regret it, and do not forget this—as long as we float in space, all sentimental walks beyond the projectile are forbidden."

Michel Ardan allowed himself to be convinced to a certain extent. He admitted that the thing was difficult but not impossible, a word which he never uttered.

The conversation passed from this subject to another, not failing him for an instant. It seemed to the three friends as though, under present conditions, ideas shot up in their brains as leaves shoot at the first warmth of spring. They felt bewildered. In the middle of the questions and answers which crossed each other, Nicholl put one question which did not find an immediate solution.

"Ah, indeed!" said he; "it is all very well to go to the moon, but how to get back again?"

His two interlocutors looked surprised. One would have thought that this possibility now occurred to them for the first time.

"What do you mean by that, Nicholl?" asked Barbicane gravely.

"To ask for means to leave a country," added Michel, "when we have not yet arrived there, seems to me rather inopportune."

"I do not say that, wishing to draw back," replied Nicholl; "but I repeat my question, and I ask, 'How shall we return?' "

"I know nothing about it," answered Barbicane.

"And I," said Michel, "if I had known how to return, I would never have started."

"There's an answer!" cried Nicholl.

"I quite approve of Michel's words," said Barbicane; "and add, that the question has no real interest. Later, when we think it is advisable to return, we will take counsel together. If the *Columbiad* is not there, the projectile will be."

"That is a step certainly. A ball without a gun!"

"The gun," replied Barbicane, "can be manufactured. The powder can be made. Neither metals, saltpeter, nor coal can fail in the depths of the moon, and we need only go 8,000 leagues in order to fall upon the terrestrial globe by virtue of the mere laws of weight."

"Enough," said Michel with animation. "Let it be no longer a question of returning: we have already entertained it too long. As to communicating with our former earthly colleagues, that will not be difficult."

"And how?"

"By means of meteors launched by lunar volcanoes."

"Well thought of, Michel," said Barbicane in a convinced tone of voice. "Laplace has calculated that a force five times greater than that of our gun would suffice to send a meteor from the moon to the earth, and there is not one volcano which has not a greater power of propulsion than that."

"Hurrah!" exclaimed Michel; "these meteors are handy postmen, and cost nothing. And how we shall be able to laugh at the post-office administration! But now I think of it—"

"What do you think of?"

"A capital idea. Why did we not fasten a thread to our projectile, and we could have exchanged telegrams with the earth?"

"The deuce!" answered Nicholl. "Do you consider the weight of a thread 250,000 miles long nothing?"

"As nothing. They could have trebled the *Columbiad*'s charge; they could have quadrupled or quintupled it!" exclaimed Michel, with whom the verb took a higher intonation each time.

"There is but one little objection to make to your proposition," replied Barbicane, "which is that, during the rotary motion of the globe, our thread would have wound itself round it like a chain on a capstan, and that it would inevitably have brought us to the ground."

"By the thirty-nine stars of the Union!" said Michel, "I have nothing but impracticable ideas to-day; ideas worthy of J. T. Maston. But I have a notion that, if we do not return to earth, J. T. Maston will be able to come to us."

"Yes, he'll come," replied Barbicane; "he is a worthy and a courageous comrade. Besides, what is easier? Is not the *Columbiad* still buried in the soil of Florida? Is cotton and nitric acid wanted wherewith to manufacture the pyroxyle? Will not the moon pass the zenith of Florida? In eighteen years' time will she not occupy exactly the same place as to-day?"

"Yes," continued Michel, "yes, Maston will come, and with him our friends Elphinstone, Blomsberry, all the members of the Gun Club, and they will be well received. And by and by they will run trains of projectiles between the earth and the moon! Hurrah for J. T. Maston!"

It is probable that, if the Hon. J. T. Maston did not hear the hurrahs uttered in his honour, his ears at least tingled. What was he doing then? Doubtless, posted in the Rocky Mountains, at the station of Long's Peak, he was trying to find the invisible projectile gravitating in space. If he was thinking of his dear companions, we must allow that they were not far behind him; and that, under the influence of a strange excitement, they were devoting to him their best thoughts.

But whence this excitement, which was evidently growing upon the tenants of the projectile? Their sobriety could not be doubted. This strange irritation of the brain, must it be attributed to the peculiar circumstances under which they found themselves, to their proximity to the orb of night, from which only a few hours separated them, to some secret influence of the moon acting upon their nervous system? Their faces were as rosy as if they had been exposed to the roaring flames of an oven; their voices resounded in loud accents; their words escaped like a champagne cork driven out by carbonic acid; their gestures became annoying, they wanted so much room to perform them; and, strange to say, they none of them noticed this great tension of the mind.

"Now," said Nicholl, in a short tone, "now that I do not know whether we shall ever return from the moon, I want to know what we are going to do there?"

"What we are going to do there?" replied Barbicane, stamping with his foot as if he was in a fencing saloon; "I do not know."

"You do not know!" exclaimed Michel, with a bellow which provoked a sonorous echo in the projectile.

"No, I have not even thought about it," retorted Barbicane, in the same loud tone.

"Well, I know," replied Michel.

"Speak, then," cried Nicholl, who could no longer contain the growling of his voice.

"I shall speak if it suits me," exclaimed Michel, seizing his companions' arms with violence.

"*It must* suit you," said Barbicane, with an eye on fire and a threatening hand. "It was you who drew us into this frightful journey, and we want to know what for."

"Yes," said the captain, "now that I do not know *where* I am going, I want to know *why* I am going."

"Why?" exclaimed Michel, jumping a yard high, "why? To take possession of the moon in the name of the United States; to add a fortieth State to the Union; to colonise the lunar regions; to cultivate them, to people them, to transport thither all the prodigies of art, of science, and industry; to civilise the Selenites, unless they are more civilised than we are; and to constitute them a republic, if they are not already one!"

"And if there are no Selenites?" retorted Nicholl, who, under the influence of this unaccountable intoxication, was very contradictory.

"Who said that there were no Selenites?" exclaimed Michel in a threatening tone.

"I do," howled Nicholl.

"Captain," said Michel, "do not repreat that insolence, or I will knock your teeth down your throat!"

The two adversaries were going to fall upon each other, and the incoherent discussion threatened to merge into a fight, when Barbicane intervened with one bound.

"Stop, miserable men," said he, separating his two companions; "if there are no Selenites, we will do without them."

"Yes," exclaimed Michel, who was not particular; "yes, we will do without them. We have only to make Selenites. Down with the Selenites!"

"The empire of the moon belongs to us," said Nicholl.

"Let us three constitute the republic."

"I will be the congress," cried Michel.

"And I the senate," retorted Nicholl.

"And Barbicane, the president," howled Michel.

"Not a president elected by the nation," replied Barbicane.

"Very well, a president elected by the congress," cried Michel; "and as I am the congress, you are unanimously elected!"

"Hurrah! hurrah! hurrah! for President Barbicane," exclaimed Nicholl.

"Hip! hip! hip!" vociferated Michel Ardan.

Then the president and the senate struck up in a tremendous voice the popular song "Yankee Doodle," while from the congress resounded the masculine tones of the "Marseillaise."

Then they struck up a frantic dance, with maniacal gestures, idiotic stampings, and somersaults like those of the boneless clowns in the circus. Diana, joining in the dance, and howling in her turn, jumped to the top of the projectile. An unaccountable flapping of wings was then heard amid most fantastic cock-crows, while five or six hens fluttered like bats against the walls.

Then the three travelling companions, acted upon by some unaccountable influence above that of intoxication, inflamed by the air which had set their respiratory apparatus on fire, fell motionless to the bottom of the projectile.

Chapter VIII

AT SEVENTY-EIGHT THOUSAND FIVE HUNDRED AND FOURTEEN LEAGUES

WHAT HAD HAPPENED? WHENCE THE CAUSE OF THIS SINGULAR INTOXICATION, THE consequences of which might have been very disastrous? A simple blunder of Michel's, which, fortunately, Nicholl was able to correct in time.

After a perfect swoon, which lasted some minutes, the captain, recovering first, soon collected his scattered senses. Although he had breakfasted only two hours before, he felt a gnawing hunger, as if he had not eaten anything for several days. Everything about him, stomach and brain, were overexcited to the highest degree. He got up and demanded from Michel a supplementary repast. Michel, utterly done up, did not answer.

Nicholl then tried to prepare some tea destined to help the absorption of a dozen sandwiches. He first tried to get some fire, and struck a match sharply. What was his surprise to see the sulphur shine with so extraordinary a brilliancy as to be almost unbearable to the eye. From the gas-burner which he lit rose a flame equal to a jet of electric light.

A revelation dawned on Nicholl's mind. That intensity of light, the physiological troubles which had arisen in him, the overexcitement of all his moral and quarrelsome faculties—he understood all.

"The oxygen!" he exclaimed.

And leaning over the air apparatus, he saw that the tap was allowing the colourless gas to escape freely, life-giving, but in its pure state producing the gravest disorders in the system. Michel had blunderingly opened the tap of the apparatus to the full.

Nicholl hastened to stop the escape of oxygen with which the atmosphere was saturated, which would have been the death of the travellers, not by suffocation, but by combustion. An hour later, the air less charged with it restored the lungs to their normal condition. By degrees the three friends recovered from their intoxication; but they were obliged to sleep themselves sobre over their oxygen as a drunkard does over his wine.

When Michel learned his share of the responsibility of this incident, he was not much disconcerted. This unexpected drunkenness broke the monotony of the journey. Many foolish things had been said while under its influence, but also quickly forgotten.

"And then," added the merry Frenchman, "I am not sorry to have tasted a little of this heady gas. Do you know, my friends, that a curious establishment might be founded with rooms of oxygen, where people whose system is weakened could for a few hours live a more active life. Fancy parties where the room was saturated with this heroic fluid, theatres where it should be kept at high pressure; what passion in the souls of the actors and spectators! what fire, what enthusiasm! And if, instead of an assembly only a whole people could be saturated, what activity in its functions, what a supplement to life it would derive. From an exhausted nation they might make a great and strong one, and I know more than one state in old Europe which ought to put itself under the regime of oxygen for the sake of its health!"

Michel spoke with so much animation that one might have fancied that the tap was still too open. But a few words from Barbicane soon shattered his enthusiasm.

"That is all very well, friend Michel," said he, "but will you inform us where these chickens came from which have mixed themselves up in our concert?"

"Those chickens?"

"Yes."

Indeed, half a dozen chickens and a fine cock were walking about, flapping their wings and chattering.

"Ah, the awkward things!" exclaimed Michel. "The oxygen has made them revolt."

"But what do you want to do with these chickens?" asked Barbicane.

"To acclimatise them in the moon, by Jove!"

"Then why did you hide them?"

"A joke, my worthy president, a simple joke, which has proved a miserable failure. I wanted to set them free on the lunar continent, without saying anything. Oh, what would have been your amazement on seeing these earthly-winged animals pecking in your lunar fields!"

"You rascal, you unmitigated rascal," replied Barbicane, "you do not want oxygen to mount to the head. You are always what we were under the influence of the gas; you are always foolish!"

"Ah, who says that we were not wise then?" replied Michel Ardan.

After this philosophical reflection, the three friends set about restoring the order of the projectile. Chickens and cock were reinstated in their coop. But while proceeding with this operation, Barbicane and his two companions had a most desired perception of a new phenomenon. From the moment of leaving the earth, their own weight, that of the projectile, and the objects it enclosed, had been subject to an increasing diminution. If they could not prove this loss of the projectile, a moment would arrive when it would be sensibly felt upon themselves and the utensils and instruments they used.

It is needless to say that a scale would not show this loss; for the weight destined to weigh the object would have lost exactly as much as the object itself; but a spring steelyard for example, the tension of which was independent of the attraction, would have given a just estimate of this loss.

We know that the attraction, otherwise called the weight, is in proportion to the densities of the bodies, and inversely as the squares of the distances. Hence this effect: If the earth had been alone in space, if the other celestial bodies had been suddenly annihilated, the projectile, according to Newton's laws, would weigh less as it got farther from the earth, but without ever losing its weight entirely, for the terrestrial attraction would always have made itself felt, at whatever distance.

But, in reality, a time must come when the projectile would no longer be subject to the law of weight, after allowing for the other celestial bodies whose effect could not be set down as zero. Indeed, the projectile's course was being traced between the earth and the moon. As it distanced the earth, the terrestrial attraction diminished: but the lunar attraction rose in proportion. There must come a point where these two attractions would neutralise each other: the projectile would possess weight no longer. If the moon's and the earth's densities had been equal, this point would have been at an equal distance between the two orbs. But taking the different densities into consideration, it was easy to reckon that this point would be situated at $\frac{47}{60}$ths of the whole journey, i. e., at 78,514 leagues from the earth. At this point, a body having no principle of speed or displacement in itself, would remain immovable forever, being attracted equally by both orbs, and not being drawn more towards one than towards the other.

Now if the projectile's impulsive force had been correctly calculated, it would attain this point without speed, having lost all trace of weight, as well as all the objects within it. What would happen then? Three hypotheses presented themselves.

1. Either it would retain a certain amount of motion, and pass the point of equal attraction, and fall upon the moon by virtue of the excess of the lunar attraction over the terrestrial.

2. Or, its speed failing, and unable to reach the point of equal attraction, it would fall upon the moon by virtue of the excess of the lunar attraction over the terrestrial.

3. Or, lastly, animated with sufficient speed to enable it to reach the neutral point, but

not sufficient to pass it, it would remain forever suspended in that spot like the pretended tomb of Mahomet, between the zenith and the nadir.

Such was their situation; and Barbicane clearly explained the consequences to his travelling companions, which greatly interested them. But how should they know when the projectile had reached this neutral point situated at that distance, especially when neither themselves, nor the objects enclosed in the projectile, would be any longer subject to the laws of weight?

Up to this time, the travellers, while admitting that this action was constantly decreasing, had not yet become sensible to its total absence.

But that day, about eleven o'clock in the morning, Nicholl having accidentally let a glass slip from his hand, the glass, instead of falling, remained suspended in the air.

"Ah!" exclaimed Michel Ardan, "that is rather an amusing piece of natural philosophy."

And immediately divers other objects, fire-arms and bottles, abandoned to themselves, held themselves up as by enchantment. Diana too, placed in space by Michel, reproduced, but without any trick, the wonderful suspension practiced by Caston and Robert Houdin. Indeed the dog did not seem to know that she was floating in air.

The three adventurous companions were surprised and stupefied, despite their scientific reasonings. They felt themselves being carried into the domain of wonders! they felt that weight was really wanting to their bodies. If they stretched out their arms, they did not attempt to fall. Their heads shook on their shoulders. Their feet no longer clung to the floor of the projectile. They were like drunken men having no stability in themselves.

Fancy has depicted men without reflection, others without shadow. But here reality, by the neutralisations of attractive forces, produced men in whom nothing had any weight, and who weighed nothing themselves.

Suddenly Michel, taking a spring, left the floor and remained suspended in the air, like Murillo's monk of the *Cusine des Anges*.

The two friends joined him instantly, and all three formed a miraculous "Ascension" in the centre of the projectile.

"Is it to be believed? is it probable? is it possible?" exclaimed Michel; "and yet it is so. Ah! if Raphael had seen us thus, what an 'Assumption' he would have thrown upon canvas!"

"The 'Assumption' cannot last," replied Barbicane. "If the projectile passes the neutral point, the lunar attraction will draw us to the moon."

"Then our feet will be upon the roof," replied Michel.

"No," said Barbicane, "because the projectile's centre of gravity is very low; it will only turn by degrees."

"Then all our portables will be upset from top to bottom, that is a fact."

"Calm yourself, Michel," replied Nicholl; "no upset is to be feared; not a thing will move, for the projectile's evolution will be imperceptible."

"Just so," continued Barbicane; "and when it has passed the point of equal attraction, its base, being the heavier, will draw it perpendicularly to the moon; but, in order that this phenomenon should take place, we must have passed the neutral line."

"Pass the neutral line," cried Michel; "then let us do as the sailors do when they cross the equator."

A slight side movement brought Michel back towards the padded side; thence he took a bottle and glasses, placed them "in space" before his companions, and, drinking merrily, they saluted the line with a triple hurrah. The influence of these attractions scarcely lasted an hour; the travellers felt themselves insensibly drawn towards the floor, and Barbicane fancied that the conical end of the projectile was varying a little from its normal direction towards the moon. By an inverse motion the base was approaching first; the lunar attraction was prevailing over the terrestrial; the fall towards the moon was beginning, almost imperceptibly as yet, but by degrees the attractive force would become stronger, the fall would be more decided, the projectile, drawn by its base, would turn its cone to the earth, and fall with ever-increasing speed on to the surface of the Selenite continent; their destination would then be attained. Now nothing could prevent the success of their enterprise, and Nicholl and Michel Ardan shared Barbicane's joy.

Then they chatted of all the phenomena which had astonished them one after the other, particularly the neutralisation of the laws of weight. Michel Ardan, always enthusiastic, drew conclusions which were purely fanciful.

"Ah, my worthy friends," he exclaimed, "what progress we should make if on earth we could throw off some of that weight, some of that chain which binds us to her; it would be the prisoner set at liberty; no more fatigue of either arms or legs. Or, if it is true that in order to fly on the earth's surface, to keep oneself suspended in the air merely by the play of the muscles, there requires a strength a hundred and fifty times greater than that which we possess, a simple act of volition, a caprice, would bear us into space, if attraction did not exist."

"Just so," said Nicholl, smiling; "if we could succeed in suppressing weight as they suppress pain by anaesthesia, that would change the face of modern society!"

"Yes," cried Michel, full of his subject, "destroy weight, and no more burdens!"

"Well said," replied Barbicane; "but if nothing had any weight, nothing would keep in its place, not even your hat on your head, worthy Michel; nor your house, whose stones only adhere by weight; nor a boat, whose stability on the waves is only caused by weight; not even the ocean, whose waves would no longer be equalised by terrestrial attraction; and lastly, not even the atmosphere, whose atoms, being no longer held in their places, would disperse in space!"

"That is tiresome," retorted Michel; "nothing like these matter-of-fact people for bringing one back to the bare reality."

"But console yourself, Michel," continued Barbicane, "for if no orb exists from whence all laws of weight are banished, you are at least going to visit one where it is much less than on the earth."

"The moon?"

"Yes, the moon, on whose surface objects weigh six times less than on the earth, a phenomenon easy to prove."

"And we shall feel it?" asked Michel.

"Evidently, as two hundred pounds will only weigh thirty pounds on the surface of the moon."

"And our muscular strength will not diminish?"

"Not at all; instead of jumping one yard high, you will rise eighteen feet high."

"But we shall be regular Herculeses in the moon!" exclaimed Michel.

"Yes," replied Nicholl; "for if the height of the Selenites is in proportion to the density of their globe, they will be scarcely a foot high."

"Lilliputians!" ejaculated Michel; "I shall play the part of Gulliver. We are going to realise the fable of the giants. This is the advantage of leaving one's own planet and overrunning the solar world."

"One moment, Michel," answered Barbicane; "if you wish to play the part of Gulliver, only visit the inferior planets, such as Mercury, Venus, or Mars, whose density is a little less than that of the earth; but do not venture into the great planets, Jupiter, Saturn, Uranus, Neptune; for there the order will be changed, and you will become Lilliputian."

"And in the sun?"

"In the sun, if its density is thirteen hundred and twenty-four thousand times greater, and the attraction is twenty-seven times greater than on the surface of our globe, keeping everything in proportion, the inhabitants ought to be at least two hundred feet high."

"By Jove!" exclaimed Michel; "I should be nothing more than a pigmy, a shrimp!"

"Gulliver with the giants," said Nicholl.

"Just so," replied Barbicane.

"And it would not be quite useless to carry some pieces of artillery to defend oneself."

"Good," replied Nicholl; "your projectiles would have no effect on the sun; they would fall back upon the earth after some minutes."

"That is a strong remark."

"It is certain," replied Barbicane; "the attraction is so great on this enormous orb, that an object weighing 70,000 pounds on the earth would weigh but 1,920 pounds on the surface of the sun. If you were to fall upon it you would weigh—let me see—about 5,000 pounds, a weight which you would never be able to raise again."

"The devil!" said Michel; "one would want a portable crane. However, we will be satisfied with the moon for the present; there at least we shall cut a great figure. We will see about the sun by and by."

Chapter IX

The Consequences of a Deviation

B ARBICANE HAD NOW NO FEAR OF THE ISSUE OF THE JOURNEY, AT LEAST AS FAR AS THE projectile's impulsive force was concerned; its own speed would carry it beyond the neutral line; it would certainly not return to earth; it would certainly not remain motionless on the line of attraction. One single hypothesis remained to be realised, the arrival of the projectile at its destination by the action of the lunar attraction.

It was in reality a fall of 8,296 leagues on an orb, it is true, where weight could only be reckoned at one-sixth of terrestrial weight; a formidable fall, nevertheless, and one against which every precaution must be taken without delay.

These precautions were of two sorts, some to deaden the shock when the projectile should touch the lunar soil, others to delay the fall, and consequently make it less violent.

To deaden the shock, it was a pity that Barbicane was no longer able to employ the means which had so ably weakened the shock at departure, that is to say, by water used as springs and the partition-breaks.

The partitions still existed but water failed, for they could not use their reserve, which was precious, in case during the first days the liquid element should be found wanting on lunar soil.

And indeed this reserve would have been quite insufficient for a spring. The layer of water stored in the projectile at the time of starting upon their journey occupied no less than three feet in depth, and spread over a surface of not less than fifty-four square feet. Besides, the cistern did not contain one-fifth part of it; they must therefore give up this efficient means of deadening the shock of arrival. Happily, Barbicane, not content with employing water, had furnished the movable disc with strong spring plugs, destined to lessen the shock against the base after the breaking of the horizontal partitions. These plugs still existed; they had only to readjust them and replace the movable disc; every piece, easy to handle, as their weight was now scarcely felt, was quickly mounted.

The different pieces were fitted without trouble, it being only a matter of bolts and screws; tools were not wanting, and soon the reinstated disc lay on steel plugs, like a table on its legs. One inconvenience resulted from the replacing of the disc, the lower window was blocked up; thus it was impossible for the travellers to observe the moon from that opening while they were being precipitated perpendicularly upon her; but they were obliged to give it up; even by the side openings they could still see vast lunar regions, as an aeronaut sees the earth from his car.

This replacing of the disc was at least an hour's work. It was past twelve when all preparations were finished. Barbicane took fresh observations on the inclination of the projectile, but to his annoyance it had not turned over sufficiently for its fall; it seemed to take a curve parallel to the lunar disc. The orb of night shone splendidly into space, while opposite, the orb of day blazed with fire.

Their situation began to make them uneasy.

"Are we reaching our destination?" said Nicholl.

"Let us act as if we were about reaching it," replied Barbicane.

"You are sceptical," retorted Michel Ardan. "We shall arrive, and that, too, quicker than we like."

This answer brought Barbicane back to his preparations, and he occupied himself with placing the contrivances intended to break their descent. We may remember the scene of the meeting held at Tampa Town, in Florida, when Captain Nicholl came forward as Barbicane's enemy and Michel Ardan's adversary. To Captain Nicholl's maintaining that the projectile would smash like glass, Michel replied that he would break their fall by means of rockets properly placed.

Thus, powerful fireworks, taking their starting-point from the base and bursting outside, could, by producing a recoil, check to a certain degree the projectile's speed. These rockets were to burn in space, it is true; but oxygen would not fail them, for they could supply themselves with it, like the lunar volcanoes, the burning of which has never yet been stopped by the want of atmosphere round the moon.

Barbicane had accordingly supplied himself with these fireworks, enclosed in little steel guns, which could be screwed on to the base of the projectile. Inside, these guns were flush with the bottom; outside, they protruded about eighteen inches. There were twenty of them. An opening left in the disc allowed them to light the match with which each was provided. All the effect was felt outside. The burning mixture had already been rammed into each gun. They had, then, nothing to do but raise the metallic buffers fixed in the base, and replace them by the guns, which fitted closely in their places.

This new work was finished about three o'clock, and after taking all these precautions there remained but to wait. But the projectile was perceptibly nearing the moon, and evidently succumbed to her influence to a certain degree; though its own velocity also drew it in an oblique direction. From these conflicting influences resulted a line which might become a tangent. But it was certain that the projectile would not fall directly on the moon; for its lower part, by reason of its weight, ought to be turned towards her.

Barbicane's uneasiness increased as he saw his projectile resist the influence of gravitation. The Unknown was opening before him, the Unknown in interplanetary space. The man of science thought he had foreseen the only three hypotheses possible—the return to the earth, the return to the moon, or stagnation on the neutral line; and here a fourth hypothesis, big with all the terrors of the Infinite, surged up inopportunely. To face it without flinching, one must be a resolute savant like Barbicane, a phlegmatic being like Nicholl, or an audacious adventurer like Michel Ardan.

Conversation was started upon this subject. Other men would have considered the question from a practical point of view; they would have asked themselves whither their projectile carriage was carrying them. Not so with these; they sought for the cause which produced this effect.

"So we have become diverted from our route," said Michel; "but why?"

"I very much fear," answered Nicholl, "that, in spite of all precautions taken, the *Columbiad* was not fairly pointed. An error, however small, would be enough to throw us out of the moon's attraction."

"Then they must have aimed badly?" asked Michel.

"I do not think so," replied Barbicane. "The perpendicularity of the gun was exact, its direction to the zenith of the spot incontestible; and the moon passing to the zenith of the spot, we ought to reach it at the full. There is another reason, but it escapes me."

"Are we not arriving too late?" asked Nicholl.

"Too late?" said Barbicane.

"Yes," continued Nicholl. "The Cambridge Observatory's note says that the transit ought to be accomplished in ninety-seven hours thirteen minutes and twenty seconds; which means to say, that *sooner* the moon will *not* be at the point indicated, and *later* it will have passed it."

"True," replied Barbicane. "But we started the 1st of December, at thirteen minutes and twenty-five seconds to eleven at night; and we ought to arrive on the 5th at midnight, at the exact moment when the moon would be full; and we are now at the 5th of December. It is now half-past three in the evening; half-past eight ought to see us at the end of our journey. Why do we not arrive?"

"Might it not be an excess of speed?" answered Nicholl; "for we know now that its initial velocity was greater than they supposed."

"No! a hundred times, no!" replied Barbicane. "An excess of speed, if the direction of the projectile had been right, would not have prevented us reaching the moon. No, there has been a deviation. We have been turned out of our course."

"By whom? by what?" asked Nicholl.

"I cannot say," replied Barbicane.

"Very well, then, Barbicane," said Michel, "do you wish to know my opinion on the subject of finding out this deviation?"

"Speak."

"I would not give half a dollar to know it. That we have deviated is a fact. Where we are going matters little; we shall soon see. Since we are being borne along in space we shall end by falling into some centre of attraction or other."

Michel Ardan's indifference did not content Barbicane. Not that he was uneasy about the future, but he wanted to know at any cost *why* his projectile had deviated.

But the projectile continued its course sideways to the moon, and with it the mass of things thrown out. Barbicane could even prove, by the elevations which served as landmarks upon the moon, which was only two thousand leagues distant, that its speed was becoming uniform—fresh proof that there was no fall. Its impulsive force still prevailed over the lunar attraction, but the projectile's course was certainly bringing it nearer to the moon, and they might hope that at a nearer point the weight, predominating, would cause a decided fall.

The three friends, having nothing better to do, continued their observations; but they could not yet determine the topographical position of the satellite; every relief was levelled under the reflection of the solar rays.

They watched thus through the side windows until eight o'clock at night. The moon had grown so large in their eyes that it filled half of the firmament. The sun on one side, and the orb of night on the other, flooded the projectile with light.

At that moment Barbicane thought he could estimate the distance which separated them from their aim at no more than 700 leagues. The speed of the projectile seemed to him to be more than 200 yards, or about 170 leagues a second. Under the centripetal force, the base of the projectile tended towards the moon; but the centrifugal still prevailed; and it was probable that its rectilineal course would be changed to a curve of some sort, the nature of which they could not at present determine.

Barbicane was still seeking the solution of his insoluble problem. Hours passed without any result. The projectile was evidently nearing the moon, but it was also evident that it would never reach her. As to the nearest distance at which it would pass her, that must be the result of two forces, attraction and repulsion, affecting its motion.

"I ask but one thing," said Michel; "that we may pass near enough to penetrate her secrets."

"Cursed be the thing that has caused our projectile to deviate from its course," cried Nicholl.

And, as if a light had suddenly broken in upon his mind, Barbicane answered, "Then cursed be the meteor which crossed our path."

"What?" said Michel Ardan.

"What do you mean?" exclaimed Nicholl.

"I mean," said Barbicane in a decided tone, "I mean that our deviation is owing solely to our meeting with this erring body."

"But it did not even brush us as it passed," said Michel.

"What does that matter? Its mass, compared to that of our projectile, was enormous, and its attraction was enough to influence our course."

"So little?" cried Nicholl.

"Yes, Nicholl; but however little it might be," replied Barbicane, "in a distance of 84,000 leagues, it wanted no more to make us miss the moon."

Chapter X

THE OBSERVERS OF THE MOON

BARBICANE HAD EVIDENTLY HIT UPON THE ONLY PLAUSIBLE REASON OF THIS DEVIATION. However slight it might have been, it had sufficed to modify the course of the projectile. It was a fatality. The bold attempt had miscarried by a fortuitous circumstance; and unless by some exceptional event, they could now never reach the moon's disc.

Would they pass near enough to be able to solve certain physical and geological questions until then insoluble? This was the question, and the only one, which occupied the minds of these bold travellers. As to the fate in store for themselves, they did not even dream of it.

But what would become of them amid these infinite solitudes, these who would soon want air? A few more days, and they would fall stifled in this wandering projectile. But some days to these intrepid fellows was a century; and they devoted all their time to observe that moon which they no longer hoped to reach.

The distance which had then separated the projectile from the satellite was estimated at about two hundred leagues. Under these conditions, as regards the visibility of the details of the disc, the travellers were farther from the moon than are the inhabitants of earth with their powerful telescopes.

Indeed, we know that the instrument mounted by Lord Rosse at Parsonstown, which magnifies 6,500 times, brings the moon to within an apparent distance of sixteen leagues. And more than that, with the powerful one set up at Long's Peak, the orb of night, magnified 48,000 times, is brought to within less than two leagues, and objects having a diameter of thirty feet are seen very distinctly. So that, at this distance, the topographical details of the moon, observed without glasses, could not be determined with precision. The eye caught the vast outline of those immense depressions inappropriately called "seas," but they could not recognise their nature. The prominence of the mountains disappeared under the splendid irradiation produced by the reflection of the solar rays. The eye, dazzled as if it was leaning over a bath of molten silver, turned from it involuntarily; but the oblong form of the orb was quite clear. It appeared like a gigantic egg, with the small end turned towards the earth. Indeed the moon, liquid and pliable in the first days of its formation, was originally a perfect sphere; but being soon drawn within the attraction of the earth, it became elongated under the influence of gravitation. In becoming a satellite, she lost her native purity of form; her centre of gravity was in advance of the centre of her figure; and from this fact some savants draw the conclusion that the air and water had taken refuge on the opposite surface of the moon, which is never seen from the earth. This alteration in the primitive form of the satellite was only perceptible for a few moments. The distance of the projectile from the moon diminished very rapidly under its speed, though that was much less than its initial velocity—but eight or nine times greater than that which propels our express trains. The oblique course of the projectile, from its very obliquity, gave Michel Ardan some hopes of striking the lunar disc at some point or other. He could not think that they would never reach it. No! he could not believe it; and this opinion he often repeated. But Barbicane, who was a better judge, always answered him with merciless logic.

"No, Michel, no! We can only reach the moon by a fall, and we are not falling. The centripetal force keeps us under the moon's influence, but the centrifugal force draws us irresistibly away from it."

This was said in a tone which quenched Michel Ardan's last hope.

The portion of the moon which the projectile was nearing was the northern hemisphere, that which the selenographic maps place below; for these maps are generally drawn after the outline given by the glasses, and we know that they reverse the objects. Such was the *Mappa Selenographica* of Bœer and Moëdler which Barbicane consulted. This northern hemisphere presented vast plains, dotted with isolated mountains.

At midnight the moon was full. At that precise moment the travellers should have alighted upon it, if the mischievous meteor had not diverted their course. The orb was exactly in the condition determined by the Cambridge Observatory. It was mathematically at its perigee, and at the zenith of the twenty-eighth parallel. An observer placed at the bottom of the enormous *Columbiad*, pointed perpendicularly to the horizon, would have framed the moon in the mouth of the gun. A straight line drawn through the axis of the piece would have passed through the centre of the orb of night. It is needless to say, that during the night of the 5th–6th of December, the travellers took not an instant's rest. Could they close their eyes when so near this new world? No! All their feelings were concentrated in one single thought:—See! Representatives of the earth, of humanity, past and present, all centered in them! It is through their eyes that the human race look at these lunar regions, and penetrate the secrets of their satellite! A strange emotion filled their hearts as they went from one window to the other. Their observations, reproduced by Barbicane, were rigidly determined. To take them, they had glasses; to correct them, maps.

As regards the optical instruments at their disposal, they had excellent marine glasses specially constructed for this journey. They possessed magnifying powers of 100. They would thus have brought the moon to within a distance (apparent) of less than 2,000 leagues from the earth. But then, at a distance which for three hours in the morning did not exceed sixty-five miles, and in a medium free from all atmospheric disturbances, these instruments could reduce the lunar surface to within less than 1,500 yards!

Chapter XI

FANCY AND REALITY

"HAVE YOU EVER SEEN THE MOON?" ASKED A PROFESSOR, IRONICALLY, OF ONE OF HIS pupils.

"No, sir!" replied the pupil, still more ironically, "but I must say I have heard it spoken of."

In one sense, the pupil's witty answer might be given by a large majority of sublunary beings. How many people have heard speak of the moon who have never seen it—at least through a glass or a telescope! How many have never examined the map of their satellite!

In looking at a selenographic map, one peculiarity strikes us. Contrary to the arrangement followed for that of the Earth and Mars, the continents occupy more particularly the southern hemisphere of the lunar globe. These continents do not show such decided, clear, and regular boundary lines as South America, Africa, and the Indian peninsula. Their angular, capricious, and deeply indented coasts are rich in gulfs and peninsulas. They remind one of the confusion in the islands of the Sound, where the land is excessively indented. If navigation ever existed on the surface of the moon, it must have been wonderfully difficult and dangerous; and we may well pity the Selenite sailors and hydrographers; the former, when they came upon these perilous coasts, the latter when they took the soundings of its stormy banks.

We may also notice that, on the lunar sphere, the south pole is much more continental than the north pole. On the latter, there is but one slight strip of land separated from other continents by vast seas. Towards the south, continents clothe almost the whole of the hemisphere. It is even possible that the Selenites have already planted the flag on one of their poles, while Franklin, Ross, Kane, Dumont, d'Urville, and Lambert have never yet been able to attain that unknown point of the terrestrial globe.

As to islands, they are numerous on the surface of the moon. Nearly all oblong or circular, and as if traced with the compass, they seem to form one vast archipelago, equal to that charming group lying between Greece and Asia Minor, and which mythology in ancient times adorned with most graceful legends. Involuntarily the names of Naxos, Tenedos, and Carpathos, rise before the mind, and we seek vainly for Ulysses' vessel or the "clipper" of the Argonauts. So at least it was in Michel Ardan's eyes. To him it was a Grecian archipelago that he saw on the map. To the eyes of his matter-of-fact companions, the aspect of these coasts recalled rather the parceled-out land of New Brunswick and Nova Scotia, and where the Frenchman discovered traces of the heroes of fable, these Americans were marking the most favourable points for the establishment of stores in the interests of lunar commerce and industry.

After wandering over these vast continents, the eye is attracted by the still greater seas. Not only their formation, but their situation and aspect remind one of the terrestrial oceans; but again, as on earth, these seas occupy the greater portion of the globe. But in point of fact, these are not liquid spaces, but plains, the nature of which the travellers hoped soon to determine. Astronomers, we must allow, have graced these pretended seas with at least odd names, which science has respected up to the present time. Michel Ardan was right when he compared this map to a "Tendre card," got up by a Scudary or a Cyrano de Bergerac. "Only," said he, "it is no longer the sentimental card of the seventeenth century; it is the card of life, very neatly divided into two parts, one feminine, the other masculine; the right hemisphere for woman, the left for man."

In speaking thus, Michel made his prosaic companions shrug their shoulders. Barbicane and Nicholl looked upon the lunar map from a very different point of view to that of their fantastic friend. Nevertheless, their fantastic friend was a little in the right. Judge for yourselves.

In the left hemisphere stretches the "Sea of Clouds," where human reason is so often shipwrecked. Not far off lies the "Sea of Rains," fed by all the fever of existence. Near this is the "Sea of Storms," where man is ever fighting against his passions, which too often gain the victory. Then, worn out by deceit, treasons, infidelity, and the whole body of terrestrial misery, what does he find at the end of his career? that vast "Sea of Humours," barely softened by some drops of the waters from the "Gulf of Dew!" Clouds, rain, storms, and humours—does the life of man contain aught but these? and is it not summed up in these four words?

The right hemisphere, "dedicated to the ladies," encloses smaller seas, whose significant names contain every incident of a feminine existence. There is the "Sea of Serenity," over which the young girl bends; "The Lake of Dreams," reflecting a joyous future; "The Sea of Nectar," with its waves of tenderness and breezes of love; "The Sea of Fruitfulness"; "The Sea of Crises"; then the "Sea of Vapours," whose dimensions are perhaps a little too confined; and lastly, that vast "Sea of Tranquillity," in which every false passion, every useless dream, every unsatisfied desire is at length absorbed, and whose waves emerge peacefully into the "Lake of Death!"

What a strange succession of names! What a singular division of the moon's two hemispheres, joined to one another like man and woman, and forming that sphere of life carried into space! And was not the fantastic Michel right in thus interpreting the fancies of the ancient astronomers? But while his imagination thus roved over "the seas," his grave companions were considering things more geographically. They were learning this new world by heart. They were measuring angles and diameters.

Chapter XII

OROGRAPHIC DETAILS

THE COURSE TAKEN BY THE PROJECTILE, AS WE HAVE BEFORE REMARKED, WAS BEARING it towards the moon's northern hemisphere. The travellers were far from the central point which they would have struck, had their course not been subject to an irremediable deviation. It was past midnight; and Barbicane then estimated the distance at seven hundred and fifty miles, which was a little greater than the length of the lunar radius, and which would diminish as it advanced nearer to the North Pole. The projectile was then not at the altitude of the equator; but across the tenth parallel, and from that latitude, carefully taken on the map to the pole, Barbicane and his two companions were able to observe the moon under the most favourable conditions. Indeed, by means of glasses, the above-named distance was reduced to little more than fourteen miles. The telescope of the Rocky Mountains brought the moon much nearer; but the terrestrial atmosphere singularly lessened its power. Thus Barbicane, posted in his projectile, with the glasses to his eyes, could seize upon details which were almost imperceptible to earthly observers.

"My friends," said the president, in a serious voice, "I do not know whither we are going; I do not know if we shall ever see the terrestrial globe again. Nevertheless, let us proceed as if our work would one day be useful to our fellow-men. Let us keep our minds free from every other consideration. We are astronomers; and this projectile is a room in the Cambridge University, carried into space. Let us make our observations!"

This said, work was begun with great exactness; and they faithfully reproduced the different aspects of the moon, at the different distances which the projectile reached.

At the time that the projectile was as high as the tenth parallel, north latitude, it seemed rigidly to follow the twentieth degree, east longitude. We must here make one important remark with regard to the map by which they were taking observations. In the selenographical maps where, on account of the reversing of the objects by the glasses, the south is above and the north below, it would seem natural that, on account of that inversion, the east should be to the left hand, and the west to the right. But it is not so. If the map were turned upside down, showing the moon as we see her, the east would be to the left, and the west to the right, contrary to that which exists on terrestrial maps. The following is the reason of this anomaly. Observers in the northern hemisphere (say in Europe) see the moon in the south—according to them. When they take observations, they turn their backs to the north, the reverse position to that which they occupy when they study a terrestrial map. As they turn their backs to the north, the east is on their left, and the west to their right. To observers in the southern hemisphere (Patagonia for example), the moon's west would be quite to their left, and the east to their right, as the south is behind them. Such is the reason of the apparent reversing of these two cardinal points, and we must bear it in mind in order to be able to follow President Barbicane's observations.

With the help of Bœer and Moëdler's *Mappa Selenographica*, the travellers were able at once to recognise that portion of the disc enclosed within the field of their glasses.

"What are we looking at, at this moment?" asked Michel.

"At the northern part of the 'Sea of Clouds,'" answered Barbicane. "We are too far off to recognise its nature. Are these plains composed of arid sand, as the first astronomer maintained? Or are they nothing but immense forests, according to M. Warren de la Rue's opinion, who gives the moon an atmosphere, though a very low and a very dense one? That we shall know by and by. We must affirm nothing until we are in a position to do so."

This "Sea of Clouds" is rather doubtfully marked out upon the maps. It is supposed that these vast plains are strewn with blocks of lava from the neighbouring volcanoes on its right, Ptolemy, Purbach, Arzachel. But the projectile was advancing, and sensibly nearing it. Soon there appeared the heights which bound this sea at this northern limit. Before them rose a mountain radiant with beauty, the top of which seemed lost in an irruption of solar rays.

"That is—?" asked Michel.

"Copernicus," replied Barbicane.

"Let us see Copernicus."

This mount, situated in 9° north latitude and 20° east longitude, rose to a height of 10,600 feet above the surface of the moon. It is quite visible from the earth; and astronomers can study it with ease, particularly during the phase between the last quarter and the new moon, because then the shadows are thrown lengthways from east to west, allowing them to measure the heights.

This Copernicus forms the most important of the radiating system, situated in the southern hemisphere, according to Tycho Brahé. It rises isolated like a gigantic lighthouse on that portion of the "Sea of Clouds," which is bounded by the "Sea of Tempests," thus lighting by its splendid rays two oceans at a time. It was a sight without an equal, those long luminous trains, so dazzling in the full moon, and which, passing the boundary chain on the north, extends to the "Sea of Rains." At one o'clock of the terrestrial morning, the projectile, like a balloon borne into space, overlooked the top of this superb mount. Barbicane could recognise perfectly its chief features. Copernicus is comprised in the series of ringed mountains of the first order, in the division of great circles. Like Kepler and Aristarchus, which overlook the "Ocean of Tempests," sometimes it appeared like a brilliant point through the cloudy light, and was taken for a volcano in activity. But it is only an extinct one—like all on that side of the moon. Its circumference showed a diameter of about twenty-two leagues. The glasses discovered traces of stratification produced by successive irruptions, and the neighbourhood was strewn with volcanic remains which still choked some of the craters.

"There exist," said Barbicane, "several kinds of circles on the surface of the moon, and it is easy to see that Copernicus belongs to the radiating class. If we were nearer, we should see the cones bristling on the inside, which in former times were so many fiery mouths. A curious arrangement, and one without an exception on the lunar disc, is that the interior surface of these circles is the reverse of the exterior, and contrary to the form taken by terrestrial craters. It follows, then, that the general curve of the bottom of these circles gives a sphere of a smaller diameter than that of the moon."

"And why this peculiar disposition?" asked Nicholl.

"We do not know," replied Barbicane.

"What splendid radiation!" said Michel. "One could hardly see a finer spectacle, I think."

"What would you say, then," replied Barbicane, "if chance should bear us towards the southern hemisphere?"

"Well, I should say that it was still more beautiful," retorted Michel Ardan.

At this moment the projectile hung perpendicularly over the circle. The circumference of Copernicus formed almost a perfect circle, and its steep escarpments were clearly defined. They could even distinguish a second ringed enclosure. Around spread a grayish plain, of a wild aspect, on which every relief was marked in yellow. At the bottom of the circle, as if enclosed in a jewel case, sparkled for one instant two or three irruptive cones, like enormous dazzling gems. Towards the north the escarpments were lowered by a depression which would probably have given access to the interior of the crater.

In passing over the surrounding plains, Barbicane noticed a great number of less important mountains; and among others a little ringed one called Guy Lussac, the breadth of which measured twelve miles.

Towards the south, the plain was very flat, without one elevation, without one projection. Towards the north, on the contrary, till where it was bounded by the "Sea of Storms," it resembled a liquid surface agitated by a storm, of which the hills and hollows formed a succession of waves suddenly congealed. Over the whole of this, and in all directions, lay the luminous lines, all converging to the summit of Copernicus.

The travellers discussed the origin of these strange rays; but they could not determine their nature any more than terrestrial observers.

"But why," said Nicholl, "should not these rays be simply spurs of mountains which reflect more vividly the light of the sun?"

"No," replied Barbicane; "if it was so, under certain conditions of the moon, these ridges would cast shadows, and they do not cast any."

And indeed, these rays only appeared when the orb of day was in opposition to the moon, and disappeared as soon as its rays became oblique.

"But how have they endeavoured to explain these lines of light?" asked Michel; "for I cannot believe that savants would ever be stranded for want of an explanation."

"Yes," replied Barbicane; "Herschel has put forward an opinion, but he did not venture to affirm it."

"Never mind. What was the opinion?"

"He thought that these rays might be streams of cooled lava which shone when the sun beat straight upon them. It may be so; but nothing can be less certain. Besides, if we pass nearer to Tycho, we shall be in a better position to find out the cause of this radiation."

"Do you know, my friends, what that plain, seen from the height we are at, resembles?" said Michel.

"No," replied Nicholl.

"Very well; with all those pieces of lava lengthened like rockets, it resembles an immense game of spelikans thrown pellmell. There wants but the hook to pull them out one by one."

"Do be serious," said Barbicane.

"Well, let us be serious," replied Michel quietly; "and instead of spelikans, let us put bones. This plain, would then be nothing but an immense cemetery, on which would repose the mortal remains of thousands of extinct generations. Do you prefer that high-flown comparison?"

"One is as good as the other," retorted Barbicane.

"My word, you are difficult to please," answered Michel.

"My worthy friend," continued the matter-of-fact Barbicane, "it matters but little what it *resembles*, when we do not know what it *is*."

"Well answered," exclaimed Michel. "That will teach me to reason with savants."

But the projectile continued to advance with almost uniform speed around the lunar disc. The travellers, we may easily imagine, did not dream of taking a moment's rest. Every minute changed the landscape which fled from beneath their gaze. About half-past one o'clock in the morning, they caught a glimpse of the tops of another mountain. Barbicane, consulting his map, recognised Eratosthenes.

It was a ringed mountain nine thousand feet high, and one of those circles so numerous on this satellite. With regard to this, Barbicane related Kepler's singular opinion on the formation of circles. According to that celebrated mathematician, these crater-like cavities had been dug by the hand of man.

"For what purpose?" asked Nicholl.

"For a very natural one," replied Barbicane. "The Selenites might have undertaken these immense works and dug these enormous holes for a refuge and shield from the solar rays which beat upon them during fifteen consecutive days."

"The Selenites are not fools," said Michel.

"A singular idea," replied Nicholl; "but it is probable that Kepler did not know the true dimensions of these circles, for the digging of them would have been the work of giants quite impossible for the Selenites."

"Why? if weight on the moon's surface is six times less than on the earth?" said Michel.

"But if the Selenites are six times smaller?" retorted Nicholl.

"And if there are *no* Selenites?" added Barbicane.

This put an end to the discussion.

Soon Eratosthenes disappeared under the horizon without the projectile being sufficiently near to allow close observation. This mountain separated the Apennines from the Carpathians. In the lunar orography they have discerned some chains of mountains, which are chiefly distributed over the northern hemisphere. Some, however, occupy certain portions of the southern hemisphere also.

About two o'clock in the morning Barbicane found that they were above the twentieth lunar parallel. The distance of the projectile from the moon was not more than six hundred miles. Barbicane, now perceiving that the projectile was steadily approaching the lunar disc, did not despair; if not of reaching her, at least of discovering the secrets of her configuration.

Chapter XIII

LUNAR LANDSCAPES

AT HALF-PAST TWO IN THE MORNING, THE PROJECTILE WAS OVER THE THIRTEENTH lunar parallel and at the effective distance of five hundred miles, reduced by the glasses to five. It still seemed impossible, however, that it could ever touch any part of the disc. Its motive speed, comparatively so moderate, was inexplicable to President Barbicane. At that distance from the moon it must have been considerable, to enable it to bear up against her attraction. Here was a phenomenon the cause of which escaped them again. Besides, time failed them to investigate the cause. All lunar relief was defiling under the eyes of the travellers, and they would not lose a single detail.

Under the glasses the disc appeared at the distance of five miles. What would an aeronaut, borne to this distance from the earth, distinguish on its surface? We cannot say, since the greatest ascension has not been more than 25,000 feet.

This, however, is an exact description of what Barbicane and his companions saw at this height. Large patches of different colours appeared on the disc. Selenographers are not agreed upon the nature of these colours. There are several, and rather vividly marked. Julius Schmidt pretends that, if the terrestrial oceans were dried up, a Selenite observer could not distinguish on the globe a greater diversity of shades between the oceans and the continental plains than those on the moon present to a terrestrial observer. According to him, the colour common to the vast plains known by the name of "seas" is a dark grey mixed with green and brown. Some of the large craters present the same appearance. Barbicane knew this opinion of the German selenographer, an opinion shared by Bœer and Moëdler. Observation has proved that right was on their side, and not on that of some astronomers who admit the existence of only grey on the moon's surface. In some parts green was very distinct, such as springs, according to Julius Schmidt, from the seas of "Serenity and Humours." Barbicane also noticed large craters, without any interior cones, which shed a bluish tint similar to the reflection of a sheet of steel freshly polished. These colours belonged really to the lunar disc, and did not result, as some astronomers say, either from the imperfection in the objective of the glasses or from the interposition of the terrestrial atmosphere.

Not a doubt existed in Barbicane's mind with regard to it, as he observed it through space, and so could not commit any optical error. He considered the establishment of this fact as an acquisition to science. Now, were these shades of green, belonging to tropical vegetation, kept up by a low dense atmosphere? He could not yet say.

Farther on, he noticed a reddish tint, quite defined. The same shade had before been observed at the bottom of an isolated enclosure, known by the name of Lichtenburg's circle, which is situated near the Hercynian mountains, on the borders of the moon; but they could not tell the nature of it.

They were not more fortunate with regard to another peculiarity of the disc, for they could not decide upon the cause of it.

Michel Ardan was watching near the president, when he noticed long white lines, vividly lighted up by the direct rays of the sun. It was a succession of luminous furrows, very different from the radiation of Copernicus not long before; they ran parallel with each other.

Michel, with his usual readiness, hastened to exclaim:

"Look there! cultivated fields!"

"Cultivated fields!" replied Nicholl, shrugging his shoulders.

"Plowed, at all events," retorted Michel Ardan; "but what laborers those Selenites must be, and what giant oxen they must harness to their plow to cut such furrows!"

"They are not furrows," said Barbicane; "they are *rifts*."

"Rifts? stuff!" replied Michel mildly; "but what do you mean by 'rifts' in the scientific world?"

Barbicane immediately enlightened his companion as to what he knew about lunar rifts. He knew that they were a kind of furrow found on every part of the disc which was not mountainous; that these furrows, generally isolated, measured from 400 to 500 leagues in length; that their breadth varied from 1,000 to 1,500 yards, and that their borders were strictly parallel; but he knew nothing more either of their formation or their nature.

Barbicane, through his glasses, observed these rifts with great attention. He noticed that their borders were formed of steep declivities; they were long parallel ramparts, and with some small amount of imagination he might have admitted the existence of long lines of fortifications, raised by Selenite engineers. Of these different rifts some were perfectly straight, as if cut by a line; others were slightly curved, though still keeping their borders parallel; some crossed each other, some cut through craters; here they wound through ordinary cavities, such as Posidonius or Petavius; there they wound through the seas, such as the "Sea of Serenity."

These natural accidents naturally excited the imaginations of these terrestrial astronomers. The first observations had not discovered these rifts. Neither Hevelius, Cassin, La Hire, nor Herschel seemed to have known them. It was Schroeter who in 1789 first drew attention to them. Others followed who studied them, as Pastorff, Gruithuysen, Bœer, and Moëdler. At this time their number amounts to seventy; but, if they have been counted, their nature has not yet been determined; they are certainly *not* fortifications, any more than they are the ancient beds of dried-up rivers; for, on one side, the waters, so slight on the moon's surface, could never have worn such drains for themselves; and, on the other, they often cross craters of great elevation.

We must, however, allow that Michel Ardan had "an idea," and that, without knowing it, he coincided in that respect with Julius Schmidt.

"Why," said he, "should not these unaccountable appearances be simply phenomena of vegetation?"

"What do you mean?" asked Barbicane quickly.

"Do not excite yourself, my worthy president," replied Michel; "might it not be possible that the dark lines forming that bastion were rows of trees regularly placed?"

"You stick to your vegetation, then?" said Barbicane.

"I like," retorted Michel Ardan, "to explain what you savants cannot explain; at least my hypotheses has the advantage of indicating why these rifts disappear, or seem to disappear, at certain seasons."

"And for what reason?"

"For the reason that the trees become invisible when they lose their leaves, and visible when they regain them."

"Your explanation is ingenious, my dear companion," replied Barbicane, "but inadmissible."

"Why?"

"Because, so to speak, there are no seasons on the moon's surface, and that, consequently, the phenomena of vegetation of which you speak cannot occur."

Indeed, the slight obliquity of the lunar axis keeps the sun at an almost equal height in every latitude. Above the equatorial regions the radiant orb almost invariably occupies the zenith, and does not pass the limits of the horizon in the polar regions; thus, according to each region, there reigns a perpetual winter, spring, summer, or autumn, as in the planet Jupiter, whose axis is but little inclined upon its orbit.

What origin do they attribute to these rifts? That is a question difficult to solve. They are certainly anterior to the formation of craters and circles, for several have introduced themselves by breaking through their circular ramparts. Thus it may be that, contemporary with the later geological epochs, they are due to the expansion of natural forces.

But the projectile had now attained the fortieth degree of lunar latitude, at a distance not exceeding 400 miles. Through the glasses objects appeared to be only four miles distant.

At this point, under their feet, rose Mount Helicon, 1,520 feet high, and round about the left rose moderate elevations, enclosing a small portion of the "Sea of Rains," under the name of the Gulf of Iris. The terrestrial atmosphere would have to be one hundred and seventy times more transparent than it is, to allow astronomers to make perfect observations on the moon's surface; but in the void in which the projectile floated no fluid interposed itself between the eye of the observer and the object observed. And more, Barbicane found himself carried to a greater distance than the most powerful telescopes had ever done before, either that of Lord Rosse or that of the Rocky Mountains. He was, therefore, under extremely favourable conditions for solving that great question of the habitability of the moon; but the solution still escaped him; he could distinguish nothing but desert beds, immense plains, and towards the north, arid mountains. Not a work betrayed the hand of man; not a ruin marked his course; not a group of animals was to be seen indicating life, even in an inferior degree. In no part was there life, in no part was there an appearance of vegetation. Of the three kingdoms which share the terrestrial globe between them, one alone was represented on the lunar, and that the mineral.

"Ah, indeed!" said Michel Ardan, a little out of countenance; "then you see no one?"

"No," answered Nicholl; "up to this time not a man, not an animal, not a tree! After all, whether the atmosphere has taken refuge at the bottom of cavities, in the midst of the circles, or even on the opposite face of the moon, we cannot decide."

"Besides," added Barbicane, "even to the most piercing eye a man cannot be distinguished farther than three and a half miles off; so that, if there are any Selenites, they can see our projectile, but we cannot see them."

Towards four in the morning, at the height of the fiftieth parallel, the distance was reduced to 300 miles. To the left ran a line of mountains capriciously shaped, lying in the full light. To the right, on the contrary, lay a black hollow resembling a vast well, unfathomable and gloomy, drilled into the lunar soil.

This hole was the "Black Lake"; it was Pluto, a deep circle which can be conveniently studied from the earth, between the last quarter and the new moon, when the shadows fall from west to east.

This black colour is rarely met with on the surface of the satellite. As yet it has only been recognised in the depths of the circle of Endymion, to the east of the "Cold Sea," in the northern hemisphere, and at the bottom of Grimaldi's circle, on the equator, towards the eastern border of the orb.

Pluto is an annular mountain, situated in 51° north latitude, and 9° east longitude. Its circuit is forty-seven miles long and thirty-two broad.

Barbicane regretted that they were not passing directly above this vast opening. There was an abyss to fathom, perhaps some mysterious phenomenon to surprise; but the projectile's course could not be altered. They must rigidly submit. They could not guide a balloon, still less a projectile, when once enclosed within its walls. Towards five in the morning the northern limits of the "Sea of Rains" was at length passed. The mounts of Condamine and Fontenelle remained—one on the right, the other on the left. That part of the disc beginning with 60° was becoming quite mountainous. The glasses brought them to within two miles, less than that separating the summit of Mont Blanc from the level of the sea. The whole region was bristling with spikes and circles. Towards the 60° Philolaus stood predominant at a height of 5,550 feet with its elliptical crater, and seen from this distance, the disc showed a very fantastical appearance. Landscapes were presented to the eye under very different conditions from those on the earth, and also very inferior to them.

The moon having no atmosphere, the consequences arising from the absence of this gaseous envelope have already been shown. No twilight on her surface; night following day and day following night with the suddenness of a lamp which is extinguished or lighted amid profound darkness—no transition from cold to heat, the temperature falling in an instant from boiling point to the cold of space.

Another consequence of this want of air is that absolute darkness reigns where the sun's rays do not penetrate. That which on earth is called diffusion of light, that luminous matter which the air holds in suspension, which creates the twilight and the daybreak, which produces the *umbrae* and *penumbrae,* and all the magic of *chiaro-oscuro,* does not exist on the moon. Hence the harshness of contrasts, which only admit of two colours, black and white. If a Selenite were to shade his eyes from the sun's rays, the sky would seem absolutely black, and the stars would shine to him as on the darkest night. Judge of the impression produced on Barbicane and his three friends by this strange scene! Their eyes were confused. They could no longer grasp the respective distances of the different plains. A lunar landscape without the softening of the phenomena of *chiaro-oscuro* could not be rendered by an earthly landscape painter: it would be spots of ink on a white page—nothing more.

This aspect was not altered even when the projectile, at the height of 80°, was only separated from the moon by a distance of fifty miles; nor even when, at five in the morning, it passed at less than twenty-five miles from the mountain of Gioja, a distance reduced by the glasses to a quarter of a mile. It seemed as if the moon might be touched by the hand! It seemed impossible that, before long, the projectile would not strike her, if only at the north pole, the brilliant arch of which was so distinctly visible on the black sky.

Michel Ardan wanted to open one of the scuttles and throw himself on to the moon's surface! A very useless attempt; for if the projectile could not attain any point whatever of the satellite, Michel, carried along by its motion, could not attain it either.

At that moment, at six o'clock, the lunar pole appeared. The disc only presented to the travellers' gaze one half brilliantly lit up, while the other disappeared in the darkness. Suddenly the projectile passed the line of demarcation between intense light and absolute darkness, and was plunged in profound night!

Chapter XIV

THE NIGHT OF THREE HUNDRED AND FIFTY-FOUR HOURS AND A HALF

AT THE MOMENT WHEN THIS PHENOMENON TOOK PLACE SO RAPIDLY, THE PROJECTILE was skirting the moon's north pole at less than twenty-five miles distance. Some seconds had sufficed to plunge it into the absolute darkness of space. The transition was so sudden, without shade, without gradation of light, without attenuation of the luminous waves, that the orb seemed to have been extinguished by a powerful blow.

"Melted, disappeared!" Michel Ardan exclaimed, aghast.

Indeed, there was neither reflection nor shadow. Nothing more was to be seen of that disc, formerly so dazzling. The darkness was complete, and rendered even more so by the rays from the stars. It was "that blackness" in which the lunar nights are ensteeped, which last three hundred and fifty-four hours and a half at each point of the disc, a long night resulting from the equality of the translatory and rotary movements of the moon. The projectile, immerged in the conical shadow of the satellite, experienced the action of the solar rays no more than any of its invisible points.

In the interior, the obscurity was complete. They could not see each other. Hence the necessity of dispelling the darkness. However desirous Barbicane might be to husband the gas, the reserve of which was small, he was obliged to ask from it a fictitious light, an expensive brilliancy which the sun then refused.

"Devil take the radiant orb!" exclaimed Michel Ardan, "which forces us to expend gas, instead of giving us his rays gratuitously."

"Do not let us accuse the sun," said Nicholl, "it is not his fault, but that of the moon, which has come and placed herself like a screen between us and it."

"It is the sun!" continued Michel.

"It is the moon!" retorted Nicholl.

An idle dispute, which Barbicane put an end to by saying:

"My friends, it is neither the fault of the sun nor of the moon; it is the fault of the *projectile*, which, instead of rigidly following its course, has awkwardly missed it. To be more just, it is the fault of that unfortunate meteor which has so deplorably altered our first direction."

"Well," replied Michel Ardan, "as the matter is settled, let us have breakfast. After a whole night of watching it is fair to build ourselves up a little."

This proposal meeting with no contradiction, Michel prepared the repast in a few minutes. But they ate for eating's sake, they drank without toasts, without hurrahs. The bold travellers being borne away into gloomy space, without their accustomed *cortége* of rays, felt a vague uneasiness in their hearts. The "strange" shadow so dear to Victor Hugo's pen bound them on all sides. But they talked over the interminable night of three hundred and fifty-four hours and a half, nearly fifteen days, which the law of physics has imposed on the inhabitants of the moon.

Barbicane gave his friends some explanation of the causes and the consequences of this curious phenomenon.

"Curious indeed," said they; "for, if each hemisphere of the moon is deprived of solar light for fifteen days, that above which we now float does not even enjoy during its long night any view of the earth so beautifully lit up. In a word she has no moon (applying this designation to our globe) but on one side of her disc. Now if this were the case with the earth—if, for example, Europe never saw the moon, and she was only visible at the antipodes, imagine to yourself the astonishment of a European on arriving in Australia."

"They would make the voyage for nothing but to see the moon!" replied Michel.

"Very well!" continued Barbicane, "that astonishment is reserved for the Selenites who inhabit the face of the moon opposite to the earth, a face which is ever invisible to our countrymen of the terrestrial globe."

"And which we should have seen," added Nicholl, "if we had arrived here when the moon was new, that is to say fifteen days later."

"I will add, to make amends," continued Barbicane, "that the inhabitants of the visible face are singularly favoured by nature, to the detriment of their brethren on the invisible face. The latter, as you see, have dark nights of 354 hours, without one single ray to break the darkness. The other, on the contrary, when the sun which has given its light for fifteen days sinks below the horizon, see a splendid orb rise on the opposite horizon. It is the earth, which is thirteen times greater than the diminutive moon that we know—the earth which developes itself at a diameter of two degrees, and which sheds a light thirteen times greater than that qualified by atmospheric strata—the earth which only disappears at the moment when the sun reappears in its turn!"

"Nicely worded!" said Michel, "slightly academical perhaps."

"It follows, then," continued Barbicane, without knitting his brows, "that the visible face of the disc must be very agreeable to inhabit, since it always looks on either the sun when the moon is full, or on the earth when the moon is new."

"But," said Nicholl, "that advantage must be well compensated by the insupportable heat which the light brings with it."

"The inconvenience, in that respect, is the same for the two faces, for the earth's light is evidently deprived of heat. But the invisible face is still more searched by the heat than the visible face. I say that for *you*, Nicholl, because Michel will probably not understand."

"Thank you," said Michel.

"Indeed," continued Barbicane, "when the invisible face receives at the same time light and heat from the sun, it is because the moon is new; that is to say, she is situated between the sun and the earth. It follows, then, considering the position which she occupies in opposition when full, that she is nearer to the sun by twice her distance from the earth; and that distance may be estimated at the two-hundredth part of that which separates the sun from the earth, or in round numbers 400,000 miles. So that invisible face is so much nearer to the sun when she receives its rays."

"Quite right," replied Nicholl.

"On the contrary," continued Barbicane.

"One moment," said Michel, interrupting his grave companion.

"What do you want?"

"I ask to be allowed to continue the explanation."

"And why?"

"To prove that I understand."

"Get along with you," said Barbicane, smiling.

"On the contrary," said Michel, imitating the tone and gestures of the president, "on the contrary, when the visible face of the moon is lit by the sun, it is because the moon is full, that is to say, opposite the sun with regard to the earth. The distance separating it from the radiant orb is then increased in round numbers to 400,000 miles, and the heat which she receives must be a little less."

"Very well said!" exclaimed Barbicane. "Do you know, Michel, that, for an amateur, you are intelligent."

"Yes," replied Michel coolly, "we are all so on the Boulevard des Italiens."

Barbicane gravely grasped the hand of his amiable companion, and continued to enumerate the advantages reserved for the inhabitants of the visible face.

Among others, he mentioned eclipses of the sun, which only take place on this side of the lunar disc; since, in order that they may take place, it is necessary for the moon to be *in opposition*. These eclipses, caused by the interposition of the earth between the moon and the sun, can last *two hours*; during which time, by reason of the rays refracted by its atmosphere, the terrestrial globe can appear as nothing but a black point upon the sun.

"So," said Nicholl, "there is a hemisphere, that invisible hemisphere which is very ill supplied, very ill treated, by nature."

"Never mind," replied Michel; "if we ever become Selenites, we will inhabit the visible face. I like the light."

"Unless, by any chance," answered Nicholl, "the atmosphere should be condensed on the other side, as certain astronomers pretend."

"That would be a consideration," said Michel.

Breakfast over, the observers returned to their post. They tried to see through the darkened scuttles by extinguishing all light in the projectile; but not a luminous spark made its way through the darkness.

One inexplicable fact preoccupied Barbicane. Why, having passed within such a short distance of the moon—about twenty-five miles only—why the projectile had not fallen? If its speed had been enormous, he could have understood that the fall would not have taken place; but, with a relatively moderate speed, that resistance to the moon's attraction could not be explained. Was the projectile under some foreign influence? Did some kind of body retain it in the ether? It was quite evident that it could never reach any point of the moon. Whither was it going? Was it going farther from, or nearing, the disc? Was it being borne in that profound darkness through the infinity of space? How could they learn, how calculate, in the midst of this night? All these questions made Barbicane uneasy, but he could not solve them.

Certainly, the invisible orb was *there*, perhaps only some few miles off; but neither he nor his companions could see it. If there was any noise on its surface, they could not hear it. Air, that medium of sound, was wanting to transmit the groanings of that moon which the Arabic legends call "a man already half granite, and still breathing."

One must allow that that was enough to aggravate the most patient observers. It was just that unknown hemisphere which was stealing from their sight. That face which fifteen days sooner, or fifteen days later, had been, or would be, splendidly illuminated by the solar rays, was then being lost in utter darkness. In fifteen days where would the projectile be? Who could say? Where would the chances of conflicting attractions have drawn it to? The disappointment of the travellers in the midst of this utter darkness may be imagined. All observation of the lunar disc was impossible. The constellations alone claimed all their attention; and we must allow that the astronomers Faye, Charconac, and Secchi, never found themselves in circumstances so favourable for their observation.

Indeed, nothing could equal the splendour of this starry world, bathed in limpid ether. Its diamonds set in the heavenly vault sparkled magnificently. The eye took in the firmament from the Southern Cross to the North Star, those two constellations which in 12,000 years, by reason of the succession of equinoxes, will resign their part of the polar stars, the one to Canopus in the southern hemisphere, the other to Wega in the northern. Imagination loses itself in this sublime Infinity, amid which the projectile was gravitating, like a new star created by the hand of man. From a natural cause, these constellations shone with a soft lustre; they did not twinkle, for there was no atmosphere which, by the intervention of its layers unequally dense and of different degrees of humidity, produces this scintillation. These stars were soft eyes, looking out into the dark night, amid the silence of absolute space.

Long did the travellers stand mute, watching the constellated firmament, upon which the moon, like a vast screen, made an enormous black hole. But at length a painful sensation drew them from their watchings. This was an intense cold, which soon covered the inside of the glass of the scuttles with a thick coating of ice. The sun was no longer warming the projectile with its direct rays, and thus it was losing the heat stored up in its walls by degrees. This heat was rapidly evaporating into space by radiation, and a considerably lower temperature was the result. The humidity of the interior was changed into ice upon contact with the glass, preventing all observation.

Nicholl consulted the thermometer, and saw that it had fallen to seventeen degrees (Centigrade) below zero.* So that, in spite of the many reasons for economising, Barbicane, after having begged light from the gas, was also obliged to beg for heat. The projectile's low temperature was no longer endurable. Its tenants would have been frozen to death.

"Well!" observed Michel, "we cannot reasonably complain of the monotony of our journey! What variety we have had, at least in temperature. Now we are blinded with light and saturated with heat, like the Indians of the Pampas! now plunged into profound darkness, amid the cold, like the Esquimaux of the north pole. No, indeed! we have no right to complain; nature does wonders in our honour."

"But," asked Nicholl, "what is the temperature outside?"

"Exactly that of the planetary space," replied Barbicane.

"Then," continued Michel Ardan, "would not this be the time to make the experiment which we dared not attempt when we were drowned in the sun's rays?"

"It is now or never," replied Barbicane, "for we are in a good position to verify the temperature of space, and see if Fourier or Pouillet's calculations are exact."

"In any case it is cold," said Michel. "See! the steam of the interior is condensing on the glasses of the scuttles. If the fall continues, the vapour of our breath will fall in snow around us."

"Let us prepare a thermometer," said Barbicane.

We may imagine that an ordinary thermometer would afford no result under the circumstances in which this instrument was to be exposed. The mercury would have been frozen in its ball, as below 42° Fahrenheit below zero it is no longer liquid. But Barbicane had furnished himself with a spirit thermometer on Wafferdin's system, which gives the minima of excessively low temperatures.

Before beginning the experiment, this instrument was compared with an ordinary one, and then Barbicane prepared to use it.

"How shall we set about it?" asked Nicholl.

"Nothing is easier," replied Michel Ardan, who was never at a loss. "We open the scuttle rapidly; throw out the instrument; it follows the projectile with exemplary docility; and a quarter of an hour after, draw it in."

"With the hand?" asked Barbicane.

*1 degree Fahrenheit.

"With the hand," replied Michel.

"Well, then, my friend, do not expose yourself," answered Barbicane, "for the hand that you draw in again will be nothing but a stump frozen and deformed by the frightful cold."

"Really!"

"You will feel as if you had had a terrible burn, like that of iron at a white heat; for whether the heat leaves our bodies briskly or enters briskly, it is exactly the same thing. Besides, I am not at all certain that the objects we have thrown out are still following us."

"Why not?" asked Nicholl.

"Because, if we are passing through an atmosphere of the slightest density, these objects will be retarded. Again, the darkness prevents our seeing if they still float around us. But in order not to expose ourselves to the loss of our thermometer, we will fasten it, and we can then more easily pull it back again."

Barbicane's advice was followed. Through the scuttle rapidly opened, Nicholl threw out the instrument, which was held by a short cord, so that it might be more easily drawn up. The scuttle had not been opened more than a second, but that second had sufficed to let in a most intense cold.

"The devil!" exclaimed Michel Ardan, "it is cold enough to freeze a white bear."

Barbicane waited until half-an-hour had elapsed, which was more than time enough to allow the instrument to fall to the level of the surrounding temperature. Then it was rapidly pulled in.

Barbicane calculated the quantity of spirits of wine overflowed into the little vial soldered to the lower part of the instrument, and said:

"A hundred and forty degrees Centigrade* below zero!"

M. Pouillet was right and Fourier wrong. That was the undoubted temperature of the starry space. Such is, perhaps, that of the lunar continents, when the orb of night has lost by radiation all the heat which fifteen days of sun have poured into her.

Chapter XV

Hyperbola or Parabola

WE MAY, PERHAPS, BE ASTONISHED TO FIND BARBICANE AND HIS COMPANIONS SO LITtle occupied with the future reserved for them in their metal prison which was bearing them through the infinity of space. Instead of asking where they were going, they passed their time making experiments, as if they had been quietly installed in their own study.

We might answer that men so strong-minded were above such anxieties—that they did not trouble themselves about such trifles—and that they had something else to do than to occupy their minds with the future.

The truth was that they were not masters of their projectile; they could neither check its course, nor alter its direction.

*218 degrees Fahrenheit below zero.

A sailor can change the head of his ship as he pleases; an aeronaut can give a vertical motion to his balloon. They, on the contrary, had no power over their vehicle. Every maneuvre was forbidden. Hence the inclination to let things alone, or as the sailors say, "let her run."

Where did they find themselves at this moment, at eight o'clock in the morning of the day called upon the earth the 6th of December? Very certainly in the neighbourhood of the moon, and even near enough for her to look to them like an enormous black screen upon the firmament. As to the distance which separated them, it was impossible to estimate it. The projectile, held by some unaccountable force, had been within four miles of grazing the satellite's north pole.

But since entering the cone of shadow these last two hours, had the distance increased or diminished? Every point of mark was wanting by which to estimate both the direction and the speed of the projectile.

Perhaps it was rapidly leaving the disc, so that it would soon quit the pure shadow. Perhaps, again, on the other hand, it might be nearing it so much that in a short time it might strike some high point on the invisible hemisphere, which would doubtlessly have ended the journey much to the detriment of the travellers.

A discussion arose on this subject, and Michel Ardan, always ready with an explanation, gave it as his opinion that the projectile, held by the lunar attraction, would end by falling on the surface of the terrestrial globe like an aerolite.

"First of all, my friend," answered Barbicane, "every aerolite does not fall to the earth; it is only a small proportion which do so; and if we had passed into an aerolite, it does not necessarily follow that we should ever reach the surface of the moon."

"But how if we get near enough?" replied Michel.

"Pure mistake," replied Barbicane. "Have you not seen shooting-stars rush through the sky by thousands at certain seasons?"

"Yes."

"Well, these stars, or rather corpuscles, only shine when they are heated by gliding over the atmospheric layers. Now, if they enter the atmosphere, they pass at least within forty miles of the earth, but they seldom fall upon it. The same with our projectile. It may approach very near to the moon, and not yet fall upon it."

"But then," asked Michel, "I shall be curious to know how our erring vehicle will act in space?"

"I see but two hypotheses," replied Barbicane, after some moments' reflection.

"What are they?"

"The projectile has the choice between two mathematical curves, and it will follow one or the other according to the speed with which it is animated, and which at this moment I cannot estimate."

"Yes," said Nicholl, "it will follow either a parabola or a hyperbola."

"Just so," replied Barbicane. "With a certain speed it will assume the parabola, and with a greater the hyperbola."

"I like those grand words," exclaimed Michel Ardan; "one knows directly what they mean. And pray what is your parabola, if you please?"

"My friend," answered the captain, "the parabola is a curve of the second order, the result of the section of a cone intersected by a plane parallel to one of the sides."

"Ah! ah!" said Michel, in a satisfied tone.

"It is very nearly," continued Nicholl, "the course described by a bomb launched from a mortar."

"Perfect! And the hyperbola?"

"The hyperbola, Michel, is a curve of the second order, produced by the intersection of a conic surface and a plane parallel to its axis, and constitutes two branches separated one from the other, both tending indefinitely in the two directions."

"Is it possible!" exclaimed Michel Ardan in a serious tone, as if they had told him of some serious event. "What I particularly like in your definition of the hyperbola (I was going to say hyperblague) is that it is still more obscure than the word you pretend to define."

Nicholl and Barbicane cared little for Michel Ardan's fun. They were deep in a scientific discussion. What curve would the projectile follow? was their hobby. One maintained the hyperbola, the other the parabola. They gave each other reasons bristling with x. Their arguments were couched in language which made Michel jump. The discussion was hot, and neither would give up his chosen curve to his adversary.

This scientific dispute lasted so long that it made Michel very impatient.

"Now, gentlemen cosines, will you cease to throw parabolas and hyperbolas at each other's heads? I want to understand the only interesting question in the whole affair. We shall follow one or the other of these curves? Good. But where will they lead us to?"

"Nowhere," replied Nicholl.

"How, nowhere?"

"Evidently," said Barbicane, "they are open curves, which may be prolonged indefinitely."

"Ah, savants!" cried Michel; "and what are either the one or the other to us from the moment we know that they equally lead us into infinite space?"

Barbicane and Nicholl could not forbear smiling. They had just been creating "art for art's sake." Never had so idle a question been raised at such an inopportune moment. The sinister truth remained that, whether hyperbolically or parabolically borne away, the projectile would never again meet either the earth or the moon.

What would become of these bold travellers in the immediate future? If they did not die of hunger, if they did not die of thirst, in some days, when the gas failed, they would die from want of air, unless the cold had killed them first. Still, important as it was to economise the gas, the excessive lowness of the surrounding temperature obliged them to consume a certain quantity. Strictly speaking, they could do without its *light*, but not without its *heat*. Fortunately the caloric generated by Reiset's and Regnaut's apparatus raised the temperature of the interior of the projectile a little, and without much expenditure they were able to keep it bearable.

But observations had now become very difficult. The dampness of the projectile was condensed on the windows and congealed immediately. This cloudiness had to be dispersed continually. In any case they might hope to be able to discover some phenomena of the highest interest.

But up to this time the disc remained dumb and dark. It did not answer the multiplicity of questions put by these ardent minds; a matter which drew this reflection from Michel, apparently a just one:

"If ever we begin this journey over again, we shall do well to choose the time when the moon is at the full."

"Certainly," said Nicholl, "that circumstance will be more favourable. I allow that the moon, immersed in the sun's rays, will not be visible during the transit, but instead we should see the earth, which would be full. And what is more, if we were drawn round the moon, as at this moment, we should at least have the advantage of seeing the invisible part of her disc magnificently lit."

"Well said, Nicholl," replied Michel Ardan. "What do you think, Barbicane?"

"I think this," answered the grave president: "If ever we begin this journey again, we shall start at the same time and under the same conditions. Suppose we had attained our end, would it not have been better to have found continents in broad daylight than a country plunged in utter darkness? Would not our first installation have been made under better circumstances? Yes, evidently. As to the invisible side, we could have visited it in our exploring expeditions on the lunar globe. So that the time of the full moon was well chosen. But we ought to have arrived at the end; and in order to have so arrived, we ought to have suffered no deviation on the road."

"I have nothing to say to that," answered Michel Ardan. "Here is, however, a good opportunity lost of observing the other side of the moon."

But the projectile was now describing in the shadow that incalculable course which no sight-mark would allow them to ascertain. Had its direction been altered, either by the influence of the lunar attraction, or by the action of some unknown star? Barbicane could not say. But a change had taken place in the relative position of the vehicle; and Barbicane verified it about four in the morning.

The change consisted in this, that the base of the projectile had turned towards the moon's surface, and was so held by a perpendicular passing through its axis. The attraction, that is to say the weight, had brought about this alteration. The heaviest part of the projectile inclined towards the invisible disc as if it would fall upon it.

Was it falling? Were the travellers attaining that much desired end? No. And the observation of a sign-point, quite inexplicable in itself, showed Barbicane that his projectile was not nearing the moon, and that it had shifted by following an almost concentric curve.

This point of mark was a luminous brightness, which Nicholl sighted suddenly, on the limit of the horizon formed by the black disc. This point could not be confounded with a star. It was a reddish incandescence which increased by degrees, a decided proof that the projectile was shifting towards it and not falling normally on the surface of the moon.

"A volcano! it is a volcano in action!" cried Nicholl; "a disembowelling of the interior fires of the moon! That world is not quite extinguished."

"Yes, an irruption," replied Barbicane, who was carefully studying the phenomenon through his night glass. "What should it be, if not a volcano?"

"But, then," said Michel Ardan, "in order to maintain that combustion, there must be air. So the atmosphere does surround that part of the moon."

"Perhaps so," replied Barbicane, "but not necessarily. The volcano, by the decomposition of certain substances, can provide its own oxygen, and thus throw flames into space. It seems to me that the deflagration, by the intense brilliancy of the substances in combustion, is produced in pure oxygen. We must not be in a hurry to proclaim the existence of a lunar atmosphere."

The fiery mountain must have been situated about the 45° south latitude on the invisible part of the disc; but, to Barbicane's great displeasure, the curve which the projectile was describing was taking it far from the point indicated by the irruption. Thus he could not determine its nature exactly. Half-an-hour after being sighted, this luminous point had disappeared behind the dark horizon; but the verification of this phenomenon was of considerable consequence in their selenographic studies. It proved that all heat had not yet disappeared from the bowels of this globe; and where heat exists, who can affirm that the vegetable kingdom, nay, even the animal kingdom itself, has not up to this time resisted all destructive influences? The existence of this volcano in irruption, unmistakably seen by these earthly savants, would doubtless give rise to many theories favourable to the grave question of the habitability of the moon.

Barbicane allowed himself to be carried away by these reflections. He forgot himself in a deep reverie in which the mysterious destiny of the lunar world was uppermost. He was seeking to combine together the facts observed up to that time, when a new incident recalled him briskly to reality. This incident was more than a cosmical phenomenon; it was a threatened danger, the consequence of which might be disastrous in the extreme.

Suddenly, in the midst of the ether, in the profound darkness, an enormous mass appeared. It was like a moon, but an incandescent moon whose brilliancy was all the more intolerable as it cut sharply on the frightful darkness of space. This mass, of a circular form, threw a light which filled the projectile. The forms of Barbicane, Nicholl, and Michel Ardan, bathed in its white sheets, assumed that livid spectral appearance which physicians produce with the fictitious light of alcohol impregnated with salt.

"By Jove!" cried Michel Ardan, "we are hideous. What is that ill-conditioned moon?"

"A meteor," replied Barbicane.

"A meteor burning in space?"

"Yes."

This shooting globe suddenly appearing in shadow at a distance of at most 200 miles, ought, according to Barbicane, to have a diameter of 2,000 yards. It advanced at a speed of about one mile and a half per second. It cut the projectile's path and must reach it in some minutes. As it approached it grew to enormous proportions.

Imagine, if possible, the situation of the travellers! It is impossible to describe it. In spite of their courage, their *sang-froid*, their carelessness of danger, they were mute, motionless with stiffened limbs, a prey to frightful terror. Their projectile, the course of which they could not alter, was rushing straight on this ignited mass, more intense than the open mouth of an oven. It seemed as though they were being precipitated towards an abyss of fire.

Barbicane had seized the hands of his two companions, and all three looked through their half-open eyelids upon that asteroid heated to a white heat. If thought was not destroyed within them, if their brains still worked amid all this awe, they must have given themselves up for lost.

Two minutes after the sudden appearance of the meteor (to them two centuries of anguish) the projectile seemed almost about to strike it, when the globe of fire burst like a bomb, but without making any noise in that void where sound, which is but the agitation of the layers of air, could not be generated.

Nicholl uttered a cry, and he and his companions rushed to the scuttle. What a sight!

What pen can describe it? What palette is rich enough in colours to reproduce so magnificent a spectacle?

It was like the opening of a crater, like the scattering of an immense conflagration. Thousands of luminous fragments lit up and irradiated space with their fires. Every size, every colour, was there intermingled. There were rays of yellow and pale yellow, red, green, gray—a crown of fireworks of all colours. Of the enormous and much-dreaded globe there remained nothing but these fragments carried in all directions, now become asteroids in their turn, some flaming like a sword, some surrounded by a whitish cloud, and others leaving behind them trains of brilliant cosmical dust.

These incandescent blocks crossed and struck each other, scattering still smaller fragments, some of which struck the projectile. Its left scuttle was even cracked by a violent shock. It seemed to be floating amid a hail of howitzer shells, the smallest of which might destroy it instantly.

The light which saturated the ether was so wonderfully intense, that Michel, drawing Barbicane and Nicholl to his window, exclaimed, "The invisible moon, visible at last!"

And through a luminous emanation, which lasted some seconds, the whole three caught a glimpse of that mysterious disc which the eye of man now saw for the first time. What could they distinguish at a distance which they could not estimate? Some lengthened bands along the disc, real clouds formed in the midst of a very confined atmosphere, from which emerged not only all the mountains, but also projections of less importance; its circles, its yawning craters, as capriciously placed as on the visible surface. Then immense spaces, no longer arid plains, but real seas, oceans, widely distributed, reflecting on their liquid surface all the dazzling magic of the fires of space; and, lastly, on the surface of the continents, large dark masses, looking like immense forests under the rapid illumination of a brilliance.

Was it an illusion, a mistake, an optical illusion? Could they give a scientific assent to an observation so superficially obtained? Dared they pronounce upon the question of its habitability after so slight a glimpse of the invisible disc?

But the lightnings in space subsided by degrees; its accidental brilliancy died away; the asteroids dispersed in different directions and were extinguished in the distance. The ether returned to its accustomed darkness; the stars, eclipsed for a moment, again twinkled in the firmament, and the disc, so hastily discerned, was again buried in impenetrable night.

Chapter XVI

THE SOUTHERN HEMISPHERE

THE PROJECTILE HAD JUST ESCAPED A TERRIBLE DANGER, AND A VERY UNFORSEEN ONE. Who would have thought of such an encounter with meteors? These erring bodies might create serious perils for the travellers. They were to them so many sand-banks upon that sea of ether which, less fortunate than sailors, they could not escape. But did these adventurers complain of space? No, not since nature had given them the splendid sight of a

cosmical meteor bursting from expansion, since this inimitable firework, which no Rug-
gieri could imitate, had lit up for some seconds the invisible glory of the moon. In that
flash, continents, seas, and forests had become visible to them. Did an atmosphere, then,
bring to this unknown face its life-giving atoms? Questions still insoluble, and forever
closed against human curiousity!

It was then half-past three in the afternoon. The projectile was following its curvi-
linear direction round the moon. Had its course again been altered by the meteor? It was
to be feared so. But the projectile must describe a curve unalterably determined by the
laws of mechanical reasoning. Barbicane was inclined to believe that this curve would be
rather a parabola than a hyperbola. But admitting the parabola, the projectile must
quickly have passed through the cone of shadow projected into space opposite the sun.
This cone, indeed, is very narrow, the angular diameter of the moon being so little when
compared with the diameter of the orb of day; and up to this time the projectile had been
floating in this deep shadow. Whatever had been its speed (and it could not have been insignificant), its period of occultation continued. That was evident, but perhaps that
would not have been the case in a supposedly rigidly parabolical trajectory—a new problem which tormented Barbicane's brain, imprisoned as he was in a circle of unknowns
which he could not unravel.

Neither of the travellers thought of taking an instant's repose. Each one watched for
an unexpected fact, which might throw some new light on their uranographic studies.
About five o'clock, Michel Ardan distributed, under the name of dinner, some pieces of
bread and cold meat, which were quickly swallowed without either of them abandoning
their scuttle, the glass of which was incessantly encrusted by the condensation of vapor.

About forty-five minutes past five in the evening, Nicholl, armed with his glass,
sighted towards the southern border of the moon, and in the direction followed by the projectile, some bright points cut upon the dark shield of the sky. They looked like a succession of sharp points lengthened into a tremulous line. They were very bright. Such
appeared the terminal line of the moon when in one of her octants.

They could not be mistaken. It was no longer a simple meteor. This luminous ridge
had neither colour nor motion. Nor was it a volcano in irruption. And Barbicane did not
hesitate to pronounce upon it.

"The sun!" he exclaimed.

"What! the sun?" answered Nicholl and Michel Ardan.

"Yes, my friends, it is the radiant orb itself lighting up the summit of the mountains
situated on the southern borders of the moon. We are evidently nearing the south pole."

"After having passed the north pole," replied Michel. "We have made the circuit of
our satellite, then?"

"Yes, my good Michel."

"Then, no more hyperbolas, no more parabolas, no more open curves to fear?"

"No, but a closed curve."

"Which is called—"

"An ellipse. Instead of losing itself in interplanetary space, it is probable that the projectile will describe an elliptical orbit around the moon."

"Indeed!"

"And that it will become *her* satellite."

"Moon of the moon!" cried Michel Ardan.

"Only, I would have you observe, my worthy friend," replied Barbicane, "that we are none the less lost for that."

"Yes, in another manner, and much more pleasantly," answered the careless Frenchman with his most amiable smile.

Chapter XVII

TYCHO

AT SIX IN THE EVENING THE PROJECTILE PASSED THE SOUTH POLE AT LESS THAN FORTY miles off, a distance equal to that already reached at the north pole. The elliptical curve was being rigidly carried out.

At this moment the travellers once more entered the blessed rays of the sun. They saw once more those stars which move slowly from east to west. The radiant orb was saluted by a triple hurrah. With its light it also sent heat, which soon pierced the metal walls. The glass resumed its accustomed appearance. The layers of ice melted as if by enchantment; and immediately, for economy's sake, the gas was put out, the air apparatus alone consuming its usual quantity.

"Ah!" said Nicholl, "these rays of heat are good. With what impatience must the Selenites wait the reappearance of the orb of day."

"Yes," replied Michel Ardan, "imbibing as it were the brilliant ether, light and heat, all life is contained in them."

At this moment the bottom of the projectile deviated somewhat from the lunar surface, in order to follow the slightly lengthened elliptical orbit. From this point, had the earth been at the full, Barbicane and his companions could have seen it, but immersed in the sun's irradiation she was quite invisible. Another spectacle attracted their attention, that of the southern part of the moon, brought by the glasses to within 450 yards. They did not again leave the scuttles, and noted every detail of this fantastical continent.

Mounts Doerful and Leibnitz formed two separate groups very near the south pole. The first group extended from the pole to the eighty-fourth parallel, on the eastern part of the orb; the second occupied the eastern border, extending from the 65° of latitude to the pole.

On their capriciously formed ridge appeared dazzling sheets, as mentioned by Père Secchi. With more certainty than the illustrious Roman astronomer, Barbicane was enabled to recognise their nature.

"They are snow," he exclaimed.

"Snow?" repeated Nicholl.

"Yes, Nicholl, snow; the surface of which is deeply frozen. See how they reflect the luminous rays. Cooled lava would never give out such intense reflection. There must then be water, there must be air on the moon. As little as you please, but the fact can no longer be contested." No, it could not be. And if ever Barbicane should see the earth again, his notes will bear witness to this great fact in his selenographic observations.

These mountains of Doerful and Leibnitz rose in the midst of plains of a medium extent, which were bounded by an indefinite succession of circles and annular ramparts. These two chains are the only ones met with in this region of circles. Comparatively but slightly marked, they throw up here and there some sharp points, the highest summit of which attains an altitude of 24,600 feet.

But the projectile was high above all this landscape, and the projections disappeared in the intense brilliancy of the disc. And to the eyes of the travellers there reappeared that original aspect of the lunar landscapes, raw in tone, without gradation of colours, and without degrees of shadow, roughly black and white, from the want of diffusion of light.

But the sight of this desolate world did not fail to captivate them by its very strangeness. They were moving over this region as if they had been borne on the breath of some storm, watching heights defile under their feet, piercing the cavities with their eyes, going down into the rifts, climbing the ramparts, sounding these mysterious holes, and levelling all cracks. But no trace of vegetation, no appearance of cities; nothing but stratification, beds of lava, overflowings polished like immense mirrors, reflecting the sun's rays with overpowering brilliancy. Nothing belonging to a *living* world—everything to a dead world, where avalanches, rolling from the summits of the mountains, would disperse noiselessly at the bottom of the abyss, retaining the motion, but wanting the sound. In any case it was the image of death, without its being possible even to say that life had ever existed there.

Michel Ardan, however, thought he recognised a heap of ruins, to which he drew Barbicane's attention. It was about the 80th parallel, in 30° longitude. This heap of stones, rather regularly placed, represented a vast fortress, overlooking a long rift, which in former days had served as a bed to the rivers of prehistorical times. Not far from that, rose to a height of 17,400 feet the annular mountain of Short, equal to the Asiatic Caucasus. Michel Ardan, with his accustomed ardor, maintained "the evidences" of his fortress. Beneath it he discerned the dismantled ramparts of a town; here the still intact arch of a portico, there two or three columns lying under their base; farther on, a succession of arches which must have supported the conduit of an aqueduct; in another part the sunken pillars of a gigantic bridge, run into the thickest parts of the rift. He distinguished all this, but with so much imagination in his glance, and through glasses so fantastical, that we must mistrust his observation. But who could affirm, who would dare to say, that the amiable fellow did not really see that which his two companions would not see?

Moments were too precious to be sacrificed in idle discussion. The Selenite city, whether imaginary or not, had already disappeared afar off. The distance of the projectile from the lunar disc was on the increase, and the details of the soil were being lost in a confused jumble. The reliefs, the circles, the craters, and the plains alone remained, and still showed their boundary lines distinctly. At this moment, to the left, lay extended one of the finest circles of lunar orography, one of the curiosities of this continent. It was Newton, which Barbicane recognised without trouble, by referring to the *Mappa Selenographica*.

Newton is situated in exactly 77° south latitude, and 16° east longitude. It forms an annular crater, the ramparts of which, rising to a height of 21,300 feet, seemed to be impassable.

Barbicane made his companions observe that the height of this mountain above the surrounding plain was far from equaling the depth of its crater. This enormous hole was beyond all measurement, and formed a gloomy abyss, the bottom of which the sun's rays could never reach. There, according to Humboldt, reigns utter darkness, which the light of the sun and the earth cannot break. Mythologists could well have made it the mouth of hell.

"Newton," said Barbicane, "is the most perfect type of these annular mountains, of which the earth possesses no sample. They prove that the moon's formation, by means of cooling, is due to violent causes; for while, under the pressure of internal fires the reliefs rise to considerable height, the depths withdraw far below the lunar level."

"I do not dispute the fact," replied Michel Ardan.

Some minutes after passing Newton, the projectile directly overlooked the annular mountains of Moret. It skirted at some distance the summits of Blancanus, and at about half-past seven in the evening reached the circle of Clavius.

This circle, one of the most remarkable of the disc, is situated in 58° south latitude, and 15° east longitude. Its height is estimated at 22,950 feet. The travellers, at a distance of twenty-four miles (reduced to four by their glasses), could admire this vast crater in its entirety.

"Terrestrial volcanoes," said Barbicane, "are but mole-hills compared with those of the moon. Measuring the old craters formed by the first irruptions of Vesuvius and Etna, we find them little more than three miles in breadth. In France the circle of Cantal measures six miles across; at Ceyland the circle of the island is forty miles, which is considered the largest on the globe. What are these diameters against that of Clavius, which we overlook at this moment?"

"What is its breadth?" asked Nicholl.

"It is 150 miles," replied Barbicane. "This circle is certainly the most important on the moon, but many others measure 150, 100, or 75 miles."

"Ah! my friends," exclaimed Michel, "can you picture to yourselves what this now peaceful orb of night must have been when its craters, filled with thunderings, vomited at the same time smoke and tongues of flame. What a wonderful spectacle then, and now what decay! This moon is nothing more than a thin carcase of fireworks, whose squibs, rockets, serpents, and suns, after a superb brilliancy, have left but sadly broken cases. Who can say the cause, the reason, the motive force of these cataclysms?"

Barbicane was not listening to Michel Ardan; he was contemplating these ramparts of Clavius, formed by large mountains spread over several miles. At the bottom of the immense cavity burrowed hundreds of small extinguished craters, riddling the soil like a colander, and overlooked by a peak 15,000 feet high.

Around the plain appeared desolate. Nothing so arid as these reliefs, nothing so sad as these ruins of mountains, and (if we may so express ourselves) these fragments of peaks and mountains which strewed the soil. The satellite seemed to have burst at this spot.

The projectile was still advancing, and this movement did not subside. Circles, craters, and uprooted mountains succeeded each other incessantly. No more plains; no more seas. A never ending Switzerland and Norway. And lastly, in the canter of this region of crevasses, the most splendid mountain on the lunar disc, the dazzling Tycho, in which posterity will ever preserve the name of the illustrious Danish astronomer.

In observing the full moon in a cloudless sky no one has failed to remark this brilliant point of the southern hemisphere. Michel Ardan used every metaphor that his imagination could supply to designate it by. To him this Tycho was a focus of light, a centre of irradiation, a crater vomiting rays. It was the tire of a brilliant wheel, an *asteria* enclosing the disc with its silver tentacles, an enormous eye filled with flames, a glory carved for Pluto's head, a star launched by the Creator's hand, and crushed against the face of the moon!

Tycho forms such a concentration of light that the inhabitants of the earth can see it without glasses, though at a distance of 240,000 miles! Imagine, then, its intensity to the eye of observers placed at a distance of only fifty miles! Seen through this pure ether, its brilliancy was so intolerable that Barbicane and his friends were obliged to blacken their glasses with the gas smoke before they could bear the splendour. Then silent, scarcely uttering an interjection of admiration, they gazed, they contemplated. All their feelings, all their impressions, were concentrated in that look, as under any violent emotion all life is concentrated at the heart.

Tycho belongs to the system of radiating mountains, like Aristarchus and Copernicus; but it is of all the most complete and decided, showing unquestionably the frightful volcanic action to which the formation of the moon is due. Tycho is situated in 43° south latitude, and 12° east longitude. Its centre is occupied by a crater fifty miles broad. It assumes a slightly elliptical form, and is surrounded by an enclosure of annular ramparts, which on the east and west overlook the outer plain from a height of 15,000 feet. It is a group of Mont Blancs, placed round one common centre and crowned by radiating beams.

What this incomparable mountain really is, with all the projections converging towards it, and the interior excrescences of its crater, photography itself could never represent. Indeed, it is during the full moon that Tycho is seen in all its splendour. Then all shadows disappear, the foreshortening of perspective disappears, and all proofs become white—a disagreeable fact; for this strange region would have been marvellous if reproduced with photographic exactness. It is but a group of hollows, craters, circles, a network of crests; then, as far as the eye could see, a whole volcanic network cast upon this encrusted soil. One can then understand that the bubbles of this central irruption have kept their first form. Crystallised by cooling, they have stereotyped that aspect which the moon formerly presented when under the Plutonian forces.

The distance which separated the travellers from the annular summits of Tycho was not so great but that they could catch the principal details. Even on the causeway forming the fortifications of Tycho, the mountains hanging on to the interior and exterior sloping flanks rose in stories like gigantic terraces. They appeared to be higher by 300 or 400 feet to the west than to the east. No system of terrestrial encampment could equal these natural fortifications. A town built at the bottom of this circular cavity would have been utterly inaccessible.

Inaccessible and wonderfully extended over this soil covered with picturesque projections! Indeed, nature had not left the bottom of this crater flat and empty. It possessed its own peculiar orography, a mountainous system, making it a world in itself. The travellers could distinguish clearly cones, central hills, remarkable positions of the soil, naturally placed to receive the *chefs-d'oeuvre* of Selenite architecture. There was marked out the place for a temple, here the ground of a forum, on this spot the plan of a palace, in another the plateau for a citadel; the whole overlooked by a central mountain of 1,500 feet. A vast circle, in which ancient Rome could have been held in its entirety ten times over.

"Ah!" exclaimed Michel Ardan, enthusiastic at the sight; "what a grand town might be constructed within that ring of mountains! A quiet city, a peaceful refuge, beyond all human misery. How calm and isolated those misanthropes, those haters of humanity might live there, and all who have a distaste for social life!"

"All! It would be too small for them," replied Barbicane simply.

Chapter XVIII

GRAVE QUESTIONS

BUT THE PROJECTILE HAD PASSED THE *ENCEINTE* OF TYCHO, AND BARBICANE AND HIS two companions watched with scrupulous attention the brilliant rays which the celebrated mountain shed so curiously over the horizon.

What was this radiant glory? What geological phenomenon had designed these ardent beams? This question occupied Barbicane's mind.

Under his eyes ran in all directions luminous furrows, raised at the edges and concave in the centre, some twelve miles, others thirty miles broad. These brilliant trains extended in some places to within 600 miles of Tycho, and seemed to cover, particularly towards the east, the north-east and the north, the half of the southern hemisphere. One of these jets extended as far as the circle of Neander, situated on the 40th meridian. Another, by a slight curve, furrowed the "Sea of Nectar," breaking against the chain of Pyrenees, after a circuit of 800 miles. Others, towards the west, covered the "Sea of Clouds" and the "Sea of Humours" with a luminous network. What was the origin of these sparkling rays, which shone on the plains as well as on the reliefs, at whatever height they might be? All started from a common centre, the crater of Tycho. They sprang from him. Herschel attributed their brilliancy to currents of lava congealed by the cold; an opinion, however, which has not been generally adopted. Other astronomers have seen in these inexplicable rays a kind of moraines, rows of erratic blocks, which had been thrown up at the period of Tycho's formation.

"And why not?" asked Nicholl of Barbicane, who was relating and rejecting these different opinions.

"Because the regularity of these luminous lines, and the violence necessary to carry volcanic matter to such distances, is inexplicable."

"Eh! by Jove!" replied Michel Ardan, "it seems easy enough to me to explain the origin of these rays."

"Indeed?" said Barbicane.

"Indeed," continued Michel. "It is enough to say that it is a vast star, similar to that produced by a ball or a stone thrown at a square of glass!"

"Well!" replied Barbicane, smiling. "And what hand would be powerful enough to throw a ball to give such a shock as that?"

"The hand is not necessary," answered Nicholl, not at all confounded; "and as to the stone, let us suppose it to be a comet."

"Ah! those much-abused comets!" exclaimed Barbicane. "My brave Michel, your explanation is not bad; but your comet is useless. The shock which produced that rent must have come from the inside of the star. A violent contraction of the lunar crust, while cooling, might suffice to imprint this gigantic star."

"A contraction! something like a lunar stomach-ache," said Michel Ardan.

"Besides," added Barbicane, "this opinion is that of an English savant, Nasmyth, and it seems to me to sufficiently explain the radiation of these mountains."

"That Nasmyth was no fool!" replied Michel.

Long did the travellers, whom such a sight could never weary, admire the splendours of Tycho. Their projectile, saturated with luminous gleams in the double irradiation of sun and moon, must have appeared like an incandescent globe. They had passed suddenly from excessive cold to intense heat. Nature was thus preparing them to become Selenites. Become Selenites! That idea brought up once more the question of the habitability of the moon. After what they had seen, could the travellers solve it? Would they decide for or against it? Michel Ardan persuaded his two friends to form an opinion, and asked them directly if they thought that men and animals were represented in the lunar world.

"I think that we can answer," said Barbicane; "but according to my idea the question ought not to be put in that form. I ask it to be put differently."

"Put it your own way," replied Michel.

"Here it is," continued Barbicane. "The problem is a double one, and requires a double solution. Is the moon *habitable?* Has the moon ever been *inhabitable?*"

"Good!" replied Nicholl. "First let us see whether the moon is habitable."

"To tell the truth, I know nothing about it," answered Michel.

"And I answer in the negative," continued Barbicane. "In her actual state, with her surrounding atmosphere certainly very much reduced, her seas for the most part dried up, her insufficient supply of water restricted, vegetation, sudden alternations of cold and heat, her days and nights of 354 hours—the moon does not seem habitable to me, nor does she seem propitious to animal development, nor sufficient for the wants of existence as we understand it."

"Agreed," replied Nicholl. "But is not the moon habitable for creatures differently organised from ourselves?"

"That question is more difficult to answer, but I will try; and I ask Nicholl if *motion* appears to him to be a necessary result of *life,* whatever be its organisation?"

"Without a doubt!" answered Nicholl.

"Then, my worthy companion, I would answer that we have observed the lunar continent at a distance of 500 yards at most, and that nothing seemed to us to move on the moon's surface. The presence of any kind of life would have been betrayed by its attendant marks, such as divers buildings, and even by ruins. And what have we seen? Everywhere and always the geological works of nature, never the work of man. If, then, there exist representatives of the animal kingdom on the moon, they must have fled to those unfathomable cavities which the eye cannot reach; which I cannot admit, for they must have left traces of their passage on those plains which the atmosphere must cover, however slightly raised it may be. These traces are nowhere visible. There remains but one hypothesis, that of a living race to which motion, which is life, is foreign."

"One might as well say, living creatures which do not live," replied Michel.

"Just so," said Barbicane, "which for us has no meaning."

"Then we may form our opinion?" said Michel.

"Yes," replied Nicholl.

"Very well," continued Michel Ardan, "the Scientific Commission assembled in the projectile of the Gun Club, after having founded their argument on facts recently observed, decide unanimously upon the question of the habitability of the moon—'*No!* the moon is not habitable.' "

This decision was consigned by President Barbicane to his note-book, where the process of the sitting of the 6th of December may be seen.

"Now," said Nicholl, "let us attack the second question, an indispensable complement of the first. I ask the honourable commission, if the moon is not habitable, has she ever been inhabited, Citizen Barbicane?"

"My friends," replied Barbicane, "I did not undertake this journey in order to form an opinion on the past habitability of our satellite; but I will add that our personal observations only confirm me in this opinion. I believe, indeed I affirm, that the moon has been inhabited by a human race organised like our own; that she has produced animals anatomically formed like the terrestrial animals: but I add that these races, human and animal, have had their day, and are now forever extinct!"

"Then," asked Michel, "the moon must be older than the earth?"

"No!" said Barbicane decidedly, "but a world which has grown old quicker, and whose formation and deformation have been more rapid. Relatively, the organising force of matter has been much more violent in the interior of the moon than in the interior of the terrestrial globe. The actual state of this cracked, twisted, and burst disc abundantly proves this. The moon and the earth were nothing but gaseous masses originally. These gases have passed into a liquid state under different influences, and the solid masses have been formed later. But most certainly our sphere was still gaseous or liquid, when the moon was solidified by cooling, and had become habitable."

"I believe it," said Nicholl.

"Then," continued Barbicane, "an atmosphere surrounded it, the waters contained within this gaseous envelope could not evaporate. Under the influence of air, water, light, solar heat, and central heat, vegetation took possession of the continents prepared to receive it, and certainly life showed itself about this period, for nature does not expend herself in vain; and a world so wonderfully formed for habitation must necessarily be inhabited."

"But," said Nicholl, "many phenomena inherent in our satellite might cramp the expansion of the animal and vegetable kingdom. For example, its days and nights of 354 hours?"

"At the terrestrial poles they last six months," said Michel.

"An argument of little value, since the poles are not inhabited."

"Let us observe, my friends," continued Barbicane, "that if in the actual state of the moon its long nights and long days created differences of temperature insupportable to organisation, it was not so at the historical period of time. The atmosphere enveloped the disc with a fluid mantle; vapour deposited itself in the shape of clouds; this natural screen tempered the ardour of the solar rays, and retained the nocturnal radiation. Light, like heat, can diffuse itself in the air; hence an equality between the influences which no longer exists, now that atmosphere has almost entirely disappeared. And now I am going to astonish you."

"Astonish us?" said Michel Ardan.

"I firmly believe that at the period when the moon was inhabited, the nights and days did not last 354 hours!"

"And why?" asked Nicholl quickly.

"Because most probably then the rotary motion of the moon upon her axis was not equal to her revolution, an equality which presents each part of her disc during fifteen days to the action of the solar rays."

"Granted," replied Nicholl, "but why should not these two motions have been equal, as they are really so?"

"Because that equality has only been determined by terrestrial attraction. And who can say that this attraction was powerful enough to alter the motion of the moon at that period when the earth was still fluid?"

"Just so," replied Nicholl; "and who can say that the moon has always been a satellite of the earth?"

"And who can say," exclaimed Michel Ardan, "that the moon did not exist before the earth?"

Their imaginations carried them away into an indefinite field of hypothesis. Barbicane sought to restrain them.

"Those speculations are too high," said he; "problems utterly insoluble. Do not let us enter upon them. Let us only admit the insufficiency of the primordial attraction; and then by the inequality of the two motions of rotation and revolution, the days and nights could have succeeded each other on the moon as they succeed each other on the earth. Besides, even without these conditions, life was possible."

"And so," asked Michel Ardan, "humanity has disappeared from the moon?"

"Yes," replied Barbicane, "after having doubtless remained persistently for millions of centuries; by degrees the atmosphere becoming rarefied, the disc became uninhabitable, as the terrestrial globe will one day become by cooling."

"By cooling?"

"Certainly," replied Barbicane; "as the internal fires became extinguished, and the incandescent matter concentrated itself, the lunar crust cooled. By degrees the consequences of these phenomena showed themselves in the disappearance of organised beings, and by the disappearance of vegetation. Soon the atmosphere was rarefied, probably withdrawn by terrestrial attraction; then aerial departure of respirable air, and disappearance of water by means of evaporation. At this period the moon becoming uninhabitable, was no longer inhabited. It was a dead world, such as we see it to-day."

"And you say that the same fate is in store for the earth?"

"Most probably."

"But when?"

"When the cooling of its crust shall have made it uninhabitable."

"And have they calculated the time which our unfortunate sphere will take to cool?"

"Certainly."

"And you know these calculations?"

"Perfectly."

"But speak, then, my clumsy savant," exclaimed Michel Ardan, "for you make me boil with impatience!"

"Very well, my good Michel," replied Barbicane quietly; "we know what diminution of temperature the earth undergoes in the lapse of a century. And according to certain calculations, this mean temperature will after a period of 400,000 years, be brought down to zero!"

"Four hundred thousand years!" exclaimed Michel. "Ah! I breathe again. Really I was frightened to hear you; I imagined that we had not more than 50,000 years to live."

Barbicane and Nicholl could not help laughing at their companion's uneasiness. Then Nicholl, who wished to end the discussion, put the second question, which had just been considered again.

"Has the moon been inhabited?" he asked.

The answer was unanimously in the affirmative. But during this discussion, fruitful in somewhat hazardous theories, the projectile was rapidly leaving the moon: the lineaments faded away from the travellers' eyes, mountains were confused in the distance; and of all the wonderful, strange, and fantastical form of the earth's satellite, there soon remained nothing but the imperishable remembrance.

Chapter XIX

A STRUGGLE AGAINST THE IMPOSSIBLE

FOR A LONG TIME BARBICANE AND HIS COMPANIONS LOOKED SILENTLY AND SADLY UPON that world which they had only seen from a distance, as Moses saw the land of Canaan, and which they were leaving without a possibility of ever returning to it. The projectile's position with regard to the moon had altered, and the base was now turned to the earth.

This change, which Barbicane verified, did not fail to surprise them. If the projectile was to gravitate round the satellite in an elliptical orbit, why was not its heaviest part turned towards it, as the moon turns hers to the earth? That was a difficult point.

In watching the course of the projectile they could see that on leaving the moon it followed a course analogous to that traced in approaching her. It was describing a very long ellipse, which would most likely extend to the point of equal attraction, where the influences of the earth and its satellite are neutralised.

Such was the conclusion which Barbicane very justly drew from facts already observed, a conviction which his two friends shared with him.

"And when arrived at this dead point, what will become of us?" asked Michel Ardan.

"We don't know," replied Barbicane.

"But one can draw some hypotheses, I suppose?"

"Two," answered Barbicane; "either the projectile's speed will be insufficient, and it will remain forever immovable on this line of double attraction—"

"I prefer the other hypothesis, whatever it may be," interrupted Michel.

"Or," continued Barbicane, "its speed will be sufficient, and it will continue its elliptical course, to gravitate forever around the orb of night."

"A revolution not at all consoling," said Michel, "to pass to the state of humble servants to a moon whom we are accustomed to look upon as our own handmaid. So that is the fate in store for us?"

Neither Barbicane nor Nicholl answered.

"You do not answer," continued Michel impatiently.

"There is nothing to answer," said Nicholl.

"Is there nothing to try?"

"No," answered Barbicane. "Do you pretend to fight against the impossible?"

"Why not? Do one Frenchman and two Americans shrink from such a word?"

"But what would you do?"

"Subdue this motion which is bearing us away."

"Subdue it?"

"Yes," continued Michel, getting animated, "or else alter it, and employ it to the accomplishment of our own ends."

"And how?"

"That is your affair. If artillerymen are not masters of their projectile they are not artillerymen. If the projectile is to command the gunner, we had better ram the gunner into the gun. My faith! fine savants! who do not know what is to become of us after inducing me—"

"Inducing you!" cried Barbicane and Nicholl. "Inducing you! What do you mean by that?"

"No recrimination," said Michel. "I do not complain; the trip has pleased me, and the projectile agrees with me; but let us do all that is humanly possible to do to fall somewhere, even if only on the moon."

"We ask no better, my worthy Michel," replied Barbicane, "but means fail us."

"We cannot alter the motion of the projectile?"

"No."

"Nor diminish its speed?"

"No."

"Not even by lightening it, as they lighten an overloaded vessel?"

"What would you throw out?" said Nicholl. "We have no ballast on board; and indeed it seems to me that if lightened it would go much quicker."

"Slower."

"Quicker."

"Neither slower nor quicker," said Barbicane, wishing to make his two friends agree; "for we float is space, and must no longer consider specific weight."

"Very well," cried Michel Ardan in a decided voice; "then their remains but one thing to do."

"What is it?" asked Nicholl.

"Breakfast," answered the cool, audacious Frenchman, who always brought up this solution at the most difficult juncture.

In any case, if this operation had no influence on the projectile's course, it could at least be tried without inconvenience, and even with success from a stomachic point of view. Certainly Michel had none but good ideas.

They breakfasted then at two in the morning; the hour mattered little. Michel served his usual repast, crowned by a glorious bottle drawn from his private cellar. If ideas did not crowd on their brains, we must despair of the Chambertin of 1853. The repast finished, observation began again. Around the projectile, at an invariable distance, were the objects which had been thrown out. Evidently, in its translatory motion round the moon, it had not passed through any atmosphere, for the specific weight of these different objects would have checked their relative speed.

On the side of the terrestrial sphere nothing was to be seen. The earth was but a day old, having been new the night before at twelve; and two days must elapse before its crescent, freed from the solar rays, would serve as a clock to the Selenites, as in its rotary movement each of its points after twenty-four hours repasses the same lunar meridian.

On the moon's side the sight was different; the orb shone in all her splendour amid innumerable constellations, whose purity could not be troubled by her rays. On the disc, the plains were already returning to the dark tint which is seen from the earth. The other part of the nimbus remained brilliant, and in the midst of this general brilliancy Tycho shone prominently like a sun.

Barbicane had no means of estimating the projectile's speed, but reasoning showed that it must uniformly decrease, according to the laws of mechanical reasoning. Having admitted that the projectile was describing an orbit around the moon, this orbit must necessarily be elliptical; science proves that it must be so. No motive body circulating round an attracting body fails in this law. Every orbit described in space is elliptical. And why should the projectile of the Gun Club escape this natural arrangement? In elliptical orbits, the attracting body always occupies one of the foci; so that at one moment the satellite is nearer, and at another farther from the orb around which it gravitates. When the earth is nearest the sun she is in her perihelion; and in her aphelion at the farthest point. Speaking of the moon, she is nearest to the earth in her perigee, and farthest from it in her apogee. To use analogous expressions, with which the astronomers' language is enriched, if the projectile remains as a satellite of the moon, we must say that it is in its "aposelene" at its farthest point, and in its "periselene" at its nearest. In the latter case, the projectile would attain its maximum of speed; and in the former its minimum. It was evidently moving towards its aposelenitical point; and Barbicane had reason to think that its speed would decrease up to this point, and then increase by degrees as it neared the moon. This speed would even become *nil*, if this point joined that of equal attraction. Barbicane studied the consequences of these different situations, and thinking what inference he could draw from them, when he was roughly disturbed by a cry from Michel Ardan.

"By Jove!" he exclaimed, "I must admit we are down-right simpletons!"

"I do not say we are not," replied Barbicane; "but why?"

"Because we have a very simple means of checking this speed which is bearing us from the moon, and we do not use it!"

"And what is the means?"

"To use the recoil contained in our rockets."

"Done!" said Nicholl.

"We have not used this force yet," said Barbicane, "it is true, but we will do so."

"When?" asked Michel.

"When the time comes. Observe, my friends, that in the position occupied by the projectile, an oblique position with regard to the lunar disc, our rockets, in slightly altering its direction, might turn it from the moon instead of drawing it nearer?"

"Just so," replied Michel.

"Let us wait, then. By some inexplicable influence, the projectile is turning its base towards the earth. It is probable that at the point of equal attraction, its conical cap will be directed rigidly towards the moon; at that moment we may hope that its speed will be *nil*; then will be the moment to act, and with the influence of our rockets we may perhaps provoke a fall directly on the surface of the lunar disc."

"Bravo!" said Michel. "What we did not do, what we could not do on our first passage at the dead point, because the projectile was then endowed with too great a speed."

"Very well reasoned," said Nicholl.

"Let us wait patiently," continued Barbicane. "Putting every chance on our side, and after having so much despaired, I may say I think we shall gain our end."

This conclusion was a signal for Michel Ardan's hips and hurrahs. And none of the audacious boobies remembered the question that they themselves had solved in the negative. No! the moon is not inhabited; no! the moon is probably not habitable. And yet they were going to try everything to reach her.

One single question remained to be solved. At what precise moment the projectile would reach the point of equal attraction, on which the travellers must play their last card. In order to calculate this to within a few seconds, Barbicane had only to refer to his notes, and to reckon the different heights taken on the lunar parallels. Thus the time necessary to travel over the distance between the dead point and the south pole would be equal to the distance separating the north pole from the dead point. The hours representing the time travelled over were carefully noted, and the calculation was easy. Barbicane found that this point would be reached at one in the morning on the night of the 7th–8th of December. So that, if nothing interfered with its course, it would reach the given point in twenty-two hours.

The rockets had primarily been placed to check the fall of the projectile upon the moon, and now they were going to employ them for a directly contrary purpose. In any case they were ready, and they had only to wait for the moment to set fire to them.

"Since there is nothing else to be done," said Nicholl, "I make a proposition."

"What is it?" asked Barbicane.

"I propose to go to sleep."

"What a motion!" exclaimed Michel Ardan.

"It is forty hours since we closed our eyes," said Nicholl. "Some hours of sleep will restore our strength."

"Never," interrupted Michel.

"Well," continued Nicholl, "everyone to his taste; I shall go to sleep." And stretching himself on the divan, he soon snored like a forty-eight pounder.

"That Nicholl has a good deal of sense," said Barbicane; "presently I shall follow his example." Some moments after his continued bass supported the captain's baritone.

"Certainly," said Michel Ardan, finding himself alone, "these practical people have sometimes most opportune ideas."

And with his long legs stretched out, and his great arms folded under his head, Michel slept in his turn.

But this sleep could be neither peaceful nor lasting, the minds of these three men were too much occupied, and some hours after, about seven in the morning, all three were on foot at the same instant.

The projectile was still leaving the moon, and turning its conical part more and more towards her.

An explicable phenomenon, but one which happily served Barbicane's ends.

Seventeen hours more, and the moment for action would have arrived.

The day seemed long. However bold the travellers might be, they were greatly impressed by the approach of that moment which would decide all—either precipitate their fall on to the moon, or forever chain them in an immutable orbit. They counted the hours as they passed too slow for their wish; Barbicane and Nicholl were obstinately plunged in their calculations, Michel going and coming between the narrow walls, and watching that impassive moon with a longing eye.

At times recollections of the earth crossed their minds. They saw once more their friends of the Gun Club, and the dearest of all, J. T. Maston. At that moment, the honourable secretary must be filling his post on the Rocky Mountains. If he could see the projectile through the glass of his gigantic telescope, what would he think? After seeing it disappear behind the moon's south pole, he would see them reappear by the north pole! They must therefore be a satellite of a satellite! Had J. T. Maston given this unexpected news to the world? Was this the *denouement* of this great enterprise?

But the day passed without incident. The terrestrial midnight arrived. The 8th of December was beginning. One hour more, and the point of equal attraction would be reached. What speed would then animate the projectile? They could not estimate it. But no error could vitiate Barbicane's calculations. At one in the morning this speed ought to be and would be *nil*.

Besides, another phenomenon would mark the projectile's stopping-point on the neutral line. At that spot the two attractions, lunar and terrestrial, would be annulled. Objects would "weigh" no more. This singular fact, which had surprised Barbicane and his companions so much in going, would be repeated on their return under the very same conditions. At this precise moment they must act.

Already the projectile's conical top was sensibly turned towards the lunar disc, presented in such a way as to utilise the whole of the recoil produced by the pressure of the rocket apparatus. The chances were in favour of the travellers. If its speed was utterly annulled on this dead point, a decided movement towards the moon would suffice, however slight, to determine its fall.

"Five minutes to one," said Nicholl.

"All is ready," replied Michel Ardan, directing a lighted match to the flame of the gas.

"Wait!" said Barbicane, holding his chronometer in his hand.

At that moment weight had no effect. The travellers felt in themselves the entire disappearance of it. They were very near the neutral point, if they did not touch it.

"One o'clock," said Barbicane.

Michel Ardan applied the lighted match to a train in communication with the rockets. No detonation was heard in the inside, for there was no air. But, through the scuttles, Barbicane saw a prolonged smoke, the flames of which were immediately extinguished.

The projectile sustained a certain shock, which was sensibly felt in the interior.

The three friends looked and listened without speaking, and scarcely breathing. One might have heard the beating of their hearts amid this perfect silence.

"Are we falling?" asked Michel Ardan, at length.

"No," said Nicholl, "since the bottom of the projectile is not turning to the lunar disc!"

At this moment, Barbicane, quitting his scuttle, turned to his two companions. He was frightfully pale, his forehead wrinkled, and his lips contracted.

"We are falling!" said he.

"Ah!" cried Michel Ardan, "on to the moon?"

"On to the earth!"

"The devil!" exclaimed Michel Ardan, adding philosophically, "well, when we came into this projectile we were very doubtful as to the ease with which we should get out of it!"

And now this fearful fall had begun. The speed retained had borne the projectile beyond the dead point. The explosion of the rockets could not divert its course. This speed in going had carried it over the neutral line, and in returning had done the same thing. The laws of physics condemned it *to pass through every point which it had already gone through*. It was a terrible fall, from a height of 160,000 miles, and no springs to break it. According to the laws of gunnery, the projectile must strike the earth with a speed equal to that with which it left the mouth of the *Columbiad*, a speed of 16,000 yards in the last second.

But to give some figures of comparison, it has been reckoned that an object thrown from the top of the towers of Notre Dame, the height of which is only 200 feet, will arrive on the pavement at a speed of 240 miles per hour. Here the projectile must strike the earth with a speed of 115,200 miles per hour.

"We are lost!" said Michel coolly.

"Very well! if we die," answered Barbicane, with a sort of religious enthusiasm, "the results of our travels will be magnificently spread. It is His own secret that God will tell us! In the other life the soul will want to know nothing, either of machines or engines! It will be identified with eternal wisdom!"

"In fact," interrupted Michel Ardan, "the whole of the other world may well console us for the loss of that inferior orb called the moon!"

Barbicane crossed his arms on his breast, with a motion of sublime resignation, saying at the same time:

"The will of heaven be done!"

Chapter XX

The Soundings of the SUSQUEHANNA

WELL, LIEUTENANT, AND OUR SOUNDINGS?"

"I think, sir, that the operation is nearing its completion," replied Lieutenant Bronsfield. "But who would have thought of finding such a depth so near in shore, and only 200 miles from the American coast?"

"Certainly, Bronsfield, there is a great depression," said Captain Blomsberry. "In this spot there is a submarine valley worn by Humboldt's current, which skirts the coast of America as far as the Straits of Magellan."

"These great depths," continued the lieutenant, "are not favourable for laying telegraphic cables. A level bottom, like that supporting the American cable between Valentia and Newfoundland, is much better."

"I agree with you, Bronsfield. With your permission, lieutenant, where are we now?"

"Sir, at this moment we have 3,508 fathoms of line out, and the ball which draws the sounding lead has not yet touched the bottom; for if so, it would have come up of itself."

"Brook's apparatus is very ingenious," said Captain Blomsberry; "it gives us very exact soundings."

"Touch!" cried at this moment one of the men at the forewheel, who was superintending the operation.

The captain and the lieutenant mounted the quarterdeck.

"What depth have we?" asked the captain.

"Three thousand six hundred and twenty-seven fathoms," replied the lieutenant, entering it in his note-book.

"Well, Bronsfield," said the captain, "I will take down the result. Now haul in the sounding line. It will be the work of some hours. In that time the engineer can light the furnaces, and we shall be ready to start as soon as you have finished. It is ten o'clock, and with your permission, lieutenant, I will turn in."

"Do so, sir; do so!" replied the lieutenant obligingly.

The captain of the *Susquehanna*, as brave a man as need be, and the humble servant of his officers, returned to his cabin, took a brandy-grog, which earned for the steward no end of praise, and turned in, not without having complimented his servant upon his making beds, and slept a peaceful sleep.

It was then ten at night. The eleventh day of the month of December was drawing to a close in a magnificent night.

The *Susquehanna*, a corvette of 500 horse-power, of the United States navy, was occupied in taking soundings in the Pacific Ocean about 200 miles off the American coast, following that long peninsula which stretches down the coast of Mexico.

The wind had dropped by degrees. There was no disturbance in the air. The pennant hung motionless from the maintop-gallant-mast truck.

Captain Jonathan Blomsberry (cousin-german of Colonel Blomsberry, one of the most ardent supporters of the Gun Club, who had married an aunt of the captain and daughter of an honourable Kentucky merchant)—Captain Blomsberry could not have wished for finer weather in which to bring to a close his delicate operations of sounding. His corvette had not even felt the great tempest, which by sweeping away the groups of clouds on the Rocky Mountains, had allowed them to observe the course of the famous projectile.

Everything went well, and with all the fervor of a Presbyterian, he did not forget to thank heaven for it. The series of soundings taken by the *Susquehanna*, had for its aim the finding of a favourable spot for the laying of a submarine cable to connect the Hawaiian Islands with the coast of America.

It was a great undertaking, due to the instigation of a powerful company. Its managing director, the intelligent Cyrus Field, purposed even covering all the islands of Oceanica with a vast electrical network, an immense enterprise, and one worthy of American genius.

To the corvette *Susquehanna* had been confided the first operations of sounding. It was on the night of the 11th–12th of December, she was in exactly 27° 7' north latitude, and 41° 37' west longitude, on the meridian of Washington.

The moon, then in her last quarter, was beginning to rise above the horizon.

After the departure of Captain Blomsberry, the lieutenant and some officers were standing together on the poop. On the appearance of the moon, their thoughts turned to that orb which the eyes of a whole hemisphere were contemplating. The best naval glasses could not have discovered the projectile wandering around its hemisphere, and yet all were pointed towards that brilliant disc which millions of eyes were looking at at the same moment.

"They have been gone ten days," said Lieutenant Bronsfield at last. "What has become of them?"

"They have arrived, lieutenant," exclaimed a young midshipman, "and they are doing what all travellers do when they arrive in a new country, taking a walk!"

"Oh! I am sure of that, if you tell me so, my young friend," said Lieutenant Bronsfield, smiling.

"But," continued another officer, "their arrival cannot be doubted. The projectile was to reach the moon when full on the 5th at midnight. We are now at the 11th of December, which makes six days. And in six times twenty-four hours, without darkness, one would have time to settle comfortably. I fancy I see my brave countrymen encamped at the bottom of some valley, on the borders of a Selenite stream, near a projectile half-buried by its fall amid volcanic rubbish, Captain Nicholl beginning his levelling operations, President Barbicane writing out his notes, and Michel Ardan embalming the lunar solitudes with the perfume of his—"

"Yes! it must be so, it is so!" exclaimed the young midshipman, worked up to a pitch of enthusiasm by this ideal description of his superior officer.

"I should like to believe it," replied the lieutenant, who was quite unmoved. "Unfortunately direct news from the lunar world is still wanting."

"Beg pardon, lieutenant," said the midshipman, "but cannot President Barbicane write?"

A burst of laughter greeted this answer.

"No letters!" continued the young man quickly. "The postal administration has something to see to there."

"Might it not be the telegraphic service that is at fault?" asked one of the officers ironically.

"Not necessarily," replied the midshipman, not at all confused. "But it is very easy to set up a graphic communication with the earth."

"And how?"

"By means of the telescope at Long's Peak. You know it brings the moon to within four miles of the Rocky Mountains, and that it shows objects on its surface of only nine feet in diameter. Very well; let our industrious friends construct a giant alphabet; let them write words three fathoms long, and sentences three miles long, and then they can send us news of themselves?"

The young midshipman, who had a certain amount of imagination, was loudly applauded; Lieutenant Bronsfield allowing that the idea was possible, but observing that if by these means they could receive news from the lunar world they could not send any from the terrestrial, unless the Selenites had instruments fit for taking distant observations at their disposal.

"Evidently," said one of the officers; "but what has become of the travellers? what they have done, what they have seen, that above all must interest us. Besides, if the experiment has succeeded (which I do not doubt), they will try it again. The *Columbiad* is still sunk in the soil of Florida. It is now only a question of powder and shot; and everytime the moon is at her zenith a cargo of visitors may be sent to her."

"It is clear," replied Lieutenant Bronsfield, "that J. T. Maston will one day join his friends."

"If he will have me," cried the midshipman, "I am ready!"

"Oh! volunteers will not be wanting," answered Bronsfield; "and if it were allowed, half of the earth's inhabitants would emigrate to the moon!"

This conversation between the officers of the *Susquehanna* was kept up until nearly one in the morning. We cannot say what blundering systems were broached, what inconsistent theories advanced by these bold spirits. Since Barbicane's attempt, nothing seemed impossible to the Americans. They had already designed an expedition, not only of savants, but of a whole colony towards the Selenite borders, and a complete army, consisting of infantry, artillery, and cavalry, to conquer the lunar world.

At one in the morning, the hauling in of the sounding-line was not yet completed; 1,670 fathoms were still out, which would entail some hours' work. According to the commander's orders, the fires had been lighted, and steam was being got up. The *Susquehanna* could have started that very instant.

At that moment (it was seventeen minutes past one in the morning) Lieutenant Bronsfield was preparing to leave the watch and return to his cabin, when his attention was attracted by a distant hissing noise. His comrades and himself first thought that this hissing was caused by the letting off of steam; but lifting their heads, they found that the noise was produced in the highest regions of the air. They had not time to question each other before the hissing became frightfully intense, and suddenly there appeared to their dazzled eyes an enormous meteor, ignited by the rapidity of its course and its friction through the atmospheric strata.

This fiery mass grew larger to their eyes, and fell, with the noise of thunder, upon the bowsprit, which it smashed close to the stem, and buried itself in the waves with a deafening roar!

A few feet nearer, and the *Susquehanna* would have foundered with all on board!

At this instant Captain Blomsberry appeared, half-dressed, and rushing on to the forecastle-deck, whither all the officers had hurried, exclaimed, "With your permission, gentlemen, what has happened?"

And the midshipman, making himself as it were the echo of the body, cried, "Commander, it is 'they' come back again!"

Chapter XXI

J. T. MASTON RECALLED

IT IS 'THEY' COME BACK AGAIN!" THE YOUNG MIDSHIPMAN HAD SAID, AND EVERYONE HAD understood him. No one doubted but that the meteor was the projectile of the Gun Club. As to the travellers which it enclosed, opinions were divided regarding their fate.

"They are dead!" said one.

"They are alive!" said another; "the crater is deep, and the shock was deadened."

"But they must have wanted air," continued a third speaker; "they must have died of suffocation."

"Burned!" replied a fourth; "the projectile was nothing but an incandescent mass as it crossed the atmosphere."

"What does it matter!" they exclaimed unanimously; "living or dead, we must pull them out!"

But Captain Blomsberry had assembled his officers, and "with their permission," was holding a council. They must decide upon something to be done immediately. The more hasty ones were for fishing up the projectile. A difficult operation, though not an impossible one. But the corvette had no proper machinery, which must be both fixed and powerful; so it was resolved that they should put in at the nearest port, and give information to the Gun Club of the projectile's fall.

This determination was unanimous. The choice of the port had to be discussed. The neighbouring coast had no anchorage on 27° latitude. Higher up, above the peninsula of Monterey, stands the important town from which it takes its name; but, seated on the borders of a perfect desert, it was not connected with the interior by a network of telegraphic wires, and electricity alone could spread these important news fast enough.

Some degrees above opened the bay of San Francisco. Through the capital of the gold country communication would be easy with the heart of the Union. And in less than two days the *Susquehanna*, by putting on high pressure, could arrive in that port. She must therefore start at once.

The fires were made up; they could set off immediately. Two thousand fathoms of line were still out, which Captain Blomsberry, not wishing to lose precious time in hauling in, resolved to cut.

"We will fasten the end to a buoy," said he, "and that buoy will show us the exact spot where the projectile fell."

"Besides," replied Lieutenant Bronsfield, "we have our situation exact—27° 7' north latitude and 41° 37' west longitude."

"Well, Mr. Bronsfield," replied the captain, "now, with your permission, we will have the line cut."

A strong buoy, strengthened by a couple of spars, was thrown into the ocean. The end of the rope was carefully lashed to it; and, left solely to the rise and fall of the billows, the buoy would not sensibly deviate from the spot.

At this moment the engineer sent to inform the captain that steam was up and they could start, for which agreeable communication the captain thanked him. The course was then given north-northeast, and the corvette, wearing, steered at full steam direct for San Francisco. It was three in the morning.

Four hundred and fifty miles to cross; it was nothing for a good vessel like the *Susquehanna*. In thirty-six hours she had covered that distance; and on the 14th of December, at twenty-seven minutes past one at night, she entered the bay of San Francisco.

At the sight of a ship of the national navy arriving at full speed, with her bowsprit broken, public curiosity was greatly roused. A dense crowd soon assembled on the quay, waiting for them to disembark.

After casting anchor, Captain Blomsberry and Lieutenant Bronsfield entered an eight-oared cutter, which soon brought them to land.

They jumped on to the quay.

"The telegraph?" they asked, without answering one of the thousand questions addressed to them.

The officer of the port conducted them to the telegraph office through a concourse of spectators. Blomsberry and Bronsfield entered, while the crowd crushed each other at the door.

Some minutes later a fourfold telegram was sent out—the first to the Naval Secretary at Washington; the second to the vice-president of the Gun Club, Baltimore; the third to the Hon. J. T. Maston, Long's Peak, Rocky Mountains; and the fourth to the sub-director of the Cambridge Observatory, Massachusetts.

It was worded as follows:

In 20° 7' north latitude, and 41° 37' west longitude, on the 12th of December, at seventeen minutes past one in the morning, the projectile of the *Columbiad* fell into the Pacific. Send instructions.

BLOMSBERRY, Commander *Susquehanna*.

Five minutes afterward the whole town of San Francisco learned the news. Before six in the evening the different States of the Union had heard the great catastrophe; and after midnight, by the cable, the whole of Europe knew the result of the great American experiment. We will not attempt to picture the effect produced on the entire world by that unexpected *denouement*.

On receipt of the telegram the Naval Secretary telegraphed to the *Susquehanna* to wait in the bay of San Francisco without extinguishing her fires. Day and night she must be ready to put to sea.

The Cambridge observatory called a special meeting; and, with that composure which distinguishes learned bodies in general, peacefully discussed the scientific bearings of the question. At the Gun Club there was an explosion. All the gunners were assembled. Vice-President the Hon. Wilcome was in the act of reading the premature despatch, in which J. T. Maston and Belfast announced that the projectile had just been seen in the gigantic reflector of Long's Peak, and also that it was held by lunar attraction, and was playing the part of undersatellite to the lunar world.

We know the truth on that point.

But on the arrival of Blomsberry's despatch, so decidedly contradicting J. T. Maston's telegram, two parties were formed in the bosom of the Gun Club. On one side were those who admitted the fall of the projectile, and consequently the return of the travellers; on the other, those who believed in the observations of Long's Peak, concluded that the commander of the *Susquehanna* had made a mistake. To the latter the pretended projectile was nothing but a meteor! nothing but a meteor, a shooting globe, which in its fall had smashed the bows of the corvette. It was difficult to answer this argument, for the speed with which it was animated must have made observation very difficult. The commander of the *Susquehanna* and her officers might have made a mistake in all good faith; one argument however, was in their favour, namely, that if the projectile had fallen on the earth, its place of meeting with the terrestrial globe could only take place on this 27° north latitude, and (taking into consideration the time that had elapsed, and the rotary motion of the earth) between the 41° and the 42° of west longitude. In any case, it was decided in the Gun Club that Blomsberry brothers, Bilsby, and Major Elphinstone should go straight to San Francisco, and consult as to the means of raising the projectile from the depths of the ocean.

These devoted men set off at once; and the railroad, which will soon cross the whole of Central America, took them as far as St. Louis, where the swift mail-coaches awaited them. Almost at the same moment in which the Secretary of Marine, the vice-president of the Gun Club, and the sub-director of the Observatory received the despatch from San Francisco, the honourable J. T. Maston was undergoing the greatest excitement he had ever experienced in his life, an excitement which even the bursting of his pet gun, which had more than once nearly cost him his life, had not caused him. We may remember that the secretary of the Gun Club had started soon after the projectile (and almost as quickly) for the station on Long's Peak, in the Rocky Mountains, J. Belfast, director of the Cambridge Observatory, accompanying him. Arrived there, the two friends had installed themselves at once, never quitting the summit of their enormous telescope. We know that this gigantic instrument had been set up according to the reflecting system, called by the English "front view." This arrangement subjected all objects to but one reflection, making the view consequently much clearer; the result was that, when they were taking observation, J. T. Maston and Belfast were placed in the *upper* part of the instrument and not in the lower, which they reached by a circular staircase, a masterpiece of lightness, while below them opened a metal well terminated by the metallic mirror, which measured two hundred and eighty feet in depth.

It was on a narrow platform placed above the telescope that the two savants passed their existence, execrating the day which hid the moon from their eyes, and the clouds which obstinately veiled her during the night.

What, then, was their delight when, after some days of waiting, on the night of the 5th of December, they saw the vehicle which was bearing their friends into space! To this delight succeeded a great deception, when, trusting to a cursory observation, they launched their first telegram to the world, erroneously affirming that the projectile had become a satellite of the moon, gravitating in an immutable orbit.

From that moment it had never shown itself to their eyes—a disappearance all the more easily explained, as it was then passing behind the moon's invisible disc; but when it was time for it to reappear on the visible disc, one may imagine the impatience of the fuming J. T. Maston and his not less impatient companion. Each minute of the night they thought they saw the projectile once more, and they did not see it. Hence constant discussions and violent disputes between them, Belfast affirming that the projectile could not be seen, J. T. Maston maintaining that "it had put his eyes out."

"It is the projectile!" repeated J. T. Maston.

"No," answered Belfast; "it is an avalanche detached from a lunar mountain."

"Well, we shall see it to-morrow."

"No, we shall not see it any more. It is carried into space."

"Yes!"

"No!"

And at these moments, when contradictions rained like hail, the well-known irritability of the secretary of the Gun Club constituted a permanent danger for the honourable Belfast. The existence of these two together would soon have become impossible; but an unforseen event cut short their everlasting discussions.

During the night, from the 14th to the 15th of December, the two irreconcilable friends were busy observing the lunar disc, J. T. Maston abusing the learned Belfast as usual, who was by his side; the secretary of the Gun Club maintaining for the thousandth time that he had just seen the projectile, and adding that he could see Michel Ardan's face looking through one of the scuttles, at the same time enforcing his argument by a series of gestures which his formidable hook rendered very unpleasant.

At this moment Belfast's servant appeared on the platform (it was ten at night) and gave him a despatch. It was the commander of the *Susquehanna*'s telegram.

Belfast tore the envelope and read, and uttered a cry.

"What!" said J. T. Maston.

"The projectile!"

"Well!"

"Has fallen to the earth!"

Another cry, this time a perfect howl, answered him. He turned towards J. T. Maston. The unfortunate man, imprudently leaning over the metal tube, had disappeared in the immense telescope. A fall of two hundred and eighty feet! Belfast, dismayed, rushed to the orifice of the reflector.

He breathed. J. T. Maston, caught by his metal hook, was holding on by one of the rings which bound the telescope together, uttering fearful cries.

Belfast called. Help was brought, tackle was let down, and they hoisted up, not without some trouble, the imprudent secretary of the Gun Club.

He reappeared at the upper orifice without hurt.

"Ah!" said he, "if I had broken the mirror?"

"You would have paid for it," replied Belfast severely.

"And that cursed projectile has fallen?" asked J. T. Maston.

"Into the Pacific!"

"Let us go!"

A quarter of an hour after the two savants were descending the declivity of the Rocky Mountains; and two days after, at the same time as their friends of the Gun Club, they arrived at San Francisco, having killed five horses on the road.

Elphinstone, the brothers Blomsberry, and Bilsby rushed towards them on their arrival.

"What shall we do?" they exclaimed.

"Fish up the projectile," replied J. T. Maston, "and the sooner the better."

Chapter XXII

RECOVERED FROM THE SEA

THE SPOT WHERE THE PROJECTILE SANK UNDER THE WAVES WAS EXACTLY KNOWN; BUT the machinery to grasp it and bring it to the surface of the ocean was still wanting. It must first be invented, then made. American engineers could not be troubled with such trifles. The grappling-irons once fixed, by their help they were sure to raise it in spite of its weight, which was lessened by the density of the liquid in which it was plunged.

But fishing-up the projectile was not the only thing to be thought of. They must act promptly in the interest of the travellers. No one doubted that they were still living.

"Yes," repeated J. T. Maston incessantly, whose confidence gained over everybody, "our friends are clever people, and they cannot have fallen like simpletons. They are alive, quite alive; but we must make haste if we wish to find them so. Food and water do not trouble me; they have enough for a long while. But air, air, that is what they will soon want; so quick, quick!"

And they did go quick. They fitted up the *Susquehanna* for her new destination. Her powerful machinery was brought to bear upon the hauling-chains. The aluminum projectile only weighed 19,250 pounds, a weight very inferior to that of the transatlantic cable which had been drawn up under similar conditions. The only difficulty was in fishing up a cylindro-conical projectile, the walls of which were so smooth as to offer no hold for the hooks. On that account Engineer Murchison hastened to San Francisco, and had some enormous grappling-irons fixed on an automatic system, which would never let the projectile go if it once succeeded in seizing it in its powerful claws. Diving-dresses were also prepared, which through this impervious covering allowed the divers to observe the bottom of the sea. He also had put on board an apparatus of compressed air very cleverly designed. There were perfect chambers pierced with scuttles, which, with water let into certain compartments, could draw it down into great depths. These apparatuses were at San Francisco, where they had been used in the construction of a submarine breakwater; and very fortunately it was so, for there was no time to construct any. But in spite of the perfection of the machinery, in spite of the ingenuity of the savants entrusted with the use of them, the success of the operation was far from being certain. How great were the chances against them, the projectile being 20,000 feet under the water! And if even it was brought to the surface, how would the travellers have borne the terrible shock which 20,000 feet of water had perhaps not sufficiently broken? At any rate they must act quickly. J. T. Maston hurried the workmen day and night. He was ready to don the diving-dress himself, or try the air apparatus, in order to reconnoitre the situation of his courageous friends.

But in spite of all the diligence displayed in preparing the different engines, in spite of the considerable sum placed at the disposal of the Gun Club by the Government of the Union, five long days (five centuries!) elapsed before the preparations were complete. During this time public opinion was excited to the highest pitch. Telegrams were exchanged incessantly throughout the entire world by means of wires and electric cables. The saving of Barbicane, Nicholl, and Michel Ardan was an international affair. Everyone who had subscribed to the Gun Club was directly interested in the welfare of the travellers.

At length the hauling-chains, the air-chambers, and the automatic grappling-irons were put on board. J. T. Maston, Engineer Murchison, and the delegates of the Gun Club, were already in their cabins. They had but to start, which they did on the 21st of December, at eight o'clock at night, the corvette meeting with a beautiful sea, a north-easterly wind, and rather sharp cold. The whole population of San Francisco was gathered on the quay, greatly excited but silent, reserving their hurrahs for the return. Steam was fully up, and the screw of the *Susquehanna* carried them briskly out of the bay.

It is needless to relate the conversations on board between the officers, sailors, and passengers. All these men had but one thought. All these hearts beat under the same emotion. While they were hastening to help them, what were Barbicane and his companions doing? What had become of them? Were they able to attempt any bold maneuvre to regain their liberty? None could say. The truth is that every attempt must have failed! Immersed nearly four miles under the ocean, this metal prison defied every effort of its prisoners.

On the 23d inst., at eight in the morning, after a rapid passage, the *Susquehanna* was due at the fatal spot. They must wait till twelve to take the reckoning exactly. The buoy to which the sounding line had been lashed had not yet been recognised.

At twelve, Captain Blomsberry, assisted by his officers who superintended the observations, took the reckoning in the presence of the delegates of the Gun Club. Then there was a moment of anxiety. Her position decided, the *Susquehanna* was found to be some minutes westward of the spot where the projectile had disappeared beneath the waves.

The ship's course was then changed so as to reach this exact point.

At forty-seven minutes past twelve they reached the buoy; it was in perfect condition, and must have shifted but little.

"At last!" exclaimed J. T. Maston.

"Shall we begin?" asked Captain Blomsberry.

"Without losing a second."

Every precaution was taken to keep the corvette almost completely motionless. Before trying to seize the projectile, Engineer Murchison wanted to find its exact position at the bottom of the ocean. The submarine apparatus destined for this expedition was supplied with air. The working of these engines was not without danger, for at 20,000 feet below the surface of the water, and under such great pressure, they were exposed to fracture, the consequences of which would be dreadful.

J. T. Maston, the brothers Blomsberry, and Engineer Murchison, without heeding these dangers, took their places in the air-chamber. The commander, posted on his bridge, superintended the operation, ready to stop or haul in the chains on the slightest signal. The screw had been shipped, and the whole power of the machinery collected on the capstan would have quickly drawn the apparatus on board. The descent began at twenty-five minutes past one at night, and the chamber, drawn under by the reservoirs full of water, disappeared from the surface of the ocean.

The emotion of the officers and sailors on board was now divided between the prisoners in the projectile and the prisoners in the submarine apparatus. As to the latter, they forgot themselves, and, glued to the windows of the scuttles, attentively watched the liquid mass through which they were passing.

The descent was rapid. At seventeen minutes past two, J. T. Maston and his companions had reached the bottom of the Pacific; but they saw nothing but an arid desert, no longer animated by either fauna or flora. By the light of their lamps, furnished with powerful reflectors, they could see the dark beds of the ocean for a considerable extent of view, but the projectile was nowhere to be seen.

The impatience of these bold divers cannot be described, and having an electrical communication with the corvette, they made a signal already agreed upon, and for the space of a mile the *Susquehanna* moved their chamber along some yards above the bottom.

Thus they explored the whole submarine plain, deceived at every turn by optical illusions which almost broke their hearts. Here a rock, there a projection from the ground, seemed to be the much-sought-for projectile; but their mistake was soon discovered, and then they were in despair.

"But where are they? where are they?" cried J. T. Maston. And the poor man called loudly upon Nicholl, Barbicane, and Michel Ardan, as if his unfortunate friends could either hear or answer him through such an impenetrable medium! The search continued under these conditions until the vitiated air compelled the divers to ascend.

The hauling in began about six in the evening, and was not ended before midnight.

"To-morrow," said J. T. Maston, as he set foot on the bridge of the corvette.

"Yes," answered Captain Blomsberry.

"And on another spot?"

"Yes."

J. T. Maston did not doubt of their final success, but his companions, no longer upheld by the excitement of the first hours, understood all the difficulty of the enterprise. What seemed easy at San Francisco, seemed here in the wide ocean almost impossible. The chances of success diminished in rapid proportion; and it was from chance alone that the meeting with the projectile might be expected.

The next day, the 24th, in spite of the fatigue of the previous day, the operation was renewed. The corvette advanced some minutes to westward, and the apparatus, provided with air, bore the same explorers to the depths of the ocean.

The whole day passed in fruitless research; the bed of the sea was a desert. The 25th brought no other result, nor the 26th.

It was disheartening. They thought of those unfortunates shut up in the projectile for twenty-six days. Perhaps at that moment they were experiencing the first approach of suffocation; that is, if they had escaped the dangers of their fall. The air was spent, and doubtless with the air all their *morale*.

"The air, possibly," answered J. T. Maston resolutely, "but their *morale* never!"

On the 28th, after two more days of search, all hope was gone. This projectile was but an atom in the immensity of the ocean. They must give up all idea of finding it.

But J. T. Maston would not hear of going away. He would not abandon the place without at least discovering the tomb of his friends. But Commander Blomsberry could no longer persist, and in spite of the exclamations of the worthy secretary, was obliged to give the order to sail.

On the 29th of December, at nine A.M., the *Susquehanna,* heading north-east, resumed her course to the bay of San Francisco.

It was ten in the morning; the corvette was under half-steam, as if regretting to leave the spot where the catastrophe had taken place, when a sailor, perched on the main-top-gallant crosstrees, watching the sea, cried suddenly:

"A buoy on the lee bow!"

The officers looked in the direction indicated, and by the help of their glasses saw that the object signalled had the appearance of one of those buoys which are used to mark the passages of bays or rivers. But, singularly to say, a flag floating on the wind surmounted its cone, which emerged five or six feet out of water. This buoy shone under the rays of the sun as if it had been made of plates of silver. Commander Blomsberry, J. T. Maston, and the delegates of the Gun Club were mounted on the bridge, examining this object straying at random on the waves.

All looked with feverish anxiety, but in silence. None dared give expression to the thoughts which came to the minds of all.

The corvette approached to within two cables' lengths of the object.

A shudder ran through the whole crew. That flag was the American flag!

At this moment a perfect howling was heard; it was the brave J. T. Maston who had just fallen all in a heap. Forgetting on the one hand that his right arm had been replaced by an iron hook, and on the other that a simple gutta percha cap covered his brain-box, he had given himself a formidable blow.

They hurried towards him, picked him up, restored him to life. And what were his first words?

"Ah! trebly brutes! quadruply idiots! quintuply boobies that we are!"

"What is it?" exclaimed everyone around him.

"What is it?"

"Come, speak!"

"It is, simpletons," howled the terrible secretary, "it is that the projectile only weighs 19,250 pounds!"

"Well?"

"And that it displaces twenty-eight tons, or in other words 56,000 pounds, and that consequently *it floats!*"

Ah! what stress the worthy man had laid on the verb "float!" And it was true! All, yes! all these savants had forgotten this fundamental law, namely, that on account of its specific lightness, the projectile, after having been drawn by its fall to the greatest depths of the ocean, must naturally return to the surface. And now it was floating quietly at the mercy of the waves.

The boats were put to sea. J. T. Maston and his friends had rushed into them! Excitement was at its height! Every heart beat loudly while they advanced to the projectile. What did it contain? Living or dead?

Living, yes! living, at least unless death had struck Barbicane and his two friends since they had hoisted the flag. Profound silence reigned on the boats. All were breathless. Eyes no longer saw. One of the scuttles of the projectile was open. Some pieces of glass remained in the frame, showing that it had been broken. This scuttle was actually five feet above the water.

A boat came alongside, that of J. T. Maston, and J. T. Maston rushed to the broken window.

At that moment they heard a clear and merry voice, the voice of Michel Ardan, exclaiming in an accent of triumph:

"White all, Barbicane, white all!"

Barbicane, Michel Ardan, and Nicholl were playing at dominoes!

Chapter XXIII

THE END

WE MAY REMEMBER THE INTENSE SYMPATHY WHICH HAD ACCOMPANIED THE TRAVellers on their departure. If at the beginning of the enterprise they had excited such emotion both in the old and new world, with what enthusiasm would they be received on their return! The millions of spectators which had beset the peninsula of Florida, would they not rush to meet these sublime adventurers? Those legions of strangers, hurrying from all parts of the globe towards the American shores, would they leave the Union without having seen Barbicane, Nicholl, and Michel Ardan? No! and the ardent passion of the public was bound to respond worthily to the greatness of the enterprise. Human creatures who had left the terrestrial sphere, and returned after this strange voyage into celestial space, could not fail to be received as the prophet Elias would be if he came back to earth. To see them first, and then to hear them, such was the universal longing.

Barbicane, Michel Ardan, Nicholl, and the delegates of the Gun Club, returning without delay to Baltimore, were received with indescribable enthusiasm. The notes of President Barbicane's voyage were ready to be given to the public. The New York *Herald* bought the manuscript at a price not yet known, but which must have been very high. Indeed, during the publication of "A Journey to the Moon," the sale of this paper amounted to five millions of copies. Three days after the return of the travellers to the earth, the slightest detail of their expedition was known. There remained nothing more but to see the heroes of this superhuman enterprise.

The expedition of Barbicane and his friends round the moon had enabled them to correct the many admitted theories regarding the terrestrial satellite. These savants had observed *de visu*, and under particular circumstances. They knew what systems should be rejected, what retained with regard to the formation of that orb, its origin, its habitability. Its past, present, and future had even given up their last secrets. Who could advance objections against conscientious observers, who at less than twenty-four miles distance had marked that curious mountain of Tycho, the strangest system of lunar orography? How answer those savants whose sight had penetrated the abyss of Pluto's circle? How contradict those bold ones whom the chances of their enterprise had borne over that invisible face of the disc, which no human eye until then had ever seen? It was now their turn to impose some limit on that selenographic science, which had reconstructed the lunar world as Cuvier did the skeleton of a fossil, and say, "The moon *was* this, a habitable world, inhabited before the earth. The moon *is* that, a world uninhabitable, and now uninhabited."

To celebrate the return of its most illustrious member and his two companions, the Gun Club decided upon giving a banquet, but a banquet worthy of the conquerors, worthy of the American people, and under such conditions that all the inhabitants of the Union could directly take part in it.

All the head lines of railroads in the States were joined by flying rails; and on all the platforms, lined with the same flags, and decorated with the same ornaments, were tables laid and all served alike. At certain hours, successively calculated, marked by electric clocks which beat the seconds at the same time, the population were invited to take their places at the banquet tables. For four days, from the 5th to the 9th of January, the trains were stopped as they are on Sundays on the railways of the United States, and every road was open. One engine only at full speed, drawing a triumphal carriage, had the right of travelling for those four days on the railroads of the United States.

The engine was manned by a driver and a stoker, and bore, by special favour, the Hon. J. T. Maston, secretary of the Gun Club. The carriage was reserved for President Barbicane, Colonel Nicholl, and Michel Ardan. At the whistle of the driver, amid the hurrahs, and all the admiring vociferations of the American language, the train left the platform of Baltimore. It travelled at a speed of one hundred and sixty miles in the hour. But what was this speed compared with that which had carried the three heroes from the mouth of the *Columbiad?*

Thus they sped from one town to the other, finding whole populations at table on their road, saluting them with the same acclamations, lavishing the same bravos! They travelled in this way through the east of the Union, Pennsylvania, Connecticut, Massachusetts, Vermont, Maine, and New Hampshire; the north and west by New York, Ohio, Michigan, and Wisconsin; returning to the south by Illinois, Missouri, Arkansas, Texas, and Louisiana; they went to the south-east by Alabama and Florida, going up by Georgia and the Carolinas, visiting the centre by Tennessee, Kentucky, Virginia, and Indiana, and, after quitting the Washington station, re-entered Baltimore, where for four days one would have thought that the United States of America were seated at one immense banquet, saluting them simultaneously with the same hurrahs! The apotheosis was worthy of these three heroes whom fable would have placed in the rank of demigods.

And now will this attempt, unprecedented in the annals of travels, lead to any practical result? Will direct communication with the moon ever be established? Will they ever lay the foundation of a travelling service through the solar world? Will they go from one planet to another, from Jupiter to Mercury, and after a while from one star to another, from the Polar to Sirius? Will this means of locomotion allow us to visit those suns which swarm in the firmament?

To such questions no answer can be given. But knowing the bold ingenuity of the Anglo-Saxon race, no one would be astonished if the Americans seek to make some use of President Barbicane's attempt.

Thus, some time after the return of the travellers, the public received with marked favour the announcement of a company, limited, with a capital of a hundred million of dollars, divided into a hundred thousand shares of a thousand dollars each, under the name of the "National Company of Interstellary Communication." President, Barbicane; vice-president, Captain Nicholl; secretary, J. T. Maston; director of movements, Michel Ardan.

And as it is part of the American temperament to foresee everything in business, even failure, the honourable Harry Trolloppe, judge commissioner, and Francis Drayton, magistrate, were nominated beforehand!

TWENTY THOUSAND LEAGUES UNDER THE SEA

Contents

Part One

I	A Shifting Reef	509
II	Pro and Con	512
III	I Form My Resolution	515
IV	Ned Land	518
V	At a Venture	521
VI	At Full Steam	524
VII	An Unknown Species of Whale	528
VIII	*Mobilis in Mobile*	532
IX	Ned Land's Tempers	536
X	The Man of the Seas	538
XI	All by Electricity	546
XII	Some Figures	549
XIII	The Black River	552
XIV	A Note of Invitation	556
XV	A Walk on the Bottom of the Sea	560
XVI	A Submarine Forest	563
XVII	Four Thousand Leagues Under the Pacific	567
XVIII	Vanikoro	570
XIX	Torres Straits	575
XX	A Few Days on Land	578
XXI	Captain Nemo's Thunderbolt	583
XXII	*"Ægri Somnia"*	589
XXIII	The Coral Kingdom	593

Part Two

I	The Indian Ocean	601
II	A Novel Proposal of Captain Nemo's	605
III	A Pearl of Ten Millions	608
IV	The Red Sea	613
V	The Arabian Tunnel	619
VI	The Grecian Archipelago	623

VII	The Mediterranean in Forty-Eight Hours	629
VIII	Vigo Bay	633
IX	A Vanished Continent	638
X	The Submarine Coal-Mines	643
XI	The Sargasso Sea	647
XII	Cachalots and Whales	650
XIII	The Iceberg	655
XIV	The South Pole	660
XV	Accident or Incident?	666
XVI	Want of Air	670
XVII	From Cape Horn to the Amazon	675
XVIII	The Poulps	679
XIX	The Gulf Stream	684
XX	From Latitude 47° 24' to Longitude 17° 28'	689
XXI	A Hecatomb	692
XXII	The Last Words of Captain Nemo	696
XXIII	Conclusion	700

PART ONE

Chapter I

A Shifting Reef

THE YEAR 1866 WAS SIGNALISED BY A REMARKABLE INCIDENT, A MYSTERIOUS AND IN-explicable phenomenon, which doubtless no one has yet forgotten. Not to mention rumours which agitated the maritime population, and excited the public mind, even in the interior of continents, seafaring men were particularly excited. Merchants, common sailors, captains of vessels, skippers, both of Europe and America, naval officers of all countries, and the governments of several states on the two continents, were deeply interested in the matter.

For some time past, vessels had been met by "an enormous thing," a long object spindle-shaped, occasionally phosphorescent, and infinitely larger and more rapid in its movements than a whale.

The facts relating to this apparition (entered in various log-books) agreed in most respects as to the shape of the object or creature in question, the untiring rapidity of its movements, its surprising power of locomotion, and the peculiar life with which it seemed endowed. If it was a cetacean, it surpassed in size all those hitherto classified in science. Taking into consideration the mean of observations made at divers times—rejecting the timid estimate of those who assigned to this object a length of two hundred feet, equally with the exaggerated opinions which set it down as a mile in width and three in length—we might fairly conclude that this mysterious being surpassed greatly all dimensions admitted by the ichthyologists of the day, if it existed at all. And that it did exist was an undeniable fact; and, with that tendency which disposes the human mind in favour of the marvellous, we can understand the excitement produced in the entire world by this supernatural apparition. As to classing it in the list of fables, the idea was out of the question.

On the 20th of July, 1866, the steamer *Governor Higginson*, of the Calcutta and Burnach Steam Navigation Company, had met this moving mass five miles off the east coast of Australia. Captain Baker thought at first that he was in the presence of an unknown sand-bank; he even prepared to determine its exact position, when two columns of water, projected by the inexplicable object, shot with a hissing noise a hundred and fifty feet up into the air. Now, unless the sand-bank had been submitted to the intermittent irruption of a geyser, the *Governor Higginson* had to do neither more nor less than with an aquatic mammal, unknown till then, which threw up from its blow-holes columns of water mixed with air and vapour.

Similar facts were observed on the 23d of July in the same year, in the Pacific Ocean, by the *Columbus*, of the West India and Pacific Steam Navigation Company. But this extraordinary cetaceous creature could transport itself from one place to another with surprising velocity; as, in an interval of three days, the *Governor Higginson* and the *Columbus* had observed it at two different points of the chart, separated by a distance of more than seven hundred nautical leagues.

Fifteen days later, two thousand miles farther off, the *Helvetia*, of the Compagnie-

Nationale, and the *Shannon*, of the Royal Mail Steamship Company, sailing to windward in that portion of the Atlantic lying between the United States and Europe, respectively signalled the monster to each other in 42° 15' N. lat. and 60° 35' W. long. In these simultaneous observations they thought themselves justified in estimating the minimum length of the mammal at more than three hundred and fifty feet, as the Shannon and Helvetia were of smaller dimensions than it, though they measured three hundred feet over all.

Now the largest whales, those which frequent those parts of the sea round the Aleutian, Kulammak, and Umgullich Islands, have never exceeded the length of sixty yards, if they attain that.

These reports arriving one after the other, with fresh observations made on board the transatlantic ship *Pereira*, a collision which occurred between the *Etna* of the Inman line and the monster, a *proces verbal* directed by the officers of the French frigate *Normandie*, a very accurate survey made by the staff of Commodore Fitz-James on board the *Lord Clyde* greatly influenced public opinion. Light-thinking people jested upon the phenomenon, but grave, practical countries, such as England, America, and Germany, treated the matter more seriously.

In every place of great resort the monster was the fashion. They sang of it in the cafés, ridiculed it in the papers, and represented it on the stage. All kinds of stories were circulated regarding it. There appeared in the papers caricatures of every gigantic and imaginary creature, from the white whale, the terrible "Moby Dick" of hyperborean regions, to the immense kraken whose tentacles could entangle a ship of five hundred tons, and hurry it into the abyss of the ocean. The legends of ancient times were even resuscitated, and the opinions of Aristotle and Pliny revived, who admitted the existence of these monsters, as well as the Norwegian tales of Bishop Pontoppidan, the accounts of Paul Heggede, and, last of all, the reports of Mr. Harrington (whose good faith no one could suspect), who affirmed that, being on board the *Castillan*, in 1857, he had seen this enormous serpent, which had never until that time frequented any other seas but those of the ancient "Constitutionnel."

Then burst forth the interminable controversy between the credulous and the incredulous in the societies of savants and scientific journals. "The question of the monster" inflamed all minds. Editors of scientific journals, quarrelling with believers in the supernatural, spilled seas of ink during this memorable campaign, some even drawing blood; for, from the sea-serpent, they came to direct personalities.

For six months war was waged with various fortune in the leading articles of the Geographical Institution of Brazil, the Royal Academy of Science of Berlin, the British Association, the Smithsonian Institution of Washington, in the discussions of the "Indian Archipelago," of the Cosmos of the Abbé Moigno, in the Mittheilungen of Petermann, in the scientific chronicles of the great journals of France and other countries. The cheaper journals replied keenly and with inexhaustible zest. These satirical writers parodied a remark of Linnæus, quoted by the adversaries of the monster, maintaining that "nature did not make fools," and adjured their contemporaries not to give the lie to nature, by admitting the existence of krakens, sea-serpents, "Moby Dicks," and other lucubrations of delirious sailors. At length an article in a well-known satirical journal by a favorite contributor, the chief of the staff, settled the monster, like Hippolytus, giving it the death-blow amid a universal burst of laughter. Wit had conquered science.

During the first months of the year 1867 the question seemed buried never to revive, when new facts were brought before the public. It was then no longer a scientific problem to be solved, but a real danger seriously to be avoided. The question took quite another shape. The monster became a small island, a rock, a reef, but a reef of indefinite and shifting proportions.

On the 5th of March, 1867, the *Moravian,* of the Montreal Ocean Company, finding herself during the night in 27° 30' lat. and 72° 15' long., struck on her starboard quarter a rock, marked in no chart for that part of the sea. Under the combined efforts of the wind and its four hundred horse-power, it was going at the rate of thirteen knots. Had it not been for the superior strength of the hull of the *Moravian,* she would have been broken by the shock, and gone down with the 237 passengers she was bringing home from Canada.

The accident happened about five o'clock in the morning, as the day was breaking. The officers of the quarter-deck hurried to the after-part of the vessel. They examined the sea with the most scrupulous attention. They saw nothing but a strong eddy about three cables' length distant, as if the surface had been violently agitated. The bearings of the place were taken exactly, and the *Moravian* continued its route without apparent damage. Had it struck on a submerged rock, or on an enormous wreck? They could not tell; but on examination of the ship's bottom when undergoing repairs, it was found that part of her keel was broken.

This fact, so grave in itself, might perhaps have been forgotten like many others, if, three weeks after, it had not been re-enacted under similar circumstances. But, thanks to the nationality of the victim of the shock, thanks to the reputation of the company to which the vessel belonged, the circumstance became extensively circulated.

The 13th of April, 1867, the sea being beautiful, the breeze favourable, the *Scotia,* of the Cunard Company's line, found herself in 15° 12' long. and 45° 37' lat. She was going at the speed of thirteen knots and a half.

At seventeen minutes past four in the afternoon, while the passengers were assembled at lunch in the great saloon, a slight shock was felt on the hull of the *Scotia,* on her quarter, a little aft of the port paddle.

The *Scotia* had not struck, but she had been struck, and seemingly by something rather sharp and penetrating than blunt. The shock had been so slight that no one had been alarmed, had it not been for the shouts of the carpenter's watch, who rushed on to the bridge, exclaiming, "We are sinking! We are sinking!" At first the passengers were much frightened, but Captain Anderson hastened to reassure them. The danger could not be imminent. The *Scotia,* divided into seven compartments by strong partitions, could brave with impunity any leak. Captain Anderson went down immediately into the hold. He found that the sea was pouring into the fifth compartment; and the rapidity of the influx proved that the force of the water was considerable. Fortunately this compartment did not hold the boilers, or the fires would have been immediately extinguished. Captain Anderson ordered the engines to be stopped at once, and one of the men went down to ascertain the extent of the injury. Some minutes afterward they discovered the existence of a large hole of two yards in diameter, in the ship's bottom. Such a leak could not be stopped; and the *Scotia,* her paddles half submerged, was obliged to continue her course. She was then three hundred miles from Cape Clear, and after three days' delay, which caused great uneasiness in Liverpool, she entered the basin of the company.

The engineers visited the *Scotia*, which was put in dry-dock. They could scarcely believe it possible; at two yards and a half below water-mark was a regular rent, in the form of an isosceles triangle. The broken place in the iron plates was so perfectly defined that it could not have been more neatly done by a punch. It was clear, then, that the instrument producing the perforation was not of a common stamp; and after having been driven with prodigious strength, and piercing an iron plate one and three-eighths inches thick, had withdrawn itself by a retrograde motion truly inexplicable.

Such was the last fact, which resulted in exciting once more the torrent of public opinion. From this moment all unlucky casualties which could not be otherwise accounted for were put down to the monster.

Upon this imaginary creature rested the responsibility of all these shipwrecks, which unfortunately were considerable; for of three thousand ships whose loss was annually recorded at Lloyd's, the number of sailing and steamships supposed to be totally lost, from the absence of all news, amounted to not less than two hundred.

Now, it was the "monster" who, justly or unjustly, was accused of their disappearance, and, thanks to it, communication between the different continents became more and more dangerous. The public demanded peremptorily that the seas should at any price be relieved from this formidable cetacean.

Chapter II

PRO AND CON

AT THE PERIOD WHEN THESE EVENTS TOOK PLACE, I HAD JUST RETURNED FROM A SCIentific research in the disagreeable territory of Nebraska, in the United States. In virtue of my office as Assistant Professor in the Museum of Natural History in Paris, the French Government had attached me to that expedition. After six months in Nebraska, I arrived in New York towards the end of March, laden with a precious collection. My departure for France was fixed for the first days in May. Meanwhile, I was occupying myself in classifying my mineralogical, botanical, and zoological riches, when the accident happened to the *Scotia*.

I was perfectly up in the subject which was the question of the day. How could I be otherwise? I had read and reread all the American and European papers without being any nearer a conclusion. This mystery puzzled me. Under the impossibility of forming an opinion, I jumped from one extreme to the other. That there really was something could not be doubted, and the incredulous were invited to put their finger on the wound of the *Scotia*.

On my arrival at New York the question was at its height. The hypothesis of the floating island, and the unapproachable sand-bank, supported by minds little competent to form a judgment, was abandoned. And, indeed, unless this shoal had a machine in its stomach, how could it change its position with such astonishing rapidity?

From the same cause, the idea of a floating hull of an enormous wreck was given up.

There remained then only two possible solutions of the question, which created two distinct parties: on one side, those who were for a monster of colossal strength; on the other, those who were for a submarine vessel of enormous motive power.

But this last hypothesis, plausible as it was, could not stand against inquiries made in both worlds. That a private gentleman should have such a machine at his command was not likely. Where, when, and how was it built? And how could its construction have been kept secret? Certainly a government might possess such a destructive machine. And in these disastrous times, when the ingenuity of man has multiplied the power of weapons of war, it was possible that, without the knowledge of others, a state might try to work such a formidable engine. After the chassepots came the torpedoes, after the torpedoes the submarine rams, then—the reaction. At least, I hope so.

But the hypothesis of a war-machine fell before the declaration of governments. As public interest was in question, and transatlantic communications suffered, their veracity could not be doubted. But how admit that the construction of this submarine boat had escaped the public eye? For a private gentleman to keep the secret under such circumstances would be very difficult, and for a state whose every act is persistently watched by powerful rivals, certainly impossible.

After inquiries made in England, France, Russia, Prussia, Spain, Italy, and America, even in Turkey, the hypothesis of a submarine monitor was definitely rejected.

Upon my arrival in New York several persons did me the honour of consulting me on the phenomenon in question. I had published in France a work in quarto, in two volumes, entitled *Mysteries of the Great Submarine Grounds*. This book, highly approved of in the learned world, gained for me a special reputation in this rather obscure branch of Natural History. My advice was asked. As long as I could deny the reality of the fact, I confined myself to a decided negative. But soon finding myself driven into a corner, I was obliged to explain myself categorically. And even "the Honorable Pierre Aronnax, Professor in the Museum of Paris," was called upon by the *New York Herald* to express a definite opinion of some sort. I did something. I spoke for want of power to hold my tongue. I discussed the question in all its forms, politically and scientifically; and I give here an extract from a carefully-studied article which I published in the number of the 30th of April. It ran as follows:

"After examining one by one the different hypotheses, rejecting all other suggestions, it becomes necessary to admit the existence of a marine animal of enormous power.

"The great depths of the ocean are entirely unknown to us. Soundings cannot reach them. What passes in those remote depths—what beings live, or can live, twelve or fifteen miles beneath the surface of the waters—what is the organisation of these animals—we can scarcely conjecture. However, the solution of the problem submitted to me may modify the form of the dilemma. Either we do know all the varieties of beings which people our planet, or we do not. If we do not know them all, if Nature still has secrets in ichthyology for us, nothing is more conformable to reason than to admit the existence of fishes, or cetaceans of other kinds, or even of new species, of an organisation formed to inhabit the strata inaccessible to soundings, and which an accident of some sort, either fantastical or capricious, has brought at long intervals to the upper level of the ocean.

"If, on the contrary, we do know all living kinds, we must necessarily seek for the animal in question among those marine beings already classed; and, in that case, I should be disposed to admit the existence of a gigantic narwhal.

"The common narwhal, or unicorn of the sea, often attains a length of sixty feet. Increase its size fivefold or tenfold, give it strength proportionate to its size, lengthen its destructive weapons, and you obtain the animal required. It will have the proportions determined by the officers of the *Shannon*, the instrument required by the perforation of the *Scotia*, and the power necessary to pierce the hull of the steamer.

"Indeed the narwhal is armed with a sort of ivory sword, a halberd, according to the expression of certain naturalists. The principal tusk has the hardness of steel. Some of these tusks have been found buried in the bodies of whales, which the unicorn always attacks with success. Others have been drawn out, not without trouble, from the bottoms of ships, which they had pierced through and through, as a gimlet pierces a barrel. The Museum of the Faculty of Medicine of Paris possesses one of these defensive weapons, two yards and a quarter in length, and fifteen inches in diameter at the base.

"Very well! Suppose this weapon to be six times stronger, and the animal ten times more powerful; launch it at the rate of twenty miles an hour, and you obtain a shock capable of producing the catastrophe required. Until further information, therefore, I shall maintain it to be a sea-unicorn of colossal dimensions, armed, not with a halberd, but with a real spur, as the armoured frigates, or the 'rams' of war, whose massiveness and motive power it would possess at the same time. Thus may this inexplicable phenomenon be explained, unless there be something over and above all that one has ever conjectured, seen, perceived, or experienced; which is just within the bounds of possibility."

These last words were cowardly on my part; but, up to a certain point, I wished to shelter my dignity as professor, and not give too much cause for laughter to the Americans, who laugh well when they do laugh. I reserved for myself a way of escape. In effect, however, I admitted the existence of the "monster." My article was warmly discussed, which procured it a high reputation. It rallied round it a certain number of partisans. The solution it proposed gave, at least, full liberty to the imagination. The human mind delights in grand conceptions of supernatural beings. And the sea is precisely their best vehicle, the only medium through which these giants (against which terrestrial animals, such as elephants or rhinoceroses, are as nothing) can be produced or developed.

The industrial and commercial papers treated the question chiefly from this point of view. The *Shipping and Mercantile Gazette*, the *Lloyd's List*, the *Packet-Boat* and the *Maritime and Colonial Review*, all papers devoted to insurance companies which threatened to raise their rates of premium, were unanimous on this point. Public opinion had been pronounced. The United States was the first in the field; and in New York they made preparations for an expedition destined to pursue this narwhal. A frigate of great speed, the *Abraham Lincoln*, was put in commission as soon as possible. The arsenals were opened to Commander Farragut, who hastened the arming of his frigate; but, as it always happens, the moment it was decided to pursue the monster, the monster did not appear. For two months no one heard it spoken of. No ship met with it. It seemed as if this unicorn knew of the plots weaving around it. It had been so much talked of, even through the Atlantic cable, that jesters pretended that this slender fly had stopped a telegram on its passage, and was making the most of it.

So when the frigate had been armed for a long campaign, and provided with formidable fishing apparatus, no one could tell what course to pursue. Impatience grew apace, when, on the 2d of June, they learned that a steamer of the line of San Francisco, from

California to Shanghai, had seen the animal three weeks before in the North Pacific Ocean. The excitement caused by this news was extreme. The ship was revictualled and well stocked with coal.

Three hours before the *Abraham Lincoln* left Brooklyn pier, I received a letter worded as follows:

> To M. Arronax, *Professor in the Museum of Paris,*
> *Fifth Avenue Hotel, New York.*

SIR: If you will consent to join the *Abraham Lincoln* in this expedition, the government of the United States will with pleasure see France represented in the enterprise. Commander Farragut has a cabin at your disposal.

> Very cordially yours,
> J. B. HOBSON,
> SECRETARY OF MARINE

Chapter III

I FORM MY RESOLUTION

THREE SECONDS BEFORE THE ARRIVAL OF J. B. HOBSON'S LETTER, I NO MORE THOUGHT of pursuing the unicorn than of attempting the passage of the North Sea. Three seconds after reading the letter of the Honourable Secretary of Marine, I felt that my true vocation, the sole end of my life, was to chase this disturbing monster, and purge it from the world.

But I had just returned from a fatiguing journey, weary, and longing for repose. I aspired to nothing more than again seeing my country, my friends, my little lodging by the Jardin des Plantes, my dear and precious collections. But nothing could keep me back! I forgot all—fatigue, friends, and collections—and accepted without hesitation the offer of the American government.

"Besides," thought I, "all roads lead back to Europe; and the unicorn may be amiable enough to hurry me towards the coast of France. This worthy animal may allow itself to be caught in the seas of Europe (for my particular benefit), and I will not bring back less than half a yard of his ivory halberd to the Museum of Natural History." But in the meanwhile I must seek this narwhal in the North Pacific Ocean, which, to return to France, was taking the road to the antipodes.

"Conseil," I called in an impatient voice.

Conseil was my servant, a true, devoted Flemish boy, who had accompanied me in all my travels. I liked him, and he returned the liking well. He was phlegmatic by nature, regular from principle, zealous from habit, evincing little disturbance at the different surprises of life, very quick with his hands, and apt at any service required of him; and, despite his name, never giving advice—even when asked for it.

Conseil had followed me for the last ten years wherever science led. Never once did he complain of the length or fatigue of a journey, never make an objection to pack his portmanteau for whatever country it might be, or however far away, whether China or Congo. Besides all this, he had good health, which defied all sickness, and solid muscles, but no nerves; good morals are understood. This boy was thirty years old, and his age to that of his master as fifteen to twenty. May I be excused for saying that I was forty years old?

But Conseil had one fault—he was ceremonious to a degree, and would never speak to me but in the third person, which was sometimes provoking.

"Conseil," said I again, beginning with feverish hands to make preparations for my departure.

Certainly, I was sure of this devoted boy. As a rule, I never asked him if it were convenient for him or not to follow me in my travels; but this time the expedition in question might be prolonged, and the enterprise might be hazardous in pursuit of an animal capable of sinking a frigate as easily as a nutshell. Here there was matter for reflection even to the most impassive man in the world. What would Conseil say?

"Conseil," I called a third time.

Conseil appeared.

"Did you call, sir?" said he, entering.

"Yes, my boy; make preparations for me and yourself too. We leave in two hours."

"As you please, sir," replied Conseil quietly.

"Not an instant to lose; lock in my trunk all travelling utensils, coats, shirts, and stockings—without counting—as many as you can, and make haste."

"And your collections, sir?" observed Conseil.

"We will think of them by and by."

"What! the archiotherium, the hyracotherium, the oreodons, the cheropotamus, and the other skins?"

"They will keep them at the hotel."

"And your live Babiroussa, sir?"

"They will feed it during our absence; besides, I will give orders to forward our menagerie to France."

"We are not returning to Paris, then?" said Conseil.

"Oh! Certainly," I answered evasively, "by making a curve."

"Will the curve please you, sir?"

"Oh! It will be nothing; not quite so direct a road, that is all. We take our passage in the *Abraham Lincoln*."

"As you think proper, sir," coolly replied Conseil.

"You see, my friend, it has to do with the monster—the famous narwhal. We are going to purge it from the seas. The author of a work in quarto, in two volumes, on the *Mysteries of the Great Submarine Grounds* cannot forbear embarking with Commander Farragut. A glorious mission, but a dangerous one! We cannot tell where we may go; these animals can be very capricious. But we will go whether or no; we have got a captain who is pretty wide awake."

I opened a credit account for Babiroussa, and, Conseil following, I jumped in a cab. Our luggage was transported to the deck of the frigate immediately. I hastened on board and asked for Commander Farragut. One of the sailors conducted me to the poop, where I found myself in the presence of a good-looking officer, who held out his hand to me.

"Monsieur Pierre Aronnax?" said he.

"Himself," replied I. "Commander Farragut?"

"You are welcome, professor; your cabin is ready for you."

I bowed, and desired to be conducted to the cabin destined for me.

The *Abraham Lincoln* had been well chosen and equipped for her new destination. She was a frigate of great speed, fitted with high-pressure engines which admitted a pressure of seven atmospheres. Under this the *Abraham Lincoln* attained the mean speed of nearly eighteen knots and a third an hour—a considerable speed, but, nevertheless, insufficient to grapple with this gigantic cetacean.

The interior arrangements of the frigate corresponded to its nautical qualities. I was well satisfied with my cabin, which was in the after-part, opening upon the gunroom.

"We shall be well off here," said I to Conseil.

"As well, by your honour's leave, as a hermit crab in the shell of a whelk," said Conseil.

I left Conseil to stow our trunks conveniently away, and remounted the poop in order to survey the preparations for departure.

At that moment Commander Farragut was ordering the last moorings to be cast loose which held the *Abraham Lincoln* to the pier of Brooklyn. So in a quarter of an hour, perhaps less, the frigate would have sailed without me. I should have missed this extraordinary, supernatural, and incredible expedition, the recital of which may well meet with some skepticism.

But Commander Farragut would not lose a day nor an hour in scouring the seas in which the animal had been sighted. He sent for the engineer.

"Is the steam full on?" asked he.

"Yes, sir," replied the engineer.

"Go ahead," cried Commander Farragut.

The quay of Brooklyn, and all that part of New York bordering on the East River, was crowded with spectators. Three cheers burst successively from five hundred thousand throats; thousands of handkerchiefs were waved above the heads of the compact mass, saluting the *Abraham Lincoln*, until she reached the waters of the Hudson, at the point of that elongated peninsula which forms the town of New York. Then the frigate, following the coast of New Jersey along the right bank of the beautiful river, covered with villas, passed between the forts, which saluted her with their heaviest guns. The *Abraham Lincoln* answered by hoisting the American colors three times, whose thirty-nine stars shone resplendent from the mizzen-peak; then modifying its speed to take the narrow channel marked by buoys placed in the inner bay formed by Sandy Hook Point, it coasted the long sandy beach, where some thousands of spectators gave it one final cheer. The escort of boats and tenders still followed the frigate, and did not leave her until they came abreast of the light-ship whose two lights marked the entrance of New York Channel.

Six bells struck, the pilot got into his boat, and rejoined the little schooner which was waiting under our lee, the fires were made up, the screw beat the waves more rapidly, the frigate skirted the low yellow coast of Long Island; and at eight bells, after having lost sight in the northwest of the lights of Fire Island, she ran at full steam on to the dark waters of the Atlantic.

Chapter IV

NED LAND

CAPTAIN FARRAGUT WAS A GOOD SEAMAN, WORTHY OF THE FRIGATE HE COMMANDED. His vessel and he were one. He was the soul of it. On the question of the cetacean there was no doubt in his mind, and he would not allow the existence of the animal to be disputed on board. He believed in it as certain good women believe in the leviathan—by faith, not by reason. The monster did exist, and he had sworn to rid the seas of it. He was a kind of knight of Rhodes, a second Dieudonné de Gozon, going to meet the serpent which desolated the island. Either Captain Farragut would kill the narwhal, or the narwhal would kill the captain. There was no third course.

The officers on board shared the opinion of their chief. They were ever chatting, discussing, and calculating the various chances of a meeting, watching narrowly the vast surface of the ocean. More than one took up his quarters voluntarily in the cross-trees, who would have cursed such a berth under any other circumstances. As long as the sun described its daily course, the rigging was crowded with sailors, whose feet were burned to such an extent by the heat of the deck as to render it unbearable; still the *Abraham Lincoln* had not yet breasted the suspected waters of the Pacific. As to the ship's company, they desired nothing better than to meet the unicorn, to harpoon it, hoist it on board, and dispatch it. They watched the sea with eager attention.

Besides, Captain Farragut had spoken of a certain sum of two thousand dollars, set apart for whoever should first sight the monster, were he cabin-boy, common seaman, or officer.

I leave you to judge how eyes were used on board the *Abraham Lincoln*.

For my own part I was not behind the others, and, left to no one my share of daily observations. The frigate might have been called the Argus, for a hundred reasons. Only one among us, Conseil, seemed to protest by his indifference against the question which so interested us all, and seemed to be out of keeping with the general enthusiasm on board.

I have said that Captain Farragut had carefully provided his ship with every apparatus for catching the gigantic cetacean. No whaler had ever been better armed. We possessed every known engine, from the harpoon thrown by the hand to the barbed arrows of the blunderbuss, and the explosive balls of the duck-gun. On the forecastle lay the perfection of a breech-loading gun, very thick at the breech, and very narrow in the bore, the model of which had been in the Exhibition of 1867. This precious weapon of American origin could throw with ease a conical projectile of nine pounds to a mean distance of ten miles.

Thus the *Abraham Lincoln* wanted for no means of destruction; and, what was better still, she had on board Ned Land, the prince of harpooners.

Ned Land was a Canadian, with an uncommon quickness of hand, and who knew no equal in his dangerous occupation. Skill, coolness, audacity, and cunning he possessed in a superior degree, and it must be a cunning whale or a singularly "cute" cachalot to escape the stroke of his harpoon.

Ned Land was about forty years of age; he was a tall man (more than six feet high),

strongly built, grave and taciturn, occasionally violent, and very passionate when contradicted. His person attracted attention, but above all the boldness of his look, which gave a
singular expression to his face.

Who calls himself Canadian calls himself French; and little communicative as Ned
Land was, I must admit that he took a certain liking for me. My nationality drew him to
me, no doubt. It was an opportunity for him to talk, and for me to hear, that old language
of Rabelais, which is still in use in some Canadian provinces. The harpooner's family was
originally from Quebec, and was already a tribe of hardy fishermen when this town belonged to France.

Little by little, Ned Land acquired a taste for chatting, and I loved to hear the recital
of his adventures in the polar seas. He related his fishing, and his combats, with natural
poetry of expression; his recital took the form of an epic poem, and I seemed to be listening to a Canadian Homer singing the Iliad of the regions of the North.

I am portraying this hardy companion as I really knew him. We are old friends now,
united in that unchangeable friendship which is born and cemented amid extreme dangers.
Ah, brave Ned! I ask no more than to live a hundred years longer, that I may have more
time to dwell the longer on your memory.

Now, what was Ned Land's opinion upon the question of the marine monster? I must
admit that he did not believe in the unicorn, and was the only one on board who did not
share that universal conviction. He even avoided the subject, which I one day thought it
my duty to press upon him. One magnificent evening, the 25th of June (that is to say, three
weeks after our departure), the frigate was abreast of Cape Blanc, thirty miles to leeward
of the coast of Patagonia. We had crossed the Tropic of Capricorn, and the Straits of Magellan opened less than seven hundred miles to the south. Before eight days were over, the
Abraham Lincoln would be ploughing the waters of the Pacific.

Seated on the poop, Ned Land and I were chatting of one thing and another as we
looked at this mysterious sea, whose great depths had up to this time been inaccessible to
the eye of man. I naturally led up the conversation to the giant unicorn, and examined the
various chances of success or failure of the expedition. But seeing that Ned Land let me
speak without saying too much himself, I pressed him more closely.

"Well, Ned," said I, "is it possible that you are not convinced of the existence of this
cetacean that we are following? Have you any particular reason for being so incredulous?"

The harpooner looked at me fixedly for some moments before answering, struck his
broad forehead with his hand (a habit of his), as if to collect himself, and said at last, "Perhaps I have, Mr. Aronnax."

"But, Ned, you, a whaler by profession, familiarized with all the great marine mammalia—you, whose imagination might easily accept the hypothesis of enormous
cetaceans—you ought to be the last to doubt under such circumstances!"

"That is just what deceives you, professor," replied Ned. "That the vulgar should believe in extraordinary comets traversing space, and in the existence of antediluvian monsters
in the heart of the globe, may well be; but neither astronomers nor geologists believe in such
chimeras. As a whaler, I have followed many a cetacean, harpooned a great number, and
killed several; but, however strong or well armed they may have been, neither their tails nor
their weapons would have been able even to scratch the iron plates of a steamer."

"But, Ned, they tell of ships which the teeth of the narwhal have pierced through and through."

"Wooden ships—that is possible," replied the Canadian; "but I have never seen it done; and, until further proof, I deny that whales, cetaceans, or sea-unicorns could ever produce the effect you describe."

"Well, Ned, I repeat it with a conviction resting on the logic of facts. I believe in the existence of a mammal powerfully organized, belonging to the branch of vertebrata, like the whales, the cachalots, or the dolphins, and furnished with a horn of defense of great penetrating power."

"Hum!" said the harpooner, shaking his head with the air of a man who would not be convinced.

"Notice one thing, my worthy Canadian," I resumed. "If such an animal is in existence, if it inhabits the depths of the ocean, if it frequents the strata lying miles below the surface of the water, it must necessarily possess an organisation the strength of which would defy all comparison."

"And why this powerful organisation?" demanded Ned.

"Because it requires incalculable strength to keep one's self in these strata and resist their pressure. Listen to me. Let us admit that the pressure of the atmosphere is represented by the weight of a column of water thirty-two feet high. In reality the column of water would be shorter, as we are speaking of sea-water, the density of which is greater than that of fresh water. Very well, when you dive, Ned, as many times thirty-two feet of water as there are above you, so many times does your body bear a pressure equal to that of the atmosphere, that is to say, 15 lbs. for each square inch of its surface. It follows, then, that at 320 feet this pressure equals that of 10 atmospheres, of 100 atmospheres at 3,200 feet, and of 1,000 atmospheres at 32,000 feet, that is, about 6 miles; which is equivalent to saying that if you could attain this depth in the ocean, each square ⅛ of an inch of the surface of your body would bear a pressure of 5,600 lbs. Ah! my brave Ned, do you know how many square inches you carry on the surface of your body?"

"I have no idea, Mr. Aronnax."

"About 6,500; and, as in reality the atmospheric pressure is about 15 lbs. to the square inch, your 6,500 square inches bear at this moment a pressure of 97,500 lbs."

"Without my perceiving it?"

"Without your perceiving it. And if you are not crushed by such a pressure, it is because the air penetrates the interior of your body with equal pressure. Hence perfect equilibrium between the interior and exterior pressure, which thus neutralise each other, and which allows you to bear it without inconvenience. But in the water it is another thing."

"Yes, I understand," replied Ned, becoming more attentive; "because the water surrounds me, but does not penetrate."

"Precisely, Ned; so that at 32 feet beneath the surface of the sea you would undergo a pressure of 97,500 lbs.; at 320 feet, ten times that pressure; at 3,200 feet, a hundred times that pressure; lastly, at 32,000 feet, a thousand times that pressure would be 97,500,000 lbs.—that is to say, that you would be flattened as if you had been drawn from the plates of a hydraulic machine!"

"The devil!" exclaimed Ned.

"Very well, my worthy harpooner, if some vertebrate, several hundred yards long, and large in proportion, can maintain itself in such depths—of those whose surface is represented by millions of square inches, that is by tens of millions of pounds, we must estimate the pressure they undergo. Consider, then, what must be the resistance of their bony structure, and the strength of their organization to withstand such pressure!"

"Why!" exclaimed Ned Land, "they must be made of iron plates eight inches thick, like the armored frigates."

"As you say, Ned. And think what destruction such a mass would cause, if hurled with the speed of an express train against the hull of a vessel."

"Yes—certainly—perhaps," replied the Canadian, shaken by these figures, but not yet willing to give in.

"Well, have I convinced you?"

"You have convinced me of one thing, sir, which is, that if such animals do exist at the bottom of the seas, they must necessarily be as strong as you say."

"But if they do not exist, mine obstinate harpooner, how explain the accident to the *Scotia*?"

Chapter V

At a Venture

THE VOYAGE OF THE *ABRAHAM LINCOLN* WAS FOR A LONG TIME MARKED BY NO SPECIAL incident. But one circumstance happened which showed the wonderful dexterity of Ned Land, and proved what confidence we might place in him.

The 30th of June, the frigate spoke some American whalers, from whom we learned that they knew nothing about the narwhal. But one of them, the captain of the *Monroe*, knowing that Ned Land had shipped on board the *Abraham Lincoln*, begged for his help in chasing a whale they had in sight. Commander Farragut, desirous of seeing Ned Land at work, gave him permission to go on board the *Monroe*. And fate served our Canadian so well that, instead of one whale, he harpooned two with a double blow, striking one straight to the heart and catching the other after some minutes' pursuit.

Decidedly, if the monster ever had to do with Ned Land's harpoon, I would not bet in its favour.

The frigate skirted the southeast coast of America with great rapidity. The 3d of July we were at the opening of the Straits of Magellan, level with Cape Vierges. But Commander Farragut would not take a tortuous passage, but doubled Cape Horn.

The ship's crew agreed with him. And certainly it was possible that they might meet the narwhal in this narrow pass. Many of the sailors affirmed that the monster could not pass there, "that he was too big for that!"

The 6th of July, about three o'clock in the afternoon, the *Abraham Lincoln*, at fifteen miles to the south, doubled the solitary island, this lost rock at the extremity of the American continent to which some Dutch sailors gave the name of their native town, Cape

Horn. The course was taken towards the north-west, and the next day the screw of the frigate was at last beating the waters of the Pacific.

"Keep your eyes open!" called out the sailors.

And they were opened widely. Both eyes and glasses, a little dazzled, it is true, by the prospect of two thousand dollars, had not an instant's repose. Day and night they watched the surface of the ocean, and even nyctalopes, whose faculty of seeing in the darkness multiplies their chances a hundredfold, would have had enough to do to gain the prize.

I, myself, for whom money had no charms, was not the least attentive on board. Giving but few minutes to my meals, but a few hours to sleep, indifferent to either rain or sunshine, I did not leave the poop of the vessel. Now leaning on the netting of the forecastle, now on the taffrail, I devoured with eagerness the soft foam which whitened the sea as far as the eye could reach; and how often have I shared the emotion of the majority of the crew when some capricious whale raised its black back above the waves! The poop of the vessel crowded in a moment. The cabins poured forth a torrent of sailors and officers, each with heaving breast and troubled eye watching the course of the cetacean. I looked, and looked, till I was nearly blind, while Conseil, always phlegmatic, kept repeating in a calm voice:

"If, sir, you would not squint so much, you would see better!"

But vain excitement! The *Abraham Lincoln* checked its speed and made for the animal signalled, a simple whale, or common cachalot, which soon disappeared amid a storm of execration.

But the weather was good. The voyage was being accomplished under the most favourable auspices. It was then the bad season in Australia, the July of that zone corresponding to our January in Europe; but the sea was beautiful and easily scanned round a vast circumference.

The 20th of July, the Tropic of Capricorn was cut by 105° of longitude, and the 27th of the same month we crossed the equator on the 110th meridian. This passed, the frigate took a more decided westerly direction, and scoured the central waters of the Pacific. Commander Farragut thought, and with reason, that it was better to remain in deep water, and keep clear of continents or islands, which the beast itself seemed to shun (perhaps because there was not enough water for him! suggested the greater part of the crew). The frigate passed at some distance from the Marquesas and the Sandwich Islands, crossed the Tropic of Cancer, and made for the China Seas. We were on the theatre of the last diversions of the monster: and, to say truth, we no longer *lived* on board. Hearts palpitated, fearfully preparing themselves for future incurable aneurism. The entire ship's crew were undergoing a nervous excitement, of which I can give no idea; they could not eat, they could not sleep: twenty times a day, a misconception or an optical illusion of some sailor seated on the taffrail would cause dreadful perspirations, and these emotions, twenty times repeated, kept us in a state of excitement so violent that a reaction was unavoidable.

And truly, reaction soon showed itself. For three months, during which a day seemed an age, the *Abraham Lincoln* furrowed all the waters of the Northern Pacific, running at whales, making sharp deviations from her course, veering suddenly from one tack to another, stopping suddenly, putting on steam, and backing ever and anon at the risk of deranging her machinery; and not one point of the Japanese or American coast was left unexplored.

The warmest partisans of the enterprise now became its most ardent detractors. Reaction mounted from the crew to the captain himself, and certainly, had it not been for the resolute determination on the part of Captain Farragut, the frigate would have headed due southward. This useless search could not last much longer. The *Abraham Lincoln* had nothing to reproach herself with, she had done her best to succeed. Never had an American ship's crew shown more zeal or patience; its failure could not be placed to their charge—there remained nothing but to return.

This was represented to the commander. The sailors could not hide their discontent, and the service suffered. I will not say there was a mutiny on board, but after a reasonable period of obstinacy, Captain Farragut (as Columbus did) asked for three days' patience. If in three days the monster did not appear, the man at the helm should give three turns of the wheel, and the *Abraham Lincoln* would make for the European seas.

This promise was made on the 2d of November. It had the effect of rallying the ship's crew. The ocean was watched with renewed attention. Each one wished for a last glance in which to sum up his remembrance. Glasses were used with feverish activity. It was a grand defiance given to the giant narwhal, and he could scarcely fail to answer the summons and "appear."

Two days passed, the steam was at half-pressure; a thousand schemes were tried to attract the attention and stimulate the apathy of the animal in case it should be met in those parts. Large quantities of bacon were trailed in the wake of the ship, to the great satisfaction (I must say) of the sharks. Small craft radiated in all directions round the *Abraham Lincoln* as she lay to, and did not leave a spot of the sea unexplored. But the night of the 4th of November arrived without the unveiling of this submarine mystery.

The next day, the 5th of November, at twelve, the delay would (morally speaking) expire; after that time, Commander Farragut, faithful to his promise, was to turn the course to the south-east and abandon forever the northern regions of the Pacific.

The frigate was then in 31° 15' north latitude and 136° 42' east longitude. The coast of Japan still remained less than two hundred miles to leeward. Night was approaching. They had just struck eight bells; large clouds veiled the face of the moon, then in its first quarter. The sea undulated peaceably under the stern of the vessel.

At that moment I was leaning forward on the starboard netting. Conseil, standing near me, was looking straight before him. The crew, perched in the ratlines, examined the horizon which contracted and darkened by degrees. Officers with their night glasses scoured the growing darkness: sometimes the ocean sparkled under the rays of the moon, which darted between two clouds, then all trace of light was lost in the darkness.

In looking at Conseil, I could see he was undergoing a little of the general influence. At least I thought so. Perhaps for the first time his nerves vibrated to a sentiment of curiosity.

"Come, Conseil," said I, "this is the last chance of pocketing the two thousand dollars."

"May I be permitted to say, sir," replied Conseil, "that I never reckoned on getting the prize; and, had the government of the Union offered a hundred thousand dollars, it would have been none the poorer."

"You are right, Conseil. It is a foolish affair after all, and one upon which we entered too lightly. What time lost, what useless emotions! We should have been back in France six months ago."

"In your little room, sir," replied Conseil, "and in your museum, sir; and I should have already classed all your fossils, sir. And the Babiroussa would have been installed in its cage in the Jardin des Plantes, and have drawn all the curious people of the capital!"

"As you say, Conseil. I fancy we shall run a fair chance of being laughed at for our pains."

"That's tolerably certain," replied Conseil quietly; "I think they will make fun of you, sir. And—must I say it—?"

"Go on, my good friend."

"Well, sir, you will only get your deserts."

"Indeed!"

"When one has the honour of being a savant as you are, sir, one should not expose one's self to——"

Conseil had not time to finish his compliment. In the midst of general silence a voice had just been heard. It was the voice of Ned Land shouting:

"Look out there! The very thing we are looking for—on our weather beam!"

Chapter VI

AT FULL STEAM

AT THIS CRY THE WHOLE SHIP'S CREW HURRIED TOWARDS THE HARPOONER—COMMANDER, officers, masters, sailors, cabin-boys; even the engineers left their engines, and the stokers their furnaces.

The order to stop her had been given, and the frigate now simply went on by her own momentum. The darkness was then profound; and however good the Canadian's eyes were, I asked myself how he had managed to see, and what he had been able to see. My heart beat as if it would break. But Ned Land was not mistaken, and we all perceived the object he pointed to. At two cables' length from the *Abraham Lincoln*, on the starboard quarter, the sea seemed to be illuminated all over. It was not a mere phosphoric phenomenon. The monster emerged some fathoms from the water, and then threw out that very intense but inexplicable light mentioned in the report of several captains. This magnificent irradiation must have been produced by an agent of great *shining* power. The luminous part traced on the sea an immense oval, much elongated, the centre of which condensed a burning heat, whose overpowering brilliancy died out by successive gradations.

"It is only a agglomeration of phosphoric particles," cried one of the officers.

"No, sir, certainly not," I replied. "Never did pholades or salpæ produce such a powerful light. That brightness is of an essentially electrical nature. Besides, see, see! It moves; it is moving forward, backward; it is darting towards us!"

A general cry arose from the frigate.

"Silence!" said the captain. "Up with the helm, reverse the engines."

The steam was shut off, and the *Abraham Lincoln*, beating to port, described a semicircle.

"Right the helm, go ahead," cried the captain.

These orders were executed, and the frigate moved rapidly from the burning light.

I was mistaken. She tried to sheer off, but the supernatural animal approached with a velocity double her own.

We gasped for breath. Stupefaction more than fear made us dumb and motionless. The animal gained on us, sporting with the waves. It made the round of the frigate, which was then making fourteen knots, and enveloped it with its electric rings like luminous dust. Then it moved away two or three miles, leaving a phosphorescent track, like those volumes of steam that the express trains leave behind. All at once from the dark line of the horizon whither it retired to gain its momentum, the monster rushed suddenly towards the *Abraham Lincoln* with alarming rapidity, stopped suddenly about twenty feet from the hull, and died out—not diving under the water, for its brilliancy did not abate—but suddenly, and as if the source of this brilliant emanation was exhausted. Then it reappeared on the other side of the vessel, as if it had turned and slid under the hull. Any moment a collision might have occurred which would have been fatal to us. However, I was astonished at the maneuvres of the frigate. She fled and did not attack.

On the captain's face, generally so impassive, was an expression of unaccountable astonishment.

"Mr. Aronnax," he said, "I do not know with what formidable being I have to deal, and I will not imprudently risk my frigate in the midst of this darkness. Besides, how attack this unknown thing, how defend one's self from it? Wait for daylight, and the scene will change."

"You have no further doubt, captain, of the nature of the animal?"

"No, sir; it is evidently a gigantic narwhal, and an electric one."

"Perhaps," added I, "one can only approach it with a gymnotus or a torpedo."

"Undoubtedly," replied the captain, "if it possesses such dreadful power, it is the most terrible animal that ever was created. That is why, sir, I must be on my guard."

The crew were on their feet all night. No one thought of sleep. The *Abraham Lincoln*, not being able to struggle with such velocity, had moderated its pace, and sailed at half speed. For its part, the narwhal, imitating the frigate, let the waves rock it at will, and seemed decided not to leave the scene of the struggle. Towards midnight, however, it disappeared, or, to use a more appropriate term, it "died out" like a large glow-worm. Had it fled? One could only fear, not hope it. But at seven minutes to one o'clock in the morning a deafening whistling was heard, like that produced by a body of water rushing with great violence.

The captain, Ned Land, and I were then on the poop, eagerly peering through the profound darkness.

"Ned Land," asked the commander, "you have often heard the roaring of whales?"

"Often, sir; but never such whales the sight of which brought me in two thousand dollars. If I can only approach within four harpoon lengths of it!"

"But to approach it," said the commander, "I ought to put a whaler at your disposal?"

"Certainly, sir."

"That will be trifling with the lives of my men."

"And mine too," simply said the harpooner.

Towards two o'clock in the morning, the burning light reappeared, not less intense, about five miles to windward of the *Abraham Lincoln*. Notwithstanding the distance, and the noise of the wind and sea, one heard distinctly the loud strokes of the animal's tail, and even its panting breath. It seemed that, at the moment that the enormous narwhal had come to take breath at the surface of the water, the air was ingulfed in its lungs, like the steam in the vast cylinders of a machine of two thousand horse-power.

"Hum!" thought I. "A whale with the strength of a cavalry regiment would be a pretty whale!"

We were on the *qui vive* till daylight, and prepared for the combat. The fishing implements were laid along the hammock nettings. The second lieutenant loaded the blunderbusses, which could throw harpoons to the distance of a mile, and long duck-guns, with explosive bullets, which inflicted mortal wounds even to the most terrible animals. Ned Land contented himself with sharpening his harpoon—a terrible weapon in his hands.

At six o'clock, day began to break; and with the first glimmer of light, the electric light of the narwhal disappeared. At seven o'clock the day was sufficiently advanced, but a very thick sea-fog obscured our view, and the best spy-glasses could not pierce it. That caused disappointment and anger.

I climbed the mizzen-mast. Some officers were already perched on the mast-heads. At eight o'clock the fog lay heavily on the waves, and its thick scrolls rose little by little. The horizon grew wider and clearer at the same time. Suddenly, just as on the day before, Ned Land's voice was heard:

"The thing itself on the port quarter!" cried the harpooner.

Every eye was turned towards the point indicated. There, a mile and a half from the frigate, a long blackish body emerged a yard above the waves. Its tail, violently agitated, produced a considerable eddy. Never did a caudal appendage beat the sea with such violence. An immense track, of dazzling whiteness, marked the passage of the animal, and described a long curve.

The frigate approached the cetacean. I examined it thoroughly.

The reports of the *Shannon* and of the *Helvetia* had rather exaggerated its size, and I estimated its length at only two hundred and fifty feet. As to its dimensions, I could only conjecture them to be admirably proportioned. While I watched this phenomenon, two jets of steam and water were ejected from its vents, and rose to the height of 120 feet; thus I ascertained its way of breathing. I concluded definitely that it belonged to the vertebrate branch, class mammalia.

The crew waited impatiently for their chief's orders. The latter, after having observed the animal attentively, called the engineer. The engineer ran to him.

"Sir," said the commander, "you have steam up?"

"Yes, sir," answered the engineer.

"Well, make up your fires and put on all steam."

Three hurrahs greeted this order. The time for the struggle had arrived. Some moments after, the two funnels of the frigate vomited torrents of black smoke, and the bridge quaked under the trembling of the boilers.

The *Abraham Lincoln*, propelled by her powerful screw, went straight at the animal. The latter allowed it to come within half a cable's length; then, as if disdaining to dive, it took a little turn, and stopped a short distance off.

This pursuit lasted nearly three-quarters of an hour, without the frigate gaining two yards on the cetacean. It was quite evident that at that rate we should never come up with it.

"Well, Mr. Land," asked the captain, "do you advise me to put the boats out to sea?"

"No, sir," replied Ned Land; "because we shall not take that beast easily."

"What shall we do then?"

"Put on more steam if you can, sir. With your leave, I mean to post myself under the bowsprit, and if we get within harpooning distance, I shall throw my harpoon."

"Go, Ned," said the captain. "Engineer, put on more pressure."

Ned Land went to his post. The fires were increased, the screw revolved forty-three times a minute, and the steam poured out of the valves. We heaved the log, and calculated that the *Abraham Lincoln* was going at the rate of $18\frac{1}{2}$ miles an hour.

But the accursed animal swam too at the rate of $18\frac{1}{2}$ minutes.

For a whole hour, the frigate kept up this pace, without gaining six feet. It was humiliating for one of the swiftest sailers in the American navy. A stubborn anger seized the crew; the sailors abused the monster, who, as before, disdained to answer them; the captain no longer contented himself with twisting his beard—he gnawed it.

The engineer was called again.

"You have turned full steam on?"

"Yes, sir," replied the engineer.

The speed of the *Abraham Lincoln* increased. Its masts trembled down to their stepping holes, and the clouds of smoke could hardly find way out of the narrow funnels.

They heaved the log a second time.

"Well?" asked the captain of the man at the wheel.

"Nineteen miles and three-tenths, sir."

"Clap on more steam."

The engineer obeyed. The manometer showed ten degrees. But the cetacean grew warm itself, no doubt; for, without straining itself, it made $19\frac{3}{10}$ miles.

What a pursuit! No, I cannot describe the emotion that vibrated through me. Ned Land kept his post, harpoon in hand. Several times the animal let us gain upon it. "We shall catch it! We shall catch it!" cried the Canadian. But just as he was going to strike the cetacean stole away with a rapidity that could not be estimated at less than thirty miles an hour, and even during our maximum of speed it bullied the frigate, going round and round it. A cry of fury broke from everyone.

At noon we were no further advanced than at eight o'clock in the morning.

The captain then decided to take more direct means.

"Ah!" said he. "That animal goes quicker than the *Abraham Lincoln*; very well! We will see whether it will escape these conical bullets. Send your men to the forecastle, sir."

The forecastle gun was immediately loaded and slewed round. But the shot passed some feet above the cetacean, which was half a mile off.

"Another more to the right," cried the commander, "and five dollars to whoever will hit that infernal beast."

An old gunner with a grey beard—that I can see now—with steady eye and grave face, went up to the gun and took a long aim. A loud report was heard, with which were mingled the cheers of the crew.

The bullet did its work; it hit the animal, but not fatally, and, sliding off the rounded surface, was lost in two miles' depth of sea.

The chase began again, and the captain, leaning towards me, said:

"I will pursue that beast till my frigate bursts up."

"Yes," answered I; "and you will be quite right to do it."

I wished the beast would exhaust itself, and not be insensible to fatigue, like a steam engine! But it was of no use. Hours passed, without its showing any signs of exhaustion.

However, it must be said in praise of the *Abraham Lincoln*, that she struggled on indefatigably. I cannot reckon the distance she made under three hundred miles during this unlucky day, November the 6th. But night came on, and overshadowed the rough ocean.

Now I thought our expedition was at an end, and that we should never again see the extraordinary animal. I was mistaken. At ten minutes to eleven in the evening, the electric light reappeared three miles to windward of the frigate, as pure, as intense as during the preceding night.

The narwhal seemed motionless; perhaps, tired with its day's work, it slept, letting itself float with the undulation of the waves. Now was a chance of which the captain resolved to take advantage.

He gave his orders. The *Abraham Lincoln* kept up half-steam, and advanced cautiously so as not to awake its adversary. It is no rare thing to meet in the middle of the ocean whales so sound asleep that they can be successfully attacked, and Ned Land had harpooned more than one during its sleep. The Canadian went to take his place again under the bowsprit.

The frigate approached noiselessly, stopped at two cables' lengths from the animal, and following its track. No one breathed; a deep silence reigned on the bridge. We were not a hundred feet from the burning focus, the light of which increased and dazzled our eyes.

At this moment, leaning on the forecastle bulwark, I saw below me Ned Land grappling the martingale in one hand, brandishing his terrible harpoon in the other, scarcely twenty feet from the motionless animal. Suddenly his arm straightened, and the harpoon was thrown; I heard the sonorous stroke of the weapon, which seemed to have struck a hard body. The electric light went out suddenly, and two enormous water-spouts broke over the bridge of the frigate, rushing like a torrent from stem to stern, overthrowing men, and breaking the lashing of the spars. A fearful shock followed, and, thrown over the rail without having time to stop myself, I fell into the sea.

Chapter VII

AN UNKNOWN SPECIES OF WHALE

THIS UNEXPECTED FALL SO STUNNED ME THAT I HAVE NO CLEAR RECOLLECTION OF MY sensations at the time. I was at first drawn down to a depth of about twenty feet. I am a good swimmer (though without pretending to rival Byron or Edgar Poe, who were masters of the art), and in that plunge I did not lose my presence of mind. Two vigorous strokes brought me to the surface of the water. My first care was to look for the frigate. Had the crew seen me disappear? Had the *Abraham Lincoln* veered round? Would the captain put out a boat? Might I hope to be saved?

The darkness was intense. I caught a glimpse of a black mass disappearing in the east, its beacon-lights dying out in the distance. It was the frigate! I was lost.

"Help! Help!" I shouted, swimming towards the *Abraham Lincoln* in desperation.

My clothes encumbered me; they seemed glued to my body, and paralyzed my movements.

I was sinking! I was suffocating!

"Help!"

This was my last cry. My mouth filled with water; I struggled against being drawn down the abyss. Suddenly my clothes were seized by a strong hand, and I felt myself quickly drawn up to the surface of the sea; and I heard, yes, I heard these words pronounced in my ear:

"If master would be so good as to lean on my shoulder, master would swim with much greater ease."

I seized with one hand my faithful Conseil's arm.

"Is it you?" said I. "You?"

"Myself," answered Conseil; "and waiting master's orders."

"That shock threw you as well as me into the sea?"

"No; but being in my master's service, I followed him."

The worthy fellow thought that was but natural.

"And the frigate?" I asked.

"The frigate?" replied Conseil, turning on his back. "I think that master had better not count too much on her."

"You think so?"

"I say that, at the time I threw myself into the sea, I heard the men at the wheel say, 'The screw and the rudder are broken.'"

"Broken?"

"Yes, broken by the monster's teeth. It is the only injury the *Abraham Lincoln* has sustained. But it is a bad lookout for us—she no longer answers her helm."

"Then we are lost!"

"Perhaps so," calmly answered Conseil. "However, we have still several hours before us, and one can do a good deal in some hours."

Conseil's imperturbable coolness set me up again. I swam more vigorously; but, cramped by my clothes, which stuck to me like a leaden weight, I felt great difficulty in bearing up. Conseil saw this.

"Will master let me make a slit?" said he; and slipping an open knife under my clothes, he ripped them up from top to bottom very rapidly. Then he cleverly slipped them off me, while I swam for both of us.

Then I did the same for Conseil, and we continued to swim near to each other.

Nevertheless, our situation was no less terrible. Perhaps our disappearance had not been noticed; and, if it had been, the frigate could not tack, being without its helm. Conseil argued on this supposition, and laid his plans accordingly. This phlegmatic boy was perfectly self-possessed. We then decided that, as our only chance of safety was being picked up by the *Abraham Lincoln*'s boats, we ought to manage so as to wait for them as long as possible. I resolved then to husband our strength, so that both should not be exhausted at the same time; and this is how we managed: while one of us lay on our back, quite still, with arms crossed, and legs stretched out, the other would swim and push the other on in front. This towing business did not last more than ten minutes each; and relieving each other thus, we could swim on for some hours, perhaps till daybreak. Poor chance! But hope is so firmly rooted in the heart of man! Moreover, there were two of us. Indeed, I declare (though it may seem improbable) if I sought to destroy all hope, if I wished to despair, I could not.

The collision of the frigate with the cetacean had occurred about eleven o'clock in the evening before. I reckoned then we should have eight hours to swim before sunrise—an operation quite practicable if we relieved each other. The sea, very calm, was in our favour. Sometimes I tried to pierce the intense darkness that was only dispelled by the phosphorescence caused by our movements. I watched the luminous waves that broke over my hand, whose mirror-like surface was spotted with silvery rings. One might have said that we were in a bath of quicksilver.

Near one o'clock in the morning, I was seized with dreadful fatigue. My limbs stiffened under the strain of violent cramp. Conseil was obliged to keep me up, and our preservation devolved on him alone. I heard the poor boy pant; his breathing became short and hurried. I found that he could not keep up much longer.

"Leave me! Leave me!" I said to him.

"Leave my master? Never!" replied he. "I would drown first."

Just then the moon appeared through the fringes of a thick cloud that the wind was driving to the east. The surface of the sea glittered with its rays. This kindly light reanimated us. My head got better again. I looked at all points of the horizon. I saw the frigate! She was five miles from us, and looked like a dark mass, hardly discernible. But no boats!

I would have cried out. But what good would it have been at such a distance? My swollen lips could utter no sounds. Conseil could articulate some words, and I heard him repeat at intervals, "Help! Help!"

Our movements were suspended for an instant; we listened. It might be only a singing in the ear, but it seemed to me as if a cry answered the cry from Conseil.

"Did you hear?" I murmured.

"Yes! Yes!"

And Conseil gave one more despairing cry.

This time there was no mistake! A human voice responded to ours! Was it the voice of another unfortunate creature, abandoned in the middle of the ocean, some other victim of the shock sustained by the vessel? Or rather was it a boat from the frigate, that was hailing us in the darkness?

Conseil made a last effort, and leaning on my shoulder, while I struck out in a desparing effort, he raised himself half out of the water, then fell back exhausted.

"What did you see?"

"I saw—" murmured he—"I saw—but do not talk—reserve all your strength!"

What had he seen? Then, I know not why, the thought of the monster came into my head for the first time! But that voice? The time is past for Jonahs to take refuge in whales' bellies! However, Conseil was towing me again. He raised his head sometimes, looked before us, and uttered a cry of recognition, which was responded to by a voice that came nearer and nearer. I scarcely heard it. My strength was exhausted; my fingers stiffened; my hand afforded me support no longer; my mouth, convulsively opening, filled with salt water. Cold crept over me. I raised my head for the last time, then I sank.

At this moment a hard body struck me. I clung to it, then I felt that I was being drawn up, that I was brought to the surface of the water, that my chest collapsed: I fainted.

It is certain that I soon came to, thanks to the vigorous rubbings that I received. I half opened my eyes.

"Conseil!" I murmured.

"Does master call me?" asked Conseil.

Just then, by the waning light of the moon, which was sinking down to the horizon, I saw a face which was not Conseil's, and which I immediately recognised.

"Ned!" I cried.

"The same, sir, who is seeking his prize!" replied the Canadian.

"Were you thrown into the sea by the shock of the frigate?"

"Yes, professor; but, more fortunate than you, I was able to find a footing almost directly upon a floating island."

"An island?"

"Or, more correctly speaking, on our gigantic narwhal."

"Explain yourself, Ned!"

"Only I soon found out why my harpoon had not entered its skin and was blunted."

"Why, Ned, why?"

"Because, professor, that beast is made of sheet-iron."

The Canadian's last words produced a sudden revolution in my brain. I wriggled myself quickly to the top of the being, or object, half out of the water, which served us for a refuge. I kicked it. It was evidently a hard, impenetrable body, and not the soft substance that forms the bodies of the great marine mammalia. But this hard body might be a bony carapace, like that of the antediluvian animals; and I should be free to class this monster among amphibious reptiles, such as tortoises or alligators.

Well, no! The blackish back that supported me was smooth, polished, without scales. The blow produced a metallic sound; and, incredible though it may be, it seemed, I might say, as if it was made of riveted plates.

There was no doubt about it! This monster, this natural phenomenon that had puzzled the learned world, and overthrown and misled the imagination of seamen of both hemispheres, was, it must be owned, a still more astonishing phenomenon, inasmuch as it was a simply human construction.

We had no time to lose, however. We were lying upon the back of a sort of submarine boat, which appeared (as far as I could judge) like a huge fish of steel. Ned Land's mind was made up on this point. Conseil and I could only agree with him.

Just then a bubbling began at the back of this strange thing (which was evidently propelled by a screw), and it began to move. We had only just time to seize hold of the upper part, which rose about seven feet out of the water, and happily its speed was not great.

"As long as it sails horizontally," muttered Ned Land, "I do not mind; but, if it takes a fancy to dive, I would not give two straws for my life."

The Canadian might have said still less. It became really necessary to communicate with the beings, whatever they were, shut up inside the machine. I searched all over the outside for an aperture, a panel, or a man-hole, to use a technical expression; but the lines of the iron rivets, solidly driven into the joints of the iron plates, were clear and uniform. Besides, the moon disappeared then, and left us in total darkness.

At last this long night passed. My indistinct remembrance prevents my describing all the impressions it made. I can only recall one circumstance. During some lulls of the wind and sea, I fancied I heard several times vague sounds, a sort of fugitive harmony produced by distant words of command. What was then the mystery of this submarine craft, of which the whole world vainly sought an explanation? What kind of beings existed in this strange boat? What mechanical agent caused its prodigious speed?

Daybreak appeared. The morning mists surrounded us, but they soon cleared off. I was about to examine the hull, which formed on deck a kind of horizontal platform, when I felt it gradually sinking.

"Oh, confound it!" cried Ned Land, kicking the resounding plate. "Open, you inhospitable rascals!"

Happily the sinking movement ceased. Suddenly a noise, like iron-works violently pushed aside, came from the interior of the boat. One iron plate was moved, a man appeared, uttered an odd cry, and disappeared immediately.

Some moments after, eight strong men with masked faces appeared noiselessly, and drew us down into their formidable machine.

Chapter VIII

MOBILIS IN MOBILE

THIS FORCIBLE ABDUCTION, SO ROUGHLY CARRIED OUT, WAS ACCOMPLISHED WITH THE rapidity of lightning. I shivered all over. Whom had we to deal with? No doubt some new sort of pirates, who explored the sea in their own way.

Hardly had the narrow panel closed upon me, when I was enveloped in darkness. My eyes, dazzled with the outer light, could distinguish nothing. I felt my naked feet cling to the rungs of an iron ladder. Ned Land and Conseil, firmly seized, followed me. At the bottom of the ladder, a door opened, and shut after us immediately with a bang.

We were alone. Where, I could not say, hardly imagine. All was black, and such a dense black that, after some minutes, my eyes had not been able to discern even the faintest glimmer.

Meanwhile, Ned Land, furious at these proceedings, gave free vent to his indignation.

"Confound it!" cried he. "Here are people who come up to the Scotch for hospitality. They only just miss being cannibals. I should not be surprised at it, but I declare that they shall not eat me without my protesting."

"Calm yourself, friend Ned, calm yourself," replied Conseil, quietly. "Do not cry out before you are hurt. We are not quite done for yet."

"Not quite," sharply replied the Canadian, "but pretty near, at all events. Things look black. Happily, my bowie-knife I have still, and I can always see well enough to use it. The first of these pirates who lays a hand on me——"

"Do not excite yourself, Ned," I said to the harpooner, "and do not compromise us by useless violence. Who knows that they will not listen to us? Let us rather try to find out where we are."

I groped about. In five steps I came to an iron wall, made of plates bolted together. Then turning back I struck against a wooden table, near which were ranged several stools. The boards of this prison were concealed under a thick mat of phoronium, which deadened the noise of the feet. The bare walls revealed no trace of window or door. Conseil, going round the reverse way, met me, and we went back to the middle of the cabin, which measured about twenty feet by ten. As to its height, Ned Land, in spite of his own great height, could not measure it.

Half an hour had already passed without our situation being bettered, when the dense darkness suddenly gave way to extreme light. Our prison was suddenly lighted—that is to say, it became filled with a luminous matter, so strong that I could not bear it at first. In its whiteness and intensity I recognised that electric light which played round the submarine boat like a magnificent phenomenon of phosphorescence. After shutting my eyes involuntarily, I opened them and saw that this luminous agent came from a half-globe, unpolished, placed in the roof of the cabin.

"At last one can see," cried Ned Land, who, knife in hand, stood on the defensive.

"Yes," said I; "but we are still in the dark about ourselves."

"Let master have patience," said the imperturbable Conseil.

The sudden lighting of the cabin enabled me to examine it minutely. It only contained a table and five stools. The invisible door might be hermetically sealed. No noise was heard. All seemed dead in the interior of this boat. Did it move, did it float on the surface of the ocean, or did it dive into its depths? I could not guess.

A noise of bolts was now heard, the door opened and two men appeared.

One was short, very muscular, broad-shouldered, with robust limbs, strong head, an abundance of black hair, thick moustache, a quick, penetrating look, and the vivacity which characterises the population of Southern France.

The second stranger merits a more detailed description. A disciple of Gratiolet or Engel would have read his face like an open book. I made out his prevailing qualities directly: self-confidence—because his head was well set on his shoulders, and his black eyes looked around with cold assurance; calmness—for his skin, rather pale, showed his coolness of blood; energy—evinced by the rapid contraction of his lofty brows; and courage—because his deep breathing denoted great power of lungs.

Whether this person was thirty-five or fifty years of age, I could not say. He was tall, had a large forehead, straight nose, a clearly cut mouth, beautiful teeth, with fine tapered hands, indicative of a highly nervous temperament. This man was certainly the most admirable specimen I had ever met. One particular feature was his eyes, rather far from each other, and which could take in nearly a quarter of the horizon at once.

This faculty—I verified it later—gave him a range of vision far superior to Ned Land's. When this stranger fixed upon an object, his eyebrows met, his large eyelids closed around so as to contract the range of his vision, and he looked as if he magnified the objects lessened by distance, as if he pierced those sheets of water so opaque to our eyes, and as if he read the very depths of the seas.

The two strangers, with caps made from the fur of the sea otter and shod with seaboots of seals' skin, were dressed in clothes of a particular texture, which allowed free movement of the limbs. The taller of the two, evidently the chief on board, examined us with great attention, without saying a word; then turning to his companion, talked with him in an unknown tongue. It was a sonorous, harmonious, and flexible dialect, the vowels seeming to admit of very varied accentuation.

The other replied by a shake of the head, and added two or three perfectly incomprehensible words. Then he seemed to question me by a look.

I replied in good French that I did not know his language; but he seemed not to understand me, and my situation became more embarrassing.

"If master were to tell our story," said Conseil, "perhaps these gentlemen may understand some words."

I began to tell our adventures, articulating each syllable clearly, and without omitting one single detail. I announced our names and rank, introducing in person Professor Aronnax, his servant Conseil, and Master Ned Land, the harpooner.

The man with the soft calm eyes listened to me quietly, even politely, and with extreme attention; but nothing in his countenance indicated that he had understood my story. When I finished he said not a word.

There remained one resource, to speak English. Perhaps they would know this almost universal language. I knew it, as well as the German language—well enough to read it fluently, but not to speak it correctly. But anyhow, we must make ourselves understood.

"Go on in your turn," I said to the harpooner; "speak your best Anglo-Saxon, and try to do better than I."

Ned did not beg off, and recommenced our story.

To his great disgust, the harpooner did not seem to have made himself more intelligible than I had. Our visitors did not stir. They evidently understood neither the language of Arago nor of Faraday.

Very much embarrassed, after having vainly exhausted our philological resources, I knew not what part to take, when Conseil said:

"If master will permit me, I will relate it in German."

But in spite of the elegant terms and good accent of the narrator, the German language had no success. At last, nonplussed, I tried to remember my first lessons, and to narrate our adventures in Latin, but with no better success. This last attempt being of no avail, the two strangers exchanged some words in their unknown language and retired.

The door shut.

"It is an infamous shame," cried Ned Land, who broke out for the twentieth time; "we speak to those rogues in French, English, German, and Latin, and not one of them has the politeness to answer!"

"Calm yourself," I said to the impetuous Ned, "anger will do no good."

"But do you see, professor," replied our irascible companion, "that we shall absolutely die of hunger in this iron cage?"

"Bah," said Conseil philosophically; "we can hold out some time yet."

"My friends," I said, "we must not despair. We have been worse off than this. Do me the favour to wait a little before forming an opinion upon the commander and crew of this boat."

"My opinion is formed," replied Ned Land sharply. "They are rascals."

"Good! And from what country?"

"From the land of rogues!"

"My brave Ned, that country is not clearly indicated on the map of the world; but I admit that the nationality of the two strangers is hard to determine. Neither English, French, nor German, that is quite certain. However, I am inclined to think that the commander and his companion were born in low latitudes. There is southern blood in them. But I cannot decide by their appearance whether they are Spaniards, Turks, Arabians, or Indians. As to their language, it is quite incomprehensible."

"There is the disadvantage of not knowing all languages," said Conseil, "or the disadvantage of not having one universal language."

As he said these words, the door opened. A steward entered. He brought us clothes, coats and trousers, made of a stuff I did not know. I hastened to dress myself, and my companions followed my example. During that time, the steward—dumb, perhaps deaf—had arranged the table, and laid three plates.

"This is something like," said Conseil.

"Bah," said the rancorous harpooner, "what do you suppose they eat here? Tortoise liver, filleted shark, and beefsteaks from sea dogs."

"We shall see," said Conseil.

The dishes, of bell metal, were placed on the table, and we took our places. Undoubtedly we had to do with civilised people, and had it not been for the electric light which flooded us, I could have fancied I was in the dining-room of the Adelphi Hotel at Liverpool, or at the Grand Hotel in Paris. I must say, however, that there was neither bread nor wine. The water was fresh and clear, but it was water and did not suit Ned Land's taste. Among the dishes which were brought to us, I recognised several fish delicately dressed; but of some, although excellent, I could give no opinion, neither could I tell to what kingdom they belonged, whether animal or vegetable. As to the dinner service, it was elegant, and in perfect taste. Each utensil, spoon, fork, knife, plate, had a letter engraved on it, with a motto above it, of which this is an exact facsimile:

MOBILIS IN MOBILE
N.

The letter N was no doubt the initial of the name of the enigmatical person who commanded at the bottom of the seas.

Ned and Conseil did not reflect much. They devoured the food, and I did likewise. I was, besides, reassured as to our fate; and it seemed evident that our hosts would not let us die of want.

However, everything has an end, everything passes away, even the hunger of people who have not eaten for fifteen hours. Our appetites satisfied, we felt overcome with sleep.

"Faith! I shall sleep well," said Conseil.

"So shall I," replied Ned Land.

My two companions stretched themselves on the cabin carpet, and were soon sound asleep. For my own part, too many thoughts crowded my brain, too many insoluble questions pressed upon me, too many fancies kept my eyes half open. Where were we? What strange power carried us on? I felt—or rather fancied I felt—the machine sinking down to the lowest beds of the sea. Dreadful nightmares beset me; I saw in these mysterious asylums a world of unknown animals, among which this submarine boat seemed to be of the same kind, living, moving, and formidable as they. Then my brain grew calmer, my imagination wandered into vague unconsciousness, and I soon fell into a deep sleep.

Chapter IX

NED LAND'S TEMPERS

HOW LONG WE SLEPT I DO NOT KNOW; BUT OUR SLEEP MUST HAVE LASTED LONG, FOR it rested us completely from our fatigues. I woke first. My companions had not moved, and were still stretched in their corner.

Hardly roused from my somewhat hard couch, I felt my brain freed, my mind clear. I then began an attentive examination of our cell. Nothing was changed inside. The prison was still a prison; the prisoners, prisoners. However, the steward, during our sleep, had cleared the table. I breathed with difficulty. The heavy air seemed to oppress my lungs. Although the cell was large, we had evidently consumed a great part of the oxygen that it contained. Indeed, each man consumes, in one hour, the oxygen contained in more than 176 pints of air, and this air, charged (as then) with a nearly equal quantity of carbonic acid, becomes unbreathable.

It became necessary to renew the atmosphere of our prison, and no doubt the whole in the submarine boat. That gave rise to a question in my mind. How would the commander of this floating dwelling-place proceed? Would he obtain air by chemical means, in getting by heat the oxygen contained in chlorate of potash, and in absorbing carbonic acid by caustic potash? Or, a more convenient, economical, and consequently more probable alternative, would he be satisfied to rise and take breath at the surface of the water, like a cetacean, and so renew for twenty-four hours the atmospheric provision?

In fact, I was already obliged to increase my respirations to eke out of this cell the little oxygen it contained, when suddenly I was refreshed by a current of pure air, and perfumed with saline emanations. It was an invigorating sea-breeze, charged with iodine. I opened my mouth wide, and my lungs saturated themselves with fresh particles.

At the same time I felt the boat rolling. The iron-plated monster had evidently just risen to the surface of the ocean to breathe, after the fashion of whales. I found out from that the mode of ventilating the boat.

When I had inhaled this air freely, I sought the conduit-pipe which conveyed to us the beneficial whiff, and I was not long in finding it. Above the door was a ventilator, through which volumes of fresh air renewed the impoverished atmosphere of the cell.

I was making my observations, when Ned and Conseil awoke almost at the same time, under the influence of this reviving air. They rubbed their eyes, stretched themselves, and were on their feet in an instant.

"Did master sleep well?" asked Conseil, with his usual politeness.

"Very well, my brave boy. And you, Mr. Land?"

"Soundly, professor. But, I don't know if I am right or not; there seems to be a sea-breeze!"

A seaman could not be mistaken, and I told the Canadian all that had passed during his sleep.

"Good!" said he. "That accounts for those roarings we heard, when the supposed narwhal sighted the *Abraham Lincoln*."

"Quite so, Master Land; it was taking breath."

"Only, Mr. Aronnax, I have no idea what o'clock it is, unless it is dinner-time."

"Dinner-time! My good fellow? Say rather breakfast-time, for we certainly have begun another day."

"So," said Conseil, "we have slept twenty-four hours?"

"That is my opinion."

"I will not contradict you," replied Ned Land. "But dinner or breakfast, the steward will be welcome, whichever he brings."

"Master Land, we must conform to the rules on board, and I suppose our appetites are in advance of the dinner-hour."

"That is just like you, friend Conseil," said Ned, impatiently. "You are never out of temper, always calm; you would return thanks before grace, and die of hunger rather than complain!"

Time was getting on, and we were fearfully hungry; and this time the steward did not appear. It was rather too long to leave us, if they really had good intentions towards us. Ned Land, tormented by the cravings of hunger, got still more angry; and notwithstanding his promise, I dreaded an explosion when he found himself with one of the crew.

For two hours more, Ned Land's temper increased; he cried, he shouted, but in vain. The walls were deaf. There was no sound to be heard in the boat; all was still as death. It did not move, for I should have felt the trembling motion of the hull under the influence of the screw. Plunged in the depths of the waters, it belonged no longer to earth—this silence was dreadful.

I felt terrified, Conseil was calm, Ned Land roared.

Just then a noise was heard outside. Steps sounded on the metal flags. The locks were turned, the door opened, and the steward appeared.

Before I could rush forward to stop him, the Canadian had thrown him down, and held him by the throat. The steward was choking under the grip of his powerful hand.

Conseil was already trying to unclasp the harpooner's hand from his half-suffocated victim, and I was going to fly to the rescue, when suddenly I was nailed to the spot by hearing these words in French:

"Be quiet, Master Land; and you, professor, will you be so good as to listen to me?"

Chapter X

THE MAN OF THE SEAS

I T WAS THE COMMANDER OF THE VESSEL WHO THUS SPOKE.

At these words, Ned Land rose suddenly. The steward, nearly strangled, tottered out on a sign from his master; but such was the power of the commander on board, that not a gesture betrayed the resentment which this man must have felt towards the Canadian. Conseil interested in spite of himself, I stupefied, awaited in silence the result of this scene.

The commander, leaning against a corner of the table with his arms folded, scanned us with profound attention. Did he hesitate to speak? Did he regret the words which he had just spoken in French? One might almost think so.

After some moments of silence, which not one of us dreamed of breaking, "Gentle-men," said he, in a calm and penetrating voice, "I speak French, English, German, and Latin equally well. I could, therefore, have answered you at our first interview, but I wished to know you first, then to reflect. The story told by each one, entirely agreeing in the main points, convinced me of your identity. I know now that chance has brought be-fore me M. Pierre Aronnax, Professor of Natural History at the Museum of Paris, en-trusted with a scientific mission abroad; Conseil, his servant; and Ned Land, of Canadian origin, harpooner on board the frigate *Abraham Lincoln* of the navy of the United States of America."

I bowed assent. It was not a question that the commander put to me. Therefore there was no answer to be made. This man expressed himself with perfect ease, without any ac-cent. His sentences were well turned, his words clear, and his fluency of speech remark-able. Yet I did not recognise in him a fellow-countryman.

He continued the conversation in these terms:

"You have doubtless thought, sir, that I have delayed long in paying you this second visit. The reason is that, your identity recognised, I wished to weigh maturely what part to act towards you. I have hesitated much. Most annoying circumstances have brought you into the presence of a man who has broken all the ties of humanity. You have come to trou-ble my existence."

"Unintentionally!" said I.

"Unintentionally?" replied the stranger, raising his voice a little. "Was it unintention-ally that the *Abraham Lincoln* pursued me all over the seas? Was it unintentionally that you took passage in this frigate? Was it unintentionally that your cannon-balls rebounded off the plating of my vessel? Was it unintentionally that Mr. Ned Land struck me with his harpoon?"

I detected a restrained irritation in these words. But to these recriminations I had a very natural answer to make, and I made it.

"Sir," said I, "no doubt you are ignorant of the discussions which have taken place concerning you in America and Europe. You do not know that divers accidents, caused by collisions with your submarine machine, have excited public feeling in the two conti-nents. I omit the hypotheses without number by which it was sought to explain the inexplicable phenomenon of which you alone possess the secret. But you must understand that, in pursuing you over the high seas of the Pacific, the *Abraham Lincoln* believed itself to be chasing some powerful sea-monster, of which it was necessary to rid the ocean at any price."

A half-smile curled the lips of the commander: then, in a calmer tone:

"M. Aronnax," he replied, "dare you affirm that your frigate would not as soon have pursued and cannonaded a submarine boat as a monster?"

This question embarrassed me, for certainly Captain Farragut might not have hesitated. He might have thought it his duty to destroy a contrivance of this kind, as he would a gigantic narwhal.

"You understand then, sir," continued the stranger, "that I have the right to treat you as enemies?"

I answered nothing, purposely. For what good would it be to discuss such a proposition, when force could destroy the best arguments?

"I have hesitated some time," continued the commander; "nothing obliged me to show you hospitality. If I chose to separate myself from you, I should have no interest in seeing you again; I could place you upon the deck of this vessel which has served you as a refuge, I could sink beneath the waters, and forget that you had ever existed. Would not that be my right?"

"It might be the right of a savage," I answered, "but not that of a civilised man."

"Professor," replied the commander quickly, "I am not what you call a civilised man! I have done with society entirely, for reasons which I alone have the right of appreciating. I do not therefore obey its laws, and I desire you never to allude to them before me again!"

This was said plainly. A flash of anger and disdain kindled in the eyes of the Unknown, and I had a glimpse of a terrible past in the life of this man. Not only had he put himself beyond the pale of human laws, but he had made himself independent of them, free in the strictest acceptation of the word, quite beyond their reach! Who then would dare to pursue him at the bottom of the sea, when, on its surface, he defied all attempts made against him? What vessel could resist the shock of his submarine monitor? What cuirass, however thick, could withstand the blows of his spur? No man could demand from him an account of his actions; God, if he believed in one—his conscience, if he had one—were the sole judges to whom he was answerable.

These reflections crossed my mind rapidly, while the stranger personage was silent, absorbed, and as if wrapped up in himself. I regarded him with fear mingled with interest, as, doubtless, Œdipus regarded the Sphinx.

After rather a long silence, the commander resumed the conversation.

"I have hesitated," said he, "but I have thought that my interest might be reconciled with that pity to which every human being has a right. You will remain on board my vessel, since fate has cast you there. You will be free; and, in exchange for this liberty, I shall only impose one single condition. Your word of honour to submit to it will suffice."

"Speak, sir," I answered. "I suppose this condition is one which a man of honour may accept?"

"Yes, sir; it is this: It is possible that certain events, unforeseen, may oblige me to consign you to your cabins for some hours or some days, as the case may be. As I desire never to use violence, I expect from you, more than all the others, a passive obedience. In thus acting, I take all the responsibility: I acquit you entirely, for I make it an impossibility for you to see what ought not to be seen. Do you accept this condition?"

Then things took place on board which, to say the least, were singular, and which ought not to be seen by people who were not placed beyond the pale of social laws. Among the surprises which the future was preparing for me, this might not be the least.

"We accept," I answered; "only I will ask your permission, sir, to address one question to you—one only."

"Speak, sir."

"You said that we should be free on board."

"Entirely."

"I ask you, then, what you mean by this liberty?"

"Just the liberty to go, to come, to see, to observe even all that passes here—save under rare circumstances—the liberty, in short, which we enjoy ourselves, my companions and I."

It was evident that we did not understand one another.

"Pardon me, sir," I resumed, "but this liberty is only what every prisoner has of pacing his prison. It cannot suffice us."

"It must suffice you, however."

"What! We must renounce forever seeing our country, our friends, our relations again?"

"Yes, sir. But to renounce that unendurable worldly yoke which men believe to be liberty is not perhaps so painful as you think."

"Well," exclaimed Ned Land, "never will I give my word of honour not to try to escape."

"I did not ask you for your word of honour, Master Land," answered the commander, coldly.

"Sir," I replied, beginning to get angry in spite of my self, "you abuse your situation towards us; it is cruelty."

"No, sir, it is clemency. You are my prisoners of war. I keep you, when I could, by a word, plunge you into the depths of the ocean. You attacked me. You came to surprise a secret which no man in the world must penetrate—the secret of my whole existence. And you think that I am going to send you back to that world which must know me no more? Never! In retaining you, it is not you whom I guard—it is myself."

These words indicated a resolution taken on the part of the commander, against which no arguments would prevail.

"So, sir," I rejoined, "you give us simply the choice between life and death?"

"Simply."

"My friends," said I, "to a question thus put, there is nothing to answer. But no word of honour binds us to the master of this vessel."

"None, sir," answered the Unknown.

Then, in a gentler tone, he continued:

"Now, permit me to finish what I have to say to you. I know you, M. Aronnax. You and your companions will not, perhaps, have so much to complain of in the chance which has bound you to my fate. You will find among the books which are my favourite study the work which you have published on 'the depths of the sea.' I have often read it. You have carried out your work as far as terrestrial science permitted you. But you do not know all—you have not seen all. Let me tell you then, professor, that you will not regret the time passed on board my vessel. You are going to visit the land of marvels."

These words of the commander had a great effect upon me. I cannot deny it. My weak point was touched; and I forgot, for a moment, that the contemplation of these sublime subjects was not worth the loss of liberty. Besides, I trusted to the future to decide this grave question. So I contented myself with saying:

"By what name ought I to address you?"

"Sir," replied the commander, "I am nothing to you but Captain Nemo; and you and your companions are nothing to me but the passengers of the *Nautilus*."

Captain Nemo called. A steward appeared. The captain gave him his orders in that strange language which I did not understand. Then, turning towards the Canadian and Conseil:

"A repast awaits you in your cabin," said he. "Be so good as to follow this man. And now, M. Aronnax, our breakfast is ready. Permit me to lead the way."

"I am at your service, captain."

I followed Captain Nemo; and as soon as I had passed through the door, I found myself in a kind of passage lighted by electricity, similar to the waist of a ship. After we had proceeded a dozen yards, a second door opened before me.

I then entered a dining-room, decorated and furnished in severe taste. High oaken sideboards, inlaid with ebony, stood at the two extremities of the room, and upon their shelves glittered china, porcelain, and glass of inestimable value.

The plate on the table sparkled in the rays which the luminous ceiling shed around while the light was tempered and softened by exquisite paintings.

In the centre of the room was a table richly laid out. Captain Nemo indicated the place I was to occupy.

The breakfast consisted of a certain number of dishes, the contents of which were furnished by the sea alone; and I was ignorant of the nature and mode of preparation of some of them. I acknowledged that they were good, but they had a peculiar flavour, which I easily became accustomed to. These different aliments appeared to me to be rich in phosphorus, and I thought they must have a marine origin.

Captain Nemo looked at me. I asked him no questions, but he guessed my thoughts, and answered of his own accord the questions which I was burning to address to him.

"The greater part of these dishes are unknown to you," he said to me. "However, you may partake of them without fear. They are wholesome and nourishing. For a long time I have renounced the food of the earth, and I am never ill now. My crew, who are healthy, are fed on the same food."

"So," said I, "all these eatables are the produce of the sea?"

"Yes, professor, the sea supplies all my wants. Sometimes I cast my nets in tow, and I draw them in ready to break. Sometimes I hunt in the midst of this element, which appears to be inaccessible to man, and quarry the game which dwells in my submarine forests. My flocks, like those of Neptune's old shepherds, graze fearlessly in the immense prairies of the ocean. I have a vast property there, which I cultivate myself, and which is always sown by the hand of the Creator of all things."

"I can understand perfectly, sir, that your nets furnish excellent fish for your table; I can understand also that you hunt aquatic game in your submarine forests; but I cannot understand at all how a particle of meat, no matter how small, can figure in your bill of fare."

"This, which you believe to be meat, professor, is nothing else than fillet of turtle. Here are also some dolphin's livers, which you take to be ragout of pork. My cook is a clever fellow, who excels in dressing these various products of the ocean. Taste all these dishes. Here is a preserve of holothuria, which a Malay would declare to be unrivalled in the world; here is a cream, of which the milk has been furnished by the cetacea, and the sugar by the great fucus of the North Sea; and, lastly, permit me to offer you some preserve of anemones, which is equal to that of the most delicious fruits."

I tasted, more from curiosity than as a connoisseur, while Captain Nemo enchanted me with his extraordinary stories.

"You like the sea, captain?"

"Yes, I love it! The sea is everything. It covers seven-tenths of the terrestrial globe. Its breath is pure and healthy. It is an immense desert, where man is never lonely, for he feels life stirring on all sides. The sea is only the embodiment of a supernatural and wonderful existence. It is nothing but love and emotion; it is the 'Living Infinite,' as one of your poets has said. In fact, professor, Nature manifests herself in it by her three kingdoms, mineral, vegetable, and animal. The sea is the vast reservoir of Nature. The globe began with sea, so to speak; and who knows if it will not end with it? In it is supreme tranquillity. The sea does not belong to despots. Upon its surface men can still exercise unjust laws, fight, tear one another to pieces, and be carried away with terrestrial horrors. But at thirty feet below its level, their reign ceases, their influence is quenched, and their power disappears. Ah! sir, live—live in the bosom of the waters! There only is independence! There I recognise no masters! There I am free!"

Captain Nemo suddenly became silent in the midst of this enthusiasm, by which he was quite carried away. For a few moments he paced up and down, much agitated. Then he became more calm, regained his accustomed coldness of expression, and turning towards me:

"Now, professor," said he, "if you wish to go over the *Nautilus*, I am at your service."

Captain Nemo rose. I followed him. A double door, contrived at the back of the dining-room, opened, and I entered a room equal in dimensions to that which I had just quitted.

It was a library. High pieces of furniture, of black violet ebony inlaid with brass, supported upon their wide shelves a great number of books uniformly bound. They followed the shape of the room, terminating at the lower part in huge divans, covered with brown leather, which were curved, to afford the greatest comfort. Light movable desks, made to slide in and out at will, allowed one to rest one's book while reading. In the centre stood an immense table, covered with pamphlets, among which were some newspapers, already of old date. The electric light flooded everything; it was shed from four unpolished globes half sunk in the volutes of the ceiling. I looked with real admiration at this room, so ingeniously fitted up, and I could scarcely believe my eyes.

"Captain Nemo," said I to my host, who had just thrown himself on one of the divans, "this is a library which would do honour to more than one of the continental palaces, and I am absolutely astounded when I consider that it can follow you to the bottom of the seas."

"Where could one find greater solitude or silence, professor?" replied Captain Nemo. "Did your study in the Museum afford you such perfect quiet?"

"No, sir; and I must confess that it is a very poor one after yours. You must have six or seven thousand volumes here."

"Twelve thousand, M. Aronnax. These are the only ties which bind me to the earth. But I had done with the world on the day when my *Nautilus* plunged for the first time beneath the waters. That day I bought my last volumes, my last pamphlets, my last papers, and from that time I wish to think that men no longer think or write. These books, professor, are at your service besides, and you can make use of them freely."

I thanked Captain Nemo, and went up to the shelves of the library. Works on science, morals, and literature abounded in every language; but I did not see one single work on political economy; that subject appeared to be strictly proscribed. Strange to say, all these books were irregularly arranged, in whatever language they were written; and this medley proved that the captain of the *Nautilus* must have read indiscriminately the books which he took up by chance.

"Sir," said I to the captain, "I thank you for having placed this library at my disposal. It contains treasures of science, and I shall profit by them."

"This room is not only a library," said Captain Nemo, "it is also a smoking-room."

"A smoking-room!" I cried. "Then one may smoke on board?"

"Certainly."

"Then, sir, I am forced to believe that you have kept up a communication with Havana."

"Not any," answered the Captain. "Accept this cigar, M. Aronnax; and, though it does not come from Havana, you will be pleased with it, if you are a connoisseur."

I took the cigar which was offered me; its shape recalled the London ones, but it seemed to be made of leaves of gold. I lighted it at a little brazier, which was supported upon an elegant bronze stem, and drew the first whiffs with the delight of a lover of smoking who has not smoked for two days.

"It is excellent," said I, "but it is not tobacco."

"No!" answered the Captain, "this tobacco comes neither from Havana nor from the East. It is a kind of sea-weed, rich in nicotine, with which the sea provides me, but somewhat sparingly."

At that moment Captain Nemo opened a door which stood opposite to that by which I had entered the library, and I passed into an immense drawing-room splendidly lighted.

It was a vast four-sided room, thirty feet long, eighteen wide, and fifteen high. A luminous ceiling, decorated with light arabesques, shed a soft clear light over all the marvels accumulated in this museum. For it was in fact a museum, in which an intelligent and prodigal hand had gathered all the treasures of nature and art, with the artistic confusion which distinguishes a painter's studio. Thirty first-rate pictures, uniformly framed, separated by bright drapery, ornamented the walls, which were hung with tapestry of severe design. I saw works of great value, the greater part of which I had admired in the special collections of Europe, and in the exhibitions of paintings. The several schools of the old masters were represented by a Madonna of Raphael, a Virgin of Leonardo da Vinci, a nymph of Corregio, a woman of Titian, an Adoration of Veronese, an Assumption of Murillo, a portrait of Holbein, a monk of Velasquez, a martyr of Ribeira, a fair of Rubens, two Flemish landscapes of Teniers, three little "genre" pictures of Gérard Dow, Metsu, and Paul Potter, two specimens of Géricault and Prudhon, and some sea-pieces of Backhuysen and Vernet. Among the works of modern painters were pictures with the signatures of Delacroix, Ingres, Decamps, Troyon, Meissonier, Daubigny, etc.; and some admirable statues in marble and bronze, after the finest antique models, stood upon pedestals in the corners of this magnificent museum. Amazement, as the captain of the *Nautilus* had predicted, had already begun to take possession of me.

"Professor," said this strange man, "you must excuse the unceremonious way in which I receive you, and the disorder of this room."

"Sir," I answered, "without seeking to know who you are, I recognise in you an artist."

"An amateur, nothing more, sir. Formerly I loved to collect these beautiful works created by the hand of man. I sought them greedily, and ferreted them out indefatigably, and I have been able to bring together some objects of great value. These are my last souvenirs of that world which is dead to me. In my eyes, your modern artists are already old; they have two or three thousand years of existence; I confound them in my own mind. Masters have no age."

"And these musicians?" said I, pointing out some works of Weber, Rossini, Mozart, Beethoven, Haydn, Meyerbeer, Hérold, Wagner, Auber, Gounod, and a number of others scattered over a large model piano organ which occupied one of the panels of the drawing-room.

"These musicians," replied Captain Nemo, "are the contemporaries of Orpheus; for in the memory of the dead all chronological differences are effaced; and I am dead, professor; as much dead as those of your friends who are sleeping six feet under the earth!"

Captain Nemo was silent, and seemed lost in a profound reverie. I contemplated him with deep interest, analysing in silence the strange expression of his countenance. Leaning on his elbow against an angle of a costly mosaic table, he no longer saw me—he had forgotten my presence.

I did not disturb this reverie, and continued my observation of the curiosities which enriched this drawing-room.

Under elegant glass cases, fixed by copper rivets, were classed and labelled the most precious productions of the sea which had ever been presented to the eye of a naturalist. My delight as a professor may be conceived.

The division containing the zoöphytes presented the most curious specimens of the two groups of polypi and echinodermes. In the first group, the tubipores, were gorgones arranged like a fan, soft sponges of Syria, ises of the Moluccas, pennatules, an admirable virgularia of the Norwegian seas, variegated unbellulairae, alcyonariae, a whole series of madrepores, which my master Milne-Edwards has so cleverly classified, among which I remarked some wonderful flabellinae, oculinae of the Island of Bourbon, the "Neptune's car" of the Antilles, superb varieties of corals, in short, every species of those curious polypi of which entire islands are formed, which will one day become continents. Of the echinodermes, remarkable for their coating of spines, asteri, sea-stars, pantacrinae, comatules, astérophons, echini, holothuri, etc., represented individually a complete collection of this group.

A somewhat nervous conchyliologist would certainly have fainted before other more numerous cases, in which were classified the specimens of molluscs. It was a collection of inestimable value, which time fails me to describe minutely. Among these specimens I will quote from memory only the elegant royal hammer-fish of the Indian Ocean, whose regular white spots stood out brightly on a red and brown ground, an imperial spondyle, bright-coloured, bristling with spines, a rare specimen in the European museums (I estimated its value at not less than £1,000); a common hammer-fish of the seas of New Holland, which is only procured with difficulty; exotic buccardia of Senegal; fragile white bivalve shells, which a breath might shatter like a soap-bubble; several varieties of the aspirgillum of Java, a kind of calcareous tube, edged with leafy folds, and much debated by amateurs; a whole series of trochi, some a greenish-yellow, found in the American seas, others a reddish-brown, natives of Australian waters; others from the Gulf of Mexico, remarkable for their imbricated shell; stellari found in the Southern Seas; and last, the rarest of all, the magnificent spur of New Zealand; and every description of delicate and fragile shells to which science has given appropriate names.

Apart, in separate compartments, were spread out chaplets of pearls of the greatest beauty, which reflected the electric light in little sparks of fire; pink pearls, torn from the pinna-marina of the Red Sea; green pearls of the haliotyde iris; yellow, blue and black pearls, the curious productions of the divers molluscs of every ocean, and certain mussels of the water-courses of the North; lastly, several specimens of inestimable value which had been gathered from the rarest pintadines. Some of these pearls were larger than a pigeon's egg, and were worth as much, and more than that which the traveller Tavernier sold to the Shah of Persia for three millions, and surpassed the one in the possession of the Imaum of Muscat, which I had believed to be unrivalled in the world.

Therefore, to estimate the value of this collection was simply impossible. Captain Nemo must have expended millions in the acquirement of these various specimens, and I was thinking what source he could have drawn from, to have been able thus to gratify his fancy for collecting, when I was interrupted by these words:

"You are examining my shells, professor? Unquestionably they must be interesting to a naturalist; but for me they have a far greater charm, for I have collected them all with my own hand, and there is not a sea on the face of the globe which has escaped my researches."

"I can understand, captain, the delight of wandering about in the midst of such riches. You are one of those who have collected their treasures themselves. No museum in Europe possesses such a collection of the produce of the ocean. But if I exhaust all my admiration upon it, I shall have none left for the vessel which carries it. I do not wish to pry into your secrets: but I must confess that this *Nautilus*, with the motive power which is confined in it, the contrivances which enable it to be worked, the powerful agent which propels it, all excite my curiosity to the highest pitch. I see suspended on the walls of this room instruments of whose use I am ignorant."

"You will find these same instruments in my own room, professor, where I shall have much pleasure in explaining their use to you. But first come and inspect the cabin which is set apart for your own use. You must see how you will be accommodated on board the *Nautilus*."

I followed Captain Nemo, who, by one of the doors opening from each panel of the drawing-room, regained the waist. He conducted me towards the bow, and there I found, not a cabin, but an elegant room, with a bed, dressing-table, and several other pieces of furniture.

I could only thank my host.

"Your room adjoins mine," said he, opening a door, "and mine opens into the drawing-room that we have just quitted."

I entered the captain's room; it had a severe, almost a monkish, aspect. A small iron bedstead, a table, some articles for the toilet; the whole lighted by a skylight. No comforts, the strictest necessaries only.

Captain Nemo pointed to a seat.

"Be so good as to sit down," he said. I seated myself, and he began thus:

Chapter XI

ALL BY ELECTRICITY

Sir," said captain nemo, showing me the instruments hanging on the walls of his room, "here are the contrivances required for the navigation of the *Nautilus*. Here, as in the drawing-room, I have them always under my eyes, and they indicate my position and exact direction in the middle of the ocean. Some are known to you, such as the thermometer, which gives the internal temperature of the *Nautilus*; the barometer, which indicates the weight of the air and foretells the changes of the weather; the hygrometer, which marks the dryness of the atmosphere; the storm-glass, the contents of which, by decomposing, announce the approach of tempests; the compass, which guides my course; the sextant, which shows the latitude by the altitude of the sun; chronometers, by which I calculate the longitude; and glasses for day and night, which I use to examine the points of the horizon, when the *Nautilus* rises to the surface of the waves."

"These are the usual nautical instruments," I replied, "and I know the use of them. But these others, no doubt, answer to the particular requirements of the *Nautilus*. This dial with movable needle is a manometer, is it not?"

"It is actually a manometer. But by communication with the water, whose external pressure it indicates, it gives our depth at the same time."

"And these other instruments, the use of which I cannot guess?"

"Here, professor, I ought to give you some explanations. Will you be kind enough to listen to me?"

He was silent for a few moments, then he said:

"There is a powerful agent, obedient, rapid, easy, which conforms to every use, and reigns supreme on board my vessel. Everything is done by means of it. It lights it, warms it, and is the soul of my mechanical apparatus. This agent is electricity."

"Electricity?" I cried in surprise.

"Yes, sir."

"Nevertheless, captain, you possess an extreme rapidity of movement, which does not agree well with the power of electricity. Until now, its dynamic force has remained under restraint, and has only been able to produce a small amount of power."

"Professor," said Captain Nemo, "my electricity is not everybody's. You know what sea-water is composed of. In a thousand grammes are found ninety-six and one-half per cent of water, and about two and two-thirds per cent of chloride of sodium; then, in a smaller quantity, chlorides of magnesium and of potassium, bromide of magnesium, sulphate of magnesia, sulphate and carbonate of lime. You see, then, that chloride of sodium forms a large part of it. So it is this sodium that I extract from the sea-water, and of which I compose my ingredients. I owe all to the ocean; it produces electricity, and electricity gives heat, light, motion, and, in a word, life to the *Nautilus*."

"But not the air you breathe?"

"Oh, I could manufacture the air necessary for my consumption, but it is useless, because I go up to the surface of the water when I please. However, if electricity does not furnish me with air to breathe, it works at least the powerful pumps that are stored in spacious reservoirs, and which enable me to prolong at need, and as long as I will, my stay in the depths of the sea. It gives a uniform and unintermittent light, which the sun does not. Now look at this clock; it is electrical, and goes with a regularity that defies the best chronometers. I have divided it into twenty-four hours, like the Italian clocks, because for me there is neither night nor day, sun nor moon, but only that factitious light that I take with me to the bottom of the sea. Look! just now, it is ten o'clock in the morning."

"Exactly."

"Another application of electricity. This dial hanging in front of us indicates the speed of the *Nautilus*. An electric thread puts it in communication with the screw, and the needle indicates the real speed. Look! now we are spinning along with a uniform speed of fifteen miles an hour."

"It is marvellous! and I see, captain, you were right to make use of this agent that takes the place of wind, water, and steam."

"We have not finished, M. Aronnax," said Captain Nemo, rising; "if you will follow me, we will examine the stern of the *Nautilus*."

Really, I knew already the anterior part of this submarine boat, of which this is the exact division, starting from the ship's head: the dining-room, five yards long, separated from the library by a water-tight partition; the library, five yards long; the large drawing-room, ten yards long, separated from the Captain's room by a second water-tight partition; the said room, five yards in length; mine, two and a half yards; and lastly, a reservoir of air, seven and a half yards, that extended to the bows. Total length thirty-five yards, or one hundred and five feet. The partitions had doors that were shut hermetically by means of India rubber instruments, and they ensured the safety of the *Nautilus* in case of a leak.

I followed Captain Nemo through the waist, and arrived at the centre of the boat. There was a sort of well that opened between two partitions. An iron ladder, fastened with an iron hook to the partition, led to the upper end. I asked the captain what the ladder was used for.

"It leads to the small boat," he said.

"What! Have you a boat?" I exclaimed, in surprise.

"Of course; an excellent vessel, light and insubmersible, that serves either as a fishing or as a pleasure boat."

"But then, when you wish to embark, you are obliged to come to the surface of the water?"

"Not at all. This boat is attached to the upper part of the hull of the *Nautilus*, and occupies a cavity made for it. It is decked, quite water-tight, and held together by solid bolts. This ladder leads to a man-hole made in the hull of the *Nautilus*, that corresponds with a similar hole made in the side of the boat. By this double opening I get into the small vessel. They shut the one belonging to the *Nautilus*; I shut the other by means of screw pressure. I undo the bolts, and the little boat goes up to the surface of the sea with prodigious rapidity. I then open the panel of the bridge, carefully shut till then; I mast it, hoist my sail, take my oars, and I'm off."

"But how do you get back on board?"

"I do not come back, M. Aronnax; the *Nautilus* comes to me."

"By your orders?"

"By my orders. An electric thread connects us. I telegraph to it, and that is enough."

"Really," I said, astonished at these marvels, "nothing can be more simple."

After having passed by the cage of the staircase that led to the platform, I saw a cabin six feet long, in which Conseil and Ned Land, enchanted with their repast, were devouring it with avidity. Then a door opened into a kitchen nine feet long, situated between the large store-rooms. There electricity, better than gas itself, did all the cooking. The streams under the furnaces gave out to the sponges of platina a heat which was regularly kept up and distributed. They also heated a distilling apparatus, which, by evaporation, furnished excellent drinkable water. Near this kitchen was a bathroom comfortably furnished, with hot and cold water taps.

Next to the kitchen was the berth-room of the vessel, sixteen feet long. But the door was shut, and I could not see the management of it, which might have given me an idea of the number of men employed on board the *Nautilus*.

At the bottom was a fourth partition, that separated this office from the engine-room. A door opened, and I found myself in the compartment where Captain Nemo—certainly an engineer of a very high order—had arranged his locomotive machinery. This engine-room, clearly lighted, did not measure less than sixty-five feet in length. It was divided into two parts; the first contained the materials for producing electricity, and the second the machinery that connected it with the screw. I examined it with great interest, in order to understand the machinery of the *Nautilus*.

"You see," said the Captain, "I use Bunsen's contrivances, not Ruhmkorff's. Those would not have been powerful enough. Bunsen's are fewer in number, but strong and large, which experience proves to be the best. The electricity produced passes forward, where it works, by electro-magnets of great size, on a system of levers and cog-wheels that transmit the movement to the axle of the screw. This one, the diameter of which is nineteen feet, and the thread twenty-three feet, performs about one hundred twenty revolutions in a second."

"And you get then?"

"A speed of fifty miles an hour."

"I have seen the *Nautilus* maneuvre before the *Abraham Lincoln*, and I have my own ideas as to its speed. But this is not enough. We must see where we go. We must be able to direct it to the right, to the left, above, below. How do you get to the great depths, where you find an increasing resistance, which is rated by hundreds of atmospheres? How do you return to the surface of the ocean? And how do you maintain yourselves in the requisite medium? Am I asking too much?"

"Not at all, professor," replied the Captain, with some hesitation; "since you may never leave this submarine boat. Come into the saloon, it is our usual study, and there you will learn all you want to know about the *Nautilus*."

Chapter XII

Some Figures

A MOMENT AFTER WE WERE SEATED ON A DIVAN IN THE SALOON SMOKING. THE CAPTAIN showed me a sketch that gave the plan, section, and elevation of the *Nautilus*. Then he began his description in these words:

"Here, M. Aronnax, are the several dimensions of the boat you are in. It is an elongated cylinder with conical ends. It is very like a cigar in shape, a shape already adopted in London in several constructions of the same sort. The length of this cylinder, from stem to stern, is exactly 232 feet, and its maximum breadth is twenty-six feet. It is not built quite like your long-voyage steamers, but its lines are sufficiently long, and its curves prolonged enough, to allow the water to slide off easily, and oppose no obstacle to its passage. These two dimensions enable you to obtain by a simple calculation the surface and cubic contents of the *Nautilus*. Its area measures 6,032 feet; and its contents about 1,500 cubic yards; that is to say, when completely immersed it displaces 50,000 feet of water, or weighs 1,500 tons.

"When I made the plans for this submarine vessel, I meant that nine-tenths should be submerged: consequently it ought only to displace nine-tenths of its bulk, that is to say, only to weigh that number of tons. I ought not, therefore, to have exceeded that weight, constructing it on the aforesaid dimensions.

"The *Nautilus* is composed of two hulls, one inside, the other outside, joined by T-shaped irons, which render it very strong. Indeed, owing to this cellular arrangement it resists like a block, as if it were solid. Its sides cannot yield; it coheres spontaneously, and not by the closeness of its rivets; and the homogeneity of its construction, due to the perfect union of the materials, enables it to defy the roughest seas.

"These two hulls are composed of steel plates, whose density is from 0.7 to 0.8 that of water. The first is not less than two inches and a half thick and weighs 394 tons. The second envelope, the keel, twenty inches high and ten thick, weighs only sixty-two tons. The engine, the ballast, the several accessories and apparatus appendages, the partitions and bulkheads, weigh 961.62 tons. Do you follow all this?"

"I do."

"Then, when the *Nautilus* is afloat under these circumstances, one-tenth is out of the water. Now, if I have made reservoirs of a size equal to this tenth, or capable of holding 150 tons, and if I fill them with water, the boat, weighing then 1,507 tons, will be completely immersed. That would happen, professor. These reservoirs are in the lower part of the *Nautilus*. I turn on taps and they fill, and the vessel sinks that had just been level with the surface."

"Well, captain, but now we come to the real difficulty. I can understand your rising to the surface; but diving below the surface, does not your submarine contrivance encounter a pressure, and consequently undergo an upward thrust of one atmosphere for every thirty feet of water, just about fifteen pounds per square inch?"

"Just so, sir."

"Then, unless you quite fill the *Nautilus*, I do not see how you can draw it down to those depths."

"Professor, you must not confound statics with dynamics or you will be exposed to grave errors. There is very little labour spent in attaining the lower regions of the ocean, for all bodies have a tendency to sink. When I wanted to find out the necessary increase of weight required to sink the *Nautilus*, I had only to calculate the reduction of volume that sea-water acquires according to the depth."

"That is evident."

"Now, if water is not absolutely incompressible, it is at least capable of very slight compression. Indeed, after the most recent calculations this reduction is only 0.000436 of an atmosphere for each thirty feet of depth. If we want to sink 3,000 feet, I should keep account of the reduction of bulk under a pressure equal to that of a column of water of a thousand feet. The calculation is easily verified. Now, I have supplementary reservoirs capable of holding a hundred tons. Therefore I can sink to a considerable depth. When I wish to rise to the level of the sea, I only let off the water, and empty all the reservoirs if I want the *Nautilus* to emerge from the tenth part of her total capacity."

I had nothing to object to these reasonings.

"I admit your calculations, captain," I replied; "I should be wrong to dispute them since daily experience confirms them; but I foresee a real difficulty in the way."

"What, sir?"

"When you are about 1,000 feet deep, the walls of the *Nautilus* bear a pressure of 100 atmospheres. If, then, just now you were to empty the supplementary reservoirs, to lighten the vessel, and to go up to the surface, the pumps must overcome the pressure of 100 atmospheres, which is 1,500 lbs. per square inch. From that a power——"

"That electricity alone can give," said the captain, hastily. "I repeat, sir, that the dynamic power of my engines is almost infinite. The pumps of the *Nautilus* have an enormous power, as you must have observed when their jets of water burst like a torrent upon the *Abraham Lincoln*. Besides, I use subsidiary reservoirs only to attain a mean depth of 750 to 1,000 fathoms, and that with a view of managing my machines. Also, when I have a mind to visit the depths of the ocean five or six miles below the surface, I make use of slower but not less infallible means."

"What are they, captain?"

"That involves my telling you how the *Nautilus* is worked."

"I am impatient to learn."

"To steer this boat to starboard or port, to turn, in a word, following a horizontal plan, I use an ordinary rudder fixed on the back of the stern post, and with one wheel and some tackle to steer by. But I can also make the *Nautilus* rise and sink, and sink and rise, by a vertical movement by means of two inclined planes fastened to its sides, opposite the centre of flotation, planes that move in every direction, and that are worked by powerful levers from the interior. If the planes are kept parallel with the boat, it moves horizontally. If slanted, the *Nautilus*, according to this inclination, and under the influence of the screw, either sinks diagonally or rises diagonally as it suits me. And even if I wish to rise more quickly to the surface, I ship the screw, and the pressure of the water causes the *Nautilus* to rise vertically like a balloon filled with hydrogen."

"Bravo, captain! But how can the steersman follow the route in the middle of the waters?"

"The steersman is placed in a glazed box, that is raised about the hull of the *Nautilus*, and furnished with lenses."

"Are these lenses capable of resisting such pressure?"

"Perfectly. Glass, which breaks at a blow, is, nevertheless, capable of offering considerable resistance. During some experiments of fishing by electric light in 1864 in the Northern Seas, we saw plates less than a third of an inch thick resist a pressure of sixteen atmospheres. Now, the glass that I use is not less than thirty times thicker."

"Granted. But, after all, in order to see, the light must exceed the darkness, and in the midst of the darkness in the water, how can you see?"

"Behind the steersman's cage is placed a powerful electric reflector, the rays from which light up the sea for half a mile in front."

"Ah! bravo, bravo, captain! Now I can account for this phosphorescence in the supposed narwhal that puzzled us so. I now ask you if the boarding of the *Nautilus* and of the *Scotia*, that has made such a noise, has been the result of a chance rencontre?"

"Quite accidental, sir. I was sailing only one fathom below the surface of the water when the shock came. It had no bad result."

"None, sir. But now, about your rencontre with the *Abraham Lincoln?*"

"Professor, I am sorry for one of the best vessels in the American navy; but they attacked me, and I was bound to defend myself. I contented myself, however, with putting the frigate *hors de combat*; she will not have any difficulty in getting repaired at the next port."

"Ah, commander! your *Nautilus* is certainly a marvellous boat."

"Yes, professor; and I love it as if it were part of myself. If danger threatens one of your vessels on the ocean, the first impression is the feeling of an abyss above and below. On the *Nautilus*, men's hearts never fail them. No defects to be afraid of, for the double shell is as firm as iron; no rigging to attend to; no sails for the wind to carry away; no boilers to burst; no fire to fear, for the vessel is made of iron, not of wood; no coal to run short, for electricity is the only mechanical agent; no collision to fear, for it alone swims in deep water; no tempest to brave, for when it dives below the water it reaches absolute tranquillity. There, sir! that is the perfection of vessels! And if it is true that the engineer has more confidence in the vessel than the builder, and the builder than the captain himself, you understand the trust I repose in my *Nautilus*; for I am at once captain, builder, and engineer."

"But how could you construct this wonderful *Nautilus* in secret?"

"Each separate portion, M. Aronnax, was brought from different parts of the globe. The keel was forged at Creusot, the shaft of the screw at Penn & Co.'s, London, the iron plates of the hull at Laird's of Liverpool, the screw itself at Scott's at Glasgow. The reservoirs were made by Cail & Co. at Paris, the engine by Krupp in Prussia, its beak in Motola's workshop in Sweden, its mathematical instruments by Hart Brothers, of New York, etc.; and each of these people had my orders under different names."

"But these parts had to be put together and arranged?"

"Professor, I had set up my workshops upon a desert island in the ocean. There my workmen, that is to say, the brave men that I instructed and educated, and myself have put together our *Nautilus*. Then, when the work was finished fire destroyed all trace of our proceedings on this island, that I could have jumped over if I had liked."

"Then the cost of this vessel is great?"

"M. Aronnax, an iron vessel costs £45 per ton. Now the *Nautilus* weighed 1,500. It came therefore to £67,500, and £80,000 more for fitting it up, and about £200,000, with the works of art and the collections it contains."

"One last question, Captain Nemo."

"Ask it, professor."

"You are rich?"

"Immensely rich, sir; and I could, without missing it, pay the national debt of France."

I stared at the singular person who spoke thus. Was he playing upon my credulity? The future would decide that.

Chapter XIII

THE BLACK RIVER

THE PORTION OF THE TERRESTRIAL GLOBE WHICH IS COVERED BY WATER IS ESTIMATED at upwards of eighty millions of acres. This fluid mass comprises two billions two hundred and fifty millions of cubic miles, forming a spherical body of a diameter of sixty leagues, the weight of which would be three quintillions of tons. To comprehend the meaning of these figures, it is necessary to observe that a quintillion is to a billion as a billion is to unity; in other words, there are as many billions in a quintillion as there are units in a billion. This mass of fluid is equal to about the quantity of water which would be discharged by all the rivers of the earth in forty thousand years.

During the geological epochs, the igneous period succeeded to the aqueous. The ocean originally prevailed everywhere. Then by degrees, in the silurian period, the tops of the mountains began to appear, the islands emerged, then disappeared in partial deluges, reappeared, became settled, formed continents, till at length the earth became geographically arranged, as we see in the present day. The solid had wrested from the liquid thirty-seven million six hundred and fifty-seven square miles, equal to twelve billions nine hundred and sixty millions of acres.

The shape of continents allows us to divide the waters into five great portions: the Arctic or Frozen Ocean, the Antarctic or Frozen Ocean, the Indian, the Atlantic, and the Pacific Oceans.

The Pacific Ocean extends from north to south between the two polar circles, and from east to west between Asia and America, over an extent of 145 degrees of longitude. It is the quietest of seas; its currents are broad and slow, it has medium tides, and abundant rain. Such was the ocean that my fate destined me first to travel over under these strange conditions.

"Sir," said Captain Nemo, "we will, if you please, take our bearings and fix the starting-point of this voyage. It is a quarter to twelve. I will go up again to the surface."

The captain pressed an electric clock three times. The pumps began to drive the water from the tanks, the needle of the manometer marked by a different pressure the ascent of the *Nautilus*, then it stopped.

"We have arrived," said the captain.

I went to the central staircase which opened on to the platform, clambered up the iron steps, and found myself on the upper part of the *Nautilus*.

The platform was only three feet out of water. The front and back of the *Nautilus* was of that spindle-shape which caused it justly to be compared to a cigar. I noticed that its iron plates, slightly overlaying each other, resembled the shell which clothes the bodies of our large terrestrial reptiles. It explained to me how natural it was, in spite of all glasses, that this boat should have been taken for a marine animal.

Towards the middle of the platform the longboat, half buried in the hull of the vessel, formed a slight excrescence. Fore and aft rose two cages of medium height with inclined sides, and partly closed by thick lenticular glasses; one destined for the steersman who directed the *Nautilus*, the other containing a brilliant lantern to give light on the road.

The sea was beautiful, the sky pure. Scarcely could the long vehicle feel the broad undulations of the ocean. A light breeze from the east rippled the surface of the waters. The horizon, free from fog, made observation easy. Nothing was in sight. Not a quicksand, not an island. A vast desert.

Captain Nemo, by the help of his sextant, took the altitude of the sun, which ought also to give the latitude. He waited for some moments till its disc touched the horizon. While taking observations not a muscle moved, the instrument could not have been more motionless in a hand of marble.

"Twelve o'clock, sir," said he. "When you like——"

I cast a last look upon the sea, slightly yellowed by the Japanese coast, and descended to the saloon.

"And now, sir, I leave you to your studies," added the captain; "our course is E.N.E., our depth is twenty-six fathoms. Here are maps on a large scale by which you may follow it. The saloon is at your disposal, and, with your permission, I will retire." Captain Nemo bowed, and I remained alone, lost in thoughts all bearing on the commander of the *Nautilus*.

For a whole hour was I deep in these reflections, seeking to pierce this mystery so interesting to me. Then my eyes fell upon the vast planisphere spread upon the table, and I placed my finger on the very spot where the given latitude and longitude crossed.

The sea has its large rivers like the continents. They are special currents known by their temperature and their colour. The most remarkable of these is known by the name of the Gulf Stream. Science has decided on the globe the direction of five principal currents: one in the North Atlantic, a second in the South, a third in the North Pacific, a fourth in the South, and a fifth in the Southern Indian Ocean. It is even probable that a sixth current existed at one time or another in the Northern Indian Ocean, when the Caspian and Aral Seas formed but one vast sheet of water.

At this point indicated on the planisphere one of these currents was rolling, the Kuro-Scivo of the Japanese, the Black River, which, leaving the Gulf of Bengal, where it is warmed by the perpendicular rays of a tropical sun, crosses the Straits of Malacca along the coast of Asia, turns into the North Pacific to the Aleutian Islands, carrying with it trunks of camphor-trees and other indigenous productions, and edging the waves of the ocean with the pure indigo of its warm water. It was this current that the *Nautilus* was to follow. I followed it with my eye; saw it lose itself in the vastness of the Pacific, and felt myself drawn with it, when Ned Land and Conseil appeared at the door of the saloon.

My two brave companions remained petrified at the sight of the wonders spread before them.

"Where are we—where are we?" exclaimed the Canadian. "In the museum at Quebec?"

"My friends," I answered, making a sign for them to enter, "you are not in Canada, but on board the *Nautilus*, fifty yards below the level of the sea."

"But, M. Aronnax," said Ned Land, "can you tell me how many men there are on board? Ten, twenty, fifty, a hundred?"

"I cannot answer you, Mr. Land; it is better to abandon for a time all idea of seizing the *Nautilus* or escaping from it. This ship is a masterpiece of modern industry, and I should be sorry not to have seen it. Many people would accept the situation forced upon us, if only to move among such wonders. So be quiet and let us try and see what passes around us."

"See!" exclaimed the harpooner. "But we can see nothing in this iron prison! We are walking—we are sailing—blindly."

Ned Land had scarcely pronounced these words when all was suddenly darkness. The luminous ceiling was gone, and so rapidly that my eyes received a painful impression.

We remained mute, not stirring, and not knowing what surprise awaited us, whether agreeable or disagreeable. A sliding noise was heard: one would have said that panels were working at the sides of the *Nautilus*.

"It is the end of the end!" said Ned Land.

Suddenly light broke at each side of the saloon, through two oblong openings. The liquid mass appeared vividly lit up by the electric gleam. Two crystal plates separated us from the sea. At first I trembled at the thought that this frail partition might break, but strong bands of copper bound them, giving an almost infinite power of resistance.

The sea was distinctly visible for a mile all round the *Nautilus*. What a spectacle! What pen can describe it? Who could paint the effects of the light through those transparent sheets of water, and the softness of the successive gradations from the lower to the superior strata of the ocean?

We know the transparency of the sea, and that its clearness is far beyond that of rock water. The mineral and organic substances which it holds in suspension heightens its transparency. In certain parts of the ocean at the Antilles, under seventy-five fathoms of water, can be seen with surprising clearness a bed of sand. The penetrating power of the solar rays does not seem to cease for a depth of one hundred and fifty fathoms. But in this middle fluid travelled over by the *Nautilus* the electric brightness was produced even in the bosom of the waves. It was no longer luminous water, but liquid light.

On each side a window opened into this unexplored abyss. The obscurity of the saloon showed to advantage the brightness outside, and we looked out as if this pure crystal had been the glass of an immense aquarium.

"You wished to see, friend Ned; well, you see now."

"Curious! curious!" muttered the Canadian, who, forgetting his ill-temper, seemed to submit to some irresistible attraction; "and one would come further than this to admire such a sight!"

"Ah!" thought I to myself. "I understand the life of this man; he has made a world apart for himself, in which he treasures all his greatest wonders."

For two whole hours an aquatic army escorted the *Nautilus*. During their games, their bounds, while rivalling each other in beauty, brightness, and velocity, I distinguished the green labre; the banded mullet, marked by a double line of black; the round-tailed goby, of a white colour, with violet spots on the back; the Japanese scombrus, a beautiful mackerel of these seas, with a blue body and silvery head; the brilliant azurors, whose name alone defies description; some banded spares, with variegated fins of blue and yellow; some aclostones, the woodcocks of the seas, some specimens of which attain a yard in length; Japanese salamanders, spider lampreys, serpents six feet long, with eyes small and lively, and a huge mouth bristling with teeth; with many other species.

Our imagination was kept at its height; interjections followed quickly on each other. Ned named the fish, and Conseil classed them. I was in ecstasies with the vivacity of their movements and the beauty of their forms. Never had it been given to me to surprise these animals, alive and at liberty, in their natural element. I will not mention all the varieties which passed before my dazzled eyes, all the collection of the seas of China and Japan. These fish, more numerous than the birds of the air, came, attracted, no doubt, by the brilliant focus of the electric light.

Suddenly there was daylight in the saloon, the iron panels closed again, and the enchanting vision disappeared. But for a long time I dreamed on till my eyes fell on the instruments hanging on the partition. The compass still showed the course to be E.N.E., the manometer indicated a pressure of five atmospheres, equivalent to a depth of twenty-five fathoms, and the electric log gave a speed of fifteen miles an hour. I expected Captain Nemo, but he did not appear. The clock marked the hour of five.

Ned Land and Conseil returned to their cabin, and I retired to my chamber. My dinner was ready. It was composed of turtle soup made of the most delicate hawksbills, of a surmullet served with puff paste (the liver of which, prepared by itself, was most delicious), and fillets of the emperor-holocanthus, the savour of which seemed to me superior even to salmon.

I passed the evening reading, writing, and thinking. Then sleep overpowered me, and I stretched myself on my couch of zostera, and slept profoundly, while the *Nautilus* was gliding rapidly through the current of the Black River.

Chapter XIV

A NOTE OF INVITATION

THE NEXT DAY WAS THE 9TH OF NOVEMBER. I AWOKE AFTER A LONG SLEEP OF TWELVE hours. Conseil came, according to custom, to know "how I passed the night," and to offer his services. He had left his friend the Canadian sleeping like a man who had never done anything else all his life. I let the worthy fellow chatter as he pleased, without caring to answer him. I was preoccupied by the absence of the captain during our sitting of the day before, and hoping to see him to-day.

As soon as I was dressed I went into the saloon. It was deserted.

I plunged into the study of the conchological treasures hidden behind the glasses. I reveled also in great herbals filled with the rarest marine plants, which, although dried up, retained their lovely colours. Among these precious hydrophytes I remarked some vorticellae pavonariae, delicate ceramies with scarlet tints, some fan-shaped agari, and some natabuli like flat mushrooms, which at one time used to be classed as zoöphytes; in short, a perfect series of algae

The whole day passed without my being honoured by a visit from Captain Nemo. The panels of the saloon did not open. Perhaps they did not wish us to tire of these beautiful things.

The course of the *Nautilus* was E.N.E., her speed twelve knots, the depth below the surface between twenty-five and thirty fathoms.

The next day, 10th of November, the same desertion, the same solitude. I did not see one of the ship's crew; Ned and Conseil spent the greater part of the day with me. They were astonished at the puzzling absence of the captain. Was this singular man ill? Had he altered his intentions with regard to us?

After all, as Conseil said, we enjoyed perfect liberty, we were delicately and abundantly fed. Our host kept to his terms of the treaty. We could not complain, and, indeed, the singularity of our fate reserved such wonderful compensation for us that we had no right to accuse it as yet.

That day I commenced the journal of these adventures which has enabled me to relate them with more scrupulous exactitude and minute detail. I wrote it on paper made from the zostera marina.

November 11th, early in the morning. The fresh air spreading over the interior of the *Nautilus* told me that we had come to the surface of the ocean to renew our supply of oxygen. I directed my steps to the central staircase, and mounted the platform.

It was six o'clock, the weather was cloudy, the sea grey, but calm. Scarcely a billow. Captain Nemo, whom I hoped to meet, would he be there? I saw no one but the steersman imprisoned in his glass cage. Seated upon the projection formed by the hull of the pinnace, I inhaled the salt breeze with delight.

By degrees the fog disappeared under the action of the sun's rays, the radiant orb rose from behind the eastern horizon. The sea flamed under its glance like a train of gunpowder. The clouds scattered in the heights were coloured with lively tints of beautiful shades, and numerous "mare's tails," which betokened wind for that day. But what was wind to this *Nautilus*, which tempests could not frighten!

I was admiring this joyous rising of the sun, so gay, and so life-giving, when I heard steps approaching the platform. I was prepared to salute Captain Nemo, but it was his second (whom I had already seen on the captain's first visit) who appeared. He advanced on the platform, not seeming to see me. With his powerful glass to his eye, he scanned every point of the horizon with great attention. This examination over, he approached the panel and pronounced a sentence in exactly these terms. I have remembered it, for every morning it was repeated under exactly the same conditions. It was thus worded:

"*Nautron respoc lorni virch.*"

What it meant I could not say.

These words pronounced, the second descended. I thought that the *Nautilus* was about to return to its submarine navigation. I regained the panel and returned to my chamber.

Five days sped thus, without any change in our situation. Every morning I mounted the platform. The same phrase was pronounced by the same individual. But Captain Nemo did not appear.

I had made up my mind that I should never see him again, when, on the 16th November, on returning to my room with Ned and Conseil, I found upon my table a note addressed to me. I opened it impatiently. It was written in a bold, clear hand, the characters rather pointed, recalling the German type. The note was worded as follows:

16th of November, 1867.

To Professor Arronax, on board the *Nautilus*:

Captain Nemo invites Professor Aronnax to a hunting-party, which will take place tomorrow morning in the forests of the Island of Crespo. He hopes that nothing will prevent the professor from being present, and he will with pleasure see him joined by his companions.

Captain Nemo, Commander of the *Nautilus*

"A hunt!" exclaimed Ned.

"And in the forests of the Island of Crespo!" added Conseil.

"Oh! then the gentleman is going on *terra firma?*" replied Ned Land.

"That seems to me to be clearly indicated," said I, reading the letter once more.

"Well, we must accept," said the Canadian. "But once more on dry ground, we shall know what to do. Indeed, I shall not be sorry to eat a piece of fresh venison."

Without seeking to reconcile what was contradictory between Captain Nemo's manifest aversion to islands and continents, and his invitation to hunt in a forest, I contented myself with replying:

"Let us first see where the Island of Crespo is."

I consulted the planisphere, and in 32° 40' north lat. and 157° 50' west long., I found a small island, recognised in 1801 by Captain Crespo, and marked in the ancient Spanish maps as Rocca de la Plata, the meaning of which is "The Silver Rock." We were then about eighteen hundred miles from our starting-point, and the course of the *Nautilus*, a little changed, was bringing it back towards the south-east.

I showed this little rock lost in the midst of the North Pacific to my companions.

"If Captain Nemo does sometimes go on dry ground," said I, "he at least chooses desert islands."

Ned Land shrugged his shoulders without speaking, and Conseil and he left me.

After supper, which was served by the steward, mute and impassible, I went to bed, not without some anxiety.

The next morning, the 17th of November, on awakening, I felt that the *Nautilus* was perfectly still. I dressed quickly and entered the saloon.

Captain Nemo was there, waiting for me. He rose, bowed, and asked me if it was convenient for me to accompany him. As he made no allusion to his absence during the last eight days, I did not mention it, and simply answered that my companions and myself were ready to follow him.

We entered the dining-room, where breakfast was served.

"M. Aronnax," said the captain, "pray share my breakfast without ceremony; we will chat as we eat. For though I promised you a walk in the forest, I did not undertake to find hotels there. So breakfast as a man who will most likely not have his dinner till very late."

I did honour to the repast. It was composed of several kinds of fish, and slices of holothuridae (excellent zoöphytes), and different sorts of seaweed. Our drink consisted of pure water, to which the captain added some drops of a fermented liquor, extracted by the Kamschatcha method from a sea-weed known under the name of Rhodomenia palmata. Captain Nemo ate at first without saying a word. Then he began:

"Sir, when I proposed to you to hunt in my submarine forest of Crespo, you evidently thought me mad. Sir, you should never judge lightly of any man."

"But, captain, believe me——"

"Be kind enough to listen, and you will then see whether you have any cause to accuse me of folly and contradiction."

"I listen."

"You know as well as I do, professor, that man can live under water, providing he carries with him a sufficient supply of breathable air. In submarine works, the workman, clad in an impervious dress, with his head in a metal helmet, receives air from above by means of forcing-pumps and regulators."

"That is a diving apparatus," said I.

"Just so; but under these conditions the man is not at liberty; he is attached to the pump which sends him air through an India rubber tube, and if we were obliged to be thus held to the *Nautilus*, we could not go far."

"And the means of getting free?" I asked.

"It is to use the Rouquayrol apparatus, invented by two of your own countrymen, which I have brought to perfection for my own use, and which will allow you to risk yourself under these new physiological conditions, without any organ whatever suffering. It consists of a reservoir of thick iron plates, in which I store the air under a pressure of fifty atmospheres. This reservoir is fixed on the back by means of braces, like a soldier's knapsack. Its upper part forms a box in which the air is kept by means of a bellows, and therefore cannot escape unless at its normal tension. In the Rouquayrol apparatus such as we use, two India rubber pipes leave this box and join a sort of tent which holds the nose and mouth; one is to introduce fresh air, the other to let out the foul, and the tongue closes one or the other according to the wants of the respirator. But I, in encountering great pressures at the bottom of the sea, was obliged to shut my head, like that of a diver in a ball of copper; and it is to this ball of copper that the two pipes, the inspirator and the expirator, open."

"Perfectly, Captain Nemo; but the air that you carry with you must soon be used; when it only contains fifteen per cent of oxygen, it is no longer fit to breathe."

"Right! But I told you, M. Aronnax, that the pumps of the *Nautilus* allow me to store the air under considerable pressure; and on those conditions, the reservoir of the apparatus can furnish breathable air for nine or ten hours."

"I have no further objections to make," I answered. "I will only ask you one thing, captain—how can you light your road at the bottom of the sea?"

"With the Ruhmkorff apparatus, M. Aronnax; one is carried on the back, the other is fastened to the waist. It is composed of a Bunsen pile, which I do not work with bichromate of potash, but with sodium. A wire is introduced which collects the electricity produced, and directs it towards a particularly made lantern. In this lantern is a spiral glass which contains a small quantity of carbonic gas. When the apparatus is at work, this gas becomes luminous, giving out a white and continuous light. Thus provided, I can breathe and I can see."

"Captain Nemo, to all my objections you make such crushing answers that I dare no longer doubt. But if I am forced to admit the Rouquayrol and Ruhmkorff apparatus, I must be allowed some reservations with regard to the gun I am to carry."

"But it is not a gun for powder," answered the captain.

"Then it is an air-gun."

"Doubtless! How would you have me manufacture gunpowder on board, without either saltpetre, sulphur, or charcoal?"

"Besides," I added, "to fire under water in a medium eight hundred and fifty-five times denser than the air, we must conquer very considerable resistance."

"That would be no difficulty. There exist guns, according to Fulton, perfected in England by Philip Coles and Burley, in France by Furcy, and in Italy by Landi, which are furnished with a peculiar system of closing, which can fire under these conditions. But I repeat, having no powder, I use air under great pressure, which the pumps of the *Nautilus* furnish abundantly."

"But this air must be rapidly used?"

"Well, have I not my Rouquayrol reservoir, which can furnish it at need? A tap is all that is required. Besides, M. Aronnax, you must see yourself that during our submarine hunt we can spend but little air and but few balls."

"But it seems to me that in this twilight, and in the midst of this fluid, which is very dense compared with the atmosphere, shots could not go far, nor easily prove mortal."

"Sir, on the contrary, with this gun every blow is mortal; and, however lightly the animal is touched, it falls as if struck by a thunderbolt."

"Why?"

"Because the balls sent by this gun are not ordinary balls, but little cases of glass (invented by Leniebroek, and Austrian chemist), of which I have a large supply. These glass cases are covered with a case of steel, and weighted with a pellet of lead; they are real Leyden bottles, into which the electricity is forced to a very high tension. With the slightest shock they are discharged, and the animal, however strong it may be, falls dead. I must tell you that these cases are size number four, and that the charge for an ordinary gun would be ten."

"I will argue no longer," I replied, rising from the table; "I have nothing left me but to take my gun. At all events, I will go where you go."

Captain Nemo then led me aft; and in passing before Ned and Conseil's cabin, I called my two companions, who followed immediately. We then came to a cell near the machinery-room, in which we put on our walking-dress.

Chapter XV

A WALK ON THE BOTTOM OF THE SEA

THIS CELL WAS, TO SPEAK CORRECTLY, THE ARSENAL AND WARDROBE OF THE *NAUTILUS*. A dozen diving apparatuses hung from the partition, waiting our use.

Ned Land, on seeing them, showed evident repugnance to dress himself in one.

"But, my worthy Ned, the forests of the island of Crespo are nothing but submarine forests."

"Good!" said the disappointed harpooner, who saw his dreams of fresh meat fade away. "And you, M. Aronnax, are you going to dress yourself in those clothes?"

"There is no alternative, Master Ned."

"As you please, sir," replied the harpooner, shrugging his shoulders; "but, as for me, unless I am forced, I will never get into one."

"No one will force you, Master Ned," said Captain Nemo.

"Is Conseil going to risk it?" asked Ned.

"I follow my master wherever he goes," replied Conseil.

At the captain's call two of the ship's crew came to help us dress in these heavy and impervious clothes, made of India rubber without seam, and constructed expressly to resist considerable pressure. One would have thought it a suit of armour, both supple and resisting. This suit formed trousers and waistcoat. The trousers were finished off with thick boots, weighted with heavy leaden soles. The texture of the waistcoat was held together by bands of copper, which crossed the chest, protecting it from the great pressure of the water, and leaving the lungs free to act; the sleeves ended in gloves, which in no way restrained the movement of the hands. There was a vast difference noticeable between these consummate apparatuses and the old cork breastplates, jackets, and other contrivances in vogue during the eighteenth century.

Captain Nemo and one of his companions (a sort of Hercules, who must have possessed great strength), Conseil, and myself were soon enveloped in the dresses. There remained nothing more to be done but to enclose our heads in the metal box. But before proceeding to this operation, I asked the captain's permission to examine the guns.

One of the *Nautilus* men gave me a simple gun, the butt end of which, made of steel hollow in the centre, was rather large. It served as a reservoir for compressed air, which a valve worked by a spring, allowed to escape into a metal tube. A box of projectiles, in a groove, in the thickness of the butt end contained about twenty of these electric balls, which by means of a spring were forced into the barrel of the gun. As soon as one shot was fired, another was ready.

"Captain Nemo," said I, "this arm is perfect, and easily handled; I only ask to be allowed to try it. But how shall we gain the bottom of the sea?"

"At this moment, professor, the *Nautilus* is stranded in five fathoms, and we have nothing to do but to start."

"But how shall we get off?"

"You shall see."

Captain Nemo thrust his head into the helmet; Conseil and I did the same, not without hearing an ironical "Good sport!" from the Canadian. The upper part of our dress terminated in a copper collar upon which was screwed the metal helmet. Three holes, protected by thick glass, allowed us to see in all directions, by simply turning our head in the interior of the head-dress. As soon as it was in position, the Rouquayrol apparatus on our backs began to act; and, for my part, I could breathe with ease.

With the Ruhmkorff lamp hanging from my belt, and the gun in my hand, I was ready to set out. But to speak the truth, imprisoned in these heavy garments, and glued to the deck by my leaden soles, it was impossible for me to take a step.

But this state of things was provided for. I felt myself being pushed into a little room contiguous to the wardrobe-room. My companions followed, towed along in the same way. I heard a water-tight door, furnished with stopper-plates, close upon us, and we were wrapped in profound darkness.

After some minutes, a loud hissing was heard. I felt the cold mount from my feet to my chest. Evidently from some part of the vessel they had, by means of a tap given entrance to the water, which was invading us, and with which the room was soon filled. A second door cut in the side of the *Nautilus* then opened. We saw a faint light. In another instant our feet trod the bottom of the sea.

And now, how can I retrace the impression left upon me by that walk under the waters? Words are impotent to relate such wonders! Captain Nemo walked in front, his companion followed some steps behind. Conseil and I remained near each other, as if an exchange of words had been possible through our metallic cases. I no longer felt the weight of my clothing, or of my shoes, of my reservoir of air, or my thick helmet, in the midst of which my head rattled like an almond in its shell.

The light, which lit the soil thirty feet below the surface of the ocean, astonished me by its power. The solar rays shone through the watery mass easily, and dissipated all colour, and I clearly distinguished objects at a distance of a hundred and fifty yards. Beyond that the tints darkened into fine gradations of ultramarine, and faded into vague obscurity. Truly this water which surrounded me was but another air denser than the terrestrial atmosphere, but almost as transparent. Above me was the calm surface of the sea. We were walking on fine, even sand, not wrinkled, as on a flat shore, which retains the impression of the billows. This dazzling carpet, really a reflector, repelled the rays of the sun with wonderful intensity, which accounted for the vibration which penetrated every atom of liquid. Shall I be believed when I say that, at the depth of thirty feet, I could see as if I was in broad daylight?

For a quarter of an hour I trod on this sand, sown with the impalpable dust of shells.

The hull of the *Nautilus,* resembling a long shoal, disappeared by degrees; but its lantern, when darkness should overtake us in the waters, would help to guide us on board by its distinct rays.

Soon forms of objects outlined in the distance were discernible. I recognised magnificent rocks, hung with a tapestry of zoöphytes of the most beautiful kind, and I was at first struck by the peculiar effect of this medium.

It was then ten in the morning; the rays of the sun struck the surface of the waves at rather an oblique angle, and at the touch of their light, decomposed by refraction as through a prism, flowers, rocks, plants, shells, and polypi were shaded at the edges by the seven solar colours. It was marvellous, a feast for the eyes, this complication of coloured tints, a perfect kaleidoscope of green, yellow, orange, violet, indigo, and blue; in one word, the whole palette of an enthusiastic colourist! Why could I not communicate to Conseil the lively sensations which were mounting to my brain, and rival him in expressions of admiration? For aught I knew, Captain Nemo and his companion might be able to exchange thoughts by means of signs previously agreed upon. So for want of better, I talked to myself; I declaimed in the copper-box which covered my head, thereby expending more air in vain words than was, perhaps, expedient.

Various kinds of isis, clusters of pure tuft-coral, prickly fungi, and anemones, formed a brilliant garden of flowers, enameled with porphitae, decked with their collarettes of blue tentacles, sea-stars studding the sandy bottom, together with asterophytons like fine lace embroidered by the hands of naiads, whose festoons were waved by the gentle undulations caused by our walk. It was a real grief to me to crush under my feet the brilliant specimens of molluscs which strewed the ground by thousands, of hammerheads, donaciae (veritable bounding shells), of staircases, and red helmet-shells, angel-wings, and many others produced by this inexhaustible ocean. But we were bound to walk, so we went on, while above our heads waved shoals of physalides leaving their tentacles to float in their train, medusae whose umbrellas of opal or rose-pink, escalloped with a band of blue, sheltered us from the rays of the sun and fiery pelagiae, which in the darkness would have strewn our path with phosphorescent light.

All these wonders I saw in the space of a quarter of a mile, scarcely stopping, and following Captain Nemo, who beckoned me on by signs. Soon the nature of the soil changed; to the sandy plain succeeded an extent of slimy mud which the Americans call "ooze," composed of equal parts of silicious and calcareous shells. We then travelled over a plain of sea-weed of wild and luxuriant vegetation. This sward was of close texture, and soft to the feet, and rivalled the softest carpet woven by the hand of man. But while verdure was spread at our feet, it did not abandon our heads. A light network of marine plants, of that inexhaustible family of sea-weeds of which more than two thousand kinds are known, grew on the surface of the water. I saw long ribbons of fucus floating, some globulars, others tuberous; laurenciae and cladostephi of most delicate foliage, and some rhodomeniae pulmatae resembling the fan of a cactus. I noticed that the green plants kept nearer the top of the sea, while the red were at a greater depth, leaving to the black or brown hydrophytes the care of forming gardens and parterres in the remote beds of the ocean.

We had quitted the *Nautilus* about an hour and a half. It was near noon; I knew by the perpendicularity of the sun's rays, which were no longer refracted. The magical colours disappeared by degrees, and the shades of emerald and sapphire were effaced. We walked with a regular step, which rang upon the ground with astonishing intensity; the slightest noise was transmitted with a quickness to which the ear is unaccustomed on the earth; indeed, water is a better conductor of sound than air, in the ratio of four to one. At this period the earth sloped downwards; the light took a uniform tint. We were at a depth of a hundred and five yards and twenty inches, undergoing a pressure of six atmospheres.

At this depth I could still see the rays of the sun, though feebly; to their intense brilliancy had succeeded a reddish twilight, the lowest state between day and night; but we could still see well enough; it was not necessary to resort to the Ruhmkorff apparatus as yet. At this moment Captain Nemo stopped; he waited till I joined him, and then pointed to an obscure mass, looming in the shadow, at a short distance.

"It is the forest of the Island of Crespo," thought I: and I was not mistaken.

Chapter XVI

A Submarine Forest

WE HAD AT LAST ARRIVED ON THE BORDERS OF THIS FOREST, DOUBTLESS ONE OF THE finest of Captain Nemo's immense domains. He looked upon it as his own, and considered he had the same right over it that the first men had in the first days of the world. And, indeed, who would have disputed with him the possession of this submarine property? What other hardier pioneer would come, hatchet in hand, to cut down the dark copses?

This forest was composed of large tree-plants; and the moment we penetrated under its vast arcades, I was struck by the singular position of their branches—a position I had not yet observed.

Not an herb which carpeted the ground, not a branch which clothed the trees, was either broken or bent, nor did they extend horizontally; all stretched up to the surface of the ocean. Not a filament, not a ribbon, however thin they might be, but kept as straight as a rod of iron. The fuci and lianas grew in rigid perpendicular lines, due to the density of the element which had produced them. Motionless, yet, when bent to one side by the hand, they directly resumed their former position. Truly it was the region of perpendicularity!

I soon accustomed myself to this fantastic position, as well as to the comparative darkness which surrounded us. The soil of the forest seemed covered with sharp blocks, difficult to avoid. The submarine flora struck me as being very perfect, and richer even than it would have been in the arctic or tropical zones, where these productions are not so plentiful. But for some minutes I involuntarily confounded the genera, taking zoöphytes for hydrophytes, animals for plants; and who would not have been mistaken? The fauna and the flora are too closely allied in this submarine world.

These plants are self-propagated, and the principle of their existence is in the water, which upholds and nourishes them. The greater number, instead of leaves, shoot forth blades of capricious shapes comprised within a scale of colours—pink, carmine, green, olive, fawn, and brown. I saw there (but not dried up, as our specimens of the *Nautilus* are) pavonari spread like a fan as if to catch the breeze; scarlet ceramies, whose luminaries extended their edible shoots of fern-shaped nereocysti, which grow to a height of fifteen feet; clusters of acetabuli, whose stems increase in size upward; and numbers of other marine plants, all devoid of flowers!

"Curious anomaly! fantastic element!" said an ingenious naturalist, "in which the animal kingdom blossoms, and the vegetable does not!"

Under these numerous shrubs (as large as trees of the temperate zone), and living under their damp shadow, were massed together real bushes of living flowers, hedges of zoöphytes, on which blossomed some zebra-meandrines, with crooked grooves; some yellow caryophylliae; and to complete the illusion, the fish-flies flew from branch to branch like a swarm of humming-birds, while yellow lepisacomthi, with bristling jaws, dactylopteri, and monocentrides rose at our feet like a flight of snipes.

In about an hour Captain Nemo gave the signal to halt. I, for my part, was not sorry, and we stretched ourselves under an arbour of alariae, the long thin blades of which stood up like arrows.

This short rest seemed delicious to me; there was nothing wanting but the charm of conversation; but, impossible to speak, impossible to answer, I only put my great copper head to Conseil's. I saw the worthy fellow's eyes glistening with delight, and, to show his satisfaction he shook himself in his breastplate of air, in the most comical way in the world.

After four hours of this walking, I was surprised not to find myself dreadfully hungry. How to account for this state of the stomach I could not tell. But instead I felt an insurmountable desire to sleep, which happens to all divers. And my eyes soon closed behind the thick glasses, and I fell into a heavy slumber, which the movement alone had prevented before. Captain Nemo and his robust companion, stretched in the clear crystal, set us the example.

How long I remained buried in this drowsiness I cannot judge; but when I woke, the sun seemed sinking towards the horizon. Captain Nemo had already risen, and I was beginning to stretch my limbs, when an unexpected apparition brought me briskly to my feet.

A few steps off, a monstrous sea-spider, about thirty-eight inches high, was watching me with squinting eyes, ready to spring upon me. Though my diver's dress was thick enough to defend me from the bite of this animal, I could not help shuddering with horror. Conseil and the sailor of the *Nautilus* awoke at this moment. Captain Nemo pointed out the hideous crustacean, which a blow from the butt end of the gun knocked over, and I saw the horrible claws of the monster writhe in terrible convulsions. This incident reminded me that other animals more to be feared might haunt these obscure depths, against whose attacks my diving-dress would not protect me. I had never thought of it before, but I now resolved to be upon my guard. Indeed, I thought that this halt would mark the termination of our walk; but I was mistaken, for, instead of returning to the *Nautilus*, Captain Nemo continued his bold excursion. The ground was still on the incline, its declivity seemed to be getting greater, and to be leading us to greater depths. It must have been about three o'clock when we reached a narrow valley, between high perpendicular walls, situated about seventy-five fathoms deep. Thanks to the perfection of our apparatus, we were forty-five fathoms below the limit which nature seems to have imposed on man as to his submarine excursions.

I say seventy-five fathoms, though I had no instrument by which to judge the distance. But I knew that even in the clearest waters the solar rays could not penetrate further. And accordingly the darkness deepened. At ten paces not an object was visible. I was groping my way, when I suddenly saw a brilliant white light. Captain Nemo had just put his electric apparatus into use; his companion did the same, and Conseil and I followed their example. By turning a screw I established a communication between the wire and the spiral glass, and the sea, lit by our four lanterns, was illuminated for a circle of thirty-six yards.

Captain Nemo was still plunging into the dark depths of the forest, whose trees were getting scarcer at every step. I noticed that vegetable life disappeared sooner than animal life. The medusae had already abandoned the arid soil, from which a great number of animals, zoöphytes, articulate, molluscs, and fishes, still obtained sustenance.

As we walked, I thought the light of our Ruhmkorff apparatus could not fail to draw some inhabitant from its dark couch. But if they did approach us, they at least kept at a respectful distance from the hunters. Several times I saw Captain Nemo stop, put his gun to his shoulder, and after some moments drop it and walk on. At last, after about four hours, this marvellous excursion came to an end. A wall of superb rocks, in an imposing mass, rose before us, a heap of gigantic blocks, an enormous, steep granite shore, forming dark grottoes, but which presented no practicable slope; it was the prop of the Island of Crespo. It was the earth! Captain Nemo stopped suddenly. A gesture of his brought us all to a halt; and, however desirous I might be to scale the wall, I was obliged to stop. Here ended Captain Nemo's domains. And he would not go beyond them. Further on was a portion of the globe he might not trample upon.

The return began. Captain Nemo had returned to the head of his little band, directing their course without hesitation. I thought we were not following the same road to return to the *Nautilus*. The new road was very steep, and consequently very painful. We approached the surface of the sea rapidly. But this return to the upper strata was not so sudden as to cause relief from the pressure too rapidly, which might have produced serious disorder in our organisation, and brought on internal lesions, so fatal to divers. Very soon light reappeared and grew, and the sun being low on the horizon, the refraction edged the different objects with a spectral ring. At ten yards and a half deep, we walked amid a shoal of little fishes of all kinds, more numerous than the birds of the air, and also more agile; but no aquatic game worthy of a shot had as yet met our gaze, when at that moment I saw the Captain shoulder his gun quickly, and follow a moving object into the shrubs. He fired—I heard a slight hissing, and a creature fell stunned at some distance from us. It was a magnificent sea-otter, an enhydrus, the only exclusively marine quadruped. This otter was five feet long, and must have been very valuable. Its skin, chestnut-brown above and silvery underneath, would have made one of those beautiful furs so sought after in the Russian and Chinese markets: the fineness and the lustre of its coat would certainly fetch £80. I admired this curious mammal, with its rounded head ornamented with short ears, its round eyes, and white whiskers like those of a cat, with webbed feet and nails, and tufted tail. This precious animal, hunted and tracked by fishermen, has now become very rare, and taken refuge chiefly in the northern parts of the Pacific, or probably its race would soon become extinct.

Captain Nemo's companion took the beast, threw it over his shoulder, and we continued our journey. For one hour a plain of sand lay stretched before us. Sometimes it rose to within two yards and some inches of the surface of the water. I then saw our image clearly reflected, drawn inversely, and above us appeared an identical group reflecting our movements and our actions; in a word, like us in every point, except that they walked with their heads downward and their feet in the air.

Another effect I noticed, which was the passage of thick clouds, which formed and vanished rapidly; but on reflection I understood that these seeming clouds were due to the varying thickness of the reeds at the bottom, and I could even see the fleecy foam which their broken tops multiplied on the water, and the shadows of large birds passing above our heads, whose rapid flight I could discern on the surface of the sea.

On this occasion I was witness to one of the finest gunshots which ever made the nerves of a hunter thrill. A large bird of great breadth of wing, clearly visible, approached, hovering over us. Captain Nemo's companion shouldered his gun and fired, when it was only a few yards above the waves. The creature fell stunned, and the force of its fall brought it within the reach of dexterous hunter's grasp. It was an albatross of the finest kind.

Our march had not been interrupted by this incident. For two hours we followed these sandy plains, then fields of algae very disagreeable to cross. Candidly, I could do no more when I saw a glimmer of light, which, for a half mile, broke the darkness of the waters. It was the lantern of the *Nautilus*. Before twenty minutes were over we should be on board, and I should be able to breathe with ease; for it seemed that my reservoir supplied air very deficient in oxygen. But I did not reckon on an accidental meeting which delayed our arrival for some time.

I had remained some steps behind, when I presently saw Captain Nemo coming hurriedly towards me. With his strong hand he bent me to the ground, his companion doing the same to Conseil. At first I knew not what to think of this sudden attack, but I was soon reassured by seeing the captain lie down beside me, and remain immovable.

I was stretched on the ground, just under the shelter of a bush of algae, when, raising my head, I saw some enormous mass, casting phosphorescent gleams, pass blusteringly by.

My blood froze in my veins as I recognised two formidable sharks which threatened us. It was a couple of tintoreas, terrible creatures, with enormous tails and a dull glassy stare, the phosphorescent matter ejected from holes pierced around the muzzle. Monstrous brutes, which would crush a whole man in their iron jaws! I did not know whether Conseil stopped to classify them; for my part, I noticed their silver bellies, and their huge mouths bristling with teeth, from a very unscientific point of view, and more as a possible victim than as a naturalist.

Happily the voracious creatures do not see well. They passed without seeing us, brushing us with their brownish fins, and we escaped by a miracle from a danger certainly greater than meeting a tiger full-face in the forest. Half an hour after, guided by the electric light, we reached the *Nautilus*. The outside door had been left open, and Captain Nemo closed it as soon as we had entered the first cell. He then pressed a knob. I heard the pumps working in the midst of the vessel. I felt the water sinking from around me, and in a few moments the cell was entirely empty. The inside door then opened, and we entered the vestry.

There our diving-dress was taken off, not without some trouble; and, fairly worn out from want of food and sleep, I returned to my room, in great wonder at this surprising excursion at the bottom of the sea.

Chapter XVII

FOUR THOUSAND LEAGUES UNDER THE PACIFIC

THE NEXT MORNING, THE 18TH OF NOVEMBER, I HAD QUITE RECOVERED FROM MY FA-tigues of the day before, and I went up on to the platform, just as the second lieutenant was uttering his daily phrase.

I was admiring the magnificent aspect of the ocean when Captain Nemo appeared. He did not seem to be aware of my presence, and began a series of astronomical observations. Then, when he had finished, he went and leaned on the cage of the watchlight, and gazed abstractedly on the ocean. In the meantime, a number of the sailors of the *Nautilus*, all strong and healthy men, had come up onto the platform. They came to draw up the nets that had been laid all night. These sailors were evidently of different nations, although the European type was visible in all of them. I recognised some unmistakable Irishmen, Frenchmen, some Slavs, and a Greek or a Candiote. They were civil, and only used that odd language among themselves, the origin of which I could not guess, neither could I question them.

The nets were hauled in. They were a large kind of "chaluts," like those on the Normandy coasts, great pockets that the waves and a chain fixed in the smaller meshes kept open. These pockets, drawn by iron poles, swept through the water, and gathered in everything in their way. That day they brought up curious specimens from those productive coasts—fishing-frogs, that, from their comical movements, have acquired the name of buffoons; black commersons, furnished with antennae; trigger-fish, encircled with red bands; orthragorisci, with very subtle venom; some olive-coloured lampreys; macrorhynci, covered with silvery scales; trichiuri, the electric power of which is equal to that of the gymnotus and cramp-fish; scaly notopteri with transverse brown bands; greenish cod; several varieties of gobies, etc.; also some larger fish; a caranx with a prominent head a yard long; several fine bonitos, streaked with blue and silver; and three splendid tunnies, which in spite of the swiftness of their motion, had not escaped the net.

I reckoned that the haul had brought in more than nine hundredweight of fish. It was a fine haul, but not to be wondered at. Indeed, the nets are let down for several hours, and enclose in their meshes an infinite variety. We had no lack of excellent food, and the rapidity of the *Nautilus* and the attraction of the electric light could always renew our supply. These several productions of the sea were immediately lowered through the panel to the steward's room, some to be eaten fresh, and others pickled.

The fishing ended, the provision of air renewed, I thought that the *Nautilus* was about to continue its submarine excursion, and was preparing to return to my room, when, without further preamble, the captain turned to me, saying:

"Professor, is not this ocean gifted with real life? It has its tempers and its gentle moods. Yesterday it slept as we did, and now it has woke after a quiet night. Look!" he continued. "It wakes under the caresses of the sun. It is going to renew its diurnal existence. It is an interesting study to watch the play of its organisation. It has a pulse, arteries, spasms; and I agree with the learned Maury, who discovered in it a circulation as real as the circulation of blood in animals.

"Yes, the ocean has indeed circulation, and to promote it, the Creator has caused things to multiply in it—caloric, salt, and animalculae."

When Captain Nemo spoke thus, he seemed altogether changed, and aroused an extraordinary emotion in me.

"Also," he added, "true existence is there; and I can imagine the foundations of nautical towns, clusters of submarine houses, which, like the *Nautilus*, would ascend every morning to breathe at the surface of the water—free towns, independent cities. Yet who knows whether some despot——"

Captain Nemo finished his sentence with a violent gesture. Then, addressing me as if to chase away some sorrowful thought:

"M. Aronnax," he asked, "do you know the depth of the ocean?"

"I only know, captain, what the principal soundings have taught us."

"Could you tell me them, so that I can suit them to my purpose?"

"These are some," I replied, "that I remember. If I am not mistaken, a depth of 8,000 yards has been found in the North Atlantic, and 2,500 yards in the Mediterranean. The most remarkable soundings have been made in the South Atlantic, near the 35th parallel, and they gave 12,000 yards, 14,000 yards, and 15,000 yards. To sum up all, it is reckoned that if the bottom of the sea were levelled, its mean depth would be about one and three-quarter leagues."

"Well, professor," replied the Captain, "we shall show you better than that I hope. As to the mean depth of this part of the Pacific, I tell you it is only 4,000 yards."

Having said this, Captain Nemo went towards the panel, and disappeared down the ladder. I followed him, and went into the large drawing-room. The screw was immediately put in motion, and the log gave twenty miles an hour.

During the days and weeks that passed, Captain Nemo was very sparing of his visits. I seldom saw him. The lieutenant pricked the ship's course regularly on the chart, so I could always tell exactly the route of the *Nautilus*.

Nearly everyday, for some time, the panels of the drawing-room were opened, and we were never tired of penetrating the mysteries of the submarine world.

The general direction of the *Nautilus* was south-east, and it kept between 100 and 150 yards of depth. One day, however, I do not know why, being drawn diagonally by means of the inclined planes, it touched the bed of the sea. The thermometer indicated a temperature of 4.25 (Cent.); a temperature that at this depth seemed common to all latitudes.

At three o'clock on the morning of the 26th of November, the *Nautilus* crossed the tropic of Cancer at 172° longitude. On the 27th instant it sighted the Sandwich Islands, where Cook died, February 14, 1779. We had then gone 4,860 leagues from our starting-point. In the morning, when I went on the platform, I saw, two miles to windward, Hawaii, the largest of the seven islands that form the group. I saw clearly the cultivated ranges, and the several mountain-chains that run parallel with the side, and the volcanoes that overtop Mouna-Rea, which rise 5,000 yards above the level of the sea. Besides other things the nets brought up, were several flabellariae and graceful polypi, that are peculiar to that part of the ocean. The direction of the *Nautilus* was still to the south-east. It crossed the equator December 1, in 142° longitude; and on the 4th of the same month, after crossing rapidly and without anything in particular occurring, we sighted the Marquesas group. I saw, three miles off, at 8° 57' latitude south, and 139° 32' west longitude. Martin's peak in Nouka-Hiva, the largest of the group that belongs to France. I only saw the woody mountains against the horizon, because Captain Nemo did not wish to bring the ship to the wind. There the nets brought up beautiful specimens of fish: choryphenes, with azure fins and tails like gold, the flesh of which is unrivalled; hologymnoses, nearly destitute of scales, but of exquisite flavour; ostorhyncs,, with bony jaws, and yellow-tinged thasards, as good as bonitos; all fish that would be of use to us. After leaving these charming islands protected by the French flag, from the 4th to the 11th of December the *Nautilus* sailed over about 2,000 miles. This navigation was remarkable for the meeting with an immense shoal of calmars, near neighbors to the cuttle. The French fishermen call them *hornets*; they belong to the cephalopod class, and to the dibranchial family, that comprehends the cuttles and the argonauts. These animals were particularly studied by students of antiquity, and they furnished numerous metaphors to the popular orators, as well as excellent dishes for the tables of the rich citizens, if one can believe Athenæus, a Greek doctor, who lived before Galen. It was during the night of the 9th or 10th of December that the *Nautilus* came across this shoal of molluscs, that are peculiarly nocturnal. One could count them by millions. They emigrate from the temperate to the warmer zones, following the track of herrings and sardines. We watched them through the thick crystal panes, swimming down the wind with great rapidity, moving by means of their locomotive tube, pursuing fish and molluscs, eating the little ones, eaten by the big ones, and tossing about in indescribable confusion the ten arms that nature has placed on their heads like a crest of pneumatic serpents. The *Nautilus*, in spite of its speed, sailed for several hours in the midst of these animals, and its nets brought in an enormous quantity, among which I recognized the nine species that D'Orbigny classed for the Pacific. One saw, while crossing, that the sea displays the most wonderful sights. They were in endless variety. The scene changed continually, and we were called upon not only to contemplate the works of the Creator in the midst of the liquid element, but to penetrate the awful mysteries of the ocean.

During the daytime of the 11th of December, I was busy reading in the large drawing-room. Ned Land and Conseil watched the luminous water through the half-open panels. The *Nautilus* was immovable. While its reservoirs were filled, it kept at a depth of 1,000 yards, a region rarely visited in the ocean, and in which large fish were seldom seen.

I was then reading a charming book by Jean Macé, "The Slaves of the Stomach," and I was learning some valuable lessons from it, when Conseil interrupted me.

"Will master come here a moment?" he said in a curious voice.

"What is the matter, Conseil?"

"I want master to look."

I rose, went, and leaned on my elbows before the panes and watched.

In a full electric light, an enormous black mass, quite immovable, was suspended in

the midst of the waters. I watched it attentively, seeking to find out the nature of this gigantic cetacean. But a sudden thought crossed my mind. "A vessel!" I said, half aloud.

"Yes," replied the Canadian, "a disabled ship that has sunk perpendicularly."

Ned Land was right; we were close to a vessel of which the tattered shrouds still hung
from their chains. The keel seemed to be in good order, and it had been wrecked at most
some few hours. Three stumps of masts, broken off about two feet above the bridge,
showed that the vessel had had to sacrifice its masts. But, lying on its side, it had filled, and
it was heeling over to port. This skeleton of what it had once been was a sad spectacle as
it lay lost under the waves; but sadder still was the sight of the bridge, where some corpses,
bound with ropes, were still lying. I counted five—four men, one of whom was standing
at the helm, and a woman standing by the poop, holding an infant in her arms. She was
quite young. I could distinguish her features, which the water had not decomposed, by the
brilliant light from the *Nautilus*. In one despairing effort, she had raised her infant above
her head, poor little thing, whose arms encircled its mother's neck. The attitude of the four
sailors was frightful, distorted as they were by their convulsive movements, while making
a last effort to free themselves from the cords that bound them to the vessel. The steersman alone, calm, with a grave, clear face, his grey hair glued to his forehead, and his hand
clutching the wheel of the helm, seemed even then to be guiding the three broken masts
through the depths of the ocean.

What a scene! We were dumb; our hearts beat fast before this shipwreck, taken as it
were from life, and photographed in its last moments. And I saw already, coming towards
it with hungry eyes, enormous sharks, attracted by the human flesh.

However, the *Nautilus*, turning, went round the submerged vessel, and in one instant
I read on the stern—*The Florida, Sunderland*.

Chapter XVIII

VANIKORO

THIS TERRIBLE SPECTACLE WAS THE FORERUNNER OF THE SERIES OF MARITIME CATAS-
trophes that the *Nautilus* was destined to meet with in its route. As long as it went
through more frequented waters, we often saw the hulls of shipwrecked vessels that were
rotting in the depths, and, deeper down, cannons, bullets, anchors, chains, and a thousand
other iron materials eaten up by rust. However, on the 11th of December, we sighted the
Pomotou Islands, the old "dangerous group" of Bougainville, that extend over a space of
500 leagues at E.S.E. to W.N.W., from the Island Ducie to that of Lazareff. This group
covers an area of 370 square leagues, and it is formed of sixty groups of islands, among
which the Gambier group is remarkable, over which France exercises sway. These are
coral islands, slowly raised, but continuous, created by the daily work of polypi. Then this
new island will be joined later on to the neighboring groups, and a fifth continent will
stretch from New Zealand and New Caledonia, and from thence to the Marquesas.

One day, when I was suggesting this theory to Captain Nemo, he replied coldly:

"The earth does not want new continents, but new men."

Chance had conducted the *Nautilus* towards the Island of Clermont-Tonnerre, one of the most curious of the group that was discovered in 1822 by Captain Bell of the *Minerva*. I could study now the madreporal system, to which are due the islands in this ocean.

Madrepores (which must not be mistaken for corals) have a tissue lined with a calcareous crust, and the modifications of its structure have induced M. Milne Edwards, my worthy master, to class them into five sections. The animalculae that the marine polypus secretes live by millions at the bottom of their cells. Their calcareous deposits become rocks, reefs, and large and small islands. Here they form a ring, surrounding a little inland lake, that communicates with the sea by means of gaps. There they make barriers of reefs like those on the coasts of New Caledonia and the various Pomotou islands. In other places, like those at Reunion and at Maurice, they raise fringed reefs, high, straight walls, near which the depth of the ocean is considerable.

Some cable-lengths off the shores of the Island of Clermont I admired the gigantic work accomplished by these microscopical workers. These walls are specially the work of those madrepores known as milleporas, porites, madrepores, and astraeas. These polypi are found particularly in the rough beds of the sea, near the surface; and consequently it is from the upper part that they begin their operations in which they bury themselves by degrees with the debris of the secretions that support them. Such is, at least, Darwin's theory, who thus explains the formation of the *atolls*, a superior theory (to my mind) to that given of the foundation of the madreporical works, summits of mountains or volcanoes, that are submerged some feet below the level of the sea.

I could observe closely these curious walls, for perpendicularly they were more than 300 yards deep, and our electric sheets lighted up this calcareous matter brilliantly. Replying to a question Conseil asked me as to the time these colossal barriers took to be raised, I astonished him much by telling him that learned men reckoned it about the eighth of an inch in a hundred years.

Towards evening Clermont-Tonnerre was lost in the distance, and the route of the *Nautilus* was sensibly changed. After having crossed the tropic of Capricorn in 135° longitude, it sailed W.N.W., making again for the tropical zone. Although the summer sun was very strong, we did not suffer from heat, for at fifteen or twenty fathoms below the surface, the temperature did not rise above from ten to twelve degrees.

On December 15, we left to the east the bewitching group of the Societies and the graceful Tahiti, queen of the Pacific. I saw in the morning, some miles to the windward, the elevated summits of the island. These waters furnished our table with excellent fish, mackerel, bonitos, and albacores, some varieties of a sea-serpent called munirophis.

On the 25th of December the *Nautilus* sailed into the midst of the New Hebrides, discovered by Quiros in 1606, and that Bougainville explored in 1768, and to which Cook gave its present name in 1773. This group is composed principally of nine large islands, that form a band of 120 leagues N.N.S. to S.S.W., between 15° and 2° south latitude, and 164° and 168° longitude. We passed tolerably near to the island of Aurou, that at noon looked like a mass of green woods, surmounted by a peak of great height.

That day being Christmas Day, Ned Land seemed to regret sorely the non-celebration of "Christmas," the family *fête* of which Protestants are so fond. I had not seen Captain Nemo for a week when, on the morning of the 27th, he came into the large drawing-room, always seeming as if he had seen you five minutes before. I was busily tracing the route of the *Nautilus* on the planisphere. The captain came up to me, put his finger on one spot on the chart, and said this single word:

"Vanikoro."

The effect was magical! It was the name of the islands on which La Perouse had been lost! I rose suddenly.

"The *Nautilus* has brought us to Vanikoro?" I asked.

"Yes, professor," said the captain.

"And I can visit the celebrated islands where the *Boussoule* and the *Astrolabe* struck?"

"If you like, professor."

"When shall we be there?"

"We are there now."

Followed by Captain Nemo, I went up on to the platform, and greedily scanned the horizon.

To the N.E. two volcanic islands emerged, of unequal size, surrounded by a coral reef that measured forty miles in circumference.

We were close to Vanikoro, really the one to which Dumont d'Urville gave the name of Isle de la Récherché, and exactly facing the little harbour of Vanou, situated in 16° 4' south latitude, and 164° 32' east longitude. The earth seemed covered with verdure from the shore to the summits in the interior, that were crowned by Mount Kapogo, 476 feet high. The *Nautilus*, having passed the outer belt of rocks by a narrow strait, found itself among breakers where the sea was from thirty to forty fathoms deep. Under the verdant shade of some mangroves I perceived some savages, who appeared greatly surprised at our approach. In the long black body, moving between wind and water, did they not see some formidable cetacean that they regarded with suspicion?

Just then Captain Nemo asked me what I knew about the wreck of La Perouse.

"Only what everyone knows, captain," I replied.

"And could you tell me what everyone knows about it?" he inquired, ironically.

"Easily."

I related to him all that the last works of Dumont d'Urville had made known—works from which the following is a brief account.

La Perouse, and his second, Captain de Langle, were sent by Louis XVI, in 1785, on a voyage of circumnavigation. They embarked in the corvettes *Boussoule* and the *Astrolabe*, neither of which were again heard of. In 1791, the French government, justly uneasy as to the fate of these two sloops, manned two large merchantmen, the *Récherché* and the *Esperance*, which left Brest the 28th of September, under the command of Bruni d'Entrecasteaux.

Two months after, they learned from Bowen, commander of the *Albemarle*, that the debris of shipwrecked vessels had been seen on the coasts of New Georgia. But D'Entrecasteaux, ignoring this communication—rather uncertain besides—directed his course towards the Admiralty Islands, mentioned in a report of Captain Hunter's as being the place where La Perouse was wrecked.

They sought in vain. The *Esperance* and the *Récherché* passed before Vanikoro without stopping there, and in fact this voyage was most disastrous, as it cost D'Entrecasteaux his life, and those of two of his lieutenants, besides several of his crew.

Captain Dillon, a shrewd old Pacific sailor, was the first to find unmistakable traces of the wrecks. On the 15th of May, 1824, his vessel, the *St. Patrick*, passed close to Tikopia, one of the New Hebrides. There a Lascar came alongside in a canoe, sold him the handle of a sword in silver that bore the print of characters engraved on the hilt. The Lascar pretended that six years before, during a stay at Vanikoro, he had seen two Europeans that belonged to some vessels that had run aground on the reefs some years ago.

Dillon guessed that he meant La Perouse, whose disappearance had troubled the whole world. He tried to get on to Vanikoro, where according to the Lascar he would find numerous debris of the wreck, but winds and tide prevented him.

Dillon returned to Calcutta. There he interested the Asiatic Society and the Indian Company in his discovery. A vessel, to which was given the name of the *Récherché*, was put at his disposal, and he set out, January 23, 1827, accompanied by a French agent.

The *Récherché*, after touching at several points in the Pacific, cast anchor before Vanikoro, July 7, 1827, in that same harbour of Vanou where the *Nautilus* was at this time.

There it collected numerous relics of the wreck—iron utensils, anchors, pulley-strops, swivel-guns, an eighteen-pound shot, fragments of astronomical instruments, a piece of crown-work, and a bronze clock, bearing this inscription: *"Bazin m'a fait,"* the mark of the foundry of the arsenal at Brest about 1785. There could be no further doubt.

Dillon, having made all inquiries, stayed in the unlucky place till October. Then he quitted Vanikoro, and directed his course towards New Zealand; put into Calcutta, April 7, 1828, and returned to France, where he was warmly welcomed by Charles X.

But at the same time, without knowing Dillon's movements, Dumont d'Urville had already set out to find the scene of the wreck. And they had learned from a whaler that some medals and a cross of St. Louis had been found in the hands of some savages of Louisiade and New Caledonia. Dumont d'Urville, commander of the *Astrolabe*, had then sailed, and two months after Dillon had left Vanikoro, he put into Hobart Town. There he learned the results of Dillon's inquiries, and found that a certain James Hobbs, second lieutenant of the *Union*, of Calcutta, after landing on an island situated 8° 18' south latitude, and 156° 30' east longitude, had seen some iron bars and red stuffs used by the natives of these parts. Dumont d'Urville, much perplexed, and not knowing how to credit the reports of low-class journals, decided to follow Dillon's track.

On the 10th of February, 1828, the *Astrolabe* appeared off Tikopia, and D'Urville took as guide and interpreter a deserter found on the island; made his way to Vanikoro, sighted it on the 12th inst., lay among the reefs until the 14th, and not until the 20th did he cast anchor within the barrier in the harbour of Vanou.

On the 23d, several officers went round the island, and brought back some unimportant trifles. The natives, adopting a system of denials and evasions, refused to take them to the unlucky place. This ambiguous conduct led them to believe that the natives had ill-treated the castaways, and indeed they seemed to fear that Dumont d'Urville had come to avenge La Perouse and his unfortunate crew.

However, on the 26th, appeased by some presents, and understanding that they had no reprisals to fear, they led M. Jacquireot to the scene of the wreck.

There, in three or four fathoms of water, between the reefs of Pacou and Vanou, lay anchors, cannons, pigs of lead and iron, embedded in the limy concretions. The large boat and the whaler belonging to the *Astrolabe* were sent to this place, and, not without some difficulty, their crews hauled up an anchor weighing 1,800 pounds, a brass gun, some pigs of iron, and two copper swivel-guns.

Dumont d'Urville, questioning the natives, learned, too, that La Perouse, after losing both his vessels on the reefs of this island, had constructed a smaller boat, only to be lost a second time. Where? No one knew.

But the French Government, fearing that Dumont d'Urville was not acquainted with Dillon's movements, had sent the sloop *Bayonnaise*, commanded by Legoarant de Tromelin, to Vanikoro, which had been stationed on the west coast of America. The *Bayonnaise* cast her anchor before Vanikoro some months after the departure of the *Astrolabe*, but found no new document; but stated that the savages had respected the monument to La Perouse. That is the substance of what I told Captain Nemo.

"So," he said, "no one knows now where the third vessel perished that was constructed by the castaways on the island of Vanikoro?"

"No one knows."

Captain Nemo said nothing, but signed to me to follow him into the large saloon. The *Nautilus* sank several yards below the waves, and the panels were opened.

I hastened to the aperture, and under the crustations of coral, covered with fungi, syphonules, alcyons, madrepores, through myriads of charming fish—girelles, glyphisidri, pompherides, diacopes, and holocentres—I recognised certain debris that the drags had not been able to tear up: iron stirrups, anchors, cannons, bullets, capstan-fittings, the stem of a ship—all objects clearly proving the wreck of some vessel, and now carpeted with living flowers.

While I was looking on this desolate scene, Captain Nemo said, in a sad voice:

"Commander La Perouse set out December 7, 1785, with his vessels *La Boussoule* and the *Astrolabe*. He first cast anchor at Botany Bay, visited the Friendly Isles, New Caledonia, then directed his course towards Santa Cruz, and put into Namouka, one of the Hapaï group. Then his vessel struck on the unknown reefs of Vanikoro. The *Boussoule*, which went first, ran aground on the southerly coast. The *Astrolabe* went to its help, and ran aground too. The first vessel was destroyed almost immediately. The second, stranded under the wind, resisted some days. The natives made the castaways welcome. They installed themselves in the island, and constructed a smaller boat with the debris of the two large ones. Some sailors stayed willingly at Vanikoro; the others, weak and ill, set out with La Perouse. They directed their course towards the Solomon Islands, and there perished, with everything, on the westerly coast of the chief island of the group, between Capes Deception and Satisfaction."

"How do you know that?"

"By this, that I found on the spot where was the last wreck."

Captain Nemo showed me a tin-plate box, stamped with the French arms, and corroded by the salt water. He opened it, and I saw a bundle of papers, yellow but still readable.

They were the instructions of the naval minister to Commander La Perouse, annotated in the margin in Louis XVI's handwriting.

"Ah! it is a fine death for a sailor!" said Captain Nemo, at last. "A coral tomb makes a quiet grave; and I trust that I and my comrades will find no other."

Chapter XIX

Torres Straits

D URING THE NIGHT OF THE 27TH OR 28TH OF DECEMBER, THE *NAUTILUS* LEFT THE shores of Vanikoro with great speed. Her course was south-westerly, and in three days she had gone over the 750 leagues that separated it from La Perouse's group and the south-east point of Papua.

Early on the 1st of January, 1863, Conseil joined me on the platform.

"Master, will you permit me to wish you a happy new year?"

"What! Conseil; exactly as if I was at Paris in my study at the Jardin des Plantes? Well, I accept your good wishes, and thank you for them. Only, I will ask you what you mean by a 'happy new year' under our circumstances? Do you mean the year that will bring us to the end of our imprisonment, or the year that sees us continue this strange voyage?"

"Really, I do not know how to answer, master. We are sure to see curious things, and for the last two months we have not had time for *ennui*. The last marvel is always the most astonishing; and, if we continue this progression, I do not know how it will end. It is my opinion that we shall never again see the like. I think, then, with no offence to master, that a happy year would be one in which we could see everything."

On January 2, we had made 11,340 miles, or 5,250 French leagues, since our starting-point in the Japan Seas. Before the ship's head stretched the dangerous shores of the coral sea, on the north-east coast of Australia. Our boat lay along some miles from the re-doubtable bank on which Cook's vessel was lost, June 10, 1770. The boat in which Cook was struck on a rock, and, if it did not sink, it was owing to a piece of coral that was broken by the shock, and fixed itself in the broken keel.

I had wished to visit the reef, 360 leagues long, against which the sea, always rough, broke with great violence, with a noise like thunder. But just then the inclined planes drew the *Nautilus* down to a great depth, and I could see nothing of the high coral walls. I had to content myself with the different specimens of fish brought up by the nets. I remarked, among others, some germons, a species of mackerel as large as a tunny, with bluish sides, and striped with transverse bands, that disappear with the animal's life. These fish fol-lowed us in shoals, and furnished us with very delicate food. We took also a large number of giltheads, about one and a half inches long, tasting like dorys; and flying pyrapeds like submarine swallows, which, in dark nights, light alternately the air and water with their phosphorescent light. Among the molluscs and zoöphytes, I found in the meshes of the net several species of alcyonarians, echini, hammers, spurs, dials, cerites, and hyalleae. The flora was represented by beautiful floating sea-weeds, laminariae, and macrocystes, im-pregnated with the mucilage that transudes through their pores; and among which I gath-ered an admirable *Nemastoma Geliniarois*, that was classed among the natural curiosities of the museum.

Two days after crossing the coral sea, January 4, we sighted the Papuan coasts. On this occasion, Captain Nemo informed me that his intention was to get into the Indian Ocean by the Strait of Torres. His communication ended there.

The Torres Straits are nearly thirty-four leagues wide; but they are obstructed by an innumerable quantity of islands, islets, breakers, and rocks, that make its navigation almost impracticable; so that Captain Nemo took all needful precautions to cross them. The *Nautilus*, floating betwixt wind and water, went at a moderate pace. Her screw, like a cetacean's tail, beat the waves slowly.

Profiting by this, I and my two companions went up on to the deserted platform. Before us was the steersman's cage, and I expected that Captain Nemo was there directing the course of the *Nautilus*. I had before me the excellent charts of the Straits of Torres, made out by the hydrographical engineer Vincendon Dumoulin. These and Captain's King's are the best charts that clear the intricacies of this strait, and I consulted them attentively. Round the *Nautilus* the sea dashed furiously. The course of the waves, that went from south-east to north-west at the rate of two and a half miles, broke on the coral that showed itself here and there.

"This is a bad sea!" remarked Ned Land.

"Detestable indeed, and one that does not suit a boat like the *Nautilus*."

"The captain must be very sure of his route, for I see there pieces of coral that would do for its keel if it only touched them slightly."

Indeed the situation was dangerous, but the *Nautilus* seemed to slide like magic off these rocks. It did not follow the routes of the *Astrolabe* and the *Boussole* exactly, for they proved fatal to Dumont d'Urville. It bore more northwards, coasted the Islands of Murray, and came back to the south-west towards Cumberland Passage. I thought it was going to pass it by, when, going back to north-west, it went through a large quantity of islands and islets little known, towards the Island Sound and Canal Mauvais.

I wondered if Captain Nemo, foolishly imprudent, would steer his vessel into that pass where Dumont d'Urville's two corvettes touched; when, swerving again, and cutting straight through to the west, he steered for the island of Gilboa.

It was then three in the afternoon. The tide began to recede, being quite full. The *Nautilus* approached the island, that I still saw, with its remarkable border of screw-pines. He stood off it at about two miles distant. Suddenly a shock overthrew me. The *Nautilus* just touched a rock, and stayed immovable, laying lightly to port side.

When I rose, I perceived Captain Nemo and his lieutenant on the platform. They were examining the situation of the vessel, and exchanging words in their incomprehensible dialect.

She was situated thus: Two miles, on the starboard side, appeared Gilboa, stretching from north to west like an immense arm; towards the south and east some coral showed itself, left by the ebb. We had run aground, and in one of those seas where the tides are middling—a sorry matter for the floating of the *Nautilus*. However, the vessel had not suffered, for her keel was solidly joined. But, if she could neither glide off nor move, she ran the risk of being forever fastened to these rocks, and then Captain Nemo's submarine vessel would be done for.

I was reflecting thus, when the captain, cool and calm, always master of himself, approached me.

"An accident?" I asked.

"No; an incident."

"But an incident that will oblige you perhaps to become an inhabitant of this land from which you flee?"

Captain Nemo looked at me curiously, and made a negative gesture, as much as to say that nothing would force him to set foot on *terra firma* again. Then he said:

"Besides, M. Aronnax, the *Nautilus* is not lost; it will carry you yet into the midst of the marvels of the ocean. Our voyage is only begun, and I do not wish to be deprived so soon of the honour of your company."

"However, Captain Nemo," I replied, without noticing the ironical turn of his phrase, "the *Nautilus* ran aground in open sea. Now the tides are not strong in the Pacific; and, if you cannot lighten the *Nautilus,* I do not see how it will be reinflated."

"The tides are not strong in the Pacific: you are right there, professor; but in Torres Straits one finds still a difference of a yard and a half between the level of high and low seas. To-day is January 4, and in five days the moon will be full. Now, I shall be very much astonished if that satellite does not raise these masses of water sufficiently, and render me a service that I should be indebted to her for."

Having said this Captain Nemo, followed by his lieutenant, redescended to the interior of the *Nautilus*. As to the vessel, it moved not, and was immovable, as if the coralline polypi had already walled it up with their indestructible cement.

"Well, sir?" said Ned Land, who came up to me after the departure of the captain.

"Well, friend Ned, we will wait patiently for the tide on the 9th instant; for it appears that the moon will have the goodness to put it off again."

"Really?"

"Really."

"And this captain is not going to cast anchor at all, since the tide will suffice?" said Conseil, simply.

The Canadian looked at Conseil, then shrugged his shoulders.

"Sir, you may believe me when I tell you that this piece of iron will navigate neither on nor under the sea again; it is only fit to be sold for its weight. I think, therefore, that the time has come to part company with Captain Nemo."

"Friend Ned, I do not despair of this stout *Nautilus,* as you do; and in four days we shall know what to hold to on the Pacific tides. Besides, flight might be possible if we were in sight of the English or Provencal coast; but on the Papuan shores, it is another thing; and it will be time enough to come to that extremity if the *Nautilus* does not recover itself again, which I look upon as a grave event."

"But do they know, at least, how to act circumspectly? There is an island; on that island there are trees; under those trees, terrestrial animals, bearers of cutlets and roast-beef, to which I would willingly give a trial."

"In this, friend Ned is right," said Conseil, "and I agree with him. Could not master obtain permission from his friend Captain Nemo to put us on land, if only so as not to lose the habit of treading on the solid parts of our planet?"

"I can ask him, but he will refuse."

"Will master risk it?" asked Conseil. "And we shall know how to rely upon the captain's amiability."

To my great surprise Captain Nemo gave me the permission I asked for, and he gave it very agreeably, without even exacting from me a promise to return to the vessel; but flight across New Guinea might be very perilous, and I should not have counselled Ned Land to attempt it. Better to be a prisoner on board the *Nautilus* than to fall into the hands of the natives.

At eight o'clock, armed with guns and hatchets, we got off the *Nautilus*. The sea was pretty calm; a slight breeze blew on land. Conseil and I rowing, we sped along quickly, and Ned steered in the straight passage that the breakers left between them. The boat was well handled, and moved rapidly.

Ned Land could not restrain his joy. He was like a prisoner that had escaped from prison, and knew not that it was necessary to re-enter it.

"Meat! We are going to eat some meat; and what meat!" he replied. "Real game! No, bread, indeed. I do not say that fish is not good; we must not abuse it; but a piece of fresh venison grilled on live coals will agreeably vary our ordinary course."

"Gourmand!" said Conseil. "He makes my mouth water."

"It remains to be seen," I said, "if these forests are full of game, and if the game is not such as will hunt the hunter himself."

"Well said, M. Aronnax," replied the Canadian, whose teeth seemed sharpened like the edge of a hatchet; "but I will eat tiger—loin of tiger—if there is no other quadruped on this island."

"Friend Ned is uneasy about it," said Conseil.

"Whatever it may be," continued Ned Land, "every animal with four paws without feathers, or with two paws without feathers, will be saluted by my first shot."

"Very well! Master Land's imprudences are beginning."

"Never fear, M. Aronnax," replied the Canadian; "I do not want twenty-five minutes to offer you a dish of my sort."

At half-past eight the *Nautilus'* boat ran softly aground, on a heavy sand, after having happily passed the coral reef that surrounds the island of Gilboa.

Chapter XX

A Few Days on Land

I WAS MUCH IMPRESSED ON TOUCHING LAND. NED LAND TRIED THE SOIL WITH HIS FEET, AS if to take possession of it. However, it was only two months before that we had become, according to Captain Nemo, "passengers on board the *Nautilus*," but, in reality, prisoners of its commander.

In a few minutes we were within musket-shot of the coast. The soil was almost entirely madreporical, but certain beds of dried-up torrents strewn with debris of granite showed that this island was of the primary formation. The whole horizon was hidden behind a beautiful curtain of forests. Enormous trees, the trunks of which attained a height of 200 feet, were tied to each other by garlands of bindweed, real natural hammocks, which a light breeze rocked. They were mimosas, focuses, casuarinae, teks, hibisci, and palm-trees, mingled together in profusion; and under the shelter of their verdant vault grew orchids, leguminous plants, and ferns.

But without noticing all these beautiful specimens of Papuan flora, the Canadian abandoned the agreeable for the useful. He discovered a cocoa-tree, beat down some of the fruit, broke them, and we drunk the milk and ate the nut with a satisfaction that protested against the ordinary food on the *Nautilus.*

"Excellent!" said Ned Land.

"Exquisite!" replied Conseil.

"And I do not think," said the Canadian, "that he would object to our introducing a cargo of cocoa-nuts on board."

"I do not think he would, but he would not taste them."

"So much the worse for him," said Conseil.

"And so much the better for us," replied Ned Land. "There will be more for us."

"One word only, Master Land," I said to the harpooner, who was beginning to ravage another cocoa-nut-tree. "Cocoa-nuts are good things, but before filling the canoe with them, it would be wise to reconnoitre and see if the island does not produce some substance not less useful. Fresh vegetables would be welcome on board the *Nautilus.*"

"Master is right," replied Conseil; "and I propose to reserve three places in our vessel: one for fruits, the other for vegetables, and the third for the venison, of which I have not yet seen the smallest specimen."

"Conseil, we must not despair," said the Canadian.

"Let us continue," I returned, "and lie in wait. Although the island seems uninhabited, it might still contain some individuals that would be less hard than we on the nature of game."

"Ho! ho!" said Ned Land, moving his jaws significantly.

"Well, Ned!" said Conseil.

"My word!" returned the Canadian, "I begin to understand the charms of anthropophagy."

"Ned! Ned! What are you saying? You, a man-eater? I should not feel safe with you, especially as I share your cabin. I might perhaps wake one day to find myself half-devoured."

"Friend Conseil, I like you much, but not enough to eat you unnecessarily."

"I would not trust you," replied Conseil. "But enough. We must absolutely bring down some game to satisfy this cannibal, or else one of these fine mornings, master will find only pieces of his servant to serve him."

While we were talking thus, we were penetrating the sombre arches of the forest, and for two hours we surveyed it in all directions.

Chance rewarded our search for eatable vegetables, and one of the most useful products of the tropical zones furnished us with precious food that we missed on board. I would speak of the bread-fruit-tree, very abundant in the island of Gilboa; and I remarked chiefly the variety destitute of seeds, which bears in Malaya the name of "rima."

Ned Land knew these fruits well. He had already eaten many during his numerous voyages, and he knew how to prepare the eatable substance. Moreover, the sight of them excited him, and he could contain himself no longer.

"Master," he said, "I shall die if I do not taste a little of this bread-fruit pie."

"Taste it, friend Ned, taste it as you want. We are here to make experiments—make them."

"It won't take long," said the Canadian.

And, provided with a lentil, he lighted a fire of dead wood that crackled joyously. During this time, Conseil and I chose the best fruits of the artocarpus. Some had not then attained a sufficient degree of maturity; and their thick skin covered a white but rather fibrous pulp. Others, the greater number yellow and gelatinous, waited only to be picked.

These fruits enclosed no kernel. Conseil brought a dozen to Ned Land, who placed them on a coal fire, after having cut them in thick slices, and while doing this repeating:

"You will see, master, how good this bread is. More so when one has been deprived of it so long. It is not even bread," added he, "but a delicate pastry. You have eaten none, master?"

"No, Ned."

"Very well, prepare yourself for a juicy thing. If you do not come for more, I am no longer the king of harpooners."

After some minutes, the part of the fruits that was exposed to the fire was completely roasted. The interior looked like a white pasty, a sort of soft crumb, the flavour of which was like that of an artichoke.

It must be confessed this bread was excellent, and I ate of it with great relish.

"What time is it now?" asked the Canadian.

"Two o'clock at least," replied Conseil.

"How time flies on firm ground!" sighed Ned Land.

"Let us be off," replied Conseil.

We returned through the forest, and completed our collection by a raid upon the cabbage-palms, that we gathered from the tops of the trees, little beans that I recognised as the "abrou" of the Malays, and yams of a superior quality.

We were loaded when we reached the boat. But Ned Land did not find his provisions sufficient. Fate, however, favoured us. Just as we were pushing off, he perceived several trees, from twenty-five to thirty feet high, a species of palm-tree. These trees, as valuable as the artocarpus, justly are reckoned among the most useful products of Malaya.

At last, at five o'clock in the evening, loaded with our riches, we quitted the shore, and half an hour after we hailed the *Nautilus*. No one appeared on our arrival. The enormous iron-plated cylinder seemed deserted. The provisions embarked, I descended to my chamber, and after supper slept soundly.

The next day, January 6, nothing new on board. Not a sound inside, not a sign of life. The boat rested along the edge, in the same place in which we had left it. We resolved to return to the island. Ned Land hoped to be more fortunate than on the day before with regard to the hunt, and wished to visit another part of the forest.

At dawn we set off. The boat, carried on by the waves that flowed to shore, reached the island in a few minutes.

We landed, and, thinking that it was better to give in to the Canadian, we followed Ned Land, whose long limbs threatened to distance us. He wound up the coast towards the west; then, fording some torrents, he gained the high plain that was bordered with admirable forests. Some kingfishers were rambling along the water-courses, but they would not let themselves be approached. Their circumspection proved to me that these birds knew what to expect from bipeds of our species, and I concluded that, if the island was not inhabited, at least human beings occasionally frequented it.

After crossing a rather large prairie, we arrived at the skirts of a little wood that was enlivened by the songs and flight of a large number of birds.

"There are only birds!" said Conseil.

"But they are eatable," replied the harpooner.

"I do not agree with you, friend Ned, for I see only parrots there."

"Friend Conseil," said Ned, gravely, "the parrot is like pheasant to those who have nothing else."

"And," I added, "this bird, suitably prepared, is worth knife and fork."

Indeed, under the thick foliage of this wood, a world of parrots were flying from branch to branch, only needing a careful education to speak the human language. For the moment, they were chattering with parrots of all colours, and grave cockatoos, who seemed to meditate upon some philosophical problem, while brilliant red lories passed like a piece of bunting carried away by the breeze; Papuans, with the finest azure colours, and in all a variety of winged things most charming to behold, but few eatable.

However, a bird peculiar to these lands, and which has never passed the limits of the Arrow and Papuan islands, was wanting in this collection. But fortune reserved it for me before long.

After passing through a moderately thick copse, we found a plain obstructed with bushes. I saw then those magnificent birds, the disposition of whose long feathers obliges them to fly against the wind. Their undulating flight, graceful aerial curves, and the shading of their colours, attracted and charmed one's looks. I had no trouble in recognising them.

"Birds of paradise!" I exclaimed.

The Malays, who carry on a great trade in these birds with the Chinese, have several means that we could not employ for taking them. Sometimes they put snares on the top of high trees that the birds of paradise prefer to frequent. Sometimes they catch them with a viscous birdlime that paralyses their movements. They even go so far as to poison the fountains that the birds generally drink from. But we were obliged to fire at them during flight, which gave us few chances to bring them down; and, indeed, we vainly exhausted one-half of our ammunition.

About eleven o'clock in the morning, the first range of mountains that form the centre of the island was traversed, and we had killed nothing. Hunger drove us on. The hunters had relied on the products of the chase, and they were wrong. Happily Conseil, to his great surprise, made a double shot and secured breakfast. He brought down a white pigeon and a wood-pigeon, which, cleverly plucked and suspended from a skewer, was roasted before a red fire of dead wood. While these interesting birds were cooking, Ned prepared the fruit of the artocarpus. Then the wood-pigeons were devoured·to the bones, and declared excellent. The nutmeg, with which they are in the habit of stuffing their crops, flavours their flesh and renders it delicious eating.

"Now, Ned, what do you miss now?"

"Some four-footed game, M. Aronnax. All these pigeons are only side-dishes and trifles; and until I have killed an animal with cutlets, I shall not be content."

"Nor I, Ned, if I do not catch a bird of paradise."

"Let us continue hunting," replied Conseil. "Let us go towards the sea. We have arrived at the first declivities of the mountains, and I think we had better regain the region of forests."

That was sensible advice, and was followed out. After walking for one hour we had attained a forest of sago-trees. Some inoffensive serpents glided away from us. The birds of paradise fled at our approach, and truly I despaired of getting near one, when Conseil, who was walking in front, suddenly bent down, uttered a triumphal cry, and came back to me bringing a magnificent specimen.

"Ah! bravo, Conseil!"

"Master is very good."

"No, my boy; you have made an excellent stroke. Take one of these living birds, and carry it in your hand."

"If master will examine it, he will see that I have not deserved great merit."

"Why, Conseil?"

"Because this bird is as drunk as a quail."

"Drunk!"

"Yes, sir; drunk with the nutmegs that it devoured under the nutmeg-tree under which I found it. See, friend Ned, see the monstrous effects of intemperance!"

"By Jove!" exclaimed the Canadian, "because I have drunk gin for two months, you must needs reproach me!"

However, I examined the curious bird. Conseil was right. The bird, drunk with the juice, was quite powerless. It could not fly; it could hardly walk.

This bird belonged to the most beautiful of the eight species that are found in Papua and in the neighboring islands. It was the "large emerald bird, the most rare kind." It measured three feet in length. Its head was comparatively small, its eyes placed near the opening of the beak, and also small. But the shades of colour were beautiful, having a yellow beak, brown feet and claws, nut-coloured wings with purple tips, pale yellow at the back of the neck and head, and emerald colour at the throat, chestnut on the breast and belly. Two horned downy nets rose from below the tail, that prolonged the long light feathers of admirable fineness, and they completed the whole of this marvellous bird, that the natives have poetically named the "bird of the sun."

But if my wishes were satisfied by the possession of the bird of paradise, the Canadian's were not yet. Happily about two o'clock Ned Land brought down a magnificent hog, from the brood of those the natives call "bari-outang." The animal came in time for us to procure real quadruped meat, and he was well received. Ned Land was very proud of his shot. The hog, hit by the electric ball, fell stone dead. The Canadian skinned and cleaned it properly, after having taken half-a-dozen cutlets, destined to furnish us with a grilled repast in the evening. Then the hunt was resumed, which was still more marked by Ned and Conseil's exploits.

Indeed, the two friends, beating the bushes, roused a herd of kangaroos, that fled and bounded along on their elastic paws. But these animals did not take to flight so rapidly but what the electric capsule could stop their course.

"Ah, professor!" cried Ned Land, who was carried away by the delights of the chase. "What excellent game! and stewed, too! What a supply for the *Nautilus!* two! three! five down! And to think that we shall eat that flesh, and that the idiots on board shall not have a crumb!"

I think that, in the excess of his joy, the Canadian, if he had not talked so much, would have killed them all. But he contented himself with a single dozen of these interesting marsupians. These animals were small. They were a species of those "kangaroo rabbits" that live habitually in the hollows of trees, and whose speed is extreme; but they are moderately fat, and furnish, at least, estimable food. We were very satisfied with the results of the hunt. Happy Ned proposed to return to this enchanting island the next day, for he wished to depopulate it of all the eatable quadrupeds. But he had reckoned without his host.

At six o'clock in the evening we had regained the shore; our boat was moored to the usual place. The *Nautilus*, like a long rock, emerged from the waves two miles from the beach. Ned Land, without waiting, occupied himself about the important dinner business. He understood all about cooking well. The "bari-outang," grilled on the coals, soon scented the air with a delicious odour.

Indeed, the dinner was excellent. Two wood-pigeons completed this extraordinary *menu*. The sago pasty, the artocarpus bread, some mangoes, half a dozen pineapples, and the liquor fermented from some cocoa-nuts, overjoyed us. I even think that my worthy companions' ideas had not all the plainness desirable.

"Suppose we do not return to the *Nautilus* this evening?" said Conseil.

"Suppose we never return?" added Ned Land.

Just then a stone fell at our feet and cut short the harpooner's proposition.

Chapter XXI

CAPTAIN NEMO'S THUNDERBOLT

WE LOOKED AT THE EDGE OF THE FOREST WITHOUT RISING, MY HAND STOPPING IN the action of putting it to my mouth, Ned Land's completing its office.

"Stones do not fall from the sky," remarked Conseil, "or they would merit the name aerolites."

A second stone, carefully aimed, that made a savoury pigeon's leg fall from Conseil's hand, gave still more weight to his observation. We all three arose, shouldered our guns, and were ready to reply to any attack.

"Are they apes?" cried Ned Land.

"Very nearly—they are savages."

"To the boat!" I said, hurrying to the sea.

It was indeed necessary to beat a retreat, for about twenty natives, armed with bows and slings appeared on the skirts of a copse that masked the horizon to the right, hardly a hundred steps from us.

Our boat was moored about sixty feet from us. The savages approached us, not running, but making hostile demonstrations. Stones and arrows fell thickly.

Ned Land had not wished to leave his provisions; and, in spite of his imminent danger, his pig on one side and kangaroos on the other, he went tolerably fast. In two minutes we were on the shore. To load the boat with provisions and arms, to push it out to sea, and ship the oars, was the work of an instant. We had not gone two cables' lengths when a hundred savages, howling and gesticulating, entered the water up to their waists. I watched to see if their apparition would attract some men from the *Nautilus* on to the platform. But no. The enormous machine, lying off, was absolutely deserted.

Twenty minutes later we were on board. The panels were open. After making the boat fast, we entered into the interior of the *Nautilus*.

I descended to the drawing-room, from whence I heard some chords. Captain Nemo was there, bending over his organ, and plunged in a musical ecstasy.

"Captain!"

He did not hear me.

"Captain!" I said again, touching his hand.

He shuddered, and, turning round, said, "Ah! it is you, professor? Well, have you had a good hunt? Have you botanised successfully?"

"Yes, captain; but we have unfortunately brought a troop of bipeds, whose vicinity troubles me."

"What bipeds?"

"Savages."

"Savages!" he echoed, ironically. "So you are astonished, Professor, at having set foot on a strange land and finding savages? Savages! where are there not any? Besides, are they worse than others, these whom you call savages?"

"But, captain——"

"How many have you counted?"

"A hundred at least."

"M. Aronnax," replied Captain Nemo, placing his fingers on the organ stops, "when all the natives of Papua are assembled on this shore, the *Nautilus* will have nothing to fear from their attacks."

The captain's fingers were then running over the keys of the instrument, and I remarked that he touched only the black keys, which gave his melodies an essentially Scotch character. Soon he had forgotten my presence, and had plunged into a reverie that I did not disturb. I went up again on to the platform—night had already fallen; for, in this low latitude, the sun sets rapidly and without twilight. I could only see the island indistinctly; but the numerous fires lighted on the beach showed that the natives did not think of leaving it. I was alone for several hours, sometimes thinking of the natives—but without any dread of them, for the imperturbable confidence of the captain was catching—sometimes forgetting them to admire the splendours of the night in the tropics. My remembrances went to France, in the train of those zodiacal stars that would shine in some hours' time. The moon shone in the midst of the constellations of the zenith.

The night slipped away without any mischance, the islanders frightened no doubt at the sight of a monster aground in the bay. The panels were open, and would have offered an easy access to the interior of the *Nautilus*.

At six o'clock in the morning of the 8th of January I went up on to the platform. The dawn was breaking. The island soon showed itself through the dissipating fogs—first the shore, then the summits.

The natives were there, more numerous than on the day before—500 or 600 perhaps—some of them, profiting by the low water, had come on to the coral, at less than two cables' lengths from the *Nautilus*. I distinguished them easily; they were true Papuans, with athletic figures, men of good race, large high foreheads—large, but not broad, and flat—and white teeth. Their woolly hair, with a reddish tinge, showed off on their black shining bodies like those of the Nubians. From the lobes of their ears, cut and distended, hung chaplets of bones. Most of these savages were naked. Among them I remarked some women, dressed from the hips to knees in quite a crinoline of herbs, that sustained a vegetable waistband. Some chiefs had ornamented their necks with a crescent and collars of glass beads, red and white; nearly all were armed with bows, arrows, and shields, and carried on their shoulders a sort of net containing those round stones which they cast from their slings with great skill. One of these chiefs, rather near to the *Nautilus*, examined it attentively. He was, perhaps, a "mado" of high rank, for he was draped in a mat of banana leaves notched round the edges, and set off with brilliant colours.

I could easily have knocked down this native, who was within a short length; but I thought that it was better to wait for real hostile demonstrations. Between Europeans and savages, it is proper for the Europeans to parry sharply, not to attack.

During low water the natives roamed about near the *Nautilus*, but were not troublesome; I heard them frequently repeat the word "Assai," and by their gestures I understood that they invited me to go on land, an invitation that I declined.

So that, on that day, the boat did not push off, to the great displeasure of Master Land, who could not complete his provisions.

This adroit Canadian employed his time in preparing the viands and meat that he had brought off the island. As for the savages, they returned to the shore about eleven o'clock in the morning, as soon as the coral tops began to disappear under the rising tide; but I saw their numbers had increased considerably on the shore. Probably they came from the neighboring islands, or very likely from Papua. However, I had not seen a single native canoe. Having nothing better to do, I thought of dragging these beautiful limpid waters, under which I saw a profusion of shells, zoöphytes, and marine plants. Moreover, it was the last day that the *Nautilus* would pass in these parts, if it float in open sea the next day, according to Captain Nemo's promise.

I therefore called Conseil, who brought me a little light drag, very like those for the oyster fishery. Now to work! For two hours we fished unceasingly, but without bringing up any rarities. The drag was filled with midas-ears, harps, melames, and particularly the most beautiful hammers I have ever seen. We also brought up some holothurias, pearl oysters, and a dozen little turtles that were reserved for the pantry on board.

But just when I expected it least, I put my hand on a wonder, I might say a natural deformity, very rarely met with. Conseil was just dragging, and his net came up filled with divers ordinary shells, when, all at once, he saw me plunge my arm quickly into the net, to draw out a shell, and heard me utter a conchological cry, that is to say, the most piercing cry that human throat can utter.

"What is the matter, sir?" he asked in surprise. "Has master been bitten?"

"No, my boy; but I would willingly have given a finger for my discovery."

"What discovery?"

"This shell," I said, holding up the object of my triumph.

"It is simply an olive porphyry, genus olive, order of the pectinibranchidae, class of gasteropods, sub-class of mollusca."

"Yes, Conseil; but instead of being rolled from right to left, this olive turns from left to right."

"Is it possible?"

"Yes, my boy; it is a left shell."

Shells are all right-handed, with rare exceptions; and when by chance their spiral is left, amateurs are ready to pay their weight in gold.

Conseil and I were absorbed in the contemplation of our treasure, and I was promising myself to enrich the museum with it, when a stone, unfortunately thrown by a native, struck against and broke the precious object in Conseil's hand. I uttered a cry of despair! Conseil took up his gun, and aimed at a savage who was poising his sling at ten yards from him. I would have stopped him, but his blow took effect, and broke the bracelet of amulets which encircled the arm of the savage.

"Conseil!" cried I; "Conseil!"

"Well, sir! do you not see that the cannibal has commenced the attack?"

"A shell is not worth the life of a man," said I.

"Ah! the scoundrel!" cried Conseil; "I would rather he had broken my shoulder!"

Conseil was in earnest, but I was not of his opinion. However, the situation had changed some minutes before, and we had not perceived. A score of canoes surrounded the *Nautilus*. These canoes, scooped out of the trunk of a tree, long, narrow, well adapted for speed, were balanced by means of a long bamboo pole, which floated on the water. They were managed by skilful, half-naked paddlers, and I watched their advance with some uneasiness. It was evident that these Papuans had already had dealings with the Europeans and knew their ships. But this long iron cylinder anchored in the bay, without masts or chimneys, what could they think of it? Nothing good, for at first they kept at a respectful distance. However, seeing it motionless, by degrees they took courage, and sought to familiarise themselves with it. Now this familiarity was precisely what it was necessary to avoid. Our arms, which were noiseless, could only produce a moderate effect on the savages, who have little respect for aught but blustering things. The thunderbolt without the reverberations of thunder would frighten man but little, though the danger lies in the lightning, not in the noise.

At this moment the canoes approached the *Nautilus*, and a shower of arrows alighted on her.

I went down to the saloon, but found no one there. I ventured to knock at the door that opened into the captain's room. "Come in," was the answer.

I entered, and found Captain Nemo deep in algebraical calculations of x and other quantities.

"I am disturbing you," said I, for courtesy's sake.

"That is true, M. Aronnax," replied the captain; "but I think you have serious reasons for wishing to see me?"

"Very grave ones; the natives are surrounding us in their canoes, and in a few minutes we shall certainly be attacked by many hundreds of savages."

"Ah!" said Captain Nemo quietly. "They are come with their canoes?"

"Yes, sir."

"Well, sir, we must close the hatches."

"Exactly, and I came to say to you——"

"Nothing can be more simple," said Captain Nemo. And pressing an electric button, he transmitted an order to the ship's crew.

"It is all done, sir," said he, after some moments. "The pinnace is ready, and the hatches are closed. You do not fear, I imagine, that these gentlemen could stave in walls on which the balls of your frigate have had no effect?"

"No, captain; but a danger still exists."

"What is that, sir?"

"It is that to-morrow, at about this hour, we must open the hatches to renew the air of the *Nautilus*. Now if, at this moment, the Papuans should occupy the platform, I do not see how you could prevent them from entering."

"Then, sir, you suppose that they will board us?"

"I am certain of it."

"Well, sir, let them come. I see no reason for hindering them. After all, these Papuans are poor creatures, and I am unwilling that my visit to the island of Gueberoan should cost the life of a single one of these wretches."

Upon that I was going away; but Captain Nemo detained me, and asked me to sit down by him. He questioned me with interest about our excursions on shore, and our hunting; and seemed not to understand the craving for meat that possessed the Canadian. Then the conversation turned on various subjects, and without being more communicative, Captain Nemo showed himself more amiable.

Among other things, we happened to speak of the situation of the *Nautilus*, run aground in exactly the same spot in this strait where Dumont d'Urville was nearly lost. Apropos of this:

"This D'Urville was one of your great sailors," said the captain to me, "one of your most intelligent navigators. He is the Captain Cook of you Frenchmen. Unfortunate man of science, after having braved the icebergs of the South Pole, the coral reefs of Oceania, the cannibals of the Pacific, to perish miserably in a railway train! If this energetic man could have reflected during the last moments of his life, what must have been uppermost in his last thoughts, do you suppose?"

So speaking, Captain Nemo seemed moved, and his emotion gave me a better opinion of him. Then, chart in hand, we reviewed the travels of the French navigator, his voyages of circumnavigation, his double detention at the South Pole, which led to the discovery of Adelaide and Louis Philippe, and fixing the hydrographical bearings of the principal islands of Oceania.

"That which your D'Urville has done on the surface of the seas," said Captain Nemo, "that have I done under them, and more easily, more completely than he. The *Astrolabe* and the *Boussole*, incessantly tossed about by the hurricane, could not be worth the *Nautilus*, quiet repository of labour that she is, truly motionless in the midst of the waters.

"To-morrow," added the captain, rising, "to-morrow, at twenty minutes to three P.M., the *Nautilus* shall float, and leave the Strait of Torres uninjured."

Having curtly pronounced these words, Captain Nemo bowed slightly. This was to dismiss me, and I went back to my room.

There I found Conseil, who wished to know the result of my interview with the captain.

"My boy," said I, "when I feigned to believe that his *Nautilus* was threatened by the natives of Papua, the captain answered me very sarcastically. I have but one thing to say to you: Have confidence in him, and go to sleep in peace."

"Have you no need of my services, sir?"

"No, my friend. What is Ned Land doing?"

"If you will excuse me, sir," answered Conseil, "friend Ned is busy making a kangaroo-pie, which will be a marvel."

I remained alone, and went to bed, but slept indifferently. I heard the noise of the savages, who stamped on the platform, uttering deafening cries. The night passed thus, without disturbing the ordinary repose of the crew. The presence of these cannibals affected them no more than the soldiers of a masked battery care for the ants that crawl over its front.

At six in the morning I rose. The hatches had not been opened. The inner air was not renewed, but the reservoirs, filled ready for any emergency, were now resorted to, and discharged several cubic feet of oxygen into the exhausted atmosphere of the *Nautilus*.

I worked in my room till noon, without having seen Captain Nemo, even for an instant. On board no preparations for departure were visible.

I waited still some time, then went into the large saloon. The clock marked half-past two. In ten minutes it would be high tide, and if Captain Nemo had not made a rash promise, the *Nautilus* would be immediately detached. If not, many months would pass ere she could leave her bed of coral.

However, some warning vibrations began to be felt in the vessel. I heard the keel grating against the rough calcareous bottom of the coral reef.

At five-and-twenty minutes to three, Captain Nemo appeared in the saloon.

"We are going to start," said he.

"Ah!" replied I.

"I have given the order to open the hatches."

"And the Papuans?"

"The Papuans?" answered Captain Nemo, slightly shrugging his shoulders.

"Will they not come inside the *Nautilus*?"

"How?"

"Only by leaping over the hatches you have opened."

"M. Aronnax," quietly answered Captain Nemo, "they will not enter the hatches of the *Nautilus* in that way, even if they were open."

I looked at the captain.

"You do not understand?" said he.

"Hardly."

"Well, come and you will see."

I directed my steps towards the central staircase. There Ned Land and Conseil were slyly watching some of the ship's crew, who were opening the hatches, while cries of rage and fearful vociferations resounded outside.

The port lids were pulled down outside. Twenty horrible faces appeared. But the first native who placed his hand on the stair-rail, struck from behind by some invisible force, I know not what, fled, uttering the most fearful cries and making the wildest contortions.

Ten of his companions followed him. They met with the same fate.

Conseil was in ecstasy. Ned Land, carried away by his violent instincts, rushed on to the staircase. But the moment he seized the rail with both hands, he, in his turn, was overthrown.

"I am struck by a thunderbolt," cried he, with an oath.

This explained all. It was no rail; but a metallic cable charged with electricity from the deck communicating with the platform. Whoever touched it felt a powerful shock—and this shock would have been mortal, if Captain Nemo had discharged into the conductor the whole force of the current. It might truly be said that between his assailants and himself he had stretched a network of electricity which none could pass with impunity.

Meanwhile, the exasperated Papuans had beaten a retreat, paralysed with terror. As for us, half-laughing, we consoled and rubbed the unfortunate Ned Land, who swore like one possessed.

But at this moment, the *Nautilus*, raised by the last waves of the tide, quitted her coral bed exactly at the fortieth minute fixed by the Captain. Her screw swept the waters slowly and majestically. Her speed increased gradually, and sailing on the surface of the ocean, she quitted safe and sound the dangerous passes of the Straits of Torres.

Chapter XXII

"ÆGRI SOMNIA"

THE FOLLOWING DAY, 10TH OF JANUARY, THE *NAUTILUS* CONTINUED HER COURSE BEtween two seas, but with such remarkable speed that I could not estimate it at less than thirty-five miles an hour. The rapidity of her screw was such that I could neither follow nor count its revolutions. When I reflected that this marvellous electric agent, after having afforded motion, heat, and light to the *Nautilus*, still protected her from outward attack, and transformed her into an ark of safety which no profane hand might touch without being thunderstricken, my admiration was unbounded, and from the structure it extended to the engineer who had called it into existence.

Our course was directed to the west, and on the 11th of January we doubled Cape Wessel, situated in 135° longitude and 10° north latitude, which forms the east point of the Gulf of Carpentaria. The reefs were still numerous, but more equalised, and marked on the chart with extreme precision. The *Nautilus* easily avoided the breakers of Money to port, and the Victoria reefs to starboard, placed at 130° longitude and on the tenth parallel which we strictly followed.

On the 13th of January, Captain Nemo arrived in the Sea of Timor, and recognised the island of that name in 122° longitude.

From this point the direction of the *Nautilus* inclined towards the south-west. Her head was set for the Indian Ocean. Where would the fancy of Captain Nemo carry us next? Would he return to the coast of Asia, or would he approach again the shores of Europe? Improbable conjectures both, for a man who fled from inhabited continents. Then, would he descend to the south? Was he going to double the Cape of Good Hope, then

Cape Horn, and finally go as far as the antarctic pole? Would he come back at last to the Pacific, where his *Nautilus* could sail free and independently? Time would show.

After having skirted the sands of Cartier, of Hibernia, Seringapatam, and Scott, last efforts of the solid against the liquid element, on the 14th of January we lost sight of land altogether. The speed of the *Nautilus* was considerably abated, and with irregular course she sometimes swam in the bosom of the waters, sometimes floated on their surface.

During this period of the voyage, Captain Nemo made some interesting experiments on the varied temperature of the sea, in different beds. Under ordinary conditions, these observations are made by means of rather complicated instruments, and with somewhat doubtful results, by means of thermometrical sounding-leads, the glasses often breaking under the pressure of the water, or an apparatus grounded on the variations of the resistance of metals to the electric currents. Results so obtained could not be correctly calculated. On the contrary, Captain Nemo went himself to test the temperature in the depths of the sea, and his thermometer, placed in communication with the different sheets of water, gave him the required degree immediately and accurately.

It was thus that, either by overloading her reservoirs, or by descending obliquely by means of her inclined planes the *Nautilus* successively attained the depth of three, four, five, seven, nine, and ten thousand yards, and the definite result of this experience was that the sea preserved an average temperature of four degrees and a half, at a depth of five thousand fathoms under all latitudes.

On the 16th of January, the *Nautilus* seemed becalmed, only a few yards beneath the surface of the waves. Her electric apparatus remained inactive, and her motionless screw left her to drift at the mercy of the currents. I supposed that the crew was occupied with interior repairs, rendered necessary by the violence of the mechanical movements of the machine.

My companions and I then witnessed a curious spectacle. The hatches of the saloon were open, and as the beacon-light of the *Nautilus* was not in action, a dim obscurity reigned in the midst of the waters. I observed the state of the sea under these conditions, and the largest fish appeared to me no more than scarcely defined shadows, when the *Nautilus* found herself suddenly transported into full light. I thought at first that the beacon had been lighted, and was casting its electric radiance into the liquid mass. I was mistaken, and after a rapid survey perceived my error.

The *Nautilus* floated in the midst of a phosphorescent bed, which, in this obscurity, became quite dazzling. It was produced by myriads of luminous animalculae, whose brilliancy was increased as they glided over the metallic hull of the vessel. I was surprised by lightning in the midst of these luminous sheets, as though they bad been rivulets of lead melted in an ardent furnace, or metallic masses brought to a white heat, so that, by force of contrast, certain portions of light appeared to cast a shade in the midst of the general ignition, from which all shade seemed banished. No; this was not the calm irradiation of our ordinary lightning. There was unusual life and vigour, this was truly living light!

In reality, it was an infinite agglomeration of coloured infusoria, of veritable globules of diaphanous jelly, provided with a thread-like tentacle, and of which as many as twenty-five thousand have been counted in less than two cubic half-inches of water; and their light was increased by the glimmering peculiar to the medusae, starfish, aurelia, and other phosphorescent zoöphytes, impregnated by the grease of the organic matter decomposed by the sea, and, perhaps, the mucus secreted by the fish.

During several hours the *Nautilus* floated in these brilliant waves, and our admiration increased as we watched the marine monsters disporting themselves like salamanders. I saw there in the midst of this fire that burns not, the swift and elegant porpoise (the indefatigable clown of the ocean), and some sword-fish ten feet long, those prophetic heralds of the hurricane, whose formidable sword would now and then strike the glass of the saloon. Then appeared the smaller fish, the variegated balista, the leaping mackerel, wolfthorn-tails, and a hundred others which striped the luminous atmosphere as they swam. This dazzling spectacle was enchanting! Perhaps some atmospheric condition increased the intensity of this phenomenon. Perhaps some storm agitated the surface of the waves. But, at this depth of some yards, the *Nautilus* was unmoved by its fury, and reposed peacefully in still water.

So we progressed, incessantly charmed by some new marvel. Conseil arranged and classed his zoöphytes, his articulata, his molluscs, his fishes. The days passed rapidly away, and I took no account of them. Ned, according to habit, tried to vary the diet on board. Like snails, we were fixed to our shells, and I declare it is easy to lead a snail's life.

Thus this life seemed easy and natural, and we thought no longer of the life we led on land; but something happened to recall us to the strangeness of our situation.

On the 18th of January, the *Nautilus* was in 105° longitude and 15° south latitude. The weather was threatening, the sea rough and rolling. There was a strong east wind. The barometer, which had been going down for some days, foreboded a coming storm. I went up on to the platform just as the second lieutenant was taking the measure of the horary angles, and waited, according to habit, till the daily phrase was said. But, on this day, it was exchanged for another phrase not less incomprehensible. Almost directly, I saw Captain Nemo appear, with a glass, looking towards the horizon.

For some minutes he was immovable, without taking his eye off the point of observation. Then he lowered his glass, and exchanged a few words with his lieutenant. The latter seemed to be a victim to some emotion that he tried in vain to repress. Captain Nemo, having more command over himself, was cool. He seemed, too, to be making some objections, to which the lieutenant replied by formal assurances; at least I concluded so by the difference of their tones and gestures. For myself, I had looked carefully in the direction indicated without seeing anything. The sky and water were lost in the clear line of the horizon.

However, Captain Nemo walked from one end of the platform to the other, without looking at me, perhaps without seeing me. His step was firm, but less regular than usual. He stopped sometimes, crossed his arms, and observed the sea. What could he be looking for on that immense expanse?

The *Nautilus* was then some hundreds of miles from the nearest coast.

The lieutenant had taken up the glass and examined the horizon steadfastly, going and coming, stamping his foot and showing more nervous agitation than his superior officer. Besides, this mystery must necessarily be solved, and before long; for, upon an order from Captain Nemo, the engine, increasing its propelling power, made the screw turn more rapidly.

Just then the lieutenant drew the captain's attention again. The latter stopped walking and directed his glass towards the place indicated. He looked long. I felt very much puzzled, and descended to the drawing-room, and took out an excellent telescope that I generally used. Then, leaning on the cage of the watch-light, that jutted out from the front of the platform, set myself to look over all the line of the sky and sea.

But my eye was no sooner applied to the glass, than it was quickly snatched out of my hands.

I turned round. Captain Nemo was before me, but I did not know him. His face was transfigured. His eyes flashed sullenly; his teeth were set; his stiff body, clinched fists, and head shrunk between his shoulders, betrayed the violent agitation that pervaded his whole frame. He did not move. My glass, fallen from his hands, had rolled at his feet.

Had I unwittingly provoked this fit of anger? Did this incomprehensible person imagine that I had discovered some forbidden secret? No; I was not the object of this hatred, for he was not looking at me; his eye was steadily fixed upon the impenetrable point of the horizon. At last Captain Nemo recovered himself. His agitation subsided. He addressed some words in a foreign language to his lieutenant, then turned to me. "M. Aronnax," he said, in rather an imperious tone, "I require you to keep one of the conditions that bind you to me."

"What is it, captain?"

"You must be confined, with your companions, until I think fit to release you."

"You are the master," I replied, looking steadily at him. "But may I ask you one question?"

"None, sir."

There was no resisting this imperious command, it would have been useless. I went down to the cabin occupied by Ned Land and Conseil, and told them the captain's determination. You may judge how this communication was received by the Canadian.

But there was not time for altercation. Four of the crew waited at the door, and conducted us to that cell where we had passed our first night on board the *Nautilus*.

Ned Land would have remonstrated, but the door was shut upon him.

"Will master tell me what this means?" asked Conseil.

I told my companions what had passed. They were as much astonished as I, and equally at a loss how to account for it.

Meanwhile, I was absorbed in my own reflections, and could think of nothing but the strange fear depicted in the captain's countenance. I was utterly at a loss to account for it, when my cogitations were disturbed by these words from Ned Land:

"Hallo! Breakfast is ready."

And indeed the table was laid. Evidently Captain Nemo had given this order at the same time that he had hastened the speed of the *Nautilus*.

"Will master permit me to make a recommendation?" asked Conseil.

"Yes, my boy."

"Well, it is that master breakfast. It is prudent, for we do not know what may happen."

"You are right, Conseil."

"Unfortunately," said Ned Land, "they have only given us the ship's fare."

"Friend Ned," asked Conseil, "what would you have said if the breakfast had been entirely forgotten?"

This argument cut short the harpooner's recriminations.

We sat down to table. The meal was eaten in silence.

Just then, the luminous globe that lighted the cell went out, and left us in total darkness. Ned Land was soon asleep, and what astonished me was that Conseil went off into a heavy sleep. I was thinking what could have caused his irresistible drowsiness, when I felt my brain becoming stupefied. In spite of my efforts to keep my eyes open, they would close. A painful suspicion seized me. Evidently soporific substances had been mixed with the food we had just taken. Imprisonment was not enough to conceal Captain Nemo's projects from us; sleep was more necessary.

I then heard the panels shut. The undulations of the sea, which caused a slight rolling motion, ceased. Had the *Nautilus* quitted the surface of the ocean? Had it gone back to the motionless bed of water? I tried to resist sleep. It was impossible. My breathing grew weak. I felt a mortal cold freeze my stiffened and half-paralysed limbs. My eyelids, like leaden caps, fell over my eyes. I could not raise them; a morbid sleep, full of hallucinations, bereft me of my being. Then the visions disappeared, and left me in complete insensibility.

Chapter XXIII

THE CORAL KINGDOM

THE NEXT DAY I WOKE WITH MY HEAD SINGULARLY CLEAR. TO MY GREAT SURPRISE, I was in my own room. My companions, no doubt, had been reinstated in their cabin, without having perceived it any more than I. Of what had passed during the night they were as ignorant as I was, and to penetrate this mystery I only reckoned upon the chances of the future.

I then thought of quitting my room. Was I free again, or a prisoner? Quite free. I opened the door, went to the half-deck, went up the central stairs. The panels, shut the evening before, were open. I went on to the platform.

Ned Land and Conseil waited there for me. I questioned them; they knew nothing. Lost in a heavy sleep in which they had been totally unconscious, they had been astonished at finding themselves in their cabin.

As for the *Nautilus*, it seemed quiet and mysterious as ever. It floated on the surface of the waves at a moderate pace. Nothing seemed changed on board.

The second lieutenant then came on to the platform, and gave the usual order below.

As for Captain Nemo, he did not appear.

Of the people on board I only saw the impassive steward, who served me with his usual dumb regularity.

About two o'clock, I was in the drawing-room, busied in arranging my notes, when the captain opened the door and appeared. I bowed. He made a slight inclination in return, without speaking. I resumed my work, hoping that he would perhaps give me some explanation of the events of the preceding night. He made none. I looked at him. He seemed fatigued; his heavy eyes had not been refreshed by sleep; his face looked very sorrowful. He walked to and fro, sat down and got up again, took up a chance book, put it down, consulted his instruments without taking his habitual notes, and seemed restless and uneasy. At last he came up to me, and said:

"Are you a doctor, M. Aronnax?"

I so little expected such a question that I stared some time at him without answering.

"Are you a doctor?" he repeated. "Several of your colleagues have studied medicine."

"Well," said I, "I am a doctor and resident surgeon to the hospital. I practised several years before entering the museum."

"Very well, sir."

My answer had evidently satisfied the captain. But not knowing what he would say next, I waited for other questions, reserving my answers according to circumstances.

"M. Aronnax, will you consent to prescribe for one of my men?" he asked.

"Is he ill?"

"Yes."

"I am ready to follow you."

"Come, then."

I own my heart beat, I do not know why. I saw certain connection between the illness of one of the crew and the events of the day before; and this mystery interested me at least as much as the sick man.

Captain Nemo conducted me to the poop of the *Nautilus*, and took me into a cabin situated near the sailors' quarters.

There, on a bed, lay a man about forty years of age, with a resolute expression of countenance, a true type of an Anglo-Saxon.

I leaned over him. He was not only ill, he was wounded. His head, swathed in bandages covered with blood, lay on a pillow. I undid the bandages, and the wounded man looked at me with his large eyes and gave no sign of pain as I did it. It was a horrible wound. The skull, shattered by some deadly weapon, left the brain exposed, which was much injured. Clots of blood had formed in the bruised and broken mass, in colour like the dregs of wine.

There was both contusion and suffusion of the brain. His breathing was slow, and some spasmodic movements of the muscles agitated his face. I felt his pulse. It was intermittent. The extremities of the body were growing cold already, and I saw death must inevitably ensue. After dressing the unfortunate man's wounds, I readjusted the bandages on his head, and turned to Captain Nemo.

"What caused this wound?" I asked.

"What does it signify?" he replied evasively. "A shock has broken one of the levers of the engine, which struck myself. But your opinion as to his state?"

I hesitated before giving it.

"You may speak," said the captain. "This man does not understand French."

I gave a last look at the wounded man.

"He will be dead in two hours."

"Can nothing save him?"

"Nothing."

Captain Nemo's hand contracted, and some tears glistened in his eyes, which I thought incapable of shedding any.

For some moments I still watched the dying man, whose life ebbed slowly. His pallor increased under the electric light that was shed over his deathbed. I looked at his intelligent forehead, furrowed with premature wrinkles, produced probably by misfortune and sorrow. I tried to learn the secret of his life from the last words that escaped his lips.

"You can go now, M. Aronnax," said the Captain.

I left him in the dying man's cabin, and returned to my room, much affected by this scene. During the whole day, I was haunted by uncomfortable suspicions, and at night I slept badly, and, between my broken dreams I fancied I heard distant sighs like the notes of a funeral psalm. Were they the prayers of the dead, murmured in that language that I could not understand?

The next morning I went on to the bridge. Captain Nemo was there before me. As soon as he perceived me he came to me.

"Professor, will it be convenient to you to make a submarine excursion to-day?"

"With my companions?" I asked.

"If they like."

"We obey your orders, captain."

"Will you be so good then, as to put on your cork-jackets?"

It was not a question of dead or dying. I rejoined Ned Land and Conseil, and told them of Captain Nemo's proposition. Conseil hastened to accept it, and this time the Canadian seemed quite willing to follow our example.

It was eight o'clock in the morning. At half-past eight we were equipped for this new excursion, and provided with two contrivances for light and breathing. The double door was open; and accompanied by Captain Nemo, who was followed by a dozen of the crew, we set foot, at a depth of about thirty feet, on the solid bottom on which the *Nautilus* rested.

A slight declivity ended in an uneven bottom, at fifteen fathoms depth. This bottom differed entirely from the one I had visited on my first excursion under the waters of the Pacific Ocean. Here, there was no fine sand, no submarine prairies, no sea-forest. I immediately recognised that marvellous region in which, on that day, the captain did the honours to us. It was the coral kingdom. In the zoöphyte branch and in the alcyon class I noticed the gorgoneae, the isidiae, and the corollariae.

The light produced a thousand charming varieties, playing in the midst of the branches that were so vividly coloured. I seemed to see the membraneous and cylindrical tubes tremble beneath the undulation of the waters. I was tempted to gather their fresh petals, ornamented with delicate tentacles, some just blown, the others budding, while a small fish, swimming swiftly, touched them slightly like flights of birds. But if my hand approached these living flowers, these animated sensitive plants, the whole colony took alarm. The white petals reentered their red cases, the flowers faded as I looked, and the bush changed into a block of stony knobs.

Chance had thrown me just by the most precious specimens of the zoöphyte. This coral was more valuable than that found in the Mediterranean, on the coasts of France, Italy, and Barbary. Its tints justified the poetical names of "Flower of Blood" and "Froth of Blood" that trade has given to its most beautiful productions. Coral is sold for £20 per ounce, and in this place the watery beds would make the fortunes of a company of coral-divers. This precious matter, often confused with other polypi, formed then the inextricable plots called "macciota," and on which I noticed several beautiful specimens of pink coral.

But soon the bushes contract, and the arborisations increase. Real petrified thickets, long joists of fantastic architecture, were disclosed before us. Captain Nemo placed himself under a dark gallery, where by a slight declivity we reached a depth of 100 yards. The light from our lamps produced sometimes magical effects, following the rough outlines of the natural arches, and pendants disposed like lustres, that were tipped with points of fire. Between the coralline shrubs I noticed other polypi not less curious—melites, and irises with articulated ramifications; also some tufts of coral, some green, others red, like sea-weed encrusted in their calcareous salts, that naturalists, after long discussion, have definitely classed in the vegetable kingdom. But following the remark of a thinking man, "there is perhaps the real point where life rises obscurely from the sleep of a stone, without detaching itself from the rough point of departure."

At last, after walking two hours, we had attained a depth of about 300 yards, that is to say, the extreme limit on which coral begins to form. But there was no isolated bush, nor modest brushwood, at the bottom of lofty trees. It was an immense forest of large mineral vegetations, enormous petrified trees, united by garlands of elegant plumarias, sea bindweed, all adorned with clouds and reflections. We passed freely under their high branches, lost in the shade of the waves, while at our feet, tubipores, meandrines, stars, fungi, and caryophyllidae formed a carpet of flowers sown with dazzling gems. What an indescribable spectacle!

Captain Nemo had stopped. I and my companions halted, and turning round, I saw his men were forming a semicircle round their chief. Watching attentively, I observed that four of them carried on their shoulders an object of an oblong shape.

We occupied in this place the centre of a vast glade surrounded by the lofty foliage of the submarine forest. Our lamps threw over this place a sort of clear twilight that singularly elongated the shadows on the ground. At the end of the glade the darkness increased, and was only relieved by little sparks reflected by the points of coral.

Ned Land and Conseil were near me. We watched, and I thought I was going to witness a strange scene. On observing the ground, I saw that it was raised in certain places by slight excrescences encrusted with limy deposits, and disposed with a regularity that betrayed the hand of man.

In the midst of the glade, on a pedestal of rocks roughly piled up, stood a cross of coral, that extended its long arms that one might have thought were made of petrified blood.

Upon a sign from Captain Nemo, one of the men advanced; and at some feet from the cross, he began to dig a hole with a pickaxe that he took from his belt. I understood all! This glade was a cemetery, this hole a tomb, this oblong object the body of the man who had died in the night! The captain and his men had come to bury their companion in this general resting-place, at the bottom of this inaccessible ocean!

The grave was being dug slowly; the fish fled on all sides while their retreat was being thus disturbed; I heard the strokes of the pickaxe, which sparkled when it hit upon some flint lost at the bottom of the waters. The hole was soon large and deep enough to receive the body. Then the bearers approached; the body, enveloped in a tissue of white byssus, was lowered into the damp grave. Captain Nemo, with his arms crossed on his breast, and all the friends of him who had loved them, knelt in prayer.

The grave was then filled in with the rubbish taken from the ground, which formed a slight mound. When this was done, Captain Nemo and his men rose; then, approaching the grave, they knelt again, and all extended their hands in sign of a last adieu. Then the funeral procession returned to the *Nautilus*, passing under the arches of the forest, in the midst of thickets, along the coral bushes, and still on the ascent. At last the fires on board appeared, and their luminous track guided us to the *Nautilus*. At one o'clock we had returned.

As soon as I had changed my clothes, I went up on to the platform, and, a prey to conflicting emotions, I sat down near the binnacle. Captain Nemo joined me. I rose and said to him:

"So, as I said he would, this man died in the night?"

"Yes, M. Aronnax."

"And he rests now, near his companions, in the coral cemetery?"

"Yes, forgotten by all else, but not by us. We dug the grave, and the polypi undertake to seal our dead for eternity." And burying his face quickly in his hands, he tried in vain to suppress a sob. Then he added: "Our peaceful cemetery is there, some hundred feet below the surface of the waves."

"Your dead sleep quietly, at least, captain, out of the reach of sharks."

"Yes, sir, of sharks and men," gravely replied the captain.

PART TWO

Chapter I

THE INDIAN OCEAN

W E NOW COME TO THE SECOND PART OF OUR JOURNEY UNDER THE SEA. THE first ended with the moving scene in the coral cemetery which left such a deep impression on my mind. Thus, in the midst of this great sea, Captain Nemo's life was passing even to his grave, which he had prepared in one of its deepest abysses. There, not one of the ocean's monsters could trouble the last sleep of the crew of the *Nautilus*, of those friends riveted to each other in death as in life. "Nor any man either," had added the captain. Still the same fierce, implacable defiance towards human society!

I could no longer content myself with the hypothesis which satisfied Conseil.

That worthy fellow persisted in seeing in the commander of the *Nautilus* one of those unknown servants who return mankind contempt for indifference. For him, he was a misunderstood genius, who, tired of earth's deceptions, had taken refuge in this inaccessible medium, where he might follow his instincts freely. To my mind, this explains but one side of Captain Nemo's character.

Indeed, the mystery of that last night, during which we had been chained in prison, the sleep, and the precaution so violently taken by the captain of snatching from my eyes the glass I had raised to sweep the horizon, the mortal wound of the man, due to an unaccountable shock of the *Nautilus*, all put me on a new track. No; Captain Nemo was not satisfied with shunning man. His formidable apparatus not only suited his instinct of freedom, but, perhaps, also the design of some terrible retaliation.

At this moment nothing is clear to me; I catch but a glimpse of light amid all the darkness, and I must confine myself to writing as events shall dictate.

That day, the 24th of January, 1868, at noon, the second officer came to take the altitude of the sun. I mounted the platform, lit a cigar, and watched the operation. It seemed to me that the man did not understand French; for several times I made remarks in a loud voice, which must have drawn from him some involuntary sign of attention, if he had understood them; but he remained undisturbed and dumb.

As he was taking observations with the sextant, one of the sailors of the *Nautilus* (the strong man who had accompanied us on our first submarine excursion to the Island of Crespo) came to clean the glasses of the lantern. I examined the fittings of the apparatus, the strength of which was increased a hundredfold by lenticular rings, placed similar to those in a lighthouse, and which projected their brilliance in a horizontal plane. The electric lamp was combined in such a way as to give its most powerful light. Indeed, it was produced in *vacuo*, which ensured both its steadiness and its intensity. This vacuum economised the graphite points between which the luminous arc was developed—an important point of economy for Captain Nemo, who could not easily have replaced them; and under these conditions their waste was imperceptible. When the *Nautilus* was ready to continue its submarine journey, I went down to the saloon. The panels were closed and the course marked direct west.

We were furrowing the waters of the Indian Ocean, a vast liquid plain, with a surface

of 1,200,000,000 of acres, and whose waters are so clear and transparent that anyone leaning over them would turn giddy. The *Nautilus* usually floated between fifty and a hundred
fathoms deep. We went on so for some days. To anyone but myself, who had a great love
for the sea, the hours would have seemed long and monotonous; but the daily walks on the
platform, when I steeped myself in the reviving air of the ocean, the sight of the rich waters through the windows of the saloon, the books in the library, the compiling of my
memoirs, took up all my time, and left me not a moment of *ennui* or weariness.

For some days we saw a great number of aquatic birds, sea-mews or gulls. Some were
cleverly killed, and, prepared in a certain way, made very acceptable water-game. Among
large-winged birds, carried a long distance from all lands, and resting upon the waves from
the fatigue of their flight, I saw some magnificent albatrosses, uttering discordant cries like
the braying of an ass, and birds belonging to the family of the longipennates. The family
of the totipalmates was represented by the sea-swallows, which caught the fish from the
surface, and by numerous phaetons, or lepturi; among others, the phaeton with red lines,
as large as a pigeon, whose white plumage, tinted with pink, shows off to advantage the
blackness of its wings.

As to the fish, they always provoked our admiration when we surprised the secrets of
their aquatic life through the open panels. I saw many kinds which I never before had a
chance of observing.

I shall notice chiefly ostracions peculiar to the Red Sea, the Indian Ocean, and that part
which washes the coast of tropical America. These fishes, like the tortoise, the armadillo,
the sea hedgehog, and the crustacea, are protected by a breastplate which is neither chalky
nor stony, but real bone. In some it takes the form of a solid triangle, in others of a solid
quadrangle. Among the triangular I saw some an inch and a half in length, with wholesome
flesh and a delicious flavour; they are brown at the tail and yellow at the fins, and I recommend their introduction into fresh water, to which a certain number of sea-fish easily accustom themselves. I would also mention quadrangular ostracions, having on the back four
large tubercles; some dotted over with white spots on the lower part of the body, and which
may be tamed like birds; trigons provided with spikes formed by the lengthening of their
bony shell, and which from their strange gruntings are called "sea-pigs"; also dromedaries
with large humps in the shape of a cone, whose flesh is very tough and leathery.

I now borrow from the daily notes of Master Conseil. "Certain fish of the genus
petrodon peculiar to those seas, with red backs and white chests, which are distinguished
by three rows of longitudinal filaments; and some electrical, seven inches long, decked in
the liveliest colours. Then, as specimens of other kinds, some ovoides, resembling an egg
of a dark brown colour, marked with white bands, and without tails; diodons, real sea por-
cupines, furnished with spikes, and capable of swelling in such a way as to look like cushions bristling with darts; hippocampi, common to every ocean; some pegasi with
lengthened snouts, which their pectoral fins, being much elongated and formed in the
shape of wings, allow, if not to fly, at least to shoot into the air; pigeon spatulae, with tails
covered with many rings of shell; macrognathi with long jaws, an excellent fish, nine
inches long, and bright with most agreeable colours; pale-coloured calliomores, with
rugged heads; and plenty of chaetodons, with long and tubular muzzles, which kill insects
by shooting them, as from an air-gun, with a single drop of water. These we may call the
fly-catchers of the seas.

"In the eighty-ninth genus of fishes, classed by Lacépède, belonging to the second lower class of bony, characterised by opercules and bronchial membranes, I remarked the scorpaena, the head of which is furnished with spikes, and which has but one dorsal fin; these creatures are covered or not, with little shells, according to the sub-class to which they belong. The second sub-class gives us specimens of didactyles fourteen or fifteen inches in length, with yellow rays, and heads of a most fantastic appearance. As to the first sub-class, it gives several specimens of that singular-looking fish appropriately called a 'sea-frog,' with large head, sometimes swollen with protuberances, bristling with spikes, and covered with tubercles; it has irregular and hideous horns; its body and tail are covered with callosities; its sting makes a dangerous wound; it is both repugnant and horrible to look at."

From the 21st to the 23d of January the *Nautilus* went at the rate of two hundred and fifty leagues in twenty-four hours, being five hundred and forty miles, or twenty-two miles an hour. If we recognised so many different varieties of fish, it was because, attracted by the electric light, they tried to follow us; the greater part, however, were soon distanced by our speed, though some kept their place in the waters of the *Nautilus* for a time. The morning of the 24th, in 12° 5' south latitude, and 94° 33' longitude, we observed Keeling Island, a madrepore formation, planted with magnificent cocoas, and which had been visited by Mr. Darwin and Captain Fitzroy. The *Nautilus* skirted the shores of this desert island for a little distance. Its nets brought up numerous specimens of polypi, and curious shells of mollusca. Some precious productions of the species of delphinulae enriched the treasures of Captain Nemo, to which I added an astraea punctifera, a kind of parasite polypus often found fixed to a shell. Soon Keeling Island disappeared from the horizon, and our course was directed to the north-west in the direction of the Indian Peninsula.

From Keeling Island our course was slower and more variable, often taking us into great depths. Several times they made use of the inclined planes, which certain internal levers placed obliquely to the water-line. In that way we went about two miles, but without ever obtaining the greatest depths of the Indian Sea, which soundings of seven thousand fathoms have never reached. As to the temperature of the lower strata, the thermometer invariably indicated 4° above zero. I only observed that, in the upper regions, the water was always colder in the high levels than at the surface of the sea.

On the 25th of January, the ocean was entirely deserted; the *Nautilus* passed the day on the surface, beating the waves with its powerful screw, and making them rebound to a great height. Who under such circumstances would not have taken it for a gigantic cetacean? Three parts of this day I spent on the platform. I watched the sea. Nothing on the horizon, till about four o'clock a steamer running west on our counter. Her masts were visible for an instant, but she could not see the *Nautilus*, being too low in the water. I fancied this steamboat belonged to the P. O. Company, which runs from Ceylon to Sydney, touching at King George's Point and Melbourne.

At five o'clock in the evening, before that fleeting twilight which binds night to day in tropical zones, Conseil and I were astonished by a curious spectacle.

It was a shoal of argonauts travelling along on the surface of the ocean. We could count several hundreds. They belonged to the tubercle kind which are peculiar to the Indian seas.

These graceful molluscs moved backwards by means of their locomotive tube, through which they propelled the water already drawn in. Of their eight tentacles, six were elongated, and stretched out floating on the water, while the other two, rolled up flat, were spread to the wind like a light sail. I saw their spiral-shaped and fluted shells, which Cuvier justly compares to an elegant skiff. A boat indeed! It bears the creature which secretes it without its adhering to it.

For nearly an hour the *Nautilus* floated in the midst of this shoal of molluscs. Then I know not what sudden fright they took; but as if at a signal every sail was furled, the arms folded, the body drawn in, the shells turned over, changing their centre of gravity, and the whole fleet disappeared under the waves. Never did the ships of a squadron maneuvre with more unity.

At that moment night fell suddenly, and the reeds, scarcely raised by the breeze, lay peaceably under the sides of the *Nautilus*.

The next day, 26th of January, we cut the equator at the eighty-second meridian and entered the northern hemisphere. During the day, a formidable troop of sharks accompanied us, terrible creatures, which multiply in these seas and make them very dangerous. They were "cestracio philippi" sharks, with brown backs and whitish bellies, armed with eleven rows of teeth—eyed sharks—their throat being marked with a large black spot surrounded with white like an eye. There were also some Isabella sharks, with rounded snouts marked with dark spots. These powerful creatures often hurled themselves at the windows of the saloon with such violence as to make us feel very insecure. At such times Ned Land was no longer master of himself. He wanted to go to the surface and harpoon the monsters, particularly certain smooth-hound sharks, whose mouth is studded with teeth like a mosaic; and large tiger-sharks nearly six yards long, the last-named of which seemed to excite him more particularly. But the *Nautilus*, accelerating her speed, easily left the most rapid of them behind.

The 27th of January, at the entrance of the vast Bay of Bengal, we met repeatedly a forbidding spectacle—dead bodies floating on the surface of the water. They were the dead of the Indian villages, carried by the Ganges to the level of the sea, and which the vultures, the only undertakers of the country, had not been able to devour. But the sharks did not fail to help them at their funereal work.

About seven o'clock in the evening, the *Nautilus*, half-immersed, was sailing in a sea of milk. At first sight the ocean seemed lactified. Was it the effect of the lunar rays? No; for the moon, scarcely two days old, was still lying hidden under the horizon in the rays of the sun. The whole sky, though lit by the sidereal rays, seemed black by contrast with the whiteness of the waters.

Conseil could not believe his eyes, and questioned me as to the cause of this strange phenomenon. Happily I was able to answer him.

"It is called a milk sea," I explained. "A large extent of white wavelets often to be seen on the coasts of Amboyna, and in these parts of the sea."

"But, sir," said Conseil, "can you tell me what causes such an effect, for I suppose the water is not really turned into milk."

"No, my boy; and the whiteness which surprises you is caused only by the presence of myriads of infusoria, a sort of luminous little worm, gelatinous and without colour, of the thickness of a hair, and whose length is not more than seven-one-thousandths of an inch. These insects adhere to one another sometimes for several leagues."

"Several leagues!" exclaimed Conseil.

"Yes, my boy; and you need not try to compute the number of these infusoria. You will not be able; for, if I am not mistaken, ships have floated on these milk seas for more than forty miles."

Towards midnight the sea suddenly resumed its usual colour; but behind us, even to the limits of the horizon, the sky reflected the whitened waves, and for a long time seemed impregnated with the vague glimmerings of an aurora borealis.

Chapter II

A Novel Proposal of Captain Nemo's

On the 28th of February, when at noon the *Nautilus* came to the surface of the sea, in 9° 4' north latitude, there was land in sight about eight miles to westward. The first thing I noticed was a range of mountains about two thousand feet high, the shapes of which were most capricious. On taking the bearings, I knew that we were nearing the island of Ceylon, the pearl which hangs from the lobe of the Indian Peninsula.

Captain Nemo and his second appeared at this moment. The captain glanced at the map. Then, turning to me, said:

"The island of Ceylon, noted for its pearl-fisheries. Would you like to visit one of them, M. Aronnax?"

"Certainly, captain."

"Well, the thing is easy. Though if we see the fisheries, we shall not see the fishermen. The annual exportation has not yet begun. Never mind, I will give orders to make for the Gulf of Manaar, where we shall arrive in the night."

The Captain said something to his second, who immediately went out. Soon the *Nautilus* returned to her native element, and the manometer showed that she was about thirty feet deep.

"Well, sir," said Captain Nemo, "you and your companions shall visit the Bank of Manaar, and if by chance some fisherman should be there, we shall see him at work."

"Agreed, captain!"

"By the by, M. Aronnax, you are not afraid of sharks?"

"Sharks!" exclaimed I.

This question seemed a very hard one.

"Well?" continued Captain Nemo.

"I admit, captain, that I am not yet very familiar with that kind of fish."

"*We* are accustomed to them," replied Captain Nemo, "and in time you will be too. However, we shall be armed, and on the road we may be able to hunt some of the tribe. It is interesting. So, till to-morrow, sir, and early."

This said in a careless tone, Captain Nemo left the saloon. Now, if you were invited to hunt the bear in the mountains of Switzerland, what would you say? "Very well! to-morrow we will go and hunt the bear." If you were asked to hunt the lion in the plains of

Atlas, or the tiger in the Indian jungles, what would you say? "Ha! ha! it seems we are going to hunt the tiger or the lion!" But when you are invited to hunt the shark in its natural element, you would perhaps reflect before accepting the invitation. As for myself, I passed my hand over my forehead, on which stood large drops of cold perspiration. "Let us reflect," said I, "and take our time. Hunting otters in submarine forests, as we did in the Island of Crespo, will pass; but going up and down at the bottom of the sea, where one is almost certain to meet sharks, is quite another thing! I know well that in certain countries, particularly in the Andaman Islands, the Negroes never hesitate to attack them with a dagger in one hand and a running noose in the other; but I also know that few who affront those creatures ever return alive. However, I am not a negro, and, if I were, I think a little hesitation in this case would not be ill-timed."

At this moment, Conseil and the Canadian entered, quite composed, and even joyous. They knew not what awaited them.

"Faith, sir," said Ned Land, "your Captain Nemo—the devil take him!—has just made us a very pleasant offer."

"Ah!" said I. "You know?"

"If agreeable to you, sir," interrupted Conseil, "the commander of the *Nautilus* has invited us to visit the magnificent Ceylon fisheries to-morrow, in your company; he did it kindly, and behaved like a real gentleman."

"He said nothing more?"

"Nothing more, sir, except that he had already spoken to you of this little walk."

"Sir," said Conseil, "would you give us some details of the pearl fishery?"

"As to the fishing itself," I asked, "or the incidents—which?"

"On the fishing," replied the Canadian; "before entering upon the ground, it is as well to know something about it."

"Very well; sit down, my friends, and I will teach you."

Ned and Conseil seated themselves on an ottoman, and the first thing the Canadian asked was:

"Sir, what is a pearl?"

"My worthy Ned," I answered, "to the poet, a pearl is a tear of the sea; to the Orientals, it is a drop of dew solidified; to the ladies, it is a jewel of an oblong shape, of a brilliancy of mother-of-pearl substance, which they wear on their fingers, their necks, or their ears; for the chemist, it is a mixture of phosphate and carbonate of lime, with a little gelatine; and lastly, for naturalists, it is simply a morbid secretion of the organ that produces the mother-of-pearl among certain bivalves."

"Branch of mollusca," said Conseil, "class of acephali, order of testacea."

"Precisely so, my learned Conseil; and, among these testacea, the earshell, the tridacnae, the turbots—in a word, all those which secrete mother-of-pearl, that is, the blue, bluish, violet, or white substance which lines the interior of their shells, are capable of producing pearls."

"Mussels too?" asked the Canadian.

"Yes, mussels of certain waters in Scotland, Wales, Ireland, Saxony, Bohemia, and France."

"Good! For the future I shall pay attention," replied the Canadian.

"But," I continued, "the particular mollusc which secretes the pearl is the *pearl-oyster*, the *Meleagrina margaritifera*, that precious pintadine. The pearl is nothing but a nacreous formation, deposited in a globular form, either adhering to the oyster shell, or buried in the folds of the creature. On the shell it is fast; in the flesh it is loose; but always has for a kernel a small, hard substance, maybe a barren egg, maybe a grain of sand, around which the pearly matter deposits itself year after year successively, and by thin concentric layers."

"Are many pearls found in the same oyster?" asked Conseil.

"Yes, my boy. There are some pintadines a perfect casket. One oyster has been mentioned, though I allow myself to doubt it, as having contained no less than a hundred and fifty sharks."

"A hundred and fifty sharks!" exclaimed Ned Land.

"Did I say sharks?" said I hurriedly. "I meant to say a hundred and fifty pearls. Sharks would not be sense."

"Certainly not," said Conseil; "but will you tell us now by what means they extract these pearls?"

"They proceed in various ways. When they adhere to the shell, the fishermen often pull them off with pincers; but the most common way is to lay the oysters on mats of the sea-weed which covers the banks. Thus they die in the open air; and at the end of ten days they are in a forward state of decomposition. They are then plunged into large reservoirs of sea-water; then they are opened and washed. Now begins the double work of the sorters. First they separate the layers of pearls, known in commerce by the name of bastard whites and bastard blacks, which are delivered in boxes of two hundred and fifty and three hundred pounds each. Then they take the parenchyma of the oyster, boil it, and pass it through a sieve in order to extract the very smallest pearls."

"The price of these pearls varies according to their size?" asked Conseil.

"Not only according to their size," I answered, "but also according to their shape, their water (that is, their colour), and their lustre: that is, that bright and diapered sparkle which makes them so charming to the eye. The most beautiful are called virgin pearls or paragons. They are formed alone in the tissue of the mollusc, are white, often opaque, and sometimes have the transparency of an opal; they are generally round or oval. The round are made into bracelets, the oval into pendants; and, being more precious, are sold singly. Those adhering to the shell of the oyster are more irregular in shape, and are sold by weight. Lastly, in a lower order are classed those small pearls known under the name of seed-pearls; they are sold by measure, and are especially used in embroidery for church ornaments."

"But," said Conseil, "is this pearl-fishery dangerous?"

"No," I answered quickly; "particularly if certain precautions are taken."

"What does one risk in such a calling?" said Ned Land. "The swallowing of some mouthfuls of sea-water?"

"As you say, Ned. By the by," said I, trying to take Captain Nemo's careless tone, "are you afraid of sharks, brave Ned?"

"I!" replied the Canadian. "A harpooner by profession? It is my trade to make light of them."

"But," said I, "it is not a question of fishing for them with an iron swivel, hoisting them into the vessel, cutting off their tails with a blow of a chopper, ripping them up, and throwing their heart into the sea!"

"Then, it is a question of—"

"Precisely."

"In the water?"

"In the water."

"Faith, with a good harpoon! You know, sir, these sharks are ill-fashioned beasts. They must turn on their bellies to seize you, and in that time—"

Ned Land had a way of saying "seize" which made my blood run cold.

"Well, and you, Conseil, what do you think of sharks?"

"Me!" said Conseil. "I will be frank, sir."

"So much the better," thought I.

"If you, sir, mean to face the sharks, I do not see why your faithful servant should not face them with you."

Chapter III

A PEARL OF TEN MILLIONS

THE NEXT MORNING AT FOUR O'CLOCK I WAS AWAKENED BY THE STEWARD, WHOM CAPtain Nemo had placed at my service. I rose hurriedly, dressed, and went into the saloon. Captain Nemo was awaiting me.

"M. Aronnax," said he, "are you ready to start?"

"I am ready."

"Then please to follow me."

"And my companions, captain?"

"They have been told, and are waiting."

"Are we not to put on our diver's dresses?" asked I.

"Not yet. I have not allowed the *Nautilus* to come too near this coast, and we are some distance from the Manaar Bank; but the boat is ready, and will take us to the exact point of disembarking, which will save us a long way. It carries our diving apparatus, which we will put on when we begin our submarine journey."

Captain Nemo conducted me to the central staircase, which led on the platform. Ned and Conseil were already there, delighted at the idea of the "pleasure party" which was preparing. Five sailors from the *Nautilus*, with their oars, waited in the boat, which had been made fast against the side.

The night was still dark. Layers of clouds covered the sky, allowing but few stars to be seen. I looked on the side where the land lay, and saw nothing but a dark line enclosing three parts of the horizon, from south-west to north-west. The *Nautilus*, having returned during the night up the western coast of Ceylon, was now west of the bay, or rather gulf, formed by the mainland and the island of Manaar. There, under the dark waters, stretched the pintadine bank, an inexhaustible field of pearls, the length of which is more than twenty miles.

Captain Nemo, Ned Land, Conseil, and I took our places in the stern of the boat. The master went to the tiller; his four companions leaned on their oars, the painter was cast off, and we sheered off.

The boat went towards the south; the oarsmen did not hurry. I noticed that their strokes, strong in the water, only followed each other every ten seconds, according to the method generally adopted in the navy. While the craft was running by its own velocity, the liquid drops struck the dark depths of the waves crisply like spats of melted lead. A little billow, spreading wide, gave a slight roll to the boat, and some samphire reeds flapped before it.

We were silent. What was Captain Nemo thinking of? Perhaps of the land he was approaching, and which he found too near to him, contrary to the Canadian's opinion, who thought it too far off. As to Conseil, he was merely there from curiosity.

About half-past five, the first tints on the horizon showed the upper line of coast more distinctly. Flat enough in the east, it rose a little to the south. Five miles still lay between us, and it was indistinct, owing to the mist on the water. At six o'clock it became suddenly daylight, with that rapidity peculiar to tropical regions, which know neither dawn nor twilight. The solar rays pierced the curtain of clouds piled up on the eastern horizon, and the radiant orb rose rapidly. I saw land distinctly, with a few trees scattered here and there. The boat neared Manaar Island, which was rounded to the south. Captain Nemo rose from his seat and watched the sea.

At a sign from him the anchor was dropped, but the chain scarcely ran, for it was little more than a yard deep, and this spot was one of the highest points of the bank of pintadines.

"Here we are, M. Aronnax," said Captain Nemo. "You see that enclosed bay? Here, in a month, will be assembled the numerous fishing-boats of the exporters, and these are the waters their divers will ransack so boldly. Happily, this bay is well situated for that kind of fishing. It is sheltered from the strongest winds; the sea is never very rough here, which makes it favourable for the diver's work. We will now put on our dresses, and begin our walk."

I did not answer, and while watching the suspected waves, began with the help of the sailors to put on my heavy sea-dress. Captain Nemo and my companions were also dressing. None of the *Nautilus* men were to accompany us on this new excursion.

Soon we were enveloped to the throat in India rubber clothing; the air apparatus fixed to our backs by braces. As to the Ruhmkorff apparatus, there was no necessity for it. Before putting my head into the copper cap, I had asked the question of the captain.

"They would be useless," he replied. "We are going to no great depth, and the solar rays will be enough to light our walk. Besides, it would not be prudent to carry the electric light in these waters; its brilliancy might attract some of the dangerous inhabitants of the coast most inopportunely."

As Captain Nemo pronounced these words, I turned to Conseil and Ned Land. But my two friends had already encased their heads in the metal cap, and they could neither hear nor answer.

One last question remained to ask of Captain Nemo.

"And our arms?" asked I. "Our guns?"

"Guns! What for? Do not mountaineers attack the bear with a dagger in their hand, and is not steel surer than lead? Here is a strong blade; put it in your belt, and we start."

I looked at my companions; they were armed like us, and, more than that, Ned Land was brandishing an enormous harpoon, which he had placed in the boat before leaving the *Nautilus*.

Then, following the captain's example, I allowed myself to be dressed in the heavy copper helmet, and our reservoirs of air were at once in activity. An instant after, we were landed, one after the other, in about two feet of water upon an even sand. Captain Nemo made a sign with his hand, and we followed him by a gentle declivity till we disappeared under the waves.

Over our feet, like coveys of snipe in a bog, rose shoals of fish, of the genus monoptera, which have no other fins but their tail. I recognised the Javanese, a real serpent two and a half feet long, of a livid colour underneath, and which might easily be mistaken for a conger eel if it were not for the golden stripes on its side. In the genus stromateus, whose bodies are very flat and oval, I saw some of the most brilliant colours, carrying their dorsal fin like a scythe; an excellent eating fish, which, dried and pickled, is known by the name of karawade; then some tranquebars, belonging to the genus apsiphoroides, whose body is covered with a shell cuirass of eight longitudinal plates.

The heightening sun lit the mass of waters more and more. The soil changed by degrees. To the fine sand succeeded a perfect causeway of boulders, covered with a carpet of molluscs and zoöphytes. Among the specimens of these branches I noticed some placenae, with thin, unequal shells, a kind of ostracion peculiar to the Red Sea and the Indian Ocean; some orange lucinae with rounded shells; rock-fish three feet and a half long, which raised themselves under the waves like hands ready to seize one. There were also some panopyres, slightly luminous; and lastly, some oculines, like magnificent fans, forming one of the richest vegetations of these seas.

In the midst of these living plants, and under the arbours of the hydrophytes, were layers of clumsy articulates, particularly some raninae, whose carapace formed a slightly rounded triangle; and some horrible-looking parthenopes.

At about seven o'clock we found ourselves at last surveying the oyster-banks, on which the pearl-oysters are reproduced by millions.

Captain Nemo pointed with his hand to the enormous heap of oysters; and I could well understand that this mine was inexhaustible, for nature's creative power is far beyond man's instinct of destruction. Ned Land, faithful to his instinct, hastened to fill a net which he carried by his side with some of the finest specimens. But we could not stop. We must follow the captain, who seemed to guide himself by paths known only to himself. The ground was sensibly rising, and sometimes, on holding up my arm, it was above the surface of the sea. Then the level of the bank would sink capriciously. Often we rounded high rocks scarped into pyramids. In their dark fractures huge crustacea, perched upon their high claws like some war-machine, watched us with fixed eyes, and under our feet crawled various kinds of annelides.

At this moment there opened before us a large grotto, dug in a picturesque heap of rocks, and carpeted with all the thick warp of the submarine flora. At first it seemed very dark to me. The solar rays seemed to be extinguished by successive gradations, until its vague transparency became nothing more than drowned light. Captain Nemo entered; we followed. My eyes soon accustomed themselves to this relative state of darkness. I could distinguish the arches springing capriciously from natural pillars, standing broad upon their granite base, like the heavy columns of Tuscan architecture. Why had our incomprehensible guide led us to the bottom of this submarine crypt? I was soon to know. After descending a rather sharp declivity, our feet trod the bottom of a kind of circular pit. There

Captain Nemo stopped, and with his hand indicated an object I had not yet perceived. It was an oyster of extraordinary dimensions, a gigantic tridacne, a goblet which could have contained a whole lake of holy water, a basin the breadth of which was more than two yards and a half, and consequently larger than that ornamenting the saloon of the *Nautilus*. I approached this extraordinary mollusc. It adhered by its byssus to a table of granite, and there, isolated, it developed itself in the calm waters of the grotto. I estimated the weight of this tridacne at 600 pounds. Such an oyster would contain 30 pounds of meat; and one must have the stomach of a Gargantua to demolish some dozens of them.

Captain Nemo was evidently acquainted with the existence of this bivalve, and seemed to have a particular motive in verifying the actual state of this tridacne. The shells were a little open; the Captain came near, and put his dagger between to prevent them from closing; then with his hand he raised the membrane with its fringed edges, which formed a cloak for the creature. There, between the folded plaits, I saw a loose pearl, whose size equalled that of a cocoa-nut. Its globular shape, perfect clearness, and admirable lustre made it altogether a jewel of inestimable value. Carried away by my curiosity, I stretched out my hand to seize it, weigh it, and touch it; but the Captain stopped me, made a sign of refusal, and quickly withdrew his dagger, and the two shells closed suddenly. I then understood Captain Nemo's intention. In leaving this pearl hidden in the mantle of the tridacne he was allowing it to grow slowly. Each year the secretions of the mollusc would add new concentric circles. I estimated its value at £500,000 at least.

After ten minutes Captain Nemo stopped suddenly. I thought he had halted previously to returning. No; by a gesture he bade us crouch beside him in a deep fracture of the rock, his hand pointed to one part of the liquid mass, which I watched attentively.

About five yards from me a shadow appeared, and sank to the ground. The disquieting idea of sharks shot through my mind, but I was mistaken; and once again it was not a monster of the ocean that we had anything to do with.

It was a man, a living man, an Indian, a fisherman, a poor devil who, I suppose, had come to glean before the harvest. I could see the bottom of his canoe anchored some feet above his head. He dived and went up successively. A stone held between his feet, cut in the shape of a sugar loaf, while a rope fastened him to his boat, helped him to descend more rapidly. This was all his apparatus. Reaching the bottom about five yards deep, he went on his knees and filled his bag with oysters picked up at random. Then he went up, emptied it, pulled up his stone, and began the operation once more, which lasted thirty seconds.

The diver did not see us. The shadow of the rock hid us from sight. And how should this poor Indian ever dream that men, beings like himself, should be there under the water watching his movements, and losing no detail of the fishing? Several times he went up in this way, and dived again. He did not carry away more than ten at each plunge, for he was obliged to pull them from the bank to which they adhered by means of their strong byssus. And how many of those oysters for which he risked his life had no pearl in them! I watched him closely; his maneuvres were regular, and for the space of half-an-hour, no danger appeared to threaten him.

I was beginning to accustom myself to the sight of this interesting fishing, when suddenly, as the Indian was on the ground, I saw him make a gesture of terror, rise, and make a spring to return to the surface of the sea.

I understood his dread. A gigantic shadow appeared just above the unfortunate diver.

It was a shark of enormous size advancing diagonally, his eyes on fire, and his jaws open. I was mute with horror and unable to move.

The voracious creature shot towards the Indian, who threw himself on one side to avoid the shark's fins; but not its tail, for it struck his chest, and stretched him on the ground.

This scene lasted but a few seconds; the shark returned, and, turning on his back, prepared himself for cutting the Indian in two, when I saw Captain Nemo rise suddenly, and then, dagger in hand, walk straight to the monster, ready to fight face to face with him. The very moment the shark was going to snap the unhappy fisherman in two, he perceived his new adversary, and, turning over, made straight towards him.

I can still see Captain Nemo's position. Holding himself well together, he waited for the shark with admirable coolness; and, when it rushed at him, threw himself on one side with wonderful quickness, avoiding the shock, and burying his dagger deep into its side. But it was not all over. A terrible combat ensued.

The shark had seemed to roar, if I might say so. The blood rushed in torrents from its wound. The sea was dyed red, and through the opaque liquid I could distinguish nothing more. Nothing more until the moment when, like lightning, I saw the undaunted captain hanging on to one of the creature's fins, struggling, as it were, hand to hand with the monster, and dealing successive blows at his enemy, yet still unable to give a decisive one.

The shark's struggles agitated the water with such fury that the rocking threatened to upset me.

I wanted to go to the captain's assistance, but, nailed to the spot with horror, I could not stir.

I saw the haggard eye; I saw the different phases of the fight. The captain fell to the earth, upset by the enormous mass which leaned upon him. The shark's jaws opened wide, like a pair of factory shears, and it would have been all over with the captain; but, quick as thought, harpoon in hand, Ned Land rushed towards the shark and struck it with its sharp point.

The waves were impregnated with a mass of blood. They rocked under the shark's movements, which beat them with indescribable fury. Ned Land had not missed his aim. It was the monster's death-rattle. Struck to the heart, it struggled in dreadful convulsions, the shock of which overthrew Conseil.

But Ned Land had disentangled the captain, who, getting up without any wound, went straight to the Indian, quickly cut the cord which held him to his stone, took him in his arms, and, with a sharp blow of his heel, mounted to the surface.

We all three followed in a few seconds, saved by a miracle, and reached the fisherman's boat.

Captain Nemo's first care was to recall the unfortunate man to life again. I did not think he could succeed. I hoped so, for the poor creature's immersion was not long; but the blow from the shark's tail might have been his death-blow.

Happily, with the captain's and Conseil's sharp friction, I saw consciousness return by degrees. He opened his eyes. What was his surprise, his terror even, at seeing four great copper heads leaning over him! And, above all, what must he have thought when Captain Nemo, drawing from the pocket of his dress a bag of pearls, placed it in his hand! This munificent charity from the man of the waters to the poor Cingalese was accepted with a trembling hand. His wondering eyes showed that he knew not to what superhuman beings he owed both fortune and life.

At a sign from the captain we regained the bank, and, following the road already traversed, came in about half-an-hour to the anchor which held the canoe of the *Nautilus* to the earth.

Once on board, we each, with the help of the sailors, got rid of the heavy copper helmets.

Captain Nemo's first word was to the Canadian.

"Thank you, Master Land," said he.

"It was in revenge, Captain," replied Ned Land. "I owed you that."

A ghastly smile passed across the captain's lips, and that was all.

"To the *Nautilus*," said he.

The boat flew over the waves. Some minutes after we met the shark's dead body floating. By the black marking of the extremity of its fins, I recognised the terrible melanopteron of the Indian seas, of the species of shark so properly called. It was more than twenty-five feet long; its enormous mouth occupied one-third of its body. It was an adult, as was known by its six rows of teeth placed in an isosceles triangle in the upper jaw.

Conseil looked at it with scientific interest, and I am sure that he placed it, and not without reason, in the cartilaginous class, of the chondropterygian order, with fixed gills, of the selacian family, in the genus of the sharks.

While I was contemplating this inert mass, a dozen of these voracious beasts appeared round the boat; and, without noticing us, threw themselves upon the dead body and fought with one another for the pieces.

At half-past eight we were again on board the *Nautilus*. There I reflected on the incidents which had taken place in our excursion to the Manaar Bank.

Two conclusions I must inevitably draw from it—one bearing upon the unparalleled courage of Captain Nemo, the other upon his devotion to a human being, a representative of that race from which he fled beneath the sea. Whatever he might say, this strange man had not yet succeeded in entirely crushing his heart.

When I made this observation to him, he answered in a slightly moved tone:

"That Indian, sir, is an inhabitant of an oppressed country; and I am still, and shall be, to my last breath, one of them!"

Chapter IV

The Red Sea

IN THE COURSE OF THE DAY OF THE 29TH OF JANUARY, THE ISLAND OF CEYLON DISAPpeared under the horizon, and the *Nautilus*, at a speed of twenty miles an hour, slid into the labyrinth of canals which separate the Maldives from the Laccadives. It coasted even the Island of Kiltan, a land originally madreporic, discovered by Vasco da Gama in 1499, and one of the nineteen principal islands of the Laccadive Archipelago, situated between 10° and 14° 30' north latitude, and 69° 50' 72" east longitude.

We had made 16,220 miles, or 7,500 (French) leagues, from our starting-point in the Japanese seas.

The next day (30th January), when the *Nautilus* went to the surface of the ocean, there was no land in sight. Its course was N.N.E., in the direction of the Sea of Oman, between Arabia and the Indian Peninsula, which serves as an outlet to the Persian Gulf. It was evidently a block without any possible egress. Where was Captain Nemo taking us to? I could not say. This, however, did not satisfy the Canadian, who that day came to me asking where we were going.

"We are going where our Captain's fancy takes us, Master Ned."

"His fancy cannot take us far, then," said the Canadian. "The Persian Gulf has no outlet; and, if we do go in, it will not be long before we are out again."

"Very well, then, we will come out again, Master Land; and if, after the Persian Gulf, the *Nautilus* would like to visit the Red Sea, the Straits of Bab-el-mandeb are there to give us entrance."

"I need not tell you, sir," said Ned Land, "that the Red Sea is as much closed as the gulf, as the Isthmus of Suez is not yet cut; and, if it was, a boat as mysterious as ours would not risk itself in a canal cut with sluices. And again, the Red Sea is not the road to take us back to Europe."

"But I never said we were going back to Europe."

"What do you suppose, then?"

"I suppose that after visiting the curious coasts of Arabia and Egypt, the *Nautilus* will go down the Indian Ocean again, perhaps cross the Channel of Mozambique, perhaps off the Mascarenhas, so as to gain the Cape of Good Hope."

"And once at the Cape of Good Hope?" asked the Canadian, with peculiar emphasis.

"Well, we shall penetrate into that Atlantic which we do not yet know. Ah! friend Ned, you are getting tired of this journey under the sea: you are surfeited with the incessantly varying spectacle of submarine wonders. For my part, I shall be sorry to see the end of a voyage which it is given to so few men to make."

For four days, till the 3d of February, the *Nautilus* scoured the Sea of Oman, at various speeds and at various depths. It seemed to go at random, as if hesitating as to which road it should follow, but we never passed the Tropic of Cancer.

In quitting this sea we sighted Muscat for an instant, one of the most important towns of the country of Oman. I admired its strange aspect, surrounded by black rocks upon which its white houses and forts stood in relief. I saw the rounded domes of its mosques, the elegant points of its minarets, its fresh and verdant terraces. But it was only a vision! The *Nautilus* soon sank under the waves of that part of the sea.

We passed along the Arabian coast of Mahrah and Hadramaut, for a distance of six miles, its undulating line of mountains being occasionally relieved by some ancient ruin. The 5th of February we at last entered the Gulf of Aden, a perfect funnel introduced into the neck of Bab-el-mandeb, through which the Indian waters entered the Red Sea.

The 6th of February, the *Nautilus* floated in sight of Aden, perched upon a promontory which a narrow isthmus joins to the mainland, a kind of inaccessible Gibraltar, the fortifications of which were rebuilt by the English after taking possession in 1839. I caught a glimpse of the octagon minarets of this town, which was at one time, according to the historian Edrisi the richest commercial magazine on the coast.

I certainly thought that Captain Nemo, arrived at this point, would back out again; but I was mistaken, for he did no such thing, much to my surprise.

The next day, the 7th of February, we entered the Straits of Bab-el-mandeb, the name of which, in the Arab tongue, means "The gate of tears."

To twenty miles in breadth, it is only thirty-two in length. And for the *Nautilus*, starting at full speed, the crossing was scarcely the work of an hour. But I saw nothing, not even the Island of Perim, with which the British Government has fortified the position of Aden. There were too many English or French steamers of the line of Suez to Bombay, Calcutta to Melbourne, and from Bourbon to the Mauritius, furrowing this narrow passage, for the *Nautilus* to venture to show itself. So it remained prudently below. At last about noon, we were in the waters of the Red Sea.

I would not even seek to understand the caprice which had decided Captain Nemo upon entering the gulf. But I quite approved of the *Nautilus* entering it. Its speed was lessened: sometimes it kept on the surface, sometimes it dived to avoid a vessel, and thus I was able to observe the upper and lower parts of this curious sea.

The 8th of February, from the first dawn of day, Mocha came in sight, now a ruined town, whose walls would fall at a gunshot, yet which shelters here and there some verdant date-trees; once an important city, containing six public markets and twenty-six mosques, and whose walls, defended by fourteen forts, formed a girdle of two miles in circumference.

The *Nautilus* then approached the African shore, where the depth of the sea was greater. There, between two waters clear as crystal, through the open panels we were allowed to contemplate the beautiful bushes of brilliant coral, and large blocks of rock clothed with a splendid fur of green algae and fuci. What an indescribable spectacle, and what variety of sites and landscapes along these sand-banks and volcanic islands which bound the Lybian coast! But where these shrubs appeared in all their beauty was on the eastern coast, which the *Nautilus* soon gained. It was on the coast of Tehama, for there not only did this display of zoöphytes flourish beneath the level of the sea, but they also formed picturesque interlacings which unfolded themselves about sixty feet above the surface, more capricious but less highly coloured than those whose freshness was kept up by the vital power of the waters.

What charming hours I passed thus at the window of the saloon! What new specimens of submarine flora and fauna did I admire under the brightness of our electric lantern!

There grew sponges of all shapes, pediculated, foliated, globular, and digital. They certainly justified the names of baskets, cups, distaffs, elk's-horns, lion's-feet, peacock's-tails, and Neptune's-gloves, which have been given to them by the fishermen, greater poets than the savants.

Other zoöphytes which multiply near the sponges consist principally of medusae of a most elegant kind. The molluscs were represented by varieties of the calmar (which, according to Orbigny, are peculiar to the Red Sea); and reptiles by the virgata turtle, of the genus cheloniae, which furnished a wholesome and delicate food for our table.

As for the fish, they were abundant and often remarkable. The following are those which the nets of the *Nautilus* brought more frequently on board:

Rays of a red-brick color, with bodies marked with blue spots, and easily recognisable by their double-spikes; some superb caranxes, marked with seven transverse bands of jet-black, blue and yellow fins, and gold and silver scales; mullets with yellow heads; gobies, and a thousand other species, common to the ocean which we had just traversed.

The 9th of February the *Nautilus* floated in the broadest part of the Red Sea, which is comprised between Souakin, on the west coast, and Koomfidah, on the east coast, with a diameter of ninety miles.

That day at noon, after the bearings were taken, Captain Nemo mounted the platform, where I happened to be, and I was determined not to let him go down again without at least pressing him regarding his ulterior projects. As soon as he saw me he approached, and graciously offered me a cigar.

"Well, sir, does this Red Sea please you? Have you sufficiently observed the wonders it covers, its fishes, its zoöphytes, its parterres of sponges, and its forests of coral? Did you catch a glimpse of the towns on its borders?"

"Yes, Captain Nemo," I replied; "and the *Nautilus* is wonderfully fitted for such a study. Ah! it is an intelligent boat!"

"Yes, sir, intelligent and invulnerable. It fears neither the terrible tempests of the Red Sea, nor its currents, nor its sand-banks."

"Certainly," said I, "this sea is quoted as one of the worst, and in the time of the ancients, if I am not mistaken, its reputation was detestable."

"Detestable, M. Aronnax. The Greek and Latin historians do not speak favourably of it, and Strabo says it is very dangerous during the Etesian winds, and in the rainy season. The Arabian Edrisi portrays it under the name of the Gulf of Colzoum, and relates that vessels perished there in great numbers on the sand-banks, and that no one would risk sailing in the night. It is, he pretends, a sea subject to fearful hurricanes, strewn with inhospitable islands, and 'which offers nothing good either on its surface or in its depths.' Such, too, is the opinion of Arrian, Agatharcides, and Artemidorus."

"One may see," I replied, "that these historians never sailed on board the *Nautilus*."

"Just so," replied the captain, smiling; "and in that respect moderns are not more advanced than the ancients. It required many ages to find out the mechanical power of steam. Who knows if, in another hundred years, we may not see a second *Nautilus?* Progress is slow, M. Aronnax."

"It is true," I answered; "your boat is at least a century before its time, perhaps an era. What a misfortune that the secret of such an invention should die with its inventor!"

Captain Nemo did not reply. After some minutes' silence he continued:

"You were speaking of the opinions of ancient historians upon the dangerous navigation of the Red Sea."

"It is true," said I; "but were not their fears exaggerated?"

"Yes and no, M. Aronnax," replied Captain Nemo, who seemed to know the Red Sea by heart. "That which is no longer dangerous for a modern vessel, well rigged, strongly built, and master of its own course, thanks to obedient steam, offered all sorts of perils to the ships of the ancients. Picture to yourself those first navigators venturing in ships made of planks sewn with the cords of the palm-trees, saturated with the grease of the sea-dog, and covered with powdered resin! They had not even instruments wherewith to take their bearings, and they went by guess among currents of which they scarcely knew anything. Under such conditions shipwrecks were, and must have been, numerous. But in our time, steamers running between Suez and the South Seas have nothing more to fear from the fury of this gulf, in spite of contrary trade winds. The captain and passengers do not prepare for their departure by offering propitiatory sacrifices; and, on their return, they no longer go ornamented with wreaths and gilt fillets to thank the gods in the neighboring temple."

"I agree with you," said I; "and steam seems to have killed all gratitude in the hearts of sailors. But, captain, since you seem to have especially studied this sea, can you tell me the origin of its name?"

"There exist several explanations on the subject, M. Aronnax. Would you like to know the opinion of a chronicler of the fourteenth century?"

"Willingly."

"This fanciful writer pretends that its name was given to it after the passage of the Israelites, when Pharaoh perished in the waves which closed at the voice of Moses."

"A poet's explanation, Captain Nemo," I replied; "but I cannot content myself with that. I ask you for your personal opinion."

"Here it is, M. Aronnax. According to my idea, we must see in this appellation of the Red Sea a translation of the Hebrew word 'Edom'; and if the ancients gave it that name, it was on account of the particular colour of its waters."

"But up to this time I have seen nothing but transparent waves and without any particular colour."

"Very likely; but as we advance to the bottom of the gulf, you will see this singular appearance. I remember seeing the Bay of Tor entirely red, like a sea of blood."

"And you attribute this colour to the presence of a microscopic sea-weed?"

"Yes; it is a mucilaginous purple matter, produced by the restless little plants known by the name of trichodesmia, and of which it requires 40,000 to occupy the space of a square 0.04 of an inch. Perhaps we shall meet some when we get to Tor."

"So, Captain Nemo, it is not the first time you have over-run the Red Sea on board the *Nautilus?*"

"No, sir."

"As you spoke a while ago of the passage of the Israelites and of the catastrophe to the Egyptians, I will ask whether you have met with the traces under the water of this great historical fact?"

"No, sir; and for a good reason."

"What is it?"

"It is, that the spot where Moses and his people passed is now so blocked up with sand that the camels can barely bathe their legs there. You can well understand that there would not be water enough for my *Nautilus.*"

"And the spot?" I asked.

"The spot is situated a little above the Isthmus of Suez, in the arm which formerly made a deep estuary when the Red Sea extended to the Salt Lakes. Now, whether this passage were miraculous or not, the Israelites, nevertheless, crossed there to reach the Promised Land, and Pharaoh's army perished precisely on that spot; and I think that excavations made in the middle of the sand would bring to light a large number of arms and instruments of Egyptian origin."

"That is evident," I replied; "and for the sake of archaeologists let us hope that these excavations will be made sooner or later, when new towns are established on the isthmus, after the construction of the Suez Canal; a canal, however, very useless to a vessel like the *Nautilus.*"

"Very likely; but useful to the whole world," said Captain Nemo. "The ancients well understood the utility of a communication between the Red Sea and the Mediterranean for their commercial affairs; but they did not think of digging a canal direct, and took the Nile as an intermediate. Very probably the canal which united the Nile to the Red Sea was begun by Sesostris, if we may believe tradition. One thing is certain, that in the year 615 before Jesus Christ, Necos undertook the works of an alimentary canal to the waters of the Nile, across the plain of Egypt, looking towards Arabia. It took four days to go up this canal, and it was so wide that two triremes could go abreast. It was carried on by Darius, the son of Hystaspes, and probably finished by Ptolemy II. Strabo saw it navigated; but its decline from the point of departure, near Bubastes, to the Red Sea was so slight that it was only navigable for a few months in the year. This canal answered all commercial purposes to the age of Antonius, when it was abandoned and blocked up with sand. Restored by order of the Caliph Omar, it was definitely destroyed in 761 or 762 by Caliph Al-Mansor, who wished to prevent the arrival of provisions to Mohammed-ben-Abdallah, who had re-volted against him. During the expedition into Egypt, your General Bonaparte discovered traces of the works in the Desert of Suez; and, surprised by the tide, he nearly perished be-fore regaining Hadjaroth, at the very place where Moses had encamped three thousand years before him."

"Well, captain, what the ancients dared not undertake, this junction between the two seas, which will shorten the road from Cadiz to India, M. Lesseps has succeeded in doing; and before long he will have changed Africa into an immense island."

"Yes, M. Aronnax; you have the right to be proud of your countryman. Such a man brings more honour to a nation than great captains. He began, like so many others, with disgust and rebuffs; but he has triumphed, for he has the genius of will. And it is sad to think that a work like that, which ought to have been an international work, and which would have sufficed to make a reign illustrious, should have succeeded by the energy of one man. All honour to M. Lesseps!"

"Yes, honour to the great citizen!" I replied, surprised by the manner in which Cap-tain Nemo had just spoken.

"Unfortunately," he continued, "I cannot take you through the Suez Canal; but you will be able to see the long jetty of Port Said after to-morrow, when we shall be in the Mediterranean."

"The Mediterranean!" I exclaimed.

"Yes, sir; does that astonish you?"

"What astonishes me is to think that we shall be there the day after to-morrow."

"Indeed?"

"Yes, captain, although by this time I ought to have accustomed myself to be sur-prised at nothing since I have been on board your boat."

"But the cause of this surprise?"

"Well! it is the fearful speed you will have to put on the *Nautilus*, if the day after to-morrow she is to be in the Mediterranean, having made the round of Africa, and doubled the Cape of Good Hope!"

"Who told you that she would make the round of Africa and double the Cape of Good Hope, sir?"

"Well, unless the *Nautilus* sails on dry land, and passes above the isthmus——"

"Or beneath it, M. Aronnax."

"Beneath it!"

"Certainly," replied Captain Nemo quietly. "A long time ago nature made under this tongue of land what man has this day made on its surface."

"What! Such a passage exists?"

"Yes; a subterranean passage, which I have named the Arabian Tunnel. It takes us beneath Suez and opens into the Gulf of Pelusium."

"But this isthmus is composed of nothing but quicksands?"

"To a certain depth. But at fifty-five yards only, there is a solid layer of rock."

"Did you discover this passage by chance?" I asked, more and more surprised.

"Chance and reasoning, sir; and by reasoning even more than by chance. Not only does this passage exist, but I have profited by it several times. Without that I should not have ventured this day into the impassable Red Sea. I noticed that in the Red Sea and in the Mediterranean there existed a certain number of fishes of a kind perfectly identical— orphidia, fiatoles, girelles, and exocoeti. Certain of the fact, I asked myself was it possible that there was no communication between the two seas? If there was, the subterranean current must necessarily run from the Red Sea to the Mediterranean, from the sole cause of difference of level. I caught a large number of fishes in the neighborhood of Suez. I passed a copper ring through their tails, and threw them back into the sea. Some months later, on the coast of Syria, I caught some of my fish ornamented with the ring. Thus the communication between the two was proved. I then sought for it with my *Nautilus*; I discovered it, ventured into it, and before long, sir, you too will have passed through my Arabian Tunnel!"

Chapter V

THE ARABIAN TUNNEL

THAT SAME EVENING, IN 21° 30′ NORTH LATITUDE, THE *NAUTILUS* FLOATED ON THE SURface of the sea, approaching the Arabian coast. I saw Djeddah, the most important counting-house of Egypt, Syria, Turkey, and India. I distinguished clearly enough its buildings, the vessels anchored at the quays, and those whose draught of water obliged them to anchor in the roads. The sun, rather low on the horizon, struck full on the houses of the town, bringing out their whiteness. Outside, some wooden cabins, and some made of reeds, showed the quarter inhabited by the Bedouins. Soon Djeddah was shut out from view by the shadows of night, and the *Nautilus* found herself under water slightly phosphorescent.

The next day, the 10th of February, we sighted several ships running to windward. The *Nautilus* returned to its submarine navigation; but at noon, when her bearings were taken, the sea being deserted, she rose again to her water-line.

Accompanied by Ned and Conseil, I seated myself on the platform. The coast on the eastern side looked like a mass faintly printed upon a damp fog.

We were leaning on the sides of the pinnace, talking of one thing and another, when Ned Land, stretching out his hand towards a spot on the sea, said:

"Do you see anything there, sir?"

"No, Ned," I replied; "but I have not your eyes, you know."

"Look well," said Ned, "there, on the starboard beam, about the height of the lantern! Do you not see a mass which seems to move?"

"Certainly," said I, after close attention; "I see something like a long black body on the top of the water."

And certainly before long the black object was not more than a mile from us. It looked like a great sand-bank deposited in the open sea. It was a gigantic dugong!

Ned Land looked eagerly. His eyes shone with covetousness at the sight of the animal. His hand seemed ready to harpoon it. One would have thought he was awaiting the moment to throw himself into the sea, and attack it in its element.

At this instant Captain Nemo appeared on the platform. He saw the dugong, understood the Canadian's attitude, and addressing him, said:

"If you held a harpoon just now, Master Land, would it not burn your hand?"

"Just so, sir."

"And you would not be sorry to go back, for one day, to your trade of a fisherman and to add this cetacean to the list of those you have already killed?"

"I should not, sir."

"Well, you can try."

"Thank you, sir," said Ned Land, his eyes flaming.

"Only," continued the captain, "I advise you for your own sake not to miss the creature."

"Is the dugong dangerous to attack?" I asked, in spite of the Canadian's shrug of the shoulders.

"Yes," replied the captain; "sometimes the animal turns upon its assailants and overturns their boat. But for Master Land, this danger is not to be feared. His eye is prompt, his arm sure."

At this moment seven men of the crew, mute and immovable as ever, mounted the platform. One carried a harpoon and a line similar to those employed in catching whales. The pinnace was lifted from the bridge, pulled from its socket, and let down into the sea. Six oarsmen took their seats, and the coxswain went to the tiller. Ned, Conseil, and I went to the back of the boat.

"You are not coming, captain?" I asked.

"No, sir; but I wish you good sport."

The boat put off, and, lifted by the six rowers, drew rapidly towards the dugong, which floated about two miles from the *Nautilus*.

Arrived some cable-lengths from the cetacean, the speed slackened, and the oars dipped noiselessly into the quiet waters. Ned Land, harpoon in hand, stood in the forepart of the boat. The harpoon used for striking the whale is generally attached to a very long cord, which runs out rapidly as the wounded creature draws it after him. But here the cord was not more than ten fathoms long, and the extremity was attached to a small barrel which, by floating, was to show the course the dugong took under the water.

I stood, and carefully watched the Canadian's adversary. This dugong, which also bears the name of the halicore, closely resembles the manatee; its oblong body terminated in a lengthened tail, and its lateral fins in perfect fingers. Its difference from the manatee consisted in its upper jaw, which was armed with two long and pointed teeth, which formed on each side diverging tusks.

This dugong, which Ned Land was preparing to attack, was of colossal dimensions; it was more than seven yards long. It did not move, and seemed to be sleeping on the waves, which circumstance made it easier to capture.

The boat approached within six yards of the animal. The oars rested on the rowlocks. I half rose. Ned Land, his body thrown a little back, brandished the harpoon in his experienced hand.

Suddenly a hissing noise was heard, and the dugong disappeared. The harpoon, although thrown with great force; had apparently only struck the water.

"Curse it!" exclaimed the Canadian furiously; "I have missed it!"

"No," said I; "the creature is wounded—look at the blood; but your weapon has not stuck in his body."

"My harpoon! My harpoon!" cried Ned Land.

The sailors rowed on, and the coxswain made for the floating barrel. The harpoon regained, we followed in pursuit of the animal.

The latter came now and then to the surface to breathe. Its wound had not weakened it, for it shot onward with great rapidity.

The boat, rowed by strong arms, flew on its track. Several times it approached within some few yards, and the Canadian was ready to strike, but the dugong made off with a sudden plunge, and it was impossible to reach it.

Imagine the passion which excited impatient Ned Land! He hurled at the unfortunate creature the most energetic expletives in the English tongue. For my part I was only vexed to see the dugong escape all our attacks.

We pursued it without relaxation for an hour, and I began to think it would prove difficult to capture, when the animal, possessed with the perverse idea of vengeance of which he had cause to repent, turned upon the pinnace and assailed us in its turn.

This maneuvre did not escape the Canadian.

"Look out!" he cried.

The coxswain said some words in his outlandish tongue, doubtless warning the men to keep on their guard.

The dugong came within twenty feet of the boat, stopped, sniffed the air briskly with its large nostrils (not pierced at the extremity, but in the upper part of its muzzle). Then taking a spring he threw himself upon us.

The pinnace could not avoid the shock, and half upset, shipped at least two tons of water, which had to be emptied; but thanks to the coxswain, we caught it sideways, not full front, so we were not quite overturned. While Ned Land, clinging to the bows, belaboured the gigantic animal with blows from his harpoon, the creature's teeth were buried in the gunwale, and it lifted the whole thing out of the water, as a lion does a roebuck. We were upset over one another, and I know not how the adventure would have ended, if the Canadian, still enraged with the beast, had not struck it to the heart.

I heard its teeth grind on the iron plate, and the dugong disappeared, carrying the harpoon with him. But the barrel soon returned to the surface, and shortly after the body of the animal, turned on its back. The boat came up with it, took it in tow, and made straight for the *Nautilus*.

It required tackle of enormous strength to hoist the dugong on to the platform. It weighed 10,000 lbs.

The next day, February 11th, the larder of the *Nautilus* was enriched by some more delicate game. A flight of sea-swallows rested on the *Nautilus*. It was a species of the *Sterna nilotica*, peculiar to Egypt; its beak is black, head grey and pointed, the eye surrounded by white spots, the back, wings, and tail of a greyish colour, the belly and throat white, and claws red. They also took some dozen of Nile ducks, a wild bird of high flavour, its throat and upper part of the head white with black spots.

About five o'clock in the evening we sighted to the north the Cape of Ras-Mohammed. This cape forms the extremity of Arabia Petraea, comprised between the Gulf of Suez and the Gulf of Acabah.

The *Nautilus* penetrated into the Strait of Jubal, which leads to the Gulf of Suez. I distinctly saw a high mountain, towering between the two gulfs of Ras-Mohammed. It was Mount Horeb, that Sinai at the top of which Moses saw God face to face.

At six o'clock the *Nautilus*, sometimes floating, sometimes immersed, passed some distance from Tor, situated at the end of the bay, the waters of which seemed tinted with red, an observation already made by Captain Nemo. Then night fell in the midst of a heavy silence, sometimes broken by the cries of the pelican and other night-birds, and the noise of the waves breaking upon the shore, chafing against the rocks, or the panting of some far-off steamer beating the waters of the gulf with its noisy paddles.

From eight to nine o'clock the *Nautilus* remained some fathoms under the water. According to my calculation we must have been very near Suez. Through the panel of the saloon I saw the bottom of the rocks brilliantly lit up by our electric lamp. We seemed to be leaving the Straits behind us more and more.

At a quarter past nine, the vessel having returned to the surface, I mounted the platform. Most impatient to pass through Captain Nemo's tunnel, I could not stay in one place, so came to breathe the fresh night-air.

Soon in the shadow I saw a pale light, half discoloured by the fog, shining about a mile from us.

"A floating lighthouse!" said someone near me.

I turned, and saw the captain.

"It is the floating light of Suez," he continued. "It will not be long before we gain the entrance of the tunnel."

"The entrance cannot be easy?"

"No, sir; for that reason I am accustomed to go into the steersman's cage, and myself direct our course. And now if you will go down, M. Aronnax, the *Nautilus* is going under the waves, and will not return to the surface until we have passed through the Arabian Tunnel."

Captain Nemo led me towards the central staircase; half-way down he opened a door, traversed the upper deck, and landed in the pilot's cage, which it may be remembered rose at the extremity of the platform. It was a cabin measuring six feet square, very much like that occupied by the pilot on the steamboats of the Mississippi or Hudson. In the midst worked a wheel, placed vertically, and caught to the tiller-rope, which ran to the back of the *Nautilus*. Four light-ports with lenticular glasses, let in a groove in the partition of the cabin, allowed the man at the wheel to see in all directions.

This cabin was dark, but soon my eyes accustomed themselves to the obscurity, and I perceived the pilot, a strong man, with his hands resting on the spokes of the wheel. Outside, the sea appeared vividly lit up by the lantern, which shed its rays from the back of the cabin to the other extremity of the platform.

"Now," said Captain Nemo, "let us try to make our passage."

Electric wires connected the pilot's cage with the machinery-room, and from there the captain could communicate simultaneously to his *Nautilus* the direction and the speed. He pressed a metal knob, and at once the speed of the screw diminished.

I looked in silence at the high straight wall we were running by at this moment, the immovable base of a massive sandy coast. We followed it thus for an hour only some few yards off.

Captain Nemo did not take his eye from the knob, suspended by its two concentric circles in the cabin. At a simple gesture, the pilot modified the course of the *Nautilus* every instant.

I had placed myself at the port scuttle, and saw some magnificent sub-structures of coral, zoöphytes, sea-weed, and fucus, agitating their enormous claws, which stretched out from the fissures of the rock.

At a quarter past ten, the captain himself took the helm. A large gallery, black and deep, opened before us. The *Nautilus* went boldly into it. A strange roaring was heard round its sides. It was the waters of the Red Sea, which the incline of the tunnel precipitated violently towards the Mediterranean. The *Nautilus* went with the torrent, rapid as an arrow, in spite of the efforts of the machinery, which, in order to offer more effective resistance, beat the waves with reversed screw.

On the walls of the narrow passage I could see nothing but brilliant rays, straight lines, furrows of fire, traced by the great speed, under the brilliant electric light. My heart beat fast.

At thirty-five minutes past ten, Captain Nemo quitted the helm, and, turning to me, said:

"The Mediterranean!"

In less than twenty minutes, the *Nautilus*, carried along by the torrent, had passed through the Isthmus of Suez.

Chapter VI

THE GRECIAN ARCHIPELAGO

THE NEXT DAY, THE 12TH OF FEBRUARY, AT THE DAWN OF DAY, THE *NAUTILUS* ROSE TO the surface. I hastened on to the platform. Three miles to the south the dim outline of Pelusium was to be seen. A torrent had carried us from one sea to another. About seven o'clock Ned and Conseil joined me.

"Well, Sir Naturalist," said the Canadian, in a slightly jovial tone, "and the Mediterranean?"

"We are floating on its surface, friend Ned."

"What!" said Conseil. "This very night?"

"Yes, this very night; in a few minutes we have passed this impassable isthmus."

"I do not believe it," replied the Canadian.

"Then you are wrong, Master Land," I continued; "this low coast which rounds off to the south is the Egyptian coast. And you, who have such good eyes, Ned, you can see the jetty of Port Said stretching into the sea."

The Canadian looked attentively.

"Certainly you are right, sir, and your captain is a first-rate man. We are in the Mediterranean. Good! Now, if you please, let us talk of our own little affair, but so that no one hears us."

I saw what the Canadian wanted, and, in any case, I thought it better to let him talk, as he wished it; so we all three went and sat down near the lantern, where we were less exposed to the spray of the blades.

"Now, Ned, we listen; what have you to tell us?"

"What I have to tell you is very simple. We are in Europe; and before Captain Nemo's caprices drag us once more to the bottom of the Polar Seas, or lead us into Oceania, I ask to leave the *Nautilus*."

I wished in no way to shackle the liberty of my companions, but I certainly felt no desire to leave Captain Nemo.

Thanks to him, and thanks to his apparatus, I was each day nearer the completion of my submarine studies; and I was rewriting my book of submarine depths in its very element. Should I ever again have such an opportunity of observing the wonders of the ocean? No, certainly not! And I could not bring myself to the idea of abandoning the *Nautilus* before the cycle of investigation was accomplished.

"Friend Ned, answer me frankly, are you tired of being on board? Are you sorry that destiny has thrown us into Captain Nemo's hands?"

The Canadian remained some moments without answering. Then, crossing his arms, he said:

"Frankly, I do not regret this journey under the seas. I shall be glad to have made it; but, now that it is made, let us have done with it. That is my idea."

"It will come to an end, Ned."

"Where and when?"

"Where I do not know, when I cannot say; or, rather, I suppose it will end when these seas have nothing more to teach us."

"Then what do you hope for?" demanded the Canadian.

"That circumstances may occur as well six months hence as now by which we may and ought to profit."

"Oh," said Ned Land, "and where shall we be in six months, if you please, Sir Naturalist?"

"Perhaps in China; you know the *Nautilus* is a rapid traveller. It goes through water as swallows through the air, or as an express on the land. It does not fear frequented seas; who can say that it may not beat the coasts of France, England, or America, on which flight may be attempted as advantageously as here."

"M. Aronnax," replied the Canadian, "your arguments are rotten at the foundation.

You speak in the future, 'We shall be there! We shall be here!' I speak in the present, 'We are here, and we must profit by it.' "

Ned Land's logic pressed me hard, and I felt myself beaten on that ground. I knew not what argument would now tell in my favour.

"Sir," continued Ned, "let us suppose an impossibility; if Captain Nemo should this day offer you your liberty, would you accept it?"

"I do not know," I answered.

"And if," he added, "the offer made you this day was never to be renewed, would you accept it?"

"Friend Ned, this is my answer. Your reasoning is against me. We must not rely on Captain Nemo's good-will. Common prudence forbids him to set us at liberty. On the other side, prudence bids us profit by the first opportunity to leave the *Nautilus*."

"Well, M. Aronnax, that is wisely said."

"Only one observation—just one. The occasion must be serious, and our first attempt must succeed; if it fails, we shall never find another, and Captain Nemo will never forgive us."

"All that is true," replied the Canadian. "But your observation applies equally to all attempts at flight, whether in two years' time, or in two days. But the question is still this: if a favourable opportunity presents itself, it must be seized."

"Agreed! And now, Ned, will you tell me what you mean by a favourable opportunity?"

"It will be that which, on a dark night, will bring the *Nautilus* a short distance from some European coast."

"And you will try and save yourself by swimming?"

"Yes, if we were near enough to the bank, and if the vessel was floating at the time. Not if the bank was far away, and the boat was under the water."

"And in that case?"

"In that case, I should seek to make myself master of the pinnace. I know how it is worked. We must get inside, and the bolts once drawn, we shall come to the surface of the water, without even the pilot, who is in the bows, perceiving our flight."

"Well, Ned, watch for the opportunity; but do not forget that a hitch will ruin us."

"I will not forget, sir."

"And now, Ned, would you like to know what I think of your project?"   •

"Certainly, M. Aronnax."

"Well, I think—I do not say I hope—I think that this favourable opportunity will never present itself."

"Why not?"

"Because Captain Nemo cannot hide from himself that we have not given up all hope of regaining our liberty, and he will be on his guard, above all, in the seas, and in the sight of European coasts."

"We shall see," replied Ned Land, shaking his head determinedly.

"And now, Ned Land," I added, "let us stop here. Not another word on the subject. The day that you are ready, come and let us know, and we will follow you. I rely entirely upon you."

Thus ended a conversation which, at no very distant time, led to such grave results. I must say here that facts seemed to confirm my foresight, to the Canadian's great despair. Did Captain Nemo distrust us in these frequented seas, or did he only wish to hide himself from the numerous vessels, of all nations, which ploughed the Mediterranean? I could not tell; but we were oftener between waters, and far from the coast. Or, if the *Nautilus* did emerge, nothing was to be seen but the pilot's cage; and sometimes it went to great depths, for, between the Grecian Archipelago and Asia Minor, we could not touch the bottom by more than a thousand fathoms.

Thus I only knew we were near the island of Carpathos, one of the Sporades, by Captain Nemo reciting these lines from Virgil:

> *Est in Carpathio Neptuni gurgite vates,*
> *Cæruleus Proteus,*

as he pointed to a spot on the planisphere.

It was indeed the ancient abode of Proteus, the old shepherd of Neptune's flocks, now the Island of Scarpanto, situated between Rhodes and Crete. I saw nothing but the granite base through the glass panels of the saloon.

The next day, the 14th of February, I resolved to employ some hours in studying the fishes of the archipelago; but for some reason or other, the panels remained hermetically sealed. Upon taking the course of the *Nautilus* I found that we were going towards Candia, the ancient Isle of Crete. At the time I embarked on the *Abraham Lincoln*, the whole of this island had risen in insurrection against the despotism of the Turks. But how the insurgents had fared since that time I was absolutely ignorant, and it was not Captain Nemo, deprived of all land communications, who could tell me.

I made no allusion to this event when that night I found myself alone with him in the saloon. Besides, he seemed to be taciturn and preoccupied. Then, contrary to his custom, he ordered both panels to be opened, and going from one to the other, observed the mass of waters attentively. To what end I could not guess; so, on my side, I employed my time in studying the fish passing before my eyes.

Among others, I remarked some gobies, mentioned by Aristotle, and commonly known by the name of sea-braches which are more particularly met with in the salt waters lying near the Delta of the Nile. Near them rolled some sea-bream, half-phosphorescent, a kind of sparus, which the Egyptians ranked among their sacred animals, whose arrival in the waters of their river announced a fertile overflow, and was celebrated by religious ceremonies. I also noticed some cheilines about nine inches long, a bony fish with transparent shell, whose livid color is mixed with red spots; they are great eaters of marine vegetation, which gives them an exquisite flavor. These cheilines were much sought after by the epicures of ancient Rome; the inside, dressed with the soft roe of the lamprey, peacocks' brains, and tongues of the phenicoptera, composed that divine dish of which Vitellius was so enamored.

Another inhabitant of these seas drew my attention, and led my mind back to recollections of antiquity. It was the remora, that fastens on to the shark's belly. This little fish, according to the ancients, hooking on to the ship's bottom, could stop its movements; and one of them, by keeping back Antony's ship during the battle of Actium, helped Augustus to gain the victory. On how little hangs the destiny of nations! I observed some fine anthiae, which belong to the order of lutjans, a fish held sacred by the Greeks, who attributed to them the power of hunting the marine monsters from waters they frequented. Their name signifies *flower,* and they justify their appellation by their shaded colors, their shades compromising the whole gamut of reds, from the paleness of the rose to the brightness of the ruby, and the fugitive tints that clouded their dorsal fin. My eyes could not leave these wonders of the sea, when they were suddenly struck by an unexpected apparition.

In the midst of the waters a man appeared, a diver, carrying at his belt a leathern purse. It was not a body abandoned to the waves; it was a living man, swimming with a strong hand, disappearing occasionally to take breath at the surface.

I turned towards Captain Nemo, and in an agitated voice exclaimed:

"A man shipwrecked! He must be saved at any price!"

The captain did not answer me, but came and leaned against the panel.

The man had approached, and with his face flattened against the glass, was looking at us.

To my great amazement, Captain Nemo signed to him. The diver answered with his hand, mounted immediately to the surface of the water, and did not appear again.

"Do not be uncomfortable," said Captain Nemo. "It is Nicholas of Cape Matapan; surnamed Pesca. He is well known in all the Cyclades. A bold diver! Water is his element, and he lives more in it than on land, going continually from one island to another, even as far as Crete."

"You know him, captain?"

"Why not, M. Aronnax?"

Saying which, Captain Nemo went towards a piece of furniture standing near the left panel of the saloon. Near this piece of furniture, I saw a chest bound with iron, on the cover of which was a copper plate, bearing the cipher of the *Nautilus* with its device.

At that moment, the captain, without noticing my presence, opened the piece of furniture, a sort of strong box, which held a great many ingots.

They were ingots of gold. From whence came this precious metal, which represented an enormous sum? Where did the Captain gather this gold from and what was he going to do with it?

I did not say one word. I looked. Captain Nemo took the ingots one by one, and arranged them methodically in the chest, which he filled entirely. I estimated the contents at more than 4,000 lbs. weight of gold, that is to say, nearly £200,000.

The chest was securely fastened, and the Captain wrote an address on the lid, in characters which must have belonged to Modern Greece.

This done, Captain Nemo pressed a knob, the wire of which communicated with the quarters of the crew. Four men appeared, and, not without some trouble, pushed the chest out of the saloon. Then I heard them hoisting it up the iron staircase by means of pulleys.

At that moment, Captain Nemo turned to me.

"And you were saying, sir?" said he.

"I was saying nothing, captain."

"Then, sir, if you will allow me, I will wish you good-night."

Whereupon he turned and left the saloon.

I returned to my room much troubled, as one may believe. I vainly tried to sleep—I sought the connecting link between the apparition of the diver and the chest filled with gold. Soon, I felt by certain movements of pitching and tossing that the *Nautilus* was leaving the depths and returning to the surface.

Then I heard steps upon the platform; and I knew they were unfastening the pinnace and launching it upon the waves. For one instant it struck the side of the *Nautilus*, then all noise ceased.

Two hours after, the same noise, the same going and coming was renewed; the boat was hoisted on board, replaced in its socket, and the *Nautilus* again plunged under the waves.

So these millions had been transported to their address. To what point of the continent? Who was Captain Nemo's correspondent?

The next day, I related to Conseil and the Canadian the events of the night, which had excited my curiosity to the highest degree. My companions were not less surprised than myself.

"But where does he take his millions to?" asked Ned Land.

To that there was no possible answer. I returned to the saloon after having breakfast, and set to work. Till five o'clock in the evening, I employed myself in arranging my notes. At that moment (ought I to attribute it to some peculiar idiosyncrasy?) I felt so great a heat that I was obliged to take off my coat of byssus! It was strange, for we were under low latitudes; and even then, the *Nautilus*, submerged as it was, ought to experience no change of temperature. I looked at the manometer; it showed a depth of sixty feet, to which atmospheric heat could never attain.

I continued my work, but the temperature rose to such a pitch as to be intolerable.

"Could there be fire on board?" I asked myself.

I was leaving the saloon, when Captain Nemo entered; he approached the thermometer, consulted it, and turning to me, said:

"Forty-two degrees."

"I have noticed it, captain," I replied; "and if it gets much hotter we cannot bear it."

"Oh, sir, it will not get better if we do not wish it."

"You can reduce it as you please, then?"

"No; but I can go farther from the stove which produces it."

"It is outward then!"

"Certainly; we are floating in a current of boiling water."

"Is it possible!" I exclaimed.

"Look."

The panels opened, and I saw the sea entirely white all round. A sulphurous smoke was curling amid the waves, which boiled like water in a copper. I placed my hand on one of the panes of glass, but the heat was so great that I quickly took it off again.

"Where are we?" I asked.

"Near the Island of Santorin, sir," replied the captain, "and just in the canal which separates Nea Kamenni from Pali Kamenni. I wished to give you a sight of the curious spectacle of a submarine irruption."

"I thought," said I, "that the formation of these new islands was ended."

"Nothing is ever ended in the volcanic parts of the sea," replied Captain Nemo; "and the globe is always being worked by subterranean fires. Already, in the nineteenth year of our era, according to Cassiodorus and Pliny, a new island, Theia (the divine), appeared in the very place where these islets have recently been formed. Then they sank under the waves, to rise again in the year 69, when they again subsided. Since that time to our days, the Plutonian work has been suspended. But, on the 3d of February, 1866, a new island, which they named George Island, emerged from the midst of the sulphurous vapour near Nea Kamenni, and settled again the 6th of the same month. Seven days after, the 13th of February, the island of Aphroessa appeared, leaving between Nea Kamenni and itself a canal ten yards broad. I was in these seas when the phenomenon occurred, and I was able therefore to observe all the different phases. The island of Aphroessa, of round form, measured 300 feet in diameter, and thirty feet in height. It was composed of black and vitreous lava, mixed with fragments of felspar. And lastly, on the 10th of March, a smaller island, called Reka, showed itself near Nea Kamenni, and since then these three have joined together, forming but one and the same island."

"And the canal in which we are at this moment?" I asked.

"Here it is," replied Captain Nemo, showing me a map of the archipelago. "You see I have marked the new islands."

I returned to the glass. The *Nautilus* was no longer moving, the heat was becoming unbearable. The sea, which till now had been white, was red, owing to the presence of salts of iron. In spite of the ship's being hermetically sealed, an insupportable smell of sulphur filled the saloon, and the brilliancy of the electricity was entirely extinguished by bright scarlet flames. I was in a bath, I was choking, I was broiled.

"We can remain no longer in this boiling water," said I to the captain.

"It would not be prudent," replied the impassive Captain Nemo.

An order was given; the *Nautilus* tacked about and left the furnace it could not brave with impunity. A quarter of an hour after we were breathing fresh air on the surface. The thought then struck me that, if Ned Land had chosen this part of the sea for our flight, we should never have come alive out of this sea of fire.

The next day, the 16th of February, we left the basin which, between Rhodes and Alexandria, is reckoned about 1,500 fathoms in depth, and the *Nautilus*, passing some distance from Cerigo, quitted the Grecian Archipelago, after having doubled Cape Matapan.

Chapter VII

The Mediterranean in Forty-Eight Hours

THE MEDITERRANEAN, THE BLUE SEA *PAR EXCELLENCE*, "THE GREAT SEA" OF THE HEbrews, "the sea" of the Greeks, the "mare nostrum" of the Romans, bordered by orange-trees, aloes, cacti, and sea-pines; embalmed with the perfume of the myrtle, surrounded by rude mountains, saturated with pure and transparent air, but incessantly worked by underground fires, a perfect battlefield in which Neptune and Pluto still dispute the empire of the world!

It is upon these banks, and on these waters, says Michelet, that man is renewed in one of the most powerful climates of the globe. But, beautiful as it was, I could only take a rapid glance at the basin whose superficial area is two million of square yards. Even Captain Nemo's knowledge was lost to me, for this enigmatical person did not appear once during our passage at full speed. I estimated the course which the *Nautilus* took under the waves of the sea at about six hundred leagues, and it was accomplished in forty-eight hours. Starting on the morning of the 16th of February from the shores of Greece, we had crossed the Straits of Gibraltar by sunrise on the 18th.

It was plain to me that this Mediterranean, enclosed in the midst of those countries which he wished to avoid, was distasteful to Captain Nemo. Those waves and those breezes brought back too many remembrances, if not too many regrets. Here he had no longer that independence and that liberty of gait which he had when in the open seas, and his *Nautilus* felt itself cramped between the close shores of Africa and Europe.

Our speed was now twenty-five miles an hour. It may be well understood that Ned Land, to his great disgust, was obliged to renounce his intended flight. He could not launch the pinnace, going at the rate of twelve or thirteen yards every second. To quit the *Nautilus* under such conditions would be as bad as jumping from a train going at full speed— an imprudent thing, to say the least of it. Besides, our vessel only mounted to the surface of the waves at night to renew its stock of air; it was steered entirely by the compass and the log.

I saw no more of the interior of this Mediterranean than a traveller by express train perceives of the landscape which flies before his eyes; that is to say, the distant horizon, and not the nearer objects which pass like a flash of lightning.

In the midst of the mass of waters brightly lit up by the electric light gilded some of those lampreys, more than a yard long, common to almost every climate. Some of the oxyrhynchi, a kind of ray five feet broad, with white belly and grey spotted back, spread out like a large shawl carried along by the current. Other rays passed so quickly that I could not see if they deserved the name of eagles which was given to them by the ancient Greeks, or the qualification of rats, toads, and bats, with which modern fishermen have loaded them. A few milander sharks, twelve feet long, and much feared by divers, struggled among them. Sea-foxes eight feet long, endowed with wonderful fineness of scent, appeared like large blue shadows. Some dorades of the shark kind, some of which measured seven feet and a half, showed themselves in their dress of blue and silver, encircled by small bands which struck sharply against the sombre tints of their fins, a fish consecrated to Venus, the eyes of which are encased in a socket of gold, a precious species, friend of all waters, fresh or salt, an inhabitant of rivers, lakes, and oceans, living in all climates, and bearing all temperatures; a race belonging to the geological era of the earth, and which has preserved all the beauty of its first days. Magnificent sturgeons, nine or ten yards long, creatures of great speed, striking the panes of glass with their strong tails, displayed their bluish backs with small brown spots; they resemble the sharks, but are not equal to them in strength, and are to be met with in all seas. But of all the diverse inhabitants of the Mediterranean, those I observed to the greatest advantage, when the *Nautilus* approached the surface, belonged to the sixty-third genus of bony fish. They were a kind of tunny, with bluish-black backs, and silvery breastplates, whose dorsal fins threw out sparkles of gold. They are said to follow in the wake of vessels whose refreshing shade they seek from the fire of a tropical sky, and they did not belie the saying, for they accompanied the *Nautilus* as they did in former times the vessel of La Perouse. For many a long hour they struggled to keep up with our vessel. I was never tired of admiring these creatures really built for speed—their small heads, their bodies lithe and cigar-shaped, which in some were more than three yards long, their pectoral fins and forked tail endowed with remarkable strength. They swam in a triangle, like certain flocks of birds, whose rapidity they equaled, and of which the ancients used to say that they understood geometry and strategy. But still they do not escape the pursuit of the provençals, who esteem them as highly as the inhabitants of the Propontis and of Italy used to do; and these precious, but blind and foolhardy creatures, perish by millions in the nets of the Marseillaise.

With regard to the species of fish common to the Atlantic and the Mediterranean, the giddy speed of the *Nautilus* prevented me from observing them with any degree of accuracy.

As to marine mammals, I thought, in passing the entrance of the Adriatic, that I saw two or three cachalots, furnished with one dorsal fin, of the genus physetera, some dolphins of the genus globicephala, peculiar to the Mediterranean, the back part of the head being marked like a zebra with small lines; also, a dozen of seals, with white bellies and black hair, known by the name of *monks*, and which really have the air of a Dominican; they are about three yards in length.

As to zoöphytes, for some instants I was able to admire a beautiful orange galeolaria, which had fastened itself to the port panel; it held on by a long filament, and was divided into an infinity of branches, terminated by the finest lace which could ever have been woven by the rivals of Arachne herself. Unfortunately, I could not take this admirable specimen; and doubtless no other Mediterranean zoöphyte would have offered itself to my observation, if, on the night of the 16th, the *Nautilus* had not, singularly enough, slackened its speed, under the following circumstances.

We were then passing between Sicily and the coast of Tunis. In the narrow space between Cape Bon and the Straits of Messina the bottom of the sea rose almost suddenly. There was a perfect bank, on which there was not more than nine fathoms of water, while on either side the depth was ninety fathoms.

The *Nautilus* had to maneuvre very carefully so as not to strike against this submarine barrier.

I showed Conseil on the map of the Mediterranean the spot occupied by this reef.

"But if you please, sir," observed Conseil, "it is like a real isthmus joining Europe to Africa."

"Yes, my boy, it forms a perfect bar to the Straits of Lybia, and the soundings of Smith have proved that in former times the continents between Cape Boco and Cape Furina were joined."

"I can well believe it," said Conseil.

"I will add," I continued, "that a similar barrier exists between Gibraltar and Ceuta, which in geological times formed the entire Mediterranean."

"What if some volcanic burst should one day raise these two barriers above the waves?"

"It is not probable, Conseil."

"Well, but allow me to finish, please, sir; if this phenomenon should take place, it will be troublesome for M. Lesseps, who has taken so much pains to pierce the isthmus."

"I agree with you; but I repeat, Conseil, this phenomenon will never happen. The violence of subterranean force is ever diminishing. Volcanoes, so plentiful in the first days of the world, are being extinguished by degrees; the internal heat is weakened, the temperature of the lower strata of the globe is lowered by a perceptible quantity every century to the detriment of our globe, for its heat is its life."

"But the sun?"

"The sun is not sufficient, Conseil. Can it give heat to a dead body?"

"Not that I know of."

"Well, my friend, this earth will one day be that cold corpse; it will become uninhabitable and uninhabited like the moon, which has long since lost all its vital heat."

"In how many centuries?"

"In some hundreds of thousands of years, my boy."

"Then," said Conseil, "we shall have time to finish our journey, that is, if Ned Land does not interfere with it."

And Conseil, reassured, returned to the study of the bank, which the *Nautilus* was skirting at a moderate speed.

There, beneath the rocky and volcanic bottom, lay outspread a living flora of sponges and reddish cydippes, which emitted a slight phosphorescent light, commonly known by the name of sea-cucumbers; and walking comatulae more than a yard long, the purple of which completely colored the water around.

The *Nautilus* having now passed the high bank on the Libyan Straits, returned to the deep waters and its accustomed speed.

From that time no more molluscs, no more articulates, no more zoöphytes; barely a few large fish passing like shadows.

During the night of the 16th and 17th of February, we had entered the second Mediterranean basin, the greatest depth of which was 1,450 fathoms. The *Nautilus*, by the action of its screw, slid down the inclined planes, and buried itself in the lowest depths of the sea.

On the 18th of February, about three o'clock in the morning, we were at the entrance of the Straits of Gibraltar. There once existed two currents—an upper one, long since recognised, which conveys the waters of the ocean into the basin of the Mediterranean; and a lower counter-current, which reasoning has now shown to exist. Indeed, the volume of water in the Mediterranean, incessantly added to by the waves of the Atlantic and by rivers falling into it, would each year raise the level of this sea, for its evaporation is not sufficient to restore the equilibrium. As it is not so, we must necessarily admit the existence of an undercurrent, which empties into the basin of the Atlantic, through the Straits of Gibraltar, the surplus waters of the Mediterranean. A fact, indeed; and it was this counter-current by which the *Nautilus* profited. It advanced rapidly by the narrow pass. For one instant I caught a glimpse of the beautiful ruins of the temple of Hercules, buried in the ground, according to Pliny, and with the low island which supports it; and a few minutes later we were floating on the Atlantic.

Chapter VIII

VIGO BAY

THE ATLANTIC! A VAST SHEET OF WATER, WHOSE SUPERFICIAL AREA COVERS TWENTY-five millions of square miles, the length of which is nine thousand miles, with a mean breadth of two thousand seven hundred—an ocean whose parallel winding shores embrace an immense circumference, watered by the largest rivers of the world, the St. Lawrence, the Mississippi, the Amazon, the Plata, the Orinoco, the Niger, the Senegal, the Elbe, the Loire, and the Rhine, which carry water from the most civilised, as well as from the most savage countries! Magnificent field of water, incessantly ploughed by vessels of every nation, sheltered by the flags of every nation, and which terminates in those two terrible points so dreaded by mariners, Cape Horn, and the Cape of Tempests.

The *Nautilus* was piercing the water with its sharp spur, after having accomplished nearly ten thousand leagues in three months and a half, a distance greater than the great circle of the earth. Where were we going now, and what was reserved for the future? The *Nautilus*, leaving the Straits of Gibraltar, had gone far out. It returned to the surface of the waves, and our daily walks on the platform were restored to us.

I mounted at once, accompanied by Ned Land and Conseil. At a distance of about twelve miles, Cape St. Vincent was dimly to be seen, forming the south-western point of the Spanish peninsula. A strong southerly gale was blowing. The sea was swollen and billowy; it made the *Nautilus* rock violently. It was almost impossible to keep one's footing on the platform, which the heavy rolls of the sea beat over every instant. So we descended after inhaling some mouthfuls of fresh air.

I returned to my room, Conseil to his cabin; but the Canadian, with a preoccupied air, followed me. Our rapid passage across the Mediterranean had not allowed him to put his project into execution, and he could not help showing his disappointment. When the door of my room was shut, he sat down and looked at me silently.

"Friend Ned," said I, "I understand you; but you cannot reproach yourself. To have attempted to leave the *Nautilus* under the circumstances would have been folly."

Ned Land did not answer; his compressed lips and frowning brow showed with him the violent possession this fixed idea had taken of his mind.

"Let us see," I continued; "we need not despair yet. We are going up the coast of Portugal again; France and England are not far off, where we can easily find refuge. Now, if the *Nautilus*, on leaving the Straits of Gibraltar, had gone to the south, if it had carried us towards regions where there were no continents, I should share your uneasiness. But we know now that Captain Nemo does not fly from civilised seas, and in some days I think you can act with security."

Ned Land still looked at me fixedly; at length his fixed lips parted, and he said, "It is for to-night."

I drew myself up suddenly. I was, I admit, little prepared for this communication. I wanted to answer the Canadian, but words would not come.

"We agreed to wait for an opportunity," continued Ned Land, "and the opportunity has arrived. This night we shall be but a few miles from the Spanish coast. It is cloudy. The wind blows freely. I have your word, M. Aronnax, and I rely upon you."

As I was silent, the Canadian approached me.

"To-night, at nine o'clock," said he. "I have warned Conseil. At that moment, Captain Nemo will be shut up in his room, probably in bed. Neither the engineers nor the ship's crew can see us. Conseil and I will gain the central staircase, and you, M. Aronnax, will remain in the library, two steps from us, waiting my signal. The oars, the mast, and the sail are in the canoe. I have even succeeded in getting some provisions. I have procured an English wrench, to unfasten the bolts which attach it to the shell of the *Nautilus*. So all is ready, till to-night."

"The sea is bad."

"That I allow," replied the Canadian; "but we must risk that. Liberty is worth paying for; besides, the boat is strong, and a few miles with a fair wind to carry us is no great thing. Who knows but by to-morrow we may be a hundred leagues away? Let circumstances only favour us, and by ten or eleven o'clock we shall have landed on some spot of *terra firma*, alive or dead. But adieu now till to-night."

With these words, the Canadian withdrew, leaving me almost dumb. I had imagined that, the chance gone, I should have time to reflect and discuss the matter. My obstinate companion had given me no time; and, after all, what could I have said to him? Ned Land was perfectly right. There was almost the opportunity to profit by. Could I retract my word, and take upon myself the responsibility of compromising the future of my companions? To-morrow Captain Nemo might take us far from all land.

At that moment a rather loud hissing noise told me that the reservoirs were filling, and that the *Nautilus* was sinking under the waves of the Atlantic.

A sad day I passed, between the desire of regaining my liberty of action, and of abandoning the wonderful *Nautilus*, and leaving my submarine studies incomplete.

What dreadful hours I passed thus; sometimes seeing myself and companions safely landed, sometimes wishing, in spite of my reason, that some unforeseen circumstance would prevent the realisation of Ned Land's project.

Twice I went to the saloon. I wished to consult the compass. I wished to see if the direction the *Nautilus* was taking was bringing us nearer or taking us farther from the coast. But no; the *Nautilus* kept in Portuguese waters.

I must therefore take my part, and prepare for flight. My luggage was not heavy; my notes, nothing more.

As to Captain Nemo, I asked myself what he would think of our escape; what trouble, what wrong it might cause him, and what he might do in case of its discovery or failure. Certainly I had no cause to complain of him; on the contrary, never was hospitality freer than his. In leaving him I could not be taxed with ingratitude. No oath bound us to him. It was on the strength of circumstances he relied, and not upon our word, to fix us forever.

I had not seen the captain since our visit to the Island of Santorin. Would chance bring me to his presence before our departure? I wished it, and I feared it at the same time. I listened if I could hear him walking the room contiguous to mine. No sound reached my ear. I felt an unbearable uneasiness. This day of waiting seemed eternal. Hours struck too slowly to keep pace with my impatience.

My dinner was served in my room as usual. I ate but little; I was too preoccupied. I left the table at seven o'clock. A hundred and twenty minutes (I counted them) still separated me from the moment in which I was to join Ned Land. My agitation redoubled. My pulse beat violently. I could not remain quiet. I went and came, hoping to calm my troubled spirit by constant movement. The idea of failure in our bold enterprise was the least painful of my anxieties; but the thought of seeing our project discovered before leaving the *Nautilus*, of being brought before Captain Nemo, irritated, or (what was worse) saddened at my desertion, made my heart beat.

I wanted to see the saloon for the last time. I descended the stairs and arrived in the museum where I had passed so many useful and agreeable hours. I looked at all its riches, all its treasures, like a man on the eve of an eternal exile, who was leaving never to return. These wonders of nature, these masterpieces of art, among which for so many days my life had been concentrated, I was going to abandon them forever! I should like to have taken a last look through the windows of the saloon into the waters of the Atlantic; but the panels were hermetically closed, and a cloak of steel separated me from that ocean which I had not yet explored.

In passing through the saloon, I came near the door, let into the angle which opened into the captain's room. To my great surprise this door was ajar. I drew back, involuntarily. If Captain Nemo should be in his room, he could see me. But, hearing no noise, I drew nearer. The room was deserted. I pushed open the door and took some steps forward. Still the same monk-like severity of aspect.

Suddenly the clock struck eight. The first beat of the hammer on the bell awoke me from my dreams. I trembled as if an invisible eye had plunged into my most secret thoughts, and I hurried from the room.

There my eye fell upon the compass. Our course was still north. The log indicated moderate speed, the manometer a depth of about sixty feet.

I returned to my room, clothed myself warmly—sea-boots, an otterskin cap, a great coat of byssus, lined with sealskin; I was ready, I was waiting. The vibration of the screw alone broke the deep silence which reigned on board. I listened attentively. Would no loud voice suddenly inform me that Ned Land had been surprised in his projected flight? A mortal dread hung over me, and I vainly tried to regain my accustomed coolness.

At a few minutes to nine, I put my ear to the captain's door. No noise. I left my room and returned to the saloon, which was half in obscurity, but deserted.

I opened the door communicating with the library. The same insufficient light, the same solitude. I placed myself near the door leading to the central staircase, and there waited for Ned Land's signal.

At that moment the trembling of the screw sensibly diminished, then it stopped entirely. The silence was now only disturbed by the beatings of my own heart. Suddenly a slight shock was felt; and I knew that the *Nautilus* had stopped at the bottom of the ocean. My uneasiness increased. The Canadian's signal did not come. I felt inclined to join Ned Land and beg of him to put off his attempt. I felt that we were not sailing under our usual conditions.

At this moment the door of the large saloon opened, and Captain Nemo appeared. He saw me, and, without further preamble, began in an amiable tone of voice:

"Ah, sir! I have been looking for you. Do you know the history of Spain?"

Now, one might know the history of one's own country by heart; but in the condition I was at the time, with troubled mind and head quite lost, I could not have said a word of it.

"Well," continued Captain Nemo, "you heard my question! Do you know the history of Spain?"

"Very slightly," I answered.

"Well, here are learned men having to learn," said the captain. "Come, sit down, and I will tell you a curious episode in this history. Sir, listen well," said he; "this history will interest you on one side, for it will answer a question which doubtless you have not been able to solve."

"I listen, captain," said I, not knowing what my interlocutor was driving at, and asking myself if this incident was bearing on our projected flight.

"Sir, if you have no objection, we will go back to 1702. You cannot be ignorant that your king, Louis XIV, thinking that the gesture of a potentate was sufficient to bring the Pyrenees under his yoke, had imposed the Duke of Anjou, his grandson, on the Spaniards. This prince reigned more or less badly under the name of Philip V, and had a strong party against him abroad. Indeed, the preceding year, the royal houses of Holland, Austria, and England had concluded a treaty of alliance at the Hague, with the intention of plucking the crown of Spain from the head of Philip V, and placing it on that of an archduke to whom they prematurely gave the title of Charles III.

"Spain must resist this coalition; but she was almost entirely unprovided with either soldiers or sailors. However, money would not fail them, provided that their galleons, laden with gold and silver from America, once entered their ports. And about the end of 1702 they expected a rich convoy which France was escorting with a fleet of twenty-three vessels, commanded by Admiral Château-Renaud, for the ships of the coalition were already beating the Atlantic. This convoy was to go to Cadiz, but the Admiral, hearing that an English fleet was cruising in those waters, resolved to make for a French port.

"The Spanish commanders of the convoy objected to this decision. They wanted to be taken to a Spanish port, and if not to Cadiz, into Vigo Bay, situated on the north-west coast of Spain, and which was not blocked.

"Admiral Chateau-Renaud had the rashness to obey this injunction, and the galleons entered Vigo Bay.

"Unfortunately, it formed an open road which could not be defended in any way. They must therefore hasten to unload the galleons before the arrival of the combined fleet; and time would not have failed them had not a miserable question of rivalry suddenly arisen.

"You are following the chain of events?" asked Captain Nemo.

"Perfectly," said I, not knowing the end proposed by this historical lesson.

"I will continue. This is what passed. The merchants of Cadiz had a privilege by which they had the right of receiving all merchandise coming from the West Indies. Now, to disembark these ingots at the port of Vigo was depriving them of their rights. They complained at Madrid, and obtained the consent of the weak-minded Philip that the convoy, without discharging its cargo, should remain sequestered in the roads of Vigo until the enemy had disappeared.

"But while coming to this decision, on the 22d of October, 1702, the English vessels arrived in Vigo Bay, when Admiral Château-Renaud, in spite of inferior forces, fought bravely. But, seeing that the treasure must fall into the enemy's hands, he burned and scuttled every galleon, which went to the bottom with their immense riches."

Captain Nemo stopped. I admit I could not see yet why this history should interest me. "Well?" I asked.

"Well, M. Aronnax," replied Captain Nemo, "we are in that Vigo Bay; and it rests with yourself whether you will penetrate its mysteries."

The captain rose, telling me to follow him. I had had time to recover. I obeyed. The saloon was dark, but through the transparent glass the waves were sparkling. I looked.

For half-a-mile around the *Nautilus* the waters seemed bathed in electric light. The sandy bottom was clean and bright. Some of the ship's crew in their diving-dresses were clearing away half-rotten barrels and empty cases from the midst of the blackened wrecks. From these cases and from these barrels escaped ingots of gold and silver, cascades of piastres and jewels. The sand was heaped up with them. Laden with their precious booty, the men returned to the *Nautilus*, disposed of their burden, and went back to this inexhaustible fishery of gold and silver.

I understood now. This was the scene of the battle of the 22d of October, 1702. Here on this very spot the galleons laden for the Spanish government had sunk. Here Captain Nemo came, according to his wants, to pack up those millions with which he burdened the *Nautilus*. It was for him and him alone America had given up her precious metals. He was heir direct, without anyone to share, in those treasures torn from the Incas and from the conquered of Ferdinand Cortez.

"Did you know, sir," he asked, smiling, "that the sea contained such riches?"

"I knew," I answered, "that they value money held in suspension in these waters at two millions."

"Doubtless; but to extract this money the expense would be greater than the profit. Here, on the contrary, I have but to pick up what man has lost—and not only in Vigo Bay, but in a thousand other spots where shipwrecks have happened, and which are marked on my submarine map. Can you understand now the source of the millions I am worth?"

"I understand, captain. But allow me to tell you that in exploring Vigo Bay you have only been beforehand with a rival society."

"And which?"

"A society which has received from the Spanish government the privilege of seeking those buried galleons. The shareholders are led on by the allurement of an enormous bounty, for they value these rich shipwrecks at five hundred millions."

"Five hundred millions they were," answered Captain Nemo, "but they are so no longer."

"Just so," said I; "and a warning to those shareholders would be an act of charity. But who knows if it would be well received? What gamblers usually regret above all is less the loss of their money, than of their foolish hopes. After all, I pity them less than the thousands of unfortunates to whom so much riches well distributed would have been profitable, while for them they will be forever barren."

I had no sooner expressed this regret than I felt that it must have wounded Captain Nemo.

"Barren!" he exclaimed, with animation. "Do you think then, sir, that these riches are lost because I gather them? Is it for myself alone, according to your idea, that I take the trouble to collect these treasures? Who told you that I did not make a good use of it? Do you think I am ignorant that there are suffering beings and oppressed races on this earth, miserable creatures to console, victims to avenge? Do you not understand?"

Captain Nemo stopped at these last words, regretting perhaps that he had spoken so much. But I had guessed that, whatever the motive which had forced him to seek independence under the sea, it had left him still a man, that his heart still beat for the sufferings of humanity, and that his immense charity was for oppressed races as well as individuals. And I then understood for whom those millions were destined, which were forwarded by Captain Nemo when the *Nautilus* was cruising in the waters of Crete.

Chapter IX

A VANISHED CONTINENT

THE NEXT MORNING, THE 19TH OF FEBRUARY, I SAW THE CANADIAN ENTER MY ROOM. I expected this visit. He looked very disappointed.

"Well, sir?" said he.

"Well, Ned, fortune was against us yesterday."

"Yes; that captain must needs stop exactly at the hour we intended leaving his vessel."

"Yes, Ned, he had business at his banker's."

"His banker's!"

"Or rather his banking-house; by that I mean the ocean, where his riches are safer than in the chests of the state."

I then related to the Canadian the incidents of the preceding night, hoping to bring him back to the idea of not abandoning the captain; but my recital had no other result than an energetically expressed regret from Ned that he had not been able to take a walk on the battlefield of Vigo on his own account.

"However," said he, "all is not ended. It is only a blow of the harpoon lost. Another time we must succeed; and to-night, if necessary——"

"In what direction is the *Nautilus* going?" I asked.

"I do not know," replied Ned.

"Well, at noon we shall see the point."

The Canadian returned to Conseil. As soon as I was dressed, I went into the saloon. The compass was not reassuring. The course of the *Nautilus* was S.S.W. We were turning our backs on Europe.

I waited with some impatience till the ship's place was pricked on the chart. At about half-past eleven the reservoirs were emptied, and our vessel rose to the surface of the ocean. I rushed towards the platform. Ned Land had preceded me. No more land in sight. Nothing but an immense sea. Some sails on the horizon, doubtless those going to San Roque in search of favourable winds for doubling the Cape of Good Hope. The weather was cloudy. A gale of wind was preparing. Ned raved, and tried to pierce the cloudy horizon. He still hoped that behind all that fog stretched the land he so longed for.

At noon the sun showed itself for an instant. The second profited by this brightness to take its height. Then the sea becoming more billowy, we descended, and the panel closed.

An hour after, upon consulting the chart, I saw the position of the *Nautilus* was marked at 16° 17' longitude, and 33° 22' latitude, at 150 leagues from the nearest coast. There was no means of flight, and I leave you to imagine the rage of the Canadian when I informed him of our situation.

For myself, I was not particularly sorry. I felt lightened of the load which had oppressed me, and was able to return with some degree of calmness to my accustomed work.

That night, about eleven o'clock, I received a most unexpected visit from Captain Nemo. He asked me very graciously if I felt fatigued from my watch of the preceding night. I answered in the negative.

"Then, M. Aronnax, I propose a curious excursion."

"Propose, captain."

"You have hitherto only visited the submarine depths by daylight, under the brightness of the sun. Would it suit you to see them in the darkness of the night?"

"Most willingly."

"I warn you, the way will be tiring. We shall have far to walk, and must climb a mountain. The roads are not well kept."

"What you say, captain, only heightens my curiosity; I am ready to follow you."

"Come then, sir, we will put on our diving-dresses."

Arrived at the robing-room, I saw that neither of my companions nor any of the ship's crew were to follow us on this excursion. Captain Nemo had not even proposed my taking with me either Ned or Conseil.

In a few moments we had put on our diving-dresses; they placed on our backs the reservoirs, abundantly filled with air, but no electric lamps were prepared. I called the captain's attention to the fact.

"They will be useless," he replied.

I thought I had not heard aright, but I could not repeat my observation, for the captain's head had already disappeared in its metal case. I finished harnessing myself. I felt them put an iron-pointed stick into my hand, and some minutes later, after going through the usual form, we set foot on the bottom of the Atlantic, at a depth of 150 fathoms. Midnight was near. The waters were profoundly dark, but Captain Nemo pointed out in the distance a reddish spot, a sort of large light shining brilliantly about two miles from the *Nautilus*. What this fire might be, what could feed it, why and how it lit up the liquid mass, I could not say. In any case, it did light our way, vaguely, it is true, but I soon accustomed myself to the peculiar darkness, and I understood, under such circumstances, the uselessness of the Ruhmkorff apparatus.

As we advanced, I heard a kind of pattering above my head. The noise redoubling, sometimes producing a continual shower, I soon understood the cause. It was rain falling violently, and crisping the surface of the waves. Instinctively the thought flashed across my mind that I should be wet through! By the water! in the midst of the water! I could not help laughing at the odd idea. But indeed, in the thick diving-dress, the liquid element is no longer felt, and one only seems to be in an atmosphere somewhat denser than the terrestrial atmosphere. Nothing more.

After half-an-hour's walk the soil became stony. Medusae, microscopic crustacea, and pennatules lit it slightly with their phosphorescent gleam. I caught a glimpse of pieces of stone covered with millions of zoöphytes and masses of sea-weed. My feet often slipped upon this viscous carpet of sea-weed, and without my iron-tipped stick I should have fallen more than once. In turning round, I could still see the whitish lantern of the *Nautilus* beginning to pale in the distance.

But the rosy light which guided us increased and lit up the horizon. The presence of this fire under water puzzled me in the highest degree. Was I going towards a natural phenomenon as yet unknown to the savants of the earth? Or even (for this thought crossed my brain) had the hand of man aught to do with this conflagration? Had he fanned this flame? Was I to meet in these depths companions and friends of Captain Nemo whom he was going to visit, and who, like him, led this strange existence? Should I find down there a whole colony of exiles who, weary of the miseries of this earth, had sought and found independence in the deep ocean? All these foolish and unreasonable ideas pursued me. And in this condition of mind, overexcited by the succession of wonders continually passing before my eyes, I should not have been surprised to meet at the bottom of the sea one of those submarine towns of which Captain Nemo dreamed.

Our road grew lighter and lighter. The white glimmer came in rays from the summit of a mountain about 800 feet high. But what I saw was simply a reflection, developed by the clearness of the waters. The source of this inexplicable light was a fire on the opposite side of the mountain.

In the midst of this stony maze, furrowing the bottom of the Atlantic, Captain Nemo advanced without hesitation. He knew this dreary road. Doubtless he had often travelled over it, and could not lose himself. I followed him with unshaken confidence. He seemed to me like a genie of the sea; and, as he walked before me, I could not help admiring his stature, which was outlined in black on the luminous horizon.

It was one in the morning when we arrived at the first slopes of the mountain; but to gain access to them we must venture through the difficult paths of a vast copse.

Yes; a copse of dead trees, without leaves, without sap, trees petrified by the action of the water, and here and there overtopped by gigantic pines. It was like a coal-pit, still standing, holding by the roots to the broken soil, and whose branches, like fine black paper cuttings, showed distinctly on the watery ceiling. Picture to yourself a forest in the Hartz hanging on to the sides of the mountain, but a forest swallowed up. The paths were encumbered with sea-weed and fucus, between which grovelled a whole world of crustacea. I went along, climbing the rocks, striding over extended trunks, breaking the sea-bind-weed which hung from one tree to the other, and frightening the fishes, which flew from branch to branch. Pressing onward, I felt no fatigue. I followed my guide, who was never tired. What a spectacle! How can I express it? How paint the aspect of those woods and rocks in this medium—their underparts dark and wild, the upper coloured with red tints, by that light which the reflecting powers of the waters doubled? We climbed rocks which fell directly after with gigantic bounds and the low growling of an avalanche. To right and left ran long, dark galleries, where sight was lost. Here opened vast glades which the hand of man seemed to have worked; and I sometimes asked myself if some inhabitant of these submarine regions would not suddenly appear to me.

But Captain Nemo was still mounting. I could not stay behind. I followed boldly. My stick gave me good help. A false step would have been dangerous on the narrow passes sloping down to the sides of the gulfs; but I walked with firm step, without feeling any giddiness. Now I jumped a crevice, the depth of which would have made me hesitate had it been among the glaciers on the land; now I ventured on the unsteady trunk of a tree, thrown across from one abyss to the other, without looking under my feet, having only eyes to admire the wild sights of this region.

There, monumental rocks, leaning on their regularly cut bases, seemed to defy all laws of equilibrium. From between their stony knees, trees sprang, like a jet under heavy pressure, and upheld others which upheld them. Natural towers, large scarps, cut perpendicularly, like a "curtain," inclined at an angle which the laws of gravitation could never have tolerated in terrestrial regions.

Two hours after quitting the *Nautilus* we had crossed the line of trees, and a hundred feet above our heads rose the top of the mountain, which cast a shadow on the brilliant irradiation of the opposite slope. Some petrified shrubs ran fantastically here and there. Fishes got up under our feet like birds in the long grass. The massive rocks were rent with impenetrable fractures, deep grottoes, and unfathomable holes, at the bottom of which formidable creatures might be heard moving. My blood curdled when I saw enormous antennae blocking my road, or some frightful claw closing with a noise in the shadow of some cavity. Millions of luminous spots shone brightly in the midst of the darkness. They were the eyes of giant crustacea crouched in their holes; giant lobsters setting themselves up like halberdiers, and moving their claws with the clicking sound of pincers; titanic crabs, pointed like a gun on its carriage; and frightful-looking poulps, interweaving their tentacles like a living nest of serpents.

We had now arrived on the first platform, where other surprises awaited me. Before us lay some picturesque ruins which betrayed the hand of man and not that of the Creator. There were vast heaps of stone, among which might be traced the vague and shadowy forms of castles and temples, clothed with a world of blossoming zoöphytes, and over which, instead of ivy, sea-weed and fucus threw a thick vegetable mantle. But what was this portion of the globe which had been swallowed by cataclysms? Who had placed those rocks and stones like cromlechs of prehistoric times? Where was I? Whither had Captain Nemo's fancy hurried me?

I would fain have asked him; not being able to, I stopped him—I seized his arm. But shaking his head, and pointing to the highest point of the mountain, he seemed to say:

"Come, come along; come higher!"

I followed, and in a few minutes I had climbed to the top, which for a circle of ten yards commanded the whole mass of rock.

I looked down the side we had just climbed. The mountain did not rise more than seven or eight hundred feet above the level of the plain; but on the opposite side it commanded from twice that height the depths of this part of the Atlantic. My eyes ranged far over a large space lit by a violent fulguration. In fact, the mountain was a volcano.

At fifty feet above the peak, in the midst of a rain of stones and scoriae, a large crater was vomiting forth torrents of lava which fell in a cascade of fire into the bosom of the liquid mass. Thus situated, this volcano lit the lower plain like an immense torch, even to the extreme limits of the horizon. I said that the submarine crater threw up lava, but no flames. Flames require the oxygen of the air to feed upon and cannot be developed under water; but streams of lava, having in themselves the principles of their incandescence, can attain a white heat, fight vigorously against the liquid element, and turn it to vapour by contact.

Rapid currents bearing all these gases in diffusion, and torrents of lava, slid to the bottom of the mountain like an eruption of Vesuvius on another Terra del Greco.

There indeed, under my eyes, ruined, destroyed, lay a town—its roofs open to the sky, its temples fallen, its arches dislocated, its columns lying on the ground, from which one would still recognise the massive character of Tuscan architecture. Further on, some remains of a gigantic aqueduct; here the high base of an Acropolis, with the floating outline of a Parthenon; there traces of a quay, as if an ancient port had formerly abutted on the borders of the ocean, and disappeared with its merchant vessels and its war-galleys. Further on again, long lines of sunken walls and broad, deserted streets—a perfect Pompeii escaped beneath the waters. Such was the sight that Captain Nemo brought before my eyes!

Where was I? Where was I? I must know at any cost. I tried to speak, but Captain Nemo stopped me by a gesture, and picking up a piece of chalkstone advanced to a rock of black basalt, and traced the one word,

ATLANTIS

What a light shot through my mind! Atlantis, the ancient Meropis of Theopompus, the Atlantis of Plato, that continent denied by Origen, Jamblichus, D'Anville, Malte-Brun, and Humboldt, who placed its disappearance among the legendary tales admitted by Posidonius, Pliny, Ammianus Marcellinus, Tertullian, Engle, Buffon, and D'Avezac. I had it there now before my eyes, bearing upon it the unexceptionable testimony of its catastrophe. The region thus engulfed was beyond Europe, Asia, and Lybia, beyond the columns of Hercules, where those powerful people, the Atlantides, lived, against whom the first wars of ancient Greeks were waged.

Thus, led by the strangest destiny, I was treading under foot the mountains of this continent, touching with my hand those ruins a thousand generations old, and contemporary with the geological epochs. I was walking on the very spot where the contemporaries of the first man had walked.

While I was trying to fix in my mind every detail of this grand landscape, Captain Nemo remained motionless, as if petrified in mute ecstasy, leaning on a mossy stone. Was he dreaming of those generations long since disappeared? Was he asking them the secret of human destiny? Was it here this strange man came to steep himself in historical recollections and live again this ancient life—he who wanted no modern one? What would I not have given to know his thoughts, to share them, to understand them! We remained for an hour at this place, contemplating the vast plains under the brightness of the lava, which was sometimes wonderfully intense. Rapid tremblings ran along the mountain caused by internal bubblings, deep noises distinctly transmitted through the liquid medium were echoed with majestic grandeur. At this moment the moon appeared through the mass of waters and threw her pale rays on the buried continent. It was but a gleam, but what an indescribable effect! The captain rose, cast one last look on the immense plain, and then bade me follow him.

We descended the mountain rapidly, and, the mineral forest once passed, I saw the lantern of the *Nautilus* shining like a star. The captain walked straight to it, and we got on board as the first rays of light whitened the surface of the ocean.

Chapter X

THE SUBMARINE COAL-MINES

THE NEXT DAY, THE 20TH OF FEBRUARY, I AWOKE VERY LATE; THE FATIGUES OF THE PRE-vious night had prolonged my sleep until eleven o'clock. I dressed quickly and hastened to find the course the *Nautilus* was taking. The instruments showed it to be still towards the south, with a speed of twenty miles an hour and a depth of fifty fathoms.

The species of fishes here did not differ much from those already noticed. There were rays of giant size, five yards long and endowed with great muscular strength, which enabled them to shoot above the waves; sharks of many kinds, among others a glaucus fifteen feet long, with triangular sharp teeth, and whose transparency rendered it almost invisible in the water; brown sagrae; humantins, prism-shaped and clad with a tuberculous hide; sturgeons, resembling their congeners of the Mediterranean; trumpet syngnathes a foot and a half long, furnished with greyish bladders, without teeth or tongue, and as supple as snakes.

Among bony fish Conseil noticed some blackish makairas about three yards long, armed at the upper jaw with a piercing sword; other bright-coloured creatures, known in the time of Aristotle by the name of the sea-dragon, which are dangerous to capture on account of the spikes on their back; also some coryphaenes with brown backs marked with little blue stripes and surrounded by a gold border; some beautiful dorades, and swordfish four-and-twenty feet long, swimming in troops, fierce animals, but rather herbivorous than carnivorous.

About four o'clock the soil, generally composed of a thick mud mixed with petrified wood, changed by degrees, and it became more stony and seemed strewn with conglomerate and pieces of basalt, with a sprinkling of lava and sulphurous obsidian. I thought that a mountainous region was succeeding the long plains; and accordingly, after a few evolutions of the *Nautilus*, I saw the southerly horizon blocked by a high wall which seemed to close all exit. Its summit evidently passed the level of the ocean. It must be a continent, or at least an island—one of the Canaries, or of the Cape Verde Islands. The bearings not being yet taken, perhaps designedly, I was ignorant of our exact position. In any case, such a wall seemed to me to mark the limits of that Atlantis of which we had in reality passed over only the smallest part.

Much longer should I have remained at the window, admiring the beauties of sea and sky, but the panels closed. At this moment the *Nautilus* arrived at the side of this high perpendicular wall. What it would do I could not guess. I returned to my room; it no longer moved. I laid myself down with the full intention of waking after a few hours' sleep; but it was eight o'clock the next day when I entered the saloon. I looked at the manometer. It told me that the *Nautilus* was floating on the surface of the ocean. Besides, I heard steps on the platform. I went to the panel. It was open; but, instead of broad daylight, as I expected, I was surrounded by profound darkness. Where were we? Was I mistaken? Was it still night? No; not a star was shining, and night has not that utter darkness.

I knew not what to think, when a voice near me said:

"Is that you, professor?"

"Ah! Captain," I answered, "where are we?"

"Underground, sir."

"Underground!" I exclaimed. "And the *Nautilus* floating still?"

"It always floats."

"But I do not understand."

"Wait a few minutes, our lantern will be lit, and, if you like light places, you will be satisfied."

I stood on the platform and waited. The darkness was so complete that I could not even see Captain Nemo; but looking to the zenith, exactly above my head, I seemed to catch an undecided gleam, a kind of twilight filling a circular hole. At this instant the lantern was lit, and its vividness dispelled the faint light. I closed my dazzled eyes for an instant, and then looked again. The *Nautilus* was stationary, floating near a mountain which formed a sort of quay. The lake then supporting it was a lake imprisoned by a circle of walls, measuring two miles in diameter and six in circumference. Its level (the manometer showed) could only be the same as the outside level, for there must necessarily be a communication between the lake and the sea. The high partitions, leaning forward on their base, grew into a vaulted roof bearing the shape of an immense funnel turned upside down, the height being about five or six hundred yards. At the summit was a circular orifice, by which I had caught the slight gleam of light, evidently daylight.

"Where are we?" I asked.

"In the very heart of an extinct volcano, the interior of which has been invaded by the sea, after some great convulsion of the earth. While you were sleeping, professor, the *Nautilus* penetrated to this lagoon by a natural canal, which opens about ten yards beneath the surface of the ocean. This is its harbour of refuge, a sure, commodious, and mysterious one, sheltered from all gales. Show me, if you can, on the coasts of any of your continents or islands, a road which can give such perfect refuge from all storms."

"Certainly," I replied, "you are in safety here, Captain Nemo. Who could reach you in the heart of a volcano? But did I not see an opening at its summit?"

"Yes; its crater, formerly filled with lava, vapour, and flames, and which now gives entrance to the life-giving air we breathe."

"But what is this volcanic mountain?"

"It belongs to one of the numerous islands with which this sea is strewn—to vessels a simple sand-bank—to us an immense cavern. Chance led me to discover it, and chance led me well."

"But of what use is this refuge, captain? The *Nautilus* wants no port."

"No, sir; but it wants electricity to make it move, and the wherewithal to make the electricity—sodium to feed the elements, coal from which to get the sodium, and a coal-mine to supply the coal. And exactly on this spot the sea covers entire forests embedded during the geological periods, now mineralised and transformed into coal; for me they are an inexhaustible mine."

"Your men follow the trade of miners here, then, Captain?"

"Exactly so. These mines extend under the waves like the mines of Newcastle. Here, in their diving-dresses, pickaxe and shovel in hand, my men extract the coal, which I do not even ask from the mines of the earth. When I burn this combustible for the manufacture of sodium, the smoke, escaping from the crater of the mountain, gives it the appearance of a still active volcano."

"And we shall see your companions at work?"

"No; not this time at least; for I am in a hurry to continue our submarine tour of the earth. So I shall content myself with drawing from the reserve of sodium I already possess. The time for loading is one day only, and we continue our voyage. So, if you wish to go over the cavern, and make the round of the lagoon, you must take advantage of to-day, M. Aronnax."

I thanked the captain and went to look for my companions, who had not yet left their cabin. I invited them to follow me without saying where we were. They mounted the platform. Conseil, who was astonished at nothing, seemed to look upon it as quite natural that he should wake under a mountain, after having fallen asleep under the waves. But Ned Land thought of nothing but finding whether the cavern had any exit. After breakfast, about ten o'clock, we went down on to the mountain.

"Here we are, once more on land," said Conseil.

"I do not call this land," said the Canadian. "And besides, we are not on it, but beneath it."

Between the walls of the mountains and the waters of the lake lay a sandy shore which, at its greatest breadth, measured five hundred feet. On this soil one might easily make the tour of the lake. But the base of the high partitions was stony ground, with volcanic locks and enormous pumice-stones lying in picturesque heaps. All these detached masses, covered with enamel, polished by the action of the subterraneous fires, shone resplendent by the light of our electric lantern. The mica-dust from the shore, rising under our feet, flew like a cloud of sparks. The bottom now rose sensibly, and we soon arrived at long circuitous slopes, or inclined planes, which took us higher by degrees; but we were obliged to walk carefully among these conglomerates, bound by no cement, the feet slipping on the glassy crystal, felspar, and quartz.

The volcanic nature of this enormous excavation was confirmed on all sides, and I pointed it out to my companions.

"Picture to yourselves," said I, "what this crater must have been when filled with boiling lava, and when the level of the incandescent liquid rose to the orifice of the mountain, as though melted on the top of a hot plate."

"I can picture it perfectly," said Conseil. "But, sir, will you tell me why the Great Architect has suspended operations, and how it is that the furnace is replaced by the quiet waters of the lake?"

"Most probably, Conseil, because some convulsion beneath the ocean produced that very opening which has served as a passage for the *Nautilus*. Then the waters of the Atlantic rushed into the interior of the mountain. There must have been a terrible struggle between the two elements, a struggle which ended in the victory of Neptune. But many ages have run out since then, and the submerged volcano is now a peaceable grotto."

"Very well," replied Ned Land; "I accept the explanation, sir; but, in our own interests, I regret that the opening of which you speak was not made above the level of the sea."

"But, friend Ned," said Conseil, "if the passage had not been under the sea, the *Nautilus* could not have gone through it."

We continued ascending. The steps became more and more perpendicular and narrow. Deep excavations, which we were obliged to cross, cut them here and there; sloping masses had to be turned. We slid upon our knees and crawled along. But Conseil's dexterity and the Canadian's strength surmounted all obstacles. At a height of about thirty-one feet the nature of the ground changed without becoming more practicable. To the conglomerate and trachyte succeeded black basalt, the first dispread in layers full of bubbles, the latter forming regular prisms, placed like a colonnade supporting the spring of the immense vault, an admirable specimen of natural architecture. Between the blocks of basalt wound long streams of lava, long since grown cold, encrusted with bituminous rays; and in some places there were spread large carpets of sulphur. A more powerful light shone through the upper crater, shedding a vague glimmer over these volcanic depressions forever buried in the bosom of this extinguished mountain. But our upward march was soon stopped at a height of about two hundred and fifty feet by impassable obstacles. There was a complete vaulted arch overhanging us, and our ascent was changed to a circular walk. At the last change vegetable life began to struggle with the mineral. Some shrubs, and even some trees, grew from the fractures of the walls. I recognised some euphorbias, with the caustic sugar coming from them; heliotropes, quite incapable of justifying their name, sadly drooped their clusters of flowers, both their colour and perfume half gone. Here and there some chrysanthemums grew timidly at the foot of an aloe with long, sickly-looking leaves. But between the streams of lava, I saw some little violets still slightly perfumed, and I admit that I smelled them with delight. Perfume is the soul of the flower, and seaflowers, those splendid hydrophytes, have no soul.

We had arrived at the foot of some sturdy dragon-trees, which had pushed aside the rocks with their strong roots, when Ned Land exclaimed:

"Ah! sir, a hive! A hive!"

"A hive!" I replied, with a gesture of incredulity.

"Yes, a hive," repeated the Canadian, "and bees humming round it."

I approached, and was bound to believe my own eyes. There at a hole bored in one of the dragon-trees were some thousands of these ingenious insects, so common in all the Canaries, and whose produce is so much esteemed. Naturally enough, the Canadian wished to gather the honey, and I could not well oppose his wish. A quantity of dry leaves, mixed with sulphur, he lit with a spark from his flint, and he began to smoke out the bees. The humming ceased by degrees, and the hive eventually yielded several pounds of the sweetest honey, with which Ned Land filled his haversack.

"When I have mixed this honey with the paste of the artocarpus," said he, "I shall be able to offer you a succulent cake."

"Upon my word," said Conseil, "it will be gingerbread."

"Never mind the gingerbread," said I; "let us continue our interesting walk."

At every turn of the path we were following, the lake appeared in all its length and breadth. The lantern lit up the whole of its peaceable surface, which knew neither ripple nor wave. The *Nautilus* remained perfectly immovable. On the platform, and on the mountain, the ship's crew were working like black shadows clearly carved against the luminous atmosphere. We were now going round the highest crest of the first layers of rock which upheld the roof. I then saw that bees were not the only representatives of the animal kingdom in the interior of this volcano. Birds of prey hovered here and there in the shadows, or fled from their nests on the top of the rocks. There were sparrow-hawks with white breasts, and kestrels, and down the slopes scampered, with their long legs, several fine fat bustards. I leave anyone to imagine the covetousness of the Canadian at the sight of this savoury game, and whether he did not regret having no gun. But he did his best to replace the lead by stones, and after several fruitless attempts, he succeeded in wounding a magnificent bird. To say that he risked his life twenty times before reaching it, is but the truth; but he managed so well that the creature joined the honey cakes in his bag. We were now obliged to descend towards the shore, the crest becoming impracticable. Above us the crater seemed to gape like the mouth of a well. From this place the sky could be clearly seen, and clouds, dissipated by the west wind, leaving behind them, even on the summit of the mountain, their misty remnants—certain proof that they were only moderately high, for the volcano did not rise more than eight hundred feet above the level of the ocean. Half-an-hour after the Canadian's last exploit we had regained the inner shore. Here the flora was represented by large carpets of marine crystal, a little umbelliferous plant very good to pickle, which also bears the name of pierce-stone and sea-fennel. Conseil gathered some bundles of it. As to the fauna, it might be counted by thousands of crustacea of all sorts, lobsters, crabs, palaemans, spider-crabs, chameleon shrimps, and a large number of shells, rockfish, and limpets. Three-quarters of an hour later, we had finished our circuitous walk and were on board. The crew had just finished loading the sodium, and the *Nautilus* could have left that instant. But Captain Nemo gave no order. Did he wish to wait until night, and leave the submarine passage secretly? Perhaps so. Whatever it might be, the next day, the *Nautilus*, having left its port, steered clear of all land at a few yards beneath the waves of the Atlantic.

Chapter XI

THE SARGASSO SEA

THAT DAY THE *NAUTILUS* CROSSED A SINGULAR PART OF THE ATLANTIC OCEAN. NO ONE can be ignorant of the existence of a current of warm water, known by the name of the Gulf Stream. After leaving the Gulf of Mexico, about twenty-five degrees of north latitude, this current divides into two arms, the principal one going towards the coast of Ireland and Norway, while the second bends to the south about the height of the Azores; then, touching the African shore, and describing a lengthened oval, returns to the Antilles. This second arm—it is rather a collar than an arm—surrounds with its circles of warm water that portion of the cold, quiet, immovable ocean called the Sargasso Sea, a perfect lake in the open Atlantic: it takes no less than three years for the great current to pass round it. Such was the region the *Nautilus* was now visiting, a perfect meadow, a close carpet of sea-weed, fucus, and tropical berries, so thick and so compact that the stem of a vessel could hardly tear its way through it. And Captain Nemo, not wishing to entangle his screw in this herbaceous mass, kept some yards beneath the surface of the waves. The name Sargasso comes from the Spanish word *sargazzo* which signifies kelp. This kelp, or berry-plant, is the principal formation of this immense bank. And this is the reason, according to the learned Maury, the author of *The Physical Geography of the Globe*, why these hydrophytes unite in the peaceful basin of the Atlantic. The only explanation which can be given, he says, seems to me to result from the experience known to all the world. Place in a vase some fragments of cork or other floating body, and give to the water in the vase a circular movement the scattered fragments will unite in a group in the centre of the liquid surface, that is to say, in the part least agitated. In the phenomenon we are considering, the Atlantic is the vase, the Gulf Stream the circular current, and the Sargasso Sea the central point at which the floating bodies unite.

I share Maury's opinion, and I was able to study the phenomenon in the very midst, where vessels rarely penetrate. Above us floated products of all kinds, heaped up among these brownish plants; trunks of trees torn from the Andes or the Rocky Mountains, and floated by the Amazon or the Mississippi; numerous wrecks, remains of keels, or ships' bottoms, side planks stove in, and so weighted with shells and barnacles that they could not again rise to the surface. And time will one day justify Maury's other opinion, that these substances thus accumulated for ages will become petrified by the action of the water, and will then form inexhaustible coal-mines—a precious reserve prepared by far-seeing nature for the moment when men shall have exhausted the mines of continents.

In the midst of this inextricable mass of plants and sea-weed, I noticed some charming pink halcyons and actiniae, with their long tentacles trailing after them; medusae, green, red, and blue and the great rhyostoms or Cuvier, the large umbrella of which was bordered and festooned with violet.

All the day of the 22d of February we passed in the Sargasso Sea, where such fish as are partial to marine plants and fuel find abundant nourishment. The next, the ocean had returned to its accustomed aspect. From this time for nineteen days, from the 23d of February to the 12th of March, the *Nautilus* kept in the middle of the Atlantic, carrying us at a constant speed of a hundred leagues in twenty-four hours. Captain Nemo evidently intended accomplishing his submarine programme, and I imagined that he intended, after doubling Cape Horn, to return to the Australian seas of the Pacific. Ned Land had cause for fear. In these large seas, void of islands, we could not attempt to leave the boat. Nor had we any means of opposing Captain Nemo's will. Our only course was to submit; but what we could neither gain by force nor cunning, I liked to think might be obtained by persuasion. This voyage ended, would he not consent to restore our liberty, under an oath never to reveal his existence—an oath of honour which we should have religiously kept? But we must consider that delicate question with the captain. But was I free to claim this liberty? Had he not himself said from the beginning, in the firmest manner, that the secret of his life exacted from him our lasting imprisonment on board the *Nautilus?* And would not my four months' silence appear to him a tacit acceptance of our situation? And would not a return to the subject result in raising suspicions which might be hurtful to our projects if at some future time a favourable opportunity offered to return to them?

During the nineteen days mentioned above, no incident of any note happened to signalise our voyage. I saw little of the captain; he was at work. In the library I often found his books left open, especially those on natural history. My work on submarine depths, conned over by him, was covered with marginal notes, often contradicting my theories and systems; but the captain contented himself with thus purging my work; it was very rare for him to discuss it with me. Sometimes I heard the melancholy tones of his organ; but only at night, in the midst of the deepest obscurity, when the *Nautilus* slept upon the deserted ocean. During this part of our voyage we sailed whole days on the surface of the waves. The sea seemed abandoned. A few sailing-vessels, on the road to India, were making for the Cape of Good Hope. One day we were followed by the boats of a whaler, who, no doubt, took us for some enormous whale of great price; but Captain Nemo did not wish the worthy fellows to lose their time and trouble, so ended the chase by plunging under the water. Our navigation continued until the 13th of March; that day the *Nautilus* was employed in taking soundings, which greatly interested me. We had then made about 13,000 leagues since our departure from the high seas of the Pacific. The bearings gave us 45° 37' south latitude, and 37° 53' west longitude. It was the same water in which Captain Denham, of the *Herald*, sounded 7,000 fathoms without finding the bottom. There, too, Lieutenant Parker, of the American frigate *Congress*, could not touch the bottom with 15,140 yards. Captain Nemo intended seeking the bottom of the ocean by a diagonal sufficiently lengthened by means of lateral planes, placed at an angle of forty-five degrees with the water-line of the *Nautilus*. Then the screw set to work at its maximum speed, its four blades beating the waves with indescribable force. Under this powerful pressure the hull of the *Nautilus* quivered like a sonorous chord, and sank regularly under the water.

At 7,000 fathoms I saw some blackish tops rising from the midst of the waters; but these summits might belong to high mountains like the Himalayas or Mont Blanc, even higher; and the depth of the abyss remained incalculable. The *Nautilus* descended still lower, in spite of the great pressure. I felt the steel plates tremble at the fastenings of the bolts; its bars bent, its partitions groaned; the windows of the saloon seemed to curve under the pressure of the waters. And this firm structure would doubtless have yielded, if, as its captain had said, it had not been capable of resistance like a solid block. In skirting the declivity of these rocks, lost under the water, I still saw some shells, some serpulae and spinorbes, still living, and some specimens of asteriads. But soon this last representative of animal life disappeared; and at the depth of more than three leagues, the *Nautilus* had passed the limits of submarine existence even as a balloon does when it rises above the respirable atmosphere. We had attained a depth of 16,000 yards (four leagues), and the sides of the *Nautilus* then bore a pressure of 1,600 atmospheres, that is to say, 3,200 pounds to each square two-fifths of an inch of its surface.

"What a situation to be in!" I exclaimed. "To over-run these deep regions where man has never trod! Look, captain, look at these magnificent rocks, these uninhabited grottoes, these lowest receptacles of the globe, where life is no longer possible! What unknown sights are here! Why should we be unable to preserve a remembrance of them?"

"Would you like to carry away more than the remembrance?" said Captain Nemo.

"What do you mean by those words?"

"I mean to say that nothing is easier than to make a photographic view of this submarine region."

I had not time to express my surprise at this new proposition, when, at Captain Nemo's call, an objective was brought into the saloon. Through the widely opened panel, the liquid mass was bright with electricity, which was distributed with such uniformity that not a shadow, not a gradation, was to be seen in our manufactured light. The *Nautilus* remained motionless, the force of its screw subdued by the inclination of its planes: the instrument was propped on the bottom of the oceanic site, and in a few seconds we had obtained a perfect negative. I here give the positive, from which may be seen those primitive rocks, which have never looked upon the light of heaven; that lowest granite which forms the foundation of the globe; those deep grottoes, woven in the stony mass whose outlines were of such sharpness, and the border lines of which are marked in black, as if done by the brush of some Flemish artist. Beyond that again, a horizon of mountains, an admirable undulating line, forming the prospective of the landscape. I cannot describe the effect of these smooth, black, polished rocks, without moss, without a spot, and of strange forms, standing solidly on the sandy carpet which sparkled under the jets of our electric light.

But the operation being over, Captain Nemo said: "Let us go up; we must not abuse our position, nor expose the *Nautilus* too long to such great pressure."

"Go up again!" I exclaimed.

"Hold well on."

I had not time to understand why the captain cautioned me thus, when I was thrown forward on to the carpet. At a signal from the captain, its screw was shipped, and its blades raised vertically; the *Nautilus* shot into the air like a balloon, rising with stunning rapidity, and cutting the mass of waters with a sonorous agitation. Nothing was visible; and in four minutes it had shot through the four leagues which separated it from the ocean, and, after emerging like a flying-fish, fell, making the waves rebound to an enormous height.

Chapter XII

CACHALOTS AND WHALES

DURING THE NIGHTS OF THE 13TH AND 14TH OF MARCH, THE *NAUTILUS* RETURNED TO its southerly course. I fancied that, when on a level with Cape Horn, he would turn the helm westward, in order to beat the Pacific seas, and so complete the tour of the world. He did nothing of the kind, but continued on his way to the southern regions. Where was he going to? To the pole? It was madness! I began to think that the captain's temerity justified Ned Land's fears. For some time past the Canadian had not spoken to me of his projects of flight; he was less communicative, almost silent. I could see that this lengthened imprisonment was weighing upon him, and I felt that rage was burning within him. When he met the captain, his eyes lit up with suppressed anger; and I feared that his natural violence would lead him into some extreme. That day, the 14th of March, Conseil and he came to me in my room. I inquired the cause of their visit.

"A simple question to ask you, sir," replied the Canadian.

"Speak, Ned."

"How many men are there on board the *Nautilus,* do you think?"

"I cannot tell, my friend."

"I should say that its working does not require a large crew."

"Certainly, under existing conditions, ten men, at the most, ought to be enough."

"Well, why should there be any more?"

"Why?" I replied, looking fixedly at Ned Land, whose meaning was easy to guess. "Because," I added, "if my surmises are correct, and if I have well understood the captain's existence, the *Nautilus* is not only a vessel' it is also a place of refuge for those who, like its commander, have broken every tie upon earth."

"Perhaps so," said Conseil; "but, in any case, the *Nautilus* can only contain a certain number of men. Could not you, sir, estimate their maximum?"

"How, Conseil?"

"By calculation; given the size of the vessel, which you know, sir, and consequently the quantity of air it contains, knowing also how much each man expends at a breath, and comparing these results with the fact that the *Nautilus* is obliged to go to the surface every twenty-four hours."

Conseil had not finished the sentence before I saw what he was driving at.

"I understand," said I; "but that calculation, though simple enough, can give but a very uncertain result."

"Never mind," said Ned Land urgently.

"Here it is, then," said I. "In one hour each man consumes the oxygen contained in twenty gallons of air; and in twenty-four, that contained in 480 gallons. We must, therefore, find how many times 480 gallons of air the *Nautilus* contains."

"Just so," said Conseil.

"Or," I continued, "the size of the *Nautilus* being 1,500 tons, and one ton holding 200 gallons, it contains 300,000 gallons of air, which, divided by 480, gives a quotient of 625. Which means to say, strictly speaking, that the air contained in the *Nautilus* would suffice for 625 men for twenty-four hours."

"Six hundred and twenty-five!" repeated Ned.

"But remember, that all of us, passengers, sailors, and officers included, would not form a tenth part of that number."

"Still too many for three men," murmured Conseil.

The Canadian shook his head, passed his hand across his forehead, and left the room without answering.

"Will you allow me to make one observation, sir?" said Conseil. "Poor Ned is longing for everything that he cannot have. His past life is always present to him; everything that we are forbidden he regrets. His head is full of old recollections. And we must understand him. What has he to do here? Nothing; he is not learned like you, sir; and has not the same taste for the beauties of the sea that we have. He would risk everything to be able to go once more into a tavern in his own country."

Certainly the monotony on board must seem intolerable to the Canadian, accustomed as he was to a life of liberty and activity. Events were rare which could rouse him to any show of spirit; but that day an event did happen which recalled the bright days of the harpooner. About eleven in the morning, being on the surface of the ocean, the *Nautilus* fell in with a troop of whales—an encounter which did not astonish me, knowing that these creatures, hunted to death, had taken refuge in high latitudes.

We were seated on the platform, with a quiet sea. The month of October in those latitudes gave us some lovely autumnal days. It was the Canadian—he could not be mistaken—who signalled a whale on the eastern horizon. Looking attentively, one might see its black back rise and fall with the waves five miles from the *Nautilus*.

"Ah!" exclaimed Ned Land, "if I was on board a whaler, now such a meeting would give me pleasure. It is one of large size. See with what strength its blow-holes throw up columns of air and steam! Confound it, why am I bound to these steel plates?"

"What, Ned," said I, "you have not forgotten your old ideas of fishing?"

"Can a whale-fisher ever forget his old trade, sir? Can he ever tire of the emotions caused by such a chase?"

"You have never fished in these seas, Ned?"

"Never, sir; in the northern only, and as much in Behring as in Davis Straits."

"Then the southern whale is still unknown to you. It is the Greenland whale you have hunted up to this time, and that would not risk passing through the warm waters of the equator. Whales are localised according to their kinds, in certain seas which they never leave. And if one of these creatures went from Behring to Davis Straits, it must be simply because there is a passage from one sea to the other, either on the American or the Asiatic side."

"In that case, as I have never fished in these seas, I do not know the kind of whale frequenting them."

"I have told you, Ned."

"A greater reason for making their acquaintance," said Conseil.

"Look! Look!" exclaimed the Canadian, "they approach; they aggravate me; they know that I cannot get at them!"

Ned stamped his feet. His hand trembled as he grasped an imaginary harpoon.

"Are these cetacea as large as those of the northern seas?" asked he.

"Very nearly, Ned."

"Because I have seen large whales, sir, whales measuring a hundred feet. I have even been told that those of Hullamoch and Umgallick, of the Aleutian Islands, are sometimes a hundred and fifty feet long."

"That seems to me exaggeration. These creatures are only balaenopterons, provided with dorsal fins; and, like the cachalots, are generally much smaller than the Greenland whale."

"Ah!" exclaimed the Canadian, whose eyes had never left the ocean. "They are coming nearer; they are in the same water as the *Nautilus*."

Then returning to the conversation, he said:

"You spoke of the cachalot as a small creature. I have heard of gigantic ones. They are intelligent cetacea. It is said of some that they cover themselves with sea-weed and fucus, and then are taken for islands. People encamp upon them, and settle there; light a fire—"

"And build houses," said Conseil.

"Yes, joker," said Ned Land. "And one fine day the creature plunges, carrying with it all the inhabitants to the bottom of the sea."

"Something like the travels of Sinbad the Sailor," I replied, laughing.

"Ah!" suddenly exclaimed Ned Land. "It is not one whale; there are ten—there are twenty—it is a whole troop! And I not able to do anything! Hands and feet tied!"

"But, friend Ned," said Conseil, "why do you not ask Captain Nemo's permission to chase them?"

Conseil had not finished his sentence when Ned Land had lowered himself through the panel to seek the captain. A few minutes afterwards the two appeared together on the platform.

Captain Nemo watched the troop of cetacea playing on the waters about a mile from the *Nautilus*.

"They are southern whales," said he; "there goes the fortune of a whole fleet of whalers."

"Well, sir," asked the Canadian, "can I not chase them, if only to remind me of my old trade of harpooner?"

"And to what purpose?" replied Captain Nemo. "Only to destroy! We have nothing to do with the whale-oil on board."

"But, sir," continued the Canadian, "in the Red Sea you allowed us to follow the dugong."

"Then it was to procure fresh meat for my crew. Here it would be killing for killing's sake. I know that is a privilege reserved for man, but I do not approve of such murderous pastime. In destroying the southern whale (like the Greenland whale, an inoffensive creature), your traders do a culpable action, Master Land. They have already depopulated the whole of Baffin's Bay, and are annihilating a class of useful animals. Leave the unfortunate cetacea alone. They have plenty of natural enemies—cachalots, swordfish, and sawfish—without *your* troubling them."

The captain was right. The barbarous and inconsiderate greed of these fishermen will one day cause the disappearance of the last whale in the ocean. Ned Land whistled "Yankee Doodle" between his teeth, thrust his hands into his pockets, and turned his back upon us. But Captain Nemo watched the troop of cetacea, and addressing me said:

"I was right in saying that whales had natural enemies enough, without counting man. These will have plenty to do before long. Do you see, M. Aronnax, about eight miles to leeward, those blackish moving points?"

"Yes, captain," I replied.

"Those are cachalots—terrible animals, which I have met in troops of two or three hundred. As to *those*, they are cruel, mischievous creatures; they would be right in exterminating them."

The Canadian turned quickly at the last words.

"Well, captain," said he, "it is still time, in the interest of the whales."

"It is useless to expose one's self, professor. The *Nautilus* will disperse them. It is armed with a steel spur as good as Master Land's harpoon, I imagine."

The Canadian did not put himself out enough to shrug his shoulders. Attack cetacea with blows of a spur! Who had ever heard of such a thing?

"Wait, M. Aronnax," said Captain Nemo. "We will show you something you have never yet seen. We have no pity for these ferocious creatures. They are nothing but mouth and teeth."

Mouth and teeth! No one could better describe the macrocephalous cachalot, which is sometimes more than seventy-five feet long. Its enormous head occupies one-third of its entire body. Better armed than the whale, whose upper jaw is furnished only with whalebone, it is supplied with twenty-five large tusks, about eight inches long, cylindrical and conical at the top, each weighing two pounds. It is in the upper part of this enormous head, in great cavities divided by cartilages, that is to be found from six to eight hundred pounds of that precious oil called spermaceti. The cachalot is a disagreeable creature, more tadpole than fish, according to Fredol's description. It is badly formed, the whole of its left side being (if we may say it) a "failure," and being only able to see with its right eye. But the formidable troop was nearing us. They had seen the whales and were preparing to attack them. One could judge beforehand that the cachalots would be victorious, not only because they were better built for attack than their inoffensive adversaries, but also because they could remain longer under water without coming to the surface. There was only just time to go to the help of the whales. The *Nautilus* went under water. Conseil, Ned Land, and I took our places before the window in the saloon, and Captain Nemo joined the pilot in his cage to work his apparatus as an engine of destruction. Soon I felt the beatings of the screw quicken, and our speed increased. The battle between the cachalots and the whales had already begun when the *Nautilus* arrived. They did not at first show any fear at the sight of this new monster joining in the conflict. But they soon had to guard against its blows. What a battle! The *Nautilus* was nothing but a formidable harpoon, brandished by the hand of its captain. It hurled itself against the fleshy mass, passing through from one part to the other, leaving behind it two quivering halves of the animal. It could not feel the formidable blows from their tails upon its sides, nor the shock which it produced itself, much more. One cachalot killed, it ran at the next, tacked on the spot that it might not miss its prey, going forward and backward, answering to its helm, plunging when the cetacean dived into the deep waters, coming up with it when it returned to the surface, striking it front or sideways, cutting or tearing in all directions and at any pace, piercing it with its terrible spur. What carnage! What a noise on the surface of the waves! What sharp hissing, and what snorting peculiar to these enraged animals! In the midst of these waters, generally so peaceful, their tails made perfect billows. For one hour this wholesale massacre continued, from which the cachalots could not escape. Several times ten or twelve united tried to crush the *Nautilus* by their weight. From the window we could see their enormous mouths, studded with tusks, and their formidable eyes. Ned Land could not contain himself, he threatened and swore at them. We could feel them clinging to our vessel like dogs worrying a wild boar in a copse. But the *Nautilus*, working its screw, carried them here and there, or to the upper levels of the ocean, without caring for their enormous weight, nor the powerful strain on the vessel. At length the mass of cachalots broke up, the waves became quiet, and I felt that we were rising to the surface. The panel opened, and we hurried on to the platform. The sea was covered with mutilated bodies. A formidable explosion could not have divided and torn this fleshy mass with more violence. We were floating amid gigantic bodies, bluish on the back and white underneath, covered with enormous protuberances. Some terrified cachalots were flying towards the horizon. The waves were dyed red for several miles, and the *Nautilus* floated in a sea of blood. Captain Nemo joined us.

"Well, Master Land?" said he.

"Well, sir," replied the Canadian, whose enthusiasm had somewhat calmed; "it is a terrible spectacle, certainly. But I am not a butcher. I am a hunter, and I call this a butchery."

"It is a massacre of mischievous creatures," replied the Captain; "and the *Nautilus* is not a butcher's knife."

"I like my harpoon better," said the Canadian.

"Everyone to his own," answered the captain, looking fixedly at Ned Land.

I feared he would commit some act of violence, which would end in sad consequences. But his anger was turned by the sight of a whale which the *Nautilus* had just come up with. The creature had not quite escaped from the cachalot's teeth. I recognised the southern whale by its flat head, which is entirely black. Anatomically, it is distinguished from the white whale and the North Cape whale by the seven cervical vertebrae, and it has two more ribs than its congeners. The unfortunate cetacean was lying on its side, riddled with holes from the bites, and quite dead. From its mutilated fin still hung a young whale which it could not save from the massacre. Its open mouth let the water flow in and out, murmuring like the waves breaking on the shore. Captain Nemo steered close to the corpse of the creature. Two of his men mounted its side, and I saw, not without surprise, that they were drawing from its breasts all the milk which they contained, that is to say, about two or three tons. The Captain offered me a cup of the milk, which was still warm. I could not help showing my repugnance to the drink; but he assured me that it was excellent, and not to be distinguished from cow's milk. I tasted it, and was of his opinion. It was a useful reserve to us, for in the shape of salt butter or cheese it would form an agreeable variety from our ordinary food. From that day I noticed with uneasiness that Ned Land's ill-will towards Captain Nemo increased, and I resolved to watch the Canadian's gestures closely.

Chapter XIII

The Iceberg

THE *NAUTILUS* WAS STEADILY PURSUING ITS SOUTHERLY COURSE, FOLLOWING THE FIFTIeth meridian with considerable speed. Did he wish to reach the pole? I did not think so, for every attempt to reach that point had hitherto failed. Again, the season was far advanced, for in the antarctic regions the 13th of March corresponds with the 13th of September of northern regions, which begin at the equinoctial season. On the 14th of March I saw floating ice in latitude 55°, merely pale bits of debris from twenty to twenty-five feet long, forming banks over which the sea curled. The *Nautilus* remained on the surface of the ocean. Ned Land, who had fished in the arctic seas, was familiar with its icebergs; but Conseil and I admired them for the first time. In the atmosphere towards the southern horizon stretched a white dazzling band. English whalers have given it the name of "ice blink." However thick the clouds may be, it is always visible, and announces the presence of an ice-pack or bank. Accordingly, larger blocks soon appeared, whose brilliancy changed with the caprices of the fog. Some of these masses showed green veins, as if long undulating lines had been traced with sulphate of copper; others resembled enormous amethysts with the light shining through them. Some reflected the light of day upon a thousand crystal facets. Others shaded with vivid calcareous reflections resembled a perfect town of marble. The more we neared the south the more these floating islands increased both in number and importance.

At sixtieth degree of latitude every pass had disappeared. But seeking carefully, Captain Nemo soon found a narrow opening, through which he boldly slipped, knowing, however, that it would close behind him. Thus, guided by this clever hand, the *Nautilus* passed through all the ice with a precision which quite charmed Conseil; icebergs or mountains, ice-fields or smooth plains, seeming to have no limits, drift ice or floating ice-packs, or plains broken up, called palches when they are circular, and streams when they are made up of long strips. The temperature was very low; the thermometer exposed to the air marked two or three degrees below zero, but we were warmly clad with fur, at the expense of the sea-bear and seal. The interior of the *Nautilus*, warmed regularly by its electric apparatus, defied the most intense cold. Besides, it would only have been necessary to go some yards beneath the waves to find a more bearable temperature. Two months earlier we should have had perpetual daylight in these latitudes; but already we had had three or four hours of night, and by and by there would be six months of darkness in these circumpolar regions. On the 15th of March we were in the latitude of New Shetland and South Orkney. The captain told me that formerly numerous tribes of seals inhabited them; but that English and American whalers, in their rage for destruction, massacred both old and young; thus, where there was once life and animation, they had left silence and death.

About eight o'clock on the morning of the 16th of March, the *Nautilus*, following the fifty-fifth meridian, cut the antarctic polar circle. Ice surrounded us on all sides, and closed the horizon. But Captain Nemo went from one opening to another, still going higher. I cannot express my astonishment at the beauties of these new regions. The ice took most surprising forms. Here the grouping formed an Oriental town, with innumerable mosques and minarets; there a fallen city thrown to the earth, as it were, by some convulsion of nature. The whole aspect was constantly changed by the oblique rays of the sun, or lost in the greyish fog amid hurricanes of snow. Detonations and falls were heard on all sides, great overthrows of icebergs, which altered the whole landscape like a diorama. Often seeing no exit, I thought we were definitely prisoners; but instinct guiding him at the slightest indication, Captain Nemo would discover a new pass. He was never mistaken when he saw the thin threads of bluish water trickling along the ice-fields; and I had no doubt that he had already ventured into the midst of these antarctic seas before. On the 16th of March, however, the ice-fields absolutely blocked our road. It was not the iceberg itself, as yet, but vast fields cemented by the cold. But this obstacle could not stop Captain Nemo: he hurled himself against it with frightful violence. The *Nautilus* entered the brittle mass like a wedge, and split it with frightful crackings. It was the battering-ram of the ancients hurled by infinite strength. The ice, thrown high in the air, fell like hail around us. By its own power of impulsion our apparatus made a canal for itself; sometimes carried away by its own impetus, it lodged on the ice-field, crushing it with its weight, and sometimes buried beneath it, dividing it by a simple pitching movement, producing large rents in it. Violent gales assailed us at this time, accompanied by thick fogs, through which, from one end of the platform to the other, we could see nothing. The wind blew sharply from all parts of the compass, and the snow lay in such hard heaps that we had to break it with blows of a pickaxe. The temperature was always at five degrees below zero; every outward part of the *Nautilus* was covered with ice. A rigged vessel would have been entangled in the blocked-up gorges. A vessel without sails, with electricity for its motive-power, and wanting no coal, could alone brave such high latitudes. At length, on the 18th of March, after many useless assaults, the *Nautilus* was positively blocked. It was no longer either streams, packs, or ice-fields, but an interminable and immovable barrier, formed by mountains soldered together.

"An iceberg!" said the Canadian to me.

I knew that to Ned Land, as well as to all other navigators who had preceded us, this was an inevitable obstacle. The sun appearing for an instant at noon, Captain Nemo took an observation as near as possible, which gave our situation at 51° 30' longitude and 67° 39' of south latitude We had advanced one degree more in this antarctic region. Of the liquid surface of the sea there was no longer a glimpse. Under the spur of the *Nautilus* lay stretched a vast plain, entangled with confused blocks. Here and there sharp points, and slender needles rising to a height of 200 feet; further on a steep shore, hewn as it were with an axe, and clothed with greyish tints; huge mirrors, reflecting a few rays of sunshine, half drowned in the fog. And over this desolate face of nature a stern silence reigned, scarcely broken by the flapping of the wings of petrels and puffins. Everything was frozen—even the noise. The *Nautilus* was then obliged to stop in its adventurous course amid these fields of ice. In spite of our efforts, in spite of the powerful means employed to break up the ice, the *Nautilus* remained immovable. Generally, when we can proceed no further, we have return still open to us; but here return was as impossible as advance, for every pass had closed behind us; and for the few moments when we were stationary, we were likely to be entirely blocked, which did indeed happen about two o'clock in the afternoon, the fresh ice forming around its sides with astonishing rapidity. I was obliged to admit that Captain Nemo was more than imprudent. I was on the platform at that moment. The captain had been observing our situation for some time past, when he said to me:

"Well, sir, what do you think of this?"

"I think that we are caught, captain."

"So, M. Aronnax, you really think that the *Nautilus* cannot disengage itself?"

"With difficulty, captain; for the season is already too far advanced for you to reckon on the breaking up of the ice."

"Ah! sir," said Captain Nemo, in an ironical tone, "you will always be the same. You see nothing but difficulties and obstacles. I affirm that not only can the *Nautilus* disengage itself, but also that it can go further still."

"Further to the south?" I asked, looking at the captain.

"Yes, sir; it shall go to the pole."

"To the pole!" I exclaimed, unable to repress a gesture of incredulity.

"Yes," replied the captain coldly, "to the antarctic pole, to that unknown point from whence springs every meridian of the globe. *You* know whether I can do as I please with the *Nautilus!*"

Yes, I knew that. I knew that this man was bold, even to rashness. But to conquer those obstacles which bristled round the South Pole, rendering it more inaccessible than the north, which had not yet been reached by the boldest navigators—was it not a mad enterprise, one which only a maniac would have conceived? It then came into my head to ask

Captain Nemo if he had ever discovered that pole which had never yet been trodden by a human creature?

"No, sir," he replied; "but we will discover it together. Where others have failed, *I* will not fail. I have never yet led my *Nautilus* so far into southern seas; but, I repeat, it shall go further yet."

"I can well believe you, captain," said I, in a slightly ironical tone. "I believe you! Let us go ahead! There are no obstacles for us! Let us smash this iceberg! Let us blow it up; and, if it resists, let us give the *Nautilus* wings to fly over it!"

"Over it, sir!" said Captain Nemo, quietly; "no, not *over* it, but *under* it!"

"Under it!" I exclaimed, a sudden idea of the captain's projects flashing upon my mind. I understood the wonderful qualities of the *Nautilus* were going to serve us in this superhuman enterprise.

"I see we are beginning to understand one another, sir," said the captain, half smiling. "You begin to see the possibility—I should say the success—of this attempt. That which is impossible for an ordinary vessel, is easy to the *Nautilus*. If a continent lies before the pole, it must stop before the continent; but if, on the contrary, the pole is washed by open sea, it will go even to the pole."

"Certainly," said I, carried away by the captain's reasoning; "if the surface of the sea is solidified by the ice, the lower depths are free by the providential law which has placed the maximum of density of the waters of the ocean one degree higher than freezing-point; and, if I am not mistaken, the portion of this iceberg which is above the water is as one to four to that which is below."

"Very nearly, sir; for one foot of iceberg above the sea there are three below it. If these ice mountains are not more than 300 feet above the surface, they are not more than 900 beneath. And what are 900 feet to the *Nautilus?*"

"Nothing, sir."

"It could even seek at greater depths that uniform temperature of sea-water, and there brave with impunity the thirty or forty degrees of surface cold."

"Just so, sir—just so," I replied, getting animated.

"The only difficulty," continued Captain Nemo, "is that of remaining several days without renewing our provision of air."

"Is that all? The *Nautilus* has vast reservoirs; we can fill them, and they will supply us with all the oxygen we want."

"Well thought of, M. Aronnax," replied the captain, smiling. "But not wishing you to accuse me of rashness, I will first give you all my objections."

"Have you any more to make?"

"Only one. It is possible, if the sea exists at the South Pole, that it may be covered; and, consequently, we shall be unable to come to the surface."

"Good, sir! but do you forget that the *Nautilus* is armed with a powerful spur, and could we not send it diagonally against these fields of ice, which would open at the shocks?"

"Ah! sir, you are full of ideas to-day."

"Besides, captain," I added, enthusiastically, "why should we not find the sea open at the South Pole as well as at the North? The frozen poles of the earth do not coincide, either in the southern or in the northern regions; and, until it is proved to the contrary, we may suppose either a continent or an ocean free from ice at these two points of the globe."

"I think so, too, M. Aronnax," replied Captain Nemo. "I only wish you to observe that, after having made so many objections to my project, you are now crushing me with arguments in its favour!"

The preparations for this audacious attempt now began. The powerful pumps of the *Nautilus* were working air into the reservoirs and storing it at high pressure. About four o'clock, Captain Nemo announced the closing of the panels on the platform. I threw one last look at the massive iceberg which we were going to cross. The weather was clear, the atmosphere pure enough, the cold very great, being twelve degrees below zero; but, the wind having gone down, this temperature was not so unbearable. About ten men mounted the sides of the *Nautilus,* armed with pickaxes to break the ice around the vessel, which was soon free. The operation was quickly performed, for the fresh ice was still very thin. We all went below. The usual reservoirs were filled with the newly liberated water, and the *Nautilus* soon descended. I had taken my place with Conseil in the saloon; through the open window we could see the lower beds of the Southern Ocean. The thermometer went up, the needle of the compass deviated on the dial. At about 900 feet, as Captain Nemo had foreseen, we were floating beneath the undulating bottom of the iceberg. But the *Nautilus* went lower still—it went to the depth of four hundred fathoms. The temperature of the water at the surface showed twelve degrees, it was now only ten; we had gained two. I need not say the temperature of the *Nautilus* was raised by its heating apparatus to a much higher degree; every maneuvre was accomplished with wonderful precision.

"We shall pass it, if you please, sir," said Conseil.

"I believe we shall," I said, in a tone of firm conviction.

In this open sea, the *Nautilus* had taken its course direct to the pole, without leaving the fifty-second meridian. From 67° 30' to 90°, twenty-two degrees and a half of latitude remained to travel; that is, about five hundred leagues. The *Nautilus* kept up a mean speed of twenty-six miles an hour—the speed of an express train. If that was kept up, in forty hours we should reach the pole.

For a part of the night the novelty of the situation kept us at the window. The sea was lit with the electric lantern; but it was deserted; fishes did not sojourn in these imprisoned waters; they only found there a passage to take them from the Antarctic Ocean to the open polar sea. Our pace was rapid; we could feel it by the quivering of the long steel body. About two in the morning, I took some hours' repose, and Conseil did the same. In crossing the waist I did not meet Captain Nemo: I supposed him to be in the pilot's cage. The next morning, the 19th of March, I took my post once more in the saloon. The electric log told me that the speed of the *Nautilus* had been slackened. It was then going towards the surface, but prudently emptying its reservoirs very slowly. My heart beat fast. Were we going to emerge and regain the open polar atmosphere? No! A shock told me that the *Nautilus* had struck the bottom of the iceberg, still very thick, judging from the deadened sound. We had in deed "struck," to use a sea expression, but in an inverse sense, and at a thousand feet deep. This would give three thousand feet of ice above us; one thousand being above the water-mark. The iceberg was then higher than at its borders—not a very reassuring fact. Several times that day the *Nautilus* tried again, and every time it struck the wall which lay like a ceiling above it. Sometimes it met with but 900 yards, only 200 of which rose above the surface. It was twice the height it was when the *Nautilus* had gone under the waves. I carefully noted the different depths, and thus obtained a submarine profile of the chain as it was developed under the water. That night no change had taken place in our situation. Still ice between four and five hundred yards in depth! It was evidently diminishing, but still what a thickness between us and the surface of the ocean! It was then eight. According to the daily custom on board the *Nautilus,* its air should have been renewed four hours ago; but I did not suffer much, although Captain Nemo had not yet made any demand upon his reserve of oxygen. My sleep was painful that night; hope and fear besieged me by turns: I rose several times. The groping of the *Nautilus* continued. About three in the morning, I noticed that the lower surface of the iceberg was only about fifty feet deep. One hundred and fifty feet now separated us from the surface of the waters. The iceberg was by degrees becoming an ice-field, the mountain a plain. My eyes never left the manometer. We were still rising diagonally to the surface, which sparkled under the electric rays. The iceberg was stretching both above and beneath into lengthening slopes; mile after mile it was getting thinner. At length, at six in the morning of that memorable day, the 19th of March, the door of the saloon opened, and Captain Nemo appeared.

"The sea is open!!" was all he said.

Chapter XIV

THE SOUTH POLE

I RUSHED ON TO THE PLATFORM. YES! THE OPEN SEA, WITH BUT A FEW SCATTERED PIECES of ice and moving icebergs—a long stretch of sea; a world of birds in the air, and myriads of fishes under those waters, which varied from intense blue to olive-green, according to the bottom. The thermometer marked three degrees centigrade above zero. It was comparatively spring, shut up as we were behind this iceberg, whose lengthened mass was dimly seen on our northern horizon.

"Are we at the pole?" I asked the captain, with a beating heart.

"I do not know," he replied. "At noon I will take our bearings."

"But will the sun show himself through this fog?" said I, looking at the leaden sky.

"However little it shows, it will be enough," replied the Captain.

About ten miles south a solitary island rose to a height of one hundred and four yards. We made for it, but carefully, for the sea might be strewn with banks. One hour afterwards we had reached it, two hours later we had made the round of it. It measured four or five miles in circumference. A narrow canal separated it from a considerable stretch of land, perhaps a continent, for we could not see its limits. The existence of this land seemed to give some colour to Maury's hypothesis. The ingenious American has remarked that, between the South Pole and the sixtieth parallel, the sea is covered with floating ice of enormous size, which is never met with in the North Atlantic. From this fact he has drawn the conclusion that the Antarctic Circle encloses considerable continents, as icebergs cannot form in open sea, but only on the coasts. According to these calculations, the mass of ice surrounding the southern pole forms a vast cap, the circumference of which must be, at least, 2,500 miles. But the *Nautilus,* for fear of running aground, had stopped about three cable-lengths from a strand over which reared a superb heap of rocks. The boat was launched; the captain, two of his men, bearing instruments, Conseil, and myself were in it. It was ten in the morning. I had not seen Ned Land. Doubtless the Canadian did not wish to admit the presence of the South Pole. A few strokes of the oar brought us to the sand, where we ran ashore. Conseil was going to jump on to the land, when I held him back.

"Sir," said I to Captain Nemo, "to you belongs the honour of first setting foot on this land."

"Yes, sir," said the captain, "and if I do not hesitate to tread this South Pole, it is because, up to this time, no human being has left a trace there."

Saying this, he jumped lightly on to the sand. His heart beat with emotion. He climbed a rock, sloping to a little promontory, and there, with his arms crossed, mute and motionless, and with an eager look, he seemed to take possession of these southern regions. After five minutes passed in this ecstasy, he turned to us.

"When you like, sir."

I landed, followed by Conseil, leaving the two men in the boat. For a long way the soil was composed of a reddish, sandy stone, something like crushed brick, scoriae, streams of lava, and pumice-stones. One could not mistake its volcanic origin. In some parts, slight curls of smoke emitted a sulphurous smell, proving that the internal fires had lost nothing of their expansive powers, though, having climbed a high acclivity, I could see no volcano for a radius of several miles. We know that in those antarctic countries, James Ross found two craters, the Erebus and Terror, in full activity, on the 167th meridian, latitude 77° 32'. The vegetation of this desolate continent seemed to me much restricted. Some lichens of the species usnea melathoxanthus lay upon the black rocks; some microscopic plants, rudimentary diatomas, a kind of cells, placed between two quartz shells; long purple and scarlet weed, supported on little swimming bladders, which the breaking of the waves brought to the shore. These constituted the meagre flora of this region. The shore was strewn with molluscs, little mussels, limpets, smooth bucards in the shape of a heart, and particularly some clios, with oblong membranous bodies, the head of which was formed of two rounded lobes. I also saw myriads of northern clios, one and a quarter inches long, of which a whale would swallow a whole world at a mouthful; and some perfect sea-butterflies, animating the waters on the skirts of the shore.

Among other zoöphytes, there appeared on the high bottoms some coral shrubs, of that kind which, according to James Ross, live in the antarctic seas to the depth of more than 1,000 yards. Then there were little kingfishers belonging to the species procellaria pelagica, as well as a large number of asteriads, peculiar to these climates, and starfish studding the soil. But where life abounded most was in the air. There thousands of birds fluttered and flew of all kinds, deafening us with their cries; others crowded the rock, looking at us as we passed by without fear, and pressing familiarly close by our feet. There were penguins, so agile in the water that they have been taken for the rapid bonitos, heavy and awkward as they are on the ground; they were uttering harsh cries, a large assembly, sober in gesture, but extravagant in clamour. Among the birds I noticed the chionis, of the long-legged family, as large as pigeons, white, with a short conical beak, and the eye framed in a red circle. Conseil laid in a stock of them, for these winged creatures, properly prepared, make an agreeable meat. Albatrosses passed in the air (the expanse of their wings being at least four yards and a half) and justly called the vultures of the ocean; some gigantic petrels, and some damiers, a kind of small duck, the underpart of whose body is black and white; then there were a whole series of petrels, some whitish with brown-bordered wings, others blue, peculiar to the antarctic seas, and so oily, as I told Conseil, that the inhabitants of the Ferroe Islands had nothing to do before lighting them, but to put a wick in.

"A little more," said Conseil, "and they would be perfect lamps! After that, we cannot expect nature to have previously furnished them with wicks!"

About half-a-mile further on, the soil was riddled with ruff's nests, a sort of laying ground, out of which many birds were issuing. Captain Nemo had some hundreds hunted. They uttered a cry like the braying of an ass, were about the size of a goose, slate colour on the body, white beneath, with a yellow line round their throats; they allowed themselves to be killed with a stone, never trying to escape. But the fog did not lift, and at eleven the sun had not yet shown itself. Its absence made me uneasy. Without it no observations were possible. How, then, could we decide whether we had reached the pole? When I rejoined Captain Nemo, I found him leaning on a piece of rock, silently watching the sky. He seemed impatient and vexed. But what was to be done? This rash and powerful man could not command the sun as he did the sea. Noon arrived without the orb of day showing itself for an instant. We could not even tell its position behind the curtain of fog; and soon the fog turned to snow.

"Till to-morrow," said the captain quietly, and we returned to the *Nautilus* amid these atmospheric disturbances.

The tempest of snow continued till the next day. It was impossible to remain on the platform. From the saloon, where I was taking notes of incidents happening during this excursion to the polar continent, I could hear the cries of petrels and albatrosses sporting in the midst of this violent storm. The *Nautilus* did not remain motionless, but skirted the coast, advancing ten miles more to the south in the half-light left by the sun as it skirted the edge of the horizon. The next day, the 20th of March, the snow had ceased. The cold was a little greater, the thermometer showing two degrees below zero. The fog was rising, and I hoped that that day our observations might be taken. Captain Nemo not having yet appeared, the boat took Conseil and myself to land. The soil was still of the same volcanic nature; everywhere were traces of lava, scoriae, and basalt; but the crater which had vomited them I could not see. Here, as lower down, this continent was alive with myriads of birds. But their rule was now divided with large troops of sea-mammals, looking at us with their soft eyes. There were several kinds of seals, some stretched on the earth, some on flakes of ice, many going in and out of the sea. They did not flee at our approach, never having had anything to do with man; and I reckoned that there were provisions there for hundreds of vessels.

"Sir," said Conseil, "will you tell me the names of these creatures?"

"They are seals and morses."

It was now eight in the morning. Four hours remained to us before the sun could be observed with advantage. I directed our steps towards a vast bay cut in the steep granite shore. There, I can aver that earth and ice were lost to sight by the numbers of sea-mammals covering them, and I involuntarily sought for old Proteus, the mythological shepherd who watched these immense flocks of Neptune. There were more seals than anything else, forming distinct groups, male and female, the father watching over his family, the mother suckling her little ones, some already strong enough to go a few steps. When they wished to change their place, they took little jumps, made by the contraction of their bodies, and helped awkwardly enough by their imperfect fin, which, as with the lamantin, their congener, forms a perfect forearm. I should say that in the water, which is their element—the spine of these creatures is flexible—with smooth and close skin and webbed feet, they swim admirably. In resting on the earth they take the most graceful attitudes. Thus the ancients, observing their soft and expressive looks, which cannot be surpassed by the most beautiful look a woman can give, their clear voluptuous eyes, their charming positions, and the poetry of their manners, metamorphosed them, the male into a triton and the female into a mermaid. I made Conseil notice the considerable development of the lobes of the brain in these interesting cetaceans. No mammal, except man, has such a quantity of cerebral matter; they are also capable of receiving a certain amount of education, are easily domesticated, and I think, with other naturalists, that if properly taught they would be of great service as fishing-dogs. The greater part of them slept on the rocks or on the sand. Among these seals, properly so called, which have no external ears (in which they differ from the otter, whose ears are prominent), I noticed several varieties of stenorhynchi about three yards long, with a white coat, bulldog heads, armed with teeth in both jaws, four incisors at the top and four at the bottom, and two large canine teeth in the shape of a "fleur de lis." Among them glided sea-elephants, a kind of seal, with short, flexible trunks. The giants of this species measured twenty feet round, and ten yards and a half in length; but they did not move as we approached.

"These creatures are not dangerous?" asked Conseil.

"No; not unless you attack them. When they have to defend their young, their rage is terrible, and it is not uncommon for them to break the fishing-boats to pieces."

"They are quite right," said Conseil.

"I do not say they are not."

Two miles further on we were stopped by the promontory which shelters the bay from the southerly winds. Beyond it we heard loud bellowings such as a troop of ruminants would produce.

"Good!" said Conseil. "A concert of bulls!"

"No; a concert of morses."

"They are fighting!"

"They are either fighting or playing."

We now began to climb the blackish rocks, amid unforeseen stumbles, and over stones which the ice made slippery. More than once I rolled over, at the expense of my loins. Conseil, more prudent or more steady, did not stumble, and helped me up, saying:

"If, sir, you would have the kindness to take wider steps, you would preserve your equilibrium better."

Arrived at the upper ridge of the promontory, I saw a vast white plain covered with morses. They were playing among themselves, and what we heard were bellowings of pleasure, not of anger.

As I passed these curious animals I could examine them leisurely, for they did not move. Their skins were thick and rugged, of a yellowish tint, approaching to red; their hair was short and scant. Some of them were four yards and a quarter long. Quieter and less timid than their congeners of the north, they did not, like them, place sentinels round the outskirts of their encampment. After examining this city of morses, I began to think of returning. It was eleven o'clock, and if Captain Nemo found the conditions favourable for observations, I wished to be present at the operation. We followed a narrow pathway running along the summit of the steep shore. At half-past eleven we had reached the place where we landed. The boat had run aground bringing the captain. I saw him standing on a block of basalt, his instruments near him, his eyes fixed on the northern horizon, near which the sun was then describing a lengthened curve. I took my place beside him, and waited without speaking. Noon arrived, and, as before, the sun did not appear. It was a fatality. Observations were still wanting. If not accomplished to-morrow, we must give up all idea of taking any. We were indeed exactly at the 20th of March. To-morrow, the 21st, would be the equinox; the sun would disappear behind the horizon for six months, and with its disappearance the long polar night would begin. Since the September equinox it had emerged from the northern horizon, rising by lengthened spirals up to the 21st of December. At this period, the summer solstice of the northern regions, it had begun to descend; and to-morrow was to shed its last rays upon them. I communicated my fears and observations to Captain Nemo.

"You are right, M. Aronnax," said he; "if to-morrow I cannot take the altitude of the sun, I shall not be able to do it for six months. But precisely because chance has led me into these seas on the 21st of March, my bearings will be easy to take, if at twelve we can see the sun."

"Why, captain?"

"Because then the orb of day describes such lengthened curves, that it is difficult to measure exactly its height above the horizon, and grave errors may be made with instruments."

"What will you do then?"

"I shall only use my chronometer," replied Captain Nemo. "If to-morrow, the 21st of March, the disc of the sun, allowing for refraction, is exactly cut by the northern horizon, it will show that I am at the South Pole."

"Just so," said I. "But this statement is not mathematically correct, because the equinox does not necessarily begin at noon."

"Very likely, sir; but the error will not be a hundred yards, and we do not want more. Till to-morrow, then!"

Captain Nemo returned on board. Conseil and I remained to survey the shore, observing and studying until five o'clock. Then I went to bed, not, however, without invoking, like the Indian, the favour of the radiant orb. The next day, the 21st of March, at five in the morning, I mounted the platform. I found Captain Nemo there.

"The weather is lightening a little," said he. "I have some hope. After breakfast we will go on shore, and choose a post for observation."

That point settled, I sought Ned Land. I wanted to take him with me. But the obstinate Canadian refused, and I saw that his taciturnity and his bad humour grew day by day. After all I was not sorry for his obstinacy under the circumstances. Indeed, there were too many seals on shore, and we ought not to lay such temptation in this unreflecting fisherman's way. Breakfast over, we went on shore. The *Nautilus* had gone some miles further up in the night. It was a whole league from the coast, above which reared a sharp peak about five hundred yards high. The boat took with me Captain Nemo, two men of the crew, and the instruments, which consisted of a chronometer, a telescope, and a barometer. While crossing, I saw numerous whales belonging to the three kinds peculiar to the southern seas: the whale, or the English "right whale," which has no dorsal fin; the "humpback," or balaenopterona, with reeved chest and large, whitish fins, which, in spite of its name, do not form wings; and the finback, of a yellowish brown, the liveliest of all the cetacea. This powerful creature is heard a long way off when he throws to a great height columns of air and vapour, which look like whirlwinds of smoke. These different mammals were disporting themselves in troops in the quiet waters; and I could see that this basin of the Antarctic Pole serves as a place of refuge to the cetacea too closely tracked by the hunters. I also noticed large medusae floating between the reeds.

At nine we landed; the sky was brightening, the clouds were flying to the south, and the fog seemed to be leaving the cold surface of the waters. Captain Nemo went towards the peak, which he doubtless meant to be his observatory. It was a painful ascent over the sharp lava and the pumice-stones, in an atmosphere often impregnated with a sulphurous smell from the smoking cracks. For a man unaccustomed to walk on land, the captain climbed the steep slopes with an agility I never saw equalled, and which a hunter would have envied. We were two hours getting to the summit of this peak, which was half porphyry and half basalt. From thence we looked upon a vast sea which, towards the north, distinctly traced its boundary line upon the sky. At our feet lay fields of dazzling whiteness. Over our heads a pale azure, free from fog. To the north the disc of the sun seemed like a ball of fire, already horned by the cutting of the horizon. From the bosom of the water rose sheaves of liquid jets by hundreds. In the distance lay the *Nautilus* like a cetacean asleep on the water. Behind us, to the south and east, an immense country and a chaotic heap of rocks and ice, the limits of which were not visible. On arriving at the summit, Captain Nemo carefully took the mean height of the barometer, for he would have to consider that in taking his observations. At a quarter to twelve, the sun, then seen only by refraction, looked like a golden disc shedding its last rays upon this deserted continent, and seas which never man had yet ploughed. Captain Nemo, furnished with a lenticular glass which, by means of a mirror, corrected the refraction, watched the orb sinking below the horizon by degrees, following a lengthened diagonal. I held the chronometer. My heart beat fast. If the disappearance of the half-disc of the sun coincided with twelve o'clock on the chronometer, we were at the pole itself.

"Twelve!" I exclaimed.

"The South Pole!" replied Captain Nemo, in a grave voice, handing me the glass, which showed the orb cut in exactly equal parts by the horizon.

I looked at the last rays crowning the peak, and the shadows mounting by degrees up its slopes. At that moment Captain Nemo, resting with his hand on my shoulder, said:

"I, Captain Nemo, on this 21st day of March, 1868, have reached the South Pole on the ninetieth degree; and I take possession of this part of the globe, equal to one-sixth of the known continents."

"In whose name, captain?"

"In my own, sir!"

Saying which, Captain Nemo unfurled a black banner, bearing an "N" in gold quartered on its bunting. Then, turning towards the orb of day, whose last rays lapped the horizon of the sea, he exclaimed:

"Adieu, sun! Disappear, thou radiant orb! Rest beneath this open sea, and let a night of six months spread its shadows over my new domains!"

Chapter XV

ACCIDENT OR INCIDENT?

T HE NEXT DAY, THE 22D OF MARCH, AT SIX IN THE MORNING, PREPARATIONS FOR DE-parture were begun. The last gleams of twilight were melting into night. The cold was great, the constellations shone with wonderful intensity. In the zenith glittered that wondrous Southern Cross—the polar bear of antarctic regions. The thermometer showed twelve degrees below zero, and when the wind freshened, it was most biting. Flakes of ice increased on the open water. The sea seemed everywhere alike. Numerous blackish patches spread on the surface, showing the formation of fresh ice. Evidently the southern basin, frozen during the six winter months, was absolutely inaccessible. What became of the whales in that time? Doubtless they went beneath the icebergs, seeking more practicable seas. As to the seals and morses, accustomed to live in a hard climate, they remained on these icy shores. These creatures have the instinct to break holes in the ice-field and to keep them open. To these holes they come for breath; when the birds, driven away by the cold, have emigrated to the north, these sea-mammals remain sole masters of the polar continent. But the reservoirs were filling with water, and the *Nautilus* was slowly descending. At 1,000 feet deep it stopped; its screw beat the waves, and it advanced straight towards the north at a speed of fifteen miles an hour. Towards night it was already floating under the immense body of the iceberg. At three in the morning I was awakened by a violent shock. I sat up in my bed and listened in the darkness, when I was thrown into the middle of the room. The *Nautilus*, after having struck, had rebounded violently. I groped along the partition, and by the staircase to the saloon, which was lit by the luminous ceiling. The furniture was upset. Fortunately the windows were firmly set, and had held fast. The pictures on the starboard side, from being no longer vertical, were clinging to the paper, while those of the port side were hanging at least a foot from the wall. The *Nautilus* was lying on its starboard side perfectly motionless. I heard footsteps, and a confusion of voices; but Captain Nemo did not appear. As I was leaving the saloon, Ned Land and Conseil entered.

"What is the matter?" said I, at once.

"I came to ask you, sir," replied Conseil.

"Confound it!" exclaimed the Canadian, "I know well enough! The *Nautilus* has struck; and, judging by the way she lies, I do not think she will right herself as she did the first time in Torres Straits."

"But," I asked, "has she at least come to the surface of the sea?"

"We do not know," said Conseil.

"It is easy to decide," I answered. I consulted the manometer. To my great surprise, it showed a depth of more than 180 fathoms. "What does that mean?" I exclaimed.

"We must ask Captain Nemo," said Conseil.

"But where shall we find him?" said Ned Land.

"Follow me," said I to my companions.

We left the saloon. There was no one in the library. At the centre staircase, by the berths of the ship's crew, there was no one. I thought that Captain Nemo must be in the pilot's cage. It was best to wait. We all returned to the saloon. For twenty minutes we remained thus, trying to hear the slightest noise which might be made on board the *Nautilus*, when Captain Nemo entered. He seemed not to see us; his face, generally so impassive, showed signs of uneasiness. He watched the compass silently, then the manometer; and, going to the planisphere, placed his finger on a spot representing the southern seas. I would not interrupt him; but, some minutes later, when he turned towards me, I said, using one of his own expressions in the Torres Straits:

"An incident, captain?"

"No, sir; an accident this time."

"Serious?"

"Perhaps."

"Is the danger immediate?"

"No."

"The *Nautilus* has stranded?"

"Yes."

"And this has happened—how?"

"From a caprice of nature, not from the ignorance of man. Not a mistake has been made in the working. But we cannot prevent equilibrium from producing its effects. We may brave human laws, but we cannot resist natural ones."

Captain Nemo had chosen a strange moment for uttering this philosophical reflection. On the whole, his answer helped me little.

"May I ask, sir, the cause of this accident?"

"An enormous block of ice, a whole mountain, has turned over," he replied. "When icebergs are undermined at their base by warmer water or reiterated shocks, their centre of gravity rises, and the whole thing turns over. This is what has happened; one of these blocks, as it fell, struck the *Nautilus*, then, gliding under its hull, raised it with irresistible force, bringing it into beds which are not so thick, where it is lying on its side."

"But can we not get the *Nautilus* off by emptying its reservoirs, that it might regain its equilibrium?"

"That, sir, is being done at this moment. You can hear the pump working. Look at the needle of the manometer; it shows that the *Nautilus* is rising, but the block of ice is floating with it; and, until some obstacle stops its ascending motion, our position cannot be altered."

Indeed, the *Nautilus* still held the same position to starboard; doubtless it would right itself when the block stopped. But at this moment who knows if we may not be frightfully crushed between the two glassy surfaces? I reflected on all the consequences of our position. Captain Nemo never took his eyes off the manometer. Since the fall of the iceberg, the *Nautilus* had risen about a hundred and fifty feet, but it still made the same angle with the perpendicular. Suddenly a slight movement was felt in the hold. Evidently it was righting a little. Things hanging in the saloon were sensibly returning to their normal position. The partitions were nearing the upright. No one spoke. With beating hearts we watched and felt the straightening. The boards became horizontal under our feet. Ten minutes passed.

"At last we have righted!" I exclaimed.

"Yes," said Captain Nemo, going to the door of the saloon.

"But are we floating?" I asked.

"Certainly," he replied; "since the reservoirs are not empty; and, when empty, the *Nautilus* must rise to the surface of the sea."

We were in open sea; but at a distance of about ten yards, on either side of the *Nautilus*, rose a dazzling wall of ice. Above and beneath the same wall: above, because the lower surface of the iceberg stretched over us like an immense ceiling: beneath, because the overturned block, having slid by degrees, had found a resting-place on the lateral walls, which kept it in that position. The *Nautilus* was really imprisoned in a perfect tunnel of ice more than twenty yards in breadth, filled with quiet water. It was easy to get out of it by going either forward or backward, and then make a free passage under the iceberg, some hundreds of yards deeper. The luminous ceiling had been extinguished, but the saloon was still resplendent with intense light. It was the powerful reflection from the glass partition sent violently back to the sheets of the lantern. I cannot describe the effect of the voltaic rays upon the great blocks so capriciously cut; upon every angle, every ridge, every facet, was thrown a different light, according to the nature of the veins running through the ice; a dazzling mine of gems, particularly of sapphires, their blue rays crossing with the green of the emerald. Here and there were opal shades of wonderful softness, running through bright spots like diamonds of fire, the brilliancy of which the eye could not bear. The power of the lantern seemed increased a hundredfold, like a lamp through the lenticular plates of a first-class lighthouse.

"How beautiful! How beautiful!" cried Conseil.

"Yes," I said, "it is a wonderful sight. Is it not, Ned?"

"Yes, confound it! Yes," answered Ned Land, "it is superb! I am mad at being obliged to admit it. No one has ever seen anything like it; but the sight may cost us dear. And, if I must say all, I think we are seeing here things which God never intended man to see."

Ned was right, it was too beautiful. Suddenly a cry from Conseil made me turn.

"What is it?" I asked.

"Shut your eyes, sir! Do not look, sir!" Saying which, Conseil clapped his hands over his eyes.

"But what is the matter, my boy?"

"I am dazzled, blinded."

My eyes turned involuntarily towards the glass, but I could not stand the fire which seemed to devour them. I understood what had happened. The *Nautilus* had put on full speed. All the quiet lustre of the ice-walls was at once changed into flashes of lightning. The fire from these myriads of diamonds was blinding. It required some time to calm our troubled looks. At last the hands were taken down.

"Faith, I should never have believed it," said Conseil.

It was then five in the morning; and at that moment a shock was felt at the bows of the *Nautilus*. I knew that its spur had struck a block of ice. It must have been a false maneuvre, for this submarine tunnel, obstructed by blocks, was not very easy navigation. I thought that Captain Nemo, by changing his course, would either turn these obstacles, or else follow the windings of the tunnel. In any case, the road before us could not be entirely blocked. But, contrary to my expectations, the *Nautilus* took a decided retrograde motion.

"We are going backwards?" said Conseil.

"Yes," I replied. "This end of the tunnel can have no egress."

"And then?"

"Then," said I, "the working is easy. We must go back again, and go out at the southern opening. That is all."

In speaking thus, I wished to appear more confident than I really was. But the retrograde motion of the *Nautilus* was increasing; and, reversing the screw, it carried us at great speed.

"It will be a hindrance," said Ned.

"What does it matter, some hours more or less, provided we get out at last?"

"Yes," repeated Ned Land, "provided we do get out at last!"

For a short time I walked from the saloon to the library. My companions were silent. I soon threw myself on an ottoman, and took a book, which my eyes over-ran mechanically. A quarter of an hour after, Conseil, approaching me, said, "Is what you are reading very interesting, sir?"

"Very interesting!" I replied.

"I should think so, sir. It is your own book you are reading."

"My book?"

And indeed I was holding in my hand the work on the *Great Submarine Depths*. I did not even dream of it. I closed the book, and returned to my walk. Ned and Conseil rose to go.

"Stay here, my friends," said I, detaining them. "Let us remain together until we are out of this block."

"As you please, sir," Conseil replied.

Some hours passed. I often looked at the instruments hanging from the partition. The manometer showed that the *Nautilus* kept at a constant depth of more than three hundred yards; the compass still pointed to south; the log indicated a speed of twenty miles an hour, which, in such a cramped space, was very great. But Captain Nemo knew that he could not hasten too much, and that minutes were worth ages to us. At twenty-five minutes past eight a second shock took place, this time from behind. I turned pale. My companions were close by my side. I seized Conseil's hand. Our looks expressed our feelings better than words. At this moment the captain entered the saloon. I went up to him.

"Our course is barred southward?" I asked.

"Yes, sir. The iceberg has shifted and closed every outlet."

"We are blocked up, then?"

"Yes."

Chapter XVI

WANT OF AIR

THUS AROUND THE *NAUTILUS*, ABOVE AND BELOW, WAS AN IMPENETRABLE WALL OF ICE. We were prisoners to the iceberg. I watched the captain. His countenance had resumed its habitual imperturbability.

"Gentlemen," he said calmly, "there are two ways of dying in the circumstances in which we are placed." (This inexplicable person had the air of a mathematical professor lecturing to his pupils.) "The first is to be crushed; the second is to die of suffocation. I do not speak of the possibility of dying of hunger, for the supply of provisions in the *Nautilus* will certainly last longer than we shall. Let us then calculate our chances."

"As to suffocation, captain," I replied, "that is not to be feared, because our reservoirs are full."

"Just so; but they will only yield two days' supply of air. Now, for thirty-six hours we have been hidden under the water, and already the heavy atmosphere of the *Nautilus* requires renewal. In forty-eight hours our reserve will be exhausted."

"Well, captain, can we be delivered before forty-eight hours?"

"We will attempt it, at least, by piercing the wall that surrounds us."

"On which side?"

"Sound will tell us. I am going to run the *Nautilus* aground on the lower bank, and my men will attack the iceberg on the side that is least thick."

Captain Nemo went out. Soon I discovered by a hissing noise that the water was entering the reservoirs. The *Nautilus* sank slowly, and rested on the ice at a depth of 350 yards, the depth at which the lower bank was immersed.

"My friends," I said, "our situation is serious, but I rely on your courage and energy."

"Sir," replied the Canadian, "I am ready to do anything for the general safety."

"Good, Ned!" and I held out my hand to the Canadian.

"I will add," he continued, "that, being as handy with the pickaxe as with the harpoon, if I can be useful to the captain, he can command my services."

"He will not refuse your help. Come, Ned!"

I led him to the room where the crew of the *Nautilus* were putting on their cork-jackets. I told the captain of Ned's proposal, which he accepted. The Canadian put on his sea-costume, and was ready as soon as his companions. When Ned was dressed, I reentered the drawing-room, where the panes of glass were open, and, posted near Conseil, I examined the ambient beds that supported the *Nautilus*. Some instants after, we saw a dozen of the crew set foot on the bank of ice, and among them Ned Land, easily known by his stature. Captain Nemo was with them. Before proceeding to dig the walls, he took the soundings, to be sure of working in the right direction. Long sounding-lines were sunk in the side walls, but after fifteen yards they were again stopped by the thick wall. It was useless to attack it on the ceiling-like surface, since the iceberg itself measured more than 400 yards in height. Captain Nemo then sounded the lower surface. There ten yards of wall separated us from the water, so great was the thickness of the ice-field. It was necessary, therefore, to cut from it a piece equal in extent to the water-line of the *Nautilus*. There was about 6,000 cubic yards to detach, so as to dig a hole by which we could descend to the ice-field. The work had begun immediately and carried on with indefatigable energy. Instead of digging round the *Nautilus*, which would have involved greater difficulty, Captain Nemo had an immense trench made at eight yards from the port quarter. Then the men set to work simultaneously with their screws on several points of its circumference. Presently the pickaxe attacked this compact matter vigorously, and large blocks were detached from the mass. By a curious effect of specific gravity, these blocks, lighter than water, fled, so to speak, to the vault of the tunnel, that increased in thickness at the top in proportion as it diminished at the base. But that mattered little, so long as the lower part grew thinner. After two hours' hard work, Ned Land came in exhausted. He and his comrades were replaced by new workers, whom Conseil and I joined. The second lieutenant of the *Nautilus* superintended us. The water seemed singularly cold, but I soon got warm handling the pickaxe. My movements were free enough, although they were made under a pressure of thirty atmospheres. When I reentered, after working two hours, to take some food and rest, I found a perceptible difference between the pure fluid with which the Rouquayrol engine supplied me and the atmosphere of the *Nautilus*, already charged with carbonic acid. The air had not been renewed for forty-eight hours, and its vivifying qualities were considerably enfeebled. However, after a lapse of twelve hours, we had only raised a block of ice one yard thick, on the marked surface, which was about 600 cubic yards! Reckoning that it took twelve hours to accomplish this much it would take five nights and four days to bring this enterprise to a satisfactory conclusion. Five nights and four days! And we have only air enough for two days in the reservoirs! "Without taking into account," said Ned, "that, even if we get out of this infernal prison, we shall also be imprisoned under the iceberg, shut out from all possible communication with the atmosphere." True enough! Who could then foresee the minimum of time necessary for our deliverance? We might be suffocated before the *Nautilus* could regain the surface of the waves! Was it destined to perish in this ice-tomb, with all those it enclosed? The situation was terrible. But everyone had looked the danger in the face, and each was determined to do his duty to the last.

As I expected, during the night a new block a yard square was carried away, and still further sank the immense hollow. But in the morning when, dressed in my cork-jacket, I traversed the slushy mass at a temperature of six or seven degrees below zero, I remarked that the side walls were gradually closing in. The beds of water furthest from the trench, that were not warmed by the men's work, showed a tendency to solidification. In presence of this new and imminent danger, what would become of our chances of safety, and how hinder the solidification of this liquid medium, that would burst the partitions of the *Nautilus* like glass?

I did not tell my companions of this new danger. What was the good of damping the energy they displayed in the painful work of escape? But when I went on board again, I told Captain Nemo of this grave complication.

"I know it," he said, in that calm tone which could counteract the most terrible apprehensions. "It is one danger more; but I see no way of escaping it; the only chance of safety is to go quicker than solidification. We must be beforehand with it, that is all."

On this day for several hours I used my pickaxe vigorously. The work kept me up. Besides, to work was to quit the *Nautilus*, and breathe directly the pure air drawn from the reservoirs, and supplied by our apparatus, and to quit the impoverished and vitiated atmosphere. Towards evening the trench was dug one yard deeper. When I returned on board, I was nearly suffocated by the carbonic acid with which the air was filled—ah! if we had only the chemical means to drive away this deleterious gas. We had plenty of oxygen; all this water contained a considerable quantity, and by dissolving it with our powerful piles, it would restore the vivifying fluid. I had thought well over it; but of what good was that, since the carbonic acid produced by our respiration had invaded every part of the vessel? To absorb it, it was necessary to fill some jars with caustic potash, and to shake them incessantly. Now this substance was wanting on board, and nothing could replace it. On that evening, Captain Nemo ought to open the taps of his reservoirs, and let some pure air into the interior of the *Nautilus*; without this precaution we could not get rid of the sense of suffocation. The next day, March 26th, I resumed my miner's work in beginning the fifth yard. The side walls and the lower surface of the iceberg thickened visibly. It was evident that they would meet before the *Nautilus* was able to disengage itself. Despair seized me for an instant, my pickaxe nearly fell from my hands. What was the good of digging if I must be suffocated, crushed by the water that was turning into stone—a punishment that the ferocity of the savages even would not have invented! Just then Captain Nemo passed near me. I touched his hand and showed him the walls of our prison. The wall to port had advanced to at least four yards from the hull of the *Nautilus*. The captain understood me, and signed me to follow him. We went on board. I took off my cork-jacket, and accompanied him into the drawing-room.

"M. Aronnax, we must attempt some desperate means, or we shall be sealed up in this solidified water as in cement."

"Yes; but what is to be done?"

"Ah! if my *Nautilus* were strong enough to bear this pressure without being crushed!"

"Well?" I asked, not catching the captain's idea.

"Do you not understand," he replied, "that this congelation of water will help us? Do you not see that by its solidification, it would burst through this field of ice that imprisons us, as, when it freezes, it bursts the hardest stones? Do you not perceive that it would be an agent of safety instead of destruction?"

"Yes, captain, perhaps. But whatever resistance to crushing the *Nautilus* possesses, it could not support this terrible pressure, and would be flattened like an iron plate."

"I know it, sir. Therefore we must not reckon on the aid of nature, but on our own exertions. We must stop this solidification. Not only will the side walls be pressed together; but there is not ten feet of water before or behind the *Nautilus*. The congelation gains on us on all sides."

"How long will the air in the reservoirs last for us to breathe on board?"

The captain looked in my face. "After to-morrow they will be empty!"

A cold sweat came over me. However, ought I to have been astonished at the answer? On March 22, the *Nautilus* was in the open polar seas. We were at 26°. For five days we had lived on the reserve on board. And what was left of the respirable air must be kept for the workers. Even now, as I write, my recollection is still so vivid that an involuntary terror seizes me and my lungs seem to be without air. Meanwhile Captain Nemo reflected silently, and evidently an idea had struck him; but he seemed to reject it. At last, these words escaped his lips:

"Boiling water!" he muttered.

"Boiling water?" I cried.

"Yes, sir. We are enclosed in a space that is relatively confined. Would not jets of boiling water, constantly injected by the pumps, raise the temperature in this part, and stay the congelation?"

"Let us try it," I said resolutely.

"Let us try it, professor."

The thermometer then stood at seven degrees outside. Captain Nemo took me to the galleys, where the vast distillatory machines stood that furnished the drinkable water by evaporation. They filled these with water, and all the electric heat from the piles was thrown through the worms bathed in the liquid. In a few minutes this water reached a hundred degrees. It was directed towards the pumps, while fresh water replaced it in proportion. The heat developed by the troughs was such that cold water, drawn up from the sea after only having gone through the machines, came boiling into the body of the pump. The injection was begun, and three hours after the thermometer marked six degrees below zero outside. One degree was gained. Two hours later the thermometer only marked four degrees.

"We shall succeed," I said to the captain, after having anxiously watched the result of the operation.

"I think," he answered, "that we shall not be crushed. We have no more suffocation to fear."

During the night the temperature of the water rose to one degree below zero. The injections could not carry it to a higher point. But as the congelation of the sea-water produces at least two degrees, I was at last reassured against the dangers of solidification.

The next day, March 27th, six yards of ice had been cleared, four yards only remaining to be cleared away. There was yet forty-eight hours' work. The air could not be renewed in the interior of the *Nautilus*. And this day would make it worse. An intolerable weight oppressed me. Towards three o'clock in the evening this feeling rose to a violent degree. Yawns dislocated my jaws. My lungs panted as they inhaled this burning fluid, which became rarefied more and more. A moral torpor took hold of me. I was powerless, almost unconscious. My brave Conseil, though exhibiting the same symptoms and suffering in the same manner, never left me. He took my hand and encouraged me, and I heard him murmur, "Oh, if I could only not breathe, so as to leave more air for my master!"

Tears came into my eyes on hearing him speak thus. If our situation to all was intolerable in the interior, with what haste and gladness would we put on our cork-jackets to work in our turn! Pickaxes sounded on the frozen ice-beds. Our arms ached, the skin was torn off our hands. But what were these fatigues, what did the wounds matter? Vital air came to the lungs! We breathed! We breathed!

All this time no one prolonged his voluntary task beyond the prescribed time. His task accomplished, each one handed in turn to his panting companions the apparatus that supplied him with life. Captain Nemo set the example, and submitted first to this severe discipline. When the time came he gave up his apparatus to another and returned to the vitiated air on board, calm, unflinching, unmurmuring.

On that day the ordinary work was accomplished with unusual vigour. Only two yards remained to be raised from the surface. Two yards only separated us from the open sea. But the reservoirs were nearly emptied of air. The little that remained ought to be kept for the workers; not a particle for the *Nautilus*. When I went back on board, I was half-suffocated. What a night! I know not how to describe it. The next day my breathing was oppressed. Dizziness accompanied the pain in my head and made me like a drunken man. My companions showed the same symptoms. Some of the crew had rattling in the throat.

On that day, the sixth of our imprisonment, Captain Nemo, finding the pickaxes work too slowly, resolved to crush the ice-bed that still separated us from the liquid sheet. This man's coolness and energy never forsook him. He subdued his physical pains by moral force.

By his orders the vessel was lightened, that is to say, raised from the ice-bed by a change of specific gravity. When it floated they towed it so as to bring it above the immense trench made on the level of the water-line. Then filling his reservoirs of water, he descended and shut himself up in the hole.

Just then all the crew came on board, and the double door of communication was shut. The *Nautilus* then rested on the bed of ice, which was not one yard thick, and which the sounding leads had perforated in a thousand places. The taps of the reservoirs were then opened, and a hundred cubic yards of water was let in, increasing the weight of the *Nautilus* to 1,800 tons. We waited, we listened, forgetting our sufferings in hope. Our safety depended on this last chance. Notwithstanding the buzzing in my head, I soon heard the humming sound under the hull of the *Nautilus*. The ice cracked with a singular noise, like tearing paper, and the *Nautilus* sank.

"We are off!" murmured Conseil in my ear.

I could not answer him. I seized his hand, and pressed it convulsively. All at once, carried away by its frightful overcharge, the *Nautilus* sank like a bullet under the waters, that is to say, it fell as if it was in a vacuum. Then all the electric force was put on the pumps, that soon began to let the water out of the reservoirs. After some minutes, our fall was stopped. Soon, too, the manometer indicated an ascending movement. The screw, going at full speed, made the iron hull tremble to its very bolts and drew us towards the north. But if this floating under the iceberg is to last another day before we reach the open sea, I shall be dead first.

Half stretched upon a divan in the library, I was suffocating. My face was purple, my lips blue, my faculties suspended. I neither saw nor heard. All notion of time had gone from my mind. My muscles could not contract. I do not know how many hours passed thus, but I was conscious of the agony that was coming over me. I felt as if I was going to die. Suddenly I came to. Some breaths of air penetrated my lungs. Had we risen to the surface of the waves? Were we free of the iceberg? No, Ned and Conseil, my two brave friends, were sacrificing themselves to save me. Some particles of air still remained at the bottom of one apparatus. Instead of using it, they had kept it for me, and while they were being suffocated, they gave me life drop by drop. I wanted to push back the thing; they held my hands, and for some moments I breathed freely. I looked at the clock; it was eleven in the morning. It ought to be the 28th of March. The *Nautilus* went at a frightful pace, forty miles an hour. It literally tore through the water. Where was Captain Nemo? Had he succumbed? Were his companions dead with him? At the moment the manometer indicated that we were not more than twenty feet from the surface. A mere plate of ice separated us from the atmosphere; could we not break it? Perhaps. In any case the *Nautilus* was going to attempt it. I felt that it was in an oblique position, lowering the stern, and raising the bows. The introduction of water had been the means of disturbing its equilibrium. Then, impelled by its powerful screw, it attacked the ice-field from beneath like a formidable battering-ram. It broke it by backing and then rushing forward against the field, which gradually gave way; and at last, dashing suddenly against it, shot forwards on the icy field, that crushed beneath its weight. The panel was opened—one might say torn off—and the pure air came in in abundance to all parts of the *Nautilus*.

Chapter XVII

From Cape Horn to the Amazon

HOW I GOT ON TO THE PLATFORM, I HAVE NO IDEA; PERHAPS THE CANADIAN HAD CARried me there. But I breathed, I inhaled the vivifying sea-air. My two companions were getting drunk with the fresh particles. The other unhappy men had been so long without food that they could not with impunity indulge in the simplest aliments that were given them. We, on the contrary, had no end to restrain ourselves; we could draw this air freely into our lungs, and it was the breeze, the breeze alone, that filled us with this keen enjoyment.

"Ah!" said Conseil. "How delightful this oxygen is! Master need not fear to breathe it. There is enough for everybody."

Ned Land did not speak, but he opened his jaws wide enough to frighten a shark. Our strength soon returned, and, when I looked round me, I saw we were alone on the platform. The foreign seamen in the *Nautilus* were contented with the air that circulated in the interior; none of them had come to drink in the open air.

The first words I spoke were words of gratitude and thankfulness to my two companions. Ned and Conseil had prolonged my life during the last hours of this long agony. All my gratitude could not repay such devotion.

"My friends," said I, "we are bound one to the other forever, and I am under infinite obligations to you."

"Which I shall take advantage of," exclaimed the Canadian.

"What do you mean?" said Conseil.

"I mean that I shall take you with me when I leave this infernal *Nautilus*."

"Well," said Conseil, "after all this, are we going right?"

"Yes," I replied, "for we are going the way of the sun, and here the sun is in the north."

"No doubt," said Ned Land; "but it remains to be seen whether he will bring the ship into the Pacific or the Atlantic Ocean, that is, into frequented or deserted seas."

I could not answer that question, and I feared that Captain Nemo would rather take us to the vast ocean that touches the coasts of Asia and America at the same time. He would thus complete the tour round the submarine world, and return to those waters in which the *Nautilus* could sail freely. We ought, before long, to settle this important point. The *Nautilus* went at a rapid pace. The polar circle was soon passed, and the course shaped for Cape Horn. We were off the American point, March 31st, at seven o'clock in the evening. Then all our past sufferings were forgotten. The remembrance of that imprisonment in the ice was effaced from our minds. We only thought of the future. Captain Nemo did not appear again either in the drawing-room or on the platform. The point shown each day on the planisphere, and, marked by the lieutenant, showed me the exact direction of the *Nautilus*. Now, on that evening, it was evident, to my great satisfaction, that we were going back to the North by the Atlantic. The next day, April 1, when the *Nautilus* ascended to the surface some minutes before noon, we sighted land to the west. It was Terra del Fuego, which the first navigators named thus from seeing the quantity of smoke that rose from the natives' huts. The coast seemed low to me, but in the distance rose high mountains. I even thought I had a glimpse of Mount Sarmiento, that rises 2,070 yards above the level of the sea, with a very pointed summit, which, according as it is misty or clear, is a sign of fine or of wet weather. At this moment, the peak was clearly defined against the sky. The *Nautilus*, diving again under the water, approached the coast, which was only some few miles off. From the glass windows in the drawing-room, I saw long sea-weeds and gigantic fuci and varech, of which the open polar sea contains so many specimens, with their sharp polished filaments; they measured about 300 yards in length—real cables, thicker than one's thumb; and having great tenacity, they are often used as ropes for vessels. Another weed known as velp, with leaves four feet long, buried in the coral concretions, hung at the bottom. It served as nest and food for myriads of crustacea and molluscs, crabs and cuttle-fish. There seals and otters had splendid repasts, eating the flesh of fish with sea-vegetables, according to the English fashion. Over this fertile and luxuriant ground the *Nautilus* passed with great rapidity. Towards evening it approached the Falkland group, the rough summits of which I recognised the following day. The depth of the sea was moderate. On the shores our nets brought in beautiful specimens of sea-weed, and particularly a certain fucus, the roots of which were filled with the best mussels in the world. Geese and ducks fell by dozens on the platform, and soon took their places in the pantry on board. With regard to fish, I observed especially specimens of the goby species, some two feet long, all over white and yellow spots. I admired also numerous medusae, and the finest of the sort, the crysaora, peculiar to the sea about the Falkland Isles. I should have liked to preserve some specimens of these delicate zoöphytes: but they are only like clouds, shadows, apparitions, that sink and evaporate, when out of their native element.

When the last heights of the Falklands had disappeared from the horizon, the *Nautilus* sank to between twenty and twenty-five yards, and followed the American coast. Captain Nemo did not show himself. Until the 3d of April we did not quit the shores of Patagonia, sometimes under the ocean, sometimes at the surface. The *Nautilus* passed beyond the large estuary formed by the mouth of the Plata, and was, on the 4th of April, fifty-six miles off Uraguay. Its direction was northwards, and followed the long windings of the coast of South America. We had then made 16,000 miles since our embarkation in the seas of Japan. About eleven o'clock in the morning the Tropic of Capricorn was crossed on the thirty-seventh meridian, and we passed Cape Frio standing out to sea. Captain Nemo, to Ned Land's great displeasure, did not like the neighborhood of the inhabited coasts of Brazil, for we went at a giddy speed. Not a fish, not a bird of the swiftest kind could follow us, and the natural curiosities of these seas escaped all observation.

This speed was kept up for several days, and in the evening of the 9th of April we sighted the most easterly point of South America that forms Cape San Roque. But then the *Nautilus* swerved again, and sought the lowest depth of a submarine valley, which is between this Cape and Sierra Leone on the African coast. This valley bifurcates to the parallel of the Antilles, and terminates at the mouth by the enormous depression of 9,000 yards. In this place, the geological basin of the ocean forms, as far as the Lesser Antilles, a cliff to three and a half miles perpendicular in height, and at the parallel of the Cape Verde Islands, another wall not less considerable, that encloses thus all the sunk continent of the Atlantic. The bottom of this immense valley is dotted with some mountains, that give to these submarine places a picturesque aspect. I speak, moreover, from the manuscript charts that were in the library of the *Nautilus*—charts evidently due to Captain Nemo's hand and made after his personal observations. For two days the desert and deep waters were visited by means of the inclined planes. The *Nautilus* was furnished with long diagonal broadsides, which carried it to all elevations. But on the 11th of April, it rose suddenly, and land appeared at the mouth of the Amazon River, a vast estuary, the embouchure of which is so considerable that it freshens the sea-water for the distance of several leagues.

The equator was crossed. Twenty miles to the west were the Guianas, a French territory, on which we could have found an easy refuge; but a stiff breeze was blowing, and the furious waves would not have allowed a single boat to face them. Ned Land understood that, no doubt, for he spoke not a word about it. For my part, I made no allusion to his schemes of flight, for I would not urge him to make an attempt that must inevitably fail. I made the time pass pleasantly by interesting studies. During the days of April 11th and 12th the *Nautilus* did not leave the surface of the sea, and the net brought in a marvellous haul of zoöphytes, fish, and reptiles. Some zoöphytes had been fished up by the chain of the nets; they were for the most part beautiful phyctallines, belonging to the actinidian family, and among other species the phyctalis protexta, peculiar to that part of the ocean, with a little cylindrical trunk, ornamented with vertical lines, speckled with red dots, crowning a marvellous blossoming of tentacles. As to the molluscs, they consisted of some I had already observed—turritellas, olive porphyras, with regular lines intercrossed, with red spots standing out plainly against the flesh; odd peteroceras, like petrified scorpions; translucid hyaleas, argonauts, cuttle-fish (excellent eating), and certain species of calmars that naturalists of antiquity have classed among the flying-fish, and that serve principally for bait for cod fishing. I had not an opportunity of studying several species of fish on these shores. Among the cartilaginous ones, petromyzons-pricka, a sort of eel, fifteen inches long, with a greenish head, violet fins, grey-blue back, brown belly, silvered and sown with bright spots, the pupil of the eye encircled with gold—a curious animal that the current of the Amazon had drawn to the sea, for they inhabit fresh waters—tuberculated streaks, with pointed snouts, and a long loose tail, armed with a long jagged sting; little sharks, a yard long, grey and whitish skin, and several rows of teeth, bent back, that are generally known by the name of pantouffles; vespertilios, a kind of red isosceles triangle, half a yard long, to which pectorals are attached by fleshy prolongations that make them look like bats, but that their horny appendage, situated near the nostrils, has given them the name of sea-unicorns; lastly, some species of balistae, the curassavian, whose spots were of a brilliant gold colour, and the capriscus of clear violet, and with varying shades like a pigeon's throat.

I end here this catalogue, which is somewhat dry, perhaps, but very exact, with a series of bony fish that I observed in passing, belonging to the apteronotes, and whose snout is white as snow, the body of a beautiful black, marked with a very long loose fleshy strip; odontognathes, armed with spikes; sardines, nine inches long, glittering with a bright silver light; a species of mackerel provided with two anal fins; centronotes of a blackish tint, that are fished for with torches, long fish, two yards in length, with fat flesh, white and firm, which, when they arc fresh, taste like eel, and when dry, like smoked salmon; labres, half red, covered with scales only at the bottom of the dorsal and anal fins; chrysoptera, on which gold and silver blend their brightness with that of the ruby and topaz; golden-tailed spares, the flesh of which is extremely delicate, and whose phosphorescent properties betray them in the midst of the waters; orange-coloured spares with long tongues; maigres, with gold caudal fins, dark thorn-tails, anableps of Surinam, etc.

Notwithstanding this "et cetera," I must not omit to mention fish that Conseil will long remember, and with good reason. One of our nets had hauled up a sort of very flat ray-fish, which, with the tail cut off, formed a perfect disc, and weighed twenty ounces. It was white underneath, red above, with large round spots of dark blue encircled with black, very glossy skin, terminating in a bilobed fin. Laid out on the platform, it struggled, tried to turn itself by convulsive movements, and made so many efforts, that one last turn had nearly sent it into the sea. But Conseil, not wishing to let the fish go, rushed to it, and, before I could prevent him, had seized it with both hands. In a moment he was overthrown, his legs in the air, and half his body paralysed, crying:

"Oh, master, master! Come to me!"

It was the first time the poor boy had not spoken to me in the third person. The Canadian and I took him up, and rubbed his contracted arms till he became sensible. The unfortunate Conseil had attacked a crampfish of the most dangerous kind, the cumana. This odd animal, in a medium conductor like water, strikes fish at several yards' distance, so great is the power of its electric organ, the two principal surfaces of which do not measure less than twenty-seven square feet. The next day, April 12th, the *Nautilus* approached the Dutch coast, near the mouth of the Maroni. There several groups of sea-cows herded together; they were manatees, that, like the dugong and the stellera, belong to the sirenian order. These beautiful animals, peaceable and inoffensive, from eighteen to twenty-one feet in length, weigh at least sixteen hundredweight. I told Ned Land and Conseil that provident nature had assigned an important *rôle* to these mammalia. Indeed, they, like the seals, are designed to graze on the submarine prairies, and thus destroy the accumulation of weed that obstructs the tropical rivers.

"And do you know," I added, "what has been the result since men have almost entirely annihilated this useful race? That the putrefied weeds have poisoned the air, and the poisoned air causes the yellow fever, that desolates these beautiful countries. Enormous vegetations are multiplied under the torrid seas, and the evil is irresistibly developed from the mouth of the Rio de la Plata to Florida. If we are to believe Toussenel, this plague is nothing to what it would be if the seas were cleaned of whales and seals. Then, infested with poulps, medusae, and cuttle-fish, they would become immense centres of infection, since their waves would not possess 'these vast stomachs that God had charged to infest the surface of the seas.' "

However, without disputing these theories, the crew of the *Nautilus* took possession of half-a-dozen manatees. They provisioned the larders with excellent flesh, superior to beef and veal. This sport was not interesting. The manatees allowed themselves to be hit without defending themselves. Several thousand pounds of meat were stored up on board to be dried. On this day, a successful haul of fish increased the stores of the *Nautilus*, so full of game were these seas. They were echeneides belonging to the third family of the malacopterygiens; their flattened discs were composed of transverse movable cartilaginous plates, by which the animal was enabled to create a vacuum, and to adhere to any object like a cupping-glass. The remora that I had observed in the Mediterranean belongs to this species. But the one of which we are speaking was the echeneis osteochera, peculiar to this sea.

The fishing over, the *Nautilus* neared the coast. About here a number of sea-turtles were sleeping on the surface of the water. It would have been difficult to capture these precious reptiles, for the least noise awakens them, and their solid shell is proof against the harpoon. But the echeneis effects their capture with extraordinary precision and certainty. This animal is, indeed, a living fish-hook, which would make the fortune of an inexperienced fisherman. The crew of the *Nautilus* tied a ring to the tail of these fish, so large as not to encumber their movements, and to this ring a long cord, lashed to the ship's side by the other end.

The echeneids, thrown into the sea, directly began their game, and fixed themselves to the breastplate of the turtles. Their tenacity was such that they were torn rather than let go their hold. The men hauled them on board, and with them the turtles to which they adhered. They took also several cacouannes a yard long, which weighed 400 lbs. Their carapace covered with large horny plates, thin, transparent, brown, with white and yellow spots, fetch a good price in the market. Besides, they were excellent in an edible point of view, as well as the fresh turtles, which have an exquisite flavor. This day's fishing brought to a close our stay on the shores of the Amazon, and by nightfall the *Nautilus* had regained the high seas.

Chapter XVIII

The Poulps

FOR SEVERAL DAYS THE *NAUTILUS* KEPT OFF FROM THE AMERICAN COAST. EVIDENTLY IT did not wish to risk the tides of the Gulf of Mexico or of the sea of the Antilles. April 16th, we sighted Martinique and Guadaloupe from a distance of about thirty miles. I saw their tall peaks for an instant. The Canadian, who counted on carrying out his projects in the Gulf, by either landing, or hailing one of the numerous boats that coast from one island to another, was quite disheartened. Flight would have been quite practicable, if Ned Land had been able to take possession of the boat without the captain's knowledge. But in the open sea it could not be thought of. The Canadian, Conseil, and I had a long conversation on this subject. For six months we had been prisoners on board the *Nautilus*. We had travelled 17,000 leagues; and, as Ned Land said, there was no reason why it should come

to an end. We could hope nothing from the captain of the *Nautilus*, but only from ourselves. Besides, for some time past he had become graver, more retired, less sociable. He
seemed to shun me. I met him rarely. Formerly, he was pleased to explain the submarine
marvels to me; now, he left me to my studies, and came no more to the saloon. What
change had come over him? For what cause? For my part, I did not wish to bury with me
my curious and novel studies. I had now the power to write the true book of the sea; and
this book, sooner or later, I wished to see daylight. Then again, in the water by the Antilles, ten yards below the surface of the waters, by the open panels, what interesting products I had to enter on my daily notes! There were, among other zoöphytes, those known
under the name of physalis pelagica, a sort of large oblong bladder, with mother-of-pearl
rays, holding out their membranes to the wind, and letting their blue tentacles float like
threads of silk; charming medusae to the eye, real nettles to the touch, that distil a corrosive fluid. There were also annelides, a yard and a half long, furnished with a pink horn,
and with 1,700 locomotive organs, that wind through the waters, and throw out in passing
all the light of the solar spectrum. There were, in the fish category, some Malabar rays,
enormous gristly things, ten feet long, weighing 600 pounds, the pectoral fin triangular in
the midst of a slightly humped back, the eyes fixed in the extremities of the face, beyond
the head, and which floated like weft, and looked sometimes like an opaque shutter on our
glass window. There were American balistae, which nature has only dressed in black and
white; gobies, with yellow fins and prominent jaw; mackerel sixteen feet long, with short-
pointed teeth, covered with small scales, belonging to the albicore species. Then, in
swarms, appeared grey mullet, covered with stripes of gold from the head to the tail, beating their resplendent fins, like masterpieces of jewelry, consecrated formerly to Diana,
particularly sought after by rich Romans, and of which the proverb says, "Whoever takes
them does not eat them." Lastly, pomacanthe dorees, ornamented with emerald bands,
dressed in velvet and silk passed before our eyes like Veronese lords; spurred spari passed
with their pectoral fins; clupanodons fifteen inches long, enveloped in their phosphorescent light; mullet beat the sea with their large jagged tails; red vendaces seemed to mow the
waves with their showy pectoral fins; and silvery selenes, worthy of their name, rose on
the horizon of the waters like so many moons with whitish rays. April 20th, we had risen
to a mean height of 1,500 yards. The land nearest us was the archipelago of the Bahamas.
There rose high submarine cliffs covered with large weeds, giant laminariae and fuci, a
perfect espalier of hydrophytes worthy of a Titan world. It was about eleven o'clock when
Ned Land drew my attention to a formidable pricking, like the sting of an ant, which was
produced by means of large sea-weeds.

"Well," I said, "these are proper caverns for poulps, and I should not be astonished to
see some of these monsters."

"What!" said Conseil. "Cuttle-fish, real cuttle-fish of the cephalopod class?"

"No," I said; "poulps of huge dimensions."

"I will never believe that such animals exist," said Ned.

"Well," said Conseil, with the most serious air in the world, "I remember perfectly to
have seen a large vessel drawn under the waves by a cephalopod's arm."

"You saw that?" said the Canadian.

"Yes, Ned."

"With your own eyes?"

"With my own eyes."

"Where, pray, might that be?"

"At St. Malo," answered Conseil.

"In the port?" said Ned ironically.

"No; in a church," replied Conseil.

"In a church!" cried the Canadian.

"Yes; friend Ned. In a picture representing the poulp in question."

"Good!" said Ned Land, bursting out laughing.

"He is quite right," I said. "I have heard of this picture; but the subject represented is taken from a legend, and you know what to think of legends in the matter of natural history. Besides, when it is a question of monsters, the imagination is apt to run wild. Not only is it supposed that these poulps can draw down vessels, but a certain Olaüs Magnus speaks of a cephalopod a mile long, that is more like an island than an animal. It is also said that the Bishop of Nidros was building an altar on an immense rock. Mass finished, the rock began to walk, and returned to the sea. The rock was a poulp. Another bishop, Pontoppidan, speaks also of a poulp on which a regiment of cavalry could maneuvre. Lastly, the ancient naturalists speak of monsters whose mouths were like gulfs, and which were too large to pass through the Straits of Gibraltar."

"But how much is true of these stories?" asked Conseil.

"Nothing, my friends; at least of that which passes the limit of truth to get to fable or legend. Nevertheless, there must be some ground for the imagination of the story-tellers. One cannot deny that poulps and cuttle-fish exist of a large species, inferior, however, to the cetaceans. Aristotle has stated the dimensions of a cuttle-fish as five cubits, or nine feet two inches. Our fishermen frequently see some that are more than four feet long. Some skeletons of poulps are preserved in the museums of Trieste and Montpellier, that measure two yards in length. Besides, according to the calculations of some naturalists, one of these animals, only six feet long, would have tentacles twenty-seven feet long. That would suffice to make a formidable monster."

"Do they fish for them in these days?" asked Ned.

"If they do not fish for them, sailors see them at least. One of my friends, Captain Paul Bos of Havre, has often affirmed that he met one of these monsters, of colossal dimensions, in the Indian seas. But the most astonishing fact, and which does not permit of the denial of the existence of these gigantic animals, happened some years ago, in 1861."

"What is the fact?" asked Ned Land.

"This is it. In 1861, to the north-east of Teneriffe, very nearly in the same latitude we are in now, the crew of the despatch-boat *Alector* perceived a monstrous cuttle-fish swimming in the waters. Captain Bouguer went near to the animal, and attacked it with harpoon and guns, without much success, for balls and harpoons glided over the soft flesh. After several fruitless attempts the crew tried to pass a slip-knot round the body of the mollusc. The noose slipped as far as the caudal fins and there stopped. They tried then to haul it on board, but its weight was so considerable that the tightness of the cord separated the tail from the body, and, deprived of this ornament, he disappeared under the water."

"Indeed! Is that a fact?"

"An indisputable fact, my good Ned. They proposed to name this poulp 'Bouguer's cuttle-fish.' "

"What length was it?" asked the Canadian.

"Did it not measure about six yards?" said Conseil, who, posted at the window, was examining again the irregular windings of the cliff.

"Precisely," I replied.

"Its head," rejoined Conseil, "was it not crowned with eight tentacles, that beat the water like a nest of serpents?"

"Precisely."

"Had not its eyes, placed at the back of its head, considerable development?"

"Yes, Conseil."

"And was not its mouth like a parrot's beak?"

"Exactly, Conseil."

"Very well! No offence to master," he replied quietly; "if this is not Bouguer's cuttle-fish, it is, at least, one of its brothers."

I looked at Conseil. Ned Land hurried to the window.

"What a horrible beast!" he cried.

I looked in my turn, and could not repress a gesture of disgust. Before my eyes was a horrible monster worthy to figure in the legends of the marvellous. It was an immense cuttle-fish, being eight yards long. It swam crossways in the direction of the *Nautilus* with great speed, watching us with its enormous staring green eyes. Its eight arms, or rather feet, fixed to its head, that have given the name of cephalopod to these animals, were twice as long as its body, and were twisted like the Furies' hair. One could see the 250 air-holes on the inner side of the tentacles. The monster's mouth, a horned beak like a parrot's, opened and shut vertically. Its tongue, a horned substance, furnished with several rows of pointed teeth, came out quivering from this veritable pair of shears. What a freak of nature—a bird's beak on a mollusc! Its spindle-like body formed a fleshy mass that might weigh 4,000 to 5,000 lbs.; the, varying colour changing with great rapidity, according to the irritation of the animal, passed successively from livid grey to reddish brown. What irritated this mollusc? No doubt the presence of the *Nautilus,* more formidable than itself, and on which its suckers or its jaws had no hold. Yet, what monsters these poulps are! What vitality the Creator has given them! What vigour in their movements! And they possess three hearts! Chance had brought us in presence of this cuttle-fish, and I did not wish to lose the opportunity of carefully studying this specimen of cephalopods. I overcame the horror that inspired me; and, taking a pencil, began to draw it.

"Perhaps this is the same which the *Alector* saw," said Conseil.

"No," replied the Canadian; "for this is whole, and the other had lost its tail."

"That is no reason," I replied. "The arms and tails of these animals are reformed by redintegration; and, in seven years, the tail of Bouguer's cuttle-fish has no doubt had time to grow."

By this time other poulps appeared at the port light. I counted seven. They formed a procession after the *Nautilus,* and I heard their beaks gnashing against the iron hull. I continued my work. These monsters kept in the water with such precision that they seemed immovable. Suddenly the *Nautilus* stopped. A shock made it tremble in every plate.

"Have we struck anything?" I asked.

"In any case," replied the Canadian, "we shall be free, for we are floating."

The *Nautilus* was floating, no doubt, but it did not move. A minute passed. Captain

Nemo, followed by his lieutenant, entered the drawing-room. I had not seen him for some time. He seemed dull. Without noticing or speaking to us, he went to the panel, looked at the poulps, and said something to his lieutenant. The latter went out. Soon the panels were shut. The ceiling was lighted. I went towards the captain.

"A curious collection of poulps?" I said.

"Yes, indeed, Mr. Naturalist," he replied; "and we are going to fight them, man to beast."

I looked at him. I thought I had not heard aright.

"Man to beast?" I repeated.

"Yes, sir. The screw is stopped. I think that the horny jaws of one of the cuttle-fish is entangled in the blades. That is what prevents our moving."

"What are you going to do?"

"Rise to the surface, and slaughter this vermin."

"A difficult enterprise."

"Yes, indeed. The electric bullets are powerless against the soft flesh, where they do not find resistance enough to go off. But we shall attack them with the hatchet."

"And the harpoon, sir," said the Canadian, "if you do not refuse my help."

"I will accept it, Master Land."

"We will follow you," I said; and following Captain Nemo, we went towards the central staircase.

There, about ten men with boarding-hatchets were ready for the attack. Conseil and I took two hatchets; Ned Land seized a harpoon. The *Nautilus* had then risen to the surface. One of the sailors, posted on the top ladder-step, unscrewed the bolts of the panels. But hardly were the screws loosed, when the panel rose with great violence, evidently drawn by the suckers of a poulp's arm. Immediately one of these arms slid like a serpent down the opening and twenty others were above. With one blow of the axe, Captain Nemo cut this formidable tentacle, that slid wriggling down the ladder. Just as we were pressing one on the other to reach the platform, two other arms, lashing the air, came down on the seaman placed before Captain Nemo, and lifted him up with irresistible power. Captain Nemo uttered a cry, and rushed out. We hurried after him.

What a scene! The unhappy man, seized by the tentacle, and fixed to the suckers, was balanced in the air at the caprice of this enormous trunk. He rattled in his throat, he was stifled, he cried, "Help! Help!" These words, *spoken in French*, startled me! I had a fellow-countryman on board, perhaps several! That heartrending cry! I shall hear it all my life. The unfortunate man was lost. Who could rescue him from that powerful pressure? However, Captain Nemo had rushed to the poulp, and with one blow of the axe had cut through one arm. His lieutenant struggled furiously against other monsters that crept on the flanks of the *Nautilus*. The crew fought with their axes. The Canadian, Conseil, and I buried our weapons in the fleshy masses; a strong smell of musk penetrated the atmosphere. It was horrible!

For one instant, I thought the unhappy man entangled with the poulp would be torn from its powerful suction. Seven of the eight arms had been cut off. One only wriggled in the air, brandishing the victim like a feather. But just as Captain Nemo and his lieutenant threw themselves on it, the animal ejected a stream of black liquid. We were blinded with it. When the cloud dispersed, the cuttle-fish had disappeared, and my unfortunate countryman with it. Ten or twelve poulps now invaded the platform and sides of the *Nautilus*. We rolled pell-mell into the midst of this nest of serpents, that wriggled on the platform in the waves of blood and ink. It seemed as though these slimy tentacles sprang up like the hydra's heads. Ned Land's harpoon, at each stroke, was plunged into the staring eyes of the cuttle-fish. But my bold companion was suddenly overturned by the tentacles of a monster he had not been able to avoid.

Ah! how my heart beat with emotion and horror! The formidable beak of a cuttle-fish was open over Ned Land. The unhappy man would be cut in two. I rushed to his succour. But Captain Nemo was before me; his axe disappeared between the two enormous jaws, and, miraculously saved, the Canadian, rising, plunged his harpoon deep into the triple heart of the poulp.

"I owed myself this revenge!" said the captain to the Canadian.

Ned bowed without replying. The combat had lasted a quarter of an hour. The monsters, vanquished and mutilated, left us at last, and disappeared under the waves. Captain Nemo, covered with blood, nearly exhausted, gazed upon the sea that had swallowed up one of his companions, and great tears gathered in his eyes.

Chapter XIX

THE GULF STREAM

THIS TERRIBLE SCENE OF THE 20TH OF APRIL NONE OF US CAN EVER FORGET. I HAVE written it under the influence of violent emotion. Since then I have revised the recital; I have read it to Conseil and to the Canadian. They found it exact as to facts, but insufficient as to effect. To paint such pictures, one must have the pen of the most illustrious of our poets, the author of "The Toilers of the Deep."

I have said that Captain Nemo wept while watching the waves; his grief was great. It was the second companion he had lost since our arrival on board, and what a death! That friend, crushed, stifled, bruised by the dreadful arms of a poulp, pounded by his iron jaws, would not rest with his comrades in the peaceful coral cemetery! In the midst of the struggle, it was the despairing cry uttered by the unfortunate man that had torn my heart. The poor Frenchman, forgetting his conventional language, had taken to his own mother tongue, to utter a last appeal! Among the crew of the *Nautilus*, associated with the body and soul of the captain, recoiling like him from all contact with men, I had a fellow-countryman. Did he alone represent France in this mysterious association, evidently composed of individuals of divers nationalities? It was one of these insoluble problems that rose up unceasingly before my mind!

Captain Nemo entered his room, and I saw him no more for some time. But that he was sad and irresolute I could see by the vessel, of which he was the soul, and which received all his impressions. The *Nautilus* did not keep on in its settled course; it floated about like a corpse at the will of the waves. It went at random. He could not tear himself away from the scene of the last struggle, from this sea that had devoured one of his men.

Ten days passed thus. It was not till the 1st of May that the *Nautilus* resumed its northerly course, after having sighted the Bahamas at the mouth of the Bahama Canal. We were then following the current from the largest river to the sea, that has its banks, its fish, and its proper temperatures. I mean the Gulf Stream. It is really a river, that flows freely to the middle of the Atlantic, and whose waters do not mix with the ocean waters. It is a salt river, saltier than the surrounding sea. Its mean depth is 1,500 fathoms, its mean breadth ten miles. In certain places the current flows with the speed of two miles and a half an hour. The body of its waters is more considerable than that of all the rivers in the globe. It was on this ocean river that the *Nautilus* then sailed.

This current carried with it all kinds of living things. Argonauts, so common in the Mediterranean, were there in quantities. Of the gristly sort, the most remarkable were the turbot, whose slender tails form nearly the third part of the body, and that looked like large lozenges twenty-five feet long; also, small sharks a yard long, with large heads, short rounded muzzles, pointed teeth in several rows, and whose bodies seemed covered with scales. Among the bony fish I noticed some grey gobies, peculiar to these waters; black giltheads, whose iris shone like fire; sirenes a yard long, with large snouts thickly set with little teeth, that uttered little cries; blue coryphaenes, in gold and silver; parrots, like the rainbows of the ocean, that could rival in color the most beautiful tropical birds; blennies with triangular heads; bluish rhombs destitute of scales; batrachoides covered with yellow transversal bands like a Greek τ; heaps of little gobies spotted with yellow; dipterodons with silvery heads and yellow tails; several specimens of salmon, mugilomores slender in shape, shining with a soft light that Lacépède consecrated to the service of his wife; and lastly, a beautiful fish, the American knight, that, decorated with all the orders and ribbons, frequents the shores of this great nation, that esteems orders and ribbons so little.

I must add that, during the night, the phosphorescent waters of the Gulf Stream rivalled the electric power of our watch-light, especially in the stormy weather that threatened us so frequently. May 8th, we were still crossing Cape Hatteras, at the height of North Carolina. The width of the Gulf Stream there is seventy-five miles, and its depth 210 yards. The *Nautilus* still went at random; all supervision seemed abandoned. I thought that, under these circumstances, escape would be possible. Indeed, the inhabited shores offered anywhere an easy refuge. The sea was incessantly ploughed by the steamers that ply between New York or Boston and the Gulf of Mexico, and over-run day and night by the little schooners coasting about the several parts of the American coast. We could hope to be picked up. It was a favourable opportunity, notwithstanding the thirty miles that separated the *Nautilus* from the coasts of the Union. One unfortunate circumstance thwarted the Canadian's plans. The weather was very bad. We were nearing those shores where tempests are so frequent, that country of water-spouts and cyclones actually engendered by the current of the Gulf Stream. To tempt the sea in a frail boat was certain destruction! Ned Land owned this himself. He fretted, seized with nostalgia that flight only could cure.

"Master," he said that day to me, "this must come to an end. I must make a clean breast of it. This Nemo is leaving land and going up to the north. But I declare to you, that I have had enough of the South Pole, and I will not follow him to the north."

"What is to be done, Ned, since flight is impracticable just now?"

"We must speak to the captain," said he; "you said nothing when we were in your native seas. I will speak, now we are in mine. When I think that before long the *Nautilus* will be by Nova Scotia, and that there near Newfoundland is a large bay, and into that bay the St. Lawrence empties itself, and that the St. Lawrence is my river, the river by Quebec, my native town—when I think of this, I feel furious, it makes my hair stand on end. Sir, I would rather throw myself into the sea! I will not stay here! I am stifled!"

The Canadian was evidently losing all patience. His vigorous nature could not stand this prolonged imprisonment. His face altered daily; his temper became more surly. I knew what he must suffer, for I was seized with nostalgia myself. Nearly seven months had passed without our having had any news from land; Captain Nemo's isolation, his altered spirits, especially since the fight with the poulps, his taciturnity, all made me view things in a different light.

"Well, sir?" said Ned, seeing I did not reply.

"Well, Ned! Do you wish me to ask Captain Nemo his intentions concerning us?"

"Yes, sir."

"Although he has already made them known?"

"Yes; I wish it settled finally. Speak for me, in my name only, if you like."

"But I so seldom meet him. He avoids me."

"That is all the more reason for you to go to see him."

I went to my room. From thence I meant to go to Captain Nemo's. It would not do to let this opportunity of meeting him slip. I knocked at the door. No answer. I knocked again, then turned the handle. The door opened, I went in. The captain was there. Bending over his work-table, he had not heard me. Resolved not to go without having spoken, I approached him. He raised his head quickly, frowned, and said roughly, "You here! What do you want?"

"To speak to you, captain."

"But I am busy, sir; I am working. I leave you at liberty to shut yourself up; cannot I be allowed the same?"

This reception was not encouraging; but I was determined to hear and answer everything.

"Sir," I said coldly, "I have to speak to you on a matter that admits of no delay."

"What is that, sir?" he replied, ironically. "Have you discovered something that has escaped me, or has the sea delivered up any new secrets?"

We were at cross-purposes. But, before I could reply, he showed me an open manuscript on his table, and said, in a more serious tone, "Here, M. Aronnax, is a manuscript written in several languages. It contains the sum of my studies of the sea; and, if it please God, it shall not perish with me. This manuscript, signed with my name, complete with the history of my life, will be shut up in a little insubmersible case. The last survivor of all of us on board the *Nautilus* will throw this case into the sea, and it will go whither it is borne by the waves."

This man's name! his history written by himself! His mystery would then be revealed someday.

"Captain," I said, "I can but approve of the idea that makes you act thus. The result of your studies must not be lost. But the means you employ seem to me to be primitive. Who knows where the winds will carry this case, and in whose hands it will fall? Could you not use some other means? Could not you, or one of yours——"

"Never, sir!" he said, hastily interrupting me.

"But I and my companions are ready to keep this manuscript in store; and, if you will put us at liberty——"

"At liberty?" said the captain, rising.

"Yes, sir; that is the subject on which I wish to question you. For seven months we have been here on board, and I ask you to-day, in the name of my companions, and in my own, if your intention is to keep us here always?"

"M. Aronnax, I will answer you to-day as I did seven months ago; whoever enters the *Nautilus* must never quit it."

"You impose actual slavery upon us!"

"Give it what name you please."

"But everywhere the slave has the right to regain his liberty."

"Who denies you this right? Have I ever tried to chain you with an oath?"

He looked at me with his arms crossed.

"Sir," I said, "to return a second time to this subject will be neither to your nor to my taste; but, as we have entered upon it, let us go through with it. I repeat, it is not only myself whom it concerns. Study is to me a relief, a diversion, a passion that could make me forget everything. Like you, I am willing to live obscure in the frail hope of bequeathing one day, to future time, the result of my labours. But it is otherwise with Ned Land. Every man, worthy of the name, deserves some consideration. Have you thought that love of liberty, hatred of slavery, can give rise to schemes of revenge in a nature like the Canadian's; that he could think, attempt, and try——"

I was silenced; Captain Nemo rose.

"Whatever Ned Land thinks of, attempts, or tries, what does it matter to me? I did not seek him! It is not for my pleasure that I keep him on board! As for you, M. Aronnax, you are one of those who can understand everything, even silence. I have nothing more to say to you. Let this first time you have come to treat of this subject be the last, for a second time I will not listen to you."

I retired. Our situation was critical. I related my conversation to my two companions.

"We know now," said Ned, "that we can expect nothing from this man. The *Nautilus* is nearing Long Island. We will escape, whatever the weather may be."

But the sky became more and more threatening. Symptoms of a hurricane became manifest. The atmosphere was becoming white and misty. On the horizon fine streaks of cirrhous clouds were succeeded by masses of cumuli. Other low clouds passed swiftly by. The swollen sea rose in huge billows. The birds disappeared, with the exception of the petrels, those friends of the storm. The barometer fell sensibly, and indicated an extreme extension of the vapours. The mixture of the storm-glass was decomposed under the influence of the electricity that pervaded the atmosphere. The tempest burst on the 18th of May, just as the *Nautilus* was floating off Long Island, some miles from the port of New York. I can describe this strife of the elements! For, instead of fleeing to the depths of the sea, Captain Nemo, by an unaccountable caprice, would brave it at the surface. The wind blew from the south-west at first. Captain Nemo, during the squalls, had taken his place on the platform. He had made himself fast, to prevent being washed overboard by the monstrous waves. I had hoisted myself up, and made myself fast also, dividing my admiration between the tempest and this extraordinary man who was coping with it. The raging sea was swept by huge cloud-drifts, which were actually saturated with the waves. The *Nau-*

tilus, sometimes lying on its side, sometimes standing up like a mast, rolled and pitched terribly. About five o'clock a torrent of rain fell, that lulled neither sea nor wind. The hurricane blew nearly forty leagues an hour. It is under these conditions that it overturns houses, breaks iron gates, displaces twenty-four pounders. However, the *Nautilus*, in the midst of the tempest, confirmed the words of a clever engineer: "There is no well-constructed hull that cannot defy the sea." This was not a resisting rock; it was a steel spindle, obedient and movable, without rigging or masts, that braved its fury with impunity. However, I watched these raging waves attentively. They measured fifteen feet in height, and 150 to 175 yards long, and their speed of propagation was thirty feet per second. Their bulk and power increased with the depth of the water. Such waves as these at the Hebrides have displaced a mass weighing 8,400 lbs. They are they which, in the tempest of December 23, 1864, after destroying the town of Yeddo, in Japan, broke the same day on the shores of America. The intensity of the tempest increased with the night. The barometer, as in 1860 at Reunion during a cyclone, fell seven-tenths at the close of day. I saw a large vessel pass the horizon struggling painfully. She was trying to lie to under half steam, to keep up above the waves. It was probably one of the steamers of the line from New York to Liverpool or Havre. It soon disappeared in the gloom. At ten o'clock in the evening the sky was on fire. The atmosphere was streaked with vivid lightning. I could not bear the brightness of it; while the captain, looking at it, seemed to envy the spirit of the tempest. A terrible noise filled the air, a complex noise, made up of the howls of the crushed waves, the roaring of the wind, and the claps of thunder. The wind veered suddenly to all points of the horizon; and the cyclone, rising in the east, returned after passing by the north, west, and south, in the inverse course pursued by the circular storms of the southern hemisphere. Ah, that Gulf Stream! It deserves its name of the King of Tempests. It is that which causes those formidable cyclones, by the difference of temperature between its air and its currents. A shower of fire had succeeded the rain. The drops of water were changed to sharp spikes. One would have thought that Captain Nemo was courting a death worthy of himself, a death by lightning. As the *Nautilus*, pitching dreadfully, raised its steel spur in the air, it seemed to act as a conductor, and I saw long sparks burst from it. Crushed and without strength I crawled to the panel, opened it, and descended to the saloon. The storm was then at its height. It was impossible to stand upright in the interior of the *Nautilus*. Captain Nemo came down about twelve. I heard the reservoirs filling by degrees, and the *Nautilus* sank slowly beneath the waves. Through the open windows in the saloon I saw large fish, terrified, passing like phantoms in the water. Some were struck before my eyes. The *Nautilus* was still descending. I thought that at about eight fathoms deep we should find a calm. But no! The upper beds were too violently agitated for that. We had to seek repose at more than twenty-five fathoms in the bowels of the deep. But there, what quiet, what silence, what peace! Who could have told that such a hurricane had been let loose on the surface of that ocean?

Chapter XX

From Latitude 47° 24' to Longitude 17° 28'

In consequence of the storm, we had been thrown eastward once more. All hope of escape on the shores of New York or St. Lawrence had faded away; and poor Ned, in despair, had isolated himself like Captain Nemo. Conseil and I, however, never left each other. I said that the *Nautilus* had gone aside to the east. I should have said (to be more exact) the north-east. For some days, it wandered first on the surface, and then beneath it, amid those fogs so dreaded by sailors. What accidents are due to these thick fogs! What shocks upon these reefs when the wind drowns the breaking of the waves! What collisions between vessels, in spite of their warning lights, whistles, and alarm-bells! And the bottoms of these seas look like a field of battle, where still lie all the conquered of the ocean; some old and already encrusted, others fresh and reflecting from their iron bands and copper plates the brilliancy of our lantern.

On the 15th of May we were at the extreme south of the Bank of Newfoundland. This bank consists of alluvia, or large heaps of organic matter, brought either from the equator by the Gulf Stream, or from the North Pole by the counter-current of cold water which skirts the American coast. There also are heaped up those erratic blocks which are carried along by the broken ice; and close by, a vast charnel-house of molluscs, which perish here by millions. The depth of the sea is not great at Newfoundland—not more than some hundreds of fathoms; but towards the south is a depression of 1,500 fathoms. There the Gulf Stream widens. It loses some of its speed and some of its temperature, but it becomes a sea.

It was on the 17th of May, about 500 miles from Heart's Content, at a depth of more than 1,400 fathoms, that I saw the electric cable lying on the bottom. Conseil, to whom I had not mentioned it, thought at first that it was a gigantic sea-serpent. But I undeceived the worthy fellow, and by way of consolation related several particulars in the laying of this cable. The first one was laid in the years 1857 and 1858; but, after transmitting about 400 telegrams, would not act any longer. In 1863 the engineers constructed an other one, measuring 2,000 miles in length, and weighing 4,500 tons, which was embarked on the *Great Eastern*. This attempt also failed.

On the 25th of May the *Nautilus*, being at a depth of more than 1,918 fathoms, was on the precise spot where the rupture occurred which ruined the enterprise. It was within 638 miles of the coast of Ireland; and at half-past two in the afternoon they discovered that communication with Europe had ceased. The electricians on board resolved to cut the cable before fishing it up, and at eleven o'clock at night they had recovered the damaged part. They made another point and spliced it, and it was once more submerged. But some days after it broke again, and in the depths of the ocean could not be recaptured. The Americans, however, were not discouraged. Cyrus Field, the bold promoter of the enterprise, as he had sunk all his own fortune, set a new subscription on foot, which was at once answered, and another cable was constructed on better principles. The bundles of conducting wires were each enveloped in gutta percha, and protected by a wadding of hemp, contained in a metallic covering. The *Great Eastern* sailed on the 13th of July, 1866. The operation worked well. But one incident occurred. Several times in unrolling the cable they observed that nails had recently been forced into it, evidently with the motive of destroying it. Captain Anderson, the officers and engineers consulted together, and had it posted up that if the offender was surprised on board, he would be thrown without further trial into the sea. From that time the criminal attempt was never repeated.

On the 23d of July the *Great Eastern* was not more than 500 miles from Newfoundland, when they telegraphed from Ireland the news of the armistice concluded between Prussia and Austria after Sadowa. On the 27th, in the midst of heavy fogs, they reached the port of Heart's Content. The enterprise was successfully terminated; and for its first despatch, young America addressed old Europe in these words of wisdom, so rarely understood: "Glory to God in the highest, and on earth peace, good-will towards men."

I did not expect to find the electric cable in its primitive state, such as it was on leaving the manufactory. The long serpent, covered with the remains of shells, bristling with foraminiferae, was encrusted with a strong coating which served as a protection against all boring molluscs. It lay quietly sheltered from the motions of the sea, and under a favourable pressure for the transmission of the electric spark which passes from Europe to America in 0.32 of a second. Doubtless this cable will last for a great length of time, for they find that the gutta percha covering is improved by the sea-water. Besides, on this level, so well chosen, the cable is never so deeply submerged as to cause it to break. The *Nautilus* followed it to the lowest depth, which was more than 2,212 fathoms, and there it lay without any anchorage and then we reached the spot where the accident had taken place in 1863. The bottom of the ocean then formed a valley about 100 miles broad, in which Mont Blanc might have been placed without its summit appearing above the waves. This valley is closed at the east by a perpendicular wall more than 2,000 yards high. We arrived there on the 28th of May, and the *Nautilus* was then not more than 120 miles from Ireland.

Was Captain Nemo going to land on the British Isles? No. To my great surprise he made for the south, once more coming back towards European seas. In rounding the Emerald Isle, for one instant I caught sight of Cape Clear, and the light which guides the thousands of vessels leaving Glasgow or Liverpool. An important question then arose in my mind. Did the *Nautilus* dare entangle itself in the Mauch? Ned Land, who had reappeared since we had been nearing land, did not cease to question me. How could I answer? Captain Nemo remained invisible. After having shown the Canadian a glimpse of American shores, was he going to show me the coast of France?

But the *Nautilus* was still going southward. On the 30th of May, it passed in sight of Land's End, between the extreme point of England and the Scilly Isles, which were left to starboard. If we wished to enter the Mauch, he must go straight to the east. He did not do so.

During the whole of the 31st of May, the *Nautilus* described a series of circles on the water, which greatly interested me. It seemed to be seeking a spot it had some trouble in finding. At noon, Captain Nemo himself came to work the ship's log. He spoke no word to me, but seemed gloomier than ever. What could sadden him thus? Was it his proximity to European shores? Had he some recollections of his abandoned country? If not, what did he feel? Remorse or regret? For a long while this thought haunted my mind, and I had a kind of presentiment that before long chance would betray the captain's secrets.

The next day, the 1st of June, the *Nautilus* continued the same process. It was evidently seeking some particular spot in the ocean. Captain Nemo took the sun's altitude as he had done the day before. The sea was beautiful, the sky clear. About eight miles to the east, a large steam vessel could be discerned on the horizon. No flag fluttered from its mast, and I could not discover its nationality. Some minutes before the sun passed the meridian, Captain Nemo took his sextant, and watched with great attention. The perfect rest of the water greatly helped the operation. The *Nautilus* was motionless; it neither rolled nor pitched.

I was on the platform when the altitude was taken, and the captain pronounced these words—"It is here."

He turned and went below. Had he seen the vessel which was changing its course and seemed to be nearing us? I could not tell. I returned to the saloon. The panels closed, I heard the hissing of the water in the reservoirs. The *Nautilus* began to sink, following a vertical line, for its screw communicated no motion to it. Some minutes later it stopped at a depth of more than 420 fathoms, resting on the ground. The luminous ceiling was darkened, then the panels were opened, and through the glass I saw the sea brilliantly illuminated by the rays of our lantern for at least half a mile round us.

I looked to the port side, and saw nothing but an immensity of quiet waters. But to starboard, on the bottom appeared a large protuberance, which at once attracted my attention. One would have thought it a ruin buried under a coating of white shells, much resembling a covering of snow. Upon examining the mass attentively, I could recognise the ever-thickening form of a vessel bare of its masts, which must have sunk. It certainly belonged to past times. This wreck, to be thus incrusted with the lime of the water, must already be able to count many years passed at the bottom of the ocean.

What was this vessel? Why did the *Nautilus* visit its tomb? Could it have been aught but a shipwreck which had drawn it under the water? I knew not what to think, when near me in a slow voice I heard Captain Nemo say:

"At one time this ship was called the *Marseillais*. It carried seventy-four guns, and was launched in 1762. In 1778, the 13th of August, commanded by La Poype-Vertrieux, it fought boldly against the *Preston*. In 1779, on the 4th of July, it was at the taking of Grenada, with the squadron of Admiral Estaing. In 1781, on the 5th of September, it took part in the battle of Comte de Grasse, in Chesapeake Bay. In 1794, the French Republic changed its name. On the 16th of April, in the same year, it joined the squadron of Villaret Joyeuse, at Brest, being entrusted with the escort of a cargo of corn coming from America, under the command of Admiral Van Stabel. On the 11th and 12th Prairal of the second year, this squadron fell in with an English vessel. Sir, to-day is the 13th Prairal, the first of June, 1868. It is now seventy-four years ago, day for day on this very spot, in latitude 47° 24', longitude 17° 28', that this vessel, after fighting heroically, losing its three masts, with the water in its hold, and the third of its crew disabled, preferred sinking with its 356 sailors to surrendering; and nailing its colours to the poop, disappeared under the waves to the cry of 'Long live the Republic!' "

"The *Avenger!*" I exclaimed.

"Yes, sir, the *Avenger!* A good name!" muttered Captain Nemo, crossing his arms.

Chapter XXI

A HECATOMB

THE WAY OF DESCRIBING THIS UNLOOKED-FOR SCENE, THE HISTORY OF THE PATRIOT ship, told at first so coldly, and the emotion with which this strange man pronounced the last words, the name of the *Avenger,* the significance of which could not escape me, all impressed itself deeply on my mind. My eyes did not leave the captain; who, with his hand stretched out to sea, was watching with a glowing eye the glorious wreck. Perhaps I was never to know who he was, from whence he came, or where he was going to, but I saw the man move, and apart from the savant. It was no common misanthropy which had shut Captain Nemo and his companions within the *Nautilus,* but a hatred, either monstrous or sublime, which time could never weaken. Did this hatred still seek for vengeance? The future would soon teach me that. But the *Nautilus* was rising slowly to the surface of the sea, and the form of the *Avenger* disappeared by degrees from my sight. Soon a slight rolling told me that we were in the open air. At that moment a dull boom was heard. I looked at the captain. He did not move.

"Captain?" said I.

He did not answer. I left him and mounted the platform. Conseil and the Canadian were already there.

"Where did that sound come from?" I asked.

"It was a gunshot," replied Ned Land.

I looked in the direction of the vessel I had already seen. It was nearing the *Nautilus,* and we could see that it was putting on steam. It was within six miles of us.

"What is that ship, Ned?"

"By its rigging, and the height of its lower masts," said the Canadian, "I bet she is a ship of war. May it reach us; and, if necessary, sink this cursed *Nautilus.*"

"Friend Ned," replied Conseil, "what harm can it do to the *Nautilus?* Can it attack it beneath the waves? Can its cannonade us at the bottom of the sea?"

"Tell me, Ned," said I, "can you recognise what country she belongs to?"

The Canadian knitted his eyebrows, dropped his eyelids, and screwed up the corners of his eyes, and for a few moments fixed a piercing look upon the vessel.

"No, sir," he replied; "I cannot tell what nation she belongs to, for she shows no colours. But I can declare she is a man-of-war, for a long pennant flutters from her main-mast."

For a quarter of an hour we watched the ship which was steaming towards us. I could not, however, believe that she could see the *Nautilus* from that distance; and still less that she could know what this submarine engine was. Soon the Canadian informed me that she was a large armoured two-decker ram. A thick black smoke was pouring from her two funnels. Her closely furled sails were stopped to her yards. She hoisted no flag at her mizzen-peak. The distance prevented us from distinguishing the colours of her pennant, which floated like a thin ribbon. She advanced rapidly. If Captain Nemo allowed her to approach, there was a chance of salvation for us.

"Sir," said Ned Land, "if that vessel passes within a mile of us, I shall throw myself into the sea, and I should advise you to do the same."

I did not reply to the Canadian's suggestion, but continued watching the ship. Whether English, French, American, or Russian, she would be sure to take us in if we could only reach her. Presently a white smoke burst from the forepart of the vessel; some seconds after the water, agitated by the fall of a heavy body, splashed the stern of the *Nautilus*, and shortly afterwards a loud explosion struck my ear.

"What! They are firing at us!" I exclaimed.

"So please you, sir," said Ned, "they have recognised the unicorn, and they are firing at us."

"But," I exclaimed, "surely they can see that there are men in the case?"

"It is, perhaps, because of that," replied Ned Land, looking at me.

A whole flood of light burst upon my mind. Doubtless they knew now how to believe the stories of the pretended monster. No doubt, on board the *Abraham Lincoln*, when the Canadian struck it with the harpoon, Commander Farragut had recognised in the supposed narwhal a submarine vessel, more dangerous than a supernatural cetacean. Yes, it must have been so; and on every sea they were now seeking this engine of destruction. Terrible indeed if, as we supposed, Captain Nemo employed the *Nautilus* in works of vengeance! On the night when we were imprisoned in that cell, in the midst of the Indian Ocean, had he not attacked some vessel? The man buried in the coral cemetery, had he not been a victim to the shock caused by the *Nautilus*? Yes, I repeat it, it must be so. One part of the mysterious existence of Captain Nemo had been unveiled; and, if his identity had not been recognised, at least, the nations united against him were no longer hunting a chimerical creature, but a man who had vowed a deadly hatred against them. All the formidable past rose before me. Instead of meeting friends on board the approaching ship, we could only expect pitiless enemies. But the shot rattled about us. Some of them struck the sea and ricochetted, losing themselves in the distance. But none touched the *Nautilus*. The vessel was not more than three miles from us. In spite of the serious cannonade, Captain Nemo did not appear on the platform; but, if one of the conical projectiles had struck the shell of the *Nautilus*, it would have been fatal. The Canadian then said, "Sir, we must do all we can to get out of this dilemma. Let us signal them. They will then, perhaps, understand that we are honest folks."

Ned Land took his handkerchief to wave in the air; but he had scarcely displayed it, when he was struck down by an iron hand, and fell, in spite of his great strength, upon the deck.

"Fool!" exclaimed the captain, "do you wish to be pierced by the spur of the *Nautilus* before it is hurled at this vessel?"

Captain Nemo was terrible to hear; he was still more terrible to see. His face was deadly pale, with a spasm at his heart. For an instant it must have ceased to beat. His pupils were fearfully contracted. He did not *speak*, he roared, as, with his body thrown forward, he wrung the Canadian's shoulders. Then, leaving him, and turning to the ship of war, whose shot was still raining around him, he exclaimed, with a powerful voice, "Ah, ship of an accursed nation, you know who I am! I do not want your colours to know you by. Look and I will show you mine!"

And on the forepart of the platform Captain Nemo unfurled a black flag, similar to the one he had placed at the South Pole. At that moment a shot struck the shell of the *Nautilus* obliquely, without piercing it; and, rebounding near the captain, was lost in the sea. He shrugged his shoulders; and, addressing me, said shortly, "Go down, you and your companions, go down!"

"Sir," I exclaimed, "are you going to attack this vessel?"

"Sir, I am going to sink it."

"You will not do that?"

"I shall do it," he replied coldly. "And I advise you not to judge me, sir. Fate has shown you what you ought not to have seen. The attack has begun; go down."

"What is this vessel?"

"You do not know? Very well! So much the better! Its nationality to you, at least, will be a secret. Go down!"

We could but obey. About fifteen of the sailors surrounded the captain, looking with implacable hatred at the vessel nearing them. One could feel that the same desire of vengeance animated every soul. I went down at the moment another projectile struck the *Nautilus,* and I heard the captain exclaim:

"Strike, mad vessel! Shower your useless shot! And then, you will not escape the spur of the *Nautilus.* But it is not here that you shall perish! I would not have your ruins mingle with those of the *Avenger!*"

I reached my room. The captain and his second had remained on the platform. The screw was set in motion, and the *Nautilus,* moving with speed, was soon beyond the reach of the ship's guns. But the pursuit continued, and Captain Nemo contented himself with keeping his distance.

About four in the afternoon, being no longer able to contain my impatience, I went to the central staircase. The panel was open, and I ventured on to the platform. The Captain was still walking up and down with an agitated step. He was looking at the ship, which was five or six miles to leeward.

He was going round it like a wild beast, and, drawing it eastward, he allowed them to pursue. But he did not attack. Perhaps he still hesitated? I wished to mediate once more. But I had scarcely spoken, when captain Nemo imposed silence, saying:

"I am the law, and I am the judge! I am the oppressed, and there is the oppressor! Through him I have lost all that I loved, cherished, and venerated—country, wife, children, father, and mother. I saw all perish! All that I hate is there! Say no more!"

I cast a last look at the man-of-war, which was putting on steam, and rejoined Ned and Conseil.

"We will fly!" I exclaimed.

"Good!" said Ned. "What is this vessel?"

"I do not know; but whatever it is, it will be sunk before night. In any case, it is better to perish with it, than be made accomplices in a retaliation the justice of which we cannot judge."

"That is my opinion too," said Ned Land coolly. "Let us wait for night."

Night arrived. Deep silence reigned on board. The compass showed that the *Nautilus* had not altered its course. It was on the surface, rolling slightly. My companions and I resolved to fly when the vessel should be near enough either to hear us or to see us; for the moon, which would be full in two or three days, shone brightly. Once on board the ship, if we could not prevent the blow which threatened it, we could, at least we would, do all that circumstances would allow. Several times I thought the *Nautilus* was preparing for attack; but Captain Nemo contented himself with allowing his adversary to approach, and then fled once more before it.

Part of the night passed without any incident. We watched the opportunity for action. We spoke little, for we were too much moved. Ned Land would have thrown himself into the sea, but I forced him to wait. According to my idea, the *Nautilus* would attack the ship at her water-line, and then it would not only be possible, but easy to fly.

At three in the morning, full of uneasiness, I mounted the platform. Captain Nemo had not left it. He was standing at the forepart near his flag, which a slight breeze displayed above his head. He did not take his eyes from the vessel. The intensity of his look seemed to attract, and fascinate, and draw it onward more surely than if he had been towing it. The moon was then passing the meridian. Jupiter was rising in the east. Amid this peaceful scene of nature, sky and ocean rivalled each other in tranquillity, the sea offering to the orbs of night the finest mirror they could ever have in which to reflect their image. As I thought of the deep calm of these elements, compared with all those passions brooding imperceptibly within the *Nautilus,* I shuddered.

The vessel was within two miles of us. It was ever nearing that phosphorescent light which showed the presence of the *Nautilus.* I could see its green and red lights, and its white lantern hanging from the large mizzen-mast. An indistinct vibration quivered through its rigging, showing that the furnaces were heated to the uttermost. Sheaves of sparks and red ashes flew from the funnels, shining in the atmosphere like stars.

I remained thus until six in the morning, without Captain Nemo noticing me. The ship stood about a mile and a half from us, and with the first dawn of day the firing began afresh. The moment could not be far off when, the *Nautilus* attacking its adversary, my companions and myself should forever leave this man. I was preparing to go down to remind them, when the second mounted the platform, accompanied by several sailors. Captain Nemo either did not or would not see them. Some steps were taken which might be called the signal for action. They were very simple. The iron balustrade around the platform was lowered, and the lantern and pilot cages were pushed within the shell until they were flush with the deck. The long surface of the steel cigar no longer offered a single point to check its maneuvres. I returned to the saloon. The *Nautilus* still floated; some streaks of light were filtering through the liquid beds. With the undulations of the waves the windows were brightened by the red streaks of the rising sun, and this dreadful day of the 2d of June had dawned.

At five o'clock, the log showed that the speed of the *Nautilus* was slackening, and I knew that it was allowing them to draw nearer. Besides, the reports were heard more distinctly, and the projectiles, labouring through the ambient water, were extinguished with a strange hissing noise.

"My friends," said I, "the moment is come. One grasp of the hand, and may God protect us!"

Ned Land was resolute, Conseil calm, myself so nervous that I knew not how to contain myself. We all passed into the library; but the moment I pushed the door opening on to the central staircase, I heard the upper panel close sharply. The Canadian rushed on to the stairs, but I stopped him. A well-known hissing noise told me that the water was running into the reservoirs, and in a few minutes the *Nautilus* was some yards beneath the surface of the waves. I understood the maneuvre. It was too late to act. The *Nautilus* did not wish to strike at the impenetrable cuirass, but below the water-line, where the metallic covering no longer protected it.

We were again imprisoned, unwilling witnesses of the dreadful drama that was preparing. We had scarcely time to reflect; taking refuge in my room, we looked at each other without speaking. A deep stupor had taken hold of my mind; thought seemed to stand still. I was in that painful state of expectation preceding a dreadful report. I waited, I listened; every sense was merged in that of hearing! The speed of the *Nautilus* was accelerated. It was preparing to rush. The whole ship trembled. Suddenly I screamed. I felt the shock, but comparatively light. I felt the penetrating power of the steel spur. I heard rattlings and scrapings. But the *Nautilus,* carried along by its propelling power, passed through the mass of the vessel like a needle through sail-cloth!

I could stand it no longer. Mad, out of my mind, I rushed from my room into the saloon. Captain Nemo was there, mute, gloomy, implacable; he was looking through the port panel. A large mass cast a shadow on the water; and that it might lose nothing of her agony, the *Nautilus* was going down into the abyss with her. Ten yards from me I saw the open shell, through which the water was rushing with the noise of thunder, then the double line of guns and the netting. The bridge was covered with black, agitated shadows.

The water was rising. The poor creatures were crowding the ratlines, clinging to the masts, struggling under water. It was a human ant-heap overtaken by the sea. Paralysed, stiffened with anguish, my hair standing on end, with eyes wide open, panting, without breath, and without voice, I too was watching! An irresistible attraction glued me to the glass! Suddenly an explosion took place. The compressed air blew up her decks, as if the magazines had caught fire. Then the unfortunate vessel sank more rapidly. Her topmast, laden with victims, now appeared; then her spars, bending under the weight of men; and, last of all, the top of her mainmast. Then the dark mass disappeared, and with it the dead crew, drawn down by the strong eddy.

I turned to Captain Nemo. That terrible avenger, a perfect archangel of hatred, was still looking. When all was over, he turned to his room, opened the door, and entered. I followed him with my eyes. On the end wall beneath his heroes, I saw the portrait of a woman still young, and two little children. Captain Nemo looked at them for some moments, stretched his arms towards them, and kneeling down burst into deep sobs.

Chapter XXII

THE LAST WORDS OF CAPTAIN NEMO

THE PANELS HAD CLOSED ON THIS DREADFUL VISION, BUT LIGHT HAD NOT RETURNED to the saloon: all was silence and darkness within the *Nautilus*. At wonderful speed, a hundred feet beneath the water, it was leaving this desolate spot. Whither was it going? To the north or south? Where was the man flying to after such dreadful retaliation? I had returned to my room, where Ned and Conseil had remained silent enough. I felt an insurmountable horror for Captain Nemo. Whatever he had suffered at the hands of these men, he had no right to punish thus. He had made me, if not an accomplice, at least a witness of his vengeance. At eleven the electric light reappeared. I passed into the saloon. It was deserted. I consulted the different instruments. The *Nautilus* was flying northward at the rate of twenty-five miles an hour, now on the surface, and now thirty feet below it. On taking the bearings by the chart, I saw that we were passing the mouth of the Manche, and that our course was hurrying us towards the northern seas at a frightful speed. That night we had crossed two hundred leagues of the Atlantic. The shadows fell, and the sea was covered with darkness until the rising of the moon. I went to my room, but could not sleep. I was troubled with a dreadful nightmare. The horrible scene of destruction was continually before my eyes. From that day, who could tell into what part of the North Atlantic basin the *Nautilus* would take us? Still with unaccountable speed, still in the midst of these northern fogs, would it touch at Spitzbergen, or on the shores of Nova Zembla? Should we explore those unknown seas, the White Sea, the Sea of Kara, the Gulf of Obi, the Archipelago of Liarrov, and the unknown coast of Asia? I could not say. I could no longer judge of the time that was passing. The clocks had been stopped on board. It seemed, as in polar countries, that night and day no longer followed their regular course. I felt myself being drawn into that strange region where the foundered imagination of Edgar Poe roamed at will. Like the fabulous Gordon Pym, at every moment I expected to see "that veiled human figure, of larger proportions than those of any inhabitant of the earth, thrown across the cataract which defends the approach to the pole." I estimated (though perhaps I may be mistaken)—I estimated this adventurous course of the *Nautilus* to have lasted fifteen or twenty days. And I know not how much longer it might have lasted, had it not been for the catastrophe which ended this voyage. Of Captain Nemo I saw nothing whatever now, nor of his second. Not a man of the crew was visible for an instant. The *Nautilus* was almost incessantly under water. When we came to the surface to renew the air, the panels opened and shut mechanically. There were no more marks on the planisphere. I knew not where we were. And the Canadian, too, his strength and patience at an end, appeared no more. Conseil could not draw a word from him, and fearing that, in a dreadful fit of madness, he might kill himself, watched him with constant devotion. One morning (what date it was I could not say) I had fallen into a heavy sleep towards the early hours, a sleep both painful and unhealthy, when I suddenly awoke. Ned Land was leaning over me, saying in a low voice, "We are going to fly."

I sat up.

"When shall we go?" I asked.

"To-night. All inspection on board the *Nautilus* seems to have ceased. All appear to be stupefied. You will be ready, sir?"

"Yes; where are we?"

"In sight of land. I took the reckoning this morning in the fog—twenty miles to the east."

"What country is it?"

"I do not know; but, whatever it is, we will take refuge there."

"Yes, Ned, yes. We will fly to-night, even if the sea should swallow us up."

"The sea is bad, the wind violent, but twenty miles in that light boat of the *Nautilus* does not frighten me. Unknown to the crew, I have been able to procure food and some bottles of water."

"I will follow you."

"But," continued the Canadian, "if I am surprised I will defend myself; I will force them to kill me."

"We will die together, friend Ned."

I had made up my mind to all. The Canadian left me. I reached the platform, on which I could with difficulty support myself against the shock of the waves. The sky was threatening; but, as land was in those thick brown shadows we must fly. I returned to the saloon, fearing and yet hoping to see Captain Nemo, wishing and yet not wishing to see him. What could I have said to him? Could I hide the involuntary horror with which he inspired me? No. It was better that I should not meet him face to face; better to forget him. And yet— How long seemed that day, the last that I should pass in the *Nautilus*. I remained alone. Ned Land and Conseil avoided speaking, for fear of betraying themselves. At six I dined, but I was not hungry; I forced myself to eat in spite of my disgust, that I might not weaken myself. At half-past six Ned Land came to my room, saying, "We shall not see each other again before our departure. At ten the moon will not be risen. We will profit by the darkness. Come to the boat; Conseil and I will wait for you."

The Canadian went out without giving me time to answer. Wishing to verify the course of the *Nautilus*, I went to the saloon. We were running N.N.E. at frightful speed, and more than fifty yards deep. I cast a last look on these wonders of nature, on the riches of art heaped up in this museum, upon the unrivalled collection destined to perish at the bottom of the sea, with him who had formed it. I wished to fix an indelible impression of it in my mind. I remained an hour thus, bathed in the light of that luminous ceiling, and passing in review those treasures shining under their glasses. Then I returned to my room.

I dressed myself in strong sea-clothing. I collected my notes, placing them carefully about me. My heart beat loudly. I could not check its pulsations. Certainly my trouble and agitation would have betrayed me to Captain Nemo's eyes. What was he doing at this moment? I listened at the door of his room. I heard steps. Captain Nemo was there. He had not gone to rest. At every moment I expected to see him appear and ask me why I wished to fly. I was constantly on the alert. My imagination magnified everything. The impression became at last so poignant that I asked myself if it would not be better to go to the captain's room, see him face to face, and brave him with look and gesture.

It was the inspiration of a madman; fortunately I resisted the desire, and stretched myself on my bed to quiet my bodily agitation. My nerves were somewhat calmer, but in my excited brain I saw over again all my existence on board the *Nautilus*; every incident, either happy or unfortunate, which had happened since my disappearance from the *Abraham Lincoln*—the submarine hunt, the Torres Straits, the savages of Papua, the running ashore, the coral cemetery, the passage of Suez, the Island of Santorin, the Cretan diver, Vigo Bay, Atlantis, the iceberg, the South Pole, the imprisonment in the ice, the fight among the poulps, the storm in the Gulf Stream, the *Avenger*, and the horrible scene of the vessel sunk with all her crew. All these events passed before my eyes like scenes in a drama. Then Captain Nemo seemed to grow enormously, his features to assume superhuman proportions. He was no longer my equal, but a man of the waters, the genie of the sea.

It was then half-past nine. I held my head between my hands to keep it from bursting.

I closed my eyes; I would not think any longer. There was another half-hour to wait, another half-hour of a nightmare, which might drive me mad.

At that moment I heard the distant strains of the organ, a sad harmony to an undefinable chant, the wail of a soul longing to break these earthly bonds. I listened with every sense, scarcely breathing; plunged, like Captain Nemo, in that musical ecstasy, which was drawing him in spirit to the end of life.

Then a sudden thought terrified me. Captain Nemo had left his room. He was in the saloon, which I must cross to fly. There I should meet him for the last time. He would see me, perhaps speak to me. A gesture of his might destroy me, a single word chain me on board.

But ten was about to strike. The moment had come for me to leave my room and join my companions.

I must not hesitate, even if Captain Nemo himself should rise before me. I opened my door carefully; and even then, as it turned on its hinges, it seemed to me to make a dreadful noise. Perhaps it only existed in my own imagination.

I crept along the dark stairs of the *Nautilus*, stopping at each step to check the beating of my heart. I reached the door of the saloon, and opened it gently. It was plunged in profound darkness. The strains of the organ sounded faintly. Captain Nemo was there. He did not see me. In the full light I do not think he would have noticed me, so entirely was he absorbed in the ecstasy.

I crept along the carpet, avoiding the slightest sound which might betray my presence. I was at least five minutes reaching the door, at the opposite side, opening into the library.

I was going to open it, when a sigh from Captain Nemo nailed me to the spot. I knew that he was rising. I could even see him, for the light from the library came through to the saloon. He came towards me silently, with his arms crossed, gliding like a spectre rather than walking. His breast was swelling with sobs; and I heard him murmur these words (the last which ever struck my ear):

"Almighty God! Enough! Enough!"

Was it a confession of remorse which thus escaped from this man's conscience?

In desperation, I rushed through the library, mounted the central staircase, and following the upper flight reached the boat. I crept through the opening, which had already admitted my two companions.

"Let us go! Let us go!" I exclaimed.

"Directly!" replied the Canadian.

The orifice in the plates of the *Nautilus* was first closed, and fastened down by means of a false key, with which Ned Land had provided himself; the opening in the boat was also closed. The Canadian began to loosen the bolts which still held us to the submarine boat.

Suddenly a noise was heard. Voices were answering each other loudly. What was the matter? Had they discovered our flight? I felt Ned Land slipping a dagger into my hand.

"Yes," I murmured, "we know how to die!"

The Canadian had stopped in his work. But one word many times repeated, a dreadful word, revealed the cause of the agitation spreading on board the *Nautilus*. It was not we the crew were looking after!

"The Maëlstrom! the Maelstrom!" I exclaimed.

The Maëlstrom! Could a more dreadful word in a more dreadful situation have sounded in our ears! We were then upon the dangerous coast of Norway. Was the *Nautilus* being drawn into this gulf at the moment our boat was going to leave its sides? We knew that at the tide the pent-up waters between the islands of Ferroe and Lofoten rush with irresistible violence, forming a whirlpool from which no vessel ever escapes. From every point of the horizon enormous waves were meeting, forming a gulf justly called the "Navel of the Ocean," whose power of attraction extends to a distance of twelve miles. There, not only vessels, but whales, are sacrificed, as well as white bears from the northern regions.

It is thither that the *Nautilus*, voluntarily or involuntarily, had been run by the captain.

It was describing a spiral, the circumference of which was lessening by degrees, and the boat, which was still fastened to its side, was carried along with giddy speed. I felt that sickly giddiness which arises from long-continued whirling round.

We were in dread. Our horror was at its height, circulation had stopped, all nervous influence was annihilated, and we were covered with cold sweat, like a sweat of agony! And what noise around our frail bark! What roarings repeated by the echo miles away! What an uproar was that of the waters broken on the sharp rocks at the bottom, where the hardest bodies are crushed, and trees worn away, "with all the fur rubbed off," according to the Norwegian phrase!

What a situation to be in! We rocked frightfully. The *Nautilus* defended itself like a human being. Its steel muscles cracked. Sometimes it seemed to stand upright, and we with it!

"We must hold on," said Ned, "and look after the bolts. We may still be saved if we stick to the *Nautilus*—"

He had not finished the words, when we heard a crashing noise, the bolts gave way, and the boat, torn from its groove, was hurled like a stone from a sling into the midst of the whirlpool.

My head struck on a piece of iron, and with the violent shock I lost all consciousness.

Chapter XXIII

CONCLUSION

THUS ENDS THE VOYAGE UNDER THE SEAS. WHAT PASSED DURING THAT NIGHT—HOW the boat escaped from the eddies of the Maëlstrom, how Ned Land, Conseil, and myself ever came out of the gulf, I cannot tell.

But when I returned to consciousness, I was lying in a fisherman's hut, on the Lofoten Isles. My two companions, safe and sound, were near me holding my hands. We embraced each other heartily.

At that moment we could not think of returning to France. The means of communication between the north of Norway and the south are rare. And I am therefore obliged to wait for the steamboat running monthly from Cape North.

And among the worthy people who have so kindly received us I revise my record of these adventures once more. Not a fact has been omitted, not a detail exaggerated. It is a faithful narrative of this incredible expedition in an element inaccessible to man, but to which Progress will one day open a road.

Shall I be believed? I do not know. And it matters little, after all. What I now affirm is, that I have a right to speak of these seas, under which, in less than ten months, I have crossed 20,000 leagues in that submarine tour of the world, which has revealed so many wonders.

But what has become of the *Nautilus?* Did it resist the pressure of the Maëlstrom? Does Captain Nemo still live? And does he still follow under the ocean those frightful retaliations? Or did he stop after the last hecatomb?

Will the waves one day carry to him this manuscript containing the history of his life? Shall I ever know the name of this man? Will the missing vessel tell us by its nationality that of Captain Nemo?

I hope so. And I also hope that his powerful vessel has conquered the sea at its most terrible gulf, and that the *Nautilus* has survived where so many other vessels have been lost! If it be so, if Captain Nemo still inhabits the ocean, his adopted country, may hatred be appeased in that savage heart! May the contemplation of so many wonders extinguish forever the spirit of vengeance! May the judge disappear, and the philosopher continue the peaceful exploration of the sea! If his destiny be strange, it is also sublime. Have I not understood it myself? Have I not lived ten months of this unnatural life? And to the question asked by Ecclesiastes 3,000 years ago, "That which is far off and exceeding deep, who can find it out?" two men alone of all now living have the right to give an answer:

CAPTAIN NEMO AND MYSELF.

AROUND THE WORLD
IN EIGHTY DAYS

CONTENTS

I   In which Phileas Fogg and Passepartout accept each other,
the one as master, the other as servant   707

II   In which Passepartout is convinced that he has at last found his ideal   709

III   In which a conversation takes place which seems likely to cost
Phileas Fogg dear   711

IV   In which Phileas Fogg astounds Passepartout, his servant   715

V   In which a new species of funds, unknown to the moneyed men,
appears on 'Change   717

VI   In which Fix, the detective, betrays a very natural impatience   719

VII   Which once more demonstrates the uselessness
of passports as aids to detectives   722

VIII   In which Passepartout talks rather more, perhaps, than is prudent   723

IX   In which the Red Sea and the Indian Ocean prove propitious
to the designs of Phileas Fogg   726

X   In which Passepartout is only too glad to get off with the
loss of his shoes   729

XI   In which Phileas Fogg secures a curious means of conveyance
at a fabulous price   731

XII   In which Phileas Fogg and his companions venture
across the Indian forests, and what ensued   736

XIII   In which Passepartout receives a new proof that fortune
favours the brave   740

XIV   In which Phileas Fogg descends the whole length of the beautiful
Valley of the Ganges without ever thinking of seeing it   744

XV   In which the bag of bank-notes disgorges some
thousands of pounds more   747

XVI   In which Fix does not seem to understand in the least
what is said to him   751

XVII   Showing what happened on the voyage from
Singapore to Hong Kong   754

XVIII   In which Phileas Fogg, Passepartout, and Fix go each
about his business   757

XIX   In which Passepartout takes a too great interest in his master,
        and what comes of it   759

XX   In which Fix comes face to face with Phileas Fogg   763

XXI   In which the master of the *Tankadere* runs great risk
        of losing a reward of two hundred pounds   767

XXII   In which Passepartout finds out that, even at the antipodes,
        it is convenient to have some money in one's pocket   771

XXIII   In which Passepartout's nose becomes outrageously long   775

XXIV   During which Mr. Fogg and party cross the Pacific Ocean   779

XXV   In which a slight glimpse is had of San Francisco   782

XXVI   In which Phileas Fogg and party travel by the Pacific Railroad   786

XXVII   In which Passepartout undergoes, at a speed of twenty miles
        an hour, a course of Mormon history   789

XXVIII In which Passepartout does not succeed in making
        anybody listen to reason   792

XXIX   In which certain incidents are narrated which are only
        to be met with on American railroads   797

XXX   In which Phileas Fogg simply does his duty   801

XXXI   In which Fix the detective considerably furthers the interests of
        Phileas Fogg   805

XXXII   In which Phileas Fogg engages in a direct struggle with
        bad fortune   808

XXXIII In which Phileas Fogg shows himself equal to the occasion   811

XXXIV   In which Phileas Fogg at last reaches London   815

XXXV   In which Phileas Fogg does not have to repeat his orders to
        Passepartout twice   817

XXXVI   In which Phileas Fogg's name is once more at a premium
        on 'Change   820

XXXVII In which it is shown that Phileas Fogg gained nothing
        by his tour around the world, unless it were happiness   822

Chapter I

In which Phileas Fogg and Passepartout accept each other, the one as master, the other as servant

MR. PHILEAS FOGG LIVED, IN 1872, AT NO. 7, SAVILLE ROW, BURLINGTON GARDENS, the house in which Sheridan died in 1814. He was one of the most noticeable members of the Reform Club, though he seemed always to avoid attracting attention; an enigmatical personage, about whom little was known, except that he was a polished man of the world. People said that he resembled Byron—at least that his head was Byronic; but he was a bearded, tranquil Byron, who might live on a thousand years without growing old.

Certainly an Englishman it was more doubtful whether Phileas Fogg was a Londoner. He was never seen on 'Change, nor at the Bank, nor in the counting-rooms of the "City"; no ships ever came into London docks of which he was the owner; he had no public employment; he had never been entered at any of the Inns of Court, either at the Temple, or Lincoln's Inn, or Gray's Inn; nor had his voice ever resounded in the Court of Chancery, or in the Exchequer, or the Queen's Bench, or the Ecclesiastical Courts. He certainly was not a manufacturer; nor was he a merchant or a gentleman farmer. His name was strange to the scientific and learned societies, and he never was known to take part in the sage deliberations of the Royal Institution or the London Institution, the Artisan's Association or the Institution of Arts and Sciences. He belonged, in fact, to none of the numerous societies which swarm in the English capital, from the Harmonic to that of the Entomologists, founded mainly for the purpose of abolishing pernicious insects.

Phileas Fogg was a member of the Reform, and that was all.

The way in which he got admission to this exclusive club was simple enough.

He was recommended by the Barings, with whom he had an open credit. His checks were regularly paid at sight from his account current, which was always flush.

Was Phileas Fogg rich? Undoubtedly. But those who knew him best could not imagine how he had made his fortune, and Mr. Fogg was the last person to whom to apply for the information. He was not lavish, nor, on the contrary, avaricious; for whenever he knew that money was needed for a noble, useful, or benevolent purpose, he supplied it quietly and sometimes anonymously. He was, in short, the least communicative of men. He talked very little and seemed all the more mysterious for his taciturn manner. His daily habits were quite open to observation; but whatever he did was so exactly the same thing that he had always done before, that the wits of the curious were fairly puzzled.

Had he travelled? It was likely, for no one seemed to know the world more familiarly; there was no spot so secluded that he did not appear to have an intimate acquaintance with it. He often corrected, with a few clear words, the thousand conjectures advanced by members of the club as to lost and unheard-of travellers, pointing out the true probabilities, and seeming as if gifted with a sort of second sight, so often did events justify his predictions. He must have travelled everywhere, at least in the spirit.

It was at least certain that Phileas Fogg had not absented himself from London for many years. Those who were honoured by a better acquaintance with him than the rest, declared that nobody could pretend to have ever seen him anywhere else. His sole pastimes were reading the papers and playing whist. He often won at this game, which, as a silent one, harmonised with his nature; but his winnings never went into his purse, being reserved as a fund for his charities. Mr. Fogg played, not to win, but for the sake of playing. The game was in his eyes a contest, a struggle with a difficulty, yet a motionless, unwearying struggle, congenial to his tastes.

Phileas Fogg was not known to have either wife or children, which may happen to the most honest people; either relatives or near friends, which is certainly more unusual. He lived alone in his house in Saville Row, whither none penetrated. A single domestic sufficed to serve him. He breakfasted and dined at the club, at hours mathematically fixed, in the same room, at the same table, never taking his meals with other members, much less bringing a guest with him; and went home at exactly midnight, only to retire at once to bed. He never used the cosy chambers which the Reform provides for its favoured members. He passed ten hours out of the twenty-four in Saville Row, either in sleeping or making his toilet. When he chose to take a walk it was with a regular step in the entrance hall with its mosaic flooring, or in the circular gallery with its dome supported by twenty red porphyry Ionic columns, and illumined by blue painted windows. When he breakfasted or dined all the resources of the club—its kitchens and pantries, its buttery and dairy—aided to crowd his table with their most succulent stores; he was served by the gravest waiters, in dress coats, and shoes with swanskin soles, who proffered the viands in special porcelain, and on the finest linen; club decanters, of a lost mould, contained his sherry, his port, and his cinnamon-spiced claret; while his beverages were refreshingly cooled with ice, brought at great cost from the American lakes.

If to live in this style is to be eccentric, it must be confessed that there is something good in eccentricity!

The mansion in Saville Row, though not sumptuous, was exceedingly comfortable. The habits of its occupant were such as to demand but little from the sole domestic, but Phileas Fogg required him to be almost superhumanly prompt and regular. On this very 2d of October he had dismissed James Forster, because that luckless youth had brought him shaving-water at eighty-four degrees Fahrenheit instead of eighty-six; and he was awaiting his successor, who was due at the house between eleven and half-past.

Phileas Fogg was seated squarely in his arm-chair, his feet close together like those of a grenadier on parade, his hands resting on his knees, his body straight, his head erect; he was steadily watching a complicated clock which indicated the hours, the minutes, the seconds, the days, the months, and the years. At exactly half-past eleven Mr. Fogg would, according to his daily habit, quit Saville Row, and repair to the Reform.

A rap at this moment sounded on the door of the cosy apartment where Phileas Fogg was seated, and James Forster, the dismissed servant, appeared.

"The new servant," said he.

A young man of thirty advanced and bowed.

"You are a Frenchman, I believe," asked Phileas Fogg, "and your name is John?"

"Jean, if monsieur pleases," replied the newcomer, "Jean Passepartout, a surname which has clung to me because I have a natural aptness for going out of one business into another. I believe I'm honest, monsieur, but, to be outspoken, I've had several trades. I've been an itinerant singer, a circus-rider, when I used to vault like Leotard, and dance on a rope like Blondin. Then I got to be a professor of gymnastics, so as to make better use of my talents; and then I was a sergeant fireman at Paris, and assisted at many a big fire. But I quitted France five years ago, and, wishing to taste the sweets of domestic life, took service as a valet here in England. Finding myself out of place, and hearing that Monsieur Phileas Fogg was the most exact and settled gentleman in the United Kingdom, I have come to monsieur in the hope of living with him a tranquil life, and forgetting even the name of Passepartout."

"Passepartout suits me," responded Mr. Fogg. "You are well recommended to me; I hear a good report of you. You know my conditions?"

"Yes, monsieur."

"Good. What time is it?"

"Twenty-two minutes after eleven," returned Passepartout, drawing an enormous silver watch from the depths of his pocket.

"You are too slow," said Mr. Fogg.

"Pardon me, monsieur, it is impossible—"

"You are four minutes too slow. No matter; it's enough to mention the error. Now from this moment, twenty-nine minutes after eleven, A.M., this Wednesday, October second, you are in my service."

Phileas Fogg got up, took his hat in his left hand, put it on his head with an automatic motion, and went off without a word.

Passepartout heard the street door shut once; it was his new master going out. He heard it shut again; it was his predecessor, James Forster, departing in his turn. Passepartout remained alone in the house in Saville Row.

Chapter II

In which Passepartout is convinced that he has at last found his ideal

"Faith," muttered Passepartout, somewhat flurried, "I've seen people at Madame Tussaud's as lively as my new master!"

Madame Tussaud's "people," let it be said, are of wax, and are much visited in London; speech is all that is wanting to make them human.

During his brief interview with Mr. Fogg, Passepartout had been carefully observing him. He appeared to be a man about forty years of age, with fine, handsome features, and a tall, well-shaped figure; his hair and whiskers were light, his forehead compact and unwrinkled, his face rather pale, his teeth magnificent. His countenance possessed in the highest degree what physiognomists call "repose in action," a quality of those who act rather than talk. Calm and phlegmatic, with a clear eye, Mr. Fogg seemed a perfect type of that English composure which Angelica Kauffmann has so skilfully represented on canvas. Seen in the various phases of his daily life, he gave the idea of being perfectly well balanced, as exactly regulated as a Leroy chronometer. Phileas Fogg was, indeed, exactitude personified, and this was betrayed even in the expression of his very hands and feet; for in men, as well as in animals, the limbs themselves are expressive of the passions.

He was so exact that he was never in a hurry, was always ready, and was economical alike of his steps and his motions. He never took one step too many, and always went to his destination by the shortest cut; he made no superfluous gestures, and was never seen to be moved or agitated. He was the most deliberate person in the world, yet always reached his destination at the exact moment.

He lived alone, and so to speak, outside of every social relation; and as he knew that in this world account must be taken of friction, and that friction retards, he never rubbed against anybody.

As for Passepartout, he was a true Parisian of Paris. Since he had abandoned his own country for England, taking service as a valet, he had in vain searched for a master after his own heart. Passepartout was by no means one of those pert dunces depicted by Molière, with a bold gaze and a nose held high in the air; he was an honest fellow, with a pleasant face, lips a trifle protruding, soft-mannered and serviceable, with a good round head, such as one likes to see on the shoulders of a friend. His eyes were blue, his complexion rubicund, his figure almost portly and well built, his body muscular and his physical powers fully developed by the exercises of his younger days. His brown hair was somewhat tumbled; for while the ancient sculptors are said to have known eighteen methods of arranging Minerva's tresses, Passepartout was familiar with but one of dressing his own: three strokes of a large-tooth comb completed his toilet.

It would be rash to predict how Passepartout's lively nature would agree with Mr. Fogg. It was impossible to tell whether the new servant would turn out as absolutely methodical as his master required: experience alone could solve the question. Passepartout had been a sort of vagrant in his early years, and now yearned for repose; but so far he had failed to find it, though he had already served in ten English houses. But he could not take root in any of these; with chagrin he found his masters invariably whimsical and irregular, constantly running about the country, or on the look-out for adventure. His last master, young Lord Longferry, Member of Parliament, after passing his nights in the Haymarket taverns, was too often brought home in the morning on policemen's shoulders. Passepartout, desirous of respecting the gentleman whom he served, ventured a mild remonstrance on such conduct; which, being ill-received, he took his leave. Hearing that Mr. Phileas Fogg was looking for a servant, and that his life was one of unbroken regularity, that he neither travelled nor stayed from home overnight, he felt sure that this would be the place he was after. He presented himself, and was accepted, as has been seen.

At half-past eleven, then, Passepartout found himself alone in the house in Saville Row. He began its inspection without delay, scouring it from cellar to garret. So clean, well arranged, solemn a mansion pleased him ; it seemed to him like a snail's shell, lighted and warmed by gas, which sufficed for both these purposes. When Passepartout reached the second story he recognised at once the room which he was to inhabit, and he was well satisfied with it. Electric bells and speaking tubes afforded communication with the lower stories; while on the mantel stood an electric clock, precisely like that in Mr. Fogg's bedchamber, both beating the same second at the same instant. "That's good, that'll do," said Passepartout to himself.

He suddenly observed, hung over the clock, a card which, upon inspection, proved to be a programme of the daily routine of the house. It comprised all that was required of the servant, from eight in the morning, exactly at which hour Phileas Fogg rose, till half-past eleven, when he left the house for the Reform Club—all the details of service, the tea and toast at twenty-three minutes past eight, the shaving-water at thirty-seven minutes past nine, and the toilet at twenty minutes before ten. Everything was regulated and foreseen that was to be done from half-past eleven A.M. till midnight, the hour at which the methodical gentleman retired.

Mr. Fogg's wardrobe was amply supplied and in the best taste. Each pair of trousers, coat, and vest bore a number, indicating the time of year and season at which they were in turn to be laid out for wearing; and the same system was applied to the master's shoes. In short, the house in Saville Row, which must have been a very temple of disorder and unrest under the illustrious but dissipated Sheridan, was cosiness, comfort, and method idealised. There was no study, nor were there books, which would have been quite useless to Mr. Fogg; for at the Reform two libraries, one of general literature and the other of law and politics, were at his service. A moderate-sized safe stood in his bedroom, constructed so as to defy fire as well as burglars; but Passepartout found neither arms nor hunting weapons anywhere; everything betrayed the most tranquil and peaceable habits.

Having scrutinised the house from top to bottom, he rubbed his hands, a broad smile overspread his features, and he said joyfully, "This is just what I wanted! Ah, we shall get on together, Mr. Fogg and I! What a domestic and regular gentleman! A real machine; well, I don't mind serving a machine."

Chapter III

IN WHICH A CONVERSATION TAKES PLACE WHICH SEEMS LIKELY TO COST PHILEAS FOGG DEAR

PHILEAS FOGG, HAVING SHUT THE DOOR OF HIS HOUSE AT HALF-PAST ELEVEN, AND HAVing put his right foot before his left five hundred and seventy-five times, and his left foot before his right five hundred and seventy-six times, reached the Reform Club, an imposing edifice in Pall Mall, which could not have cost less than three millions. He repaired at once to the dining-room, the nine windows of which open upon a tasteful garden, where the trees were already gilded with an autumn colouring; and took his place at the habitual table, the cover of which had already been laid for him. His breakfast consisted of a side-dish, a broiled fish with Reading sauce, a scarlet slice of roast beef garnished with mushrooms, a rhubarb and gooseberry tart, and a morsel of Cheshire cheese, the whole being washed down with several cups of tea, for which the Reform is famous. He rose at thirteen minutes to one, and directed his steps towards the large hall, a sumptuous apartment adorned with lavishly-framed paintings. A flunkey handed him an uncut *Times*, which he proceeded to cut with a skill which betrayed familiarity with this delicate operation. The perusal of this paper absorbed Phileas Fogg until a quarter before four, whilst the *Stan-*

dard, his next task, occupied him till the dinner hour. Dinner passed as breakfast had done, and Mr. Fogg reappeared in the reading-room and sat down to the *Pall Mall* at twenty minutes before six. Half-an-hour later several members of the Reform came in and drew up to the fireplace, where a coal fire was steadily burning. They were Mr. Fogg's usual partners at whist: Andrew Stuart, an engineer; John Sullivan and Samuel Fallentin, bankers; Thomas Flanagan, a brewer; and Gauthier Ralph, one of the directors of the Bank of England; all rich and highly respectable personages, even in a club which comprises the princes of English trade and finance.

"Well, Ralph," said Thomas Flanagan, "what about that robbery?"

"Oh," replied Stuart; "the bank will lose the money."

"On the contrary," broke in Ralph, "I hope we may put our hands on the robber. Skilful detectives have been sent to all the principal ports of America and the Continent, and he'll be a clever fellow if he slips through their fingers."

"But have you got the robber's description?" asked Stuart.

"In the first place, he is no robber at all," returned Ralph, positively.

"What! a fellow who makes off with fifty-five thousand pounds, no robber?"

"No."

"Perhaps he's a manufacturer, then."

"The *Daily Telegraph* says that he is a gentleman."

It was Phileas Fogg, whose head now emerged from behind his newspapers, who made this remark. He bowed to his friends, and entered into the conversation. The affair which formed its subject, and which was town talk, had occurred three days before at the Bank of England. A package of bank-notes, to the value of fifty-five thousand pounds, had been taken from the principal cashier's table, that functionary being at the moment engaged in registering the receipt of three shillings and sixpence. Of course he could not have his eyes everywhere. Let it be observed that the Bank of England reposes a touching confidence in the honesty of the public. There are neither guards nor gratings to protect its treasures; gold, silver, bank-notes are freely exposed, at the mercy of the first comer. A keen observer of English customs relates that, being in one of the rooms of the Bank one day, he had the curiosity to examine a gold ingot weighing some seven or eight pounds. He took it up, scrutinised it, passed it to his neighbour, he to the next man, and so on until the ingot, going from hand to hand, was transferred to the end of a dark entry; nor did it return to its place for half-an-hour. Meanwhile, the cashier had not so much as raised his head. But in the present instance things had not gone so smoothly. The package of notes not being found when five o'clock sounded from the ponderous clock in the "drawing office," the amount was passed to the account of profit and loss. As soon as the robbery was discovered, picked detectives hastened off to Liverpool, Glasgow, Havre, Suez, Brindisi, New York, and other ports, inspired by the proffered reward of two thousand pounds, and five per cent on the sum that might be recovered. Detectives were also charged with narrowly watching those who arrived at or left London by rail, and a judicial examination was at once entered upon.

There were real grounds for supposing, as the *Daily Telegraph* said, that the thief did not belong to a professional band. On the day of the robbery a well-dressed gentleman of polished manners, and with a well-to-do air, had been observed going to and fro in the paying-room, where the crime was committed. A description of him was easily procured and sent to the detectives; and some hopeful spirits, of whom Ralph was one, did not despair of his apprehension. The papers and clubs were full of the affair, and everywhere people were discussing the probabilities of a successful pursuit; and the Reform Club was especially agitated, several of its members being Bank officials.

Ralph would not concede that the work of the detectives was likely to be in vain, for he thought that the prize offered would greatly stimulate their zeal and activity. But Stuart was far from sharing this confidence; and, as they placed themselves at the whist-table, they continued to argue the matter. Stuart and Flanagan played together, while Phileas Fogg had Fallentin for his partner. As the game proceeded the conversation ceased, excepting between the rubbers, when it revived again.

"I maintain," said Stuart, "that the chances are in favour of the thief, who must be a shrewd fellow."

"Well, but where can he fly to?" asked Ralph. "No country is safe for him."

"Pshaw!"

"Where could he go, then?"

"Oh, I don't know that. The world is big enough."

"It was once," said Phileas Fogg, in a low tone. "Cut, sir," he added, handing the cards to Thomas Flanagan.

The discussion fell during the rubber, after which Stuart took up its thread.

"What do you mean by 'once'? Has the world grown smaller?"

"Certainly," returned Ralph. "I agree with Mr. Fogg. The world has grown smaller, since a man can now go round it ten times more quickly than a hundred years ago. And that is why the search for this thief will be more likely to succeed."

"And also why the thief can get away more easily."

"Be so good as to play, Mr. Stuart," said Phileas Fogg.

But the incredulous Stuart was not convinced, and when the hand was finished, said eagerly: "You have a strange way, Ralph, of proving that the world has grown smaller. So, because you can go round it in three months—"

"In eighty days," interrupted Phileas Fogg.

"That is true, gentlemen," added John Sullivan. "Only eighty days, now that the section between Rothal and Allahabad, on the Great Indian Peninsula Railway, has been opened. Here is the estimate made by the *Daily Telegraph:*

From London to Suez via Mont Cenis and Brindisi, by rail and steamboats	7 days
From Suez to Bombay, by steamer	13 "
From Bombay to Calcutta, by rail	3 "
From Calcutta to Hong Kong, by steamer	13 "
From Hong Kong to Yokohama (Japan), by steamer	6 "
From Yokohama to San Francisco, by steamer	22 "
From San Francisco to New York, by rail	7 "
From New York to London, by steamer and rail	9 "
TOTAL	80 days

"Yes, in eighty days!" exclaimed Stuart, who in his excitement made a false deal. "But that doesn't take into account bad weather, contrary winds, shipwrecks, railway accidents, and so on."

"All included," returned Phileas Fogg, continuing to play despite the discussion.

"But suppose the Hindoos or Indians pull up the rails," replied Stuart; "suppose they stop the trains, pillage the luggage-vans, and scalp the passengers!"

"All included," calmly retorted Fogg; adding, as he threw down the cards, "Two trumps."

Stuart, whose turn it was to deal, gathered them up, and went on: "You are right, theoretically, Mr. Fogg, but practically—"

"Practically also, Mr. Stuart."

"I'd like to see you do it in eighty days."

"It depends on you. Shall we go?"

"Heaven preserve me! But I would wager four thousand pounds that such a journey, made under these conditions, is impossible."

"Quite possible, on the contrary," returned Mr. Fogg.

"Well, make it, then!"

"The journey round the world in eighty days?"

"Yes."

"I should like nothing better."

"When?"

"At once. Only I warn you that I shall do it at your expense."

"It's absurd!" cried Stuart, who was beginning to be annoyed at the persistency of his friend. "Come, let's go on with the game."

"Deal over again, then," said Phileas Fogg. "There's a false deal."

Stuart took up the pack with a feverish hand; then suddenly put them down again.

"Well, Mr. Fogg," said he, "it shall be so; I will wager the four thousand on it."

"Calm yourself, my dear Stuart," said Fallentin. "It's only a joke."

"When I say I'll wager," returned Stuart, "I mean it."

"All right," said Mr. Fogg; and turning to the others he continued: "I have a deposit of twenty thousand at Barings which I will willingly risk upon it."

"Twenty thousand pounds!" cried Sullivan. "Twenty thousand pounds, which you would lose by a single accidental delay!"

"The unforeseen does not exist," quietly replied Phileas Fogg.

"But, Mr. Fogg, eighty days are only the estimate of the least possible time in which the journey can be made."

"A well-used minimum suffices for everything."

"But, in order not to exceed it, you must jump mathematically from the trains upon the steamers, and from the steamers upon the trains again."

"I will jump—mathematically."

"You are joking."

"A true Englishman doesn't joke when he is talking about so serious a thing as a wager," replied Phileas Fogg, solemnly. "I will bet twenty thousand pounds against anyone who wishes that I will make the tour of the world in eighty days or less; in nineteen hundred and twenty hours, or a hundred and fifteen thousand two hundred minutes. Do you accept?"

"We accept," replied Messrs. Stuart, Fallentin, Sullivan, Flanagan, and Ralph, after consulting each other.

"Good," said Mr. Fogg. "The train leaves for Dover at a quarter before nine. I will take it."

"This very evening?" asked Stuart.

"This very evening," returned Phileas Fogg. He took out and consulted a pocket almanac, and added, "As to-day is Wednesday, the second of October, I shall be due in London, in this very room of the Reform Club, on Saturday, the twenty-first of December, at a quarter before nine P.M.; or else the twenty thousand pounds, now deposited in my name at Baring's, will belong to you, in fact and in right, gentlemen. Here is a check for the amount."

A memorandum of the wager was at once drawn up and signed by the six parties, during which Phileas Fogg preserved a stoical composure. He certainly did not bet to win, and had only staked the twenty thousand pounds, half of his fortune, because he foresaw that he might have to expend the other half to carry out this difficult, not to say unattainable, project. As for his antagonists, they seemed much agitated; not so much by the value of their stake, as because they had some scruples about betting under conditions so difficult to their friend.

The clock struck seven, and the party offered to suspend the game so that Mr. Fogg might make his preparations for departure.

"I am quite ready now," was his tranquil response. "Diamonds are trumps: be so good as to play, gentlemen."

Chapter IV

In which Phileas Fogg astounds Passepartout, his servant

Having won twenty guineas at whist, and taken leave of his friends, Phileas Fogg, at twenty-five minutes past seven, left the Reform Club.

Passepartout, who had conscientiously studied the program of his duties, was more than surprised to see his master guilty of the inexactness of appearing at this unaccustomed hour; for, according to rule, he was not due in Saville Row until precisely midnight.

Mr. Fogg repaired to his bedroom, and called out, "Passepartout!"

Passepartout did not reply. It could not be he who was called; it was not the right hour.

"Passepartout!" repeated Mr. Fogg, without raising his voice.

Passepartout made his appearance.

"I've called you twice," observed his master.

"But it is not midnight," responded the other, showing his watch.

"I know it; I don't blame you. We start for Dover and Calais in ten minutes."

A puzzled grin overspread Passepartout's round face; clearly he had not comprehended his master.

"Monsieur is going to leave home?"

"Yes," returned Phileas Fogg. "We are going round the world."

Passepartout opened wide his eyes, raised his eyebrows, held up his hands, and seemed about to collapse, so overcome was he with stupefied astonishment.

"Round the world!" he murmured.

"In eighty days," responded Mr. Fogg. "So we haven't a moment to lose."

"But the trunks?" gasped Passepartout, unconsciously swaying his head from right to left.

"We'll have no trunks; only a carpet-bag, with two shirts and three pairs of stockings for me, and the same for you. We'll buy our clothes on the way. Bring down my mackintosh and travelling-cloak, and some stout shoes, though we shall do little walking. Make haste!"

Passepartout tried to reply, but could not. He went out, mounted to his own room, fell into a chair, and muttered: "That's good, that is! And I, who wanted to remain quiet!"

He mechanically set about making the preparations for departure. Around the world in eighty days! Was his master a fool? No. Was this a joke, then? They were going to Dover; good. To Calais; good again. After all, Passepartout, who had been away from France five years, would not be sorry to set foot on his native soil again. Perhaps they would go as far as Paris, and it would do his eyes good to see Paris once more. But surely a gentleman so chary of his steps would stop there; no doubt—but, then, it was none the less true that he was going away, this so domestic person hitherto!

By eight o'clock Passepartout had packed the modest carpet-bag, containing the wardrobes of his master and himself; then, still troubled in mind, he carefully shut the door of his room, and descended to Mr. Fogg.

Mr. Fogg was quite ready. Under his arm might have been observed a red-bound copy of "Bradshaw's Continental Railway Steam Transit and General Guide," with its time-tables showing the arrival and departure of steamers and railways. He took the carpet-bag, opened it, and slipped into it a goodly roll of Bank of England notes, which would pass wherever he might go.

"You have forgotten nothing?" asked he.

"Nothing, monsieur."

"My mackintosh and cloak?"

"Here they are."

"Good. Take this carpet-bag," handing it to Passepartout. "Take good care of it, for there are twenty thousand pounds in it."

Passepartout nearly dropped the bag, as if the twenty thousand pounds were in gold, and weighed him down.

Master and man then descended, the street door was double-locked, and at the end of Saville Row they took a cab and drove rapidly to Charing Cross. The cab stopped before the railway station at twenty minutes past eight. Passepartout jumped off the box and followed his master, who, after paying the cabman, was about to enter the station, when a poor beggar-woman, with a child in her arms, her naked feet smeared with mud, her head covered with a wretched bonnet, from which hung a tattered feather, and her shoulders shrouded in a ragged shawl, approached, and mournfully asked for alms.

Mr. Fogg took out the twenty guineas he had just won at whist, and handed them to the beggar, saying, "Here, my good woman. I'm glad that I met you"; and passed on.

Passepartout had a moist sensation about the eyes; his master's action touched his susceptible heart.

Two first-class tickets for Paris having been speedily purchased, Mr. Fogg was crossing the station to the train, when he perceived his five friends of the Reform.

"Well, gentlemen," said he, "I'm off, you see; and, if you will examine my passport when I get back, you will be able to judge whether I have accomplished the journey agreed upon."

"Oh, that would be quite unnecessary, Mr. Fogg," said Ralph politely. "We will trust your word, as a gentleman of honour."

"You do not forget when you are due in London again?" asked Stuart.

"In eighty days; on Saturday, the twenty-first of December, 1872, at a quarter before nine P.M. Good-by, gentlemen."

Phileas Fogg and his servant seated themselves in a first-class carriage at twenty minutes before nine; five minutes later the whistle screamed, and the train slowly glided out of the station.

The night was dark, and a fine, steady rain was falling. Phileas Fogg, snugly ensconced in his corner, did not open his lips. Passepartout, not yet recovered from his stupefaction, clung mechanically to the carpet-bag, with its enormous treasure.

Just as the train was whirling through Sydenham, Passepartout suddenly uttered a cry of despair.

"What's the matter?" asked Mr. Fogg.

"Alas! In my hurry—I—I forgot—"

"What?"

"To turn off the gas in my room!"

"Very well, young man," returned Mr. Fogg, coolly; "it will burn—at your expense."

Chapter V

IN WHICH A NEW SPECIES OF FUNDS, UNKNOWN TO THE MONEYED MEN, APPEARS ON 'CHANGE

PHILEAS FOGG RIGHTLY SUSPECTED THAT HIS DEPARTURE FROM LONDON WOULD CREATE a lively sensation at the West End. The news of the bet spread through the Reform Club, and afforded an exciting topic of conversation to its members. From the Club it soon got into the papers throughout England. The boasted "tour of the world" was talked about, disputed, argued with as much warmth as if the subject were another Alabama claim. Some took sides with Phileas Fogg, but the large majority shook their heads and declared against him; it was absurd, impossible, they declared, that the tour of the world could be made, except theoretically and on paper, in this minimum of time, and with the existing means of travelling. The *Times, Standard, Morning Post,* and *Daily News,* and twenty other highly respectable newspapers scouted Mr. Fogg's project as madness; the *Daily Telegraph* alone hesitatingly supported him. People in general thought him a lunatic, and blamed his Reform Club friends for having accepted a wager which betrayed the mental aberration of its proposer.

Articles no less passionate than logical appeared on the question, for geography is one of the pet subjects of the English; and the columns devoted to Phileas Fogg's venture were eagerly devoured by all classes of readers. At first some rash individuals, principally of the gentler sex, espoused his cause, which became still more popular when the *Illustrated London News* came out with his portrait, copied from a photograph in the Reform Club. A few readers of the *Daily Telegraph* even dared to say, "Why not, after all? Stranger things have come to pass."

At last a long article appeared, on the 7th of October, in the bulletin of the Royal Geographical Society, which treated the question from every point of view, and demonstrated the utter folly of the enterprise.

Everything, it said, was against the travellers, every obstacle imposed alike by man and by nature. A miraculous agreement of the times of departure and arrival, which was impossible, was absolutely necessary to his success. He might, perhaps, reckon on the arrival of trains at the designated hours, in Europe, where the distances were relatively moderate; but when he calculated upon crossing India in three days, and the United States in seven, could he rely beyond misgiving upon accomplishing his task? There were accidents to machinery, the liability of trains to run off the line, collisions, bad weather, the blocking up by snow—were not all these against Phileas Fogg? Would he not find himself, when travelling by steamer in winter, at the mercy of the winds and fogs? Is it uncommon for the best ocean steamers to be two or three days behind time? But a single delay would suffice to fatally break the chain of communication; should Phileas Fogg once miss, even by an hour, a steamer, he would have to wait for the next, and that would irrevocably render his attempt vain.

This article made a great deal of noise, and being copied into all the papers, seriously depressed the advocates of the rash tourist.

Everybody knows that England is the world of betting men, who are of a higher class than mere gamblers; to bet is in the English temperament. Not only the members of the Reform, but the general public, made heavy wagers for or against Phileas Fogg, who was set down in the betting books as if he were a race-horse. Bonds were issued, and made their appearance on 'Change; "Phileas Fogg bonds" were offered at par or at a premium, and a great business was done in them. But five days after the article in the bulletin of the Geographical Society appeared, the demand began to subside: "Phileas Fogg" declined. They were offered by packages, at first of five, then of ten, until at last nobody would take less than twenty, fifty, a hundred!

Lord Albemarle, an elderly paralytic gentleman, was now the only advocate of Phileas Fogg left. This noble lord, who was fastened to his chair, would have given his fortune to be able to make the tour of the world, if it took ten years; and he bet five thousand pounds on Phileas Fogg. When the folly as well as the uselessness of the adventure was pointed out to him, he contented himself with replying, "If the thing is feasible, the first to do it ought to be an Englishman."

The Fogg party dwindled more and more, everybody was going against him, and the bets stood a hundred and fifty and two hundred to one; and a week after his departure an incident occurred which deprived him of backers at any price.

The commissioner of police was sitting in his office at nine o'clock one evening, when the following telegraphic despatch was put into his hands:

SUEZ TO LONDON

Rowan, Commissioner of Police, Scotland Yard:
I've found the bank robber, Phileas Fogg. Send with out delay warrant of arrest to Bombay.

FIX, DETECTIVE

The effect of this despatch was instantaneous. The polished gentleman disappeared to give place to the bank robber. His photograph, which was hung with those of the rest of the members at the Reform Club, was minutely examined, and it betrayed, feature by feature, the description of the robber which had been provided to the police. The mysterious habits of Phileas Fogg were recalled; his solitary ways, his sudden departure; and it seemed clear that, in undertaking a tour around the world on the pretext of a wager, he had had no other end in view than to elude the detectives, and throw them off his track.

Chapter VI

IN WHICH FIX, THE DETECTIVE,
BETRAYS A VERY NATURAL IMPATIENCE

THE CIRCUMSTANCES UNDER WHICH THIS TELEGRAPHIC DESPATCH ABOUT PHILEAS FOGG was sent were as follows:

The steamer *Mongolia,* belonging to the Peninsular and Oriental Company, built of iron, of two thousand eight hundred tons burden, and five hundred horse-power, was due at eleven o'clock A.M. on Wednesday, the 9th of October, at Suez. The *Mongolia* plied regularly between Brindisi and Bombay via the Suez Canal, and was one of the fastest steamers belonging to the company, always making more than ten knots an hour between Brindisi and Suez, and nine and a half between Suez and Bombay.

Two men were promenading up and down the wharves, among the crowd of natives and strangers who were sojourning at this once straggling village—now, thanks to the enterprise of M. Lesseps, a fast-growing town. One was the British consul at Suez, who, despite the prophecies of the English Government, and the unfavourable predictions of Stephenson, was in the habit of seeing, from his office window, English ships daily passing to and fro on the great canal, by which the old roundabout route from England to India by the Cape of Good Hope was abridged by at least a half. The other was a small, slight-built personage, with a nervous, intelligent face, and bright eyes peering out from under eyebrows which he was incessantly twitching. He was just now manifesting unmistakable signs of impatience, nervously pacing up and down, and unable to stand still for a moment. This was Fix, one of the detectives who had been despatched from England in search of the bank robber; it was his task to narrowly watch every passenger who arrived at Suez, and to follow up all who seemed to be suspicious characters, or bore a resemblance to the description of the criminal, which he had received two days before from the police head-quarters at London. The detective was evidently inspired by the hope of obtaining the splendid reward which would be the prize of success, and awaited with a feverish impatience, easy to understand, the arrival of the steamer *Mongolia*.

"So you say, consul," asked he for the twentieth time, "that this steamer is never behind time?"

"No, Mr. Fix," replied the consul. "She was bespoken yesterday at Port Said, and the rest of the way is of no account to such a craft. I repeat that the *Mongolia* has been in advance of the time required by the company's regulations, and gained the prize awarded for excess of speed."

"Does she come directly from Brindisi?"

"Directly from Brindisi; she takes on the Indian mails there, and she left there Saturday at five P.M. Have patience, Mr. Fix; she will not be late. But really I don't see how, from the description you have, you will be able to recognise your man, even if he is on board the *Mongolia*."

"A man rather feels the presence of these fellows, consul, than recognises them. You must have a scent for them, and a scent is like a sixth sense which combines hearing, seeing, and smelling. I've arrested more than one of these gentlemen in my time, and if my thief is on board, I'll answer for it, he'll not slip through my fingers."

"I hope so, Mr. Fix, for it was a heavy robbery."

"A magnificent robbery, consul; fifty-five thousand pounds! We don't often have such windfalls. Burglars are getting to be so contemptible nowadays! A fellow gets hung for a handful of shillings!"

"Mr. Fix," said the consul, "I like your way of talking, and hope you'll succeed; but I fear you will find it far from easy. Don't you see, the description which you have there has a singular resemblance to an honest man?"

"Consul," remarked the detective, dogmatically, "great robbers *always* resemble honest folks. Fellows who have rascally faces have only one course to take, and that is to remain honest; otherwise they would be arrested offhand. The artistic thing is, to unmask honest countenances; it's no light task, I admit, but a real art."

Mr. Fix evidently was not wanting in a tinge of self-conceit.

Little by little the scene on the quay became more animated; sailors of various nations, merchants, shipbrokers, porters, fellahs, bustled to and fro as if the steamer were immediately expected. The weather was clear, and slightly chilly. The minarets of the town loomed above the houses in the pale rays of the sun. A jetty pier, some two thousand yards along, extended into the roadstead. A number of fishing-smacks and coasting boats, some retaining the fantastic fashion of ancient galleys, were discernible on the Red Sea.

As he passed among the busy crowd, Fix, according to habit, scrutinised the passers-by with a keen, rapid glance.

It was now half-past ten.

"The steamer doesn't come!" he exclaimed, as the port clock struck.

"She can't be far off now," returned his companion.

"How long will she stop at Suez?"

"Four hours; long enough to get in her coal. It is thirteen hundred and ten miles from Suez to Aden, at the other end of the Red Sea, and she has to take in a fresh coal supply."

"And does she go from Suez directly to Bombay?"

"Without putting in anywhere."

"Good," said Fix. "If the robber is on board he will no doubt get off at Suez, so as to reach the Dutch or French colonies in Asia by some other route. He ought to know that he would not be safe an hour in India, which is English soil."

"Unless," objected the consul, "he is exceptionally shrewd. An English criminal, you know, is always better concealed in London than anywhere else."

This observation furnished the detective food for thought, and meanwhile the consul went away to his office. Fix, left alone, was more impatient than ever, having a presentiment that the robber was on board the *Mongolia*. If he had indeed left London intending to reach the New World he would naturally take the route via India, which was less watched and more difficult to watch than that of the Atlantic. But Fix's reflections were soon interrupted by a succession of sharp whistles, which announced the arrival of the *Mongolia*. The porters and fellahs rushed down the quay, and a dozen boats pushed off from the shore to go and meet the steamer. Soon her gigantic hull appeared passing along between the banks, and eleven o'clock struck as she anchored in the road. She brought an unusual number of passengers, some of whom remained on deck to scan the picturesque panorama of the town, while the greater part disembarked in the boats, and landed on the quay.

Fix took up a position, and carefully examined each face and figure which made its appearance. Presently one of the passengers, after vigourously pushing his way through the importunate crowd of porters, came up to him and politely asked if he could point out the English consulate, at the same time showing a passport which he wished to have visaed. Fix instinctively took the passport, and with a rapid glance read the description of its bearer. An involuntary motion of surprise nearly escaped him, for the description in the passport was identical with that of the bank robber which he had received from Scotland Yard.

"Is this your passport?" asked he.

"No, it's my master's."

"And your master is—"

"He stayed on board."

"But he must go to the consul's in person, so as to establish his identity."

"Oh, is that necessary?"

"Quite indispensable."

"And where is the consulate?"

"There, on the corner of the square," said Fix, pointing to a house two hundred steps off.

"I'll go and fetch my master, who won't be much pleased, however, to be disturbed."

The passenger bowed to Fix, and returned to the steamer.

Chapter VII

WHICH ONCE MORE DEMONSTRATES THE USELESSNESS OF PASSPORTS AS AIDS TO DETECTIVES

THE DETECTIVE PASSED DOWN THE QUAY, AND RAPIDLY MADE HIS WAY TO THE CONSUL'S office, where he was at once admitted to the presence of that official.

"Consul," said he, without preamble, "I have strong reasons for believing that my man is a passenger on the *Mongolia*." And he narrated what had just passed concerning the passport.

"Well, Mr. Fix," replied the consul; "I shall not be sorry to see the rascal's face; but perhaps he won't come here—that is, if he is the person you suppose him to be. A robber doesn't quite like to leave traces of his flight behind him; and, besides, he is not obliged to have his passport countersigned."

"If he is as shrewd as I think he is, consul, he will come."

"To have his passport visaed?"

"Yes. Passports are only good for annoying honest folks, and aiding in the flight of rogues. I assure you it will be quite the thing for him to do; but I hope you will not visa the passport."

"Why not? If the passport is genuine I have no right to refuse."

"Still, I must keep this man here until I can get a warrant to arrest him from London."

"Ah, that's your look-out. But I cannot—"

The consul did not finish his sentence, for as he spoke a knock was heard at the door, and two strangers entered, one of whom was the servant whom Fix had met on the quay. The other, who was his master, held out his passport with the request that the consul would do him the favour to visa it. The consul took the document and carefully read it, whilst Fix observed, or rather devoured, the stranger with his eyes from a corner of the room.

"You are Mr. Phileas Fogg?" said the consul, after reading the passport.

"I am."

"And this man is your servant?"

"He is; a Frenchman, named Passepartout."

"You are from London?"

"Yes."

"And you are going—"

"To Bombay."

"Very good, sir. You know that a visa is useless, and that no passport is required?"

"I know it, sir," replied Phileas Fogg; "but I wish to prove, by your visa, that I came by Suez."

"Very well, sir."

The consul proceeded to sign and date the passport, after which he added his official seal. Mr. Fogg paid the customary fee, coldly bowed, and went out, followed by his servant.

"Well?" queried the detective.

"Well, he looks and acts like a perfectly honest man," replied the consul.

"Possibly; but that is not the question. Do you think, consul, that this phelgmatic gentleman resembles, feature by feature, the robber whose description I have received?"

"I concede that; but then, you know, all descriptions—"

"I'll make certain of it," interrupted Fix. "The servant seems to me less mysterious than the master; besides, he's a Frenchman, and can't help talking. Excuse me for a little while, consul."

Fix started off in search of Passepartout.

Meanwhile Mr. Fogg, after leaving the consulate, repaired to the quay, gave some orders to Passepartout, went off to the *Mongolia* in a boat, and descended to his cabin. He took up his note-book, which contained the following memoranda:—

Left London, Wednesday, October 2d, at 8:45 P.M.

Reached Paris, Thursday, October 3d, at 7:20 A.M.

Left Paris, Thursday, at 8:40 A.M.

Reached Turin by Mont Cenis, Friday, October 4th, at 6:35 A.M.

Left Turin, Friday, at 7:20 A.M.

Arrived at Brindisi, Saturday, October 5th, at 4 P.M.

Sailed on the *Mongolia*, Saturday, at 5 P.M.

Reached Suez, Wednesday, October 9th, at 11 A.M.

Total of hours spent, 158½; or, in days, six days and a half.

These dates were inscribed in an itinerary divided into columns, indicating the month, the day of the month, and the day for the stipulated and actual arrivals at each principal point—Paris, Brindisi, Suez, Bombay, Calcutta, Singapore, Hong Kong, Yokohama, San Francisco, New York, and London—from the 2d of October to the 21st of December; and giving a space for setting down the gain made or the loss suffered on arrival at each locality. This methodical record thus contained an account of everything needed, and Mr. Fogg always knew whether he was behindhand or in advance of his time. On this Friday, October 9th, he noted his arrival at Suez, and observed that he had as yet neither gained nor lost. He sat down quietly to breakfast in his cabin, never once thinking of inspecting the town, being one of those Englishmen who are wont to see foreign countries through the eyes of their domestics.

Chapter VIII

IN WHICH PASSEPARTOUT TALKS RATHER MORE,
PERHAPS, THAN IS PRUDENT

FIX SOON REJOINED PASSEPARTOUT, WHO WAS LOUNGING AND LOOKING ABOUT ON THE quay, as if he did not feel that he, at least, was obliged not to see anything.

"Well, my friend," said the detective, coming up with him, "is your passport visaed?"

"Ah, it's you, is it, monsieur?" responded Passepartout. "Thanks, yes, the passport is all right."

"And you are looking about you?"

"Yes; but we travel so fast that I seem to be journeying in a dream. So this is Suez?"

"Yes."

"In Egypt?"

"Certainly, in Egypt."

"And in Africa?"

"In Africa."

"In Africa!" repeated Passepartout. "Just think, monsieur, I had no idea that we should go farther than Paris; and all that I saw of Paris was between twenty minutes past seven and twenty minutes before nine in the morning, between the Northern and the Lyons stations, through the windows of a car, and in a driving rain! How I regret not having seen once more Père la Chaise and the circus in the Champs Elysées!"

"You are in a great hurry, then?"

"I am not, but my master is. By the way, I must buy some shoes and shirts. We came away without trunks, only with a carpet-bag."

"I will show you an excellent shop for getting what you want."

"Really, monsieur, you are very kind."

And they walked off together, Passepartout chatting volubly as they went along.

"Above all," said he; "don't let me lose the steamer."

"You have plenty of time; it's only twelve o'clock."

Passepartout pulled out his big watch. "Twelve!" he exclaimed; "why it's only eight minutes before ten."

"Your watch is slow."

"My watch? A family watch, monsieur, which has come down from my great-grandfather! It doesn't vary five minutes in the year, it's a perfect chronometer, look you."

"I see how it is," said Fix. "You have kept London time, which is two hours behind that of Suez. You ought to regulate your watch at noon in each country."

"I regulate my watch? Never!"

"Well, then, it will not agree with the sun."

"So much the worse for the sun, monsieur. The sun will be wrong, then!"

And the worthy fellow returned the watch to its fob with a defiant gesture. After a few minutes' silence, Fix resumed: "You left London hastily, then?"

"I rather think so! Last Friday at eight o'clock in the evening, Monsieur Fogg came home from his club, and three-quarters of an hour afterwards we were off."

"But where is your master going?"

"Always straight ahead. He is going round the world."

"Round the world?" cried Fix.

"Yes, and in eighty days! He says it is on a wager; but, between us, I don't believe a word of it. That wouldn't be common sense. There's something else in the wind."

"Ah! Mr. Fogg is a character, is he?"

"I should say he was."

"Is he rich?"

"No doubt, for he is carrying an enormous sum in brand-new bank-notes with him. And he doesn't spare the money on the way, either: he has offered a large reward to the engineer of the *Mongolia* if he gets us to Bombay well in advance of time."

"And you have known your master a long time?"

"Why, no; I entered his service the very day we left London."

The effect of these replies upon the already suspicious and excited detective may be imagined. The hasty departure from London soon after the robbery; the large sum carried by Mr. Fogg; his eagerness to reach distant countries; the pretext of an eccentric and fool-hardy bet—all confirmed Fix in his theory. He continued to pump poor Passepartout, and learned that he really knew little or nothing of his master, who lived a solitary existence in London, was said to be rich, though no one knew whence came his riches, and was mysterious and impenetrable in his affairs and habits. Fix felt sure that Phileas Fogg would not land at Suez, but was really going on to Bombay.

"Is Bombay far from here?" asked Passepartout.

"Pretty far. It is a ten days' voyage by sea."

"And in what country is Bombay?"

"India."

"In Asia?"

"Certainly."

"The deuce! I was going to tell you—there's one thing that worries me—my burner!"

"What burner?"

"My gas-burner, which I forgot to turn off, and which is at this moment burning—at my expense. I have calculated, monsieur, that I lose two shillings every four and twenty hours, exactly sixpence more than I earn; and you will understand that the longer our journey—"

Did Fix pay any attention to Passepartout's trouble about the gas? It is not probable. He was not listening, but was cogitating a project. Passepartout and he had now reached the shop, where Fix left his companion to make his purchases, after recommending him not to miss the steamer, and hurried back to the consulate. Now that he was fully convinced Fix had quite recovered his equanimity.

"Consul," said he, "I have no longer any doubt. I have spotted my man. He passes himself off as an odd stick, who is going round the world in eighty days."

"Then he's a sharp fellow," returned the consul, "and counts on returning to London after putting the police of the two countries off his track."

"We'll see about that," replied Fix.

"But are you not mistaken?"

"I am not mistaken."

"Why was this robber so anxious to prove, by the visa, that he had passed through Suez?"

"Why? I have no idea; but listen to me."

He reported in a few words the most important parts of his conversation with Passepartout.

"In short," said the consul, "appearances are wholly against this man. And what are you going to do?"

"Send a despatch to London for a warrant of arrest to be despatched instantly to Bombay, take passage on board the *Mongolia,* follow my rogue to India, and there, on English ground, arrest him politely, with my warrant in my hand, and my hand on his shoulder."

Having uttered these words with a cool, careless air, the detective took leave of the consul, and repaired to the telegraph office, whence he sent the despatch which we have seen to the London police office. A quarter of an hour later found Fix, with a small bag in his hand, proceeding on board the *Mongolia;* and ere many moments longer, the noble steamer rode out at full steam upon the waters of the Red Sea.

Chapter IX

IN WHICH THE RED SEA AND THE INDIAN OCEAN PROVE PROPITIOUS TO THE DESIGNS OF PHILEAS FOGG

THE DISTANCE BETWEEN SUEZ AND ADEN IS PRECISELY THIRTEEN HUNDRED AND TEN miles, and the regulations of the company allow the steamers one hundred and thirty-eight hours in which to traverse it. The *Mongolia*, thanks to the vigourous exertions of the engineer, seemed likely, so rapid was her speed, to reach her destination considerably within that time. The greater part of the passengers from Brindisi were bound for India—some for Bombay, others for Calcutta by way of Bombay, the nearest route thither, now that a railway crosses the Indian peninsula. Among the passengers was a number of officials and military officers of various grades, the latter being either attached to the regular British forces, or commanding the Sepoy troops and receiving high salaries ever since the central government has assumed the powers of the East India Company: for the sub-lieutenants get 280*l.*, brigadiers, 2,400*l.*, and generals of divisions, 4,000*l.* What with the military men, a number of rich young Englishmen on their travels, and the hospitable efforts of the purser, the time passed quickly on the *Mongolia*. The best of fare was spread upon the cabin tables at breakfast, lunch, dinner, and the eight o'clock supper, and the ladies scrupulously changed their toilets twice a day; and the hours were whirled away, when the sea was tranquil, with music, dancing, and games.

But the Red Sea is full of caprice, and often boisterous, like most long and narrow gulfs. When the wind came from the African or Asian coast the *Mongolia*, with her long hull, rolled fearfully. Then the ladies speedily disappeared below; the pianos were silent; singing and dancing suddenly ceased. Yet the good ship ploughed straight on, unretarded by wind or wave, towards the straits of Bab-el-Mandeb. What was Phileas Fogg doing all this time? It might be thought that, in his anxiety, he would be constantly watching the changes of the wind, the disorderly raging of the billows—every chance, in short, which might force the *Mongolia* to slacken her speed, and thus interrupt his journey. But if he thought of these possibilities, he did not betray the fact by any outward sign.

Always the same impassible member of the Reform Club, whom no incident could surprise, as unvarying as the ship's chronometers, and seldom having the curiosity even to go upon the deck, he passed through the memorable scenes of the Red Sea with cold indifference; did not care to recognise the historic towns and villages which, along its borders, raised their picturesque outlines against the sky; and betrayed no fear of the dangers of the Arabic Gulf, which the old historians always spoke of with horror, and upon which the ancient navigators never ventured without propitiating the gods by ample sacrifices.

How did this eccentric personage pass his time on the *Mongolia?* He made his four hearty meals everyday, regardless of the most persistent rolling and pitching on the part of the steamer; and he played whist indefatigably, for he had found partners as enthusiastic in the game as himself. A tax-collector, on the way to his post at Goa; the Rev. Decimus Smith, returning to his parish at Bombay; and a brigadier-general of the English army, who was about to rejoin his brigade at Benares, made up the party, and, with Mr. Fogg, played whist by the hour together in absorbing silence.

As for Passepartout, he, too, had escaped seasickness, and took his meals conscientiously in the forward cabin. He rather enjoyed the voyage, for he was well fed and well lodged, took a great interest in the scenes through which they were passing, and consoled himself with the delusion that his master's whim would end at Bombay. He was pleased, on the day after leaving Suez, to find on deck the obliging person with whom he had walked and chatted on the quays.

"If I am not mistaken," said he, approaching this person with his most amiable smile, "you are the gentleman who so kindly volunteered to guide me at Suez?"

"Ah! I quite recognise you. You are the servant of the strange Englishman—"

"Just so, Monsieur—"

"Fix."

"Monsieur Fix," resumed Passepartout, "I'm charmed to find you on board. Where are you bound?"

"Like you, to Bombay."

"That's capital! Have you made this trip before?"

"Several times. I am one of the agents of the Peninsula Company."

"Then you know India?"

"Why—yes," replied Fix, who spoke cautiously.

"A curious place, this India?"

"Oh, very curious. Mosques, minarets, temples, fakirs, pagodas, tigers, snakes, elephants! I hope you will have ample time to see the sights."

"I hope so, Monsieur Fix. You see, a man of sound sense ought not to spend his life jumping from a steamer upon a railway train, and from a railway train upon a steamer again, pretending to make the tour of the world in eighty days! No; all these gymnastics, you may be sure, will cease at Bombay."

"And Mr. Fogg is getting on well?" asked Fix, in the most natural tone in the world.

"Quite well, and I too. I eat like a famished ogre; it's the sea-air."

"But I never see your master on deck."

"Never; he hasn't the least curiosity."

"Do you know, Mr. Passepartout, that this pretended tour in eighty days may conceal some secret errand—perhaps a diplomatic mission?"

"Faith, Monsieur Fix, I assure you I know nothing about it, nor would I give half-a-crown to find out."

After this meeting, Passepartout and Fix got into the habit of chatting together, the latter making it a point to gain the worthy man's confidence. He frequently offered him a glass of whisky or pale ale in the steamer bar-room, which Passepartout never failed to accept with graceful alacrity, mentally pronouncing Fix the best of good fellows.

Meanwhile the *Mongolia* was pushing forward rapidly; on the 13th, Mocha, surrounded by its ruined walls whereon date-trees were growing, was sighted, and on the mountains beyond were espied vast coffee-fields. Passepartout was ravished to behold this celebrated place, and thought that, with its circular walls and dismantled fort, it looked like an immense coffee cup and saucer. The following night they passed through the Strait of Bab-el-Mandeb, which means in Arabic "The Bridge of Tears," and the next day they put in at Steamer Point, north-west of Aden harbor, to take in coal. This matter of fuelling steamers is a serious one at such distances from the coal mines; it costs the Peninsular Company some eight hundred thousand pounds a year. In these distant seas, coal is worth three or four pounds sterling a ton.

The *Mongolia* had still sixteen hundred and fifty miles to traverse before reaching Bombay, and was obliged to remain four hours at Steamer Point to coal up. But this delay, as it was foreseen, did not affect Phileas Fogg's program; besides, the *Mongolia*, instead of reaching Aden on the morning of the 15th, when she was due, arrived there on the evening of the 14th, a gain of fifteen hours.

Mr. Fogg and his servant went ashore at Aden to have the passport again visaed; Fix, unobserved, followed them. The visa procured, Mr. Fogg returned on board to resume his former habits; while Passepartout, according to custom, sauntered about among the mixed population of Somanlis, Banyans, Parsees, Jews, Arabs, and Europeans who comprise the twenty-five thousand inhabitants of Aden. He gazed with wonder upon the fortifications which make this place the Gibraltar of the Indian Ocean, and the vast cisterns where the English engineers were still at work, two thousand years after the engineers of Solomon.

"Very curious, *very* curious," said Passepartout to himself, on returning to the steamer. "I see that it is by no means useless to travel, if a man wants to see something new." At six P.M. the *Mongolia* slowly moved out of the roadstead, and was soon once more on the Indian Ocean. She had a hundred and sixty-eight hours in which to reach Bombay, and the sea was favourable, the wind being in the north-west, and all sails aiding the engine. The steamer rolled but little, the ladies, in fresh toilets, reappeared on deck, and the singing and dancing were resumed. The trip was being accomplished most successfully, and Passepartout was enchanted with the congenial companion which chance had secured him in the person of the delightful Fix. On Sunday, October 20th, towards noon, they came in sight of the Indian coast: two hours later the pilot came on board. A range of hills lay against the sky in the horizon, and soon the rows of palms which adorn Bombay came distinctly into view. The steamer entered the road formed by the islands in the bay, and at half-past four she hauled up at the quays of Bombay.

Phileas Fogg was in the act of finishing the thirty-third rubber of the voyage, and his partner and himself having, by a bold stroke, captured all thirteen of the tricks, concluded this fine campaign with a brilliant victory.

The *Mongolia* was due at Bombay on the 22d; she arrived on the 20th. This was again to Phileas Fogg of two days since his departure from London, and he calmly entered the fact in the itinerary, in the column of gains.

Chapter X

IN WHICH PASSEPARTOUT IS ONLY TOO GLAD TO GET OFF WITH THE LOSS OF HIS SHOES

EVERYBODY KNOWS THAT THE GREAT REVERSED TRIANGLE OF LAND, WITH ITS BASE IN the north and its apex in the south, which is called India, embraces fourteen hundred thousand square miles, upon which is spread unequally a population of one hundred and eighty millions of souls. The British Crown exercises a real and despotic dominion over the larger portion of this vast country, and has a governor-general stationed at Calcutta, governors at Madras, Bombay, and in Bengal, and a lieutenant-governor at Agra.

But British India, properly so called, only embraces seven hundred thousand square miles, and a population of from one hundred to one hundred and ten millions of inhabitants. A considerable portion of India is still free from British authority; and there are certain ferocious rajahs in the interior who are absolutely independent. The celebrated East India Company was all-powerful from 1756, when the English first gained a foothold on the spot where now stands the city of Madras, down to the time of the great Sepoy insurrection. It gradually annexed province after province, purchasing them of the native chiefs, whom it seldom paid, and appointed the governor-general and his subordinates, civil and military. But the East India Company has now passed away, leaving the British possessions in India directly under the control of the Crown. The aspect of the country, as well as the manners and distinctions of race, is daily changing.

Formerly one was obliged to travel in India by the old cumbrous methods of going on foot or on horseback, in palanquins or unwieldly coaches; now, fast steamboats ply on the Indus and the Ganges, and a great railway, with branch lines joining the main line at many points on its route, traverses the peninsula from Bombay to Calcutta in three days. This railway does not run in a direct line across India. The distance between Bombay and Calcutta, as the bird flies, is only from one thousand to eleven hundred miles; but the deflections of the road increase this distance by more than a third.

The general route of the Great Indian Peninsula Railway is as follows:—Leaving Bombay, it passes through Salcette, crossing to the continent opposite Tannah, goes over the chain of the Western Ghauts, runs thence north-east as far as Burhampoor, skirts the nearly independent territory of Bundelcund, ascends to Allahabad, turns thence eastwardly, meeting the Ganges at Benares, then departs from the river a little, and, descending south-eastward by Burdivan and the French town of Chandernagor, has its terminus at Calcutta.

The passengers of the *Mongolia* went ashore at half-past four P.M.; at exactly eight the train would start for Calcutta.

Mr. Fogg, after bidding good-by to his whist partners, left the steamer, gave his servant several errands to do, urged it upon him to be at the station promptly at eight, and, with his regular step, which beat to the second, like an astronomical clock, directed his steps to the passport office. As for the wonders of Bombay—its famous city hall, its splendid library, its forts and docks, its bazaars, mosques, synagogues, its Armenian churches, and the noble pagoda on Malebar Hill with its two polygonal towers—he cared not a straw to see them. He would not deign to examine even the masterpieces of Elephanta, or the mysterious hypogea, concealed south-east from the docks, or those fine remains of Buddhist architecture, the Kanherian grottoes of the island of Salcette.

Having transacted his business at the passport office, Phileas Fogg repaired quietly to the railway station, where he ordered dinner. Among the dishes served up to him, the landlord especially recommended a certain giblet of "native rabbit," on which he prided himself.

Mr. Fogg accordingly tasted the dish, but, despite its spiced sauce, found it far from palatable. He rang for the landlord, and on his appearance, said, fixing his clear eyes upon him, "Is this rabbit, sir?"

"Yes, my lord," the rogue boldly replied, "rabbit from the jungles."

"And this rabbit did not mew when he was killed?"

"Mew, my lord! what, a rabbit mew! I swear to you—"

"Be so good, landlord, as not to swear, but remember this: cats were formerly considered, in India, as sacred animals. That was a good time."

"For the cats, my lord?"

"Perhaps for the travellers as well!"

After which Mr. Fogg quietly continued his dinner. Fix had gone on shore shortly after Mr. Fogg, and his first destination was the headquarters of the Bombay police. He made himself known as a London detective, told his business at Bombay, and the position of affairs relative to the supposed robber, and nervously asked if a warrant had arrived from London. It had not reached the office; indeed, there had not yet been time for it to arrive. Fix was sorely disappointed, and tried to obtain an order of arrest from the director of the Bombay police. This the director refused, as the matter concerned the London office, which alone could legally deliver the warrant. Fix did not insist, and was fain to resign himself to await the arrival of the important document; but he was determined not to lose sight of the mysterious rogue as long as he stayed in Bombay. He did not doubt for a moment, any more than Passepartout, that Phileas Fogg would remain there, at least until it was time for the warrant to arrive.

Passepartout, however, had no sooner heard his master's orders on leaving the *Mongolia*, than he saw at once that they were to leave Bombay as they had done Suez and Paris, and that the journey would be extended at least as far as Calcutta, and perhaps beyond that place. He began to ask himself if this bet that Mr. Fogg talked about was not really in good earnest, and whether his fate was not in truth forcing him, despite his love of repose, around the world in eighty days!

Having purchased the usual quota of shirts and shoes, he took a leisurely promenade about the streets, where crowds of people of many nationalities—Europeans, Persians with pointed caps, Banyas with round turbans, Sindes with square bonnets, Parsees with black mitres, and long-robed Armenians—were collected. It happened to be the day of a Parsee festival. These descendants of the sect of Zoroaster—the most thrifty, civilised, intelligent, and austere of the East Indians, among whom are counted the richest native merchants of Bombay—were celebrating a sort of religious carnival, with processions and shows, in the midst of which Indian dancing-girls, clothed in rose-colored gauze, looped up with gold and silver, danced airily, but with perfect modesty, to the sound of viols and the clanging of tambourines. It is needless to say that Passepartout watched these curious ceremonies with staring eyes and gaping mouth, and that his countenance was that of the greenest booby imaginable.

Unhappily for his master, as well as himself, his curiosity drew him unconsciously farther off than he intended to go. At last, having seen the Parsee carnival wind away in the distance, he was turning his steps towards the station, when he happened to espy the splendid pagoda on Malebar Hill, and was seized with an irresistible desire to see its interior. He was quite ignorant that it is forbidden to Christians to enter certain Indian temples, and that even the faithful must not go in without first leaving their shoes outside the door. It may be said here that the wise policy of the British Government severely punishes a disregard of the practices of the native religions.

Passepartout, however, thinking no harm, went in like a simple tourist, and was soon lost in admiration of the splendid Brahmin ornamentation which everywhere met his eyes, when of a sudden he found himself sprawling on the sacred flagging. He looked up to behold three enraged priests, who forthwith fell upon him, tore off his shoes, and began to beat him with loud, savage exclamations. The agile Frenchman was soon upon his feet again, and lost no time in knocking down two of his long-gowned adversaries with his fists and a vigourous application of his toes; then, rushing out of the pagoda as fast as his legs could carry him, he soon escaped the third priest by mingling with the crowd in the streets.

At five minutes before eight, Passepartout, hatless, shoeless, and having in the squabble lost his package of shirts and shoes, rushed breathlessly into the station.

Fix, who had followed Mr. Fogg to the station, and saw that he was really going to leave Bombay, was there, upon the platform. He had resolved to follow the supposed robber to Calcutta, and farther, if necessary. Passepartout did not observe the detective, who stood in an obscure corner; but Fix heard him relate his adventures in a few words to Mr. Fogg.

"I hope that this will not happen again," said Phileas Fogg, coldly, as he got into the train. Poor Passepartout, quite crestfallen, followed his master without a word. Fix was on the point of entering another carriage, when an idea struck him which induced him to alter his plan.

"No, I'll stay," muttered he. "An offence has been committed on Indian soil. I've got my man."

Just then the locomotive gave a sharp screech, and the train passed out into the darkness of the night.

Chapter XI

IN WHICH PHILEAS FOGG SECURES A CURIOUS MEANS OF CONVEYANCE AT A FABULOUS PRICE

THE TRAIN HAD STARTED PUNCTUALLY. AMONG THE PASSENGERS WERE A NUMBER OF officers, Government officials, and opium and indigo merchants, whose business called them to the eastern coast. Passepartout rode in the same carriage with his master, and a third passenger occupied a seat opposite to them. This was Sir Francis Cromarty, one of Mr. Fogg's whist partners on the *Mongolia*, now on his way to join his corps at Benares. Sir Francis was a tall, fair man of fifty, who had greatly distinguished himself in the last Sepoy revolt. He made India his home, only paying brief visits to England at rare intervals; and was almost as familiar as a native with the customs, history, and character of India and its people. But Phileas Fogg, who was not travelling, but only describing a circumference, took no pains to enquire into these subjects; he was a solid body, traversing an orbit around the terrestrial globe, according to the laws of rational mechanics. He was at this moment calculating in his mind the number of hours spent since his departure from London, and, had it been in his nature to make a useless demonstration, would have rubbed his hands for satisfaction. Sir Francis Cromarty had observed the oddity of his travelling companion—although the only opportunity he had for studying him had been while he was dealing the cards, and between two rubbers—and questioned himself whether a human heart really beat beneath this cold exterior, and whether Phileas Fogg had any sense of the beauties of nature. The brigadier-general was free to mentally confess, that, of all the eccentric persons he had ever met, none was comparable to this product of the exact sciences.

Phileas Fogg had not concealed from Sir Francis his design of going around the world, nor the circumstances under which he set out; and the general only saw in the wager a useless eccentricity and a lack of sound common sense. In the way this strange gentleman was going on, he would leave the world without having done any good to himself or anybody else.

An hour after leaving Bombay the train had passed the viaducts and the Island of Salcette, and had got into the open country. At Callyan they reached the junction of the branch line which descends towards south-eastern India by Kandallah and Pounah; and, passing Pauwell, they entered the defiles of the mountains, with their basalt bases, and their summits crowned with thick and verdant forests. Phileas Fogg and Sir Francis Cromarty exchanged a few words from time to time, and now Sir Francis, reviving the conversation, observed, "Some years ago, Mr. Fogg, you would have met with a delay at this point which would probably have lost you your wager."

"How so, Sir Francis?"

"Because the railway stopped at the base of these mountains, which the passengers were obliged to cross in palanquins or on ponies to Kandallah, on the other side."

"Such a delay would not have deranged my plans in the least," said Mr. Fogg. "I have constantly foreseen the likelihood of certain obstacles."

"But, Mr. Fogg," pursued Sir Francis, "you run the risk of having some difficulty about this worthy fellow's adventure at the pagoda." Passepartout, his feet comfortably wrapped in his travelling-blanket, was sound asleep, and did not dream that anybody was talking about him. "The Government is very severe upon that kind of offence. It takes particular care that the religious customs of the Indians should be respected, and if your servant were caught—"

"Very well, Sir Francis," replied Mr. Fogg; "if he had been caught he would have been condemned and punished, and then would have quietly returned to Europe. I don't see how this affair could have delayed his master."

The conversation fell again. During the night the train left the mountains behind, and passed Nassik, and the next day proceeded over the flat, well-cultivated country of the

Khandeish, with its straggling villages, above which rose the minarets of the pagodas. This fertile territory is watered by numerous small rivers and limpid streams, mostly tributaries of the Godavery.

Passepartout, on waking and looking out, could not realise that he was actually crossing India in a railway train. The locomotive, guided by an English engineer and fed with English coal, threw out its smoke upon cotton, coffee, nutmeg, clove, and pepper plantations, while the steam curled in spirals around groups of palm-trees, in the midst of which were seen picturesque bungalows, viharis (a sort of abandoned monasteries), and marvelous temples enriched by the exhaustless ornamentation of Indian architecture. Then they came upon vast tracts extending to the horizon, with jungles inhabited by snakes and tigers, which fled at the noise of the train; succeeded by forests penetrated by the railway, and still haunted by elephants which, with pensive eyes, gazed at the train as it passed. The travellers crossed, beyond Malligaum, the fatal country so often stained with blood by the sectaries of the goddess Kali. Not far off rose Ellora, with its graceful pagodas, and the famous Aurungabad, capital of the ferocious Aureng-Zeb, now the chief town of one of the detached provinces of the kingdom of the Nizam. It was thereabouts that Feringhea, the Thuggee chief, king of the stranglers, held his sway. These ruffians, united by a secret bond, strangled victims of every age in honour of the goddess Death, without ever shedding blood; there was a period when this part of the country could scarcely be travelled over without corpses being found in every direction. The English Government has succeeded in greatly diminishing these murders, though the Thuggees still exist, and pursue the exercise of their horrible rites.

At half-past twelve the train stopped at Burhampoor, where Passepartout was able to purchase some Indian slippers, ornamented with false pearls, in which, with evident vanity, he proceeded to encase his feet. The travellers made a hasty breakfast and started off for Assurghur, after skirting for a little the banks of the small river Tapty, which empties into the Gulf of Cambray, near Surat.

Passepartout was now plunged into absorbing reverie. Up to his arrival at Bombay, he had entertained hopes that their journey would end there; but now that they were plainly whirling across India at full speed, a sudden change had come over the spirit of his dreams. His old vagabond nature returned to him; the fantastic ideas of his youth once more took possession of him. He came to regard his master's project as intended in good earnest, believed in the reality of the bet, and therefore in the tour of the world, and the necessity of making it without fail within the designated period. Already he began to worry about possible delays, and accidents which might happen on the way. He recognised himself as being personally interested in the wager, and trembled at the thought that he might have been the means of losing it by his unpardonable folly of the night before. Being much less cool-headed than Mr. Fogg, he was much more restless, counting and recounting the days passed over, uttering maledictions when the train stopped, and accusing it of sluggishness, and mentally blaming Mr. Fogg for not having bribed the engineer. The worthy fellow was ignorant that, while it was possible by such means to hasten the rate of a steamer, it could not be done on the railway.

The train entered the defiles of the Sutpour Mountains, which separate the Khandeish from Bundelcund, towards evening. The next day Sir Francis Cromarty asked Passepartout what time it was; to which, on consulting his watch, he replied that it was three in the morning. This famous timepiece, always regulated on the Greenwich meridian, which was now some seventy-seven degrees westward, was at least four hours slow. Sir Francis corrected Passepartout's time, whereupon the latter made the same remark that he had done to Fix; and upon the general insisting that the watch should be regulated in each new meridian, since he was constantly going eastward, that is in the face of the sun, and therefore the days were shorter by four minutes for each degree gone over, Passepartout obstinately refused to alter his watch, which he kept at London time. It was an innocent delusion which could harm no one.

The train stopped, at eight o'clock, in the midst of a glade some fifteen miles beyond Rothal, where there were several bungalows, and workmen's cabins. The conductor, passing along the carriages, shouted, "Passengers will get out here!"

Phileas Fogg looked at Sir Francis Cromarty for an explanation; but the general could not tell what meant a halt in the midst of this forest of dates and acacias.

Passepartout, not less surprised, rushed out and speedily returned, crying: "Monsieur, no more railway!"

"What do you mean?" asked Sir Francis.

"I mean to say that the train isn't going on."

The general at once stepped out, while Phileas Fogg calmly followed him, and they proceeded together to the conductor.

"Where are we?" asked Sir Francis.

"At the hamlet of Kholby."

"Do we stop here?"

"Certainly. The railway isn't finished."

"What! not finished?"

"No. There's still a matter of fifty miles to be laid from here to Allahabad, where the line begins again."

"But the papers announced the opening of the railway throughout."

"What would you have, officer? The papers were mistaken."

"Yet you sell tickets from Bombay to Calcutta," retorted Sir Francis, who was growing warm.

"No doubt," replied the conductor; "but the passengers know that they must provide means of transportation for themselves from Kholby to Allahabad."

Sir Francis was furious. Passepartout would willingly have knocked the conductor down, and did not dare to look at his master.

"Sir Francis," said Mr. Fogg, quietly, "we will, if you please, look about for some means of conveyance to Allahabad."

"Mr. Fogg, this is a delay greatly to your disadvantage."

"No, Sir Francis; it was foreseen."

"What! You knew that the way—"

"Not at all; but I knew that some obstacle or other would sooner or later arise on my route. Nothing, therefore, is lost. I have two days, which I have already gained, to sacrifice. A steamer leaves Calcutta for Hong Kong at noon, on the 25th. This is the 22d, and we shall reach Calcutta in time."

There was nothing to say to so confident a response.

It was but too true that the railway came to a termination at this point. The papers were like some watches, which have a way of getting too fast, and had been premature in their announcement of the completion of the line. The greater part of the travellers were aware of this interruption, and leaving the train, they began to engage such vehicles as the village could provide—four-wheeled palkigharis, wagons drawn by zebus, carriages that looked like perambulating pagodas, palanquins, ponies, and what not.

Mr. Fogg and Sir Francis Cromarty, after searching the village from end to end, came back without having found anything.

"I shall go afoot," said Phileas Fogg.

Passepartout, who had now rejoined his master, made a wry grimace, as he thought of his magnificent, but too frail Indian shoes. Happily he too had been looking about him, and, after a moment's hesitation, said, "Monsieur, I think I have found a means of conveyance."

"What?"

"An elephant! An elephant that belongs to an Indian who lives but a hundred steps from here."

"Let's go and see the elephant," replied Mr. Fogg.

They soon reached a small hut, near which, enclosed within some high palings, was the animal in question. An Indian came out of the hut, and, at their request, conducted them within the enclosure. The elephant, which its owner had reared, not for a beast of burden, but for war-like purposes, was half domesticated. The Indian had begun already, by often irritating him, and feeding him every three months on sugar and butter, to impart to him a ferocity not in his nature, this method being often employed by those who train the Indian elephants for battle. Happily, however, for Mr. Fogg, the animal's instruction in this direction had not gone far, and the elephant still preserved his natural gentleness. Kiouni—this was the name of the beast—could doubtless travel rapidly for a long time, and, in default of any other means of conveyance, Mr. Fogg resolved to hire him. But elephants are far from cheap in India, where they are becoming scarce; the males, which alone are suitable for circus shows, are much sought, especially as but few of them are domesticated. When, therefore, Mr. Fogg proposed to the Indian to hire Kiouni, he refused pointblank. Mr. Fogg persisted, offering the excessive sum of ten pounds an hour for the loan of the beast to Allahabad. Refused. Twenty pounds? Refused also. Forty pounds? Still refused. Passepartout jumped at each advance; but the Indian declined to be tempted. Yet the offer was an alluring one, for, supposing it took the elephant fifteen hours to reach Allahabad, his owner would receive no less than six hundred pounds sterling.

Phileas Fogg, without getting in the least flurried, then proposed to purchase the animal outright, and at first offered a thousand pounds for him. The Indian, perhaps thinking he was going to make a great bargain, still refused.

Sir Francis Cromarty took Mr. Fogg aside, and begged him to reflect before he went any further; to which the gentleman replied that he was not in the habit of acting rashly, that a bet of twenty thousand pounds was at stake, that the elephant was absolutely necessary to him, and that he would secure him if he had to pay twenty times his value. Returning to the Indian, whose small, sharp eyes, glistening with avarice, betrayed that with him it was only a question of how great a price he could obtain, Mr. Fogg offered first twelve hundred, then fifteen hundred, eighteen hundred, two thousand pounds. Passepartout, usually so rubicund, was fairly white with suspense.

At two thousand pounds the Indian yielded.

"What a price, good heaven!" cried Passepartout, "for an elephant!"

It only remained now to find a guide, which was comparatively easy. A young Parsee, with an intelligent face, offered his services, which Mr. Fogg accepted, promising so generous a reward as to materially stimulate his zeal. The elephant was led out and equipped. The Parsee, who was an accomplished elephant driver, covered his back with a sort of saddle-cloth, and attached to each of his flanks some curiously uncomfortable howdahs.

Phileas Fogg paid the Indian with some bank-notes which he extracted from the famous carpet-bag, a proceeding that seemed to deprive poor Passepartout of his vitals. Then he offered to carry Sir Francis to Allahabad, which the brigadier gratefully accepted, as one traveller the more would not be likely to fatigue the gigantic beast. Provisions were purchased at Kholby and, while Sir Francis and Mr. Fogg took the howdahs on either side, Passepartout got astride the saddle-cloth between them. The Parsee perched himself on the elephant's neck, and at nine o'clock they set out from the village, the animal marching off through the dense forest of palms by the shortest cut.

Chapter XII

IN WHICH PHILEAS FOGG AND HIS COMPANIONS VENTURE ACROSS THE INDIAN FORESTS, AND WHAT ENSUED

IN ORDER TO SHORTEN THE JOURNEY, THE GUIDE PASSED TO THE LEFT OF THE LINE WHERE the railway was still in process of being built. This line, owing to the capricious turnings of the Vindhia Mountains, did not pursue a straight course. The Parsee, who was quite familiar with the roads and paths in the district, declared that they would gain twenty miles by striking directly through the forest.

Phileas Fogg and Sir Francis Cromarty, plunged to the neck in the peculiar howdahs provided for them, were horribly jostled by the swift trotting of the elephant, spurred on as he was by the skilful Parsee; but they endured the discomfort with true British phlegm, talking little, and scarcely able to catch a glimpse of each other. As for Passepartout, who was mounted on the beast's back, and received the direct force of each concussion as he trod along, he was very careful, in accordance with his master's advice, to keep his tongue from between his teeth, as it would otherwise have been bitten off short. The worthy fellow bounced from the elephant's neck to his rump, and vaulted like a clown on a springboard; yet he laughed in the midst of his bouncing, and from time to time took a piece of sugar out of his pocket, and inserted it in Kiouni's trunk, who received it without in the least slackening his regular trot.

After two hours the guide stopped the elephant, and gave him an hour for rest, during which Kiouni, after quenching his thirst at a neighbouring spring, set to devouring the branches and shrubs round about him. Neither Sir Francis nor Mr. Fogg regretted the delay, and both descended with a feeling of relief. "Why, he's made of iron!" exclaimed the general, gazing admiringly on Kiouni.

"Of forged iron," replied Passepartout, as he set about preparing a hasty breakfast.

At noon the Parsee gave the signal of departure. The country soon presented a very savage aspect. Copses of dates and dwarf-palms succeeded the dense forests; then vast, dry plains, dotted with scanty shrubs, and sown with great blocks of syenite. All this portion of Bundelcund, which is little frequented by travellers, is inhabited by a fanatical population, hardened in the most horrible practices of the Hindoo faith. The English have not been able to secure complete dominion over this territory, which is subjected to the influence of rajahs, whom it is almost impossible to reach in their inaccessible mountain fastnesses. The travellers several times saw bands of ferocious Indians, who, when they perceived the elephant striding across country, made angry and threatening motions. The Parsee avoided them as much as possible. Few animals were observed on the route; even the monkeys hurried from their path with contortions and grimaces which convulsed Passepartout with laughter.

In the midst of his gayety, however, one thought troubled the worthy servant. What would Mr. Fogg do with the elephant, when he got to Allahabad? Would he carry him on with him? Impossible! The cost of transporting him would make him ruinously expensive. Would he sell him, or set him free? The estimable beast certainly deserved some consideration. Should Mr. Fogg choose to make him, Passepartout, a present of Kiouni, he would be very much embarrassed; and these thoughts did not cease worrying him for a long time.

The principal chain of the Vindhias was crossed by eight in the evening, and another halt was made on the northern slope, in a ruined bungalow. They had gone nearly twenty-five miles that day, and an equal distance still separated them from the station of Allahabad.

The night was cold. The Parsee lit a fire in the bungalow with a few dry branches, and the warmth was very grateful. The provisions purchased at Kholby sufficed for supper, and the travellers ate ravenously. The conversation, beginning with a few disconnected phrases, soon gave place to loud and steady snores. The guide watched Kiouni, who slept standing, bolstering himself against the trunk of a large tree. Nothing occurred during the night to disturb the slumberers, although occasional growls from panthers and chatterings of monkeys broke the silence; the more formidable beasts made no cries or hostile demonstration against the occupants of the bungalow. Sir Francis slept heavily, like an honest soldier overcome with fatigue. Passepartout was wrapped in uneasy dreams of the bouncing of the day before. As for Mr. Fogg, he slumbered as peacefully as if he had been in his serene mansion in Saville Row.

The journey was resumed at six in the morning; the guide hoped to reach Allahabad by evening. In that case, Mr. Fogg would only lose a part of the forty-eight hours saved since the beginning of the tour. Kiouni, resuming his rapid gait, soon descended the lower spurs of the Vindhias, and towards noon they passed by the village of Kallenger, on the Cani, one of the branches of the Ganges. The guide avoided inhabited places, thinking it safer to keep to the open country, which lies along the first depressions of the basin of the great river. Allahabad was now only twelve miles to the north-east. They stopped under a clump of bananas, the fruit of which, as healthy as bread and as succulent as cream, was amply partaken of and appreciated.

At two o'clock the guide entered a thick forest which extended several miles; he preferred to travel under cover of the woods. They had not as yet had any unpleasant encounters, and the journey seemed on the point of being successfully accomplished, when the elephant, becoming restless, suddenly stopped.

It was then four o'clock.

"What's the matter?" asked Sir Francis, putting out his head.

"I don't know, officer," replied the Parsee, listening attentively to a confused murmur which came through the thick branches.

The murmur soon became more distinct; it now seemed like a distant concert of human voices accompanied by brass instruments. Passepartout was all eyes and ears. Mr. Fogg patiently waited without a word. The Parsee jumped to the ground, fastened the elephant to a tree, and plunged into the thicket. He soon returned, saying—

"A procession of Brahmins is coming this way. We must prevent their seeing us, if possible."

The guide unloosed the elephant and led him into a thicket, at the same time asking the travellers not to stir. He held himself ready to bestride the animal at a moment's notice, should flight become necessary; but he evidently thought that the procession of the faithful would pass without perceiving them amid the thick foliage, in which they were wholly concealed.

The discordant tones of the voices and instruments drew nearer, and now droning songs mingled with the sound of the tambourines and cymbals. The head of the procession soon appeared beneath the trees, a hundred paces away; and the strange figures who performed the religious ceremony were easily distinguished through the branches. First came the priests, with mitres on their heads, and clothed in long lace robes. They were surrounded by men, women, and children, who sang a kind of lugubrious psalm, interrupted at regular intervals by the tambourines and cymbals; while behind them was drawn a car with large wheels, the spokes of which represented serpents entwined with each other. Upon the car, which was drawn by four richly caparisoned zebus, stood a hideous statue with four arms, the body coloured a dull red, with haggard eyes, dishevelled hair, protruding tongue, and lips tinted with betel. It stood upright upon the figure of a prostrate and headless giant.

Sir Francis, recognising the statue, whispered, "The goddess Kali; the goddess of love and death."

"Of death, perhaps," muttered back Passepartout, "but of love—that ugly old hag? Never!"

The Parsee made a motion to keep silence.

A group of old fakirs were capering and making a wild ado round the statue; these were striped with ochre, and covered with cuts whence their blood issued drop by drop— stupid fanatics, who, in the great Indian ceremonies, still throw themselves under the wheels of Juggernaut. Some Brahmins, clad in all the sumptuousness of Oriental apparel, and leading a woman who faltered at every step, followed. This woman was young, and as fair as a European. Her head and neck, shoulders, ears, arms, hands, and toes, were loaded down with jewels and gems—with bracelets, earrings, and rings; while a tunic bordered with gold, and covered with a light muslin robe betrayed the outline of her form.

The guards who followed the young woman presented a violent contrast to her, armed as they were with naked sabres hung at their waists, and long damascened pistols, and bearing a corpse on a palanquin. It was the body of an old man, gorgeously arrayed in the habiliments of a rajah, wearing, as in life, a turban embroidered with pearls, a robe of tissue of silk and gold, a scarf of cashmere sewed with diamonds, and the magnificent weapons of a Hindoo prince. Next came the musicians and a rearguard of capering fakirs, whose cries sometimes drowned the noise of the instruments; these closed the procession.

Sir Francis watched the procession with a sad countenance, and, turning to the guide, said, "A suttee."

The Parsee nodded, and put his finger to his lips. The procession slowly wound under the trees, and soon its last ranks disappeared in the depths of the wood. The songs gradually died away; occasionally cries were heard in the distance, until at last all was silence again.

Phileas Fogg had heard what Sir Francis said, and, as soon as the procession had disappeared, asked: "What is a 'suttee'?"

"A suttee," returned the general, "is a human sacrifice, but a voluntary one. The woman you have just seen will be burned to-morrow at the dawn of day."

"Oh, the scoundrels!" cried Passepartout, who could not repress his indignation.

"And the corpse?" asked Mr. Fogg.

"Is that of the prince, her husband," said the guide; "an independent rajah of Bundelcund."

"Is it possible," resumed Phileas Fogg, his voice betraying not the least emotion, "that these barbarous customs still exist in India, and that the English have been unable to put a stop to them?"

"These sacrifices do not occur in the larger portion of India," replied Sir Francis; "but we have no power over these savage territories, and especially here in Bundelcund. The whole district north of the Vindhias is the theatre of incessant murders and pillage."

"The poor wretch!" exclaimed Passepartout, "to be burned alive!"

"Yes," returned Sir Francis, "burned alive. And if she were not, you cannot conceive what treatment she would be obliged to submit to from her relatives. They would shave off her hair, feed her on a scanty allowance of rice, treat her with contempt; she would be looked upon as an unclean creature, and would die in some corner, like a scurvy dog. The prospect of so frightful an existence drives these poor creatures to the sacrifice much more than love or religious fanaticism. Sometimes, however, the sacrifice is really voluntary, and it requires the active interference of the Government to prevent it. Several years ago, when I was living at Bombay, a young widow asked permission of the governor to be burned along with her husband's body; but, as you may imagine, he refused. The woman left the town, took refuge with an independent rajah, and there carried out her self-devoted purpose."

While Sir Francis was speaking, the guide shook his head several times, and now said: "The sacrifice which will take place to-morrow at dawn is not a voluntary one."

"How do you know?"

"Everybody knows about this affair in Bundelcund."

"But the wretched creature did not seem to be making any resistance," observed Sir Francis.

"That was because they had intoxicated her with fumes of hemp and opium."

"But where are they taking her?"

"To the pagoda of Pillaji, two miles from here; she will pass the night there."

"And the sacrifice will take place—"

"To-morrow, at the first light of dawn."

The guide now led the elephant out of the thicket, and leaped upon his neck. Just at the moment that he was about to urge Kiouni forward with a peculiar whistle, Mr. Fogg stopped him, and, turning to Sir Francis Cromarty, said, "Suppose we save this woman."

"Save the woman, Mr. Fogg!"

"I have yet twelve hours to spare; I can devote them to that."

"Why, you are a man of heart!"

"Sometimes," replied Phileas Fogg, quietly; "when I have the time."

Chapter XIII

IN WHICH PASSEPARTOUT RECEIVES A NEW PROOF THAT FORTUNE FAVOURS THE BRAVE

THE PROJECT WAS A BOLD ONE, FULL OF DIFFICULTY, PERHAPS IMPRACTICABLE. MR. Fogg was going to risk life, or at least liberty, and therefore the success of his tour. But he did not hesitate, and he found in Sir Francis Cromarty an enthusiastic ally.

As for Passepartout, he was ready for anything that might be proposed. His master's idea charmed him; he perceived a heart, a soul, under that icy exterior. He began to love Phileas Fogg.

There remained the guide: what course would he adopt? Would he not take part with the Indians? In default of his assistance, it was necessary to be assured of his neutrality.

Sir Francis frankly put the question to him.

"Officers," replied the guide, "I am a Parsee, and this woman is a Parsee. Command me as you will."

"Excellent!" said Mr. Fogg.

"However," resumed the guide; "it is certain, not only that we shall risk our lives, but horrible tortures, if we are taken."

"That is foreseen," replied Mr. Fogg. "I think we must wait till night before acting."

"I think so," said the guide.

The worthy Indian then gave some account of the victim, who, he said, was a celebrated beauty of the Parsee race, and the daughter of a wealthy Bombay merchant. She had received a thoroughly English education in that city, and, from her manners and intelligence, would be thought a European. Her name was Aouda. Left an orphan, she was married against her will to the old rajah of Bundelcund; and, knowing the fate that awaited her, she escaped, was retaken, and devoted by the rajah's relatives, who had an interest in her death, to the sacrifice from which it seemed she could not escape.

The Parsee's narrative only confirmed Mr. Fogg and his companions in their generous design. It was decided that the guide should direct the elephant towards the pagoda of Pillaji, which he accordingly approached as quickly as possible. They halted, half-an-hour afterwards, in a copse, some five hundred feet from the pagoda, where they were well concealed; but they could hear the groans and cries of the fakirs distinctly.

They then discussed the means of getting at the victim. The guide was familiar with the pagoda of Pillaji, in which, as he declared, the young woman was imprisoned. Could they enter any of its doors while the whole party of Indians was plunged in a drunken sleep, or was it safer to attempt to make a hole in the walls? This could only be determined at the moment and the place themselves; but it was certain that the abduction must be made that night, and not when, at break of day, the victim was led to her funeral pyre. Then no human intervention could save her.

As soon as night fell, about six o'clock, they decided to make a reconnaissance around the pagoda. The cries of the fakirs were just ceasing; the Indians were in the act of plunging themselves into the drunkenness caused by liquid opium mingled with hemp, and it might be possible to slip between them to the temple itself.

The Parsee, leading the others, noiselessly crept through the wood, and in ten minutes they found themselves on the banks of a small stream, whence, by the light of the rosin torches, they perceived a pyre of wood, on the top of which lay the embalmed body of the rajah, which was to be burned with his wife. The pagoda, whose minarets loomed above the trees in the deepening dusk, stood a hundred steps away.

"Come!" whispered the guide.

He slipped more cautiously than ever through the brush, followed by his companions; the silence around was only broken by the low murmuring of the wind among the branches.

Soon the Parsee stopped on the borders of the glade, which was lit up by the torches. The ground was covered by groups of the Indians, motionless in their drunken sleep; it seemed a battle-field strewn with the dead. Men, women, and children lay together.

In the background, among the trees, the pagoda of Pillaji loomed indistinctly. Much to the guide's disappointment, the guards of the rajah, lighted by torches, were watching at the doors and marching to and fro with naked sabres; probably the priests, too, were watching within.

The Parsee, now convinced that it was impossible to force an entrance to the temple, advanced no farther, but led his companions back again. Phileas Fogg and Sir Francis Cromarty also saw that nothing could be attempted in that direction. They stopped, and engaged in a whispered colloquy.

"It is only eight now," said the brigadier, "and these guards may also go to sleep."

"It is not impossible," returned the Parsee.

They lay down at the foot of a tree, and waited.

The time seemed long; the guide ever and anon left them to take an observation on the edge of the wood, but the guards watched steadily by the glare of the torches, and a dim light crept through the windows of the pagoda.

They waited till midnight; but no change took place among the guards, and it became apparent that their yielding to sleep could not be counted on. The other plan must be carried out; an opening in the walls of the pagoda must be made. It remained to ascertain whether the priests were watching by the side of their victim as assiduously as were the soldiers at the door.

After a last consultation, the guide announced that he was ready for the attempt, and advanced, followed by the others. They took a roundabout way, so as to get at the pagoda on the rear. They reached the walls about half-past twelve, without having met anyone; here there was no guard, nor were there either windows or doors.

The night was dark. The moon, on the wane, scarcely left the horizon, and was covered with heavy clouds; the height of the trees deepened the darkness.

It was not enough to reach the walls; an opening in them must be accomplished, and to attain this purpose the party only had their pocketknives. Happily the temple walls were built of brick and wood, which could be penetrated with little difficulty; after one brick had been taken out, the rest would yield easily.

They set noiselessly to work, and the Parsee on one side and Passepartout on the other began to loosen the bricks so as to make an aperture two feet wide. They were getting on rapidly, when suddenly a cry was heard in the interior of the temple, followed almost instantly by other cries replying from the outside. Passepartout and the guide stopped. Had they been heard? Was the alarm being given? Common prudence urged them to retire, and they did so, followed by Phileas Fogg and Sir Francis. They again hid themselves in the wood, and waited till the disturbance, whatever it might be, ceased, holding themselves ready to resume their attempt without delay. But, awkwardly enough, the guards now appeared at the rear of the temple, and there installed themselves, in readiness to prevent a surprise.

It would be difficult to describe the disappointment of the party, thus interrupted in their work. They could not now reach the victim; how, then, could they save her? Sir Francis shook his fists, Passepartout was beside himself, and the guide gnashed his teeth with rage. The tranquil Fogg waited, without betraying any emotion.

"We have nothing to do but to go away," whispered Sir Francis.

"Nothing but to go away," echoed the guide.

"Stop," said Fogg. "I am only due at Allahabad to-morrow before noon."

"But what can you hope to do?" asked Sir Francis. "In a few hours it will be daylight, and—"

"The chance which now seems lost may present itself at the last moment."

Sir Francis would have liked to read Phileas Fogg's eyes.

What was this cool Englishman thinking of? Was he planning to make a rush for the young woman at the very moment of the sacrifice, and boldly snatch her from her executioners?

This would be utter folly, and it was hard to admit that Fogg was such a fool. Sir Francis consented, however, to remain to the end of this terrible drama. The guide led them to the rear of the glade, where they were able to observe the sleeping groups.

Meanwhile Passepartout, who had perched himself on the lower branches of a tree, was resolving an idea which had at first struck him like a flash, and which was now firmly lodged in his brain.

He had commenced by saying to himself, "What folly!" and then he repeated, "Why not, after all? It's a chance—perhaps the only one; and with such sots!" Thinking thus, he slipped, with the suppleness of a serpent, to the lowest branches, the ends of which bent almost to the ground.

The hours passed, and the lighter shades now announced the approach of day, though it was not yet light. This was the moment. The slumbering multitude became animated, the tambourines sounded, songs and cries arose; the hour of the sacrifice had come. The doors of the pagoda swung open, and a bright light escaped from its interior, in the midst of which Mr. Fogg and Sir Francis espied the victim. She seemed, having shaken off the stupor of intoxication, to be striving to escape from her executioner. Sir Francis's heart throbbed; and convulsively seizing Mr. Fogg's hand, found in it an open knife. Just at this moment the crowd began to move. The young woman had again fallen into a stupor caused by the fumes of hemp, and passed among the fakirs, who escorted her with their wild, religious cries.

Phileas Fogg and his companions, mingling in the rear ranks of the crowd, followed; and in two minutes they reached the banks of the stream, and stopped fifty paces from the pyre, upon which still lay the rajah's corpse. In the semi-obscurity they saw the victim, quite senseless, stretched out beside her husband's body. Then a torch was brought, and the wood, soaked with oil, instantly took fire.

At this moment Sir Francis and the guide seized Phileas Fogg, who, in an instant of mad generosity, was about to rush upon the pyre. But he had quickly pushed them aside, when the whole scene suddenly changed. A cry of terror arose. The whole multitude prostrated themselves, terror-stricken, on the ground.

The old rajah was not dead, then, since he rose of a sudden, like a spectre, took up his wife in his arms, and descended from the pyre in the midst of the clouds of smoke, which only heightened his ghostly appearance.

Fakirs and soldiers and priests, seized with instant terror, lay there with their faces on the ground, not daring to lift their eyes and behold such a prodigy.

The inanimate victim was borne along by the vigourous arms which supported her, and which she did not seem in the least to burden. Mr. Fogg and Sir Francis stood erect, the Parsee bowed his head, and Passepartout was, no doubt, scarcely less stupefied.

The resuscitated rajah approached Sir Francis and Mr. Fogg, and, in an abrupt tone, said, "Let us be off!"

It was Passepartout himself, who had slipped upon the pyre in the midst of the smoke and, profiting by the still overhanging darkness, had delivered the young woman from death! It was Passepartout who, playing his part with a happy audacity, had passed through the crowd amid the general terror.

A moment after all four of the party had disappeared in the woods, and the elephant was bearing them away at a rapid pace. But the cries and noise, and a ball which whizzed through Phileas Fogg's hat, apprised them that the trick had been discovered.

The old rajah's body, indeed, now appeared upon the burning pyre; and the priests, recovered from their terror, perceived that an abduction had taken place. They hastened into the forest, followed by the soldiers, who fired a volley after the fugitives; but the latter rapidly increased the distance between them, and ere long found themselves beyond the reach of the bullets and arrows.

Chapter XIV

IN WHICH PHILEAS FOGG DESCENDS THE WHOLE LENGTH OF THE BEAUTIFUL VALLEY OF THE GANGES WITHOUT EVER THINKING OF SEEING IT

THE RASH EXPLOIT HAD BEEN ACCOMPLISHED; AND FOR AN HOUR PASSEPARTOUT laughed gaily at his success. Sir Francis pressed the worthy fellow's hand, and his master said, "Well done!" which, from him, was high commendation; to which Passepartout replied that all the credit of the affair belonged to Mr. Fogg. As for him, he had only been struck with a "queer" idea; and he laughed to think that for a few moments he, Passepartout, the ex-gymnast, ex-sergeant fireman, had been the spouse of a charming woman, a venerable, embalmed rajah! As for the young Indian woman, she had been unconscious throughout of what was passing, and now, wrapped up in a travelling-blanket, was reposing in one of the howdahs.

The elephant, thanks to the skillful guidance of the Parsee, was advancing rapidly through the still darksome forest, and, an hour after leaving the pagoda, had crossed a vast plain. They made a halt at seven o'clock, the young woman being still in a state of complete prostration. The guide made her drink a little brandy and water, but the drowsiness which stupefied her could not yet be shaken off. Sir Francis, who was familiar with the effects of the intoxication produced by the fumes of hemp, reassured his companions on her account. But he was more disturbed at the prospect of her future fate. He told Phileas Fogg that, should Aouda remain in India, she would inevitably fall again into the hands of her executioners. These fanatics were scattered throughout the county, and would, despite the English police, recover their victim at Madras, Bombay, or Calcutta. She would only be safe by quitting India forever.

Phileas Fogg replied that he would reflect upon the matter.

The station at Allahabad was reached about ten o'clock, and the interrupted line of railway being resumed, would enable them to reach Calcutta in less than twenty-four hours. Phileas Fogg would thus be able to arrive in time to take the steamer which left Calcutta the next day, October 25th, at noon, for Hong Kong.

The young woman was placed in one of the waiting-rooms of the station, whilst Passepartout was charged with purchasing for her various articles of toilet, a dress, shawl, and some furs; for which his master gave him unlimited credit. Passepartout started off forthwith, and found himself in the streets of Allahabad, that is, the "City of God," one of the most venerated in India, being built at the junction of the two sacred rivers, Ganges and Jumna, the waters of which attract pilgrims from every part of the peninsula. The Ganges, according to the legends of the Ramayana, rises in heaven, whence owing to Brahma's agency, it descends to the earth.

Passepartout made it a point, as he made his purchases, to take a good look at the city. It was formerly defended by a noble fort, which has since become a state prison; its commerce has dwindled away, and Passepartout in vain looked about him for such a bazaar as he used to frequent in Regent Street. At last he came upon an elderly, crusty Jew, who sold second-hand articles, and from whom he purchased a dress of Scotch stuff, a large mantle, and a fine otterskin pelisse, for which he did not hesitate to pay seventy-five pounds. He then returned triumphantly to the station.

The influence to which the priests of Pillaji had subjected Aouda began gradually to yield, and she became more herself, so that her fine eyes resumed all their soft Indian expression.

When the poet-king, Ucaf Uddaul, celebrates the charms of the queen of Ahmehnagara, he speaks thus:

"Her shining tresses, divided in two parts, encircle the harmonious contour of her white and delicate cheeks, brilliant in their glow and freshness. Her ebony brows have the form and charm of the bow of Kama, the god of love, and beneath her long silken lashes the purest reflections and a celestial light swim, as in the sacred lakes of Himalaya, in the black pupils of her great clear eyes. Her teeth, fine, equal, and white, glitter between her smiling lips like dewdrops in a passion-flower's half-enveloped breast. Her delicately formed ears, her vermilion hands, her little feet, curved and tender as the lotus-bud, glitter with the brilliancy of the loveliest pearls of Ceylon, the most dazzling diamonds of Golconda. Her narrow and supple waist, which a hand may clasp around, sets forth the outline of her rounded figure and the beauty of her bosom, where youth in its flower displays the wealth of its treasures; and beneath the silken folds of her tunic she seems to have been modelled in pure silver by the god-like hand of Vicvarcarma, the immortal sculptor."

It is enough to say, without applying this poetical rhapsody to Aouda, that she was a charming woman, in all the European acceptation of the phrase. She spoke English with great purity, and the guide had not exaggerated in saying that the young Parsee had been transformed by her bringing up.

The train was about to start from Allahabad, and Mr. Fogg proceeded to pay the guide the price agreed upon for his service, and not a farthing more; which astonished Passepartout, who remembered all that his master owed to the guide's devotion. He had, indeed, risked his life in the adventure at Pillaji, and if he should be caught afterward by the Indians, he would with difficulty escape their vengeance. Kiouni, also, must be disposed of. What should be done with the elephant, which had been so dearly purchased? Phileas Fogg had already determined this question.

"Parsee," said he to the guide, "you have been serviceable and devoted. I have paid for your service, but not for your devotion. Would you like to have this elephant? He is yours."

The guide's eyes glistened.

"Your honour is giving me a fortune!" cried he.

"Take him, guide," returned Mr. Fogg, "and I shall still be your debtor."

"Good!" exclaimed Passepartout; "take him, friend. Kiouni is a brave and faithful beast." And, going up to the elephant, he gave him several lumps of sugar, saying, "Here, Kiouni, here, here."

The elephant grunted out his satisfaction, and, clasping Passepartout around the waist with his trunk, lifted him as high as his head. Passepartout, not in the least alarmed, caressed the animal, which replaced him gently on the ground.

Soon after, Phileas Fogg, Sir Francis Cromarty, and Passepartout, installed in a carriage with Aouda, who had the best seat, were whirling at full speed towards Benares. It was a run of eighty miles, and was accomplished in two hours. During the journey, the young woman fully recovered her senses. What was her astonishment to find herself in this carriage, on the railway, dressed in European habiliments, and with travellers who were quite strangers to her! Her companions first set about fully reviving her with a little liquor, and then Sir Francis narrated to her what had passed, dwelling upon the courage with which Phileas Fogg had not hesitated to risk his life to save her, and recounting the happy sequel of the venture, the result of Passepartout's rash idea. Mr. Fogg said nothing; while Passepartout, abashed, kept repeating that "it wasn't worth telling."

Aouda pathetically thanked her deliverers, rather with tears than words; her fine eyes interpreted her gratitude better than her lips. Then, as her thoughts strayed back to the scene of the sacrifice, and recalled the dangers which still menaced her, she shuddered with terror.

Phileas Fogg understood what was passing in Aouda's mind, and offered, in order to reassure her, to escort her to Hong Kong, where she might remain safely until the affair was hushed up—an offer which she eagerly and gratefully accepted. She had, it seems, a Parsee relation, who was one of the principal merchants of Hong Kong, which is wholly an English city, though on an island on the Chinese coast.

At half-past twelve the train stopped at Benares. The Brahmin legends assert that this city is built on the site of the ancient Casi, which, like Mahomet's tomb, was once suspended between heaven and earth; though the Benares of to-day, which the Orientalists call the Athens of India, stands quite unpoetically on the solid earth. Passepartout caught glimpses of its brick houses and clay huts, giving an aspect of desolation to the place, as the train entered it.

Benares was Sir Francis Cromarty's destination, the troops he was rejoining being encamped some miles northward of the city. He bade adieu to Phileas Fogg, wishing him all success, and expressing the hope that he would come that way again in a less original but more profitable fashion. Mr. Fogg lightly pressed him by the hand. The parting of Aouda, who did not forget what she owed to Sir Francis, betrayed more warmth; and, as for Passepartout, he received a hearty shake of the hand from the gallant general.

The railway, on leaving Benares, passed for a while along the valley of the Ganges. Through the windows of their carriage the travellers had glimpses of the diversified landscape of Behar, with its mountains clothed in verdure, its fields of barley, wheat, and corn, its jungles peopled with green alligators, its neat villages and its still thickly-leaved forests. Elephants were bathing in the waters of the sacred river, and groups of Indians, despite the advanced season and chilly air, were performing solemnly their pious ablutions. These were fervent Brahmins, the bitterest foes of Buddhism, their deities being Vishnu, the solar god, Shiva, the divine impersonation of natural forces, and Brahma, the supreme ruler of priests and legislators. What would these divinities think of India, anglicised as it is to-day, with steamers whistling and scudding along the Ganges, frightening the gulls which float upon its surface, the turtles swarming along its banks, and the faithful dwelling upon its borders?

The panorama passed before their eyes like a flash, save when the steam concealed it fitfully from the view; the travellers could scarcely discern the fort of Chupenie, twenty miles south-westward from Benares, the ancient stronghold of the rajahs of Behar; or Ghazipur and its famous rose-water factories; or the tomb of Lord Cornwallis, rising on the left bank of the Ganges; the fortified town of Buxar, or Patna, a large manufacturing and trading place, where is held the principal opium market of India; or Monghir, a more than European town, for it is as English as Manchester or Birmingham, with its iron foundries, edge-tool factories, and high chimneys puffing clouds of black smoke heavenward.

Night came on; the train passed on at full speed, in the midst of the roaring of the tigers, bears, and wolves which fled before the locomotive; and the marvels of Bengal, Golconda, ruined Gour, Murshedabad, the ancient capital, Burdwan, Hugly, and the French town of Chandernagor, where Passepartout would have been proud to see his country's flag flying, were hidden from their view in the darkness.

Calcutta was reached at seven in the morning, and the packet left for Hong Kong at noon; so that Phileas Fogg had five hours before him.

According to his journal, he was due at Calcutta on the 25th of October, and that was the exact date of his actual arrival. He was therefore neither behindhand nor ahead of time. The two days gained between London and Bombay had been lost, as has been seen, in the journey across India. But it is not to be supposed that Phileas Fogg regretted them.

Chapter XV

IN WHICH THE BAG OF BANK-NOTES DISGORGES SOME THOUSANDS OF POUNDS MORE

THE TRAIN ENTERED THE STATION, AND PASSEPARTOUT, JUMPING OUT FIRST, WAS FOL-lowed by Mr. Fogg, who assisted his fair companion to descend. Phileas Fogg intended to proceed at once to the Hong Kong steamer, in order to get Aouda comfortably settled for the voyage. He was unwilling to leave her while they were still on dangerous ground.

Just as he was leaving the station a policeman came up to him, and said, "Mr. Phileas Fogg?"

"I am he."

"Is this man your servant?" added the policeman, pointing to Passepartout.

"Yes."

"Be so good, both of you, as to follow me."

Mr. Fogg betrayed no surprise whatever. The policeman was a representative of the law, and law is sacred to an Englishman. Passepartout tried to reason about the matter, but the policeman tapped him with his stick, and Mr. Fogg made him a signal to obey.

"May this young lady go with us?" asked he.

"She may," replied the policeman.

Mr. Fogg, Aouda, and Passepartout were conducted to a "palki-gari," a sort of four-wheeled carriage, drawn by two horses, in which they took their places and were driven away. No one spoke during the twenty minutes which elapsed before they reached their destination. They first passed through the "black town," with its narrow streets, its miserable, dirty huts, and squalid population; then through the "European town," which presented a relief in its bright brick mansions, shaded by cocoa-nut-trees and bristling with masts, where, although it was early morning, elegantly dressed horsemen and handsome equipages were passing back and forth.

The carriage stopped before a modest-looking house, which, however, did not have the appearance of a private mansion. The policeman having requested his prisoners—for so, truly, they might be called—to descend, conducted them into a room with barred windows, and said: "You will appear before Judge Obadiah at half-past eight."

He then retired, and closed the door.

"Why, we are prisoners!" exclaimed Passepartout, falling into a chair.

Aouda, with an emotion she tried to conceal, said to Mr. Fogg: "Sir, you must leave me to my fate! It is on my account that you receive this treatment; it is for having saved me!"

Phileas Fogg contented himself with saying that it was impossible. It was quite unlikely that he should be arrested for preventing a suttee. The complainants would not dare present themselves with such a charge. There was some mistake. Moreover, he would not in any event abandon Aouda, but would escort her to Hong Kong.

"But the steamer leaves at noon!" observed Passepartout, nervously.

"We shall be on board by noon," replied his master, placidly.

It was said so positively, that Passepartout could not help muttering to himself, "Parbleu, that's certain! Before noon we shall be on board." But he was by no means reassured.

At half-past eight the door opened, the policeman appeared, and, requesting them to follow him, led the way to an adjoining hall. It was evidently a court-room, and a crowd of Europeans and natives already occupied the rear of the apartment.

Mr. Fogg and his two companions took their places on a bench opposite the desks of the magistrate and his clerk. Immediately after, Judge Obadiah, a fat, round man, followed by the clerk, entered. He proceeded to take down a wig which was hanging on a nail, and put it hurriedly on his head.

"The first case," said he; then, putting his hand to his head, he exclaimed, "Heh! This is not my wig!"

"No, your worship," returned the clerk, "it is mine."

"My dear Mr. Oysterpuff, how can a judge give a wise sentence in a clerk's wig?"

The wigs were exchanged.

Passepartout was getting nervous, for the hands on the face of the big clock over the judge seemed to go around with terrible rapidity.

"The first case," repeated Judge Obadiah.

"Phileas Fogg?" demanded Oysterpuff.

"I am here," replied Mr. Fogg.

"Passepartout?"

"Present!" responded Passepartout.

"Good," said the judge. "You have been looked for, prisoners, for two days on the trains from Bombay."

"But of what are we accused?" asked Passepartout, impatiently.

"You are about to be informed."

"I am an English subject, sir," said Mr. Fogg, "and I have the right—"

"Have you been ill-treated?"

"Not at all."

"Very well; let the complainants come in."

A door was swung open by order of the judge and three Indian priests entered.

"That's it," muttered Passepartout; "these are the rogues who were going to burn our young lady."

The priests took their places in front of the judge, and the clerk proceeded to read in a loud voice, a complaint of sacrilege against Phileas Fogg and his servant, who were accused of having violated a place held consecrated by the Brahmin religion.

"You hear the charge?" asked the judge.

"Yes, sir," replied Mr. Fogg, consulting his watch, "and I admit it."

"You admit it?"

"I admit it, and I wish to hear these priests admit, in their turn, what they were going to do at the pagoda of Pillaji."

The priests looked at each other; they did not seem to understand what was said.

"Yes," cried Passepartout, warmly; "at the pagoda of Pillaji, where they were on the point of burning their victim."

The judge stared with astonishment, and the priests were stupefied.

"What victim?" said Judge Obadiah. "Burn whom? In Bombay itself?"

"Bombay?" cried Passepartout.

"Certainly. We are not talking of the pagoda of Pillaji, but of the pagoda of Malebar Hill, at Bombay."

"And as a proof," added the clerk, "here are the desecrator's very shoes, which he left behind him."

Whereupon he placed a pair of shoes on his desk.

"My shoes!" cried Passepartout, in his surprise permitting this imprudent exclamation to escape him.

The confusion of master and man, who had quite forgotten the affair at Bombay, for which they were now detained at Calcutta, may be imagined.

Fix, the detective, had foreseen the advantage which Passepartout's escapade gave him, and, delaying his departure for twelve hours, had consulted the priests of Malebar Hill. Knowing that the English authorities dealt very severely with this kind of misdemeanor, he promised them a goodly sum in damages, and sent them forward to Calcutta by the next train. Owing to the delay caused by the rescue of the young widow, Fix and the priests reached the Indian capital before Mr. Fogg and his servant, the magistrates having been already warned by a despatch to arrest them should they arrive. Fix's disappointment when he learned that Phileas Fogg had not made his appearance in Calcutta, may be imagined. He made up his mind that the robber had stopped somewhere on the route and taken refuge in the southern provinces. For twenty-four hours Fix watched the station with feverish anxiety; at last he was rewarded by seeing Mr. Fogg and Passepartout arrive, accompanied by a young woman, whose presence he was wholly at a loss to explain. He hastened for a policeman; and this was how the party came to be arrested and brought before Judge Obadiah.

Had Passepartout been a little less preoccupied, he would have espied the detective ensconced in a corner of the court-room, watching the proceedings with an interest easily understood; for the warrant had failed to reach him at Calcutta, as it had done at Bombay and Suez.

Judge Obadiah had unfortunately caught Passepartout's rash exclamation, which the poor fellow would have given the world to recall.

"The facts are admitted?" asked the judge.

"Admitted," replied Mr. Fogg, coldly.

"Inasmuch," resumed the judge, "as the English law protects equally and sternly the religions of the Indian people, and as the man Passepartout has admitted that he violated the sacred pagoda of Malebar Hill, at Bombay, on the 20th of October, I condemn the said Passepartout to imprisonment for fifteen days and a fine of three hundred pounds."

"Three hundred pounds!" cried Passepartout, startled at the largeness of the sum.

"Silence!" shouted the constable.

"And inasmuch," continued the judge, "as it is not proved that the act was not done by the connivance of the master with the servant, and as the master in any case must be held responsible for the acts of his paid servant, I condemn Phileas Fogg to a week's imprisonment and a fine of one hundred and fifty pounds."

Fix rubbed his hands softly with satisfaction; if Phileas Fogg could be detained in Calcutta a week, it would be more than time for the warrant to arrive. Passepartout was stupefied. This sentence ruined his master. A wager of twenty thousand pounds lost, because he, like a precious fool, had gone into that abominable pagoda!

Phileas Fogg, as self-composed as if the judgment did not in the least concern him, did not even lift his eyebrows while it was being pronounced. Just as the clerk was calling the next case, he rose, and said, "I offer bail."

"You have that right," returned the judge.

Fix's blood ran cold, but he resumed his composure when he heard the judge announce that the bail required for each prisoner would be one thousand pounds.

"I will pay it at once," said Mr. Fogg, taking a roll of bank-bills from the carpet-bag, which Passepartout had by him, and placing them on the clerk's desk.

"This sum will be restored to you upon your release from prison," said the judge. "Meanwhile, you are liberated on bail."

"Come!" said Phileas Fogg to his servant.

"But let them at least give me back my shoes!" cried Passepartout, angrily.

"Ah, these are pretty dear shoes!" he muttered, as they were handed to him. "More than a thousand pounds apiece; besides, they pinch my feet."

Mr. Fogg, offering his arm to Aouda, then departed, followed by the crestfallen Passepartout. Fix still nourished hopes that the robber would not, after all, leave the two thousand pounds behind him, but would decide to serve out his week in jail, and issued forth on Mr. Fogg's traces. That gentleman took a carriage, and the party were soon landed on one of the quays.

The *Rangoon* was moored half-a-mile off in the harbour, its signal of departure hoisted at the mast-head. Eleven o'clock was striking; Mr. Fogg was an hour in advance of time. Fix saw them leave the carriage and push off in a boat for the steamer, and stamped his feet with disappointment.

"The rascal is off, after all!" he exclaimed. "Two thousand pounds sacrificed! He's as prodigal as a thief! I'll follow him to the end of the world if necessary; but at the rate he is going on, the stolen money will soon be exhausted."

The detective was not far wrong in making this conjecture. Since leaving London, what with travelling expenses, bribes, the purchase of the elephant, bails, and fines, Mr. Fogg had already spent more than five thousand pounds on the way, and the percentage of the sum recovered from the bank robber, promised to the detectives, was rapidly diminishing.

Chapter XVI

IN WHICH FIX DOES NOT SEEM TO UNDERSTAND
IN THE LEAST WHAT IS SAID TO HIM

THE *RANGOON*—ONE OF THE PENINSULAR AND ORIENTAL COMPANY'S BOATS PLYING IN the Chinese and Japanese seas—was a screw steamer, built of iron, weighing about seventeen hundred and seventy tons, and with engines of four hundred horse-power. She was as fast, but not as well fitted up, as the *Mongolia*, and Aouda was not as comfortably provided for on board of her as Phileas Fogg could have wished. However, the trip from Calcutta to Hong Kong only comprised some three thousand five hundred miles, occupying from ten to twelve days, and the young woman was not difficult to please.

During the first days of the journey Aouda became better acquainted with her protector, and constantly gave evidence of her deep gratitude for what he had done. The phlegmatic gentleman listened to her, apparently at least, with coldness, neither his voice nor his manner betraying the slightest emotion; but he seemed to be always on the watch that nothing should be wanting to Aouda's comfort. He visited her regularly each day at certain hours, not so much to talk himself as to sit and hear her talk. He treated her with the strictest politeness, but with the precision of an automaton, the movements of which had been arranged for this purpose. Aouda did not quite know what to make of him, though Passepartout had given her some hints of his master's eccentricity, and made her smile by telling her of the wager which was sending him round the world. After all, she owed Phileas Fogg her life, and she always regarded him through the exalting medium of her gratitude.

Aouda confirmed the Parsee guide's narrative of her touching history. She did, indeed, belong to the highest of the native races of India. Many of the Parsee merchants have made great fortunes there by dealing in cotton; and one of them, Sir Jametsee Jeejeebhoy, was made a baronet by the English government. Aouda was a relative of this great man, and it was his cousin, Jeejeeh, whom she hoped to join at Hong Kong. Whether she would find a protector in him she could not tell; but Mr. Fogg essayed to calm her anxieties, and to assure her that everything would be mathematically—he used the very word—arranged. Aouda fastened her great eyes, "clear as the sacred lakes of the Himalaya," upon him; but the intractable Fogg, as reserved as ever, did not seem at all inclined to throw himself into this lake.

The first few days of the voyage passed prosperously, amid favourable weather and propitious winds, and they soon came in sight of the great Andaman, the principal of the islands in the Bay of Bengal, with its picturesque Saddle Peak, two thousand four hundred feet high, looming above the waters. The steamer passed along near the shores, but the savage Papuans, who are in the lowest scale of humanity, but are not, as has been asserted, cannibals, did not make their appearance.

The panorama of the islands, as they steamed by them, was superb. Vast forests of palms, arecs, bamboo, teakwood, of the gigantic mimosa, and tree-like ferns covered the foreground, while behind, the graceful outlines of the mountains were traced against the sky; and along the coasts swarmed by thousands the precious swallows whose nests furnish a luxurious dish to the tables of the Celestial Empire. The varied landscape afforded by the Andaman Islands was soon passed, however, and the *Rangoon* rapidly approached the Straits of Malacca, which gave access to the China seas.

What was detective Fix, so unluckily drawn on from country to country, doing all this while? He had managed to embark on the *Rangoon* at Calcutta without being seen by Passepartout, after leaving orders that, if the warrant should arrive, it should be forwarded to him at Hong Kong; and he hoped to conceal his presence to the end of the voyage. It would have been difficult to explain why he was on board without awaking Passepartout's suspicions, who thought him still at Bombay. But necessity impelled him, nevertheless, to renew his acquaintance with the worthy servant, as will be seen.

All the detective's hopes and wishes were now centred on Hong Kong; for the steamer's stay at Singapore would be too brief to enable him to take any steps there. The arrest must be made at Hong Kong, or the robber would probably escape him forever. Hong Kong was the last English ground on which he would set foot; beyond, China, Japan, America offered to Fogg an almost certain refuge. If the warrant should at last make its appearance at Hong Kong, Fix could arrest him and give him into the hands of the local police, and there would be no further trouble. But beyond Hong Kong, a simple warrant would be of no avail; an extradition warrant would be necessary, and that would result in delays and obstacles, of which the rascal would take advantage to elude justice.

Fix thought over these probabilities during the long hours which he spent in his cabin, and kept repeating to himself, "Now, either the warrant will be at Hong Kong, in which case I shall arrest my man, or it will not be there; and this time it is absolutely necessary that I should delay his departure. I have failed at Bombay, and I have failed at Calcutta; if I fail at Hong Kong, my reputation is lost. Cost what it may, I *must succeed!* But how shall I prevent his departure, if that should turn out to be my last resource?"

Fix made up his mind that, if worst came to worse, he would make a confidant of Passepartout, and tell him what kind of a fellow his master really was. That Passepartout was not Fogg's accomplice, he was very certain. The servant, enlightened by his disclosure, and afraid of being himself implicated in the crime, would doubtless become an ally of the detective. But this method was a dangerous one, only to be employed when everything else had failed. A word from Passepartout to his master would ruin all. The detective was therefore in a sore strait. But suddenly a new idea struck him. The presence of Aouda on the *Rangoon,* in company with Phileas Fogg, gave him new material for reflection.

Who was this woman? What combination of events had made her Fogg's travelling companion? They had evidently met somewhere between Bombay and Calcutta; but where? Had they met accidentally, or had Fogg gone into the interior purposely in quest of this charming damsel? Fix was fairly puzzled. He asked himself whether there had not been a wicked elopement; and this idea so impressed itself upon his mind that he determined to make use of the supposed intrigue. Whether the young woman were married or not, he would be able to create such difficulties for Mr. Fogg at Hong Kong, that he could not escape by paying any amount of money.

But could he even wait till they reached Hong Kong? Fogg had an abominable way of jumping from one boat to another, and, before anything could be effected, might get full underway again for Yokohama.

Fix decided that he must warn the English authorities, and signal the *Rangoon* before her arrival. This was easy to do, since the steamer stopped at Singapore, whence there is a telegraphic wire to Hong Kong. He finally resolved, moreover, before acting more positively, to question Passepartout. It would not be difficult to make him talk; and, as there was no time to lose, Fix prepared to make himself known.

It was now the 30th of October, and on the following day the *Rangoon* was due at Singapore.

Fix emerged from his cabin and went on deck. Passepartout was promenading up and down in the forward part of the steamer. The detective rushed forward with every appearance of extreme surprise, and exclaimed, "You here, on the *Rangoon?*"

"What, Monsieur Fix, are you on board?" returned the really astonished Passepartout, recognising his crony of the *Mongolia*. "Why, I left you at Bombay, and here you are, on the way to Hong Kong! Are you going round the world too?"

"No, no," replied Fix; "I shall stop at Hong Kong—at least for some days."

"Hum!" said Passepartout, who seemed for an instant perplexed. "But how is it I have not seen you on board since we left Calcutta?"

"Oh, a trifle of seasickness—I've been staying in my berth. The Gulf of Bengal does not agree with me as well as the Indian Ocean. And how is Mr. Fogg?"

"As well and as punctual as ever, not a day behind time! But, Monsieur Fix, you don't know that we have a young lady with us."

"A young lady?" replied the detective, not seeming to comprehend what was said.

Passepartout thereupon recounted Aouda's history, the affair at the Bombay pagoda, the purchase of the elephant for two thousand pounds, the rescue, the arrest and sentence of the Calcutta court, and the restoration of Mr. Fogg and himself to liberty on bail. Fix, who was familiar with the last events, seemed to be equally ignorant of all that Passepartout related; and the latter was charmed to find so interested a listener.

"But does your master propose to carry this young woman to Europe?"

"Not at all. We are simply going to place her under the protection of one of her relatives, a rich merchant at Hong Kong."

"Nothing to be done there," said Fix to himself, concealing his disappointment. "A glass of gin, Mr. Passepartout?"

"Willingly, Monsieur Fix. We must at least have a friendly glass on board the *Rangoon*."

Chapter XVII

SHOWING WHAT HAPPENED ON THE VOYAGE
FROM SINGAPORE TO HONG KONG

THE DETECTIVE AND PASSEPARTOUT MET OFTEN ON DECK AFTER THIS INTERVIEW, though Fix was reserved, and did not attempt to induce his companion to divulge any more facts concerning Mr. Fogg. He caught a glimpse of that mysterious gentleman once or twice; but Mr. Fogg usually confined himself to the cabin, where he kept Aouda company, or according to his inveterate habit, took a hand at whist.

Passepartout began very seriously to conjecture what strange chance kept Fix still on the route that his master was pursuing. It was really worth considering why this certainly very amiable and complacent person, whom he had first met at Suez, had then encountered on board the *Mongolia*, who disembarked at Bombay, which he announced as his destination, and now turned up so unexpectedly on the *Rangoon*, was following Mr. Fogg's tracks step by step. What was Fix's object? Passepartout was ready to wager his Indian shoes—which he religiously preserved—that Fix would also leave Hong Kong at the same time with them, and probably on the same steamer.

Passepartout might have cudgeled his brain for a century without hitting upon the real object which the detective had in view. He could never have imagined that Phileas Fogg was being tracked as a robber around the globe. But as it is in human nature to attempt the solution of every mystery, Passepartout suddenly discovered an explanation of Fix's movements, which was in truth far from unreasonable. Fix, he thought, could only be an agent of Mr. Fogg's friends at the Reform Club, sent to follow him up, and to ascertain that he really went around the world as had been agreed upon.

"It's clear!" repeated the worthy servant to himself, proud of his shrewdness. "He's a spy sent to keep us in view! That isn't quite the thing, either, to be spying on Mr. Fogg, who is so honourable a man! Ah, gentlemen of the Reform, this shall cost you dear!"

Passepartout, enchanted with his discovery, resolved to say nothing to his master, lest he should be justly offended at this mistrust on the part of his adversaries. But he determined to chaff Fix, when he had the chance, with mysterious allusions, which, however, need not betray his real suspicions.

During the afternoon of Wednesday, October 30th, the *Rangoon* entered the Strait of Malacca, which separates the peninsula of that name from Sumatra. The mountainous and craggy islets intercepted the beauties of this noble island from the view of the travellers. The *Rangoon* weighed anchor at Singapore the next day at four A.M., to receive coal, having gained half-a-day on the prescribed time of her arrival. Phileas Fogg noted this gain in his journal, and then, accompanied by Aouda, who betrayed a desire for a walk on shore, disembarked.

Fix, who suspected Mr. Fogg's every movement, followed them cautiously, without being himself perceived; while Passepartout, laughing in his sleeve at Fix's maneuvres, went about his usual errands.

The island of Singapore is not imposing in aspect, for there are no mountains; yet its appearance is not without attractions. It is a park checkered by pleasant highways and avenues. A handsome carriage, drawn by a sleek pair of New Holland horses, carried Phileas Fogg and Aouda into the midst of rows of palms with brilliant foliage, and of clove-trees, whereof the cloves form the heart of a half-open flower. Pepper plants replaced the prickly hedges of European fields; sago-bushes, large ferns with gorgeous branches, varied the aspect of this tropical clime; while nutmeg-trees in full foliage filled the air with a penetrating perfume. Agile and grinning bands of monkeys skipped about in the trees, nor were tigers wanting in the jungles.

After a drive of two hours through the country, Aouda and Mr. Fogg returned to the town, which is a vast collection of heavy-looking, irregular houses, surrounded by charming gardens rich in tropical fruits and plants; and at ten o'clock they re-embarked, closely followed by the detective, who had kept them constantly in sight.

Passepartout, who had been purchasing several dozen mangoes—a fruit as large as good-sized apples, of a dark-brown colour outside and a bright red within, and whose white pulp, melting in the mouth, affords gourmands a delicious sensation—was waiting for them on deck. He was only too glad to offer some mangoes to Aouda, who thanked him very gracefully for them.

At eleven o'clock the *Rangoon* rode out of Singapore harbour, and in a few hours the high mountains of Malacca, with their forests inhabited by the most beautifully-furred tigers in the world, were lost to view. Singapore is distant some thirteen hundred miles from the island of Hong Kong, which is a little English colony near the Chinese coast. Phileas Fogg hoped to accomplish the journey in six days, so as to be in time for the steamer which would leave on the 6th of November for Yokohama, the principal Japanese port.

The *Rangoon* had a large quota of passengers, many of whom disembarked at Singapore, among them a number of Indians, Ceylonese, Chinamen, Malays, and Portuguese, mostly second-class travellers.

The weather, which had hitherto been fine, changed with the last quarter of the moon. The sea rolled heavily, and the wind at intervals rose almost to a storm, but happily blew from the south-west, and thus aided the steamer's progress. The captain as often as possible put up his sails, and under the double action of steam and sail the vessel made rapid progress along the coasts of Anam and Cochin China. Owing to the defective construction of the *Rangoon*, however, unusual precautions became necessary in unfavorable weather; but the loss of time which resulted from this cause, while it nearly drove Passepartout out of his senses, did not seem to affect his master in the least. Passepartout blamed the captain, the engineer, and the crew, and consigned all who were connected with the ship to the land where the pepper grows. Perhaps the thought of the gas, which was remorselessly burning at his expense in Saville Row, had something to do with his hot impatience.

"You are in a great hurry, then," said Fix to him one day, "to reach Hong Kong?"

"A very great hurry!"

"Mr. Fogg, I suppose, is anxious to catch the steamer for Yokohama?"

"Terribly anxious."

"You believe in this journey around the world, then?"

"Absolutely. Don't you, Mr. Fix?"

"I? I don't believe a word of it."

"You're a sly dog!" said Passepartout, winking at him.

This expression rather disturbed Fix, without his knowing why. Had the Frenchman guessed his real purpose? He knew not what to think. But how could Passepartout have discovered that he was a detective? Yet, in speaking as he did, the man evidently meant more than he expressed.

Passepartout went still further the next day; he could not hold his tongue.

"Mr. Fix," said he, in a bantering tone; "shall we be so unfortunate as to lose you when we get to Hong Kong?"

"Why," responded Fix, a little embarrassed, "I don't know; perhaps—"

"Ah, if you would only go on with us! An agent of the Peninsular Company, you know, can't stop on the way! You were only going to Bombay, and here you are in China. America is not far off, and from America to Europe is only a step."

Fix looked intently at his companion, whose countenance was as serene as possible, and laughed with him. But Passepartout persisted in chaffing him by asking him if he made much by his present occupation.

"Yes, and no," returned Fix; "there is good and bad luck in such things. But you must understand that I don't travel at my own expense."

"Oh, I am quite sure of that!" cried Passepartout, laughing heartily.

Fix, fairly puzzled, descended to his cabin and gave himself up to his reflections. He was evidently suspected; somehow or other the Frenchman had found out that he was a detective. But had he told his master? What part was he playing in all this: was he an accomplice or not? Was the game, then, up? Fix spent several hours turning these things over in his mind, sometimes thinking that all was lost, then persuading himself that Fogg was ignorant of his presence, and then undecided what course it was best to take.

Nevertheless, he preserved his coolness of mind, and at last resolved to deal plainly with Passepartout. If he did not find it practicable to arrest Fogg at Hong Kong, and if Fogg made preparations to leave that last foothold of English territory, he, Fix, would tell Passepartout all. Either the servant was the accomplice of his master, and in this case the master knew of his operations, and he should fail; or else the servant knew nothing about the robbery, and then his interest would be to abandon the robber.

Such was the situation between Fix and Passepartout. Meanwhile Phileas Fogg moved about above them in the most majestic and unconscious indifference. He was passing methodically in his orbit around the world, regardless of the lesser stars which gravitated around him. Yet there was nearby what the astronomers would call a disturbing star, which might have produced an agitation in this gentleman's heart. But no! the charms of Aouda failed to act, to Passepartout's great surprise; and the disturbances, if they existed, would have been more difficult to calculate than those of Uranus which led to the discovery of Neptune.

It was everyday an increasing wonder to Passepartout, who read in Aouda's eyes the depths of her gratitude to his master. Phileas Fogg, though brave and gallant, must be, he thought, quite heartless. As to the sentiment which this journey might have awakened in him, there was clearly no trace of such a thing; while poor Passepartout existed in perpetual reveries.

One day he was leaning on the railing of the engine-room, and was observing the engine, when a sudden pitch of the steamer threw the screw out of the water. The steam came hissing out of the valves; and this made Passepartout indignant.

"The valves are not sufficiently charged!" he exclaimed. "We are not going. Oh, these English! If this was an American craft, we should blow up, perhaps, but we should at all events go faster!"

Chapter XVIII

IN WHICH PHILEAS FOGG, PASSEPARTOUT, AND FIX GO EACH ABOUT HIS BUSINESS

THE WEATHER WAS BAD DURING THE LATTER DAYS OF THE VOYAGE. THE WIND, OBSTI-nately remaining in the north-west, blew a gale, and retarded the steamer. The *Rangoon* rolled heavily, and the passengers became impatient of the long, monstrous waves which the wind raised before their path. A sort of tempest arose on the 3d of November, the squall knocking the vessel about with fury, and the waves running high. The *Rangoon* reefed all her sails, and even the rigging proved too much, whistling and shaking amid the squall. The steamer was forced to proceed slowly, and the captain estimated that she would reach Hong Kong twenty hours behind time, and more if the storm lasted.

Phileas Fogg gazed at the tempestuous sea, which seemed to be struggling especially to delay him, with his habitual tranquillity. He never changed countenance for an instant, though a delay of twenty hours, by making him too late for the Yokohama boat, would almost inevitably cause the loss of the wager. But this man of nerve manifested neither impatience nor annoyance; it seemed as if the storm were a part of his program, and had been foreseen. Aouda was amazed to find him as calm as he had been from the first time she saw him.

Fix did not look at the state of things in the same light. The storm greatly pleased him. His satisfaction would have been complete had the *Rangoon* been forced to retreat before the violence of wind and waves. Each delay filled him with hope, for it became more and more probable that Fogg would be obliged to remain some days at Hong Kong; and now the heavens themselves became his allies, with the gusts and squalls. It mattered not that they made him seasick—he made no account of this inconvenience; and whilst his body was writhing under their effects, his spirit bounded with hopeful exultation.

Passepartout was enraged beyond expression by the unpropitious weather. Every-thing had gone so well till now! Earth and sea had seemed to be at his master's service; steamers and railways obeyed him; wind and steam united to speed his journey. Had the hour of adversity come? Passepartout was as much excited as if the twenty thousand pounds were to come from his own pocket. The storm exasperated him, the gale made him furious, and he longed to lash the obstinate sea into obedience. Poor fellow! Fix carefully concealed from him his own satisfaction, for, had he betrayed it, Passepartout could scarcely have restrained himself from personal violence.

Passepartout remained on deck as long as the tempest lasted, being unable to remain quiet below, and taking it into his head to aid the progress of the ship by lending a hand with the crew. He overwhelmed the captain, officers, and sailors, who could not help laughing at his impatience, with all sorts of questions. He wanted to know exactly how long the storm was going to last; whereupon he was referred to the barometer, which seemed to have no intention of rising. Passepartout shook it, but with no perceptible effect; for neither shaking nor maledictions could prevail upon it to change its mind.

On the 4th, however, the sea became more calm, and the storm lessened its violence; the wind veered southward, and was once more favourable. Passepartout cleared up with the weather. Some of the sails were unfurled, and the *Rangoon* resumed its most rapid speed. The time lost could not, however, be regained. Land was not signaled until five o'clock on the morning of the 6th; the steamer was due on the 5th. Phileas Fogg was twenty-four hours behindhand, and the Yokohama steamer would, of course, be missed.

The pilot went on board at six, and took his place on the bridge, to guide the *Rangoon* through the channels to the port of Hong Kong. Passepartout longed to ask him if the steamer had left for Yokohama; but he dared not, for he wished to preserve the spark of hope, which still remained, till the last moment. He had confided his anxiety to Fix, who—the sly rascal!—tried to console him by saying that Mr. Fogg would be in time if he took the next boat; but this only put Passepartout in a passion.

Mr. Fogg, bolder than his servant, did not hesitate to approach the pilot, and tranquilly ask him if he knew when a steamer would leave Hong Kong for Yokohama.

"At high tide to-morrow morning," answered the pilot.

"Ah!" said Mr. Fogg, without betraying any astonishment.

Passepartout, who heard what passed, would willingly have embraced the pilot, while Fix would have been glad to twist his neck.

"What is the steamer's name?" asked Mr. Fogg.

"The *Carnatic*."

"Ought she not to have gone yesterday?"

"Yes, sir; but they had to repair one of her boilers, and so her departure was postponed till to-morrow."

"Thank you," returned Mr. Fogg, descending mathematically to the saloon.

Passepartout clasped the pilot's hand and shook it heartily in his delight, exclaiming, "Pilot, you are the best of good fellows!"

The pilot probably does not know to this day why his responses won him this enthusiastic greeting. He remounted the bridge, and guided the steamer through the flotilla of junks, tankas, and fishing-boats which crowd the harbor of Hong Kong.

At one o'clock the *Rangoon* was at the quay, and the passengers were going ashore.

Chance had strangely favoured Phileas Fogg, for, had not the *Carnatic* been forced to lie over for repairing her boilers, she would have left on the 6th of November, and the passengers for Japan would have been obliged to await for a week the sailing of the next steamer. Mr. Fogg was, it is true, twenty-four hours behind his time; but this could not seriously imperil the remainder of his tour.

The steamer which crossed the Pacific from Yokohama to San Francisco made a direct connection with that from Hong Kong, and it could not sail until the latter reached Yokohama; and if Mr. Fogg was twenty-four hours late on reaching Yokohama, this time would no doubt be easily regained in the voyage of twenty-two days across the Pacific. He found himself, then, about twenty-four hours behindhand, thirty-five days after leaving London.

The *Carnatic* was announced to leave Hong Kong at five the next morning. Mr. Fogg had sixteen hours in which to attend to his business there, which was to deposit Aouda safely with her wealthy relative.

On landing, he conducted her to a palanquin, in which they repaired to the Club Hotel. A room was engaged for the young woman, and Mr. Fogg, after seeing that she wanted for nothing, set out in search of her cousin Jeejeeh. He instructed Passepartout to remain at the hotel until his return, that Aouda might not be left entirely alone.

Mr. Fogg repaired to the Exchange, where, he did not doubt, everyone would know so wealthy and considerable a personage as the Parsee merchant. Meeting a broker, he made the enquiry, to learn that Jeejeeh had left China two years before, and, retiring from business with an immense fortune, had taken up his residence in Europe—in Holland, the broker thought, with the merchants of which country he had principally traded. Phileas Fogg returned to the hotel, begged a moment's conversation with Aouda, and, without more ado, apprised her that Jeejeeh was no longer at Hong Kong, but probably in Holland.

Aouda at first said nothing. She passed her hand across her forehead, and reflected a few moments. Then, in her sweet, soft voice, she said: "What ought I to do, Mr. Fogg?"

"It is very simple," responded the gentleman. "Go on to Europe."

"But I cannot intrude——"

"You do not intrude, nor do you in the least embarrass my project. Passepartout!"

"Monsieur."

"Go to the *Carnatic*, and engage three cabins."

Passepartout, delighted that the young woman, who was very gracious to him, was going to continue the journey with them, went off at a brisk gait to obey his master's order.

Chapter XIX

IN WHICH PASSEPARTOUT TAKES A TOO GREAT INTEREST IN HIS MASTER, AND WHAT COMES OF IT

HONG KONG IS AN ISLAND WHICH CAME INTO THE POSSESSION OF THE ENGLISH BY THE treaty of Nankin, after the war of 1842; and the colonising genius of the English has created upon it an important city and an excellent port. The island is situated at the mouth of the Canton River, and is separated by about sixty miles from the Portuguese town of Macao, on the opposite coast. Hong Kong has beaten Macao in the struggle for the Chinese trade, and now the greater part of the transportation of Chinese goods finds its dépôt at the former place. Docks, hospitals, wharves, a Gothic cathedral, a Government house, macadamised streets give to Hong Kong the appearance of a town in Kent or Surrey transferred by some strange magic to the antipodes.

Passepartout wandered, with his hands in his pockets, towards the Victoria port, gazing as he went at the curious palanquins and other modes of conveyance, and the groups of Chinese, Japanese, and Europeans who passed to and fro in the streets. Hong Kong seemed to him not unlike Bombay, Calcutta, and Singapore, since, like them, it betrayed everywhere the evidence of English supremacy. At the Victoria port he found a confused mass of ships of all nations: English, French, American, and Dutch, men-of-war and trading vessels, Japanese and Chinese junks, sempas, tankas, and flower-boats, which formed so many floating parterres. Passepartout noticed in the crowd a number of the natives who seemed very old and were dressed in yellow. On going into a barber's to get shaved he learned that these ancient men were all at least eighty years old, at which age they are permitted to wear yellow, which is the Imperial colour. Passepartout, without exactly knowing why, thought this very funny.

On reaching the quay where they were to embark on the *Carnatic*, he was not astonished to find Fix walking up and down. The detective seemed very much disturbed and disappointed.

"This is bad," muttered Passepartout, "for the gentlemen of the Reform Club!" He accosted Fix with a merry smile, as if he had not perceived that gentleman's chagrin. The detective had, indeed, good reasons to inveigh against the bad luck which pursued him. The warrant had not come! It was certainly on the way, but as certainly it could not now reach Hong Kong for several days; and this being the last English territory on Mr. Fogg's route, the robber would escape, unless he could manage to detain him.

"Well, Monsieur Fix," said Passepartout, "have you decided to go on with us as far as America?"

"Yes," returned Fix, through his set teeth.

"Good!" exclaimed Passepartout, laughing heartily. "I knew you could not persuade yourself to separate from us. Come and engage your berth."

They entered the steamer office and secured cabins for four persons. The clerk, as he gave them the tickets, informed them that, the repairs on the *Carnatic* having been completed, the steamer would leave that very evening, and not next morning as had been announced.

"That will suit my master all the better," said Passepartout. "I will go and let him know."

Fix now decided to make a bold move; he resolved to tell Passepartout all. It seemed to be the only possible means of keeping Phileas Fogg several days longer at Hong Kong. He accordingly invited his companion into a tavern which caught his eye on the quay. On entering, they found themselves in a large room handsomely decorated, at the end of which was a large camp-bed furnished with cushions. Several persons lay upon this bed in a deep sleep. At the same tables which were arranged about the room some thirty customers were drinking English beer, porter, gin, and brandy; smoking, the while, long red clay pipes stuffed with little balls of opium mingled with essence of rose. From time to time one of the smokers, overcome with the narcotic, would slip under the table, whereupon the waiters, taking him by the head and feet, carried and laid him upon the bed. The bed already supported twenty of these stupefied sots.

Fix and Passepartout saw that they were in a smoking-house haunted by those wretched, cadaverous, idiotic creatures, to whom the English merchants sell every year the miserable drug called opium, to the amount of one million four hundred thousand pounds—thousands devoted to one of the most despicable vices which afflict humanity!

The Chinese Government has in vain attempted to deal with the evil by stringent laws. It passed gradually from the rich, to whom it was at first exclusively reserved, to the lower classes, and then its ravages could not be arrested. Opium is smoked everywhere, at all times, by men and women, in the Celestial Empire; and, once accustomed to it, the victims cannot dispense with it, except by suffering horrible bodily contortions and agonies. A great smoker can smoke as many as eight pipes a day; but he dies in five years. It was in one of these dens that Fix and Passepartout, in search of a friendly glass, found themselves. Passepartout had no money, but willingly accepted Fix's invitation in the hope of returning the obligation at some future time.

They ordered two bottles of port, to which the Frenchman did ample justice, whilst Fix observed him with close attention. They chatted about the journey, and Passepartout was especially merry at the idea that Fix was going to continue it with them. When the bottles were empty, however, he rose to go and tell his master of the change in the time of the sailing of the *Carnatic*.

Fix caught him by the arm, and said, "Wait a moment."

"What for, Mr. Fix?"

"I want to have a serious talk with you."

"A serious talk!" cried Passepartout, drinking up the little wine that was left in the bottom of his glass. "Well, we'll talk about it to-morrow; I haven't time now."

"Stay! What I have to say concerns your master."

Passepartout, at this, looked attentively at his companion. Fix's face seemed to have a singular expression. He resumed his seat.

"What is it that you have to say?"

Fix placed his hand upon Passepartout's arm, and, lowering his voice, said, "You have guessed who I am?"

"Parbleu!" said Passepartout, smiling.

"Then I'm going to tell you everything—"

"Now that I know everything, my friend! Ah! that's very good. But go on, go on. First, though, let me tell you that those gentlemen have put themselves to a useless expense."

"Useless!" said Fix. "You speak confidently. It's clear that you don't know how large the sum is."

"Of course I do," returned Passepartout. "Twenty thousand pounds."

"Fifty-five thousand!" answered Fix, pressing his companion's hand.

"What!" cried the Frenchman. "Has Monsieur Fogg dared—fifty-five thousand pounds! Well, there's all the more reason for not losing an instant," he continued, getting up hastily.

Fix pushed Passepartout back in his chair, and resumed: "Fifty-five thousand pounds; and if I succeed, I get two thousand pounds. If you'll help me, I'll let you have five hundred of them."

"Help you?" cried Passepartout, whose eyes were standing wide open.

"Yes; help me keep Mr. Fogg here for two or three days."

"Why, what are you saying? Those gentlemen are not satisfied with following my master and suspecting his honour, but they must try to put obstacles in his way! I blush for them!"

"What do you mean?"

"I mean that it is a piece of shameful trickery. They might as well waylay Mr. Fogg and put his money in their pockets!"

"That's just what we count on doing."

"It's a conspiracy, then," cried Passepartout, who became more and more excited as the liquor mounted in his head, for he drank without perceiving it. "A real conspiracy! And gentlemen, too. Bah!"

Fix began to be puzzled.

"Members of the Reform Club!" continued Passepartout. "You must know, Monsieur Fix, that my master is an honest man, and that, when he makes a wager, he tries to win it fairly!"

"But who do you think I am?" asked Fix, looking at him intently.

"Parbleu! An agent of the members of the Reform Club, sent out here to interrupt my master's journey. But, though I found you out some time ago, I've taken good care to say nothing about it to Mr. Fogg."

"He knows nothing, then?"

"Nothing," replied Passepartout, again emptying his glass.

The detective passed his hand across his forehead, hesitating before he spoke again. What should he do? Passepartout's mistake seemed sincere, but it made his design more difficult. It was evident that the servant was not the master's accomplice, as Fix had been inclined to suspect.

"Well," said the detective to himself, "as he is not an accomplice, he will help me."

He had no time to lose: Fogg must be detained at Hong Kong, so he resolved to make a clean breast of it.

"Listen to me," said Fix abruptly. "I am not, as you think, an agent of the members of the Reform Club—"

"Bah!" retorted Passepartout, with an air of raillery.

"I am a police detective, sent out here by the London office."

"You, a detective?"

"I will prove it. Here is my commission."

Passepartout was speechless with astonishment when Fix displayed this document, the genuineness of which could not be doubted.

"Mr. Fogg's wager," resumed Fix, "is only a pretext, of which you and the gentlemen of the Reform are dupes. He had a motive for securing your innocent complicity."

"But why?"

"Listen. On the 28th of last September a robbery of fifty-five thousand pounds was committed at the Bank of England by a person whose description was fortunately secured. Here is his description; it answers exactly to that of Mr. Phileas Fogg."

"What nonsense!" cried Passepartout, striking the table with his fist. "My master is the most honourable of men!"

"How can you tell? You know scarcely anything about him. You went into his service the day he came away; and he came away on a foolish pretext, without trunks, and carrying a large amount in bank-notes. And yet you are bold enough to assert that he is an honest man!"

"Yes, yes," repeated the poor fellow, mechanically.

"Would you like to be arrested as his accomplice?"

Passepartout, overcome by what he had heard, held his head between his hands, and did not dare to look at the detective. Phileas Fogg, the savior of Aouda, that brave and generous man, a robber! And yet how many presumptions there were against him! Passepartout essayed to reject the suspicions which forced themselves upon his mind; he did not wish to believe that his master was guilty.

"Well, what do you want of me?" said he, at last, with an effort.

"See here," replied Fix; "I have tracked Mr. Fogg to this place, but as yet I have failed to receive the warrant of arrest for which I sent to London. You must help me to keep him here in Hong Kong—"

"I! But I—"

"I will share with you the two thousand pounds reward offered by the Bank of England."

"Never!" replied Passepartout, who tried to rise, but fell back, exhausted in mind and body.

"Mr. Fix," he stammered; "even should what you say be true—if my master is really the robber you are seeking for—which I deny—I have been, am, in his service; I have seen his generosity and goodness; and I will never betray him—not for all the gold in the world. I come from a village where they don't eat that kind of bread!"

"You refuse?"

"I refuse."

"Consider that I've said nothing," said Fix; "and let us drink."

"Yes; let us drink!"

Passepartout felt himself yielding more and more to the effects of the liquor. Fix, seeing that he must, at all hazards, be separated from his master, wished to entirely overcome him. Some pipes full of opium lay upon the table. Fix slipped one into Passepartout's hand. He took it, put it between his lips, lit it, drew several puffs, and his head, becoming heavy under the influence of the narcotic, fell upon the table.

"At last!" said Fix, seeing Passepartout unconscious. "Mr. Fogg will not be informed of the *Carnatic*'s departure; and, if he is, he will have to go without this cursed Frenchman!"

And, after paying his bill, Fix left the tavern.

Chapter XX

IN WHICH FIX COMES FACE TO FACE WITH PHILEAS FOGG

WHILE THESE EVENTS WERE PASSING AT THE OPIUM-HOUSE, MR. FOGG, UNCONSCIOUS of the danger he was in of losing the steamer, was quietly escorting Aouda about the streets of the English quarter, making the necessary purchases for the long voyage before them. It was all very well for an Englishman like Mr. Fogg to make the tour of the world with a carpet-bag; a lady could not be expected to travel comfortably under such conditions. He acquitted his task with characteristic serenity, and invariably replied to the remonstrances of his fair companion, who was confused by his patience and generosity—

"It is in the interest of my journey—a part of my programme."

The purchases made, they returned to the hotel, where they dined at a sumptuously served *table-d'hôte;* after which Aouda, shaking hands with her protector after the English fashion, retired to her room for rest. Mr. Fogg absorbed himself throughout the evening in the perusal of the *Times* and *Illustrated London News.*

Had he been capable of being astonished at anything, it would have been not to see his servant return at bed-time. But, knowing that the steamer was not to leave for Yokohama until the next morning, he did not disturb himself about the matter. When Passepartout did not appear the next morning to answer his master's bell, Mr. Fogg, not betraying the least vexation, contented himself with taking his carpet-bag, calling Aouda, and sending for a palanquin.

It was then eight o'clock; at half-past nine, it being then high tide, the *Carnatic* would leave the harbor. Mr. Fogg and Aouda got into the palanquin, their luggage being brought after on a wheelbarrow, and half-an-hour later stepped upon the quay whence they were to embark. Mr. Fogg then learned that the *Carnatic* had sailed the evening before. He had expected to find not only the steamer, but his domestic, and was forced to give up both; but no sign of disappointment appeared on his face, and he merely remarked to Aouda, "It is an accident, madam; nothing more."

At this moment a man who had been observing him attentively approached. It was Fix, who, bowing, addressed Mr. Fogg: "Were you not, like me, sir, a passenger by the *Rangoon,* which arrived yesterday?"

"I was, sir," replied Mr. Fogg coldly. "But I have not the honour—"

"Pardon me; I thought I should find your servant here."

"Do you know where he is, sir?" asked Aouda anxiously.

"What!" responded Fix, feigning surprise. "Is he not with you?"

"No," said Aouda. "He has not made his appearance since yesterday. Could he have gone on board the *Carnatic* without us?"

"Without you, madam?" answered the detective. "Excuse me, did you intend to sail in the *Carnatic?*"

"Yes, sir."

"So did I, madam, and I am excessively disappointed. The *Carnatic,* its repairs being completed, left Hong Kong twelve hours before the stated time, without any notice being given; and we must now wait a week for another steamer."

As he said "a week" Fix felt his heart leap for joy. Fogg detained at Hong Kong a week! There would be time for the warrant to arrive, and fortune at last favoured the representative of the law. His horror may be imagined when he heard Mr. Fogg say, in his placid voice, "But there are other vessels besides the *Carnatic,* it seems to me, in the harbor of Hong Kong."

And, offering his arm to Aouda, he directed his steps towards the docks in search of some craft about to start. Fix, stupefied, followed; it seemed as if he were attached to Mr. Fogg by an invisible thread. Chance, however, appeared really to have abandoned the man it had hitherto served so well. For three hours Phileas Fogg wandered about the docks, with the determination, if necessary, to charter a vessel to carry him to Yokohama; but he could only find vessels which were loading or unloading, and which could not therefore set sail. Fix began to hope again.

But Mr. Fogg, far from being discouraged, was continuing his search, resolved not to stop if he had to resort to Macao, when he was accosted by a sailor on one of the wharves.

"Is your honour looking for a boat?"

"Have you a boat ready to sail?"

"Yes, your honour; a pilot-boat—No. 43—the best in the harbour."

"Does she go fast?"

"Between eight and nine knots the hour. Will you look at her?"

"Yes."

"Your honour will be satisfied with her. Is it for a sea excursion?"

"No; for a voyage."

"A voyage?"

"Yes; will you agree to take me to Yokohama?"

The sailor leaned on the railing, opened his eyes wide, and said, "Is your honour joking?"

"No. I have missed the *Carnatic,* and I must get to Yokohama by the 14th at the latest, to take the boat for San Francisco."

"I am sorry," said the sailor; "but it is impossible."

"I offer you a hundred pounds per day, and an additional reward of two hundred pounds if I reach Yokohama in time."

"Are you in earnest?"

"Very much so."

The pilot walked away a little distance, and gazed out to sea, evidently struggling between the anxiety to gain a large sum and the fear of venturing so far. Fix was in mortal suspense.

Mr. Fogg turned to Aouda and asked her, "You would not be afraid, would you, madam?"

"Not with you, Mr. Fogg," was her answer.

The pilot now returned, shuffling his hat in his hands.

"Well, pilot?" said Mr. Fogg.

"Well, your honour," replied he; "I could not risk myself, my men, or my little boat of scarcely twenty tons on so long a voyage at this time of year. Besides, we could not reach Yokohama in time, for it is sixteen hundred and sixty miles from Hong Kong."

"Only sixteen hundred," said Mr. Fogg.

"It's the same thing."

Fix breathed more freely.

"But," added the pilot; "it might be arranged another way."

Fix ceased to breathe at all.

"How?" asked Mr. Fogg.

"By going to Nagasaki, at the extreme south of Japan, or even to Shanghai, which is only eight hundred miles from here. In going to Shanghai we should not be forced to sail wide of the Chinese coast, which would be a great advantage, as the currents run northward, and would aid us."

"Pilot," said Mr. Fogg, "I must take the American steamer at Yokohama, and not at Shanghai or Nagasaki."

"Why not?" returned the pilot. "The San Francisco steamer does not start from Yokohama. It puts in at Yokohama and Nagasaki, but it starts from Shanghai."

"You are sure of that?"

"Perfectly."

"And when does the boat leave Shanghai?"

"On the 11th, at seven in the evening. We have, therefore, four days before us, that is ninety-six hours; and in that time, if we had good luck and a south-west wind, and the sea was calm, we could make those eight hundred miles to Shanghai."

"And you could go—"

"In an hour; as soon as provisions could be got aboard and the sails put up."

"It is a bargain. Are you the master of the boat?"

"Yes; John Bunsby, master of the *Tankadere*."

"Would you like some earnest-money?"

"If it would not put your honour out—"

"Here are two hundred pounds on account. Sir," added Phileas Fogg, turning to Fix, "if you would like to take advantage—"

"Thanks, sir; I was about to ask the favour."

"Very well. In half-an-hour we shall go on board."

"But poor Passepartout?" urged Aouda, who was much disturbed by the servant's disappearance.

"I shall do all I can to find him," replied Phileas Fogg.

While Fix, in a feverish, nervous state, repaired to the pilot-boat the others directed their course to the police-station at Hong Kong. Phileas Fogg there gave Passepartout's description, and left a sum of money to be spent in the search for him. The same formalities having been gone through at the French consulate, and the palanquin having stopped at the hotel for the luggage, which had been sent back there, they returned to the wharf.

It was now three o'clock; and pilot-boat No. 43, with its crew on board, and its provisions stored away, was ready for departure.

The *Tankadere* was a neat little craft of twenty tons, as gracefully built as if she were a racing yacht. Her shining copper sheathing, her galvanised iron-work, her deck, white as ivory, betrayed the pride taken by John Bunsby in making her presentable. Her two masts leaned a trifle backward; she carried brigantine, foresail, storm-jib, and standing-jib, and was well rigged for running before the wind; and she seemed capable of brisk speed, which, indeed, she had already proved by gaining several prizes in pilot-boat races. The crew of the *Tankadere* was composed of John Bunsby, the master, and four hardy mariners, who were familiar with the Chinese seas. John Bunsby himself, a man of forty-five or thereabouts, vigorous, sunburned, with a sprightly expression of the eye, and energetic and self-reliant countenance, would have inspired confidence in the most timid.

Phileas Fogg and Aouda went on board, where they found Fix already installed. Below deck was a square cabin, of which the walls bulged out in the form of cots, above a circular divan; in the centre was a table provided with a swinging lamp. The accommodation was confined, but neat.

"I am sorry to have nothing better to offer you," said Mr. Fogg to Fix, who bowed without responding.

The detective had a feeling akin to humiliation in profiting by the kindness of Mr. Fogg.

"It's certain," thought he, "though rascal as he is, he is a polite one!"

The sails and the English flag were hoisted at ten minutes past three. Mr. Fogg and Aouda, who were seated on deck, cast a last glance at the quay, in the hope of espying Passepartout. Fix was not without his fears lest chance should direct the steps of the unfortunate servant, whom he had so badly treated, in this direction; in which case an explanation the reverse of satisfactory to the detective must have ensued. But the Frenchman did not appear, and, without doubt, was still lying under the stupefying influence of the opium.

John Bunsby, master, at length gave the order to start, and the *Tankadere*, taking the wind under her brigantine, foresail, and standing-jib, bounded briskly forward over the waves.

Chapter XXI

IN WHICH THE MASTER OF THE TANKADERE RUNS GREAT RISK OF LOSING A REWARD OF TWO HUNDRED POUNDS

THIS VOYAGE OF EIGHT HUNDRED MILES WAS A PERILOUS VENTURE, ON A CRAFT OF twenty tons, and at that season of the year, the Chinese seas are usually boisterous, subject to terrible gales of wind, and especially during the equinoxes; and it was now early November.

It would clearly have been to the master's advantage to carry his passengers to Yokohama, since he was paid a certain sum per day; but he would have been rash to attempt such a voyage, and it was imprudent even to attempt to reach Shanghai. But John Bunsby believed in the *Tankadere*, which rode on the waves like a sea-gull; and perhaps he was not wrong.

Late in the day they passed through the capricious channels of Hong Kong, and the *Tankadere*, impelled by favourable winds, conducted herself admirably.

"I do not need, pilot," said Phileas Fogg, when they got into the open sea, "to advise you to use all possible speed."

"Trust me, your honour. We are carrying all the sail the wind will let us. The poles would add nothing, and are only used when we are going into port."

"Its your trade, not mine, pilot, and I confide in you."

Phileas Fogg, with body erect and legs wide apart, standing like a sailor, gazed without staggering at the swelling waters. The young woman, who was seated aft, was profoundly affected as she looked out upon the ocean, darkening now with the twilight, on which she had ventured in so frail a vessel. Above her head rustled the white sails, which seemed like great white wings. The boat, carried forward by the wind, seemed to be flying in the air.

Night came. The moon was entering her first quarter, and her insufficient light would soon die out in the mist on the horizon. Clouds were rising from the east, and already overcast a part of the heavens.

The pilot had hung out his lights, which was very necessary in these seas crowded with vessels bound landward; for collisions are not uncommon occurrences, and, at the speed she was going the least shock would shatter the gallant little craft.

Fix, seated in the bow, gave himself up to meditation. He kept apart from his fellow-travellers, knowing Mr. Fogg's taciturn tastes; besides, he did not quite like to talk to the man whose favours he had accepted. He was thinking, too, of the future. It seemed certain that Fogg would not stop at Yokohama, but would at once take the boat for San Francisco; and the vast extent of America would ensure him impunity and safety. Fogg's plan appeared to him the simplest in the world. Instead of sailing directly from England to the United States, like a common villain, he had traversed three-quarters of the globe, so as to gain the American continent more surely; and there, after throwing the police off his track, he would quietly enjoy himself with the fortune stolen from the bank. But, once in the United States, what should he, Fix, do? Should he abandon this man? No, a hundred times no! Until he had secured his extradition, he would not lose sight of him for an hour. It was his duty, and he would fulfil it to the end. At all events, there was one thing to be thankful for; Passe-partout was not with his master; and it was above all important, after the confidences Fix had imparted to him, that the servant should never have speech with his master.

Phileas Fogg was also thinking of Passepartout, who had so strangely disappeared. Looking at the matter from every point of view, it did not seem to him impossible that, by some mistake, the man might have embarked on the *Carnatic* at the last moment; and this was also Aouda's opinion, who regretted very much the loss of the worthy fellow to whom she owed so much. They might then find him at Yokohama; for, if the *Carnatic* was carrying him thither, it would be easy to ascertain if he had been on board.

A brisk breeze arose about ten o'clock; but, though it might have been prudent to take in a reef, the pilot, after carefully examining the heavens, let the craft remain rigged as before. The *Tankadere* bore sail admirably, as she drew a great deal of water, and everything was prepared for high speed in case of a gale.

Mr. Fogg and Aouda descended into the cabin at midnight, having been already preceded by Fix, who had lain down on one of the cots. The pilot and crew remained on deck all night.

At sunrise the next day, which was November 8th, the boat had made more than one hundred miles. The log indicated a mean speed of between eight and nine miles. The *Tankadere* still carried all sail, and was accomplishing her greatest capacity of speed. If the wind held as it was, the chances would be in her favour. During the day she kept along the coast, where the currents were favourable; the coast, irregular in profile, and visible sometimes across the clearings, was at most five miles distant. The sea was less boisterous, since the wind came off land—a fortunate circumstance for the boat, which would suffer, owing to its small tonnage, by a heavy surge on the sea.

The breeze subsided a little towards noon, and set in from the south-west. The pilot put up his poles, but took them down again within two hours, as the wind freshened up anew.

Mr. Fogg and Aouda, happily unaffected by the roughness of the sea, ate with a good appetite, Fix being invited to share their repast, which he accepted with secret chagrin. To travel at this man's expense and live upon his provisions was not palatable to him. Still, he was obliged to eat, and so he ate.

When the meal was over, he took Mr. Fogg apart, and said, "Sir"—this "sir" scorched his lips, and he had to control himself to avoid collaring this "gentleman,"—"sir, you have been very kind to give me a passage on this boat. But, though my means will not admit of my expending them as freely as you, I must ask to pay my share—"

"Let us not speak of that, sir," replied Mr. Fogg.

"But, if I insist—"

"No, sir," repeated Mr. Fogg, in a tone which did not admit of a reply. "This enters into my general expenses."

Fix, as he bowed, had a stifled feeling, and going forward, where he ensconced himself, did not open his mouth for the rest of the day.

Meanwhile they were progressing famously, and John Bunsby was in high hope. He several times assured Mr. Fogg that they would reach Shanghai in time; to which that gentleman responded that he counted upon it. The crew set to work in good earnest, inspired by the reward to be gained. There was not a sheet which was not tightened, not a sail which was not vigorously hoisted; not a lurch could be charged to the man at the helm. They worked as desperately as if they were contesting in a Royal Yacht regatta.

By evening, the log showed that two hundred and twenty miles had been accomplished from Hong Kong, and Mr. Fogg might hope that he would be able to reach Yokohama without recording any delay in his journal; in which case, the only misadventure which had overtaken him since he left London would not seriously affect his journey.

The *Tankadere* entered the Straits of Fo-Kien, which separate the island of Formosa from the Chinese coast, in the small hours of the night, and crossed the Tropic of Cancer. The sea was very rough in the straits, full of eddies formed by the counter-currents, and the chopping waves broke her course, whilst it became very difficult to stand on deck.

At daybreak the wind began to blow hard again, and the heavens seemed to predict a gale. The barometer announced a speedy change, the mercury rising and falling capriciously; the sea also, in the south-east, raised long surges which indicated a tempest. The sun had set the evening before in a red mist, in the midst of the phosphorescent scintillations of the ocean.

John Bunsby long examined the threatening aspect of the heavens, muttering indistinctly between his teeth. At last he said in a low voice to Mr. Fogg, "Shall I speak out to your honour?"

"Of course."

"Well, we are going to have a squall."

"Is the wind north or south?" asked Mr. Fogg quietly.

"South. Look! a typhoon is coming up."

"Glad it's a typhoon from the south, for it will carry us forward."

"Oh, if you take it that way," said John Bunsby, "I've nothing more to say." John Bunsby's suspicions were confirmed. At a less advanced season of the year the typhoon, according to a famous meteorologist, would have passed away like a luminous cascade of electric flame; but in the winter equinox, it was to be feared that it would burst upon them with great violence.

The pilot took his precautions in advance. He reefed all sail, the pole-masts were dispensed with; all hands went forward to the bows. A single triangular sail, of strong canvas, was hoisted as a storm-jib, so as to hold the wind from behind. Then they waited.

John Bunsby had requested his passengers to go below; but this imprisonment in so narrow a space, with little air, and the boat bouncing in the gale, was far from pleasant. Neither Mr. Fogg, Fix, nor Aouda consented to leave the deck.

The storm of rain and wind descended upon them towards eight o'clock. With but its bit of sail, the *Tankadere* was lifted like a feather by a wind, an idea of whose violence can scarcely be given. To compare her speed to four times that of a locomotive going on full steam would be below the truth.

The boat scudded thus northward during the whole day, borne on by monstrous waves, preserving always, fortunately, a speed equal to theirs. Twenty times she seemed almost to be submerged by these mountains of water which rose behind her; but the adroit management of the pilot saved her. The passengers were often bathed in spray, but they submitted to it philosophically. Fix cursed it, no doubt; but Aouda, with her eyes fastened upon her protector, whose coolness amazed her, showed herself worthy of him, and bravely weathered the storm. As for Phileas Fogg, it seemed just as if the typhoon were a part of his program.

Up to this time the *Tankadere* had always held her course to the north; but towards evening the wind, veering three-quarters, bore down from the north-west. The boat, now lying in the trough of the waves, shook and rolled terribly; the sea struck her with fearful violence. At night the tempest increased in violence. John Bunsby saw the approach of darkness and the rising of the storm with dark misgivings. He thought a while, and then asked his crew if it was not time to slacken speed. After a consultation he approached Mr. Fogg, and said, "I think, your honour, that we should do well to make for one of the ports on the coast."

"I think so too."

"Ah!" said the pilot. "But which one?"

"I know of but one," returned Mr. Fogg tranquilly.

"And that is—"

"Shanghai."

The pilot, at first, did not seem to comprehend; he could scarcely realise so much determination and tenacity. Then he cried, "Well—yes! Your honour is right. To Shanghai!"

So the *Tankadere* kept steadily on her northward track.

The night was really terrible; it would be a miracle if the craft did not founder. Twice it could have been all over with her if the crew had not been constantly on the watch. Aouda was exhausted, but did not utter a complaint. More than once Mr. Fogg rushed to protect her from the violence of the waves.

Day reappeared. The tempest still raged with undiminished fury; but the wind now returned to the south-east. It was a favourable change, and the *Tankadere* again bounded forward on this mountainous sea, though the waves crossed each other, and imparted shocks and counter-shocks which would have crushed a craft less solidly built. From time to time the coast was visible through the broken mist, but no vessel was in sight. The *Tankadere* was alone upon the sea.

There were some signs of a calm at noon, and these became more distinct as the sun descended towards the horizon. The tempest had been as brief as terrific. The passengers, thoroughly exhausted, could now eat a little, and take some repose.

The night was comparatively quiet. Some of the sails were again hoisted, and the speed of the boat was very good. The next morning at dawn they espied the coast, and John Bunsby was able to assert that they were not one hundred miles from Shanghai. A hundred miles, and only one day to traverse them! That very evening Mr. Fogg was due at Shanghai, if he did not wish to miss the steamer to Yokohama. Had there been no storm, during which several hours were lost, they would be at this moment within thirty miles of their destination.

The wind grew decidedly calmer, and happily the sea fell with it. All sails were now hoisted, and at noon the *Tankadere* was within forty-five miles of Shanghai. There remained yet six hours in which to accomplish that distance. All on board feared that it could not be done, and everyone—Phileas Fogg, no doubt, excepted—felt his heart beat with impatience. The boat must keep up an average of nine miles an hour, and the wind was becoming calmer every moment! It was a capricious breeze, coming from the coast, and after it passed the sea became smooth. Still, the *Tankadere* was so light, and her fine sails caught the fickle zephyrs so well, that, with the aid of the current, John Bunsby found himself at six o'clock not more than ten miles from the mouth of the Shanghai River. Shanghai itself is situated at least twelve miles up the stream. At seven they were still three miles from Shanghai. The pilot swore an angry oath; the reward of two hundred pounds was evidently on the point of escaping him. He looked at Mr. Fogg. Mr. Fogg was perfectly tranquil; and yet his whole fortune was at this moment at stake.

At this moment, also, a long black funnel crowned with wreaths of smoke, appeared on the edge of the waters. It was the American steamer, leaving for Yokohama at the appointed time.

"Confound her!" cried John Bunsby, pushing back the rudder with a desperate jerk.

"Signal her!" said Phileas Fogg quietly.

A small brass cannon stood on the forward deck of the *Tankadere*, for making signals in the fogs. It was loaded to the muzzle; but just as the pilot was about to apply a red-hot coal to the touch-hole, Mr. Fogg said, "Hoist your flag!"

The flag was run up at half-mast, and, this being the signal of distress, it was hoped that the American steamer, perceiving it, would change her course a little, so as to succour the pilot-boat.

"Fire!" said Mr. Fogg. And the booming of the little cannon resounded in the air.

Chapter XXII

IN WHICH PASSEPARTOUT FINDS OUT THAT, EVEN AT THE ANTIPODES, IT IS CONVENIENT TO HAVE SOME MONEY IN ONE'S POCKET

THE *CARNATIC*, SETTING SAIL FROM HONG KONG AT HALF-PAST SIX ON THE 7TH OF NOvember, directed her course at full steam towards Japan. She carried a large cargo and a well-filled cabin of passengers. Two state-rooms in the rear were, however, unoccupied—those which had been engaged by Phileas Fogg.

The next day a passenger with a half-stupefied eye, staggering gait, and disordered hair, was seen to emerge from the second cabin, and to totter to a seat on deck.

It was Passepartout; and what had happened to him was as follows: Shortly after Fix left the opium den, two waiters had lifted the unconscious Passepartout, and had carried him to the bed reserved for the smokers. Three hours later, pursued even in his dreams by a fixed idea, the poor fellow awoke, and struggled against the stupefying influence of the narcotic. The thought of a duty unfulfilled shook off his torpor, and he hurried from the abode of drunkenness. Staggering and holding himself up by keeping against the walls, falling down, and creeping up again, and irresistibly impelled by a kind of instinct, he kept crying out, "The *Carnatic!* the *Carnatic!*"

The steamer lay puffing alongside the quay, on the point of starting. Passepartout had but few steps to go; and, rushing upon the plank, he crossed it, and fell unconscious on the deck, just as the *Carnatic* was moving off. Several sailors, who were evidently accustomed to this sort of scene, carried the poor Frenchman down into the second cabin, and Passepartout did not wake until they were one hundred and fifty miles away from China. Thus he found himself the next morning on the deck of the *Carnatic,* and eagerly inhaling the exhilarating sea-breeze. The pure air sobered him. He began to collect his senses, which he found a difficult task; but at last he recalled the events of the evening before, Fix's revelation, and the opium-house.

"It is evident," said he to himself, "that I have been abominably drunk! What will Mr. Fogg say? At least I have not missed the steamer, which is the most important thing."

Then, as Fix occurred to him: "As for that rascal, I hope we are well rid of him, and that he has not dared, as he proposed, to follow us on board the *Carnatic.* A detective on the track of Mr. Fogg, accused of robbing the Bank of England! Pshaw! Mr. Fogg is no more a robber than I am a murderer."

Should he divulge Fix's real errand to his master? Would it do to tell the part the detective was playing? Would it not be better to wait until Mr. Fogg reached London again, and then impart to him that an agent of the metropolitan police had been following him around the world, and have a good laugh over it? No doubt; at least, it was worth considering. The first thing to do was to find Mr. Fogg, and apologise for his singular behaviour.

Passepartout got up and proceeded, as well as he could with the rolling of the steamer, to the after-deck. He saw no one who resembled either his master or Aouda. "Good!" muttered he; "Aouda has not got up yet, and Mr. Fogg has probably found some partners at whist."

He descended to the saloon. Mr. Fogg was not there. Passepartout had only, however, to ask the purser the number of his master's state-room. The purser replied that he did not know any passenger by the name of Fogg.

"I beg your pardon," said Passepartout persistently. "He is a tall gentleman, quiet, and not very talkative, and has with him a young lady—"

"There is no young lady on board," interrupted the purser. "Here is a list of the passengers; you may see for yourself."

Passepartout scanned the list, but his master's name was not upon it. All at once an idea struck him.

"Ah! am I on the *Carnatic?*"

"Yes."

"On the way to Yokohama?"

"Certainly."

Passepartout had for an instant feared that he was on the wrong boat; but, though he was really on the *Carnatic*, his master was not there.

He fell thunderstruck on a seat. He saw it all now. He remembered that the time of sailing had been changed, that he should have informed his master of that fact, and that he had not done so. It was his fault, then, that Mr. Fogg and Aouda had missed the steamer. Yes, but it was still more the fault of the traitor who, in order to separate him from his master, and detain the latter at Hong Kong, had inveigled him into getting drunk! He now saw the detective's trick; and at this moment Mr. Fogg was certainly ruined, his bet was lost, and he himself perhaps arrested and imprisoned! At this thought Passepartout tore his hair. Ah, if Fix ever came within his reach, what a settling of accounts there would be!

After his first depression, Passepartout became calmer, and began to study his situation. It was certainly not an enviable one. He found himself on the way to Japan, and what should he do when he got there? His pocket was empty; he had not a solitary shilling—not so much as a penny. His passage had fortunately been paid for in advance; and he had five or six days in which to decide upon his future course. He fell to at meals with an appetite, and ate for Mr. Fogg, Aouda, and himself. He helped himself as generously as if Japan were a desert, where nothing to eat was to be looked for.

At dawn on the 13th the *Carnatic* entered the port of Yokohama. This is an important way-station in the Pacific, where all the mail-steamers, and those carrying travellers between North America, China, Japan, and the Oriental islands, put in. It is situated in the bay of Yeddo, and at but a short distance from that second capital of the Japanese Empire, and the residence of the Tycoon, the civil Emperor, before the Mikado, the spiritual Emperor, absorbed his office in his own. The *Carnatic* anchored at the quay near the custom-house, in the midst of a crowd of ships bearing the flags of all nations.

Passepartout went timidly ashore on this so curious territory of the Sons of the Sun. He had nothing better to do than, taking chance for his guide, to wander aimlessly through the streets of Yokohama. He found himself at first in a thoroughly European quarter, the houses having low fronts, and being adorned with verandas, beneath which he caught glimpses of neat peristyles. This quarter occupied, with its streets, squares, docks, and warehouses, all the space between the "promontory of the Treaty" and the river. Here, as at Hong Kong and Calcutta, were mixed crowds of all races—Americans and English, Chinamen and Dutchmen, mostly merchants ready to buy or sell anything. The Frenchman felt himself as much alone among them as if he had dropped down in the midst of Hottentots.

He had, at least, one resource—to call on the French and English consuls at Yokohama for assistance. But he shrank from telling the story of his adventures, intimately connected as it was with that of his master; and, before doing so, he determined to exhaust all other means of aid. As chance did not favour him in the European quarter, he penetrated that inhabited by the native Japanese, determined, if necessary, to push on to Yeddo.

The Japanese quarter of Yokohama is called Benten, after the goddess of the sea, who is worshipped on the islands round about. There Passepartout beheld beautiful fir and cedar groves, sacred gates of a singular architecture, bridges half hid in the midst of bamboos and reeds, temples shaded by immense cedar-trees, holy retreats where were sheltered Buddhist priests and sectaries of Confucius, and interminable streets, where a perfect harvest of rose-tinted and red-cheeked children, who looked as if they had been cut out of

Japanese screens, and who were playing in the midst of short-legged poodles and yellowish cats, might have been gathered.

The streets were crowded with people. Priests were passing in processions, beating their dreary tambourines; police and custom-house officers with pointed hats encrusted with lac, and carrying two sabres hung to their waists; soldiers, clad in blue cotton with white stripes, and bearing guns; the Mikado's guards, enveloped in silken doublets, hauberks, and coats of mail; and numbers of military folk of all ranks—for the military profession is as much respected in Japan as it is despised in China—went hither and thither in groups and pairs. Passepartout saw, too, begging friars, long-robed pilgrims, and simple civilians, with their warped and jet-black hair, big heads, long busts, slender legs, short stature, and complexions varying from copper-color to a dead white, but never yellow, like the Chinese, from whom the Japanese widely differ. He did not fail to observe the curious equipages—carriages and palanquins, barrows supplied with sails, and litters made of bamboo; nor the women—whom he thought not especially handsome—who took little steps with their little feet, whereon they wore canvas shoes, straw sandals, and clogs of worked wood, and who displayed tight-looking eyes, flat chests, teeth fashionably blackened, and gowns crossed with silken scarfs, tied in an enormous knot behind—an ornament which the modern Parisian ladies seem to have borrowed from the dames of Japan.

Passepartout wandered for several hours in the midst of this motley crowd, looking in at the windows of the rich and curious shops, the jewelery establishments glittering with quaint Japanese ornaments, the restaurants decked with streamers and banners, the teahouses, where the odorous beverage was being drunk with "saki," a liquor concocted from the fermentation of rice, and the comfortable smoking-houses, where they were puffing, not opium, which is almost unknown in Japan, but a very fine, stringy tobacco. He went on till he found himself in the fields, in the midst of vast rice plantations. There he saw dazzling camelias expanding themselves, with flowers which were giving forth their last colours and perfumes, not on bushes, but on trees; and within bamboo enclosures, cherry-, plum-, and apple-trees, which the Japanese cultivate rather for their blossoms than their fruit, and which queerly-fashioned grinning scarecrows protected from the sparrows, pigeons, ravens, and other voracious birds. On the branches of the cedars were perched large eagles; amid the foliage of the weeping willows were herons, solemnly standing on one leg; and on every hand were crows, ducks, hawks, wild birds, and a multitude of cranes, which the Japanese consider sacred, and which to their minds symbolise long life and prosperity.

As he was strolling alone, Passepartout espied some violets among the shrubs.

"Good!" said he; "I'll have some supper."

But, on smelling them, he found that they were odorless.

"No chance there," thought he.

The worthy fellow had certainly taken good care to eat as hearty a breakfast as possible before leaving the *Carnatic;* but as he had been walking about all day, the demands of hunger were becoming importunate. He observed that the butchers' stalls contained neither mutton, goat, nor pork; and knowing also that it is a sacrilege to kill cattle, which are preserved solely for farming, he made up his mind that meat was far from plentiful in Yokohama—nor was he mistaken; and in default of butcher's meat, he could have wished for a quarter of wild boar or deer, a partridge, or some quails, some game or fish, which, with rice, the Japanese eat almost exclusively. But he found it necessary to keep up a stout heart, and to postpone the meal he craved till the following morning. Night came, and Passepartout re-entered the native quarter, where he wandered through the streets, lit by vari-coloured lanterns, looking on at the dancers who were executing skilful steps and boundings, and the astrologers who stood in the open air with their telescopes. Then he came to the harbour, which was lit up by the rosin torches of the fishermen, who were fishing from their boats.

The streets at last became quiet, and the patrol, the officers of which, in their splendid costumes, and surrounded by their suites, Passepartout thought seemed like ambassadors, succeeded the bustling crowd. Each time a company passed, Passepartout chuckled, and said to himself: "Good! another Japanese embassy departing for Europe!"

Chapter XXIII

IN WHICH PASSEPARTOUT'S NOSE BECOMES OUTRAGEOUSLY LONG

THE NEXT MORNING POOR, JADED, FAMISHED PASSEPARTOUT SAID TO HIMSELF THAT HE must get something to eat at all hazards, and the sooner he did so the better. He might, indeed, sell his watch; but he would have starved first. Now or never he must use the strong, if not melodious voice which nature had bestowed upon him. He knew several French and English songs, and resolved to try them upon the Japanese, who must be lovers of music, since they were forever pounding on their cymbals, tam-tams, and tambourines, and could not but appreciate European talent.

It was, perhaps, rather early in the morning to get up a concert, and the audience, prematurely aroused from their slumbers, might not, possibly, pay their entertainer with coin bearing the Mikado's features. Passepartout therefore decided to wait several hours; and, as he was sauntering along, it occurred to him that he would seem rather too well dressed for a wandering artist. The idea struck him to change his garments for clothes more in harmony with his project; by which he might also get a little money to satisfy the immediate cravings of hunger. The resolution taken, it remained to carry it out.

It was only after a long search that Passepartout discovered a native dealer in old clothes, to whom he applied for an exchange. The man liked the European costume, and ere long Passepartout issued from his shop accoutred in an old Japanese coat, and a sort of one-sided turban, faded with long use. A few small pieces of silver, moreover, jingled in his pocket.

"Good!" thought he. "I will imagine I am at the Carnival!"

His first care, after being thus "Japanesed," was to enter a tea-house of modest appearance, and upon half a bird and a little rice, to breakfast like a man for whom dinner was as yet a problem to be solved.

"Now," thought he, when he had eaten heartily, "I mustn't lose my head. I can't sell this costume again for one still more Japanese. I must consider how to leave this country of the Sun, of which I shall not retain the most delightful of memories, as quickly as possible."

It occurred to him to visit the steamers which were about to leave for America. He would offer himself as a cook or servant, in payment of his passage and meals. Once at San Francisco, he would find some means of going on. The difficulty was, how to traverse the four thousand seven hundred miles of the Pacific which lay between Japan and the New World.

Passepartout was not the man to let an idea go begging, and directed his steps towards the docks. But, as he approached them, his project, which at first had seemed so simple, began to grow more and more formidable to his mind. What need would they have of a cook or servant on an American steamer, and what confidence would they put in him, dressed as he was? What references could he give?

As he was reflecting in this wise, his eyes fell upon an immense placard which a sort of clown was carrying through the streets. This placard, which was in English, read as follows:

ACROBATIC JAPANESE TROUPE,

HONORABLE WILLIAM BATULCAR, PROPRIETOR,

LAST PRESENTATIONS,

PRIOR TO THEIR DEPARTURE TO THE UNITED STATES,

OF THE LONG NOSES! LONG NOSES!

UNDER THE DIRECT PATRONAGE OF THE GOD TINGOU!

GREAT ATTRACTION!

"The United States!" said Passepartout; "that's just what I want!"

He followed the clown, and soon found himself once more in the Japanese quarter. A quarter of an hour later he stopped before a large cabin, adorned with several clusters of streamers, the exterior walls of which were designed to represent, in violent colours and without perspective, a company of jugglers.

This was the Honorable William Batulcar's establishment. That gentleman was a sort of Barnum, the director of a troupe of mountebanks, jugglers, clowns, acrobats, equilibrists, and gymnasts, who, according to the placard, was giving his last performances before leaving the Empire of the Sun for the States of the Union.

Passepartout entered and asked for Mr. Batulcar, who straightway appeared in person.

"What do you want?" said he to Passepartout, whom he at first took for a native.

"Would you like a servant, sir?" asked Passepartout.

"A servant!" cried Mr. Batulcar, caressing the thick grey beard which hung from his chin. "I already have two who are obedient and faithful, have never left me, and serve me for their nourishment—and here they are," added he, holding out his two robust arms, furrowed with veins as large as the strings of a bass-viol.

"So I can be of no use to you?"

"None."

"The devil! I should so like to cross the Pacific with you!"

"Ah!" said the Honorable Mr. Batulcar. "You are no more a Japanese than I am a monkey! Why are you dressed up in that way?"

"A man dresses as he can."

"That's true. You are a Frenchman, aren't you?"

"Yes; a Parisian of Paris."

"Then you ought to know how to make grimaces?"

"Why," replied Passepartout, a little vexed that his nationality should cause this question; "we Frenchmen know how to make grimaces, it is true—but not any better than the Americans do."

"True. Well, if I can't take you as a servant, I can as a clown. You see, my friend, in France they exhibit foreign clowns, and in foreign parts French clowns."

"Ah!"

"You are pretty strong, eh?"

"Especially after a good meal."

"And you can sing?"

"Yes," returned Passepartout, who had formerly been wont to sing in the streets.

"But can you sing standing on your head, with a top spinning on your left foot, and a sabre balanced on your right?"

"Humph! I think so," replied Passepartout, recalling the exercises of his younger days.

"Well, that's enough," said the Honourable William Batulcar.

The engagement was concluded there and then.

Passepartout had at last found something to do. He was engaged to act in the celebrated Japanese troupe. It was not a very dignified position, but within a week he would be on his way to San Francisco.

The performance, so noisily announced by the Honorable Mr. Batulcar, was to commence at three o'clock, and soon the deafening instruments of a Japanese orchestra resounded at the door. Passepartout, though he had not been able to study or rehearse a part, was designated to lend the aid of his sturdy shoulders in the great exhibition of the "human pyramid," executed by the Long Noses of the god Tingou. This "great attraction" was to close the performance.

Before three o'clock the large shed was invaded by the spectators, comprising Europeans and natives, Chinese and Japanese, men, women, and children, who precipitated themselves upon the narrow benches and into the boxes opposite inside, and were vigorously performing on their gongs, tam-tams, flutes, bones, tambourines, and immense drums.

The performance was much like all acrobatic displays; but it must be confessed that the Japanese are the first equilibrists in the world.

One, with a fan and some bits of paper, performed the graceful trick of the butterflies and the flowers; another traced in the air, with the odorous smoke of his pipe, a series of blue words, which composed a compliment to the audience; while a third juggled with some lighted candles, which he extinguished successively as they passed his lips, and relit again without interrupting for an instant his juggling. Another reproduced the most singular combinations with a spinning-top; in his hands the revolving tops seemed to be animated with a life of their own in their interminable whirling; they ran over pipe-stems, the edges of sabres, wires, and even hairs stretched across the stage; they turned around on the edges of large glasses, crossed bamboo ladders, dispersed into all the corners, and produced strange musical effects by the combination of their various pitches of tone. The jugglers tossed them in the air, threw them like shuttlecocks with wooden battledores, and yet they kept on spinning; they put them into their pockets, and took them out still whirling as before.

It is useless to describe the astonishing performances of the acrobats and gymnasts. The turning on ladders, poles, balls, barrels, &c., was executed with wonderful precision.

But the principal attraction was the exhibition of the Long Noses, a show to which Europe is as yet a stranger.

The Long Noses form a peculiar company, under the direct patronage of the god Tingou. Attired after the fashion of the Middle Ages, they bore upon their shoulders a splendid pair of wings; but what especially distinguished them was the long noses which were fastened to their faces, and the uses which they made of them. These noses were made of bamboo, and were five, six, and even ten feet long, some straight, others curved, some ribboned, and some having imitation warts upon them. It was upon these appendages, fixed tightly on their real noses, that they performed their gymnastic exercises. A dozen of these sectaries of Tingou lay flat upon their backs, while others, dressed to represent lightning-rods, came and frolicked on their noses, jumping from one to another, and performing the most skilful leapings and somersaults.

As a last scene, a "human pyramid" had been announced, in which fifty Long Noses were to represent the Car of Juggernaut. But, instead of forming a pyramid by mounting each other's shoulders, the artists were to group themselves on top of the noses. It happened that the performer who had hitherto formed the base of the Car had quitted the troup, and as, to fill this part, only strength and adroitness were necessary, Passepartout had been chosen to take his place.

The poor fellow really felt sad when—melancholy reminiscence of his youth!—he donned his costume, adorned with vari-colored wings, and fastened to his natural feature a false nose six feet long. But he cheered up when he thought that this nose was winning him something to eat.

He went upon the stage, and took his place beside the rest who were to compose the base of the Car of Juggernaut. They all stretched themselves on the floor, their noses pointing to the ceiling. A second group of artists disposed themselves on these long appendages, then a third above these, then a fourth, until a human monument reaching to the very cornices of the theatre soon arose on top of the noses. This elicited loud applause in the midst of which the orchestra was just striking up a deafening air, when the pyramid tottered, the balance was lost, one of the lower noses vanished from the pyramid, and the human monument was shattered like a castle built of cards!

It was Passepartout's fault. Abandoning his position, clearing the footlights without the aid of his wings, and clambering up to the right-hand gallery, he fell at the feet of one of the spectators, crying, "Ah, my master! my master!"

"You here?"

"Myself."

"Very well; then let us go to the steamer, young man!"

Mr. Fogg, Aouda, and Passepartout passed through the lobby of the theatre to the outside, where they encountered the Honorable Mr. Batulcar, furious with rage. He demanded damages for the "breakage" of the pyramid; and Phileas Fogg appeased him by giving him a handful of bank-notes.

At half-past six, the very hour of departure, Mr. Fogg and Aouda, followed by Passepartout, who in his hurry had retained his wings, and nose six feet long, stepped upon the American steamer.

Chapter XXIV

DURING WHICH MR. FOGG AND PARTY
CROSS THE PACIFIC OCEAN

WHAT HAPPENED WHEN THE PILOT-BOAT CAME IN SIGHT OF SHANGHAI WILL BE EASily guessed. The signals made by the *Tankadere* had been seen by the captain of the Yokohama steamer, who, espying the flag at half-mast, had directed his course towards the little craft. Phileas Fogg, after paying the stipulated price of his passage to John Busby, and rewarding that worthy with the additional sum of five hundred and fifty pounds, ascended the steamer with Aouda and Fix; and they started at once for Nagasaki and Yokohama.

They reached their destination on the morning of the 14th of November. Phileas Fogg lost no time in going on board the *Carnatic*, where he learned, to Aouda's great delight—and perhaps to his own, though he betrayed no emotion—that Passepartout, a Frenchman, had really arrived on her the day before.

The San Francisco steamer was announced to leave that very evening, and it became necessary to find Passepartout, if possible, without delay. Mr. Fogg applied in vain to the French and English consuls, and, after wandering through the streets a long time, began to despair of finding his missing servant. Chance, or perhaps a kind of presentiment, at last led him into the Honorable Mr. Batulcar's theatre. He certainly would not have recognised Passepartout in the eccentric mountebank's costume; but the latter, lying on his back, perceived his master in the gallery. He could not help starting, which so changed the position of his nose as to bring the "pyramid" pell-mell upon the stage.

All this Passepartout learned from Aouda, who recounted to him what had taken place on the voyage from Hong Kong to Shanghai on the *Tankadere*, in company with one Mr. Fix.

Passepartout did not change countenance on hearing this name. He thought that the time had not yet arrived to divulge to his master what had taken place between the detective and himself; and in the account he gave of his absence, he simply excused himself for having been overtaken by drunkenness, in smoking opium at a tavern in Hong Kong.

Mr. Fogg heard this narrative coldly, without a word; and then furnished his man with funds necessary to obtain clothing more in harmony with his position. Within an hour the Frenchman had cut off his nose and parted with his wings, and retained nothing about him which recalled the sectary of the god Tingou.

The steamer which was about to depart from Yokohama to San Francisco belonged to the Pacific Mail Steamship Company, and was named the *General Grant*. She was a large paddle-wheel steamer of two thousand five hundred tons, well equipped and very fast. The massive walking-beam rose and fell above the deck; at one end a piston-rod worked up and down; and at the other was a connecting-rod which, in changing the rectilinear motion to a circular one, was directly connected with the shaft of the paddles. The *General Grant* was rigged with three masts, giving a large capacity for sails, and thus materially aiding the steam power. By making twelve miles an hour, she would cross the ocean in twenty-one days. Phileas Fogg was therefore justified in hoping that he would reach San Francisco by the 2d of December, New York by the 11th, and London on the 20th—thus gaining several hours on the fatal date of the 21st of December.

There was a full complement of passengers on board, among them English, many Americans, a large number of Coolies on their way to California, and several East Indian officers, who were spending their vacation in making the tour of the world. Nothing of moment happened on the voyage; the steamer, sustained on its large paddles, rolled but little, and the Pacific almost justified its name. Mr. Fogg was as calm and taciturn as ever. His young companion felt herself more and more attached to him by other ties than gratitude; his silent but generous nature impressed her more than she thought; and it was almost unconsciously that she yielded to emotions which did not seem to have the least effect upon her protector. Aouda took the keenest interest in his plans, and became impatient at any incident which seemed likely to retard his journey.

She often chatted with Passepartout, who did not fail to perceive the state of the lady's heart; and, being the most faithful of domestics, he never exhausted his eulogies of Phileas Fogg's honesty, generosity, and devotion. He took pains to calm Aouda's doubts of a successful termination of the journey, telling her that the most difficult part of it had passed, that now they were beyond the fantastic countries of Japan and China, and were fairly on their way to civilised places again. A railway train from San Francisco to New York, and a transatlantic steamer from New York to Liverpool, would doubtless bring them to the end of this impossible journey round the world within the period agreed upon.

On the ninth day after leaving Yokohama, Phileas Fogg had traversed exactly one-half of the terrestrial globe. The *General Grant* passed, on the 23d of November, the one hundred and eightieth meridian, and was at the very antipodes of London. Mr. Fogg had, it is true, exhausted fifty-two of the eighty days in which he was to complete the tour, and there were only twenty-eight left. But, though he was only half-way by the difference of meridians, he had really gone over two-thirds of the whole journey; for he had been obliged to make long circuits from London to Aden, from Aden to Bombay, from Calcutta to Singapore, and from Singapore to Yokohama. Could he have followed without deviation the fiftieth parallel, which is that of London, the whole distance would only have been about twelve thousand miles; whereas he would be forced, by the irregular methods of locomotion, to traverse twenty-six thousand, of which he had, on the 23d of November, accomplished seventeen thousand five hundred. And now the course was a straight one, and Fix was no longer there to put obstacles in their way!

It happened also, on the 23d of November, that Passepartout made a joyful discovery. It will be remembered that the obstinate fellow had insisted on keeping his famous family watch at London time, and on regarding that of the countries he had passed through as quite false and unreliable. Now, on this day, though he had not changed the hands, he found that his watch exactly agreed with the ship's chronometers. His triumph was hilarious. He would have liked to know what Fix would say if he were aboard!

"The rogue told me a lot of stories," repeated Passepartout, "about the meridians, the sun, and the moon! Moon, indeed! moonshine more likely! If one listened to that sort of people, a pretty sort of time one would keep! I was sure that the sun would some day regulate itself by my watch!"

Passepartout was ignorant that, if the face of his watch had been divided into twenty-four hours, like the Italian clocks, he would have no reason for exultation; for the hands of his watch would then, instead of as now indicating nine o'clock in the morning, indicate nine o'clock in the evening, that is the twenty-first hour after midnight—precisely the difference between London time and that of the one hundred and eightieth meridian. But if Fix had been able to explain this purely physical effect, Passepartout would not have admitted, even if he had comprehended it. Moreover, if the detective had been on board at that moment, Passepartout would have joined issue with him on a quite different subject, and in an entirely different manner.

Where was Fix at that moment?

He was actually on board the *General Grant*.

On reaching Yokohama, the detective, leaving Mr. Fogg, whom he expected to meet again during the day, had repaired at once to the English consulate, where he at last found the warrant of arrest. It had followed him from Bombay, and had come by the *Carnatic*, on which steamer he himself was supposed to be. Fix's disappointment may be imagined when he reflected that the warrant was now useless. Mr. Fogg had left English ground, and it was now necessary to procure his extradition!

"Well," thought Fix, after a moment of anger, "my warrant is not good here, but it will be in England. The rogue evidently intends to return to his own country, thinking he has thrown the police off his track. Good! I will follow him across the Atlantic. As for the money, Heaven grant there may be some left! But the fellow has already spent in travelling, rewards, trials, bail, elephants, and all sorts of charges, more than five thousand pounds. Yet, after all, the Bank is rich!"

His course decided on, he went on board the *General Grant*, and was there when Mr. Fogg and Aouda arrived. To his utter amazement, he recognised Passepartout, despite his theatrical disguise. He quickly concealed himself in his cabin, to avoid an awkward explanation, and hoped—thanks to the number of passengers—to remain unperceived by Mr. Fogg's servant.

On that very day, however, he met Passepartout face to face on the forward deck. The latter, without a word, made a rush for him, grasped him by the throat, and, much to the amusement of a group of Americans, who immediately began to bet on him, administered to the detective a perfect volley of blows, which proved the great superiority of French over English pugilistic skill.

When Passepartout had finished, he found himself relieved and comforted. Fix got up in a somewhat rumpled condition, and, looking at his adversary, coldly said, "Have you done?"

"For this time—yes."

"Then let me have a word with you."

"But I—"

"In your master's interest."

Passepartout seemed to be vanquished by Fix's coolness, for he quietly followed him, and they sat down aside from the rest of the passengers.

"You have given me a thrashing," said Fix. "Good. I expected it. Now, listen to me. Up to this time I have been Mr. Fogg's adversary. I am now in his game."

"Aha!" cried Passepartout; "you are convinced he is an honest man?"

"No," replied Fix coldly, "I think him a rascal. Sh! don't budge, and let me speak. As long as Mr. Fogg was on English ground, it was for my interest to detain him there until my warrant of arrest arrived. I did everything I could to keep him back. I sent the Bombay priests after him, I got you intoxicated at Hong Kong, I separated you from him, and I made him miss the Yokohama steamer."

Passepartout listened, with closed fists.

"Now," resumed Fix, "Mr. Fogg seems to be going back to England. Well, I will follow him there. But hereafter I will do as much to keep obstacles out of his way as I have done up to this time to put them in his path. I've changed my game, you see, and simply because it was for my interest to change it. Your interest is the same as mine; for it is only in England that you will ascertain whether you are in the service of a criminal or an honest man."

Passepartout listened very attentively to Fix, and was convinced that he spoke with entire good faith.

"Are we friends?" asked the detective.

"Friends?—no," replied Passepartout; "but allies, perhaps. At the least sign of treason, however, I'll twist your neck for you."

"Agreed," said the detective quietly.

Eleven days later, on the 3d of December, the *General Grant* entered the bay of the Golden Gate, and reached San Francisco.

Mr. Fogg had neither gained nor lost a single day.

Chapter XXV

IN WHICH A SLIGHT GLIMPSE IS HAD OF SAN FRANCISCO

IT WAS SEVEN IN THE MORNING WHEN MR. FOGG, AOUDA, AND PASSEPARTOUT SET FOOT upon the American continent, if this name can be given to the floating quay upon which they disembarked. These quays, rising and falling with the tide, thus facilitate the loading and unloading of vessels. Alongside them were clippers of all sizes, steamers of all nationalities, and the steamboats, with several decks rising one above the other, which ply on the Sacramento and its tributaries. There were also heaped up the products of a commerce which extends to Mexico, Chile, Peru, Brazil, Europe, Asia, and all the Pacific islands.

Passepartout, in his joy on reaching at last the American continent, thought he would manifest it by executing a perilous vault in fine style; but, tumbling upon some worm-eaten planks, he fell through them. Put out of countenance by the manner in which he thus "set foot" upon the New World, he uttered a loud cry, which so frightened the innumerable cormorants and pelicans that are always perched upon these movable quays, that they flew noisily away.

Mr. Fogg, on reaching shore, proceeded to find out at what hour the first train left for New York, and learned that this was at six o'clock P.M.; he had, therefore, an entire day to spend in the Californian capital. Taking a carriage at a charge of three dollars, he and Aouda entered it, while Passepartout mounted the box beside the driver, and they set out for the International Hotel.

From his exalted position Passepartout observed with much curiosity the wide streets, the low, evenly ranged houses, the Anglo-Saxon Gothic churches, the great docks, the palatial wooden and brick warehouses, the numerous conveyances, omnibuses, horse-cars, and upon the side-walks, not only Americans and Europeans, but Chinese and Indians. Passepartout was surprised at all he saw. San Francisco was no longer the legendary city of 1849—a city of banditti, assassins, and incendiaries, who had flocked hither in crowds in pursuit of plunder; a paradise of outlaws, where they gambled with gold-dust, a revolver in one hand and a bowie-knife in the other: it was now a great commercial emporium.

The lofty tower of its City Hall overlooked the whole panorama of the streets and avenues, which cut each other at right angles, and in the midst of which appeared pleasant, verdant squares, while beyond appeared the Chinese quarter, seemingly imported from the Celestial Empire in a toy-box. Sombreros and red shirts and plumed Indians were rarely to be seen; but there were silk hats and black coats everywhere worn by a multitude of nervously active, gentlemanly-looking men. Some of the streets—especially Montgomery Street, which is to San Francisco what Regent Street is to London, the Boulevard des Italiens to Paris, and Broadway to New York—were lined with splendid and spacious stores, which exposed in their windows the products of the entire world.

When Passepartout reached the International Hotel, it did not seem to him as if he had left England at all.

The ground floor of the hotel was occupied by a large bar, a sort of restaurant freely open to all passers-by, who might partake of dried beef, oyster soup, biscuits, and cheese, without taking out their purses. Payment was made only for the ale, porter, or sherry which was drunk. This seemed "very American" to Passepartout. The hotel refreshment-rooms were comfortable, and Mr. Fogg and Aouda, installing themselves at a table, were abundantly served on diminutive plates by negroes of darkest hue.

After breakfast, Mr. Fogg, accompanied by Aouda, started for the English consulate to have his passport visaed. As he was going out, he met Passepartout, who asked him if it would not do well, before taking the train, to purchase some dozens of Enfield rifles and Colt's revolvers. He had been listening to stories of attacks upon the trains by the Sioux and Pawnees. Mr. Fogg thought it a useless precaution, but told him to do as he thought best, and went on to the consulate.

He had not proceeded two hundred steps, however, when, "by the greatest chance in the world," he met Fix. The detective seemed wholly taken by surprise. What! Had Mr. Fogg and himself crossed the Pacific together, and not met on the steamer! At least Fix felt honoured to behold once more the gentleman to whom he owed so much, and as his business recalled him to Europe, he should be delighted to continue the journey in such pleasant company.

Mr. Fogg replied that the honour would be his; and the detective—who was determined not to lose sight of him—begged permission to accompany them in their walk about San Francisco—a request which Mr. Fogg readily granted.

They soon found themselves in Montgomery Street, where a great crowd was collected; the side-walks, street, horse-car rails, the shop-doors, the windows of the houses, and even the roofs, were full of people. Men were going about carrying large posters, and flags and streamers were floating in the wind; while loud cries were heard on every hand.

"Hurrah for Camerfield!"

"Hurrah for Mandiboy!"

It was a political meeting; at least so Fix conjectured, who said to Mr. Fogg, "Perhaps we had better not mingle with the crowd. There may be danger in it."

"Yes," returned Mr. Fogg; "and blows, even if they are political, are still blows."

Fix smiled at this remark; and in order to be able to see without being jostled about, the party took up a position on the top of a flight of steps situated at the upper end of Montgomery Street. Opposite them, on the other side of the street, between a coal wharf and a petroleum warehouse, a large platform had been erected in the open air, towards which the current of the crowd seemed to be directed.

For what purpose was this meeting? What was the occasion of this excited assemblage? Phileas Fogg could not imagine. Was it to nominate some high official—a governor or member of Congress? It was not improbable, so agitated was the multitude before them.

Just at this moment there was an unusual stir in the human mass. All the hands were raised in the air. Some, tightly closed, seemed to disappear suddenly in the midst of the cries—an energetic way, no doubt, of casting a vote. The crowd swayed back, the banners and flags wavered, disappeared an instant, then reappeared in tatters. The undulations of the human surge reached the steps, while all the heads floundered on the surface like a sea agitated by a squall. Many of the black hats disappeared, and the greater part of the crowd seemed to have diminished in height.

"It is evidently a meeting," said Fix, "and its object must be an exciting one. I should not wonder if it were about the Alabama, despite the fact that that question is settled."

"Perhaps," replied Mr. Fogg simply.

"At least, there are two champions in presence of each other, the Honorable Mr. Camerfield and the Honorable Mr. Mandiboy."

Aouda, leaning upon Mr. Fogg's arm, observed the tumultuous scene with surprise, while Fix asked a man near him what the cause of it all was. Before the man could reply, a fresh agitation arose; hurrahs and excited shouts were heard; the staffs of the banners began to be used as offensive weapons; and fists flew about in every direction. Thumps were exchanged from the tops of the carriages and omnibuses which had been blocked up in the crowd. Boots and shoes went whirling through the air, and Mr. Fogg thought he even heard the crack of revolvers mingling in the din. The rout approached the stairway, and flowed over the lower step. One of the parties had evidently been repulsed; but the mere lookers-on could not tell whether Mandiboy or Camerfield had gained the upper hand.

"It would be prudent for us to retire," said Fix, who was anxious that Mr. Fogg should not receive any injury, at least until they got back to London. "If there is any question about England in all this, and we were recognised, I fear it would go hard with us."

"An English subject—" began Mr. Fogg.

He did not finish his sentence; for a terrific hubbub now arose on the terrace behind the flight of steps where they stood, and there were frantic shouts of, "Hurrah for Mandiboy! Hip, hip, hurrah!"

It was a band of voters coming to the rescue of their allies, and taking the Camerfield forces in flank. Mr. Fogg, Aouda, and Fix found themselves between two fires; it was too late to escape. The torrent of men, armed with loaded canes and sticks, was irresistible. Phileas Fogg and Fix were roughly hustled in their attempts to protect their fair companion; the former, as cool as ever, tried to defend himself with the weapons which nature has placed at the end of every Englishman's arm, but in vain. A big brawny fellow with a red beard, flushed face, and broad shoulders, who seemed to be the chief of the band, raised his clenched fist to strike Mr. Fogg, whom he would have given a crushing blow, had not Fix rushed in and received it in his stead. An enormous bruise immediately made its appearance under the detective's silk hat, which was completely smashed in.

"Yankee!" exclaimed Mr. Fogg, darting a contemptuous look at the ruffian.

"Englishman!" returned the other. "We will meet again!"

"When you please."

"What is your name?"

"Phileas Fogg. And yours?"

"Colonel Stamp Proctor."

The human tide now swept by, after overturning Fix, who speedily got upon his feet again, though with tattered clothes. Happily, he was not seriously hurt. His travelling overcoat was divided into two unequal parts, and his trousers resembled those of certain Indians, which fit less compactly than they are easy to put on. Aouda had escaped unharmed, and Fix alone bore marks of the fray in his black and blue bruise.

"Thanks," said Mr. Fogg to the detective, as soon as they were out of the crowd.

"No thanks are necessary," replied. Fix "but let us go."

"Where?"

"To a tailor's."

Such a visit was, indeed, opportune. The clothing of both Mr. Fogg and Fix was in rags, as if they had themselves been actively engaged in the contest between Camerfield and Mandiboy. An hour after, they were once more suitably attired, and with Aouda returned to the International Hotel.

Passepartout was waiting for his master, armed with half-a-dozen six-barrelled revolvers. When he perceived Fix, he knit his brows; but Aouda having, in a few words, told him of their adventure, his countenance resumed its placid expression. Fix evidently was no longer an enemy, but an ally; he was faithfully keeping his word.

Dinner over, the coach which was to convey the passengers and their luggage to the station drew up to the door. As he was getting in, Mr. Fogg said to Fix, "You have not seen this Colonel Proctor again?"

"No."

"I will come back to America to find him," said Phileas Fogg calmly. "It would not be right for an Englishman to permit himself to be treated in that way, without retaliating."

The detective smiled, but did not reply. It was clear that Mr. Fogg was one of those Englishmen who, while they do not tolerate duelling at home, fight abroad when their honour is attacked.

At a quarter before six the travellers reached the station, and found the train ready to depart. As he was about to enter it, Mr. Fogg called a porter, and said to him: "My friend, was there not some trouble to-day in San Francisco?"

"It was a political meeting, sir," replied the porter.

"But I thought there was a great deal of disturbance in the streets."

"It was only a meeting assembled for an election."

"The election of a general-in-chief, no doubt?" asked Mr. Fogg.

"No, sir; of a justice of the peace."

Phileas Fogg got into the train, which started off at full speed.

Chapter XXVI

IN WHICH PHILEAS FOGG AND PARTY
TRAVEL BY THE PACIFIC RAILROAD

"FROM OCEAN TO OCEAN"—SO SAY THE AMERICANS; AND THESE FOUR WORDS COMPOSE the general designation of the "great trunk line" which crosses the entire width of the United States. The Pacific Railroad is, however, really divided into two distinct lines: the Central Pacific, between San Francisco and Ogden, and the Union Pacific, between Ogden and Omaha. Five main lines connect Omaha with New York.

New York and San Francisco are thus united by an uninterrupted metal ribbon, which measures no less than three thousand seven hundred and eighty-six miles. Between Omaha and the Pacific the railway crosses a territory which is still infested by Indians and wild beasts, and a large tract which the Mormons, after they were driven from Illinois in 1845, began to colonise.

The journey from New York to San Francisco consumed, formerly, under the most favourable conditions, at least six months. It is now accomplished in seven days.

It was in 1862 that, in spite of the Southern members of Congress, who wished a more southerly route, it was decided to lay the road between the forty-first and forty-second parallels. President Lincoln himself fixed the end of the line at Omaha, in Nebraska. The work was at once commenced, and pursued with true American energy; nor did the rapidity with which it went on injuriously affect its good execution. The road grew, on the prairies, a mile and a half a day. A locomotive, running on the rails laid down the evening before, brought the rails to be laid on the morrow, and advanced upon them as fast as they were put in position.

The Pacific Railroad is joined by several branches in Iowa, Kansas, Colorado, and Oregon. On leaving Omaha, it passes along the left bank of the Platte River as far as the junction of its northern branch, follows its southern branch, crosses the Laramie territory and the Wahsatch Mountains, turns the Great Salt Lake, and reaches Salt Lake City, the Mormon capital, plunges into the Tuilla Valley, across the American Desert, Cedar and Humboldt Mountains, the Sierra Nevada, and descends, via Sacramento, to the Pacific—its grade, even on the Rocky Mountains, never exceeding one hundred and twelve feet to the mile.

Such was the road to be traversed in seven days, which would enable Phileas Fogg—at least, so he hoped—to take the Atlantic steamer at New York on the 11th for Liverpool.

The car which he occupied was a sort of long omnibus on eight wheels, and with no compartments in the interior. It was supplied with two rows of seats, perpendicular to the direction of the train on either side of an aisle which conducted to the front and rear platforms. These platforms were found throughout the train, and the passengers were able to pass from one end of the train to the other. It was supplied with saloon cars, balcony cars, restaurants, and smoking cars; theatre cars alone were wanting, and they will have these someday.

Book and news dealers, sellers of edibles, drinkables, and cigars, who seemed to have plenty of customers, were continually circulating in the aisles.

The train left Oakland station at six o'clock. It was already night, cold and cheerless, the heavens being overcast with clouds which seemed to threaten snow. The train did not proceed rapidly; counting the stoppages, it did not run more than twenty miles an hour, which was a sufficient speed, however, to enable it to reach Omaha within its designated time.

There was but little conversation in the car, and soon many of the passengers were overcome with sleep. Passepartout found himself beside the detective; but he did not talk to him. After recent events, their relations with each other had grown somewhat cold; there could no longer be mutual sympathy or intimacy between them. Fix's manner had not changed; but Passepartout was very reserved, and ready to strangle his former friend on the slightest provocation.

Snow began to fall an hour after they started, a fine snow, however, which happily could not obstruct the train; nothing could be seen from the windows but a vast, white sheet, against which the smoke of the locomotive had a greyish aspect.

At eight o'clock a steward entered the car and announced that the time for going to bed had arrived; and in a few minutes the car was transformed into a dormitory. The backs of the seats were thrown back, bedsteads carefully packed were rolled out by an ingenious system, berths were suddenly improvised, and each traveller had soon at his disposition a comfortable bed, protected from curious eyes by thick curtains. The sheets were clean and the pillows soft. It only remained to go to bed and sleep—which everybody did—while the train sped on across the State of California.

The country between San Francisco and Sacramento is not very hilly. The Central Pacific, taking Sacramento for its starting-point, extends eastward to meet the road from Omaha. The line from San Francisco to Sacramento runs in a north-easterly direction, along the American River, which empties into San Pablo Bay. The one hundred and twenty miles between these cities were accomplished in six hours, and towards midnight, while fast asleep, the travellers passed through Sacramento; so that they saw nothing of that important place, the seat of the State government, with its fine quays, its broad streets, its noble hotels, squares, and churches.

The train, on leaving Sacramento, and passing the junction, Roclin, Auburn, and Colfax, entered the range of the Sierra Nevada. Cisco was reached at seven in the morning; and an hour later the dormitory was transformed into an ordinary car, and the travellers could observe the picturesque beauties of the mountain region through which they were steaming. The railway track wound in and out among the passes, now approaching the mountain-sides, now suspended over precipices, avoiding abrupt angles by bold curves, plunging into narrow defiles, which seemed to have no outlet. The locomotive, its great funnel emitting a weird light, with its sharp bell, and its cow-catcher extended like a spur, mingled its shrieks and bellowings with the noise of torrents and cascades, and twined its smoke among the branches of the gigantic pines.

There were few or no bridges or tunnels on the route. The railway turned around the sides of the mountains, and did not attempt to violate nature by taking the shortest cut from one point to another.

The train entered the State of Nevada through the Carson Valley about nine o'clock, going always north-easterly; and at midday reached Reno, where there was a delay of twenty minutes for breakfast.

From this point the road, running along Humboldt River, passed northward for several miles by its banks; then it turned eastward, and kept by the river until it reached the Humboldt Range, nearly at the extreme eastern limit of Nevada.

Having breakfasted, Mr. Fogg and his companions resumed their places in the car, and observed the varied landscape which unfolded itself as they passed along: the vast prairies, the mountains lining the horizon, and the creeks with their frothy, foaming streams. Sometimes a great herd of buffaloes, massing together in the distance, seemed like a movable dam. These innumerable multitudes of ruminating beasts often form an insurmountable obstacle to the passage of the trains; thousands of them have been seen passing over the track for hours together, in compact ranks. The locomotive is then forced to stop and wait till the road is once more clear.

This happened, indeed, to the train in which Mr. Fogg was travelling. About twelve o'clock a troop of ten or twelve thousand head of buffalo encumbered the track. The locomotive, slackening in speed, tried to clear the way with its cow-catcher; but the mass of animals was too great. The buffaloes marched along with a tranquil gait, uttering now and then deafening bellowings. There was no use of interrupting them, for, having taken a particular direction, nothing can moderate and change their course; it is a torrent of living flesh which no dam could contain.

The travellers gazed on this curious spectacle from the platforms; but Phileas Fogg, who had the most reason of all to be in a hurry, remained in his seat, and waited philosophically until it should please the buffaloes to get out of the way.

Passepartout was furious at the delay they occasioned, and longed to discharge his arsenal of revolvers upon them.

"What a country!" cried he. "Mere cattle stop the trains, and go by in a procession, just as if they were not impeding travel! Parbleu! I should like to know if Mr. Fogg foresaw *this* mishap in his programme! And here's an engineer who doesn't dare to run the locomotive into this herd of beasts!"

The engineer did not try to overcome the obstacle, and he was wise. He would have crushed the first buffaloes, no doubt, with the cow-catcher; but the locomotive, however powerful, would soon have been checked, the train would inevitably have been thrown off the track, and would then have been helpless.

The best course was to wait patiently, and regain the lost time by greater speed when the obstacle was removed. The procession of buffaloes lasted three full hours, and it was night before the track was clear. The last ranks of the herd were now passing over the rails, while the first had already disappeared below the southern horizon.

It was eight o'clock when the train passed through the defiles of the Humboldt Range, and half-past nine when it penetrated Utah, the region of the Great Salt Lake, the singular colony of the Mormons.

Chapter XXVII

In which Passepartout undergoes, at a speed of twenty miles an hour, a course of Mormon history

DURING THE NIGHT OF THE 5TH OF DECEMBER, THE TRAIN RAN SOUTH-EASTERLY FOR about fifty miles; then rose an equal distance in a north-easterly direction, towards the Great Salt Lake.

Passepartout, about nine o'clock, went out upon the platform to take the air. The weather was cold, the heavens grey, but it was not snowing. The sun's disc, enlarged by the mist, seemed an enormous ring of gold, and Passepartout was amusing himself by calculating its value in pounds sterling, when he was diverted from this interesting study by a strange-looking personage who made his appearance on the platform.

This personage, who had taken the train at Elko, was tall and dark, with black moustaches, black stockings, a black silk hat, a black waistcoat, black trousers, a white cravat, and dog-skin gloves. He might have been taken for a clergyman. He went from one end of the train to the other, and affixed to the door of each car a notice written in manuscript.

Passepartout approached and read one of these notices, which stated that Elder William Hitch, Mormon missionary, taking advantage of his presence on train No. 48, would deliver a lecture on Mormonism in car No. 117, from eleven to twelve o'clock; and that he invited all who were desirous of being instructed concerning the mysteries of the religion of the "Latter Day Saints" to attend.

"I'll go," said Passepartout to himself. He knew nothing of Mormonism except the custom of polygamy, which is its foundation.

The news spread quickly through the train, which contained about one hundred passengers, thirty of whom, at most, attracted by the notice, ensconced themselves in car No. 117. Passepartout took one of the front seats. Neither Mr. Fogg nor Fix cared to attend.

At the appointed hour Elder William Hitch rose, and, in an irritated voice, as if he had already been contradicted, said, "I tell you that Joe Smith is a martyr, that his brother Hiram is a martyr; and that the persecutions of the United States Government against the prophets will also make a martyr of Brigham Young. Who dares to say the contrary?"

No one ventured to gainsay the missionary, whose excited tone contrasted curiously with his naturally calm visage. No doubt his anger arose from the hardships to which the Mormons were actually subjected. The government had just succeeded, with some difficulty, in reducing these independent fanatics to its rule. It had made itself master of Utah, and subjected that territory to the laws of the Union, after imprisoning Brigham Young on a charge of rebellion and polygamy. The disciples of the prophet had since redoubled their efforts, and resisted, by words at least, the authority of Congress. Elder Hitch, as is seen, was trying to make proselytes on the very railway trains.

Then, emphasising his words with his loud voice and frequent gestures, he related the history of the Mormons from Biblical times: how that, in Israel, a Mormon prophet of the tribe of Joseph published the annals of the new religion, and bequeathed them to his son Mormon; how, many centuries later, a translation of this precious book, which was written in Egyptian, was made by Joseph Smith, Junior, a Vermont farmer, who revealed himself as a mystical prophet in 1825; and how, in short, the celestial messenger appeared to him in an illuminated forest, and gave him the annals of the Lord.

Several of the audience, not being much interested in the missionary's narrative, here left the car; but Elder Hitch, continuing his lecture, related how Smith, Junior, with his father, two brothers, and a few disciples, founded the church of the "Latter Day Saints," which, adopted not only in America, but in England, Norway and Sweden, and Germany, counts many artisans, as well as men engaged in the liberal professions, among its members; how a colony was established in Ohio, a temple erected there at a cost of two hundred thousand dollars, and a town built at Kirkland; how Smith became an enterprising banker, and received from a simple mummy showman a papyrus scroll written by Abraham and several famous Egyptians.

The Elder's story became somewhat wearisome, and his audience grew gradually less, until it was reduced to twenty passengers. But this did not disconcert the enthusiast, who proceeded with the story of Joseph Smith's bankruptcy in 1837, and how his ruined creditors gave him a coat of tar and feathers; his reappearance some years afterward, more honourable and honoured than ever, at Independence, Missouri, the chief of a flourishing colony of three thousand disciples, and his pursuit thence by outraged Gentiles, and retirement into the Far West.

Ten hearers only were now left, among them honest Passepartout, who was listening with all his ears. Thus he learned that, after long persecutions, Smith reappeared in Illinois, and in 1839 founded a community at Nauvoo, on the Mississippi, numbering twenty-five thousand souls, of which he became mayor, chief justice, and general-in-chief; that he announced himself, in 1843, as a candidate for the Presidency of the United States; and that finally, being drawn into ambuscade at Carthage, he was thrown into prison, and assassinated by a band of men disguised in masks.

Passepartout was now the only person left in the car, and the Elder, looking him full in the face, reminded him that, two years after the assassination of Joseph Smith, the inspired prophet, Brigham Young, his successor, left Nauvoo for the banks of the Great Salt Lake, where, in the midst of that fertile region, directly on the route of the emigrants who crossed Utah on their way to California, the new colony, thanks to the polygamy practiced by the Mormons, had flourished beyond expectation.

"And this," added Elder William Hitch, "this is why the jealousy of Congress has been aroused against us! Why have the soldiers of the Union invaded the soil of Utah? Why has Brigham Young, our chief, been imprisoned, in contempt of all justice? Shall we yield to force? Never! Driven from Vermont, driven from Illinois, driven from Ohio, driven from Missouri, driven from Utah, we shall yet find some independent territory on which to plant our tents. And you, my brother," continued the Elder, fixing his angry eyes upon his single auditor, "will you not plant yours there, too, under the shadow of our flag?"

"No!" replied Passepartout courageously, in his turn retiring from the car, and leaving the Elder to preach to vacancy.

During the lecture the train had been making good progress, and towards half-past twelve it reached the north-west border of the Great Salt Lake. Thence the passengers could observe the vast extent of this interior sea, which is also called the Dead Sea, and into which flows an American Jordan. It is a picturesque expanse, framed in lofty crags in large strata, encrusted with white salt—a superb sheet of water, which was formerly of larger extent than now, its shores having encroached with the lapse of time, and thus at once reduced its breadth and increased its depth.

The Salt Lake, seventy miles long and thirty-five wide, is situated three miles eight hundred feet above the sea. Quite different from Lake Asphaltite, whose depression is twelve hundred feet below the sea, it contains considerable salt, and one-quarter of the weight of its water is solid matter, its specific weight being 1,170, and, after being distilled, 1,000. Fishes are of course unable to live in it, and those which descend through the Jordan, the Weber, and other streams, soon perish.

The country around the lake was well cultivated, for the Mormons are mostly farmers; while ranches and pens for domesticated animals, fields of wheat, corn, and other cereals, luxuriant prairies, hedges of wild rose, clumps of acacias and milk-wort, would have been seen six months later. Now the ground was covered with a thin powdering of snow.

The train reached Ogden at two o'clock, where it rested for six hours, Mr. Fogg and his party had time to pay a visit to Salt Lake City, connected with Ogden by a branch road; and they spent two hours in this strikingly American town, built on the pattern of other cities of the Union, like a checker-board, "with the sombre sadness of right angles," as Victor Hugo expresses it. The founder of the City of the Saints could not escape from the taste for symmetry which distinguishes the Anglo-Saxons. In this strange country, where the people are certainly not up to the level of their institutions, everything is done "squarely"—cities, houses, and follies.

The travellers, then, were promenading, at three o'clock, about the streets of the town built between the banks of the Jordan and the spurs of the Wahsatch Range. They saw few or no churches, but the prophet's mansion, the court-house, and the arsenal, blue-brick houses with verandas and porches, surrounded by gardens bordered with acacias, palms, and locusts. A clay and pebble wall, built in 1853, surrounded the town; and in the principal street were the market and several hotels adorned with pavilions. The place did not seem thickly populated. The streets were almost deserted, except in the vicinity of the Temple, which they only reached after having traversed several quarters surrounded by palisades. There were many women, which was easily accounted for by the "peculiar institution" of the Mormons; but it must not be supposed that all the Mormons are polygamists. They are free to marry or not, as they please; but it is worth noting that it is mainly the female citizens of Utah who are anxious to marry, as, according to the Mormon religion, maiden ladies are not admitted to the possession of its highest joys. These poor creatures seemed to be neither well off nor happy. Some—the more well-to-do, no doubt—wore short, open, black silk dresses, under a hood or modest shawl; others were habited in Indian fashion.

Passepartout could not behold without a certain fright these women, charged, in groups, with conferring happiness on a single Mormon. His common sense pitied, above all, the husband. It seemed to him a terrible thing to have to guide so many wives at once across the vicissitudes of life, and to conduct them, as it were, in a body to the Mormon paradise, with the prospect of seeing them in the company of the glorious Smith, who doubtless was the chief ornament of that delightful place, to all eternity. He felt decidedly repelled from such a vocation, and he imagined—perhaps he was mistaken—that the fair ones of Salt Lake City cast rather alarming glances on his person. Happily, his stay there was but brief. At four the party found themselves again at the station, took their places in the train, and the whistle sounded for starting. Just at the moment, however, that the locomotive wheels began to move, cries of "Stop! stop!" were heard.

Trains, like time and tide, stop for no one. The gentleman who uttered the cries was evidently a belated Mormon. He was breathless with running. Happily for him, the station had neither gates nor barriers. He rushed along the track, jumped on the rear platform of the train, and fell exhausted into one of the seats.

Passepartout, who had been anxiously watching this amateur gymnast, approached him with lively interest, and learned that he had taken flight after an unpleasant domestic scene.

When the Mormon had recovered his breath, Passepartout ventured to ask him politely how many wives he had; for, from the manner in which he had decamped, it might be thought that he had twenty at least.

"One, sir," replied the Mormon, raising his arms heavenward—"one, and that was enough!"

Chapter XXVIII

IN WHICH PASSEPARTOUT DOES NOT SUCCEED IN MAKING ANYBODY LISTEN TO REASON

THE TRAIN, ON LEAVING GREAT SALT LAKE AT OGDEN, PASSED NORTHWARD FOR AN hour as far as Weber River, having completed nearly nine hundred miles from San Francisco. From this point it took an easterly direction towards the jagged Wahsatch Mountains. It was in the section included between this range and the Rocky Mountains that the American engineers found the most formidable difficulties in laying the road, and that the government granted a subsidy of forty-eight thousand dollars per mile, instead of sixteen thousand allowed for the work done on the plains. But the engineers, instead of violating nature, avoided its difficulties by winding around, instead of penetrating the rocks. One tunnel only, fourteen thousand feet in length, was pierced in order to arrive at the great basin.

The track up to this time had reached its highest elevation at the Great Salt Lake. From this point it described a long curve, descending towards Bitter Creek Valley, to rise again to the dividing ridge of the waters between the Atlantic and the Pacific. There were many creeks in this mountainous region, and it was necessary to cross Muddy Creek, Green Creek, and others, upon culverts.

Passepartout grew more and more impatient as they went on, while Fix longed to get out of this difficult region, and was more anxious than Phileas Fogg himself to be beyond the danger of delays and accidents, and set foot on English soil.

At ten o'clock at night the train stopped at Fort Bridger station, and twenty minutes later entered Wyoming Territory, following the valley of Bitter Creek throughout. The next day, December 7th, they stopped for a quarter of an hour at Green River station. Snow had fallen abundantly during the night, but, being mixed with rain, it had half melted, and did not interrupt their progress. The bad weather, however, annoyed Passepartout; for the accumulation of snow, by blocking the wheels of the cars, would certainly have been fatal to Mr. Fogg's tour.

"What an idea!" he said to himself. "Why did my master make this journey in winter? Couldn't he have waited for the good season to increase his chances?"

While the worthy Frenchman was absorbed in the state of the sky and the depression of the temperature, Aouda was experiencing fears from a totally different cause.

Several passengers had got off at Green River, and were walking up and down the platforms; and among these Aouda recognised Colonel Stamp Proctor, the same who had so grossly insulted Phileas Fogg at the San Francisco meeting. Not wishing to be recognised, the young woman drew back from the window, feeling much alarm at her discovery. She was attached to the man who, however coldly, gave her daily evidences of the most absolute devotion. She did not comprehend, perhaps, the depth of the sentiment with which her protector inspired her, which she called gratitude, but which, though she was unconscious of it, was really more than that. Her heart sank within her when she recognised the man whom Mr. Fogg desired, sooner or later, to call to account for his conduct. Chance alone, it was clear, had brought Colonel Proctor on this train; but there he was, and it was necessary, at all hazards, that Phileas Fogg should not perceive his adversary.

Aouda seized a moment when Mr. Fogg was asleep to tell Fix and Passepartout whom she had seen.

"That Proctor on this train!" cried Fix. "Well, reassure yourself, madam; before he settles with Mr. Fogg, he has got to deal with me! It seems to me that I was the more insulted of the two."

"And besides," added Passepartout, "I'll take charge of him, colonel as he is."

"Mr. Fix," resumed Aouda, "Mr. Fogg will allow no one to avenge him. He said that he would come back to America to find this man. Should he perceive Colonel Proctor, we could not prevent a collision which might have terrible results. He must not see him."

"You are right, madam," replied Fix; "a meeting between them might ruin all. Whether he were victorious or beaten, Mr. Fogg would be delayed, and—"

"And," added Passepartout, "that would play the game of the gentlemen of the Reform Club. In four days we shall be in New York. Well, if my master does not leave this car during those four days, we may hope that chance will not bring him face to face with this confounded American. We must, if possible, prevent his stirring out of it."

The conversation dropped. Mr. Fogg had just woke up, and was looking out of the window. Soon after Passepartout, without being heard by his master or Aouda, whispered to the detective, "Would you really fight for him?"

"I would do anything," replied Fix, in a tone which betrayed determined will, "to get him back living to Europe!"

Passepartout felt something like a shudder shoot through his frame, but his confidence in his master remained unbroken.

Was there any means of detaining Mr. Fogg in the car, to avoid a meeting between him and the colonel? It ought not to be a difficult task, since that gentleman was naturally sedentary and little curious. The detective, at least, seemed to have found a way; for, after a few moments, he said to Mr. Fogg, "These are long and slow hours, sir, that we are passing on the railway."

"Yes," replied Mr. Fogg; "but they pass."

"You were in the habit of playing whist," resumed Fix, "on the steamers."

"Yes; but it would be difficult to do so here. I have neither cards nor partners."

"Oh, but we can easily buy some cards, for they are sold on all the American trains. And as for partners, if madam plays—"

"Certainly, sir," Aouda quickly replied; "I understand whist. It is part of an English education."

"I myself have some pretensions to playing a good game. Well, here are three of us, and a dummy—"

"As you please, sir," replied Phileas Fogg, heartily glad to resume his favourite pastime—even on the railway.

Passepartout was despatched in search of the steward, and soon returned with two packs of cards, some pins, counters, and a shelf covered with cloth.

The game commenced. Aouda understood whist sufficiently well, and even received some compliments on her playing from Mr. Fogg. As for the detective, he was simply an adept, and worthy of being matched against his present opponent.

"Now," thought Passepartout, "we've got him. He won't budge."

At eleven in the morning the train had reached the dividing ridge of the waters at Bridger Pass, seven thousand five hundred and twenty-four feet above the level of the sea, one of the highest points attained by the track in crossing the Rocky Mountains. After going about two hundred miles, the travellers at last found themselves on one of those vast plains which extend to the Atlantic, and which nature has made so propitious for laying the iron road.

On the declivity of the Atlantic basin the first streams, branches of the North Platte River, already appeared. The whole northern and eastern horizon was bounded by the immense semicircular curtain which is formed by the southern portion of the Rocky Mountains, the highest being Laramie Peak. Between this and the railway extended vast plains, plentifully irrigated. On the right rose the lower spurs of the mountainous mass which extends southward to the sources of the Arkansas River, one of the great tributaries of the Missouri.

At half-past twelve the travellers caught sight for an instant of Fort Halleck, which commands that section; and in a few more hours the Rocky Mountains were crossed. There was reason to hope, then, that no accident would mark the journey through this difficult country. The snow had ceased falling, and the air became crisp and cold. Large birds, frightened by the locomotive, rose and flew off in the distance. No wild beast appeared on the plain. It was a desert in its vast nakedness.

After a comfortable breakfast, served in the car, Mr. Fogg and his partners had just resumed whist, when a violent whistling was heard, and the train stopped. Passepartout put his head out of the door, but saw nothing to cause the delay; no station was in view.

Aouda and Fix feared that Mr. Fogg might take it into his head to get out; but that gentleman contented himself with saying to his servant, "See what is the matter."

Passepartout rushed out of the car. Thirty or forty passengers had already descended, amongst them Colonel Stamp Proctor.

The train had stopped before a red signal which blocked the way. The engineer and conductor were talking excitedly with a signal-man, whom the station-master at Medicine Bow, the next stopping-place, had sent on before. The passengers drew around and took part in the discussion, in which Colonel Proctor, with his insolent manner, was conspicuous.

Passepartout, joining the group, heard the signal-man say, "No! you can't pass. The bridge at Medicine Bow is shaky, and would not bear the weight of the train."

This was a suspension-bridge thrown over some rapids, about a mile from the place where they now were. According to the signal-man, it was in a ruinous condition, several of the iron wires being broken; and it was impossible to risk the passage. He did not in any way exaggerate the condition of the bridge. It may be taken for granted that, rash as the Americans usually are, when they are prudent there is good reason for it.

Passepartout, not daring to apprise his master of what he heard, listened with set teeth, immovable as a statue.

"Hum!" cried Colonel Proctor; "but we are not going to stay here, I imagine, and take root in the snow?"

"Colonel," replied the conductor, "we have telegraphed to Omaha for a train, but it is not likely that it will reach Medicine Bow is less than six hours."

"Six hours!" cried Passepartout.

"Certainly," returned the conductor. "Besides, it will take us as long as that to reach Medicine Bow on foot."

"But it is only a mile from here," said one of the passengers.

"Yes, but it's on the other side of the river."

"And can't we cross that in a boat?" asked the colonel.

"That's impossible. The creek is swelled by the rains. It is a rapid, and we shall have to make a circuit of ten miles to the north to find a ford."

The colonel launched a volley of oaths, denouncing the railway company and the conductor; and Passepartout, who was furious, was not disinclined to make common cause with him. Here was an obstacle, indeed, which all his master's bank-notes could not remove.

There was a general disappointment among the passengers, who, without reckoning the delay, saw themselves compelled to trudge fifteen miles over a plain covered with snow. They grumbled and protested, and would certainly have thus attracted Phileas Fogg's attention if he had not been completely absorbed in his game.

Passepartout found that he could not avoid telling his master what had occurred, and, with hanging head he was turning towards the car, when the engineer—a true Yankee, named Forster—called out, "Gentlemen, perhaps there is a way, after all, to get over."

"On the bridge?" asked a passenger.

"On the bridge."

"With our train?"

"With our train."

Passepartout stopped short, and eagerly listened to the engineer.

"But the bridge is unsafe," urged the conductor.

"No matter," replied Forster; "I think that by putting on the very highest speed we might have a chance of getting over."

"The devil!" muttered Passepartout.

But a number of the passengers were at once attracted by the engineer's proposal, and Colonel Proctor was especially delighted, and found the plan a very feasible one. He told stories about engineers leaping their trains over rivers without bridges, by putting on full steam; and many of those present avowed themselves of the engineer's mind.

"We have fifty chances out of a hundred of getting over," said one.

"Eighty! ninety!"

Passepartout was astounded, and, though ready to attempt anything to get over Medicine Creek, thought the experiment proposed a little too American. "Besides," thought he, "there's still a more simple way, and it does not even occur to any of these people! Sir," said he aloud to one of the passengers, "the engineer's plan seems to me a little dangerous, but—"

"Eighty chances!" replied the passenger, turning his back on him.

"I know it," said Passepartout, turning to another passenger, "but a simple idea—"

"Ideas are no use," returned the American, shrugging his shoulders, "as the engineer assures us that we can pass."

"Doubtless," urged Passepartout, "we can pass, but perhaps it would be more prudent—"

"What! Prudent!" cried Colonel Proctor, whom this word seemed to excite prodigiously. "At full speed, don't you see, at full speed!"

"I know—I see," repeated Passepartout; "but it would be, if not more prudent, since that word displeases you, at least more natural—"

"Who! What! What's the matter with this fellow?" cried several.

The poor fellow did not know to whom to address himself.

"Are you afraid?" asked Colonel Proctor.

"I afraid! Very well; I will show these people that a Frenchman can be as American as they!"

"All aboard!" cried the conductor.

"Yes, all aboard!" repeated Passepartout, and immediately. "But they can't prevent me from thinking that it would be more natural for us to cross the bridge on foot, and let the train come after!"

But no one heard this sage reflection, nor would anyone have acknowledged its justice. The passengers resumed their places in the cars. Passepartout took his seat without telling what had passed. The whist-players were quite absorbed in their game.

The locomotive whistled vigorously; the engineer, reversing the steam, backed the train for nearly a mile—retiring, like a jumper, in order to take a longer leap. Then, with another whistle, he began to move forward; the train increased its speed, and soon its rapidity became frightful; a prolonged screech issued from the locomotive; the piston worked up and down twenty strokes to the second. They perceived that the whole train, rushing on at the rate of a hundred miles an hour, hardly bore upon the rails at all.

And they passed over! It was like a flash. No one saw the bridge. The train leaped, so to speak, from one bank to the other, and the engineer could not stop it until it had gone five miles beyond the station. But scarcely had the train passed the river, when the bridge, completely ruined, fell with a crash into the rapids of Medicine Bow.

Chapter XXIX

IN WHICH CERTAIN INCIDENTS ARE NARRATED WHICH ARE ONLY TO BE MET WITH ON AMERICAN RAILROADS

THE TRAIN PURSUED ITS COURSE, THAT EVENING, WITHOUT INTERRUPTION, PASSING Fort Saunders, crossing Cheyenne Pass, and reaching Evans Pass. The road here attained the highest elevation of the journey, eight thousand and ninety-one feet above the level of the sea. The travellers had now only to descend to the Atlantic by limitless plains, levelled by nature. A branch of the "grand trunk" led off southward to Denver, the capital of Colorado. The country round about is rich in gold and silver, and more than fifty thousand inhabitants are already settled there.

Thirteen hundred and eighty-two miles had been passed over from San Francisco, in three days and three nights; four days and nights more would probably bring them to New York. Phileas Fogg was not as yet behind-hand.

During the night Camp Walbach was passed on the left; Lodge Pole Creek ran parallel with the road, marking the boundary between the territories of Wyoming and Colorado. They entered Nebraska at eleven, passed near Sedgwick, and touched at Julesburg, on the southern branch of the Platte River.

It was here that the Union Pacific Railroad was inaugurated on the 23d of October, 1867, by the chief engineer, General Dodge. Two powerful locomotives, carrying nine cars of invited guests, amongst whom was Thomas C. Durant, vice-president of the road, stopped at this point; cheers were given, the Sioux and Pawnees performed an imitation Indian battle, fireworks were let off, and the first number of the *Railway Pioneer* was printed by a press brought on the train. Thus was celebrated the inauguration of this great railroad, a mighty instrument of progress and civilisation, thrown across the desert, and destined to link together cities and towns which do not yet exist. The whistle of the locomotive, more powerful than Amphion's lyre, was about to bid them rise from American soil.

Fort McPherson was left behind at eight in the morning, and three hundred and fifty-seven miles had yet to be traversed before reaching Omaha. The road followed the capricious windings of the southern branch of the Platte River, on its left bank. At nine the train stopped at the important town of North Platte, built between the two arms of the river, which rejoin each other around it and form a single artery—a large tributary whose waters empty into the Missouri a little above Omaha.

The one hundred and first meridian was passed.

Mr. Fogg and his partners had resumed their game; no one—not even the dummy—complained of the length of the trip. Fix had begun by winning several guineas, which he seemed likely to lose; but he showed himself a not less eager whist-player than Mr. Fogg. During the morning, chance distinctly favoured that gentleman. Trumps and honours were showered upon his hands.

Once, having resolved on a bold stroke, he was on the point of playing a spade, when a voice behind him said, "I should play a diamond."

Mr. Fogg, Aouda, and Fix raised their heads, and beheld Colonel Proctor.

Stamp Proctor and Phileas Fogg recognised each other at once.

"Ah! it's you, is it, Englishman?" cried the colonel; "it's you who are going to play a spade!"

"And who plays it," replied Phileas Fogg coolly, throwing down the ten of spades.

"Well, it pleases me to have it diamonds," replied Colonel Proctor, in an insolent tone.

He made a movement as if to seize the card which had just been played, adding, "You don't understand anything about whist."

"Perhaps I do, as well as another," said Phileas Fogg, rising.

"You have only to try, son of John Bull," replied the colonel.

Aouda turned pale, and her blood ran cold. She seized Mr. Fogg's arm and gently pulled him back. Passepartout was ready to pounce upon the American, who was staring insolently at his opponent. But Fix got up, and going to Colonel Proctor said, "You forget that it is I with whom you have to deal, sir; for it was I whom you not only insulted, but struck!"

"Mr. Fix," said Mr. Fogg, "pardon me, but this affair is mine, and mine only. The colonel has again insulted me, by insisting that I should not play a spade, and he shall give me satisfaction for it."

"When and where you will," replied the American, "and with whatever weapon you choose."

Aouda in vain attempted to retain Mr. Fogg; as vainly did the detective endeavour to make the quarrel his. Passepartout wished to throw the colonel out of the window, but a sign from his master checked him. Phileas Fogg left the car, and the American followed him upon the platform.

"Sir," said Mr. Fogg to his adversary, "I am in a great hurry to get back to Europe, and any delay whatever will be greatly to my disadvantage."

"Well, what's that to me?" replied Colonel Proctor.

"Sir," said Mr. Fogg, very politely, "after our meeting at San Francisco, I determined to return to America and find you as soon as I had completed the business which called me to England."

"Really!"

"Will you appoint a meeting for six months hence?"

"Why not ten years hence?"

"I say six months," returned Phileas Fogg, "and I shall be at the place of meeting promptly."

"All this is an evasion," cried Stamp Proctor. "Now or never!"

"Very good. You are going to New York?"

"No."

"To Chicago?"

"No."

"To Omaha?"

"What difference is it to you? Do you know Plum Creek?"

"No," replied Mr. Fogg.

"It's the next station. The train will be there in an hour, and will stop there ten minutes. In ten minutes several revolver-shots could be exchanged."

"Very well," said Mr. Fogg. "I will stop at Plum Creek."

"And I guess you'll stay there too," added the American insolently.

"Who knows?" replied Mr. Fogg, returning to the car as coolly as usual. He began to reassure Aouda, telling her that blusterers were never to be feared, and begged Fix to be his second at the approaching duel, a request which the detective could not refuse. Mr. Fogg resumed the interrupted game with perfect calmness.

At eleven o'clock the locomotive's whistle announced that they were approaching Plum Creek station. Mr. Fogg rose, and, followed by Fix, went out upon the platform. Passepartout accompanied him, carrying a pair of revolvers. Aouda remained in the car, as pale as death.

The door of the next car opened, and Colonel Proctor appeared on the platform, attended by a Yankee of his own stamp as his second. But just as the combatants were about to step from the train, the conductor hurried up, and shouted, "You can't get off, gentlemen!"

"Why not?" asked the colonel.

"We are twenty minutes late, and we shall not stop."

"But I am going to fight a duel with this gentleman."

"I am sorry," said the conductor; "but we shall be off at once. There's the bell ringing now."

The train started.

"I'm really very sorry, gentlemen," said the conductor. "Under any other circumstances I should have been happy to oblige you. But, after all, as you have not had time to fight here, why not fight as we go along?"

"That wouldn't be convenient, perhaps, for this gentleman," said the colonel, in a jeering tone.

"It would be perfectly so," replied Phileas Fogg.

"Well, we are really in America," thought Passepartout, "and the conductor is a gentleman of the first order!"

So muttering, he followed his master.

The two combatants, their seconds, and the conductor passed through the cars to the rear of the train. The last car was only occupied by a dozen passengers, whom the conductor politely asked if they would not be so kind as to leave it vacant for a few moments, as two gentlemen had an affair of honour to settle. The passengers granted the request with alacrity, and straightaway disappeared on the platform.

The car, which was some fifty feet long, was very convenient for their purpose. The adversaries might march on each other in the aisle, and fire at their ease. Never was duel more easily arranged. Mr. Fogg and Colonel Proctor, each provided with two six-barrelled revolvers, entered the car. The seconds, remaining outside, shut them in. They were to begin firing at the first whistle of the locomotive. After an interval of two minutes, what remained of the two gentlemen would be taken from the car.

Nothing could be more simple. Indeed, it was all so simple that Fix and Passepartout felt their hearts beating as if they would crack. They were listening for the whistle agreed upon, when suddenly savage cries resounded in the air, accompanied by reports which certainly did not issue from the car where the duellists were. The reports continued in front and the whole length of the train. Cries of terror proceeded from the interior of the cars.

Colonel Proctor and Mr. Fogg, revolvers in hand, hastily quitted their prison, and rushed forward where the noise was most clamorous. They then perceived that the train was attacked by a band of Sioux.

This was not the first attempt of these daring Indians, for more than once they had way-laid trains on the road. A hundred of them had, according to their habit, jumped upon the steps without stopping the train, with the ease of a clown mounting a horse at full gallop.

The Sioux were armed with guns, from which came the reports, to which the passengers, who were almost all armed, responded by revolver-shots.

The Indians had first mounted the engine, and half stunned the engineer and stoker with blows from their muskets. A Sioux chief, wishing to stop the train, but not knowing how to work the regulator, had opened wide instead of closing the steam-valve, and the locomotive was plunging forward with terrific velocity.

The Sioux had at the same time invaded the cars, skipping like enraged monkeys over the roofs, thrusting open the doors, and fighting hand to hand with the passengers. Penetrating the baggage-car, they pillaged it, throwing the trunks out of the train. The cries and shots were constant.

The travellers defended themselves bravely; some of the cars were barricaded, and sustained a siege, like moving forts, carried along at a speed of a hundred miles an hour.

Aouda behaved courageously from the first. She defended herself like a true heroine with a revolver, which she shot through the broken windows whenever a savage made his appearance. Twenty Sioux had fallen mortally wounded to the ground, and the wheels crushed those who fell upon the rails as if they had been worms. Several passengers, shot or stunned, lay on the seats.

It was necessary to put an end to the struggle, which had lasted for ten minutes, and which would result in the triumph of the Sioux if the train was not stopped. Fort Kearney station, where there was a garrison, was only two miles distant; but, that once passed, the Sioux would be masters of the train between Fort Kearney and the station beyond.

The conductor was fighting beside Mr. Fogg, when he was shot and fell. At the same moment he cried, "Unless the train is stopped in five minutes, we are lost!"

"It shall be stopped," said Phileas Fogg, preparing to rush from the car.

"Stay, monsieur," cried Passepartout; "I will go."

Mr. Fogg had not time to stop the brave fellow, who, opening a door unperceived by the Indians, succeeded in slipping under the car; and while the struggle continued, and the balls whizzed across each other over his head, he made use of his old acrobatic experience, and with amazing agility worked his way under the cars, holding on to the chains, aiding himself by the brakes and edges of the sashes, creeping from one car to another with marvellous skill, and thus gaining the forward end of the train.

There, suspended by one hand between the baggage-car and the tender, with the other he loosened the safety chains; but, owing to the traction, he would never have succeeded in unscrewing the yoking-bar, had not a violent concussion jolted this bar out. The train, now detached from the engine, remained a little behind, whilst the locomotive rushed forward with increased speed.

Carried on by the force already acquired, the train still moved for several minutes; but the brakes were worked, and at last they stopped, less than a hundred feet from Kearney station.

The soldiers of the fort, attracted by the shots, hurried up; the Sioux had not expected them, and decamped in a body before the train entirely stopped.

But when the passengers counted each other on the station platform several were found missing; among others the courageous Frenchman, whose devotion had just saved them.

Chapter XXX

IN WHICH PHILEAS FOGG SIMPLY DOES HIS DUTY

THREE PASSENGERS—INCLUDING PASSEPARTOUT—HAD DISAPPEARED. HAD THEY BEEN killed in the struggle? Were they taken prisoners by the Sioux? It was impossible to tell.

There were many wounded, but none mortally. Colonel Proctor was one of the most seriously hurt; he had fought bravely, and a ball had entered his groin. He was carried into the station with the other wounded passengers, to receive such attention as could be of avail.

Aouda was safe; and Phileas Fogg, who had been in the thickest of the fight, had not received a scratch. Fix was slightly wounded in the arm. But Passepartout was not to be found, and tears coursed down Aouda's cheeks.

All the passengers had got out of the train, the wheels of which were stained with blood. From the tires and spokes hung ragged pieces of flesh. As far as the eye could reach on the white plain behind, red trails were visible. The last Sioux were disappearing in the south, along the banks of the Republican River.

Mr. Fogg, with folded arms, remained motionless. He had a serious decision to make. Aouda, standing near him, looked at him without speaking, and he understood her look. If his servant was a prisoner, ought he not to risk everything to rescue him from the Indians? "I will find him, living or dead," said he quietly to Aouda.

"Ah, Mr.—Mr. Fogg!" cried she, clasping his hands and covering them with tears.

"Living," added Mr. Fogg, "if we do not lose a moment."

Phileas Fogg, by this resolution, inevitably sacrificed himself; he pronounced his own doom. The delay of a single day would make him lose the steamer at New York, and his bet would be certainly lost. But as he thought, "It is my duty," he did not hesitate.

The commanding officer of Fort Kearney was there. A hundred of his soldiers had placed themselves in a position to defend the station, should the Sioux attack it.

"Sir," said Mr. Fogg to the captain, "three passengers have disappeared."

"Dead?" asked the captain.

"Dead or prisoners; that is the uncertainty which must be solved. Do you propose to pursue the Sioux?"

"That's a serious thing to do, sir," returned the captain. "These Indians may retreat beyond the Arkansas, and I cannot leave the fort unprotected."

"The lives of three men are in question, sir," said Phileas Fogg.

"Doubtless; but can I risk the lives of fifty men to save three?"

"I don't know whether you can, sir; but you ought to do so."

"Nobody here," returned the other, "has a right to teach me my duty."

"Very well," said Mr. Fogg, coldly. "I will go alone."

"You, sir!" cried Fix, coming up; "you go alone in pursuit of the Indians?"

"Would you have me leave this poor fellow to perish—him to whom everyone present owes his life? I shall go."

"No, sir, you shall not go alone," cried the captain, touched in spite of himself. "No! you are a brave man. Thirty volunteers!" he added, turning to the soldiers.

The whole company started forward at once. The captain had only to pick his men. Thirty were chosen, and an old sergeant placed at their head.

"Thanks, captain," said Mr. Fogg.

"Will you let me go with you?" asked Fix.

"Do as you please, sir. But if you wish to do me a favour, you will remain with Aouda. In case anything should happen to me—"

A sudden pallor overspread the detective's face. Separate himself from the man whom he had so persistently followed step by step! Leave him to wander about in this desert! Fix gazed attentively at Mr. Fogg, and, despite his suspicions and of the struggle which was going on within him, he lowered his eyes before that calm and frank look.

"I will stay," said he.

A few moments after, Mr. Fogg pressed the young woman's hand, and, having confided to her his precious carpet-bag, went off with the sergeant and his little squad. But, before going, he had said to the soldiers, "My friends, I will divide five thousand dollars among you, if we save the prisoners."

It was then a little past noon.

Aouda retired to a waiting-room, and there she waited alone, thinking of the simple and noble generosity, the tranquil courage of Phileas Fogg. He had sacrificed his fortune, and was now risking his life, all without hesitation, from duty, in silence.

Fix did not have the same thoughts, and could scarcely conceal his agitation. He walked feverishly up and down the platform, but soon resumed his outward composure. He now saw the folly of which he had been guilty in letting Fogg go alone. What! This man, whom he had just followed around the world, was permitted now to separate himself from him! He began to accuse and abuse himself, and, as if he were director of police, administered to himself a sound lecture for his greenness.

"I have been an idiot!" he thought, "and this man will see it. He has gone, and won't come back! But how is it that I, Fix, who have in my pocket a warrant for his arrest, have been so fascinated by him? Decidedly, I am nothing but an ass!"

So reasoned the detective, while the hours crept by all too slowly. He did not know what to do. Sometimes he was tempted to tell Aouda all; but he could not doubt how the young woman would receive his confidences. What course should he take? He thought of pursuing Fogg across the vast white plains; it did not seem impossible that he might overtake him. Footsteps were easily printed on the snow! But soon, under a new sheet, every imprint would be effaced.

Fix became discouraged. He felt a sort of insurmountable longing to abandon the game altogether. He could now leave Fort Kearney station, and pursue his journey homeward in peace.

Towards two o'clock in the afternoon, while it was snowing hard, long whistles were heard approaching from the east. A great shadow, preceded by a wild light, slowly advanced, appearing still larger through the mist, which gave it a fantastic aspect. No train was expected from the east, neither had there been time for the succor asked for by telegraph to arrive; the train from Omaha to San Francisco was not due till the next day. The mystery was soon explained.

The locomotive, which was slowly approaching with deafening whistles, was that which, having been detached from the train, had continued its route with such terrific rapidity, carrying off the unconscious engineer and stoker. It had run several miles, when, the fire becoming low for want of fuel, the steam had slackened; and it had finally stopped an hour after, some twenty miles beyond Fort Kearney. Neither the engineer nor the stoker was dead, and, after remaining for some time in their swoon, had come to themselves. The train had then stopped. The engineer, when he found himself in the desert, and the locomotive without cars, understood what had happened. He could not imagine how the locomotive had become separated from the train; but he did not doubt that the train left behind was in distress.

He did not hesitate what to do. It would be prudent to continue on to Omaha, for it would be dangerous to return to the train, which the Indians might still be engaged in pillaging. Nevertheless, he began to rebuild the fire in the furnace; the pressure again mounted, and the locomotive returned, running backward to Fort Kearney. This it was which was whistling in the mist.

The travellers were glad to see the locomotive resume its place at the head of the train. They could now continue the journey so terribly interrupted.

Aouda, on seeing the locomotive come up, hurried out of the station, and asked the conductor, "Are you going to start?"

"At once, madam."

"But the prisoners—our unfortunate fellow-travellers—"

"I cannot interrupt the trip," replied the conductor. "We are already three hours behind time."

"And when will another train pass here from San Francisco?"

"To-morrow evening, madam."

"To-morrow evening! But then it will be too late! We must wait—"

"It is impossible," responded the conductor. "If you wish to go, please get in."

"I will not go," said Aouda.

Fix had heard this conversation. A little while before, when there was no prospect of proceeding on the journey, he had made up his mind to leave Fort Kearney; but now that the train was there, ready to start, and he had only to take his seat in the car, an irresistible influence held him back. The station platform burned his feet, and he could not stir. The conflict in his mind again began; anger and failure stifled him. He wished to struggle on to the end.

Meanwhile the passengers and some of the wounded, among them Colonel Proctor, whose injuries were serious, had taken their places in the train. The buzzing of the overheated boiler was heard, and the steam was escaping from the valves. The engineer whistled, the train started, and soon disappeared, mingling its white smoke with the eddies of the densely falling snow.

The detective had remained behind.

Several hours passed. The weather was dismal, and it was very cold. Fix sat motionless on a bench in the station; he might have been thought asleep. Aouda, despite the storm, kept coming out of the waiting-room, going to the end of the platform, and peering through the tempest of snow, as if to pierce the mist which narrowed the horizon around her, and to hear, if possible, some welcome sound. She heard and saw nothing. Then she would return, chilled through, to issue out again after the lapse of a few moments, but always in vain.

Evening came, and the little band had not returned. Where could they be? Had they found the Indians, and were they having a conflict with them, or were they still wandering amid the mist? The commander of the fort was anxious, though he tried to conceal his apprehensions. As night approached, the snow fell less plentifully, but it became intensely cold. Absolute silence rested on the plains. Neither flight of bird nor passing of beast troubled the perfect calm.

Throughout the night Aouda, full of sad forebodings, her heart stifled with anguish, wandered about on the verge of the plains. Her imagination carried her far off, and showed her innumerable dangers. What she suffered through the long hours it would be impossible to describe.

Fix remained stationary in the same place, but did not sleep. Once a man approached and spoke to him, and the detective merely replied by shaking his head.

Thus the night passed. At dawn the half-extinguished disc of the sun rose above a misty horizon ; but it was now possible to recognise objects two miles off. Phileas Fogg and the squad had gone southward; in the south all was still vacancy. It was then seven o'clock.

The captain, who was really alarmed, did not know what course to take.

Should he send another detachment to the rescue of the first? Should he sacrifice more men, with so few chances of saving those already sacrificed? His hesitation did not last long, however. Calling one of his lieutenants, he was on the point of ordering a reconnaissance, when gunshots were heard. Was it a signal? The soldiers rushed out of the fort, and half-a-mile off they perceived a little band returning in good order.

Mr. Fogg was marching at their head, and just behind him were Passepartout and the other two travellers, rescued from the Sioux.

They had met and fought the Indians ten miles south of Fort Kearney. Shortly before the detachment arrived, Passepartout and his companions had begun to struggle with their captors, three of whom the Frenchman had felled with his fists, when his master and the soldiers hastened up to their relief.

All were welcomed with joyful cries. Phileas Fogg distributed the reward he had promised to the soldiers, while Passepartout, not without reason, muttered to himself, "It must certainly be confessed that I cost my master dear!"

Fix, without saying a word, looked at Mr. Fogg, and it would have been difficult to analyse the thoughts which struggled within him. As for Aouda, she took her protector's hand and pressed it in her own, too much moved to speak.

Meanwhile, Passepartout was looking about for the train; he thought he should find it there, ready to start for Omaha, and he hoped that the time lost might be regained.

"The train! the train!" cried he.

"Gone," replied Fix.

"And when does the next train pass here?" said Phileas Fogg.

"Not till this evening."

"Ah!" returned the impassible gentleman quietly.

Chapter XXXI

IN WHICH FIX THE DETECTIVE CONSIDERABLY FURTHERS THE INTERESTS OF PHILEAS FOGG

PHILEAS FOGG FOUND HIMSELF TWENTY HOURS BEHIND TIME. PASSEPARTOUT, THE INvoluntary cause of this delay, was desperate. He had ruined his master!

At this moment the detective approached Mr. Fogg, and, looking him intently in the face, said—

"Seriously, sir, are you in great haste?"

"Quite seriously."

"I have a purpose in asking," resumed Fix. "Is it absolutely necessary that you should be in New York on the 11th, before nine o'clock in the evening, the time that the steamer leaves for Liverpool?"

"It is absolutely necessary."

"And, if your journey had not been interrupted by these Indians, you would have reached New York on the morning of the 11th?"

"Yes; with eleven hours to spare before the steamer left."

"Good! you are therefore twenty hours behind. Twelve from twenty leaves eight. You must regain eight hours. Do you wish to try to do so?"

"On foot?" asked Mr. Fogg.

"No; on a sledge," replied Fix. "On a sledge with sails. A man has proposed such a method to me."

It was the man who had spoken to Fix during the night, and whose offer he had refused.

Phileas Fogg did not reply at once; but Fix having pointed out the man, who was walking up and down in front of the station, Mr. Fogg went up to him. An instant after, Mr. Fogg and the American, whose name was Mudge, entered a hut built just below the fort.

There Mr. Fogg examined a curious vehicle, a kind of frame on two long beams, a little raised in front like the runners of a sledge, and upon which there was room for five or six persons. A high mast was fixed on the frame, held firmly by metallic lashings, to which was attached a large brigantine sail. This mast held an iron stay upon which to hoist a jib-sail. Behind, a sort of rudder served to guide the vehicle. It was, in short, a sledge rigged like a sloop. During the winter, when the trains are blocked up by the snow, these sledges make extremely rapid journeys across the frozen plains from one station to another. Provided with more sails than a cutter, and with the wind behind them, they slip over the surface of the prairies with a speed equal if not superior to that of the express trains.

Mr. Fogg readily made a bargain with the owner of this land-craft. The wind was favourable, being fresh, and blowing from the west. The snow had hardened, and Mudge was very confident of being able to transport Mr. Fogg in a few hours to Omaha. Thence the trains eastward run frequently to Chicago and New York. It was not impossible that the lost time might yet be recovered; and such an opportunity was not to be rejected.

Not wishing to expose Aouda to the discomforts of travelling in the open air, Mr. Fogg proposed to leave her with Passepartout at Fort Kearney, the servant taking upon himself to escort her to Europe by a better route and under more favourable conditions. But Aouda refused to separate from Mr. Fogg, and Passepartout was delighted with her decision; for nothing could induce him to leave his master while Fix was with him.

It would be difficult to guess the detective's thoughts. Was this conviction shaken by Phileas Fogg's return, or did he still regard him as an exceedingly shrewd rascal, who, his journey around the world completed, would think himself absolutely safe in England? Perhaps Fix's opinion of Phileas Fogg was somewhat modified; but he was nevertheless resolved to do his duty, and to hasten the return of the whole party to England as much as possible.

At eight o'clock the sledge was ready to start. The passengers took their places on it, and wrapped themselves up closely in their travelling-cloaks. The two great sails were hoisted, and under the pressure of the wind the sledge slid over the hardened snow with a velocity of forty miles an hour.

The distance between Fort Kearney and Omaha, as the birds fly, is at most two hundred miles. If the wind held good, the distance might be traversed in five hours; if no accident happened the sledge might reach Omaha by one o'clock.

What a journey! The travellers, huddled close together, could not speak for the cold, intensified by the rapidity at which they were going. The sledge sped on as lightly as a boat over the waves. When the breeze came skimming the earth, the sledge seemed to be lifted off the ground by its sails. Mudge, who was at the rudder, kept in a straight line, and by a turn of his hand checked the lurches which the vehicle had a tendency to make. All the sails were up, and the jib was so arranged as not to screen the brigantine. A topmast was hoisted, and another jib, held out to the wind, added its force to the other sails. Although the speed could not be exactly estimated, the sledge could not be going at less than forty miles an hour.

"If nothing breaks," said Mudge, "we shall get there!"

Mr. Fogg had made it for Mudge's interest to reach Omaha within the time agreed on, by the offer of a handsome reward.

The prairie, across which the sledge was moving in a straight line, was as flat as a sea. It seemed like a vast frozen lake. The railroad which ran through this section ascended from the south-west to the north-west by Great Island, Columbus, an important Nebraska town, Schuyler, and Fremont, to Omaha. It followed throughout the right bank of the Platte River. The sledge, shortening this route, took a chord of the arc described by the railway. Mudge was not afraid of being stopped by the Platte River, because it was frozen. The road, then, was quite clear of obstacles, and Phileas Fogg had but two things to fear—an accident to the sledge, and a change or calm in the wind.

But the breeze, far from lessening its force, blew as if to bend the mast, which, however, the metallic lashings held firmly. These lashings, like the chords of a stringed instrument, resounded as if vibrated by a violin bow. The sledge slid along in the midst of a plaintively intense melody.

"Those chords give the fifth and the octave," said Mr. Fogg.

These were the only words he uttered during the journey. Aouda, cozily packed in furs and cloaks, was sheltered as much as possible from the attacks of the freezing wind. As for Passepartout, his face was as red as the sun's disc when it sets in the mist, and he labouriously inhaled the biting air. With his natural buoyancy of spirits, he began to hope again. They would reach New York on the evening, if not on the morning, of the 11th, and there was still some chances that it would be before the steamer sailed for Liverpool.

Passepartout even felt a strong desire to grasp his ally, Fix, by the hand. He remembered that it was the detective who procured the sledge, the only means of reaching Omaha in time; but, checked by some presentiment, he kept his usual reserve. One thing, however, Passepartout would never forget, and that was the sacrifice which Mr. Fogg had made, without hesitation, to rescue him from the Sioux. Mr. Fogg had risked his fortune and his life. No! His servant would never forget that!

While each of the party was absorbed in reflections so different, the sledge flew fast over the vast carpet of snow. The creeks it passed over were not perceived. Fields and streams disappeared under the uniform whiteness. The plain was absolutely deserted. Between the Union Pacific road and the branch which unites Kearney with Saint Joseph it formed a great uninhabited island. Neither village, station, nor fort appeared. From time to time they sped by some phantom-like tree, whose white skeleton twisted and rattled in the wind. Sometimes flocks of wild birds rose, or bands of gaunt, famished, ferocious prairie-wolves ran howling after the sledge. Passepartout, revolver in hand, held himself ready to fire on those which came too near. Had an accident then happened to the sledge, the travellers, attacked by these beasts, would have been in the most terrible danger; but it held on its even course, soon gained on the wolves, and ere long left the howling band at a safe distance behind.

About noon Mudge perceived by certain landmarks that he was crossing the Platte River. He said nothing, but he felt certain that he was now within twenty miles of Omaha. In less than an hour he left the rudder and furled his sails, whilst the sledge, carried forward by the great impetus the wind had given it, went on half-a-mile further with its sails unspread.

It stopped at last, and Mudge, pointing to a mass of roofs white with snow, said: "We have got there!"

Arrived! Arrived at the station which is in daily communication, by numerous trains, with the Atlantic seaboard!

Passepartout and Fix jumped off, stretched their stiffened limbs, and aided Mr. Fogg and the young woman to descend from the sledge. Phileas Fogg generously rewarded Mudge, whose hand Passepartout warmly grasped, and the party directed their steps to the Omaha railway station.

The Pacific Railroad proper finds its terminus at this important Nebraska town. Omaha is connected with Chicago by the Chicago and Rock Island Railroad, which runs directly east, and passes fifty stations.

A train was ready to start when Mr. Fogg and his party reached the station, and they only had time to get into the cars. They had seen nothing of Omaha; but Passepartout confessed to himself that this was not to be regretted, as they were not travelling to see the sights.

The train passed rapidly across the State of Iowa, by Council Bluffs, Des Moines, and Iowa City. During the night it crossed the Mississippi at Davenport, and by Rock Island entered Illinois. The next day, which was the 10th, at four in the evening, it reached Chicago, already risen from its ruins, and more proudly seated than ever on the borders of its beautiful Lake Michigan.

Nine hundred miles separated Chicago from New York; but trains are not wanting at Chicago. Mr. Fogg passed at once from one to the other, and the locomotive of the Pittsburgh, Fort Wayne, and Chicago Railway left at full speed, as if it fully comprehended that that gentleman had no time to lose. It traversed Indiana, Ohio, Pennsylvania, and New Jersey like a flash, rushing through towns with antique names, some of which had streets and car-tracks, but as yet no houses. At last the Hudson came into view; and at a quarter-past eleven in the evening of the 11th, the train stopped in the station on the right bank of the river, before the very pier of the Cunard line.

The *China*, for Liverpool, had started three-quarters of an hour before!

Chapter XXXII

IN WHICH PHILEAS FOGG ENGAGES IN A DIRECT STRUGGLE WITH BAD FORTUNE

THE *CHINA*, IN LEAVING, SEEMED TO HAVE CARRIED OFF PHILEAS FOGG'S LAST HOPE. None of the other steamers were able to serve his projects. The *Pereire*, of the French Transatlantic Company, whose admirable steamers are equal to any in speed and comfort, did not leave until the 14th; the Hamburg boats did not go directly to Liverpool or London, but to Havre; and the additional trip from Havre to Southampton would render Phileas Fogg's last efforts of no avail. The Inman steamer did not depart till the next day, and could not cross the Atlantic in time to save the wager.

Mr. Fogg learned all this in consulting his "Bradshaw," which gave him the daily movements of the transatlantic steamers.

Passepartout was crushed; it overwhelmed him to lose the boat by three-quarters of an hour. It was his fault, for, instead of helping his master, he had not ceased putting obstacles in his path! And when he recalled all the incidents of the tour, when he counted up the sums expended in pure loss and on his own account, when he thought that the immense stake, added to the heavy charges of this useless journey, would completely ruin Mr. Fogg, he overwhelmed himself with bitter self-accusations. Mr. Fogg, however, did not reproach him; and, on leaving the Cunard pier, only said: "We will consult about what is best to-morrow. Come."

The party crossed the Hudson in the Jersey City ferryboat, and drove in a carriage to the St. Nicholas Hotel, on Broadway. Rooms were engaged, and the night passed, briefly to Phileas Fogg, who slept profoundly, but very long to Aouda and the others, whose agitation did not permit them to rest.

The next day was the 12th of December. From seven in the morning of the 12th, to a quarter before nine in the evening of the 21st, there were nine days, thirteen hours, and forty-five minutes. If Phileas Fogg had left in the *China*, one of the fastest steamers on the Atlantic, he would have reached Liverpool, and then London, within the period agreed upon.

Mr. Fogg left the hotel alone, after giving Passepartout instructions to await his return, and inform Aouda to be ready at an instant's notice. He proceeded to the banks of the Hudson, and looked about among the vessels moored or anchored in the river, for any that were about to depart. Several had departure signals, and were preparing to put to sea at morning tide; for in this immense and admirable port there is not one day in a hundred that vessels do not set out for every quarter of the globe. But they were mostly sailing vessels, of which, of course, Phileas Fogg could make no use.

He seemed about to give up all hope, when he espied, anchored at the Battery, a cable's length off at most, a trading vessel, with a screw, well shaped, whose funnel, puffing a cloud of smoke, indicated that she was getting ready for departure.

Phileas Fogg hailed a boat, got into it, and soon found himself on board the *Henrietta*, iron-hulled, wood-built above. He ascended to the deck, and asked for the captain, who forthwith presented himself. He was a man of fifty, a sort of sea-wolf, with big eyes, a complexion of oxidised copper, red hair and thick neck, and a growling voice.

"The captain?" asked Mr. Fogg.

"I am the captain."

"I am Phileas Fogg, of London."

"And I am Andrew Speedy, of Cardiff."

"You are going to put to sea?"

"In an hour."

"You are bound for—"

"Bordeaux."

"And your cargo?"

"No freight. Going in ballast."

"Have you any passengers?"

"No passengers. Never have passengers. Too much in the way."

"Is your vessel a swift one?"

"Between eleven and twelve knots. The *Henrietta*, well known."

"Will you carry me and three other persons to Liverpool?"

"To Liverpool? Why not to China?"

"I said Liverpool."

"No!"

"No?"

"No. I am setting out for Bordeaux, and shall go to Bordeaux."

"Money is no object?"

"None."

The captain spoke in a tone which did not admit of a reply.

"But the owners of the *Henrietta*—" resumed Phileas Fogg.

"The owners are myself," replied the captain. "The vessel belongs to me."

"I will freight it for you."

"No."

"I will buy it of you."

"No."

Phileas Fogg did not betray the least disappointment; but the situation was a grave one. It was not at New York as at Hong Kong, nor with the captain of the *Henrietta* as with the captain of the *Tankadere*. Up to this time money had smoothed away every obstacle. Now money failed.

Still, some means must be found to cross the Atlantic on a boat, unless by balloon— which would have been venturesome, besides not being capable of being put in practice. It seemed that Phileas Fogg had an idea, for he said to the captain, "Well, will you carry me to Bordeaux?"

"No, not if you paid me two hundred dollars."

"I offer you two thousand."

"Apiece?"

"Apiece."

"And there are four of you?"

"Four."

Captain Speedy began to scratch his head. There were eight thousand dollars to gain, without changing his route; for which it was well worth conquering the repugnance he had for all kinds of passengers. Besides, passengers at two thousand dollars are no longer passengers, but valuable merchandise. "I start at nine o'clock," said Captain Speedy, simply. "Are you and your party ready?"

"We will be on board at nine o'clock," replied, no less simply, Mr. Fogg.

It was half-past eight. To disembark from the *Henrietta*, jump into a hack, hurry to the St. Nicholas, and return with Aouda, Passepartout, and even the inseparable Fix, was the work of a brief time, and was performed by Mr. Fogg with the coolness which never abandoned him. They were on board when the *Henrietta* made ready to weigh anchor.

When Passepartout heard what this last voyage was going to cost, he uttered a prolonged "Oh!" which extended throughout his vocal gamut.

As for Fix, he said to himself that the Bank of England would certainly not come out of this affair well indemnified. When they reached England, even if Mr. Fogg did not throw some handfuls of bank-bills into the sea, more than seven thousand pounds would have been spent!

Chapter XXXIII

IN WHICH PHILEAS FOGG SHOWS HIMSELF
EQUAL TO THE OCCASION

AN HOUR AFTER, THE *HENRIETTA* PASSED THE LIGHTHOUSE WHICH MARKS THE ENTRANCE of the Hudson, turned the point of Sandy Hook, and put to sea. During the day she skirted Long Island, passed Fire Island, and directed her course rapidly eastward.

At noon the next day, a man mounted the bridge to ascertain the vessel's position. It might be thought that this was Captain Speedy. Not the least in the world. It was Phileas Fogg, Esquire. As for Captain Speedy, he was shut up in his cabin under lock and key, and was uttering loud cries, which signified an anger at once pardonable and excessive.

What had happened was very simple. Phileas Fogg wished to go to Liverpool, but the captain would not carry him there. Then Phileas Fogg had taken passage for Bordeaux, and, during the thirty hours he had been on board, had so shrewdly managed with his bank-notes that the sailors and stokers, who were only an occasional crew, and were not on the best terms with the captain, went over to him in a body. This was why Phileas Fogg was in command instead of Captain Speedy; why the captain was a prisoner in his cabin; and why, in short, the *Henrietta* was directing her course towards Liverpool. It was very clear, to see Mr. Fogg manage the craft, that he had been a sailor.

How the adventure ended will be seen anon. Aouda was anxious, though she said nothing. As for Passepartout, he thought Mr. Fogg's maneuvre simply glorious. The captain had said "between eleven and twelve knots," and the *Henrietta* confirmed his prediction.

If, then—for there were "ifs" still—the sea did not become too boisterous, if the wind did not veer round to the east, if no accident happened to the boat or its machinery, the *Henrietta* might cross the three thousand miles from New York to Liverpool in the nine days, between the 12th and the 21st of December. It is true that, once arrived, the affair on board the *Henrietta*, added to that of the Bank of England, might create more difficulties for Mr. Fogg than he imagined or could desire.

During the first days, they went along smoothly enough. The sea was not very unpropitious, the wind seemed stationary in the north-east, the sails were hoisted, and the *Henrietta* ploughed across the waves like a real transatlantic steamer.

Passepartout was delighted. His master's last exploit, the consequences of which he ignored, enchanted him. Never had the crew seen so jolly and dexterous a fellow. He formed warm friendships with the sailors, and amazed them with his acrobatic feats. He thought they managed the vessel like gentlemen, and that the stokers fired up like heroes. His loquacious good-humor infected everyone. He had forgotten the past, its vexations and delays. He only thought of the end, so nearly accomplished; and sometimes he boiled over with impatience, as if heated by the furnaces of the *Henrietta*. Often, also, the worthy fellow revolved around Fix, looking at him with a keen, distrustful eye; but he did not speak to him, for their old intimacy no longer existed.

Fix, it must be confessed, understood nothing of what was going on. The conquest of the *Henrietta*, the bribery of the crew, Fogg managing the boat like a skilled seaman, amazed and confused him. He did not know what to think. For, after all, a man who began by stealing fifty-five thousand pounds might end by stealing a vessel; and Fix was not unnaturally inclined to conclude that the *Henrietta*, under Fogg's command, was not going to Liverpool at all, but to some part of the world where the robber, turned into a pirate, would quietly put himself in safety. The conjecture was at least a plausible one, and the detective began to seriously regret that he had embarked in the affair.

As for Captain Speedy, he continued to howl and growl in his cabin; and Passepartout, whose duty it was to carry him his meals, courageous as he was, took the greatest precautions. Mr. Fogg did not seem even to know that there was a captain on board.

On the 13th they passed the edge of the Banks of Newfoundland, a dangerous locality; during the winter, especially, there are frequent fogs and heavy gales of wind. Ever since the evening before, the barometer, suddenly falling, had indicated an approaching change in the atmosphere; and during the night the temperature varied, the cold became sharper, and the wind veered to the south-east.

This was a misfortune. Mr. Fogg, in order not to deviate from his course, furled his sails and increased the force of the steam; but the vessel's speed slackened, owing to the state of the sea, the long waves of which broke against the stern. She pitched violently, and this retarded her progress. The breeze little by little swelled into a tempest, and it was to be feared that the *Henrietta* might not be able to maintain herself upright on the waves.

Passepartout's visage darkened with the skies, and for two days the poor fellow experienced constant fright. But Phileas Fogg was a bold mariner, and knew how to maintain headway against the sea; and he kept on his course, without even decreasing his steam. The *Henrietta*, when she could not rise upon the waves, crossed them, swamping her deck, but passing safely. Sometimes the screw rose out of the water, beating its protruding end, when a mountain of water raised the stern above the waves; but the craft always kept straight ahead.

The wind, however, did not grow as boisterous as might have been feared; it was not one of those tempests which burst, and rush on with a speed of ninety miles an hour. It continued fresh, but, unhappily, it remained obstinately in the south-east, rendering the sails useless.

The 16th of December was the seventy-fifth day since Phileas Fogg's departure from London, and the *Henrietta* had not yet been seriously delayed. Half of the voyage was almost accomplished, and the worst localities had been passed. In summer, success would have been well-nigh certain. In winter, they were at the mercy of the bad season. Passepartout said nothing; but he cherished hope in secret, and comforted himself with the reflection that, if the wind failed them, they might still count on the steam.

On this day the engineer came on deck, went up to Mr. Fogg, and began to speak earnestly with him. Without knowing why—it was a presentiment, perhaps—Passepartout became vaguely uneasy. He would have given one of his ears to hear with the other what the engineer was saying. He finally managed to catch a few words, and was sure he heard his master say, "You are certain of what you tell me?"

"Certain, sir," replied the engineer. "You must remember that, since we started, we have kept up hot fires in all our furnaces and, though we had coal enough to go on short steam from New York to Bordeaux, we haven't enough to go with all steam from New York to Liverpool."

"I will consider," replied Mr. Fogg.

Passepartout understood it all; he was seized with mortal anxiety. The coal was giving out! "Ah, if my master can get over that," muttered he, "he'll be a famous man!" He could not help imparting to Fix what he had overheard.

"Then you believe that we really are going to Liverpool?"

"Of course."

"Ass!" replied the detective, shrugging his shoulders and turning on his heel.

Passepartout was on the point of vigorously resenting the epithet, the reason of which he could not for the life of him comprehend; but he reflected that the unfortunate Fix was probably very much disappointed and humiliated in his self-esteem, after having so awkwardly followed a false scent around the world, and refrained.

And now what course would Phileas Fogg adopt? It was difficult to imagine. Nevertheless he seemed to have decided upon one, for that evening he sent for the engineer, and said to him, "Feed all the fires until the coal is exhausted."

A few moments after, the funnel of the *Henrietta* vomited forth torrents of smoke. The vessel continued to proceed with all steam on; but on the 18th, the engineer, as he had predicted, announced that the coal would give out in the course of the day.

"Do not let the fires go down," replied Mr. Fogg. "Keep them up to the last. Let the valves be filled."

Towards noon Phileas Fogg, having ascertained their position, called Passepartout, and ordered him to go for Captain Speedy. It was as if the honest fellow had been commanded to unchain a tiger. He went to the poop, saying to himself, "He will be like a madman!"

In a few moments, with cries and oaths, a bomb appeared on the poop-deck. The bomb was Captain Speedy. It was clear that he was on the point of bursting. "Where are we?" were the first words his anger permitted him to utter. Had the poor man be an apoplectic, he could never have recovered from his paroxysm of wrath.

"Where are we?" he repeated, with purple face.

"Seven hundred and seven miles from Liverpool," replied Mr. Fogg, with imperturbable calmness.

"Pirate!" cried Captain Speedy.

"I have sent for you, sir——"

"Pickaroon!"

"——Sir," continued Mr. Fogg, "to ask you to sell me your vessel."

"No! By all the devils, no!"

"But I shall be obliged to burn her."

"Burn the *Henrietta!*"

"Yes; at least the upper part of her. The coal has given out."

"Burn my vessel!" cried Captain Speedy, who could scarcely pronounce the words. "A vessel worth fifty thousand dollars!"

"Here are sixty thousand," replied Phileas Fogg, handing the captain a roll of bank-bills. This had a prodigious effect on Andrew Speedy. An American can scarcely remain unmoved at the sight of sixty thousand dollars. The captain forgot in an instant his anger, his imprisonment, and all his grudges against his passenger. The *Henrietta* was twenty years old; it was a great bargain. The bomb would not go off after all. Mr. Fogg had taken away the match.

"And I shall still have the iron hull," said the captain in a softer tone.

"The iron hull and the engine. Is it agreed?"

"Agreed."

And Andrew Speedy, seizing the bank-notes, counted them and consigned them to his pocket.

During this colloquy, Passepartout was as white as a sheet, and Fix seemed on the point of having an apoplectic fit. Nearly twenty thousand pounds had been expended, and Fogg left the hull and engine to the captain, that is, near the whole value of the craft! It was true, however, that fifty-five thousand pounds had been stolen from the Bank.

When Andrew Speedy had pocketed the money, Mr. Fogg said to him, "Don't let this astonish you, sir. You must know that I shall lose twenty thousand pounds, unless I arrive in London by a quarter before nine on the evening of the 21st of December. I missed the steamer at New York, and as you refused to take me to Liverpool—"

"And I did well!" cried Andrew Speedy; "for I have gained at least forty thousand dollars by it!" He added, more sedately, "Do you know one thing, Captain—"

"Fogg."

"Captain Fogg, you've got something of the Yankee about you."

And, having paid his passenger what he considered a high compliment, he was going away, when Mr. Fogg said, "The vessel now belongs to me?"

"Certainly, from the keel to the truck of the masts—all the wood, that is."

"Very well. Have the interior seats, bunks, and frames pulled down, and burn them."

It was necessary to have dry wood to keep the steam up to the adequate pressure, and on that day the poop, cabins, bunks, and the spare deck were sacrificed. On the next day, the 19th of December, the masts, rafts, and spars were burned; the crew worked lustily, keeping up the fires. Passepartout hewed, cut, and sawed away with all his might. There was a perfect rage for demolition.

The railings, fittings, the greater part of the deck, and top sides disappeared on the 20th, and the Henrietta was now only a flat hulk. But on this day they sighted the Irish coast and Fastnet Light. By ten in the evening they were passing Queenstown. Phileas Fogg had only twenty-four hours more in which to get to London; that length of time was necessary to reach Liverpool, with all steam on. And the steam was about to give out altogether!

"Sir," said Captain Speedy, who was now deeply interested in Mr. Fogg's project, "I really commiserate you. Everything is against you. We are only opposite Queenstown."

"Ah," said Mr. Fogg, "is that place where we see the lights Queenstown?"

"Yes."

"Can we enter the harbour?"

"Not under three hours. Only at high tide."

"Stay," replied Mr. Fogg calmly, without betraying in his features that by a supreme inspiration he was about to attempt once more to conquer ill-fortune.

Queenstown is the Irish port at which the transatlantic steamers stop to put off the mails. These mails are carried to Dublin by express trains always held in readiness to start; from Dublin they are sent on to Liverpool by the most rapid boats, and thus gain twelve hours on the Atlantic steamers.

Phileas Fogg counted on gaining twelve hours in the same way. Instead of arriving at

Liverpool the next evening by the *Henrietta*, he would be there by noon, and would therefore have time to reach London before a quarter before nine in the evening.

The *Henrietta* entered Queenstown Harbour at one o'clock in the morning, it then being high tide; and Phileas Fogg, after being grasped heartily by the hand by Captain Speedy, left that gentleman on the levelled hulk of his craft, which was still worth half what he had sold it for.

The party went on shore at once. Fix was greatly tempted to arrest Mr. Fogg on the spot; but he did not. Why? What struggle was going on within him? Had he changed his mind about "his man"? Did he understand that he had made a grave mistake? He did not, however, abandon Mr. Fogg. They all got upon the train, which was just ready to start, at half-past one; at dawn of day they were in Dublin; and they lost no time in embarking on a steamer which, disdaining to rise upon the waves, invariably cut through them.

Phileas Fogg at last disembarked on the Liverpool quay, at twenty minutes before twelve, December 21st. He was only six hours distant from London.

But at this moment Fix came up, put his hand upon Mr. Fogg's shoulder, and, showing his warrant, said, "You are really Phileas Fogg?"

"I am."

"I arrest you in the Queen's name!"

Chapter XXXIV

IN WHICH PHILEAS FOGG AT LAST REACHES LONDON

PHILEAS FOGG WAS IN PRISON. HE HAD BEEN SHUT UP IN THE CUSTOM-HOUSE, AND HE was to be transferred to London the next day.

Passepartout, when he saw his master arrested, would have fallen upon Fix had he not been held back by some policemen. Aouda was thunderstruck at the suddenness of an event which she could not understand. Passepartout explained to her how it was that the honest and courageous Fogg was arrested as a robber. The young woman's heart revolted against so heinous a charge, and when she saw that she could attempt or do nothing to save her protector, she wept bitterly.

As for Fix, he had arrested Mr. Fogg because it was his duty, whether Mr. Fogg were guilty or not.

The thought then struck Passepartout, that he was the cause of this new misfortune! Had he not concealed Fix's errand from his master? When Fix revealed his true character and purpose, why had he not told Mr. Fogg? If the latter had been warned, he would no doubt have given Fix proof of his innocence, and satisfied him of his mistake; at least, Fix would not have continued his journey at the expense and on the heels of his master, only to arrest him the moment he set foot on English soil. Passepartout wept till he was blind, and felt like blowing his brains out.

Aouda and he had remained, despite the cold, under the portico of the custom-house. Neither wished to leave the place; both were anxious to see Mr. Fogg again.

That gentleman was really ruined, and that at the moment when he was about to attain his end. This arrest was fatal. Having arrived at Liverpool at twenty minutes before twelve on the 21st of December, he had till a quarter before nine that evening to reach the Reform Club, that is, nine hours and a quarter; the journey from Liverpool to London was six hours.

If anyone, at this moment, had entered the custom-house, he would have found Mr. Fogg seated, motionless, calm, and without apparent anger, upon a wooden bench. He was not, it is true, resigned; but this last blow failed to force him into an outward betrayal of any emotion. Was he being devoured by one of those secret rages, all the more terrible because contained, and which only burst forth, with an irresistible force, at the last moment? No one could tell. There he sat, calmly waiting—for what? Did he still cherish hope? Did he still believe, now that the door of this prison was closed upon him, that he would succeed?

However that may have been, Mr. Fogg carefully put his watch upon the table, and observed its advancing hands. Not a word escaped his lips, but his look was singularly set and stern. The situation, in any event, was a terrible one, and might be thus stated: If Phileas Fogg was honest he was ruined; if he was a knave, he was caught.

Did escape occur to him? Did he examine to see if there were any practicable outlet from his prison? Did he think of escaping from it? Possibly; for once he walked slowly around the room. But the door was locked, and the window heavily barred with iron rods. He sat down again, and drew his journal from his pocket. On the line where these words were written, "December 21st, Saturday, Liverpool," he added, "80th day, 11.40 A.M.," and waited.

The custom-house clock struck one. Mr. Fogg observed that his watch was two hours too fast.

Two hours! Admitting that he was at this moment taking an express train, he could reach London and the Reform Club by a quarter before nine, P.M. His forehead slightly wrinkled.

At thirty-three minutes past two he heard a singular noise outside, then a hasty opening of doors. Passepartout's voice was audible, and immediately after that of Fix. Phileas Fogg's eyes brightened for an instant.

The door swung open, and he saw Passepartout, Aouda, and Fix, who hurried towards him.

Fix was out of breath, and his hair was in disorder. He could not speak. "Sir," he stammered, "Sir—forgive me—a most—unfortunate resemblance—robber arrested three days ago—you—are free!"

Phileas Fogg was free! He walked to the detective, looked him steadily in the face, and with the only rapid motion he had ever made in his life, or which he ever would make, drew back his arms, and with the precision of a machine, knocked Fix down.

"Well hit!" cried Passepartout, "Parbleu! that's what you might call a good application of English fists!"

Fix, who found himself on the floor, did not utter a word. He had only received his deserts. Mr. Fogg, Aouda, and Passepartout left the custom-house without delay, got into a cab, and in a few moments descended at the station.

Phileas Fogg asked if there was an express train about to leave for London. It was forty minutes past two. The express train had left thirty-five minutes before.

Phileas Fogg then ordered a special train.

There were several rapid locomotives on hand; but the railway arrangements did not permit the special train to leave until three o'clock.

At that hour Phileas Fogg, having stimulated the engineer by the offer of a generous reward, at last set out towards London with Aouda and his faithful servant.

It was necessary to make the journey in five hours and a half; and this would have been easy on a clear road throughout. But there were forced delays, and when Mr. Fogg stepped from the train at the terminus, all the clocks in London were striking ten minutes before nine.*

Having made the tour of the world, he was behindhand five minutes. He had lost the wager!

Chapter XXXV

IN WHICH PHILEAS FOGG DOES NOT HAVE TO REPEAT HIS ORDERS TO PASSEPARTOUT TWICE

THE DWELLERS IN SAVILLE ROW WOULD HAVE BEEN SURPRISED, THE NEXT DAY, IF THEY had been told that Phileas Fogg had returned home. His doors and windows were still closed; no appearance of change was visible.

After leaving the station, Mr. Fogg gave Passepartout instructions to purchase some provisions, and quietly went to his domicile.

He bore his misfortune with his habitual tranquillity. Ruined! And by the blundering of the detective! After having steadily traversed that long journey, overcome a hundred obstacles, braved many dangers, and still found time to do some good on his way, to fail near the goal by a sudden event which he could not have foreseen, and against which he was unarmed; it was terrible! But a few pounds were left of the large sum he had carried with him. There only remained of his fortune the twenty thousand pounds deposited at Barings, and this amount he owed to his friends of the Reform Club. So great had been the expense of his tour, that, even had he won, it would not have enriched him; and it is probable that he had not sought to enrich himself, being a man who rather laid wagers for honour's sake than for the stake proposed. But this wager totally ruined him.

Mr. Fogg's course, however, was fully decided upon; he knew what remained for him to do.

A room in the house in Saville Row was set apart for Aouda, who was overwhelmed with grief at her protector's misfortune. From the words which Mr. Fogg dropped, she saw that he was meditating some serious project.

Knowing that Englishmen governed by a fixed idea sometimes resort to the desperate expedient of suicide, Passepartout kept a narrow watch upon his master, though he carefully concealed the appearance of so doing.

*A somewhat remarkable eccentricity on the part of the London clocks!—TRANSLATOR.

First of all, the worthy fellow had gone up to his room, and had extinguished the gas-burner, which had been burning for eighty days. He had found in the letter-box a bill from the gas company, and he thought it more than time to put a stop to this expense, which he had been doomed to bear.

The night passed. Mr. Fogg went to bed, but did he sleep? Aouda did not once close her eyes. Passepartout watched all night, like a faithful dog, at his master's door.

Mr. Fogg called him in the morning, and told him to get Aouda's breakfast, and a cup of tea and a chop for himself. He desired Aouda to excuse him from breakfast and dinner, as his time would be absorbed all day in putting his affairs to rights. In the evening he would ask permission to have a few moments' conversation with the young lady.

Passepartout, having received his orders, had nothing to do but obey them. He looked at his imperturbable master, and could scarcely bring his mind to leave him. His heart was full, and his conscience tortured by remorse; for he accused himself more bitterly than ever of being the cause of the irretrievable disaster. Yes! if he had warned Mr. Fogg, and had betrayed Fix's projects to him, his master would certainly not have given the detective passage to Liverpool, and then—

Passepartout could hold in no longer.

"My master! Mr. Fogg!" he cried, "why do you not curse me? It was my fault that—"

"I blame no one," returned Phileas Fogg, with perfect calmness. "Go!"

Passepartout left the room, and went to find Aouda, to whom he delivered his master's message.

"Madam," he added, "I can do nothing myself—nothing! I have no influence over my master; but you, perhaps—"

"What influence could I have?" replied Aouda. "Mr. Fogg is influenced by no one. Has he ever understood that my gratitude to him is overflowing? Has he ever read my heart? My friend, he must not be left alone an instant! You say he is going to speak with me this evening?"

"Yes, madam; probably to arrange for your protection and comfort in England."

"We shall see," replied Aouda, becoming suddenly pensive.

Throughout this day (Sunday) the house in Saville Row was as if uninhabited, and Phileas Fogg, for the first time since he had lived in that house, did not set out for his club when Westminster clock struck half-past eleven.

Why should he present himself at the Reform? His friends no longer expected him there. As Phileas Fogg had not appeared in the saloon on the evening before (Saturday, the 21st of December, at a quarter before nine), he had lost his wager. It was not even necessary that he should go to his bankers for the twenty thousand pounds; for his antagonists already had his check in their hands, and they had only to fill it out and send it to the Barings to have the amount transferred to their credit.

Mr. Fogg, therefore, had no reason for going out, and so he remained at home. He shut himself up in his room, and busied himself putting his affairs in order. Passepartout continually ascended and descended the stairs. The hours were long for him. He listened at his master's door, and looked through the keyhole, as if he had a perfect right so to do, and as if he feared that something terrible might happen at any moment. Sometimes he thought of Fix, but no longer in anger. Fix, like all the world, had been mistaken in Phileas

Fogg, and had only done his duty in tracking and arresting him; while he, Passepartout—. This thought haunted him, and he never ceased cursing his miserable folly.

Finding himself too wretched to remain alone, he knocked at Aouda's door, went into her room, seated himself, without speaking, in a corner, and looked ruefully at the young woman. Aouda was still pensive.

About half-past seven in the evening Mr. Fogg sent to know if Aouda would receive him, and in a few moments he found himself alone with her.

Phileas Fogg took a chair, and sat down near the fireplace, opposite Aouda. No emotion was visible on his face. Fogg returned was exactly the Fogg who had gone away; there was the same calm, the same impassibility.

He sat several minutes without speaking; then, bending his eyes on Aouda, "Madam," said he, "will you pardon me for bringing you to England?"

"I, Mr. Fogg!" replied Aouda, checking the pulsations of her heart.

"Please let me finish," returned Mr. Fogg. "When I decided to bring you far away from the country which was so unsafe for you, I was rich, and counted on putting a portion of my fortune at your disposal; then your existence would have been free and happy. But now I am ruined."

"I know it, Mr. Fogg," replied Aouda; "and I ask you in my turn, will you forgive me for having followed you, and—who knows?—for having, perhaps, delayed you, and thus contributed to your ruin?"

"Madam, you could not remain in India, and your safety could only be assured by bringing you to such a distance that your persecutors could not take you."

"So, Mr. Fogg," resumed Aouda, "not content with rescuing me from a terrible death, you thought yourself bound to secure my comfort in a foreign land?"

"Yes, madam; but circumstances have been against me. Still, I beg to place the little I have left at your service."

"But what will become of you, Mr. Fogg?"

"As for me, madam," replied the gentleman, coldly, "I have need of nothing."

"But how do you look upon the fate, sir, which awaits you?"

"As I am in the habit of doing."

"At least," said Aouda, "want should not overtake a man like you. Your friends—"

"I have no friends, madam."

"Your relatives—"

"I have no longer any relatives."

"I pity you, then, Mr. Fogg, for solitude is a sad thing, with no heart to which to confide your griefs. They say, though, that misery itself, shared by two sympathetic souls, may be borne with patience."

"They say so, madam."

"Mr. Fogg," said Aouda, rising and seizing his hand, "do you wish at once a kinswoman and friend? Will you have me for your wife?"

Mr. Fogg, at this, rose in his turn. There was an unwonted light in his eyes, and a slight trembling of his lips. Aouda looked into his face. The sincerity, rectitude, firmness, and sweetness of this soft glance of a noble woman, who could dare all to save him to whom she owed all, at first astonished, then penetrated him. He shut his eyes for an instant, as if to avoid her look. When he opened them again, "I love you!" he said, simply. "Yes, by all that is holiest, I love you, and I am entirely yours!"

"Ah!" cried Aouda, pressing his hand to her heart.

Passepartout was summoned and appeared immediately. Mr. Fogg still held Aouda's hand in his own; Passepartout understood, and his big, round face became as radiant as the tropical sun at its zenith.

Mr. Fogg asked him if it was not too late to notify the Reverend Samuel Wilson, of Marylebone Parish, that evening.

Passepartout smiled his most genial smile, and said, "Never too late."

It was five minutes past eight.

"Will it be for to-morrow, Monday?"

"For to-morrow, Monday," said Mr. Fogg, turning to Aouda.

"Yes; for to-morrow, Monday," she replied.

Passepartout hurried off as fast as his legs could carry him.

Chapter XXXVI

IN WHICH PHILEAS FOGG'S NAME IS ONCE MORE AT A PREMIUM ON 'CHANGE

IT IS TIME TO RELATE WHAT A CHANGE TOOK PLACE IN ENGLISH PUBLIC OPINION, WHEN it transpired that the real bank-robber, a certain James Strand, had been arrested, on the 17th of December, at Edinburgh. Three days before, Phileas Fogg had been a criminal, who was being desperately followed up by the police; now he was an honourable gentleman, mathematically pursuing his eccentric journey around the world.

The papers resumed their discussion about the wager; all those who had laid bets, for or against him, revived their interest, as if by magic; the "Phileas Fogg bonds" again became negotiable, and many new wagers were made. Phileas Fogg's name was once more at a premium on 'Change.

His five friends of the Reform Club passed these three days in a state of feverish suspense. Would Phileas Fogg, whom they had forgotten, reappear before their eyes! Where was he at this moment? The 17th of December, the day of James Strand's arrest, was the seventy-sixth since Phileas Fogg's departure, and no news of him had been received. Was he dead? Had he abandoned the effort, or was he continuing his journey along the route agreed upon? And would he appear on Saturday, the 21st of December, at a quarter before nine in the evening, on the threshold of the Reform Club saloon?

The anxiety in which, for three days, London society existed, cannot be described. Telegrams were sent to America and Asia for news of Phileas Fogg. Messengers were despatched to the house in Saville Row morning and evening. No news. The police were ignorant of what had become of the detective, Fix, who had so unfortunately followed up a false scent. Bets increased, nevertheless, in number and value. Phileas Fogg, like a racehorse, was drawing near his last turning-point. The bonds were quoted, no longer at a hundred below par, but at twenty, at ten, and at five; and paralytic old Lord Albemarle bet even in his favour.

A great crowd was collected in Pall Mall and the neighbouring streets on Saturday evening; it seemed like a multitude of brokers permanently established around the Reform Club. Circulation was impeded, and everywhere disputes, discussions, and financial transactions were going on. The police had great difficulty in keeping back the crowd, and as the hour when Phileas Fogg was due approached, the excitement rose to its highest pitch.

The five antagonists of Phileas Fogg had met in the great saloon of the club. John Sullivan and Samuel Fallentin, the bankers, Andrew Stuart, the engineer, Gauthier Ralph, the director of the Bank of England, and Thomas Flanagan, the brewer, one and all waited anxiously.

When the clock indicated twenty minutes past eight, Andrew Stuart got up, saying, "Gentlemen, in twenty minutes the time agreed upon between Mr. Fogg and ourselves will have expired."

"What time did the last train arrive from Liverpool?" asked Thomas Flanagan.

"At twenty-three minutes past seven," replied Gauthier Ralph; "and the next does not arrive till ten minutes after twelve."

"Well, gentlemen," resumed Andrew Stuart, "if Phileas Fogg had come in the seven twenty-three train, he would have got here by this time. We can, therefore, regard the bet as won."

"Wait; don't let us be too hasty," replied Samuel Fallentin. "You know that Mr. Fogg is very eccentric. His punctuality is well known; he never arrives too soon, or too late; and I should not be surprised if he appeared before us at the last minute."

"Why," said Andrew Stuart nervously, "if I should see him, I should not believe it was he."

"The fact is," resumed Thomas Flanagan, "Mr. Fogg's project was absurdly foolish. Whatever his punctuality, he could not prevent the delays which were certain to occur; and a delay of only two or three days would be fatal to his tour."

"Observe, too," added John Sullivan, "that we have received no intelligence from him, though there are telegraphic lines all along his route."

"He has lost, gentleman," said Andrew Stuart—"he has a hundred times lost! You know, besides, that the *China*—the only steamer he could have taken from New York to get here in time—arrived yesterday. I have seen a list of the passengers, and the name of Phileas Fogg is not among them. Even if we admit that fortune has favoured him, he can scarcely have reached America. I think he will be at least twenty days behindhand, and that Lord Albemarle will lose a cool five thousand."

"It is clear," replied Gauthier Ralph; "and we have nothing to do but to present Mr. Fogg's check at the Barings to-morrow."

At this moment, the hands of the club clock pointed to twenty minutes to nine.

"Five minutes more," said Andrew Stuart.

The five gentlemen looked at each other. Their anxiety was becoming intense; but, not wishing to betray it, they readily assented to Mr. Fallentin's proposal of a rubber.

"I wouldn't give up my four thousand of the bet," said Andrew Stuart, as he took his seat, "for three thousand nine hundred and ninety-nine."

The clock indicated eighteen minutes to nine.

The players took up their cards, but could not keep their eyes off the clock. Certainly, however secure they felt, minutes had never seemed so long to them!

"Seventeen minutes to nine," said Thomas Flanagan, as he cut the cards which Ralph handed to him.

Then there was a moment of silence. The great saloon was perfectly quiet; but the murmurs of the crowd outside were heard, with now and then a shrill cry. The pendulum beat the seconds, which each player eagerly counted, as he listened, with mathematical regularity.

"Sixteen minutes to nine!" said John Sullivan, in a voice which betrayed his emotion.

One minute more, and the wager would be won. Andrew Stuart and his partners suspended their game. They left their cards, and counted the seconds.

At the fortieth second, nothing. At the fiftieth, still nothing.

At the fifty-fifth, a loud cry was heard in the street, followed by applause, hurrahs, and some fierce growls.

The players rose from their seats.

At the fifty-seventh second the door of the saloon opened; and the pendulum had not beat the sixtieth second when Phileas Fogg appeared, followed by an excited crowd who had forced their way through the club doors, and in his calm voice, said, "Here I am, gentlemen!"

Chapter XXXVII

IN WHICH IT IS SHOWN THAT PHILEAS FOGG GAINED NOTHING BY HIS TOUR AROUND THE WORLD, UNLESS IT WERE HAPPINESS

YES; PHILEAS FOGG IN PERSON.

The reader will remember that at five minutes past eight in the evening about five and twenty hours after the arrival of the travellers in London—Passepartout had been sent by his master to engage the services of the Reverend Samuel Wilson in a certain marriage ceremony, which was to take place the next day.

Passepartout went on his errand enchanted. He soon reached the clergyman's house, but found him not at home. Passepartout waited a good twenty minutes, and when he left the reverend gentleman, it was thirty-five minutes past eight. But in what a state he was! With his hair in disorder, and without his hat, he ran along the street as never man was seen to run before, overturning passers-by, rushing over the side-walk like a water-spout.

In three minutes he was in Saville Row again, and staggered breathlessly into Mr. Fogg's room.

He could not speak.

"What is the matter?" asked Mr. Fogg.

"My master!" gasped Passepartout—"marriage—impossible—"

"Impossible?"

"Impossible—for to-morrow."

"Why so?"

"Because to-morrow—is Sunday!"

"Monday," replied Mr. Fogg.

"No—to-day—is Saturday."

"Saturday? Impossible!"

"Yes, yes, yes, yes!" cried Passepartout. "You have made a mistake of one day! We arrived twenty-four hours ahead of time; but there are only ten minutes left!"

Passepartout had seized his master by the collar, and was dragging him along with irresistible force.

Phileas Fogg, thus kidnapped, without having time to think, left his house, jumped into a cab, promised a hundred pounds to the cabman, and, having run over two dogs and overturned five carriages, reached the Reform Club.

The clock indicated a quarter before nine when he appeared in the great saloon.

Phileas Fogg had accomplished the journey around the world in eighty days!

Phileas Fogg had won his wager of twenty thousand pounds!

How was it that a man so exact and fastidious could have made this error of a day? How came he to think that he had arrived in London on Saturday, the twenty-first day of December, when it was really Friday, the twentieth, the seventy-ninth day only from his departure?

The cause of the error is very simple.

Phileas Fogg had, without suspecting it, gained one day on his journey, and this merely because he had travelled constantly *eastward;* he would, on the contrary, have lost a day had he gone in the opposite direction, that is, *westward*.

In journeying eastward he had gone towards the sun, and the days therefore diminished for him as many times four minutes as he crossed degrees in this direction. There are three hundred and sixty degrees, multiplied by four minutes, gives precisely twenty-four hours—that is, the day unconsciously gained. In other words, while Phileas Fogg, going eastward, saw the sun pass the meridian *eighty* times, his friends in London only saw it pass the meridian *seventy-nine* times. This is why they awaited him at the Reform Club on Saturday, and not Sunday, as Mr. Fogg thought.

And Passepartout's famous family watch, which had always kept London time, would have betrayed this fact, if it had marked the days as well as the hours and the minutes!

Phileas Fogg, then, had won the twenty thousand pounds; but as he had spent nearly nineteen thousand on the way, the pecuniary gain was small. His object was, however, to be victorious, and not to win money. He divided the one thousand pounds that remained between Passepartout and the unfortunate Fix, against whom he cherished no grudge. He deducted, however, from Passepartout's share the cost of the gas which had burned in his room for nineteen hundred and twenty hours, for the sake of regularity.

That evening, Mr. Fogg, as tranquil and phlegmatic as ever, said to Aouda: "Is our marriage still agreeable to you?"

"Mr. Fogg," replied she, "it is for me to ask that question. You were ruined, but now you are rich again."

"Pardon me, madam; my fortune belongs to you. If you had not suggested our marriage, my servant would not have gone to the Reverend Samuel Wilson's, I should not have been apprised of my error, and—"

"Dear Mr. Fogg!" said the young woman.

"Dear Aouda!" replied Phileas Fogg.

It need not be said that the marriage took place forty-eight hours after, and that Passepartout, glowing and dazzling, gave the bride away. Had he not saved her, and was he not entitled to this honour?

The next day, as soon as it was light, Passepartout rapped vigourously at his master's door. Mr. Fogg opened it, and asked, "What's the matter, Passepartout?"

"What is it, sir? Why, I've just this instant found out—"

"What?"

"That we might have made the tour of the world in only seventy-eight days."

"No doubt," returned Mr. Fogg, "by not crossing India. But if I had not crossed India, I should not have saved Aouda; she would not have been my wife, and—"

Mr. Fogg quietly shut the door.

Phileas Fogg had won his wager, and had made his journey around the world in eighty days. To do this he had employed every means of conveyance—steamers, railways, carriages, yachts, trading-vessels, sledges, elephants. The eccentric gentleman had throughout displayed all his marvelous qualities of coolness and exactitude. But what then? What had he really gained by all this trouble? What had he brought back from this long and weary journey?

Nothing, say you? Perhaps so; nothing but a charming woman, who, strange as it may appear, made him the happiest of men!

Truly, would you not for less than that make the tour around the world?

THE MYSTERIOUS ISLAND

CONTENTS

Part I—Dropped from the Clouds

    I   The Storm of 1865—Voices in the Air—A Balloon Carried Away
by a Whirlwind—Five Passengers—What Happened in the Car   837

    II   An Incident in the War of Secession—The Engineer Cyrus Harding—
Gideon Spilett—The Negro Neb—Pencroft the Sailor—The Night
Rendezvous—Departure in the Storm   841

    III   Five O'Clock in the Evening—The Missing One—Neb's Despair—
Search Towards the North—The Islet—A Dreadful Night—A Fog
in the Morning—Neb Swims—Sight of Land—Fording the Channel 846

    IV   Lithodomes—The River's Mouth—The Chimneys—Continued
Researches—The Forest of Evergreens—Waiting for the Ebb—
On the Heights—The Raft—Return to the Shore   851

    V   Arranging the Chimneys—How to Procure Fire—A Box of Matches—
Search on the Shore—Return of the Reporter and Neb—A Single
Match—A Roaring Fire—The First Supper, and Night on Shore   856

    VI   The Inventory of the Castaways—Nothing—Burned Linen—An
Expedition to the Forest—Flight of the Jacamar—Traces of Deer—
Couroucous—Grouse—A Curious Fishing-Line   861

    VII   Neb Has Not Yet Returned—The Reporter's Reflections—Supper—
A Threatening Night—The Tempest Is Frightful—They Rush Out into
the Night—Struggle Against the Wind and Rain—Eight Miles from
the First Encampment   866

    VIII   Is Cyrus Harding Living?—Neb's Recital—Footprints—An
Unanswerable Question—Cyrus Harding's First Words—Identifying
the Footsteps—Return to the Chimneys—Pencroft Startled!   871

    IX   Cyrus Is Here—Pencroft's Attempts—Rubbing Wood—Island or
Continent—The Engineer's Projects—In What Part of the Pacific
Ocean—In the Midst of the Forests—The Stone Pine—Chasing a
Capybara—An Auspicious Smoke   877

X   The Engineer's Invention—The Question Which Engrosses the
        Thoughts of Cyrus Harding—Departure for the Mountain—
        Volcanic Soil—Tragopans—Sheep—The First Plateau—
        Encampment for the Night—The Summit of the Cone   883

XI   At the Summit of the Cone—The Interior of the Crater—Sea All
        Round—No Land in Sight—A Bird's-Eye View of the Coast—
        Hydrography and Orology—Is the Island Inhabited—Christening
        the Bays, Gulfs, Capes, Rivers, etc.—Lincoln Island   889

XII   Regulating the Watches—Pencroft Is Satisfied—A Suspicious
        Smoke—Course of Red Creek—The Flora of Lincoln Island—The
        Fauna—Mountain Pheasants—Chasing Kangaroos—An Agouti—
        Lake Grant—Return to the Chimneys   895

XIII   What Is Found upon Top—Manufacturing Bows and Arrows—
        A Brick-Field—A Pottery—Different Cooking Utensils—The First
        Boiled Meat—Wormwood—The Southern Cross—An Important
        Astronomical Observation   901

XIV   Measuring the Cliff—An Application of the Theorem of Similar
        Triangles—Latitude of the Island—Excursion to the North—An
        Oyster-Bed—Plans for the Future—The Sun Passing the Meridian—
        The Longitude of Lincoln Island   907

XV   It Is Decided to Winter on the Island—A Metallic Question—
        Exploring Safety Island—A Seal Hunt—Capture of an Echidua—
        A Koala—What Is Called the Catalan Method—Manufacturing
        Iron—How Steel Is Obtained   913

XVI   The Question of a Dwelling Is Again Discussed—Pencroft's Fancies—
        Exploring to the North of the Lake—The Northern Edge of the
        Plateau—Snakes—Extremity of the Lake—Top's Uneasiness—
        Top Swimming—A Combat under the Water—The Dugong   918

XVII   Visit to the Lake—The Indicating Current—Cyrus Harding's
        Projects—The Fat of the Dugong—Employing Shistose Pyrites—
        Sulphate of Iron—How Glycerine is Made—Soap—Saltpeter—
        Sulphuric Acid—Azotic Acid—The New Fall   923

XVIII   Pencroft Now Doubts Nothing—The Outlet of the Lake—A
        Subterranean Descent—The Way Through the Granite—Top
        Disappears—The Central Cavern—The Lower Well—Mystery—
        Using the Pickaxe—The Return   929

XIX   Cyrus Harding's Project—The Front of Granite House—The Rope
        Ladder—Pencroft's Dreams—Aromatic Herbs—A Natural Warren—
        Water for the New Dwelling—View from the Windows of Granite
        House   934

XX   The Rainy Season—The Question of Clothes—A Seal Hunt—
        Manufacturing Candles—Work in Granite House—The Two
        Bridges—Return from a Visit to the Oyster-Bed—What Herbert
        Finds in His Pocket   939

XXI   Some Degrees below Zero—Exploring the Marshy Part to the South-
        east—The Wolf-Fox—View of the Sea—A Conversation on the Future
        of the Pacific Ocean—The Incessant Work of the Coral Insects—What
        Our Globe Will Become—The Chase—Tadorn's Fens   944

XXII   Traps—Foxes—Peccaries—The Wind Changes to the North-west—
        Snowstorm—Basket-Makers—The Severest Cold—Maple Sugar—
        The Mysterious Well—An Exploration Planned—The Leaden
        Bullet   949

Part II—Abandoned
    I   Conversation on the Subject of the Bullet—Construction of a Canoe—
        Hunting—At the Top of a Kauri—Nothing to Attest the Presence of
        Man—Neb and Herbert's Prize—Turning a Turtle—The Turtle
        Disappears—Cyrus Harding's Explanation   959

    II First Trial of the Canoe—A Wreck on the Coast—Towing—Flotsam
        Point—Inventory of the Case: Tools, Weapons, Instruments, Clothes,
        Books, Utensils—What Pencroft Misses—The Gospel—A Verse from
        the Sacred Book   964

    III The Start—The Rising Tide—Elms and Different Plants—The
        Jacamar—Aspect of the Forest—Gigantic Eucalypti—The Reason
        They are Called "Fever-Trees"—Troops of Monkeys—A Waterfall—
        The Night Encampment   970

    IV Journey to the Coast—Troops of Monkeys—A New River—
        The Reason the Tide Was Not Felt—A Woody Shore—Reptile
        Promontory—Herbert Envies Gideon Spilett—Explosion of
        Bamboos   976

    V   Proposal to Return by the Southern Shore—Configuration of the
        Coast—Searching for the Supposed Wreck—A Wreck in the Air—

Discovery of a Small Natural Port—At Midnight on the Banks
of the Mercy—The Canoe Adrift   981

VI   Pencroft's Halloos—A Night in the Chimneys—Herbert's Arrows—
The Captain's Project—An Unexpected Explanation—What Has
Happened in Granite House—How a New Servant Enters the Service
of the Colonists   988

VII   Plans—A Bridge over the Mercy—Mode Adopted for Making an
Island of Prospect Heights—The Drawbridge—Harvest—
The Stream—The Poultry-Yard—A Pigeon-House—The Two
Onagers—The Cart—Excursion to Port Balloon   994

VIII   Linen—Shoes of Seal-Leather—Manufacture of Pyroxyle—
Gardening—Fishing—Turtle-Eggs—Improvement of Master Jup—
The Corral—Musmon Hunt—New Animal and Vegetable
Possessions—Recollections of Their Native Land   999

IX   Bad Weather—The Hydraulic Lift—Manufacture of Glassware—
The Bread-Tree—Frequent Visits to the Corral—Increase of the
Flock—The Reporter's Question—Exact Position of Lincoln Island—
Pencroft's Proposal   1005

X   Boat-Building—Second Crop of Corn—Hunting Koalas—A New
Plant, More Pleasant Than Useful—Whale in Sight—A Harpoon from
the Vineyard—Cutting Up the Whale—Use for the Bones—End of the
Month of May—Pencroft Has Nothing Left to Wish for   1010

XI   Winter—Felling Wood—The Mill—Pencroft's Fixed Idea—The
Bones—To What Use an Albatross May be Put—Fuel for the Future—
Top and Jup—Storms—Damage to the Poultry-Yard—Excursion
to the Marsh—Cyrus Harding Alone—Exploring the Well   1015

XII   The Rigging of the Vessel—An Attack from Foxes—Jup Wounded—
Jup Cured—Completion of the Boat—Pencroft's Triumph—
The Bonadventure's Trial Trip to the South of the Island—
An Unexpected Document   1022

XIII   Departure Decided Upon—Conjectures—Preparations—The Three
Passengers—First Night—Second Night—Tabor Island—Searching
the Shore—Searching the Wood—No One—Animals—Plants—
A Dwelling—Deserted   1029

XIV   The Inventory—Night—A Few Letters—Continuation of the
       Search—Plants and Animals—Herbert in Great Danger—On Board—
       The Departure—Bad Weather—A Gleam of Reason—Lost on the
       Sea—A Timely Light   1035

XV   The Return—Discussion—Cyrus Harding and the Stranger—Port
       Balloon—The Engineer's Devotion—A Touching Incident—
       Tears Flow   1041

XVI   A Mystery to be Cleared Up—The Stranger's First Words—Twelve
       Years on the Islet—Avowal Which Escapes Him—The
       Disappearance—Cyrus Harding's Confidence—Construction of a
       Mill—The First Bread—An Act of Devotion—Honest Hands   1046

XVII   Still Alone—The Stranger's Request—The Farm Established at the
       Corral—Twelve Years Ago—The Boatswain's Mate of the Britannia—
       Left on Tabor Island—Cyrus Harding's Hand—The Mysterious
       Document   1053

XVIII Conversation—Cyrus Harding and Gideon Spilett—An Idea of the
       Engineer's—The Electric Telegraph—The Wires—The Battery—
       The Alphabet—Fine Season—Prosperity of the Colony—Photography—
       An Appearance of Snow—Two Years in Lincoln Island   1060

XIX   Recollections of Their Native Land—Probable Future—Project for
       Surveying the Coasts of the Island—Departure on the 16th of April—
       Sea-View of Reptile End—The Basaltic Rocks of the Western Coast—
       Bad Weather—Night Comes On—New Incident   1066

XX   A Night at Sea—Shark Gulf—Confidences—Preparations for Winter—
       Forwardness of the Bad Season—Severe Cold—Work in the Interior—
       In Six Months—A Photographic Negative—Unexpected Incident   1071

Part III—The Secret of the Island
   I   Lost or Saved—Ayrton Summoned—Important Discussion—It is not
       the Duncan—Suspicious Vessel—Precautions to Be Taken—
       The Ship Approaches—A Cannon-Shot—The Brig Anchors in
       Sight of the Island—Night Comes On   1081

   II Discussions—Presentiments—Ayrton's Proposal—It is Accepted—
       Ayrton and Pencroft on Grant Islet—Convicts from Norfolk Island—
       Ayrton's Heroic Attempt—His Return—Six Against Fifty   1087

III   The Mist Rises—The Engineer's Preparations—Three Posts—
      Ayrton and Pencroft—The First Boat—Two Other Boats—On the
      Islet—Six Convicts Land—The Brig Weighs Anchor—The *Speedy's*
      Guns—A Desperate Situation—Unexpected Catastrophe   1093

IV   The Colonists on the Beach—Ayrton and Pencroft Work amid the
      Wreck—Conversation during Breakfast—Pencroft's Arguments—
      Minute Examination of the Brig's Hull—The Powder-Magazine
      Untouched—New Riches—The Last of the Wreck—A Broken
      Piece of Cylinder   1100

V   The Engineer's Declaration—Pencroft's Grand Hypothesis—An Aerial
      Battery—The Four Cannons—The Surviving Convicts—Ayrton's
      Hesitation—Cyrus Harding's Generous Sentiments—
      Pencroft's Regret   1106

VI   Expeditions Planned—Ayrton at the Corral—Visit to Port Balloon—
      Pencroft's Observations on Board the *Bonadventure*—Despatch Sent to
      the Corral—No Reply from Ayrton—Departure the Next Day—The
      Reason Why the Wire Did Not Work—A Report   1112

VII   The Reporter and Pencroft in the Corral—Herbert's Wound—
      The Sailor's Despair—Consultation Between the Reporter and the
      Engineer—Mode of Treatment—Hope Not Abandoned—How Is Neb
      to Be Warned—A Sure and Faithful Messenger—Neb's Reply   1118

VIII The Convicts in the Neighborhood of the Corral—Provisional
      Establishment—Continuation of the Treatment of Herbert—
      Pencroft's First Rejoicings—Conversation on Past Events—What the
      Future Has in Reserve—Cyrus Harding's Ideas on This Subject 1123

IX   No News of Neb—A Proposal from Pencroft and the Reporter,
      Which Is Not Accepted—Several Sorties by Gideon Spilett—
      A Rag of Cloth—A Message—Hasty Departure—Arrival on the
      Plateau of Prospect Heights   1126

X   Herbert Carried to Granite House—Neb Relates All That Has
      Happened—Harding's Visit to the Plateau—Ruin and Devastation—
      The Colonists Baffled by Herbert's Illness—Willow Bark—A Deadly
      Fever—Top Barks Again!   1131

XI   Inexplicable Mystery—Herbert's Convalescence—The Parts of the
      Island to Be Explored—Preparations for Departure—First Day—

Night—Second Day—Kauries—A Couple of Cassowaries—
Footprints in the Forest—Arrival at Reptile Point   1136

XII   Exploration of the Serpentine Peninsula—Encampment at the Mouth
       of Falls River—Gideon Spilett and Pencroft Reconnoitre—Their
       Return—Forward, All!—An Open Door—A Lighted Window—
       By the Light of the Moon!   1141

XIII   Ayrton's Story—Plans of His Former Accomplices—Their Installation
       in the Corral—The Avenging Justice of Lincoln Island—The
       Bonadventure—Researches around Mount Franklin—The Upper
       Valleys—A Subterranean Volcano—Pencroft's Opinion—At the
       Bottom of the Crater—Return   1147

XIV   Three Years Have Passed—The New Vessel—What Is Agreed On—
       Prosperity of the Colony—The Dockyard—Cold of the Southern
       Hemisphere—Washing Linen—Mount Franklin   1153

XV   The Awakening of the Volcano—The Fine Season—Continuation of
       Work—The Evening of the 15th of October—A Telegram—
       A Question—An Answer—Departure for the Corral—The Notice—
       The Additional Wire—The Basalt Coast—At High Tide—At Low
       Tide—The Cavern—A Dazzling Light   1159

XVI   Captain Nemo—His First Words—The History of the Recluse—
       His Adventures—His Sentiments—His Comrades—Submarine Life—
       Alone—The Last Refuge of the Nautilus in Lincoln Island—
       The Mysterious Genius of the Island   1167

XVII   Last Moments of Captain Nemo—Wishes of the Dying Man—
       A Parting Gift to His Friends of a Day—Captain Nemo's Coffin—
       Advice to the Colonists—The Supreme Moment—At the Bottom
       of the Sea   1173

XVIII Reflections of the Colonists—Their Labours of Reconstruction
       Resumed—The 1st of January, 1869—A Cloud over the Summit of the
       Volcano—First Warnings of an Irruption—Ayrton and Cyrus Harding
       at the Corral—Exploration of the Dakkar Grotto—What Captain
       Nemo Had Confided to the Engineer   1178

XIX   Cyrus Harding Gives an Account of His Exploration—The
       Construction of the Ship Pushed Forward—A Last Visit to the
       Corral—The Battle Between Fire and Water—All That Remains of the

Island—It is Decided to Launch the Vessel—The Night of the 8th of
March   1186

XX   An Isolated Rock in the Pacific—The Last Refuge of the Colonists of
     Lincoln Island—Death Their Only Prospect—Unexpected Succor—
     Why and How It Arrives—A Last Kindness—An Island on *Terra
     Firma*—The Tomb of Captain Prince Dakkar Nemo   1193

PART I

DROPPED FROM THE CLOUDS

Chapter I

THE STORM OF 1865—VOICES IN THE AIR—A BALLOON
CARRIED AWAY BY A WHIRLWIND—FIVE PASSENGERS—
WHAT HAPPENED IN THE CAR

A RE WE RISING AGAIN?" "NO. ON THE CONTRARY." "ARE WE DESCENDING?"
"Worse than that, captain! we are falling!" "For Heaven's sake heave out the
ballast!" "There! the last sack is empty!" "Does the balloon rise?" "No!" "I hear
a noise like the dashing of waves!" "The sea is below the car! It cannot be more than 500
feet from us!" "Overboard with every weight! . . . everything!"

Such were the loud and startling words which resounded through the air, above the
vast watery desert of the Pacific, about four o'clock in the evening of the 23d of March,
1865.

Few can possibly have forgotten the terrible storm from the north-east, in the middle
of the equinox of that year. The tempest raged without intermission from the 18th to the
26th of March. Its ravages were terrible in America, Europe, and Asia, covering a distance
of eighteen hundred miles, and extending obliquely to the equator from the thirty-fifth
north parallel to the fortieth south parallel. Towns were overthrown, forests uprooted,
coasts devastated by the mountains of water which were precipitated on them, vessels cast
on the shore, which the published accounts numbered by hundreds, whole districts levelled
by water-spouts which destroyed everything they passed over, several thousand people
crushed on land or drowned at sea; such were the traces of its fury, left by this devastating
tempest. It surpassed in disasters those which so frightfully ravaged Havana and
Guadalupe, one on the 25th of October, 1810, the other on the 26th of July, 1825.

But while so many catastrophes were taking place on land and at sea, a drama not less
exciting was being enacted in the agitated air.

In fact, a balloon, as a ball might be carried on the summit of a water-spout, had been
taken into the circling movement of a column of air and had traversed space at the rate of
ninety miles an hour, turning round and round as if seized by some aerial maëlstrom.

Beneath the lower point of the balloon, swung a car, containing five passengers,
scarcely visible in the midst of the thick vapour mingled with spray which hung over the
surface of the ocean.

Whence, it may be asked, had come that plaything of the tempest? From what part of
the world did it rise? It surely could not have started during the storm. But the storm has
raged five days already, and the first symptoms were manifested on the 18th. It cannot be
doubted that the balloon came from a great distance, for it could not have travelled less
than two thousand miles in twenty-four hours.

At any rate the passengers, destitute of all marks for their guidance, could not have
possessed the means of reckoning the route traversed since their departure. It was a remarkable fact that, although in the very midst of the furious tempest, they did not suffer
from it. They were thrown about and whirled round and round without feeling the rota-

tion in the slightest degree, or being sensible that they were removed from a horizontal position.

Their eyes could not pierce through the thick mist which had gathered beneath the car. Dark vapour was all around them. Such was the density of the atmosphere that they could not be certain whether it was day or night. No reflection of light, no sound from inhabited land, no roaring of the ocean could have reached them, through the obscurity, while suspended in those elevated zones. Their rapid descent alone had informed them of the dangers which they ran from the waves. However, the balloon, lightened of heavy articles, such as ammunition, arms, and provisions, had risen into the higher layers of the atmosphere, to a height of 4,500 feet. The voyagers, after having discovered that the sea extended beneath them, and thinking the dangers above less dreadful than those below, did not hesitate to throw overboard even their most useful articles, while they endeavoured to lose no more of that fluid, the life of their enterprise, which sustained them above the abyss.

The night passed in the midst of alarms which would have been death to less energetic souls. Again the day appeared and with it the tempest began to moderate. From the beginning of that day, the 24th of March, it showed symptoms of abating. At dawn, some of the lighter clouds had risen into the more lofty regions of the air. In a few hours the wind had changed from a hurricane to a fresh breeze, that is to say, the rate of the transit of the atmospheric layers was diminished by half. It was still what sailors call "a close-reefed topsail breeze," but the commotion in the elements had not the less considerably diminished.

Towards eleven o'clock, the lower region of the air was sensibly clearer. The atmosphere threw off that chilly dampness which is felt after the passage of a great meteor. The storm did not seem to have gone farther to the west. It appeared to have exhausted itself. Could it have passed away in electric sheets, as is sometimes the case with regard to the typhoons of the Indian Ocean?

But at the same time, it was also evident that the balloon was again slowly descending with a regular movement. It appeared as if it were, little by little, collapsing, and that its case was lengthening and extending, passing from a spherical to an oval form. Towards midday the balloon was hovering above the sea at a height of only 2,000 feet. It contained 50,000 cubic feet of gas, and, thanks to its capacity, it could maintain itself a long time in the air, although it should reach a great altitude or might be thrown into a horizontal position.

Perceiving their danger, the passengers cast away the last articles which still weighed down the car, the few provisions they had kept, everything, even to their pocketknives, and one of them, having hoisted himself on to the circles which united the cords of the net, tried to secure more firmly the lower point of the balloon.

It was, however, evident to the voyagers that the gas was failing, and that the balloon could no longer be sustained in the higher regions. They must infallibly perish!

There was not a continent, nor even an island, visible beneath them. The watery expanse did not present a single speck of land, not a solid surface upon which their anchor could hold.

It was the open sea, whose waves were still dashing with tremendous violence! It was the ocean, without any visible limits, even for those whose gaze, from their commanding position, extended over a radius of forty miles. The vast liquid plain, lashed without mercy by the storm, appeared as if covered with herds of furious chargers, whose white and di-shevelled crests were streaming in the wind. No land was in sight, not a solitary ship could be seen. It was necessary at any cost to arrest their downward course, and to prevent the balloon from being engulfed in the waves. The voyagers directed all their energies to this urgent work. But, notwithstanding their efforts, the balloon still fell, it was also suddenly overthrown, following the direction of the wind, that is to say, from the north-east to the south-west.

Frightful indeed was the situation of these unfortunate men. They were evidently no longer masters of the machine. All their attempts were useless. The case of the balloon col-lapsed more and more. The gas escaped without any possibility of retaining it. Their descent was visibly accelerated, and soon after midday the car hung within 600 feet of the ocean.

It was impossible to prevent the escape of gas, which rushed through a large rent in the silk. By lightening the car of all the articles which it contained, the passengers had been able to prolong their suspension in the air for a few hours. But the inevitable catastrophe could only be retarded, and if land did not appear before night, voyagers, car, and balloon must to a certainty vanish beneath the waves.

They now resorted to the only remaining expedient. They were truly dauntless men, who knew how to look death in the face. Not a single murmur escaped from their lips. They were determined to struggle to the last minute, to do anything to retard their fall. The car was only a sort of willow basket, unable to float, and there was not the slightest possibility of maintaining it on the surface of the sea.

Two more hours passed and the balloon was scarcely 400 feet above the water.

At that moment a loud voice, the voice of a man whose heart was inaccessible to fear, was heard. To this voice responded others not less determined. "Is everything thrown out?" "No, here are still 2,000 dollars in gold." A heavy bag immediately plunged into the sea. "Does the balloon rise?" "A little, but it will not be long before it falls again." "What still remains to be thrown out?" "Nothing." "Yes! the car!" "Let us catch hold of the net, and into the sea with the car."

This was, in fact, the last and only mode of lightening the balloon. The ropes which held the car were cut, and the balloon, after its fall, mounted 2,000 feet.

The five voyagers had hoisted themselves into the net, and clung to the meshes, gaz-ing at the abyss.

The delicate sensibility of balloons is well known. It is sufficient to throw out the lightest article to produce a difference in its vertical position. The apparatus in the air is like a balance of mathematical precision. It can be thus easily understood that when it is lightened of any considerable weight its movement will be impetuous and sudden. So it happened on this occasion. But after being suspended for an instant aloft, the balloon began to redescend, the gas escaping by the rent which it was impossible to repair.

The men had done all that men could do. No human efforts could save them now. They must trust to the mercy of Him who rules the elements.

At four o'clock the balloon was only 500 feet above the surface of the water.

A loud barking was heard. A dog accompanied the voyagers, and was held pressed close to his master in the meshes of the net.

"Top has seen something," cried one of the men. Then immediately a loud voice shouted—

"Land! land!" The balloon, which the wind still drove towards the south-west, had since daybreak gone a considerable distance, which might be reckoned by hundreds of miles, and a tolerably high land had, in fact, appeared in that direction. But this land was still thirty miles off. It would not take less than an hour to get to it, and then there was the chance of falling to leeward.

An hour! Might not the balloon before that be emptied of all the fluid it yet retained?

Such was the terrible question! The voyagers could distinctly see that solid spot which they must reach at any cost. They were ignorant of what it was, whether an island or a continent, for they did not know to what part of the world the hurricane had driven them. But they must reach this land, whether inhabited or desolate, whether hospitable or not.

It was evident that the balloon could no longer support itself! Several times already had the crests of the enormous billows licked the bottom of the net, making it still heavier, and the balloon only half rose, like a bird with a wounded wing. Half-an-hour later the land was not more than a mile off, but the balloon, exhausted, flabby, hanging in great folds, had gas in its upper part alone. The voyagers, clinging to the net, were still too heavy for it, and soon, half plunged into the sea, they were beaten by the furious waves. The balloon-case bulged out again, and the wind, taking it, drove it along like a vessel. Might it not possibly thus reach the land?

But, when only two fathoms off, terrible cries resounded from four pairs of lungs at once. The balloon, which had appeared as if it would never again rise, suddenly made an unexpected bound, after having been struck by a tremendous sea. As if it had been at that instant relieved of a new part of its weight, it mounted to a height of 1,500 feet, and there it met a current of wind, which instead of taking it directly to the coast, carried it in a nearly parallel direction.

At last, two minutes later, it reapproached obliquely, and finally fell on a sandy beach, out of the reach of the waves.

The voyagers, aiding each other, managed to disengage themselves from the meshes of the net. The balloon, relieved from their weight, was taken by the wind, and like a wounded bird which revives for an instant, disappeared into space.

But the car had contained five passengers, with a dog, and the balloon only left four on the shore.

The missing person had evidently been swept off by the sea, which had just struck the net, and it was owing to this circumstance that the lightened balloon rose the last time, and then soon after reached the land. Scarcely had the four castaways set foot on firm ground, than they all, thinking of the absent one, simultaneously exclaimed, "Perhaps he will try to swim to land! Let us save him! let us save him!"

Chapter II

AN INCIDENT IN THE WAR OF SECESSION—THE ENGINEER CYRUS HARDING—GIDEON SPILETT—THE NEGRO NEB— PENCROFT THE SAILOR—THE NIGHT RENDEZVOUS— DEPARTURE IN THE STORM

THOSE WHOM THE HURRICANE HAD JUST THROWN ON THIS COAST WERE NEITHER AERO-nauts by profession nor amateurs. They were prisoners of war whose boldness had induced them to escape in this extraordinary manner.

A hundred times they had almost perished! A hundred times had they almost fallen from their torn balloon into the depths of the ocean. But Heaven had reserved them for a strange destiny, and after having, on the 20th of March, escaped from Richmond, besieged by the troops of General Ulysses Grant, they found themselves seven thousand miles from the capital of Virginia, which was the principal stronghold of the South, during the terrible war of Secession. Their aerial voyage had lasted five days.

The curious circumstances which led to the escape of the prisoners were as follows:

That same year, in the month of February, 1865, in one of the coups-de-main by which General Grant attempted, though in vain, to possess himself of Richmond, several of his officers fell into the power of the enemy and were detained in the town. One of the most distinguished was Captain Cyrus Harding. He was a native of Massachusetts, a first-class engineer, to whom the government had confided, during the war, the direction of the railways, which were so important at that time. A true Northerner, thin, bony, lean, about forty-five years of age; his close-cut hair and his beard, of which he only kept a thick mustache, were already getting grey. He had one of those finely-developed heads which appear made to be struck on a medal, piercing eyes, a serious mouth, the physiognomy of a clever man of the military school. He was one of those engineers who began by handling the hammer and pickaxe, like generals who first act as common soldiers. Besides mental power, he also possessed great manual dexterity. His muscles exhibited remarkable proofs of tenacity. A man of action as well as a man of thought, all he did was without effort to one of his vigourous and sanguine temperament. Learned, clear-headed, and practical, he fulfilled in all emergencies those three conditions which united ought to ensure human success—activity of mind and body, impetuous wishes, and powerful will. He might have taken for his motto that of William of Orange in the 17th century: "I can undertake and persevere even without hope of success." Cyrus Harding was courage personified. He had been in all the battles of that war. After having begun as a volunteer at Illinois, under Ulysses Grant, he fought at Paducah, Belmont, Pittsburg Landing, at the siege of Corinth, Port Gibson, Black River, Chattanooga, the Wilderness, on the Potomac, everywhere and valiantly, a soldier worthy of the general who said, "I never count my dead!" And hundreds of times Captain Harding had almost been among those who were not counted by the terrible Grant; but in these combats where he never spared himself, fortune favoured him till the moment when he was wounded and taken prisoner on the field of battle near

Richmond. At the same time and on the same day another important personage fell into the hands of the Southerners. This was no other than Gideon Spilett, a reporter for the *New York Herald,* who had been ordered to follow the changes of the war in the midst of the Northern armies.

Gideon Spilett was one of that race of indomitable English or American chroniclers, like Stanley and others, who stop at nothing to obtain exact information, and transmit it to their journal in the shortest possible time. The newspapers of the Union, such as the *New York Herald,* are formed of actual powers, and their reporters are their representatives. Gideon Spilett ranked among the first of those reporters: a man of great merit, energetic, prompt and ready for anything, full of ideas, having travelled over the whole world, soldier and artist, enthusiastic in council, resolute in action, caring neither for trouble, fatigue, nor danger, when in pursuit of information, for himself first, and then for his journal, a perfect treasury of knowledge on all sorts of curious subjects, of the unpublished, of the unknown, and of the impossible. He was one of those intrepid observers who write under fire, "reporting" among bullets, and to whom every danger is welcome.

He also had been in all the battles, in the first rank, revolver in one hand, note-book in the other; grapeshot never made his pencil tremble. He did not fatigue the wires with incessant telegrams, like those who speak when they have nothing to say, but each of his notes, short, decisive, and clear, threw light on some important point. Besides, he was not wanting in humour. It was he who, after the affair of the Black River, determined at any cost to keep his place at the wicket of the telegraph office, and after having announced to his journal the result of the battle, telegraphed for two hours the first chapters of the Bible. It cost the *New York Herald* two thousand dollars, but the *New York Herald* published the first intelligence.

Gideon Spilett was tall. He was rather more than forty years of age. Light whiskers bordering on red surrounded his face. His eye was steady, lively, rapid in its changes. It was the eye of a man accustomed to take in at a glance all the details of a scene. Well built, he was inured to all climates, like a bar of steel hardened in cold water.

For ten years Gideon Spilett had been the reporter of the *New York Herald,* which he enriched by his letters and drawings, for he was as skilful in the use of the pencil as of the pen. When he was captured, he was in the act of making a description and sketch of the battle. The last words in his note-book were these: "A Southern rifleman has just taken aim at me, but—" The Southerner notwithstanding missed Gideon Spilett, who, with his usual fortune, came out of this affair without a scratch.

Cyrus Harding and Gideon Spilett, who did not know each other except by reputation, had both been carried to Richmond. The engineer's wounds rapidly healed, and it was during his convalescence that he made acquaintance with the reporter. The two men then learned to appreciate each other. Soon their common aim had but one object, that of escaping, rejoining Grant's army, and fighting together in the ranks of the Federals.

The two Americans had from the first determined to seize every chance; but although they were allowed to wander at liberty in the town, Richmond was so strictly guarded, that escape appeared impossible. In the meanwhile Captain Harding was rejoined by a servant who was devoted to him in life and in death. This intrepid fellow was a negro born on the engineer's estate, of a slave father and mother, but to whom Cyrus, who was an Abolitionist from conviction and heart, had long since given his freedom. The once slave, though free, would not leave his master. He would have died for him. He was a man of about thirty, vigourous, active, clever, intelligent, gentle, and calm, sometimes naive, always merry, obliging, and honest. His name was Nebuchadnezzar, but he only answered to the familiar abbreviation of Neb.

When Neb heard that his master had been made prisoner, he left Massachusetts without hesitating an instant, arrived before Richmond, and by dint of stratagem and shrewdness, after having risked his life twenty times over, managed to penetrate into the besieged town. The pleasure of Harding on seeing his servant, and the joy of Neb at finding his master, can scarcely be described.

But though Neb had been able to make his way into Richmond, it was quite another thing to get out again, for the Northern prisoners were very strictly watched. Some extraordinary opportunity was needed to make the attempt with any chance of success, and this opportunity not only did not present itself, but was very difficult to find.

Meanwhile Grant continued his energetic operations. The victory of Petersburg had been very dearly bought. His forces, united to those of Butler, had as yet been unsuccessful before Richmond, and nothing gave the prisoners any hope of a speedy deliverance.

The reporter, to whom his tedious captivity did not offer a single incident worthy of note, could stand it no longer. His usually active mind was occupied with one sole thought—how he might get out of Richmond at any cost. Several times had he even made the attempt, but was stopped by some insurmountable obstacle. However, the siege continued; and if the prisoners were anxious to escape and join Grant's army, certain of the besieged were no less anxious to join the Southern forces. Among them was one Jonathan Forster, a determined Southerner. The truth was, that if the prisoners of the Secessionists could not leave the town, neither could the Secessionists themselves while the Northern army invested it. The Governor of Richmond for a long time had been unable to communicate with General Lee, and he very much wished to make known to him the situation of the town, so as to hasten the march of the army to their relief. This Jonathan Forster accordingly conceived the idea of rising in a balloon, so as to pass over the besieging lines, and in that way reach the Secessionist camp.

The Governor authorised the attempt. A balloon was manufactured and placed at the disposal of Forster, who was to be accompanied by five other persons. They were furnished with arms in case they might have to defend themselves when they alighted, and provisions in the event of their aerial voyage being prolonged.

The departure of the balloon was fixed for the 18th of March. It should be effected during the night, with a north-west wind of moderate force, and the aeronauts calculated that they would reach General Lee's camp in a few hours.

But this north-west wind was not a simple breeze. From the 18th it was evident that it was changing to a hurricane. The tempest soon became such that Forster's departure was deferred, for it was impossible to risk the balloon and those whom it carried in the midst of the furious elements.

The balloon, inflated on the great square of Richmond, was ready to depart on the first abatement of the wind, and, as may be supposed, the impatience among the besieged to see the storm moderate was very great.

The 18th, the 19th of March passed without any alteration in the weather. There was even great difficulty in keeping the balloon fastened to the ground, as the squalls dashed it furiously about.

The night of the 19th passed, but the next morning the storm blew with redoubled force. The departure of the balloon was impossible.

On that day the engineer, Cyrus Harding, was accosted in one of the streets of Richmond by a person whom he did not in the least know. This was a sailor named Pencroft, a man of about thirty-five or forty years of age, strongly built, very sunburned, and possessed of a pair of bright sparkling eyes and a remarkably good physiognomy. Pencroft was an American from the North, who had sailed all the ocean over, and who had gone through every possible and almost impossible adventure that a being with two feet and no wings could encounter. It is needless to say that he was a bold, dashing fellow, ready to dare anything and was astonished at nothing. Pencroft at the beginning of the year had gone to Richmond on business, with a young boy of fifteen from New Jersey, son of a former captain, an orphan, whom he loved as if he had been his own child. Not having been able to leave the town before the first operations of the siege, he found himself shut up, to his great disgust; but, not accustomed to succumb to difficulties, he resolved to escape by some means or other. He knew the engineer-officer by reputation; he knew with what impatience that determined man chafed under his restraint. On this day he did not, therefore, hesitate to accost him, saying, without circumlocution, "Have you had enough of Richmond, captain?"

The engineer looked fixedly at the man who spoke, and who added, in a low voice—

"Captain Harding, will you try to escape?"

"When?" asked the engineer quickly, and it was evident that this question was uttered without consideration, for he had not yet examined the stranger who addressed him. But after having with a penetrating eye observed the open face of the sailor, he was convinced that he had before him an honest man.

"Who are you?" he asked briefly.

Pencroft made himself known.

"Well," replied Harding, "and in what way do you propose to escape?"

"By that lazy balloon which is left there doing nothing, and which looks to me as if it was waiting on purpose for us—"

There was no necessity for the sailor to finish his sentence. The engineer understood him at once. He seized Pencroft by the arm, and dragged him to his house. There the sailor developed his project, which was indeed extremely simple. They risked nothing but their lives in its execution. The hurricane was in all its violence, it is true, but so clever and daring an engineer as Cyrus Harding knew perfectly well how to manage a balloon. Had he himself been as well acquainted with the art of sailing in the air as he was with the navigation of a ship, Pencroft would not have hesitated to set out, of course taking his young friend Herbert with him; for, accustomed to brave the fiercest tempests of the ocean, he was not to be hindered on account of the hurricane.

Captain Harding had listened to the sailor without saying a word, but his eyes shone with satisfaction. Here was the long-sought-for opportunity—he was not a man to let it pass. The plan was feasible, though, it must be confessed, dangerous in the extreme. In the night, in spite of their guards, they might approach the balloon, slip into the car, and then cut the cords which held it. There was no doubt that they might be killed, but on the other hand they might succeed, and without this storm!—Without this storm the balloon would have started already and the looked-for opportunity would not have then presented itself.

"I am not alone!" said Harding at last.

"How many people do you wish to bring with you?" asked the sailor.

"Two; my friend Spilett, and my servant Neb."

"That will be three," replied Pencroft; "and with Herbert and me five. But the balloon will hold six—"

"That will be enough, we will go," answered Harding in a firm voice.

This "we" included Spilett, for the reporter, as his friend well knew, was not a man to draw back, and when the project was communicated to him he approved of it unreservedly. What astonished him was, that so simple an idea had not occurred to him before. As to Neb, he followed his master wherever his master wished to go.

"This evening, then," said Pencroft, "we will all meet out there."

"This evening, at ten o'clock," replied Captain Harding; "and Heaven grant that the storm does not abate before our departure."

Pencroft took leave of the two friends, and returned to his lodging, where young Herbert Brown had remained. The courageous boy knew of the sailor's plan, and it was not without anxiety that he awaited the result of the proposal being made to the engineer. Thus five determined persons were about to abandon themselves to the mercy of the tempestuous elements!

No! the storm did not abate, and neither Jonathan Forster nor his companions dreamed of confronting it in that frail car.

It would be a terrible journey. The engineer only feared one thing, it was that the balloon, held to the ground and dashed about by the wind, would be torn into shreds. For several hours he roamed round the nearly-deserted square, surveying the apparatus. Pencroft did the same on his side, his hands in his pockets, yawning now and then like a man who did not know how to kill the time, but really dreading, like his friend, either the escape or destruction of the balloon. Evening arrived. The night was dark in the extreme. Thick mists passed like clouds close to the ground. Rain fell mingled with snow. It was very cold. A mist hung over Richmond. It seemed as if the violent storm had produced a truce between the besiegers and the besieged, and that the cannon were silenced by the louder detonations of the storm. The streets of the town were deserted. It had not even appeared necessary in that horrible weather to place a guard in the square, in the midst of which plunged the balloon. Everything favoured the departure of the prisoners, but what might possibly be the termination of the hazardous voyage they contemplated in the midst of the furious elements?—

"Dirty weather!" exclaimed Pencroft, fixing his hat firmly on his head with a blow of his fist; "but pshaw, we shall succeed all the same!"

At half-past nine, Harding and his companions glided from different directions into the square, which the gas-lamps, extinguished by the wind, had left in total obscurity. Even the enormous balloon, almost beaten to the ground, could not be seen. Independently of the sacks of ballast, to which the cords of the net were fastened, the car was held by a strong cable passed through a ring in the pavement. The five prisoners met by the car. They had not been perceived, and such was the darkness that they could not even see each other.

Without speaking a word, Harding, Spilett, Neb, and Herbert took their places in the car, while Pencroft by the engineer's order detached successively the bags of ballast. It was the work of a few minutes only, and the sailor rejoined his companions.

The balloon was then only held by the cable, and the engineer had nothing to do but to give the word.

At that moment a dog sprang with a bound into the car. It was Top, a favourite of the engineer. The faithful creature, having broken his chain, had followed his master. He, however, fearing that its additional weight might impede their ascent, wished to send away the animal.

"One more will make but little difference, poor beast!" exclaimed Pencroft, heaving out two bags of sand, and as he spoke letting go the cable; the balloon ascending in an oblique direction, disappeared, after having dashed the car against two chimneys, which it threw down as it swept by them.

Then, indeed, the full rage of the hurricane was exhibited to the voyagers. During the night the engineer could not dream of descending, and when day broke, even a glimpse of the earth below was intercepted by fog.

Five days had passed when a partial clearing allowed them to see the wide extending ocean beneath their feet, now lashed into the maddest fury by the gale.

Our readers will recollect what befell these five daring individuals who set out on their hazardous expedition in the balloon on the 20th of March. Five days afterwards four of them were thrown on a desert coast, seven thousand miles from their country! But one of their number was missing, the man who was to be their guide, their leading spirit, the engineer, Captain Harding! The instant they had recovered their feet, they all hurried to the beach in the hopes of rendering him assistance.*

Chapter III

FIVE O'CLOCK IN THE EVENING—THE MISSING ONE—
NEB'S DESPAIR—SEARCH TOWARDS THE NORTH—THE ISLET—
A DREADFUL NIGHT—A FOG IN THE MORNING—NEB SWIMS—
SIGHT OF LAND—FORDING THE CHANNEL

THE ENGINEER, THE MESHES OF THE NET HAVING GIVEN WAY, HAD BEEN CARRIED OFF by a wave. His dog also had disappeared. The faithful animal had voluntarily leaped out to help his master. "Forward," cried the reporter; and all four, Spilett, Herbert, Pencroft, and Neb, forgetting their fatigue, began their search. Poor Neb shed bitter tears, giving way to despair at the thought of having lost the only being he loved on earth.

Only two minutes had passed from the time when Cyrus Harding disappeared to the

*On the 5th of April Richmond fell into the hands of Grant; the revolt of the Secessionists was suppressed, Lee retreated to the West, and the cause of the Federals triumphed.

moment when his companions set foot on the ground. They had hopes therefore of arriving in time to save him. "Let us look for him! let us look for him!" cried Neb.

"Yes, Neb," replied Gideon Spilett, "and we will find him too!"

"Living, I trust!"

"Still living!"

"Can he swim?" asked Pencroft.

"Yes," replied Neb, "and besides, Top is there."

The sailor, observing the heavy surf on the shore, shook his head.

The engineer had disappeared to the north of the shore, and nearly half-a-mile from the place where the castaways had landed. The nearest point of the beach he could reach was thus fully that distance off.

It was then nearly six o'clock. A thick fog made the night very dark. The castaways proceeded towards the north of the land on which chance had thrown them, an unknown region, the geographical situation of which they could not even guess. They were walking upon a sandy soil, mingled with stones, which appeared destitute of any sort of vegetation. The ground, very unequal and rough, was in some places perfectly riddled with holes, making walking extremely painful. From these holes escaped every minute great birds of clumsy flight, which flew in all directions. Others, more active, rose in flocks and passed in clouds over their heads. The sailor thought he recognised gulls and cormorants, whose shrill cries rose above the roaring of the sea.

From time to time the castaways stopped and shouted, then listened for some response from the ocean, for they thought that if the engineer had landed, and they had been near to the place, they would have heard the barking of the dog Top, even should Harding himself have been unable to give any sign of existence. They stopped to listen, but no sound arose above the roaring of the waves and the dashing of the surf. The little band then continued their march forward, searching into every hollow of the shore.

After walking for twenty minutes, the four castaways were suddenly brought to a standstill by the sight of foaming billows close to their feet. The solid ground ended here. They found themselves at the extremity of a sharp point on which the sea broke furiously.

"It is a promontory," said the sailor; "we must retrace our steps, holding towards the right, and we shall thus gain the mainland."

"But if he is there," said Neb, pointing to the ocean, whose waves shone of a snowy white in the darkness. "Well, let us call again," and all uniting their voices, they gave a vigourous shout, but there came no reply. They waited for a lull, then began again; still no reply.

The castaways accordingly returned, following the opposite side of the promontory, over a soil equally sandy and rugged. However, Pencroft observed that the shore was more equal, that the ground rose, and he declared that it was joined by a long slope to a hill, whose massive front he thought that he could see looming indistinctly through the mist. The birds were less numerous on this part of the shore; the sea was also less tumultuous, and they observed that the agitation of the waves was diminished. The noise of the surf was scarcely heard. This side of the promontory evidently formed a semicircular bay, which the sharp point sheltered from the breakers of the open sea. But to follow this direction was to go south, exactly opposite to that part of the coast where Harding might have landed. After a walk of a mile and a half, the shore presented no curve which would permit them to return to the north. This promontory, of which they had turned the point, must be attached to the mainland. The castaways, although their strength was nearly exhausted, still marched courageously forward, hoping every moment to meet with a sudden angle which would set them in the first direction. What was their disappointment, when, after trudging nearly two miles, having reached an elevated point composed of slippery rocks, they found themselves again stopped by the sea.

"We are on an islet," said Pencroft, "and we have surveyed it from one extremity to the other."

The sailor was right; they had been thrown, not on a continent, not even on an island, but on an islet which was not more than two miles in length, with even a less breadth.

Was this barren spot the desolate refuge of sea-birds, strewn with stones and destitute of vegetation, attached to a more important archipelago? It was impossible to say. When the voyagers from their car saw the land through the mist, they had not been able to reconnoitre it sufficiently. However, Pencroft, accustomed with his sailor eyes to piece through the gloom, was almost certain that he could clearly distinguish in the west confused masses which indicated an elevated coast. But they could not in the dark determine whether it was a single island, or connected with others. They could not leave it either, as the sea surrounded them; they must therefore put off till the next day their search for the engineer, from whom, alas! not a single cry had reached them to show that he was still in existence.

"The silence of our friend proves nothing," said the reporter. "Perhaps he has fainted or is wounded, and unable to reply directly, so we will not despair."

The reporter then proposed to light a fire on a point of the islet, which would serve as a signal to the engineer. But they searched in vain for wood or dry brambles; nothing but sand and stones were to be found. The grief of Neb and his companions, who were all strongly attached to the intrepid Harding, can be better pictured than described. It was too evident that they were powerless to help him. They must wait with what patience they could for daylight. Either the engineer had been able to save himself, and had already found a refuge on some point of the coast, or he was lost forever! The long and painful hours passed by. The cold was intense. The castaways suffered cruelly, but they scarcely perceived it. They did not even think of taking a minute's rest. Forgetting everything but their chief, hoping or wishing to hope on, they continued to walk up and down on this sterile spot, always returning to its northern point, where they could approach nearest to the scene of the catastrophe. They listened, they called, and then uniting their voices, they endeavoured to raise even a louder shout than before, which would be transmitted to a great distance. The wind had now fallen almost to a calm, and the noise of the sea began also to subside. One of Neb's shouts even appeared to produce an echo. Herbert directed Pencroft's attention to it, adding, "That proves that there is a coast to the west, at no great distance." The sailor nodded; besides, his eyes could not deceive him. If he had discovered land, however indistinct it might appear, land was sure to be there. But that distant echo was the only response produced by Neb's shouts, while a heavy gloom hung over all the part east of the island.

Meanwhile, the sky was clearing little by little. Towards midnight the stars shone out, and if the engineer had been there with his companions he would have remarked that these stars did not belong to the northern hemisphere. The polar star was not visible, the constellations were not those which they had been accustomed to see in the United States; the Southern Cross glittered brightly in the sky.

The night passed away. Towards five o'clock in the morning of the 25th of March, the sky began to lighten; the horizon still remained dark, but with daybreak a thick mist rose from the sea, so that the eye could scarcely penetrate beyond twenty feet or so from where they stood. At length the fog gradually unrolled itself in great heavily moving waves.

It was unfortunate, however, that the castaways could distinguish nothing around them. While the gaze of the reporter and Neb were cast upon the ocean, the sailor and Herbert looked eagerly for the coast in the west. But not a speck of land was visible. "Never mind," said Pencroft, "though I do not see the land, I feel it . . . it is there . . . there . . . as sure as the fact that we are no longer at Richmond." But the fog was not long in rising. It was only a fine-weather mist. A hot sun soon penetrated to the surface of the island. About half-past six, three-quarters of an hour after sunrise, the mist became more transparent. It grew thicker above, but cleared away below. Soon the isle appeared as if it had descended from a cloud, then the sea showed itself around them, spreading far away towards the east, but bounded on the west by an abrupt and precipitous coast.

Yes! the land was there. Their safety was at least provisionally ensured. The islet and the coast were separated by a channel about half-a-mile in breadth, through which rushed an extremely rapid current.

However, one of the castaways, following the impulse of his heart, immediately threw himself into the current, without consulting his companions, without saying a single word. It was Neb. He was in haste to be on the other side, and to climb towards the north. It had been impossible to hold him back. Pencroft called him in vain. The reporter prepared to follow him, but Pencroft stopped him. "Do you want to cross the channel?" he asked. "Yes," replied Spilett. "All right!" said the seaman; "wait a bit; Neb is well able to carry help to his master. If we venture into the channel, we risk being carried into the open sea by the current, which is running very strong; but, if I'm not wrong, it is ebbing. See, the tide is going down over the sand. Let us have patience, and at low water it is possible we may find a fordable passage." "You are right," replied the reporter, "we will not separate more than we can help."

During this time Neb was struggling vigourously against the current. He was crossing in an oblique direction. His black shoulders could be seen emerging at each stroke. He was carried down very quickly, but he also made way towards the shore. It took more than half-an-hour to cross from the islet to the land, and he reached the shore several hundred feet from the place which was opposite to the point from which he had started.

Landing at the foot of a high wall of granite, he shook himself vigourously; and then, setting off running, soon disappeared behind a rocky point, which projected to nearly the height of the northern extremity of the islet.

Neb's companions had watched his daring attempt with painful anxiety, and when he was out of sight, they fixed their attention on the land where their hope of safety lay, while eating some shell-fish with which the sand was strewn. It was a wretched repast, but still it was better than nothing. The opposite coast formed one vast bay, terminating on the south by a very sharp point, which was destitute of all vegetation, and was of a very wild aspect. This point abutted on the shore in a grotesque outline of high granite rocks. Towards the north, on the contrary, the bay widened, and a more rounded coast appeared, trending from the south-west to the north-east, and terminating in a slender cape. The distance between these two extremities, which made the bow of the bay, was about eight miles. Half-a-mile from the shore rose the islet, which somewhat resembled the carcass of a gigantic whale. Its extreme breadth was not more than a quarter of a mile.

Opposite the islet, the beach consisted first of sand, covered with black stones, which were now appearing little by little above the retreating tide. The second level was separated by a perpendicular granite cliff, terminated at the top by an unequal edge at a height of at least 300 feet. It continued thus for a length of three miles, ending suddenly on the right with a precipice which looked as if cut by the hand of man. On the left, above the promontory, this irregular and jagged cliff descended by a long slope of conglomerated rocks till it mingled with the ground of the southern point. On the upper plateau of the coast not a tree appeared. It was a flat table-land like that above Cape Town at the Cape of Good Hope, but of reduced proportions; at least so it appeared seen from the islet. However, verdure was not wanting to the right beyond the precipice. They could easily distinguish a confused mass of great trees, which extended beyond the limits of their view. This verdure relieved the eye, so long wearied by the continued ranges of granite. Lastly, beyond and above the plateau, in a north-westerly direction and at a distance of at least seven miles, glittered a white summit which reflected the sun's rays. It was that of a lofty mountain, capped with snow.

The question could not at present be decided whether this land formed an island, or whether it belonged to a continent. But on beholding the convulsed masses heaped upon the left, no geologist would have hesitated to give them a volcanic origin, for they were unquestionably the work of subterranean convulsions.

Gideon Spilett, Pencroft, and Herbert attentively examined this land, on which they might perhaps have to live many long years; on which indeed they might even die, should it be out of the usual track of vessels, as was too likely to be the case.

"Well," asked Herbert, "what do you say, Pencroft?"

"There is some good and some bad, as in everything," replied the sailor. "We shall see. But now the ebb is evidently making. In three hours we will attempt the passage, and once on the other side, we will try to get out of this scrape, and I hope may find the captain." Pencroft was not wrong in his anticipations. Three hours later at low tide, the greater part of the sand forming the bed of the channel was uncovered. Between the islet and the coast there only remained a narrow channel which would no doubt be easy to cross.

About ten o'clock, Gideon Spilett and his companions stripped themselves of their clothes, which they placed in bundles on their heads, and then ventured into the water, which was not more than five feet deep. Herbert, for whom it was too deep, swam like a fish, and got through capitally. All three arrived without difficulty on the opposite shore. Quickly drying themselves in the sun, they put on their clothes, which they had preserved from contact with the water, and sat down to take counsel together what to do next.

Chapter IV

LITHODOMES—THE RIVER'S MOUTH—THE CHIMNEYS—
CONTINUED RESEARCHES—THE FOREST OF EVERGREENS—
WAITING FOR THE EBB—ON THE HEIGHTS—THE RAFT—
RETURN TO THE SHORE

ALL AT ONCE THE REPORTER SPRANG UP, AND TELLING THE SAILOR THAT HE WOULD RE-join them at that same place, he climbed the cliff in the direction which the negro Neb had taken a few hours before. Anxiety hastened his steps, for he longed to obtain news of his friend, and he soon disappeared round an angle of the cliff. Herbert wished to accompany him.

"Stop here, my boy," said the sailor; "we have to prepare an encampment, and to try and find rather better grub than these shell-fish. Our friends will want something when they come back. There is work for everybody."

"I am ready," replied Herbert.

"All right," said the sailor; "that will do. We must set about it regularly. We are tired, cold, and hungry; therefore we must have shelter, fire, and food. There is wood in the forest, and eggs in nests; we have only to find a house."

"Very well," returned Herbert, "I will look for a cave among the rocks, and I shall be sure to discover some hole into which we can creep."

"All right," said Pencroft; "go on, my boy."

They both walked to the foot of the enormous wall over the beach, far from which the tide had now retreated; but instead of going towards the north, they went southward. Pencroft had remarked, several hundred feet from the place at which they landed, a narrow cutting, out of which he thought a river or stream might issue. Now, on the one hand it was important to settle themselves in the neighbourhood of a good stream of water, and on the other it was possible that the current had thrown Cyrus Harding on the shore there.

The cliff, as has been said, rose to a height of three hundred feet, but the mass was unbroken throughout, and even at its base, scarcely washed by the sea, it did not offer the smallest fissure which would serve as a dwelling. It was a perpendicular wall of very hard granite, which even the waves had not worn away. Towards the summit fluttered myriads of sea-fowl, and especially those of the web-footed species with long, flat, pointed beaks—a clamorous tribe, bold in the presence of man, who probably for the first time thus invaded their domains. Pencroft recognised the skua and other gulls among them, the voracious little sea-mew, which in great numbers nestled in the crevices of the granite. A shot fired among this swarm would have killed a great number, but to fire a shot a gun was needed, and neither Pencroft nor Herbert had one; besides this, gulls and sea-mews are scarcely eatable, and even their eggs have a detestable taste. However, Herbert who had gone forward a little more to the left, soon came upon rocks covered with sea-weed, which, some hours later, would be hidden by the high tide. On these rocks, in the midst of slippery wrack, abounded bivalve shell-fish, not to be despised by starving people. Herbert called Pencroft, who ran up hastily.

"Why! here are mussels!" cried the sailor; "these will do instead of eggs!"

"They are not mussels," replied Herbert, who was attentively examining the molluscs attached to the rocks; "they are lithodomes."

"Are they good to eat?" asked Pencroft.

"Perfectly so."

"Then let us eat some lithodomes."

The sailor could rely upon Herbert; the young boy was well up in natural history, and always had had quite a passion for the science. His father had encouraged him in it, by letting him attend the lectures of the best professors in Boston, who were very fond of the intelligent, industrious lad. And his turn for natural history was, more than once in the course of time, of great use, and he was not mistaken in this instance. These lithodomes were oblong shells, suspended in clusters and adhering very tightly to the rocks. They belong to that species of molluscous perforators which excavate holes in the hardest stone; their shell is rounded at both ends, a feature which is not remarked in the common mussel.

Pencroft and Herbert made a good meal of the lithodomes, which were then half opened to the sun. They ate them as oysters, and as they had a strong peppery taste, they were palatable without condiments of any sort.

Their hunger was thus appeased for the time, but not their thirst, which increased after eating these naturally-spiced molluscs. They had then to find fresh water, and it was not likely that it would be wanting in such a capriciously uneven region. Pencroft and Herbert, after having taken the precaution of collecting an ample supply of lithodomes, with which they filled their pockets and handkerchiefs, regained the foot of the cliff.

Two hundred paces farther they arrived at the cutting, through which, as Pencroft had guessed, ran a stream of water, whether fresh or not was to be ascertained. At this place the wall appeared to have been separated by some violent subterranean force. At its base was hollowed out a little creek, the farthest part of which formed a tolerably sharp angle. The water-course at that part measured one hundred feet in breadth, and its two banks on each side were scarcely twenty feet high. The river became strong almost directly between the two walls of granite, which began to sink above the mouth; it then suddenly turned and disappeared beneath a wood of stunted trees half-a-mile off.

"Here is the water, and yonder is the wood we require!" said Pencroft. "Well, Herbert, now we only want the house."

The water of the river was limpid. The sailor ascertained that at this time—that is to say, at low tide, when the rising floods did not reach it—it was sweet. This important point established, Herbert looked for some cavity which would serve them as a retreat, but in vain; everywhere the wall appeared smooth, plain, and perpendicular.

However, at the mouth of the water-course and above the reach of the high tide, the convulsions of nature had formed, not a grotto, but a pile of enormous rocks, such as are often met with in granite countries and which bear the name of "Chimneys."

Pencroft and Herbert penetrated quite far in among the rocks, by sandy passages in which light was not wanting, for it entered through the openings which were left between the blocks, of which some were only sustained by a miracle of equilibrium; but with the light came also air—a regular corridor-gale—and with the wind the sharp cold from the exterior. However, the sailor thought that by stopping-up some of the openings with a mixture of stones and sand, the Chimneys could be rendered habitable. Their geometrical plan represented the typographical sign "&," which signifies *"et cetera"* abridged, but by isolating the upper mouth of the sign, through which the south and west winds blew so strongly, they could succeed in making the lower part of use.

"Here's our work," said Pencroft, "and if we ever see Captain Harding again, he will know how to make something of this labyrinth."

"We shall see him again, Pencroft," cried Herbert, "and when he returns he must find a tolerable dwelling here. It will be so, if we can make a fireplace in the left passage and keep an opening for the smoke."

"So we can, my boy," replied the sailor, "and these Chimneys will serve our turn. Let us set to work, but first come and get a store of fuel. I think some branches will be very useful in stopping up these openings, through which the wind shrieks like so many fiends."

Herbert and Pencroft left the Chimneys, and, turning the angle, they began to climb the left bank of the river. The current here was quite rapid, and drifted down some dead wood. The rising tide—and it could already be perceived—must drive it back with force to a considerable distance. The sailor then thought that they could utilise this ebb and flow for the transport of heavy objects.

After having walked for a quarter of an hour, the sailor and the boy arrived at the angle which the river made in turning towards the left. From this point its course was pursued through a forest of magnificent trees. These trees still retained their verdure, notwithstanding the advanced season, for they belonged to the family of "coniferae," which is spread over all the regions of the globe, from northern climates to the tropics. The young naturalist recognised especially the "deodara," which are very numerous in the Himalayan zone, and which spread around them a most agreeable odor. Between these beautiful trees sprang up clusters of firs, whose opaque open parasol boughs spread wide around. Among the long grass, Pencroft felt that his feet were crushing dry branches which crackled like fireworks.

"Well, my boy," said he to Herbert, "if I don't know the name of these trees, at any rate I reckon that we may call them 'burning wood,' and just now that's the chief thing we want."

"Let us get a supply," replied Herbert, who immediately set to work.

The collection was easily made. It was not even necessary to lop the trees, for enormous quantities of dead wood were lying at their feet; but if fuel was not wanting, the means of transporting it was not yet found. The wood, being very dry, would burn rapidly; it was therefore necessary to carry to the Chimneys a considerable quantity, and the loads of two men would not be sufficient. Herbert remarked this.

"Well, my boy," replied the sailor, "there must be some way of carrying this wood; there is always a way of doing everything. If we had a cart or a boat, it would be easy enough."

"But we have the river," said Herbert.

"Right," replied Pencroft; "the river will be to us like a road which carries of itself, and rafts have not been invented for nothing."

"Only," observed Herbert, "at this moment our road is going the wrong way, for the tide is rising!"

"We shall be all right if we wait till it ebbs," replied the sailor, "and then we will trust it to carry our fuel to the Chimneys. Let us get the raft ready."

The sailor, followed by Herbert, directed his steps towards the river. They both carried, each in proportion to his strength, a load of wood bound in fagots. They found on the bank also a great quantity of dead branches in the midst of grass, among which the foot of man had probably never before trod. Pencroft began directly to make his raft. In a kind of little bay, created by a point of the shore which broke the current, the sailor and the lad placed some good-sized pieces of wood, which they had fastened together with dry creepers. A raft was thus formed, on which they stacked all they had collected, sufficient, indeed, to have loaded at least twenty men. In an hour the work was finished, and the raft moored to the bank, awaited the turning of the tide.

There were still several hours to be occupied, and with one consent Pencroft and Herbert resolved to gain the upper plateau, so as to have a more extended view of the surrounding country.

Exactly two hundred feet behind the angle formed by the river, the wall, terminated by a fall of rocks, died away in a gentle slope to the edge of the forest. It was a natural staircase. Herbert and the sailor began their ascent; thanks to the vigour of their muscles they reached the summit in a few minutes, and proceeded to the point above the mouth of the river.

On attaining it, their first look was cast upon the ocean which not long before they had traversed in such a terrible condition. They observed, with emotion, all that part to the north of the coast on which the catastrophe had taken place. It was there that Cyrus Harding had disappeared. They looked to see if some portion of their balloon, to which a man might possibly cling, yet existed. Nothing! The sea was but one vast watery desert. As to the coast, it was solitary also. Neither the reporter nor Neb could be anywhere seen. But it was possible that at this time they were both too far away to be perceived.

"Something tells me," cried Herbert, "that a man as energetic as Captain Harding would not let himself be drowned like other people. He must have reached some point of the shore; don't you think so, Pencroft?"

The sailor shook his head sadly. He little expected ever to see Cyrus Harding again; but wishing to leave some hope to Herbert: "Doubtless, doubtless," said he; "our engineer is a man who would get out of a scrape to which anyone else would yield."

In the meantime he examined the coast with great attention. Stretched out below them was the sandy shore, bounded on the right of the river's mouth by lines of breakers. The rocks which were visible appeared like amphibious monsters reposing in the surf. Beyond the reef, the sea sparkled beneath the sun's rays. To the south a sharp point closed the horizon, and it could not be seen if the land was prolonged in that direction, or if it ran southeast and south-west, which would have made this coast a very long peninsula. At the northern extremity of the bay the outline of the shore was continued to a great distance in a wider curve. There the shore was low, flat, without cliffs, and with great banks of sand, which the tide left uncovered. Pencroft and Herbert then returned towards the west. Their attention was first arrested by the snow-topped mountain which rose at a distance of six or seven miles. From its first declivities to within two miles of the coast were spread vast masses of wood, relieved by large green patches, caused by the presence of evergreen-trees. Then, from the edge of this forest to the shore extended a plain, scattered irregularly with groups of trees. Here and there on the left sparkled through glades the waters of the little river; they could trace its winding course back towards the spurs of the mountain, among which it seemed to spring. At the point where the sailor had left his raft of wood, it began to run between the two high granite walls; but if on the left bank the wall remained clear and abrupt, on the right bank, on the contrary, it sank gradually, the massive sides changed to isolated rocks, the rocks to stones, the stones to shingle running to the extremity of the point.

"Are we on an island?" murmured the sailor.

"At any rate, it seems to be big enough," replied the lad.

"An island, ever so big, is an island all the same!" said Pencroft.

But this important question could not yet be answered. A more perfect survey will be required to settle the point. As to the land itself, island or continent, it appeared fertile, agreeable in its aspect, and varied in its productions.

"This is satisfactory," observed Pencroft; "and in our misfortune, we must thank Providence for it."

"God be praised!" responded Herbert, whose pious heart was full of gratitude to the Author of all things.

Pencroft and Herbert examined for some time the country on which they had been cast; but it was difficult to guess after so hasty an inspection what the future had in store for them.

They then returned, following the southern crest of the granite platform, bordered by a long fringe of jagged rocks, of the most whimsical shapes. Some hundreds of birds lived there nestled in the holes of the stone; Herbert, jumping over the rocks, startled a whole flock of these winged creatures.

"Oh!" cried he, "those are not gulls nor sea-mews!"

"What are they then?" asked Pencroft.

"Upon my word, one would say they were pigeons!"

"Just so, but these are wild or rock pigeons. I recognise them by the double band of black on the wing, by the white tail, and by their slate-colored plumage. But if the rock-pigeon is good to eat, its eggs must be excellent, and we will soon see how many they may have left in their nests!"

"We will not give them time to hatch, unless it is in the shape of an omelet!" replied Pencroft merrily.

"But what will you make your omelet in?" asked Herbert; "in your hat?"

"Well!" replied the sailor, "I am not quite conjuror enough for that; we must come down to eggs in the shell, my boy, and I will undertake to despatch the hardest!"

Pencroft and Herbert attentively examined the cavities in the granite, and they really found eggs in some of the hollows. A few dozen being collected, were packed in the sailor's handkerchief, and as the time when the tide would be full was approaching, Pencroft and Herbert began to redescend towards the water-course. When they arrived there, it was an hour after midday. The tide had already turned. They must now avail themselves of the ebb to take the wood to the mouth. Pencroft did not intend to let the raft go away in the current without guidance, neither did he mean to embark on it himself to steer it. But a sailor is never at a loss when there is a question of cables or ropes, and Pencroft rapidly twisted a cord, a few fathoms long, made of dry creepers. This vegetable cable was fastened to the after-part of the raft, and the sailor held it in his hand while Herbert, pushing off the raft with a long pole, kept it in the current. This succeeded capitally. The enormous load of wood drifted down the current. The bank was very equal; there was no fear that the raft would run aground, and before two o'clock they arrived at the river's mouth, a few paces from the Chimneys.

Chapter V

ARRANGING THE CHIMNEYS—HOW TO PROCURE FIRE—A BOX OF MATCHES—SEARCH ON THE SHORE—RETURN OF THE REPORTER AND NEB—A SINGLE MATCH—A ROARING FIRE— THE FIRST SUPPER, AND NIGHT ON SHORE

PENCROFT'S FIRST CARE, AFTER UNLOADING THE RAFT, WAS TO RENDER THE CAVE HABitable by stopping up all the holes which made it draughty. Sand, stones, twisted branches, wet clay, closed up the galleries open to the south winds. One narrow and winding opening at the side was kept, to lead out the smoke and to make the fire draw. The cave was thus divided into three or four rooms, if such dark dens with which a donkey would scarcely have been contented deserved the name. But they were dry, and there was space to stand upright, at least in the principal room, which occupied the centre. The floor was covered with fine sand, and taking all in all they were well pleased with it for want of a better.

"Perhaps," said Herbert, while he and Pencroft were working, "our companions have found a superior place to ours."

"Very likely," replied the seaman; "but, as we don't know, we must work all the same. Better to have two strings to one's bow than no string at all!"

"Oh!" exclaimed Herbert, "how jolly it will be if they were to find Captain Harding and were to bring him back with them!"

"Yes, indeed!" said Pencroft, "that was a man of the right sort."

"Was!" exclaimed Herbert, "do you despair of ever seeing him again?"

"God forbid!" replied the sailor. Their work was soon done, and Pencroft declared himself very well satisfied.

"Now," said he, "our friends can come back when they like. They will find a good enough shelter."

They now had only to make a fireplace and to prepare the supper—an easy task. Large flat stones were placed on the ground at the opening of the narrow passage which had been kept. This, if the smoke did not take the heat out with it, would be enough to maintain an equal temperature inside. Their wood was stowed away in one of the rooms, and the sailor laid in the fireplace some logs and brushwood. The seaman was busy with this, when Herbert asked him if he had any matches.

"Certainly," replied Pencroft, "and I may say happily, for without matches or tinder we should be in a fix."

"Still we might get fire as the savages do," replied Herbert, "by rubbing two bits of dry stick one against the other."

"All right; try, my boy, and let's see if you can do anything besides exercising your arms."

"Well, it's a very simple proceeding, and much used in the islands of the Pacific."

"I don't deny it," replied Pencroft, "but the savages must know how to do it or employ a peculiar wood, for more than once I have tried to get fire in that way, but I could never manage it. I must say I prefer matches. By the by, where are my matches?"

Pencroft searched in his waistcoat for the box, which was always there, for he was a confirmed smoker. He could not find it; he rummaged the pockets of his trousers, but, to his horror, he could nowhere discover the box.

"Here's a go!" said he, looking at Herbert. "The box must have fallen out of my pocket and got lost! Surely, Herbert, you must have something—a tinder-box—anything that can possibly make fire!"

"No, I haven't, Pencroft."

The sailor rushed out, followed by the boy. On the sand, among the rocks, near the river's bank, they both searched carefully, but in vain. The box was of copper, and therefore would have been easily seen.

"Pencroft," asked Herbert, "didn't you throw it out of the car?"

"I knew better than that," replied the sailor; "but such a small article could easily disappear in the tumbling about we have gone through. I would rather even have lost my pipe! Confound the box! Where can it be?"

"Look here, the tide is going down," said Herbert; "let's run to the place where we landed."

It was scarcely probable that they would find the box, which the waves had rolled about among the pebbles, at high tide, but it was as well to try. Herbert and Pencroft walked rapidly to the point where they had landed the day before, about two hundred feet from the cave. They hunted there, among the shingle, in the clefts of the rocks, but found nothing. If the box had fallen at this place it must have been swept away by the waves. As the sea went down, they searched every little crevice with no result. It was a grave loss in their circumstances, and for the time irreparable. Pencroft could not hide his vexation; he looked very anxious, but said not a word. Herbert tried to console him by observing, that if they had found the matches, they would, very likely, have been wetted by the sea and useless.

"No, my boy," replied the sailor; "they were in a copper box which shut very tightly; and now what are we to do?"

"We shall certainly find some way of making a fire," said Herbert. "Captain Harding or Mr. Spilett will not be without them."

"Yes," replied Pencroft; "but in the meantime we are without fire, and our companions will find but a sorry repast on their return."

"But," said Herbert quickly, "do you think it possible that they have no tinder or matches?"

"I doubt it," replied the sailor, shaking his head, "for neither Neb nor Captain Harding smoke, and I believe that Mr. Spilett would rather keep his note-book than his match-box."

Herbert did not reply. The loss of the box was certainly to be regretted, but the boy was still sure of procuring fire in some way or other. Pencroft, more experienced, did not think so, although he was not a man to trouble himself about a small or great grievance. At any rate, there was only one thing to be done—to await the return of Neb and the reporter; but they must give up the feast of hard eggs which they had meant to prepare, and a meal of raw flesh was not an agreeable prospect either for themselves or for the others.

Before returning to the cave, the sailor and Herbert, in the event of fire being positively unattainable, collected some more shell-fish, and then silently retraced their steps to their dwelling.

Pencroft, his eyes fixed on the ground, still looked for his box. He even climbed up the left bank of the river from its mouth to the angle where the raft had been moored. He returned to the plateau, went over it in every direction, searched among the high grass on the border of the forest, all in vain.

It was five in the evening when he and Herbert re-entered the cave. It is useless to say that the darkest corners of the passages were ransacked before they were obliged to give it up in despair. Towards six o'clock, when the sun was disappearing behind the high lands of the west, Herbert, who was walking up and down on the strand, signalised the return of Neb and Spilett.

They were returning alone! . . . The boy's heart sank; the sailor had not been deceived in his forebodings; the engineer, Cyrus Harding, had not been found!

The reporter, on his arrival, sat down on a rock, without saying anything. Exhausted with fatigue, dying of hunger, he had not strength to utter a word.

As to Neb, his red eyes showed how he had cried, and the tears which he could not restrain told too clearly that he had lost all hope.

The reporter recounted all that they had done in their attempt to recover Cyrus Harding. He and Neb had surveyed the coast for a distance of eight miles, and consequently much beyond the place where the balloon had fallen the last time but one, a fall which was followed by the disappearance of the engineer and the dog Top. The shore was solitary; not a vestige of a mark. Not even a pebble recently displaced; not a trace on the sand; not a human footstep on all that part of the beach. It was clear that that portion of the shore had never been visited by a human being. The sea was as deserted as the land, and it was there, a few hundred feet from the coast, that the engineer must have found a tomb.

As Spilett ended his account, Neb jumped up, exclaiming in a voice which showed how hope struggled within him, "No! he is not dead! he can't be dead! It might happen to anyone else, but never to him! He could get out of anything!" Then his strength forsaking him, "Oh! I can do no more!" he murmured.

"Neb," said Herbert, running to him, "we will find him! God will give him back to us! But in the meantime you are hungry, and you must eat something."

So saying, he offered the poor negro a few handfuls of shell-fish, which was indeed wretched and insufficient food. Neb had not eaten anything for several hours, but he refused them. He could not, would not live without his master.

As to Gideon Spilett, he devoured the shell-fish, then he laid himself down on the sand, at the foot of a rock. He was very weak, but calm. Herbert went up to him, and taking his hand, "Sir," said he, "we have found a shelter which will be better than lying here. Night is advancing. Come and rest! To-morrow we will search farther."

The reporter got up, and guided by the boy went towards the cave. On the way, Pencroft asked him in the most natural tone, if by chance he happened to have a match or two.

The reporter stopped, felt in his pockets, but finding nothing said, "I had some, but I must have thrown them away."

The seaman then put the same question to Neb and received the same answer.

"Confound it!" exclaimed the sailor.

The reporter heard him and seizing his arm, "Have you no matches?" he asked.

"Not one, and no fire in consequence."

"Ah!" cried Neb, "if my master was here, he would know what to do!"

The four castaways remained motionless, looking uneasily at each other. Herbert was the first to break the silence by saying, "Mr. Spilett, you are a smoker and always have matches about you; perhaps you haven't looked well, try again, a single match will be enough!"

The reporter hunted again in the pockets of his trousers, waistcoat, and great-coat, and at last to Pencroft's great joy, no less to his extreme surprise, he felt a tiny piece of wood entangled in the lining of his waistcoat. He seized it with his fingers through the stuff, but he could not get it out. If this was a match and a single one, it was of great importance not to rub off the phosphorus.

"Will you let me try?" said the boy, and very cleverly, without breaking it, he managed to draw out the wretched yet precious little bit of wood which was of such great importance to these poor men. It was unused.

"Hurrah!" cried Pencroft; "it is as good as having a whole cargo!" He took the match, and, followed by his companions, entered the cave.

This small piece of wood, of which so many in an inhabited country are wasted with indifference and are of no value, must here be used with the greatest caution.

The sailor first made sure that it was quite dry; that done, "We must have some paper," said he.

"Here," replied Spilett, after some hesitation tearing a leaf out of his note-book.

Pencroft took the piece of paper which the reporter held out to him, and knelt down before the fireplace. Some handfuls of grass, leaves, and dry moss were placed under the fagots and disposed in such a way that the air could easily circulate, and the dry wood would rapidly catch fire.

Pencroft then twisted the piece of paper into the shape of a cone, as smokers do in a high wind, and poked it in among the moss. Taking a small, rough stone, he wiped it carefully, and with a beating heart, holding his breath, he gently rubbed the match. The first attempt did not produce any effect. Pencroft had not struck hard enough, fearing to rub off the phosphorus.

"No, I can't do it," said he, "my hand trembles, the match has missed fire; I cannot, I will not!" and rising, he told Herbert to take his place.

Certainly the boy had never in all his life been so nervous. Prometheus going to steal the fire from heaven could not have been more anxious. He did not hesitate, however, but struck the match directly.

A little spluttering was heard and a tiny blue flame sprang up, making a choking smoke. Herbert quickly turned the match so as to augment the flame, and then slipped it into the paper cone, which in a few seconds too caught fire, and then the moss.

A minute later the dry wood crackled and a cheerful flame, assisted by the vigourous blowing of the sailor, sprang up in the midst of the darkness.

"At last!" cried Pencroft, getting up; "I was never so nervous before in all my life!"

The flat stones made a capital fireplace. The smoke went quite easily out at the narrow passage, the chimney drew, and an agreeable warmth was not long in being felt.

They must now take great care not to let the fire go out, and always to keep some embers alight. It only needed care and attention, as they had plenty of wood and could renew their store at any time.

Pencroft's first thought was to use the fire by preparing a more nourishing supper than a dish of shell-fish. Two dozen eggs were brought by Herbert. The reporter leaning up in a corner, watched these preparations without saying anything. A threefold thought weighed on his mind. Was Cyrus still alive? If he was alive, where was he? If he had survived from his fall, how was it that he had not found some means of making known his existence? As to Neb, he was roaming about the shore. He was like a body without a soul.

Pencroft knew fifty ways of cooking eggs, but this time he had no choice, and was obliged to content himself with roasting them under the hot cinders. In a few minutes the cooking was done, and the seaman invited the reporter to take his share of the supper. Such was the first repast of the castaways on this unknown coast. The hard eggs were excellent, and as eggs contain everything indispensable to man's nourishment, these poor people thought themselves well off, and were much strengthened by them. Oh! if only one of them had not been missing at this meal! If the five prisoners who escaped from Richmond had been all there, under the piled-up rocks, before this clear, crackling fire on the dry sand, what thanksgivings must they have rendered to Heaven! But the most ingenious, the most learned, he who was their unquestioned chief, Cyrus Harding, was, alas! missing, and his body had not even obtained a burial-place.

Thus passed the 25th of March. Night had come on. Outside could be heard the howling of the wind and the monotonous sound of the surf breaking on the shore. The waves rolled the shingle backwards and forwards with a deafening noise.

The reporter retired into a dark corner after having shortly noted down the occurrences of the day; the first appearance of this new land, the loss of their leader, the exploration of the coast, the incident of the matches, etc.; and then overcome by fatigue, he managed to forget his sorrow in sleep. Herbert went to sleep directly. As to the sailor, he passed the night with one eye on the fire, on which he did not spare fuel. But one of the castaways did not sleep in the cave. The inconsolable, despairing Neb, notwithstanding all that his companions could say to induce him to take some rest, wandered all night long on the shore calling on his master.

Chapter VI

THE INVENTORY OF THE CASTAWAYS—NOTHING— BURNED LINEN—AN EXPEDITION TO THE FOREST—FLIGHT OF THE JACAMAR—TRACES OF DEER—COUROUCOUS— GROUSE—A CURIOUS FISHING-LINE

THE INVENTORY OF THE ARTICLES POSSESSED BY THESE CASTAWAYS FROM THE CLOUDS, thrown upon a coast which appeared to be uninhabited, was soon made out. They had nothing, save the clothes which they were wearing at the time of the catastrophe. We must mention, however, a note-book and a watch which Gideon Spilett had kept, doubtless by inadvertence, not a weapon, not a tool, not even a pocketknife; for while in the car they had thrown out everything to lighten the balloon. The imaginary heroes of Daniel De Foe or of Wyss, as well as Selkirk and Raynal shipwrecked on Juan Fernandez and on the archipelago of the Aucklands, were never in such absolute destitution. Either they had abundant resources from their stranded vessels, in grain, cattle, tools, ammunition, or else some things were thrown upon the coast which supplied them with all the first necessities of life. But here, not any instrument whatever, not a utensil. From nothing they must supply themselves with everything.

And yet, if Cyrus Harding had been with them, if the engineer could have brought his practical science, his inventive mind to bear on their situation, perhaps all hope would not have been lost. Alas! they must hope no longer again to see Cyrus Harding. The castaways could expect nothing but from themselves and from that Providence which never abandons those whose faith is sincere.

But ought they to establish themselves on this part of the coast, without trying to know to what continent it belonged, if it was inhabited, or if they were on the shore of a desert island?

It was an important question, and should be solved with the shortest possible delay. From its answer they would know what measures to take. However, according to Pencroft's advice, it appeared best to wait a few days before commencing an exploration. They must, in fact, prepare some provisions and procure more strengthening food than eggs and molluscs. The explorers, before undertaking new fatigues, must first of all recruit their strength.

The Chimneys offered a retreat sufficient for the present. The fire was lighted, and it was easy to preserve some embers. There were plenty of shell-fish and eggs among the rocks and on the beach. It would be easy to kill a few of the pigeons which were flying by hundreds about the summit of the plateau, either with sticks or stones. Perhaps the trees of the neighbouring forest would supply them with eatable fruit. Lastly, the sweet water was there.

It was accordingly settled that for a few days they would remain at the Chimneys so as to prepare themselves for an expedition, either along the shore or into the interior of the country. This plan suited Neb particularly. As obstinate in his ideas as in his presentiments, he was in no haste to abandon this part of the coast, the scene of the catastrophe. He did not, he would not believe in the loss of Cyrus Harding. No, it did not seem to him possible that such a man had ended in this vulgar fashion, carried away by a wave, drowned in the floods, a few hundred feet from a shore. As long as the waves had not cast up the body of the engineer, as long as he, Neb, had not seen with his eyes, touched with his hands the corpse of his master, he would not believe in his death! And this idea rooted itself deeper than ever in his determined heart. An illusion perhaps, but still an illusion to be respected, and one which the sailor did not wish to destroy. As for him, he hoped no longer, but there was no use in arguing with Neb. He was like the dog who will not leave the place where his master is buried, and his grief was such that most probably he would not survive him.

This same morning, the 26th of March, at daybreak, Neb had set out on the shore in a northerly direction, and he had returned to the spot where the sea, no doubt, had closed over the unfortunate Harding.

That day's breakfast was composed solely of pigeon's eggs and lithodomes. Herbert had found some salt deposited by evaporation in the hollows of the rocks, and this mineral was very welcome.

The repast ended, Pencroft asked the reporter if he wished to accompany Herbert and himself to the forest, where they were going to try to hunt. But on consideration, it was thought necessary that someone should remain to keep in the fire, and to be at hand in the highly improbable event of Neb requiring aid. The reporter accordingly remained behind.

"To the chase, Herbert," said the sailor. "We shall find ammunition on our way, and cut our weapons in the forest." But at the moment of starting, Herbert observed, that since they had no tinder, it would perhaps be prudent to replace it by another substance.

"What?" asked Pencroft.

"Burned linen," replied the boy. "That could in case of need serve for tinder."

The sailor thought it very sensible advice. Only it had the inconvenience of necessitating the sacrifice of a piece of handkerchief. Notwithstanding, the thing was well worthwhile trying, and a part of Pencroft's large checked handkerchief was soon reduced to the state of a half-burned rag. This inflammable material was placed in the central chamber at the bottom of a little cavity in the rock, sheltered from all wind and damp.

It was nine o'clock in the morning. The weather was threatening and the breeze blew from the south-east. Herbert and Pencroft turned the angle of the Chimneys, not without having cast a look at the smoke which, just at that place, curled round a point of rock: they ascended the left bank of the river.

Arrived at the forest, Pencroft broke from the first tree two stout branches which he transformed into clubs, the ends of which Herbert rubbed smooth on a rock. Oh! what would they not have given for a knife!

The two hunters now advanced among the long grass, following the bank. From the turning which directed its course to the south-west, the river narrowed gradually and the channel lay between high banks, over which the trees formed a double arch. Pencroft, lest they should lose themselves, resolved to follow the course of the stream, which would always lead them back to the point from which they started. But the bank was not without some obstacles: here, the flexible branches of the trees bent level with the current; there, creepers and thorns which they had to break down with their sticks. Herbert often glided among the broken stumps with the agility of a young cat, and disappeared in the underwood. But Pencroft called him back directly, begging him not to wander away. Meanwhile, the sailor attentively observed the disposition and nature of the surrounding country. On the left bank, the ground, which was flat and marshy, rose imperceptibly towards the interior. It looked there like a network of liquid threads which doubtless reached the river by some underground drain. Sometimes a stream ran through the underwood, which they crossed without difficulty. The opposite shore appeared to be more uneven, and the valley of which the river occupied the bottom was more clearly visible. The hill, covered with trees disposed in terraces, intercepted the view. On the right bank walking would have been difficult, for the declivities fell suddenly, and the trees bending over the water were only sustained by the strength of their roots.

It is needless to add that this forest, as well as the coast already surveyed, was destitute of any sign of human life. Pencroft only saw traces of quadrupeds, fresh footprints of animals, of which he could not recognise the species. In all probability, and such was also Herbert's opinion, some had been left by formidable wild beasts which doubtless would give them some trouble; but nowhere did they observe the mark of an axe on the trees, nor the ashes of a fire, nor the impression of a human foot. On this they might probably congratulate themselves, for on any land in the middle of the Pacific the presence of man was perhaps more to be feared than desired. Herbert and Pencroft speaking little, for the difficulties of the way were great, advanced very slowly, and after walking for an hour they had scarcely gone more than a mile. As yet the hunt had not been successful. However, some birds sang and fluttered in the foliage, and appeared very timid, as if man had inspired them with an instinctive fear. Among others, Herbert described, in a marshy part of the forest, a bird with a long pointed beak, closely resembling the king-fisher, but its plumage was not fine, though of a metallic brilliancy.

"That must be a jacamar," said Herbert, trying to get nearer.

"This will be a good opportunity to taste jacamar," replied the sailor, "if that fellow is in a humour to be roasted!"

Just then, a stone cleverly thrown by the boy, struck the creature on the wing, but the blow did not disable it, and the jacamar ran off and disappeared in an instant.

"How clumsy I am!" cried Herbert.

"No, no, my boy!" replied the sailor. "The blow was well aimed; many a one would have missed it altogether! Come, don't be vexed with yourself. We shall catch it another day!"

As the hunters advanced, the trees were found to be more scattered, many being magnificent, but none bore eatable fruit. Pencroft searched in vain for some of those precious palm-trees which are employed in so many ways in domestic life, and which have been found as far as the fortieth parallel in the northern hemisphere, and to the thirty-fifth only in the southern hemisphere. But this forest was only composed of coniferae, such as deodaras, already recognised by Herbert, the Douglas pine, similar to those which grow on the north-west coast of America, and splendid firs, measuring a hundred and fifty feet in height.

At this moment a flock of birds, of a small size and pretty plumage, with long glancing tails, dispersed themselves among the branches strewing their feathers, which covered the ground as with fine down. Herbert picked up a few of these feathers, and after having examined them—

"These are couroucous," said he.

"I should prefer a moor-cock or guinea-fowl," replied Pencroft, "still, if they are good to eat—"

"They are good to eat, and also their flesh is very delicate," replied Herbert. "Besides, if I don't mistake, it is easy to approach and kill them with a stick."

The sailor and the lad, creeping among the grass, arrived at the foot of a tree, whose lower branches were covered with little birds. The couroucous were waiting the passage of insects which served for their nourishment. Their feathery feet could be seen clasping the slender twigs which supported them.

The hunters then rose, and using their sticks like scythes, they mowed down whole rows of these couroucous, who never thought of flying away, and stupidly allowed themselves to be knocked off. A hundred were already heaped on the ground, before the others made up their minds to fly.

"Well," said Pencroft, "here is game, which is quite within the reach of hunters like us. We have only to put out our hands and take it!"

The sailor having strung the couroucous like larks on flexible twigs, they then continued their exploration. The stream here made a bend towards the south, but this detour was probably not prolonged, for the river must have its source in the mountain, and be supplied by the melting of the snow which covered the sides of the central cone.

The particular object of their expedition was, as has been said, to procure the greatest possible quantity of game for the inhabitants of the Chimneys. It must be acknowledged that as yet this object had not been attained. So the sailor actively pursued his researches, though he exclaimed, when some animal which he had not even time to recognise fled into the long grass, "If only we had had the dog Top!" But Top had disappeared at the same time as his master, and had probably perished with him.

Towards three o'clock new flocks of birds were seen through certain trees, at whose aromatic berries they were pecking, those of the juniper-tree among others. Suddenly a loud trumpet call resounded through the forest. This strange and sonorous cry was produced by the ruffed grouse or the "tétra," of the United States. They soon saw several couples, whose plumage was rich chestnut-brown mottled with dark brown, and tail of the same colour. Herbert recognised the males by the two wing-like appendages raised on the neck. Pencroft determined to get hold of at least one of these gallinaceae, which were as large as a fowl, and whose flesh is better than that of a pullet. But it was difficult, for they would not allow themselves to be approached. After several fruitless attempts, which resulted in nothing but scaring the tétras, the sailor said to the lad—

"Decidedly, since we can't kill them on the wing, we must try to take them with a line."

"Like a fish?" cried Herbert, much surprised at the proposal.

"Like a fish," replied the sailor quite seriously. Pencroft had found among the grass half a dozen tétras' nests, each having three or four eggs. He took great care not to touch these nests, to which their proprietors would not fail to return. It was around these that he meant to stretch his lines, not snares, but real fishing-lines. He took Herbert to some distance from the nests, and there prepared his singular apparatus with all the care which a disciple of Izaak Walton would have used. Herbert watched the work with great interest, though rather doubting its success. The lines were made of fine creepers, fastened one to the other, of the length of fifteen or twenty feet. Thick, strong thorns, the points bent back (which were supplied from a dwarf acacia bush) were fastened to the ends of the creepers, by way of hooks. Large red worms, which were crawling on the ground, furnished bait.

This done, Pencroft, passing among the grass and concealing himself skilfully, placed the end of his lines armed with hooks near the tétras' nests; then he returned, took the other ends and hid with Herbert behind a large tree. There they both waited patiently; though, it must be said, that Herbert did not reckon much on the success of the inventive Pencroft.

A whole half-hour passed, but then, as the sailor had surmised, several couple of tétras returned to their nests. They walked along, pecking the ground, and not suspecting in any way the presence of the hunters, who, besides, had taken care to place themselves to leeward of the gallinaceae.

The lad felt at this moment highly interested. He held his breath, and Pencroft, his eyes staring, his mouth open, his lips advanced, as if about to taste a piece of tétra, scarcely breathed.

Meanwhile, the birds walked about among the hooks, without taking any notice of them. Pencroft then gave little tugs which moved the bait as if the worms had been still alive.

The sailor undoubtedly felt much greater anxiety than does the fisherman, for he does not see his prey coming through the water. The jerks attracted the attention of the gallinaceae, and they attacked the hooks with their beaks. Three voracious tétras swallowed at the same moment bait and hook. Suddenly with a smart jerk, Pencroft "struck" his line, and a flapping of wings showed that the birds were taken.

"Hurrah!" he cried, rushing towards the game, of which he made himself master in an instant.

Herbert clapped his hands. It was the first time that he had ever seen birds taken with a line, but the sailor modestly confessed that it was not his first attempt, and that besides he could not claim the merit of invention.

"And at any rate," added he, "situated as we are, we must hope to hit upon many other contrivances."

The tétras were fastened by their claws, and Pencroft, delighted at not having to appear before their companions with empty hands, and observing that the day had begun to decline, judged it best to return to their dwelling.

The direction was indicated by the river, whose course they had only to follow, and, towards six o'clock, tired enough with their excursion, Herbert and Pencroft arrived at the Chimneys.

Chapter VII

NEB HAS NOT YET RETURNED—THE REPORTER'S REFLECTIONS—
SUPPER—A THREATENING NIGHT—
THE TEMPEST IS FRIGHTFUL—THEY RUSH OUT INTO THE
NIGHT—STRUGGLE AGAINST THE WIND AND RAIN—
EIGHT MILES FROM THE FIRST ENCAMPMENT

GIDEON SPILETT WAS STANDING MOTIONLESS ON THE SHORE, HIS ARMS CROSSED, GAZing over the sea, the horizon of which was lost towards the east in a thick black cloud which was spreading rapidly towards the zenith. The wind was already strong, and increased with the decline of day. The whole sky was of a threatening aspect, and the first symptoms of a violent storm were clearly visible.

Herbert entered the Chimneys, and Pencroft went towards the reporter. The latter, deeply absorbed, did not see him approach.

"We are going to have a dirty night, Mr. Spilett!" said the sailor: "Petrels delight in wind and rain."

The reporter, turning at the moment, saw Pencroft, and his first words were—

"At what distance from the coast would you say the car was, when the waves carried off our companion?"

The sailor had not expected this question. He reflected an instant and replied—

"Two cables' lengths at the most."

"But what is a cable's length?" asked Gideon Spilett.

"About a hundred and twenty fathoms, or six hundred feet."

"Then," said the reporter, "Cyrus Harding must have disappeared twelve hundred feet at the most from the shore?"

"About that," replied Pencroft.

"And his dog also?"

"Also."

"What astonishes me," rejoined the reporter, "while admitting that our companion has perished, is that Top has also met his death, and that neither the body of the dog nor of his master has been cast on the shore!"

"It is not astonishing, with such a heavy sea," replied the sailor. "Besides, it is possible that currents have carried them farther down the coast."

"Then, it is your opinion that our friend has perished in the waves?" again asked the reporter.

"That is my opinion."

"My own opinion," said Gideon Spilett, "with due deference to your experience, Pencroft, is that in the double fact of the absolute disappearance of Cyrus and Top, living or dead, there is something unaccountable and unlikely."

"I wish I could think like you, Mr. Spilett," replied Pencroft; "unhappily, my mind is made upon this point." Having said this, the sailor returned to the Chimneys. A good fire crackled on the hearth. Herbert had just thrown on an armful of dry wood, and the flame cast a bright light into the darkest parts of the passage.

Pencroft immediately began to prepare the dinner. It appeared best to introduce something solid into the bill of fare, for all needed to get up their strength. The strings of couroucous were kept for the next day, but they plucked a couple of tétras, which were soon spitted on a stick, and roasting before a blazing fire.

At seven in the evening Neb had not returned. The prolonged absence of the negro made Pencroft very uneasy. It was to be feared that he had met with an accident on this unknown land, or that the unhappy fellow had been driven to some act of despair. But Herbert drew very different conclusions from this absence. According to him, Neb's delay was caused by some new circumstances which had induced him to prolong his search. Also, everything new must be to the advantage of Cyrus Harding. Why had Neb not returned unless hope still detained him? Perhaps he had found some mark, a footstep, a trace which had put him in the right path. Perhaps he was at this moment on a certain track. Perhaps even he was near his master.

Thus the lad reasoned. Thus he spoke. His companions let him talk. The reporter alone approved with a gesture. But what Pencroft thought most probable was, that Neb had pushed his researches on the shore farther than the day before, and that he had not as yet had time to return.

Herbert, however, agitated by vague presentiments, several times manifested an intention to go to meet Neb. But Pencroft assured him that that would be a useless course, that in the darkness and deplorable weather he could not find any traces of Neb, and that it would be much better to wait. If Neb had not made his appearance by the next day, Pencroft would not hesitate to join him in his search.

Gideon Spilett approved of the sailor's opinion that it was best not to divide, and Herbert was obliged to give up his project; but two large tears fell from his eyes.

The reporter could not refrain from embracing the generous boy.

Bad weather now set in. A furious gale from the south-east passed over the coast. The sea roared as it beat over the reef. Heavy rain was dashed by the storm into particles like dust. Ragged masses of vapour drove along the beach, on which the tormented shingles sounded as if poured out in cart-loads, while the sand raised by the wind added as it were mineral dust to that which was liquid, and rendered the united attack insupportable. Between the river's mouth and the end of the cliff, eddies of wind whirled and gusts from this maëlstrom lashed the water which ran through the narrow valley. The smoke from the fireplace was also driven back through the opening, filling the passages and rendering them uninhabitable.

Therefore, as the tétras were cooked, Pencroft let the fire die away, and only preserved a few embers buried under the ashes.

At eight o'clock Neb had not appeared, but there was no doubt that the frightful weather alone hindered his return, and that he must have taken refuge in some cave, to await the end of the storm or at least the return of day. As to going to meet him, or attempting to find him, it was impossible.

The game constituted the only dish at supper; the meat was excellent, and Pencroft and Herbert, whose long excursion had rendered them very hungry, devoured it with infinite satisfaction.

Their meal concluded, each retired to the corner in which he had rested the preceding night, and Herbert was not long in going to sleep near the sailor, who had stretched himself beside the fireplace.

Outside, as the night advanced, the tempest also increased in strength, until it was equal to that which had carried the prisoners from Richmond to this land in the Pacific. The tempests which are frequent during the seasons of the equinox, and which are so prolific in catastrophes, are above all terrible over this immense ocean, which opposes no obstacle to their fury. No description can give an idea of the terrific violence of the gale as it beat upon the unprotected coast.

Happily the pile of rocks which formed the Chimneys was solid. It was composed of enormous blocks of granite, a few of which, insecurely balanced, seemed to tremble on their foundations, and Pencroft could feel rapid quiverings under his head as it rested on the rock. But he repeated to himself, and rightly, that there was nothing to fear, and that their retreat would not give way. However he heard the noise of stones torn from the summit of the plateau by the wind, falling down on to the beach. A few even rolled on to the upper part of the Chimneys, or flew off in fragments when they were projected perpendicularly. Twice the sailor rose and entrenched himself at the opening of the passage, so as to take a look in safety at the outside. But there was nothing to be feared from these showers, which were not considerable, and he returned to his couch before the fireplace, where the embers glowed beneath the ashes.

Notwithstanding the fury of the hurricane, the uproar of the tempest, the thunder, and the tumult, Herbert slept profoundly. Sleep at last took possession of Pencroft, whom a seafaring life had habituated to anything. Gideon Spilett alone was kept awake by anxiety. He reproached himself with not having accompanied Neb. It was evident that he had not abandoned all hope. The presentiments which had troubled Herbert did not cease to agitate him also. His thoughts were concentrated on Neb. Why had Neb not returned? He tossed about on his sandy couch, scarcely giving a thought to the struggle of the elements. Now and then, his eyes, heavy with fatigue, closed for an instant, but some sudden thought reopened them almost immediately.

Meanwhile the night advanced, and it was perhaps two hours from morning, when Pencroft, then sound asleep, was vigourously shaken.

"What's the matter?" he cried, rousing himself, and collecting his ideas with the promptitude usual to seamen.

The reporter was leaning over him, and saying—

"Listen, Pencroft, listen!"

The sailor strained his ears, but could hear no noise beyond those caused by the storm.

"It is the wind," said he.

"No," replied Gideon Spilett, listening again, "I thought I heard—"

"What?"

"The barking of a dog!"

"A dog!" cried Pencroft, springing up.

"Yes—barking—"

"It's not possible!" replied the sailor. "And besides, how, in the roaring of the storm—"

"Stop—listen—" said the reporter.

Pencroft listened more attentively, and really thought he heard, during a lull, distant barking.

"Well!" said the reporter, pressing the sailor's hand.

"Yes—yes!" replied Pencroft.

"It is Top! It is Top!" cried Herbert, who had just awoke; and all three rushed towards the opening of the Chimneys. They had great difficulty in getting out. The wind drove them back. But at last they succeeded, and could only remain standing by leaning against the rocks. They looked about, but could not speak. The darkness was intense. The sea, the sky, the land were all mingled in one black mass. Not a speck of light was visible.

The reporter and his companions remained thus for a few minutes, overwhelmed by the wind, drenched by the rain, blinded by the sand.

Then, in a pause of the tumult, they again heard the barking, which they found must be at some distance.

It could only be Top! But was he alone or accompanied? He was most probably alone, for, if Neb had been with him, he would have made his way more directly towards the Chimneys. The sailor squeezed the reporter's hand, for he could not make himself heard, in a way which signified "Wait!" then he re-entered the passage.

An instant after he issued with a lighted fagot, which he threw into the darkness, whistling shrilly.

It appeared as if this signal had been waited for; the barking immediately came nearer, and soon a dog bounded into the passage. Pencroft, Herbert, and Spilett entered after him.

An armful of dry wood was thrown on the embers. The passage was lighted up with a bright flame.

"It is Top!" cried Herbert.

It was indeed Top, a magnificent Anglo-Norman, who derived from these two races crossed the swiftness of foot and the acuteness of smell which are the pre-eminent qualities of coursing dogs. It was the dog of the engineer, Cyrus Harding. But he was alone! Neither Neb nor his master accompanied him!

How was it that his instinct had guided him straight to the Chimneys, which he did not know? It appeared inexplicable, above all, in the midst of this black night and in such a tempest! But what was still more inexplicable was, that Top was neither tired, nor exhausted, nor even soiled with mud or sand!—Herbert had drawn him towards him, and was patting his head, the dog rubbing his neck against the lad's hands.

"If the dog is found, the master will be found also!" said the reporter.

"God grant it!" responded Herbert. "Let us set off! Top will guide us!"

Pencroft did not make any objection. He felt that Top's arrival contradicted his conjectures. "Come along then!" said he.

Pencroft carefully covered the embers on the hearth. He placed a few pieces of wood among them, so as to keep in the fire until their return. Then, preceded by the dog, who seemed to invite them by short barks to come with him, and followed by the reporter and the boy, he dashed out, after having put up in his handkerchief the remains of the supper.

The storm was then in all its violence, and perhaps at its height. Not a single ray of light from the moon pierced through the clouds. To follow a straight course was difficult.

It was best to rely on Top's instinct. They did so. The reporter and Herbert walked behind the dog, and the sailor brought up the rear. It was impossible to exchange a word. The rain was not very heavy, but the wind was terrific.

However, one circumstance favoured the seaman and his two companions. The wind being south-east, consequently blew on their backs. The clouds of sand, which otherwise would have been insupportable, from being received behind, did not in consequence impede their progress. In short, they sometimes went faster than they liked, and had some difficulty in keeping their feet; but hope gave them strength, for it was not at random that they made their way along the shore. They had no doubt that Neb had found his master, and that he had sent them the faithful dog. But was the engineer living, or had Neb only sent for his companions that they might render the last duties to the corpse of the unfortunate Harding?

After having passed the precipice, Herbert, the reporter, and Pencroft prudently stepped aside to stop and take breath. The turn of the rocks sheltered them from the wind, and they could breathe after this walk or rather run of a quarter of an hour.

They could now hear and reply to each other, and the lad having pronounced the name of Cyrus Harding, Top gave a few short barks, as much as to say that his master was saved.

"Saved, isn't he?" repeated Herbert; "saved, Top?"

And the dog barked in reply.

They once more set out. The tide began to rise, and urged by the wind it threatened to be unusually high, as it was a spring tide. Great billows thundered against the reef with such violence that they probably passed entirely over the islet, then quite invisible. The mole no longer protected the coast, which was directly exposed to the attacks of the open sea.

As soon as the sailor and his companions left the precipice, the wind struck them again with renewed fury. Though bent under the gale they walked very quickly, following Top, who did not hesitate as to what direction to take.

They ascended towards the north, having on their left an interminable extent of billows, which broke with a deafening noise, and on their right a dark country, the aspect of which it was impossible to guess. But they felt that it was comparatively flat, for the wind passed completely over them, without being driven back as it was when it came in contact with the cliff.

At four o'clock in the morning, they reckoned that they had cleared about five miles. The clouds were slightly raised, and the wind, though less damp, was very sharp and cold. Insufficiently protected by their clothing, Pencroft, Herbert and Spilett suffered cruelly, but not a complaint escaped their lips. They were determined to follow Top, wherever the intelligent animal wished to lead them.

Towards five o'clock day began to break. At the zenith, where the fog was less thick, grey shades bordered the clouds; under an opaque belt, a luminous line clearly traced the horizon. The crests of the billows were tipped with a wild light, and the foam regained its whiteness. At the same time on the left the hilly parts of the coast could be seen, though very indistinctly.

At six o'clock day had broken. The clouds rapidly lifted. The seaman and his companions were then about six miles from the Chimneys. They were following a very flat shore bounded by a reef of rocks, whose heads scarcely emerged from the sea, for they were in deep water. On the left, the country appeared to be one vast extent of sandy downs, bristling with thistles. There was no cliff, and the shore offered no resistance to the ocean but a chain of irregular hillocks. Here and there grew two or three trees, inclined towards the west, their branches projecting in that direction. Quite behind, in the southwest, extended the border of the forest.

At this moment, Top became very excited. He ran forward, then returned, and seemed to entreat them to hasten their steps. The dog then left the beach, and guided by his wonderful instinct, without showing the least hesitation, went straight in among the downs. They followed him. The country appeared an absolute desert. Not a living creature was to be seen.

The downs, the extent of which was large, were composed of hillocks and even of hills, very irregularly distributed. They resembled a Switzerland modelled in sand, and only an amazing instinct could have possibly recognised the way.

Five minutes after having left the beach, the reporter and his two companions arrived at a sort of excavation, hollowed out at the back of a high mound. There Top stopped, and gave a loud, clear bark. Spilett, Herbert, and Pencroft dashed into the cave.

Neb was there, kneeling beside a body extended on a bed of grass—

The body was that of the engineer, Cyrus Harding.

Chapter VIII

IS CYRUS HARDING LIVING?—NEB'S RECITAL—FOOTPRINTS—
AN UNANSWERABLE QUESTION—CYRUS HARDING'S FIRST
WORDS—IDENTIFYING THE FOOTSTEPS—RETURN TO THE
CHIMNEYS—PENCROFT STARTLED!

NEB DID NOT MOVE. PENCROFT ONLY UTTERED ONE WORD.

"Living?" he cried.

Neb did not reply. Spilett and the sailor turned pale. Herbert clasped his hands, and remained motionless. The poor negro, absorbed in his grief, evidently had neither seen his companions nor heard the sailor speak.

The reporter knelt down beside the motionless body, and placed his ear to the engineer's chest, having first torn open his clothes.

A minute—an age!—passed, during which he endeavoured to catch the faintest throb of the heart.

Neb had raised himself a little and gazed without seeing. Despair had completely changed his countenance. He could scarcely be recognised, exhausted with fatigue, broken with grief. He believed his master was dead.

Gideon Spilett at last rose, after a long and attentive examination.

"He lives!" said he.

Pencroft knelt in his turn beside the engineer, he also heard a throbbing, and even felt a slight breath on his cheek.

Herbert at a word from the reporter ran out to look for water. He found, a hundred feet off, a limpid stream, which seemed to have been greatly increased by the rains, and which filtered through the sand; but nothing in which to put the water, not even a shell among the downs. The lad was obliged to content himself with dipping his handkerchief in the stream, and with it hastened back to the grotto.

Happily the wet handkerchief was enough for Gideon Spilett, who only wished to wet the engineer's lips. The cold water produced an almost immediate effect. His chest heaved and he seemed to try to speak.

"We will save him!" exclaimed the reporter.

At these words hope revived in Neb's heart. He undressed his master to see if he was wounded, but not so much as a bruise was to be found, either on the head, body, or limbs, which was surprising, as he must have been dashed against the rocks; even the hands were uninjured, and it was difficult to explain how the engineer showed no traces of the efforts which he must have made to get out of reach of the breakers.

But the explanation would come later. When Cyrus was able to speak he would say what had happened. For the present the question was, how to recall him to life, and it appeared likely that rubbing would bring this about; so they set to work with the sailor's jersey.

The engineer, revived by this rude shampooing, moved his arm slightly, and began to breathe more regularly. He was sinking from exhaustion, and certainly, had not the reporter and his companions arrived, it would have been all over with Cyrus Harding.

"You thought your master was dead, didn't you?" said the seaman to Neb.

"Yes! quite dead!" replied Neb, "and if Top had not found you, and brought you here, I should have buried my master, and then have lain down on his grave to die!"

It had indeed been a narrow escape for Cyrus Harding!

Neb then recounted what had happened. The day before, after having left the Chimneys at daybreak, he had ascended the coast in a northerly direction, and had reached that part of the shore which he had already visited.

There, without any hope he acknowledged, Neb had searched the beach, among the rocks, on the sand, for the smallest trace to guide him. He examined particularly that part of the beach which was not covered by the high tide, for near the sea the water would have obliterated all marks. Neb did not expect to find his master living. It was for a corpse that he searched, a corpse which he wished to bury with his own hands!

He sought long in vain. This desert coast appeared never to have been visited by a human creature. The shells, those which the sea had not reached, and which might be met with by millions above high-water mark, were untouched. Not a shell was broken.

Neb then resolved to walk along the beach for some miles. It was possible that the waves had carried the body to quite a distant point. When a corpse floats a little distance from a low shore, it rarely happens that the tide does not throw it up, sooner or later. This Neb knew, and he wished to see his master again for the last time.

"I went along the coast for another two miles, carefully examining the beach, both at high and low water, and I had despaired of finding anything, when yesterday, above five in the evening, I saw footprints on the sand."

"Footprints?" exclaimed Pencroft.

"Yes!" replied Neb.

"Did these footprints begin at the water's edge?" asked the reporter.

"No," replied Neb, "only above high-water mark, for the others must have been washed out by the tide."

"Go on, Neb," said Spilett.

"I went half crazy when I saw these footprints. They were very clear and went towards the downs. I followed them for a quarter of a mile, running, but taking care not to destroy them. Five minutes after, as it was getting dark, I heard the barking of a dog. It was Top, and Top brought me here, to my master!"

Neb ended his account by saying what had been his grief at finding the inanimate body, in which he vainly sought for the least sign of life. Now that he had found him dead he longed for him to be alive. All his efforts were useless! Nothing remained to be done but to render the last duties to the one whom he had loved so much! Neb then thought of his companions. They, no doubt, would wish to see the unfortunate man again. Top was there. Could he not rely on the sagacity of the faithful animal? Neb several times pronounced the name of the reporter, the one among his companions whom Top knew best. Then he pointed to the south, and the dog bounded off in the direction indicated to him.

We have heard how, guided by an instinct which might be looked upon almost as supernatural, Top had found them.

Neb's companions had listened with great attention to this account.

It was unaccountable to them how Cyrus Harding, after the efforts which he must have made to escape from the waves by crossing the rocks, had not received even a scratch. And what could not be explained either was how the engineer had managed to get to this cave in the downs, more than a mile from the shore.

"So, Neb," said the reporter, "it was not you who brought your master to this place."

"No, it was not I," replied the negro.

"It's very clear that the captain came here by himself," said Pencroft.

"It is clear in reality," observed Spilett, "but it is not credible!"

The explanation of this fact could only be procured from the engineer's own lips, and they must wait for that till speech returned. Rubbing had re-established the circulation of the blood. Cyrus Harding moved his arm again, then his head, and a few incomprehensible words escaped him.

Neb, who was bending over him, spoke, but the engineer did not appear to hear, and his eyes remained closed. Life was only exhibited in him by movement, his senses had not as yet been restored.

Pencroft much regretted not having either fire, or the means of procuring it, for he had, unfortunately, forgotten to bring the burned linen, which would easily have ignited from the sparks produced by striking together two flints. As to the engineer's pockets, they were entirely empty, except that of his waistcoat, which contained his watch. It was necessary to carry Harding to the Chimneys, and that as soon as possible. This was the opinion of all.

Meanwhile, the care which was lavished on the engineer brought him back to consciousness sooner than they could have expected. The water with which they wetted his lips revived him gradually. Pencroft also thought of mixing with the water some moisture from the tétra's flesh which he had brought. Herbert ran to the beach and returned with two large bivalve shells. The sailor concocted something which he introduced between the lips of the engineer, who eagerly drinking it opened his eyes.

Neb and the reporter were leaning over him.

"My master! my master!" cried Neb.

The engineer heard him. He recognised Neb and Spilett, then his other two companions, and his hand slightly pressed theirs.

A few words again escaped him, which showed what thoughts were, even then, troubling his brain. This time he was understood. Undoubtedly they were the same words he had before attempted to utter.

"Island or continent?" he murmured.

"Bother the continent," cried Pencroft hastily; "there is time enough to see about that, captain! we don't care for anything, provided you are living."

The engineer nodded faintly, and then appeared to sleep.

They respected this sleep, and the reporter began immediately to make arrangements for transporting Harding to a more comfortable place. Neb, Herbert, and Pencroft left the cave and directed their steps towards a high mound crowned with a few distorted trees. On the way the sailor could not help repeating—

"Island or continent! To think of that, when at one's last gasp! What a man!"

Arrived at the summit of the mound, Pencroft and his two companions set to work, with no other tools than their hands, to despoil of its principal branches a rather sickly tree, a sort of marine fir; with these branches they made a litter, on which, covered with grass and leaves, they could carry the engineer.

This occupied them nearly forty minutes, and it was ten o'clock when they returned to Cyrus Harding whom Spilett had not left.

The engineer was just awaking from the sleep, or rather from the drowsiness, in which they had found him. The colour was returning to his cheeks, which till now had been as pale as death. He raised himself a little, looked around him, and appeared to ask where he was.

"Can you listen to me without fatigue, Cyrus?" asked the reporter.

"Yes," replied the engineer.

"It's my opinion," said the sailor, "that Captain Harding will be able to listen to you still better, if he will have some more tétra jelly—for we have tétras, captain," added he, presenting him with a little of this jelly, to which he this time added some of the flesh.

Cyrus Harding ate a little of the tétra, and the rest was divided among his companions, who found it but a meager breakfast, for they were suffering extremely from hunger.

"Well!" said the sailor, "there is plenty of food at the Chimneys, for you must know, captain, that down there, in the south, we have a house, with rooms, beds, and fireplace, and in the pantry, several dozen of birds, which our Herbert calls couroucou. Your litter is ready, and as soon as you feel strong enough we will carry you home."

"Thanks, my friend," replied the engineer; "wait another hour or two, and then we will set out. And now speak, Spilett."

The reporter then told him all that had occurred. He recounted all the events with which Cyrus was unacquainted, the last fall of the balloon, the landing on this unknown land, which appeared a desert (whatever it was, whether island or continent), the discovery of the Chimneys, the search for him, not forgetting of course Neb's devotion, the intelligence exhibited by the faithful Top, as well as many other matters.

"But," asked Harding, in a still feeble voice, "you did not, then, pick me upon the beach?"

"No," replied the reporter.

"And did you not bring me to this cave?"

"No."

"At what distance is this cave from the sea?"

"About a mile," replied Pencroft; "and if you are astonished, captain, we are not less surprised ourselves at seeing you in this place!"

"Indeed," said the engineer, who was recovering gradually, and who took great interest in these details, "indeed it is very singular!"

"But," resumed the sailor, "can you tell us what happened after you were carried off by the sea?"

Cyrus Harding considered. He knew very little. The wave had torn him from the balloon net. He sank at first several fathoms. On returning to the surface, in the half light, he felt a living creature struggling near him. It was Top, who had sprung to his help. He saw nothing of the balloon, which, lightened both of his weight and that of the dog, had darted away like an arrow.

There he was, in the midst of the angry sea, at a distance which could not be less than half-a-mile from the shore. He attempted to struggle against the billows by swimming vigourously. Top held him up by his clothes; but a strong current seized him and drove him towards the north, and after half-an-hour of exertion, he sank, dragging Top with him into the depths. From that moment to the moment in which he recovered to find himself in the arms of his friends he remembered nothing.

"However," remarked Pencroft, "you must have been thrown on to the beach, and you must have had strength to walk here, since Neb found your footmarks!"

"Yes . . . of course . . ." replied the engineer, thoughtfully; "and you found no traces of human beings on this coast?"

"Not a trace," replied the reporter; "besides, if by chance you had met with some deliverer there, just in the nick of time, why should he have abandoned you after having saved you from the waves?"

"You are right, my dear Spilett. Tell me, Neb," added the engineer, turning to his servant, "it was not you who . . . you can't have had a moment of unconsciousness . . . during which . . . no, that's absurd. . . . Do any of the footsteps still remain?" asked Harding.

"Yes, master," replied Neb; "here, at the entrance, at the back of the mound, in a place sheltered from the rain and wind. The storm has destroyed the others."

"Pencroft," said Cyrus Harding, "will you take my shoe and see if it fits exactly to the footprints?"

The sailor did as the engineer requested. While he and Herbert, guided by Neb, went to the place where the footprints were to be found, Cyrus remarked to the reporter—

"It is a most extraordinary thing!"

"Perfectly inexplicable!" replied Gideon Spilett.

"But do not dwell upon it just now, my dear Spilett, we will talk about it by and by."

A moment after the others entered.

There was no doubt about it. The engineer's shoe fitted exactly to the footmarks. It was therefore Cyrus Harding who had left them on the sand.

"Come," said he, "I must have experienced this unconsciousness which I attributed to Neb. I must have walked like a somnambulist, without any knowledge of my steps, and Top must have guided me here, after having dragged me from the waves . . . Come, Top! Come, old dog!"

The magnificent animal bounded barking to his master, and caresses were lavished on him. It was agreed that there was no other way of accounting for the rescue of Cyrus Harding, and that Top deserved all the honour of the affair.

Towards twelve o'clock, Pencroft having asked the engineer if they could now remove him, Harding, instead of replying, and by an effort which exhibited the most energetic will, got up. But he was obliged to lean on the sailor, or he would have fallen.

"Well done!" cried Pencroft; "bring the captain's litter."

The litter was brought; the transverse branches had been covered with leaves and long grass. Harding was laid on it, and Pencroft, having taken his place at one end and Neb at the other, they started towards the coast. There was a distance of eight miles to be accomplished; but, as they could not go fast, and it would perhaps be necessary to stop frequently, they reckoned that it would take at least six hours to reach the Chimneys. The wind was still strong, but fortunately it did not rain. Although lying down, the engineer, leaning on his elbow, observed the coast, particularly inland. He did not speak, but he gazed; and, no doubt, the appearance of the country, with its inequalities of ground, its forests, its various productions, were impressed on his mind. However, after travelling for two hours, fatigue overcame him, and he slept.

At half-past five the little band arrived at the precipice, and a short time after at the Chimneys.

They stopped, and the litter was placed on the sand; Cyrus Harding was sleeping profoundly, and did not awake.

Pencroft, to his extreme surprise, found that the terrible storm had quite altered the aspect of the place. Important changes had occurred; great blocks of stone lay on the beach, which was also covered with a thick carpet of sea-weed, algae, and wrack. Evidently the sea, passing over the islet, had been carried right up to the foot of the enormous curtain of granite. The soil in front of the cave had been torn away by the violence of the waves. A horrid presentiment flashed across Pencroft's mind. He rushed into the passage, but returned almost immediately, and stood motionless, staring at his companions. . . . The fire was out; the drowned cinders were nothing but mud; the burned linen, which was to have served as tinder, had disappeared! The sea had penetrated to the end of the passages, and everything was overthrown and destroyed in the interior of the Chimneys!

Chapter IX

CYRUS IS HERE—PENCROFT'S ATTEMPTS—RUBBING WOOD—
ISLAND OR CONTINENT—THE ENGINEER'S PROJECTS—IN WHAT
PART OF THE PACIFIC OCEAN—IN THE MIDST OF THE FORESTS—
THE STONE PINE—CHASING A CAPYBARA—
AN AUSPICIOUS SMOKE

IN A FEW WORDS, GIDEON SPILETT, HERBERT, AND NEB WERE MADE ACQUAINTED WITH what had happened. This accident, which appeared so very serious to Pencroft, produced different effects on the companions of the honest sailor.

Neb, in his delight at having found his master, did not listen, or rather, did not care to trouble himself with what Pencroft was saying.

Herbert shared in some degree the sailor's feelings.

As to the reporter, he simply replied—

"Upon my word, Pencroft, it's perfectly indifferent to me!"

"But, I repeat, that we haven't any fire!"

"Pooh!"

"Nor any means of relighting it!"

"Nonsense!"

"But I say, Mr. Spilett—"

"Isn't Cyrus here?" replied the reporter.

"Is not our engineer alive? He will soon find some way of making fire for us!"

"With what?"

"With nothing."

What had Pencroft to say? He could say nothing, for, in the bottom of his heart he shared the confidence which his companions had in Cyrus Harding. The engineer was to them a microcosm, a compound of every science, a possessor of all human knowledge. It was better to be with Cyrus in a desert island, than without him in the most flourishing town in the United States. With him they could want nothing; with him they would never despair. If these brave men had been told that a volcanic irruption would destroy the land, that this land would be engulfed in the depths of the Pacific, they would have imperturbably replied—

"Cyrus is here!"

While in the palanquin, however, the engineer had again relapsed into unconsciousness, which the jolting to which he had been subjected during his journey had brought on, so that they could not now appeal to his ingenuity. The supper must necessarily be very meager. In fact, all the tétras' flesh had been consumed, and there no longer existed any means of cooking more game. Besides, the couroucou which had been reserved had disappeared. They must consider what was to be done.

First of all, Cyrus Harding was carried into the central passage. There they managed to arrange for him a couch of sea-weed which still remained almost dry. The deep sleep which had overpowered him would no doubt be more beneficial to him than any nourishment.

Night had closed in, and the temperature, which had modified when the wind shifted to the north-west, again became extremely cold. Also, the sea having destroyed the partitions which Pencroft had put up in certain places in the passages, the Chimneys, on account of the draughts, had become scarcely habitable. The engineer's condition would, therefore, have been bad enough, if his companions had not carefully covered him with their coats and waistcoats.

Supper, this evening, was of course composed of the inevitable lithodomes, of which Herbert and Neb picked up a plentiful supply on the beach. However, to these molluscs, the lad added some edible sea-weed, which he gathered on high rocks, whose sides were only washed by the sea at the time of high tides. This sea-weed, which belongs to the order of Sucacae, of the genus Sargussum, produces, when dry, a gelatinous matter, rich and nutritious. The reporter and his companions, after having eaten a quantity of lithodomes, sucked the sargussum, of which the taste was very tolerable. It is used in parts of the East very considerably by the natives. "Never mind!" said the sailor, "the captain will help us soon." Meanwhile the cold became very severe, and unhappily they had no means of defending themselves from it.

The sailor, extremely vexed, tried in all sorts of ways to procure fire. Neb helped him in this work. He found some dry moss, and by striking together two pebbles he obtained some sparks, but the moss, not being inflammable enough, did not take fire, for the sparks were really only incandescent, and not at all of the same consistency as those which are emitted from flint when struck in the same manner. The experiment, therefore, did not succeed.

Pencroft, although he had no confidence in the proceeding, then tried rubbing two pieces of dry wood together, as savages do. Certainly, the movement which he and Neb gave themselves, if they had been transformed into heat, according to the new theory, would have been enough to heat the boiler of a steamer! It came to nothing. The bits of wood became hot, to be sure, but much less so than the operators themselves.

After working an hour, Pencroft, who was in a complete state of perspiration, threw down the pieces of wood in disgust.

"I can never be made to believe that savages light their fires in this way, let them say what they will," he exclaimed. "I could sooner light my arms by rubbing them against each other!"

The sailor was wrong to despise the proceeding. Savages often kindle wood by means of rapid rubbing. But every sort of wood does not answer for the purpose, and besides, there is "the knack," following the usual expression, and it is probable that Pencroft had not "the knack."

Pencroft's ill humour did not last long. Herbert had taken the bits of wood which he had turned down, and was exerting himself to rub them. The hardy sailor could not restrain a burst of laughter on seeing the efforts of the lad to succeed where he had failed.

"Rub, my boy, rub!" said he.

"I am rubbing," replied Herbert, laughing, "but I don't pretend to do anything else but warm myself instead of shivering, and soon I shall be as hot as you are, my good Pencroft!"

This soon happened. However, they were obliged to give up, for this night at least, the attempt to procure fire. Gideon Spilett repeated, for the twentieth time, that Cyrus Harding would not have been troubled for so small a difficulty. And, in the meantime, he stretched himself in one of the passages on his bed of sand. Herbert, Neb, and Pencroft did the same, while Top slept at his master's feet.

Next day, the 28th of March, when the engineer awoke, about eight in the morning, he saw his companions around him watching his sleep, and, as on the day before, his first words were:—

"Island or continent?"

This was his uppermost thought.

"Well!" replied Pencroft, "we don't know anything about it, captain!"

"You don't know yet?"

"But we shall know," rejoined Pencroft, "when you have guided us into the country."

"I think I am able to try it," replied the engineer, who, without much effort, rose and stood upright.

"That's capital!" cried the sailor.

"I feel dreadfully weak," replied Harding. "Give me something to eat, my friends, and it will soon go off. You have fire, haven't you?"

This question was not immediately replied to. But, in a few seconds—

"Alas! we have no fire," said Pencroft, "or rather, captain, we have it no longer!"

And the sailor recounted all that had passed the day before. He amused the engineer by the history of the single match, then his abortive attempt to procure fire in the savages' way.

"We shall consider," replied the engineer, "and if we do not find some substance similar to tinder—"

"Well?" asked the sailor.

"Well, we will make matches."

"Chemicals?"

"Chemicals!"

"It is not more difficult than that," cried the reporter, striking the sailor on the shoulder.

The latter did not think it so simple, but he did not protest. All went out. The weather had become very fine. The sun was rising from the sea's horizon, and touched with golden spangles the prismatic rugosities of the huge precipice.

Having thrown a rapid glance around him, the engineer seated himself on a block of stone. Herbert offered him a few handfuls of shell-fish and sargussum, saying—

"It is all that we have, Captain Harding."

"Thanks, my boy," replied Harding; "it will do—for this morning at least."

He ate the wretched food with appetite, and washed it down with a little fresh water, drawn from the river in an immense shell.

His companions looked at him without speaking. Then, feeling somewhat refreshed, Cyrus Harding crossed his arms, and said—

"So, my friends, you do not know yet whether fate has thrown us on an island, or on a continent?"

"No, captain," replied the boy.

"We shall know to-morrow," said the engineer; "till then, there is nothing to be done."

"Yes," replied Pencroft.

"What?"

"Fire," said the sailor, who, also, had a fixed idea.

"We will make it, Pencroft," replied Harding.

"While you were carrying me yesterday, did I not see in the west a mountain which commands the country?"

"Yes," replied Spilett, "a mountain which must be rather high—"

"Well," replied the engineer, "we will climb to the summit to-morrow, and then we shall see if this land is an island or a continent. Till then, I repeat, there is nothing to be done."

"Yes, fire!" said the obstinate sailor again.

"But he will make us a fire!" replied Gideon Spilett, "only have a little patience, Pencroft!"

The seaman looked at Spilett in a way which seemed to say, "If it depended upon you to do it, we wouldn't taste roast meat very soon"; but he was silent.

Meanwhile Captain Harding had made no reply. He appeared to be very little troubled by the question of fire. For a few minutes he remained absorbed in thought; then again speaking—

"My friends," said he, "our situation is, perhaps, deplorable; but, at any rate, it is very plain. Either we are on a continent, and then, at the expense of greater or less fatigue, we shall reach some inhabited place, or we are on an island. In the latter case, if the island is inhabited, we will try to get out of the scrape with the help of its inhabitants; if it is desert, we will try to get out of the scrape by ourselves."

"Certainly, nothing could be plainer," replied Pencroft.

"But, whether it is an island or a continent," asked Gideon Spilett, "whereabouts do you think, Cyrus, this storm has thrown us?"

"I cannot say exactly," replied the engineer, "but I presume it is some land in the Pacific. In fact, when we left Richmond, the wind was blowing from the north-east, and its very violence greatly proves that it could not have varied. If the direction has been maintained from the north-east to the south-west, we have traversed the States of North Carolina, of South Carolina, of Georgia, the Gulf of Mexico, Mexico, itself, in its narrow part, then a part of the Pacific Ocean. I cannot estimate the distance traversed by the balloon at less than six to seven thousand miles, and, even supposing that the wind had varied half a quarter, it must have brought us either to the archipelago of Mendava, either on the Pomotous, or even, if it had a greater strength than I suppose, to the land of New Zealand. If the last hypothesis is correct, it will be easy enough to get home again. English or Maoris, we shall always find someone to whom we can speak. If, on the contrary, this is the coast of a desert island in some tiny archipelago, perhaps we shall be able to reconnoitre it from the summit of that peak which overlooks the country, and then we shall see how best to establish ourselves here as if we are never to go away."

"Never?" cried the reporter. "You say 'Never,' my dear Cyrus?"

"Better to put things at the worst at first," replied the engineer, "and reserve the best for a surprise."

"Well said," remarked Pencroft. "It is to be hoped, too, that this island, if it be one, is not situated just out of the course of ships; that would be really unlucky!"

"We shall not know what we have to rely on until we have first made the ascent of the mountain," replied the engineer.

"But to-morrow, captain," asked Herbert, "shall you be in a state to bear the fatigue of the ascent?"

"I hope so," replied the engineer, "provided you and Pencroft, my boy, show yourselves quick and clever hunters."

"Captain," said the sailor, "since you are speaking of game, if, on my return, I was as certain of being able to roast it as I am of bringing it back—"

"Bring it back all the same, Pencroft," replied Harding.

It was then agreed that the engineer and the reporter were to pass the day at the Chimneys, so as to examine the shore and the upper plateau. Neb, Herbert, and the sailor were to return to the forest, renew their store of wood, and lay violent hands on every creature, feathered or hairy, which might come within their reach.

They set out accordingly about ten o'clock in the morning, Herbert confident, Neb joyous, Pencroft murmuring aside—

"If, on my return, I find a fire at the house, I shall believe that the thunder itself came to light it." All three climbed the bank; and arrived at the angle made by the river, the sailor, stopping, said to his two companions—

"Shall we begin by being hunters or wood-men?"

"Hunters," replied Herbert. "There is Top already in quest."

"We will hunt, then," said the sailor, "and afterwards we can come back and collect our wood."

This agreed to, Herbert, Neb, and Pencroft, after having torn three sticks from the trunk of a young fir, followed Top, who was bounding about among the long grass.

This time, the hunters, instead of following the course of the river, plunged straight into the heart of the forest. There were still the same trees, belonging, for the most part, to the pine family. In certain places, less crowded, growing in clumps, these pines exhibited considerable dimensions, and appeared to indicate, by their development, that the country was situated in a higher latitude than the engineer had supposed. Glades, bristling with stumps worn away by time, were covered with dry wood, which formed an inexhaustible store of fuel. Then, the glade passed, the underwood thickened again, and became almost impenetrable.

It was difficult enough to find the way among the groups of trees, without any beaten track. So the sailor from time to time broke off branches which might be easily recognised. But, perhaps, he was wrong not to follow the water-course, as he and Herbert had done on their first excursion, for after walking an hour not a creature had shown itself. Top, running under the branches, only roused birds which could not be approached. Even the couroucous were invisible, and it was probable that the sailor would be obliged to return to the marshy part of the forest, in which he had so happily performed his tétra fishing.

"Well, Pencroft," said Neb, in a slightly sarcastic tone, "if this is all the game which you promised to bring back to my master, it won't need a large fire to roast it!"

"Have patience," replied the sailor, "it isn't the game which will be wanting on our return."

"Have you not confidence in Captain Harding?"

"Yes."

"But you don't believe that he will make fire?"

"I shall believe it when the wood is blazing in the fireplace."

"It will blaze, since my master has said so."

"We shall see!"

Meanwhile, the sun had not reached the highest point in its course above the horizon. The exploration, therefore, continued, and was usefully marked by a discovery which Herbert made of a tree whose fruit was edible. This was the stone-pine, which produces an excellent almond, very much esteemed in the temperate regions of America and Europe. These almonds were in a perfect state of maturity, and Herbert described them to his companions, who feasted on them.

"Come," said Pencroft, "sea-weed by way of bread, raw mussels for meat, and almonds for dessert, that's certainly a good dinner for those who have not a single match in their pocket!"

"We mustn't complain," said Herbert.

"I am not complaining, my boy," replied Pencroft, "only I repeat, that meat is a little too much economised in this sort of meal."

"Top has found something!" cried Neb, who ran towards a thicket, in the midst of which the dog had disappeared, barking. With Top's barking were mingled curious gruntings.

The sailor and Herbert had followed Neb. If there was game there this was not the time to discuss how it was to be cooked, but rather, how they were to get hold of it.

The hunters had scarcely entered the bushes when they saw Top engaged in a struggle with an animal which he was holding by the ear. This quadruped was a sort of pig nearly two feet and a half long, of a blackish brown colour, lighter below, having hard scanty hair; its toes, then strongly fixed in the ground, seemed to be united by a membrane. Herbert recognised in this animal the capybara, that is to say, one of the largest members of the rodent order.

Meanwhile, the capybara did not struggle against the dog. It stupidly rolled its eyes, deeply buried in a thick bed of fat. Perhaps it saw men for the first time.

However, Neb having tightened his grasp on his stick, was just going to fell the pig, when the latter, tearing itself from Top's teeth, by which it was only held by the tip of its ear, uttered a vigourous grunt, rushed upon Herbert, almost overthrew him, and disappeared in the wood.

"The rascal!" cried Pencroft.

All three directly darted after Top, but at the moment when they joined him the animal had disappeared under the waters of a large pond shaded by venerable pines.

Neb, Herbert, and Pencroft stopped, motionless. Top plunged into the water, but the capybara, hidden at the bottom of the pond, did not appear.

"Let us wait," said the boy, "for he will soon come to the surface to breathe."

"Won't he drown?" asked Neb.

"No," replied Herbert, "since he has webbed feet, and is almost an amphibious animal. But watch him."

Top remained in the water. Pencroft and his two companions went to different parts of the bank, so as to cut off the retreat of the capybara, which the dog was looking for beneath the water.

Herbert was not mistaken. In a few minutes the animal appeared on the surface of the water. Top was upon it in a bound, and kept it from plunging again. An instant later the capybara, dragged to the bank, was killed by a blow from Neb's stick.

"Hurrah!" cried Pencroft, who was always ready with this cry of triumph.

"Give me but a good fire, and this pig shall be gnawed to the bones!"

Pencroft hoisted the capybara on his shoulders, and judging by the height of the sun that it was about two o'clock, he gave the signal to return.

Top's instinct was useful to the hunters, who, thanks to the intelligent animal, were enabled to discover the road by which they had come. Half-an-hour later they arrived at the river.

Pencroft soon made a raft of wood, as he had done before, though if there was no fire it would be a useless task, and the raft following the current, they returned towards the Chimneys.

But the sailor had not gone fifty paces when he stopped, and again uttering a tremendous hurrah, pointed towards the angle of the cliff—

"Herbert! Neb! Look!" he shouted.

Smoke was escaping and curling up among the rocks.

Chapter X

The Engineer's Invention—The Question Which Engrosses the Thoughts of Cyrus Harding—Departure for the Mountain—Volcanic Soil—Tragopans—Sheep— The First Plateau—Encampment for the Night— The Summit of the Cone

I N A FEW MINUTES THE THREE HUNTERS WERE BEFORE A CRACKLING FIRE. THE CAPTAIN and the reporter were there. Pencroft looked from one to the other, his capybara in his hand, without saying a word.

"Well, yes, my brave fellow," cried the reporter.

"Fire, real fire, which will roast this splendid pig perfectly, and we will have a feast presently!"

"But who lighted it?" asked Pencroft.

"The sun!"

Gideon Spilett was quite right in his reply. It was the sun which had furnished the heat which so astonished Pencroft. The sailor could scarcely believe his eyes, and he was so amazed that he did not think of questioning the engineer.

"Had you a burning-glass, sir?" asked Herbert of Harding.

"No, my boy," replied he, "but I made one."

And he showed the apparatus which served for a burning-glass. It was simply two glasses which he had taken from his own and the reporter's watches. Having filled them with water and rendered their edges adhesive by means of a little clay, he thus fabricated a regular burning-glass, which, concentrating the solar rays on some very dry moss, soon caused it to blaze.

The sailor considered the apparatus; then he gazed at the engineer without saying a word, only a look plainly expressed his opinion that if Cyrus Harding was not a magician, he was certainly no ordinary man. At last speech returned to him, and he cried—

"Note that, Mr. Spilett, note that down on your paper!"

"It is noted," replied the reporter.

Then, Neb helping him, the seaman arranged the spit, and the capybara, properly cleaned, was soon roasting like a suckling-pig before a clear, crackling fire.

The Chimneys had again become more habitable, not only because the passages were warmed by the fire, but because the partitions of wood and mud had been re-established.

It was evident that the engineer and his companions had employed their day well. Cyrus Harding had almost entirely recovered his strength, and had proved it by climbing to the upper plateau. From this point his eye, accustomed to estimate heights and distances, was fixed for a long time on the cone, the summit of which he wished to reach the next day. The mountain, situated about six miles to the north-west, appeared to him to measure 3,500 feet above the level of the sea. Consequently the gaze of an observer posted on its summit would extend over a radius of at least fifty miles. Therefore it was probable that Harding could easily solve the question of "island or continent," to which he attached so much importance.

They supped capitally. The flesh of the capybara was declared excellent. The sargussum and the almonds of the stone-pine completed the repast, during which the engineer spoke little. He was preoccupied with projects for the next day.

Once or twice Pencroft gave forth some ideas upon what it would be best to do; but Cyrus Harding, who was evidently of a methodical mind, only shook his head without uttering a word.

"To-morrow," he repeated, "we shall know what we have to depend upon, and we will act accordingly."

The meal ended, fresh armfuls of wood were thrown on the fire, and the inhabitants of the Chimneys, including the faithful Top, were soon buried in a deep sleep. No incident disturbed this peaceful night, and the next day, the 29th of March, fresh and active they awoke, ready to undertake the excursion which must determine their fate.

All was ready for the start. The remains of the capybara would be enough to sustain Harding and his companions for at least twenty-four hours. Besides, they hoped to find more food on the way. As the glasses had been returned to the watches of the engineer and reporter, Pencroft burned a little linen to serve as tinder. As to flint, that would not be wanting in these regions of Plutonic origin. It was half-past seven in the morning when the explorers, armed with sticks, left the Chimneys. Following Pencroft's advice, it appeared best to take the road already traversed through the forest, and to return by another route. It was also the most direct way to reach the mountain. They turned the south angle and followed the left bank of the river, which was abandoned at the point where it formed an elbow towards the south-west. The path, already trodden under the evergreen trees, was found, and at nine o'clock Cyrus Harding and his companions had reached the western border of the forest. The ground, till then, very little undulated, boggy at first, dry and sandy afterwards, had a gentle slope, which ascended from the shore towards the interior of the country. A few very timid animals were seen under the forest trees. Top quickly started them, but his master soon called him back, for the time had not come to commence hunting, that would be attended to later. The engineer was not a man who would allow himself to be diverted from his fixed idea. It might even have been said that he did not observe the country at all, either in its configuration or in its natural productions, his great aim being to climb the mountain before him, and therefore straight towards it he went. At ten o'clock a halt of a few minutes was made. On leaving the forest, the mountain system of the country appeared before the explorers. The mountain was composed of two cones; the first, truncated at a height of about two thousand five hundred feet, was sustained by buttresses, which appeared to branch out like the talons of an immense claw set on the ground. Between these were narrow valleys, bristling with trees, the last clumps of which rose to the top of the lowest cone. There appeared to be less vegetation on that side of the mountain which was exposed to the north-east, and deep fissures could be seen which, no doubt, were water-courses.

On the first cone rested a second, slightly rounded, and placed a little on one side, like a great round hat cocked over the ear. A Scotchman would have said, "His bonnet was a thocht ajee." It appeared formed of bare earth, here and there pierced by reddish rocks.

They wished to reach the second cone, and proceeding along the ridge of the spurs seemed to be the best way by which to gain it.

"We are on volcanic ground," Cyrus Harding had said, and his companions following him began to ascend by degrees on the back of a spur, which, by a winding and consequently more accessible path, joined the first plateau.

The ground had evidently been convulsed by subterranean force. Here and there stray blocks, numerous debris of basalt and pumice-stone, were met with. In isolated groups rose fir-trees, which, some hundred feet lower, at the bottom of the narrow gorges, formed massive shades almost impenetrable to the sun's rays.

During this first part of the ascent, Herbert remarked on the footprints which indicated the recent passage of large animals.

"Perhaps these beasts will not let us pass by willingly," said Pencroft.

"Well," replied the reporter, who had already hunted the tiger in India, and the lion in Africa, "we shall soon learn how successfully to encounter them. But in the meantime we must be upon our guard!"

They ascended but slowly.

The distance, increased by detours and obstacles which could not be surmounted directly, was long. Sometimes, too, the ground suddenly fell, and they found themselves on the edge of a deep chasm which they had to go round. Thus, in retracing their steps so as to find some practicable path, much time was employed and fatigue undergone for nothing. At twelve o'clock, when the small band of adventurers halted for breakfast at the foot of a large group of firs, near a little stream which fell in cascades, they found themselves still half-way from the first plateau, which most probably they would not reach till nightfall. From this point the view of the sea was much extended, but on the right the high promontory prevented their seeing whether there was land beyond it. On the left, the sight extended several miles to the north; but, on the north-west, at the point occupied by the explorers, it was cut short by the ridge of a fantastically-shaped spur, which formed a powerful support of the central cone.

At one o'clock the ascent was continued. They slanted more towards the south-west and again entered among thick bushes. There under the shade of the trees fluttered several couples of gallinaceae belonging to the pheasant species. They were tragopans, ornamented by a pendant skin which hangs over their throats, and by two small, round horns planted behind the eyes. Among these birds, which were about the size of a fowl, the female was uniformly brown, while the male was gorgeous in his red plumage, decorated with white spots. Gideon Spilett, with a stone cleverly and vigourously thrown, killed one of these tragopans, on which Pencroft, made hungry by the fresh air, had cast greedy eyes.

After leaving the region of bushes, the party, assisted by resting on each other's shoulders, climbed for about a hundred feet up a steep acclivity and reached a level place, with very few trees, where the soil appeared volcanic. It was necessary to ascend by zigzags to make the slope more easy, for it was very steep, and the footing being exceedingly precarious required the greatest caution. Neb and Herbert took the lead, Pencroft the rear, the captain and the reporter between them. The animals which frequented these heights—and there were numerous traces of them—must necessarily belong to those races of sure foot and supple spine, chamois or goat. Several were seen, but this was not the name Pencroft gave them, for all of a sudden—"Sheep!" he shouted.

All stopped about fifty feet from half-a-dozen animals of a large size, with strong horns bent back and flattened towards the point, with a woolly fleece, hidden under long silky hair of a tawny colour.

They were not ordinary sheep, but a species usually found in the mountainous regions of the temperate zone, to which Herbert gave the name of the musmon.

"Have they legs and chops?" asked the sailor.

"Yes," replied Herbert.

"Well, then, they are sheep!" said Pencroft.

The animals, motionless among the blocks of basalt, gazed with an astonished eye, as if they saw human bipeds for the first time. Then their fears suddenly aroused, they disappeared, bounding over the rocks.

"Good-by, till we meet again!" cried Pencroft, as he watched them, in such a comical tone that Cyrus Harding, Gideon Spilett, Herbert, and Neb could not help laughing.

The ascent was continued. Here and there were traces of lava. Sulphur springs sometimes stopped their way, and they had to go round them. In some places the sulphur had formed crystals among other substances, such as whitish cinders made of an infinity of little feldspar crystals.

In approaching the first plateau formed by the truncating of the lower cone, the difficulties of the ascent were very great. Towards four o'clock the extreme zone of the trees had been passed. There only remained here and there a few twisted, stunted pines, which must have had a hard life in resisting at this altitude the high winds from the open sea. Happily for the engineer and his companions the weather was beautiful, the atmosphere tranquil; for a high breeze at an elevation of three thousand feet would have hindered their proceedings. The purity of the sky at the zenith was felt through the transparent air. A perfect calm reigned around them. They could not see the sun, then hid by the vast screen of the upper cone, which masked the half-horizon of the west, and whose enormous shadow stretching to the shore increased as the radiant luminary sank in its diurnal course. Vapours—mist rather than clouds—began to appear in the east, and assume all the prismatic colours under the influence of the solar rays.

Five hundred feet only separated the explorers from the plateau, which they wished to reach so as to establish there an encampment for the night, but these five hundred feet were increased to more than two miles by the zigzags which they had to describe. The soil, as it were, slid under their feet. The slope often presented such an angle that they slipped when the stones worn by the air did not give a sufficient support. Evening came on by degrees, and it was almost night when Cyrus Harding and his companions, much fatigued by an ascent of seven hours, arrived at the plateau of the first cone. It was then necessary to prepare an encampment, and to restore their strength by eating first and sleeping afterwards. This second stage of the mountain rose on a base of rocks, among which it would be easy to find a retreat. Fuel was not abundant. However, a fire could be made by means of the moss and dry brushwood, which covered certain parts of the plateau. While the sailor was preparing his hearth with stones which he put to this use, Neb and Herbert occupied themselves with getting a supply of fuel. They soon returned with a load of brushwood. The steel was struck, the burned linen caught the sparks of flint, and, under Neb's breath, a crackling fire showed itself in a few minutes under the shelter of the rocks. Their object in lighting a fire was only to enable them to withstand the cold temperature of the night, as it was not employed in cooking the bird, which Neb kept for the next day. The remains of the capybara and some dozens of the stone-pine almonds formed their supper. It was not half-past six when all was finished.

Cyrus Harding then thought of exploring in the half-light the large circular layer which supported the upper cone of the mountain. Before taking any rest, he wished to know if it was possible to get round the base of the cone in the case of its sides being too steep and its summit being inaccessible. This question preoccupied him, for it was possible that from the way the hat inclined, that is to say, towards the north, the plateau was not practicable. Also, if the summit of the mountain could not be reached on one side, and if, on the other, they could not get round the base of the cone, it would be impossible to survey the western part of the country, and their object in making the ascent would in part be altogether unattained.

The engineer, accordingly, regardless of fatigue, leaving Pencroft and Neb to arrange the beds, and Gideon Spilett to note the incidents of the day, began to follow the edge of the plateau, going towards the north. Herbert accompanied him.

The night was beautiful and still, the darkness was not yet deep. Cyrus Harding and the boy walked near each other, without speaking. In some places the plateau opened before them, and they passed without hindrance. In others, obstructed by rocks, there was only a narrow path, in which two persons could not walk abreast. After a walk of twenty minutes, Cyrus Harding and Herbert were obliged to stop. From this point the slope of the two cones became one. No shoulder here separated the two parts of the mountain. The slope, being inclined almost seventy degrees, the path became impracticable.

But if the engineer and the boy were obliged to give up thoughts of following a circular direction, in return an opportunity was given for ascending the cone.

In fact, before them opened a deep hollow. It was the rugged mouth of the crater, by which the irruptive liquid matter had escaped at the periods when the volcano was still in activity. Hardened lava and crusted scoria formed a sort of natural staircase of large steps, which would greatly facilitate the ascent to the summit of the mountain.

Harding took all this in at a glance, and without hesitating, followed by the lad, he entered the enormous chasm in the midst of an increasing obscurity.

There was still a height of a thousand feet to overcome. Would the interior acclivities of the crater be practicable? It would soon be seen. The persevering engineer resolved to continue his ascent until he was stopped. Happily these acclivities wound up the interior of the volcano and favoured their ascent.

As to the volcano itself, it could not be doubted that it was completely extinct. No smoke escaped from its sides; not a flame could be seen in the dark hollows; not a roar, not a mutter, no trembling even issued from this black well, which perhaps reached far into the bowels of the earth. The atmosphere inside the crater was filled with no sulphurous vapour. It was more than the sleep of a volcano; it was its complete extinction. Cyrus Harding's attempt would succeed.

Little by little, Herbert and he climbing up the sides of the interior, saw the crater widen above their heads. The radius of this circular portion of the sky, framed by the edge of the cone, increased obviously. At each step, as it were, that the explorers made, fresh stars entered the field of their vision. The magnificent constellations of the southern sky shone resplendently. At the zenith glittered the splendid Antares in the Scorpion, and not far the β in the Centaur, which is believed to be the nearest star to the terrestrial globe. Then, as the crater widened, appeared Fomalhaut of the Fish, the Southern Triangle, and lastly, nearly at the Antarctic Pole, the glittering Southern Cross, which replaces the Polar Star of the Northern Hemisphere.

It was nearly eight o'clock when Cyrus Harding and Herbert set foot on the highest ridge of the mountain at the summit of the cone.

It was then perfectly dark, and their gaze could not extend over a radius of two miles. Did the sea surround this unknown land, or was it connected in the west with some continent of the Pacific? It could not yet be made out. Towards the west, a cloudy belt, clearly visible at the horizon, increased the gloom, and the eye could not discover if the sky and water were blended together in the same circular line.

But at one point of the horizon a vague light suddenly appeared, which descended slowly in proportion as the cloud mounted to the zenith.

It was the slender crescent moon, already almost disappearing; but its light was sufficient to show clearly the horizontal line, then detached from the cloud, and the engineer could see its reflection trembling for an instant on a liquid surface. Cyrus Harding seized the lad's hand, and in a grave voice—

"An island!" said he, at the moment when the lunar crescent disappeared beneath the waves.

Chapter XI

AT THE SUMMIT OF THE CONE—THE INTERIOR OF THE CRATER—SEA ALL ROUND—NO LAND IN SIGHT—A BIRD'S-EYE VIEW OF THE COAST—HYDROGRAPHY AND OROLOGY—IS THE ISLAND INHABITED—CHRISTENING THE BAYS, GULFS, CAPES, RIVERS, ETC.—LINCOLN ISLAND

HALF-AN-HOUR LATER CYRUS HARDING AND HERBERT HAD RETURNED TO THE EN-campment. The engineer merely told his companions that the land upon which fate had thrown them was an island, and that the next day they would consult. Then each set-tled himself as well as he could to sleep, and in that rocky hole, at a height of two thou-sand five hundred feet above the level of the sea, through a peaceful night, the islanders enjoyed profound repose.

The next day, the 30th of March, after a hasty breakfast, which consisted solely of the roasted tragopan, the engineer wished to climb again to the summit of the volcano, so as more attentively to survey the island upon which he and his companions were imprisoned for life perhaps, should the island be situated at a great distance from any land, or if it was out of the course of vessels which visited the archipelagoes of the Pacific Ocean. This time his companions followed him in the new exploration. They also wished to see the is-land, on the productions of which they must depend for the supply of all their wants.

It was about seven o'clock in the morning when Cyrus Harding, Herbert, Pencroft, Gideon Spilett, and Neb quitted the encampment. No one appeared to be anxious about their situation. They had faith in themselves, doubtless, but it must be observed that the basis of this faith was not the same with Harding as with his companions. The engineer had confidence, because he felt capable of extorting from this wild country everything necessary for the life of himself and his companions; the latter feared nothing, just because Cyrus Harding was with them. Pencroft especially, since the incident of the relighted fire, would not have despaired for an instant, even if he was on a bare rock, if the engineer was with him on the rock.

"Pshaw!" said he, "we left Richmond without permission from the authorities! It will be hard if we don't manage to get away some day or other from a place where certainly no one will detain us!"

Cyrus Harding followed the same road as the evening before. They went round the cone by the plateau which formed the shoulder, to the mouth of the enormous chasm. The weather was magnificent. The sun rose in a pure sky and flooded with his rays all the east-ern side of the mountain.

The crater was reached. It was just what the engineer had made it out to be in the dark; that is to say, a vast funnel which extended, widening, to a height of a thousand feet above the plateau. Below the chasm, large thick streaks of lava wound over the sides of the mountain, and thus marked the course of the irruptive matter to the lower valleys which furrowed the northern part of the island.

The interior of the crater, whose inclination did not exceed thirty-five to forty degrees, presented no difficulties nor obstacles to the ascent. Traces of very ancient lava were noticed, which probably had overflowed the summit of the cone, before this lateral chasm had opened a new way to it.

As to the volcanic chimney which established a communication between the subterranean layers and the crater, its depth could not be calculated with the eye, for it was lost in obscurity. But there was no doubt as to the complete extinction of the volcano.

Before eight o'clock Harding and his companions were assembled at the summit of the crater, on a conical mound which swelled the northern edge.

"The sea, the sea everywhere!" they cried, as if their lips could not restrain the words which made islanders of them.

The sea, indeed, formed an immense circular sheet of water all around them! Perhaps, on climbing again to the summit of the cone, Cyrus Harding had had a hope of discovering some coast, some island shore, which he had not been able to perceive in the dark the evening before. But nothing appeared on the farthest verge of the horizon, that is to say over a radius of more than fifty miles. No land in sight. Not a sail. Over all this immense space the ocean alone was visible—the island occupied the centre of a circumference which appeared to be infinite.

The engineer and his companions, mute and motionless, surveyed for some minutes every point of the ocean, examining it to its most extreme limits. Even Pencroft, who possessed a marvelous power of sight, saw nothing; and certainly if there had been land at the horizon, if it appeared only as an indistinct vapour, the sailor would undoubtedly have found it out, for nature had placed regular telescopes under his eyebrows.

From the ocean their gaze returned to the island which they commanded entirely, and the first question was put by Gideon Spilett in these terms:—

"About what size is this island?"

Truly, it did not appear large in the midst of the immense ocean.

Cyrus Harding reflected a few minutes; he attentively observed the perimeter of the island, taking into consideration the height at which he was placed; then—

"My friends," said he, "I do not think I am mistaken in giving to the shore of the island a circumference of more than a hundred miles."

"And consequently an area?"

"That is difficult to estimate," replied the engineer, "for it is so uneven."

If Cyrus Harding was not mistaken in his calculation, the island had almost the extent of Malta or Zante, in the Mediterranean, but it was at the same time much more irregular and less rich in capes, promontories, point, bays, or creeks. Its strange form caught the eye, and when Gideon Spilett, on the engineer's advice, had drawn the outline, they found that it resembled some fantastic animal, a monstrous leviathan, which lay sleeping on the surface of the Pacific.

This was in fact the exact shape of the island, which it is of consequence to know, and a tolerably correct map of it was immediately drawn by the reporter.

The east part of the shore, where the castaways had landed, formed a wide bay, terminated by a sharp cape, which had been concealed by a high point from Pencroft on his first exploration. At the north-east two other capes closed the bay, and between them ran a narrow gulf, which looked like the half-open jaws of a formidable dog-fish.

From the north-east to the south-west the coast was rounded, like the flattened cranium of an animal, rising again, forming a sort of protuberance which did not give any particular shape to this part of the island, of which the centre was occupied by the volcano.

From this point the shore ran pretty regularly north and south, broken at two-thirds of its perimeter by a narrow creek, from which it ended in a long tail, similar to the caudal appendage of a gigantic alligator.

This tail formed a regular peninsula, which stretched more than thirty miles into the sea, reckoning from the cape south-east of the island, already mentioned; it curled round, making an open road-stead, which marked out the lower shore of this strangely-formed land.

At the narrowest part, that is to say between the Chimneys and the creek on the western shore, which corresponded to it in latitude, the island only measured ten miles; but its greatest length, from the jaws at the north-east to the extremity of the tail of the south-west, was not less than thirty miles.

As to the interior of the island, its general aspect was this—very woody throughout the southern part from the mountain to the shore, and arid and sandy in the northern part. Between the volcano and the east coast Cyrus Harding and his companions were surprised to see a lake, bordered with green trees, the existence of which they had not suspected. Seen from this height, the lake appeared to be on the same level as the ocean, but, on reflection, the engineer explained to his companions that the altitude of this little sheet of water must be about three hundred feet, because the plateau, which was its basin, was but a prolongation of the coast.

"Is it a freshwater lake?" asked Pencroft.

"Certainly," replied the engineer, "for it must be fed by the water which flows from the mountain."

"I see a little river which runs into it," said Herbert, pointing out a narrow stream, which evidently took its source somewhere in the west.

"Yes," said Harding; "and since this stream feeds the lake, most probably on the side near the sea there is an outlet by which the surplus water escapes. We shall see that on our return."

This little winding water-course and the river already mentioned constituted the water-system, at least such as it was displayed to the eyes of the explorers. However, it was possible that under the masses of trees which covered two-thirds of the island, forming an immense forest, other rivers ran towards the sea. It might even be inferred that such was the case, so rich did this region appear in the most magnificent specimens of the flora of the temperate zones. There was no indication of running water in the north, though perhaps there might be stagnant water among the marshes in the north-east; but that was all, in addition to the downs, sand, and aridity which contrasted so strongly with the luxuriant vegetation of the rest of the island.

The volcano did not occupy the central part; it rose, on the contrary, in the north-western region, and seemed to mark the boundary of the two zones. At the south-west, at the south, and the south-east, the first part of the spurs were hidden under masses of verdure. At the north, on the contrary, one could follow their ramifications, which died away on the sandy plains. It was on this side that, at the time when the mountain was in a state of irruption, the discharge had worn away a passage, and a large heap of lava had spread to the narrow jaw which formed the north-eastern gulf.

Cyrus Harding and his companions remained an hour at the top of the mountain. The island was displayed under their eyes, like a plan in relief with different tints, green for the forests, yellow for the sand, blue for the water. They viewed it in its *tout-ensemble*, nothing remained concealed but the ground hidden by verdure, the hollows of the valleys, and the interior of the volcanic chasms.

One important question remained to be solved, and the answer would have a great effect upon the future of the castaways.

Was the island inhabited?

It was the reporter who put this question, to which after the close examination they had just made, the answer seemed to be in the negative.

Nowhere could the work of a human hand be perceived. Not a group of huts, not a solitary cabin, not a fishery on the shore. No smoke curling in the air betrayed the presence of man. It is true, a distance of nearly thirty miles separated the observers from the extreme points, that is, of the tail which extended to the south-west, and it would have been difficult, even to Pencroft's eyes, to discover a habitation there. Neither could the curtain of verdure, which covered three-quarters of the island, be raised to see if it did not shelter some straggling village. But in general the islanders live on the shores of the narrow spaces which emerge above the waters of the Pacific, and this shore appeared to be an absolute desert.

Until a more complete exploration, it might be admitted that the island was uninhabited. But was it frequented, at least occasionally, by the natives of neighbouring islands? It was difficult to reply to this question. No land appeared within a radius of fifty miles. But fifty miles could be easily crossed, either by Malay proas or by the large Polynesian canoes. Everything depended on the position of the island, of its isolation in the Pacific, or of its proximity to archipelagoes. Would Cyrus Harding be able to find out their latitude and longitude without instruments? It would be difficult. In the doubt, it was best to take precautions against a possible descent of neighbouring natives.

The exploration of the island was finished, its shape determined, its features made out, its extent calculated, the water and mountain systems ascertained. The disposition of the forests and plains had been marked in a general way on the reporter's plan. They had now only to descend the mountain slopes again, and explore the soil, in the triple point of view, of its mineral, vegetable, and animal resources.

But before giving his companions the signal for departure, Cyrus Harding said to them in a calm, grave voice—

Here, my friends, is the small corner of land upon which the hand of the Almighty has thrown us. We are going to live here; a long time, perhaps. Perhaps, too, unexpected help will arrive, if some ship passes by chance. I say by chance, because this is an unimportant island; there is not even a port in which ships could anchor, and it is to be feared that it is situated out of the route usually followed, that is to say, too much to the south for the ships which frequent the archipelagoes of the Pacific, and too much to the north for those which go to Australia by doubling Cape Horn. I wish to hide nothing of our position from you—"

"And you are right, my dear Cyrus," replied the reporter, with animation. "You have to deal with men. They have confidence in you, and you can depend upon them. Is it not so, my friends?"

"I will obey you in everything, captain," said Herbert, seizing the engineer's hand.

"My master always, and everywhere!" cried Neb.

"As for me," said the sailor, "if I ever grumble at work, my name's not Jack Pencroft, and if you like, captain, we will make a little America of this island! We will build towns, we will establish railways, start telegraphs, and one fine day, when it is quite changed, quite put in order and quite civilised, we will go and offer it to the government of the Union. Only, I ask one thing."

"What is that?" said the reporter.

"It is, that we do not consider ourselves castaways, but colonists, who have come here to settle." Harding could not help smiling, and the sailor's idea was adopted. He then thanked his companions, and added, that he would rely on their energy and on the aid of Heaven.

"Well, now let us set off to the Chimneys!" cried Pencroft.

"One minute, my friends," said the engineer. "It seems to me it would be a good thing to give a name to this island, as well as to the capes, promontories, and water-courses, which we can see."

"Very good," said the reporter. "In the future, that will simplify the instructions which we shall have to give and follow."

"Indeed," said the sailor, "already it is something to be able to say where one is going, and where one has come from. At least, it looks like somewhere."

"The Chimneys, for example," said Herbert.

"Exactly!" replied Pencroft. "That name was the most convenient, and it came to me quite of myself. Shall we keep the name of the Chimneys for our first encampment, captain?"

"Yes, Pencroft, since you have so christened it."

"Good! as for the others, that will be easy," returned the sailor, who was in high spirits. "Let us give them names, as the Robinsons did, whose story Herbert has often read to me; Providence Bay, Whale Point, Cape Disappointment!"

"Or, rather, the names of Captain Harding," said Herbert, "of Mr. Spilett, of Neb!—"

"My name!" cried Neb, showing his sparkling white teeth.

"Why not?" replied Pencroft. "Port Neb, that would do very well! And Cape Gideon—"

"I should prefer borrowing names from our country," said the reporter, "which would remind us of America."

"Yes, for the principal ones," then said Cyrus Harding; "for those of the bays and seas, I admit it willingly. We might give to that vast bay on the east the name of Union Bay, for example; to that large hollow on the south, Washington Bay; to the mountain upon which we are standing, that of Mount Franklin; to that lake which is extended under our eyes, that of Lake Grant; nothing could be better, my friends. These names will recall our country, and those of the great citizens who have honoured it; but for the rivers, gulfs, capes, and promontories, which we perceive from the top of this mountain, rather let us choose names which will recall their particular shape. They will impress themselves better on our memory, and at the same time will be more practical. The shape of the island is so strange that we shall not be troubled to imagine what it resembles. As to the streams which we do not know as yet, in different parts of the forest which we shall explore later, the creeks which afterwards will be discovered, we can christen them as we find them. What do you think, my friends?"

The engineer's proposal was unanimously agreed to by his companions. The island was spread out under their eyes like a map, and they had only to give names to all its angles and points. Gideon Spilett would write them down, and the geographical nomenclature of the island would be definitely adopted.

First of all, they named the two bays and the mountain, Union Bay, Washington Bay, and Mount Franklin, as the engineer had suggested.

"Now," said the reporter, "to this peninsula at the south-west of the island, I propose to give the name of Serpentine Peninsula, and that of Reptile-end to the bent tail which terminates it, for it is just like a reptile's tail."

"Adopted," said the engineer.

"Now," said Herbert, pointing to the other extremity of the island, "let us call this gulf which is so singularly like a pair of open jaws, Shark Gulf."

"Capital!" cried Pencroft, "and we can complete the resemblance by naming the two parts of the jaws Mandible Cape."

"But there are two capes," observed the reporter.

"Well," replied Pencroft, "we can have North Mandible Cape and South Mandible Cape."

"They are inscribed," said Spilett.

"There is only the point at the south-eastern extremity of the island to be named," said Pencroft.

"That is, the extremity of Union Bay?" asked Herbert.

"Claw Cape," cried Neb directly, who also wished to be godfather to some part of his domain.

In truth, Neb had found an excellent name, for this cape was very like the powerful claw of the fantastic animal which this singularly-shaped island represented.

Pencroft was delighted at the turn things had taken, and their imaginations soon gave to the river which furnished the settlers with drinking water and near which the balloon had thrown them, the name of the Mercy, in true gratitude to Providence. To the islet upon which the castaways had first landed, the name of Safety Island; to the plateau which crowned the high granite precipice above the Chimneys, and from whence the gaze could embrace the whole of the vast bay, the name of Prospect Heights.

Lastly, all the masses of impenetrable wood which covered the Serpentine Peninsula were named the forests of the Far West.

The nomenclature of the visible and known parts of the island was thus finished, and later, they would complete it as they made fresh discoveries.

As to the points of the compass, the engineer had roughly fixed them by the height and position of the sun, which placed Union Bay and Prospect Heights to the east. But the next day, by taking the exact hour of the rising and setting of the sun, and by marking its position between this rising and setting, he reckoned to fix the north of the island exactly, for, in consequence of its situation in the southern hemisphere, the sun, at the precise moment of its culmination, passed in the north and not in the south, as, in its apparent movement, it seems to do, to those places situated in the northern hemisphere.

Everything was finished, and the settlers had only to descend Mount Franklin to re-turn to the Chimneys, when Pencroft cried out—

"Well! we are preciously stupid!"

"Why?" asked Gideon Spilett, who had closed his note-book and risen to depart.

"Why! our island! we have forgotten to christen it!"

Herbert was going to propose to give it the engineer's name and all his companions would have applauded him, when Cyrus Harding said simply—

"Let us give it the name of a great citizen, my friend; of him who now struggles to de-fend the unity of the American Republic! Let us call it Lincoln Island!"

The engineer's proposal was replied to by three hurrahs.

And that evening, before sleeping, the new colonists talked of their absent country; they spoke of the terrible war which stained it with blood; they could not doubt that the South would soon be subdued, and that the cause of the North, the cause of justice, would triumph, thanks to Grant, thanks to Lincoln!

Now this happened the 30th of March, 1865. They little knew that sixteen days after-wards a frightful crime would be committed in Washington, and that on Good Friday Abraham Lincoln would fall by the hand of a fanatic.

Chapter XII

REGULATING THE WATCHES—PENCROFT IS SATISFIED—A SUSPICIOUS SMOKE—COURSE OF RED CREEK—THE FLORA OF LINCOLN ISLAND—THE FAUNA—MOUNTAIN PHEASANTS— CHASING KANGAROOS—AN AGOUTI—LAKE GRANT— RETURN TO THE CHIMNEYS

THEY NOW BEGAN THE DESCENT OF THE MOUNTAIN. CLIMBING DOWN THE CRATER, THEY went round the cone and reached their encampment of the previous night. Pencroft thought it must be breakfast-time, and the watches of the reporter and engineer were therefore consulted to find out the hour.

That of Gideon Spilett had been preserved from the sea-water, as he had been thrown at once on the sand out of reach of the waves. It was an instrument of excellent quality, a perfect pocket chronometer, which the reporter had not forgotten to wind up carefully everyday.

As to the engineer's watch, it, of course, had stopped during the time which he had passed on the downs.

The engineer now wound it up, and ascertaining by the height of the sun that it must be about nine o'clock in the morning, he put his watch at that hour.

Gideon Spilett was about to do the same, when the engineer, stopping his hand, said—

"No, my dear Spilett, wait. You have kept the Richmond time, have you not?"

"Yes, Cyrus."

"Consequently, your watch is set by the meridian of that town, which is almost that of Washington?"

"Undoubtedly."

"Very well, keep it thus. Content yourself with winding it up very exactly, but do not touch the hands. This may be of use to us."

"What will be the good of that?" thought the sailor.

They ate, and so heartily, that the store of game and almonds was totally exhausted. But Pencroft was not at all uneasy, they would supply themselves on the way. Top, whose share had been very much to his taste, would know how to find some fresh game among the brushwood. Moreover, the sailor thought of simply asking the engineer to manufacture some powder and one or two fowling-pieces; he supposed there would be no difficulty in that.

On leaving the plateau, the captain proposed to his companions to return to the Chimneys by a new way. He wished to reconnoitre Lake Grant, so magnificently framed in trees. They therefore followed the crest of one of the spurs, between which the creek* that supplied the lake probably had its source. In talking, the settlers already employed the names which they had just chosen, which singularly facilitated the exchange of their ideas. Herbert and Pencroft—the one young and the other very boyish—were enchanted, and while walking, the sailor said—

"Hey, Herbert! how capital it sounds! It will be impossible to lose ourselves, my boy, since, whether we follow the way to Lake Grant, or whether we join the Mercy through the woods of the Far West, we shall be certain to arrive at Prospect Heights, and, consequently, at Union Bay!"

It had been agreed, that without forming a compact band, the settlers should not stray away from each other. It was very certain that the thick forests of the island were inhabited by dangerous animals, and it was prudent to be on their guard. In general, Pencroft, Herbert, and Neb walked first, preceded by Top, who poked his nose into every bush. The reporter and the engineer went together, Gideon Spilett ready to note every incident, the engineer silent for the most part, and only stepping aside to pick up sometimes one thing, sometimes another, a mineral or vegetable substance, which he put into his pocket without making any remark.

"What can he be picking up?" muttered Pencroft. "I have looked in vain for anything that's worth the trouble of stooping for."

Towards ten o'clock the little band descended the last declivities of Mount Franklin. As yet the ground was scantily strewn with bushes and trees. They were walking over yellowish calcinated earth, forming a plain of nearly a mile long, which extended to the edge of the wood. Great blocks of that basalt, which, according to Bischof, takes three hundred and fifty millions of years to cool, strewed the plain, very confused in some places. However, there were here no traces of lava, which was spread more particularly over the northern slopes.

Cyrus Harding expected to reach, without incident, the course of the creek, which he supposed flowed under the trees at the border of the plain, when he saw Herbert running hastily back, while Neb and the sailor were hiding behind the rocks.

*An American name for a small water-course.

"What's the matter, my boy?" asked Spilett.

"Smoke," replied Herbert. "We have seen smoke among the rocks, a hundred paces from us."

"Men in this place?" cried the reporter.

"We must avoid showing ourselves before knowing with whom we have to deal," replied Cyrus Harding. "I trust that there are no natives on this island; I dread them more than anything else. Where is Top?"

"Top is on before."

"And he doesn't bark?"

"No."

"That is strange. However, we must try to call him back."

In a few moments, the engineer, Gideon Spilett, and Herbert had rejoined their two companions, and like them, they kept out of sight behind the heaps of basalt.

From thence they clearly saw smoke of a yellowish colour rising in the air.

Top was recalled by a slight whistle from his master, and the latter, signing to his companions to wait for him, glided away among the rocks. The colonists, motionless, anxiously awaited the result of this exploration, when a shout from the engineer made them hasten forward. They soon joined him, and were at once struck with a disagreeable odor which impregnated the atmosphere.

The odor, easily recognised, was enough for the engineer to guess what the smoke was which at first, not without cause, had startled him.

"This fire," said he, "or rather, this smoke is produced by nature alone. There is a sulphur spring there, which will effectually cure all our sore throats."

"Captain!" cried Pencroft. "What a pity that I haven't got a cold!"

The settlers then directed their steps towards the place from which the smoke escaped. They there saw a sulphur spring which flowed abundantly between the rocks, and its waters discharged a strong sulphuric acid odor, after having absorbed the oxygen of the air.

Cyrus Harding, dipping in his hand, felt the water oily to the touch. He tasted it and found it rather sweet. As to its temperature, that he estimated at ninety-five degrees Fahrenheit. Herbert having asked on what he based this calculation—

"Its quite simple, my boy," said he, "for, in plunging my hand into the water, I felt no sensation either of heat or cold. Therefore it has the same temperature as the human body, which is about ninety-five degrees."

The sulphur spring not being of any actual use to the settlers, they proceeded towards the thick border of the forest, which began some hundred paces off.

There, as they had conjectured, the waters of the stream flowed clear and limpid between high banks of red earth, the colour of which betrayed the presence of oxide of iron. From this colour, the name of Red Creek was immediately given to the water-course.

It was only a large stream, deep and clear, formed of the mountain water, which, half river, half torrent, here rippling peacefully over the sand, there chafing against the rocks or dashing down in a cascade, ran towards the lake, over a distance of a mile and a half, its breadth varying from thirty to forty feet. Its waters were sweet, and it was supposed that those of the lake were so also. A fortunate circumstance, in the event of their finding on its borders a more suitable dwelling than the Chimneys.

As to the trees, which some hundred feet downwards shaded the banks of the creek, they belonged, for the most part, to the species which abound in the temperate zone of America and Tasmania, and no longer to those coniferae observed in that portion of the island already explored to some miles from Prospect Heights. At this time of the year, the commencement of the month of April, which represents the month of October, in this hemisphere, that is, the beginning of autumn, they were still in full leaf. They consisted principally of casuarinas and eucalypti, some of which next year would yield a sweet manna, similar to the manna of the East. Clumps of Australian cedars rose on the sloping banks, which were also covered with the high grass called "tussac" in New Holland; but the cocoa-nut, so abundant in the archipelagoes of the Pacific, seemed to be wanting in the island, the latitude, doubtless, being too low.

"What a pity!" said Herbert, "such a useful tree, and which has such beautiful nuts!"

As to the birds, they swarmed among the scanty branches of the eucalypti and casuarinas, which did not hinder the display of their wings. Black, white, or grey cockatoos, paroquets, with plumage of all colours, kingfishers of a sparkling green and crowned with red, blue lories, and various other birds appeared on all sides, as through a prism, fluttering about and producing a deafening clamor. Suddenly, a strange concert of discordant voices resounded in the midst of a thicket. The settlers heard successively the song of birds, the cry of quadrupeds, and a sort of clacking which they might have believed to have escaped from the lips of a native. Neb and Herbert rushed towards the bush, forgetting even the most elementary principles of prudence. Happily, they found there, neither a formidable wild beast nor a dangerous native, but merely half-a-dozen mocking and singing birds, known as mountain pheasants. A few skilful blows from a stick soon put an end to their concert, and procured excellent food for the evening's dinner.

Herbert also discovered some magnificent pigeons with bronzed wings, some superbly crested, others draped in green, like their congeners at Port-Macquarie; but it was impossible to reach them, or the crows and magpies which flew away in flocks.

A charge of small shot would have made great slaughter among these birds, but the hunters were still limited to sticks and stones, and these primitive weapons proved very insufficient.

Their insufficiency was still more clearly shown when a troop of quadrupeds, jumping, bounding, making leaps of thirty feet, regular flying mammiferae, fled over the thickets, so quickly and at such a height, that one would have thought that they passed from one tree to another like squirrels.

"Kangaroos!" cried Herbert.

"Are they good to eat?" asked Pencroft.

"Stewed," replied the reporter, "their flesh is equal to the best venison!—"

Gideon Spilett had not finished this exciting sentence when the sailor, followed by Neb and Herbert, darted on the kangaroos tracks. Cyrus Harding called them back in vain. But it was in vain too for the hunters to pursue such agile game, which went bounding away like balls. After a chase of five minutes, they lost their breath, and at the same time all sight of the creatures, which disappeared in the wood. Top was not more successful than his masters.

"Captain," said Pencroft, when the engineer and the reporter had rejoined them, "Captain, you see quite well we can't get on unless we make a few guns. Will that be possible?"

"Perhaps," replied the engineer, "but we will begin by first manufacturing some bows and arrows, and I don't doubt that you will become as clever in the use of them as the Australian hunters."

"Bows and arrows!" said Pencroft scornfully. "That's all very well for children!"

"Don't be proud, friend Pencroft," replied the reporter. "Bows and arrows were sufficient for centuries to stain the earth with blood. Powder is but a thing of yesterday, and war is as old as the human race—unhappily!"

"Faith, that's true, Mr. Spilett," replied the sailor, "and I always speak too quickly. You must excuse me!"

Meanwhile, Herbert constant to his favourite science, Natural History, reverted to the kangaroos, saying—

"Besides, we had to deal just now with the species which is most difficult to catch. They were giants with long grey fur; but if I am not mistaken, there exist black and red kangaroos, rock kangaroos, and rat kangaroos, which are more easy to get hold of. It is reckoned that there are about a dozen species—"

"Herbert," replied the sailor sententiously, "there is only one species of kangaroos to me, that is 'kangaroo on the spit,' and it's just the one we haven't got this evening!"

They could not help laughing at Master Pencroft's new classification. The honest sailor did not hide his regret at being reduced for dinner to the singing pheasants, but fortune once more showed itself obliging to him.

In fact, Top, who felt that his interest was concerned went and ferreted everywhere with an instinct doubled by a ferocious appetite. It was even probable that if some piece of game did fall into his clutches, none would be left for the hunters, if Top was hunting on his own account; but Neb watched him and he did well.

Towards three o'clock the dog disappeared in the brushwood, and gruntings showed that he was engaged in a struggle with some animal. Neb rushed after him, and soon saw Top eagerly devouring a quadruped, which ten seconds later would have been past recognizing in Top's stomach. But fortunately the dog had fallen upon a brood, and besides the victim he was devouring, two other rodents—the animals in question belonged to that order—lay strangled on the turf.

Neb reappeared triumphantly holding one of the rodents in each hand. Their size exceeded that of a rabbit, their hair was yellow, mingled with green spots, and they had the merest rudiments of tails.

The citizens of the Union were at no loss for the right name of these rodents. They were maras, a sort of agouti, a little larger than their congeners of tropical countries, regular American rabbits, with long ears, jaws armed on each side with five molars, which distinguish the agouti.

"Hurrah!" cried Pencroft, "the roast has arrived! and now we can go home."

The walk, interrupted for an instant, was resumed. The limpid waters of the Red Creek flowed under an arch of casuarinas, banksias, and gigantic gum-trees. Superb lilacs rose to a height of twenty feet. Other arborescent species, unknown to the young naturalist, bent over the stream, which could be heard murmuring beneath the bowers of verdure.

Meanwhile the stream grew much wider, and Cyrus Harding supposed that they would soon reach its mouth. In fact, on emerging from beneath a thick clump of beautiful trees, it appeared all at once.

The explorers had arrived on the western shore of Lake Grant. The place was well worth looking at. This extent of water, of a circumference of nearly seven miles and an area of two hundred and fifty acres, reposed in a border of diversified trees. Towards the east, through a curtain of verdure, picturesquely raised in some places, sparkled an horizon of sea. The lake was curved at the north, which contrasted with the sharp outline of its lower part. Numerous aquatic birds frequented the shores of this little Ontario, in which the thousand isles of its American namesake were represented by a rock which emerged from its surface, some hundred feet from the southern shore. There lived in harmony several couples of kingfishers perched on a stone, grave, motionless, watching for fish, then darting down, they plunged in with a sharp cry, and reappeared with their prey in their beaks. On the shores and on the islets, strutted wild ducks, pelicans, water-hens, red-beaks, philedons, furnished with a tongue like a brush, and one or two specimens of the splendid menura, the tail of which expands gracefully like a lyre.

As to the water of the lake, it was sweet, limpid, rather dark, and from certain bubblings, and the concentric circles which crossed each other on the surface, it could not be doubted that it abounded in fish.

"This lake is really beautiful!" said Gideon Spilett. "We could live on its borders!"

"We will live there!" replied Harding.

The settlers, wishing to return to the Chimneys by the shortest way, descended towards the angle formed on the south by the junction of the lake's bank. It was not without difficulty that they broke a path through the thickets and brushwood which had never been put aside by the hand of mm, and they thus went towards the shore, so as to arrive at the north of Prospect Heights. Two miles were cleared in this direction, and then, after they had passed the last curtain of trees, appeared the plateau, carpeted with thick turf, and beyond that the infinite sea.

To return to the Chimneys, it was enough to cross the plateau obliquely for the space of a mile, and then to descend to the elbow formed by the first detour of the Mercy. But the engineer desired to know how and where the overplus of the water from the lake escaped, and the exploration was prolonged under the trees for a mile and a half towards the north. It was most probable that an overfall existed somewhere, and doubtless through a cleft in the granite. This lake was only, in short, an immense centre basin, which was filled by degrees by the creek, and its waters must necessarily pass to the sea by some fall. If it was so, the engineer thought that it might perhaps be possible to utilise this fall and borrow its power, actually lost without profit to anyone. They continued then to follow the shores of Lake Grant by climbing the plateau; but, after having gone a mile in this direction, Cyrus Harding had not been able to discover the overfall, which, however, must exist somewhere.

It was then half-past four. In order to prepare for dinner it was necessary that the settlers should return to their dwelling. The little band retraced their steps, therefore, and by the left bank of the Mercy Cyrus Harding and his companions arrived at the Chimneys.

The fire was lighted, and Neb and Pencroft, on whom the functions of cooks naturally devolved, to the one in his quality of negro, to the other in that of sailor, quickly prepared some broiled agouti, to which they did great justice.

The repast at length terminated; at the moment when each one was about to give himself up to sleep, Cyrus Harding drew from his pocket little specimens of different sorts of minerals, and just said—

"My friends, this is iron mineral, this a pyrite, this is clay, this is lime, and this is coal. Nature gives us these things. It is our business to make a right use of them. To-morrow we will commence operations."

Chapter XIII

What Is Found upon Top—Manufacturing Bows and Arrows—A Brick-Field—A Pottery—Different Cooking Utensils—The First Boiled Meat— Wormwood—The Southern Cross—An Important Astronomical Observation

WELL, CAPTAIN, WHERE ARE WE GOING TO BEGIN?" ASKED PENCROFT NEXT MORNING of the engineer.

"At the beginning," replied Cyrus Harding.

And in fact, the settlers were compelled to begin "at the very beginning." They did not possess even the tools necessary for making tools, and they were not even in the condition of nature, who, "having time, husbands her strength." They had no time, since they had to provide for the immediate wants of their existence, and though, profiting by acquired experience, they had nothing to invent, still they had everything to make; their iron and their steel were as yet only in the state of minerals, their earthenware in the state of clay, their linen and their clothes in the state of textile material.

It must be said, however, that the settlers were "men" in the complete and higher sense of the word. The engineer Harding could not have been seconded by more intelligent companions, nor with more devotion and zeal. He had tried them. He knew their abilities.

Gideon Spilett, a talented reporter, having learned everything so as to be able to speak of everything, would contribute largely with his head and hands to the colonisation of the island. He would not draw back from any task: a determined sportsman, he would make a business of what till then had only been a pleasure to him.

Herbert, a gallant boy, already remarkably well informed in the natural sciences, would render greater service to the common cause.

Neb was devotion personified. Clever, intelligent, indefatigable, robust, with iron health, he knew a little about the work of the forge, and could not fail to be very useful in the colony.

As to Pencroft, he had sailed over every sea, a carpenter in the dockyards in Brooklyn, assistant tailor in the vessels of the state, gardener, cultivator, during his holidays, etc., and like all seamen, fit for anything, he knew how to do everything.

It would have been difficult to unite five men, better fitted to struggle against fate, more certain to triumph over it.

"At the beginning," Cyrus Harding had said. Now this beginning of which the engineer spoke was the construction of an apparatus which would serve to transform the natural substances. The part which heat plays in these transformations is known. Now fuel, wood or coal, was ready for immediate use, an oven must be built to use it.

"What is this oven for?" asked Pencroft.

"To make the pottery which we have need of," replied Harding.

"And of what shall we make the oven?"

"With bricks."

"And the bricks?"

"With clay. Let us start, my friends. To save trouble, we will establish our manufactory at the place of production. Neb will bring provisions, and there will be no lack of fire to cook the food."

"No," replied the reporter; "but if there is a lack of food, for want of instruments for the chase?"

"Ah, if we only had a knife!" cried the sailor.

"Well?" asked Cyrus Harding.

"Well! I would soon make a bow and arrows, and then there could be plenty of game in the larder!"

"Yes, a knife, a sharp blade—" said the engineer, as if he was speaking to himself.

At this moment his eyes fell upon Top, who was running about on the shore. Suddenly Harding's face became animated.

"Top, here," said he.

The dog came at his master's call. The latter took Top's head between his hands, and unfastening the collar which the animal wore round his neck, he broke it in two, saying—

"There are two knives, Pencroft!"

Two hurrahs from the sailor was the reply. Top's collar was made of a thin piece of tempered steel. They had only to sharpen it on a piece of sandstone, then to raise the edge on a finer stone. Now sandstone was abundant on the beach, and two hours after the stock of tools in the colony consisted of two sharp blades, which were easily fixed in solid handles.

The production of these their first tools was hailed as a triumph. It was indeed a valuable result of their labor, and a very opportune one. They set out. Cyrus Harding proposed that they should return to the western shore of the lake, where the day before he had noticed the clayey ground of which he possessed a specimen. They therefore followed the bank of the Mercy, traversed Prospect Heights, and after a walk of five miles or more they reached a glade, situated two hundred feet from Lake Grant.

On the way Herbert had discovered a tree, the branches of which the Indians of South America employ for making their bows. It was the crejimba, of the palm family, which does not bear edible fruit. Long straight branches were cut, the leaves stripped off; it was shaped, stronger in the middle, more slender at the extremities, and nothing remained to be done but to find a plant fit to make the bow-string. This was the "hibiscus heterophyllus," which furnishes fibres of such remarkable tenacity that they have been compared to the tendons of animals. Pencroft thus obtained bows of tolerable strength, for which he only wanted arrows. These were easily made with straight stiff branches, without knots, but the points with which they must be armed, that is to say, a substance to serve in lieu of iron, could not be met with so easily. But Pencroft said, that having done his part of the work, chance would do the rest.

The settlers arrived on the ground which had been discovered the day before. Being composed of the sort of clay which is used for making bricks and tiles, it was very useful for the work in question. There was no great difficulty in it. It was enough to scour the clay with sand, then to mould the bricks and bake them by the heat of a wood fire.

Generally bricks are formed in moulds, but the engineer contented himself with making them by hand. All that day and the day following were employed in this work. The clay, soaked in water, was mixed by the feet and hands of the manipulators, and then divided into pieces of equal size. A practiced workman can make, without a machine, about ten thousand bricks in twelve hours; but in their two days' work the five brick-makers on Lincoln Island had not made more than three thousand, which were ranged near each other, until the time when their complete desiccation would permit them to be used in building the oven, that is to say, in three or four days.

It was on the 2d of April that Harding had employed himself in fixing the orientation of the island, or, in other words, the precise spot where the sun rose. The day before he had noted exactly the hour when the sun disappeared beneath the horizon, making allowance for the refraction. This morning he noted, no less exactly, the hour at which it reappeared. Between this setting and rising twelve hours, twenty-four minutes passed. Then, six hours, twelve minutes after its rising, the sun on this day would exactly pass the meridian, and the point of the sky which it occupied at this moment would be the north.*

At the said hour, Cyrus marked this point, and putting in a line with the sun two trees which would serve him for marks, he thus obtained an invariable meridian for his ulterior operations.

The settlers employed the two days before the oven was built in collecting fuel. Branches were cut all round the glade, and they picked up all the fallen wood under the trees. They were also able to hunt with greater success, since Pencroft now possessed some dozen arrows armed with sharp points. It was Top who had furnished these points, by bringing in a porcupine, rather inferior eating, but of great value, thanks to the quills with which it bristled. These quills were fixed firmly at the ends of the arrows, the flight of which was made more certain by some cockatoos' feathers. The reporter and Herbert soon became very skilful archers. Game of all sorts in consequence abounded at the Chimneys, capybaras, pigeons, agouties, grouse, etc. The greater part of these animals were killed in the part of the forest on the left bank of the Mercy, to which they gave the name of Jacamar Wood, in remembrance of the bird which Pencroft and Herbert had pursued when on their first exploration.

This game was eaten fresh, but they preserved some capybara hams, by smoking them above a fire of green wood, after having perfumed them with sweet-smelling leaves. However, this food, although very strengthening, was always roast upon roast, and the party

---

* Indeed at this time of the year and in this latitude the sun rises at 33 minutes past 5 in the morning, and sets at 17 minutes past 6 in the evening.

would have been delighted to hear some soup bubbling on the hearth, but they must wait till a pot could be made, and, consequently, till the oven was built.

During these excursions, which were not extended far from the brick-field, the hunters could discern the recent passage of animals of a large size, armed with powerful claws, but they could not recognise the species. Cyrus Harding advised them to be very careful, as the forest probably enclosed many dangerous beasts.

And he did right. Indeed, Gideon Spilett and Herbert one day saw an animal which resembled a jaguar. Happily the creature did not attack them, or they might not have escaped without a severe wound. As soon as he could get a regular weapon, that is to say, one of the guns which Pencroft begged for, Gideon Spilett resolved to make desperate war against the ferocious beasts, and exterminate them from the island.

The Chimneys during these few days was not made more comfortable, for the engineer hoped to discover, or build if necessary, a more convenient dwelling. They contented themselves with spreading moss and dry leaves on the sand of the passages, and on these primitive couches the tired workers slept soundly.

They also reckoned the days they had passed on Lincoln Island, and from that time kept a regular account. The 5th of April, which was Wednesday, was twelve days from the time when the wind threw the castaways on this shore.

On the 6th of April, at daybreak, the engineer and his companions were collected in the glade, at the place where they were going to perform the operation of baking the bricks. Naturally this had to be in the open air, and not in a kiln, or rather, the agglomeration of bricks made an enormous kiln, which would bake itself. The fuel, made of well-prepared fagots, was laid on the ground and surrounded with several rows of dried bricks, which soon formed an enormous cube, to the exterior of which they contrived air-holes. The work lasted all day, and it was not till the evening that they set fire to the fagots. No one slept that night, all watching carefully to keep up the fire.

The operation lasted forty-eight hours, and succeeded perfectly. It then became necessary to leave the smoking mass to cool, and during this time Neb and Pencroft, guided by Cyrus Harding, brought, on a hurdle made of interlaced branches, loads of carbonate of lime and common stones, which were very abundant, to the north of the lake. These stones, when decomposed by heat, made a very strong quicklime, greatly increased by slacking, at least as pure as if it had been produced by the calcination of chalk or marble. Mixed with sand the lime made excellent mortar.

The result of these different works was, that, on the 9th of April, the engineer had at his disposal a quantity of prepared lime and some thousands of bricks.

Without losing an instant, therefore, they began the construction of a kiln to bake the pottery, which was indispensable for their domestic use. They succeeded without much difficulty. Five days after, the kiln was supplied with coal, which the engineer had discovered lying open to the sky towards the mouth of the Red Creek, and the first smoke escaped from a chimney twenty feet high. The glade was transformed into a manufactory, and Pencroft was not far wrong in believing that from this kiln would issue all the products of modern industry.

In the meantime what the settlers first manufactured was a common pottery in which to cook their food. The chief material was clay, to which Harding added a little lime and quartz. This paste made regular "pipe-clay," with which they manufactured bowls, cups moulded on stones of a proper size, great jars and pots to hold water, etc. The shape of these objects was clumsy and defective, but after they had been baked in a high temperature, the kitchen of the Chimneys was provided with a number of utensils, as precious to the settlers as the most beautifully enamelled china. We must mention here that Pencroft, desirous to know if the clay thus prepared was worthy of its name of pipe-clay, made some large pipes, which he thought charming, but for which, alas! he had no tobacco, and that was a great privation to Pencroft. "But tobacco will come, like everything else!" he repeated, in a burst of absolute confidence.

This work lasted till the 15th of April, and the time was well employed. The settlers, having become potters, made nothing but pottery. When it suited Cyrus Harding to change them into smiths, they would become smiths. But the next day being Sunday, and also Easter Sunday, all agreed to sanctify the day by rest. These Americans were religious men, scrupulous observers of the precepts of the Bible, and their situation could not but develop sentiments of confidence towards the Author of all things.

On the evening of the 15th of April they returned to the Chimneys, carrying with them the pottery, the furnace being extinguished until they could put it to a new use. Their return was marked by a fortunate incident; the engineer discovered a substance which replaced tinder. It is known that a spongy, velvety flesh is procured from a certain mushroom of the genus polyporous. Properly prepared, it is extremely inflammable, especially when it has been previously saturated with gunpowder, or boiled in a solution of nitrate or chlorate of potash. But, till then, they had not found any of these polypores or even any of the morels which could replace them. On this day, the engineer, seeing a plant belonging to the wormwood genus, the principal species of which are absinthe, balm-mint, tarragon, etc., gathered several tufts, and, presenting them to the sailor, said—

"Here, Pencroft, this will please you."

Pencroft looked attentively at the plant, covered with long silky hair, the leaves being clothed with soft down.

"What's that, captain?" asked Pencroft. "Is it tobacco?"

"No," replied Harding, "it is wormwood; Chinese wormwood to the learned, but to us it will be tinder."

When the wormwood was properly dried it provided them with a very inflammable substance, especially afterwards when the engineer had impregnated it with nitrate of potash, of which the island possessed several beds, and which is in truth saltpeter.

The colonists had a good supper that evening. Neb prepared some agouti soup, a smoked capybara ham, to which was added the boiled tubercules of the "caladium macrorhizum," an herbaceous plant of the arum family. They had an excellent taste, and were very nutritious, being something similar to the substance which is sold in England under the name of "Portland sago"; they were also a good substitute for bread, which the settlers in Lincoln Island did not yet possess.

When supper was finished, before sleeping, Harding and his companions went to take the air on the beach. It was eight o'clock in the evening; the night was magnificent. The moon, which had been full five days before, had not yet risen, but the horizon was already silvered by those soft, pale shades which might be called the dawn of the moon. At the southern zenith glittered the circum-polar constellations, and above all the Southern Cross, which some days before the engineer had greeted on the summit of Mount Franklin.

Cyrus Harding gazed for some time at this splendid constellation, which has at its summit and at its base two stars of the first magnitude, at its left arm a star of the second, and at its right arm a star of the third magnitude.

Then, after some minutes' thought—

"Herbert," he asked of the lad, "is not this the 15th of April?"

"Yes, captain," replied Herbert.

"Well, if I am not mistaken, to-morrow will be one of the four days in the year in which the real time is identical with average time; that is to say, my boy, that to-morrow, to within some seconds, the sun will pass the meridian just at midday by the clocks. If the weather is fine I think that I shall obtain the longitude of the island with an approximation of some degrees."

"Without instruments, without sextant?" asked Gideon Spilett.

"Yes," replied the engineer. "Also, since the night is clear, I will try, this very evening, to obtain our latitude by calculating the height of the Southern Cross, that is, from the southern pole above the horizon. You understand, my friends, that before undertaking the work of installation in earnest it is not enough to have found out that this land is an island; we must, as nearly as possible, know at what distance it is situated, either from the American continent or Australia, or from the principal archipelagoes of the Pacific."

"In fact," said the reporter, "instead of building a house it would be more important to build a boat, if by chance we are not more than a hundred miles from an inhabited coast."

"That is why," returned Harding, "I am going to try this evening to calculate the latitude of Lincoln Island, and to-morrow, at midday, I will try to calculate the longitude."

If the engineer had possessed a sextant, an apparatus with which the angular distance of objects can be measured with great precision, there would have been no difficulty in the operation. This evening by the height of the pole, the next day by the passing of the sun at the meridian, he would obtain the position of the island. But as they had not one he would have to supply the deficiency.

Harding then entered the Chimneys. By the light of the fire he cut two little flat rulers, which he joined together at one end so as to form a pair of compasses, whose legs could separate or come together. The fastening was fixed with a strong acacia thorn which was found in the wood pile. This instrument finished, the engineer returned to the beach, but as it was necessary to take the height of the pole from above a clear horizon, that is, a sea horizon, and as Claw Cape hid the southern horizon, he was obliged to look for a more suitable station. The best would evidently have been the shore exposed directly to the south; but the Mercy would have to be crossed, and that was a difficulty. Harding resolved, in consequence, to make his observation from Prospect Heights, taking into consideration its height above the level of the sea—a height which he intended to calculate next day by a simple process of elementary geometry.

The settlers, therefore, went to the plateau, ascending the left bank of the Mercy, and placed themselves on the edge which looked north-west and south-east, that is, above the curiously-shaped rocks which bordered the river.

This part of the plateau commanded the heights of the left bank, which sloped away to the extremity of Claw Cape, and to the southern side of the island. No obstacle intercepted their gaze, which swept the horizon in a semicircle from the cape to Reptile End.

To the south the horizon, lighted by the first rays of the moon, was very clearly defined against the sky.

At this moment the Southern Cross presented itself to the observer in an inverted position, the star Alpha marking its base, which is nearer to the southern pole.

This constellation is not situated as near to the antarctic pole as the Polar Star is to the arctic pole. The star Alpha is about twenty-seven degrees from it, but Cyrus Harding knew this and made allowance for it in his calculation. He took care also to observe the moment when it passed the meridian below the pole, which would simplify the operation.

Cyrus Harding pointed one leg of the compasses to the horizon, the other to Alpha, and the space between the two legs gave him the angular distance which separated Alpha from the horizon. In order to fix the angle obtained, he fastened with thorns the two pieces of wood on a third placed transversely, so that their separation should be properly maintained.

That done, there was only the angle to calculate by bringing back the observation to the level of the sea, taking into consideration the depression of the horizon, which would necessitate measuring the height of the cliff. The value of this angle would give the height of Alpha, and consequently that of the pole above the horizon, that is to say, the latitude of the island, since the latitude of a point of the globe is always equal to the height of the pole above the horizon of this point.

The calculations were left for the next day, and at ten o'clock everyone was sleeping soundly.

Chapter XIV

MEASURING THE CLIFF—AN APPLICATION OF THE THEOREM
OF SIMILAR TRIANGLES—LATITUDE OF THE ISLAND—
EXCURSION TO THE NORTH—AN OYSTER-BED—PLANS FOR
THE FUTURE—THE SUN PASSING THE MERIDIAN—
THE LONGITUDE OF LINCOLN ISLAND

THE NEXT DAY, THE 16TH OF APRIL, AND EASTER SUNDAY, THE SETTLERS ISSUED FROM the Chimneys at daybreak, and proceeded to wash their linen. The engineer intended to manufacture soap as soon as he could procure the necessary materials—soda or potash, fat or oil. The important question of renewing their wardrobe would be treated of in the proper time and place. At any rate their clothes would last at least six months longer, for they were strong, and could resist the wear of manual labor. But all would depend on the situation of the island with regard to inhabited land. This would be settled to-day if the weather permitted.

The sun rising above a clear horizon, announced a magnificent day, one of those beautiful autumn days which are like the last farewells of the warm season.

It was now necessary to complete the observations of the evening before by measuring the height of the cliff above the level of the sea.

"Shall you not need an instrument similar to the one which you used yesterday?" said Herbert to the engineer.

"No, my boy," replied the latter, "we are going to proceed differently, but in as precise a way."

Herbert, wishing to learn everything he could, followed the engineer to the beach. Pencroft, Neb, and the reporter remained behind and occupied themselves in different ways.

Cyrus Harding had provided himself with a straight stick, twelve feet long, which he had measured as exactly as possible by comparing it with his own height, which he knew to a hair. Herbert carried a plumb-line which Harding had given him, that is to say, a simple stone fastened to the end of a flexible fibre. Having reached a spot about twenty feet from the edge of the beach, and nearly five hundred feet from the cliff, which rose perpendicularly, Harding thrust the pole two feet into the sand, and wedging it up carefully, he managed, by means of the plumb-line, to erect it perpendicularly with the plane of the horizon.

That done, he retired the necessary distance, when, lying on the sand, his eye glanced at the same time at the top of the pole and the crest of the cliff. He carefully marked the place with a little stick.

Then addressing Herbert—

"Do you know the first principles of geometry?" he asked.

"Slightly, captain," replied Herbert, who did not wish to put himself forward.

"You remember what are the properties of two similar triangles?"

"Yes," replied Herbert; "their homologous sides are proportional."

"Well, my boy, I have just constructed two similar right-angled triangles; the first, the smallest, has for its sides the perpendicular pole, the distance which separates the little stick from the foot of the pole, and my visual ray for hypothenuse; the second has for its sides the perpendicular cliff, the height of which we wish to measure, the distance which separates the little stick from the bottom of the cliff, and my visual ray also forms its hypothenuse, which proves to be prolongation of that of the first triangle."

"Ah, captain, I understand!" cried Herbert.

"As the distance from the stick to the pole is to the distance from the stick to the base of the cliff, so is the height of the pole to the height of the cliff."

"Just so, Herbert," replied the engineer; "and when we have measured the two first distances, knowing the height of the pole, we shall only have a sum in proportion to do, which will give us the height of the cliff, and will save us the trouble of measuring it directly."

The two horizontal distances were found out by means of the pole, whose length above the sand was exactly ten feet.

The first distance was fifteen feet between the stick and the place where the pole was thrust into the sand.

The second distance between the stick and the bottom of the cliff was five hundred feet.

These measurements finished, Cyrus Harding and the lad returned to the Chimneys.

The engineer then took a flat stone which he had brought back from one of his previous excursions, a sort of slate, on which it was easy to trace figures with a sharp shell. He then proved the following proportions:—

$$15:500::10:x$$
$$500 \text{ x } 10 = 5000$$
$$\frac{5000}{15} = 333.3$$

From which it was proved that the granite cliff measured 333 feet in height.

Cyrus Harding then took the instrument which he had made the evening before, the space between its two legs giving the angular distance between the star Alpha and the horizon. He measured, very exactly, the opening of this angle on a circumference which he divided into 360 equal parts. Now, this angle by adding to it the twenty-seven degrees which separated Alpha from the antarctic pole, and by reducing to the level of the sea the height of the cliff on which the observation had been made, was found to be fifty-three degrees. These fifty-three degrees being subtracted from ninety degrees—the distance from the pole to the equator—there remained thirty-seven degrees. Cyrus Harding concluded, therefore, that Lincoln Island was situated on the thirty-seventh degree of the southern latitude, or taking into consideration through the imperfection of the performance, an error of five degrees, that it must be situated between the thirty-fifth and the fortieth parallel.

There was only the longitude to be obtained, and the position of the island would be determined, The engineer hoped to attempt this the same day, at twelve o'clock, at which moment the sun would pass the meridian.

It was decided that Sunday should be spent in a walk, or rather an exploring expedition, to that side of the island between the north of the lake and Shark Gulf, and if there was time they would push their discoveries to the northern side of Cape South Mandible. They would breakfast on the downs, and not return till evening.

At half-past eight the little band was following the edge of the channel. On the other side, on Safety Islet, numerous birds were gravely strutting. They were divers, easily recognised by their cry, which much resembles the braying of a donkey. Pencroft only considered them in an eatable point of view, and learned with some satisfaction that their flesh, though blackish, is not bad food.

Great amphibious creatures could also be seen crawling on the sand; seals, doubtless, who appeared to have chosen the islet for a place of refuge. It was impossible to think of those animals in an alimentary point of view, for their oily flesh is detestable; however, Cyrus Harding observed them attentively, and without making known his idea, he announced to his companions that very soon they would pay a visit to the islet. The beach was strewn with innumerable shells, some of which would have rejoiced the heart of a conchologist; there were, among others, the phasianella, the terebratula, etc. But what would be of more use, was the discovery, by Neb, at low tide, of a large oyster-bed, among the rocks, nearly five miles from the Chimneys.

"Neb will not have lost his day," cried Pencroft, looking at the spacious oyster-bed.

"It is really a fortunate discovery," said the reporter, "and as it is said that each oyster produces yearly from fifty to sixty thousand eggs, we shall have an inexhaustible supply there."

"Only I believe that the oyster is not very nourishing," said Herbert.

"No," replied Harding. "The oyster contains very little nitrogen, and if a man lived exclusively on them, he would have to eat not less than fifteen to sixteen dozen a day."

"Capital!" replied Pencroft. "We might swallow dozens and dozens without exhausting the bed. Shall we take some for breakfast?"

And without waiting for a reply to this proposal, knowing that it would be approved of, the sailor and Neb detached a quantity of the molluscs. They put them in a sort of net of hibiscus fibre, which Neb had manufactured, and which already contained food; they then continued to climb the coast between the downs and the sea.

From time to time Harding consulted his watch, so as to be prepared in time for the solar observation, which had to be made exactly at midday.

All that part of the island was very barren as far as the point which closed Union Bay, and which had received the name of Cape South Mandible. Nothing could be seen there but sand and shells, mingled with debris of lava. A few sea-birds frequented this desolate coast, gulls, great albatrosses, as well as wild duck, for which Pencroft had a great fancy. He tried to knock some over with an arrow, but without result, for they seldom perched, and he could not hit them on the wing.

This led the sailor to repeat to the engineer—

"You see, captain, so long as we have not one or two fowling-pieces, we shall never get anything!"

"Doubtless, Pencroft," replied the reporter, "but it depends on you. Procure us some iron for the barrels, steel for the hammers, saltpeter, coal and sulphur for powder, mercury and nitric acid for the fulminate, and lead for the shot, and the captain will make us first-rate guns."

"Oh!" replied the engineer, "we might, no doubt, find all these substances on the island, but a gun is a delicate instrument, and needs very particular tools. However, we shall see later!"

"Why," cried Pencroft, "were we obliged to throw overboard all the weapons we had with us in the car, all our implements, even our pocketknives?"

"But if we had not thrown them away, Pencroft, the balloon would have thrown us to the bottom of the sea!" said Herbert.

"What you say is true, my boy," replied the sailor.

Then passing to another idea—

"Think," said he, "how astounded Jonathan Forster and his companions must have been when, next morning, they found the place empty, and the machine flown away!"

"I am utterly indifferent about knowing what they may have thought," said the reporter.

"It was all my idea, that!" said Pencroft, with a satisfied air.

"A splendid idea, Pencroft!" replied Gideon Spilett, laughing, "and which has placed us where we are."

"I would rather be here than in the hands of the Southerners," cried the sailor, "especially since the captain has been kind enough to come and join us again."

"So would I, truly!" replied the reporter. "Besides, what do we want? Nothing."

"If that is not—everything!" replied Pencroft, laughing and shrugging his shoulders. "But, someday or other, we shall find means of going away!"

"Sooner, perhaps, than you imagine, my friends," remarked the engineer, "if Lincoln Island is but a medium distance from an inhabited island, or from a continent. We shall know in an hour. I have not a map of the Pacific, but my memory has preserved a very clear recollection of its southern part. The latitude which I obtained yesterday placed New Zealand to the west of Lincoln Island, and the coast of Chile to the east. But between these two countries, there is a distance of at least six thousand miles. It has, therefore, to be determined what point in this great space the island occupies, and this the longitude will give us presently, with a sufficient approximation, I hope."

"Is not the archipelago of the Pomoutous the nearest point to us in latitude?" asked Herbert.

"Yes," replied the engineer, "but the distance which separates us from it is more than twelve hundred miles."

"And that way?" asked Neb, who followed the conversation with extreme interest, pointing to the south.

"That way, nothing," replied Pencroft.

"Nothing, indeed," added the engineer.

"Well, Cyrus," asked the reporter, "if Lincoln Island is not more than two or three thousand miles from New Zealand or Chile?"

"Well," replied the engineer, "instead of building a house we will build a boat, and Master Pencroft shall be put in command—"

"Well then," cried the sailor, "I am quite ready to be captain—as soon as you can make a craft that's able to keep at sea!"

"We shall do it, if it is necessary," replied Cyrus Harding.

But while these men, who really hesitated at nothing, were talking, the hour approached at which the observation was to be made. What Cyrus Harding was to do to ascertain the passage of the sun at the meridian of the island, without an instrument of any sort, Herbert could not guess.

The observers were then about six miles from the Chimneys, not far from that part of the downs in which the engineer had been found after his enigmatical preservation. They halted at this place and prepared for breakfast, for it was half-past eleven. Herbert went for some fresh water from a stream which ran near, and brought it back in a jug, which Neb had provided.

During these preparations Harding arranged everything for his astronomical observation. He chose a clear place on the shore, which the ebbing tide had left perfectly level. This bed of fine sand was as smooth as ice, not a grain out of place. It was of little importance whether it was horizontal or not, and it did not matter much whether the stick six feet high, which was planted there, rose perpendicularly. On the contrary, the engineer inclined it towards the south, that is to say, in the direction of the coast opposite to the sun, for it must not be forgotten that the settlers in Lincoln Island, as the island was situated in the southern hemisphere, saw the radiant planet describe its diurnal arc above the northern, and not above the southern horizon.

Herbert now understood how the engineer was going to proceed to ascertain the culmination of the sun, that is to say its passing the meridian of the island or, in other terms, the south if the place. It was by means of the shadow cast on the sand by the stick, a way which, for want of an instrument, would give him a suitable approach to the result which he wished to obtain.

In fact, the moment when this shadow would reach its minimum of length would be exactly twelve o'clock, and it would be enough to watch the extremity of the shadow, so as to ascertain the instant when, after having successively diminished, it began to lengthen. By inclining his stick to the side opposite to the sun, Cyrus Harding made the shadow longer, and consequently its modifications would be more easily ascertained. In fact, the longer the needle of a dial is, the more easily can the movement of its point be followed. The shadow of the stick was nothing but the needle of a dial.

Whe he thought the moment had come, Cyrus Harding knelt on the sand, and with little wooden pegs, which he stuck into the sand, he began to mark the successive diminutions of the stick's shadow. His companions, bending over him, watched the operation with extreme interest. The reporter held his chronometer in his hand, ready to tell the hour which it marked when the shadow would be at its shortest. Moreover, as Cyrus Harding was working on the 16th of April, the day on which the true and the average time are identical, the hour given by Gideon Spilett would be the true hour then at Washington, which would simplify the calculation. Meanwhile as the sun slowly advanced, the shadow slowly diminished, and when it appeared to Cyrus Harding that it was beginning to increase, he asked, "What o'clock is it?"

"One minute past five," replied Gideon Spilett directly. They had now only to calculate the operation. Nothing could be easier. It could be seen that there existed, in round numbers, a difference of five hours between the meridian of Washington and that of Lincoln Island, that is to say, it was midday in Lincoln Island when it was already five o'clock in the evening in Washington. Now the sun, in its apparent movement round the earth, traverses one degree in four minutes, or fifteen degrees an hour. Fifteen degrees multiplied by five hours give seventy-five degrees.

Then, since Washington is 77° 3' 11", as much as to say seventy-seven degrees counted from the meridian of Greenwich—which the Americans take for their starting-point for longitudes concurrently with the English—it followed that the island must be situated seventy-seven and seventy-five degrees west of the meridian of Greenwich, that is to say, on the hundred and fifty-second degree of west longitude.

Cyrus Harding announced this result to his companions, and taking into consideration errors of observation, as he had done for the latitude, he believed he could positively affirm that the position of Lincoln Island was between the thirty-fifth and the thirty-seventh parallel, and between the hundred and fiftieth and the hundred and fifty-fifth meridian to the west of the meridian of Greenwich.

The possible fault which he attributed to errors in the observation was, it may be seen, of five degrees on both sides, which, at sixty miles to a degree, would give an error of three hundred miles in latitude and longitude for the exact position.

But this error would not influence the determination which it was necessary to take. It was very evident that Lincoln Island was at such a distance from every country or island that it would be too hazardous to attempt to reach one in a frail boat.

In fact, this calculation placed it at least twelve hundred miles from Tahiti and the islands of the archipelago of the Pomoutous, more than eighteen hundred miles from New Zealand, and more than four thousand five hundred miles from the American coast!

And when Cyrus Harding consulted his memory, he could not remember in any way that such an island occupied, in that part of the Pacific, the situation assigned to Lincoln Island.

Chapter XV

IT IS DECIDED TO WINTER ON THE ISLAND—A METALLIC QUESTION—EXPLORING SAFETY ISLAND—A SEAL HUNT— CAPTURE OF AN ECHIDUA—A KOALA—WHAT IS CALLED THE CATALAN METHOD—MANUFACTURING IRON— HOW STEEL IS OBTAINED

THE NEXT DAY, THE 17TH OF APRIL, THE SAILOR'S FIRST WORDS WERE ADDRESSED TO Gideon Spilett.

"Well, sir," he asked, "what shall we do to-day?"

"What the captain pleases," replied the reporter.

Till then the engineer's companions had been brick-makers and potters, now they were to become metallurgists.

The day before, after breakfast, they had explored as far as the point of Mandible Cape, seven miles distant from the Chimneys. There, the long series of downs ended, and the soil had a volcanic appearance. There were no longer high cliffs as at Prospect Heights, but a strange and capricious border which surrounded the narrow gulf between the two capes, formed of mineral matter, thrown up by the volcano. Arrived at this point the settlers retraced their steps, and at nightfall entered the Chimneys; but they did not sleep before the question of knowing whether they could think of leaving Lincoln Island or not was definitely settled.

The twelve hundred miles which separated the island from the Pomoutous Island was a considerable distance. A boat could not cross it, especially at the approach of the bad season. Pencroft had expressly declared this. Now, to construct a simple boat, even with the necessary tools, was a difficult work, and the colonists not having tools they must begin by making hammers, axes, adzes, saws, augers, planes, etc., which would take some time. It was decided, therefore, that they would winter at Lincoln Island, and that they would seek for a more comfortable dwelling than the Chimneys, in which to pass the winter months.

Before anything else could be done it was necessary to make the iron ore, of which the engineer had observed some traces in the north-west part of the island, fit for use by converting it either into iron or into steel.

Metals are not generally found in the ground in a pure state. For the most part they are combined with oxygen or sulphur. Such was the case with the two specimens which Cyrus

Harding had brought back, one of magnetic iron, not carbonated, the other a pyrite, also called sulphuret of iron. It was, therefore, the first, the oxide of iron, which they must reduce with coal, that is to say, get rid of the oxygen, to obtain it in a pure state. This reduction is made by subjecting the ore with coal to a high temperature, either by the rapid and easy Catalan method, which has the advantage of transforming the ore into iron in a single operation, or by the blast furnace, which first smelts the ore, then changes it into iron, by carrying away the three to four per cent of coal, which is combined with it.

Now Cyrus Harding wanted iron, and he wished to obtain it as soon as possible. The ore which he had picked up was in itself very pure and rich. It was the oxydulous iron, which is found in confused masses of a deep grey colour; it gives a black dust, crystallised in the form of the regular octahedron. Native lodestones consist of this ore, and iron of the first quality is made in Europe from that with which Sweden and Norway are so abundantly supplied. Not far from this vein was the vein of coal already made use of by the settlers. The ingredients for the manufacture being close together would greatly facilitate the treatment of the ore. This is the cause of the wealth of the mines in Great Britain, where the coal aids the manufacture of the metal extracted from the same soil at the same time as itself.

"Then, captain," said Pencroft, "we are going to work iron ore?"

"Yes, my friend," replied the engineer, "and for that—something which will please you—we must begin by having a seal hunt on the islet."

"A seal hunt!" cried the sailor, turning towards Gideon Spilett. "Are seals needed to make iron?"

"Since Cyrus has said so!" replied the reporter.

But the engineer had already left the Chimneys, and Pencroft prepared for the seal hunt, without having received any other explanation.

Cyrus Harding, Herbert, Gideon Spilett, Neb, and the sailor were soon collected on the shore, at a place where the channel left a ford passable at low tide. The hunters could therefore traverse it without getting wet higher than the knee.

Harding then put his foot on the islet for the first, and his companions for the second time.

On their landing some hundreds of penguins looked fearlessly at them. The hunters, armed with sticks, could have killed them easily, but they were not guilty of such useless massacre, as it was important not to frighten the seals, who were lying on the sand several cable lengths off. They also respected certain innocent-looking birds, whose wings were reduced to the state of stumps, spread out like fins, ornamented with feathers of a scaly appearance. The settlers, therefore, prudently advanced towards the north point, walking over ground riddled with little holes, which formed nests for the sea-birds. Towards the extremity of the islet appeared great black heads floating just above the water, having exactly the appearance of rocks in motion.

These were the seals which were to be captured. It was necessary, however, first to allow them to land, for with their close, short hair, and their fusiform conformation, being excellent swimmers, it is difficult to catch them in the sea, while on land their short, webbed feet prevent their having more than a slow, waddling movement.

Pencroft knew the habits of these creatures, and he advised waiting till they were stretched on the sand, when the sun, before long, would send them to sleep. They must then manage to cut off their retreat and knock them on the head.

The hunters, having concealed themselves behind the rocks, waited silently.

An hour passed before the seals came to play on the sand. They could count half-a-dozen. Pencroft and Herbert then went round the point of the islet, so as to take them in the rear, and cut off their retreat. During this time Cyrus Harding, Spilett, and Neb, crawling behind the rocks, glided towards the future scene of combat.

All at once the tall figure of the sailor appeared. Pencroft shouted. The engineer and his two companions threw themselves between the sea and the seals. Two of the animals soon lay dead on the sand, but the rest regained the sea in safety.

"Here are the seals required, captain!" said the sailor, advancing towards the engineer.

"Capital," replied Harding. "We will make bellows of them!"

"Bellows!" cried Pencroft. "Well! these are lucky seals!"

It was, in fact, a blowing-machine, necessary for the treatment of the ore that the engineer wished to manufacture with the skins of the amphibious creatures. They were of a medium size, for their length did not exceed six feet. They resembled a dog about the head.

As it was useless to burden themselves with the weight of both the animals, Neb and Pencroft resolved to skin them on the spot, while Cyrus Harding and the reporter continued to explore the islet.

The sailor and the negro cleverly performed the operation, and three hours afterwards Cyrus Harding had at his disposal two seals' skins, which he intended to use in this state, without subjecting them to any tanning process.

The settlers waited till the tide was again low, and crossing the channel they entered the Chimneys.

The skins had then to be stretched on a frame of wood and sewn by means of fibres so as to preserve the air without allowing too much to escape. Cyrus Harding had nothing but the two steel blades from Top's collar, and yet he was so clever, and his companions aided him with so much intelligence, that three days afterwards the little colony's stock of tools was augmented by a blowing-machine, destined to inject the air into the midst of the ore when it should be subjected to heat—an indispensable condition to the success of the operation.

On the morning of the 20th of April began the "metallic period," as the reporter called it in his notes. The engineer had decided, as has been said, to operate near the veins both of coal and ore. Now, according to his observations, these veins were situated at the foot of the north-east spurs of Mount Franklin, that is to say, a distance of six miles from their home. It was impossible, therefore, to return everyday to the Chimneys, and it was agreed that the little colony should camp under a hut of branches, so that the important operation could be followed night and day.

This settled, they set out in the morning. Neb and Pencroft dragged the bellows on a hurdle; also a quantity of vegetables and animals, which they besides could renew on the way.

The road led through Jacamar Wood, which they traversed obliquely from south-east to north-west, and in the thickest part. It was necessary to beat a path, which would in the future form the most direct road to Prospect Heights and Mount Franklin. The trees, belonging to the species already discovered, were magnificent. Herbert found some new ones, among others some which Pencroft called "sham leeks"; for, in spite of their size, they were of the same liliaceous family as the onion, chive, shallot, or asparagus. These trees produce ligneous roots which, when cooked, are excellent; from them, by fermentation, a very agreeable liquor is made. They therefore made a good store of the roots.

The journey through the wood was long; it lasted the whole day, and so allowed plenty of time for examining the flora and fauna. Top, who took special charge of the fauna, ran through the grass and brushwood, putting up all sorts of game. Herbert and Gideon Spilett killed two kangaroos with bows and arrows, and also an animal which strongly resembled both a hedgehog and an ant-eater. It was like the first because it rolled itself into a ball, and bristled with spines, and the second because it had sharp claws, a long slender snout which terminated in a bird's beak, and an extendible tongue, covered with little thorns which served to hold the insects.

"And when it is in the pot," asked Pencroft naturally, "what will it be like?"

"An excellent piece of beef," replied Herbert.

"We will not ask more from it," replied the sailor,

During this excursion they saw several wild boars, which however, did not offer to attack the little band, and it appeared as if they would not meet with any dangerous beasts; when, in a thick part of the wood, the reporter thought he saw, some paces from him, among the lower branches of a tree, an animal which he took for a bear, and which he very tranquilly began to draw. Happily for Gideon Spilett, the animal in question did not belong to the redoubtable family of the plantigrades. It was only a koala, better known under the name of the sloth, being about the size of a large dog, and having stiff hair of a dirty colour, the paws armed with strong claws, which enabled it to climb trees and feed on the leaves. Having identified the animal, which they did not disturb, Gideon Spilett erased "bear" from the title of his sketch, putting koala in its place, and the journey was resumed.

At five o'clock in the evening, Cyrus Harding gave the signal to halt. They were now outside the forest, at the beginning of the powerful spurs which supported Mount Franklin towards the west. At a distance of some hundred feet flowed the Red Creek, and consequently plenty of fresh water was within their reach.

The camp was soon organised. In less than an hour, on the edge of the forest, among the trees, a hut of branches interlaced with creepers, and pasted over with clay, offered a tolerable shelter. Their geological researches were put off till the next day. Supper was prepared, a good fire blazed before the hut, the roast turned, and at eight o'clock, while one of the settlers watched to keep up the fire, in case any wild beasts should prowl in the neighbourhood, the others slept soundly.

The next day, the 21st of April, Cyrus Harding accompanied by Herbert, went to look for the soil of ancient formation, on which he had already discovered a specimen of ore. They found the vein above ground, near the source of the creek, at the foot of one of the north-eastern spurs. This ore, very rich in iron, enclosed in its fusible vein-stone, was perfectly suited to the mode of reduction which the engineer intended to employ; that is, the Catalan method, but simplified, as it is used in Corsica. In fact, the Catalan method, properly so called, requires the construction of kilns and crucibles, in which the ore and the coal, placed in alternate layers, are transformed and reduced. But Cyrus Harding intended to economise these constructions, and wished simply to form, with the ore and the coal, a cubic mass, to the centre of which he would direct the wind from his bellows. Doubtless, it was the proceeding employed by Tubal Cain, and the first metallurgists of the inhabited world. Now that which had succeeded with the grandson of Adam, and which still yielded good results in countries rich in ore and fuel, could not but succeed with the settlers in Lincoln Island.

The coal, as well as the ore, was collected without trouble on the surface of the ground. They first broke the ore into little pieces, and cleansed them with the hand from the impurities which soiled their surface. Then coal and ore were arranged in heaps and in successive layers, as the charcoal-burner does with the wood which he wishes to carbonise. In this way, under the influence of the air projected by the blowing-machine, the coal would be transformed into carbonic acid, then into oxide of carbon, its use being to reduce the oxide of iron, that is to say, to rid it of the oxygen.

Thus the engineer proceeded. The bellows of sealskin, furnished at its extremity with a nozzle of clay, which had been previously fabricated in the pottery kiln, was established near the heap of ore. Moved by a mechanism which consisted of a frame, cords of fibre and counterpoise, he threw into the mass an abundance of air, which by raising the temperature also concurred with the chemical transformation to produce in time pure iron.

The operation was difficult. All the patience, all the ingenuity of the settlers was needed; but at last it succeeded, and the result was a lump of iron, reduced to a spongy state, which it was necessary to shingle and fagot, that is to say, to forge so as to expel from it the liquefied vein-stone. These amateur smiths had, of course, no hammer; but they were in no worse a situation than the first metallurgist, and therefore did what, no doubt, he had to do.

A handle was fixed to the first lump, and was used as a hammer to forge the second on a granite anvil, and thus they obtained a coarse but useful metal. At length, after many trials and much fatigue, on the 25th of April several bars of iron were forged, and transformed into tools, crowbars, pincers, pickaxes, spades, etc., which Pencroft and Neb declared to be real jewels.

But the metal was not yet in its most serviceable state, that is, of steel. Now steel is a combination of iron and coal, which is extracted, either from the liquid ore, by taking from it the excess of coal, or from the iron by adding to it the coal which was wanting. The first, obtained by the decarburation of the metal, gives natural or puddled steel; the second, produced by the carburation of the iron, gives steel of cementation.

It was the last which Cyrus Harding intended to forge, as he possessed iron in a pure state. He succeeded by heating the metal with powdered coal in a crucible which had previously been manufactured from clay suitable for the purpose.

He then worked this steel, which is malleable both when hot or cold, with the hammer. Neb and Pencroft, cleverly directed, made hatchets, which, heated red-hot, and plunged suddenly into cold water, acquired an excellent temper.

Other instruments, of course roughly fashioned, were also manufactured; blades for planes, axes, hatchets, pieces of steel to be transformed into saws, chisels; then iron for spades, pickaxes, hammers, nails, etc. At last, on the 5th of May, the metallic period ended, the smiths returned to the Chimneys, and new work would soon authorise them to take a fresh title.

Chapter XVI

THE QUESTION OF A DWELLING IS AGAIN DISCUSSED—
PENCROFT'S FANCIES—EXPLORING TO THE NORTH OF THE LAKE—
THE NORTHERN EDGE OF THE PLATEAU—SNAKES—EXTREMITY
OF THE LAKE—TOP'S UNEASINESS—TOP SWIMMING—
A COMBAT UNDER THE WATER—THE DUGONG

IT WAS THE 6TH OF MAY, A DAY WHICH CORRESPONDS TO THE 6TH OF NOVEMBER IN THE countries of the northern hemisphere. The sky had been obscured for some days, and it was of importance to make preparations for the winter. However, the temperature was not as yet much lower, and a centigrade thermometer, transported to Lincoln Island, would still have marked an average of ten to twelve degrees above zero. This was not surprising, since Lincoln Island, probably situated between the thirty-fifth and fortieth parallel, would be subject, in the southern hemisphere, to the same climate as Sicily or Greece in the northern hemisphere. But as Greece and Sicily have severe cold, producing snow and ice, so doubtless would Lincoln Island in the severest part of the winter, and it was advisable to provide against it.

In any case if cold did not yet threaten them, the rainy season would begin, and on this lonely island, exposed to all the fury of the elements, in mid-ocean, bad weather would be frequent, and probably terrible. The question of a more comfortable dwelling than the Chimneys must therefore be seriously considered and promptly resolved on.

Pencroft, naturally, had some predilection for the retreat which he had discovered, but he well understood that another must be found. The Chimneys had been already visited by the sea, under circumstances which are known, and it would not do to be exposed again to a similar accident.

"Besides," added Cyrus Harding, who this day was talking of these things with his companions, "we have some precautions to take."

"Why? The island is not inhabited," said the reporter.

"That is probable," replied the engineer, "although we have not yet explored the interior; but if no human beings are found, I fear that dangerous animals may abound. It is necessary to guard against a possible attack, so that we shall not be obliged to watch every night, or to keep up a fire. And then, my friends, we must foresee everything. We are here in a part of the Pacific often frequented by Malay pirates—"

"What!" said Herbert, "at such a distance from land?"

"Yes, my boy," replied the engineer. "These pirates are bold sailors as well as formidable enemies, and we must take measures accordingly."

"Well," replied Pencroft, "we will fortify ourselves against savages with two legs as well as against savages with four. But, captain, will it not be best to explore every part of the island before undertaking anything else?"

"That would be best," added Gideon Spilett.

"Who knows if we might not find on the opposite side one of the caverns which we have searched for in vain here?"

"That is true," replied the engineer, "but you forget, my friends, that it will be necessary to establish ourselves in the neighbourhood of a water-course, and that, from the summit of Mount Franklin, we could not see towards the west, either stream or river. Here, on the contrary, we are placed between the Mercy and Lake Grant, an advantage which must not be neglected. And, besides, this side, looking towards the east, is not exposed as the other is to the trade-winds, which in this hemisphere blow from the north-west."

"Then, captain," replied the sailor, "let us build a house on the edge of the lake. Neither bricks nor tools are wanting now. After having been brick-makers, potters, smelters, and smiths, we shall surely know how to be masons!"

"Yes, my friend; but before coming to any decision we must consider the matter thoroughly. A natural dwelling would spare us much work, and would be a surer retreat, for it would be as well defended against enemies from the interior as those from outside."

"That is true, Cyrus," replied the reporter, "but we have already examined all that mass of granite, and there is not a hole, not a cranny!"

"No, not one!" added Pencroft. "Ah, if we were able to dig out a dwelling in that cliff, at a good height, so as to be out of the reach of harm, that would be capital! I can see that on the front which looks seaward, five or six rooms—"

"With windows to light them!" said Herbert, laughing.

"And a staircase to climb up to them!" added Neb.

"You are laughing," cried the sailor, "and why? What is there impossible in what I propose? Haven't we got pickaxes and spades? Won't Captain Harding be able to make powder to blow up the mine? Isn't it true, captain, that you will make powder the very day we want it?"

Cyrus Harding listened to the enthusiastic Pencroft developing his fanciful projects. To attack this mass of granite, even by a mine, was Herculean work, and it was really vexing that nature could not help them at their need. But the engineer did not reply to the sailor except by proposing to examine the cliff more attentively, from the mouth of the river to the angle which terminated it on the north.

They went out, therefore, and the exploration was made with extreme care over an extent of nearly two miles. But in no place, in the bare, straight cliff, could any cavity be found. The nests of the rock pigeons which fluttered at its summit were only, in reality, holes bored at the very top, and on the irregular edge of the granite.

It was a provoking circumstance, and as to attacking this cliff, either with pickaxe or with powder, so as to effect a sufficient excavation, it was not to be thought of. It so happened that, on all this part of the shore, Pencroft had discovered the only habitable shelter, that is to say, the Chimneys, which now had to be abandoned.

The exploration ended, the colonists found themselves at the north angle of the cliff, where it terminated in long slopes which died away on the shore. From this place, to its extreme limit in the west, it only formed a sort of declivity, a thick mass of stones, earth, and sand, bound together by plants, bushes, and grass, inclined at an angle of only forty-five degrees. Clumps of trees grew on these slopes, which were also carpeted with thick grass. But the vegetation did not extend far, and a long, sandy plain, which began at the foot of these slopes, reached to the beach.

Cyrus Harding thought, not without reason, that the overplus of the lake must overflow on this side. The excess of water furnished by the Red Creek must also escape by some channel or other. Now the engineer had not yet found this channel on any part of the shore already explored, that is to say, from the mouth of the stream on the west of Prospect Heights.

The engineer now proposed to his companions to climb the slope, and to return to the Chimneys by the heights, while exploring the northern and eastern shores of the lake. The proposal was accepted, and in a few minutes Herbert and Neb were on the upper plateau. Cyrus Harding, Gideon Spilett, and Pencroft followed with more sedate steps.

The beautiful sheet of water glittered through the trees under the rays of the sun. In this direction the country was charming. The eye feasted on the groups of trees. Some old trunks, bent with age, showed black against the verdant grass which covered the ground. Crowds of brilliant cockatoos screamed among the branches, moving prisms, hopping from one bough to another.

The settlers instead of going directly to the north bank of the lake, made a circuit round the edge of the plateau, so as to join the mouth of the creek on its left bank. It was a detour of more than a mile and a half. Walking was easy, for the trees widely spread, left a considerable space between them. The fertile zone evidently stopped at this point, and vegetation would be less vigorous in the part between the course of the creek and the Mercy.

Cyrus Harding and his companions walked over this new ground with great care. Bows, arrows, and sticks with sharp iron points were their only weapons. However, no wild beast showed itself, and it was probable that these animals frequented rather the thick forests in the south; but the settlers had the disagreeable surprise of seeing Top stop before a snake of great size, measuring from fourteen to fifteen feet in length. Neb killed it by a blow from his stick. Cyrus Harding examined the reptile, and declared it not venomous, for it belonged to that species of diamond serpents which the natives of New South Wales rear. But it was possible that others existed whose bite was mortal, such as the deaf vipers with forked tails, which rise up under the feet, or those winged snakes, furnished with two ears, which enable them to proceed with great rapidity. Top, the first moment of surprise over, began a reptile chase with such eagerness, that they feared for his safety. His master called him back directly.

The mouth of the Red Creek, at the place where it entered into the lake, was soon reached. The explorers recognised on the opposite shore the point which they had visited on their descent from Mount Franklin. Cyrus Harding ascertained that the flow of water into it from the creek was considerable. Nature must therefore have provided some place for the escape of the overplus. This doubtless formed a fall, which, if it could be discovered, would be of great use.

The colonists, walking apart, but not straying far from each other, began to skirt the edge of the lake, which was very steep. The water appeared to be full of fish, and Pencroft resolved to make some fishing-rods, so as to try and catch some.

The north-east point was first to be doubled. It might have been supposed that the discharge of water was at this place, for the extremity of the lake was almost on a level with the edge of the plateau. But no signs of this were discovered, and the colonists continued to explore the bank, which, after a slight bend, descended parallel to the shore.

On this side the banks were less woody, but clumps of trees, here and there, added to the picturesqueness of the country. Lake Grant was viewed from thence in all its extent, and no breath disturbed the surface of its waters. Top, in beating the bushes, put up flocks of birds of different kinds, which Gideon Spilett and Herbert saluted with arrows. One was hit by the lad, and fell into some marshy grass. Top rushed forward, and brought a beautiful swimming bird, of a slate colour, short beak, very developed frontal plate, and wings edged with white. It was a "coot," the size of a large partridge, belonging to the group of macro-dactyls which form the transition between the order of wading birds and that of palmipeds. Sorry game, in truth, and its flavour is far from pleasant. But Top was not so particular in these things as his masters, and it was agreed that the coot should be for his supper.

The settlers were now following the eastern bank of the lake, and they would not be long in reaching the part which they already knew. The engineer was much surprised at not seeing any indication of the discharge of water. The reporter and the sailor talked with him, and he could not conceal his astonishment.

At this moment Top, who had been very quiet till then, gave signs of agitation. The intelligent animal went backwards and forwards on the shore, stopped suddenly, and looked at the water, one paw raised, as if he was pointing at some invisible game; then he barked furiously, and was suddenly silent.

Neither Cyrus Harding nor his companions had at first paid any attention to Top's be-haviour; but the dog's barking soon became so frequent that the engineer noticed it.

"What is there there, Top?" he asked.

The dog bounded towards his master, seeming to be very uneasy, and then rushed again towards the bank. Then, all at once, he plunged into the lake.

"Here, Top!" cried Cyrus Harding, who did not like his dog to venture into the treacherous water.

"What's happening down there?" asked Pencroft, examining the surface of the lake.

"Top smells some amphibious creature," replied Herbert.

"An alligator, perhaps," said the reporter.

"I do not think so," replied Harding. "Alligators are only met with in regions less el-evated in latitude."

Meanwhile Top had returned at his master's call, and had regained the shore: but he could not stay quiet; he plunged in among the tall grass, and guided by instinct, he ap-peared to follow some invisible being which was slipping along under the surface of the water. However the water was calm, not a ripple disturbed its surface. Several times the settlers stopped on the bank, and observed it attentively. Nothing appeared. There was some mystery there.

The engineer was puzzled.

"Let us pursue this exploration to the end," said he.

Half-an-hour after they had all arrived at the south-east angle of the lake, on Prospect Heights. At this point the examination of the banks of the lake was considered finished, and yet the engineer had not been able to discover how and where the waters were dis-charged. "There is no doubt this overflow exists," he repeated, "and since it is not visible it must go through the granite cliff at the west!"

"But what importance do you attach to knowing that, my dear Cyrus?" asked Gideon Spilett.

"Considerable importance," replied the engineer; "for if it flows through the cliff there is probably some cavity, which it would be easy to render habitable after turning away the water."

"But is it not possible, captain, that the water flows away at the bottom of the lake," said Herbert, "and that it reaches the sea by some subterranean passage?"

"That might be," replied the engineer, "and should it be so we shall be obliged to build our house ourselves, since nature has not done it for us."

The colonists were about to begin to traverse the plateau to return to the Chimneys, when Top gave new signs of agitation. He barked with fury, and before his master could restrain him, he had plunged a second time into the lake.

All ran towards the bank. The dog was already more than twenty feet off, and Cyrus was calling him back, when an enormous head emerged from the water, which did not appear to be deep in that place.

Herbert recognised directly the species of amphibian to which the tapering head, with large eyes, and adorned with long silky mustaches, belonged.

"A lamantin!" he cried.

It was not a lamantin, but one of that species of the order of cetaceans, which bear the name of the "dugong," for its nostrils were open at the upper part of its snout. The enormous animal rushed on the dog, who tried to escape by returning towards the shore. His master could do nothing to save him, and before Gideon Spilett or Herbert thought of bending their bows, Top, seized by the dugong, had disappeared beneath the water.

Neb, his iron-tipped spear in his hand, wished to go to Top's help, and attack the dangerous animal in its own element.

"No, Neb," said the engineer, restraining his courageous servant.

Meanwhile, a struggle was going on beneath the water, an inexplicable struggle, for in his situation Top could not possibly resist; and judging by the bubbling of the surface it must be also a terrible struggle, and could not but terminate in the death of the dog! But suddenly, in the middle of a foaming circle, Top reappeared. Thrown in the air by some unknown power, he rose ten feet above the surface of the lake, fell again into the midst of the agitated waters, and then soon gained the shore, without any severe wounds, miraculously saved.

Cyrus Harding and his companions could not understand it. What was not less inexplicable was that the struggle still appeared to be going on. Doubtless, the dugong, attacked by some powerful animal, after having released the dog, was fighting on its own account. But it did not last long. The water became red with blood, and the body of the dugong, emerging from the sheet of scarlet which spread around, soon stranded on a little beach at the south angle of the lake. The colonists ran towards it. The dugong was dead. It was an enormous animal, fifteen or sixteen feet long, and must have weighed from three to four thousand pounds. At its neck was a wound, which appeared to have been produced by a sharp blade.

What could the amphibious creature have been, who, by this terrible blow had destroyed the formidable dugong? No one could tell, and much interested in this incident, Harding and his companions returned to the Chimneys.

Chapter XVII

VISIT TO THE LAKE—THE INDICATING CURRENT—CYRUS
HARDING'S PROJECTS—THE FAT OF THE DUGONG—EMPLOYING
SHISTOSE PYRITES—SULPHATE OF IRON—HOW GLYCERINE IS
MADE—SOAP—SALTPETER—SULPHURIC ACID—
AZOTIC ACID—THE NEW FALL

THE NEXT DAY, THE 7TH OF MAY, HARDING AND GIDEON SPILETT, LEAVING NEB TO PRE-
pare breakfast, climbed Prospect Heights, while Herbert and Pencroft ascended by
the river, to renew their store of wood.

The engineer and the reporter soon reached the little beach on which the dugong had
been stranded. Already flocks of birds had attacked the mass of flesh, and had to be driven
away with stones, for Cyrus wished to keep the fat for the use of the colony. As to the animal's flesh, it would furnish excellent food, for in the islands of the Malay Archipelago
and elsewhere, it is especially reserved for the table of the native princes. But that was
Neb's affair.

At this moment Cyrus Harding had other thoughts. He was much interested in the incident of the day before. He wished to penetrate the mystery of that submarine combat,
and to ascertain what monster could have given the dugong so strange a wound. He remained at the edge of the lake, looking, observing; but nothing appeared under the tranquil waters, which sparkled in the first rays of the rising sun.

At the beach, on which lay the body of the dugong, the water was tolerably shallow,
but from this point the bottom of the lake sloped gradually, and it was probable that the
depth was considerable in the centre. The lake might be considered as a large centre basin,
which was filled by the water from the Red Creek.

"Well, Cyrus," said the reporter, "there seems to be nothing suspicious in this water."

"No, my dear Spilett," replied the engineer, "and I really do not know how to account
for the incident of yesterday."

"I acknowledge," returned Spilett, "that the wound given this creature is, at least,
very strange, and I cannot explain either how Top was so vigorously cast up out of the
water. One could have thought that a powerful arm hurled him up, and that the same arm
with a dagger killed the dugong!"

"Yes," replied the engineer, who had become thoughtful; "there is something there
that I cannot understand. But do you better understand either, my dear Spilett, in what way
I was saved myself—how I was drawn from the waves, and carried to the downs? No! Is
it not true? Now, I feel sure that there is some mystery there, which, doubtless, we shall
discover some day. Let us observe, but do not dwell on these singular incidents before our
companions. Let us keep our remarks to ourselves, and continue our work."

It will be remembered that the engineer had not as yet been able to discover the place
where the surplus water escaped, but he knew it must exist somewhere. He was much surprised to see a strong current at this place. By throwing in some bits of wood he found that

it set towards the southern angle. He followed the current, and arrived at the south point of the lake.

There was there a sort of depression in the water, as if it was suddenly lost in some fissure in the ground.

Harding listened; placing his ear to the level of the lake, he very distinctly heard the noise of a subterranean fall.

"There," said he, rising, "is the discharge of the water; there, doubtless, by a passage in the granite cliff, it joins the sea, through cavities which we can use to our profit. Well, I can find it!"

The engineer cut a long branch, stripped it of its leaves, and plunging it into the angle between the two banks, he found that there was a large hole one foot only beneath the surface of the water. This hole was the opening so long looked for in vain, and the force of the current was such that the branch was torn from the engineer's hands and disappeared.

"There is no doubt about it now," repeated Harding. "There is the outlet, and I will lay it open to view!"

"How?" asked Gideon Spilett.

"By lowering the level of the water of the lake three feet."

"And how will you lower the level?"

"By opening another outlet larger than this."

"At what place, Cyrus?"

"At the part of the bank nearest the coast."

"But it is a mass of granite!" observed Spilett.

"Well," replied Cyrus Harding, "I will blow up the granite, and the water escaping, will subside, so as to lay bare this opening—"

"And make a waterfall, by falling on to the beach," added the reporter.

"A fall that we shall make use of!" replied Cyrus. "Come, come!"

The engineer hurried away his companion, whose confidence in Harding was such that he did not doubt the enterprise would succeed. And yet, how was this granite wall to be opened without powder, and with imperfect instruments? Was not this work upon which the engineer was so bent above their strength?

When Harding and the reporter entered the Chimneys, they found Herbert and Pencroft unloading their raft of wood.

"The woodmen have just finished, captain." said the sailor, laughing, "and when you want masons—"

"Masons—no, but chemists," replied the engineer.

"Yes," added the reporter, "we are going to blow up the island—"

"Blow up the island?" cried Pencroft.

"Part of it, at least," replied Spilett.

"Listen to me, my friends," said the engineer. And he made known to them the result of his observations.

According to him, a cavity, more or less considerable, must exist in the mass of granite which supported Prospect Heights, and he intended to penetrate into it. To do this, the opening through which the water rushed must first be cleared, and the level lowered by making a larger outlet. Therefore an explosive substance must be manufactured, which would make a deep trench in some other part of the shore. This was what Harding was going to attempt with the minerals which nature placed at his disposal.

It is useless to say with what enthusiasm all, especially Pencroft, received this project. To employ great means, open the granite, create a cascade, that suited the sailor. And he would just as soon be a chemist as a mason or boot-maker, since the engineer wanted chemicals. He would be all that they liked, "even a professor of dancing and deportment," said he to Neb, if that was ever necessary.

Neb and Pencroft were first of all told to extract the grease from the dugong, and to keep the flesh, which was destined for food. Such perfect confidence had they in the engineer, that they set out directly, without even asking a question. A few minutes after them, Cyrus Harding, Herbert, and Gideon Spilett, dragging the hurdle, went towards the vein of coals, where those shistose pyrites abound which are met with in the most recent transition soil, and of which Harding had already found a specimen. All the day being employed in carrying a quantity of these stones to the Chimneys, by evening they had several tons.

The next day, the 8th of May, the engineer began his manipulations. These shistose pyrites being composed principally of coal, flint, alumina, and sulphuret of iron—the latter in excess—it was necessary to separate the sulphuret of iron, and transform it into sulphate as rapidly as possible. The sulphate obtained, the sulphuric acid could then be extracted.

This was the object to be attained. Sulphuric acid is one of the agents the most frequently employed, and the manufacturing importance of a nation can be measured by the consumption which is made of it. This acid would later be of great use to the settlers, in the manufacturing of candles, tanning skins, etc., but this time the engineer reserved it for another use.

Cyrus Harding chose, behind the Chimneys, a site where the ground was perfectly level. On this ground he placed a layer of branches and chopped wood, on which were piled some pieces of shistose pyrites, buttressed one against the other, the whole being covered with a thin layer of pyrites, previously reduced to the size of a nut.

This done, they set fire to the wood, the heat was communicated to the shist, which soon kindled, since it contains coal and sulphur. Then new layers of bruised pyrites were arranged so as to form an immense heap, the exterior of which was covered with earth and grass, several air-holes being left, as if it was a stack of wood which was to be carbonised to make charcoal.

They then left the transformation to complete itself, and it would not take less than ten or twelve days for the sulphuret of iron to be changed to sulphate of iron and the alumina into sulphate of alumina, two equally soluble substances, the others, flint, burned coal, and cinders, not being so.

While this chemical work was going on, Cyrus Harding proceeded with other operations, which were pursued with more than zeal—it was eagerness.

Neb and Pencroft had taken away the fat from the dugong, and placed it in large earthen pots. It was then necessary to separate the glycerine from the fat by saponifying it. Now, to obtain this result, it had to be treated either with soda or lime. In fact, one or other of these substances, after having attacked the fat, would form a soap by separating the glycerine, and it was just this glycerine which the engineer wished to obtain. There was no want of lime, only treatment by lime would give calcareous soap, insoluble, and consequently useless, while treatment by soda would furnish, on the contrary, a soluble soap, which could be put to domestic use. Now, a practical man, like Cyrus Harding, would rather try to obtain soda. Was this difficult? No; for marine plants abounded on the shore, glass-wort, ficoides, and all those fucaceae which form wrack. A large quantity of these plants was collected, first dried, then burned in holes in the open air. The combustion of these plants was kept up for several days, and the result was a compact grey mass, which has been long known under the name of "natural soda."

This obtained, the engineer treated the fat with soda, which gave both a soluble soap and that neutral substance glycerine.

But this was not all. Cyrus Harding still needed, in view of his future preparation, another substance, azote of potash, which is better known under the name of salt niter, or of saltpeter.

Cyrus Harding could have manufactured this substance by treating the carbonate of potash, which would be easily extracted from the cinders of the vegetables, by azotic acid. But this acid was wanting, and he would have been in some difficulty, if nature had not happily furnished the saltpeter, without giving them any other trouble than that of picking it up. Herbert found a vein of it at the foot of Mount Franklin, and they had nothing to do but purify this salt.

These different works lasted a week. They were finished before the transformation of the sulphuret into sulphate of iron had been accomplished. During the following days the settlers had time to construct a furnace of bricks of a particular arrangement, to serve for the distillation of the sulphate of iron when it had been obtained. All this was finished about the 18th of May, nearly at the time when the chemical transformation terminated. Gideon Spilett, Herbert, Neb, and Pencroft, skilfully directed by the engineer, had become most clever workmen. Before all masters, necessity is the one most listened to, and who teaches the best.

When the heap of pyrites had been entirely reduced by fire, the result of the operation, consisting of sulphate of iron, sulphate of alumina, flint, remains of coal, and cinders was placed in a basinful of water. They stirred this mixture, let it settle, then decanted it, and obtained a clear liquid containing in solution sulphate of iron and sulphate of alumina, the other matters remaining solid, since they are insoluble. Lastly, this liquid being partly evaporated, crystals of sulphate of iron were deposited, and the not evaporated liquid, which contained the sulphate of alumina, was thrown away.

Cyrus Harding had now at his disposal a large quantity of these sulphate of iron crystals, from which the sulphuric acid had to be extracted. The making of sulphuric acid is a very expensive manufacture. Considerable works are necessary—a special set of tools, an apparatus of platina, leaden chambers, unassailable by the acid, and in which the transformation is performed, etc. The engineer had none of these at his disposal, but he knew that, in Bohemia especially, sulphuric acid is manufactured by very simple means, which have also the advantage of producing it to a superior degree of concentration. It is thus that the acid known under the name of Nordhausen acid is made.

To obtain sulphuric acid, Cyrus Harding had only one operation to make, to calcine the sulphate of iron crystals in a close vase, so that the sulphuric acid should distil in vapour, which vapour, by condensation, would produce the acid.

The crystals were placed in pots, and the heat from the furnace would distil the sulphuric acid. The operation was successfully completed, and on the 20th of May, twelve days after commencing it, the engineer was the possessor of the agent which later he hoped to use in so many different ways.

Now, why did he wish for this agent? Simply to produce azotic acid; and that was easy, since saltpeter, attacked by sulphuric acid, gives this acid by distillation.

But, after all, how was he going to employ this azotic acid? His companions were still ignorant of this, for he had not informed them of the result at which he aimed.

However, the engineer had nearly accomplished his purpose, and by a last operation he would procure the substance which had given so much trouble.

Taking some azotic acid, he mixed it with glycerine, which had been previously concentrated by evaporation, subjected to the water-bath, and he obtained, without even employing a refrigerant mixture, several pints of an oily yellow mixture.

This last operation Cyrus Harding had made alone, in a retired place, at a distance from the Chimneys, for he feared the danger of an explosion, and when he showed a bottle of this liquid to his friends, he contented himself with saying—

"Here is nitro-glycerine!"

It was really this terrible production, of which the explosive power is perhaps tenfold that of ordinary powder, and which has already caused so many accidents. However, since a way has been found to transform it into dynamite, that is to say, to mix with it some solid substance, clay or sugar, porous enough to hold it, the dangerous liquid has been used with some security. But dynamite was not yet known at the time when the settlers worked on Lincoln Island.

"And is it that liquid that is going to blow up our rocks?" said Pencroft incredulously.

"Yes, my friend," replied the engineer, "and this nitro-glycerine will produce so much the more effect, as the granite is extremely hard, and will oppose a greater resistance to the explosion."

"And when shall we see this, captain?"

"To-morrow, as soon as we have dug a hole for the mine," replied the engineer.

The next day, the 21st of May, at daybreak, the miners went to the point which formed the eastern shore of Lake Grant, and was only five hundred feet from the coast. At this place, the plateau inclined downwards from the waters, which were only restrained by their granite case. Therefore, if this case was broken, the water would escape by the opening and form a stream, which, flowing over the inclined surface of the plateau, would rush on to the beach. Consequently, the level of the lake would be greatly lowered, and the opening where the water escaped would be exposed, which was their final aim.

Under the engineer's directions, Pencroft, armed with a pickaxe, which he handled skilfully and vigourously, attacked the granite. The hole was made on the point of the shore, slanting, so that it should meet a much lower level than that of the water of the lake. In this way the explosive force, by scattering the rock, would open a large place for the water to rush out.

The work took some time, for the engineer, wishing to produce a great effect, intended to devote not less than seven quarts of nitro-glycerine to the operation. But Pencroft, relieved by Neb, did so well, that towards four o'clock in the evening, the mine was finished.

Now the question of setting fire to the explosive substance was raised. Generally, nitro-glycerine is ignited by amorces of fulminate, which in bursting cause the explosion. A shock is therefore needed to produce the explosion, for, simply lighted, this substance would burn without exploding.

Cyrus Harding would certainly have been able to fabricate an amorce. In default of fulminate, he could easily obtain a substance similar to gun-cotton, since he had azotic acid at his disposal. This substance, pressed in a cartridge, and introduced among the nitro-glycerine, would burst by means of a match, and cause the explosion.

But Cyrus Harding knew that nitro-glycerine would explode by a shock. He resolved to employ this means, and try another way, if this did not succeed.

In fact, the blow of a hammer on a few drops of nitro-glycerine, spread out on a hard surface, was enough to create an explosion. But the operator could not be there to give the blow, without becoming a victim to the operation. Harding, therefore, thought of suspending a mass of iron, weighing several pounds, by means of a fibre, to an upright just above the mine. Another long fibre, previously impregnated with sulphur, was attached to the middle of the first, by one end, while the other lay on the ground several feet distant from the mine. The second fibre being set on fire, it would burn till it reached the first. This catching fire in its turn, would break, and the mass of iron would fall on the nitro-glycerine. This apparatus being then arranged, the engineer, after having sent his companions to a distance, filled the hole, so that the nitro-glycerine was on a level with the opening; then he threw a few drops of it on the surface of the rock, above which the mass of iron was already suspended.

This done, Harding lit the end of the sulphured fibre, and leaving the place, he returned with his companions to the Chimneys.

The fibre was intended to burn five and twenty minutes, and, in fact, five and twenty minutes afterwards a most tremendous explosion was heard. The island appeared to tremble to its very foundation. Stones were projected in the air as if by the irruption of a volcano. The shock produced by the displacing of the air was such, that the rocks of the Chimneys shook. The settlers, although they were more than two miles from the mine, were thrown on the ground.

They rose, climbed the plateau, and ran towards the place where the bank of the lake must have been shattered by the explosion.

A cheer escaped them! A large rent was seen in the granite! A rapid stream of water rushed foaming across the plateau and dashed down a height of three hundred feet on to the beach!

Chapter XVIII

PENCROFT NOW DOUBTS NOTHING—THE OUTLET OF THE LAKE—
A SUBTERRANEAN DESCENT—THE WAY THROUGH THE GRANITE—
TOP DISAPPEARS—THE CENTRAL CAVERN—THE LOWER WELL—
MYSTERY—USING THE PICKAXE—THE RETURN

CYRUS HARDING'S PROJECT HAD SUCCEEDED, BUT, ACCORDING TO HIS USUAL HABIT HE showed no satisfaction; with closed lips and a fixed look, he remained motionless. Herbert was in ecstasies, Neb bounded with joy, Pencroft nodded his great head, murmuring these words—

"Come, our engineer gets on capitally!"

The nitro-glycerine had indeed acted powerfully. The opening which it had made was so large that the volume of water which escaped through this new outlet was at least treble that which before passed through the old one. The result was, that a short time after the operation the level of the lake would be lowered two feet, or more.

The settlers went to the Chimneys to take some pickaxes, iron-tipped spears, string made of fibres, flint and steel; they then returned to the plateau, Top accompanying them.

On the way the sailor could not help saying to the engineer—

"Don't you think, captain, that by means of that charming liquid you have made, one could blow up the whole of our island?"

"Without any doubt, the island, continents, and the world itself," replied the engineer. "It is only a question of quantity."

"Then could you not use this nitro-glycerine for loading fire-arms?" asked the sailor.

"No, Pencroft; for it is too explosive a substance. But it would be easy to make some gun-cotton, or even ordinary powder, as we have azotic acid, saltpeter, sulphur, and coal. Unhappily, it is the guns which we have not got."

"Oh, captain," replied the sailor, "with a little determination—"

Pencroft had erased the word "impossible" from the dictionary of Lincoln Island.

The settlers, having arrived at Prospect Heights, went immediately towards that point of the lake near which was the old opening now uncovered. This outlet had now become practicable, since the water no longer rushed through it, and it would doubtless be easy to explore the interior.

In a few minutes the settlers had reached the lower point of the lake, and a glance showed them that the object had been attained.

In fact, in the side of the lake, and now above the surface of the water, appeared the long-looked-for opening. A narrow ridge, left bare by the retreat of the water, allowed them to approach it. This orifice was nearly twenty feet in width, but scarcely two in height. It was like the mouth of a drain at the edge of the pavement, and therefore did not offer an easy passage to the settlers; but Neb and Pencroft, taking their pickaxes, soon made it of a suitable height.

The engineer then approached, and found that the sides of the opening, in its upper part at least, had not a slope of more than from thirty to thirty-five degrees. It was there-fore practicable, and, provided that the declivity did not increase, it would be easy to de-scend even to the level of the sea. If then, as was probable, some vast cavity existed in the interior of the granite, it might, perhaps, be of great use.

"Well, captain, what are we stopping for?" asked the sailor, impatient to enter the nar-row passage. "You see Top has got before us!"

"Very well," replied the engineer. "But we must see our way. Neb, go and cut some resinous branches."

Neb and Herbert ran to the edge of the lake, shaded with pines and other green trees, and soon returned with some branches, which they made into torches. The torches were lighted with flint and steel, and Cyrus Harding leading, the settlers ventured into the dark passage, which the overplus of the lake had formerly filled.

Contrary to what might have been supposed, the diameter of the passage increased as the explorers proceeded, so that they very soon were able to stand upright. The granite, worn by the water for an infinite time, was very slippery, and falls were to be dreaded. But the settlers were all attached to each other by a cord, as is frequently done in ascending mountains. Happily some projections of the granite, forming regular steps, made the de-scent less perilous. Drops, still hanging from the rocks, shone here and there under the light of the torches, and the explorers guessed that the sides were clothed with innumer-able stalactites. The engineer examined this black granite. There was not a stratum, not a break in it. The mass was compact, and of an extremely close grain. The passage dated, then, from the very origin of the island. It was not the water which little by little had hol-lowed it. Pluto and not Neptune had bored it with his own hand, and on the wall traces of an irruptive work could be distinguished, which all the washing of the water had not been able totally to efface.

The settlers descended very slowly. They could not but feel a certain awe, in this ven-turing into these unknown depths, for the first time visited by human beings. They did not speak, but they thought; and the thought came to more than one, that some polypus or other gigantic cephalopod might inhabit the interior cavities, which were in communica-tion with the sea. However, Top kept at the head of the little band, and they could rely on the sagacity of the dog, who would not fail to give the alarm if there was any need for it.

After having descended about a hundred feet, following a winding road, Harding who was walking on before, stopped, and his companions came up with him. The place where they had halted was wider, so as to form a cavern of moderate dimensions. Drops of water fell from the vault, but that did not prove that they oozed through the rock. They were simply the last traces left by the torrent which had so long thundered through this cavity, and the air there was pure though slightly damp, but producing no mephitic exhalation.

"Well, my dear Cyrus," said Gideon Spilett, "here is a very secure retreat, well hid in the depths of the rock, but it is, however, uninhabitable."

"Why uninhabitable?" asked the sailor.

"Because it is too small and too dark."

"Couldn't we enlarge it, hollow it out, make openings to let in light and air?" replied Pencroft, who now thought nothing impossible.

"Let us go on with our exploration," said Cyrus Harding. "Perhaps lower down, na-ture will have spared us this labor."

"We have only gone a third of the way," observed Herbert.

"Nearly a third," replied Harding, "for we have descended a hundred feet from the opening, and it is not impossible that a hundred feet farther down—"

"Where is Top?" asked Neb, interrupting his master.

They searched the cavern, but the dog was not there.

"Most likely he has gone on," said Pencroft.

"Let us join him," replied Harding.

The descent was continued. The engineer carefully observed all the deviations of the passage, and notwithstanding so many detours, he could easily have given an account of its general direction, which went towards the sea.

The settlers had gone some fifty feet farther, when their attention was attracted by distant sounds which came up from the depths. They stopped and listened. These sounds, carried through the passage as through an acoustic tube, came clearly to the ear.

"That is Top barking!" cried Herbert.

"Yes," replied Pencroft, "and our brave dog is barking furiously!"

"We have our iron-tipped spears," said Cyrus Harding. "Keep on your guard, and forward!"

"It is becoming more and more interesting," murmured Gideon Spilett in the sailor's ear, who nodded. Harding and his companions rushed to the help of their dog. Top's barking became more and more perceptible, and it seemed strangely fierce. Was he engaged in a struggle with some animal whose retreat he had disturbed? Without thinking of the danger to which they might be exposed, the explorers were now impelled by an irresistible curiosity, and in a few minutes, sixteen feet lower they rejoined Top.

There the passage ended in a vast and magnificent cavern. Top was running backwards and forwards, barking furiously. Pencroft and Neb, waving their torches, threw the light into every crevice; and at the same time, Harding, Gideon Spilett, and Herbert, their spears raised, were ready for any emergency which might arise. The enormous cavern was empty. The settlers explored it in every direction. There was nothing there, not an animal, not a human being; and yet Top continued to bark. Neither caresses nor threats could make him be silent.

"There must be a place somewhere, by which the waters of the lake reached the sea," said the engineer.

"Of course," replied Pencroft, "and we must take care not to tumble into a hole."

"Go, Top, go!" cried Harding.

The dog, excited by his master's words, ran towards the extremity of the cavern, and there redoubled his barking.

They followed him, and by the light of the torches, perceived the mouth of a regular well in the granite. It was by this that the water escaped; and this time it was not an oblique and practicable passage, but a perpendicular well, into which it was impossible to venture.

The torches were held over the opening: nothing could be seen. Harding took a lighted branch, and threw it into the abyss. The blazing resin, whose illuminating power increased still more by the rapidity of its fall, lighted up the interior of the well, but yet nothing appeared. The flame then went out with a slight hiss, which showed that it had reached the water, that is to say, the level of the sea.

The engineer, calculating the time employed in its fall, was able to calculate the depth of the well, which was found to be about ninety feet.

The floor of the cavern must thus be situated ninety feet above the level of the sea.

"Here is our dwelling," said Cyrus Harding.

"But it was occupied by some creature," replied Gideon Spilett, whose curiosity was not yet satisfied.

"Well, the creature, amphibious or otherwise, has made off through this opening," replied the engineer, "and has left the place for us."

"Never mind," added the sailor, "I should like very much to be Top, just for a quarter of an hour, for he doesn't bark for nothing!"

Cyrus Harding looked at his dog, and those of his companions who were near him might have heard him murmur these words—

"Yes, I believe that Top knows more than we do about a great many things."

However, the wishes of the settlers were for the most part satisfied. Chance, aided by the marvelous sagacity of their leader, had done them great service. They had now at their disposal a vast cavern, the size of which could not be properly calculated by the feeble light of their torches, but it would certainly be easy to divide it into rooms, by means of brick partitions, or to use it, if not as a house, at least as a spacious apartment. The water which had left it could not return. The place was free.

Two difficulties remained; firstly, the possibility of lighting this excavation in the midst of solid rock; secondly, the necessity of rendering the means of access more easy. It was useless to think of lighting it from above, because of the enormous thickness of the granite which composed the ceiling; but perhaps the outer wall next the sea might be pierced. Cyrus Harding, during the descent, had roughly calculated its obliqueness, and consequently the length of the passage, and was therefore led to believe that the outer wall could not be very thick. If light was thus obtained, so would a means of access, for it would be as easy to pierce a door as windows, and to establish an exterior ladder.

Harding made known his ideas to his companions.

"Then, captain, let us set to work!" replied Pencroft. "I have my pickaxe, and I shall soon make my way through this wall. Where shall I strike?"

"Here," replied the engineer, showing the sturdy sailor a considerable recess in the side, which would much diminish the thickness.

Pencroft attacked the granite, and for half-an-hour, by the light of the torches, he made the splinters fly around him. Neb relieved him, then Spilett took Neb's place.

This work had lasted two hours, and they began to fear that at this spot the wall would not yield to the pickaxe, when at a last blow, given by Gideon Spilett, the instrument, passing through the rock, fell outside.

"Hurrah! hurrah!" cried Pencroft.

The wall only measured there three feet in thickness.

Harding applied his eye to the aperture, which overlooked the ground from a height of eighty feet. Before him was extended the sea-coast, the islet, and beyond the open sea.

Floods of light entered by this hole, inundating the splendid cavern and producing a magic effect! On its left side it did not measure more than thirty feet in height and breadth, but on the right it was enormous, and its vaulted roof rose to a height of more than eighty feet.

In some places granite pillars, irregularly disposed, supported the vaulted roof, as those in the nave of a cathedral, here forming lateral piers, there elliptical arches, adorned with pointed mouldings, losing themselves in dark bays, amid the fantastic arches of which glimpses could be caught in the shade, covered with a profusion of projections formed like so many pendants. This cavern was a picturesque mixture of all the styles of Byzantine, Roman, or Gothic architecture ever produced by the hand of man. And yet this was only the work of nature. She alone had hollowed this fairy Alhambra in a mass of granite.

The settlers were overwhelmed with admiration. Where they had only expected to find a narrow cavity, they had found a sort of marvelous palace, and Neb had taken off his hat, as if he had been transported into a temple!

Cries of admiration issued from every mouth. Hurrahs resounded, and the echo was repeated again and again till it died away in the dark naves.

"Ah, my friends!" exclaimed Cyrus Harding, "when we have lighted the interior of this place, and have arranged our rooms and storehouses in the left part, we shall still have this splendid cavern, which we will make our study and our museum!"

"And we will call it?—" asked Herbert.

"Granite House," replied Harding; a name which his companions again saluted with a cheer.

The torches were now almost consumed, and as they were obliged to return by the passage to reach the summit of the plateau, it was decided to put off the work necessary for the arrangement of their new dwelling till the next day.

Before departing, Cyrus Harding leaned once more over the dark well, which descended perpendicularly to the level of the sea. He listened attentively. No noise was heard, not even that of the water, which the undulations of the surge must sometimes agitate in its depths. A flaming branch was again thrown in. The sides of the well were lighted up for an instant, but as at the first time, nothing suspicious was seen.

If some marine monster had been surprised unawares by the retreat of the water, he would by this time have regained the sea by the subterranean passage, before the new opening had been offered to him.

Meanwhile, the engineer was standing motionless, his eyes fixed on the gulf, without uttering a word.

The sailor approached him, and touching his arm, "Captain!" said he.

"What do you want, my friend?" asked the engineer, as if he had returned from the land of dreams.

"The torches will soon go out."

"Forward!" replied Cyrus Harding.

The little band left the cavern and began to ascend through the dark passage. Top closed the rear, still growling every now and then. The ascent was painful enough. The settlers rested a few minutes in the upper grotto, which made a sort of landing-place half-way up the long granite staircase. Then they began to climb again.

Soon fresher air was felt. The drops of water, dried by evaporation, no longer sparkled on the walls. The flaring torches began to grow dim. The one which Neb carried went out, and if they did not wish to find their way in the dark, they must hasten.

This was done, and a little before four o'clock, at the moment when the sailor's torch went out in its turn, Cyrus Harding and his companions passed out of the passage.

Chapter XIX

CYRUS HARDING'S PROJECT—THE FRONT OF GRANITE HOUSE—
THE ROPE LADDER—PENCROFT'S DREAMS—AROMATIC HERBS—
A NATURAL WARREN—WATER FOR THE NEW DWELLING—
VIEW FROM THE WINDOWS OF GRANITE HOUSE

THE NEXT DAY, THE 22D OF MAY, THE ARRANGEMENT OF THEIR NEW DWELLING WAS commenced. In fact, the settlers longed to exchange the insufficient shelter of the Chimneys for this large and healthy retreat, in the midst of solid rock, and sheltered from the water both of the sea and sky. Their former dwelling was not, however, to be entirely abandoned, for the engineer intended to make a manufactory of it for important works. Cyrus Harding's first care was to find out the position of the front of Granite House from the outside. He went to the beach, and as the pickaxe when it escaped from the hands of the reporter must have fallen perpendicularly to the foot of the cliff, the finding it would be sufficient to show the place where the hole had been pierced in the granite.

The pickaxe was easily found, and the hole could be seen in a perpendicular line above the spot where it was stuck in the sand. Some rock pigeons were already flying in and out of the narrow opening; they evidently thought that Granite House had been discovered on purpose for them. It was the engineer's intention to divide the right portion of the cavern into several rooms, preceded by an entrance passage, and to light it by means of five windows and a door, pierced in the front. Pencroft was much pleased with the five windows, but he could not understand the use of the door, since the passage offered a natural staircase, through which it would always be easy to enter Granite House.

"My friend," replied Harding, "if it is easy for us to reach our dwelling by this passage, it will be equally easy for others besides us. I mean, on the contrary, to block up that opening, to seal it hermetically, and, if it is necessary, to completely hide the entrance, by making a dam, and thus causing the water of the lake to rise."

"And how shall we get in?" asked the sailor.

"By an outside ladder," replied Cyrus Harding, "a rope ladder, which, once drawn up, will render access to our dwelling impossible."

"But why so many precautions?" asked Pencroft. "As yet we have seen no dangerous animals. As to our island being inhabited by natives, I don't believe it!"

"Are you quite sure of that, Pencroft?" asked the engineer, looking at the sailor.

"Of course we shall not be quite sure, till we have explored it in every direction," replied Pencroft.

"Yes," said Harding, "for we know only a small portion of it as yet. But at any rate, if we have no enemies in the interior, they may come from the exterior, for parts of the Pacific are very dangerous. We must be provided against every contingency."

Cyrus Harding spoke wisely; and without making any further objection, Pencroft prepared to execute his orders.

The front of Granite House was then to be lighted by five windows and a door, besides a large bay window and some smaller oval ones, which would admit plenty of light to enter into the marvellous nave which was to be their chief room. This façade, situated at a height of eighty feet above the ground, was exposed to the east, and the rising sun saluted it with its first rays. It was found to be just at that part of the cliff which was between the projection at the mouth of the Mercy and a perpendicular line traced above the heap of rocks which formed the Chimneys. Thus the winds from the north-east would only strike it obliquely, for it was protected by the projection. Besides, until the window-frames were made, the engineer meant to close the openings with thick shutters, which would prevent either wind or rain from entering, and which could be concealed in need.

The first work was to make the openings. This would have taken too long with the pickaxe alone, and it is known that Harding was an ingenious man. He had still a quantity of nitro-glycerine at his disposal, and he employed it usefully. By means of this explosive substance the rock was broken open at the very places chosen by the engineer. Then, with the pickaxe and spade, the windows and doors were properly shaped, the jagged edges were smoothed off, and a few days after the beginning of the work, Granite House was abundantly lighted by the rising sun, whose rays penetrated into its most secret recesses. Following the plan proposed by Cyrus Harding, the space was to be divided into five compartments looking out on the sea; to the right, an entry with a door, which would meet the ladder; then a kitchen, thirty feet long; a dining-room, measuring forty feet; a sleeping-room, of equal size; and lastly, a "Visitor's room," petitioned for by Pencroft, and which was next to the great hall. These rooms, or rather this suite of rooms, would not occupy all the depth of the cave. There would be also a corridor and a store-house, in which their tools, provisions, and stores would be kept. All the productions of the island, the flora as well as the fauna, were to be there in the best possible state of preservation, and completely sheltered from the damp. There was no want of space, so that each object could be methodically arranged. Besides, the colonists had still at their disposal the little grotto above the great cavern, which was like the garret of the new dwelling.

This plan settled, it had only to be put into execution. The miners became brick-makers again, then the bricks were brought to the foot of Granite House. Till then, Harding and his companions had only entered the cavern by the long passage. This mode of communication obliged them first to climb Prospect Heights, making a detour by the river's bank, and then to descend two hundred feet through the passage, having to climb as far when they wished to return to the plateau. This was a great loss of time, and was also very fatiguing. Cyrus Harding, therefore, resolved to proceed without any further delay to the fabrication of a strong rope ladder, which, once raised, would render Granite House completely inaccessible.

This ladder was manufactured with extreme care, and its uprights, formed of the twisted fibres of a species of cane, had the strength of a thick cable. As to the rounds, they were made of a sort of red cedar, with light, strong branches; and this apparatus was wrought by the masterly hand of Pencroft.

Other ropes were made with vegetable fibres, and a sort of crane with a tackle was fixed at the door. In this way bricks could easily be raised into Granite House. The transport of the materials being thus simplified, the arrangement of the interior could begin immediately. There was no want of lime, and some thousands of bricks were there ready to be used. The framework of the partitions was soon raised, very roughly at first, and in a short time, the cave was divided into rooms and storehouses, according to the plan agreed upon.

These different works progressed rapidly under the direction of the engineer, who himself handled the hammer and the trowel. No labour came amiss to Cyrus Harding, who thus set an example to his intelligent and zealous companions. They worked with confidence, even gaily, Pencroft always having some joke to crack, sometimes carpenter, sometimes rope-maker, sometimes mason, while he communicated his good-humour to all the members of their little world. His faith in the engineer was complete; nothing could disturb it. He believed him capable of undertaking anything and succeeding in everything. The question of boots and clothes—assuredly a serious question—that of light during the winter months, utilizing the fertile parts of the island, transforming the wild flora into cultivated flora, it all appeared easy to him; Cyrus Harding helping, everything would be done in time. He dreamed of canals facilitating the transport of the riches of the ground; workings of quarries and mines; machines for every industrial manufacture; railroads; yes, railroads! of which a network would certainly one day cover Lincoln Island.

The engineer let Pencroft talk. He did not put down the aspirations of this brave heart. He knew how communicable confidence is; he even smiled to hear him speak, and said nothing of the uneasiness for the future which he felt. In fact, in that part of the Pacific, out of the course of vessels, it was to be feared that no help would ever come to them. It was on themselves, on themselves alone, that the settlers must depend, for the distance of Lincoln Island from all other land was such, that to hazard themselves in a boat, of a necessarily inferior construction, would be a serious and perilous thing.

"But," as the sailor said, "they quite took the wind out of the sails of the Robinsons, for whom everything was done by a miracle."

In fact, they were energetic; an energetic man will succeed where an indolent one would vegetate and inevitably perish.

Herbert distinguished himself in these works. He was intelligent and active; understanding quickly, he performed well; and Cyrus Harding became more and more attached to the boy. Herbert had a lively and reverent love for the engineer. Pencroft saw the close sympathy which existed between the two, but he was not in the least jealous. Neb was Neb: he was what he would be always, courage, zeal, devotion, self-denial personified. He had the same faith in his master that Pencroft had, but he showed it less vehemently. When the sailor was enthusiastic, Neb always looked as if he would say, "Nothing could be more natural." Pencroft and he were great friends.

As to Gideon Spilett, he took part in the common work, and was not less skilful in it than his companions, which always rather astonished the sailor. A "journalist," clever, not only in understanding, but in performing everything.

The ladder was finally fixed on the 28th of May. There were not less than a hundred rounds in this perpendicular height of eighty feet. Harding had been able, fortunately, to divide it in two parts, profiting by an overhanging of the cliff which made a projection forty feet above the ground. This projection, carefully levelled by the pickaxe, made a sort of platform, to which they fixed the first ladder, of which the oscillation was thus diminished one-half, and a rope permitted it to be raised to the level of Granite House. As to the second ladder, it was secured both at its lower part, which rested on the projection, and at its upper end, which was fastened to the door. In short the ascent had been made much easier. Besides, Cyrus Harding hoped later to establish an hydraulic apparatus, which would avoid all fatigue and loss of time, for the inhabitants of Granite House.

The settlers soon became habituated to the use of this ladder. They were light and active, and Pencroft, as a sailor, accustomed to run up the masts and shrouds, was able to give them lessons. But it was also necessary to give them to Top. The poor dog, with his four paws, was not formed for this sort of exercise. But Pencroft was such a zealous master, that Top ended by properly performing his ascents, and soon mounted the ladder as readily as his brethren in the circus. It need not be said that the sailor was proud of his pupil. However, more than once Pencroft hoisted him on his back, which Top never complained of.

It must be mentioned here, that during these works, which were actively conducted, for the bad season was approaching, the alimentary question was not neglected. Everyday, the reporter and Herbert, who had been voted purveyors to the colony, devoted some hours to the chase. As yet, they only hunted in Jacamar Wood, on the left of the river, because, for want of a bridge or boat, the Mercy had not yet been crossed. All the immense woods, to which the name of the Forests of the Far West had been given, were not explored. They reserved this important excursion for the first fine days of the next spring. But Jacamar Wood was full of game; kangaroos and boars abounded, and the hunters' iron-tipped spears and bows and arrows did wonders. Besides, Herbert discovered towards the south-west point of the lagoon a natural warren, a slightly damp meadow, covered with willows and aromatic herbs which scented the air, such as thyme, basil, savory, all the sweet-scented species of the labiated plants, which the rabbits appeared to be particularly fond of.

On the reporter observing that since the table was spread for the rabbits, it was strange that the rabbits themselves should be wanting, the two sportsmen carefully explored the warren. At any rate, it produced an abundance of useful plants, and a naturalist would have had a good opportunity of studying many specimens of the vegetable kingdom. Herbert gathered several shoots of the basil, rosemary, balm, betony, etc., which possess different medicinal properties, some pectoral, astringent, febrifuge, others anti-spasmodic, or anti-rheumatic. When, afterwards, Pencroft asked the use of this collection of herbs—

"For medicine," replied the lad, "to treat us when we are ill."

"Why should we be ill, since there are no doctors in the island?" asked Pencroft quite seriously.

There was no reply to be made to that, but the lad went on with his collection all the same, and it was well received at Granite House. Besides these medicinal herbs, he added a plant known in North America as "Oswego tea," which made an excellent beverage.

At last, by searching thoroughly, the hunters arrived at the real site of the warren. There the ground was perforated like a sieve.

"Here are the burrows!" cried Herbert.

"Yes," replied the reporter, "so I see."

"But are they inhabited?"

"That is the question."

This was soon answered. Almost immediately, hundreds of little animals, similar to rabbits, fled in every direction, with such rapidity that even Top could not overtake them. Hunters and dog ran in vain, these rodents escaped them easily. But the reporter resolved not to leave the place, until he had captured at least half-a-dozen of the quadrupeds. He wished to stock their larder first, and domesticate those which they might take later. It would not have been difficult to do this, with a few snares stretched at the openings of the burrows. But at this moment they had neither snares, nor anything to make them of. They must, therefore, be satisfied with visiting each hole, and rummaging in it with a stick, hoping by dint of patience to do what could not be done in any other way.

At last, after half-an-hour, four rodents were taken in their holes. They were similar to their European brethren, and are commonly known by the name of American rabbits.

This produce of the chase was brought back to Granite House, and figured at the evening repast. The tenants of the warren were not at all to be despised, for they were delicious. It was a valuable resource of the colony, and it appeared to be inexhaustible.

On the 31st of May the partitions were finished. The rooms had now only to be furnished, and this would be work for the long winter days. A chimney was established in the first room, which served as a kitchen. The pipe destined to conduct the smoke outside gave some trouble to these amateur bricklayers. It appeared simplest to Harding to make it of brick clay; as creating an outlet for it to the upper plateau was not to be thought of, a hole was pierced in the granite above the window of the kitchen, and the pipe met it like that of an iron stove. Perhaps the winds which blew directly against the façade would make the chimney smoke, but these winds were rare, and besides, Master Neb, the cook, was not so very particular about that.

When these interior arrangements were finished, the engineer occupied himself in blocking up the outlet by the lake, so as to prevent any access by that way. Masses of rock were rolled to the entrance and strongly cemented together. Cyrus Harding did not yet realise his plan of drowning this opening under the waters of the lake, by restoring them to their former level by means of a dam. He contented himself with hiding the obstruction with grass and shrubs, which were planted in the interstices of the rocks, and which next spring would sprout thickly. However, he used the waterfall so as to lead a small stream of fresh water to the new dwelling. A little trench, made below their level, produced this result; and this derivation from a pure and inexhaustible source yielded twenty-five or thirty gallons a day. There would never be any want of water at Granite House. At last all was finished, and it was time, for the bad season was near. Thick shutters closed the windows of the façade, until the engineer had time to make glass.

Gideon Spilett had very artistically arranged on the rocky projections around the windows plants of different kinds, as well as long streaming grass, so that the openings were picturesquely framed in green, which had a pleasing effect.

The inhabitants of this solid, healthy, and secure dwelling, could not but be charmed with their work. The view from the windows extended over a boundless horizon, which was closed by the two Mandible Capes on the north, and Claw Cape on the south. All Union Bay was spread before them. Yes, our brave settlers had reason to be satisfied, and Pencroft was lavish in his praise of what he humourously called, "his apartments on the fifth floor above the ground!"

Chapter XX

THE RAINY SEASON—THE QUESTION OF CLOTHES—A SEAL
HUNT—MANUFACTURING CANDLES—WORK IN GRANITE HOUSE—
THE TWO BRIDGES—RETURN FROM A VISIT TO THE OYSTER-
BED—WHAT HERBERT FINDS IN HIS POCKET

THE WINTER SEASON SET IN WITH THE MONTH OF JUNE, WHICH CORRESPONDS WITH THE month of December in the northern hemisphere. It began with showers and squalls, which succeeded each other without intermission. The tenants of Granite House could appreciate the advantages of a dwelling which sheltered them from the inclement weather. The Chimneys would have been quite insufficient to protect them against the rigour of winter, and it was to be feared that the high tides would make another irruption. Cyrus Harding had taken precautions against this contingency, so as to preserve as much as possible the forge and furnace which were established there.

During the whole of the month of June the time was employed in different occupations, which excluded neither hunting nor fishing, the larder being, therefore, abundantly supplied. Pencroft, so soon as he had leisure, proposed to set some traps, from which he expected great results. He soon made some snares with creepers, by the aid of which the warren henceforth everyday furnished its quota of rodents. Neb employed nearly all his time in salting or smoking meat, which ensured their always having plenty of provisions. The question of clothes was now seriously discussed, the settlers having no other garments than those they wore when the balloon threw them on the island. These clothes were warm and good; they had taken great care of them as well as of their linen, and they were perfectly whole, but they would soon need to be replaced. Moreover, if the winter was severe, the settlers would suffer greatly from cold.

On this subject the ingenuity of Harding was at fault. They must provide for their most pressing wants, settle their dwelling, and lay in a store of food; thus the cold might come upon them before the question of clothes had been settled. They must therefore make up their minds to pass this first winter without additional clothing. When the fine season came round again, they would regularly hunt those musmons which had been seen on the expedition to Mount Franklin, and the wool once collected, the engineer would know how to make it into strong warm stuff. . . . How? he would consider.

"Well, we are free to roast ourselves at Granite House!" said Pencroft. "There are heaps of fuel, and no reason for sparing it."

"Besides," added Gideon Spilett, "Lincoln Island is not situated under a very high latitude, and probably the winters here are not severe. Did you not say, Cyrus, that this thirty-fifth parallel corresponded to that of Spain in the other hemisphere?"

"Doubtless," replied the engineer, "but some winters in Spain are very cold! No want of snow and ice; and perhaps Lincoln Island is just as rigourously tried. However, it is an island, and as such, I hope that the temperature will be more moderate."

"Why, captain?" asked Herbert.

"Because the sea, my boy, may be considered as an immense reservoir, in which is stored the heat of the summer. When winter comes, it restores this heat, which ensures for the regions near the ocean a medium temperature, less high in summer, but less low in winter."

"We shall prove that," replied Pencroft. "But I don't want to bother myself about whether it will be cold or not. One thing is certain, that is that the days are already short, and the evenings long. Suppose we talk about the question of light."

"Nothing is easier," replied Harding.

"To talk about?" asked the sailor.

"To settle."

"And when shall we begin?"

"To-morrow, by having a seal hunt."

"To make candles?"

"Yes."

Such was the engineer's project; and it was quite feasible, since he had lime and sulphuric acid, while the amphibians of the islet would furnish the fat necessary for the manufacture.

They were now at the 4th of June. It was Whit Sunday, and they agreed to observe this feast. All work was suspended, and prayers were offered to Heaven. But these prayers were now thanksgivings. The settlers in Lincoln Island were no longer the miserable castaways thrown on the islet. They asked for nothing more—they gave thanks. The next day, the 5th of June, in rather uncertain weather, they set out for the islet. They had to profit by the low tide to cross the Channel, and it was agreed that they would construct, for this purpose, as well as they could, a boat which would render communication so much easier, and would also permit them to ascend the Mercy, at the time of their grand exploration of the south-west of the island, which was put off till the first fine days.

The seals were numerous, and the hunters, armed with their iron-tipped spears, easily killed half-a-dozen. Neb and Pencroft skinned them, and only brought back to Granite House their fat and skin, this skin being intended for the manufacture of boots.

The result of the hunt was this: nearly three hundred pounds of fat, all to be employed in the fabrication of candles.

The operation was extremely simple, and if it did not yield absolutely perfect results, they were at least very useful. Cyrus Harding would only have had at his disposal sulphuric acid, but by heating this acid with the neutral fatty bodies, he could separate the glycerine; then from this new combination, he easily separated the olein, the margarin, and the stearin, by employing boiling water. But to simplify the operation, he preferred to saponify the fat by means of lime. By this he obtained a calcareous soap, easy to decompose by sulphuric acid, which precipitated the lime into the state of sulphate, and liberated the fatty acids.

From these three acids—oleic, margaric, and stearic—the first, being liquid, was driven out by a sufficient pressure. As to the two others, they formed the very substance of which the candles were to be moulded.

This operation did not last more than four and twenty hours. The wicks, after several trials, were made of vegetable fibres, and dipped in the liquified substance, they formed regular stearic candles, moulded by the hand, which only wanted whiteness and polish.

They would not doubtless have the advantages of the wicks which are impregnated with boracic acid, and which vitrify as they burn and are entirely consumed, but Cyrus Harding having manufactured a beautiful pair of snuffers, these candles would be greatly appreciated during the long evenings in Granite House.

During this month there was no want of work in the interior of their new dwelling. The joiners had plenty to do. They improved their tools, which were very rough, and added others also.

Scissors were made among other things, and the settlers were at last able to cut their hair, and also to shave, or at least trim their beards. Herbert had none, Neb but little, but their companions were bristling in a way which justified the making of the said scissors.

The manufacture of a hand-saw cost infinite trouble, but at last an instrument was obtained which, when vigourously handled, could divide the ligneous fibres of the wood. They then made tables, seats, cupboards, to furnish the principal rooms, and bedsteads, of which all the bedding consisted of grass mattresses. The kitchen, with its shelves, on which rested the cooking utensils, its brick stove, looked very well, and Neb worked away there as earnestly as if he was in a chemist's laboratory.

But the joiners had soon to be replaced by carpenters. In fact, the waterfall created by the explosion rendered the construction of two bridges necessary, one on Prospect Heights, the other on the shore. Now the plateau and the shore were transversely divided by a water-course, which had to be crossed to reach the northern part of the island. To avoid it the colonists had been obliged to make a considerable detour, by climbing up to the source of the Red Creek. The simplest thing was to establish on the plateau, and on the shore, two bridges from twenty to five and twenty feet in length. All the carpenter's work that was needed was to clear some trees of their branches: this was a business of some days. Directly the bridges were established, Neb and Pencroft profited by them to go to the oyster-bed which had been discovered near the downs. They dragged with them a sort of rough cart, which replaced the former inconvenient hurdle, and brought back some thousands of oysters, which soon increased among the rocks and formed a bed at the mouth of the Mercy. These molluscs were of excellent quality, and the colonists consumed some daily.

It has been seen that Lincoln Island, although its inhabitants had as yet only explored a small portion of it, already contributed to almost all their wants. It was probable that if they hunted into its most secret recesses, in all the wooded part between the Mercy and Reptile Point, they would find new treasures.

The settlers in Lincoln Island had still one privation. There was no want of meat, nor of vegetable products; those ligneous roots which they had found, when subjected to fermentation, gave them an acid drink, which was preferable to cold water; they also made sugar, without canes or beetroots, by collecting the liquor which distils from the "acer saccharinum," a sort of maple-tree, which flourishes in all the temperate zones, and of which the island possessed a great number; they made a very agreeable tea by employing the herbs brought from the warren; lastly, they had an abundance of salt, the only mineral which is used in food, . . . but bread was wanting.

Perhaps in time the settlers could replace this want by some equivalent, it was possible that they might find the sago or the breadfruit-tree among the forests of the south, but they had not as yet met with these precious trees. However, Providence came directly to their aid, in an infinitesimal proportion it is true, but Cyrus Harding, with all his intelligence, all his ingenuity, would never have been able to produce that which, by the greatest chance, Herbert one day found in the lining of his waistcoat, which he was occupied in setting to rights.

On this day, as it was raining in torrents, the settlers were assembled in the great hall in Granite House, when the lad cried out all at once—

"Look here, captain—a grain of corn!"

And he showed his companions a grain—a single grain—which from a hole in his pocket had got into the lining of his waistcoat.

The presence of this grain was explained by the fact that Herbert, when at Richmond, used to feed some pigeons, of which Pencroft had made him a present.

"A grain of corn?" said the engineer quickly.

"Yes, captain; but one, only one!"

"Well, my boy," said Pencroft, laughing, "we're getting on capitally, upon my word! What shall we make with one grain of corn?"

"We will make bread of it," replied Cyrus Harding.

"Bread, cakes, tarts!" replied the sailor. "Come, the bread that this grain of corn will make won't choke us very soon!"

Herbert, not attaching much importance to his discovery, was going to throw away the grain in question; but Harding took it, examined it, found that it was in good condition, and looking the sailor full in the face—"Pencroft," he asked quietly, "do you know how many ears one grain of corn can produce?"

"One, I suppose!" replied the sailor, surprised at the question.

"Ten, Pencroft! And do you know how many grains one ear bears?"

"No, upon my word."

"About eighty!" said Cyrus Harding. "Then, if we plant this grain, at the first crop we shall reap eight hundred grains which at the second will produce six hundred and forty thousand; at the third, five hundred and twelve millions; at the fourth, more than four hundred thousands of millions! There is the proportion."

Harding's companions listened without answering. These numbers astonished them. They were exact, however.

"Yes, my friends," continued the engineer, "such are the arithmetical progressions of prolific nature; and yet what is this multiplication of the grain of corn, of which the ear only bears eight hundred grains, compared to the poppy-plant, which bears thirty-two thousand seeds; to the tobacco-plant, which produces three hundred and sixty thousand? In a few years, without the numerous causes of destruction, which arrests their fecundity, these plants would overrun the earth."

But the engineer had not finished his lecture.

"And now, Pencroft," he continued, "do you know how many bushels four hundred thousand millions of grains would make?"

"No," replied the sailor; "but what I do know is, that I am nothing better than a fool!"

"Well, they would make more than three millions, at a hundred and thirty thousand a bushel, Pencroft."

"Three millions!" cried Pencroft.

"Three millions."

"In four years?"

"In four years," replied Cyrus Harding, "and even in two years, if, as I hope, in this latitude we can obtain two crops a year."

At that, according to his usual custom, Pencroft could not reply otherwise than by a tremendous hurrah.

"So, Herbert," added the engineer, "you have made a discovery of great importance to us. Everything, my friends, everything can serve us in the condition in which we are. Do not forget that, I beg of you."

"No, captain, no, we shan't forget it," replied Pencroft; "and if ever I find one of those tobacco-seeds, which multiply by three hundred and sixty thousand, I assure you I won't throw it away! And now, what must we do?"

"We must plant this grain," replied Herbert.

"Yes," added Gideon Spilett, "and with every possible care, for it bears in itself our future harvests."

"Provided it grows!" cried the sailor.

"It will grow," replied Cyrus Harding.

This was the 20th of June. The time was then propitious for sowing this single precious grain of corn. It was first proposed to plant it in a pot, but upon reflection it was decided to leave it to nature, and confide it to the earth. This was done that very day, and it is needless to add, that every precaution was taken that the experiment might succeed.

The weather having cleared, the settlers climbed the height above Granite House. There, on the plateau, they chose a spot, well sheltered from the wind, and exposed to all the heat of the midday sun. The place was cleared, carefully weeded, and searched for insects and worms; then a bed of good earth, improved with a little lime, was made; it was surrounded by a railing; and the grain was buried in the damp earth.

Did it not seem as if the settlers were laying the first stone of some edifice? It recalled to Pencroft the day on which he lighted his only match, and all the anxiety of the operation. But this time the thing was more serious. In fact, the castaways would have been always able to procure fire, in some mode or other, but no human power could supply another grain of corn, if unfortunately this should be lost!

Chapter XXI

Some Degrees below Zero—Exploring the Marshy Part
to the South-east—The Wolf-Fox—View of the Sea—A
Conversation on the Future of the Pacific Ocean—The
Incessant Work of the Coral Insects—What Our Globe
Will Become—The Chase—Tadorn's Fens

FROM THIS TIME PENCROFT DID NOT LET A SINGLE DAY PASS WITHOUT GOING TO VISIT what he gravely called his "corn-field." And woe to the insects which dared to venture there! No mercy was shown them.

Towards the end of the month of June, after incessant rain, the weather became decidedly colder, and on the 29th a Fahrenheit thermometer would certainly have announced only twenty degrees above zero, that is considerably below the freezing-point. The next day, the 30th of June, the day which corresponds to the 31st of December in the northern year, was a Friday. Neb remarked that the year finished on a bad day, but Pencroft replied that naturally the next would begin on a good one, which was better.

At any rate it commenced by very severe cold. Ice accumulated at the mouth of the Mercy, and it was not long before the whole expanse of the lake was frozen.

The settlers had frequently been obliged to renew their store of wood. Pencroft also had wisely not waited till the river was frozen, but had brought enormous rafts of wood to their destination. The current was an indefatigable moving power, and it was employed in conveying the floating wood to the moment when the frost enchained it. To the fuel which was so abundantly supplied by the forest, they added several cartloads of coal, which had to be brought from the foot of the spurs of Mount Franklin. The powerful heat of the coal was greatly appreciated in the low temperature, which on the 4th of July fell to eight degrees of Fahrenheit, that is, thirteen degrees below zero. A second fireplace had been established in the dining-room, where they all worked together at their different avocations. During this period of cold, Cyrus Harding had great cause to congratulate himself on having brought to Granite House the little stream of water from Lake Grant. Taken below the frozen surface, and conducted through the passage, it preserved its fluidity, and arrived at an interior reservoir which had been hollowed out at the back part of the store-room, while the overflow ran through the well to the sea.

About this time, the weather being extremely dry, the colonists, clothed as warmly as possible, resolved to devote a day to the exploration of that part of the island between the Mercy and Claw Cape. It was a wide extent of marshy land, and they would probably find good sport, for water-birds ought to swarm there.

They reckoned that it would be about eight or nine miles to go there, and as much to return, so that the whole of the day would be occupied. As an unknown part of the island was about to be explored, the whole colony took part in the expedition. Accordingly, on the 5th of July, at six o'clock in the morning, when day had scarcely broken, Cyrus Harding, Gideon Spilett, Herbert, Neb, and Pencroft, armed with spears, snares, bows and arrows, and provided with provisions, left Granite House, preceded by Top, who bounded before them.

Their shortest way was to cross the Mercy on the ice, which then covered it.

"But," as the engineer justly observed, "that could not take the place of a regular bridge!" So, the construction of a regular bridge was noted in the list of future works.

It was the first time that the settlers had set foot on the right bank of the Mercy, and ventured into the midst of those gigantic and superb coniferae now sprinkled over with snow.

But they had not gone half-a-mile when from a thicket a whole family of quadrupeds, who had made a home there, disturbed by Top, rushed forth into the open country.

"Ah! I should say those are foxes!" cried Herbert, when he saw the troop rapidly decamping.

They were foxes, but of a very large size, who uttered a sort of barking, at which Top seemed to be very much astonished, for he stopped short in the chase, and gave the swift animals time to disappear.

The dog had reason to be surprised, as he did not know Natural History. But, by their barking, these foxes, with reddish-grey hair, black tails terminating in a white tuft, had betrayed their origin. So Herbert was able, without hesitating, to give them their real name of "Arctic foxes." They are frequently met with in Chile, in the Falkland Islands, and in all parts of America traversed by the thirtieth and fortieth parallels. Herbert much regretted that Top had not been able to catch one of these carnivora.

"Are they good to eat?" asked Pencroft, who only regarded the representatives of the fauna in the island from one special point of view.

"No," replied Herbert; "but zoologists have not yet found out if the eye of these foxes is diurnal or nocturnal, or whether it is correct to class them in the genus dog, properly so called."

Harding could not help smiling on hearing the lad's reflection, which showed a thoughtful mind. As to the sailor, from the moment when he found that the foxes were not classed in the genus eatable, they were nothing to him. However, when a poultry-yard was established at Granite House, he observed that it would be best to take some precautions against a probable visit from these four-legged plunderers, and no one disputed this.

After having turned the point, the settlers saw a long beach washed by the open sea. It was then eight o'clock in the morning. The sky was very clear, as it often is after prolonged cold; but warmed by their walk, neither Harding nor his companions felt the sharpness of the atmosphere too severely. Besides there was no wind, which made it much more bearable. A brilliant sun, but without any calorific action, was just issuing from the ocean. The sea was as tranquil and blue as that of a Mediterranean gulf, when the sky is clear. Claw Cape, bent in the form of a yataghan, tapered away nearly four miles to the southeast. To the left the edge of the marsh was abruptly ended by a little point. Certainly, in this part of Union Bay, which nothing sheltered from the open sea, not even a sand-bank, ships beaten by the east winds would have found no shelter. They perceived by the tranquillity of the sea, in which no shallows troubled the waters, by its uniform colour, which was stained by no yellow shades, by the absence of even a reef, that the coast was steep and that the ocean there covered a deep abyss. Behind in the west, but at a distance of four miles, rose the first trees of the forests of the Far West. They might have believed themselves to be on the desolate coast of some island in the Antarctic regions which the ice had invaded. The colonists halted at this place for breakfast. A fire of brushwood and dried sea-weed was lighted, and Neb prepared the breakfast of cold meat, to which he added some cups of Oswego tea.

While eating they looked around them. This part of Lincoln Island was very sterile, and contrasted with all the western part. The reporter was thus led to observe that if chance had thrown them at first on the shore, they would have had but a deplorable idea of their future domain.

"I believe that we should not have been able to reach it," replied the engineer, "for the sea is deep, and there is not a rock on which we could have taken refuge. Before Granite House, at least, there were sand-banks, an islet, which multiplied our chances of safety. Here, nothing but the depths!"

"It is singular enough," remarked Spilett, "that this comparatively small island should present such varied ground. This diversity of aspect, logically only belongs to continents of a certain extent. One would really say, that the western part of Lincoln Island, so rich and so fertile, is washed by the warm waters of the Gulf of Mexico, and that its shores to the north and the south-east extend over a sort of Arctic sea."

"You are right, my dear Spilett," replied Cyrus Harding, "I have also observed this. I think the form and also the nature of this island strange. It is a summary of all the aspects which a continent presents, and I should not be surprised if it was a continent formerly."

"What! a continent in the middle of the Pacific?" cried Pencroft.

"Why not?" replied Cyrus Harding. "Why should not Australia, New Ireland, Australasia, united to the archipelagoes of the Pacific, have once formed a sixth part of the world, as important as Europe or Asia, as Africa or the two Americas? To my mind, it is quite possible that all these islands, emerging from this vast ocean, are but the summits of a continent, now submerged, but which was above the waters at an ante-historic period."

"As the Atlantis was formerly," replied Herbert.

"Yes, my boy . . . if, however, it has existed."

"And would Lincoln Island have been a part of that continent?" asked Pencroft.

"It is probable," replied Cyrus Harding, "and that would sufficiently explain the variety of productions which are seen on its surface."

"And the great number of animals which still inhabit it," added Herbert.

"Yes, my boy," replied the engineer, "and you furnish me with an argument to support my theory. It is certain, after what we have seen, that animals are numerous in this island, and what is more strange, that the species are extremely varied. There is a reason for that, and to me it is that Lincoln Island may have formerly been a part of some vast continent which had gradually sunk below the Pacific."

"Then, some fine day," said Pencroft, who did not appear to be entirely convinced, "the rest of this ancient continent may disappear in its turn, and there will be nothing between America and Asia."

"Yes," replied Harding, "there will be new continents which millions and millions of animalculae are building at this moment."

"And what are these masons?" asked Pencroft.

"Coral insects," replied Cyrus Harding. "By constant work they made the island of Clermont-Tonnerre, and numerous other coral islands in the Pacific Ocean. Forty-seven millions of these insects are needed to weigh a grain, and yet, with the sea-salt they absorb, the solid elements of water which they assimilate, these animalculae produce limestone, and this limestone forms enormous submarine erections, of which the hardness and solidity equal granite. Formerly, at the first periods of creation, nature employing fire, heaved up the land, but now she entrusts to these microscopic creatures the task of replacing this agent, of which the dynamic power in the interior of the globe has evidently diminished— which is proved by the number of volcanoes on the surface of the earth, now actually extinct. And I believe that centuries succeeding to centuries, and insects to insects, this Pacific may one day be changed into a vast continent, which new generations will inhabit and civilise in their turn."

"That will take a long time," said Pencroft.

"Nature has time for it," replied the engineer.

"But what would be the use of new continents?" asked Herbert. "It appears to me that the present extent of habitable countries is sufficient for humanity. Yet nature does nothing uselessly."

"Nothing uselessly, certainly," replied the engineer, "but this is how the necessity of new continents for the future, and exactly on the tropical zone occupied by the coral islands, may be explained. At least to me this explanation appears plausible."

"We are listening, captain," said Herbert.

"This is my idea: philosophers generally admit that some day our globe will end, or rather that animal and vegetable life will no longer be possible, because of the intense cold to which it will be subjected. What they are not agreed upon, is the cause of this cold. Some think that it will arise from the falling of the temperature, which the sun will experience after millions of years; others, from the gradual extinction of the fires in the interior of our globe, which have a greater influence on it than is generally supposed. I hold to this last hypothesis, grounding it on the fact that the moon is really a cold star, which is no longer habitable, although the sun continues to throw on its surface the same amount of heat. If, then, the moon has become cold, it is because the interior fires to which, as do all the stars of the stellar world, it owes its origin, are completely extinct. Lastly, whatever may be the cause, our globe will become cold someday, but this cold will only operate gradually. What will happen, then? The temperate zones, at a more or less distant period, will not be more habitable than the polar regions now are. Then the population of men, as well as the animals, will flow towards the latitudes which are more directly under the solar influence. An immense emigration will be performed. Europe, Central Asia, North America, will gradually be abandoned, as well as Australasia and the lower parts of South America. The vegetation will follow the human emigration. The flora will retreat towards the Equator at the same time as the fauna. The central parts of South America and Africa will be the continents chiefly inhabited. The Laplanders and the Samoides will find the climate of the polar regions on the shores of the Mediterranean. Who can say, that at this period, the equatorial regions will not be too small, to contain and nourish terrestrial humanity? Now, may not provident nature, so as to give refuge to all the vegetable and animal emigration, be at present laying the foundation of a new continent under the Equator, and may she not have entrusted these insects with the construction of it? I have often thought of all these things, my friends, and I seriously believe that the aspect of our globe will someday be completely changed; that by the raising of new continents the sea will cover the old, and that, in future ages, a Columbus will go to discover the islands of Chimborazo, of the Himalaya, or of Mont Blanc, remains of a submerged America, Asia, and Europe. Then these new continents will become, in their turn, uninhabitable; heat will die away, as does the heat from a body when the soul has left it; and life will disappear from the globe, if not forever, at least for a period. Perhaps then, our spheroid will rest—will be left to death—to revive some day under superior conditions! But all that, my friends, is the secret of the Author of all things; and beginning by the work of the insects, I have perhaps let myself be carried too far, in investigating the secrets of the future."

"My dear Cyrus," replied Spilett, "these theories are prophecies to me, and they will be accomplished some day."

"That is the secret of God," said the engineer.

"All that is well and good," then said Pencroft, who had listened with all his might, "but will you tell me, captain, if Lincoln Island has been made by your insects?"

"No," replied Harding; "it is of a purely volcanic origin."

"Then it will disappear someday?"

"That is probable."

"I hope we won't be here then."

"No, don't be uneasy, Pencroft; we shall not be here then, as we have no wish to die here, and hope to get away some time."

"In the meantime," replied Gideon Spilett, "let us establish ourselves here as if forever. There is no use in doing things by halves."

This ended the conversation. Breakfast was finished, the exploration was continued, and the settlers arrived at the border of the marshy region. It was a marsh of which the extent, to the rounded coast which terminated the island at the south-east, was about twenty square miles. The soil was formed of clayey flint-earth, mingled with vegetable matter, such as the remains of rushes, reeds, grass, etc. Here and there beds of grass, thick as a carpet, covered it. In many places icy pools sparkled in the sun. Neither rain nor any river, increased by a sudden swelling, could supply these ponds. They therefore naturally concluded that the marsh was fed by the infiltrations of the soil, and it was really so. It was also to be feared that during the heat miasmas would arise, which might produce fevers.

Above the aquatic plants, on the surface of the stagnant water, fluttered numbers of birds. Wild duck, teal, snipe lived there in flocks, and those fearless birds allowed themselves to be easily approached.

One shot from a gun would certainly have brought down some dozen of the birds, they were so close together. The explorers were, however, obliged to content themselves with bows and arrows. The result was less, but the silent arrow had the advantage of not frightening the birds, while the noise of fire-arms would have dispersed them to all parts of the marsh. The hunters were satisfied, for this time, with a dozen ducks, which had white bodies with a band of cinnamon, a green head, wings black, white, and red, and flattened beak. Herbert called them tadorns. Top helped in the capture of these birds, whose name was given to this marshy part of the island. The settlers had here an abundant reserve of aquatic game. At some future time they meant to explore it more carefully, and it was probable that some of the birds there might be domesticated, or at least brought to the shores of the lake, so that they would be more within their reach.

About five o'clock in the evening Cyrus Harding and his companions retraced their steps to their dwelling by traversing Tadorn's Fens, and crossed the Mercy on the ice-bridge.

At eight in the evening they all entered Granite House.

Chapter XXII

TRAPS—FOXES—PECCARIES—THE WIND CHANGES TO THE
NORTH-WEST—SNOWSTORM—BASKET-MAKERS—THE SEVEREST
COLD—MAPLE SUGAR—THE MYSTERIOUS WELL—AN
EXPLORATION PLANNED—THE LEADEN BULLET

THIS INTENSE COLD LASTED TILL THE 15TH OF AUGUST, WITHOUT, HOWEVER, PASSING the degree of Fahrenheit already mentioned. When the atmosphere was calm, the low temperature was easily borne, but when the wind blew, the poor settlers, insufficiently clothed, felt it severely. Pencroft regretted that Lincoln Island was not the home of a few families of bears rather than of so many foxes and seals.

"Bears," said he, "are generally very well dressed, and I ask no more than to borrow for the winter the warm cloaks which they have on their backs."

"But," replied Neb, laughing, "perhaps the bears would not consent to give you their cloaks, Pencroft. These beasts are not St. Martins."

"We would make them do it, Neb, we would make them," replied Pencroft, in quite an authoritative tone.

But these formidable carnivora did not exist in the island, or at any rate they had not yet shown themselves.

In the meanwhile, Herbert, Pencroft, and the reporter occupied themselves with making traps on Prospect Heights and at the border of the forest.

According to the sailor, any animal, whatever it was, would be a lawful prize, and the rodents or carnivora which might get into the new snares would be well received at Granite House.

The traps were besides extremely simple; being pits dug in the ground, a platform of branches and grass above, which concealed the opening, and at the bottom some bait, the scent of which would attract animals. It must be mentioned also, that they had not been dug at random, but at certain places where numerous footprints showed that quadrupeds frequented the ground. They were visited everyday, and at three different times, during the first days, specimens of those Antarctic foxes which they had already seen on the right bank of the Mercy were found in them.

"Why, there are nothing but foxes in this country!" cried Pencroft, when for the third time he drew one of the animals out of the pit. Looking at it in great disgust, he added, "beasts which are good for nothing!"

"Yes," said Gideon Spilett, "they are good for something!"

"And what is that?"

"To make bait to attract other creatures!"

The reporter was right, and the traps were henceforward baited with the foxes' carcasses.

The sailor had also made snares from the long tough fibres of a certain plant, and they were even more successful than the traps. Rarely a day passed without some rabbits from the warren being caught. It was always rabbit, but Neb knew how to vary his sauces, and the settlers did not think of complaining.

However, once or twice in the second week of August, the traps supplied the hunters with other animals more useful than foxes, namely, several of those small wild boars which had already been seen to the north of the lake. Pencroft had no need to ask if these beasts were eatable. He could see that by their resemblance to the pig of America and Europe.

"But these are not pigs," said Herbert to him, "I warn you of that, Pencroft."

"My boy," replied the sailor, bending over the trap and drawing out one of these representatives of the family of *sus* by the little appendage which served it as a tail. "Let me believe that these are pigs!"

"Why?"

"Because that pleases me!"

"Are you very fond of pig then, Pencroft?"

"I am very fond of pig," replied the sailor, "particularly of its feet, and if it had eight instead of four, I should like it twice as much!"

As to the animals in question, they were peccaries belonging to one of the four species which are included in the family, and they were also of the species of Tajacu, recognisable by their deep colour and the absence of those long teeth with which the mouths of their congeners are armed. These peccaries generally live in herds, and it was probable that they abounded in the woody parts of the island.

At any rate, they were eatable from head to foot, and Pencroft did not ask more from them.

Towards the 15th of August, the state of the atmosphere was suddenly moderated by the wind shifting to the north-west. The temperature rose some degrees, and the accumulated vapour in the air was not long in resolving into snow. All the island was covered with a sheet of white, and showed itself to its inhabitants under a new aspect. The snow fell abundantly for several days, and it soon reached a thickness of two feet.

The wind also blew with great violence, and at the height of Granite House the sea could be heard thundering against the reefs. In some places, the wind, eddying round the corners, formed the snow into tall whirling columns, resembling those water-spouts which turn round on their base, and which vessels attack with a shot from a gun. However, the storm, coming from the north-west, blew across the island, and the position of Granite House preserved it from a direct attack.

But in the midst of this snow-storm, as terrible as if it had been produced in some polar country, neither Cyrus Harding nor his companions could, notwithstanding their wish for it, venture forth, and they remained shut up for five days, from the 20th to the 25th of August. They could hear the tempest raging in Jacamar Woods, which would surely suffer from it. Many of the trees would no doubt be torn up by the roots, but Pencroft consoled himself by thinking that he would not have the trouble of cutting them down.

"The wind is turning woodman, let it alone," he repeated.

Besides, there was no way of stopping it, if they had wished to do so.

How grateful the inhabitants of Granite House then were to Heaven for having prepared for them this solid and immovable retreat! Cyrus Harding had also his legitimate share of thanks, but after all, it was Nature who had hollowed out this vast cavern, and he had only discovered it. There all were in safety, and the tempest could not reach them. If they had constructed a house of bricks and wood on Prospect Heights, it certainly would not have resisted the fury of this storm. As to the Chimneys, it must have been absolutely uninhabitable, for the sea, passing over the islet, would beat furiously against it. But here, in Granite House, in the middle of a solid mass, over which neither the sea nor air had any influence, there was nothing to fear.

During these days of seclusion the settlers did not remain inactive.

There was no want of wood, cut up into planks, in the store-room, and little by little they completed their furnishing; constructing the most solid of tables and chairs, for material was not spared. Neb and Pencroft were very proud of this rather heavy furniture, which they would not have changed on any account.

Then the carpenters became basket-makers, and they did not succeed badly in this new manufacture. At the point of the lake which projected to the north, they had discovered an osier-bed in which grew a large number of purple osiers. Before the rainy season, Pencroft and Herbert had cut down these useful shrubs, and their branches, well prepared, could now be effectively employed. The first attempts were somewhat crude, but in consequence of the cleverness and intelligence of the workmen, by consulting, and recalling the models which they had seen, and by emulating each other, the possessions of the colony were soon increased by several baskets of different sizes. The store-room was provided with them, and in special baskets Neb placed his collection of rhizomes, stone-pine almonds, etc.

During the last week of the month of August the weather moderated again. The temperature fell a little, and the tempest abated. The colonists sallied out directly. There was certainly two feet of snow on the shore, but they were able to walk without much difficulty on the hardened surface. Cyrus Harding and his companions climbed Prospect Heights.

What a change! The woods, which they had left green, especially in the part at which the firs predominated, had disappeared under a uniform colour. All was white, from the summit of Mount Franklin to the shore, the forests, the plains, the lake, the river. The waters of the Mercy flowed under a roof of ice, which, at each rising and ebbing of the tide, broke up with loud crashes. Numerous birds fluttered over the frozen surface of the lake. Ducks and snipe, teal and guillemots were assembled in thousands. The rocks among which the cascade flowed were bristling with icicles. One might have said that the water escaped by a monstrous gargoyle, ornamented as grotesquely as an artist of the Renaissance. As to the damage caused by the storm in the forest, that could not as yet be ascertained, they must wait till the snowy covering was dissipated.

Gideon Spilett, Pencroft, and Herbert did not miss this opportunity of going to visit their traps. They did not find them easily, under the snow with which they were covered. They had also to be careful not to fall into one or other of them, which would have been both dangerous and humiliating; to be taken in their own snares! But happily they avoided this unpleasantness, and found their traps perfectly intact. No animal had fallen into them, and yet the footprints in the neighbourhood were very numerous, among others, certain very clear marks of claws. Herbert did not hesitate to affirm that some animal of the feline species had passed there, which justified the engineer's opinion that dangerous beasts existed in Lincoln Island. These animals doubtless generally lived in the forests of the Far West, but pressed by hunger, they had ventured as far as Prospect Heights. Perhaps they had smelled out the inhabitants of Granite House.

"Now, what are these feline creatures?" asked Pencroft.

"They are tigers," replied Herbert.

"I thought those beasts were only found in hot countries?"

"On the new continent," replied the lad, "they are found from Mexico to the Pampas of Buenos Aires. Now, as Lincoln Island is nearly under the same latitude as the provinces of La Plata, it is not surprising that tigers are to be met with in it."

"Well, we must look out for them," replied Pencroft.

However, the snow soon disappeared, quickly dissolving under the influence of the rising temperature. Rain fell, and the sheet of white soon vanished. Notwithstanding the bad weather, the settlers renewed their stores of different things, stone-pine almonds, rhizomes, syrup from the maple-tree, for the vegetable part; rabbits from the warren, agoutis, and kangaroos for the animal part. This necessitated several excursions into the forest, and they found that a great number of trees had been blown down by the last hurricane. Pencroft and Neb also pushed with the cart as far as the vein of coal, and brought back several tons of fuel. They saw in passing that the pottery kiln had been severely damaged by the wind, at least six feet of it having been blown off.

At the same time as the coal, the store of wood was renewed at Granite House, and they profited by the current of the Mercy having again become free, to float down several rafts. They could see that the cold period was not ended.

A visit was also paid to the Chimneys, and the settlers could not but congratulate themselves on not having been living there during the hurricane. The sea had left unquestionable traces of its ravages. Sweeping over the islet, it had furiously assailed the passages, half filling them with sand, while thick beds of sea-weed covered the rocks. While Neb, Herbert, and Pencroft hunted or collected wood, Cyrus Harding and Gideon Spilett busied themselves in putting the Chimneys to rights, and they found the forge and the bellows almost unhurt, protected as they had been from the first by the heaps of sand.

The store of fuel had not been made uselessly. The settlers had not done with the rigourous cold. It is known that, in the northern hemisphere, the month of February is principally distinguished by rapid fallings of the temperature. It is the same in the southern hemisphere, and the end of the month of August, which is the February of North America, does not escape this climatic law.

About the 25th, after another change from snow to rain, the wind shifted to the southeast, and the cold became, suddenly, very severe. According to the engineer's calculation, the mercurial column of a Fahrenheit thermometer would not have marked less than eight degrees below zero, and this intense cold, rendered still more painful by a sharp gale, lasted for several days. The colonists were again shut up in Granite House, and as it was necessary to hermetically seal all the openings of the façade, only leaving a narrow passage for renewing the air, the consumption of candles was considerable. To economise them, the cavern was often only lighted by the blazing hearths, on which fuel was not spared. Several times, one or other of the settlers descended to the beach in the midst of ice which the waves heaped up at each tide, but they soon climbed up again to Granite House, and it was not without pain and difficulty that their hands could hold to the rounds of the ladder. In consequence of the intense cold, their fingers felt as if burned when they touched the rounds. To occupy the leisure hours, which the tenants of Granite House now had at their disposal, Cyrus Harding undertook an operation which could be performed indoors.

We know that the settlers had no other sugar at their disposal than the liquid substance which they drew from the maple, by making deep incisions in the tree. They contented themselves with collecting this liquor in jars and employing it in this state for different culinary purposes, and the more so, as on growing old, this liquid began to become white and to be of a syrupy consistence.

But there was something better to be made of it, and one day Cyrus Harding announced to his companions that they were going to turn into refiners.

"Refiners!" replied Pencroft. "That is rather a warm trade, I think."

"Very warm," answered the engineer.

"Then it will be seasonable!" said the sailor.

This word refining need not awake in the mind thoughts of an elaborate manufactory with apparatus and numerous workmen. No! to crystallise this liquor, only an extremely easy operation is required. Placed on the fire in large earthen pots, it was simply subjected to evaporation, and soon a scum arose to its surface. As soon as this began to thicken, Neb carefully removed it with a wooden spatula; this accelerated the evaporation, and at the same time prevented it from contracting an empyreumatic flavour.

After boiling for several hours on a hot fire, which did as much good to the operators as the substance operated upon, the latter was transformed into a thick syrup. This syrup was poured into clay moulds, previously fabricated in the kitchen stove, and to which they had given various shapes. The next day this syrup had become cold, and formed cakes and tablets. This was sugar of rather a reddish colour, but nearly transparent and of a delicious taste.

The cold continued to the middle of September, and the prisoners in Granite House began to find their captivity rather tedious. Nearly everyday they attempted sorties which they could not prolong. They constantly worked at the improvement of their dwelling. They talked while working. Harding instructed his companions in many things, principally explaining to them the practical applications of science. The colonists had no library at their disposal; but the engineer was a book which was always at hand, always open at the page which one wanted, a book which answered all their questions, and which they often consulted. The time thus passed away pleasantly, these brave men not appearing to have any fears for the future.

However, all were anxious to see, if not the fine season, at least the cessation of the insupportable cold. If only they had been clothed in a way to meet it, how many excursions they would have attempted, either to the downs or to Tadorn's Fens! Game would have been easily approached, and the chase would certainly have been most productive. But Cyrus Harding considered it of importance that no one should injure his health, for he had need of all his hands, and his advice was followed.

But it must be said, that the one who was most impatient of this imprisonment, after

Pencroft perhaps, was Top. The faithful dog found Granite House very narrow. He ran backwards and forwards from one room to another, showing in his way how weary he was of being shut up. Harding often remarked that when he approached the dark well which communicated with the sea, and of which the orifice opened at the back of the store-room, Top uttered singular growlings. He ran round and round this hole, which had been covered with a wooden lid. Sometimes even he tried to put his paws under the lid, as if he wished to raise it. He then yelped in a peculiar way, which showed at once anger and uneasiness.

The engineer observed this maneuvre several times.

What could there be in this abyss to make such an impression on the intelligent animal? The well led to the sea, that was certain. Could narrow passages spread from it through the foundations of the island? Did some marine monster come from time to time, to breathe at the bottom of this well? The engineer did not know what to think, and could not refrain from dreaming of many strange improbabilities. Accustomed to go far into the regions of scientific reality, he would not allow himself to be drawn into the regions of the strange and almost of the supernatural; but yet how to explain why Top, one of those sensible dogs who never waste their time in barking at the moon, should persist in trying with scent and hearing to fathom this abyss, if there was nothing there to cause his uneasiness? Top's conduct puzzled Cyrus Harding even more than he cared to acknowledge to himself.

At all events, the engineer only communicated his impressions to Gideon Spilett, for he thought it useless to explain to his companions the suspicions which arose from what perhaps was only Top's fancy.

At last the cold ceased. There had been rain, squalls mingled with snow, hailstorms, gusts of wind, but these inclemencies did not last. The ice melted, the snow disappeared; the shore, the plateau, the banks of the Mercy, the forest, again became practicable. This return of spring delighted the tenants of Granite House, and they soon only passed it in the hours necessary for eating and sleeping.

They hunted much in the second part of September, which led Pencroft to again entreat for the fire-arms, which he asserted had been promised by Cyrus Harding. The latter, knowing well that without special tools it would be nearly impossible for him to manufacture a gun which would be of any use, still drew back and put off the operation to some future time, observing in his usual dry way, that Herbert and Spilett had become very skilful archers, so that many sorts of excellent animals, agouties, kangaroos, capybaras, pigeons, bustards, wild ducks, snipes, in short, game both with fur and feathers, fell victims to their arrows, and that, consequently, they could wait. But the obstinate sailor would listen to nothing of this, and he would give the engineer no peace till he promised to satisfy his desire. Gideon Spilett, however, supported Pencroft.

"If, which may be doubted," said he, "the island is inhabited by wild beasts, we must think how to fight with and exterminate them. A time may come when this will be our first duty."

But at this period, it was not the question of fire-arms which occupied Harding, but that of clothes. Those which the settlers wore had passed this winter, but they would not last until next winter. Skins of carnivora or the wool of ruminants must be procured at any price, and since there were plenty of musmons, it was agreed to consult on the means of forming a flock which might be brought up for the use of the colony. An enclosure for the domestic animals, a poultry-yard for the birds, in a word to establish a sort of farm in the island, such were the two important projects for the fine season.

In consequence and in view of these future establishments, it became of much importance that they should penetrate into all the yet unknown parts of Lincoln Island, that is to say, through that thick forest which extended on the right bank of the Mercy, from its mouth to the extremity of the Serpentine Peninsula, as well as on the whole of its western side. But this needed settled weather, and a month must pass before this exploration could be profitably undertaken.

They therefore waited with some impatience, when an incident occurred which increased the desire the settlers had to visit the whole of their domain.

It was the 24th of October. On this day, Pencroft had gone to visit his traps, which he always kept properly baited. In one of them he found three animals which would be very welcome for the larder. They were a female peccary and her two young ones.

Pencroft then returned to Granite House, enchanted with his capture, and, as usual, he made a great show of his game.

"Come, we shall have a grand feast, captain!" he exclaimed. "And you too, Mr. Spilett, you will eat some!"

"I shall be very happy," replied the reporter; "but what is it that I am going to eat?"

"Suckling-pig."

"Oh, indeed, suckling-pig, Pencroft? To hear you, I thought that you were bringing back a young partridge stuffed with truffles!"

"What?" cried Pencroft. "Do you mean to say that you turn up your nose at suckling-pig?'

"No," replied Gideon Spilett, without showing any enthusiasm; "provided one doesn't eat too much—"

"That's right, that's right," returned the sailor, who was not pleased whenever he heard his chase made light of. "You like to make objections. Seven months ago, when we landed on the island, you would have been only too glad to have met with such game!"

"Well, well," replied the reporter, "man is never perfect, nor contented."

"Now," said Pencroft, "I hope that Neb will distinguish himself. Look here! These two little peccaries are not more than three months old! They will be as tender as quails! Come along, Neb, come! I will look after the cooking myself."

And the sailor, followed by Neb, entered the kitchen, where they were soon absorbed in their culinary labors.

They were allowed to do it in their own way. Neb, therefore, prepared a magnificent repast—the two little peccaries, kangaroo soup, a smoked ham, stone-pine almonds, Oswego tea; in fact, all the best that they had, but among all the dishes figured in the first rank the savory peccaries.

At five o'clock dinner was served in the dining-room of Granite House. The kangaroo soup was smoking on the table. They found it excellent.

To the soup succeeded the peccaries, which Pencroft insisted on carving himself, and of which he served out monstrous portions to each of the guests.

These suckling-pigs were really delicious, and Pencroft was devouring his share with great gusto, when all at once a cry and an oath escaped him.

"What's the matter?" asked Cyrus Harding.

"The matter? the matter is that I have just broken a tooth!" replied the sailor.

"What, are there pebbles in your peccaries?" said Gideon Spilett.

"I suppose so," replied Pencroft, drawing from his lips the object which had cost him a grinder!—

It was not a pebble—it was a leaden bullet.

PART II

ABANDONED

Chapter I

CONVERSATION ON THE SUBJECT OF THE BULLET—CONSTRUCTION
OF A CANOE—HUNTING—AT THE TOP OF A KAURI—NOTHING TO
ATTEST THE PRESENCE OF MAN—NEB AND HERBERT'S PRIZE—
TURNING A TURTLE—THE TURTLE DISAPPEARS—CYRUS
HARDING'S EXPLANATION

IT WAS NOW EXACTLY SEVEN MONTHS SINCE THE BALLOON VOYAGERS HAD BEEN THROWN
on Lincoln Island. During that time, notwithstanding the researches they had made,
no human being had been discovered. No smoke even had betrayed the presence of
man on the surface of the island. No vestiges of his handiwork showed that either at an
early or at a late period had man lived there. Not only did it now appear to be uninhabited
by any but themselves, but the colonists were compelled to believe that it never had been
inhabited. And now, all this scaffolding of reasonings fell before a simple ball of metal,
found in the body of an inoffensive rodent! In fact, this bullet must have issued from a fire-
arm, and who but a human being could have used such a weapon?

When Pencroft had placed the bullet on the table, his companions looked at it with intense astonishment. All the consequences likely to result from this incident, notwithstanding its apparent insignificance, immediately took possession of their minds. The sudden
apparition of a supernatural being could not have startled them more completely.

Cyrus Harding did not hesitate to give utterance to the suggestions which this fact, at
once surprising and unexpected, could not fail to raise in his mind. He took the bullet,
turned it over and over, rolled it between his finger and thumb; then, turning to Pencroft,
he asked—

"Are you sure that the peccary wounded by this bullet was not more than three
months old?"

"Not more, captain," replied Pencroft. "It was still sucking its mother when I found
it in the trap."

"Well," said the engineer, "that proves that within three months a gun-shot was fired
in Lincoln Island."

"And that a bullet," added Gideon Spilett, "wounded, though not mortally, this little
animal."

"That is unquestionable," said Cyrus Harding, "and these are the deductions which
must be drawn from this incident: that the island was inhabited before our arrival, or that
men have landed here within three months. Did these men arrive here voluntarily or involuntarily, by disembarking on the shore or by being wrecked? This point can only be
cleared up later. As to what they were, Europeans or Malays, enemies or friends of our
race, we cannot possibly guess; and if they still inhabit the island, or if they have left it,
we know not. But these questions are of too much importance to be allowed to remain
long unsettled."

"No! a hundred times no! a thousand times no!" cried the sailor, springing up from the table. "There are no other men than ourselves on Lincoln Island! By my faith! The island isn't large and if it had been inhabited, we should have seen some of the inhabitants long before this!"

"In fact, the contrary would be very astonishing," said Herbert.

"But it would be much more astonishing, I should think," observed the reporter, "that this peccary had been born with a bullet in its inside!"

"At least," said Neb seriously, "if Pencroft has not had——"

"Look here, Neb," burst out Pencroft. "Do you think I could have a bullet in my jaw for five or six months without finding it out? Where could it be hidden?" he asked, opening his mouth to show the two-and-thirty teeth with which it was furnished. "Look well, Neb, and if you find one hollow tooth in this set, I will let you pull out half-a-dozen!"

"Neb's supposition is certainly inadmissible," replied Harding, who, notwithstanding the gravity of his thoughts, could not restrain a smile. "It is certain that a gun has been fired in the island, within three months at most. But I am inclined to think that the people who landed on this coast were only here a very short time ago, or that they just touched here; for if, when we surveyed the island from the summit of Mount Franklin, it had been inhabited, we should have seen them or we should have been seen ourselves. It is, therefore, probable that within only a few weeks castaways have been thrown by a storm on some part of the coast. However that may be, it is of consequence to us to have this point settled."

"I think that we should act with caution," said the reporter.

"Such is my advice," replied Cyrus Harding, "for it is to be feared that Malay pirates have landed on the island!"

"Captain," asked the sailor, "would it not be a good plan, before setting out, to build a canoe in which we could either ascend the river, or, if we liked, coast round the inland? It will not do to be unprovided."

"Your idea is good, Pencroft," replied the engineer, "but we cannot wait for that. It would take at least a month to build a boat."

"Yes, a real boat," replied the sailor; "but we do not want one for a sea voyage, and in five days at the most, I will undertake to construct a canoe fit to navigate the Mercy."

"Five days," cried Neb, "to build a boat?"

"Yes, Neb; a boat in the Indian fashion."

"Of wood?" asked the negro, looking still unconvinced.

"Of wood," replied Pencroft, "of rather of bark. I repeat, captain, that in five days the work will be finished!"

"In five days, then, be it," replied the engineer.

"But till that time we must be very watchful," said Herbert.

"Very watchful indeed, my friends," replied Harding; "and I beg you to confine your hunting excursions to the neighbourhood of Granite House."

The dinner ended less gaily than Pencroft had hoped.

So, then, the island was, or had been, inhabited by others than the settlers. Proved as it was by the incident of the bullet, it was hereafter an unquestionable fact, and such a discovery could not but cause great uneasiness among the colonists.

Cyrus Harding and Gideon Spilett, before sleeping, conversed long about the matter. They asked themselves if by chance this incident might not have some connection with the inexplicable way in which the engineer had been saved, and the other peculiar circumstances which had struck them at different times. However, Cyrus Harding, after having discussed the pros and cons of the question, ended by saying—

"In short, would you like to know my opinion, my dear Spilett?"

"Yes, Cyrus."

"Well, then, it is this: however minutely we explore the island, we shall find nothing."

The next day Pencroft set to work. He did not mean to build a boat with boards and planking, but simply a flat-bottomed canoe, which would be well suited for navigating the Mercy—above all, for approaching its source, where the water would naturally be shallow. Pieces of bark, fastened one to the other, would form a light boat; and in case of natural obstacles, which would render a portage necessary, it would be easily carried. Pencroft intended to secure the pieces of bark by means of nails, to ensure the canoe being water-tight.

It was first necessary to select the trees which would afford a strong and supple bark for the work. Now the last storm had brought down a number of large birch-trees, the bark of which would be perfectly suited for their purpose. Some of these trees lay on the ground, and they had only to be barked, which was the most difficult thing of all, owing to the imperfect tools which the settlers possessed. However, they overcame all difficulties.

While the sailor, seconded by the engineer, thus occupied himself without losing an hour, Gideon Spilett and Herbert were not idle.

They were made purveyors to the colony. The reporter could not but admire the boy, who had acquired great skill in handling the bow and spear. Herbert also showed great courage and much of that presence of mind which may justly be called "the reasoning of bravery." These two companions of the chase, remembering Cyrus Harding's recommendations, did not go beyond a radius of two miles round Granite House; but the borders of the forest furnished a sufficient tribute of agoutis, capybaras, kangaroos, peccaries, etc.; and if the result from the traps was less than during the cold, still the warren yielded its accustomed quota, which might have fed all the colony in Lincoln Island.

Often during these excursions, Herbert talked with Gideon Spilett on the incident of the bullet, and the deductions which the engineer drew from it, and one day—it was the 26th of October—he said—

"But, Mr. Spilett, do you not think it very extraordinary that, if any castaways have landed on the island, they have not yet shown themselves near Granite House?"

"Very astonishing if they are still here," replied the reporter, "but not astonishing at all if they are here no longer!"

"So you think that these people have already quitted the island?" returned Herbert.

"It is more than probable, my boy; for if their stay was prolonged, and above all, if they were still here, some accident would have at last betrayed their presence."

"But if they were able to go away," observed the lad, "they could not have been castaways."

"No, Herbert; or, at least, they were what might be called provisional castaways. It is very possible that a storm may have driven them to the island without destroying their vessel, and that, the storm over, they went away again."

"I must acknowledge one thing," said Herbert, "it is that Captain Harding appears rather to fear than desire the presence of human beings on our island."

"In short," responded the reporter, "there are only Malays who frequent these seas, and those fellows are ruffians which it is best to avoid."

"It is not impossible, Mr. Spilett," said Herbert, "that someday or other we may find traces of their landing."

"I do not say no, my boy. A deserted camp, the ashes of a fire, would put us on the track, and this is what we will look for in our next expedition."

The day on which the hunters spoke thus, they were in a part of the forest near the Mercy, remarkable for its beautiful trees. There, among others, rose, to a height of nearly 200 feet above the ground, some of those superb coniferae, to which, in New Zealand, the natives give the name of Kauris.

"I have an idea, Mr. Spilett," said Herbert. "If I were to climb to the top of one of these kauris, I could survey the country for an immense distance round."

"The idea is good," replied the reporter; "but could you climb to the top of those giants?"

"I can at least try," replied Herbert.

The light and active boy then sprang on the first branches, the arrangement of which made the ascent of the kauri easy, and in a few minutes he arrived at the summit, which emerged from the immense plain of verdure.

From this elevated situation his gaze extended over all the southern portion of the island, from Claw Cape on the south-east, to Reptile End on the south-west. To the north-west rose Mount Franklin, which concealed a great part of the horizon.

But Herbert, from the height of his observatory, could examine all the yet unknown portion of the island, which might have given shelter to the strangers whose presence they suspected.

The lad looked attentively. There was nothing in sight on the sea, not a sail, neither on the horizon nor near the island. However, as the bank of trees hid the shore, it was possible that a vessel, especially if deprived of her masts, might lie close to the land and thus be invisible to Herbert.

Neither in the forests of the Far West was anything to be seen. The wood formed an impenetrable screen, measuring several square miles, without a break or an opening. It was impossible even to follow the course of the Mercy, or to ascertain in what part of the mountain it took its source. Perhaps other creeks also ran towards the west, but they could not be seen.

But at last, if all indication of an encampment escaped Herbert's sight could he not even catch a glimpse of smoke, the faintest trace of which would be easily discernible in the pure atmosphere?

For an instant Herbert thought he could perceive a slight smoke in the west, but a more attentive examination showed that he was mistaken. He strained his eyes in every direction, and his sight was excellent. No, decidedly there was nothing there.

Herbert descended to the foot of the kauri, and the two sportsmen returned to Granite House. There Cyrus Harding listened to the lad's account, shook his head and said nothing. It was very evident that no decided opinion could be pronounced on this question until after a complete exploration of the island.

Two days after—the 28th of October—another incident occurred, for which an explanation was again required.

While strolling along the shore about two miles from Granite House, Herbert and Neb were fortunate enough to capture a magnificent specimen of the order of chelonia. It was a turtle of the species Midas, the edible green turtle, so called from the colour both of its shell and fat.

Herbert caught sight of this turtle as it was crawling among the rocks to reach the sea.

"Help, Neb, help!" he cried.

Neb ran up.

"What a fine animal!" said Neb; "but how are we to catch it?"

"Nothing is easier, Neb," replied Herbert. "We have only to turn the turtle on its back, and it cannot possibly get away. Take your spear and do as I do."

The reptile, aware of danger, had retired between its carapace and plastron. They no longer saw its head or feet, and it was motionless as a rock.

Herbert and Neb then drove their sticks underneath the animal, and by their united efforts managed without difficulty to turn it on its back. The turtle, which was three feet in length, would have weighed at least four hundred pounds.

"Capital!" cried Neb; "this is something which will rejoice friend Pencroft's heart."

In fact, the heart of friend Pencroft could not fail to be rejoiced, for the flesh of the turtle, which feeds on wrackgrass, is extremely savory. At this moment the creature's head could be seen, which was small, flat, but widened behind by the large temporal fossae hidden under the long roof.

"And now, what shall we do with our prize?" said Neb. "We can't drag it to Granite House!"

"Leave it here, since it cannot turn over," replied Herbert, "and we will come back with the cart to fetch it."

"That is the best plan."

However, for greater precaution, Herbert took the trouble, which Neb deemed superfluous, to wedge up the animal with great stones; after which the two hunters returned to Granite House, following the beach, which the tide had left uncovered. Herbert, wishing to surprise Pencroft, said nothing about the "superb specimen of a chelonian" which they had turned over on the sand; but, two hours later, he and Neb returned with the cart to the place where they had left it. The "superb specimen of a chelonian" was no longer there!

Neb and Herbert stared at each other first; then they stared about them. It was just at this spot that the turtle had been left. The lad even found the stones which he had used, and therefore he was certain of not being mistaken.

"Well!" said Neb, "these beasts can turn themselves over, then?"

"It appears so," replied Herbert, who could not understand it at all, and was gazing at the stones scattered on the sand.

"Well, Pencroft will be disgusted!"

"And Captain Harding will perhaps be very perplexed how to explain this disappearance," thought Herbert.

"Look here," said Neb, who wished to hide his ill-luck, "we won't speak about it."

"On the contrary, Neb, we must speak about it," replied Herbert.

And the two, taking the cart, which there was now no use for, returned to Granite House.

Arrived at the dock-yard, where the engineer and the sailor were working together, Herbert recounted what had happened.

"Oh! the stupids!" cried the sailor, "to have let at least fifty meals escape!"

"But, Pencroft," replied Neb, "it wasn't our fault that the beast got away; as I tell you, we had turned it over on its back!"

"Then you didn't turn it over enough!" returned the obstinate sailor.

"Not enough!" cried Herbert.

And he told how he had taken care to wedge up the turtle with stones.

"It is a miracle, then!" replied Pencroft.

"I thought, captain," said Herbert, "that turtles, once placed on their backs, could not regain their feet, especially when they are of a large size?'

"That is true, my boy," replied Cyrus Harding.

"Then how did it manage?"

"At what distance from the sea did you leave this turtle?" asked the engineer, who, having suspended his work, was reflecting on this incident.

"Fifteen feet at the most," replied Herbert.

"And the tide was low at the time?"

"Yes, captain."

"Well," replied the engineer, "what the turtle could not do on the sand it might have been able to do in the water. It turned over when the tide overtook it, and then quietly returned to the deep sea."

"Oh! what stupids we were!" cried Neb.

"That is precisely what I had the honour of telling you before!" returned the sailor.

Cyrus Harding had given this explanation, which, no doubt, was admissible. But was he himself convinced of the accuracy of this explanation? It cannot be said that he was.

Chapter II

FIRST TRIAL OF THE CANOE—A WRECK ON THE COAST— TOWING—FLOTSAM POINT—INVENTORY OF THE CASE: TOOLS, WEAPONS, INSTRUMENTS, CLOTHES, BOOKS, UTENSILS— WHAT PENCROFT MISSES—THE GOSPEL— A VERSE FROM THE SACRED BOOK

ON THE 9TH OF OCTOBER THE BARK CANOE WAS ENTIRELY FINISHED. PENCROFT HAD kept his promise, and a light boat, the shell of which was joined together by the flexible twigs of the crejimba, had been constructed in five days. A seat in the stern, a second seat in the middle to preserve the equilibrium, a third seat in the bows, rowlocks for the two oars, a scull to steer with, completed the little craft, which was twelve feet long, and did not weigh more than two hundred pounds.

The operation of launching it was extremely simple. The canoe was carried to the beach and laid on the sand before Granite House, and the rising tide floated it. Pencroft, who leaped in directly, maneuvred it with the scull and declared it to be just the thing for the purpose to which they wished to put it.

"Hurrah!" cried the sailor, who did not disdain to celebrate thus his own triumph. "With this we could go round—"

"The world?" asked Gideon Spilett.

"No, the island. Some stones for ballast, a mast and a sail, which the captain will make for us someday, and we shall go splendidly! Well, captain—and you, Mr. Spilett; and you, Herbert; and you, Neb—aren't you coming to try our new vessel? Come along! we must see if it will carry all five of us!"

This was certainly a trial which ought to be made. Pencroft soon brought the canoe to the shore by a narrow passage among the rocks, and it was agreed that they should make a trial of the boat that day by following the shore as far as the first point at which the rocks of the south ended.

As they embarked, Neb cried—

"But your boat leaks rather, Pencroft."

"That's nothing, Neb," replied the sailor; "the wood will get seasoned. In two days there won't be a single leak, and our boat will have no more water in her than there is in the stomach of a drunkard. Jump in!"

They were soon all seated, and Pencroft shoved off. The weather was magnificent, the sea as calm as if its waters were contained within the narrow limits of a lake. Thus the boat could proceed with as much security as if it was ascending the tranquil current of the Mercy.

Neb took one of the oars, Herbert the other, and Pencroft remained in the stern in order to use the scull.

The sailor first crossed the channel, and steered close to the southern point of the islet. A light breeze blew from the south. No roughness was found either in the channel or the green sea. A long swell, which the canoe scarcely felt, as it was heavily laden, rolled regularly over the surface of the water. They pulled out about half-a-mile distant from the shore, that they might have a good view of Mount Franklin.

Pencroft afterwards returned towards the mouth of the river. The boat then skirted the shore, which, extending to the extreme point, hid all Tadorn's Fens.

This point, of which the distance was increased by the irregularity of the coast, was nearly three miles from the Mercy. The settlers resolved to go to its extremity, and only go beyond it as much as was necessary to take a rapid survey of the coast as far as Claw Cape.

The canoe followed the windings of the shore, avoiding the rocks which fringed it, and which the rising tide began to cover. The cliff gradually sloped away from the mouth of the river to the point. This was formed of granite rocks, capriciously distributed, very different from the cliff at Prospect Heights, and of an extremely wild aspect. It might have been said that an immense cartload of rocks had been emptied out there. There was no vegetation on this sharp promontory, which projected two miles from the forest, and it thus represented a giant's arm stretched out from a leafy sleeve.

The canoe, impelled by the two oars, advanced without difficulty. Gideon Spilett, pencil in one hand and note-book in the other, sketched the coast in bold strokes. Neb, Herbert, and Pencroft chatted, while examining this part of their domain, which was new to them, and, in proportion as the canoe proceeded towards the south, the two Mandible Capes appeared to move, and surround Union Bay more closely.

As to Cyrus Harding, he did not speak; he simply gazed, and by the mistrust which his look expressed, it appeared that he was examining some strange country.

In the meanwhile, after a voyage of three-quarters of an hour, the canoe reached the extremity of the point, and Pencroft was preparing to return, when Herbert, rising, pointed to a black object, saying—

"What do I see down there on the beach?"

All eyes turned towards the point indicated.

"Why," said the reporter, "there is something. It looks like part of a wreck half buried in the sand."

"Ah!" cried Pencroft, "I see what it is!"

"What?" asked Neb.

"Barrels, barrels, which perhaps are full," replied the sailor.

"Pull to the shore, Pencroft!" said Cyrus.

A few strokes of the oar brought the canoe into a little creek, and its passengers leaped on shore.

Pencroft was not mistaken. Two barrels were there, half buried in the sand, but still firmly attached to a large chest, which, sustained by them, had floated to the moment when it stranded on the beach.

"There has been a wreck, then, in some part of the island," said Herbert.

"Evidently," replied Spilett.

"But what's in this chest?" cried Pencroft, with very natural impatience. "What's in this chest? It is shut up, and nothing to open it with! Well, perhaps a stone—"

And the sailor, raising a heavy block, was about to break in one of the sides of the chest, when the engineer arrested his hand.

"Pencroft," said he, "can you restrain your impatience for one hour only?"

"But, captain, just think! Perhaps there is everything we want in there!"

"We shall find that out, Pencroft," replied the engineer; "but trust to me, and do not break the chest, which may be useful to us. We must convey it to Granite House, where we can open it easily, and without breaking it. It is quite prepared for a voyage; and, since it has floated here, it may just as well float to the mouth of the river."

"You are right, captain, and I was wrong, as usual," replied the sailor.

The engineer's advice was good. In fact, the canoe probably would not have been able to contain the articles possibly enclosed in the chest, which doubtless was heavy, since two empty barrels were required to buoy it up. It was, therefore, much better to tow it to the beach at Granite House.

And now, whence had this chest come? That was the important question. Cyrus Harding and his companions looked attentively around them, and examined the shore for several hundred steps. No other articles or pieces of wreck could be found. Herbert and Neb climbed a high rock to survey the sea, but there was nothing in sight—neither a dismasted vessel nor a ship under sail.

However, there was no doubt that there had been a wreck. Perhaps this incident was connected with that of the bullet? Perhaps strangers had landed on another part of the island? Perhaps they were still there? But the thought which came naturally to the settlers was, that these strangers could not be Malay pirates, for the chest was evidently of American or European make.

All the party returned to the chest, which was of an unusually large size. It was made of oak wood, very carefully closed and covered with a thick hide, which was secured by copper nails. The two great barrels, hermetically sealed, but which sounded hollow and empty, were fastened to its sides by strong ropes, knotted with a skill which Pencroft directly pronounced sailors alone could exhibit. It appeared to be in a perfect state of preservation, which was explained by the fact that it had stranded on a sandy beach, and not among rocks. They had no doubt whatever, on examining it carefully, that it had not been long in the water, and that its arrival on this coast was recent. The water did not appear to have penetrated to the inside, and the articles which it contained were no doubt uninjured.

It was evident that this chest had been thrown overboard from some dismasted vessel driven towards the island, and that, in the hope that it would reach the land, where they might afterwards find it, the passengers had taken the precaution to buoy it up by means of this floating apparatus.

"We will tow this chest to Granite House," said the engineer, "where we can make an inventory of its contents; then, if we discover any of the survivors from the supposed wreck, we can return it to those to whom it belongs. If we find no one—"

"We will keep it for ourselves!" cried Pencroft. "But what in the world can there be in it?"

The sea was already approaching the chest, and the high tide would evidently float it. One of the ropes which fastened the barrels was partly unlashed and used as a cable to unite the floating apparatus with the canoe. Pencroft and Neb then dug away the sand with their oars, so as to facilitate the moving of the chest, towing which the boat soon began to double the point, to which the name of Flotsam Point was given.

The chest was heavy, and the barrels were scarcely sufficient to keep it above water. The sailor also feared every instant that it would get loose and sink to the bottom of the sea. But happily his fears were not realised, and an hour and a half after they set out—all that time had been taken up in going a distance of three miles—the boat touched the beach below Granite House.

Canoe and chest were then hauled upon the sand; and as the tide was then going out, they were soon left high and dry. Neb, hurrying home, brought back some tools with which to open the chest in such a way that it might be injured as little as possible, and they proceeded to its inventory. Pencroft did not try to hide that he was greatly excited.

The sailor began by detaching the two barrels, which, being in good condition, would of course be of use. Then the locks were forced with a cold chisel and hammer, and the lid thrown back. A second casing of zinc lined the interior of the chest, which had been evidently arranged that the articles which it enclosed might under any circumstances be sheltered from damp.

"Oh!" cried Neb, "suppose it's jam!"

"I hope not," replied the reporter.

"If only there was—" said the sailor in a low voice.

"What?" asked Neb, who overheard him.

"Nothing!"

The covering of zinc was torn off and thrown back over the sides of the chest, and by degrees numerous articles of very varied character were produced and strewn about on the sand. At each new object Pencroft uttered fresh hurrahs, Herbert clapped his hands, and Neb danced—like a nigger. There were books which made Herbert wild with joy, and cooking utensils which Neb covered with kisses!

In short, the colonists had reason to be extremely satisfied, for this chest contained tools, weapons, instruments, clothes, books; and this is the exact list of them as stated in Gideon Spilett's note-book:—

Tools:—3 knives with several blades, 2 woodmen's axes, 2 carpenter's hatchets, 3 planes, 2 adzes, 1 twibil or mattock, 6 chisels, 2 files, 3 hammers, 3 gimlets, 2 augers, 10 bags of nails and screws, 3 saws of different sizes, 2 boxes of needles.

Weapons:—2 flint-lock guns, 2 for percussion caps, 2 breech-loader carbines, 5 boarding cutlasses, 4 sabres, 2 barrels of powder, each containing twenty-five pounds; 12 boxes of percussion caps.

Instruments:—1 sextant, 1 double opera-glass, 1 telescope, 1 box of mathematical instruments, 1 mariner's compass, 1 Fahrenheit thermometer, 1 aneroid barometer, 1 box containing a photographic apparatus, object-glass, plates, chemicals, etc.

Clothes:—2 dozen shirts of a peculiar material resembling wool, but evidently of a vegetable origin; 3 dozen stockings of the same material.

Utensils:—1 iron pot, 6 copper saucepans, 3 iron dishes, 10 metal plates, 2 kettles, 1 portable stove, 6 table-knives.

Books:—1 Bible, 1 atlas, 1 dictionary of the different Polynesian idioms, 1 dictionary of natural science, in six volumes; 3 reams of white paper, 2 books with blank pages.

"It must be allowed," said the reporter, after the inventory had been made, "that the owner of this chest was a practical man! Tools, weapons, instruments, clothes, utensils, books—nothing is wanting! It might really be said that he expected to be wrecked, and had prepared for it beforehand."

"Nothing is wanting, indeed," murmured Cyrus Harding thoughtfully.

"And for a certainty," added Herbert, "the vessel which carried this chest and its owner was not a Malay pirate!"

"Unless," said Pencroft, "the owner had been taken prisoner by pirates—"

"That is not admissible," replied the reporter. "It is more probable that an American or European vessel has been driven into this quarter, and that her passengers, wishing to save necessaries at least, prepared this chest and threw it overboard."

"Is that your opinion, captain?" asked Herbert.

"Yes, my boy," replied the engineer, "that may have been the case. It is possible that at the moment, or in expectation of a wreck, they collected into this chest different articles of the greatest use in hopes of finding it again on the coast—"

"Even the photographic box!" exclaimed the sailor incredulously.

"As to that apparatus," replied Harding, "I do not quite see the use of it; and a more complete supply of clothes or more abundant ammunition would have been more valuable to us as well as to any other castaways!"

"But isn't there any mark or direction on these instruments, tools, or books, which would tell us something about them?" asked Gideon Spilett.

That might be ascertained. Each article was carefully examined, especially the books, instruments and weapons. Neither the weapons nor the instruments, contrary to the usual custom, bore the name of the maker; they were, besides, in a perfect state, and did not appear to have been used. The same peculiarity marked the tools and utensils; all were new, which proved that the articles had not been taken by chance and thrown into the chest, but, on the contrary, that the choice of things had been well considered and arranged with care. This was also indicated by the second case of metal which had preserved them from damp, and which could not have been soldered in a moment of haste.

As to the dictionaries of natural science and Polynesian idioms, both were English; but they neither bore the name of the publisher nor the date of publication.

The same with the Bible printed in English, in quarto, remarkable from a typographical point of view, and which appeared to have been often used.

The atlas was a magnificent work, comprising maps of every country in the world, and several planispheres arranged upon Mercator's projection, and of which the nomenclature was in French—but which also bore neither date nor name of publisher.

There was nothing, therefore, on these different articles by which they could be traced, and nothing consequently of a nature to show the nationality of the vessel which must have recently passed these shores.

But, wherever the chest might have come from, it was a treasure to the settlers on Lincoln Island. Till then, by making use of the productions of nature, they had created everything for themselves, and, thanks to their intelligence, they had managed without difficulty. But did it not appear as if Providence had wished to reward them by sending them these productions of human industry? Their thanks rose unanimously to Heaven.

However, one of them was not quite satisfied: it was Pencroft. It appeared that the chest did not contain something which he evidently held in great esteem, for in proportion as they approached the bottom of the box, his hurrahs diminished in heartiness, and, the inventory finished, he was heard to mutter these words:—

"That's all very fine, but you can see that there is nothing for me in that box!"

This led Neb to say—

"Why, friend Pencroft, what more do you expect?"

"Half a pound of tobacco," replied Pencroft seriously, "and nothing would have been wanting to complete my happiness!"

No one could help laughing at this speech of the sailor's.

But the result of this discovery of the chest was, that it was now more than ever necessary to explore the island thoroughly. It was therefore agreed that the next morning at break of day they should set out, by ascending the Mercy so as to reach the western shore. If any castaways had landed on the coast, it was to be feared they were without resources, and it was therefore the more necessary to carry help to them without delay.

During the day the different articles were carried to Granite House, where they were methodically arranged in the great hall.

This day—the 29th of October—happened to be a Sunday, and, before going to bed, Herbert asked the engineer if he would not read them something from the Gospel.

"Willingly," replied Cyrus Harding.

He took the sacred volume, and was about to open it, when Pencroft stopped him, saying—

"Captain, I am superstitious. Open at random and read the first verse which your eye falls upon. We will see if it applies to our situation."

Cyrus Harding smiled at the sailor's idea, and, yielding to his wish, he opened exactly at a place where the leaves were separated by a marker.

Immediately his eyes were attracted by a cross which, made with a pencil, was placed against the eighth verse of the seventh chapter of the Gospel of St. Matthew. He read the verse, which was this:—

"For everyone that asketh receiveth; and he that seeketh findeth."

Chapter III

The Start—The Rising Tide—Elms and Different Plants— The Jacamar—Aspect of the Forest—Gigantic Eucalypti— The Reason They are Called "Fever-Trees"—Troops of Monkeys—A Waterfall—The Night Encampment

THE NEXT DAY, THE 30TH OF OCTOBER, ALL WAS READY FOR THE PROPOSED EXPLORING expedition, which recent events had rendered so necessary. In fact, things had so come about that the settlers in Lincoln Island no longer needed help for themselves, but were even able to carry it to others.

It was therefore agreed that they should ascend the Mercy as far as the river was navigable. A great part of the distance would thus be traversed without fatigue, and the explorers could transport their provisions and arms to an advanced point in the west of the island.

It was necessary to think not only of the things which they should take with them, but also of those which they might have by chance to bring back to Granite House. If there had been a wreck on the coast, as was supposed, there would be many things cast up, which would be lawfully their prizes. In the event of this, the cart would have been of more use than the light canoe, but it was heavy and clumsy to drag, and therefore more difficult to use; this led Pencroft to express his regret that the chest had not contained, besides "his half-pound of tobacco," a pair of strong New Jersey horses, which would have been very useful to the colony!

The provisions, which Neb had already packed up, consisted of a store of meat and of several gallons of beer, that is to say enough to sustain them for three days, the time which Harding assigned for the expedition. They hoped besides to supply themselves on the road, and Neb took care not to forget the portable stove.

The only tools the settlers took were the two woodmen's axes, which they could use to cut a path through the thick forests, as also the instruments, the telescope and pocket-compass.

For weapons they selected the two flint-lock guns, which were likely to be more useful to them than the percussion fowling-pieces, the first only requiring flints which could be easily replaced, and the latter needing fulminating caps, a frequent use of which would soon exhaust their limited stock. However, they took also one of the carbines and some cartridges. As to the powder, of which there was about fifty pounds in the barrel, a small supply of it had to be taken, but the engineer hoped to manufacture an explosive substance which would allow them to husband it. To the fire-arms were added the five cutlasses well sheathed in leather, and, thus supplied, the settlers could venture into the vast forest with some chance of success.

It is useless to add that Pencroft, Herbert, and Neb, thus armed, were at the summit of their happiness, although Cyrus Harding made them promise not to fire a shot unless it was necessary.

At six in the morning the canoe put off from the shore; all had embarked, including Top, and they proceeded to the mouth of the Mercy.

The tide had begun to come up half-an-hour before. For several hours, therefore, there would be a current, which it was well to profit by, for later the ebb would make it difficult to ascend the river. The tide was already strong, for in three days the moon would be full, and it was enough to keep the boat in the centre of the current, where it floated swiftly along between the high banks without its being necessary to increase its speed by the aid of the oars. In a few minutes the explorers arrived at the angle formed by the Mercy, and exactly at the place where, seven months before, Pencroft had made his first raft of wood.

After this sudden angle the river widened and flowed under the shade of great evergreen firs.

The aspect of the banks was magnificent. Cyrus Harding and his companions could not but admire the lovely effects so easily produced by nature with water and trees. As they advanced the forest element diminished. On the right bank of the river grew magnificent specimens of the ulmaceae tribe, the precious elm, so valuable to builders, and which withstands well the action of water. Then there were numerous groups belonging to the same family, among others one in particular, the fruit of which produces a very useful oil. Further on, Herbert remarked the lardizabala, a twining shrub which, when bruised in water, furnishes excellent cordage; and two or three ebony trees of a beautiful black, crossed with capricious veins.

From time to time, in certain places where the landing was easy, the canoe was stopped, when Gideon Spilett, Herbert, and Pencroft, their guns in their hands, and preceded by Top, jumped on shore. Without expecting game, some useful plant might be met with, and the young naturalist was delighted with discovering a sort of wild spinach, belonging to the order of chenopodiaceae, and numerous specimens of cruciferae, belonging to the cabbage tribe, which it would certainly be possible to cultivate by transplanting. There were cresses, horse-radish, turnips, and lastly, little branching hairy stalks, scarcely more than three feet high, which produced brownish grains.

"Do you know what this plant is?" asked Herbert of the sailor.

"Tobacco!" cried Pencroft, who evidently had never seen his favourite plant except in the bowl of his pipe.

"No, Pencroft," replied Herbert; "this is not tobacco, it is mustard."

"Mustard be hanged!" returned the sailor; "but if by chance you happen to come across a tobacco-plant, my boy, pray don't scorn that!"

"We shall find it someday!" said Gideon Spilett.

"Well!" exclaimed Pencroft, "when that day comes, I do not know what more will be wanting in our island!"

These different plants, which had been carefully rooted up, were carried to the canoe, where Cyrus Harding had remained buried in thought.

The reporter, Herbert, and Pencroft in this manner frequently disembarked, sometimes on the right bank, sometimes on the left bank of the Mercy.

The latter was less abrupt, but the former more wooded. The engineer ascertained by consulting his pocket-compass that the direction of the river from the first turn was obviously south-west and north-east, and nearly straight for a length of about three miles. But it was to be supposed that this direction changed beyond that point, and that the Mercy continued to the north-west, towards the spurs of Mount Franklin, among which the river rose.

During one of these excursions, Gideon Spilett managed to get hold of two couples of living gallinaceae. They were birds with long, thin beaks, lengthened necks, short wings, and without any appearance of a tail. Herbert rightly gave them the name of tinamons, and it was resolved that they should be the first tenants of their future poultry-yard.

But till then the guns had not spoken, and the first report which awoke the echoes of the forest of the Far West was provoked by the appearance of a beautiful bird, resembling the kingfisher.

"I recognise him!" cried Pencroft, and it seemed as if his gun went off by itself.

"What do you recognise?" asked the reporter.

"The bird which escaped us on our first excursion, and from which we gave the name to that part of the forest."

"A jacamar!" cried Herbert.

It was indeed a jacamar, of which the plumage shines with a metallic luster. A shot brought it to the ground, and Top carried it to the canoe. At the same time half-a-dozen lories were brought down. The lory is of the size of a pigeon, the plumage dashed with green, part of the wings crimson, and its crest bordered with white. To the young boy belonged the honour of this shot, and he was proud enough of it. Lories are better food than the jacamar, the flesh of which is rather tough, but it was difficult to persuade Pencroft that he had not killed the king of eatable birds. It was ten o'clock in the morning when the canoe reached a second angle of the Mercy, nearly five miles from its mouth. Here a halt was made for breakfast under the shade of some splendid trees. The river still measured from sixty to seventy feet in breadth, and its bed from five to six feet in depth. The engineer had observed that it was increased by numerous affluents, but they were unnavigable, being simply little streams. As to the forest, including Jacamar Wood, as well as the forests of the Far West, it extended as far as the eye could reach. In no place, either in the depths of the forests or under the trees on the banks of the Mercy, was the presence of man revealed. The explorers could not discover one suspicious trace. It was evident that the woodman's axe had never touched these trees, that the pioneer's knife had never severed the creepers hanging from one trunk to another in the midst of tangled brushwood and long grass. If castaways had landed on the island, they could not have yet quitted the shore, and it was not in the woods that the survivors of the supposed shipwreck should be sought.

The engineer therefore manifested some impatience to reach the western coast of Lincoln Island, which was at least five miles distant according to his estimation.

The voyage was continued, and as the Mercy appeared to flow not towards the shore, but rather towards Mount Franklin, it was decided that they should use the boat as long as there was enough water under its keel to float it. It was both fatigue spared and time gained, for they would have been obliged to cut a path through the thick wood with their axes. But soon the flow completely failed them, either the tide was going down, and it was about the hour, or it could no longer be felt at this distance from the mouth of the Mercy. They had therefore to make use of the oars, Herbert and Neb each took one, and Pencroft took the scull. The forest soon became less dense, the trees grew further apart and often quite isolated. But the further they were from each other the more magnificent they appeared, profiting, as they did, by the free, pure air which circulated around them.

What splendid specimens of the flora of this latitude! Certainly their presence would have been enough for a botanist to name without hesitation the parallel which traversed Lincoln Island.

"Eucalypti!" cried Herbert.

They were, in fact, those splendid trees, the giants of the extratropical zone, the congeners of the Australian and New Zealand eucalyptus, both situated under the same latitude as Lincoln Island. Some rose to a height of two hundred feet. Their trunks at the base measured twenty feet in circumference, and their bark was covered by a network of furrows containing a red, sweet-smelling gum. Nothing is more wonderful or more singular than those enormous specimens of the order of the myrtaceae, with their leaves placed vertically and not horizontally, so that an edge and not a surface looks upwards, the effect being that the sun's rays penetrate more freely among the trees.

The ground at the foot of the eucalypti was carpeted with grass, and from the bushes escaped flights of little birds, which glittered in the sunlight like winged rubies.

"These are something like trees!" cried Neb; "but are they good for anything?"

"Pooh!" replied Pencroft. "Of course there are vegetable giants as well as human giants, and they are no good, except to show themselves at fairs!"

"I think that you are mistaken, Pencroft," replied Gideon Spilett, "and that the wood of the eucalyptus has begun to be very advantageously employed in cabinet-making."

"And I may add," said Herbert, "that the eucalyptus belongs to a family which comprises many useful members; the guava-tree, from whose fruit guava jelly is made; the clove-tree, which produces the spice; the pomegranate-tree, which bears pomegranates; the Eugeacia Cauliflora, the fruit of which is used in making a tolerable wine; the Ugui myrtle, which contains an excellent alcoholic liquor; the Caryophyllus myrtle, of which the bark forms an esteemed cinnamon; the Eugenia Pimenta, from whence comes Jamaica pepper; the common myrtle, from whose buds and berries spice is sometimes made; the Eucalyptus manifera, which yields a sweet sort of manna; the Guinea Eucalyptus, the sap of which is transformed into beer by fermentation; in short, all those trees known under the name of gum-trees or iron-bark-trees in Australia, belong to this family of the myrtaceae, which contains forty-six genera and thirteen hundred species!"

The lad was allowed to run on, and he delivered his little botanical lecture with great animation. Cyrus Harding listened smiling, and Pencroft with an indescribable feeling of pride.

"Very good, Herbert," replied Pencroft, "but I could swear that all those useful specimens you have just told us about are none of them giants like these!"

"That is true, Pencroft."

"That supports what I said," returned the sailor, "namely, that these giants are good for nothing!"

"There you are wrong, Pencroft," said the engineer; "these gigantic eucalypti, which shelter us, are good for something."

"And what is that?"

"To render the countries which they inhabit healthy. Do you know what they are called in Australia and New Zealand?"

"No, captain."

"They are called 'fever-trees.' "

"Because they give fevers?"

"No, because they prevent them!"

"Good. I must note that," said the reporter.

"Note it then, my dear Spilett; for it appears proved that the presence of the eucalyptus is enough to neutralise miasmas. This natural antidote has been tried in certain countries in the middle of Europe and the north of Africa, where the soil was absolutely unhealthy, and the sanitary condition of the inhabitants has been gradually ameliorated. No more intermittent fevers prevail in the regions now covered with forests of the myrtaceae. This fact is now beyond doubt, and it is a happy circumstance for us settlers in Lincoln Island."

"Ah! what an island! What a blessed island!" cried Pencroft. "I tell you, it wants nothing—unless it is—"

"That will come, Pencroft, that will be found," replied the engineer; "but now we must continue our voyage and push on as far as the river will carry our boat!"

The exploration was therefore continued for another two miles in the midst of country covered with eucalypti, which predominated in the woods of this portion of the island. The space which they occupied extended as far as the eye could reach on each side of the Mercy, which wound along between high green banks. The bed was often obstructed by long weeds, and even by pointed rocks, which rendered the navigation very difficult. The action of the oars was prevented, and Pencroft was obliged to push with a pole. They found also that the water was becoming shallower and shallower, and that the canoe must soon stop. The sun was already sinking towards the horizon, and the trees threw long shadows on the ground. Cyrus Harding, seeing that he could not hope to reach the western coast of the island in one journey, resolved to camp at the place where any further navigation was prevented by want of water. He calculated that they were still five or six miles from the coast, and this distance was too great for them to attempt during the night in the midst of unknown woods.

The boat was pushed on through the forest, which gradually became thicker again, and appeared also to have more inhabitants; for if the eyes of the sailor did not deceive him, he thought he saw bands of monkeys springing among the trees. Sometimes even two or three of these animals stopped at a little distance from the canoe and gazed at the settlers without manifesting any terror, as if, seeing men for the first time, they had not yet learned to fear them. It would have been easy to bring down one of these quadrumani with a gunshot, and Pencroft was greatly tempted to fire, but Harding opposed so useless a massacre. This was prudent, for the monkeys, or apes rather, appearing to be very powerful and extremely active, it was useless to provoke an unnecessary aggression, and the creatures might, ignorant of the power of the explorers' fire-arms, have attacked them. It is true that the sailor considered the monkeys from a purely alimentary point of view, for those animals which are herbivorous make very excellent game; but since they had an abundant supply of provisions, it was a pity to waste their ammunition.

Towards four o'clock, the navigation of the Mercy became exceedingly difficult, for its course was obstructed by aquatic plants and rocks. The banks rose higher and higher, and already they were approaching the spurs of Mount Franklin. The source could not be far off, since it was fed by the water from the southern slopes of the mountain.

"In a quarter of an hour," said the sailor, "we shall be obliged to stop, captain."

"Very well, we will stop, Pencroft, and we will make our encampment for the night."

"At what distance are we from Granite House?" asked Herbert.

"About seven miles," replied the engineer, "taking into calculation, however, the detours of the river, which has carried us to the north-west."

"Shall we go on?" asked the reporter.

"Yes, as long as we can," replied Cyrus Harding. "To-morrow, at break of day, we will leave the canoe, and in two hours I hope we shall cross the distance which separates us from the coast, and then we shall have the whole day in which to explore the shore."

"Go ahead!" replied Pencroft.

But soon the boat grated on the stony bottom of the river, which was now not more than twenty feet in breadth. The trees met like a bower overhead, and caused a half-darkness. They also heard the noise of a waterfall, which showed that a few hundred feet up the river there was a natural barrier.

Presently, after a sudden turn of the river, a cascade appeared through the trees. The canoe again touched the bottom, and in a few minutes it was moored to a trunk near the right bank.

It was nearly five o'clock. The last rays of the sun gleamed through the thick foliage and glanced on the little waterfall, making the spray sparkle with all the colours of the rainbow. Beyond that, the Mercy was lost in the brushwood, where it was fed from some hidden source. The different streams which flowed into it increased it to a regular river further down, but here it was simply a shallow, limpid brook.

It was agreed to camp here, as the place was charming. The colonists disembarked, and a fire was soon lighted under a clump of trees, among the branches of which Cyrus Harding and his companions could, if it was necessary, take refuge for the night.

Supper was quickly devoured, for they were very hungry, and then there was only sleeping to think of. But, as roarings of rather a suspicious nature had been heard during the evening, a good fire was made up for the night, so as to protect the sleepers with its crackling flames. Neb and Pencroft also watched by turns, and did not spare fuel. They thought they saw the dark forms of some wild animals prowling round the camp among the bushes, but the night passed without incident, and the next day, the 31st of October, at five o'clock in the morning, all were on foot, ready for a start.

Chapter IV

JOURNEY TO THE COAST—TROOPS OF MONKEYS—A NEW RIVER—
THE REASON THE TIDE WAS NOT FELT—A WOODY SHORE—
REPTILE PROMONTORY—HERBERT ENVIES GIDEON SPILETT—
EXPLOSION OF BAMBOOS

IT WAS SIX O' CLOCK IN THE MORNING WHEN THE SETTLERS, AFTER A HASTY BREAKFAST, set out to reach by the shortest way, the western coast of the island. And how long would it take to do this? Cyrus Harding had said two hours, but of course that depended on the nature of the obstacles they might meet with. As it was probable that they would have to cut a path through the grass, shrubs, and creepers, they marched axe in hand, and with guns also ready, wisely taking warning from the cries of the wild beasts heard in the night.

The exact position of the encampment could be determined by the bearing of Mount Franklin, and as the volcano arose in the north at a distance of less than three miles, they had only to go straight towards the south-west to reach the western coast. They set out, having first carefully secured the canoe. Pencroft and Neb carried sufficient provision for the little band for at least two days. It would not thus be necessary to hunt. The engineer advised his companions to refrain from firing, that their presence might not be betrayed to anyone near the shore. The first hatchet blows were given among the brushwood in the midst of some mastic-trees, a little above the cascade; and his compass in his hand, Cyrus Harding led the way.

The forest here was composed for the most part of trees which had already been met with near the lake and on Prospect Heights. There were deodars, Douglas firs, casuarinas, gum-trees, eucalypti, hibiscus, cedars, and other trees, generally of a moderate size, for their number prevented their growth.

Since their departure, the settlers had descended the slopes which constituted the mountain system of the island, on to a dry soil, but the luxuriant vegetation of which indicated it to be watered either by some subterranean marsh or by some stream. However, Cyrus Harding did not remember having seen, at the time of his excursion to the crater, any other water-courses but the Red Creek and the Mercy.

During the first part of their excursion, they saw numerous troops of monkeys who exhibited great astonishment at the sight of men, whose appearance was so new to them. Gideon Spilett jokingly asked whether these active and merry quadrupeds did not consider him and his companions as degenerate brothers.

And certainly, pedestrians, hindered at each step by bushes, caught by creepers, barred by trunks of trees, did not shine beside those supple animals, who, bounding from branch to branch, were hindered by nothing on their course. The monkeys were numerous, but happily they did not manifest any hostile disposition.

Several pigs, agoutis, kangaroos, and other rodents were seen, also two or three koalas, at which Pencroft longed to have a shot.

"But," said he, "you may jump and play just now; we shall have one or two words to say to you on our way back!"

At half-past nine the way was suddenly found to be barred by an unknown stream, from thirty to forty feet broad, whose rapid current dashed foaming over the numerous rocks which interrupted its course. This creek was deep and clear, but it was absolutely unnavigable.

"We are cut off!" cried Neb.

"No," replied Herbert, "it is only a stream, and we can easily swim over."

"What would be the use of that?" returned Harding. "This creek evidently runs to the sea. Let us remain on this side and follow the bank, and I shall be much astonished if it does not lead us very quickly to the coast. Forward!"

"One minute," said the reporter. "The name of this creek, my friends? Do not let us leave our geography incomplete."

"All right!" said Pencroft.

"Name it, my boy," said the engineer, addressing the lad.

"Will it not be better to wait until we have explored it to its mouth?" answered Herbert.

"Very well," replied Cyrus Harding. "Let us follow it as fast as we can without stopping."

"Still another minute!" said Pencroft.

"What's the matter?" asked the reporter.

"Though hunting is forbidden, fishing is allowed, I suppose," said the sailor.

"We have no time to lose," replied the engineer.

"Oh! five minutes!" replied Pencroft, "I only ask for five minutes to use in the interest of our breakfast!"

And Pencroft, lying down on the bank, plunged his arm into the water, and soon pulled up several dozen of fine crayfish from among the stones.

"These will be good!" cried Neb, going to the sailor's aid.

"As I said, there is everything in this island, except tobacco!" muttered Pencroft with a sigh.

The fishing did not take five minutes, for the crayfish were swarming in the creek. A bag was filled with the crustaceae, whose shells were of a cobalt blue. The settlers then pushed on.

They advanced more rapidly and easily along the bank of the river than in the forest. From time to time they came upon the traces of animals of a large size who had come to quench their thirst at the stream, but none were actually seen, and it was evidently not in this part of the forest that the peccary had received the bullet which had cost Pencroft a grinder.

In the meanwhile, considering the rapid current, Harding was led to suppose that he and his companions were much farther from the western coast than they had at first supposed. In fact, at this hour, the rising tide would have turned back the current of the creek, if its mouth had only been a few miles distant. Now, this effect was not produced, and the water pursued its natural course. The engineer was much astonished at this, and frequently consulted his compass, to assure himself that some turn of the river was not leading them again into the Far West.

However, the creek gradually widened and its waters became less tumultuous. The trees on the right bank were as close together as on the left bank, and it was impossible to distinguish anything beyond them; but these masses of wood were evidently uninhabited, for Top did not bark, and the intelligent animal would not have failed to signal the presence of any stranger in the neighbourhood.

At half-past ten, to the great surprise of Cyrus Harding, Herbert, who was a little in front, suddenly stopped and exclaimed—

"The sea!"

In a few minutes more, the whole western shore of the island lay extended before the eyes of the settlers.

But what a contrast between this and the eastern coast, upon which chance had first thrown them. No granite cliff, no rocks, not even a sandy beach. The forest reached the shore, and the tall trees bending over the water were beaten by the waves. It was not such a shore as is usually formed by nature, either by extending a vast carpet of sand, or by grouping masses of rock, but a beautiful border consisting of the most splendid trees. The bank was raised a little above the level of the sea, and on this luxuriant soil, supported by a granite base, the fine forest trees seemed to be as firmly planted as in the interior of the island.

The colonists were then on the shore of an unimportant little harbour, which would scarcely have contained even two or three fishing-boats. It served as a neck to the new creek, of which the curious thing was that its waters, instead of joining the sea by a gentle slope, fell from a height of more than forty feet, which explained why the rising tide was not felt up the stream. In fact, the tides of the Pacific, even at their maximum elevation, could never reach the level of the river, and, doubtless, millions of years would pass before the water would have worn away the granite and hollowed a practicable mouth.

It was settled that the name of Falls River should be given to this stream. Beyond, towards the north, the forest border was prolonged for a space of nearly two miles; then the trees became scarcer, and beyond that again the picturesque heights described a nearly straight line, which ran north and south. On the contrary, all the part of the shore between Falls River and Reptile End was a mass of wood, magnificent trees, some straight, others bent, so that the long sea-swell bathed their roots. Now, it was this coast, that is, all the Serpentine Peninsula, that was to be explored, for this part of the shore offered a refuge to castaways, which the other wild and barren side must have refused.

The weather was fine and clear, and from a height of a hillock on which Neb and Pencroft had arranged breakfast, a wide view was obtained. There was, however, not a sail in sight; nothing could be seen along the shore as far as the eye could reach. But the engineer would take nothing for granted until he had explored the coast to the very extremity of the Serpentine Peninsula.

Breakfast was soon despatched, and at half-past eleven the captain gave the signal for departure. Instead of proceeding over the summit of a cliff or along a sandy beach, the settlers were obliged to remain under cover of the trees so that they might continue on the shore.

The distance which separated Falls River from Reptile End was about twelve miles. It would have taken the settlers four hours to do this, on a clear ground and without hurrying themselves; but as it was they needed double the time, for what with trees to go round, bushes to cut down, and creepers to chop away, they were impeded at every step, these obstacles greatly lengthening their journey.

There was, however, nothing to show that a shipwreck had taken place recently. It is true that, as Gideon Spilett observed, any remains of it might have drifted out to sea, and they must not take it for granted that because they could find no traces of it, a ship had not been cast away on the coast.

The reporter's argument was just, and besides, the incident of the bullet proved that a shot must have been fired in Lincoln Island within three months.

It was already five o'clock, and there were still two miles between the settlers and the extremity of the Serpentine Peninsula. It was evident that after having reached Reptile End, Harding and his companions would not have time to return before dark to their encampment near the source of the Mercy. It would therefore be necessary to pass the night on the promontory. But they had no lack of provisions, which was lucky, for there were no animals on the shore, though birds, on the contrary, abounded—jacamars, couroucous, tragopans, grouse, lories, parrots, cockatoos, pheasants, pigeons, and a hundred others. There was not a tree without a nest, and not a nest which was not full of flapping wings.

Towards seven o'clock the weary explorers arrived at Reptile End. Here the seaside forest ended, and the shore resumed the customary appearance of a coast, with rocks, reefs, and sands. It was possible that something might be found here, but darkness came on, and the further exploration had to be put off to the next day.

Pencroft and Herbert hastened on to find a suitable place for their camp. Among the last trees of the forest of the Far West, the boy found several thick clumps of bamboos.

"Good," said he; "this is a valuable discovery."

"Valuable?" returned Pencroft.

"Certainly," replied Herbert. "I may say, Pencroft, that the bark of the bamboo, cut into flexible laths, is used for making baskets; that this bark, mashed into a paste, is used for the manufacture of Chinese paper; that the stalks furnish, according to their size, canes and pipes and are used for conducting water; that large bamboos make excellent material for building, being light and strong, and being never attacked by insects. I will add that by sawing the bamboo in two at the joint, keeping for the bottom the part of the transverse film which forms the joint, useful cups are obtained, which are much in use among the Chinese. No! you don't care for that. But—"

"But what?"

"But I can tell you, if you are ignorant of it, that in India these bamboos are eaten like asparagus."

"Asparagus thirty feet high!" exclaimed the sailor. "And are they good?"

"Excellent," replied Herbert. "Only it is not the stems of thirty feet high which are eaten, but the young shoots."

"Perfect, my boy, perfect!" replied Pencroft.

"I will also add that the pith of the young stalks, preserved in vinegar, makes a good pickle."

"Better and better, Herbert!"

"And lastly, that the bamboos exude a sweet liquor which can be made into a very agreeable drink."

"Is that all?" asked the sailor.

"That is all!"

"And they don't happen to do for smoking?"

"No, my poor Pencroft."

Herbert and the sailor had not to look long for a place in which to pass the night. The rocks, which must have been violently beaten by the sea under the influence of the winds of the south-west, presented many cavities in which shelter could be found against the night air. But just as they were about to enter one of these caves a loud roaring arrested them.

"Back!" cried Pencroft. "Our guns are only loaded with small shot, and beasts which can roar as loud as that would care no more for it than for grains of salt!" And the sailor, seizing Herbert by the arm, dragged him behind a rock, just as a magnificent animal showed itself at the entrance of the cavern.

It was a jaguar of a size at least equal to its Asiatic congeners, that is to say, it measured five feet from the extremity of its head to the beginning of its tail. The yellow colour of its hair was relieved by streaks and regular oblong spots of black, which contrasted with the white of its chest. Herbert recognised it as the ferocious rival of the tiger, as formidable as the puma, which is the rival of the largest wolf!

The jaguar advanced and gazed around him with blazing eyes, his hair bristling as if this was not the first time he had scented men.

At this moment the reporter appeared round a rock, and Herbert, thinking that he had not seen the jaguar, was about to rush towards him, when Gideon Spilett signed to him to remain where he was. This was not his first tiger, and advancing to within ten feet of the animal he remained motionless, his gun to his shoulder, without moving a muscle. The jaguar collected itself for a spring, but at that moment a shot struck it in the eyes, and it fell dead.

Herbert and Pencroft rushed towards the jaguar. Neb and Harding also ran up, and they remained for some instants contemplating the animal as it lay stretched on the ground, thinking that its magnificent skin would be a great ornament to the hall at Granite House.

"Oh, Mr. Spilett, how I admire and envy you!" cried Herbert, in a fit of very natural enthusiasm.

"Well, my boy," replied the reporter, "you could have done the same."

"I! with such coolness!—"

"Imagine to yourself, Herbert, that the jaguar is only a hare, and you would fire as quietly as possible."

"That is," rejoined Pencroft, "that it is not more dangerous than a hare!"

"And now," said Gideon Spilett, "since the jaguar has left its abode, I do not see, my friends, why we should not take possession of it for the night."

"But others may come," said Pencroft.

"It will be enough to light a fire at the entrance of the cavern," said the reporter, "and no wild beasts will dare to cross the threshold."

"Into the jaguar's house, then!" replied the sailor, dragging after him the body of the animal.

While Neb skinned the jaguar, his companions collected an abundant supply of dry wood from the forest, which they heaped up at the cave.

Cyrus Harding, seeing the clump of bamboos, cut a quantity, which he mingled with the other fuel.

This done, they entered the grotto, of which the floor was strewn with bones, the guns were carefully loaded, in case of a sudden attack, they had supper, and then just before they lay down to rest, the heap of wood piled at the entrance was set fire to. Immediately, a regular explosion, or rather a series of reports, broke the silence! The noise was caused by the bamboos, which, as the flames reached them, exploded like fireworks. The noise was enough to terrify even the boldest of wild beasts.

It was not the engineer who had invented this way of causing loud explosions, for, according to Marco Polo, the Tartars have employed it for many centuries to drive away from their encampments the formidable wild beasts of Central Asia.

Chapter V

Proposal to Return by the Southern Shore— Configuration of the Coast—Searching for the Supposed Wreck—A Wreck in the Air—Discovery of a Small Natural Port—At Midnight on the Banks of the Mercy— The Canoe Adrift

CYRUS HARDING AND HIS COMPANIONS SLEPT LIKE INNOCENT MARMOTS IN THE CAVE which the jaguar had so politely left at their disposal.

At sunrise all were on the shore at the extremity of the promontory, and their gaze was directed towards the horizon, of which two-thirds of the circumference were visible. For the last time the engineer could ascertain that not a sail nor the wreck of a ship was on the sea, and even with the telescope nothing suspicious could be discovered.

There was nothing either on the shore, at least, in the straight line of three miles which formed the south side of the promontory, for beyond that, rising ground hid the rest of the coast, and even from the extremity of the Serpentine Peninsula Claw Cape could not be seen.

The southern coast of the island still remained to be explored. Now should they undertake it immediately, and devote this day to it?

This was not included in their first plan. In fact, when the boat was abandoned at the sources of the Mercy, it had been agreed that after having surveyed the west coast, they should go back to it, and return to Granite House by the Mercy. Harding then thought that the western coast would have offered refuge, either to a ship in distress, or to a vessel in her regular course; but now, as he saw that this coast presented no good anchorage, he wished to seek on the south what they had not been able to find on the west.

Gideon Spilett proposed to continue the exploration, that the question of the supposed wreck might be completely settled, and he asked at what distance Claw Cape might be from the extremity of the peninsula.

"About thirty miles," replied the engineer, "if we take into consideration the curvings of the coast."

"Thirty miles!" returned Spilett. "That would be a long day's march. Nevertheless, I think that we should return to Granite House by the south coast."

"But," observed Herbert, "from Claw Cape to Granite House there must be at least another ten miles.

"Make it forty miles in all," replied the engineer, "and do not hesitate to do it. At least we should survey the unknown shore, and then we shall not have to begin the exploration again."

"Very good," said Pencroft. "But the boat?"

"The boat has remained by itself for one day at the sources of the Mercy," replied Gideon Spilett; "it may just as well stay there two days! As yet, we have had no reason to think that the island is infested by thieves!"

"Yet," said the sailor, "when I remember the history of the turtle, I am far from confident of that."

"The turtle! the turtle!" replied the reporter. "Don't you know that the sea turned it over?"

"Who knows?" murmured the engineer.

"But—" said Neb.

Neb had evidently something to say, for he opened his mouth to speak and yet said nothing.

"What do you want to say, Neb?" asked the engineer.

"If we return by the shore to Claw Cape," replied Neb, "after having doubled the Cape, we shall be stopped—"

"By the Mercy! of course," replied Herbert, "and we shall have neither bridge nor boat by which to cross."

"But, captain," added Pencroft, "with a few floating trunks we shall have no difficulty in crossing the river."

"Never mind," said Spilett, "it will be useful to construct a bridge if we wish to have an easy access to the Far West!"

"A bridge!" cried Pencroft. "Well, is not the captain the best engineer in his profession? He will make us a bridge when we want one. As to transporting you this evening to the other side of the Mercy, and that without wetting one thread of your clothes, I will take care of that. We have provisions for another day, and besides we can get plenty of game. Forward!"

The reporter's proposal, so strongly seconded by the sailor, received general approbation, for each wished to have their doubts set at rest, and by returning by Claw Cape the exploration would be ended. But there was not an hour to lose, for forty miles was a long march, and they could not hope to reach Granite House before night.

At six o'clock in the morning the little band set out. As a precaution the guns were loaded with ball, and Top, who led the van, received orders to beat about the edge of the forest.

From the extremity of the promontory which formed the tail of the peninsula the coast was rounded for a distance of five miles, which was rapidly passed over, without even the most minute investigations bringing to light the least trace of any old or recent landings; no debris, no mark of an encampment, no cinders of a fire, nor even a footprint!

From the point of the peninsula on which the settlers now were their gaze could extend along the south-west. Twenty-five miles off the coast terminated in the Claw Cape, which loomed dimly through the morning mists, and which, by the phenomenon of the mirage, appeared as if suspended between land and water.

Between the place occupied by the colonists and the other side of the immense bay, the shore was composed, first, of a tract of low land, bordered in the background by trees; then the shore became more irregular, projecting sharp points into the sea, and finally ended in the black rocks which, accumulated in picturesque disorder, formed Claw Cape.

Such was the development of this part of the island, which the settlers took in at a glance, while stopping for an instant.

"If a vessel ran in here," said Pencroft, "she would certainly be lost. Sand-banks and reefs everywhere! Bad quarters!"

"But at least something would be left of the ship," observed the reporter.

"There might be pieces of wood on the rocks, but nothing on the sands," replied the sailor.

"Why?"

"Because the sands are still more dangerous than the rocks, for they swallow up everything that is thrown on them. In a few days the hull of a ship of several hundred tons would disappear entirely in there!"

"So, Pencroft," asked the engineer, "if a ship has been wrecked on these banks, is it not astonishing that there is now no trace of her remaining?"

"No, captain, with the aid of time and tempest. However, it would be surprising, even in this case, that some of the masts or spars should not have been thrown on the beach, out of reach of the waves."

"Let us go on with our search, then," returned Cyrus Harding.

At one o'clock the colonists arrived at the other side of Washington Bay, they having now gone a distance of twenty miles.

They then halted for breakfast.

Here began the irregular coast, covered with lines of rocks and sand-banks. The long sea-swell could be seen breaking over the rocks in the bay, forming a foamy fringe. From this point to Claw Cape the beach was very narrow between the edge of the forest and the reefs.

Walking was now more difficult, on account of the numerous rocks which encumbered the beach. The granite cliff also gradually increased in height, and only the green tops of the trees which crowned it could be seen.

After half-an-hour's rest, the settlers resumed their journey, and not a spot among the rocks was left unexamined. Pencroft and Neb even rushed into the surf whenever any object attracted their attention. But they found nothing, some curious formations of the rocks having deceived them. They ascertained, however, that eatable shellfish abounded there, but these could not be of any great advantage to them until some easy means of communication had been established between the two banks of the Mercy, and until the means of transport had been perfected.

Nothing therefore which threw any light on the supposed wreck could be found on this shore, yet an object of any importance, such as the hull of a ship, would have been seen directly, or any of her masts and spars would have been washed on shore, just as the chest had been, which was found twenty miles from here. But there was nothing.

Towards three o'clock Harding and his companions arrived at a snug little creek. It formed quite a natural harbour, invisible from the sea, and was entered by a narrow channel.

At the back of this creek some violent convulsion had torn up the rocky border, and a cutting, by a gentle slope, gave access to an upper plateau, which might be situated at least ten miles from Claw Cape, and consequently four miles in a straight line from Prospect Heights. Gideon Spilett proposed to his companions that they should make a halt here. They agreed readily, for their walk had sharpened their appetites; and although it was not their usual dinner-hour, no one refused to strengthen himself with a piece of venison. This luncheon would sustain them till their supper, which they intended to take at Granite House. In a few minutes the settlers, seated under a clump of fine sea-pines, were devouring the provisions which Neb produced from his bag.

This spot was raised from fifty to sixty feet above the level of the sea. The view was very extensive, but beyond the cape it ended in Union Bay. Neither the islet nor Prospect Heights were visible, and could not be from thence, for the rising ground and the curtain of trees closed the northern horizon.

It is useless to add that notwithstanding the wide extent of sea which the explorers could survey, and though the engineer swept the horizon with his glass, no vessel could be found.

The shore was of course examined with the same care from the edge of the water to the cliff, and nothing could be discovered even with the aid of the instrument.

"Well," said Gideon Spilett, "it seems we must make up our minds to console ourselves with thinking that no one will come to dispute with us the possession of Lincoln Island!"

"But the bullet," cried Herbert. "That was not imaginary, I suppose!"

"Hang it, no!" exclaimed Pencroft, thinking of his absent tooth.

"Then what conclusion may be drawn?" asked the reporter.

"This," replied the engineer, "that three months or more ago, a vessel, either voluntarily or not, came here."

"What! then you admit, Cyrus, that she was swallowed up without leaving any trace?" cried the reporter.

"No, my dear Spilett; but you see that if it is certain that a human being set foot on the island, it appears no less certain that he has now left it."

"Then, if I understand you right, captain," said Herbert, "the vessel has left again?"

"Evidently."

"And we have lost an opportunity to get back to our country?" said Neb.

"I fear so."

"Very well, since the opportunity is lost, let us go on; it can't be helped," said Pencroft, who felt home-sickness for Granite House.

But just as they were rising, Top was heard loudly barking; and the dog issued from the wood, holding in his mouth a rag soiled with mud.

Neb seized it. It was a piece of strong cloth!

Top still barked, and by his going and coming, seemed to invite his master to follow him into the forest.

"Now there's something to explain the bullet!" exclaimed Pencroft.

"A castaway!" replied Herbert.

"Wounded, perhaps!" said Neb.

"Or dead!" added the reporter.

All ran after the dog, among the tall pines on the border of the forest. Harding and his companions made ready their fire-arms, in case of an emergency.

They advanced some way into the wood, but to their great disappointment, they as yet saw no signs of any human being having passed that way. Shrubs and creepers were uninjured, and they had even to cut them away with the axe, as they had done in the deepest recesses of the forest. It was difficult to fancy that any human creature had ever passed there, but yet Top went backwards and forwards, not like a dog who searches at random, but like a dog being endowed with a mind, who is following up an idea.

In about seven or eight minutes Top stopped in a glade surrounded with tall trees. The settlers gazed around them, but saw nothing, neither under the bushes nor among the trees.

"What is the matter, Top?" said Cyrus Harding.

Top barked louder, bounding about at the foot of a gigantic pine. All at once Pencroft shouted—

"Ho, splendid! capital!"

"What is it?" asked Spilett.

"We have been looking for a wreck at sea or on land!"

"Well?"

"Well; and here we've found one in the air!"

And the sailor pointed to a great white rag, caught in the top of the pine, a fallen scrap of which the dog had brought to them.

"But that is not a wreck!" cried Gideon Spilett.

"I beg your pardon!" returned Pencroft.

"Why? is it—?"

"It is all that remains of our airy boat, of our balloon, which has been caught up aloft there, at the top of that tree!"

Pencroft was not mistaken, and he gave vent to his feelings in a tremendous hurrah, adding—

"There is good cloth! There is what will furnish us with linen for years. There is what will make us handkerchiefs and shirts! Ha, ha, Mr. Spilett, what do you say to an island where shirts grow on the trees?"

It was certainly a lucky circumstance for the settlers in Lincoln Island that the balloon, after having made its last bound into the air, had fallen on the island and thus given them the opportunity of finding it again, whether they kept the case under its present form, or whether they wished to attempt another escape by it, or whether they usefully employed the several hundred yards of cotton, which was of fine quality. Pencroft's joy was therefore shared by all.

But it was necessary to bring down the remains of the balloon from the tree, to place it in security, and this was no slight task. Neb, Herbert, and the sailor, climbing to the summit of the tree, used all their skill to disengage the now reduced balloon.

The operation lasted two hours, and then not only the case, with its valve, its springs, its brasswork, lay on the ground, but the net, that is to say a considerable quantity of ropes and cordage, and the circle and the anchor. The case, except for the fracture, was in good condition, only the lower portion being torn.

It was a fortune which had fallen from the sky.

"All the same, captain," said the sailor, "if we ever decide to leave the island, it won't be in a balloon, will it? These air-boats won't go where we want them to go, and we have had some experience in that way! Look here, we will build a craft of some twenty tons, and then we can make a mainsail, a foresail, and a jib out of that cloth. As to the rest of it, that will help to dress us."

"We shall see, Pencroft," replied Cyrus Harding; "we shall see."

"In the meantime, we must put it in a safe place," said Neb.

They certainly could not think of carrying this load of cloth, ropes, and cordage, to Granite House, for the weight of it was very considerable, and while waiting for a suitable vehicle in which to convey it, it was of importance that this treasure should not be left longer exposed to the mercies of the first storm. The settlers, uniting their efforts, managed to drag it as far as the shore, where they discovered a large rocky cavity, which owing to its position could not be visited either by the wind or rain.

"We needed a locker, and now we have one," said Pencroft; "but as we cannot lock it up, it will be prudent to hide the opening. I don't mean from two-legged thieves, but from those with four paws!"

At six o'clock, all was stowed away, and after having given the creek the very suitable name of "Port Balloon," the settlers pursued their way along Claw Cape. Pencroft and the engineer talked of the different projects which it was agreed to put into execution with the briefest possible delay. It was necessary first of all to throw a bridge over the Mercy, so as to establish an easy communication with the south of the island; then the cart must be taken to bring back the balloon, for the canoe alone could not carry it, then they would build a decked boat, and Pencroft would rig it as a cutter, and they would be able to undertake voyages of circumnavigation round the island, etc.

In the meanwhile night came on, and it was already dark when the settlers reached Flotsam Point, the place where they had discovered the precious chest.

The distance between Flotsam Point and Granite House was another four miles, and it was midnight when, after having followed the shore to the mouth of the Mercy, the settlers arrived at the first angle formed by the Mercy.

There the river was eighty feet in breadth, which was awkward to cross, but as Pencroft had taken upon himself to conquer this difficulty, he was compelled to do it. The settlers certainly had reason to be pretty tired. The journey had been long, and the task of getting down the balloon had not rested either their arms or legs. They were anxious to reach Granite House to eat and sleep, and if the bridge had been constructed, in a quarter of an hour they would have been at home.

The night was very dark. Pencroft prepared to keep his promise by constructing a sort of raft, on which to make the passage of the Mercy. He and Neb, armed with axes, chose two trees near the water, and began to attack them at the base.

Cyrus Harding and Spilett, seated on the bank, waited till their companions were ready for their help, while Herbert roamed about, though without going to any distance. All at once, the lad, who had strolled by the river, came running back, and, pointing up the Mercy, exclaimed—

"What is floating there?"

Pencroft stopped working, and seeing an indistinct object moving through the gloom—

"A canoe!" cried he.

All approached, and saw to their extreme surprise, a boat floating down the current.

"Boat ahoy!" shouted the sailor, without thinking that perhaps it would be best to keep silence.

No reply. The boat still drifted onward, and it was not more than twelve feet off, when the sailor exclaimed—

"But it is our own boat! she has broken her moorings, and floated down the current. I must say she has arrived very opportunely."

"Our boat?" murmured the engineer.

Pencroft was right. It was indeed the canoe, of which the rope had undoubtedly broken, and which had come alone from the sources of the Mercy. It was very important to seize it before the rapid current should have swept it away out of the mouth of the river, but Neb and Pencroft cleverly managed this by means of a long pole.

The canoe touched the shore. The engineer leaped in first, and found, on examining the rope, that it had been really worn through by rubbing against the rocks.

"Well," said the reporter to him, in a low voice, "this is a strange thing."

"Strange indeed!" returned Cyrus Harding.

Strange or not, it was very fortunate. Herbert, the reporter, Neb, and Pencroft, embarked in turn. There was no doubt about the rope having been worn through, but the astonishing part of the affair was, that the boat should arrive just at the moment when the settlers were there to seize it on its way, for a quarter of an hour earlier or later it would have been lost in the sea.

If they had been living in the time of genii, this incident would have given them the right to think that the island was haunted by some supernatural being, who used his power in the service of the castaways!

A few strokes of the oar brought the settlers to the mouth of the Mercy. The canoe was hauled upon the beach near the Chimneys, and all proceeded towards the ladder of Granite House.

But at that moment, Top barked angrily, and Neb, who was looking for the first steps, uttered a cry.

There was no longer a ladder!

Chapter VI

PENCROFT'S HALLOOS—A NIGHT IN THE CHIMNEYS—
HERBERT'S ARROWS—THE CAPTAIN'S PROJECT—AN UNEXPECTED
EXPLANATION—WHAT HAS HAPPENED IN GRANITE HOUSE—
HOW A NEW SERVANT ENTERS THE SERVICE OF THE COLONISTS

CYRUS HARDING STOOD STILL, WITHOUT SAYING A WORD. HIS COMPANIONS SEARCHED in the darkness on the wall, in case the wind should have moved the ladder, and on the ground, thinking that it might have fallen down. . . . But the ladder had quite disappeared. As to ascertaining if a squall had blown it on the landing-place, half-way up, that was impossible in the dark.

"If it is a joke," cried Pencroft, "it is a very stupid one; to come home and find no staircase to go up to your room by, for weary men, there is nothing to laugh at that I can see."

Neb could do nothing but cry out "Oh! oh! oh!"

"I begin to think that very curious things happen in Lincoln Island!" said Pencroft.

"Curious?" replied Gideon Spilett, "not at all, Pencroft, nothing can be more natural. Someone has come during our absence, taken possession of our dwelling and drawn up the ladder."

"Someone," cried the sailor. "But who?"

"Who but the hunter who fired the bullet?" replied the reporter.

"Well, if there is anyone up there," replied Pencroft, who began to lose patience, "I will give them a hail, and they must answer."

And in a stentorian voice the sailor gave a prolonged "Halloo!" which was echoed again and again from the cliff and rocks.

The settlers listened and they thought they heard a sort of chuckling laugh, of which they could not guess the origin. But no voice replied to Pencroft, who in vain repeated his vigourous shouts.

There was something indeed in this to astonish the most apathetic of men, and the settlers were not men of that description. In their situation every incident had its importance, and, certainly, during the seven months which they had spent on the island, they had not before met with anything of so surprising a character.

Be that as it may, forgetting their fatigue in the singularity of the event, they remained below Granite House, not knowing what to think, not knowing what to do, questioning each other without any hope of a satisfactory reply, everyone starting some supposition each more unlikely than the last. Neb bewailed himself, much disappointed at not being able to get into his kitchen, for the provisions which they had had on their expedition were exhausted, and they had no means of renewing them.

"My friends," at last said Cyrus Harding, "there is only one thing to be done at present, wait for day, and then act according to circumstances. But let us go to the Chimneys. There we shall be under shelter, and if we cannot eat, we can at least sleep."

"But who is it that has played us this cool trick?" again asked Pencroft, unable to make up his mind to retire from the spot.

Whoever it was, the only thing practicable was to do as the engineer proposed, to go to the Chimneys and there wait for day. In the meanwhile Top was ordered to mount guard below the windows of Granite House, and when Top received an order he obeyed it without any questioning. The brave dog therefore remained at the foot of the cliff while his master with his companions sought a refuge among the rocks.

To say that the settlers, notwithstanding their fatigue, slept well on the sandy floor of the Chimneys would not be true. It was not only that they were extremely anxious to find out the cause of what had happened, whether it was the result of an accident which would be discovered at the return of day, or whether on the contrary it was the work of a human being; but they also had very uncomfortable beds. That could not be helped, however, for in some way or other at that moment their dwelling was occupied, and they could not possibly enter it.

Now Granite House was more than their dwelling, it was their warehouse. There were all the stores belonging to the colony, weapons, instruments, tools, ammunition, provisions, etc. To think that all that might be pillaged and that the settlers would have all their work to do over again, fresh weapons and tools to make, was a serious matter. Their uneasiness led one or other of them also to go out every few minutes to see if Top was keeping good watch. Cyrus Harding alone waited with his habitual patience, although his strong mind was exasperated at being confronted with such an inexplicable fact, and he was provoked at himself for allowing a feeling to which he could not give a name, to gain an influence over him. Gideon Spilett shared his feelings in this respect, and the two conversed together in whispers of the inexplicable circumstance which baffled even their intelligence and experience.

"It is a joke," said Pencroft; "it is a trick someone has played us. Well, I don't like such jokes, and the joker had better look out for himself, if he falls into my hands, I can tell him."

As soon as the first gleam of light appeared in the east, the colonists, suitably armed, repaired to the beach under Granite House. The rising sun now shone on the cliff and they could see the windows, the shutters of which were closed, through the curtains of foliage.

All here was in order; but a cry escaped the colonists when they saw that the door, which they had closed on their departure, was now wide open.

Someone had entered Granite House—there could be no more doubt about that.

The upper ladder, which generally hung from the door to the landing, was in its place, but the lower ladder was drawn up and raised to the threshold. It was evident that the intruders had wished to guard themselves against a surprise.

Pencroft hailed again.

No reply.

"The beggars," exclaimed the sailor. "There they are sleeping quietly as if they were in their own house. Hallo there, you pirates, brigands, robbers, sons of John Bull!"

When Pencroft, being a Yankee, treated anyone to the epithet of "son of John Bull," he considered he had reached the last limits of insult.

The sun had now completely risen, and the whole façade of Granite House became illuminated by his rays; but in the interior as well as on the exterior all was quiet and calm.

The settlers asked if Granite House was inhabited or not, and yet the position of the ladder was sufficient to show that it was; it was also certain that the inhabitants, whoever they might be, had not been able to escape. But how were they to be got at?

Herbert then thought of fastening a cord to an arrow, and shooting the arrow so that it should pass between the first rounds of the ladder which hung from the threshold. By means of the cord they would then be able to draw down the ladder to the ground, and so re-establish the communication between the beach and Granite House. There was evidently nothing else to be done, and, with a little skill, this method might succeed. Very fortunately bows and arrows had been left at the Chimneys, where they also found a quantity of light hibiscus cord. Pencroft fastened this to a well-feathered arrow. Then Herbert fixing it to his bow, took a careful aim for the lower part of the ladder.

Cyrus Harding, Gideon Spilett, Pencroft, and Neb drew back, so as to see if anything appeared at the windows. The reporter lifted his gun to his shoulder and covered the door.

The bow was bent, the arrow flew, taking the cord with it, and passed between the two last rounds.

The operation had succeeded.

Herbert immediately seized the end of the cord, but, at that moment when he gave it a pull to bring down the ladder, an arm, thrust suddenly out between the wall and the door, grasped it and dragged it inside Granite House.

"The rascals!" shouted the sailor. "If a ball can do anything for you, you shall not have long to wait for it."

"But who was it?" asked Neb.

"Who was it? Didn't you see?"

"No."

"It was a monkey, a sapaso, an orang-outang, a baboon, a gorilla, a sagoin. Our dwelling has been invaded by monkeys, who climbed up the ladder during our absence."

And, at this moment, as if to bear witness to the truth of the sailor's words, two or three quadrumana showed themselves at the windows, from which they had pushed back the shutters, and saluted the real proprietors of the place with a thousand hideous grimaces.

"I knew that it was only a joke," cried Pencroft; "but one of the jokers shall pay the penalty for the rest."

So saying, the sailor, raising his piece, took a rapid aim at one of the monkeys and fired. All disappeared, except one who fell mortally wounded on the beach. This monkey, which was of a large size, evidently belonged to the first order of the quadrumana. Whether this was a chimpanzee, an orang-outang, or a gorilla, he took rank among the anthropoid apes, who are so called from their resemblance to the human race. However, Herbert declared it to be an orang-outang.

"What a magnificent beast!" cried Neb.

"Magnificent, if you like," replied Pencroft; "but still I do not see how we are to get into our house."

"Herbert is a good marksman," said the reporter, "and his bow is here. He can try again."

"Why, these apes are so cunning," returned Pencroft; "they won't show themselves again at the windows and so we can't kill them; and when I think of the mischief they may do in the rooms and store-house——"

"Have patience," replied Harding; "these creatures cannot keep us long at bay."

"I shall not be sure of that till I see them down here," replied the sailor. "And now, captain, do you know how many dozens of these fellows are up there?"

It was difficult to reply to Pencroft, and as for the young boy making another attempt, that was not easy; for the lower part of the ladder had been drawn again into the door, and when another pull was given, the line broke and the ladder remained firm. The case was really perplexing. Pencroft stormed. There was a comic side to the situation, but he did not think it funny at all. It was certain that the settlers would end by reinstating themselves in their domicile and driving out the intruders, but when and how? this is what they were not able to say.

Two hours passed, during which the apes took care not to show themselves, but they were still there, and three or four times a nose or a paw was poked out at the door or windows, and was immediately saluted by a gunshot.

"Let us hide ourselves," at last said the engineer. "Perhaps the apes will think we have gone quite away and will show themselves again. Let Spilett and Herbert conceal themselves behind those rocks and fire on all that may appear."

The engineer's orders were obeyed, and while the reporter and the lad, the best marksmen in the colony, posted themselves in a good position, but out of the monkeys' sight, Neb, Pencroft, and Cyrus climbed the plateau and entered the forest in order to kill some game, for it was now time for breakfast and they had no provisions remaining.

In half-an-hour the hunters returned with a few rock pigeons, which they roasted as well as they could. Not an ape had appeared. Gideon Spilett and Herbert went to take their share of the breakfast, leaving Top to watch under the windows. They then, having eaten, returned to their post.

Two hours later, their situation was in no degree improved. The quadrumana gave no sign of existence, and it might have been supposed that they had disappeared; but what seemed more probable was that, terrified by the death of one of their companions, and frightened by the noise of the fire-arms, they had retreated to the back part of the house or probably even into the store-room. And when they thought of the valuables which this store-room contained, the patience so much recommended by the engineer, fast changed into great irritation, and there certainly was room for it.

"Decidedly it is too bad," said the reporter; "and the worst of it is, there is no way of putting an end to it."

"But we must drive these vagabonds out somehow," cried the sailor. "We could soon get the better of them, even if there are twenty of the rascals; but for that, we must meet them hand to hand. Come now, is there no way of getting at them?"

"Let us try to enter Granite House by the old opening at the lake," replied the engineer.

"Oh!" shouted the sailor, "and I never thought of that."

This was in reality the only way by which to penetrate into Granite House so as to fight with and drive out the intruders. The opening was, it is true, closed up with a wall of cemented stones, which it would be necessary to sacrifice, but that could easily be rebuilt.

Fortunately, Cyrus Harding had not as yet effected his project of hiding this opening by raising the waters of the lake, for the operation would then have taken some time.

It was already past twelve o'clock, when the colonists, well armed and provided with picks and spades, left the Chimneys, passed beneath the windows of Granite House, after telling Top to remain at his post, and began to ascend the left bank of the Mercy, so as to reach Prospect Heights.

But they had not made fifty steps in this direction, when they heard the dog barking furiously.

And all rushed down the bank again.

Arrived at the turning, they saw that the situation had changed.

In fact, the apes, seized with a sudden panic, from some unknown cause, were trying to escape. Two or three ran and clambered from one window to another with the agility of acrobats. They were not even trying to replace the ladder, by which it would have been easy to descend; perhaps in their terror they had forgotten this way of escape. The colonists, now being able to take aim without difficulty, fired. Some, wounded or killed, fell back into the rooms, uttering piercing cries. The rest, throwing themselves out, were dashed to pieces in their fall, and in a few minutes, so far as they knew, there was not a living quadrumana in Granite House.

At this moment the ladder was seen to slip over the threshold, then unroll and fall to the ground.

"Hullo!" cried the sailor, "this is queer!"

"Very strange!" murmured the engineer, leaping first up the ladder.

"Take care, captain!" cried Pencroft, "perhaps there are still some of these rascals. . . ."

"We shall soon see," replied the engineer, without stopping however.

All his companions followed him, and in a minute they had arrived at the threshold. They searched everywhere. There was no one in the rooms nor in the store-house, which had been respected by the band of quadrumana.

"Well now, and the ladder," cried the sailor; "who can the gentleman have been who sent us that down?"

But at that moment a cry was heard, and a great orang, who had hidden himself in the passage, rushed into the room, pursued by Neb.

"Ah, the robber!" cried Pencroft.

And hatchet in hand, he was about to cleave the head of the animal, when Cyrus Harding seized his arm, saying—

"Spare him, Pencroft."

"Pardon this rascal?"

"Yes! it was he who threw us the ladder!"

And the engineer said this in such a peculiar voice that it was difficult to know whether he spoke seriously or not.

Nevertheless, they threw themselves on the orang, who defended himself gallantly, but was soon overpowered and bound.

"There!" said Pencroft. "And what shall we make of him, now we've got him?"

"A servant!" replied Herbert.

The lad was not joking in saying this, for he knew how this intelligent race could be turned to account.

The settlers then approached the ape and gazed at it attentively. He belonged to the family of anthropoid apes, of which the facial angle is not much inferior to that of the Australians and Hottentots. It was an orang-outang, and as such, had neither the ferocity of the gorilla, nor the stupidity of the baboon. It is to this family of the anthropoid apes that so many characteristics belong which prove them to be possessed of an almost human intelligence. Employed in houses, they can wait at table, sweep rooms, brush clothes, clean boots, handle a knife, fork, and spoon properly, and even drink wine . . . doing everything as well as the best servant that ever walked upon two legs. Buffon possessed one of these apes, who served him for a long time as a faithful and zealous servant.

The one which had been seized in the hall of Granite House was a great fellow, six feet high, with an admirably poportioned frame, a broad chest, head of a moderate size, the facial angle reaching sixty-five degrees, round skull, projecting nose, skin covered with soft glossy hair, in short, a fine specimen of the anthropoids. His eyes, rather smaller than human eyes, sparkled with intelligence; his white teeth glittered under his mustache, and he wore a little curly brown beard.

"A handsome fellow!" said Pencroft; "if we only knew his language, we could talk to him."

"But, master," said Neb, "are you serious? Are we going to take him as a servant?"

"Yes, Neb," replied the engineer, smiling. "But you must not be jealous."

"And I hope he will make an excellent servant," added Herbert. "He appears young, and will be easy to educate, and we shall not be obliged to use force to subdue him, nor draw his teeth, as is sometimes done. He will soon grow fond of his masters if they are kind to him."

"And they will be," replied Pencroft, who had forgotten all his rancor against "the jokers."

Then, approaching the orang—

"Well, old boy!" he asked, "how are you?"

The orang replied by a little grunt which did not show any anger.

"You wish to join the colony?" again asked the sailor. "You are going to enter the service of Captain Cyrus Harding?"

Another respondent grunt was uttered by the ape.

"And you will be satisfied with no other wages than your food?"

Third affirmative grunt.

"This conversation is slightly monotonous," observed Gideon Spilett.

"So much the better," replied Pencroft; "the best servants are those who talk the least. And then, no wages, do you hear, my boy? We will give you no wages at first, but we will double them afterwards if we are pleased with you."

Thus the colony was increased by a new member. As to his name the sailor begged that in memory of another ape which he had known, he might be called Jupiter, and Jup for short.

And so, without more ceremony, Master Jup was installed in Granite House.

Chapter VII

PLANS—A BRIDGE OVER THE MERCY—MODE ADOPTED FOR
MAKING AN ISLAND OF PROSPECT HEIGHTS—THE
DRAWBRIDGE—HARVEST—THE STREAM—THE POULTRY-
YARD—A PIGEON-HOUSE—THE TWO ONAGERS—
THE CART—EXCURSION TO PORT BALLOON

THE SETTLERS IN LINCOLN ISLAND HAD NOW REGAINED THEIR DWELLING, WITHOUT having been obliged to reach it by the old opening, and were therefore spared the trouble of mason's work. It was certainly lucky, that at the moment they were about to set out to do so, the apes had been seized with that terror, no less sudden than inexplicable, which had driven them out of Granite House. Had the animals discovered that they were about to be attacked from another direction? This was the only explanation of their sudden retreat.

During the day the bodies of the apes were carried into the wood, where they were buried; then the settlers busied themselves in repairing the disorder caused by the intruders, disorder but not damage, for although they had turned everything in the rooms topsy-turvy, yet they had broken nothing. Neb relighted his stove, and the stores in the larder furnished a substantial repast, to which all did ample justice.

Jup was not forgotten, and he ate with relish some stone-pine almonds and rhizome roots, with which he was abundantly supplied. Pencroft had unfastened his arms, but judged it best to have his legs tied until they were more sure of his submission.

Then, before retiring to rest, Harding and his companions seated round their table, discussed those plans, the execution of which was most pressing. The most important and most urgent was the establishment of a bridge over the Mercy, so as to form a communication with the southern part of the island and Granite House; then the making of an enclosure for the musmons or other woolly animals which they wished to capture.

These two projects would help to solve the difficulty as to their clothing, which was now serious. The bridge would render easy the transport of the balloon case, which would furnish them with linen, and the inhabitants of the enclosure would yield wool which would supply them with winter clothes.

As to the enclosure, it was Cyrus Harding's intention to establish it at the sources of the Red Creek, where the ruminants would find fresh and abundant pasture. The road between Prospect Heights and the sources of the stream was already partly beaten, and with a better cart than the first, the material could be easily conveyed to the spot, especially if they could manage to capture some animals to draw it.

But though there might be no inconvenience in the enclosure being so far from Granite House, it would not be the same with the poultry-yard, to which Neb called the attention of the colonists. It was indeed necessary that the birds should be close within reach of the cook, and no place appeared more favourable for the establishment of the said poultry-yard than that portion of the banks of the lake which was close to the old opening.

Water-birds would prosper there as well as others, and the couple of tinamous taken in their last excursion would be the first to be domesticated.

The next day, the 3d of November, the new works were begun by the construction of the bridge, and all hands were required for this important task. Saws, hatchets, and hammers were shouldered by the settlers, who, now transformed into carpenters, descended to the shore.

There Pencroft observed—

"Suppose, that during our absence, Master Jup takes it into his head to draw up the ladder which he so politely returned to us yesterday?"

"Let us tie its lower end down firmly," replied Cyrus Harding.

This was done by means of two stakes securely fixed in the sand. Then the settlers, ascending the left bank of the Mercy, soon arrived at the angle formed by the river.

There they halted, in order to ascertain if the bridge could be thrown across. The place appeared suitable.

In fact, from this spot, to Port Balloon, discovered the day before on the southern coast, there was only a distance of three miles and a half, and from the bridge to the Port, it would be easy to make a good cart-road which would render the communication between Granite House and the south of the island extremely easy.

Cyrus Harding now imparted to his companions a scheme for completely isolating Prospect Heights so as to shelter it from the attacks both of quadrupeds and quadrumana. In this way, Granite House, the Chimneys, the poultry-yard, and all the upper part of the plateau which was to be used for cultivation, would be protected against the depredations of animals. Nothing could be easier than to execute this project, and this is how the engineer intended to set to work.

The plateau was already defended on three sides by water-courses, either artificial or natural. On the north-west, by the shores of Lake Grant, from the entrance of the passage to the breach made in the banks of the lake for the escape of the water.

On the north, from this breach to the sea, by the new water-course which had hollowed out a bed for itself across the plateau and shore, above and below the fall, and it would be enough to dig the bed of this creek a little deeper to make it impracticable for animals, on all the eastern border by the sea itself, from the mouth of the aforesaid creek to the mouth of the Mercy.

Lastly, on the south, from the mouth to the turn of the Mercy where the bridge was to be established.

The western border of the plateau now remained between the turn of the river and the southern angle of the lake, a distance of about a mile, which was open to all comers. But nothing could be easier than to dig a broad deep ditch, which could be filled from the lake, and the overflow of which would throw itself by a rapid fall into the bed of the Mercy. The level of the lake would, no doubt, be somewhat lowered by this fresh discharge of its waters, but Cyrus Harding had ascertained that the volume of water in the Red Creek was considerable enough to allow of the execution of this project.

"So then," added the engineer, "Prospect Heights will become a regular island, being surrounded with water on all sides, and only communicating with the rest of our domain by the bridge which we are about to throw across the Mercy, the two little bridges already established above and below the fall; and, lastly, two other little bridges which must be constructed, one over the canal which I propose to dig, the other across to the left bank of the Mercy. Now, if these bridges can be raised at will, Prospect Heights will be guarded from any surprise."

The bridge was the most urgent work. Trees were selected, cut down, stripped of their branches, and cut into beams, joists, and planks. The end of the bridge which rested on the right bank of the Mercy was to be firm, but the other end on the left bank was to be movable, so that it might be raised by means of a counterpoise, as some canal bridges are managed.

This was certainly a considerable work, and though it was skilfully conducted, it took some time, for the Mercy at this place was eighty feet wide. It was therefore necessary to fix piles in the bed of the river so as to sustain the floor of the bridge and establish a pile-driver to act on the tops of these piles, which would thus form two arches and allow the bridge to support heavy loads.

Happily there was no want of tools with which to shape the wood, nor of iron-work to make it firm, nor of the ingenuity of a man who had a marvelous knowledge of the work, nor lastly, the zeal of his companions, who in seven months had necessarily acquired great skill in the use of their tools; and it must be said that not the least skilful was Gideon Spilett, who in dexterity almost equaled the sailor himself. "Who would ever have expected so much from a newspaper man!" thought Pencroft.

The construction of the Mercy bridge lasted three weeks of regular hard work. They even breakfasted on the scene of their labors, and the weather being magnificent, they only returned to Granite House to sleep.

During this period it may be stated that Master Jup grew more accustomed to his new masters, whose movements he always watched with very inquisitive eyes. However, as a precautionary measure, Pencroft did not as yet allow him complete liberty, rightly wishing to wait until the limits of the plateau should be settled by the projected works. Top and Jup were good friends and played willingly together, but Jup did everything solemnly.

On the 20th of November the bridge was finished. The movable part, balanced by the counterpoise, swung easily, and only a slight effort was needed to raise it; between its hinge and the last cross-bar on which it rested when closed, there existed a space of twenty feet, which was sufficiently wide to prevent any animals from crossing.

The settlers now began to talk of fetching the balloon-case, which they were anxious to place in perfect security; but to bring it, it would be necessary to take a cart to Port Balloon, and consequently, necessary to beat a road through the dense forests of the Far West. This would take some time. Also, Neb and Pencroft having gone to examine into the state of things at Port Balloon, and reported that the stock of cloth would suffer no damage in the grotto where it was stored, it was decided that the work at Prospect Heights should not be discontinued.

"That," observed Pencroft, "will enable us to establish our poultry-yard under better conditions, since we need have no fear of visits from foxes nor the attacks of other beasts."

"Then," added Neb, "we can clear the plateau, and transplant wild plants to it."

"And prepare our second corn-field!" cried the sailor with a triumphant air.

In fact, the first corn-field sown with a single grain had prospered admirably, thanks to Pencroft's care. It had produced the ten ears foretold by the engineer, and each ear containing eighty grains, the colony found itself in possession of eight hundred grains, in six months, which promised a double harvest each year.

These eight hundred grains, except fifty, which were prudently reserved, were to be sown in a new field, but with no less care than was bestowed on the single grain.

The field was prepared, then surrounded with a strong palisade, high and pointed, which quadrupeds would have found difficulty in leaping. As to birds, some scarecrows, due to Pencroft's ingenious brain, were enough to frighten them. The seven hundred and fifty grains deposited in very regular furrows were then left for nature to do the rest.

On the 21st of November, Cyrus Harding began to plan the canal which was to close the plateau on the west, from the south angle of Lake Grant to the angle of the Mercy. There was there two or three feet of vegetable earth, and below that granite. It was therefore necessary to manufacture some more nitro-glycerine, and the nitro-glycerine did its accustomed work. In less than a fortnight a ditch, twelve feet wide and six deep, was dug out in the hard ground of the plateau. A new trench was made by the same means in the rocky border of the lake, forming a small stream, to which they gave the name of Creek Glycerine, and which was thus an affluent of the Mercy. As the engineer had predicted, the level of the lake was lowered, though very slightly. To complete the enclosure the bed of the stream on the beach was considerably enlarged, and the sand supported by means of stakes.

By the end of the first fortnight of December these works were finished, and Prospect Heights—that is to say, a sort of irregular pentagon, having a perimeter of nearly four miles, surrounded by a liquid belt—was completely protected from depredators of every description.

During the month of December, the heat was very great. In spite of it, however, the settlers continued their work, and as they were anxious to possess a poultry-yard they forthwith commenced it.

It is useless to say that since the enclosing of the plateau had been completed, Master Jup had been set at liberty. He did not leave his masters, and evinced no wish to escape. He was a gentle animal, though very powerful and wonderfully active. He was already taught to make himself useful by drawing loads of wood and carting away the stones which were extracted from the bed of Creek Glycerine.

The poultry-yard occupied an area of two hundred square yards, on the south-eastern bank of the lake. It was surrounded by a palisade, and in it were constructed various shelters for the birds which were to populate it. These were simply built of branches and divided into compartments, made ready for the expected guests.

The first were the two tinamous, which were not long in having a number of young ones; they had for companions half-a-dozen ducks, accustomed to the borders of the lake. Some belonged to the Chinese species, of which the wings open like a fan, and which by the brilliancy of their plumage rival the golden pheasants. A few days afterwards, Herbert snared a couple of gallinaceae, with spreading tails composed of long feathers, magnificent alectors, which soon became tame. As to pelicans, kingfishers, water-hens, they came of themselves to the shores of the poultry-yard, and this little community, after some disputes, cooing, screaming, clucking, ended by settling down peacefully, and increased in encouraging proportion for the future use of the colony.

Cyrus Harding, wishing to complete his performance, established a pigeon-house in a corner of the poultry-yard. There he lodged a dozen of those pigeons which frequented the rocks of the plateau. These birds soon became accustomed to returning every evening to their new dwelling, and showed more disposition to domesticate themselves than their congeners, the wood-pigeons.

Lastly, the time had come for turning the balloon-case to use, by cutting it up to make shirts and other articles; for as to keeping it in its present form, and risking themselves in a balloon filled with gas, above a sea of the limits of which they had no idea, it was not to be thought of.

It was necessary to bring the case to Granite House, and the colonists employed themselves in rendering their heavy cart lighter and more manageable. But though they had a vehicle, the moving power was yet to be found.

But did there not exist in the island some animal which might supply the place of the horse, ass, or ox? That was the question.

"Certainly," said Pencroft, "a beast of burden would be very useful to us until the captain has made a steam cart, or even an engine, for someday we shall have a railroad from Granite House to Port Balloon, with a branch line to Mount Franklin!"

One day, the 23d of December, Neb and Top were heard shouting and barking, each apparently trying who could make the most noise. The settlers, who were busy at the Chimneys, ran, fearing some vexatious incident.

What did they see? Two fine animals of a large size, who had imprudently ventured on the plateau, when the bridges were open. One would have said they were horses, or at least donkeys, male and female, of a fine shape, dove-colored, the legs and tail white, striped with black on the head and neck. They advanced quietly without showing any uneasiness, and gazed at the men, in whom they could not as yet recognise their future masters.

"These are onagers!" cried Herbert, "animals something between the zebra and the conaga!"

"Why not donkeys?" asked Neb.

"Because they have not long ears, and their shape is more graceful!"

"Donkeys or horses," interrupted Pencroft, "they are 'moving powers,' as the captain would say, and as such must be captured!"

The sailor, without frightening the animals, crept through the grass to the bridge over Creek Glycerine, lowered it, and the onagers were prisoners.

Now, should they seize them with violence and master them by force? No. It was decided that for a few days they should be allowed to roam freely about the plateau, where there was an abundance of grass, and the engineer immediately began to prepare a stable near the poultry-yard, in which the onagers might find food, with a good litter, and shelter during the night.

This done, the movements of the two magnificent creatures were left entirely free, and the settlers avoided even approaching them so as to terrify them. Several times, however, the onagers appeared to wish to leave the plateau, too confined for animals accustomed to the plains and forests. They were then seen following the water-barrier which everywhere presented itself before them, uttering short neighs, then galloping through the grass, and becoming calmer, they would remain entire hours gazing at the woods, from which they were cut off forever!

In the meantime harness of vegetable fibre had been manufactured, and some days after the capture of the onagers, not only the cart was ready, but a straight road, or rather a cutting, had been made through the forests of the Far West, from the angle of the Mercy to Port Balloon. The cart might then be driven there, and towards the end of December they tried the onagers for the first time.

Pencroft had already coaxed the animals to come and eat out of his hand, and they allowed him to approach without making any difficulty, but once harnessed they reared and could with difficulty be held in. However, it was not long before they submitted to this new service, for the onager, being less refractory than the zebra, is frequently put in harness in the mountainous regions of Southern Africa, and it has even been acclimatised in Europe, under zones of a relative coolness.

On this day all the colony, except Pencroft who walked at the animals' heads, mounted the cart, and set out on the road to Port Balloon.

Of course they were jolted over the somewhat rough road, but the vehicle arrived without any accident, and was soon loaded with the case and rigging of the balloon.

At eight o'clock that evening the cart, after passing over the Mercy bridge, descended the left bank of the river, and stopped on the beach. The onagers being unharnessed, were thence led to their stable, and Pencroft before going to sleep gave vent to his feelings in a deep sigh of satisfaction that awoke all the echoes of Granite House.

Chapter VIII

LINEN—SHOES OF SEAL-LEATHER—MANUFACTURE OF PYROXYLE—GARDENING—FISHING—TURTLE-EGGS— IMPROVEMENT OF MASTER JUP—THE CORRAL—MUSMON HUNT— NEW ANIMAL AND VEGETABLE POSSESSIONS—RECOLLECTIONS OF THEIR NATIVE LAND

THE FIRST WEEK OF JANUARY WAS DEVOTED TO THE MANUFACTURE OF THE LINEN GARments required by the colony. The needles found in the box were used by sturdy if not delicate fingers, and we may be sure that what was sewn was sewn firmly.

There was no lack of thread, thanks to Cyrus Harding's idea of re-employing that which had been already used in the covering of the balloon. This with admirable patience was all unpicked by Gideon Spilett and Herbert, for Pencroft had been obliged to give this work up, as it irritated him beyond measure; but he had no equal in the sewing part of the business. Indeed, everybody knows that sailors have a remarkable aptitude for tailoring.

The cloth of which the balloon-case was made was then cleaned by means of soda and potash, obtained by the incineration of plants, in such a way that the cotton, having got rid of the varnish, resumed its natural softness and elasticity; then, exposed to the action of the atmosphere, it soon became perfectly white. Some dozen shirts and socks—the latter not knitted, of course, but made of cotton—were thus manufactured. What a comfort it was to the settlers to clothe themselves again in clean linen, which was doubtless rather rough, but they were not troubled about that! and then to go to sleep between sheets, which made the couches at Granite House into quite comfortable beds!

It was about this time also that they made boots of seal-leather, which were greatly needed to replace the shoes and boots brought from America. We may be sure that these new shoes were large enough and never pinched the feet of the wearers.

With the beginning of the year 1866 the heat was very great, but the hunting in the forests did not stand still. Agouties, peccaries, capybaras, kangaroos, game of all sorts, actually swarmed there, and Spilett and Herbert were too good marksmen ever to throw away their shot uselessly.

Cyrus Harding still recommended them to husband the ammunition, and he took measures to replace the powder and shot which had been found in the box, and which he wished to reserve for the future. How did he know where chance might one day cast his companions and himself in the event of their leaving their domain? They should, then, prepare for the unknown future by husbanding their ammunition and by substituting for it some easily renewable substance.

To replace lead, of which Harding had found no traces in the island, he employed granulated iron, which was easy to manufacture. These bullets, not having the weight of leaden bullets, were made larger, and each charge contained less, but the skill of the sportsmen made up this deficiency. As to powder, Cyrus Harding would have been able to make that also, for he had at his disposal saltpeter, sulphur, and coal; but this preparation requires extreme care, and without special tools it is difficult to produce it of a good quality. Harding preferred, therefore, to manufacture pyroxyle, that is to say gun-cotton, a substance in which cotton is not indispensable, as the elementary tissue of vegetables may be used, and this is found in an almost pure state, not only in cotton, but in the textile fibres of hemp and flax, in paper, the pith of the elder, etc. Now, the elder abounded in the island towards the mouth of Red Creek, and the colonists had already made coffee of the berries of these shrubs, which belong to the family of the caprifoliaceae.

The only thing to be collected, therefore, was elder-pith, for as to the other substance necessary for the manufacture of pyroxyle, it was only fuming azotic acid. Now, Harding having sulphuric acid at his disposal, had already been easily able to produce azotic acid by attacking the saltpeter with which nature supplied him. He accordingly resolved to manufacture and employ pyroxyle, although it has some inconveniences, that is to say, a great inequality of effect, an excessive inflammability, since it takes fire at one hundred and seventy degrees instead of two hundred and forty, and lastly, an instantaneous deflagration which might damage the fire-arms. On the other hand, the advantages of pyroxyle consist in this, that it is not injured by damp, that it does not make the gun-barrels dirty, and that its force is four times that of ordinary powder.

To make pyroxyle, the cotton must be immersed in the fuming azotic acid for a quarter of an hour, then washed in cold water and dried. Nothing could be more simple.

Cyrus Harding had only at his disposal the ordinary azotic acid and not the fuming or monohydrate azotic acid, that is to say, acid which emits white vapours when it comes in contact with damp air; but by substituting for the latter ordinary azotic acid, mixed, in the proportion of from three to five volumes of concentrated sulphuric acid, the engineer obtained the same result. The sportsmen of the island therefore soon had a perfectly prepared substance, which, employed discreetly, produced admirable results.

About this time the settlers cleared three acres of the plateau, and the rest was preserved in a wild state, for the benefit of the onagers. Several excursions were made into the Jacamar Wood and the forests of the Far West, and they brought back from thence a large collection of wild vegetables, spinach, cress, radishes, and turnips, which careful culture would soon improve, and which would temper the regimen on which the settlers had till then subsisted. Supplies of wood and coal were also carted. Each excursion was at the same time a means of improving the roads, which gradually became smoother under the wheels of the cart.

The rabbit-warren still continued to supply the larder of Granite House. As fortunately it was situated on the other side of Creek Glycerine, its inhabitants could not reach the plateau nor ravage the newly-made plantation. The oyster-bed among the rocks was frequently renewed and furnished excellent molluscs. Besides that, the fishing, either in the lake or the Mercy, was very profitable, for Pencroft had made some lines, armed with iron hooks, with which they frequently caught fine trout, and a species of fish whose silvery sides were speckled with yellow, and which were also extremely savory. Master Neb, who was skilled in the culinary art, knew how to vary agreeably the bill of fare. Bread alone was wanting at the table of the settlers, and as has been said, they felt this privation greatly.

The settlers hunted too the turtles which frequented the shores of Cape Mandible. At this place the beach was covered with little mounds, concealing perfectly spherical turtles' eggs, with white hard shells, the albumen of which does not coagulate as that of birds' eggs. They were hatched by the sun, and their number was naturally considerable, as each turtle can lay annually two hundred and fifty.

"A regular egg-field," observed Gideon Spilett, "and we have nothing to do but to pick them up."

But not being contented with simply the produce, they made chase after the producers, the result of which was that they were able to bring back to Granite House a dozen of these chelonians, which were really valuable from an alimentary point of view. The turtle soup, flavoured with aromatic herbs, often gained well-merited praises for its preparer, Neb.

We must here mention another fortunate circumstance by which new stores for the winter were laid in. Shoals of salmon entered the Mercy, and ascended the country for several miles. It was the time at which the females, going to find suitable places in which to spawn, precede the males and make a great noise through the fresh water. A thousand of these fish, which measured about two feet and a half in length, came up the river, and a large quantity were retained by fixing dams across the stream. More than a hundred were thus taken, which were salted and stored for the time when winter, freezing up the streams, would render fishing impracticable. By this time the intelligent Jup was raised to the duty of valet. He had been dressed in a jacket, white linen breeches, and an apron, the pockets of which were his delight. The clever orang had been marvelously trained by Neb, and any one would have said that the negro and the ape understood each other when they talked together. Jup had besides a real affection for Neb, and Neb returned it. When his services were not required, either for carrying wood or for climbing to the top of some tree, Jup passed the greatest part of his time in the kitchen, where he endeavoured to imitate Neb in all that he saw him do. The black showed the greatest patience and even extreme zeal in instructing his pupil, and the pupil exhibited remarkable intelligence in profiting by the lessons he received from his master.

Judge then of the pleasure Master Jup gave to the inhabitants of Granite House when, without their having had any idea of it, he appeared one day, napkin on his arm, ready to wait at table. Quick, attentive, he acquitted himself perfectly, changing the plates, bringing dishes, pouring out water, all with a gravity which gave intense amusement to the settlers, and which enraptured Pencroft.

"Jup, some soup!"

"Jup, a little agouti!"

"Jup, a plate!"

"Jup! Good Jup! Honest Jup!"

Nothing was heard but that, and Jup without ever being disconcerted, replied to everyone, watched for everything, and he shook his head in a knowing way when Pencroft, referring to his joke of the first day, said to him—

"Decidedly, Jup, your wages must be doubled."

It is useless to say that the orang was now thoroughly domesticated at Granite House, and that he often accompanied his masters to the forest without showing any wish to leave them. It was most amusing to see him walking with a stick which Pencroft had given him, and which he carried on his shoulder like a gun. If they wished to gather some fruit from the summit of a tree, how quickly he climbed for it. If the wheel of the cart stuck in the mud, with what energy did Jup with a single heave of his shoulder put it right again.

"What a jolly fellow he is!" cried Pencroft often. "If he was as mischievous as he is good, there would be no doing anything with him!"

It was towards the end of January the colonists began their labours in the centre of the island. It had been decided that a corral should be established near the sources of the Red Creek, at the foot of Mount Franklin, destined to contain the ruminants, whose presence would have been troublesome at Granite House, and especially for the musmons, who were to supply the wool for the settlers' winter garments.

Each morning, the colony, sometimes entire, but more often represented only by Harding, Herbert, and Pencroft, proceeded to the sources of the Creek, a distance of not more than five miles, by the newly beaten road to which the name of Corral Road had been given.

There a site was chosen, at the back of the southern ridge of the mountain. It was a meadow-land, dotted here and there with clumps of trees, and watered by a little stream, which sprung from the slopes which closed it in on one side. The grass was fresh, and it was not too much shaded by the trees which grew about it. This meadow was to be surrounded by a palisade, high enough to prevent even the most agile animals from leaping over. This enclosure would be large enough to contain a hundred musmons and wild goats, with all the young ones they might produce.

The perimeter of the corral was then traced by the engineer, and they would then have proceeded to fell the trees necessary for the construction of the palisade, but as the opening up of the road had already necessitated the sacrifice of a considerable number, those were brought and supplied a hundred stakes, which were firmly fixed in the ground.

At the front part of the palisade a large entrance was reserved, and closed with strong folding-doors.

The construction of this corral did not take less than three weeks, for besides the palisade, Cyrus Harding built large sheds, in which the animals could take shelter. These buildings had also to be made very strong, for musmons are powerful animals, and their first fury was to be feared. The stakes, sharpened at their upper end and hardened by fire, had been fixed by means of cross-bars, and at regular distances props assured the solidity of the whole.

The corral finished, a raid had to be made on the pastures frequented by the ruminants. This was done on the 7th of February, on a beautiful summer's day, and everyone took part in it. The onagers, already well trained, were ridden by Spilett and Herbert, and were of great use.

The maneuvre consisted simply in surrounding the musmons and goats, and gradually narrowing the circle around them. Cyrus Harding, Pencroft, Neb, and Jup, posted themselves in different parts of the wood, while the two cavaliers and Top galloped in a radius of half-a-mile round the corral.

The musmons were very numerous in this part of the island. These fine animals were as large as deer; their horns were stronger than those of the ram, and their grey-coloured fleece was mixed with long hair.

This hunting day was very fatiguing. Such going and coming, and running and riding and shouting! Of a hundred musmons which had been surrounded, more than two-thirds escaped, but at last, thirty of these animals and ten wild goats were gradually driven back towards the corral, the open door of which appearing to offer a means of escape, they rushed in and were prisoners.

In short, the result was satisfactory, and the settlers had no reason to complain. There was no doubt that the flock would prosper, and that at no distant time not only wool but hides would be abundant.

That evening the hunters returned to Granite House quite exhausted. However, notwithstanding their fatigue, they returned the next day to visit the corral. The prisoners had been trying to overthrow the palisade, but of course had not succeeded, and were not long in becoming more tranquil.

During the month of February, no event of any importance occurred. The daily labours were pursued methodically, and, as well as improving the roads to the corral and to Port Balloon, a third was commenced, which, starting from the enclosure, proceeded towards the western coast. The yet unknown portion of Lincoln Island was that of the wood-covered Serpentine Peninsula, which sheltered the wild beasts, from which Gideon Spilett was so anxious to clear their domain.

Before the cold season should appear the most assiduous care was given to the cultivation of the wild plants which had been transplanted from the forest to Prospect Heights. Herbert never returned from an excursion without bringing home some useful vegetable. One day, it was some specimens of the chicory tribe, the seeds of which by pressure yield an excellent oil; another, it was some common sorrel, whose antiscorbutic qualities were not to be despised; then, some of those precious tubers, which have at all times been cultivated in South America, potatoes, of which more than two hundred species are now known. The kitchen garden, now well stocked and carefully defended from the birds, was divided into small beds, where grew lettuces, kidney potatoes, sorrel, turnips, radishes, and other cruciferae. The soil on the plateau was particularly fertile, and it was hoped that the harvests would be abundant.

They had also a variety of different beverages, and so long as they did not demand wine, the most hard to please would have had no reason to complain. To the Oswego tea, and the fermented liquor extracted from the roots of the dragonnier, Harding had added a regular beer, made from the young shoots of the spruce-fir, which, after having been boiled and fermented, made that agreeable drink called by the Anglo-Americans spring-beer.

Towards the end of the summer, the poultry-yard was possessed of a couple of fine bustards, which belonged to the houbara species, characterised by a sort of feathery mantle; a dozen shovelers, whose upper mandible was prolonged on each side by a membraneous appendage; and also some magnificent cocks, similar to the Mozambique cocks, the comb, caruncle, and epidermis being black. So far, everything had succeeded, thanks to the activity of these courageous and intelligent men. Nature did much for them, doubtless; but faithful to the great precept, they made a right use of what a bountiful Providence gave them.

After the heat of these warm summer days, in the evening when their work was finished and the sea-breeze began to blow, they liked to sit on the edge of Prospect Heights, in a sort of veranda, covered with creepers, which Neb had made with his own hands. There they talked, they instructed each other, they made plans, and the rough good-humor of the sailor always amused this little world, in which the most perfect harmony had never ceased to reign.

They often spoke of their country, of their dear and great America. What was the result of the War of Secession? It could not have been greatly prolonged. Richmond had doubtless soon fallen into the hands of General Grant. The taking of the capital of the Confederates must have been the last action of this terrible struggle. Now the North had triumphed in the good cause, how welcome would have been a newspaper to the exiles in Lincoln Island! For eleven months all communication between them and the rest of their fellow-creatures had been interrupted, and in a short time the 24th of March would arrive, the anniversary of the day on which the balloon had thrown them on this unknown coast. They were then mere castaways, not even knowing how they should preserve their miserable lives from the fury of the elements! And now, thanks to the knowledge of their captain, and their own intelligence, they were regular colonists, furnished with arms, tools, and instruments; they had been able to turn to their profit the animals, plants, and minerals of the island, that is to say, the three kingdoms of Nature.

Yes; they often talked of all these things and formed still more plans for the future.

As to Cyrus Harding he was for the most part silent, and listened to his companions more often than he spoke to them. Sometimes he smiled at Herbert's ideas or Pencroft's nonsense, but always and everywhere he pondered over those inexplicable facts, that strange enigma, of which the secret still escaped him!

Chapter IX

BAD WEATHER—THE HYDRAULIC LIFT—MANUFACTURE OF
GLASSWARE—THE BREAD-TREE—FREQUENT VISITS TO THE
CORRAL—INCREASE OF THE FLOCK—THE REPORTER'S
QUESTION—EXACT POSITION OF LINCOLN ISLAND—
PENCROFT'S PROPOSAL

THE WEATHER CHANGED DURING THE FIRST WEEK OF MARCH. THERE HAD BEEN A FULL moon at the commencement of the month, and the heat was still excessive. The atmosphere was felt to be full of electricity, and a period of some length of tempestuous weather was to be feared.

Indeed, on the 2d, peals of thunder were heard, the wind blew from the east, and hail rattled against the façade of Granite House like volleys of grapeshot. The door and windows were immediately closed, or everything in the rooms would have been drenched. On seeing these hailstones, some of which were the size of a pigeon's egg, Pencroft's first thought was that his corn-field was in serious danger.

He directly rushed to his field, where little green heads were already appearing, and by means of a great cloth, he managed to protect his crop.

This bad weather lasted a week, during which time the thunder rolled without cessation in the depths of the sky.

The colonists, not having any pressing work out of doors, profited by the bad weather to work at the interior of Granite House, the arrangement of which was becoming more complete from day to day. The engineer made a turning-lathe, with which he turned several articles both for the toilet and the kitchen, particularly buttons, the want of which was greatly felt. A gun-rack had been made for the fire-arms, which were kept with extreme care, and neither tables nor cupboards were left incomplete. They sawed, they planed, they filed, they turned; and during the whole of this bad season, nothing was heard but the grinding of tools or the humming of the turning-lathe which responded to the growling of the thunder.

Master Jup had not been forgotten, and he occupied a room at the back, near the store-room, a sort of cabin with a cot always full of good litter, which perfectly suited his taste.

"With good old Jup there is never any quarreling," often repeated Pencroft, "never any improper reply. What a servant, Neb, what a servant!"

Of course Jup was now well used to service. He brushed their clothes, he turned the spit, he waited at table, he swept the rooms, he gathered wood, and he performed another admirable piece of service which delighted Pencroft—he never went to sleep without first coming to tuck up the worthy sailor in his bed.

As to the health of the members of the colony, bipeds or bimana, quadrumana or quadrupeds, it left nothing to be desired. With their life in the open air, on this salubrious soil, under that temperate zone, working both with head and hands, they could not suppose that illness would ever attack them.

All were indeed wonderfully well. Herbert had already grown two inches in the year. His figure was forming and becoming more manly, and he promised to be an accomplished man, physically as well as morally. Besides he improved himself during the leisure hours which manual occupations left to him; he read the books found in the case; and after the practical lessons which were taught by the very necessity of their position, he found in the engineer for science, and the reporter for languages, masters who were delighted to complete his education.

The tempest ended about the 9th of March, but the sky remained covered with clouds during the whole of this last summer month. The atmosphere, violently agitated by the electric commotions, could not recover its former purity, and there was almost invariably rain and fog, except for three or four fine days on which several excursions were made. About this time the female onager gave birth to a young one which belonged to the same sex as its mother, and which throve capitally. In the corral, the flock of musmons had also increased, and several lambs already bleated in the sheds, to the great delight of Neb and Herbert, who had each their favourite among these newcomers. An attempt was also made for the domestication of the peccaries, which succeeded well. A sty was constructed under the poultry-yard, and soon contained several young ones in the way to become civilised, that is to say, to become fat under Neb's care. Master Jup, entrusted with carrying them their daily nourishment, leavings from the kitchen, etc., acquitted himself conscientiously of his task. He sometimes amused himself at the expense of his little pensioners by tweaking their tails; but this was mischief, and not wickedness, for these little twisted tails amused him like a plaything, and his instinct was that of a child. One day in this month of March, Pencroft, talking to the engineer, reminded Cyrus Harding of a promise which the latter had not as yet had time to fulfil.

"You once spoke of an apparatus which would take the place of the long ladders at Granite House, captain," said he; "won't you make it someday?"

"Nothing will be easier; but is this a really useful thing?"

"Certainly, captain. After we have given ourselves necessaries, let us think a little of luxury. For us it may be luxury, if you like, but for things it is necessary. It isn't very convenient to climb up a long ladder when one is heavily loaded."

"Well, Pencroft, we will try to please you," replied Cyrus Harding.

"But you have no machine at your disposal."

"We will make one."

"A steam machine?"

"No, a water machine."

And, indeed, to work his apparatus there was already a natural force at the disposal of the engineer which could be used without great difficulty. For this, it was enough to augment the flow of the little stream which supplied the interior of Granite House with water. The opening among the stones and grass was then increased, thus producing a strong fall at the bottom of the passage, the overflow from which escaped by the inner well. Below this fall the engineer fixed a cylinder with paddles, which was joined on the exterior with a strong cable rolled on a wheel, supporting a basket. In this way, by means of a long rope reaching to the ground, which enabled them to regulate the motive power, they could rise in the basket to the door of Granite House.

It was on the 17th of March that the lift acted for the first time, and gave universal satisfaction. Henceforward all the loads, wood, coal, provisions, and even the settlers themselves, were hoisted by this simple system, which replaced the primitive ladder, and, as may be supposed, no one thought of regretting the change. Top particularly was enchanted with this improvement, for he had not, and never could have possessed Master Jup's skill in climbing ladders, and often it was on Neb's back, or even on that of the orang that he had been obliged to make the ascent to Granite House. About this time, too, Cyrus Harding attempted to manufacture glass, and he at first put the old pottery-kiln to this new use. There were some difficulties to be encountered; but, after several fruitless attempts, he succeeded in setting up a glass manufactory, which Gideon Spilett and Herbert, his usual assistants, did not leave for several days. As to the substances used in the composition of glass, they are simply sand, chalk, and soda, either carbonate or sulphate. Now the beach supplied sand, lime supplied chalk, sea-weeds supplied soda, pyrites supplied sulphuric acid, and the ground supplied coal to heat the kiln to the wished-for temperature. Cyrus Harding thus soon had everything ready for setting to work.

The tool, the manufacture of which presented the most difficulty, was the pipe of the glass-maker, an iron tube, five or six feet long, which collects on one end the material in a state of fusion. But by means of a long, thin piece of iron rolled up like the barrel of a gun, Pencroft succeeded in making a tube soon ready for use.

On the 28th of March the tube was heated. A hundred parts of sand, thirty-five of chalk, forty of sulphate of soda, mixed with two or three parts of powdered coal, composed the substance, which was placed in crucibles. When the high temperature of the oven had reduced it to a liquid, or rather a pasty state, Cyrus Harding collected with the tube a quantity of the paste: he turned it about on a metal plate, previously arranged, so as to give it a form suitable for blowing, then he passed the tube to Herbert, telling him to blow at the other extremity.

And Herbert, swelling out his cheeks, blew so much and so well into the tube—taking care to twirl it round at the same time—that his breath dilated the glassy mass. Other quantities of the substance in a state of fusion were added to the first, and in a short time the result was a bubble which measured a foot in diameter. Harding then took the tube out of Herbert's hands, and, giving to it a pendulous motion, he ended by lengthening the malleable bubble so as to give it a cylindro-conic shape.

The blowing operation had given a cylinder of glass terminated by two hemispheric caps, which were easily detached by means of a sharp iron dipped in cold water; then, by the same proceeding, this cylinder was cut lengthways, and after having been rendered malleable by a second heating, it was extended on a plate and spread out with a wooden roller.

The first pane was thus manufactured, and they had only to perform this operation fifty times to have fifty panes. The windows at Granite House were soon furnished with panes; not very white, perhaps, but still sufficiently transparent.

As to bottles and tumblers, that was only play. They were satisfied with them, besides, just as they came from the end of the tube. Pencroft had asked to be allowed to "blow" in his turn, and it was great fun for him; but he blew so hard that his productions took the most ridiculous shapes, which he admired immensely.

Cyrus Harding and Herbert, while hunting one day, had entered the forest of the Far West, on the left bank of the Mercy, and, as usual, the lad was asking a thousand questions of the engineer, who answered them heartily. Now, as Harding was not a sportsman, and as, on the other side, Herbert was talking chemistry and natural philosophy, numbers of kangaroos, capybaras, and agouties came within range, which, however, escaped the lad's gun; the consequence was that the day was already advanced, and the two hunters were in danger of having made a useless excursion, when Herbert, stopping, and uttering a cry of joy, exclaimed—

"Oh, Captain Harding, do you see that tree?" and he pointed to a shrub, rather than a tree, for it was composed of a single stem, covered with a scaly bark, which bore leaves streaked with little parallel veins.

"And what is this tree which resembles a little palm?" asked Harding.

"It is a 'cycas revoluta,' of which I have a picture in our dictionary of Natural History!" said Herbert.

"But I can't see any fruit on this shrub!" observed his companion.

"No, captain," replied Herbert; "but its stem contains a flour with which nature has provided us all ready ground."

"It is, then, the bread-tree?"

"Yes, the bread-tree."

"Well, my boy," replied the engineer, "this is a valuable discovery, since our wheat harvest is not yet ripe; I hope that you are not mistaken!"

Herbert was not mistaken: he broke the stem of a cycas, which was composed of a glandulous tissue, containing a quantity of floury pith, traversed with woody fibre, separated by rings of the same substance, arranged concentrically. With this fecula was mingled a mucilaginous juice of disagreeable flavour, but which it would be easy to get rid of by pressure. This cellular substance was regular flour of a superior quality, extremely nourishing; its exportation was formerly forbidden by the Japanese laws.

Cyrus Harding and Herbert, after having examined that part of the Far West where the cycas grew, took their bearings, and returned to Granite House, where they made known their discovery.

The next day the settlers went to collect some, and returned to Granite House with an ample supply of cycas stems. The engineer constructed a press, with which to extract the mucilaginous juice mingled with the fecula, and he obtained a large quantity of flour, which Neb soon transformed into cakes and puddings. This was not quite real wheaten bread, but it was very like it.

Now, too, the onager, the goats, and the sheep in the corral furnished daily the milk necessary to the colony. The cart, or rather a sort of light carriole which had replaced it, made frequent journeys to the corral, and when it was Pencroft's turn to go he took Jup, and let him drive, and Jup, cracking his whip, acquitted himself with his customary intelligence.

Everything prospered, as well in the corral as in Granite House, and certainly the settlers, if it had not been that they were so far from their native land, had no reason to complain. They were so well suited to this life, and were, besides, so accustomed to the island, that they could not have left its hospitable soil without regret!

And yet so deeply is the love of his country implanted in the heart of man, that if a ship had unexpectedly come in sight of the island, the colonists would have made signals, would have attracted her attention, and would have departed!

It was the 1st of April, a Sunday, Easter Day, which Harding and his companions sanctified by rest and prayer. The day was fine, such as an October day in the northern hemisphere might be.

All, towards the evening after dinner, were seated under the veranda on the edge of Prospect Heights, and they were watching the darkness creeping up from the horizon. Some cups of the infusion of elder-berries, which took the place of coffee, had been served by Neb. They were speaking of the island and of its isolated situation in the Pacific, which led Gideon Spilett to say—

"My dear Cyrus, have you ever, since you possessed the sextant found in the case, again taken the position of our island?"

"No," replied the engineer.

"But it would perhaps be a good thing to do it with this instrument, which is more perfect than that which you before used."

"What is the good?" said Pencroft. "The island is quite comfortable where it is!"

"Well, who knows," returned the reporter, "who knows but that we may be much nearer inhabited land than we think?"

"We shall know to-morrow," replied Cyrus Harding, "and if it had not been for the occupations which left me no leisure, we should have known it already."

"Good!" said Pencroft. "The captain is too good an observer to be mistaken, and, if it has not moved from its place, the island is just where he put it."

"We shall see."

On the next day, therefore, by means of the sextant, the engineer made the necessary observations to verify the position which he had already obtained, and this was the result of his operation. His first observation had given him the situation of Lincoln Island—

In west longitude: from 150° to 155°;
In south latitude: from 30° to 35°.

The second gave exactly:

In longitude: 150° 30'
In south latitude: 34° 57'.

So then, notwithstanding the imperfection of his apparatus, Cyrus Harding had operated with so much skill that his error did not exceed five degrees.

"Now," said Gideon Spilett, "since we possess an atlas as well as a sextant, let us see, my dear Cyrus, the exact position which Lincoln Island occupies in the Pacific."

Herbert fetched the atlas, and the map of the Pacific was opened, and the engineer, compass in hand, prepared to determine their position.

Suddenly the compasses stopped, and he exclaimed—

"But an island exists in this part of the Pacific already!"

"An island?" cried Pencroft.

"Tabor Island."

"An important island?"

"No, an islet lost in the Pacific, and which perhaps has never been visited."

"Well, we will visit it," said Pencroft.

"We?"

"Yes, captain. We will build a decked boat, and I will undertake to steer her. At what distance are we from this Tabor Island?"

"About a hundred and fifty miles to the north-east," replied Harding.

"A hundred and fifty miles! And what's that?" returned Pencroft. "In forty-eight hours, with a good wind, we should sight it!"

And, on this reply, it was decided that a vessel should be constructed in time to be launched towards the month of next October, on the return of the fine season.

Chapter X

BOAT-BUILDING—SECOND CROP OF CORN—HUNTING KOALAS— A NEW PLANT, MORE PLEASANT THAN USEFUL—WHALE IN SIGHT—A HARPOON FROM THE VINEYARD—CUTTING UP THE WHALE—USE FOR THE BONES—END OF THE MONTH OF MAY— PENCROFT HAS NOTHING LEFT TO WISH FOR

WHEN PENCROFT HAD ONCE GOT A PLAN IN HIS HEAD, HE HAD NO PEACE TILL IT WAS executed. Now he wished to visit Tabor Island, and as a boat of a certain size was necessary for this voyage, he determined to build one.

What wood should he employ? Elm or fir, both of which abounded in the island? They decided for the fir, as being easy to work, but which stands water as well as the elm.

These details settled, it was agreed that since the fine season would not return before six months, Cyrus Harding and Pencroft should work alone at the boat. Gideon Spilett and Herbert were to continue to hunt, and neither Neb nor Master Jup, his assistant, were to leave the domestic duties which had devolved upon them.

Directly the trees were chosen, they were felled, stripped of their branches, and sawn into planks as well as sawyers would have been able to do it. A week after, in the recess between the Chimneys and the cliff, a dockyard was prepared, and a keel five-and-thirty feet long, furnished with a stern-post at the stern and a stem at the bows, lay along the sand.

Cyrus Harding was not working in the dark at this new trade. He knew as much about ship-building as about nearly everything else, and he had at first drawn the model of his ship on paper. Besides, he was ably seconded by Pencroft, who, having worked for several years in a dockyard at Brooklyn, knew the practical part of the trade. It was not until after careful calculation and deep thought that the timbers were laid on the keel.

Pencroft, as may be believed, was all eagerness to carry out his new enterprise, and would not leave his work for an instant.

A single thing had the honour of drawing him, but for one day only, from his dock-yard. This was the second wheat-harvest, which was gathered in on the 15th of April. It was as much a success as the first, and yielded the number of grains which had been predicted.

"Five bushels, captain," said Pencroft, after having scrupulously measured his treasure.

"Five bushels," replied the engineer; "and a hundred and thirty thousand grains a bushel will make six hundred and fifty thousand grains."

"Well, we will sow them all this time," said the sailor, "except a little in reserve."

"Yes, Pencroft, and if the next crop gives a proportionate yield, we shall have four thousand bushels."

"And shall we eat bread?"

"We shall eat bread."

"But we must have a mill."

"We will make one."

The third corn-field was very much larger than the two first, and the soil, prepared with extreme care, received the precious seed. That done, Pencroft returned to his work.

During this time Spilett and Herbert hunted in the neighbourhood, and they ventured deep into the still unknown parts of the Far West, their guns loaded with ball, ready for any dangerous emergency. It was a vast thicket of magnificent trees, crowded together as if pressed for room. The exploration of these dense masses of wood was difficult in the extreme, and the reporter never ventured there without the pocket-compass, for the sun scarcely pierced through the thick foliage, and it would have been very difficult for them to retrace their way. It naturally happened that game was more rare in those situations where there was hardly sufficient room to move; two or three large herbivorous animals were however killed during the last fortnight of April. These were koalas, specimens of which the settlers had already seen to the north of the lake, and which stupidly allowed themselves to be killed among the thick branches of the trees in which they took refuge. Their skins were brought back to Granite House, and there, by the help of sulphuric acid, they were subjected to a sort of tanning process which rendered them capable of being used.

On the 30th of April, the two sportsmen were in the depth of the Far West, when the reporter, preceding Herbert a few paces, arrived in a sort of clearing, into which the trees more sparsely scattered had permitted a few rays to penetrate. Gideon Spilett was at first surprised at the odor which exhaled from certain plants with straight stalks, round and branchy, bearing grape-like clusters of flowers and very small berries. The reporter broke off one or two of these stalks and returned to the lad, to whom he said—

"What can this be, Herbert?"

"Well, Mr. Spilett," said Herbert, "this is a treasure which will secure you Pencroft's gratitude forever."

"Is it tobacco?"

"Yes, and though it may not be of the first quality, it is none the less tobacco!"

"Oh, good old Pencroft! Won't he be pleased! But we must not let him smoke it all, he must give us our share."

"Ah! an idea occurs to me, Mr, Spilett," replied Herbert. "Don't let us say anything to Pencroft yet; we will prepare these leaves, and one fine day we will present him with a pipe already filled!"

"All right, Herbert, and on that day our worthy companion will have nothing left to wish for in this world."

The reporter and the lad secured a good store of the precious plant, and then returned to Granite House, where they smuggled it in with as much precaution as if Pencroft had been the most vigilant and severe of custom-house officers.

Cyrus Harding and Neb were taken into confidence, and the sailor suspected nothing during the whole time, necessarily somewhat long, which was required in order to dry the small leaves, chop them up, and subject them to a certain torrefaction on hot stones. This took two months; but all these manipulations were successfully carried on unknown to Pencroft, for, occupied with the construction of his boat, he only returned to Granite House at the hour of rest.

For some days they had observed an enormous animal two or three miles out in the open sea swimming around Lincoln Island. This was a whale of the largest size, which apparently belonged to the southern species, called the "Cape Whale."

"What a lucky chance it would be if we could capture it!" cried the sailor. "Ah! if we only had a proper boat and a good harpoon, I would say 'After the beast,' for he would be well worth the trouble of catching!"

"Well, Pencroft," observed Harding, "I should much like to watch you handling a harpoon. It would be very interesting."

"I am astonished," said the reporter, "to see a whale in this comparatively high latitude."

"Why so, Mr. Spilett?" replied Herbert. "We are exactly in that part of the Pacific which English and American whalemen call the whale-field, and it is here, between New Zealand and South America, that the whales of the southern hemisphere are met with in the greatest numbers."

And Pencroft returned to his work, not without uttering a sigh of regret, for every sailor is a born fisherman, and if the pleasure of fishing is in exact proportion to the size of the animal, one can judge how a whaler feels in sight of a whale. And if this had only been for pleasure! But they could not help feeling how valuable such a prize would have been to the colony, for the oil, the fat, and the bones would have been put to many uses.

Now it happened that this whale appeared to have no wish to leave the waters of the island. Therefore, whether from the windows of Granite House, or from Prospect Heights, Herbert and Gideon Spilett, when they were not hunting, or Neb, unless presiding over his fires, never left the telescope, but watched all the animal's movements. The cetacean, having entered far into Union Bay, made rapid furrows across it from Mandible Cape to Claw Cape, propelled by its enormously powerful flukes, on which it supported itself, and making its way through the water at the rate little short of twelve knots an hour. Sometimes also it approached so near to the island that it could be clearly distinguished. It was the southern whale, which is completely black, the head being more depressed than that of the northern whale.

They could also see it throwing up from its air-holes to a great height a cloud of vapour, or of water, for, strange as it may appear, naturalists and whalers are not agreed on this subject. Is it air or is it water which is thus driven out? It is generally admitted to be vapour, which, condensing suddenly by contact with the cold air, falls again as rain.

However, the presence of this mammifer preoccupied the colonists. It irritated Pencroft especially, as he could think of nothing else while at work. He ended by longing for it, like a child for a thing which it has been denied. At night he talked about it in his sleep, and certainly if he had had the means of attacking it, if the sloop had been in a fit state to put to sea, he would not have hesitated to set out in pursuit.

But what the colonists could not do for themselves chance did for them, and on the 3d of May shouts from Neb, who had stationed himself at the kitchen window, announced that the whale was stranded on the beach of the island.

Herbert and Gideon Spilett, who were just about to set out hunting, left their guns, Pencroft threw down his axe, and Harding and Neb joining their companions, all rushed towards the scene of action.

The stranding had taken place on the beach of Flotsam Point, three miles from Granite House, and at high tide. It was therefore probable that the cetacean would not be able to extricate itself easily; at any rate it was best to hasten, so as to cut off its retreat if necessary. They ran with pickaxes and iron-tipped poles in their hands, passed over the Mercy bridge, descended the right bank of the river, along the beach, and in less than twenty minutes the settlers were close to the enormous animal, above which flocks of birds already hovered.

"What a monster!" cried Neb.

And the exclamation was natural, for it was a southern whale, eighty feet long, a giant of the species, probably not weighing less than a hundred and fifty thousand pounds!

In the meanwhile, the monster thus stranded did not move, nor attempt by struggling to regain the water while the tide was still high.

It was dead, and a harpoon was sticking out of its left side.

"There are whalers in these quarters, then?" said Gideon Spilett directly.

"Oh, Mr. Spilett, that doesn't prove anything!" replied Pencroft. "Whales have been known to go thousands of miles with a harpoon in the side, and this one might even have been struck in the north of the Atlantic and come to die in the south of the Pacific, and it would be nothing astonishing."

Pencroft, having torn the harpoon from the animal's side, read this inscription on it:

MARIA STELLA,
VINEYARD

"A vessel from the Vineyard! A ship from my country!" he cried. "The *Maria Stella!* A fine whaler, 'pon my word; I know her well! Oh, my friends, a vessel from the Vineyard!—a whaler from the Vineyard!"*

And the sailor brandishing the harpoon, repeated, not without emotion, the name which he loved so well—the name of his birthplace.

But as it could not be expected that the *Maria Stella* would come to reclaim the animal harpooned by her, they resolved to begin cutting it up before decomposition should commence. The birds, who had watched this rich prey for several days, had determined to take possession of it without further delay, and it was necessary to drive them off by firing at them repeatedly.

The whale was a female, and a large quantity of milk was taken from it, which, ac-

* A port in the State of New York.

cording to the opinion of the naturalist Duffenbach, might pass for cow's milk, and, indeed, it differs from it neither in taste, colour, nor density.

Pencroft had formerly served on board a whaling-ship, and he could methodically direct the operation of cutting up—a sufficiently disagreeable operation lasting three days, but from which the settlers did not flinch, not even Gideon Spilett, who, as the sailor said, would end by making a "real good castaway."

The blubber, cut in parallel slices of two feet and a half in thickness, then divided into pieces which might weigh about a thousand pounds each, was melted down in large earthen pots brought to the spot, for they did not wish to taint the environs of Granite House, and in this fusion it lost nearly a third of its weight.

But there was an immense quantity of it; the tongue alone yielded six thousand pounds of oil, and the lower lip four thousand. Then, besides the fat, which would ensure for a long time a store of stearine and glycerine, there were still the bones, for which a use could doubtless be found, although there were neither umbrellas nor stays used at Granite House. The upper part of the mouth of the cetacean was, indeed, provided on both sides with eight hundred horny blades, very elastic, of a fibrous texture, and fringed at the edge like great combs, at which the teeth, six feet long, served to retain the thousands of animalculae, little fish, and molluscs, on which the whale fed.

The operation finished, to the great satisfaction of the operators, the remains of the animal were left to the birds, who would soon make every vestige of it disappear, and their usual daily occupations were resumed by the inmates of Granite House.

However, before returning to the dockyard, Cyrus Harding conceived the idea of fabricating certain machines, which greatly excited the curiosity of his companions. He took a dozen of the whale's bones, cut them into six equal parts, and sharpened their ends.

"This machine is not my own invention, and it is frequently employed by the Aleutian hunters in Russian America. You see these bones, my friends; well, when it freezes, I will bend them, and then wet them with water till they are entirely covered with ice, which will keep them bent, and I will strew them on the snow, having previously covered them with fat. Now, what will happen if a hungry animal swallows one of these baits? Why, the heat of his stomach will melt the ice, and the bone, springing straight, will pierce him with its sharp points."

"Well! I do call that ingenious!" said Pencroft.

"And it will spare the powder and shot," rejoined Cyrus Harding.

"That will be better than traps!" added Neb.

In the meanwhile the boat-building progressed, and towards the end of the month half the planking was completed. It could already be seen that her shape was excellent, and that she would sail well.

Pencroft worked with unparallelled ardour, and only a sturdy frame could have borne such fatigue; but his companions were preparing in secret a reward for his labors, and on the 31st of May he was to meet with one of the greatest joys of his life.

On that day, after dinner, just as he was about to leave the table, Pencroft felt a hand on his shoulder.

It was the hand of Gideon Spilett, who said—

"One moment, Master Pencroft, you mustn't sneak off like that! You've forgotten your dessert."

"Thank you, Mr. Spilett," replied the sailor, "I am going back to my work."

"Well, a cup of coffee, my friend?"

"Nothing more."

"A pipe, then?"

Pencroft jumped up, and his great good-natured face grew pale when he saw the reporter presenting him with a ready-filled pipe, and Herbert with a glowing coal.

The sailor endeavoured to speak, but could not get out a word; so, seizing the pipe, he carried it to his lips, then applying the coal, he drew five or six great whiffs. A fragrant blue cloud soon arose, and from its depths a voice was heard repeating excitedly—

"Tobacco! real tobacco!"

"Yes, Pencroft," returned Cyrus Harding, "and very good tobacco too!"

"O, divine Providence! sacred Author of all things!" cried the sailor. "Nothing more is now wanting to our island."

And Pencroft smoked, and smoked, and smoked.

"And who made this discovery?" he asked at length. "You, Herbert, no doubt?"

"No, Pencroft, it was Mr. Spilett."

"Mr. Spilett!" exclaimed the sailor, seizing the reporter, and clasping him to his breast with such a squeeze that he had never felt anything like it before.

"Oh, Pencroft," said Spilett, recovering his breath at last, "a truce for one moment. You must share your gratitude with Herbert, who recognised the plant, with Cyrus, who prepared it, and with Neb, who took a great deal of trouble to keep our secret."

"Well, my friends, I will repay you someday," replied the sailor. "Now we are friends for life."

Chapter XI

WINTER—FELLING WOOD—THE MILL—PENCROFT'S FIXED IDEA—THE BONES—TO WHAT USE AN ALBATROSS MAY BE PUT—FUEL FOR THE FUTURE—TOP AND JUP—STORMS—DAMAGE TO THE POULTRY-YARD—EXCURSION TO THE MARSH—CYRUS HARDING ALONE—EXPLORING THE WELL

WINTER ARRIVED WITH THE MONTH OF JUNE, WHICH IS THE DECEMBER OF THE NORTHern zones, and the great business was the making of warm and solid clothing.

The musmons in the corral had been stripped of their wool, and this precious textile material was now to be transformed into stuff.

Of course Cyrus Harding, having at his disposal neither carders, combers, polishers, stretchers, twisters, mule-jenny, nor self-acting machine to spin the wool, nor loom to weave it, was obliged to proceed in a simpler way, so as to do without spinning and weaving. And indeed he proposed to make use of the property which the filaments of wool possess when subjected to a powerful pressure of mixing together, and of manufacturing by this simple process the material called felt. This felt could then be obtained by a simple operation which, if it diminished the flexibility of the stuff, increased its power of retaining heat in proportion. Now the wool furnished by the musmons was composed of very short hairs, and was in a good condition to be felted.

The engineer, aided by his companions, including Pencroft, who was once more obliged to leave his boat, commenced the preliminary operations, the object of which was to rid the wool of that fat and oily substance with which it is impregnated, and which is called grease. This cleaning was done in vats filled with water, which was maintained at the temperature of seventy degrees, and in which the wool was soaked for four and twenty hours; it was then thoroughly washed in baths of soda, and, when sufficiently dried by pressure, it was in a state to be compressed, that is to say, to produce a solid material, rough, no doubt, and such as would have no value in a manufacturing centre of Europe or America, but which would be highly esteemed in the Lincoln Island markets.

This sort of material must have been known from the most ancient times, and, in fact, the first woolen stuffs were manufactured by the process which Harding was now about to employ. Where Harding's engineering qualifications now came into play was in the construction of the machine for pressing the wool; for he knew how to turn ingeniously to profit the mechanical force, hitherto unused, which the waterfall on the beach possessed to move a fulling-mill.

Nothing could be more rudimentary. The wool was placed in troughs, and upon it fell in turns heavy wooden mallets; such was the machine in question, and such it had been for centuries until the time when the mallets were replaced by cylinders of compression, and the material was no longer subjected to beating, but to regular rolling.

The operation, ably directed by Cyrus Harding, was a complete success. The wool, previously impregnated with a solution of soap, intended on the one hand to facilitate the interlacing, the compression, and the softening of the wool, and on the other to prevent its diminution by the beating, issued from the mill in the shape of thick felt cloth. The roughnesses with which the staple of wool is naturally filled were so thoroughly entangled and interlaced together that a material was formed equally suitable either for garments or bedclothes. It was certainly neither merino, muslin, cashmere, rep, satin, alpaca, cloth, nor flannel. It was "Lincolnian felt," and Lincoln Island possessed yet another manufacture. The colonists had now warm garments and thick bedclothes, and they could without fear await the approach of the winter of 1866–67.

The severe cold began to be felt about the 20th of June, and, to his great regret, Pencroft was obliged to suspend his boat-building, which he hoped to finish in time for next spring.

The sailor's great idea was to make a voyage of discovery to Tabor Island, although Harding could not approve of a voyage simply for curiosity's sake, for there was evidently nothing to be found on this desert and almost arid rock. A voyage of a hundred and fifty miles in a comparatively small vessel, over unknown seas, could not but cause him some anxiety. Suppose that their vessel, once out at sea, should be unable to reach Tabor Island, and could not return to Lincoln Island, what would become of her in the midst of the Pacific, so fruitful of disasters?

Harding often talked over this project with Pencroft, and he found him strangely bent upon undertaking this voyage, for which determination he himself could give no sufficient reason.

"Now," said the engineer one day to him, "I must observe, my friend, that after having said so much, in praise of Lincoln Island, after having spoken so often of the sorrow you would feel if you were obliged to forsake it, you are the first to wish to leave it."

"Only to leave it for a few days," replied Pencroft, "only for a few days, captain. Time to go and come back, and see what that islet is like!"

"But it is not nearly as good as Lincoln Island."

"I know that beforehand."

"Then why venture there?"

"To know what is going on in Tabor Island."

"But nothing is going on there; nothing could happen there."

"Who knows?"

"And if you are caught in a hurricane?"

"There is no fear of that in the fine season," replied Pencroft. "But, captain, as we must provide against everything, I shall ask your permission to take Herbert only with me on this voyage."

"Pencroft," replied the engineer, placing his hand on the sailor's shoulder, "if any misfortune happens to you, or to this lad, whom chance has made our child, do you think we could ever cease to blame ourselves?"

"Captain Harding," replied Pencroft, with unshaken confidence, "we shall not cause you that sorrow. Besides, we will speak further of this voyage, when the time comes to make it. And I fancy, when you have seen our tight-rigged little craft, when you have observed how she behaves at sea, when we sail round our island, for we will do so together—I fancy, I say, that you will no longer hesitate to let me go. I don't conceal from you that your boat will be a masterpiece."

"Say 'our' boat, at least, Pencroft," replied the engineer, disarmed for the moment. The conversation ended thus, to be resumed later on, without convincing either the sailor or the engineer.

The first snow fell towards the end of the month of June. The corral had previously been largely supplied with stores, so that daily visits to it were not requisite; but it was decided that more than a week should never be allowed to pass without someone going to it.

Traps were again set, and the machines manufactured by Harding were tried. The bent whalebones, imprisoned in a case of ice, and covered with a thick outer layer of fat, were placed on the border of the forest at a spot where animals usually passed on their way to the lake.

To the engineer's great satisfaction, this invention, copied from the Aleutian fishermen, succeeded perfectly. A dozen foxes, a few wild boars, and even a jaguar, were taken in this way, the animals being found dead, their stomachs pierced by the unbent bones.

An incident must here be related, not only as interesting in itself, but because it was the first attempt made by the colonists to communicate with the rest of mankind.

Gideon Spilett had already several times pondered whether to throw into the sea a letter enclosed in a bottle, which currents might perhaps carry to an inhabited coast, or to confide it to pigeons.

But how could it be seriously hoped that either pigeons or bottles could cross the distance of twelve hundred miles which separated the island from any inhabited land? It would have been pure folly.

But on the 30th of June the capture was effected, not without difficulty, of an albatross, which a shot from Herbert's gun had slightly wounded in the foot. It was a magnificent bird, measuring ten feet from wing to wing, and which could traverse seas as wide as the Pacific.

Herbert would have liked to keep this superb bird, as its wound would soon heal, and he thought he could tame it; but Spilett explained to him that they should not neglect this opportunity of attempting to communicate by this messenger with the lands of the Pacific; for if the albatross had come from some inhabited region, there was no doubt but that it would return there so soon as it was set free.

Perhaps in his heart Gideon Spilett, in whom the journalist sometimes came to the surface, was not sorry to have the opportunity of sending forth to take its chance an exciting article relating the adventures of the settlers in Lincoln Island. What a success for the authorised reporter of the *New York Herald*, and for the number which should contain the article, if it should ever reach the address of its editor, the Honorable James Bennett!

Gideon Spilett then wrote out a concise account, which was placed in a strong waterproof bag, with an earnest request to whoever might find it to forward it to the office of the *New York Herald*. This little bag was fastened to the neck of the albatross, and not to its foot, for these birds are in the habit of resting on the surface of the sea; then liberty was given to this swift courier of the air, and it was not without some emotion that the colonists watched it disappear in the misty west.

"Where is he going to?" asked Pencroft.

"Towards New Zealand," replied Herbert.

"A good voyage to you," shouted the sailor, who himself did not expect any great result from this mode of correspondence.

With the winter, work had been resumed in the interior of Granite House, mending clothes and different occupations, among others making the sails for their vessel, which were cut from the inexhaustible balloon-case.

During the month of July the cold was intense, but there was no lack of either wood or coal. Cyrus Harding had established a second fireplace in the dining-room, and there the long winter evenings were spent. Talking while they worked, reading when the hands remained idle, the time passed with profit to all.

It was real enjoyment to the settlers when in their room, well lighted with candles, well warmed with coal, after a good dinner, elder-berry coffee smoking in the cups, the pipes giving forth an odoriferous smoke, they could hear the storm howling without. Their comfort would have been complete, if complete comfort could ever exist for those who are far from their fellow-creatures, and without any means of communication with them. They often talked of their country, of the friends whom they had left, of the grandeur of the American Republic, whose influence could not but increase; and Cyrus Harding, who had been much mixed up with the affairs of the Union, greatly interested his auditors by his recitals, his views, and his prognostics.

It chanced one day that Spilett was led to say—

"But now, my dear Cyrus, all this industrial and commercial movement to which you predict a continual advance, does it not run the danger of being sooner or later completely stopped?"

"Stopped! And by what?"

"By the want of coal, which may justly be called the most precious of minerals."

"Yes, the most precious indeed," replied the engineer; "and it would seem that nature wished to prove that it was so by making the diamond, which is simply pure carbon crystallised."

"You don't mean to say, captain," interrupted Pencroft, "that we burn diamonds in our stoves in the shape of coal?"

"No, my friend," replied Harding.

"However," resumed Gideon Spilett, "you do not deny that someday the coal will be entirely consumed?"

"Oh! the veins of coal are still considerable, and the hundred thousand miners who annually extract from them a hundred millions of hundredweights have not nearly exhausted them."

"With the increasing consumption of coal," replied Gideon Spilett, "it can be foreseen that the hundred thousand workmen will soon become two hundred thousand, and that the rate of extraction will be doubled."

"Doubtless; but after the European mines, which will be soon worked more thoroughly with new machines, the American and Australian mines will for a long time yet provide for the consumption in trade."

"For how long a time?" asked the reporter.

"For at least two hundred and fifty or three hundred years."

"That is reassuring for us, but a bad look-out for our great-grandchildren!" observed Pencroft.

"They will discover something else," said Herbert.

"It is to be hoped so," answered Spilett, "for without coal there would be no machinery, and without machinery there would be no railways, no steamers, no manufactories, nothing of that which is indispensable to modern civilisation!"

"But what will they find?" asked Pencroft. "Can you guess, captain?"

"Nearly, my friend."

"And what will they burn instead of coal?"

"Water," replied Harding.

"Water!" cried Pencroft, "water as fuel for steamers and engines! water to heat water!"

"Yes, but water decomposed into its primitive elements," replied Cyrus Harding, "and decomposed doubtless, by electricity, which will then have become a powerful and manageable force, for all great discoveries, by some inexplicable laws, appear to agree and become complete at the same time. Yes, my friends, I believe that water will one day be employed as fuel, that hydrogen and oxygen which constitute it, used singly or together, will furnish an inexhaustible source of heat and light, of an intensity of which coal is not capable. Someday the coal-rooms of steamers and the tenders of locomotives will, instead of coal, be stored with these two condensed gases, which will burn in the furnaces with enormous calorific power. There is, therefore, nothing to fear. As long as the earth is inhabited it will supply the wants of its inhabitants, and there will be no want of either light or heat as long as the productions of the vegetable, mineral or animal kingdoms do not fail us. I believe, then, that when the deposits of coal are exhausted we shall heat and warm ourselves with water. Water will be the coal of the future."

"I should like to see that," observed the sailor.

"You were born too soon, Pencroft," returned Neb, who only took part in the discussion by these words.

However, it was not Neb's speech which interrupted the conversation, but Top's barking, which broke out again with that strange intonation which had before perplexed the engineer. At the same time Top began to run round the mouth of the well, which opened at the extremity of the interior passage.

"What can Top be barking in that way for?" asked Pencroft.

"And Jup be growling like that?" added Herbert.

In fact the orang, joining the dog, gave unequivocal signs of agitation, and, singular to say, the two animals appeared more uneasy than angry.

"It is evident," said Gideon Spilett, "that this well is in direct communication with the sea, and that some marine animal comes from time to time to breathe at the bottom."

"That's evident," replied the sailor, "and there can be no other explanation to give. Quiet there, Top!" added Pencroft, turning to the dog, "and you, Jup, be off to your room!"

The ape and the dog were silent. Jup went off to bed, but Top remained in the room, and continued to utter low growls at intervals during the rest of the evening. There was no further talk on the subject, but the incident, however, clouded the brow of the engineer.

During the remainder of the month of July there was alternate rain and frost. The temperature was not so low as during the preceding winter, and its maximum did not exceed eight degrees Fahrenheit. But although this winter was less cold, it was more troubled by storms and squalls; the sea besides often endangered the safety of the Chimneys. At times it almost seemed as if an undercurrent raised these monstrous billows which thundered against the wall of Granite House.

When the settlers, leaning from their windows, gazed on the huge watery masses breaking beneath their eyes, they could not but admire the magnificent spectacle of the ocean in its impotent fury. The waves rebounded in dazzling foam, the beach entirely disappearing under the raging flood, and the cliff appearing to emerge from the sea itself, the spray rising to a height of more than a hundred feet.

During these storms it was difficult and even dangerous to venture out, owing to the frequently falling trees; however, the colonists never allowed a week to pass without having paid a visit to the corral. Happily, this enclosure, sheltered by the south-eastern spur of Mount Franklin, did not greatly suffer from the violence of the hurricanes, which spared its trees, sheds, and palisades; but the poultry-yard on Prospect Heights, being directly exposed to the gusts of wind from the east, suffered considerable damage. The pigeon-house was twice unroofed and the paling blown down. All this required to be remade more solidly than before, for, as may be clearly seen, Lincoln Island was situated in one of the most dangerous parts of the Pacific. It really appeared as if it formed the central point of vast cyclones, which beat it perpetually as the whip does the top, only here it was the top which was motionless and the whip which moved. During the first week of the month of August the weather became more moderate, and the atmosphere recovered the calm which it appeared to have lost forever. With the calm the cold again became intense, and the thermometer fell to eight degrees Fahrenheit, below zero.

On the 3d of August an excursion which had been talked of for several days was made into the south-eastern part of the island, towards Tadorn Marsh. The hunters were tempted by the aquatic game which took up their winter quarters there. Wild duck, snipe, teal and grebe abounded there, and it was agreed that a day should be devoted to an expedition against these birds.

Not only Gideon Spilett and Herbert, but Pencroft and Neb also took part in this excursion. Cyrus Harding alone, alleging some work as an excuse, did not join them, but remained at Granite House.

The hunters proceeded in the direction of Port Balloon, in order to reach the marsh, after having promised to be back by the evening. Top and Jup accompanied them. As soon as they had passed over the Mercy Bridge, the engineer raised it and returned, intending to put into execution a project for the performance of which he wished to be alone.

Now this project was to minutely explore the interior well, the mouth of which was on a level with the passage of Granite House, and which communicated with the sea, since it formerly supplied a way to the waters of the lake.

Why did Top so often run round this opening? Why did he utter such strange barks when a sort of uneasiness seemed to draw him towards this well? Why did Jup join Top in a sort of common anxiety? Had this well branches besides the communication with the sea? Did it spread towards other parts of the island? This is what Cyrus Harding wished to know. He had resolved, therefore, to attempt the exploration of the well during the absence of his companions, and an opportunity for doing so had now presented itself.

It was easy to descend to the bottom of the well by employing the rope ladder which had not been used since the establishment of the lift. The engineer drew the ladder to the hole, the diameter of which measured nearly six feet, and allowed it to unroll itself after having securely fastened its upper extremity. Then, having lighted a lantern, taken a revolver, and placed a cutlass in his belt, he began the descent.

The sides were everywhere entire; but points of rock jutted out here and there, and by means of these points it would have been quite possible for an active creature to climb to the mouth of the well.

The engineer remarked this; but although he carefully examined these points by the light of his lantern, he could find no impression, no fracture which could give any reason to suppose that they had either recently or at any former time been used as a staircase. Cyrus Harding descended deeper, throwing the light of his lantern on all sides.

He saw nothing suspicious.

When the engineer had reached the last rounds he came upon the water, which was then perfectly calm. Neither at its level nor in any other part of the well, did any passage open which could lead to the interior of the cliff. The wall which Harding struck with the hilt of his cutlass sounded solid. It was compact granite, through which no living being could force a way. To arrive at the bottom of the well and then climb up to its mouth it was necessary to pass through the channel under the rocky subsoil of the beach, which placed it in communication with the sea, and this was only possible for marine animals. As to the question of knowing where this channel ended, at what point of the shore, and at what depth beneath the water, it could not be answered.

Then Cyrus Harding, having ended his survey, re-ascended, drew up the ladder, covered the mouth of the well, and returned thoughtfully to the dining-room, saying to himself—

"I have seen nothing, and yet there *is* something there!"

Chapter XII

THE RIGGING OF THE VESSEL—AN ATTACK FROM FOXES—JUP
WOUNDED—JUP CURED—COMPLETION OF THE BOAT—
PENCROFT'S TRIUMPH—THE BONADVENTURE'S TRIAL TRIP TO
THE SOUTH OF THE ISLAND—AN UNEXPECTED DOCUMENT

IN THE EVENING THE HUNTERS RETURNED, HAVING ENJOYED GOOD SPORT, AND BEING LITerally loaded with game; indeed, they had as much as four men could possibly carry. Top wore a necklace of teal and Jup wreaths of snipe round his body.

"Here, master," cried Neb; "here's something to employ our time! Preserved and made into pies we shall have a welcome store! But I must have someone to help me. I count on you, Pencroft."

"No, Neb," replied the sailor; "I have the rigging of the vessel to finish and to look after, and you will have to do without me."

"And you, Mr. Herbert?"

"I must go to the corral to-morrow, Neb," replied the lad.

"It will be you then, Mr. Spilett, who will help me?"

"To oblige you, Neb, I will," replied the reporter; "but I warn you that if you disclose your receipts to me, I shall publish them."

"Whenever you like, Mr. Spilett," replied Neb; "whenever you like."

And so the next day Gideon Spilett became Neb's assistant and was installed in his culinary laboratory. The engineer had previously made known to him the result of the exploration which he had made the day before, and on this point the reporter shared Harding's opinion, that although he had found nothing, a secret still remained to be discovered!

The frost continued for another week, and the settlers did not leave Granite House unless to look after the poultry-yard. The dwelling was filled with appetizing odours, which were emitted from the learned manipulation of Neb and the reporter. But all the results of the chase were not made into preserved provisions; and as the game kept perfectly in the intense cold, wild duck and other fowl were eaten fresh, and declared superior to all other aquatic birds in the known world.

During this week, Pencroft, aided by Herbert, who handled the sail-maker's needle with much skill, worked with such energy that the sails of the vessel were finished. There was no want of cordage. Thanks to the rigging which had been discovered with the case of the balloon, the ropes and cables from the net were all of good quality, and the sailor turned them all to account. To the sails were attached strong bolt ropes, and there still remained enough from which to make the halyards, shrouds, and sheets, etc. The blocks were manufactured by Cyrus Harding under Pencroft's directions by means of the turning lathe. It therefore happened that the rigging was entirely prepared before the vessel was finished. Pencroft also manufactured a flag, that flag so dear to every true American, containing the stars and stripes of their glorious Union. The colours for it were supplied from certain plants used in dyeing, and which were very abundant in the island; only to the thirty-seven stars, representing the thirty-seven States of the Union, which shine on the American flag, the sailor added a thirty-eighth, the star of "the State of Lincoln," for he considered his island as already united to the great republic. "And," said he, "it is so already in heart, if not in deed!"

In the meantime, the flag was hoisted at the central window of Granite House, and the settlers saluted it with three cheers.

The cold season was now almost at an end, and it appeared as if this second winter was to pass without any unusual occurrence, when on the night of the 11th of August, the plateau of Prospect Heights was menaced with complete destruction.

After a busy day the colonists were sleeping soundly, when towards four o'clock in the morning they were suddenly awakened by Top's barking.

The dog was not this time barking near the mouth of the well, but at the threshold of the door, at which he was scratching as if he wished to burst it open. Jup was also uttering piercing cries.

"Hello, Top!" cried Neb, who was the first awake. But the dog continued to bark more furiously than ever.

"What's the matter now?" asked Harding.

And all dressing in haste rushed to the windows, which they opened.

Beneath their eyes was spread a sheet of snow which looked grey in the dim light. The settlers could see nothing, but they heard a singular yelping noise away in the darkness. It was evident that the beach had been invaded by a number of animals which could not be seen.

"What are they?" cried Pencroft.

"Wolves, jaguars, or apes?" replied Neb.

"They have nearly reached the plateau," said the reporter.

"And our poultry-yard," exclaimed Herbert, "and our garden!"

"Where can they have crossed?" asked Pencroft.

"They must have crossed the bridge on the shore," replied the engineer, "which one of us must have forgotten to close."

"True," said Spilett, "I remember having left it open."

"A fine job you have made of it, Mr. Spilett," cried the sailor.

"What is done cannot be undone," replied Cyrus Harding. "We must consult what it will now be best to do."

Such were the questions and answers which were rapidly exchanged between Harding and his companions. It was certain that the bridge had been crossed, that the shore had been invaded by animals, and that whatever they might be they could by ascending the left bank of the Mercy reach Prospect Heights. They must therefore be advanced against quickly and fought with if necessary.

"But what are these beasts?" was asked a second time, as the yelpings were again heard more loudly than before. These yelps made Herbert start, and he remembered having heard them before during his first visit to the sources of the Red Creek.

"They are culpeux foxes!" he exclaimed.

"Forward!" shouted the sailor.

And all arming themselves with hatchets, carbines, and revolvers, threw themselves into the lift and soon set foot on the shore.

Culpeux are dangerous animals when in great numbers and irritated by hunger, nevertheless the colonists did not hesitate to throw themselves into the midst of the troop, and their first shots vividly lighting up the darkness made their assailants draw back.

The chief thing was to hinder these plunderers from reaching the plateau, for the garden and the poultry-yard would then have been at their mercy, and immense, perhaps irreparable mischief, would inevitably be the result, especially with regard to the corn-field. But as the invasion of the plateau could only be made by the left bank of the Mercy, it was sufficient to oppose the culpeux on the narrow bank between the river and the cliff of granite.

This was plain to all, and, by Cyrus Harding's orders, they reached the spot indicated by him, while the culpeux rushed fiercely through the gloom. Harding, Gideon Spilett, Herbert, Pencroft and Neb posted themselves in impregnable line. Top, his formidable jaws open, preceded the colonists, and he was followed by Jup, armed with knotty cudgel, which he brandished like a club.

The night was extremely dark, it was only by the flashes from the revolvers as each person fired that they could see their assailants, who were at least a hundred in number, and whose eyes were glowing like hot coals.

"They must not pass!" shouted Pencroft.

"They shall not pass!" returned the engineer.

But if they did not pass it was not for want of having attempted it. Those in the rear pushed on the foremost assailants, and it was an incessant struggle with revolvers and hatchets. Several culpeux already lay dead on the ground, but their number did not appear to diminish, and it might have been supposed that reinforcements were continually arriving over the bridge.

The colonists were soon obliged to fight at close quarters, not without receiving some wounds, though happily very slight ones. Herbert had, with a shot from his revolver, rescued Neb, on whose back a colpeo had sprung like a tiger cat. Top fought with actual fury, flying at the throats of the foxes and strangling them instantaneously. Jup wielded his weapon valiantly, and it was in vain that they endeavoured to keep him in the rear. Endowed doubtless with sight which enabled him to pierce the obscurity, he was always in the thick of the fight, uttering from time to time a sharp hissing sound, which was with him the sign of great rejoicing.

At one moment he advanced so far, that by the light from a revolver he was seen surrounded by five or six large culpeux, with whom he was coping with great coolness.

However, the struggle was ended at last, and victory was on the side of the settlers, but not until they had fought for two long hours! The first signs of the approach of day doubtless determined the retreat of their assailants, who scampered away towards the north, passing over the bridge, which Neb ran immediately to raise. When day had sufficiently lighted up the field of battle, the settlers counted as many as fifty dead bodies scattered about on the shore.

"And Jup!" cried Pencroft; "where is Jup?" Jup had disappeared. His friend Neb called him, and for the first time Jup did not reply to his friend's call.

Everyone set out in search of Jup, trembling lest he should be found among the slain; they cleared the place of the bodies which stained the snow with their blood. Jup was found in the midst of a heap of culpeux whose broken jaws and crushed bodies showed that they had to do with the terrible club of the intrepid animal.

Poor Jup still held in his hand the stump of his broken cudgel, but deprived of his weapon he had been overpowered by numbers, and his chest was covered with severe wounds.

"He is living," cried Neb, who was bending over him.

"And we will save him," replied the sailor. "We will nurse him as if he was one of ourselves."

It appeared as if Jup understood, for he leaned his head on Pencroft's shoulder as if to thank him. The sailor was wounded himself, but his wound was insignificant, as were those of his companions; for thanks to their fire-arms they had been almost always able to keep their assailants at a distance. It was therefore only the orang whose condition was serious.

Jup, carried by Neb and Pencroft, was placed in the lift, and only a slight moan now and then escaped his lips. He was gently drawn up to Granite House. There he was laid on a mattress taken from one of the beds, and his wounds were bathed with the greatest care. It did not appear that any vital part had been reached, but Jup was very weak from loss of blood, and a high fever soon set in after his wounds had been dressed. He was laid down, strict diet was imposed, "just like a real person," as Neb said, and they made him swallow several cups of a cooling drink, for which the ingredients were supplied from the vegetable medicine chest of Granite House. Jup was at first restless, but his breathing gradually became more regular, and he was left sleeping quietly. From time to time Top, walking on tip-toe, as one might say, came to visit his friend, and seemed to approve of all the care that had been taken of him. One of Jup's hands hung over the side of his bed, and Top licked it with a sympathizing air.

They employed the day in interring the dead, who were dragged to the forest of the Far West, and there buried deep.

This attack, which might have had such serious consequences, was a lesson to the settlers, who from this time never went to bed until one of their number had made sure that all the bridges were raised, and that no invasion was possible.

However, Jup, after having given them serious anxiety for several days, began to recover. His constitution brought him through, the fever gradually subsided, and Gideon Spilett, who was a bit of a doctor, pronounced him quite out of danger. On the 16th of August, Jup began to eat. Neb made him nice little sweet dishes, which the invalid discussed with great relish, for if he had a pet failing it was that of being somewhat of a gourmand, and Neb had never done anything to cure him of this fault.

"What would you have?" said he to Gideon Spilett, who sometimes expostulated with him for spoiling the ape. "Poor Jup has no other pleasure than that of the palate, and I am only too glad to be able to reward his services in this way!"

Ten days after having taken to his bed, on the 21st of August, Master Jup arose. His wounds were healed, and it was evident that he would not be long in regaining his usual strength and agility. Like all convalescents, he was tremendously hungry, and the reporter allowed him to eat as much as he liked, for he trusted to that instinct, which is too often wanting in reasoning beings, to keep the orang from any excess. Neb was delighted to see his pupil's appetite returning.

"Eat away, my Jup," said he, "and don't spare anything; you have shed your blood for us, and it is the least I can do to make you strong again!"

On the 25th of August Neb's voice was heard calling to his companions.

"Captain, Mr. Spilett, Mr. Herbert, Pencroft, come! come!"

The colonists, who were together in the dining-room, rose at Neb's call, who was then in Jup's room.

"What's the matter?" asked the reporter.

"Look," replied Neb, with a shout of laughter. And what did they see? Master Jup smoking calmly and seriously, sitting cross-legged like a Turk at the entrance to Granite House!

"My pipe," cried Pencroft. "He has taken my pipe! Hello, my honest Jup, I make you a present of it! Smoke away, old boy, smoke away!"

And Jup gravely puffed out clouds of smoke which seemed to give him great satisfaction. Harding did not appear to be much astonished at this incident, and he cited several examples of tame apes, to whom the use of tobacco had become quite familiar.

But from this day Master Jup had a pipe of his own, the sailor's ex-pipe, which was hung in his room near his store of tobacco. He filled it himself, lighted it with a glowing coal, and appeared to be the happiest of quadrumana. It may readily be understood that this similarity of tastes of Jup and Pencroft served to tighten the bonds of friendship which already existed between the honest ape and the worthy sailor.

"Perhaps he is really a man," said Pencroft sometimes to Neb. "Should you be surprised to hear him beginning to speak to us someday?"

"My word, no," replied Neb. "What astonishes me is that he hasn't spoken to us before, for now he wants nothing but speech!"

"It would amuse me all the same," resumed the sailor, "if some fine day he said to me, 'Suppose we change pipes, Pencroft.'"

"Yes," replied Neb, "what a pity he was born dumb!"

With the month of September the winter ended, and the works were again eagerly commenced. The building of the vessel advanced rapidly, she was already completely decked over, and all the inside parts of the hull were firmly united with ribs bent by means of steam, which answered all the purposes of a mould.

As there was no want of wood, Pencroft proposed to the engineer to give a double lining to the hull, so as to completely ensure the strength of the vessel.

Harding, not knowing what the future might have in store for them, approved the sailor's idea of making the craft as strong as possible. The interior and deck of the vessel was entirely finished towards the 15th of September. For calking the seams they made oakum of dry sea-weed, which was hammered in between the planks; then these seams were covered with boiling tar, which was obtained in great abundance from the pines in the forest.

The management of the vessel was very simple. She had from the first been ballasted with heavy blocks of granite walled up, in a bed of lime, twelve thousand pounds of which they stowed away.

A deck was placed over this ballast, and the interior was divided into two cabins; two benches extended along them and served also as lockers. The foot of the mast supported the partition which separated the two cabins, which were reached by two hatchways let into the deck.

Pencroft had no trouble in finding a tree suitable for the mast. He chose a straight young fir, with no knots, and which he had only to square at the step, and round off at the top. The iron-work of the mast, the rudder and the hull had been roughly but strongly forged at the Chimneys. Lastly, yards, masts, boom, spars, oars, etc., were all furnished by the first week in October, and it was agreed that a trial trip should be taken round the island, so as to ascertain how the vessel would behave at sea, and how far they might depend upon her.

During all this time the necessary works had not been neglected. The corral was enlarged, for the flock of musmons and goats had been increased by a number of young ones, who had to be housed and fed. The colonists had paid visits also to the oyster bed, the warren, the coal and iron mines, and to the till then unexplored districts of the Far West forest, which abounded in game. Certain indigenous plants were discovered, and those fit for immediate use contributed to vary the vegetable stores of Granite House.

They were a species of ficoide, some similar to those of the Cape, with eatable fleshy leaves, others bearing seeds containing a sort of flour.

On the 10th of October the vessel was launched. Pencroft was radiant with joy, the operation was perfectly successful; the boat completely rigged, having been pushed on rollers to the water's edge, was floated by the rising tide, amid the cheers of the colonists, particularly of Pencroft, who showed no modesty on this occasion. Besides his importance was to last beyond the finishing of the vessel, since, after having built her, he was to command her. The grade of captain was bestowed upon him with the approbation of all. To satisfy Captain Pencroft, it was now necessary to give a name to the vessel, and, after many propositions had been discussed, the votes were all in favour of the *Bonadventure*. As soon as the *Bonadventure* had been lifted by the rising tide, it was seen that she lay evenly in the water, and would be easily navigated. However, the trial trip was to be made that very day, by an excursion off the coast. The weather was fine, the breeze fresh, and the sea smooth, especially towards the south coast, for the wind was blowing from the north-west.

"All hands on board," shouted Pencroft; but breakfast was first necessary, and it was thought best to take provisions on board, in the event of their excursion being prolonged until the evening.

Cyrus Harding was equally anxious to try the vessel, the model of which had originated with him, although on the sailor's advice he had altered some parts of it, but he did not share Pencroft's confidence in her, and as the latter had not again spoken of the voyage to Tabor Island, Harding hoped he had given it up. He would have indeed great reluctance in letting two or three of his companions venture so far in so small a boat, which was not of more than fifteen tons' burden.

At half-past ten everybody was on board, even Top and Jup, and Herbert weighed the anchor, which was fast in the sand near the mouth of the Mercy. The sail was hoisted, the Lincolnian flag floated from the mast-head, and the *Bonadventure*, steered by Pencroft, stood out to sea.

The wind blowing out of Union Bay she ran before it, and thus showed her owners, much to their satisfaction, that she possessed a remarkably fast pair of heels, according to Pencroft's mode of speaking. After having doubled Flotsam Point and Claw Cape, the captain kept her close hauled, so as to sail along the southern coast of the island, when it was found she sailed admirably within five points of the wind. All hands were enchanted, they had a good vessel, which, in case of need, would be of great service to them, and with fine weather and a fresh breeze the voyage promised to be charming.

Pencroft now stood off the shore, three or four miles across from Port Balloon. The island then appeared in all its extent and under a new aspect, with the varied panorama of its shore from Claw Cape to Reptile End, the forests in which dark firs contrasted with the young foliage of other trees and overlooked the whole, and Mount Franklin whose lofty head was still whitened with snow.

"How beautiful it is!" cried Herbert.

"Yes, our island is beautiful and good," replied Pencroft. "I love it as I loved my poor mother. It received us poor and destitute, and now what is wanting to us five fellows who fell on it from the sky?"

"Nothing," replied Neb; "nothing, captain."

And the two brave men gave three tremendous cheers in honour of their island!

During all this time Gideon Spilett, leaning against the mast, sketched the panorama which was developed before his eyes.

Cyrus Harding gazed on it in silence.

"Well, Captain Harding," asked Pencroft, "what do you think of our vessel?"

"She appears to behave well," replied the engineer.

"Good! And do you think now that she could undertake a voyage of some extent?"

"What voyage, Pencroft?"

"One to Tabor Island, for instance."

"My friend," replied Harding, "I think that in any pressing emergency we need not hesitate to trust ourselves to the *Bonadventure* even for a longer voyage; but you know I should see you set off to Tabor Island with great uneasiness, since nothing obliges you to go there."

"One likes to know one's neighbours," returned the sailor, who was obstinate in his idea. "Tabor Island is our neighbour, and the only one! Politeness requires us to go at least to pay a visit."

"By Jove," said Spilett, "our friend Pencroft has become very particular about the proprieties all at once!"

"I am not particular about anything at all," retorted the sailor, who was rather vexed by the engineer's opposition, but who did not wish to cause him anxiety.

"Consider, Pencroft," resumed Harding, "you cannot go alone to Tabor Island."

"One companion will be enough for me."

"Even so," replied the engineer, "you will risk depriving the colony of Lincoln Island of two settlers out of five."

"Out of six," answered Pencroft; "you forget Jup."

"Out of seven," added Neb; "Top is quite worth another."

"There is no risk at all in it, captain," replied Pencroft.

"That is possible, Pencroft; but I repeat it is to expose ourselves uselessly."

The obstinate sailor did not reply, and let the conversation drop, quite determined to resume it again. But he did not suspect that an incident would come to his aid and change into an act of humanity that which was at first only a doubtful whim.

After standing off the shore the *Bonadventure* again approached it in the direction of Port Balloon. It was important to ascertain the channels between the sand-banks and reefs, that buoys might be laid down, since this little creek was to be the harbor.

They were not more than half-a-mile from the coast, and it was necessary to tack to beat against the wind. The *Bonadventure* was then going at a very moderate rate, as the breeze, partly intercepted by the high land, scarcely swelled her sails, and the sea, smooth as glass, was only rippled now and then by passing gusts.

Herbert had stationed himself in the bows that he might indicate the course to be followed among the channels, when all at once he shouted—

"Luff, Pencroft, luff!"

"What's the matter," replied the sailor; "a rock?"

"No—wait," said Herbert; "I don't quite see. Luff again—right—now."

So saying, Herbert, leaning over the side, plunged his arm into the water, and pulled it out, exclaiming—

"A bottle!"

He held in his hand a corked bottle which he had just seized a few cables' length from the shore.

Cyrus Harding took the bottle. Without uttering a single word he drew the cork, and took from it a damp paper, on which were written these words:—

"Castaway. . . . Tabor Island: 153° W. long., 37° 11' S. lat."

Chapter XIII

DEPARTURE DECIDED UPON—CONJECTURES—PREPARATIONS— THE THREE PASSENGERS—FIRST NIGHT—SECOND NIGHT— TABOR ISLAND—SEARCHING THE SHORE— SEARCHING THE WOOD—NO ONE—ANIMALS—PLANTS— A DWELLING—DESERTED

A CASTAWAY!" EXCLAIMED PENCROFT; "LEFT ON THIS TABOR ISLAND NOT TWO HUNDRED miles from us! Ah, Captain Harding, you won't now oppose my going."

"No, Pencroft," replied Cyrus Harding; "and you shall set out as soon as possible."

"To-morrow?"

"To-morrow!"

The engineer still held in his hand the paper which he had taken from the bottle. He contemplated it for some instants, then resumed—

"From this document, my friends, from the way in which it is worded, we may conclude this: first, that the castaway on Tabor Island is a man possessing a considerable knowledge of navigation, since he gives the latitude and longitude of the island exactly as we ourselves found it, and to a second of approximation; secondly, that he is either English or American, as the document is written in the English language."

"That is perfectly logical," answered Spilett; "and the presence of this castaway explains the arrival of the case on the shores of our island. There must have been a wreck, since there is a castaway. As to the latter, whoever he may be, it is lucky for him that Pencroft thought of building this boat and of trying her this very day, for a day later and this bottle might have been broken on the rocks."

"Indeed," said Herbert, "it is a fortunate chance that the *Bonadventure* passed exactly where the bottle was still floating!"

"Does not this appear strange to you?" asked Harding of Pencroft.

"It appears fortunate, that's all," answered the sailor. "Do you see anything extraordinary in it, captain? The bottle must go somewhere, and why not here as well as anywhere else?"

"Perhaps you are right, Pencroft," replied the engineer; "and yet—"

"But," observed Herbert, "there's nothing to prove that this bottle has been floating long in the sea."

"Nothing," replied Gideon Spilett, "and the document appears even to have been recently written. What do you think about it, Cyrus?"

"It is difficult to say, and besides we shall soon know," replied Harding.

During this conversation Pencroft had not remained inactive. He had put the vessel about, and the *Bonadventure*, all sails set, was running rapidly towards Claw Cape.

Everyone was thinking of the castaway on Tabor Island. Should they be in time to save him? This was a great event in the life of the colonists! They themselves were but castaways, but it was to be feared that another might not have been so fortunate, and their duty was to go to his succor.

Claw Cape was doubled, and about four o'clock the *Bonadventure* dropped her anchor at the mouth of the Mercy.

That same evening the arrangements for the new expedition were made. It appeared best that Pencroft and Herbert, who knew how to work the vessel, should undertake the voyage alone. By setting out the next day, the 10th of October, they would arrive on the 13th, for with the present wind it would not take more than forty-eight hours to make this passage of a hundred and fifty miles. One day in the island, three or four to return, they might hope therefore that on the 17th they would again reach Lincoln Island. The weather was fine, the barometer was rising, the wind appeared settled, everything then was in favour of these brave men whom an act of humanity was taking far from their island.

Thus it had been agreed that Cyrus Harding, Neb, and Gideon Spilett should remain at Granite House, but an objection was raised, and Spilett, who had not forgotten his business as reporter to the *New York Herald*, having declared that he would go by swimming rather than lose such an opportunity, he was admitted to take a part in the voyage.

The evening was occupied in transporting on board the *Bonadventure* articles of bedding, utensils, arms, ammunition, a compass, provisions for a week, and this business being rapidly accomplished the colonists ascended to Granite House.

The next day, at five o'clock in the morning, the farewells were said, not without some emotion on both sides, and Pencroft setting sail made towards Claw Cape, which had to be doubled in order to proceed to the south-west.

The *Bonadventure* was already a quarter of a mile from the coast when the passengers perceived on the heights of Granite House two men waving their farewells; they were Cyrus Harding and Neb.

"Our friends," exclaimed Spilett, "this is our first separation for fifteen months."

Pencroft, the reporter and Herbert waved in return, and Granite House soon disappeared behind the high rocks of the Cape.

During the first part of the day the *Bonadventure* was still in sight of the southern coast of Lincoln Island, which soon appeared just like a green basket, with Mount Franklin rising from the centre. The heights, diminished by distance, did not present an appearance likely to tempt vessels to touch there. Reptile End was passed in about an hour, though at a distance of about ten miles.

At this distance it was no longer possible to distinguish anything of the Western Coast, which stretched away to the ridges of Mount Franklin, and three hours after the last of Lincoln Island sank below the horizon.

The *Bonadventure* behaved capitally. Bounding over the waves she proceeded rapidly on her course. Pencroft had hoisted the foresail, and steering by the compass followed a rectilinear direction. From time to time Herbert relieved him at the helm, and the lad's hand was so firm that the sailor had not a point to find fault with.

Gideon Spilett chatted sometimes with one, sometimes with the other, if wanted he lent a hand with the ropes, and Captain Pencroft was perfectly satisfied with his crew.

In the evening the crescent moon, which would not be in its first quarter until the 16th, appeared in the twilight and soon set again. The night was dark but starry, and the next day again promised to be fine.

Pencroft prudently lowered the foresail, not wishing to be caught by a sudden gust while carrying too much canvas; it was perhaps an unnecessary precaution on such a calm night, but Pencroft was a prudent sailor and cannot be blamed for it.

The reporter slept part of the night. Pencroft and Herbert took turns for a spell of two hours each at the helm. The sailor trusted Herbert as he would himself, and his confidence was justified by the coolness and judgment of the lad. Pencroft gave him his directions as a commander to his steersman, and Herbert never allowed the *Bonadventure* to swerve even a point. The night passed quietly, as did the day of the 12th of October. A south-easterly direction was strictly maintained. Unless the *Bonadventure* fell in with some unknown current she would come exactly within sight of Tabor Island.

As to the sea over which the vessel was then sailing, it was absolutely deserted. Now and then a great albatross or frigate bird passed within gunshot, and Gideon Spilett wondered if it was to one of them that he had confided his last letter addressed to the *New York Herald*. These birds were the only beings that appeared to frequent this part of the ocean between Tabor and Lincoln Islands.

"And yet," observed Herbert, "this is the time that whalers usually proceed towards the southern part of the Pacific. Indeed I do not think there could be a more deserted sea than this."

"It is not quite so deserted as all that," replied Pencroft.

"What do you mean?" asked the reporter.

"We are on it. Do you take our vessel for a wreck and us for porpoises?"

And Pencroft laughed at his joke.

By the evening, according to calculation, it was thought that the *Bonadventure* had accomplished a distance of a hundred and twenty miles since her departure from Lincoln Island, that is to say in thirty-six hours, which would give her a speed of between three and four knots an hour. The breeze was very slight and might soon drop altogether. However, it was hoped that the next morning by break of day, if the calculation had been correct and the course true, they would sight Tabor Island.

Neither Gideon Spilett, Herbert, nor Pencroft slept that night. In the expectation of the next day they could not but feel some emotion. There was so much uncertainty in their enterprise! Were they near Tabor Island? Was the island still inhabited by the castaway to whose succor they had come? Who was this man? Would not his presence disturb the little colony till then so united? Besides, would he be content to exchange his prison for another? All these questions, which would no doubt be answered the next day, kept them in suspense, and at the dawn of day they all fixed their gaze on the western horizon.

"Land!" shouted Pencroft at about six o'clock in the morning.

And it was impossible that Pencroft should be mistaken, it was evident that land was there. Imagine the joy of the little crew of the *Bonadventure*. In a few hours they would land on the beach of the island!

The low coast of Tabor Island, scarcely emerging from the sea, was not more than fifteen miles distant.

The head of the *Bonadventure*, which was a little to the south of the island, was set directly towards it, and as the sun mounted in the east, its rays fell upon one or two headlands.

"This is a much less important isle than Lincoln Island," observed Herbert, "and is probably due like ours to some submarine convulsion."

At eleven o'clock the *Bonadventure* was not more than two miles off, and Pencroft, while looking for a suitable place at which to land, proceeded very cautiously through the unknown waters. The whole of the island could now be surveyed, and on it could be seen groups of gum and other large trees, of the same species as those growing on Lincoln Island. But the astonishing thing was that no smoke arose to show that the island was inhabited, not a signal appeared on any point of the shore whatever!

And yet the document was clear enough; there was a castaway, and this castaway should have been on the watch.

In the meanwhile the *Bonadventure* entered the winding channels among the reefs, and Pencroft observed every turn with extreme care. He had put Herbert at the helm, posting himself in the bows, inspecting the water, while he held the halliard in his hand, ready to lower the sail at a moment's notice. Gideon Spilett with his glass eagerly scanned the shore, though without perceiving anything.

However, at about twelve o'clock the keel of the *Bonadventure* grated on the bottom. The anchor was let go, the sails furled, and the crew of the little vessel landed.

And there was no reason to doubt that this was Tabor Island, since according to the most recent charts there was no island in this part of the Pacific between New Zealand and the American Coast.

The vessel was securely moored, so that there should be no danger of her being carried away by the receding tide; then Pencroft and his companions, well armed, ascended the shore, so as to gain an elevation of about two hundred and fifty or three hundred feet which rose at a distance of half-a-mile.

"From the summit of that hill," said Spilett, "we can no doubt obtain a complete view of the island, which will greatly facilitate our search."

"So as to do here," replied Herbert, "that which Captain Harding did the very first thing on Lincoln Island, by climbing Mount Franklin."

"Exactly so," answered the reporter, "and it is the best plan of proceeding."

While thus talking the explorers had advanced along a clearing which terminated at the foot of the hill. Flocks of rock-pigeons and sea-swallows, similar to those of Lincoln Island, fluttered around them. Under the woods which skirted the glade on the left they could hear the bushes rustling and see the grass waving, which indicated the presence of timid animals, but still nothing to show that the island was inhabited.

Arrived at the foot of the hill, Pencroft, Spilett, and Herbert climbed it in a few minutes, and gazed anxiously round the horizon.

They were on an islet, which did not measure more than six miles in circumference, its shape not much bordered by capes or promontories, bays or creeks, being a lengthened oval. All around, the lonely sea extended to the limits of the horizon. No land nor even a sail was in sight.

This woody islet did not offer the varied aspects of Lincoln Island, arid and wild in one part, but fertile and rich in the other. On the contrary this was a uniform mass of verdure, out of which rose two or three hills of no great height. Obliquely to the oval of the island ran a stream through a wide meadow falling into the sea on the west by a narrow mouth.

"The domain is limited," said Herbert.

"Yes," rejoined Pencroft: "It would have been too small for us."

"And moreover," said the reporter, "it appears to be uninhabited."

"Indeed," answered Herbert, "nothing here betrays the presence of man."

"Let us go down," said Pencroft, "and search."

The sailor and his two companions returned to the shore, to the place where they had left the *Bonadventure*.

They had decided to make the tour of the island on foot, before exploring the interior; so that not a spot should escape their investigations. The beach was easy to follow, and only in some places was their way barred by large rocks, which, however, they easily passed round. The explorers proceeded towards the south, disturbing numerous flocks of sea-birds and herds of seals, which threw themselves into the sea as soon as they saw the strangers at a distance.

"Those beasts yonder," observed the reporter, "do not see men for the first time. They fear them, therefore they must know them."

An hour after their departure they arrived on the southern point of the islet, terminated by a sharp cape, and proceeded towards the north along the western coast, equally formed by sand and rocks, the background bordered with thick woods.

There was not a trace of a habitation in any part, not the print of a human foot on the shore of the island, which after four hours' walking had been gone completely round.

It was to say the least very extraordinary, and they were compelled to believe that Tabor Island was not or was no longer inhabited. Perhaps, after all, the document was already several months or several years old, and it was possible in this case, either that the castaway had been enabled to return to his country, or that he had died of misery.

Pencroft, Spilett, and Herbert, forming more or less probable conjectures, dined rapidly on board the *Bonadventure* so as to be able to continue their excursion until nightfall. This was done at five o'clock in the evening, at which hour they entered the wood.

Numerous animals fled at their approach, being principally, one might say, only goats and pigs, which it was easy to see belonged to European species.

Doubtless some whaler had landed them on the island, where they had rapidly increased. Herbert resolved to catch one or two living, and take them back to Lincoln Island.

It was no longer doubtful that men at some period or other had visited this islet, and this became still more evident when paths appeared trodden through the forest, felled trees, and everywhere traces of the hand of man; but the trees were becoming rotten, and had been felled many years ago; the marks of the axe were velveted with moss, and the grass grew long and thick on the paths, so that it was difficult to find them.

"But," observed Gideon Spilett, "this not only proves that men have landed on the island, but also that they lived on it for some time. Now, who were these men? How many of them remain?"

"The document," said Herbert, "only spoke of one castaway."

"Well, if he is still on the island," replied Pencroft, "it is impossible but that we shall find him."

The exploration was continued. The sailor and his companions naturally followed the route which cut diagonally across the island, and they were thus obliged to follow the stream which flowed towards the sea.

If the animals of European origin, if works due to a human hand, showed incontestably that men had already visited the island, several specimens of the vegetable kingdom did not prove it less. In some places, in the midst of clearings, it was evident that the soil had been planted with culinary plants, at probably the same distant period.

What, then, was Herbert's joy, when he recognised potatoes, chicory, sorrel, carrots, cabbages, and turnips, of which it was sufficient to collect the seed to enrich the soil of Lincoln Island.

"Capital, jolly!" exclaimed Pencroft. "That will suit Neb as well as us. Even if we do not find the castaway, at least our voyage will not have been useless, and God will have rewarded us."

"Doubtless," replied Gideon Spilett, "but to see the state in which we find these plantations, it is to be feared that the island has not been inhabited for some time."

"Indeed," answered Herbert, "an inhabitant, whoever he was, could not have neglected such an important culture!"

"Yes," said Pencroft, "the castaway has gone."

"We must suppose so."

"It must then be admitted that the document has already a distant date?"

"Evidently."

"And that the bottle only arrived at Lincoln Island after having floated in the sea a long time."

"Why not?" returned Pencroft. "But night is coming on," added he, "and I think that it will be best to give up the search for the present."

"Let us go on board, and to-morrow we will begin again," said the reporter.

This was the wisest course, and it was about to be followed when Herbert, pointing to a confused mass among the trees, exclaimed—

"A hut!"

All three immediately ran towards the dwelling. In the twilight it was just possible to see that it was built of planks and covered with a thick tarpaulin.

The half-closed door was pushed open by Pencroft, who entered with a rapid step.

The hut was empty!

Chapter XIV

THE INVENTORY—NIGHT—A FEW LETTERS—CONTINUATION OF
THE SEARCH—PLANTS AND ANIMALS—HERBERT IN GREAT
DANGER—ON BOARD—THE DEPARTURE—BAD WEATHER—A
GLEAM OF REASON—LOST ON THE SEA—A TIMELY LIGHT

PENCROFT, HERBERT, AND GIDEON SPILETT REMAINED SILENT IN THE MIDST OF THE darkness.

Pencroft shouted loudly.

No reply was made.

The sailor then struck a light and set fire to a twig. This lighted for a minute a small room, which appeared perfectly empty. At the back was a rude fireplace, with a few cold cinders, supporting an armful of dry wood. Pencroft threw the blazing twig on it, the wood crackled and gave forth a bright light.

The sailor and his two companions then perceived a disordered bed, of which the damp and yellow coverlets proved that it had not been used for a long time. In the corner of the fireplace were two kettles, covered with rust, and an overthrown pot. A cupboard, with a few mouldy sailor's clothes; on the table a tin plate and a Bible, eaten away by damp; in a corner a few tools, a spade, pickaxe, two fowling-pieces, one of which was broken; on a plank, forming a shelf, stood a barrel of powder, still untouched, a barrel of shot, and several boxes of caps, all thickly covered with dust, accumulated, perhaps, by many long years.

"There is no one here," said the reporter.

"No one," replied Pencroft.

"It is a long time since this room has been inhabited," observed Herbert.

"Yes, a very long time!" answered the reporter.

"Mr. Spilett," then said Pencroft, "instead of returning on board, I think that it would be well to pass the night in this hut."

"You are right, Pencroft," answered Gideon Spilett, "and if its owner returns, well! perhaps he will not be sorry to find the place taken possession of."

"He will not return," said the sailor, shaking his head.

"You think that he has quitted the island?" asked the reporter.

"If he had quitted the island he would have taken away his weapons and his tools," replied Pencroft. "You know the value which castaways set on such articles as these, the last remains of a wreck. No! no!" repeated the sailor, in a tone of conviction; "no, he has not left the island! If he had escaped in a boat made by himself, he would still less have left these indispensable and necessary articles. No! he is on the island!"

"Living?" asked Herbert.

"Living or dead. But if he is dead, I suppose he has not buried himself, and so we shall at least find his remains!"

It was then agreed that the night should be passed in the deserted dwelling, and a store of wood found in a corner was sufficient to warm it. The door closed, Pencroft, Herbert and Spilett remained there, seated on a bench, talking little but wondering much. They were in a frame of mind to imagine anything or expect anything. They listened eagerly for sounds outside. The door might have opened suddenly, and a man presented himself to them without their being in the least surprised, notwithstanding all that the hut revealed of abandonment, and they had their hands ready to press the hands of this man, this castaway, this unknown friend, for whom friends were waiting.

But no voice was heard, the door did not open. The hours thus passed away.

How long the night appeared to the sailor and his companions! Herbert alone slept for two hours, for at his age sleep is a necessity. They were all three anxious to continue their exploration of the day before, and to search the most secret recesses of the islet! The inferences deduced by Pencroft were perfectly reasonable, and it was nearly certain that, as the hut was deserted, and the tools, utensils, and weapons were still there, the owner had succumbed. It was agreed, therefore, that they should search for his remains, and give them at least Christian burial.

Day dawned; Pencroft and his companions immediately proceeded to survey the dwelling. It had certainly been built in a favourable situation, at the back of a little hill, sheltered by five or six magnificent gum-trees. Before its front and through the trees the axe had prepared a wide clearing, which allowed the view to extend to the sea. Beyond a lawn, surrounded by a wooden fence falling to pieces, was the shore, on the left of which was the mouth of the stream.

The hut had been built of planks, and it was easy to see that these planks had been obtained from the hull or deck of a ship. It was probable that a disabled vessel had been cast on the coast of the island, that one at least of the crew had been saved, and that by means of the wreck this man, having tools at his disposal, had built the dwelling.

And this became still more evident when Gideon Spilett, after having walked round the hut, saw on a plank, probably one of those which had formed the armour of the wrecked vessel, these letters already half effaced:

Br—tan—a

"Britannia," exclaimed Pencroft, whom the reporter had called; "it is a common name for ships, and I could not say if she was English or American!"

"It matters very little, Pencroft!"

"Very little indeed," answered the sailor, "and we will save the survivor of her crew if he is still living, to whatever country he may belong. But before beginning our search again let us go on board the *Bonadventure*."

A sort of uneasiness had seized Pencroft upon the subject of his vessel. Should the island be inhabited after all, and should someone have taken possession of her? But he shrugged his shoulders at such an unreasonable supposition. At any rate the sailor was not sorry to go to breakfast on board. The road already trodden was not long, scarcely a mile. They set out on their walk, gazing into the wood and thickets through which goats and pigs fled in hundreds.

Twenty minutes after leaving the hut Pencroft and his companions reached the western coast of the island, and saw the *Bonadventure* held fast by her anchor, which was buried deep in the sand.

Pencroft could not restrain a sigh of satisfaction. After all this vessel was his child, and it is the right of fathers to be often uneasy when there is no occasion for it.

They returned on board, breakfasted, so that it should not be necessary to dine until very late; then the repast being ended, the exploration was continued and conducted with the most minute care. Indeed, it was very probable that the only inhabitant of the island had perished. It was therefore more for the traces of a dead than of a living man that Pencroft and his companions searched. But their searches were vain, and during the half of that day they sought to no purpose among the thickets of trees which covered the islet. There was then scarcely any doubt that, if the castaway was dead, no trace of his body now remained, but that some wild beast had probably devoured it to the last bone.

"We will set off to-morrow at daybreak," said Pencroft to his two companions, as about two o'clock they were resting for a few minutes under the shade of a clump of firs.

"I should think that we might without scruple take the utensils which belonged to the castaway," added Herbert.

"I think so, too," returned Gideon Spilett, "and these arms and tools will make up the stores of Granite House. The supply of powder and shot is also most important."

"Yes," replied Pencroft, "but we must not forget to capture a couple or two of those pigs, of which Lincoln Island is destitute—"

"Nor to gather those seeds," added Herbert, "which will give us all the vegetables of the Old and the New Worlds."

"Then perhaps it would be best," said the reporter, "to remain a day longer on Tabor Island, so as to collect all that may be useful to us."

"No, Mr. Spilett," answered Pencroft, "I will ask you to set off to-morrow at daybreak. The wind seems to me to be likely to shift to the west, and after having had a fair wind for coming we shall have a fair wind for going back."

"Then do not let us lose time," said Herbert, rising.

"We won't waste time," returned Pencroft. "You, Herbert, go and gather the seeds, which you know better than we do. While you do that, Mr. Spilett and I will go and have a pig hunt, and even without Top I hope we shall manage to catch a few!"

Herbert accordingly took the path which led towards the cultivated part of the islet, while the sailor and the reporter entered the forest.

Many specimens of the porcine race fled before them, and these animals, which were singularly active, did not appear to be in a humour to allow themselves to be approached.

However, after an hour's chase, the hunters had just managed to get hold of a couple lying in a thicket, when cries were heard resounding from the north part of the island. With the cries were mingled terrible yells, in which there was nothing human.

Pencroft and Gideon Spilett were at once on their feet, and the pigs by this movement began to run away, at the moment when the sailor was getting ready the rope to bind them.

"That's Herbert's voice," said the reporter.

"Run!" exclaimed Pencroft.

And the sailor and Spilett immediately ran at full speed towards the spot from whence the cries proceeded.

They did well to hasten, for at a turn of the path near a clearing they saw the lad thrown on the ground and in the grasp of a savage being, apparently a gigantic ape, who was about to do him some great harm.

To rush on this monster, throw him on the ground in his turn, snatch Herbert from him, then bind him securely, was the work of a minute for Pencroft and Gideon Spilett. The sailor was of Herculean strength, the reporter also very powerful, and in spite of the monster's resistance he was firmly tied so that he could not even move.

"You are not hurt, Herbert?" asked Spilett.

"No, no!"

"Oh, if this ape had wounded him!" exclaimed Pencroft.

"But he is not an ape," answered Herbert.

At these words Pencroft and Gideon Spilett looked at the singular being who lay on the ground. Indeed it was not an ape; it was a human being, a man. But what a man! A savage in all the horrible acceptation of the word, and so much the more frightful that he seemed fallen to the lowest degree of brutishness!

Shaggy hair, untrimmed beard descending to the chest, the body almost naked except a rag round the waist, wild eyes, enormous hands with immensely long nails, skin the colour of mahogany, feet as hard as if made of horn—such was the miserable creature who yet had a claim to be called a man. But it might justly be asked if there were yet a soul in this body, or if the brute instinct alone survived in it!

"Are you quite sure that this is a man, or that he has ever been one?" said Pencroft to the reporter.

"Alas! there is no doubt about it," replied Spilett.

"Then this must be the castaway?" asked Herbert.

"Yes," replied Gideon Spilett, "but the unfortunate man has no longer anything human about him!"

The reporter spoke the truth. It was evident that if the castaway had ever been a civilised being, solitude had made him a savage, or worse, perhaps a regular man of the woods. Hoarse sounds issued from his throat between his teeth, which were sharp as the teeth of a wild beast made to tear raw flesh.

Memory must have deserted him long before, and for a long time also he had forgotten how to use his gun and tools, and he no longer knew how to make a fire! It could be seen that he was active and powerful, but the physical qualities had been developed in him to the injury of the moral qualities. Gideon Spilett spoke to him. He did not appear to understand or even to hear. And yet on looking into his eyes, the reporter thought he could see that all reason was not extinguished in him. However, the prisoner did not struggle, nor even attempt to break his bonds. Was he overwhelmed by the presence of men whose fellow he had once been? Had he found in some corner of his brain a fleeting remembrance which recalled him to humanity? If free, would he attempt to fly, or would he remain? They could not tell, but they did not make the experiment; and after gazing attentively at the miserable creature—

"Whoever he may be," remarked Gideon Spilett, "whoever he may have been, and whatever he may become, it is our duty to take him with us to Lincoln Island."

"Yes, yes!" replied Herbert, "and perhaps with care we may arouse in him some gleam of intelligence."

"The soul does not die," said the reporter, "and it would be a great satisfaction to rescue one of God's creatures from brutishness."

Pencroft shook his head doubtfully.

"We must try at any rate," returned the reporter; "humanity commands us."

It was indeed their duty as Christians and civilised beings. All three felt this, and they well knew that Cyrus Harding would approve of their acting thus.

"Shall we leave him bound?" asked the sailor.

"Perhaps he would walk if his feet were unfastened," said Herbert.

"Let us try," replied Pencroft.

The cords which shackled the prisoner's feet were cut off, but his arms remained securely fastened. He got up by himself and did not manifest any desire to run away. His hard eyes darted a piercing glance at the three men, who walked near him, but nothing denoted that he recollected being their fellow, or at least having been so. A continual hissing sound issued from his lips, his aspect was wild, but he did not attempt to resist.

By the reporter's advice the unfortunate man was taken to the hut. Perhaps the sight of the things that belonged to him would make some impression on him! Perhaps a spark would be sufficient to revive his obscured intellect, to rekindle his dulled soul. The dwelling was not far off. In a few minutes they arrived there, but the prisoner remembered nothing, and it appeared that he had lost consciousness of everything.

What could they think of the degree of brutishness into which this miserable being had fallen, unless that his imprisonment on the islet dated from a very distant period and after having arrived there a rational being solitude had reduced him to this condition.

The reporter then thought that perhaps the sight of fire would have some effect on him, and in a moment one of those beautiful flames, that attract even animals, blazed upon the hearth. The sight of the flame seemed at first to fix the attention of the unhappy object, but soon he turned away and the look of intelligence faded. Evidently there was nothing to be done, for the time at least, but to take him on board the *Bonadventure*. This was done, and he remained there in Pencroft's charge.

Herbert and Spilett returned to finish their work; and some hours after they came back to the shore, carrying the utensils and guns, a store of vegetables, of seeds, some game, and two couple of pigs.

All was embarked, and the *Bonadventure* was ready to weigh anchor and sail with the morning tide.

The prisoner had been placed in the forecabin, where he remained quiet, silent, apparently deaf and dumb.

Pencroft offered him something to eat, but he pushed away the cooked meat that was presented to him and which doubtless did not suit him. But on the sailor showing him one of the ducks which Herbert had killed, he pounced on it like a wild beast, and devoured it greedily.

"You think that he will recover his senses?" asked Pencroft. "It is not impossible that our care will have an effect upon him, for it is solitude that has made him what he is, and from this time forward he will be no longer alone."

"The poor man must no doubt have been in this state for a long time," said Herbert.

"Perhaps," answered Gideon Spilett.

"About what age is he?" asked the lad.

"It is difficult to say," replied the reporter, "for it is impossible to see his features under the thick beard which covers his face, but he is no longer young, and I suppose he might be about fifty."

"Have you noticed, Mr. Spilett, how deeply sunk his eyes are?" asked Herbert.

"Yes, Herbert, but I must add that they are more human than one could expect from his appearance."

"However, we shall see," replied Pencroft, "and I am anxious to know what opinion Captain Harding will have of our savage. We went to look for a human creature, and we are bringing back a monster! After all, we did what we could."

The night passed, and whether the prisoner slept or not could not be known, but at any rate, although he had been unbound, he did not move. He was like a wild animal, which appears stunned at first by its capture, and becomes wild again afterwards.

At daybreak the next morning, the 15th of October, the change of weather predicted by Pencroft occurred. The wind having shifted to the north-west favoured the return of the *Bonadventure*, but at the same time it freshened, which might render navigation more difficult.

At five o'clock in the morning the anchor was weighed. Pencroft took a reef in the main-sail, and steered towards the north-east, so as to sail straight for Lincoln Island.

The first day of the voyage was not marked by any incident. The prisoner remained quiet in the forecabin, and as he had been a sailor it appeared that the motion of the vessel might produce on him a salutary reaction. Did some recollection of his former calling return to him? However that might be, he remained tranquil, astonished rather than depressed.

The next day the wind increased, blowing more from the north, consequently in a less favourable direction for the *Bonadventure*. Pencroft was soon obliged to sail close-hauled, and without saying anything about it he began to be uneasy at the state of the sea, which frequently broke over the bows. Certainly, if the wind did not moderate, it would take a longer time to reach Lincoln Island than it had taken to make Tabor Island.

Indeed, on the morning of the 17th, the *Bonadventure* had been forty-eight hours at sea, and nothing showed that she was near the island. It was impossible, besides, to estimate the distance traversed, or to trust to the reckoning for the direction, as the speed had been very irregular.

Twenty-four hours after there was yet no land in sight. The wind was right ahead and the sea very heavy. The sails were close-reefed, and they tacked frequently. On the 18th, a wave swept completely over the *Bonadventure*; and if the crew had not taken the precaution of lashing themselves to the deck, they would have been carried away.

On this occasion Pencroft and his companions, who were occupied with loosing themselves, received unexpected aid from the prisoner, who emerged from the hatchway as if his sailor's instinct had suddenly returned, broke a piece out of the bulwarks with a spar so as to let the water which filled the deck escape. Then the vessel being clear, he descended to his cabin without having uttered a word. Pencroft, Gideon Spilett, and Herbert, greatly astonished, let him proceed.

Their situation was truly serious, and the sailor had reason to fear that he was lost on the wide sea without any possibility of recovering his course.

The night was dark and cold. However, about eleven o'clock, the wind fell, the sea went down, and the speed of the vessel, as she labored less, greatly increased.

Neither Pencroft, Spilett, nor Herbert thought of taking an hour's sleep. They kept a sharp look-out, for either Lincoln Island could not be far distant and would be sighted at daybreak, or the *Bonadventure*, carried away by currents, had drifted so much that it would be impossible to rectify her course. Pencroft, uneasy to the last degree, yet did not despair, for he had a gallant heart, and grasping the tiller he anxiously endeavoured to pierce the darkness which surrounded them.

About two o'clock in the morning he started forward—

"A light! a light!" he shouted.

Indeed, a bright light appeared twenty miles to the north-east. Lincoln Island was there, and this fire, evidently lighted by Cyrus Harding, showed them the course to be followed. Pencroft, who was bearing too much to the north, altered his course and steered towards the fire, which burned brightly above the horizon like a star of the first magnitude.

Chapter XV

The Return—Discussion—Cyrus Harding and the Stranger—Port Balloon—The Engineer's Devotion— A Touching Incident—Tears Flow

THE NEXT DAY, THE 20TH OF OCTOBER, AT SEVEN O'CLOCK IN THE MORNING, AFTER A voyage of four days, the *Bonadventure* gently glided up to the beach at the mouth of the Mercy.

Cyrus Harding and Neb, who had become very uneasy at the bad weather and the prolonged absence of their companions, had climbed at daybreak to the plateau of Prospect Heights, and they had at last caught sight of the vessel which had been so long in returning.

"God be praised! there they are!" exclaimed Cyrus Harding.

As to Neb in his joy, he began to dance, to twirl round, clapping his hands and shouting, "Oh! my master!" A more touching pantomime than the finest discourse.

The engineer's first idea, on counting the people on the deck of the *Bonadventure*, was that Pencroft had not found the castaway of Tabor Island, or at any rate that the unfortunate man had refused to leave his island and change one prison for another.

Indeed Pencroft, Gideon Spilett, and Herbert were alone on the deck of the *Bonadventure*.

The moment the vessel touched, the engineer and Neb were waiting on the beach, and before the passengers had time to leap on to the sand, Harding said: "We have been very uneasy at your delay, my friends! Did you meet with any accident?"

"No," replied Gideon Spilett; "on the contrary, everything went wonderfully well. We will tell you all about it."

"However," returned the engineer, "your search has been unsuccessful, since you are only three, just as you went!"

"Excuse me, captain," replied the sailor, "we are four."

"You have found the castaway?"

"Yes."

"And you have brought him?"

"Yes."

"Living?"

"Yes."

"Where is he? Who is he?"

"He is," replied the reporter, "or rather he was a man! There, Cyrus, that is all we can tell you!"

The engineer was then informed of all that had passed during the voyage, and under what conditions the search had been conducted; how the only dwelling in the island had long been abandoned; how at last a castaway had been captured, who appeared no longer to belong to the human species.

"And that's just the point," added Pencroft, "I don't know if we have done right to bring him here."

"Certainly you have, Pencroft," replied the engineer quickly.

"But the wretched creature has no sense!"

"That is possible at present," replied Cyrus Harding, "but only a few months ago the wretched creature was a man like you and me. And who knows what will become of the survivor of us after a long solitude on this island? It is a great misfortune to be alone, my friends; and it must be believed that solitude can quickly destroy reason, since you have found this poor creature in such a state!"

"But, captain," asked Herbert, "what leads you to think that the brutishness of the unfortunate man began only a few months back?"

"Because the document we found had been recently written," answered the engineer, "and the castaway alone can have written it."

"Always supposing," observed Gideon Spilett, "that it had not been written by a companion of this man, since dead."

"That is impossible, my dear Spilett."

"Why so?" asked the reporter.

"Because the document would then have spoken of two castaways," replied Harding, "and it mentioned only one."

Herbert then in a few words related the incidents of the voyage, and dwelt on the curious fact of the sort of passing gleam in the prisoner's mind, when for an instant in the height of the storm he had become a sailor.

"Well, Herbert," replied the engineer, "you are right to attach great importance to this fact. The unfortunate man cannot be incurable, and despair has made him what he is; but here he will find his fellow-men, and since there is still a soul in him, this soul we shall save!"

The castaway of Tabor Island, to the great pity of the engineer and the great astonishment of Neb, was then brought from the cabin which he occupied in the forepart of the *Bonadventure*; when once on land he manifested a wish to run away.

But Cyrus Harding approaching, placed his hand on his shoulder with a gesture full of authority, and looked at him with infinite tenderness. Immediately the unhappy man, submitting to a superior will, gradually became calm, his eyes fell, his head bent, and he made no more resistance.

"Poor fellow!" murmured the engineer.

Cyrus Harding had attentively observed him. To judge by his appearance this miserable being had no longer anything human about him, and yet Harding, as had the reporter already, observed in his look an indefinable trace of intelligence.

It was decided that the castaway, or rather the stranger as he was thenceforth termed by his companions, should live in one of the rooms of Granite House, from which, however, he could not escape. He was led there without difficulty, and with careful attention, it might, perhaps, be hoped that some day he would be a companion to the settlers in Lincoln Island.

Cyrus Harding, during breakfast, which Neb had hastened to prepare, as the reporter, Herbert, and Pencroft were dying of hunger, heard in detail all the incidents which had marked the voyage of exploration to the islet. He agreed with his friends on this point, that the stranger must be either English or American, the name Britannia leading them to suppose this, and, besides, through the bushy beard, and under the shaggy, matted hair, the engineer thought he could recognise the characteristic features of the Anglo-Saxon.

"But, by the by," said Gideon Spilett, addressing Herbert, "you never told us how you met this savage, and we know nothing, except that you would have been strangled, if we had not happened to come up in time to help you!"

"Upon my word," answered Herbert, "it is rather difficult to say how it happened. I was, I think, occupied in collecting my plants, when I heard a noise like an avalanche falling from a very tall tree. I scarcely had time to look round. This unfortunate man, who was without doubt concealed in a tree, rushed upon me in less time than I take to tell you about it, and unless Mr. Spilett and Pencroft—"

"My boy!" said Cyrus Harding, "you ran a great danger, but, perhaps, without that, the poor creature would have still hidden himself from your search, and we should not have had a new companion."

"You hope, then, Cyrus, to succeed in reforming the man?" asked the reporter.

"Yes," replied the engineer.

Breakfast over, Harding and his companions left Granite House and returned to the beach. They there occupied themselves in unloading the *Bonadventure*, and the engineer, having examined the arms and tools, saw nothing which could help them to establish the identity of the stranger.

The capture of pigs, made on the islet, was looked upon as being very profitable to Lincoln Island, and the animals were led to the sty, where they soon became at home.

The two barrels, containing the powder and shot, as well as the box of caps, were very welcome. It was agreed to establish a small powder-magazine, either outside Granite House or in the Upper Cavern, where there would be no fear of explosion. However, the use of pyroxyle was to be continued, for this substance giving excellent results, there was no reason for substituting ordinary powder.

When the unloading of the vessel was finished—

"Captain," said Pencroft, "I think it would be prudent to put our *Bonadventure* in a safe place."

"Is she not safe at the mouth of the Mercy?" asked Cyrus Harding.

"No, captain," replied the sailor. "Half of the time she is stranded on the sand, and that works her. She is a famous craft, you see, and she behaved admirably during the squall which struck us on our return."

"Could she not float in the river?"

"No doubt, captain, she could; but there is no shelter there, and in the east winds, I think that the *Bonadventure* would suffer much from the surf."

"Well, where would you put her, Pencroft?"

"In Port Balloon," replied the sailor. "That little creek, shut in by rocks, seems to me to be just the harbour we want."

"Is it not rather far?"

"Pooh! it is not more than three miles from Granite House, and we have a fine straight road to take us there!"

"Do it then, Pencroft, and take your *Bonadventure* there," replied the engineer, "and yet I would rather have her under our more immediate protection. When we have time, we must make a little harbour for her."

"Famous!" exclaimed Pencroft. "A harbour with a lighthouse, a pier, and a dock! Ah! really with you, captain, everything becomes easy."

"Yes, my brave Pencroft," answered the engineer, "but on condition, however, that you help me, for you do as much as three men in all our work."

Herbert and the sailor then re-embarked on board the *Bonadventure*, the anchor was weighed, the sail hoisted, and the wind drove her rapidly towards Claw Cape. Two hours after, she was reposing on the tranquil waters of Port Balloon.

During the first days passed by the stranger in Granite House, had he already given them reason to think that his savage nature was becoming tamed? Did a brighter light burn in the depths of that obscured mind? In short, was the soul returning to the body?

Yes, to a certainty, and to such a degree, that Cyrus Harding and the reporter wondered if the reason of the unfortunate man had ever been totally extinguished. At first, accustomed to the open air, to the unrestrained liberty which he had enjoyed on Tabor Island, the stranger manifested a sullen fury, and it was feared that he might throw himself onto the beach, out of one of the windows of Granite House. But gradually he became calmer, and more freedom was allowed to his movements.

They had reason to hope, and to hope much. Already, forgetting his carnivorous instincts, the stranger accepted a less bestial nourishment than that on which he fed on the islet, and cooked meat did not produce in him the same sentiment of repulsion which he had showed on board the *Bonadventure*. Cyrus Harding had profited by a moment when he was sleeping, to cut his hair and matted beard, which formed a sort of mane and gave him such a savage aspect. He had also been clothed more suitably, after having got rid of the rag which covered him. The result was that, thanks to these attentions, the stranger resumed a more human appearance, and it even seemed as if his eyes had become milder. Certainly, when formerly lighted up by intelligence, this man's face must have had a sort of beauty.

Everyday, Harding imposed on himself the task of passing some hours in his company. He came and worked near him, and occupied himself in different things, so as to fix his attention. A spark, indeed, would be sufficient to reillumine that soul, a recollection crossing that brain to recall reason. That had been seen, during the storm, on board the *Bonadventure!* The engineer did not neglect either to speak aloud, so as to penetrate at the same time by the organs of hearing and sight the depths of that torpid intelligence. Sometimes one of his companions, sometimes another, sometimes all joined him. They spoke most often of things belonging to the navy, which must interest a sailor.

At times, the stranger gave some slight attention to what was said, and the settlers were soon convinced that he partly understood them. Sometimes the expression of his countenance was deeply sorrowful, a proof that he suffered mentally, for his face could not be mistaken; but he did not speak, although at different times, however, they almost thought that words were about to issue from his lips. At all events, the poor creature was quite quiet and sad!

But was not his calm only apparent? Was not his sadness only the result of his seclusion? Nothing could yet be ascertained. Seeing only certain objects and in a limited space, always in contact with the colonists, to whom he would soon become accustomed, having no desires to satisfy, better fed, better clothed, it was natural that his physical nature should gradually improve; but was he penetrated with the sense of a new life? or rather, to employ a word which would be exactly applicable to him, was he not becoming tamed, like an animal in company with his master? This was an important question, which Cyrus Harding was anxious to answer, and yet he did not wish to treat his invalid roughly! Would he ever be a convalescent?

How the engineer observed him every moment! How he was on the watch for his soul, if one may use the expression! How he was ready to grasp it! The settlers followed with real sympathy all the phases of the cure undertaken by Harding. They aided him also in this work of humanity, and all, except perhaps the incredulous Pencroft, soon shared both his hope and his faith.

The calm of the stranger was deep, as has been said, and he even showed a sort of attachment for the engineer, whose influence he evidently felt. Cyrus Harding resolved then to try him, by transporting him to another scene, from that ocean which formerly his eyes had been accustomed to contemplate, to the border of the forest, which might perhaps recall those where so many years of his life had been passed!

"But," said Gideon Spilett, "can we hope that he will not escape, if once set at liberty?"

"The experiment must be tried," replied the engineer.

"Well!" said Pencroft. "When that fellow is outside, and feels the fresh air, he will be off as fast as his legs can carry him!"

"I do not think so," returned Harding.

"Let us try," said Spilett.

"We will try," replied the engineer.

This was on the 30th of October, and consequently the castaway of Tabor Island had been a prisoner in Granite House for nine days. It was warm, and a bright sun darted its rays on the island. Cyrus Harding and Pencroft went to the room occupied by the stranger, who was found lying near the window and gazing at the sky.

"Come, my friend," said the engineer to him.

The stranger rose immediately. His eyes were fixed on Cyrus Harding, and he followed him, while the sailor marched behind them, little confident as to the result of the experiment.

Arrived at the door, Harding and Pencroft made him take his place in the lift, while

Neb, Herbert, and Gideon Spilett waited for them before Granite House. The lift descended, and in a few moments all were united on the beach.

The settlers went a short distance from the stranger, so as to leave him at liberty.

He then made a few steps towards the sea, and his look brightened with extreme animation, but he did not make the slightest attempt to escape. He was gazing at the little waves which, broken by the islet, rippled on the sand.

"This is only the sea," observed Gideon Spilett, "and possibly it does not inspire him with any wish to escape!"

"Yes," replied Harding, "we must take him to the plateau, on the border of the forest. There the experiment will be more conclusive."

"Besides, he could not run away," said Neb, "since the bridge is raised."

"Oh!" said Pencroft, "that isn't a man to be troubled by a stream like Creek Glycerine! He could cross it directly, at a single bound!"

"We shall soon see," Harding contented himself with replying, his eyes not quitting those of his patient.

The latter was then led towards the mouth of the Mercy, and all climbing the left bank of the river, reached Prospect Heights.

Arrived at the spot on which grew the first beautiful trees of the forest, their foliage slightly agitated by the breeze, the stranger appeared greedily to drink in the penetrating odor which filled the atmosphere, and a long sigh escaped from his chest.

The settlers kept behind him, ready to seize him if he made any movement to escape!

And, indeed, the poor creature was on the point of springing into the creek which separated him from the forest, and his legs were bent for an instant as if for a spring, but almost immediately he stepped back, half sank down, and a large tear fell from his eyes.

"Ah!" exclaimed Cyrus Harding, "you have become a man again, for you can weep!"

Chapter XVI

A MYSTERY TO BE CLEARED UP—THE STRANGER'S FIRST
WORDS—TWELVE YEARS ON THE ISLET—AVOWAL WHICH ESCAPES
HIM—THE DISAPPEARANCE—CYRUS HARDING'S CONFIDENCE—
CONSTRUCTION OF A MILL—THE FIRST BREAD—AN ACT OF
DEVOTION—HONEST HANDS

YES! THE UNFORTUNATE MAN HAD WEPT! SOME RECOLLECTION DOUBTLESS HAD FLASHED across his brain, and to use Cyrus Harding's expression, by those tears he was once more a man.

The colonists left him for some time on the plateau, and withdrew themselves to a short distance, so that he might feel himself free; but he did not think of profiting by this liberty, and Harding soon brought him back to Granite House. Two days after this occurrence, the stranger appeared to wish gradually to mingle with their common life. He evidently heard and understood, but no less evidently was he strangely determined not to speak to the colonists; for one evening, Pencroft, listening at the door of his room, heard these words escape from his lips:—

"No! here! I! never!"

The sailor reported these words to his companions.

"There is some painful mystery there!" said Harding.

The stranger had begun to use the laboring tools, and he worked in the garden. When he stopped in his work, as was often the case, he remained retired within himself, but on the engineer's recommendation, they respected the reserve which he apparently wished to keep. If one of the settlers approached him, he drew back, and his chest heaved with sobs, as if overburdened!

Was it remorse that overwhelmed him thus? They were compelled to believe so, and Gideon Spilett could not help one day making this observation—

"If he does not speak it is because he has, I fear, things too serious to be told!"

They must be patient and wait.

A few days later, on the 3d of November, the stranger, working on the plateau, had stopped, letting his spade drop to the ground, and.Harding, who was observing him from a little distance, saw that tears were again flowing from his eyes. A sort of irresistible pity led him towards the unfortunate man, and he touched his arm lightly.

"My friend!" said he.

The stranger tried to avoid his look, and Cyrus Harding having endeavoured to take his hand, he drew back quickly.

"My friend," said Harding in a firmer voice, "look at me, I wish it!"

The stranger looked at the engineer, and seemed to be under his power, as a subject under the influence of a mesmerist. He wished to run away. But then his countenance suddenly underwent a transformation. His eyes flashed. Words struggled to escape from his lips. He could no longer contain himself! . . . At last he folded his arms; then, in a hollow voice—

"Who are you?" he asked Cyrus Harding.

"Castaways, like you," replied the engineer, whose emotion was deep. "We have brought you here, among your fellow-men."

"My fellow-men! . . . I have none!"

"You are in the midst of friends."

"Friends!—for me! friends!" exclaimed the stranger, hiding his face in his hands. "No—never—leave me! leave me!"

Then he rushed to the side of the plateau which overlooked the sea, and remained there a long time motionless.

Harding rejoined his companions and related to them what had just happened.

"Yes! there is some mystery in that man's life," said Gideon Spilett, "and it appears as if he had only re-entered society by the path of remorse."

"I don't know what sort of a man we have brought here," said the sailor. "He has secrets—"

"Which we will respect," interrupted Cyrus Harding quickly. "If he has committed any crime, he has most fearfully expiated it, and in our eyes he is absolved."

For two hours the stranger remained alone on the shore, evidently under the influence of recollections which recalled all his past life—a melancholy life doubtless—and the colonists, without losing sight of him, did not attempt to disturb his solitude. However, after two hours, appearing to have formed a resolution, he came to find Cyrus Harding. His eyes were red with the tears he had shed, but he wept no longer. His countenance expressed deep humility. He appeared anxious, timorous, ashamed, and his eyes were constantly fixed on the ground.

"Sir," said he to Harding, "your companions and you, are you English?"

"No," answered the engineer, "we are Americans."

"Ah!" said the stranger, and he murmured, "I prefer that!"

"And you, my friend?" asked the engineer.

"English," replied he hastily.

And as if these few words had been difficult to say, he retreated to the beach, where he walked up and down between the cascade and the mouth of the Mercy, in a state of extreme agitation.

Then, passing one moment close to Herbert, he stopped and in a stifled voice—

"What month?" he asked.

"December," replied Herbert.

"What year?"

"1866."

"Twelve years! twelve years!" he exclaimed.

Then he left him abruptly.

Herbert reported to the colonists the questions and answers which had been made.

"This unfortunate man," observed Gideon Spilett, "was no longer acquainted with either months or years!"

"Yes!" added Herbert, "and he had been twelve years already on the islet when we found him there!"

"Twelve years!" rejoined Harding. "Ah! twelve years of solitude, after a wicked life, perhaps, may well impair a man's reason!"

"I am induced to think," said Pencroft, "that this man was not wrecked on Tabor Island, but that in consequence of some crime he was left there."

"You must be right, Pencroft," replied the reporter, "and if it is so it is not impossible that those who left him on the island may return to fetch him someday!"

"And they will no longer find him," said Herbert.

"But then," added Pencroft, "they must return, and—"

"My friends," said Cyrus Harding, "do not let us discuss this question until we know more about it. I believe that the unhappy man has suffered, that he has severely expiated his faults, whatever they may have been, and that the wish to unburden himself stifles him. Do not let us press him to tell us his history! He will tell it to us doubtless, and when we know it, we shall see what course it will be best to follow. He alone besides can tell us, if he has more than a hope, a certainty, of returning someday to his country, but I doubt it!"

"And why?" asked the reporter.

"Because that, in the event of his being sure of being delivered at a certain time, he would have waited the hour of his deliverance and would not have thrown this document into the sea. No, it is more probable that he was condemned to die on that islet, and that he never expected to see his fellow-creatures again!"

"But," observed the sailor, "there is one thing which I cannot explain."

"What is it?"

"If this man had been left for twelve years on Tabor Island, one may well suppose that he had been several years already in the wild state in which we found him!"

"That is probable," replied Cyrus Harding.

"It must then be many years since he wrote that document!"

"No doubt, and yet the document appears to have been recently written!"

"Besides, how do you know that the bottle which enclosed the document may not have taken several years to come from Tabor Island to Lincoln Island?"

"That is not absolutely impossible," replied the reporter.

"Might it not have been a long time already on the coast of the island?"

"No," answered Pencroft, "for it was still floating. We could not even suppose that after it had stayed for any length of time on the shore, it would have been swept off by the sea, for the south coast is all rocks, and it would certainly have been smashed to pieces there!"

"That is true," rejoined Cyrus Harding thoughtfully.

"And then," continued the sailor, "if the document was several years old, if it had been shut up in that bottle for several years, it would have been injured by damp. Now, there is nothing of the kind, and it was found in a perfect state of preservation."

The sailor's reasoning was very just, and pointed out an incomprehensible fact, for the document appeared to have been recently written, when the colonists found it in the bottle. Moreover, it gave the latitude and longitude of Tabor Island correctly, which implied that its author had a more complete knowledge of hydrography than could be expected of a common sailor.

"There is in this, again, something unaccountable," said the engineer, "but we will not urge our companion to speak. When he likes, my friends, then we shall be ready to hear him!"

During the following days the stranger did not speak a word, and did not once leave the precincts of the plateau. He worked away, without losing a moment, without taking a minute's rest, but always in a retired place. At meal times he never came to Granite House, although invited several times to do so, but contented himself with eating a few raw vegetables. At nightfall he did not return to the room assigned to him, but remained under some clump of trees, or when the weather was bad crouched in some cleft of the rocks. Thus he lived in the same manner as when he had no other shelter than the forests of Tabor Island, and as all persuasion to induce him to improve his life was in vain, the colonists waited patiently. And the time was near, when, as it seemed, almost involuntarily urged by his conscience, a terrible confession escaped him.

On the 10th of November, about eight o'clock in the evening, as night was coming on, the stranger appeared unexpectedly before the settlers, who were assembled under the veranda. His eyes burned strangely, and he had quite resumed the wild aspect of his worst days.

Cyrus Harding and his companions were astounded on seeing that, overcome by some terrible emotion, his teeth chattered like those of a person in a fever. What was the matter with him? Was the sight of his fellow-creatures insupportable to him? Was he weary of this return to a civilised mode of existence? Was he pining for his former savage life? It appeared so, as soon he was heard to express himself in these incoherent sentences:—

"Why am I here?. . . By what right have you dragged me from my islet?. . . Do you think there could be any tie between you and me?. . . Do you know who I am—what I have done—why I was there—alone? And who told you that I was not abandoned there—that I was not condemned to die there? . . . Do you know my past?. . . How do you know that I have not stolen, murdered—that I am not a wretch—an accursed being—only fit to live like a wild beast far from all—speak—do you know it?"

The colonists listened without interrupting the miserable creature, from whom these broken confessions escaped, as it were, in spite of himself. Harding wishing to calm him, approached him, but he hastily drew back.

"No! no!" he exclaimed; "one word only—am I free?"

"You are free," answered the engineer.

"Farewell, then!" he cried, and fled like a madman.

Neb, Pencroft, and Herbert ran also towards the edge of the wood—but they returned alone.

"We must let him alone!" said Cyrus Harding.

"He will never come back!" exclaimed Pencroft.

"He will come back," replied the engineer.

Many days passed; but Harding—was it a sort of presentiment?—persisted in the fixed idea that sooner or later the unhappy man would return.

"It is the last revolt of his wild nature," said he, "which remorse has touched, and which renewed solitude will terrify."

In the meanwhile, works of all sorts were continued, as well on Prospect Heights as at the corral, where Harding intended to build a farm. It is unnecessary to say that the seeds collected by Herbert on Tabor Island had been carefully sown. The plateau thus formed one immense kitchen-garden, well laid out and carefully tended, so that the arms of the settlers were never in want of work. There was always something to be done. As the esculents increased in number, it became necessary to enlarge the simple beds, which threatened to grow into regular fields and replace the meadows. But grass abounded in other parts of the island, and there was no fear of the onagers being obliged to go on short allowance. It was well worthwhile, besides, to turn Prospect Heights into a kitchen-garden, defended by its deep belt of creeks, and to remove them to the meadows, which had no need of protection against the depredations of quadrumana and quadrupeds.

On the 15th of November, the third harvest was gathered in. How wonderfully had the field increased in extent, since eighteen months ago, when the first grain of wheat was sown! The second crop of six hundred thousand grains produced this time four thousand bushels, or five hundred millions of grains!

The colony was rich in corn, for ten bushels alone were sufficient for sowing every year to produce an ample crop for the food both of men and beasts. The harvest was completed, and the last fortnight of the month of November was devoted to the work of converting it into food for man. In fact, they had corn, but not flour, and the establishment of a mill was necessary. Cyrus Harding could have utilised the second fall which flowed into the Mercy to establish his motive power, the first being already occupied with moving the felting mill, but, after some consultation, it was decided that a simple windmill should be built on Prospect Heights. The building of this presented no more difficulty than the building of the former, and it was moreover certain that there would be no want of wind on the plateau, exposed as it was to the sea-breezes.

"Not to mention," said Pencroft, "that the windmill will be more lively and will have a good effect in the landscape!"

They set to work by choosing timber for the frame and machinery of the mill. Some large stones, found at the north of the lake, could be easily transformed into millstones, and as to the sails, the inexhaustible case of the balloon furnished the necessary material.

Cyrus Harding made his model, and the site of the mill was chosen a little to the right of the poultry-yard, near the shore of the lake. The frame was to rest on a pivot supported with strong timbers, so that it could turn with all the machinery it contained according as the wind required it. The work advanced rapidly. Neb and Pencroft had become very skilful carpenters, and had nothing to do but to copy the models provided by the engineer.

Soon a sort of cylindrical box, in shape like a pepper-pot, with a pointed roof, rose on the spot chosen. The four frames which formed the sails had been firmly fixed in the centre beam, so as to form a certain angle with it, and secured with iron clamps. As to the different parts of the internal mechanism, the box destined to contain the two millstones, the fixed stone and the moving stone, the hopper, a sort of large square trough, wide at the top, narrow at the bottom, which would allow the grain to fall on the stones, the oscillating spout intended to regulate the passing of the grain, and lastly the bolting machine, which by the operation of sifting, separates the bran from the flour, were made without difficulty. The tools were good, and the work not difficult, for in reality, the machinery of a mill is very simple. This was only a question of time.

Everyone had worked at the construction of the mill, and on the 1st of December it was finished. As usual, Pencroft was delighted with his work, and had no doubt that the apparatus was perfect.

"Now for a good wind," said he, "and we shall grind our first harvest splendidly!"

"A good wind, certainly," answered the engineer, "but not too much, Pencroft."

"Pooh! our mill would only go the faster!"

"There is no need for it to go so very fast," replied Cyrus Harding. "It is known by experience that the greatest quantity of work is performed by a mill when the number of turns made by the sails in a minute is six times the number of feet traversed by the wind in a second. A moderate breeze, which passes over twenty-four feet to the second, will give sixteen turns to the sails during a minute, and there is no need of more."

"Exactly!" cried Herbert, "a fine breeze is blowing from the north-east, which will soon do our business for us."

There was no reason for delaying the inauguration of the mill, for the settlers were eager to taste the first piece of bread in Lincoln Island. On this morning two or three bushels of wheat were ground, and the next day at breakfast a magnificent loaf, a little heavy perhaps, although raised with yeast, appeared on the table at Granite House. Everyone munched away at it with a pleasure which may be easily understood.

In the meanwhile, the stranger had not reappeared. Several times Gideon Spilett and Herbert searched the forest in the neighbourhood of Granite House, without meeting or finding any trace of him. They became seriously uneasy at this prolonged absence. Certainly, the former savage of Tabor Island could not be perplexed how to live in the forest, abounding in game, but was it not to be feared that he had resumed his habits, and that this freedom would revive in him his wild instincts? However, Harding, by a sort of presentiment, doubtless, always persisted in saying that the fugitive would return.

"Yes, he will return!" he repeated with a confidence which his companions could not share. "When this unfortunate man was on Tabor Island, he knew himself to be alone! Here, he knows that fellow-men are awaiting him! Since he has partially spoken of his past life, the poor penitent will return to tell the whole, and from that day he will belong to us!"

The event justified Cyrus Harding's predictions. On the 3d of December, Herbert had left the plateau to go and fish on the southern bank of the lake. He was unarmed, and till then had never taken any precautions for defence, as dangerous animals had not shown themselves on that part of the island.

Meanwhile, Pencroft and Neb were working in the poultry-yard, while Harding and the reporter were occupied at the Chimneys in making soda, the store of soap being exhausted.

Suddenly cries resounded—

"Help! help!"

Cyrus Harding and the reporter, being at too great a distance, had not been able to hear the shouts. Pencroft and Neb, leaving the poultry-yard in all haste, rushed towards the lake.

But before then, the stranger, whose presence at this place no one had suspected, crossed Creek Glycerine, which separated the plateau from the forest, and bounded up the opposite bank.

Herbert was there face to face with a fierce jaguar, similar to the one which had been killed on Reptile End. Suddenly surprised, he was standing with his back against a tree, while the animal gathering itself together was about to spring.

But the stranger, with no other weapon than a knife, rushed on the formidable animal, who turned to meet this new adversary.

The struggle was short. The stranger possessed immense strength and activity. He seized the jaguar's throat with one powerful hand, holding it as in a vise, without heeding the beast's claws which tore his flesh, and with the other he plunged his knife into its heart.

The jaguar fell. The stranger kicked away the body, and was about to fly at the moment when the settlers arrived on the field of battle, but Herbert, clinging to him, cried—

"No, no! you shall not go!"

Harding advanced towards the stranger, who frowned when he saw him approaching. The blood flowed from his shoulder under his torn shirt, but he took no notice of it.

"My friend," said Cyrus Harding, "we have just contracted a debt of gratitude to you. To save our boy you have risked your life!"

"My life!" murmured the stranger. "What is that worth? Less than nothing!"

"You are wounded?"

"It is no matter."

"Will you give me your hand?"

And as Herbert endeavoured to seize the hand which had just saved him, the stranger folded his arms, his chest heaved, his look darkened, and he appeared to wish to escape, but making a violent effort over himself, and in an abrupt tone—

"Who are you?" he asked, "and what do you claim to be to me?"

It was the colonists' history which he thus demanded, and for the first time. Perhaps this history recounted, he would tell his own.

In a few words Harding related all that had happened since their departure from Richmond; how they had managed, and what resources they now had at their disposal.

The stranger listened with extreme attention.

Then the engineer told who they all were, Gideon Spilett, Herbert, Pencroft, Neb, himself, and, he added, that the greatest happiness they had felt since their arrival in Lincoln Island was on the return of the vessel from Tabor Island, when they had been able to include among them a new companion.

At these words the stranger's face flushed, his head sunk on his breast, and confusion was depicted on his countenance.

"And now that you know us," added Cyrus Harding, "will you give us your hand?"

"No," replied the, stranger in a hoarse voice; "no! You are honest men! And I—"

Chapter XVII

STILL ALONE—THE STRANGER'S REQUEST—THE FARM ESTABLISHED AT THE CORRAL—TWELVE YEARS AGO— THE BOATSWAIN'S MATE OF THE BRITANNIA—LEFT ON TABOR ISLAND—CYRUS HARDING'S HAND— THE MYSTERIOUS DOCUMENT

THESE LAST WORDS JUSTIFIED THE COLONISTS' PRESENTIMENT. THERE HAD BEEN SOME mournful past, perhaps expiated in the sight of men, but from which his conscience had not yet absolved him. At any rate the guilty man felt remorse, he repented, and his new friends would have cordially pressed the hand which they sought; but he did not feel himself worthy to extend it to honest men! However, after the scene with the jaguar, he did not return to the forest, and from that day did not go beyond the enclosure of Granite House.

What was the mystery of his life? Would the stranger one day speak of it? Time alone could show. At any rate, it was agreed that his secret should never be asked from him, and that they would live with him as if they suspected nothing.

For some days their life continued as before. Cyrus Harding and Gideon Spilett worked together, sometimes chemists, sometimes experimentalists. The reporter never left the engineer except to hunt with Herbert, for it would not have been prudent to allow the lad to ramble alone in the forest; and it was very necessary to be on their guard. As to Neb and Pencroft, one day at the stables and poultry-yard, another at the corral, without reckoning work in Granite House, they were never in want of employment.

The stranger worked alone, and he had resumed his usual life, never appearing at meals, sleeping under the trees in the plateau, never mingling with his companions. It really seemed as if the society of those who had saved him was insupportable to him!

"But then," observed Pencroft, "why did he entreat the help of his fellow-creatures? Why did he throw that paper into the sea?"

"He will tell us why," invariably replied Cyrus Harding.

"When?"

"Perhaps sooner than you think, Pencroft."

And, indeed, the day of confession was near.

On the 10th of December, a week after his return to Granite House, Harding saw the stranger approaching, who, in a calm voice and humble tone, said to him: "Sir, I have a request to make of you."

"Speak," answered the engineer, "but first let me ask you a question."

At these words the stranger reddened, and was on the point of withdrawing. Cyrus Harding understood what was passing in the mind of the guilty man, who doubtless feared that the engineer would interrogate him on his past life.

Harding held him back.

"Comrade," said he, "we are not only your companions but your friends. I wish you to believe that, and now I will listen to you."

The stranger pressed his hand over his eyes. He was seized with a sort of trembling, and remained a few moments without being able to articulate a word.

"Sir," said he at last, "I have come to beg you to grant me a favour."

"What is it?"

"You have, four or five miles from here, a corral for your domesticated animals. These animals need to be taken care of. Will you allow me to live there with them?"

Cyrus Harding gazed at the unfortunate man for a few moments with a feeling of deep commiseration; then—

"My friend," said he, "the corral has only stables hardly fit for animals."

"It will be good enough for me, sir."

"My friend," answered Harding, "we will not constrain you in anything. You wish to live at the corral, so be it. You will, however, be always welcome at Granite House. But since you wish to live at the corral we will make the necessary arrangements for your being comfortably established there."

"Never mind that, I shall do very well."

"My friend," answered Harding, who always intentionally made use of this cordial appellation, "you must let us judge what it will be best to do in this respect."

"Thank you, sir," replied the stranger as he withdrew.

The engineer then made known to his companions the proposal which had been made to him, and it was agreed that they should build a wooden house at the corral, which they would make as comfortable as possible.

That very day the colonists repaired to the corral with the necessary tools, and a week had not passed before the house was ready to receive its tenant. It was built about twenty feet from the sheds, and from there it was easy to overlook the flock of sheep, which then numbered more than eighty. Some furniture, a bed, table, bench, cupboard, and chest were manufactured, and a gun, ammunition, and tools were carried to the corral.

The stranger, however, had seen nothing of his new dwelling, and he had allowed the settlers to work there without him, while he occupied himself on the plateau, wishing, doubtless, to put the finishing stroke to his work. Indeed, thanks to him, all the ground was dug up and ready to be sowed when the time came.

It was on the 20th of December that all the arrangements at the corral were completed. The engineer announced to the stranger that his dwelling was ready to receive him, and the latter replied that he would go and sleep there that very evening.

On this evening the colonists were gathered in the dining-room of Granite House. It was then eight o'clock, the hour at which their companion was to leave them. Not wishing to trouble him by their presence, and thus imposing on him the necessity of saying farewells which might perhaps be painful to him, they had left him alone and ascended to Granite House.

Now, they had been talking in the room for a few minutes, when a light knock was heard at the door. Almost immediately the stranger entered, and without any preamble—

"Gentlemen," said he, "before I leave you, it is right that you should know my history. I will tell it you."

These simple words profoundly impressed Cyrus Harding and his companions.

The engineer rose.

"We ask you nothing, my friend," said he; "it is your right to be silent."

"It is my duty to speak."

"Sit down, then."

"No, I will stand."

"We are ready to hear you," replied Harding.

The stranger remained standing in a corner of the room, a little in the shade. He was bareheaded, his arms folded across his chest, and it was in this posture that in a hoarse voice, speaking like someone who obliges himself to speak, he gave the following recital, which his auditors did not once interrupt:—

"On the 20th of December, 1854, a steam-yacht, belonging to a Scotch nobleman, Lord Glenarvan, anchored off Cape Bermouilli, on the western coast of Australia, in the thirty-seventh parallel. On board this yacht were Lord Glenarvan and his wife, a major in the English army, a French geographer, a young girl, and a young boy. These two last were the children of Captain Grant, whose ship, the *Britannia*, had been lost, crew and cargo, a year before. The *Duncan* was commanded by Captain John Mangles, and manned by a crew of fifteen men.

"This is the reason the yacht at this time lay off the coast of Australia. Six months before, a bottle, enclosing a document written in English, German, and French, had been found in the Irish Sea, and picked up by the *Duncan*. This document stated in substance that there still existed three survivors from the wreck of the *Britannia*, that these survivors were Captain Grant and two of his men, and that they had found refuge on some land, of which the document gave the latitude, but of which the longitude, effaced by the sea, was no longer legible.

"This latitude was 37° 11' south; therefore, the longitude being unknown, if they followed the thirty-seventh parallel over continents and seas, they would be certain to reach the spot inhabited by Captain Grant and his two companions. The English Admiralty having hesitated to undertake this search, Lord Glenarvan resolved to attempt everything to find the captain. He communicated with Mary and Robert Grant, who joined him. The

Duncan yacht was equipped for the distant voyage, in which the nobleman's family and the captain's children wished to take part, and the *Duncan*, leaving Glasgow, proceeded towards the Atlantic, passed through the Straits of Magellan, and ascended the Pacific as far as Patagonia, where, according to a previous interpretation of the document, they supposed that Captain Grant was a prisoner among the Indians.

"The *Duncan* disembarked her passengers on the western coast of Patagonia, and sailed to pick them up again on the eastern coast at Cape Corrientes. Lord Glenarvan traversed Patagonia, following the thirty-seventh parallel, and having found no trace of the captain, he re-embarked on the 13th of November, so as to pursue his search through the Ocean.

"After having unsuccessfully visited the islands of Tristan d'Acunha and Amsterdam, situated in her course, the *Duncan*, as I have said, arrived at Cape Bermouilli, on the Australian coast, on the 20th of December, 1854.

"It was Lord Glenarvan's intention to traverse Australia as he had traversed America, and he disembarked. A few miles from the coast was established a farm, belonging to an Irishman, who offered hospitality to the travellers. Lord Glenarvan made known to the Irishman the cause which had brought him to these parts, and asked if he knew whether a three-masted English vessel, the *Britannia*, had been lost less than two years before on the west coast of Australia.

"The Irishman had never heard of this wreck, but, to the great surprise of the bystanders, one of his servants came forward and said—

" 'My lord, praise and thank God! If Captain Grant is still living, he is living on the Australian shores.'

" 'Who are you?' asked Lord Glenarvan.

" 'A Scotchman like yourself, my lord,' replied the man; 'I am one of Captain Grant's crew—one of the castaways of the *Britannia*.'

"This man was called Ayrton. He was, in fact, the boatswain's mate of the *Britannia*, as his papers showed. But, separated from Captain Grant at the moment when the ship struck upon the rocks, he had till then believed that the captain with all his crew had perished, and that he, Ayrton, was the sole survivor of the *Britannia*.

" 'Only,' he added, 'it was not on the west coast, but on the east coast of Australia that the vessel was lost, and if Captain Grant is still living, as his document indicates, he is a prisoner among the natives, and it is on the other coast that he must be looked for.'

"This man spoke in a frank voice and with a confident look; his words could not be doubted. The irishman, in whose service he had been for more than a year, answered for his trustworthiness. Lord Glenarvan, therefore, believed in the fidelity of this man and, by his advice, resolved to cross Australia, following the thirty-seventh parallel. Lord Glenarvan, his wife, the two children, the major, the Frenchman, Captain Mangles, and a few sailors composed the little band under the command of Ayrton, while the *Duncan*, under charge of the mate, Tom Austin, proceeded to Melbourne, there to await Lord Glenarvan's instructions.

"They set out on the 23d of December, 1854.

"It is time to say that Ayrton was a traitor. He was, indeed, the boatswain's mate of the *Britannia*, but, after some dispute with his captain, he endeavoured to incite the crew to mutiny and seize the ship, and Captain Grant had landed him, on the 8th of April, 1852, on the west coast of Australia, and then sailed, leaving him there, as was only just.

"Therefore this wretched man knew nothing of the wreck of the *Britannia*; he had just heard of it from Glenarvan's account. Since his abandonment, he had become, under the name of Ben Joyce, the leader of the escaped convicts; and if he boldly maintained that the wreck had taken place on the east coast, and led Lord Glenarvan to proceed in that direction, it was that he hoped to separate him from his ship, seize the *Duncan,* and make the yacht a pirate in the Pacific."

Here the stranger stopped for a moment. His voice trembled, but he continued—

"The expedition set out and proceeded across Australia. It was inevitably unfortunate, since Ayrton, or Ben Joyce, as he may be called, guided it, sometimes preceded, sometimes followed by his band of convicts, who had been told what they had to do.

"Meanwhile, the *Duncan* had been sent to Melbourne for repairs. It was necessary, then, to get Lord Glenarvan to order her to leave Melbourne and go to the east coast of Australia, where it would be easy to seize her. After having led the expedition near enough to the coast, in the midst of vast forests with no resources, Ayrton obtained a letter, which he was charged to carry to the mate of the *Duncan*—a letter which ordered the yacht to repair immediately to the east coast, to Twofold Bay, that is to say a few days' journey from the place where the expedition had stopped. It was there that Ayrton had agreed to meet his accomplices, and two days after gaining possession of the letter, he arrived at Melbourne.

"So far the villain had succeeded in his wicked design. He would be able to take the *Duncan* into Twofold Bay, where it would be easy for the convicts to seize her, and her crew massacred, Ben Joyce would become master of the seas. . . . But it pleased God to prevent the accomplishment of these terrible projects.

"Ayrton, arrived at Melbourne, delivered the letter to the mate, Tom Austin, who read it and immediately set sail, but judge of Ayrton's rage and disappointment, when the next day he found that the mate was taking the vessel, not to the east coast of Australia, to Twofold Bay, but to the east coast of New Zealand. He wished to stop him, but Austin showed him the letter! . . . And indeed, by a providential error of the French geographer, who had written the letter, the east coast of New Zealand was mentioned as the place of destination.

"All Ayrton's plans were frustrated! He became outrageous. They put him in irons. He was then taken to the coast of New Zealand, not knowing what would become of his accomplices, or what would become of Lord Glenarvan.

"The *Duncan* cruised about on this coast until the 3d of March. On that day Ayrton heard the report of guns. The guns on the *Duncan* were being fired, and soon Lord Glenarvan and his companions came on board.

"This is what had happened.

"After a thousand hardships, a thousand dangers, Lord Glenarvan had accomplished his journey, and arrived on the east coast of Australia, at Twofold Bay. 'No *Duncan!*' He telegraphed to Melbourne. They answered, '*Duncan* sailed on the 18th instant. Destination unknown.'

"Lord Glenarvan could only arrive at one conclusion; that his honest yacht had fallen into the hands of Ben Joyce, and had become a pirate vessel!

"However, Lord Glenarvan would not give up. He was a bold and generous man. He embarked in a merchant vessel, sailed to the west coast of New Zealand, traversed it along the thirty-seventh parallel, without finding any trace of Captain Grant; but on the other side, to his great surprise, and by the will of Heaven, he found the *Duncan*, under command of the mate, who had been waiting for him for five weeks!

"This was on the 3d of March, 1855. Lord Glenarvan was now on board the *Duncan*, but Ayrton was there also. He appeared before the nobleman, who wished to extract from him all that the villain knew about Captain Grant. Ayrton refused to speak. Lord Glenarvan then told him, that at the first port they put into, he would be delivered up to the English authorities. Ayrton remained mute.

"The *Duncan* continued her voyage along the thirty-seventh parallel. In the meanwhile, Lady Glenarvan undertook to vanquish the resistance of the ruffian.

"At last, her influence prevailed, and Ayrton, in exchange for what he could tell, proposed that Lord Glenarvan should leave him on some island in the Pacific, instead of giving him up to the English authorities. Lord Glenarvan, resolving to do anything to obtain information about Captain Grant, consented.

"Ayrton then related all his life, and it was certain that he knew nothing from the day on which Captain Grant had landed him on the Australian coast.

"Nevertheless, Lord Glenarvan kept the promise which he had given. The *Duncan* continued her voyage and arrived at Tabor Island. It was there that Ayrton was to be landed, and it was there also that, by a veritable miracle, they found Captain Grant and two men, exactly on the thirty-seventh parallel.

"The convict, then, went to take their place on this desert islet, and at the moment he left the yacht these words were pronounced by Lord Glenarvan:—

" 'Here, Ayrton, you will be far from any land, and without any possible communication with your fellow-creatures. You cannot escape from this islet on which the *Duncan* leaves you. You will be alone, under the eye of a God who reads the depths of the heart, but you will be neither lost nor forgotten, as was Captain Grant. Unworthy as you are to be remembered by men, men will remember you. I know where you are Ayrton, and I know where to find you. I will never forget it!

"And the *Duncan*, making sail, soon disappeared. This was 18th of March, 1855.*

"Ayrton was alone, but he had no want of either ammunition, weapons, tools, or seeds.

"At his, the convict's disposal, was the house built by honest Captain Grant. He had only to live and expiate in solitude the crimes which he had committed.

"Gentlemen, he repented, he was ashamed of his crimes and was very miserable! He said to himself, that if men came someday to take him from that islet, he must be worthy to return among them! How he suffered, that wretched man! How he labored to recover himself by work! How he prayed to be reformed by prayer! For two years, three years, this went on, but Ayrton, humbled by solitude, always looking for some ship to appear on the horizon, asking himself if the time of expiation would soon be complete, suffered as none other suffered! Oh! how dreadful was this solitude, to a heart tormented by remorse!

---

* The events which have just been briefly related are taken from a work which some of our readers have no doubt read, and which is entitled. "Captain Grant's Children." They will remark on this occasion, as well as later, some discrepancy in the dates; but later again, they will understand why the real dates were not at first given.

"But doubtless Heaven had not sufficiently punished this unhappy man, for he felt that he was gradually becoming a savage! He felt that brutishness was gradually gaining on him!

"He could not say if it was after two or three years of solitude, but at last he became the miserable creature you found!

"I have no need to tell you, gentlemen, that Ayrton, Ben Joyce, and I, are the same."

Cyrus Harding and his companions rose at the end of this account. It is impossible to say how much they were moved! What misery, grief, and despair lay revealed before them!

"Ayrton," said Harding, rising, "you have been a great criminal, but Heaven must certainly think that you have expiated your crimes! That has been proved by your having been brought again among your fellow-creatures. Ayrton, you are forgiven! And now you will be our companion?"

Ayrton drew back.

"Here is my hand!" said the engineer.

Ayrton grasped the hand which Harding extended to him, and great tears fell from his eyes.

"Will you live with us?" asked Cyrus Harding.

"Captain Harding, leave me some time longer," replied Ayrton, "leave me alone in the hut in the corral!"

"As you like, Ayrton," answered Cyrus Harding. Ayrton was going to withdraw, when the engineer addressed one more question to him:—

"One word more, my friend. Since it was your intention to live alone, why did you throw into the sea the document which put us on your track?"

"A document?" repeated Ayrton, who did not appear to know what he meant.

"Yes, the document which we found enclosed in a bottle, giving us the exact position of Tabor Island!"

Ayrton passed his hand over his brow, then after having thought, "I never threw any document into the sea!" he answered.

"Never," exclaimed Pencroft.

"Never!"

And Ayrton, bowing, reached the door and departed.

Chapter XVIII

CONVERSATION—CYRUS HARDING AND GIDEON SPILETT—AN
IDEA OF THE ENGINEER'S—THE ELECTRIC TELEGRAPH—THE
WIRES—THE BATTERY—THE ALPHABET—FINE SEASON—
PROSPERITY OF THE COLONY—PHOTOGRAPHY—AN APPEARANCE
OF SNOW—TWO YEARS IN LINCOLN ISLAND

POOR MAN!" SAID HERBERT, WHO HAD RUSHED TO THE DOOR, BUT RETURNED, HAVING
seen Ayrton slide down the rope on the lift and disappear in the darkness.

"He will come back," said Cyrus Harding.

"Come, now, captain," exclaimed Pencroft, "what does that mean? What! wasn't it
Ayrton who threw that bottle into the sea? Who was it then?"

Certainly, if ever a question was necessary to be made, it was that one!

"It was he," answered Neb, "only the unhappy man was half mad."

"Yes!" said Herbert, "and he was no longer conscious of what he was doing."

"It can only be explained in that way, my friends," replied Harding quickly, "and I understand now how Ayrton was able to point out exactly the situation of Tabor Island, since
the events which had preceded his being left on the island had made it known to him."

"However," observed Pencroft, "if he was not yet a brute when he wrote that document, and if he threw it into the sea seven or eight years ago, how is it that the paper has
not been injured by damp?"

"That proves," answered Cyrus Harding, "that Ayrton was deprived of intelligence
at a more recent time than he thinks."

"Of course it must be so," replied Pencroft, "without that the fact would be
unaccountable."

"Unaccountable indeed," answered the engineer, who did not appear desirous to prolong the conversation.

"But has Ayrton told the truth?" asked the sailor.

"Yes," replied the reporter. "The story which he has told is true in every point. I remember quite well the account in the newspapers of the yacht expedition undertaken by
Lord Glenarvan, and its result."

"Ayrton has told the truth," added Harding. "Do not doubt it, Pencroft, for it was
painful to him. People tell the truth when they accuse themselves like that!"

The next day—the 21st of December—the colonists descended to the beach, and
having climbed the plateau they found nothing of Ayrton. He had reached his house in the
corral during the night and the settlers judged it best not to agitate him by their presence.
Time would doubtless perform what sympathy had been unable to accomplish.

Herbert, Pencroft, and Neb resumed their ordinary occupations. On this day the same
work brought Harding and the reporter to the workshop at the Chimneys.

"Do you know, my dear Cyrus," said Gideon Spilett, "that the explanation you gave
yesterday on the subject of the bottle has not satisfied me at all! How can it be supposed

that the unfortunate man was able to write that document and throw the bottle into the sea without having the slightest recollection of it?"

"Nor was it he who threw it in, my dear Spilett."

"You think then—"

"I think nothing, I know nothing!" interrupted Cyrus Harding. "I am content to rank this incident among those which I have not been able to explain to this day!"

"Indeed, Cyrus," said Spilett, "these things are incredible! Your rescue, the case stranded on the sand, Top's adventure, and lastly this bottle . . . Shall we never have the answer to these enigmas?"

"Yes!" replied the engineer quickly, "yes, even if I have to penetrate into the bowels of this island!"

"Chance will perhaps give us the key to this mystery!"

"Chance! Spilett! I do not believe in chance, any more than I believe in mysteries in this world. There is a reason for everything unaccountable which has happened here, and that reason I shall discover. But in the meantime we must work and observe."

The month of January arrived. The year 1867 commenced. The summer occupations were assiduously continued. During the days which followed, Herbert and Spilett having gone in the direction of the corral, ascertained that Ayrton had taken possession of the habitation which had been prepared for him. He busied himself with the numerous flock confided to his care, and spared his companions the trouble of coming every two or three days to visit the corral. Nevertheless, in order not to leave Ayrton in solitude for too long a time, the settlers often paid him a visit.

It was not unimportant either, in consequence of some suspicions entertained by the engineer and Gideon Spilett, that this part of the island should be subject to a surveillance of some sort, and that Ayrton, if any incident occurred unexpectedly, should not neglect to inform the inhabitants of Granite House of it.

Nevertheless it might happen that something would occur which it would be necessary to bring rapidly to the engineer's knowledge. Independently of facts bearing on the mystery of Lincoln Island, many others might happen, which would call for the prompt interference of the colonists—such as the sighting of a vessel, a wreck on the western coast, the possible arrival of pirates, etc.

Therefore Cyrus Harding resolved to put the corral in instantaneous communication with Granite House.

It was on the 10th of January that he made known his project to his companions.

"Why! how are you going to manage that, captain?" asked Pencroft. "Do you by chance happen to think of establishing a telegraph?"

"Exactly so," answered the engineer.

"Electric?" cried Herbert.

"Electric," replied Cyrus Harding. "We have all the necessary materials for making a battery, and the most difficult thing will be to stretch the wires, but by means of a draw-plate I think we shall manage it."

"Well, after that," returned the sailor, "I shall never despair of seeing ourselves some-day rolling along on a railway!"

They then set to work, beginning with the most difficult thing, for, if they failed in that, it would be useless to manufacture the battery and other accessories.

The iron of Lincoln Island, as has been said, was of excellent quality, and consequently very fit for being drawn out. Harding commenced by manufacturing a draw-plate, that is to say, a plate of steel, pierced with conical holes of different sizes, which would successively bring the wire to the wished-for tenacity. This piece of steel, after having been tempered, was fixed in as firm a way as possible in a solid framework planted in the ground, only a few feet from the great fall, the motive power of which the engineer intended to utilise. In fact as the fulling-mill was there, although not then in use, its beam moved with extreme power would serve to stretch out the wire by rolling it round itself. It was a delicate operation, and required much care. The iron, prepared previously in long thin rods, the ends of which were sharpened with the file, having been introduced into the largest hole of the draw-plate, was drawn out by the beam which wound it round itself, to a length of twenty-five or thirty feet, then unrolled, and the same operation was performed successively through the holes of a less size. Finally, the engineer obtained wires from forty to fifty feet long, which could be easily fastened together and stretched over the distance of five miles, which separated the corral from the bounds of Granite House.

It did not take more than a few days to perform this work, and indeed as soon as the machine had been commenced, Cyrus Harding left his companions to follow the trade of wire-drawers, and occupied himself with manufacturing his battery.

It was necessary to obtain a battery with a constant current. It is known that the elements of modern batteries are generally composed of retort coal, zinc, and copper. Copper was absolutely wanting to the engineer, who, notwithstanding all his researches, had never been able to find any trace of it in Lincoln Island, and was therefore obliged to do without it. Retort coal, that is to say, the hard graphite which is found in the retorts of gas manufactories, after the coal has been dehydrogenised, could have been obtained, but it would have been necessary to establish a special apparatus, involving great labor. As to zinc, it may be remembered that the case found at Flotsam Point was lined with this metal, which could not be better utilised than for this purpose.

Cyrus Harding, after mature consideration, decided to manufacture a very simple battery, resembling as nearly as possible that invented by Becquerel in 1820, and in which zinc only is employed. The other substances, azotic acid and potash, were all at his disposal.

The way in which the battery was composed was as follows, and the results were to be attained by the reaction of acid and potash on each other. A number of glass bottles were made and filled with azotic acid. The engineer corked them by means of a stopper through which passed a glass tube, bored at its lower extremity, and intended to be plunged into the acid by means of a clay stopper secured by a rag. Into this tube, through its upper extremity, he poured a solution of potash, previously obtained by burning and reducing to ashes various plants, and in this way the acid and potash could act on each other through the clay.

Cyrus Harding then took two slips of zinc, one of which was plunged into azotic acid, the other into a solution of potash. A current was immediately produced, which was transmitted from the slip of zinc in the bottle to that in the tube, and the two slips having been connected by a metallic wire the slip in the tube became the positive pole, and that in the bottle the negative pole of the apparatus. Each bottle, therefore, produced as many currents as united would be sufficient to produce all the phenomena of the electric telegraph. Such was the ingenious and very simple apparatus constructed by Cyrus Harding, an apparatus which would allow them to establish a telegraphic communication between Granite House and the corral.

On the 6th of February was commenced the planting along the road to the corral, of posts furnished with glass insulators, and intended to support the wire. A few days after, the wire was extended, ready to produce the electric current at a rate of twenty thousand miles a second.

Two batteries had been manufactured, one for Granite House, the other for the corral; for if it was necessary the corral should be able to communicate with Granite House it might also be useful that Granite House should be able to communicate with the corral.

As to the receiver and manipulator, they were very simple. At the two stations the wire was wound round a magnet, that is to say, round a piece of soft iron surrounded with a wire. The communication was thus established between the two poles; the current, starting from the positive pole, traversed the wire, passed through the magnet which was temporarily magnetised, and returned through the earth to the negative pole. If the current was interrupted, the magnet immediately became unmagnetised. It was sufficient to place a plate of soft iron before the magnet, which, attracted during the passage of the current, would fall back when the current was interrupted. This movement of the plate thus obtained, Harding could easily fasten to it a needle arranged on a dial, bearing the letters of the alphabet, and in this way communicate from one station to the other.

All was completely arranged by the 12th of February. On this day, Harding, having sent the current through the wire, asked if all was going on well at the corral, and received in a few moments a satisfactory reply from Ayrton. Pencroft was wild with joy, and every morning and evening he sent a telegram to the corral, which always received an answer.

This mode of communication presented two very real advantages: firstly, because it enabled them to ascertain that Ayrton was at the corral; and secondly, that he was thus not left completely isolated. Besides, Cyrus Harding never allowed a week to pass without going to see him, and Ayrton came from time to time to Granite House, where he always found a cordial welcome.

The fine season passed away in the midst of the usual work. The resources of the colony, particularly in vegetables and corn, increased from day to day, and the plants brought from Tabor Island had succeeded perfectly.

The plateau of Prospect Heights presented an encouraging aspect. The fourth harvest had been admirable and it may be supposed that no one thought of counting whether the four hundred thousand millions of grains duly appeared in the crop. However, Pencroft had thought of doing so, but Cyrus Harding having told him that even if he managed to count three hundred grains a minute, or nine thousand an hour, it would take him nearly five thousand five hundred years to finish his task, the honest sailor considered it best to give up the idea.

The weather was splendid, the temperature very warm in the daytime, but in the evening the sea-breezes tempered the heat of the atmosphere and procured cool nights for the inhabitants of Granite House. There were, however, a few storms, which, although they were not of long duration, swept over Lincoln Island with extraordinary fury. The lightning blazed and the thunder continued to roll for some hours.

At this period the little colony was extremely prosperous.

The tenants of the poultry-yard swarmed, and they lived on the surplus, but it became necessary to reduce the population to a more moderate number. The pigs had already produced young, and it may be understood that their care for these animals absorbed a great part of Neb and Pencroft's time. The onagers, who had two pretty colts, were most often mounted by Gideon Spilett and Herbert, who had become an excellent rider under the reporter's instruction, and they also harnessed them to the cart either for carrying wood and coal to Granite House, or different mineral productions required by the engineer.

Several expeditions were made about this time into the depths of the Far West forests. The explorers could venture there without having anything to fear from the heat, for the sun's rays scarcely penetrated through the thick foliage spreading above their heads. They thus visited all the left bank of the Mercy, along which ran the road from the corral to the mouth of Falls River.

But in these excursions the settlers took care to be well armed, for they met with savage wild boars, with which they often had a tussle. They also, during this season, made fierce war against the jaguars. Gideon Spilett had vowed a special hatred against them, and his pupil Herbert seconded him well. Armed as they were, they no longer feared to meet one of those beasts. Herbert's courage was superb, and the reporter's *sang froid* astonishing. Already twenty magnificent skins ornamented the dining-room of Granite House, and if this continued, the jaguar race would soon be extinct in the island, the object aimed at by the hunters.

The engineer sometimes took part in the expeditions made to the unknown parts of the island, which he surveyed with great attention. It was for other traces than those of animals that he searched the thickets of the vast forest, but nothing suspicious ever appeared. Neither Top nor Jup, who accompanied him, ever betrayed by their behaviour that there was anything strange there, and yet more than once again the dog barked at the mouth of the well, which the engineer had before explored without result.

At this time Gideon Spilett, aided by Herbert, took several views of the most picturesque parts of the island, by means of the photographic apparatus found in the cases, and of which they had not as yet made any use.

This apparatus, provided with a powerful object-glass, was very complete. Substances necessary for the photographic reproduction, collodion for preparing the glass plate, nitrate of silver to render it sensitive, hyposulfate of soda to fix the prints obtained, chloride of ammonium in which to soak the paper destined to give the positive proof, acetate of soda and chloride of gold in which to immerse the paper, nothing was wanting. Even the papers were there, all prepared, and before laying in the printing-frame upon the negatives, it was sufficient to soak them for a few minutes in the solution of nitrate of silver.

The reporter and his assistant became in a short time very skilful operators, and they obtained fine views of the country, such as the island, taken from Prospect Heights with Mount Franklin in the distance, the mouth of the Mercy, so picturesquely framed in high rocks, the glade and the corral, with the spurs of the mountain in the background, the curious development of Claw Cape, Flotsam Point, etc.

Nor did the photographers forget to take the portraits of all the inhabitants of the island, leaving out no one.

"It multiplies us," said Pencroft.

And the sailor was enchanted to see his own countenance, faithfully reproduced, ornamenting the walls of Granite House, and he stopped as willingly before this exhibition as he would have done before the richest shop-windows in Broadway.

But it must be acknowledged that the most successful portrait was incontestably that of Master Jup. Master Jup had sat with a gravity not to be described, and his portrait was life-like!

"He looks as if he was just going to grin!" exclaimed Pencroft.

And if Master Jup had not been satisfied, he would have been very difficult to please; but he was quite contented and contemplated his own countenance with a sentimental air which expressed some small amount of conceit.

The summer heat ended with the month of March. The weather was sometimes rainy, but still warm. The month of March, which corresponds to the September of northern latitudes, was not so fine as might have been hoped. Perhaps it announced an early and rigourous winter.

It might have been supposed one morning—the 21st—that the first snow had already made its appearance. In fact Herbert looking early from one of the windows of Granite House, exclaimed—

"Hallo! the islet is covered with snow!"

"Snow at this time?" answered the reporter, joining the boy.

Their companions were soon beside them, but could only ascertain one thing, that not only the islet but all the beach below Granite House was covered with one uniform sheet of white.

"It must be snow!" said Pencroft.

"Or rather it's very like it!" replied Neb.

"But the thermometer marks fifty-eight degrees!" observed Gideon Spilett.

Cyrus Harding gazed at the sheet of white without saying anything, for he really did not know how to explain this phenomenon, at this time of year and in such a temperature.

"By Jove!" exclaimed Pencroft, "all our plants will be frozen!"

And the sailor was about to descend, when he was preceded by the nimble Jup, who slid down to the sand.

But the orang had not touched the ground, when the snowy sheet arose and dispersed in the air in such innumerable flakes that the light of the sun was obscured for some minutes.

"Birds!" cried Herbert.

They were indeed swarms of sea-birds, with dazzling white plumage. They had perched by thousands on the islet and on the shore, and they disappeared in the distance, leaving the colonists amazed as if they had been present at some transformation scene, in which summer succeeded winter at the touch of a fairy's wand. Unfortunately the change had been so sudden, that neither the reporter nor the lad had been able to bring down one of these birds, of which they could not recognise the species.

A few days after came the 26th of March, the day on which, two years before, the castaways from the air had been thrown upon Lincoln Island.

Chapter XIX

RECOLLECTIONS OF THEIR NATIVE LAND—PROBABLE FUTURE—
PROJECT FOR SURVEYING THE COASTS OF THE ISLAND—DEPARTURE
ON THE 16TH OF APRIL—SEA-VIEW OF REPTILE END—THE
BASALTIC ROCKS OF THE WESTERN COAST—BAD WEATHER—
NIGHT COMES ON—NEW INCIDENT

TWO YEARS ALREADY! AND FOR TWO YEARS THE COLONISTS HAD HAD NO COMMUNICA-
tion with their fellow-creatures! They were without news from the civilised world,
lost on this island, as completely as if they had been on the most minute star of the celestial hemisphere!

What was now happening in their country? The picture of their native land was always before their eyes, the land torn by civil war at the time they left it, and which the
Southern rebellion was perhaps still staining with blood! It was a great sorrow to them, and
they often talked together of these things, without ever doubting however that the cause
of the North must triumph, for the honour of the American Confederation.

During these two years not a vessel had passed in sight of the island; or, at least, not
a sail had been seen. It was evident that Lincoln Island was out of the usual track, and also
that it was unknown—as was besides proved by the maps—for though there was no port,
vessels might have visited it for the purpose of renewing their store of water. But the surrounding ocean was deserted as far as the eye could reach, and the colonists must rely on
themselves for regaining their native land.

However, one chance of rescue existed, and this chance was discussed one day on the
first week of April, when the colonists were gathered together in the dining-room of
Granite House.

They had been talking of America, of their native country, which they had so little
hope of ever seeing again.

"Decidedly we have only one way," said Spilett, "one single way for leaving Lincoln
Island, and that is, to build a vessel large enough to sail several hundred miles. It appears
to me, that when one has built a boat it is just as easy to build a ship!"

"And in which we might go to the Pomatous," added Herbert, "just as easily as we
went to Tabor Island."

"I do not say no," replied Pencroft, who had always the casting vote in maritime questions; "I do not say no, although it is not exactly the same thing to make a long as a short
voyage! If our little craft had been caught in any heavy gale of wind during the voyage to
Tabor Island, we should have known that land was at no great distance either way; but
twelve hundred miles is a pretty long way, and the nearest land is at least that distance!"

"Would you not, in that case, Pencroft, attempt the adventure?" asked the reporter.

"I will attempt anything that is desired, Mr. Spilett," answered the sailor, "and you
know well that I am not a man to flinch!"

"Remember, besides, that we number another sailor amongst us now," remarked Neb.

"Who is that?" asked Pencroft.

"Ayrton."

"That is true," replied Herbert.

"If he will consent to come," said Pencroft.

"Nonsense!" returned the reporter; "do you think that if Lord Glenarvan's yacht had appeared at Tabor Island, while he was still living there, Ayrton would have refused to depart?"

"You forget, my friends," then said Cyrus Harding, "that Ayrton was not in possession of his reason during the last years of his stay there. But that is not the question. The point is to know if we may count among our chances of being rescued, the return of the Scotch vessel. Now, Lord Glenarvan promised Ayrton that he would return to take him off from Tabor Island when he considered that his crimes were expiated, and I believe that he will return."

"Yes," said the reporter, "and I will add that he will return soon, for it is twelve years since Ayrton was abandoned."

"Well!" answered Pencroft, "I agree with you that the nobleman will return, and soon too. But where will he touch? At Tabor Island, and not at Lincoln Island."

"That is the more certain," replied Herbert, "as Lincoln Island is not even marked on the map."

"Therefore, my friends," said the engineer, "we ought to take the necessary precautions for making our presence and that of Ayrton on Lincoln Island known at Tabor Island."

"Certainly," answered the reporter, "and nothing is easier than to place in the hut, which was Captain Grant's and Ayrton's dwelling, a notice which Lord Glenarvan and his crew cannot help finding, giving the position of our island."

"It is a pity," remarked the sailor, "that we forgot to take that precaution on our first visit to Tabor Island."

"And why should we have done it?" asked Herbert. "At that time we did not know Ayrton's history; we did not know that anyone was likely to come someday to fetch him, and when we did know his history, the season was too advanced to allow us to return then to Tabor Island."

"Yes," replied Harding, "it was too late, and we must put off the voyage until next spring."

"But suppose the Scotch yacht comes before that," said Pencroft.

"That is not probable," replied the engineer, "for Lord Glenarvan would not choose the winter season to venture into these seas. Either he has already returned to Tabor Island, since Ayrton has been with us, that is to say, during the last five months and has left again; or he will not come till later, and it will be time enough in the first fine October days to go to Tabor Island, and leave a notice there."

"We must allow," said Neb, "that it will be very unfortunate if the *Duncan* has returned to these parts only a few months ago!"

"I hope that it is not so," replied Cyrus Harding, "and that Heaven has not deprived us of the best chance which remains to us."

"I think," observed the reporter, "that at any rate we shall know what we have to depend on when we have been to Tabor Island, for if the yacht has returned there, they will necessarily have left some traces of their visit."

"That is evident," answered the engineer. "So then, my friends, since we have this chance of returning to our country, we must wait patiently, and if it is taken from us we shall see what will be best to do."

"At any rate," remarked Pencroft, "it is well understood that if we do leave Lincoln Island in some way or another, it will not be because we were uncomfortable there!"

"No, Pencroft," replied the engineer, "it will be because we are far from all that a man holds dearest in the world, his family, his friends, his native land!"

Matters being thus decided, the building of a vessel large enough to sail either to the Archipelagoes in the north, or to New Zealand in the west, was no longer talked of, and they busied themselves in their accustomed occupations, with a view to wintering a third time in Granite House.

However, it was agreed that before the stormy weather came on, their little vessel should be employed in making a voyage round the island. A complete survey of the coast had not yet been made, and the colonists had but an imperfect idea of the shore to the west and north, from the mouth of Falls River to the Mandible Capes, as well as of the narrow bay between them, which opened like a shark's jaws.

The plan of this excursion was proposed by Pencroft, and Cyrus Harding fully acquiesced in it, for he himself wished to see this part of his domain.

The weather was variable, but the barometer did not fluctuate by sudden movements, and they could therefore count on tolerable weather. However, during the first week of April, after a sudden barometrical fall, a renewed rise was marked by a heavy gale of wind, lasting five or six days; then the needle of the instrument remained stationary at a height of twenty-nine inches and nine-tenths, and the weather appeared propitious for an excursion.

The departure was fixed for the 16th of April, and the *Bonadventure*, anchored in Port Balloon, was provisioned for a voyage which might be of some duration.

Cyrus Harding informed Ayrton of the projected expedition, and proposed that he should take part in it, but Ayrton preferring to remain on shore, it was decided that he should come to Granite House during the absence of his companions. Master Jup was ordered to keep him company, and made no remonstrance.

On the morning of the 16th of April all the colonists, including Top, embarked. A fine breeze blew from the south-west, and the *Bonadventure* tacked on leaving Port Balloon so as to reach Reptile End. Of the ninety miles which the perimeter of the island measured, twenty included the south coast between the port and the promontory. The wind being right ahead it was necessary to hug the shore.

It took the whole day to reach the promontory, for the vessel on leaving port had only two hours of ebb tide and had therefore to make way for six hours against the flood. It was nightfall before the promontory was doubled.

The sailor then proposed to the engineer that they should continue sailing slowly with two reefs in the sail. But Harding preferred to anchor a few cable-lengths from the shore, so as to survey that part of the coast during the day. It was agreed also that as they were anxious for a minute exploration of the coast they should not sail during the night, but would always, when the weather permitted it, be at anchor near the shore.

The night was passed under the promontory, and the wind having fallen, nothing disturbed the silence. The passengers, with the exception of the sailor, scarcely slept as well on board the *Bonadventure* as they would have done in their rooms at Granite House, but they did sleep however. Pencroft set sail at break of day, and by going on the larboard tack they could keep close to the shore.

The colonists knew this beautiful wooded coast, since they had already explored it on foot, and yet it again excited their admiration. They coasted along as close in as possible, so as to notice everything, avoiding always the trunks of trees which floated here and there. Several times also they anchored, and Gideon Spilett took photographs of the superb scenery.

About noon the *Bonadventure* arrived at the mouth of Falls River. Beyond, on the left bank, a few scattered trees appeared, and three miles further even these dwindled into solitary groups among the western spurs of the mountain, whose arid ridge sloped down to the shore.

What a contrast between the northern and southern part of the coast! In proportion as one was woody and fertile so was the other rugged and barren! It might have been designated as one of those iron coasts, as they are called in some countries, and its wild confusion appeared to indicate that a sudden crystallisation had been produced in the yet liquid basalt of some distant geological sea. These stupendous masses would have terrified the settlers if they had been cast at first on this part of the island! They had not been able to perceive the sinister aspect of this shore from the summit of Mount Franklin, for they overlooked it from too great a height, but viewed from the sea it presented a wild appearance which could not perhaps be equaled in any corner of the globe.

The *Bonadventure* sailed along this coast for the distance of half-a-mile. It was easy to see that it was composed of blocks of all sizes, from twenty to three hundred feet in height, and of all shapes, round like towers, prismatic like steeples, pyramidal like obelisks, conical like factory chimneys. An iceberg of the Polar seas could not have been more capricious in its terrible sublimity! Here, bridges were thrown from one rock to another; there, arches like those of a wave, into the depths of which the eye could not penetrate; in one place, large vaulted excavations presented a monumental aspect; in another, a crowd of columns, spires, and arches, such as no Gothic cathedral ever possessed. Every caprice of nature, still more varied than those of the imagination, appeared on this grand coast, which extended over a length of eight or nine miles.

Cyrus Harding and his companions gazed, with a feeling of surprise bordering on stupefaction. But, although they remained silent, Top, not being troubled with feelings of this sort, uttered barks which were repeated by the thousand echoes of the basaltic cliff. The engineer even observed that these barks had something strange in them, like those which the dog had uttered at the mouth of the well in Granite House.

"Let us go close in," said he.

And the *Bonadventure* sailed as near as possible to the rocky shore. Perhaps some cave, which it would be advisable to explore, existed there? But Harding saw nothing, not a cavern, not a cleft which could serve as a retreat to any being whatever, for the foot of the cliff was washed by the surf. Soon Top's barks ceased, and the vessel continued her course at a few cable-lengths from the coast.

In the north-west part of the island the shore became again flat and sandy. A few trees here and there rose above a low, marshy ground, which the colonists had already surveyed, and in violent contrast to the other desert shore, life was again manifested by the presence of myriads of water-fowl. That evening the *Bonadventure* anchored in a small bay to the north of the island, near the land, such was the depth of water there. The night passed quietly, for the breeze died away with the last light of day, and only rose again with the first streaks of dawn.

As it was easy to land, the usual hunters of the colony, that is to say, Herbert and Gideon Spilett, went for a ramble of two hours or so, and returned with several strings of wild duck and snipe. Top had done wonders, and not a bird had been lost, thanks to his zeal and cleverness.

At eight o'clock in the morning the *Bonadventure* set sail, and ran rapidly towards North Mandible Cape, for the wind was right astern and freshening rapidly.

"However," observed Pencroft, "I should not be surprised if a gale came up from the west. Yesterday the sun set in a very red-looking horizon, and now, this morning, those mares-tails don't forebode anything good."

These mares-tails are cirrus clouds, scattered in the zenith, their height from the sea being less than five thousand feet. They look like light pieces of cotton wool, and their presence usually announces some sudden change in the weather.

"Well," said Harding, "let us carry as much sail as possible, and run for shelter into Shark Gulf. I think that the *Bonadventure* will be safe there."

"Perfectly," replied Pencroft, "and besides, the north coast is merely sand, very uninteresting to look at."

"I shall not be sorry," resumed the engineer, "to pass not only to-night but to-morrow in that bay, which is worth being carefully explored."

"I think that we shall be obliged to do so, whether we like it or not," answered Pencroft, "for the sky looks very threatening towards the west. Dirty weather is coming on!"

"At any rate we have a favourable wind for reaching Cape Mandible," observed the reporter.

"A very fine wind," replied the sailor; "but we must tack to enter the gulf, and I should like to see my way clear in these unknown quarters."

"Quarters which appear to be filled with rocks," added Herbert, "if we judge by what we saw on the south coast of Shark Gulf."

"Pencroft," said Cyrus Harding, "do as you think best, we will leave it to you."

"Don't make your mind uneasy, captain," replied the sailor, "I shall not expose myself needlessly! I would rather a knife were run into my ribs than a sharp rock into those of my *Bonadventure!*"

That which Pencroft called ribs was the part of his vessel under water, and he valued it more than his own skin.

"What o'clock is it?" asked Pencroft.

"Ten o'clock," replied Gideon Spilett.

"And what distance is it to the Cape, captain?"

"About fifteen miles," replied the engineer.

"That's a matter of two hours and a half," said the sailor, "and we shall be off the Cape between twelve and one o'clock. Unluckily, the tide will be turning at that moment, and will be ebbing out of the gulf. I am afraid that it will be very difficult to get in, having both wind and tide against us."

"And the more so that it is a full moon to-day," remarked Herbert, "and these April tides are very strong."

"Well, Pencroft," asked Cyrus Harding, "can you not anchor off the Cape?"

"Anchor near land, with bad weather coming on!" exclaimed the sailor. "What are you thinking of, captain? We should run aground to a certainty!"

"What will you do then?"

"I shall try to keep in the offing until the flood, that is to say, till about seven in the evening, and if there is still light enough I will try to enter the gulf; if not, we must stand off and on during the night, and we will enter to-morrow at sunrise."

"As I told you, Pencroft, we will leave it to you," answered Harding.

"Ah!" said Pencroft, "if there was only a lighthouse on the coast, it would be much more convenient for sailors."

"Yes," replied Herbert, "and this time we shall have no obliging engineer to light a fire to guide us into port!"

"Why, indeed, my dear Cyrus," said Spilett, "we have never thanked you for it; but frankly, without that fire we should never have been able to reach—"

"A fire?" asked Harding, much astonished at the reporter's words.

"We mean, captain," answered Pencroft, "that on board the *Bonadventure* we were very anxious during the few hours before our return, and we should have passed to windward of the island, if it had not been for the precaution you took of lighting a fire the night of the 19th of October, on Prospect Heights."

"Yes, yes! That was a lucky idea of mine!" replied the engineer.

"And this time," continued the sailor, "unless the idea occurs to Ayrton, there will be no one to do us that little service!"

"No! no one!" answered Cyrus Harding.

A few minutes after, finding himself alone in the bows of the vessel with the reporter, the engineer bent down and whispered—

"If there is one thing certain in this world, Spilett, it is that I never lighted any fire during the night of the 19th of October, neither on Prospect Heights nor on any other part of the island!"

Chapter XX

A Night at Sea—Shark Gulf—Confidences—Preparations for Winter—Forwardness of the Bad Season—Severe Cold—Work in the Interior—In Six Months—A Photographic Negative—Unexpected Incident

THINGS HAPPENED AS PENCROFT HAD PREDICTED, HE BEING SELDOM MISTAKEN IN HIS prognostications. The wind rose, and from a fresh breeze it soon increased to a regular gale; that is to say, it acquired a speed of from forty to forty-five miles an hour, before which a ship in the open sea would have run under close-reefed topsails. Now, as it was nearly six o'clock when the *Bonadventure* reached the gulf, and as at that moment the tide turned, it was impossible to enter. They were therefore compelled to stand off, for even if he had wished to do so, Pencroft could not have gained the mouth of the Mercy. Hoisting the jib to the mainmast by way of a storm-sail, he hove to, putting the head of the vessel towards the land.

Fortunately, although the wind was strong the sea, being sheltered by the land, did not run very high. They had then little to fear from the waves, which always endanger small craft. The *Bonadventure* would doubtlessly not have capsized, for she was well ballasted, but enormous masses of water falling on the deck might injure her if her timbers could not sustain them. Pencroft, as a good sailor, was prepared for anything. Certainly, he had great confidence in his vessel, but nevertheless he awaited the return of day with some anxiety.

During the night, Cyrus Harding and Gideon Spilett had no opportunity for talking together, and yet the words pronounced in the reporter's ear by the engineer were well worth being discussed, together with the mysterious influence which appeared to reign over Lincoln Island. Gideon Spilett did not cease from pondering over this new and inexplicable incident—the appearance of a fire on the coast of the island. The fire had actually been seen! His companions, Herbert and Pencroft, had seen it with him! The fire had served to signalise the position of the island during that dark night, and they had not doubted that it was lighted by the engineer's hand; and here was Cyrus Harding expressly declaring that he had never done anything of the sort! Spilett resolved to recur to this incident as soon as the *Bonadventure* returned, and to urge Cyrus Harding to acquaint their companions with these strange facts. Perhaps it would be decided to make in common a complete investigation of every part of Lincoln Island.

However that might be, on this evening no fire was lighted on these yet unknown shores, which formed the entrance to the gulf, and the little vessel stood off during the night.

When the first streaks of dawn appeared in the western horizon, the wind, which had slightly fallen, shifted two points, and enabled Pencroft to enter the narrow gulf with greater ease. Towards seven o'clock in the morning, the *Bonadventure*, weathering the North Mandible Cape, entered the strait and glided on to the waters, so strangely enclosed in the frame of lava.

"Well," said Pencroft, "this bay would make admirable roads, in which a whole fleet could lie at their ease!"

"What is especially curious," observed Harding, "is that the gulf has been formed by two rivers of lava, thrown out by the volcano, and accumulated by successive irruptions. The result is that the gulf is completely sheltered on all sides, and I believe that even in the stormiest weather, the sea here must be as calm as a lake."

"No doubt," returned the sailor, "since the wind has only that narrow entrance between the two capes to get in by, and, besides, the north cape protects that of the south in a way which would make the entrance of gusts very difficult. I declare our *Bonadventure* could stay here from one end of the year to the other, without even dragging at her anchor!"

"It is rather large for her!" observed the reporter.

"Well! Mr. Spilett," replied the sailor, "I agree that it is too large for the *Bonadventure*, but if the fleets of the Union were in want of a harbor in the Pacific, I don't think they would ever find a better place than this!"

"We are in the shark's mouth," remarked Neb, alluding to the form of the gulf.

"Right into its mouth, my honest Neb!" replied Herbert, "but you are not afraid that it will shut upon us, are you?"

"No, Mr. Herbert," answered Neb, "and yet this gulf here doesn't please me much! It has a wicked look!"

"Hallo!" cried Pencroft, "here is Neb turning up his nose at my gulf, just as I was thinking of presenting it to America!"

"But, at any rate, is the water deep enough?" asked the engineer, "for a depth sufficient for the keel of the *Bonadventure* would not be enough for those of our iron-clads."

"That is easily found out," replied Pencroft.

And the sailor sounded with a long cord, which served him as a lead-line, and to which was fastened a lump of iron. This cord measured nearly fifty fathoms, and its entire length was unrolled without finding any bottom.

"There," exclaimed Pencroft, "our iron-clads can come here after all! They would not run aground!"

"Indeed," said Gideon Spilett, "this gulf is a regular abyss, but, taking into consideration the volcanic origin of the island, it is not astonishing that the sea should offer similar depressions."

"One would say too," observed Herbert, "that these cliffs were perfectly perpendicular; and I believe that at their foot, even with a line five or six times longer, Pencroft would not find bottom."

"That is all very well," then said the reporter, "but I must point out to Pencroft that his harbor is wanting in one very important respect!"

"And what is that, Mr. Spilett?"

"An opening, a cutting of some sort, to give access to the interior of the island. I do not see a spot on which we could land."

And, in fact, the steep lava cliffs did not afford a single place suitable for landing. They formed an insuperable barrier, recalling, but with more wildness, the fiords of Norway. The *Bonadventure,* coasting as close as possible along the cliffs, did not discover even a projection which would allow the passengers to leave the deck.

Pencroft consoled himself by saying that with the help of a mine they could soon open out the cliff when that was necessary, and then, as there was evidently nothing to be done in the gulf, he steered his vessel towards the strait and passed out at about two o'clock in the afternoon.

"Ah!" said Neb, uttering a sigh of satisfaction.

One might really say that the honest negro did not feel at his ease in those enormous jaws.

The distance from Mandible Cape to the mouth of the Mercy was not more than eight miles. The head of the *Bonadventure* was put towards Granite House, and a fair wind filling her sails, she ran rapidly along the coast.

To the enormous lava rocks succeeded soon those capricious sand dunes, among which the engineer had been so singularly recovered, and which sea-birds frequented in thousands.

About four o'clock, Pencroft leaving the point of the islet on his left, entered the channel which separated it from the coast, and at five o'clock the anchor of the *Bonadventure* was buried in the sand at the mouth of the Mercy.

The colonists had been absent three days from their dwelling. Ayrton was waiting for them on the beach, and Jup came joyously to meet them, giving vent to deep grunts of satisfaction.

A complete exploration of the coast of the island had now been made, and no suspicious appearances had been observed. If any mysterious being resided on it, it could only be under cover of the impenetrable forest of the Serpentine Peninsula, to which the colonists had not yet directed their investigations.

Gideon Spilett discussed these things with the engineer, and it was agreed that they should direct the attention of their companions to the strange character of certain incidents which had occurred on the island, and of which the last was the most unaccountable.

However, Harding, returning to the fact of a fire having been kindled on the shore by an unknown hand, could not refrain from repeating for the twentieth time to the reporter—

"But are you quite sure of having seen it? Was it not a partial irruption of the volcano, or perhaps some meteor?"

"No, Cyrus," answered the reporter, "it was certainly a fire lighted by the hand of man. Besides; question Pencroft and Herbert. They saw it as I saw it myself, and they will confirm my words."

In consequence, therefore, a few days after, on the 25th of April, in the evening, when the settlers were all collected on Prospect Heights, Cyrus Harding began by saying—

"My friends, I think it my duty to call your attention to certain incidents which have occurred in the island, on the subject of which I shall be happy to have your advice. These incidents are, so to speak, supernatural—"

"Supernatural!" exclaimed the sailor, emitting a volume of smoke from his mouth. "Can it be possible that our island is supernatural?"

"No, Pencroft, but mysterious, most certainly," replied the engineer; "unless you can explain that which Spilett and I have until now failed to understand."

"Speak away, captain," answered the sailor.

"Well, have you understood," then said the engineer, "how was it that after falling into the sea, I was found a quarter of a mile into the interior of the island, and that, without my having any consciousness of my removal there?"

"Unless, being unconscious—" said Pencroft.

"That is not admissible," replied the engineer. "But to continue. Have you understood how Top was able to discover your retreat five miles from the cave in which I was lying?"

"The dog's instinct—" observed Herbert.

"Singular instinct!" returned the reporter, "since notwithstanding the storm of rain and wind which was raging during that night, Top arrived at the Chimneys, dry and without a speck of mud!"

"Let us continue," resumed the engineer. "Have you understood how our dog was so strangely thrown up out of the water of the lake, after his struggle with the dugong?"

"No! I confess, not at all," replied Pencroft, "and the wound which the dugong had in its side, a wound which seemed to have been made with a sharp instrument; that can't be understood, either."

"Let us continue again," said Harding. "Have you understood, my friends, how that bullet got into the body of the young peccary; how that case happened to be so fortunately stranded, without there being any trace of a wreck; how that bottle containing the document presented itself so opportunely, during our first sea-excursion; how our canoe, having broken its moorings, floated down the current of the Mercy and rejoined us at the very moment we needed it; how after the ape invasion the ladder was so obligingly thrown down from Granite House; and lastly, how the document, which Ayrton asserts was never written by him, fell into our hands?"

As Cyrus Harding thus enumerated, without forgetting one, the singular incidents which had occurred in the island, Herbert, Neb, and Pencroft stared at each other, not knowing what to reply, for this succession of incidents, grouped thus for the first time, could not but excite their surprise to the highest degree.

" 'Pon my word," said Pencroft at last, "you are right, captain, and it is difficult to explain all these things!"

"Well, my friends," resumed the engineer, "a last fact has just been added to these, and it is no less incomprehensible than the others!"

"What is it, captain?" asked Herbert quickly.

"When you were returning from Tabor Island, Pencroft," continued the engineer, "you said that a fire appeared on Lincoln Island?"

"Certainly," answered the sailor.

"And you are quite certain of having seen this fire?"

"As sure as I see you now."

"You also, Herbert?"

"Why, captain," cried Herbert, "that fire was blazing like a star of the first magnitude!"

"But was it not a star?" urged the engineer.

"No," replied Pencroft, "for the sky was covered with thick clouds, and at any rate a star would not have been so low on the horizon. But Mr. Spilett saw it as well as we, and he will confirm our words."

"I will add," said the reporter, "that the fire was very bright, and that it shot up like a sheet of lightning."

"Yes, yes! exactly," added Herbert, "and it was certainly placed on the heights of Granite House."

"Well, my friends," replied Cyrus Harding, "during the night of the 19th of October, neither Neb nor I lighted any fire on the coast."

"You did not!" exclaimed Pencroft, in the height of his astonishment, not being able to finish his sentence.

"We did not leave Granite House," answered Cyrus Harding, "and if a fire appeared on the coast, it was lighted by another hand than ours!"

Pencroft, Herbert, and Neb were stupefied. No illusion could be possible, and a fire had actually met their eyes during the night of the 19th of October.

Yes! they had to acknowledge it, a mystery existed! An inexplicable influence, evidently favourable to the colonists, but very irritating to their curiosity, was executed always in the nick of time on Lincoln Island. Could there be some being hidden in its profoundest recesses? It was necessary at any cost to ascertain this.

Harding also reminded his companions of the singular behaviour of Top and Jup when they prowled round the mouth of the well, which placed Granite House in communication with the sea, and he told them that he had explored the well, without discovering anything suspicious. The final resolve taken, in consequence of this conversation, by all the members of the colony, was that as soon as the fine season returned they would thoroughly search the whole of the island.

But from that day Pencroft appeared to be anxious. He felt as if the island which he had made his own personal property belonged to him entirely no longer, and that he shared it with another master, to whom, willing or not, he felt subject. Neb and he often talked of those unaccountable things, and both, their natures inclining them to the marvellous, were not far from believing that Lincoln Island was under the dominion of some supernatural power.

In the meanwhile, the bad weather came with the month of May, the November of the northern zones. It appeared that the winter would be severe and forward. The preparations for the winter season were therefore commenced without delay.

Nevertheless, the colonists were well prepared to meet the winter, however hard it might be. They had plenty of felt clothing, and the musmons, very numerous by this time, had furnished an abundance of wool necessary for the manufacture of this warm material.

It is unnecessary to say that Ayrton had been provided with this comfortable clothing. Cyrus Harding proposed that he should come to spend the bad season with them in Granite House, where he would be better lodged than at the corral, and Ayrton promised to do so, as soon as the last work at the corral was finished. He did this towards the middle of April. From that time Ayrton shared the common life, and made himself useful on all occasions; but still humble and sad, he never took part in the pleasures of his companions.

For the greater part of this, the third winter which the settlers passed in Lincoln Island, they were confined to Granite House. There were many violent storms and frightful tempests, which appeared to shake the rocks to their very foundations. Immense waves threatened to overwhelm the island, and certainly any vessel anchored near the shore would have been dashed to pieces. Twice, during one of these hurricanes, the Mercy swelled to such a degree as to give reason to fear that the bridges would be swept away, and it was necessary to strengthen those on the shore, which disappeared under the foaming waters, when the sea beat against the beach.

It may well be supposed that such storms, comparable to water-spouts in which were mingled rain and snow, would cause great havoc on the plateau of Prospect Heights. The mill and the poultry-yard particularly suffered. The colonists were often obliged to make immediate repairs, without which the safety of the birds would have been seriously threatened.

During the worst weather, several jaguars and troops of quadrumana ventured to the edge of the plateau, and it was always to be feared that the most active and audacious would, urged by hunger, manage to cross the stream, which besides, when frozen, offered them an easy passage. Plantations and domestic animals would then have been infallibly destroyed, without a constant watch, and it was often necessary to make use of the guns to keep those dangerous visitors at a respectful distance. Occupation was not wanting to the colonists, for without reckoning their out-door cares, they had always a thousand plans for the fitting up of Granite House.

They had also some fine sporting excursions, which were made during the frost in the vast Tadorn Marsh. Gideon Spilett and Herbert, aided by Jup and Top, did not miss a shot in the midst of myriads of wild duck, snipe, teal, and others. The access to these hunting-grounds was easy; besides, whether they reached them by the road to Port Balloon, after having passed the Mercy Bridge, or by turning the rocks from Flotsam Point, the hunters were never distant from Granite House more than two or three miles.

Thus passed the four winter months, which were really rigourous, that is to say, June, July, August, and September. But, in short, Granite House did not suffer much from the inclemency of the weather, and it was the same with the corral, which, less exposed than the plateau, and sheltered partly by Mount Franklin, only received the remains of the hurricanes, already broken by the forests and the high rocks of the shore. The damages there were consequently of small importance, and the activity and skill of Ayrton promptly repaired them, when some time in October he returned to pass a few days in the corral.

During this winter, no fresh inexplicable incident occurred. Nothing strange happened, although Pencroft and Neb were on the watch for the most insignificant facts to which they attached any mysterious cause. Top and Jup themselves no longer growled round the well or gave any signs of uneasiness. It appeared, therefore, as if the series of supernatural incidents was interrupted, although they often talked of them during the evenings in Granite House, and they remained thoroughly resolved that the island should be searched, even in those parts the most difficult to explore. But an event of the highest importance, and of which the consequences might be terrible, momentarily diverted from their projects Cyrus Harding and his companions.

It was the month of October. The fine season was swiftly returning. Nature was reviving; and among the evergreen foliage of the coniferae which formed the border of the wood, already appeared the young leaves of the banksias, deodars, and other trees.

It may be remembered that Gideon Spilett and Herbert had, at different times, taken photographic views of Lincoln Island.

Now, on the 17th of this month of October, towards three o'clock in the afternoon, Herbert, enticed by the charms of the sky, thought of reproducing Union Bay, which was opposite to Prospect Heights, from Cape Mandible to Claw Cape.

The horizon was beautifully clear, and the sea, undulating under a soft breeze, was as calm as the waters of a lake, sparkling here and there under the sun's rays.

The apparatus had been placed at one of the windows of the dining-room at Granite House, and consequently overlooked the shore and the bay. Herbert proceeded as he was accustomed to do, and the negative obtained, he went away to fix it by means of the chemicals deposited in a dark nook of Granite House.

Returning to the bright light, and examining it well, Herbert perceived on his negative an almost imperceptible little spot on the sea-horizon. He endeavoured to make it disappear by reiterated washing, but could not accomplish it.

"It is a flaw in the glass," he thought.

And then he had the curiosity to examine this flaw with a strong magnifier which he unscrewed from one of the telescopes.

But he had scarcely looked at it, when he uttered a cry, and the glass almost fell from his hands.

Immediately running to the room in which Cyrus Harding then was, he extended the negative and magnifier towards the engineer, pointing out the little spot.

Harding examined it; then seizing his telescope he rushed to the window.

The telescope, after having slowly swept the horizon, at last stopped on the looked-for spot, and Cyrus Harding, lowering it, pronounced one word only—

"A vessel!"

And in fact a vessel was in sight, off Lincoln Island!

PART III

THE SECRET OF THE ISLAND

Chapter I

Lost or Saved—Ayrton Summoned—Important
Discussion—It is not the DUNCAN—Suspicious Vessel—
Precautions to Be Taken—The Ship Approaches—
A Cannon-Shot—The Brig Anchors in Sight of the
Island—Night Comes On

It was now two years and a half since the castaways from the balloon had been thrown on Lincoln Island, and during that period there had been no communication between them and their fellow-creatures. Once the reporter had attempted to communicate with the inhabited world by confiding to a bird a letter which contained the secret of their situation, but that was a chance on which it was impossible to reckon seriously. Ayrton, alone, under the circumstances which have been related, had come to join the little colony. Now, suddenly, on this day, the 17th of October, other men had unexpectedly appeared in sight of the island, on that deserted sea!

There could be no doubt about it! A vessel was there! But would she pass on, or would she put into port? In a few hours the colonists would definitely know what to expect.

Cyrus Harding and Herbert having immediately called Gideon Spilett, Pencroft, and Neb into the dining-room of Granite House, told them what had happened. Pencroft, seizing the telescope, rapidly swept the horizon, and stopping on the indicated point, that is to say, on that which had made the almost imperceptible spot on the photographic negative—

"I'm blessed but it is really a vessel!" he exclaimed, in a voice which did not express any great amount of satisfaction.

"Is she coming here?" asked Gideon Spilett.

"Impossible to say anything yet," answered Pencroft, "for her rigging alone is above the horizon, and not a bit of her hull can be seen."

"What is to be done?" asked the lad.

"Wait," replied Harding.

And for a considerable time the settlers remained silent, given up to all the thoughts, all the emotions, all the fears, all the hopes, which were aroused by this incident—the most important which had occurred since their arrival in Lincoln Island. Certainly, the colonists were not in the situation of castaways abandoned on a sterile islet, constantly contending against a cruel nature for their miserable existence, and incessantly tormented by the longing to return to inhabited countries. Pencroft and Neb, especially, who felt themselves at once so happy and so rich, would not have left their island without regret. They were accustomed, besides, to this new life in the midst of the domain which their intelligence had as it were civilised. But at any rate this ship brought news from the world, perhaps even from their native land. It was bringing fellow-creatures to them, and it may be conceived how deeply their hearts were moved at the sight!

From time to time Pencroft took the glass and rested himself at the window. From thence he very attentively examined the vessel, which was at a distance of twenty miles to the east. The colonists had as yet, therefore, no means of signalising their presence. A flag would not have been perceived; a gun would not have been heard; a fire would not have been visible. However, it was certain that the island, overtopped by Mount Franklin, could not escape the notice of the vessel's look-out. But why was the ship coming there? Was it simple chance which brought it to that part of the Pacific, where the maps mentioned no land except Tabor Island, which itself was out of the route usually followed by vessels from the Polynesian Archipelagoes, from New Zealand, and from the American coast? To this question, which each one asked himself, a reply was suddenly made by Herbert.

"Can it be the *Duncan?*" he cried.

The *Duncan*, as has been said, was Lord Glenarvan's yacht, which had left Ayrton on the islet, and which was to return there someday to fetch him. Now, the islet was not so far distant from Lincoln Island, but that a vessel, standing for the one, could pass in sight of the other. A hundred and fifty miles only separated them in longitude, and seventy in latitude.

"We must tell Ayrton," said Gideon Spilett, "and send for him immediately. He alone can say if it is the *Duncan.*"

This was the opinion of all, and the reporter, going to the telegraphic apparatus which placed the corral in communication with Granite House, sent this telegram:—"Come with all possible speed."

In a few minutes the bell sounded.

"I am coming," replied Ayrton.

Then the settlers continued to watch the vessel.

"If it is the *Duncan*," said Herbert, "Ayrton will recognise her without difficulty, since he sailed on board her for some time."

"And if he recognises her," added Pencroft, "it will agitate him exceedingly!"

"Yes," answered Cyrus Harding; "but now Ayrton is worthy to return on board the *Duncan*, and pray Heaven that it is indeed Lord Glenarvan's yacht, for I should be suspicious of any other vessel. These are ill-famed seas, and I have always feared a visit from Malay pirates to our island."

"We could defend it,'," cried Herbert.

"No doubt, my boy," answered the engineer smiling, "but it would be better not to have to defend it."

"A useless observation," said Spilett. "Lincoln Island is unknown to navigators, since it is not marked even on the most recent maps. Do you not think, Cyrus, that that is a sufficient motive for a ship, finding herself unexpectedly in sight of new land, to try and visit rather than avoid it?"

"Certainly," replied Pencroft.

"I think so too," added the engineer. "It may even be said that it is the duty of a captain to come and survey any land or island not yet known, and Lincoln Island is in this position."

"Well," said Pencroft, "suppose this vessel comes and anchors there a few cable-lengths from our island, what shall we do?"

This sudden question remained at first without any reply. But Cyrus Harding, after some moments' thought, replied in the calm tone which was usual to him—

"What we shall do, my friends? What we ought to do is this:—we will communicate with the ship, we will take our passage on board her, and we will leave our island, after having taken possession of it in the name of the United States. Then we will return with any who may wish to follow us to colonise it definitely, and endow the American Republic with a useful station in this part of the Pacific Ocean!"

"Hurrah!" exclaimed Pencroft, "and that will be no small present which we shall make to our country! The colonisation is already almost finished; names are given to every part of the island; there is a natural port, fresh water, roads, a telegraph, a dockyard, and manufactories; and there will be nothing to be done but to inscribe Lincoln Island on the maps!"

"But if anyone seizes it in our absence?" observed Gideon Spilett.

"Hang it!" cried the sailor. "I would rather remain all alone to guard it: and trust to Pencroft, they shouldn't steal it from him, like a watch from the pocket of a swell!"

For an hour it was impossible to say with any certainty whether the vessel was or was not standing towards Lincoln Island. She was nearer, but in what direction was she sailing? This Pencroft could not determine. However, as the wind was blowing from the northeast, in all probability the vessel was sailing on the starboard tack. Besides, the wind was favourable for bringing her towards the island, and, the sea being calm, she would not be afraid to approach although the shallows were not marked on the chart.

Towards four o'clock—an hour after he had been sent for—Ayrton arrived at Granite House. He entered the dining-room saying—

"At your service, gentlemen."

Cyrus Harding gave him his hand, as was his custom to do, and, leading him to the window—

"Ayrton," said he, "we have begged you to come here for an important reason. A ship is in sight of the island."

Ayrton at first paled slightly, and for a moment his eyes became dim; then, leaning out the window, he surveyed the horizon, but could see nothing.

"Take this telescope," said Spilett, "and look carefully, Ayrton, for it is possible that this ship may be the *Duncan* come to these seas for the purpose of taking you home again."

"The *Duncan!*" murmured Ayrton. "Already?" This last word escaped Ayrton's lips as if involuntarily, and his head drooped upon his hands.

Did not twelve years' solitude on a desert island appear to him a sufficient expiation? Did not the penitent yet feel himself pardoned, either in his own eyes or in the eyes of others?

"No," said he, "no! it cannot be the *Duncan!*"

"Look, Ayrton," then said the engineer, "for it is necessary that we should know beforehand what to expect."

Ayrton took the glass and pointed it in the direction indicated. During some minutes he examined the horizon without moving, without uttering a word. Then—

"It is indeed a vessel," said he, "but I do not think she is the *Duncan*."

"Why do you not think so?" asked Gideon Spilett.

"Because the *Duncan* is a steam-yacht, and I cannot perceive any trace of smoke either above or near that vessel."

"Perhaps she is simply sailing," observed Pencroft. "The wind is favourable for the direction which she appears to be taking, and she may be anxious to economise her coal, being so far from land."

"It is possible that you may be right, Mr. Pencroft," answered Ayrton, "and that the vessel has extinguished her fires. We must wait until she is nearer, and then we shall soon know what to expect."

So saying, Ayrton sat down in a corner of the room and remained silent. The colonists again discussed the strange ship, but Ayrton took no part in the conversation. All were in such a mood that they found it impossible to continue their work. Gideon Spilett and Pencroft were particularly nervous, going, coming, not able to remain still in one place. Herbert felt more curiosity. Neb alone maintained his usual calm manner. Was not his country that where his master was? As to the engineer, he remained plunged in deep thought, and in his heart feared rather than desired the arrival of the ship. In the meanwhile, the vessel was a little nearer the island. With the aid of the glass, it was ascertained that she was a brig, and not one of those Malay proas, which are generally used by the pirates of the Pacific. It was, therefore, reasonable to believe that the engineer's apprehensions would not be justified, and that the presence of this vessel in the vicinity of the island was fraught with no danger. Pencroft, after a minute examination, was able positively to affirm that the vessel was rigged as a brig, and that she was standing obliquely towards the coast, on the starboard tack, under her topsails and top-gallant-sails. This was confirmed by Ayrton. But by continuing in this direction she must soon disappear behind Claw Cape, as the wind was from the south-west, and to watch her it would be then necessary to ascend the height of Washington Bay, near Port Balloon—a provoking circumstance, for it was already five o'clock in the evening, and the twilight would soon make any observation extremely difficult.

"What shall we do when night comes on?" asked Gideon Spilett. "Shall we light a fire, so as to signal our presence on the coast?"

This was a serious question, and yet, although the engineer still retained some of his presentiments, it was answered in the affirmative. During the night the ship might disappear and leave forever, and, this ship gone, would another ever return to the waters of Lincoln Island? Who could foresee what the future would then have in store for the colonists?

"Yes," said the reporter, "we ought to make known to that vessel, whoever she may be, that the island is inhabited. To neglect the opportunity which is offered to us might be to create everlasting regrets."

It was therefore decided that Neb and Pencroft should go to Port Balloon, and that there, at nightfall, they should light an immense fire, the blaze of which would necessarily attract the attention of the brig.

But at the moment when Neb and the sailor were preparing to leave Granite House, the vessel suddenly altered her course, and stood directly for Union Bay. The brig was a good sailer, for she approached rapidly. Neb and Pencroft put off their departure, therefore, and the glass was put into Ayrton's hands, that he might ascertain for certain whether the ship was or was not the *Duncan*. The Scotch yacht was also rigged as a brig. The question was, whether a chimney could be discerned between the two masts of the vessel, which was now at a distance of only five miles.

The horizon was still very clear. The examination was easy, and Ayrton soon let the glass fall again, saying—

"It is not the *Duncan!* It could not be her!"

Pencroft again brought the brig within the range of the telescope, and could see that she was of between three and four hundred tons burden, wonderfully narrow, well-masted, admirably built, and must be a very rapid sailer. But to what nation did she belong? That was difficult to say.

"And yet," added the sailor, "a flag is floating from her peak, but I cannot distinguish the colours of it."

"In half-an-hour we shall be certain about that," answered the reporter. "Besides, it is very evident that the intention of the captain of this ship is to land, and, consequently, if not to-day, to-morrow at the latest, we shall make his acquaintance."

"Never mind!" said Pencroft. "It is best to know whom we have to deal with, and I shall not be sorry to recognise that fellow's colours!"

And, while thus speaking, the sailor never left the glass. The day began to fade, and with the day the breeze fell also. The brig's ensign hung in folds, and it became more and more difficult to observe it.

"It is not the American flag," said Pencroft from time to time, "nor the English, the red of which could be easily seen, nor the French or German colours, nor the white flag of Russia, nor the yellow of Spain. One would say it was all one colour. Let's see: in these seas, what do we generally meet with? The Chilean flag?—but that is tri-color. Brazilian?—it is green. Japanese?—it is yellow and black, while this—"

At that moment the breeze blew out the unknown flag. Ayrton seizing the telescope which the sailor had put down, put it to his eye, and in a hoarse voice—

"The black flag!" he exclaimed.

And indeed the sombre bunting was floating from the mast of the brig, and they had now good reason for considering her to be a suspicious vessel!

Had the engineer, then, been right in his presentiments? Was this a pirate vessel? Did she scour the Pacific, competing with the Malay proas which still infest it? For what had she come to look at the shores of Lincoln Island? Was it to them an unknown island, ready to become a magazine for stolen cargoes? Had she come to find on the coast a sheltered port for the winter months? Was the settlers' honest domain destined to be transformed into an infamous refuge—the headquarters of the piracy of the Pacific?

All these ideas instinctively presented themselves to the colonists' imaginations. There was no doubt, besides, of the signification which must be attached to the colour of the hoisted flag. It was that of pirates! It was that which the *Duncan* would have carried, had the convicts succeeded in their criminal design! No time was lost before discussing it.

"My friends," said Cyrus Harding, "perhaps this vessel only wishes to survey the coast of the island. Perhaps her crew will not land. There is a chance of it. However that may be, we ought to do everything we can to hide our presence here. The windmill on Prospect Heights is too easily seen. Let Ayrton and Neb go and take down the sails. We must also conceal the windows of Granite House with thick branches. All the fires must be extinguished, so that nothing may betray the presence of men on the island."

"And our vessel?" said Herbert.

"Oh," answered Pencroft, "she is sheltered in Port Balloon, and I defy any of those rascals there to find her!"

The engineer's orders were immediately executed. Neb and Ayrton ascended the plateau, and took the necessary precautions to conceal any indication of a settlement. While they were thus occupied, their companions went to the border of Jacamar Wood, and brought back a large quantity of branches and creepers, which would at some distance appear as natural foliage, and thus disguise the windows in the granite cliff. At the same time, the ammunition and guns were placed ready so as to be at hand in case of an unexpected attack.

When all these precautions had been taken—

"My friends," said Harding, and his voice betrayed some emotion, "if the wretches endeavour to seize Lincoln Island, we shall defend it—shall we not?"

"Yes, Cyrus," replied the reporter, "and if necessary we will die to defend it!"

The engineer extended his hand to his companions, who pressed it warmly.

Ayrton remained in his corner, not joining the colonists. Perhaps he, the former convict, still felt himself unworthy to do so!

Cyrus Harding understood what was passing in Ayrton's mind, and going to him—

"And you, Ayrton," he asked, "what will you do?"

"My duty," answered Ayrton.

He then took up his station near the window and gazed through the foliage.

It was now half-past seven. The sun had disappeared twenty minutes ago behind Granite House. Consequently the eastern horizon was becoming obscured. In the meanwhile the brig continued to advance towards Union Bay. She was now not more than two miles off, and exactly opposite the plateau of Prospect Heights, for after having tacked off Claw Cape, she had drifted towards the north in the current of the rising tide. One might have said that at this distance she had already entered the vast bay, for a straight line drawn from Claw Cape to Cape Mandible would have rested on her starboard quarter.

Was the brig about to penetrate far into the bay? That was the first question. When once in the bay, would she anchor there? That was the second. Would she not content herself with only surveying the coast, and stand out to sea again without landing her crew? They would know this in an hour. The colonists could do nothing but wait.

Cyrus Harding had not seen the suspected vessel hoist the black flag without deep anxiety. Was it not a direct menace against the work which he and his companions had till now conducted so successfully? Had these pirates—for the sailors of the brig could be nothing else—already visited the island, since on approaching it they had hoisted their colours. Had they formerly invaded it, so that certain unaccountable peculiarities might be explained in this way? Did there exist in the as yet unexplored parts some accomplice ready to enter into communication with them?

To all these questions which he mentally asked himself, Harding knew not what to reply; but he felt that the safety of the colony could not but be seriously threatened by the arrival of the brig.

However, he and his companions were determined to fight to the last gasp. It would have been very important to know if the pirates were numerous and better armed than the colonists. But how was this information to be obtained?

Night fell. The new moon had disappeared. Profound darkness enveloped the island and the sea. No light could pierce through the heavy piles of clouds on the horizon. The wind had died away completely with the twilight. Not a leaf rustled on the trees, not a ripple murmured on the shore. Nothing could be seen of the ship, all her lights being extinguished, and if she was still in sight of the island, her whereabouts could not be discovered.

"Well! who knows?" said Pencroft. "Perhaps that cursed craft will stand off during the night, and we shall see nothing of her at daybreak."

As if in reply to the sailor's observation, a bright light flashed in the darkness, and a cannon-shot was heard.

The vessel was still there and had guns on board.

Six seconds elapsed between the flash and the report.

Therefore the brig was about a mile and a quarter from the coast.

At the same time, the chains were heard rattling through the hawse-holes.

The vessel had just anchored in sight of Granite House!

Chapter II

DISCUSSIONS—PRESENTIMENTS—AYRTON'S PROPOSAL—IT IS ACCEPTED—AYRTON AND PENCROFT ON GRANT ISLET—CONVICTS FROM NORFOLK ISLAND—AYRTON'S HEROIC ATTEMPT—HIS RETURN—SIX AGAINST FIFTY

THERE WAS NO LONGER ANY DOUBT AS TO THE PIRATES' INTENTIONS. THEY HAD dropped anchor at a short distance from the island, and it was evident that the next day by means of their boats they purposed to land on the beach!

Cyrus Harding and his companions were ready to act, but, determined though they were, they must not forget to be prudent. Perhaps their presence might still be concealed in the event of the pirates contenting themselves with landing on the shore without examining the interior of the island. It might be, indeed, that their only intention was to obtain fresh water from the Mercy, and it was not impossible that the bridge, thrown across a mile and a half from the mouth, and the manufactory at the Chimneys might escape their notice.

But why was that flag hoisted at the brig's peak? What was that shot fired for? Pure bravado doubtless, unless it was a sign of the act of taking possession. Harding knew now that the vessel was well armed. And what had the colonists of Lincoln Island to reply to the pirates' guns? A few muskets only.

"However," observed Cyrus Harding, "here we are in an impregnable position. The enemy cannot discover the mouth of the outlet, now that it is hidden under reeds and grass, and consequently it would be impossible for them to penetrate into Granite House."

"But our plantations, our poultry-yard, our corral, all, everything!" exclaimed Pencroft, stamping his foot. "They may spoil everything, destroy everything in a few hours!"

"Everything, Pencroft," answered Harding, "and we have no means of preventing them."

"Are they numerous? that is the question," said the reporter. "If they are not more than a dozen, we shall be able to stop them, but forty, fifty, more perhaps!"

"Captain Harding," then said Ayrton, advancing towards the engineer, "will you give me leave?"

"For what, my friend?"

"To go to that vessel to find out the strength of her crew."

"But Ayrton—" answered the engineer, hesitating, "you will risk your life—"

"Why not, sir?"

"That is more than your duty."

"I have more than my duty to do," replied Ayrton.

"Will you go to the ship in the boat?" asked Gideon Spilett.

"No, sir, but I will swim. A boat would be seen where a man may glide between wind and water."

"Do you know that the brig is a mile and a quarter from the shore?" said Herbert.

"I am a good swimmer, Mr. Herbert."

"I tell you it is risking your life," said the engineer.

"That is no matter," answered Ayrton. "Captain Harding, I ask this as a favour. Perhaps it will be a means of raising me in my own eyes!"

"Go, Ayrton," replied the engineer, who felt sure that a refusal would have deeply wounded the former convict, now become an honest man.

"I will accompany you," said Pencroft.

"You mistrust me!" said Ayrton quickly.

Then more humbly—

"Alas!"

"No! no!" exclaimed Harding with animation, "no, Ayrton, Pencroft does not mistrust you. You interpret his words wrongly."

"Indeed," returned the sailor, "I only propose to accompany Ayrton as far as the islet. It may be, although it is scarcely possible, that one of these villains has landed, and in that case two men will not be too many to hinder him from giving the alarm. I will wait for Ayrton on the islet, and he shall go alone to the vessel, since he has proposed to do so." These things agreed to, Ayrton made preparations for his departure. His plan was bold, but it might succeed, thanks to the darkness of the night. Once arrived at the vessel's side, Ayrton, holding on to the main-chains, might reconnoitre the number and perhaps overhear the intentions of the pirates.

Ayrton and Pencroft, followed by their companions, descended to the beach. Ayrton undressed and rubbed himself with grease, so as to suffer less from the temperature of the water, which was still cold. He might, indeed, be obliged to remain in it for several hours.

Pencroft and Neb, during this time, had gone to fetch the boat, moored a few hundred feet higher up, on the bank of the Mercy, and by the time they returned, Ayrton was ready to start. A coat was thrown over his shoulders, and the settlers all came round him to press his hand.

Ayrton then shoved off with Pencroft in the boat.

It was half-past ten in the evening when the two adventurers disappeared in the darkness. Their companions returned to wait at the Chimneys.

The channel was easily traversed, and the boat touched the opposite shore of the islet. This was not done without precaution, for fear lest the pirates might be roaming about there. But after a careful survey, it was evident that the islet was deserted. Ayrton then, followed by Pencroft, crossed it with a rapid step, scaring the birds nestled in the holes of the rocks; then, without hesitating, he plunged into the sea, and swam noiselessly in the direction of the ship, in which a few lights had recently appeared, showing her exact situation. As to Pencroft, he crouched down in a cleft of the rock, and awaited the return of his companion.

In the meanwhile, Ayrton, swimming with a vigourous stroke, glided through the sheet of water without producing the slightest ripple. His head just emerged above it and his eyes were fixed on the dark hull of the brig, from which the lights were reflected in the water. He thought only of the duty which he had promised to accomplish, and nothing of the danger which he ran, not only on board the ship, but in the sea, often frequented by sharks. The current bore him along and he rapidly receded from the shore.

Half-an-hour afterwards, Ayrton, without having been either seen or heard, arrived at the ship and caught hold of the main-chains. He took breath, then, hoisting himself up, he managed to reach the extremity of the cutwater. There were drying several pairs of sailors' trousers. He put on a pair. Then settling himself firmly, he listened. They were not sleeping on board the brig. On the contrary, they were talking, singing, laughing. And these were the sentences, accompanied with oaths, which principally struck Ayrton:—

"Our brig is a famous acquisition."

"She sails well, and merits her name of the *Speedy*."

"She would show all the navy of Norfolk a clean pair of heels."

"Hurrah for her captain!"

"Hurrah for Bob Harvey!"

What Ayrton felt when he overheard this fragment of conversation may be understood when it is known that in this Bob Harvey he recognised one of his old Australian companions, a daring sailor, who had continued his criminal career. Bob Harvey had seized, on the shores of Norfolk Island, this brig, which was loaded with arms, ammunition, utensils, and tools of all sorts, destined for one of the Sandwich Islands. All his gang had gone on board, and pirates after having been convicts, these wretches, more ferocious than the Malays themselves, scoured the Pacific, destroying vessels, and massacring their crews.

The convicts spoke loudly, they recounted their deeds, drinking deeply at the same time, and this is what Ayrton gathered. The actual crew of the *Speedy* was composed solely of English prisoners, escaped from Norfolk Island.

Here it may be well to explain what this island was. In 29° 2' south latitude, and 165° 42' east longitude, to the east of Australia, is found a little island, six miles in circumference, overlooked by Mount Pitt, which rises to a height of 1,100 feet above the level of the sea. This is Norfolk Island, once the seat of an establishment in which were lodged the most intractable convicts from the English penitentiaries. They numbered 500, under an iron discipline, threatened with terrible punishments, and were guarded by 150 soldiers, and 150 employed under the orders of the governor. It would be difficult to imagine a collection of greater ruffians. Sometimes—although very rarely—notwithstanding the extreme surveillance of which they were the object, many managed to escape, and seizing vessels which they surprised, they infested the Polynesian Archipelagoes.*

Thus had Bob Harvey and his companions done. Thus had Ayrton formerly wished to do. Bob Harvey had seized the brig *Speedy*, anchored in sight of Norfolk Island; the crew had been massacred; and for a year this ship had scoured the Pacific, under the command of Harvey, now a pirate, and well known to Ayrton!

* Norfolk Island has long since been abandoned as a penal settlement.

The convicts were, for the most part, assembled under the poop; but a few, stretched on the deck, were talking loudly.

The conversation still continued amid shouts and libations. Ayrton learned that chance alone had brought the *Speedy* in sight of Lincoln Island; Bob Harvey had never yet set foot on it; but, as Cyrus Harding had conjectured, finding this unknown land in his course, its position being marked on no chart, he had formed the project of visiting it, and, if he found it suitable, of making it the brig's headquarters.

As to the black flag hoisted at the *Speedy's* peak, and the gun which had been fired, in imitation of men-of-war when they lower their colours, it was pure piratical bravado. It was in no way a signal, and no communication yet existed between the convicts and Lincoln Island.

The settlers' domain was now menaced with terrible danger. Evidently the island, with its water, its harbor, its resources of all kinds so increased in value by the colonists, and the concealment afforded by Granite House, could not but be convenient for the convicts; in their hands it would become an excellent place of refuge, and, being unknown, it would assure them, for a long time perhaps, impunity and security. Evidently, also, the lives of the settlers would not be respected, and Bob Harvey and his accomplices' first care would be to massacre them without mercy. Harding and his companions had, therefore, not even the choice of flying and hiding themselves in the island, since the convicts intended to reside there, and since, in the event of the *Speedy* departing on an expedition, it was probable that some of the crew would remain on shore, so as to settle themselves there. Therefore, it would be necessary to fight, to destroy every one of these scoundrels, unworthy of pity, and against whom any means would be right. So thought Ayrton, and he well knew that Cyrus Harding would be of his way of thinking.

But was resistance and, in the last place, victory possible? That would depend on the equipment of the brig, and the number of men which she carried.

This Ayrton resolved to learn at any cost, and as an hour after his arrival the vociferations had begun to die away, and as a large number of the convicts were already buried in a drunken sleep, Ayrton did not hesitate to venture onto the *Speedy's* deck, which the extinguished lanterns now left in total darkness. He hoisted himself onto the cutwater, and by the bowsprit arrived at the forecastle. Then, gliding among the convicts stretched here and there, he made the round of the ship, and found that the *Speedy* carried four guns, which would throw shot of from eight to ten pounds in weight. He found also, on touching them that these guns were breech-loaders. They were, therefore, of modern make, easily used, and of terrible effect.

As to the men lying on the deck, they were about ten in number, but it was to be supposed that more were sleeping down below. Besides, by listening to them, Ayrton had understood that there were fifty on board. That was a large number for the six settlers of Lincoln Island to contend with! But now, thanks to Ayrton's devotion, Cyrus Harding would not be surprised, he would know the strength of his adversaries, and would make his arrangements accordingly.

There was nothing more for Ayrton to do but to return, and render to his companions an account of the mission with which he had charged himself, and he prepared to regain the bows of the brig, so that he might let himself down into the water.

But to this man, whose wish was, as he had said, to do more than his duty, there came an heroic thought. This was to sacrifice his own life, but save the island and the colonists. Cyrus Harding evidently could not resist fifty ruffians, all well armed, who, either by penetrating by main force into Granite House, or by starving out the besieged, could obtain from them what they wanted. And then he thought of his preservers—those who had made him again a man, and an honest man, those to whom he owed all—murdered without pity, their works destroyed, their island turned into a pirates' den! He said to himself that he, Ayrton, was the principal cause of so many disasters, since his old companion, Bob Harvey, had but realised his own plans, and a feeling of horror took possession of him. Then he was seized with an irresistible desire to blow up the brig, and with her, all whom she had on board. He would perish in the explosion, but he would have done his duty.

Ayrton did not hesitate. To reach the powder-room, which is always situated in the after-part of a vessel, was easy. There would be no want of powder in a vessel which followed such a trade, and a spark would be enough to destroy it in an instant.

Ayrton stole carefully along the between-decks, strewn with numerous sleepers, overcome more by drunkenness than sleep. A lantern was lighted at the foot of the mainmast, round which was hung a gun-rack, furnished with weapons of all sorts.

Ayrton took a revolver from the rack, and assured himself that it was loaded and primed. Nothing more was needed to accomplish the work of destruction. He then glided towards the stern, so as to arrive under the brig's poop at the powder-magazine.

It was difficult to proceed along the dimly lighted deck without stumbling over some half-sleeping convict, who retorted by oaths and kicks. Ayrton was, therefore, more than once obliged to halt. But at last he arrived at the partition dividing the after-cabin, and found the door opening into the magazine itself.

Ayrton, compelled to force it open, set to work. It was a difficult operation to perform without noise, for he had to break a padlock. But under his vigourous hand, the padlock broke, and the door was open.

At that moment a hand was laid on Ayrton's shoulder.

"What are you doing here?" asked a tall man, in a harsh voice, who, standing in the shadow, quickly threw the light of a lantern in Ayrton's face.

Ayrton drew back. In the rapid flash of the lantern, he had recognised his former accomplice, Bob Harvey, who could not have known him, as he must have thought Ayrton long since dead.

"What are you doing here?" again said Bob Harvey, seizing Ayrton by the waistband.

But Ayrton, without replying, wrenched himself from his grasp and attempted to rush into the magazine. A shot fired into the midst of the powder-casks, and all would be over!

"Help, lads!" shouted Bob Harvey.

At his shout two or three pirates awoke, jumped up, and, rushing on Ayrton, endeavoured to throw him down. He soon extricated himself from their grasp. He fired his revolver, and two of the convicts fell, but a blow from a knife which he could not ward off made a gash in his shoulder.

Ayrton perceived that he could no longer hope to carry out his project. Bob Harvey had reclosed the door of the powder-magazine, and a movement on the deck indicated a general awakening of the pirates. Ayrton must reserve himself to fight at the side of Cyrus Harding. There was nothing for him but flight!

But was flight still possible? It was doubtful, yet Ayrton resolved to dare everything in order to rejoin his companions.

Four barrels of the revolver were still undischarged. Two were fired—one, aimed at Bob Harvey, did not wound him, or at any rate only slightly, and Ayrton, profiting by the momentary retreat of his adversaries, rushed towards the companion-ladder to gain the deck. Passing before the lantern, he smashed it with a blow from the butt of his revolver. A profound darkness ensued, which favoured his flight. Two or three pirates, awakened by the noise, were descending the ladder at the same moment. A fifth shot from Ayrton laid one low, and the others drew back, not understanding what was going on. Ayrton was on deck in two bounds, and three seconds later, having discharged his last barrel in the face of a pirate who was about to seize him by the throat, he leaped over the bulwarks into the sea.

Ayrton had not made six strokes before shots were splashing around him like hail.

What were Pencroft's feelings, sheltered under a rock on the islet! what were those of Harding, the reporter, Herbert, and Neb, crouched in the Chimneys, when they heard the reports on board the brig! They rushed out on to the beach, and, their guns shouldered, they stood ready to repel any attack.

They had no doubt about it themselves! Ayrton, surprised by the pirates, had been murdered, and, perhaps, the wretches would profit by the night to make a descent on the island!

Half-an-hour was passed in terrible anxiety. The firing had ceased, and yet neither Ayrton nor Pencroft had reappeared. Was the islet invaded? Ought they not to fly to the help of Ayrton and Pencroft? But how? The tide being high at that time, rendered the channel impassable. The boat was not there! We may imagine the horrible anxiety which took possession of Harding and his companions!

At last, towards half-past twelve, a boat, carrying two men, touched the beach. It was Ayrton, slightly wounded in the shoulder, and Pencroft, safe and sound, whom their friends received with open arms.

All immediately took refuge in the Chimneys. There Ayrton recounted all that had passed, even to his plan for blowing up the brig, which he had attempted to put into execution.

All hands were extended to Ayrton, who did not conceal from them that their situation was serious. The pirates had been alarmed. They knew that Lincoln Island was inhabited. They would land upon it in numbers and well armed. They would respect nothing. Should the settlers fall into their hands, they must expect no mercy!

"Well, we shall know how to die!" said the reporter.

"Let us go in and watch," answered the engineer.

"Have we any chance of escape, captain?" asked the sailor.

"Yes, Pencroft."

"Hum! six against fifty!"

"Yes! six! without counting—"

"Who?" asked Pencroft.

Cyrus did not reply, but pointed upwards.

Chapter III

THE MIST RISES—THE ENGINEER'S PREPARATIONS—THREE POSTS—AYRTON AND PENCROFT—THE FIRST BOAT—TWO OTHER BOATS—ON THE ISLET—SIX CONVICTS LAND— THE BRIG WEIGHS ANCHOR—THE SPEEDY'S GUNS— A DESPERATE SITUATION—UNEXPECTED CATASTROPHE

THE NIGHT PASSED WITHOUT INCIDENT. THE COLONISTS WERE ON THE *QUI VIVE*, AND did not leave their post at the Chimneys. The pirates, on their side, did not appear to have made any attempt to land. Since the last shots fired at Ayrton not a report, not even a sound, had betrayed the presence of the brig in the neighbourhood of the island. It might have been fancied that she had weighed anchor, thinking that she had to deal with her match, and had left the coast.

But it was no such thing, and when day began to dawn the settlers could see a confused mass through the morning mist. It was the *Speedy*.

"These, my friends," said the engineer, "are the arrangements which appear to me best to make before the fog completely clears away. It hides us from the eyes of the pirates, and we can act without attracting their attention. The most important thing is, that the convicts should believe that the inhabitants of the island are numerous, and consequently capable of resisting them. I therefore propose that we divide into three parties. The first of which shall be posted at the Chimneys, the second at the mouth of the Mercy. As to the third, I think it would be best to place it on the islet, so as to prevent, or at all events delay, any attempt at landing. We have the use of two rifles and four muskets. Each of us will be armed, and, as we are amply provided with powder and shot, we need not spare our fire. We have nothing to fear from the muskets nor even from the guns of the brig. What can they do against these rocks? And, as we shall not fire from the windows of Granite House, the pirates will not think of causing irreparable damage by throwing shell against it. What is to be feared is, the necessity of meeting hand-to-hand, since the convicts have numbers on their side. We must therefore try to prevent them from landing, but without discovering ourselves. Therefore, do not economise the ammunition. Fire often, but with a sure aim. We have each eight or ten enemies to kill, and they must be killed!"

Cyrus Harding had clearly represented their situation, although he spoke in the calmest voice, as if it was a question of directing a piece of work and not ordering a battle. His companions approved these arrangements without even uttering a word. There was nothing more to be done but for each to take his place before the fog should be completely dissipated. Neb and Pencroft immediately ascended to Granite House and brought back a sufficient quantity of ammunition. Gideon Spilett and Ayrton, both very good marksmen, were armed with the two rifles, which carried nearly a mile. The four other muskets were divided among Harding, Neb, Pencroft, and Herbert.

The posts were arranged in the following manner:—

Cyrus Harding and Herbert remained in ambush at the Chimneys, thus commanding the shore to the foot of Granite House.

Gideon Spilett and Neb crouched among the rocks at the mouth of the Mercy, from which the drawbridges had been raised, so as to prevent anyone from crossing in a boat or landing on the opposite shore.

As to Ayrton and Pencroft, they shoved off in the boat, and prepared to cross the channel and to take up two separate stations on the islet. In this way, shots being fired from four different points at once, the convicts would be led to believe that the island was both largely peopled and strongly defended.

In the event of a landing being effected without their having been able to prevent it, and also if they saw that they were on the point of being cut off by the brig's boat, Ayrton and Pencroft were to return in their boat to the shore and proceed towards the threatened spot.

Before starting to occupy their posts, the colonists for the last time wrung each other's hands.

Pencroft succeeded in controlling himself sufficiently to suppress his emotion when he embraced Herbert, his boy! and then they separated.

In a few moments Harding and Herbert on one side, the reporter and Neb on the other, had disappeared behind the rocks, and five minutes later Ayrton and Pencroft, having without difficulty crossed the channel, disembarked on the islet and concealed themselves in the clefts of its eastern shore.

None of them could have been seen, for they themselves could scarcely distinguish the brig in the fog.

It was half-past six in the morning.

Soon the fog began to clear away, and the topmasts of the brig issued from the vapour. For some minutes great masses rolled over the surface of the sea, then a breeze sprang up, which rapidly dispelled the mist.

The *Speedy* now appeared in full view, with a spring on her cable, her head to the north, presenting her larboard side to the island. Just as Harding had calculated, she was not more than a mile and a quarter from the coast.

The sinister black flag floated from the peak.

The engineer, with his telescope, could see that the four guns on board were pointed at the island. They were evidently ready to fire at a moment's notice.

In the meanwhile the *Speedy* remained silent. About thirty pirates could be seen moving on the deck. A few more on the poop; two others posted in the shrouds, and armed with spy-glasses, were attentively surveying the island.

Certainly, Bob Harvey and his crew would not be able easily to give an account of what had happened during the night on board the brig. Had this half-naked man, who had forced the door of the powder-magazine, and with whom they had struggled, who had six times discharged his revolver at them, who had killed one and wounded two others, escaped their shot? Had he been able to swim to shore? Whence did he come? What had been his object? Had his design really been to blow up the brig, as Bob Harvey had thought? All this must be confused enough to the convicts' minds. But what they could no longer doubt was that the unknown island before which the *Speedy* had cast anchor was inhabited, and that there was, perhaps, a numerous colony ready to defend it. And yet no one was to be seen, neither on the shore, nor on the heights. The beach appeared to be absolutely deserted. At any rate, there was no trace of dwellings. Had the inhabitants fled into the interior? Thus probably the pirate captain reasoned, and doubtless, like a prudent man, he wished to reconnoitre the locality before he allowed his men to venture there.

During an hour and a half, no indication of attack or landing could be observed on board the brig. Evidently Bob Harvey was hesitating. Even with his strongest telescopes he could not have perceived one of the settlers crouched among the rocks. It was not even probable that his attention had been awakened by the screen of green branches and creepers hiding the windows of Granite House, and showing rather conspicuously on the bare rock. Indeed, how could he imagine that a dwelling was hollowed out, at that height, in the solid granite? From Claw Cape to the Mandible Capes, in all the extent of Union Bay, there was nothing to lead him to suppose that the island was or could be inhabited.

At eight o'clock, however, the colonists observed a movement on board the *Speedy*. A boat was lowered, and seven men jumped into her. They were armed with muskets; one took the yoke-lines, four others the oars, and the two others, kneeling in the bows, ready to fire, reconnoitred the island. Their object was no doubt to make an examination but not to land, for in the latter case they would have come in larger numbers. The pirates from their look-out could have seen that the coast was sheltered by an islet, separated from it by a channel half-a-mile in width. However, it was soon evident to Cyrus Harding, on observing the direction followed by the boat, that they would not attempt to penetrate into the channel, but would land on the islet.

Pencroft and Ayrton, each hidden in a narrow cleft of the rock, saw them coming directly towards them, and waited till they were within range.

The boat advanced with extreme caution. The oars only dipped into the water at long intervals. It could now be seen that one of the convicts held a lead-line in his hand, and that he wished to fathom the depth of the channel hollowed out by the current of the Mercy. This showed that it was Bob Harvey's intention to bring his brig as near as possible to the coast. About thirty pirates, scattered in the rigging, followed every movement of the boat, and took the bearings of certain landmarks which would allow them to approach without danger. The boat was not more than two cable-lengths off the islet when she stopped. The man at the tiller stood up and looked for the best place at which to land.

At that moment two shots were heard. Smoke curled up from among the rocks of the islet. The man at the helm and the man with the lead-line fell backwards into the boat. Ayrton's and Pencroft's balls had struck them both at the same moment.

Almost immediately a louder report was heard, a cloud of smoke issued from the brig's side, and a ball, striking the summit of the rock which sheltered Ayrton and Pencroft, made it fly in splinters, but the two marksmen remained unhurt.

Horrible imprecations burst from the boat, which immediately continued its way. The man who had been at the tiller was replaced by one of his comrades, and the oars were rapidly plunged into the water. However, instead of returning on board as might have been expected, the boat coasted along the islet, so as to round its southern point. The pirates pulled vigourously at their oars that they might get out of range of the bullets.

They advanced to within five cable-lengths of that part of the shore terminated by Flotsam Point, and after having rounded it in a semicircular line, still protected by the brig's guns, they proceeded towards the mouth of the Mercy.

Their evident intention was to penetrate into the channel, and cut off the colonists posted on the islet, in such a way, that whatever their number might be, being placed between the fire from the boat and the fire from the brig, they would find themselves in a very disadvantageous position.

A quarter of an hour passed while the boat advanced in this direction. Absolute silence, perfect calm reigned in the air and on the water.

Pencroft and Ayrton, although they knew they ran the risk of being cut off, had not left their post, both that they did not wish to show themselves as yet to their assailants, and expose themselves to the *Speedy*'s guns, and that they relied on Neb and Gideon Spilett, watching at the mouth of the river, and on Cyrus Harding and Herbert, in ambush among the rocks at the Chimneys.

Twenty minutes after the first shots were fired, the boat was less than two cable-lengths off the Mercy. As the tide was beginning to rise with its accustomed violence, caused by the narrowness of the straits, the pirates were drawn towards the river, and it was only by dint of hard rowing that they were able to keep in the middle of the channel. But, as they were passing within good range of the mouth of the Mercy, two balls saluted them, and two more of their number were laid in the bottom of the boat. Neb and Spilett had not missed their aim.

The brig immediately sent a second ball on the post betrayed by the smoke, but without any other result than that of splintering the rock.

The boat now contained only three able men. Carried on by the current, it shot through the channel with the rapidity of an arrow, passed before Harding and Herbert, who, not thinking it within range, withheld their fire, then, rounding the northern point of the islet with the two remaining oars, they pulled towards the brig.

Hitherto the settlers had nothing to complain of. Their adversaries had certainly had the worst of it. The latter already counted four men seriously wounded if not dead; they, on the contrary, unwounded, had not missed a shot. If the pirates continued to attack them in this way, if they renewed their attempt to land by means of a boat, they could be destroyed one by one.

It was now seen how advantageous the engineer's arrangements had been. The pirates would think that they had to deal with numerous and well-armed adversaries, whom they could not easily get the better of.

Half-an-hour passed before the boat, having to pull against the current, could get alongside the *Speedy*. Frightful cries were heard when they returned on board with the wounded, and two or three guns were fired with no results.

But now about a dozen other convicts, maddened with rage, and possibly by the effect of the evening's potations, threw themselves into the boat. A second boat was also lowered, in which eight men took their places, and while the first pulled straight for the islet, to dislodge the colonists from thence the second maneuvred so as to force the entrance of the Mercy.

The situation was evidently becoming very dangerous for Pencroft and Ayrton, and they saw that they must regain the mainland.

However, they waited till the first boat was within range, when two well-directed balls threw its crew into disorder. Then, Pencroft and Ayrton, abandoning their posts, under fire from the dozen muskets, ran across the islet at full speed, jumped into their boat, crossed the channel at the moment the second boat reached the southern end, and ran to hide themselves in the Chimneys.

They had scarcely rejoined Cyrus Harding and Herbert, before the islet was overrun with pirates in every direction. Almost at the same moment, fresh reports resounded from the Mercy station, to which the second boat was rapidly approaching. Two, out of the eight men who manned her, were mortally wounded by Gideon Spilett and Neb, and the boat herself, carried irresistibly onto the reefs, was stove in at the mouth of the Mercy. But the six survivors, holding their muskets above their heads to preserve them from contact with the water, managed to land on the right bank of the river. Then, finding they were exposed to the fire of the ambush there, they fled in the direction of Flotsam Point, out of range of the balls.

The actual situation was this: on the islet were a dozen convicts, of whom some were no doubt wounded, but who had still a boat at their disposal; on the island were six, but who could not by any possibility reach Granite House, as they could not cross the river, all the bridges being raised.

"Hallo," exclaimed Pencroft as he rushed into the Chimneys, "hallo, captain! What do you think of it, now?"

"I think," answered the engineer, "that the combat will now take a new form, for it cannot be supposed that the convicts will be so foolish as to remain in a position so unfavourable for them!"

"They won't cross the channel," said the sailor. "Ayrton and Mr. Spilett's rifles are there to prevent them. You know that they carry more than a mile!"

"No doubt," replied Herbert; "but what can two rifles do against the brig's guns?"

"Well, the brig isn't in the channel yet, I fancy!" said Pencroft.

"But suppose she does come there?" said Harding.

"That's impossible, for she would risk running aground and being lost!"

"It is possible," said Ayrton. "The convicts might profit by the high tide to enter the channel, with the risk of grounding at low tide, it is true; but then, under the fire from her guns, our posts would be no longer tenable."

"Confound them!" exclaimed Pencroft, "it really seems as if the blackguards were preparing to weigh anchor."

"Perhaps we shall be obliged to take refuge in Granite House!" observed Herbert.

"We must wait!" answered Cyrus Harding.

"But Mr. Spilett and Neb?" said Pencroft.

"They will know when it is best to rejoin us. Be ready, Ayrton. It is yours and Spilett's rifles which must speak now."

It was only too true. The *Speedy* was beginning to weigh her anchor, and her intention was evidently to approach the islet. The tide would be rising for an hour and a half, and the ebb current being already weakened, it would be easy for the brig to advance. But as to entering the channel, Pencroft, contrary to Ayrton's opinion, could not believe that she would dare to attempt it.

In the meanwhile, the pirates who occupied the islet had gradually advanced to the opposite shore, and were now only separated from the mainland by the channel.

Being armed with muskets alone, they could do no harm to the settlers, in ambush at the Chimneys and the mouth of the Mercy; but, not knowing the latter to be supplied with long range rifles, they on their side did not believe themselves to be exposed. Quite uncovered, therefore, they surveyed the islet, and examined the shore.

Their illusion was of short duration. Ayrton's and Gideon Spilett's rifles then spoke, and no doubt imparted some very disagreeable intelligence to two of the convicts, for they fell backwards.

Then there was a general helter-skelter. The ten others, not even stopping to pick up their dead or wounded companions, fled to the other side of the islet, tumbled into the boat which had brought them, and pulled away with all their strength.

"Eight less!" exclaimed Pencroft. "Really, one would have thought that Mr. Spilett and Ayrton had given the word to fire together!"

"Gentlemen," said Ayrton, as he reloaded his gun, "this is becoming more serious. The brig is making sail!"

"The anchor is weighed!" exclaimed Pencroft.

"Yes, and she is already moving."

In fact, they could distinctly hear the creaking of the windlass. The *Speedy* was at first held by her anchor; then, when that had been raised, she began to drift towards the shore. The wind was blowing from the sea; the jib and the foretopsail were hoisted, and the vessel gradually approached the island.

From the two posts of the Mercy and the Chimneys they watched her without giving a sign of life, but not without some emotion. What could be more terrible for the colonists than to be exposed, at a short distance, to the brig's guns, without being able to reply with any effect? How could they then prevent the pirates from landing?

Cyrus Harding felt this strongly, and he asked himself what it would be possible to do. Before long, he would be called upon for his determination. But what was it to be? To shut themselves up in Granite House, to be besieged there, to remain there for weeks, for months even, since they had an abundance of provisions? So far good! But after that? The pirates would not the less be masters of the island, which they would ravage at their pleasure, and in time, they would end by having their revenge on the prisoners in Granite House.

However, one chance yet remained; it was that Bob Harvey, after all, would not venture his ship into the channel, and that he would keep outside the islet. He would be still separated from the coast by half-a-mile, and at that distance his shot could not be very destructive.

"Never!" repeated Pencroft, "Bob Harvey will never, if he is a good seaman, enter that channel! He knows well that it would risk the brig, if the sea got up ever so little! And what would become of him without his vessel?"

In the meanwhile the brig approached the islet, and it could be seen that she was endeavouring to make the lower end. The breeze was light, and as the current had then lost much of its force, Bob Harvey had absolute command over his vessel.

The route previously followed by the boats had allowed her to reconnoitre the channel, and she boldly entered it.

The pirate's design was now only too evident; he wished to bring her broadside to bear on the Chimneys and from there to reply with shell and ball to the shot which had till then decimated her crew.

Soon the *Speedy* reached the point of the islet; she rounded it with ease; the mainsail was braced up, and the brig hugging the wind, stood across the mouth of the Mercy.

"The scoundrels! they are coming!" said Pencroft.

At that moment, Cyrus Harding, Ayrton, the sailor, and Herbert, were rejoined by Neb and Gideon Spilett.

The reporter and his companion had judged it best to abandon the post at the Mercy, from which they could do nothing against the ship, and they had acted wisely. It was better that the colonists should be together at the moment when they were about to engage in a decisive action. Gideon Spilett and Neb had arrived by dodging behind the rocks, though not without attracting a shower of bullets, which had not, however, reached them.

"Spilett! Neb!" cried the engineer. "You are not wounded?"

"No," answered the reporter, "a few bruises only from the ricochet! But that cursed brig has entered the channel!"

"Yes," replied Pencroft, "and in ten minutes she will have anchored before Granite House!"

"Have you formed any plan, Cyrus?" asked the reporter.

"We must take refuge in Granite House while there is still time, and the convicts cannot see us."

"That is my opinion, too," replied Gideon Spilett, "but once shut up—"

"We must be guided by circumstances," said the engineer.

"Let us be off, then, and make haste!" said the reporter.

"Would you not wish, captain, that Ayrton and I should remain here?" asked the sailor.

"What would be the use of that, Pencroft?" replied Harding. "No. We will not separate!"

There was not a moment to be lost. The colonists left the Chimneys. A bend of the cliff prevented them from being seen by those in the brig, but two or three reports, and the crash of bullets on the rock, told them that the *Speedy* was at no great distance.

To spring into the lift, hoist themselves up to the door of Granite House, where Top and Jup had been shut up since the evening before, to rush into the large room, was the work of a minute only.

It was quite time, for the settlers, through the branches, could see the *Speedy*, surrounded with smoke, gliding up the channel. The firing was incessant, and shot from the four guns struck blindly, both on the Mercy post, although it was not occupied, and on the Chimneys. The rocks were splintered, and cheers accompanied each discharge. However, they were hoping that Granite House would be spared, thanks to Harding's precaution of concealing the windows when a shot, piercing the door, penetrated into the passage.

"We are discovered!" exclaimed Pencroft.

The colonists had not, perhaps, been seen, but it was certain that Bob Harvey had thought proper to send a ball through the suspected foliage which concealed that part of the cliff. Soon he redoubled his attack, when another ball having torn away the leafy screen, disclosed a gaping aperture in the granite.

The colonists' situation was desperate. Their retreat was discovered. They could not oppose any obstacle to these missiles, nor protect the stone, which flew in splinters around them. There was nothing to be done but to take refuge in the upper passage of Granite House, and leave their dwelling to be devastated, when a deep roar was heard, followed by frightful cries!

Cyrus Harding and his companions rushed to one of the windows—

The brig irresistibly raised on a sort of water-spout, had just split in two, and in less than ten seconds she was swallowed up with all her criminal crew!

Chapter IV

THE COLONISTS ON THE BEACH—AYRTON AND PENCROFT WORK AMID THE WRECK—CONVERSATION DURING BREAKFAST— PENCROFT'S ARGUMENTS—MINUTE EXAMINATION OF THE BRIG'S HULL—THE POWDER-MAGAZINE UNTOUCHED—NEW RICHES— THE LAST OF THE WRECK—A BROKEN PIECE OF CYLINDER

S HE HAS BLOWN UP!" CRIED HERBERT.

"Yes! blown up, just as if Ayrton had set fire to the powder!" returned Pencroft, throwing himself into the lift together with Neb and the lad.

"But what has happened?" asked Gideon Spilett, quite stunned by this unexpected catastrophe.

"Oh! this time, we shall know—" answered the engineer quickly.

"What shall we know?—"

"Later! later! Come, Spilett. The main point is that these pirates have been exterminated!"

And Cyrus Harding, hurrying away the reporter and Ayrton, joined Pencroft, Neb, and Herbert on the beach.

Nothing could be seen of the brig, not even her masts. After having been raised by the water-spout, she had fallen on her side, and had sunk in that position, doubtless in consequence of some enormous leak. But as in that place the channel was not more than twenty feet in depth, it was certain that the sides of the submerged brig would reappear at low water.

A few things from the wreck floated on the surface of the water, a raft could be seen consisting of spare spars, coops of poultry with their occupants still living, boxes and barrels, which gradually came to the surface, after having escaped through the hatchways, but no pieces of the wreck appeared, neither planks from the deck, nor timber from the hull— which rendered the sudden disappearance of the *Speedy* perfectly inexplicable.

However, the two masts, which had been broken and escaped from the shrouds and stays came up, and with their sails, some furled and the others spread. But it was not necessary to wait for the tide to bring up these riches, and Ayrton and Pencroft jumped into the boat with the intention of towing the pieces of wreck either to the beach or to the islet. But just as they were shoving off, an observation from Gideon Spilett arrested them.

"What about those six convicts who disembarked on the right bank of the Mercy?" said he.

In fact, it would not do to forget that the six men whose boat had gone to pieces on the rocks, had landed at Flotsam Point.

They looked in that direction. None of the fugitives were visible. It was probable that, having seen their vessel engulfed in the channel, they had fled into the interior of the island.

"We will deal with them later," said Harding. "As they are armed, they will still be dangerous; but as it is six against six, the chances are equal. To the most pressing business first."

Ayrton and Pencroft pulled vigorously towards the wreck.

The sea was calm and the tide very high, as there had been a new moon but two days before. A whole hour at least would elapse before the hull of the brig could emerge from the water of the channel.

Ayrton and Pencroft were able to fasten the masts and spars by means of ropes, the ends of which were carried to the beach. There, by the united efforts of the settlers the pieces of wreck were hauled up. Then the boat picked up all that was floating, coops, barrels, and boxes, which were immediately carried to the Chimneys.

Several bodies floated also. Among them, Ayrton recognised that of Bob Harvey, which he pointed out to his companion, saying with some emotion—

"That is what I have been, Pencroft."

"But what you are no longer, brave Ayrton!" returned the sailor warmly.

It was singular enough that so few bodies floated. Only five or six were counted, which were already being carried by the current towards the open sea. Very probably the convicts had not had time to escape, and the ship lying over on her side, the greater number of them had remained below. Now the current, by carrying the bodies of these miserable men out to sea, would spare the colonists the sad task of burying them in some corner of their island.

For two hours, Cyrus Harding and his companions were solely occupied in hauling up the spars on to the sand, and then in spreading the sails, which were perfectly uninjured, to dry. They spoke little, for they were absorbed in their work, but what thoughts occupied their minds!

The possession of this brig, or rather all that she contained, was a perfect mine of wealth. In fact, a ship is like a little world in miniature, and the stores of the colony would be increased by a large number of useful articles. It would be, on a large scale, equivalent to the chest found at Flotsam Point.

"And besides," thought Pencroft, "why should it be impossible to refloat the brig? If she has only a leak, that may be stopped up; a vessel from three to four hundred tons, why she is a regular ship compared to our *Bonadventure!* And we could go a long distance in her! We could go anywhere we liked! Captain Harding, Ayrton and I must examine her! She would be well worth the trouble!"

In fact, if the brig was still fit to navigate, the colonists' chances of returning to their native land were singularly increased. But, to decide this important question, it was necessary to wait until the tide was quite low, so that every part of the brig's hull might be examined.

When their treasures had been safely conveyed on shore, Harding and his companions agreed to devote some minutes to breakfast. They were almost famished; fortunately, the larder was not far off, and Neb was noted for being an expeditious cook. They breakfasted, therefore, near the Chimneys, and during their repast, as may be supposed, nothing was talked of but the event which had so miraculously saved the colony.

"Miraculous is the word," repeated Pencroft, "for it must be acknowledged that those rascals blew up just at the right moment! Granite House was beginning to be uncomfortable as a habitation!"

"And can you guess, Pencroft," asked the reporter, "how it happened, or what can have occasioned the explosion?"

"Oh! Mr. Spilett, nothing is more simple," answered Pencroft. "A convict vessel is not disciplined like a man-of-war! Convicts are not sailors. Of course the powder-magazine was open, and as they were firing incessantly, some careless or clumsy fellow just blew up the vessel!"

"Captain Harding," said Herbert, "what astonishes me is that the explosion has not produced more effect. The report was not loud, and besides there are so few planks and timbers torn out. It seems as if the ship had rather foundered than blown up."

"Does that astonish you, my boy?" asked the engineer.

"Yes, captain."

"And it astonishes me also, Herbert," replied he, "but when we visit the hull of the brig, we shall no doubt find the explanation of the matter."

"Why, captain," said Pencroft, "you don't suppose that the *Speedy* simply foundered like a ship which has struck on a rock?"

"Why not," observed Neb, "if there are rocks in the channel?"

"Nonsense, Neb," answered Pencroft, "you did not look at the right moment. An instant before she sank, the brig, as I saw perfectly well, rose on an enormous wave, and fell back on her larboard side. Now, if she had only struck, she would have sunk quietly and gone to the bottom like an honest vessel."

"It was just because she was not an honest vessel!" returned Neb.

"Well, we shall soon see, Pencroft," said the engineer.

"We shall soon see," rejoined the sailor, "but I would wager my head there are no rocks in the channel. Look here, captain, to speak candidly, do you mean to say that there is anything marvellous in the occurrence?"

Cyrus Harding did not answer.

"At any rate," said Gideon Spilett, "whether rock or explosion, you will agree, Pencroft, that it occurred just in the nick of time!"

"Yes! yes!" replied the sailor, "but that is not the question. I ask Captain Harding if he sees anything supernatural in all this."

"I cannot say, Pencroft," said the engineer. "That is all the answer I can make."

A reply which did not satisfy Pencroft at all. He stuck to "an explosion," and did not wish to give it up. He would never consent to admit that in that channel, with its fine sandy bed, just like the beach, which he had often crossed at low water, there could be an unknown rock.

And besides, at the time the brig foundered, it was high water, that is to say, there was enough water to carry the vessel clear over any rocks which would not be uncovered at low tide. Therefore, there could not have been a collision. Therefore, the vessel had not struck. Therefore, she had blown up.

And it must be confessed that the sailor's arguments were not without reason.

Towards half-past one, the colonists embarked in the boat to visit the wreck. It was to be regretted that the brig's two boats had not been saved; but one, as has been said, had gone to pieces at the mouth of the Mercy, and was absolutely useless; the other had disappeared when the brig went down, and had not again been seen, having doubtless been crushed.

The hull of the *Speedy* was just beginning to issue from the water. The brig was lying right over on her side, for her masts being broken, pressed down by the weight of the ballast displaced by the shock, the keel was visible along her whole length. She had been regularly turned over by the inexplicable but frightful submarine action, which had been at the same time manifested by an enormous water-spout.

The settlers rowed round the hull, and in proportion as the tide went down, they could ascertain, if not the cause which had occasioned the catastrophe, at least the effect produced.

Towards the bows, on both sides of the keel, seven or eight feet from the beginning of the stem, the sides of the brig were frightfully torn. Over a length of at least twenty feet there opened two large leaks, which would be impossible to stop up. Not only had the copper sheathing and the planks disappeared, reduced, no doubt, to powder, but also the ribs, the iron bolts, and treenails which united them. From the entire length of the hull to the stern the false keel had been separated with unaccountable violence, and the keel itself, torn from the carline in several places, was split in all its length.

"I've a notion!" exclaimed Pencroft, "that this vessel will be difficult to get afloat again."

"It will be impossible," said Ayrton.

"At any rate," observed Gideon Spilett to the sailor, "the explosion, if there has been one, has produced singular effects! It has split the lower part of the hull, instead of blowing up the deck and topsides! These great rents appear rather to have been made by a rock than by the explosion of a powder-magazine."

"There is not a rock in the channel!" answered the sailor. "I will admit anything you like, except the rock."

"Let us try to penetrate into the interior of the brig," said the engineer; "perhaps we shall then know what to think of the cause of her destruction."

This was the best thing to be done, and it was agreed, besides, to take an inventory of all the treasures on board, and to arrange for their preservation.

Access to the interior of the brig was now easy. The tide was still going down and the deck was practicable. The ballast, composed of heavy masses of iron, had broken through in several places. The noise of the sea could be heard as it rushed out at the holes in the hull.

Cyrus Harding and his companions, hatchets in hand, advanced along the shattered deck. Cases of all sorts encumbered it, and, as they had been but a very short time in the water, their contents were perhaps uninjured.

They then busied themselves in placing all this cargo in safety. The water would not return for several hours, and these hours must be employed in the most profitable way.

Ayrton and Pencroft had, at the entrance made in the hull, discovered tackle, which would serve to hoist up the barrels and chests. The boat received them and transported them to the shore. They took the articles as they came, intending to sort them afterwards.

At any rate, the settlers saw at once, with extreme satisfaction, that the brig possessed a very varied cargo—an assortment of all sorts of articles, utensils, manufactured goods, and tools—such as the ships which make the great coasting-trade of Polynesia are usually laden with. It was probable that they would find a little of everything, and they agreed that it was exactly what was necessary for the colony of Lincoln Island.

However—and Cyrus Harding observed it in silent astonishment—not only, as has been said, had the hull of the brig enormously suffered from the shock, whatever it was, that had occasioned the catastrophe, but the interior arrangements had been destroyed, especially towards the bows. Partitions and stanchions were smashed, as if some tremendous shell had burst in the interior of the brig. The colonists could easily go fore and aft, after having removed the cases as they were extricated. They were not heavy bales, which would have been difficult to remove, but simple packages, of which the stowage, besides, was no longer recognisable.

The colonists then reached the stern of the brig—the part formerly surmounted by the poop. It was there that, following Ayrton's directions, they must look for the powder-magazine. Cyrus Harding thought that it had not exploded; that it was possible some barrels might be saved, and that the powder, which is usually enclosed in metal coverings might not have suffered from contact with the water.

This, in fact, was just what had happened. They extricated from among a large number of shot twenty barrels, the insides of which were lined with copper. Pencroft was convinced by the evidence of his own eyes that the destruction of the *Speedy* could not be attributed to an explosion. That part of the hull in which the magazine was situated was, moreover, that which had suffered least.

"It may be so," said the obstinate sailor; "but as to a rock, there is not one in the channel!"

"Then, how did it happen?" asked Herbert.

"I don't know," answered Pencroft, "Captain Harding doesn't know, and nobody knows or ever will know!"

Several hours had passed during these researches, and the tide began to flow. Work must be suspended for the present. There was no fear of the brig being carried away by the sea, for she was already fixed as firmly as if moored by her anchors.

They could, therefore, without inconvenience, wait until the next day to resume operations; but, as to the vessel itself, she was doomed, and it would be best to hasten to save the remains of her hull, as she would not be long in disappearing in the quicksands of the channel.

It was now five o'clock in the evening. It had been a hard day's work for the men. They ate with good appetite, and, notwithstanding their fatigue, they could not resist, after dinner, their desire of inspecting the cases which composed the cargo of the *Speedy*.

Most of them contained clothes, which, as may be believed, were well received. There were enough to clothe a whole colony—linen for everyone's use, shoes for everyone's feet.

"We are too rich!" exclaimed Pencroft, "But what are we going to do with all this?"

And every moment burst forth the hurrahs of the delighted sailor when he caught sight of the barrels of gunpowder, fire-arms and side-arms, balls of cotton, implements of husbandry, carpenter's, joiner's, and blacksmith's tools, and boxes of all kinds of seeds, not in the least injured by their short sojourn in the water. Ah, two years before, how these things would have been prized! And now, even though the industrious colonists had provided themselves with tools, these treasures would find their use.

There was no want of space in the store-rooms of Granite House, but that daytime would not allow them to stow away the whole. It would not do also to forget that the six survivors of the *Speedy's* crew had landed on the island, for they were in all probability scoundrels of the deepest dye, and it was necessary that the colonists should be on their guard against them. Although the bridges over the Mercy were raised, the convicts would not be stopped by a river or a stream, and, rendered desperate, these wretches would be capable of anything.

They would see later what plan it would be best to follow; but in the meantime it was necessary to mount guard over cases and packages heaped up near the Chimneys, and thus the settlers employed themselves in turn during the night.

The morning came, however, without the convicts having attempted any attack. Master Jup and Top, on guard at the foot of Granite House, would have quickly given the alarm. The three following days—the 19th, 20th, and 21st of October—were employed in saving everything of value, or of any use whatever, either from the cargo or rigging of the brig. At low tide they overhauled the hold—at high tide they stowed away the rescued articles. A great part of the copper sheathing had been torn from the hull, which everyday sank lower. But before the sand had swallowed the heavy things which had fallen through the bottom, Ayrton and Pencroft, diving to the bed of the channel, recovered the chains and anchors of the brig, the iron of her ballast, and even four guns, which, floated by means of empty casks, were brought to shore.

It may be seen that the arsenal of the colony had gained by the wreck, as well as the store-rooms of Granite House. Pencroft, always enthusiastic in his projects, already spoke of constructing a battery to command the channel and the mouth of the river. With four guns, he engaged to prevent any fleet, "however powerful it might be," from venturing into the waters of Lincoln Island!

In the meantime, when nothing remained of the brig but a useless hulk, bad weather came on, which soon finished her. Cyrus Harding had intended to blow her up, so as to collect the remains on the shore, but a strong gale from the north-east and a heavy sea compelled him to economise his powder.

In fact, on the night of the 23d, the hull entirely broke up, and some of the wreck was cast upon the beach.

As to the papers on board, it is useless to say that, although he carefully searched the lockers of the poop, Harding did not discover any trace of them. The pirates had evidently destroyed everything that concerned either the captain or the owners of the *Speedy*, and, as the name of her port was not painted on her counter, there was nothing which would tell them her nationality. However, by the shape of her boats Ayrton and Pencroft believed that the brig was of English build.

A week after the castrophe—or, rather, after the fortunate, though inexplicable, event to which the colony owed its preservation—nothing more could be seen of the vessel, even at low tide. The wreck had disappeared, and Granite House was enriched by nearly all it had contained.

However, the mystery which enveloped its strange destruction would doubtless never have been cleared away if, on the 30th of November, Neb, strolling on the beach, had not found a piece of a thick iron cylinder, bearing traces of explosion. The edges of this cylinder were twisted and broken, as if they had been subjected to the action of some explosive substance.

Neb brought this piece of metal to his master, who was then occupied with his companions in the workshop of the Chimneys.

Cyrus Harding examined the cylinder attentively, then, turning to Pencroft—

"You persist, my friend," said he, "in maintaining that the *Speedy* was not lost in consequence of a collision?"

"Yes, captain," answered the sailor. "You know as well as I do that there are no rocks in the channel."

"But suppose she had run against this piece of iron?" said the engineer, showing the broken cylinder.

"What, that bit of pipe!" exclaimed Pencroft in a tone of perfect incredulity.

"My friends," resumed Harding, "you remember that before she foundered the brig rose on the summit of a regular water-spout?"

"Yes, captain," replied Herbert.

"Well, would you like to know what occasioned that water-spout? It was this," said the engineer, holding up the broken tube.

"That?" returned Pencroft.

"Yes! This cylinder is all that remains of a torpedo!"

"A torpedo!" exclaimed the engineer's companions.

"And who put the torpedo there?" demanded Pencroft, who did not like to yield.

"All that I can tell you is, that it was not I," answered Cyrus Harding; "but it was there, and you have been able to judge of its incomparable power!"

Chapter V

The Engineer's Declaration—Pencroft's Grand Hypothesis—An Aerial Battery—The Four Cannons—The Surviving Convicts—Ayrton's Hesitation—Cyrus Harding's Generous Sentiments—Pencroft's Regret

So, then, all was explained by the submarine explosion of this torpedo. Cyrus Harding could not be mistaken, as, during the war of the Union, he had had occasion to try these terrible engines of destruction. It was under the action of this cylinder, charged with some explosive substance, nitro-glycerine, picrate, or some other material of the same nature, that the water of the channel had been raised like a dome, the bottom of the brig crushed in, and she had sunk instantly, the damage done to her hull being so considerable that it was impossible to refloat her. The *Speedy* had not been able to withstand a torpedo that would have destroyed an iron-clad as easily as a fishing-boat!

Yes! all was explained, everything—except the presence of the torpedo in the waters of the channel!

"My friends, then," said Cyrus Harding, "we can no longer be in doubt as to the presence of a mysterious being, a castaway like us, perhaps, abandoned on our island, and I say this in order that Ayrton may be acquainted with all the strange events which have occurred during these two years. Who this beneficent stranger is, whose intervention has, so fortunately for us, been manifested on many occasions, I cannot imagine. What his object can be in acting thus, in concealing himself after rendering us so many services, I cannot understand. But his services are not the less real, and are of such a nature that only a man possessed of prodigious power, could render them. Ayrton is indebted to him as much as we are, for, if it was the stranger who saved me from the waves after the fall from the balloon, evidently it was he who wrote the document, who placed the bottle in the channel, and who has made known to us the situation of our companion. I will add that it was he who guided that chest, provided with everything we wanted, and stranded it on Flotsam Point; that it was he who lighted that fire on the heights of the island, which permitted you to land; that it was he who fired that bullet found in the body of the peccary; that it was he who immersed that torpedo in the channel, which destroyed the brig; in a word, that all those inexplicable events, for which we could not assign a reason, are due to this mysterious being. Therefore, whoever he may be, whether shipwrecked, or exiled on our island, we shall be ungrateful, if we think ourselves freed from gratitude towards him. We have contracted a debt, and I hope that we shall one day pay it."

"You are right in speaking thus, my dear Cyrus," replied Gideon Spilett. "Yes, there is an almost all-powerful being, hidden in some part of the island, and whose influence has been singularly useful to our colony. I will add that the unknown appears to possess means of action which border on the supernatural, if in the events of practical life the supernatural were recognisable. Is it he who is in secret communication with us by the well in Granite House, and has he thus a knowledge of all our plans? Was it he who threw us that bottle, when the vessel made her first cruise? Was it he who threw Top out of the lake, and killed the dugong? Was it he, who as everything leads us to believe, saved you from the waves, and that under circumstances in which anyone else would not have been able to act? If it was he, he possesses a power which renders him master of the elements."

The reporter's reasoning was just, and everyone felt it to be so.

"Yes," rejoined Cyrus Harding, "if the intervention of a human being is not more questionable for us, I agree that he has at his disposal means of action beyond those possessed by humanity. There is a mystery still, but if we discover the man, the mystery will be discovered also. The question, then, is, ought we to respect the *incognito* of this generous being, or ought we to do everything to find him out? What is your opinion on the matter?"

"My opinion," said Pencroft, "is that, whoever he may be, he is a brave man, and he has my esteem!"

"Be it so," answered Harding, "but that is not an answer, Pencroft."

"Master," then said Neb, "my idea is, that we may search as long as we like for this gentleman whom you are talking about, but that we shall not discover him till he pleases."

"That's not bad, what you say, Neb," observed Pencroft.

"I am of Neb's opinion," said Gideon Spilett, "but that is no reason for not attempting the adventure. Whether we find this mysterious being or not, we shall at least have fulfilled our duty towards him."

"And you, my boy, give us your opinion," said the engineer, turning to Herbert.

"Oh," cried Herbert, his countenance full of animation, "how I should like to thank him, he who saved you first, and who has now saved us!"

"Of course, my boy," replied Pencroft, "so would I and all of us. I am not inquisitive, but I would give one of my eyes to see this individual face to face! It seems to me that he must be handsome, tall, strong, with a splendid beard, radiant hair, and that he must be seated on the clouds, a great ball in his hands!"

"But, Pencroft," answered Spilett, "you are describing a picture of the Creator."

"Possibly, Mr. Spilett," replied the sailor, "but that is how I imagine him!"

"And you, Ayrton?" asked the engineer.

"Captain Harding," replied Ayrton, "I can give you no better advice in this matter. Whatever you do will be best, when you wish me to join you in your researches, I am ready to follow you."

"I thank you, Ayrton," answered Cyrus Harding, "but I should like a more direct answer to the question I put to you. You are our companion; you have already endangered your life several times for us, and you, as well as the rest, ought to be consulted in the matter of any important decision. Speak, therefore."

"Captain Harding," replied Ayrton, "I think that we ought to do everything to discover this unknown benefactor. Perhaps he is alone. Perhaps he is suffering. Perhaps he has a life to be renewed. I, too, as you said, have a debt of gratitude to pay him. It was he, it could be only he who must have come to Tabor Island, who found there the wretch you knew, and who made known to you that there was an unfortunate man there to be saved. Therefore it is, thanks to him, that I have become a man again. No, I will never forget him!"

"That is settled, then," said Cyrus Harding. "We will begin our researches as soon as possible. We will not leave a corner of the island unexplored. We will search into its most secret recesses, and will hope that our unknown friend will pardon us in consideration of our intentions!"

For several days the colonists were actively employed in haymaking and the harvest. Before putting their project of exploring the yet unknown parts of the island into execution, they wished to get all possible work finished. It was also the time for collecting the various vegetables from the Tabor Island plants. All was stowed away, and happily there was no want of room in Granite House, in which they might have housed all the treasures of the island. The products of the colony were there, methodically arranged, and in a safe place, as may be believed, sheltered as much from animals as from man.

There was no fear of damp in the middle of that thick mass of granite. Many natural excavations situated in the upper passage were enlarged either by pickaxe or mine, and Granite House thus became a general warehouse, containing all the provisions, arms, tools, and spare utensils—in a word, all the stores of the colony.

As to the guns obtained from the brig, they were pretty pieces of ordnance, which, at Pencroft's entreaty, were hoisted by means of tackle and pulleys, right up into Granite

House; embrasures were made between the windows, and the shining muzzles of the guns could soon be seen through the granite cliff. From this height they commanded all Union Bay. It was like a little Gibraltar, and any vessel anchored off the islet would inevitably be exposed to the fire of this aerial battery.

"Captain," said Pencroft one day, it was the 8th of November, "now that our fortifications are finished, it would be a good thing if we tried the range of our guns."

"Do you think that is useful?" asked the engineer.

"It is more than useful, it is necessary! Without that how are we to know to what distance we can send one of those pretty shot with which we are provided?"

"Try them, Pencroft," replied the engineer. "However, I think that in making the experiment, we ought to employ, not the ordinary powder, the supply of which, I think, should remain untouched, but the pyroxyle which will never fail us."

"Can the cannon support the shock of the pyroxyle?" asked the reporter, who was not less anxious than Pencroft to try the artillery of Granite House.

"I believe so. However," added the engineer, "we will be prudent."

The engineer was right in thinking that the guns were of excellent make. Made of forged steel, and breech-loaders, they ought consequently to be able to bear a considerable charge, and also have an enormous range. In fact, as regards practical effect, the transit described by the ball ought to be as extended as possible, and this tension could only be obtained under the condition that the projectile should be impelled with a very great initial velocity.

"Now," said Harding to his companions, "the initial velocity is in proportion to the quantity of powder used. In the fabrication of these pieces, everything depends on employing a metal with the highest possible power of resistance, and steel is incontestably that metal of all others which resists the best. I have, therefore, reason to believe that our guns will bear without risk the expansion of the pyroxyle gas, and will give excellent results."

"We shall be a great deal more certain of that when we have tried them!" answered Pencroft.

It is unnecessary to say that the four cannons were in perfect order. Since they had been taken from the water, the sailor had bestowed great care upon them. How many hours he had spent, in rubbing, greasing, and polishing them, and in cleaning the mechanism! And now the pieces were as brilliant as if they had been on board a frigate of the United States' Navy.

On this day, therefore, in presence of all the members of the colony, including Master Jup and Top, the four cannon were successively tried. They were charged with pyroxyle, taking into consideration its explosive power, which, as has been said, is four times that of ordinary powder: the projectile to be fired was cylindro-conic.

Pencroft, holding the end of the quick-match, stood ready to fire.

At Harding's signal, he fired. The shot, passing over the islet, fell into the sea at a distance which could not be calculated with exactitude.

The second gun was pointed at the rocks at the end of Flotsam Point, and the shot, striking a sharp rock nearly three miles from Granite House, made it fly into splinters. It was Herbert who had pointed this gun and fired it, and very proud he was of his first shot. Pencroft only was prouder than he! Such a shot, the honour of which belonged to his dear boy.

The third shot, aimed this time at the downs forming the upper side of Union Bay, struck the sand at a distance of four miles, then having ricocheted, was lost in the sea in a cloud of spray.

For the fourth piece Cyrus Harding slightly increased the charge, so as to try its extreme range. Then, all standing aside for fear of its bursting, the match was lighted by means of a long cord.

A tremendous report was heard, but the piece had held good, and the colonists rushing to the windows, saw the shot graze the rocks of Mandible Cape, nearly five miles from Granite House, and disappear in Shark Gulf.

"Well, captain," exclaimed Pencroft, whose cheers might have rivaled the reports themselves, "what do you say of our battery? All the pirates in the Pacific have only to present themselves before Granite House! Not one can land there now without our permission!"

"Believe me, Pencroft," replied the engineer, "it would be better not to have to make the experiment."

"Well," said the sailor, "what ought to be done with regard to those six villains who are roaming about the island? Are we to leave them to overrun our forests, our fields, our plantations? These pirates are regular jaguars, and it seems to me we ought not to hesitate to treat them as such! What do you think, Ayrton?" added Pencroft, turning to his companion.

Ayrton hesitated at first to reply, and Cyrus Harding regretted that Pencroft had so thoughtlessly put this question. And he was much moved when Ayrton replied in a humble tone—

"I have been one of those jaguars, Mr. Pencroft. I have no right to speak."

And with a slow step he walked away.

Pencroft understood.

"What a brute I am!" he exclaimed. "Poor Ayrton! He has as much right to speak here as anyone!"

"Yes," said Gideon Spilett, "but his reserve does him honour, and it is right to respect the feeling which he has about his sad past."

"Certainly, Mr. Spilett," answered the sailor, "and there is no fear of my doing so again. I would rather bite my tongue off than cause Ayrton any pain! But to return to the question. It seems to me that these ruffians have no right to any pity, and that we ought to rid the island of them as soon as possible."

"Is that your opinion, Pencroft?" asked the engineer.

"Quite my opinion."

"And before hunting them mercilessly, you would not wait until they had committed some fresh act of hostility against us?"

"Isn't what they have done already enough?" asked Pencroft, who did not understand these scruples.

"They may adopt other sentiments!" said Harding, "and perhaps repent."

"They repent!" exclaimed the sailor, shrugging his shoulders.

"Pencroft, think of Ayrton!" said Herbert, taking the sailor's hand. "He became an honest man again!"

Pencroft looked at his companions one after the other. He had never thought of his proposal being met with any objection. His rough nature could not allow that they ought to come to terms with the rascals who had landed on the island with Bob Harvey's accomplices, the murderers of the crew of the *Speedy,* and he looked upon them as wild beasts which ought to be destroyed without delay and without remorse.

"Come!" said be. "Everybody is against me! You wish to be generous to those villains! Very well; I hope we mayn't repent it!"

"What danger shall we run," said Herbert, "if we take care to be always on our guard?"

"Hum!" observed the reporter, who had not given any decided opinion. "They are six and well armed. If they each lay hid in a corner, and each fired at one of us, they would soon be masters of the colony!"

"Why have they not done so?" said Herbert. "No doubt because it was not their interest to do it. Besides, we are six also."

"Well, well!" replied Pencroft, whom no reasoning could have convinced. "Let us leave these good people to do what they like, and don't think anything more about them!"

"Come, Pencroft," said Neb, "don't make yourself out so bad as all that! Suppose one of these unfortunate men were here before you, within good range of your guns, you would not fire."

"I would fire on him as I would on a mad dog, Neb," replied Pencroft coldly.

"Pencroft," said the engineer, "you have always shown much deference to my advice; will you, in this matter, yield to me?"

"I will do as you please, Captain Harding," answered the sailor, who was not at all convinced.

"Very well, wait, and we will not attack them unless we are attacked first."

Thus their behaviour towards the pirates was agreed upon, although Pencroft augured nothing good from it. They were not to attack them, but were to be on their guard. After all, the island was large and fertile. If any sentiment of honesty yet remained in the bottom of their hearts, these wretches might perhaps be reclaimed. Was it not their interest in the situation in which they found themselves to begin a new life? At any rate, for humanity's sake alone, it would be right to wait. The colonists would no longer as before, be able to go and come without fear. Hitherto they had only wild beasts to guard against, and now six convicts of the worst description, perhaps, were roaming over their island. It was serious, certainly, and to less brave men, it would have been security lost! No matter! At present, the colonists had reason on their side against Pencroft. Would they be right in the future? That remained to be seen.

Chapter VI

EXPEDITIONS PLANNED—AYRTON AT THE CORRAL—VISIT TO
PORT BALLOON—PENCROFT'S OBSERVATIONS ON BOARD THE
BONADVENTURE—DESPATCH SENT TO THE CORRAL—NO
REPLY FROM AYRTON—DEPARTURE THE NEXT DAY—THE REASON
WHY THE WIRE DID NOT WORK—A REPORT

HOWEVER, THE CHIEF BUSINESS OF THE COLONISTS WAS TO MAKE THAT COMPLETE EXploration of the island which had been decided upon, and which would have two objects: to discover the mysterious being whose existence was now indisputable, and at the same time to find out what had become of the pirates, what retreat they had chosen, what sort of life they were leading, and what was to be feared from them. Cyrus Harding wished to set out without delay; but as the expedition would be of some days' duration, it appeared best to load the cart with different materials and tools in order to facilitate the organisation of the encampments. One of the onagers, however, having hurt its leg, could not be harnessed at present, and a few days' rest was necessary. The departure was, therefore, put off for a week, until the 20th of November. The month of November in this latitude corresponds to the month of May in the northern zones. It was, therefore, the fine season. The sun was entering the tropic of Capricorn, and gave the longest days in the year. The time was, therefore, very favourable for the projected expedition, which, if it did not accomplish its principal object, would at any rate be fruitful in discoveries, especially of natural productions, since Harding proposed to explore those dense forests of the Far West, which stretched to the extremity of the Serpentine Peninsula.

During the nine days which preceded their departure, it was agreed that the work on Prospect Heights should be finished off.

Moreover, it was necessary for Ayrton to return to the corral, where the domesticated animals required his care. It was decided that he should spend two days there, and return to Granite House after having liberally supplied the stables.

As he was about to start, Harding asked him if he would not like one of them to accompany him, observing that the island was less safe than formerly. Ayrton replied that this was unnecessary, as he was enough for the work, and that besides he apprehended no danger. If anything occurred at the corral, or in the neighbourhood, he could instantly warn the colonists by sending a telegram to Granite House.

Ayrton departed at dawn on the 9th, taking the cart drawn by one onager, and two hours after, the electric wire announced that he had found all in order at the corral.

During these two days Harding busied himself in executing a project which would completely guard Granite House against any surprise. It was necessary to completely conceal the opening of the old outlet, which was already walled up and partly hidden under grass and plants, at the southern angle of Lake Grant. Nothing was easier, since if the level of the lake was raised two or three feet, the opening would be quite beneath it. Now, to raise this level they had only to establish a dam at the two openings made by the lake, and by which were fed Creek Glycerine and Falls River.

The colonists worked with a will, and the two dams which besides did not exceed eight feet in width by three in height, were rapidly erected by means of well-cemented blocks of stone.

This work finished, it would have been impossible to guess that at that part of the lake, there existed a subterranean passage through which the overflow of the lake formerly escaped.

Of course the little stream which fed the reservoir of Granite House and worked the lift, had been carefully preserved, and the water could not fail. The lift once raised, this sure and comfortable retreat would be safe from any surprise.

This work had been so quickly done, that Pencroft, Gideon Spilett, and Herbert found time to make an expedition to Port Balloon. The sailor was very anxious to know if the little creek in which the *Bonadventure* was moored, had been visited by the convicts.

"These gentlemen," he observed, "landed on the south coast, and if they followed the shore, it is to be feared that they may have discovered the little harbour, and in that case, I wouldn't give half-a-dollar for our *Bonadventure*."

Pencroft's apprehensions were not without foundation, and a visit to Port Balloon appeared to be very desirable. The sailor and his companions set off on the 10th of November, after dinner, well armed. Pencroft, ostentatiously slipping two bullets into each barrel of his rifle, shook his head in a way which betokened nothing good to anyone who approached too near to him, whether "man or beast," as he said. Gideon Spilett and Herbert also took their guns, and about three o'clock all three left Granite House.

Neb accompanied them to the turn of the Mercy, and after they had crossed, he raised the bridge. It was agreed that a gunshot should announce the colonists' return, and that at the signal Neb should return and re-establish the communication between the two banks of the river.

The little band advanced directly along the road which led to the southern coast of the island. This was only a distance of three miles and a half, but Gideon Spilett and his companions took two hours to traverse it. They examined all the border of the road, the thick forest, as well as Tabor Marsh. They found no trace of the fugitives who, no doubt, not having yet discovered the number of the colonists, or the means of defence which they had at their disposal, had gained the less accessible parts of the island.

Arrived at Port Balloon, Pencroft saw with extreme satisfaction that the *Bonadventure* was tranquilly floating in the narrow creek. However, Port Balloon was so well hidden among high rocks, that it could scarcely be discovered either from the land or the sea.

"Come," said Pencroft, "the blackguards have not been there yet. Long grass suits reptiles best, and evidently we shall find them in the Far West."

"And it's very lucky, for if they had found the *Bonadventure*," added Herbert, "they would have gone off in her, and we should have been prevented from returning to Tabor Island."

"Indeed," remarked the reporter, "it will be important to take a document there which will make known the situation of Lincoln Island, and Ayrton's new residence, in case the Scotch yacht returns to fetch him."

"Well, the *Bonadventure* is always there, Mr. Spilett," answered the sailor. "She and her crew are ready to start at a moment's notice!"

"I think, Pencroft, that that is a thing to be done after our exploration of the island is finished. It is possible after all that the stranger, if we manage to find him, may know as much about Tabor Island as about Lincoln Island. Do not forget that he is certainly the author of the document, and he may, perhaps, know how far we may count on the return of the yacht!"

"But!" exclaimed Pencroft, "who in the world can he be? The fellow knows us and we know nothing about him! If he is a simple castaway, why should he conceal himself! We are honest men, I suppose, and the society of honest men isn't unpleasant to anyone. Did he come here voluntarily? Can he leave the island if he likes? Is he here still? Will he remain any longer?"

Chatting thus, Pencroft, Gideon Spilett, and Herbert got on board and looked about the deck of the *Bonadventure*. All at once, the sailor having examined the bitts to which the cable of the anchor was secured—

"Hallo," he cried, "this is queer!"

"What is the matter, Pencroft?" asked the reporter.

"The matter is, that it was not I who made this knot!"

And Pencroft showed a rope which fastened the cable to the bitt itself.

"What, it was not you?" asked Gideon Spilett.

"No! I can swear to it. This is a reef knot, and I always make a running bowline."

"You must be mistaken, Pencroft."

"I am not mistaken!" declared the sailor. "My hand does it so naturally, and one's hand is never mistaken!"

"Then can the convicts have been on board?" asked Herbert.

"I know nothing about that," answered Pencroft, "but what is certain, is that someone has weighed the *Bonadventure's* anchor and dropped it again! And look here, here is another proof! The cable of the anchor has been run out, and its service is no longer at the hawse-hole. I repeat that someone has been using our vessel!"

"But if the convicts had used her, they would have pillaged her, or rather gone off with her."

"Gone off! where to—to Tabor Island?" replied Pencroft. "Do you think they would risk themselves in a boat of such small tonnage?"

"We must, besides, be sure that they know of the islet," rejoined the reporter.

"However that may be," said the sailor, "as sure as my name is Bonadventure Pencroft, of the Vineyard, our *Bonadventure* has sailed without us!"

The sailor was so positive that neither Gideon Spilett nor Herbert could dispute his statement. It was evident that the vessel had been moved, more or less, since Pencroft had brought her to Port Balloon. As to the sailor, he had not the slightest doubt that the anchor had been raised and then dropped again. Now, what was the use of these two maneuvres, unless the vessel had been employed in some expedition?

"But how was it we did not see the *Bonadventure* pass in the sight of the island?" observed the reporter, who was anxious to bring forward every possible objection.

"Why, Mr. Spilett," replied the sailor, "they would only have to start in the night with a good breeze, and they would be out of sight of the island in two hours."

"Well," resumed Gideon Spilett, "I ask again, what object could the convicts have had in using the *Bonadventure*, and why, after they had made use of her, should they have brought her back to port?"

"Why, Mr. Spilett," replied the sailor, "we must put that among the unaccountable things, and not think anything more about it. The chief thing is that the *Bonadventure* was there, and she is there now. Only, unfortunately, if the convicts take her a second time, we shall very likely not find her again in her place!"

"Then, Pencroft," said Herbert, "would it not be wisest to bring the *Bonadventure* off to Granite House?"

"Yes and no," answered Pencroft, "or rather no. The mouth of the Mercy is a bad place for a vessel, and the sea is heavy there."

"But by hauling her upon the sand, to the foot of the Chimneys?"

"Perhaps yes," replied Pencroft. "At any rate, since we must leave Granite House for a long expedition, I think the *Bonadventure* will be safer here during our absence, and we shall do best to leave her here until the island is rid of these blackguards."

"That is exactly my opinion," said the reporter. "At any rate in the event of bad weather, she will not be exposed here as she would be at the mouth of the Mercy."

"But suppose the convicts pay her another visit," said Herbert.

"Well, my boy," replied Pencroft, "not finding her here, they would not be long in finding her on the sands of Granite House, and, during our absence, nothing could hinder them from seizing her! I agree, therefore, with Mr. Spilett, that she must be left in Port Balloon. But, if on our return we have not rid the island of those rascals, it will be prudent to bring our boat to Granite House, until the time when we need not fear any unpleasant visits."

"That's settled. Let us be off," said the reporter.

Pencroft, Herbert, and Gideon Spilett, on their return to Granite House, told the engineer all that had passed, and the latter approved of their arrangements both for the present and the future. He also promised the sailor that he would study that part of the channel situated between the islet and the coast, so as to ascertain if it would not be possible to make an artificial harbor there by means of dams. In this way, the *Bonadventure* would be always within reach, under the eyes of the colonists, and if necessary, under lock and key.

That evening a telegram was sent to Ayrton, requesting him to bring from the corral a couple of goats, which Neb wished to acclimatise to the plateau. Singularly enough, Ayrton did not acknowledge the receipt of the despatch, as he was accustomed to do. This could not but astonish the engineer. But it might be that Ayrton was not at that moment in the corral, or even that he was on his way back to Granite House. In fact, two days had already passed since his departure, and it had been decided that on the evening of the 10th or at the latest the morning of the 11th, he should return. The colonists waited, therefore, for Ayrton to appear on Prospect Heights. Neb and Herbert even watched at the bridge so as to be ready to lower it the moment their companion presented himself.

But up to ten in the evening, there were no signs of Ayrton. It was, therefore, judged best to send a fresh despatch, requiring an immediate reply.

The bell of the telegraph at Granite House remained mute.

The colonists' uneasiness was great. What had happened? Was Ayrton no longer at the corral, or if he was still there, had he no longer control over his movements? Could they go to the corral in this dark night?

They consulted. Some wished to go, the others to remain.

"But," said Herbert, "perhaps some accident has happened to the telegraphic apparatus, so that it works no longer?"

"That may be," said the reporter.

"Wait till to-morrow," replied Cyrus Harding. "It is possible, indeed, that Ayrton has not received our despatch, or even that we have not received his."

They waited, of course not without some anxiety.

At dawn of day, the 11th of November, Harding again sent the electric current along the wire and received no reply.

He tried again: the same result.

"Off to the corral," said he.

"And well armed!" added Pencroft.

It was immediately decided that Granite House should not be left alone and that Neb should remain there. After having accompanied his friends to Creek Glycerine, he raised the bridge; and waiting behind a tree he watched for the return of either his companions or Ayrton.

In the event of the pirates presenting themselves and attempting to force the passage, he was to endeavour to stop them by firing on them, and as a last resource he was to take refuge in Granite House, where, the lift once raised, he would be in safety.

Cyrus Harding, Gideon Spilett, Herbert, and Pencroft were to repair to the corral, and if they did not find Ayrton, search the neighbouring woods.

At six o'clock in the morning, the engineer and his three companions had passed Creek Glycerine, and Neb posted himself behind a small mound crowned by several dragoniners, on the left bank of the stream.

The colonists, after leaving the plateau of Prospect Heights, immediately took the road to the corral. They shouldered their guns, ready to fire on the slightest hostile demonstration. The two rifles and the two guns had been loaded with ball.

The wood was thick on each side of the road and might easily have concealed the convicts, who owing to their weapons would have been really formidable.

The colonists walked rapidly and in silence. Top preceded them, sometimes running on the road, sometimes taking a ramble into the wood, but always quiet and not appearing to fear anything unusual. And they could be sure that the faithful dog would not allow them to be surprised, but would bark at the least appearance of danger.

Cyrus Harding and his companions followed beside the road the wire which connected the corral with Granite House. After walking for nearly two miles, they had not as yet discovered any explanation of the difficulty. The posts were in good order, the wire regularly extended. However, at that moment the engineer observed that the wire appeared to be slack, and on arriving at post No. 74, Herbert, who was in advance stopped, exclaiming—

"The wire is broken!"

His companions hurried forward and arrived at the spot where the lad was standing. The post was rooted up and lying across the path. The unexpected explanation of the difficulty was here, and it was evident that the despatches from Granite House had not been received at the corral, nor those from the corral at Granite House.

"It wasn't the wind that blew down this post," observed Pencroft.

"No," replied Gideon Spilett. "The earth has been dug up round its foot, and it has been torn up by the hand of man."

"Besides, the wire is broken," added Herbert, showing that the wire had been snapped.

"Is the fracture recent?" asked Harding.

"Yes," answered Herbert, "it has certainly been done quite lately."

"To the corral! to the corral!" exclaimed the sailor.

The colonists were now half-way between Granite House and the corral, having still two miles and a half to go. They pressed forward with redoubled speed.

Indeed, it was to be feared that some serious accident had occurred in the corral. No doubt, Ayrton might have sent a telegram which had not arrived, but this was not the reason why his companions were so uneasy, for, a more unaccountable circumstance, Ayrton, who had promised to return the evening before, had not reappeared. In short, it was not without a motive that all communication had been stopped between the corral and Granite House, and who but the convicts could have any interest in interrupting this communication?

The settlers hastened on, their hearts oppressed with anxiety. They were sincerely attached to their new companion. Were they to find him struck down by the hands of those of whom he was formerly the leader?

Soon they arrived at the place where the road led along the side of the little stream which flowed from the Red Creek and watered the meadows of the corral. They then moderated their pace so that they should not be out of breath at the moment when a struggle might be necessary. Their guns were in their hands ready cocked. The forest was watched on every side. Top uttered sullen groans which were rather ominous.

At last the palisade appeared through the trees. No trace of any damage could be seen. The gate was shut as usual. Deep silence reigned in the corral. Neither the accustomed bleating of the sheep nor Ayrton's voice could be heard.

"Let us enter," said Cyrus Harding.

And the engineer advanced, while his companions, keeping watch about twenty paces behind him, were ready to fire at a moment's notice.

Harding raised the inner latch of the gate and was about to push it back, when Top barked loudly. A report sounded and was responded to by a cry of pain.

Herbert, struck by a bullet, lay stretched on the ground.

Chapter VII

THE REPORTER AND PENCROFT IN THE CORRAL—HERBERT'S
WOUND—THE SAILOR'S DESPAIR—CONSULTATION BETWEEN THE
REPORTER AND THE ENGINEER—MODE OF TREATMENT—HOPE
NOT ABANDONED—HOW IS NEB TO BE WARNED—A SURE AND
FAITHFUL MESSENGER—NEB'S REPLY

A T HERBERT'S CRY, PENCROFT, LETTING HIS GUN FALL, RUSHED TOWARDS HIM.
"They have killed him!" he cried. "My boy! They have killed him!"

Cyrus Harding and Gideon Spilett ran to Herbert.

The reporter listened to ascertain if the poor lad's heart was still beating.

"He lives," said he, "but he must be carried—"

"To Granite House? that is impossible!" replied the engineer.

"Into the corral, then!" said Pencroft.

"In a moment," said Harding.

And he ran round the left corner of the palisade. There he found a convict, who aiming at him, sent a ball through his hat. In a few seconds, before he had even time to fire his second barrel, he fell, struck to the heart by Harding's dagger, more sure even than his gun.

During this time, Gideon Spilett and the sailor hoisted themselves over the palisade, leaped into the enclosure, threw down the props which supported the inner door, ran into the empty house, and soon, poor Herbert was lying on Ayrton's bed. In a few moments, Harding was by his side.

On seeing Herbert senseless, the sailor's grief was terrible. He sobbed, he cried, he tried to beat his head against the wall. Neither the engineer nor the reporter could calm him. They themselves were choked with emotion. They could not speak.

However, they knew that it depended on them to rescue from death the poor boy who was suffering beneath their eyes. Gideon Spilett had not passed through the many incidents by which his life had been checkered without acquiring some slight knowledge of medicine. He knew a little of everything, and several times he had been obliged to attend to wounds produced either by a sword-bayonet or shot. Assisted by Cyrus Harding, he proceeded to render the aid Herbert required.

The reporter was immediately struck by the complete stupor in which Herbert lay, a stupor owing either to the hemorrhage, or to the shock, the ball having struck a bone with sufficient force to produce a violent concussion.

Herbert was deadly pale, and his pulse so feeble that Spilett only felt it beat at long intervals, as if it was on the point of stopping.

These symptoms were very serious.

Herbert's chest was laid bare, and the blood having been stanched with handkerchiefs, it was bathed with cold water.

The contusion, or rather the contused wound appeared—an oval below the chest between the third and fourth ribs. It was there that Herbert had been hit by the bullet.

Cyrus Harding and Gideon Spilett then turned the poor boy over; as they did so, he uttered a moan so feeble that they almost thought it was his last sigh.

Herbert's back was covered with blood from another contused wound, by which the ball had immediately escaped.

"God be praised!" said the reporter, "the ball is not in the body, and we shall not have to extract it."

"But the heart?" asked Harding.

"The heart has not been touched; if it had been, Herbert would be dead!"

"Dead!" exclaimed Pencroft, with a groan.

The sailor had only heard the last words uttered by the reporter.

"No, Pencroft," replied Cyrus Harding, "no! He is not dead. His pulse still beats. He has even uttered a moan. But for your boy's sake, calm yourself. We have need of all our self-possession. Do not make us lose it, my friend."

Pencroft was silent, but a reaction set in, and great tears rolled down his cheeks.

In the meanwhile, Gideon Spilett endeavoured to collect his ideas, and proceed methodically. After his examination he had no doubt that the ball, entering in front, between the seventh and eighth ribs, had issued behind between the third and fourth. But what mischief had the ball committed in its passage? What important organs had been reached? A professional surgeon would have had difficulty in determining this at once, and still more so the reporter.

However, he knew one thing, this was that he would have to prevent the inflammatory strangulation of the injured parts, then to contend with the local inflammation and fever which would result from the wound, perhaps mortal! Now, what styptics, what antiphlogistics ought to be employed? By what means could inflammation be prevented?

At any rate, the most important thing was that the two wounds should be dressed without delay. It did not appear necessary to Gideon Spilett that a fresh flow of blood should be caused by bathing them in tepid water, and compressing their lips. The hemorrhage had been very abundant, and Herbert was already too much enfeebled by the loss of blood.

The reporter, therefore, thought it best to simply bathe the two wounds with cold water.

Herbert was placed on his left side, and was maintained in that position.

"He must not be moved." said Gideon Spilett. "He is in the most favourable position for the wounds in his back and chest to suppurate easily, and absolute rest is necessary."

"What! can't we carry him to Granite House?" asked Pencroft.

"No, Pencroft," replied the reporter.

"I'll pay the villains off!" cried the sailor, shaking his fist in a menacing manner.

"Pencroft!" said Cyrus Harding.

Gideon Spilett had resumed his examination of the wounded boy. Herbert was still so frightfully pale, that the reporter felt anxious.

"Cyrus," said he, "I am not a surgeon. I am in terrible perplexity. You must aid me with your advice, your experience!"

"Take courage, my friend," answered the engineer, pressing the reporter's hand. "Judge coolly. Think only of this: Herbert must be saved!"

These words restored to Gideon Spilett that self-possession which he had lost in a moment of discouragement on feeling his great responsibility. He seated himself close to the bed. Cyrus Harding stood near. Pencroft had torn up his shirt, and was mechanically making lint.

Spilett then explained to Cyrus Harding that he thought he ought first of all to stop the hemorrhage, but not close the two wounds, or cause their immediate cicatrisation, for there had been internal perforation, and the suppuration must not be allowed to accumulate in the chest.

Harding approved entirely, and it was decided that the two wounds should be dressed without attempting to close them by immediate coaptation.

And now did the colonists possess an efficacious agent to act against the inflammation which might occur?

Yes. They had one, for nature had generously lavished it. They had cold water, that is to say, the most powerful sedative that can be employed against inflammation of wounds, the most efficacious therapeutic agent in grave cases, and the one which is now adopted by all physicians. Cold water has, moreover, the advantage of leaving the wound in absolute rest, and preserving it from all premature dressing, a considerable advantage, since it has been found by experience that contact with the air is dangerous during the first days.

Gideon Spilett and Cyrus Harding reasoned thus with their simple good sense, and they acted as the best surgeon would have done. Compresses of linen were applied to poor Herbert's two wounds, and were kept constantly wet with cold water.

The sailor had at first lighted a fire in the hut, which was not wanting in things necessary for life. Maple sugar, medicinal plants, the same which the lad had gathered on the banks of Lake Grant, enabled them to make some refreshing drinks, which they gave him without his taking any notice of it. His fever was extremely high, and all that day and night passed without his becoming conscious.

Herbert's life hung on a thread, and this thread might break at any moment. The next day, the 12th of November, the hopes of Harding and his companions slightly revived. Herbert had come out of his long stupor. He opened his eyes, he recognised Cyrus Harding, the reporter, and Pencroft. He uttered two or three words. He did not know what had happened. They told him, and Spilett begged him to remain perfectly still, telling him that his life was not in danger, and that his wounds would heal in a few days. However, Herbert scarcely suffered at all, and the cold water with which they were constantly bathed, prevented any inflammation of the wounds. The suppuration was established in a regular way, the fever did not increase, and it might now be hoped that this terrible wound would not involve any catastrophe. Pencroft felt the swelling of his heart gradually subside. He was like a sister of mercy, like a mother by the bed of her child.

Herbert dozed again, but his sleep appeared more natural.

"Tell me again that you hope, Mr. Spilett," said Pencroft. "Tell me again that you will save Herbert!"

"Yes, we will save him!" replied the reporter. "The wound is serious, and, perhaps, even the ball has traversed the lungs, but the perforation of this organ is not fatal."

"God bless you!" answered Pencroft.

As may be believed, during the four-and-twenty hours they had been in the corral, the colonists had no other thought than that of nursing Herbert. They did not think either of the danger which threatened them should the convicts return, or of the precautions to be taken for the future.

But on this day, while Pencroft watched by the sick-bed, Cyrus Harding and the reporter consulted as to what it would be best to do.

First of all they examined the corral. There was not a trace of Ayrton. Had the unhappy man been dragged away by his former accomplices? Had he resisted, and been overcome in the struggle? This last supposition was only too probable. Gideon Spilett, at the moment he scaled the palisade, had clearly seen some one of the convicts running along the southern spur of Mount Franklin, towards whom Top had sprung. It was one of those whose object had been so completely defeated by the rocks at the mouth of the Mercy. Besides, the one killed by Harding, and whose body was found outside the enclosure, of course belonged to Bob Harvey's crew.

As to the corral, it had not suffered any damage. The gates were closed, and the animals had not been able to disperse in the forest. Nor could they see traces of any struggle, any devastation, either in the hut, or in the palisade. The ammunition only, with which Ayrton had been supplied, had disappeared with him.

"The unhappy man has been surprised," said Harding, "and as he was a man to defend himself, he must have been overpowered."

"Yes, that is to be feared!" said the reporter. "Then, doubtless, the convicts installed themselves in the corral where they found plenty of everything, and only fled when they saw us coming. It is very evident, too, that at this moment Ayrton, whether living or dead, is not here!"

"We shall have to beat the forest," said the engineer, "and rid the island of these wretches. Pencroft's presentiments were not mistaken, when he wished to hunt them as wild beasts. That would have spared us all these misfortunes!"

"Yes," answered the reporter, "but now we have the right to be merciless!"

"At any rate," said the engineer, "we are obliged to wait some time, and to remain at the corral until we can carry Herbert without danger to Granite House."

"But Neb?" asked the reporter.

"Neb is in safety."

"But if, uneasy at our absence, he would venture to come?"

"He must not come!" returned Cyrus Harding quickly. "He would be murdered on the road!"

"It is very probable, however, that he will attempt to rejoin us!"

"Ah, if the telegraph still acted, he might be warned! But that is impossible now! As to leaving Pencroft and Herbert here alone, we could not do it! Well, I will go alone to Granite House."

"No, no! Cyrus," answered the reporter, "you must not expose yourself! Your courage would be of no avail. The villains are evidently watching the corral, they are hidden in the thick woods which surround it, and if you go we shall soon have to regret two misfortunes instead of one!"

"But Neb?" repeated the engineer. "It is now four-and-twenty hours since he has had any news of us! He will be sure to come!"

"And as he will be less on his guard than we should be ourselves," added Spilett, "he will be killed!"

"Is there really no way of warning him?"

While the engineer thought, his eyes fell on Top, who, going backwards and forwards seemed to say—

"Am not I here?"

"Top!" exclaimed Cyrus Harding.

The animal sprang at his master's call.

"Yes, Top will go," said the reporter, who had understood the engineer.

"Top can go where we cannot! He will carry to Granite House the news of the corral, and he will bring back to us that from Granite House!"

"Quick!" said Harding. "Quick!"

Spilett rapidly tore a leaf from his note-book, and wrote these words:—

"Herbert wounded. We are at the corral. Be on your guard. Do not leave Granite House. Have the convicts appeared in the neighbourhood? Reply by Top."

This laconic note contained all that Neb ought to know, and at the same time asked all that the colonists wished to know. It was folded and fastened to Top's collar in a conspicuous position.

"Top, my dog," said the engineer, caressing the animal, "Neb, Top! Neb! Go, go!"

Top bounded at these words. He understood, he knew what was expected of him. The road to the corral was familiar to him. In less than an hour he could clear it, and it might be hoped that where neither Cyrus Harding nor the reporter could have ventured without danger, Top, running among the grass or in the wood, would pass unperceived.

The engineer went to the gate of the corral and opened it.

"Neb, Top! Neb!" repeated the engineer, again pointing in the direction of Granite House.

Top sprang forwards, then almost immediately disappeared.

"He will get there!" said the reporter.

"Yes, and he will come back, the faithful animal!"

"What o'clock is it?" asked Gideon Spilett.

"Ten."

"In an hour he may be here. We will watch for his return."

The gate of the corral was closed. The engineer and the reporter re-entered the house. Herbert was still in a sleep. Pencroft kept the compresser always wet. Spilett, seeing there was nothing he could do at that moment, busied himself in preparing some nourishment, while attentively watching that part of the enclosure against the hill, at which an attack might be expected.

The settlers awaited Top's return with much anxiety. A little before eleven o'clock, Cyrus Harding and the reporter, rifle in hand, were behind the gate, ready to open it at the first bark of their dog.

They did not doubt that if Top had arrived safely at Granite House, Neb would have sent him back immediately.

They had both been there for about ten minutes, when a report was heard, followed by repeated barks.

The engineer opened the gate, and seeing smoke a hundred feet off in the wood, he fired in that direction.

Almost immediately Top bounded into the corral, and the gate was quickly shut.

"Top, Top!" exclaimed the engineer, taking the dog's great honest head between his hands.

A note was fastened to his neck, and Cyrus Harding read these words, traced in Neb's large writing:—

"No pirates in the neighbourhood of Granite House. I will not stir. Poor Mr. Herbert!"

Chapter VIII

THE CONVICTS IN THE NEIGHBORHOOD OF THE CORRAL— PROVISIONAL ESTABLISHMENT—CONTINUATION OF THE TREATMENT OF HERBERT—PENCROFT'S FIRST REJOICINGS— CONVERSATION ON PAST EVENTS—WHAT THE FUTURE HAS IN RESERVE—CYRUS HARDING'S IDEAS ON THIS SUBJECT

SO THE CONVICTS WERE STILL THERE, WATCHING THE CORRAL, AND DETERMINED TO KILL the settlers one after the other. There was nothing to be done but to treat them as wild beasts. But great precautions must be taken, for just now the wretches had the advantage on their side, seeing, and not being seen, being able to surprise by the suddenness of their attack, yet not to be surprised themselves. Harding made arrangements, therefore, for living in the corral, of which the provisions would last for a tolerable length of time. Ayrton's house had been provided with all that was necessary for existence, and the convicts, scared by the arrival of the settlers, had not had time to pillage it. It was probable, as Gideon Spilett observed, that things had occurred as follows:—The six convicts, disembarking on the island, had followed the southern shore, and after having traversed the double shore of the Serpentine Peninsula, not being inclined to venture into the Far West woods, they had reached the mouth of Falls River. From this point, by following the right bank of the watercourse, they would arrive at the spurs of Mount Franklin, among which they would naturally seek a retreat, and they could not have been long in discovering the corral, then uninhabited. There they had regularly installed themselves, awaiting the moment to put their abominable schemes into execution. Ayrton's arrival had surprised them, but they had managed to overpower the unfortunate man, and—the rest may be easily imagined!

Now, the convicts—reduced to five, it is true, but well armed—were roaming the woods, and to venture there was to expose themselves to their attacks, which could be neither guarded against nor prevented.

"Wait! There is nothing else to be done!" repeated Cyrus Harding. "When Herbert is cured, we can organise a general battue of the island, and have satisfaction of these convicts. That will be the object of our grand expedition at the same time—"

"As the search for our mysterious protector," added Gideon Spilett, finishing the engineer's sentence. "Ah, it must be acknowledged, my dear Cyrus, that this time his protection was wanting at the very moment when it was most necessary to us!"

"Who knows?" replied the engineer.

"What do you mean?" asked the reporter.

"That we are not at the end of our trouble yet, my dear Spilett, and that his powerful intervention may, perhaps, have another opportunity of exercising itself. But that is not the question now. Herbert's life before everything."

This was the colonists' saddest thought. Several days passed, and the poor boy's state was happily no worse. Cold water, always kept at a suitable temperature, had completely prevented the inflammation of the wounds. It even seemed to the reporter that this water, being slightly sulphurous—which was explained by the neighbourhood of the volcano— had a more direct action on the healing. The suppuration was much less abundant, and— thanks to the incessant care by which he was surrounded!—Herbert returned to life, and his fever abated. He was besides subjected to a severe diet, and consequently his weakness was and would be extreme; but there was no want of refreshing drinks, and absolute rest was of the greatest benefit to him. Cyrus Harding, Gideon Spilett, and Pencroft had become very skilful in dressing the lad's wounds. All the linen in the house had been sacrificed. Herbert's wounds, covered with compresses and lint, were pressed neither too much nor too little, so as to cause their cicatrisation without determining on inflammatory reaction. The reporter used extreme care in the dressing, knowing well the importance of it, and repeating to his companions that which most surgeons willingly admit, that it is perhaps rarer to see a dressing well done than an operation well performed.

In ten days, on the 22d of November, Herbert was considerably better. He had begun to take some nourishment. The colour was returning to his cheeks, and his bright eyes smiled at his nurses. He talked a little, notwithstanding Pencroft's efforts, who talked incessantly to prevent him from beginning to speak, and told him the most improbable stories. Herbert had questioned him on the subject of Ayrton, whom he was astonished not to see near him, thinking that he was at the corral. But the sailor, not wishing to distress Herbert, contented himself by replying that Ayrton had rejoined Neb, so as to defend Granite House.

"Humph!" said Pencroft, "these pirates! they are gentlemen who have no right to any consideration! And the captain wanted to win them by kindness! I'll send them some kindness, but in the shape of a good bullet!"

"And have they not been seen again?" asked Herbert.

"No, my boy," answered the sailor, "but we shall find them, and when you are cured we shall see if the cowards who strike us from behind will dare to meet us face to face!"

"I am still very weak, my poor Pencroft!"

"Well! your strength will return gradually! What's a ball through the chest? Nothing but a joke! I've seen many, and I don't think much of them!"

At last things appeared to be going on well, and if no complication occurred, Herbert's recovery might be regarded as certain. But what would have been the condition of the colonists if his state had been aggravated—if, for example, the ball had remained in his body, if his arm or his leg had had to be amputated?

"No," said Spilett more than once, "I have never thought of such a contingency without shuddering!"

"And yet, if it had been necessary to operate," said Harding one day to him, "you would not have hesitated?"

"No, Cyrus!" said Gideon Spilett, "but thank God that we have been spared this complication!"

As in so many other conjectures, the colonists had appealed to the logic of that simple good sense of which they had made use so often, and once more, thanks to their general knowledge, it had succeeded! But might not a time come when all their science would be at fault? They were alone on the island. Now, men in all states of society are necessary to each other. Cyrus Harding knew this well, and sometimes he asked himself if some circumstance might not occur which they would be powerless to surmount. It appeared to him besides, that he and his companions, till then so fortunate, had entered into an unlucky period. During the two years and a half which had elapsed since their escape from Richmond, it might be said that they had had everything their own way. The island had abundantly supplied them with minerals, vegetables, animals, and as Nature had constantly loaded them, their science had known how to take advantage of what she offered them.

The well-being of the colony was therefore complete. Moreover, in certain occurrences an inexplicable influence had come to their aid! . . . But all that could only be for a time.

In short, Cyrus Harding believed that fortune had turned against them.

In fact, the convicts' ship had appeared in the waters of the island, and if the pirates had been, so to speak, miraculously destroyed, six of them, at least, had escaped the catastrophe. They had disembarked on the island, and it was almost impossible to get at the five who survived. Ayrton had no doubt been murdered by these wretches, who possessed fire-arms, and at the first use that they had made of them, Herbert had fallen, wounded almost mortally. Were these the first blows aimed by adverse fortune at the colonists? This was often asked by Harding. This was often repeated by the reporter; and it appeared to him also that the intervention, so strange, yet so efficacious, which till then had served them so well, had now failed them. Had this mysterious being, whatever he was, whose existence could not be denied, abandoned the island? Had he in his turn succumbed?

No reply was possible to these questions. But it must not be imagined that because Harding and his companions spoke of these things, they were men to despair. Far from that. They looked their situation in the face, they analysed the chances, they prepared themselves for any event, they stood firm and straight before the future, and if adversity was at last to strike them, it would find in them men prepared to struggle against it.

Chapter IX

No News of Neb—A Proposal from Pencroft and the
Reporter, Which Is Not Accepted—Several Sorties by
Gideon Spilett—A Rag of Cloth—A Message—Hasty
Departure—Arrival on the Plateau of Prospect Heights

THE CONVALESCENCE OF THE YOUNG INVALID WAS REGULARLY PROGRESSING. ONE
thing only was now to be desired, that his state would allow him to be brought to
Granite House. However well built and supplied the corral house was, it could not be so
comfortable as the healthy granite dwelling. Besides, it did not offer the same security, and
its tenants, notwithstanding their watchfulness, were here always in fear of some shot from
the convicts. There, on the contrary, in the middle of that impregnable and inaccessible
cliff, they would have nothing to fear, and any attack on their persons would certainly fail.
They therefore waited impatiently for the moment when Herbert might be moved without
danger from his wound, and they were determined to make this move, although the communication through Jacamar Wood was very difficult.

They had no news from Neb, but were not uneasy on that account. The courageous
negro, well entrenched in the depths of Granite House, would not allow himself to be surprised. Top had not been sent again to him, as it appeared useless to expose the faithful dog
to some shot which might deprive the settlers of their most useful auxiliary.

They waited, therefore, although they were anxious to be reunited at Granite House.
It pained the engineer to see his forces divided, for it gave great advantage to the pirates.
Since Ayrton's disappearance they were only four against five, for Herbert could not yet
be counted, and this was not the least care of the brave boy, who well understood the trouble of which he was the cause.

The question of knowing how, in their condition, they were to act against the pirates,
was thoroughly discussed on the 29th of November by Cyrus Harding, Gideon Spilett,
and Pencroft, at a moment when Herbert was asleep and could not hear them.

"My friends," said the reporter, after they had talked of Neb and of the impossibility
of communicating with him, "I think, like you, that to venture on the road to the corral
would be to risk receiving a gunshot without being able to return it. But do you not think
that the best thing to be done now is to openly give chase to these wretches?"

"That is just what I was thinking," answered Pencroft. "I believe we're not fellows to
be afraid of a bullet, and as for me, if Captain Harding approves, I'm ready to dash into
the forest! Why, hang it, one man is equal to another!"

"But is he equal to five?" asked the engineer.

"I will join Pencroft," said the reporter, "and both of us, well armed and accompanied
by Top—"

"My dear Spilett, and you, Pencroft," answered Harding, "let us reason coolly. If the
convicts were hid in one spot of the island, if we knew that spot, and had only to dislodge

them, I would undertake a direct attack; but is there not occasion to fear, on the contrary, that they are sure to fire the first shot?"

"Well, captain," cried Pencroft, "a bullet does not always reach its mark."

"That which struck Herbert did not miss, Pencroft," replied the engineer. "Besides, observe that if both of you left the corral I should remain here alone to defend it. Do you imagine that the convicts will not see you leave it, that they will not allow you to enter the forest, and that they will not attack it during your absence, knowing that there is no one here but a wounded boy and a man?"

"You are right, captain," replied Pencroft, his chest swelling with sullen anger. "You are right; they will do all they can to retake the corral, which they know to be well stored; and alone you could not hold it against them."

"Oh, if we were only at Granite House!"

"If we were at Granite House," answered the engineer, "the case would be very different. There I should not be afraid to leave Herbert with one, while the other three went to search the forests of the island. But we are at the corral, and it is best to stay here until we can leave it together."

Cyrus Harding's reasoning was unanswerable, and his companions understood it well.

"If only Ayrton was still one of us!" said Gideon Spilett. "Poor fellow! his return to social life will have been but of short duration."

"If he is dead," added Pencroft, in a peculiar tone.

"Do you hope, then, Pencroft, that the villains have spared him?" asked Gideon Spilett.

"Yes, if they had any interest in doing so."

"What! you suppose that Ayrton, finding his old companions, forgetting all that he owes us—"

"Who knows?" answered the sailor, who did not hazard this shameful supposition without hesitating.

"Pencroft," said Harding, taking the sailor's arm, "that is a wicked idea of yours, and you will distress me much if you persist in speaking thus. I will answer for Ayrton's fidelity."

"And I also," added the reporter quickly.

"Yes, yes, captain, I was wrong," replied Pencroft; "it was a wicked idea indeed that I had, and nothing justifies it. But what can I do? I'm not in my senses. This imprisonment in the corral wearies me horribly, and I have never felt so excited as I do now."

"Be patient, Pencroft," replied the engineer. "How long will it be, my dear Spilett, before you think Herbert may be carried to Granite House?"

"That is difficult to say, Cyrus," answered the reporter, "for any imprudence might involve terrible consequences. But his convalescence is progressing, and if he continues to gain strength, in eight days from now—well, we shall see."

Eight days! That would put off the return to Granite House until the first days of December. At this time two months of spring had already passed. The weather was fine, and the heat began to be great. The forests of the island were in full leaf, and the time was approaching when the usual crops ought to be gathered. The return to the plateau of

Prospect Heights would, therefore, be followed by extensive agricultural labors, interrupted only by the projected expedition through the island.

It can, therefore, be well understood how injurious this seclusion in the corral must be to the colonists.

But if they were compelled to bow before necessity, they did not do so without impatience.

Once or twice the reporter ventured out into the road and made the tour of the palisade. Top accompanied him, and Gideon Spilett, his gun cocked, was ready for any emergency.

He met with no misadventure and found no suspicious traces. His dog would have warned him of any danger, and, as Top did not bark, it might be concluded that there was nothing to fear at the moment at least, and that the convicts were occupied in another part of the island.

However, on his second sortie, on the 27th of November, Gideon Spilett, who had ventured a quarter of a mile into the woods, towards the south of the mountain, remarked that Top scented something. The dog had no longer his unconcerned manner; he went backwards and forwards, ferreting among the grass and bushes as if his smell had revealed some suspicious object to him.

Gideon Spilett followed Top, encouraged him, excited him by his voice, while keeping a sharp look-out, his gun ready to fire, and sheltering himself behind the trees. It was not probable that Top scented the presence of man, for in that case, he would have announced it by half-uttered, sullen, angry barks. Now, as he did not growl, it was because danger was neither near nor approaching.

Nearly five minutes passed thus, Top rummaging, the reporter following him prudently when, all at once, the dog rushed towards a thick bush, and drew out a rag.

It was a piece of cloth, stained and torn, which Spilett immediately brought back to the corral. There it was examined by the colonists, who found that it was a fragment of Ayrton's waistcoat, a piece of that felt, manufactured solely by the Granite House factory.

"You see, Pencroft," observed Harding, "there has been resistance on the part of the unfortunate Ayrton. The convicts have dragged him away in spite of himself! Do you still doubt his honesty?"

"No, captain," answered the sailor, "and I repented of my suspicion a long time ago! But it seems to me that something may be learned from the incident."

"What is that?" asked the reporter.

"It is that Ayrton was not killed at the corral! That they dragged him away living, since he has resisted. Therefore, perhaps, he is still living!"

"Perhaps, indeed," replied the engineer, who remained thoughtful.

This was a hope, to which Ayrton's companions could still hold. Indeed, they had before believed that, surprised in the corral, Ayrton had fallen by a bullet, as Herbert had fallen. But if the convicts had not killed him at first, if they had brought him living to another part of the island, might it not be admitted that he was still their prisoner? Perhaps, even, one of them had found in Ayrton his old Australian companion Ben Joyce, the chief of the escaped convicts. And who knows but that they had conceived the impossible hope of bringing back Ayrton to themselves? He would have been very useful to them, if they had been able to make him turn traitor!

This incident was, therefore, favourably interpreted at the corral, and it no longer appeared impossible that they should find Ayrton again. On his side, if he was only a prisoner, Ayrton would no doubt do all he could to escape from the hands of the villains, and this would be a powerful aid to the settlers!

"At any rate," observed Gideon Spilett, "if happily Ayrton did manage to escape, he would go directly to Granite House, for he could not know of the attempted assassination of which Herbert has been a victim, and consequently would never think of our being imprisoned in the corral."

"Oh! I wish that he was there, at Granite House!" cried Pencroft, "and that we were there, too! For, although the rascals can do nothing to our house, they may plunder the plateau, our plantations, our poultry-yard!"

Pencroft had become a thorough farmer, heartily attached to his crops. But it must be said that Herbert was more anxious than any to return to Granite House, for he knew how much the presence of the settlers was needed there. And it was he who was keeping them at the corral! Therefore, one idea occupied his mind—to leave the corral, and when! He believed he could bear removal to Granite House. He was sure his strength would return more quickly in his room, with the air and sight of the sea!

Several times he pressed Gideon Spilett, but the latter, fearing, with good reason, that Herbert's wounds, half healed, might reopen on the way, did not give the order to start.

However, something occurred which compelled Cyrus Harding and his two friends to yield to the lad's wish, and God alone knew that this determination might cause them grief and remorse.

It was the 29th of November, seven o'clock in the evening. The three settlers were talking in Herbert's room, when they heard Top utter quick barks.

Harding, Pencroft, and Spilett seized their guns and ran out of the house. Top, at the foot of the palisade, was jumping, barking, but it was with pleasure, not anger.

"Someone is coming."

"Yes."

"It is not an enemy!"

"Neb, perhaps?"

"Or Ayrton?"

These words had hardly been exchanged between the engineer and his two companions when a body leaped over the palisade and fell on the ground inside the corral.

It was Jup, Master Jup in person, to whom Top immediately gave a most cordial reception.

"Jup!" exclaimed Pencroft.

"Neb has sent him to us," said the reporter.

"Then," replied the engineer, "he must have some note on him."

Pencroft rushed up to the orang. Certainly if Neb had any important matter to communicate to his master he could not employ a more sure or more rapid messenger, who could pass where neither the colonists could, nor even Top himself.

Cyrus Harding was not mistaken. At Jup's neck hung a small bag, and in this bag was found a little note traced by Neb's hand.

The despair of Harding and his companions may be imagined when they read these words:—

Friday, six o'clock in the morning.
Plateau invaded by convicts.

NEB

They gazed at each other without uttering a word, then they re-entered the house. What were they to do? The convicts on Prospect Heights! that was disaster, devastation, ruin.

Herbert, on seeing the engineer, the reporter, and Pencroft re-enter, guessed that their situation was aggravated, and when he saw Jup, he no longer doubted that some misfortune menaced Granite House.

"Captain Harding," said he, "I must go; I can bear the journey. I must go."

Gideon Spilett approached Herbert; then, having looked at him—

"Let us go, then!" said he.

The question was quickly decided whether Herbert should be carried on a litter or in the cart which had brought Ayrton to the corral. The motion of the litter would have been more easy for the wounded lad, but it would have necessitated two bearers, that is to say, there would have been two guns less for defence if an attack was made on the road. Would they not, on the contrary, by employing the cart leave every arm free? Was it impossible to place the mattress on which Herbert was lying in it, and to advance with so much care that any jolt should be avoided? It could be done.

The cart was brought. Pencroft harnessed the onager. Cyrus Harding and the reporter raised Herbert's mattress and placed it on the bottom of the cart. The weather was fine. The sun's bright rays glanced through the trees.

"Are the guns ready?" asked Cyrus Harding.

They were. The engineer and Pencroft, each armed with a double-barrelled gun, and Gideon Spilett carrying his rifle, had nothing to do but start.

"Are you comfortable, Herbert?" asked the engineer.

"Ah, captain," replied the lad, "don't be uneasy, I shall not die on the road!"

While speaking thus, it could be seen that the poor boy had called up all his energy, and by the energy of a powerful will had collected his failing strength.

The engineer felt his heart sink painfully. He still hesitated to give the signal for departure; but that would have driven Herbert to despair—killed him perhaps.

"Forward!" said Harding.

The gate of the corral was opened. Jup and Top, who knew when to be silent, ran in advance. The cart came out, the gate was reclosed, and the onager, led by Pencroft, advanced at a slow pace.

Certainly, it would have been safer to have taken a different road than that which led straight from the corral to Granite House, but the cart would have met with great difficulties in moving under the trees. It was necessary, therefore, to follow this way, although it was well known to the convicts.

Cyrus Harding and Gideon Spilett walked one on each side of the cart, ready to answer to any attack. However, it was not probable that the convicts would have yet left the plateau of Prospect Heights.

Neb's note had evidently been written and sent as soon as the convicts had shown themselves there. Now, this note was dated six o'clock in the morning, and the active orang, accustomed to come frequently to the corral, had taken scarcely three-quarters of an hour to cross the five miles which separated it from Granite House. They would, therefore, be safe at that time, and if there was any occasion for firing, it would probably not be until they were in the neighbourhood of Granite House. However, the colonists kept a strict watch. Top and Jup, the latter armed with his club, sometimes in front, sometimes beating the wood at the sides of the road, signalised no danger.

The cart advanced slowly under Pencroft's guidance. It had left the corral at half-past seven. An hour after, four out of the five miles had been cleared, without any incident having occurred. The road was as deserted as all that part of the Jacamar Wood which lay between the Mercy and the lake. There was no occasion for any warning. The wood appeared as deserted as on the day when the colonists first landed on the island.

They approached the plateau. Another mile and they would see the bridge over Creek Glycerine. Cyrus Harding expected to find it in its place; supposing that the convicts would have crossed it, and that, after having passed one of the streams which enclosed the plateau, they would have taken the precaution to lower it again, so as to keep open a retreat.

At length an opening in the trees allowed the sea-horizon to be seen. But the cart continued its progress, for not one of its defenders thought of abandoning it.

At that moment Pencroft stopped the onager, and in a hoarse voice—

"Oh! the villains!" he exclaimed.

And he pointed to a thick smoke rising from the mill, the sheds, and the buildings at the poultry-yard.

A man was moving about in the midst of the smoke. It was Neb.

His companions uttered a shout. He heard, and ran to meet them.

The convicts had left the plateau nearly half-an-hour before, having devastated it!

"And Mr. Herbert?" asked Neb.

Gideon Spilett returned to the cart.

Herbert had lost consciousness!

Chapter X

HERBERT CARRIED TO GRANITE HOUSE—NEB RELATES ALL THAT HAS HAPPENED—HARDING'S VISIT TO THE PLATEAU— RUIN AND DEVASTATION—THE COLONISTS BAFFLED BY HERBERT'S ILLNESS—WILLOW BARK—A DEADLY FEVER— TOP BARKS AGAIN!

OF THE CONVICTS, THE DANGERS WHICH MENACED GRANITE HOUSE, THE RUINS WITH which the plateau was covered, the colonists thought no longer. Herbert's critical state outweighed all other considerations. Would the removal prove fatal to him by causing some internal injury? The reporter could not affirm it, but he and his companions almost despaired of the result. The cart was brought to the bend of the river. There some branches, disposed as a litter, received the mattress on which lay the unconscious Herbert. Ten minutes after, Cyrus Harding, Spilett, and Pencroft were at the foot of the cliff, leaving Neb to take the cart on to the plateau of Prospect Heights. The lift was put in motion, and Herbert was soon stretched on his bed in Granite House.

What cares were lavished on him to bring him back to life! He smiled for a moment on finding himself in his room, but could scarcely even murmur a few words, so great was his weakness. Gideon Spilett examined his wounds. He feared to find them reopened, having been imperfectly healed. There was nothing of the sort. From whence, then, came this prostration? Why was Herbert so much worse? The lad then fell into a kind of feverish sleep, and the reporter and Pencroft remained near the bed. During this time, Harding told Neb all that had happened at the corral, and Neb recounted to his master the events of which the plateau had just been the theatre.

It was only during the preceding night that the convicts had appeared on the edge of the forest, at the approaches to Creek Glycerine. Neb, who was watching near the poultry-yard, had not hesitated to fire at one of the pirates, who was about to cross the stream; but in the darkness he could not tell whether the man had been hit or not. At any rate, it was not enough to frighten away the band, and Neb had only just time to get up to Granite House, where at least he was in safety.

But what was he to do there? How prevent the devastations with which the convicts threatened the plateau? Had Neb any means by which to warn his master? And, besides, in what situation were the inhabitants of the corral themselves? Cyrus Harding and his companions had left on the 11th of November, and it was now the 29th. It was, therefore, nineteen days since Neb had had other news than that brought by Top—disastrous news: Ayrton disappeared, Herbert severely wounded, the engineer, reporter, and sailor, as it were, imprisoned in the corral!

What was he to do? asked poor Neb. Personally he had nothing to fear, for the convicts could not reach him in Granite House. But the buildings, the plantations, all their arrangements at the mercy of the pirates! Would it not be best to let Cyrus Harding judge of what he ought to do, and to warn him, at least, of the danger which threatened him?

Neb then thought of employing Jup, and confiding a note to him. He knew the orang's great intelligence, which had been often put to the proof. Jup understood the word corral, which had been frequently pronounced before him, and it may be remembered, too, that he had often driven the cart thither in company with Pencroft. Day had not yet dawned. The active orang would know how to pass unperceived through the woods, of which the convicts, besides, would think he was a native.

Neb did not hesitate. He wrote the note, he tied it to Jup's neck, he brought the ape to the door of Granite House, from which he let down a long cord to the ground; then, several times he repeated these words—

"Jup, Jup! corral, corral!"

The creature understood, seized the cord, glided rapidly down to the beach, and disappeared in the darkness without the convicts' attention having been in the least excited.

"You did well, Neb," said Harding, "but perhaps in not warning us you would have done still better!"

And, in speaking thus, Cyrus Harding thought of Herbert, whose recovery the removal had so seriously checked.

Neb ended his account. The convicts had not appeared at all on the beach. Not knowing the number of the island's inhabitants, they might suppose that Granite House was defended by a large party. They must have remembered that during the attack by the brig numerous shot had been fired both from the lower and upper rocks, and no doubt they did not wish to expose themselves. But the plateau of Prospect Heights was open to them, and not covered by the fire of Granite House. They gave themselves up, therefore, to their instinct of destruction—plundering, burning, devastating everything—and only retiring half-an-hour before the arrival of the colonists, whom they believed still confined in the corral.

On their retreat, Neb hurried out. He climbed the plateau at the risk of being perceived and fired at, tried to extinguish the fire which was consuming the buildings of the poultry-yard, and had struggled, though in vain, against it until the cart appeared at the edge of the wood.

Such had been these serious events. The presence of the convicts constituted a permanent source of danger to the settlers in Lincoln Island, until then so happy, and who might now expect still greater misfortunes.

Spilett remained in Granite House with Herbert and Pencroft, while Cyrus Harding, accompanied by Neb, proceeded to judge for himself of the extent of the disaster.

It was fortunate that the convicts had not advanced to the foot of Granite House. The workshop at the Chimneys would in that case not have escaped destruction. But after all, this evil would have been more easily reparable than the ruins accumulated on the plateau of Prospect Heights. Harding and Neb proceeded towards the Mercy, and ascended its left bank without meeting with any trace of the convicts; nor on the other side of the river, in the depths of the wood, could they perceive any suspicious indications.

Besides, it might be supposed that in all probability either the convicts knew of the return of the settlers to Granite House, by having seen them pass on the road from the corral, or, after the devastation of the plateau, they had penetrated into Jacamar Wood, following the course of the Mercy, and were thus ignorant of their return.

In the former case, they must have returned towards the corral, now without defenders, and which contained valuable stores.

In the latter, they must have regained their encampment, and would wait an opportunity to recommence the attack.

It was, therefore, possible to prevent them, but any enterprise to clear the island was now rendered difficult by reason of Herbert's condition. Indeed, their whole force would have been barely sufficient to cope with the convicts, and just now no one could leave Granite House.

The engineer and Neb arrived on the plateau. Desolation reigned everywhere. The fields had been trampled over; the ears of wheat, which were nearly full-grown, lay on the ground. The other plantations had not suffered less.

The kitchen-garden was destroyed. Happily, Granite House possessed a store of seed which would enable them to repair these misfortunes.

As to the wall and buildings of the poultry-yard and the onagers' stable, the fire had destroyed all. A few terrified creatures roamed over the plateau. The birds, which during the fire had taken refuge on the waters of the lake, had already returned to their accustomed spot, and were dabbling on the banks. Everything would have to be reconstructed.

Cyrus Harding's face, which was paler than usual, expressed an internal anger which he commanded with difficulty, but he did not utter a word. Once more he looked at his devastated fields, and at the smoke which still rose from the ruins, then he returned to Granite House.

The following days were the saddest of any that the colonists had passed on the island! Herbert's weakness visibly increased. It appeared that a more serious malady, the consequence of the profound physiological disturbance he had gone through, threatened to declare itself, and Gideon Spilett feared such an aggravation of his condition that he would be powerless to fight against it!

In fact, Herbert remained in an almost continuous state of drowsiness, and symptoms of delirium began to manifest themselves. Refreshing drinks were the only remedies at the colonists' disposal. The fever was not as yet very high, but it soon appeared that it would probably recur at regular intervals. Gideon Spilett first recognised this on the 6th of December.

The poor boy, whose fingers, nose, and ears had become extremely pale, was at first seized with slight shiverings, horripilations, and tremblings. His pulse was weak and irregular, his skin dry, his thirst intense. To this soon succeeded a hot fit; his face became flushed; his skin reddened; his pulse quick; then a profuse perspiration broke out, after which the fever seemed to diminish. The attack had lasted nearly five hours.

Gideon Spilett had not left Herbert, who, it was only too certain was now seized by an intermittent fever, and this fever must be cured at any cost before it should assume a more serious aspect.

"And in order to cure it," said Spilett to Cyrus Harding, "we need a febrifuge."

"A febrifuge—" answered the engineer. "We have neither Peruvian bark, nor sulphate of quinine."

"No," said Gideon Spilett, "but there are willows on the border of the lake, and the bark of the willow might, perhaps, prove to be a substitute for quinine."

"Let us try it without losing a moment," replied Cyrus Harding.

The bark of the willow has, indeed, been justly considered as a succedaneum for Peruvian bark, as has also that of the horse-chestnut-tree, the leaf of the holly, the snakeroot, etc. It was evidently necessary to make trial of this substance, although not so valuable as Peruvian bark, and to employ it in its natural state, since they had no means for extracting its essence.

Cyrus Harding went himself to cut from the trunk of a species of black willow, a few pieces of bark; he brought them back to Granite House, and reduced them to a powder, which was administered that same evening to Herbert.

The night passed without any important change. Herbert was somewhat delirious, but the fever did not reappear in the night, and did not return either during the following day.

Pencroft again began to hope. Gideon Spilett said nothing. It might be that the fever was not quotidian, but tertian, and that it would return next day. Therefore, he awaited the next day with the greatest anxiety.

It might have been remarked besides that during this period Herbert remained utterly prostrate, his head weak and giddy. Another symptom alarmed the reporter to the highest degree. Herbert's liver became congested, and soon a more intense delirium showed that his brain was also affected.

Gideon Spilett was overwhelmed by this new complication. He took the engineer aside. "It is a malignant fever," said he.

"A malignant fever!" cried Harding. "You are mistaken, Spilett. A malignant fever does not declare itself spontaneously; its germ must previously have existed."

"I am not mistaken," replied the reporter. "Herbert no doubt contracted the germ of this fever in the marshes of the island. He has already had one attack; should a second come on and should we not be able to prevent a third, he is lost."

"But the willow bark?"

"That is insufficient," answered the reporter, "and the third attack of a malignant fever, which is not arrested by means of quinine, is always fatal."

Fortunately, Pencroft heard nothing of this conversation or he would have gone mad.

It may be imagined what anxiety the engineer and the reporter suffered during the day of the 7th of December and the following night.

Towards the middle of the day the second attack came on. The crisis was terrible. Herbert felt himself sinking. He stretched his arms towards Cyrus Harding, towards Spilett, towards Pencroft. He was so young to die! The scene was heartrending. They were obliged to send Pencroft away.

The fit lasted five hours. It was evident that Herbert could not survive a third.

The night was frightful. In his delirium Herbert uttered words which went to the hearts of his companions. He struggled with the convicts, he called to Ayrton, he poured forth entreaties to that mysterious being—that powerful unknown protector—whose image was stamped upon his mind; then he again fell into a deep exhaustion which completely prostrated him. Several times Gideon Spilett thought that the poor boy was dead.

The next day, the 8th of December, was but a succession of the fainting fits. Herbert's thin hands clutched the sheets. They had administered further doses of pounded bark, but the reporter expected no result from it.

"If before to-morrow morning we have not given him a more energetic febrifuge," said the reporter, "Herbert will be dead."

Night arrived—the last night, it was too much to be feared, of the good, brave, intelligent boy, so far in advance of his years, and who was loved by all as their own child. The only remedy which existed against this terrible malignant fever, the only specific which could overcome it, was not to be found in Lincoln Island.

During the night of the 8th of December, Herbert was seized by a more violent delirium. His liver was fearfully congested, his brain affected, and already it was impossible for him to recognise anyone.

Would he live until the next day, until that third attack which must infallibly carry him off? It was not probable. His strength was exhausted, and in the intervals of fever he lay as one dead.

Towards three o'clock in the morning Herbert uttered a piercing cry. He seemed to be torn by a supreme convulsion. Neb, who was near him, terrified, ran into the next room where his companions were watching.

Top, at that moment, barked in a strange manner.

All rushed in immediately and managed to restrain the dying boy, who was endeavouring to throw himself out of his bed, while Spilett, taking his arm, felt his pulse gradually quicken.

It was five in the morning. The rays of the rising sun began to shine in at the windows of Granite House. It promised to be a fine day, and this day was to be poor Herbert's last!

A ray glanced on the table placed near the bed.

Suddenly Pencroft, uttering a cry, pointed to the table.

On it lay a little oblong box, of which the cover bore these words:—
"Sulphate of Quinine."

Chapter XI

INEXPLICABLE MYSTERY—HERBERT'S CONVALESCENCE—THE PARTS OF THE ISLAND TO BE EXPLORED—PREPARATIONS FOR DEPARTURE—FIRST DAY—NIGHT—SECOND DAY—KAURIES— A COUPLE OF CASSOWARIES—FOOTPRINTS IN THE FOREST— ARRIVAL AT REPTILE POINT

GIDEON SPILETT TOOK THE BOX AND OPENED IT. IT CONTAINED NEARLY TWO HUNDRED grains of a white powder, a few particles of which he carried to his lips. The extreme bitterness of the substance precluded all doubt; it was certainly the precious extract of quinine, that pre-eminent antifebrile.

This powder must be administered to Herbert without delay. How it came there might be discussed later.

"Some coffee!" said Spilett.

In a few moments Neb brought a cup of the warm infusion. Gideon Spilett threw into it about eighteen grains of quinine, and they succeeded in making Herbert drink the mixture.

There was still time, for the third attack of the malignant fever had not yet shown itself. How they longed to be able to add that it would not return!

Besides, it must be remarked, the hopes of all had now revived. The mysterious influence had been again exerted, and in a critical moment, when they had despaired of it.

In a few hours Herbert was much calmer. The colonists could now discuss this incident. The intervention of the stranger was more evident than ever. But how had he been able to penetrate during the night into Granite House? It was inexplicable, and, in truth, the proceedings of the genius of the island were not less mysterious than was that genius himself. During this day the sulphate of quinine was administered to Herbert every three hours.

The next day some improvement in Herbert's condition was apparent. Certainly, he was not out of danger, intermittent fevers being subject to frequent and dangerous relapses, but the most assiduous care was bestowed on him. And besides, the specific was at hand; nor, doubtless, was he who had brought it far distant! and the hearts of all were animated by returning hope.

This hope was not disappointed. Ten days after, on the 20th of December, Herbert's convalescence commenced.

He was still weak, and strict diet had been imposed upon him, but no access of fever supervened. And then, the poor boy submitted with such docility to all the prescriptions ordered him! He longed so to get well!

Pencroft was as a man who has been drawn up from the bottom of an abyss. Fits of joy approaching delirium seized him. When the time for the third attack had passed by, he nearly suffocated the reporter in his embrace. Since then, he always called him Dr. Spilett.

The real doctor, however, remained undiscovered.

"We will find him!" repeated the sailor.

Certainly, this man, whoever he was, might expect a somewhat too energetic embrace from the worthy Pencroft!

The month of December ended, and with it the year 1867, during which the colonists of Lincoln Island had of late been so severely tried. They commenced the year 1868 with magnificent weather, great heat, and a tropical temperature, delightfully cooled by the sea-breeze. Herbert's recovery progressed, and from his bed, placed near one of the windows of Granite House, he could inhale the fresh air, charged with ozone, which could not fail to restore his health. His appetite returned, and what numberless delicate, savoury little dishes Neb prepared for him!

"It is enough to make one wish to have a fever oneself!" said Pencroft.

During all this time, the convicts did not once appear in the vicinity of Granite House. There was no news of Ayrton, and though the engineer and Herbert still had some hopes of finding him again, their companions did not doubt but that the unfortunate man had perished. However, this uncertainty could not last, and when once the lad should have recovered, the expedition, the result of which must be so important, would be undertaken. But they would have to wait a month, perhaps, for all the strength of the colony must be put into requisition to obtain satisfaction from the convicts.

However, Herbert's convalescence progressed rapidly. The congestion of the liver had disappeared, and his wounds might be considered completely healed.

During the month of January, important work was done on the plateau of Prospect Heights; but it consisted solely in saving as much as was possible from the devastated crops, either of corn or vegetables. The grain and the plants were gathered, so as to provide a new harvest for the approaching half-season. With regard to rebuilding the poultry-yard, wall, or stables, Cyrus Harding preferred to wait. While he and his companions were in pursuit of the convicts, the latter might very probably pay another visit to the plateau, and it would be useless to give them an opportunity of recommencing their work of destruction. When the island should be cleared of these miscreants, they would set about rebuilding. The young convalescent began to get up in the second week of January, at first for one hour a day, then two, then three. His strength visibly returned, so vigourous was his constitution. He was now eighteen years of age. He was tall, and promised to become a man of noble and commanding presence. From this time his recovery, while still requiring care—and Dr. Spilett was very strict—made rapid progress. Towards the end of the month, Herbert was already walking about on Prospect Heights, and the beach.

He derived, from several sea-baths, which he took in company with Pencroft and Neb, the greatest possible benefit. Cyrus Harding thought he might now settle the day for their departure, for which the 15th of February was fixed. The nights, very clear at this time of year, would be favourable to the researches they intended to make all over the island.

The necessary preparations for this exploration were now commenced, and were important, for the colonists had sworn not to return to Granite House until their twofold object had been achieved; on the one hand, to exterminate the convicts, and rescue Ayrton, if he was still living; on the other, to discover who it was that presided so effectually over the fortunes of the colony.

Of Lincoln Island, the settlers knew thoroughly all the eastern coast from Claw Cape to the Mandible Capes, the extensive Tadorn Marsh, the neighbourhood of Lake Grant, Jacamar Wood, between the road to the corral and the Mercy, the courses of the Mercy and Red Creek, and lastly, the spurs of Mount Franklin, among which the corral had been established.

They had explored, though only in an imperfect manner, the vast shore of Washington Bay from Claw Cape to Reptile End, the woody and marshy border of the west coast, and the interminable downs, ending at the open mouth of Shark Gulf. But they had in no way surveyed the woods which covered the Serpentine Peninsula, all to the right of the Mercy, the left bank of Falls River, and the wilderness of spurs and valleys which supported three-quarters of the base of Mount Franklin, to the east, the north, and the west, and where doubtless many secret retreats existed. Consequently, many millions of acres of the island had still escaped their investigations.

It was, therefore, decided that the expedition should be carried through the Far West, so as to include all that region situated on the right of the Mercy.

It might, perhaps, be better worthwhile to go direct to the corral, where it might be supposed that the convicts had again taken refuge, either to pillage or to establish themselves there. But either the devastation of the corral would have been an accomplished fact by this time, and it would be too late to prevent it, or it had been the convicts' interest to entrench themselves there, and there would be still time to go and turn them out on their return.

Therefore, after some discussion, the first plan was adhered to, and the settlers resolved to proceed through the wood to Reptile End. They would make their way with their hatchets, and thus lay the first draft of a road which would place Granite House in communication with the end of the peninsula for a length of from sixteen to seventeen miles.

The cart was in good condition. The onagers, well rested, could go a long journey. Provisions, camp effects, a portable stove, and various utensils were packed in the cart, as also weapons and ammunition, carefully chosen from the now complete arsenal of Granite House. But it was necessary to remember that the convicts were, perhaps, roaming about the woods, and that in the midst of these thick forests a shot might quickly be fired and received. It was therefore resolved that the little band of settlers should remain together and not separate under any pretext whatever.

It was also decided that no one should remain at Granite House. Top and Jup themselves were to accompany the expedition; the inaccessible dwelling needed no guard. The 14th of February, eve of the departure, was Sunday. It was consecrated entirely to repose, and thanksgivings addressed by the colonists to the Creator. A place in the cart was reserved for Herbert, who, though thoroughly convalescent, was still a little weak. The next morning, at daybreak, Cyrus Harding took the necessary measures to protect Granite House from any invasion. The ladders, which were formerly used for the ascent, were brought to the Chimneys and buried deep in the sand, so that they might be available on the return of the colonists, for the machinery of the lift had been taken to pieces, and nothing of the apparatus remained. Pencroft stayed the last in Granite House in order to finish this work, and he then lowered himself down by means of a double rope held below, and which, when once hauled down, left no communication between the upper landing and the beach.

The weather was magnificent.

"We shall have a warm day of it," said the reporter, laughing.

"Pooh! Dr. Spilett," answered Pencroft, "we shall walk under the shade of the trees and shan't even see the sun!"

"Forward!" said the engineer.

The cart was waiting on the beach before the Chimneys. The reporter made Herbert take his place in it during the first hours at least of the journey, and the lad was obliged to submit to his doctor's orders.

Neb placed himself at the onagers' heads. Cyrus Harding, the reporter, and the sailor, walked in front. Top bounded joyfully along. Herbert offered a seat in his vehicle to Jup, who accepted it without ceremony. The moment for departure had arrived, and the little band set out.

The cart first turned the angle of the mouth of the Mercy, then, having ascended the left bank for a mile, crossed the bridge, at the other side of which commenced the road to Port Balloon, and there the explorers, leaving this road on their left, entered the cover of the immense woods which formed the region of the Far West.

For the first two miles the widely scattered trees allowed the cart to pass with ease; from time to time it became necessary to cut away a few creepers and bushes, but no serious obstacle impeded the progress of the colonists.

The thick foliage of the trees threw a grateful shade on the ground. Deodars, Douglas-firs, casuarinas, banksias, gum-trees, dragon-trees, and other well-known species, succeeded each other far as the eye could reach. The feathered tribes of the island were all represented—tétras, jacamars, pheasants, lories, as well as the chattering cockatoos, parrots, and paroquets. Agouties, kangaroos, and capybaras fled swiftly at their approach; and all this reminded the settlers of the first excursions they had made on their arrival at the island.

"Nevertheless," observed Cyrus Harding, "I notice that these creatures, both birds and quadrupeds, are more timid than formerly. These woods have, therefore, been recently traversed by the convicts, and we shall certainly find some traces of them."

And, in fact, in several places they could distinguish traces, more or less recent, of the passage of a band of men—here branches broken off the trees, perhaps to mark out the way; there the ashes of a fire, and footprints in clayey spots; but nothing which appeared to belong to a settled encampment.

The engineer had recommended his companions to refrain from hunting. The reports of the fire-arms might give the alarm to the convicts, who were, perhaps, roaming through the forest. Moreover, the hunters would necessarily ramble some distance from the cart, which it was dangerous to leave unguarded.

In the after-part of the day, when about six miles from Granite House, their progress became much more difficult. In order to make their way through some thickets, they were obliged to cut down trees. Before entering such places Harding was careful to send in Top and Jup, who faithfully accomplished their commission, and when the dog and orang returned without giving any warning, there was evidently nothing to fear, either from convicts or wild beasts, two varieties of the animal kingdom, whose ferocious instincts placed them on the same level. On the evening of the first day the colonists encamped about nine miles from Granite House, on the border of a little stream falling into the Mercy, and of the existence of which they had till then been ignorant; it evidently, however, belonged to the hydrographical system to which the soil owed its astonishing fertility. The settlers made a hearty meal, for their appetites were sharpened, and measures were then taken that the night might be passed in safety. If the engineer had had only to deal with wild beasts, jaguars or others, he would have simply lighted fires all around his camp, which would have sufficed for its defence; but the convicts would be rather attracted than terrified by the flames, and it was, therefore, better to be surrounded by the profound darkness of night.

The watch was, however, carefully organised. Two of the settlers were to watch together, and every two hours it was agreed that they should be relieved by their comrades. And so, notwithstanding his wish to the contrary, Herbert was exempted from guard, Pencroft and Gideon Spilett in one party, the engineer and Neb in another, mounted guard in turns over the camp.

The night, however, was but of few hours. The darkness was due rather to the thickness of the foliage than to the disappearance of the sun. The silence was scarcely disturbed by the howling of jaguars and the chattering of the monkeys, the latter appearing to particularly irritate Master Jup. The night passed without incident, and on the next day, the 15th of February, the journey through the forest, rather tedious than difficult, was continued. This day they could not accomplish more than six miles, for every moment they were obliged to cut a road with their hatchets.

Like true settlers, the colonists spared the largest and most beautiful trees, which would besides have cost immense labour to fell, and the small ones only were sacrificed, but the result was that the road took a very winding direction, and lengthened itself by numerous detours.

During the day Herbert discovered several new specimens not before met with in the island, such as the tree-fern, with its leaves spread out like the waters of a fountain, locust-trees, on the long pods of which the onagers browsed greedily, and which supplied a sweet pulp of excellent flavour. There, too, the colonists again found groups of magnificent kauries, their cylindrical trunks, crowded with a cone of verdure, rising to a height of two hundred feet. These were the tree-kings of New Zealand, as celebrated as the cedars of Lebanon.

As to the fauna, there was no addition to those species already known to the hunters. Nevertheless, they saw, though unable to get near them, a couple of those large birds peculiar to Australia, a sort of cassowary, called emu, five feet in height, and with brown plumage, which belong to the tribe of waders. Top darted after them as fast as his four legs could carry him, but the emus distanced him with ease, so prodigious was their speed.

As to the traces left by the convicts, a few more were discovered. Some footprints found near an apparently recently extinguished fire were attentively examined by the settlers. By measuring them one after the other, according to their length and breadth, the marks of five men's feet were easily distinguished. The five convicts had evidently camped on this spot; but—and this was the object of so minute an examination—a sixth footprint could not be discovered, which in that case would have been that of Ayrton.

"Ayrton was not with them!" said Herbert.

"No," answered Pencroft, "and if he was not with them, it was because the wretches had already murdered him! but then these rascals have not a den to which they may be tracked like tigers!"

"No," replied the reporter, "it is more probable that they wander at random, and it is their interest to rove about until the time when they will be masters of the island!"

"The masters of the island!" exclaimed the sailor; "the masters of the island! . . ." he repeated, and his voice was choked, as if his throat was seized in an iron grasp. Then in a calmer tone, "Do you know, Captain Harding," said he, "what the ball is which I have rammed into my gun?"

"No, Pencroft!"

"It is the ball that went through Herbert's chest, and I promise you it won't miss its mark!"

But this just retaliation would not bring Ayrton back to life, and from the examination of the footprints left in the ground, they must, alas! conclude that all hopes of ever seeing him again must be abandoned.

That evening they encamped fourteen miles from Granite House, and Cyrus Harding calculated that they could not be more than five miles from Reptile Point.

And, indeed, the next day the extremity of the peninsula was reached, and the whole length of the forest had been traversed; but there was nothing to indicate the retreat in which the convicts had taken refuge, nor that, no less secret, which sheltered the mysterious unknown.

Chapter XII

EXPLORATION OF THE SERPENTINE PENINSULA—ENCAMPMENT AT THE MOUTH OF FALLS RIVER—GIDEON SPILETT AND PENCROFT RECONNOITRE—THEIR RETURN—FORWARD, ALL!— AN OPEN DOOR—A LIGHTED WINDOW— BY THE LIGHT OF THE MOON!

THE NEXT DAY, THE 18TH OF FEBRUARY, WAS DEVOTED TO THE EXPLORATION OF ALL that wooded region forming the shore from Reptile End to Falls River. The colonists were able to search this forest thoroughly, for, as it was comprised between the two shores of the Serpentine Peninsula, it was only from three to four miles in breadth. The trees, both by their height and their thick foliage, bore witness to the vegetative power of the soil, more astonishing here than in any other part of the island. One might have said that a corner from the virgin forests of America or Africa had been transported into this temperate zone. This led them to conclude that the superb vegetation found a heat in this soil, damp in its upper layer, but warmed in the interior by volcanic fires, which could not belong to a temperate climate. The most frequently occurring trees were kauries and eucalypti of gigantic dimensions.

But the colonists' object was not simply to admire the magnificent vegetation. They knew already that in this respect Lincoln Island would have been worthy to take the first rank in the Canary group, to which the first name given was that of the Happy Isles. Now, alas! their island no longer belonged to them entirely; others had taken possession of it, miscreants polluted its shores, and they must be destroyed to the last man.

No traces were found on the western coast, although they were carefully sought for. No more footprints, no more broken branches, no more deserted camps.

"This does not surprise me," said Cyrus Harding to his companions. "The convicts first landed on the island in the neighbourhood of Flotsam Point, and they immediately plunged into the Far West forests, after crossing Tadorn Marsh. They then followed almost the same route that we took on leaving Granite House. This explains the traces we found in the wood. But, arriving on the shore, the convicts saw at once that they would discover no suitable retreat there, and it was then that, going northwards again, they came upon the corral."

"Where they have perhaps returned," said Pencroft.

"I do not think so," answered the engineer, "for they would naturally suppose that our researches would be in that direction. The corral is only a store-house to them, and not a definitive encampment."

"I am of Cyrus' opinion," said the reporter, "and I think that it is among the spurs of Mount Franklin that the convicts will have made their lair."

"Then, captain, straight to the corral!" cried Pencroft. "We must finish them off, and till now we have only lost time!"

"No, my friend," replied the engineer; "you forget that we have a reason for wishing to know if the forests of the Far West do not contain some habitation. Our exploration has a double object, Pencroft. If, on the one hand, we have to chastise crime, we have, on the other, an act of gratitude to perform."

"That was well said, captain," replied the sailor, "but, all the same, it is my opinion that we shall not find the gentleman until he pleases."

And truly Pencroft only expressed the opinion of all. It was probable that the stranger's retreat was not less mysterious than was he himself.

That evening the cart halted at the mouth of Falls River. The camp was organised as usual, and the customary precautions were taken for the night. Herbert, become again the healthy and vigourous lad he was before his illness, derived great benefit from this life in the open air, between the sea-breezes and the vivifying air from the forests. His place was no longer in the cart, but at the head of the troop.

The next day, the 19th of February, the colonists, leaving the shore, where, beyond the mouth, basalts of every shape were so picturesquely piled up, ascended the river by its left bank. The road had been already partly cleared in their former excursions made from the corral to the west coast. The settlers were now about six miles from Mount Franklin.

The engineer's plan was this:—To minutely survey the valley forming the bed of the river, and to cautiously approach the neighbourhood of the corral; if the corral was occupied, to seize it by force; if it was not, to entrench themselves there and make it the centre of the operations which had for their object the exploration of Mount Franklin.

This plan was unanimously approved by the colonists, for they were impatient to regain entire possession of their island.

They made their way then along the narrow valley separating two of the largest spurs of Mount Franklin. The trees, crowded on the river's bank, became rare on the upper slopes of the mountain. The ground was hilly and rough, very suitable for ambushes, and over which they did not venture without extreme precaution. Top and Jup skirmished on the flanks, springing right and left through the thick brushwood, and emulating each other in intelligence and activity. But nothing showed that the banks of the stream had been recently frequented—nothing announced either the presence or the proximity of the convicts. Towards five in the evening the cart stopped nearly 600 feet from the palisade. A semicircular screen of trees still hid it.

It was necessary to reconnoitre the corral, in order to ascertain if it was occupied. To go there openly, in broad daylight, when the convicts were probably in ambush, would be to expose themselves, as poor Herbert had done, to the fire-arms of the ruffians. It was better, then, to wait until night came on.

However, Gideon Spilett wished without further delay to reconnoitre the approaches to the corral, and Pencroft, who was quite out of patience, volunteered to accompany him.

"No, my friends," said the engineer, "wait till night. I will not allow one of you to expose himself in open day."

"But, captain—" answered the sailor, little disposed to obey.

"I beg of you, Pencroft," said the engineer.

"Very well!" replied the sailor, who vented his anger in another way, by bestowing on the convicts the worst names in his maritime vocabulary.

The colonists remained, therefore, near the cart, and carefully watched the neighbouring parts of the forest.

Three hours passed thus. The wind had fallen, and absolute silence reigned under the great trees. The snapping of the smallest twig, a footstep on the dry leaves, the gliding of a body among the grass, would have been heard without difficulty. All was quiet. Besides, Top, lying on the grass, his head stretched out on his paws, gave no sign of uneasiness. At eight o'clock the day appeared far enough advanced for the reconnaissance to be made under favourable conditions. Gideon Spilett declared himself ready to set out accompanied by Pencroft. Cyrus Harding consented. Top and Jup were to remain with the engineer, Herbert, and Neb, for a bark or a cry at a wrong moment would give the alarm.

"Do not be imprudent," said Harding to the reporter and Pencroft, "you have not to gain possession of the corral, but only to find out whether it is occupied or not."

"All right," answered Pencroft.

And the two departed.

Under the trees, thanks to the thickness of their foliage, the obscurity rendered any object invisible beyond a radius of from thirty to forty feet. The reporter and Pencroft, halting at any suspicious sound, advanced with great caution.

They walked a little distance apart from each other so as to offer a less mark for a shot. And, to tell the truth, they expected every moment to hear a report. Five minutes after leaving the cart, Gideon Spilett and Pencroft arrived at the edge of the wood before the clearing beyond which rose the palisade.

They stopped. A few straggling beams still fell on the field clear of trees. Thirty feet distant was the gate of the corral, which appeared to be closed. This thirty feet, which it was necessary to cross from the wood to the palisade, constituted the dangerous zone, to coin a term: in fact, one or more bullets fired from behind the palisade might knock over anyone who ventured on to this zone. Gideon Spilett and the sailor were not men to draw back, but they knew that any imprudence on their part, of which they would be the first victims, would fall afterwards on their companions. If they themselves were killed, what would become of Harding, Neb, and Herbert?

But Pencroft, excited at feeling himself so near the corral where he supposed the convicts had taken refuge, was about to press forward, when the reporter held him back with a grasp of iron.

"In a few minutes it will be quite dark," whispered Spilett in the sailor's ear, "then will be the time to act."

Pencroft, convulsively clasping the butt-end of his gun, restrained his energies, and waited, swearing to himself.

Soon the last of the twilight faded away. Darkness, which seemed as if it issued from the dense forest, covered the clearing. Mount Franklin rose like an enormous screen before the western horizon, and night spread rapidly over all, as it does in regions of low latitudes. Now was the time.

The reporter and Pencroft, since posting themselves on the edge of the wood, had not once lost sight of the palisade. The corral appeared to be absolutely deserted. The top of the palisade formed a line, a little darker than the surrounding shadow, and nothing disturbed its distinctness. Nevertheless, if the convicts were there, they must have posted one of their number to guard against any surprise.

Spilett grasped his companion's hand, and both crept towards the corral, their guns ready to fire.

They reached the gate without the darkness being illuminated by a single ray of light.

Pencroft tried to push open the gate, which, as the reporter and he had supposed, was closed. However, the sailor was able to ascertain that the outer bars had not been put up. It might, then, be concluded that the convicts were there in the corral, and that very probably they had fastened the gate in such a way that it could not be forced open.

Gideon Spilett and Pencroft listened.

Not a sound could be heard inside the palisade. The musmons and the goats, sleeping no doubt in their huts, in no way disturbed the calm of night.

The reporter and the sailor hearing nothing, asked themselves whether they had not better scale the palisades and penetrate into the corral. This would have been contrary to Cyrus Harding's instructions.

It is true that the enterprise might succeed, but it might also fail. Now, if the convicts were suspecting nothing, if they knew nothing of the expedition against them, if, lastly, there now existed a chance of surprising them, ought this chance to be lost by inconsiderately attempting to cross the palisades?

This was not the reporter's opinion. He thought it better to wait until all the settlers were collected together before attempting to penetrate into the corral. One thing was certain, that it was possible to reach the palisade without being seen, and also that it did not appear to be guarded. This point settled, there was nothing to be done but to return to the cart, where they would consult.

Pencroft probably agreed with this decision, for he followed the reporter without making any objection when the latter turned back to the wood.

In a few minutes the engineer was made acquainted with the state of affairs.

"Well," said he, after a little thought, "I now have reason to believe that the convicts are not in the corral."

"We shall soon know," said Pencroft, "when we have scaled the palisade."

"To the corral, my friends!" said Cyrus Harding.

"Shall we leave the cart in the wood?" asked Neb.

"No," replied the engineer, "it is our wagon of ammunition and provisions, and, if necessary, it would serve as an entrenchment."

"Forward, then!" said Gideon Spilett.

The cart emerged from the wood and began to roll noiselessly towards the palisade. The darkness was now profound, the silence as complete as when Pencroft and the reporter crept over the ground. The thick grass completely muffled their footsteps.

The colonists held themselves ready to fire. Jup, at Pencroft's orders, kept behind. Neb led Top in a leash, to prevent him from bounding forward.

The clearing soon came in sight. It was deserted. Without hesitating, the little band moved towards the palisade. In a short space of time the dangerous zone was passed. Not a shot had been fired. When the cart reached the palisade, it stopped. Neb remained at the onagers' heads to hold them. The engineer, the reporter, Herbert, and Pencroft, proceeded to the door, in order to ascertain if it was barricaded inside.

It was open!

"What do you say now?" asked the engineer, turning to the sailor and Spilett.

Both were stupefied.

"I can swear," said Pencroft, "that this gate was shut just now!"

The colonists now hesitated. Were the convicts in the corral when Pencroft and the reporter made their reconnaissance? It could not be doubted, as the gate then closed could only have been opened by them. Were they still there, or had one of their number just gone out?

All these questions presented themselves simultaneously to the minds of the colonists, but how could they be answered?

At that moment, Herbert, who had advanced a few steps into the enclosure, drew back hurriedly, and seized Harding's hand.

"What's the matter?" asked the engineer.

"A light!"

"In the house?"

"Yes!"

All five advanced and indeed, through the window fronting them, they saw glimmering a feeble light. Cyrus Harding made up his mind rapidly. "It is our only chance," said he to his companions, "of finding the convicts collected in this house, suspecting nothing! They are in our power! Forward!" The colonists crossed through the enclosure, holding their guns ready in their hands. The cart had been left outside under the charge of Jup and Top, who had been prudently tied to it.

Cyrus Harding, Pencroft, and Gideon Spilett on one side, Herbert and Neb on the other, going along by the palisade, surveyed the absolutely dark and deserted corral.

In a few moments they were near the closed door of the house.

Harding signed to his companions not to stir, and approached the window, then feebly lighted by the inner light.

He gazed into the apartment.

On the table burned a lantern. Near the table was the bed formerly used by Ayrton. On the bed lay the body of a man.

Suddenly Cyrus Harding drew back, and in a hoarse voice—

"Ayrton!" he exclaimed.

Immediately the door was forced rather than opened, and the colonists rushed into the room.

Ayrton appeared to be asleep. His countenance showed that he had long and cruelly suffered. On his wrists and ankles could be seen great bruises.

Harding bent over him.

"Ayrton!" cried the engineer, seizing the arm of the man whom he had just found again under such unexpected circumstances.

At this exclamation Ayrton opened his eyes, and, gazing at Harding, then at the others—

"You!" he cried, "you?"

"Ayrton! Ayrton!" repeated Harding.

"Where am I?"

"In the house in the corral!"

"Alone?"

"Yes!"

"But they will come back!" cried Ayrton. "Defend yourselves! defend yourselves!"

And he fell back exhausted.

"Spilett," exclaimed the engineer, "we may be attacked at any moment. Bring the cart into the corral. Then barricade the door, and all come back here."

Pencroft, Neb, and the reporter hastened to execute the engineer's orders. There was not a moment to be lost. Perhaps even now the cart was in the hands of the convicts!

In a moment the reporter and his two companions had crossed the corral and reached the gate of the palisade behind which Top was heard growling sullenly.

The engineer, leaving Ayrton for an instant, came out ready to fire. Herbert was at his side. Both surveyed the crest of the spur overlooking the corral. If the convicts were lying in ambush there, they might knock the settlers over one after the other.

At that moment the moon appeared in the east, above the black curtain of the forest, and a white sheet of light spread over the interior of the enclosure. The corral, with its clumps of trees, the little stream which watered it, its wide carpet of grass, was suddenly illuminated. From the side of the mountain, the house and a part of the palisade stood out white in the moonlight. On the opposite side towards the door, the enclosure remained dark.

A black mass soon appeared. This was the cart entering the circle of light, and Cyrus Harding could hear the noise made by the door, as his companions shut it and fastened the interior bars.

But, at that moment, Top, breaking loose, began to bark furiously and rush to the back of the corral, to the right of the house.

"Be ready to fire, my friends!" cried Harding.

The colonists raised their pieces and waited the moment to fire.

Top still barked, and Jup, running towards the dog, uttered shrill cries.

The colonists followed him, and reached the borders of the little stream, shaded by large trees. And there, in the bright moonlight, what did they see? Five corpses, stretched on the bank!

They were those of the convicts who, four months previously, had landed on Lincoln Island!

Chapter XIII

AYRTON'S STORY—PLANS OF HIS FORMER ACCOMPLICES—THEIR
INSTALLATION IN THE CORRAL—THE AVENGING JUSTICE OF
LINCOLN ISLAND—THE BONADVENTURE—RESEARCHES
AROUND MOUNT FRANKLIN—THE UPPER VALLEYS—A
SUBTERRANEAN VOLCANO—PENCROFT'S OPINION—AT THE
BOTTOM OF THE CRATER—RETURN

HOW HAD IT HAPPENED? WHO HAD KILLED THE CONVICTS? WAS IT AYRTON? NO, FOR A moment before he was dreading their return.

But Ayrton was now in a profound stupor, from which it was no longer possible to rouse him. After uttering those few words he had again become unconscious, and had fallen back motionless on the bed.

The colonists, a prey to a thousand confused thoughts, under the influence of violent excitement, waited all night, without leaving Ayrton's house, or returning to the spot where lay the bodies of the convicts. It was very probable that Ayrton would not be able to throw any light on the circumstances under which the bodies had been found, since he himself was not aware that he was in the corral. But at any rate he would be in a position to give an account of what had taken place before this terrible execution. The next day Ayrton awoke from his torpor, and his companions cordially manifested all the joy they felt, on seeing him again, almost safe and sound, after a hundred and four days' separation.

Ayrton then in a few words recounted what had happened, or, at least, as much as he knew.

The day after his arrival at the corral, on the 10th of last November, at nightfall, he was surprised by the convicts, who had scaled the palisade. They bound and gagged him; then he was led to a dark cavern, at the foot of Mount Franklin, where the convicts had taken refuge.

His death had been decided upon, and the next day the convicts were about to kill him, when one of them recognised him and called him by the name which he bore in Australia. The wretches had no scruples as to murdering Ayrton! They spared Ben Joyce!

But from that moment Ayrton was exposed to the importunities of his former accomplices. They wished him to join them again, and relied upon his aid to enable them to gain possession of Granite House, to penetrate into that hitherto inaccessible dwelling, and to become masters of the island, after murdering the colonists!

Ayrton remained firm. The once convict, now repentant and pardoned, would rather die than betray his companions. Ayrton—bound, gagged, and closely watched—lived in this cave for four months.

Nevertheless the convicts had discovered the corral a short time after their arrival in the island, and since then they had subsisted on Ayrton's stores, but did not live at the corral.

On the 11th of November, two of the villains, surprised by the colonists' arrival, fired at Herbert, and one of them returned, boasting of having killed one of the inhabitants of the island; but he returned alone. His companion, as is known, fell by Cyrus Harding's dagger.

Ayrton's anxiety and despair may be imagined when he learned the news of Herbert's death. The settlers were now only four, and, as it seemed, at the mercy of the convicts. After this event, and during all the time that the colonists, detained by Herbert's illness, remained in the corral, the pirates did not leave their cavern, and even after they had pillaged the plateau of Prospect Heights, they did not think it prudent to abandon it.

The ill-treatment inflicted on Ayrton was now redoubled. His hands and feet still bore the bloody marks of the cords which bound him day and night. Every moment he expected to be put to death, nor did it appear possible that he could escape.

Matters remained thus until the third week of February. The convicts, still watching for a favourable opportunity, rarely quitted their retreat, and only made a few hunting excursions, either to the interior of the island, or the south coast.

Ayrton had no further news of his friends, and relinquished all hope of ever seeing them again. At last, the unfortunate man, weakened by ill-treatment, fell into a prostration so profound that sight and hearing failed him. From that moment, that is to say, since the last two days, he could give no information whatever of what had occurred.

"But, Captain Harding," he added, "since I was imprisoned in that cavern, how is it that I find myself in the corral?"

"How is it that the convicts are lying yonder dead, in the middle of the enclosure?" answered the engineer.

"Dead!" cried Ayrton, half rising from his bed, notwithstanding his weakness.

His companions supported him. He wished to get up, and with their assistance he did so. They then proceeded together towards the little stream.

It was now broad daylight.

There, on the bank, in the position in which they had been stricken by death in its most instantaneous form, lay the corpses of the five convicts!

Ayrton was astounded. Harding and his companions looked at him without uttering a word. On a sign from the engineer, Neb and Pencroft examined the bodies, already stiffened by the cold.

They bore no apparent trace of any wound.

Only, after carefully examining them, Pencroft found on the forehead of one, on the chest of another, on the back of this one, on the shoulder of that, a little red spot, a sort of scarcely visible bruise, the cause of which it was impossible to conjecture.

"It is there that they have been struck!" said Cyrus Harding.

"But with what weapon?" cried the reporter.

"A weapon, lightning-like in its effects, and of which we have not the secret!"

"And who has struck the blow?" asked Pencroft.

"The avenging power of the island," replied Harding, "he who brought you here, Ayrton, whose influence has once more manifested itself, who does for us all that which we cannot do for ourselves, and who, his will accomplished, conceals himself from us."

"Let us make search for him, then!" exclaimed Pencroft.

"Yes, we will search for him," answered Harding, "but we shall not discover this powerful being who performs such wonders, until he pleases to call us to him!"

This invisible protection, which rendered their own action unavailing, both irritated and piqued the engineer. The relative inferiority which it proved was of a nature to wound a haughty spirit. A generosity evinced in such a manner as to elude all tokens of gratitude, implied a sort of disdain for those on whom the obligation was conferred, which in Cyrus Harding's eyes marred, in some degree, the worth of the benefit.

"Let us search," he resumed, "and God grant that we may someday be permitted to prove to this haughty protector that he has not to deal with ungrateful people! What would I not give could we repay him, by rendering him in our turn, although at the price of our lives, some signal service!"

From this day, the thoughts of the inhabitants of Lincoln Island were solely occupied with the intended search. Everything incited them to discover the answer to this enigma, an answer which could only be the name of a man endowed with a truly inexplicable, and in some degree superhuman power.

In a few minutes, the settlers re-entered the house, where their influence soon restored to Ayrton his moral and physical energy.

Neb and Pencroft carried the corpses of the convicts into the forest, some distance from the corral, and buried them deep in the ground.

Ayrton was then made acquainted with the facts which had occurred during his seclusion. He learned Herbert's adventures, and through what various trials the colonists had passed. As to the settlers, they had despaired of ever seeing Ayrton again, and had been convinced that the convicts had ruthlessly murdered him.

"And now," said Cyrus Harding, as he ended his recital, "a duty remains for us to perform. Half of our task is accomplished, but although the convicts are no longer to be feared, it is not owing to ourselves that we are once more masters of the island."

"Well!" answered Gideon Spilett, "let us search all this labyrinth of the spurs of Mount Franklin. We will not leave a hollow, not a hole unexplored! Ah! if ever a reporter found himself face to face with a mystery, it is I who now speak to you, my friends!"

"And we will not return to Granite House until we have found our benefactor," said Herbert.

"Yes," said the engineer, "we will do all that it is humanly possible to do, but I repeat we shall not find him until he himself permits us."

"Shall we stay at the corral?" asked Pencroft.

"We shall stay here," answered Harding. "Provisions are abundant, and we are here in the very centre of the circle we have to explore. Besides, if necessary, the cart will take us rapidly to Granite House."

"Good!" answered the sailor. "Only I have a remark to make."

"What is it?"

"Here is the fine season getting on, and we must not forget that we have a voyage to make."

"A voyage?" said Gideon Spilett.

"Yes, to Tabor Island," answered Pencroft. "It is necessary to carry a notice there to point out the position of our island and say that Ayrton is here in case the Scotch yacht should come to take him off. Who knows if it is not already too late?"

"But, Pencroft," asked Ayrton, "how do you intend to make this voyage?"

"In the *Bonadventure*."

"The *Bonadventure*!" exclaimed Ayrton. "She no longer exists."

"My *Bonadventure* exists no longer!" shouted Pencroft, bounding from his seat.

"No," answered Ayrton. "The convicts discovered her in her little harbor only eight days ago, they put to sea in her, and——"

"And?" said Pencroft, his heart beating.

"And not having Bob Harvey to steer her, they ran on the rocks, and the vessel went to pieces."

"Oh, the villains, the cutthroats, the infamous scoundrels!" exclaimed Pencroft.

"Pencroft," said Herbert, taking the sailor's hand, "we will build another *Bonadventure*—a larger one. We have all the iron-work—all the rigging of the brig at our disposal."

"But do you know," returned Pencroft, "that it will take at least five or six months to build a vessel of from thirty to forty tons?"

"We can take our time," said the reporter, "and we must give up the voyage to Tabor Island for this year."

"Oh, my *Bonadventure*! my poor *Bonadventure*!" cried Pencroft, almost broken-hearted at the destruction of the vessel of which he was so proud.

The loss of the *Bonadventure* was certainly a thing to be lamented by the colonists, and it was agreed that this loss should be repaired as soon as possible. This settled, they now occupied themselves with bringing their researches to bear on the most secret parts of the island.

The exploration was commenced at daybreak on the 19th of February, and lasted an entire week. The base of the mountain, with its spurs and their numberless ramifications, formed a labyrinth of valleys and elevations. It was evident that there, in the depths of these narrow gorges, perhaps even in the interior of Mount Franklin itself, was the proper place to pursue their researches. No part of the island could have been more suitable to conceal a dwelling whose occupant wished to remain unknown. But so irregular was the formation of the valleys that Cyrus Harding was obliged to conduct the exploration in a strictly methodical manner.

The colonists first visited the valley opening to the south of the volcano, and which first received the waters of Falls River. There Ayrton showed them the cavern where the convicts had taken refuge, and in which he had been imprisoned until his removal to the corral. This cavern was just as Ayrton had left it. They found there a consider-able quantity of ammunition and provisions, conveyed thither by the convicts in order to form a reserve.

The whole of the valley bordering on the cave, shaded by fir and other trees, was thoroughly explored, and on turning the point of the south-western spur, the colonists entered a narrower gorge similar to the picturesque columns of basalt on the coast. Here the trees were fewer. Stones took the place of grass. Goats and musmons gambolled among the rocks. Here began the barren part of the island. It could already be seen that, of the numerous valleys branching off at the base of Mount Franklin, three only were wooded and rich in pasturage like that of the corral, which bordered on the west on the Falls River valley, and on the east on the Red Creek valley. These two streams, which lower down became rivers by the absorption of several tributaries, were formed by all the springs of the mountain and thus caused the fertility of its southern part. As to the Mercy, it was more directly fed from ample springs concealed under the cover of Jacamar Wood, and it was by springs of this nature, spreading in a thousand streamlets, that the soil of the Serpentine Peninsula was watered.

Now, of these three well-watered valleys, either might have served as a retreat to some solitary who would have found there everything necessary for life. But the settlers had already explored them, and in no part had they discovered the presence of man.

Was it then in the depths of those barren gorges, in the midst of the piles of rock, in the rugged northern ravines, among the streams of lava, that this dwelling and its occupant would be found?

The northern part of Mount Franklin was at its base composed solely of two valleys, wide, not very deep, without any appearance of vegetation, strewn with masses of rock, paved with lava, and varied with great blocks of mineral. This region required a long and careful exploration. It contained a thousand cavities, comfortless no doubt, but perfectly concealed and difficult of access.

The colonists even visited dark tunnels, dating from the volcanic period, still black from the passage of the fire, and penetrated into the depths of the mountain. They traversed these sombre galleries, waving lighted torches; they examined the smallest excavations; they sounded the shallowest depths, but all was dark and silent. It did not appear that the foot of man had ever before trodden these ancient passages, or that his arm had ever displaced one of these blocks, which remained as the volcano had cast them up above the waters, at the time of the submersion of the island.

However, although these passages appeared to be absolutely deserted, and the obscurity was complete, Cyrus Harding was obliged to confess that absolute silence did not reign there.

On arriving at the end of one of these gloomy caverns, extending several hundred feet into the interior of the mountain, he was surprised to hear a deep rumbling noise, increased in intensity by the sonorousness of the rocks.

Gideon Spilett, who accompanied him, also heard these distant mutterings, which indicated a revivification of the subterranean fires. Several times both listened, and they agreed that some chemical process was taking place in the bowels of the earth.

"Then the volcano is not totally extinct?" said the reporter.

"It is possible that since our exploration of the crater," replied Cyrus Harding, "some change has occurred. Any volcano, although considered extinct, may evidently again burst forth."

"But if an irruption of Mount Franklin occurred," asked Spilett, "would there not be some danger to Lincoln Island?"

"I do not think so," answered the reporter. "The crater, that is to say, the safety-valve, exists, and the overflow of smoke and lava, would escape, as it did formerly, by this customary outlet."

"Unless the lava opened a new way for itself towards the fertile parts of the island!"

"And why, my dear Spilett," answered Cyrus Harding, "should it not follow the road naturally traced out for it?"

"Well, volcanoes are capricious," returned the reporter.

"Notice," answered the engineer, "that the inclination of Mount Franklin favours the flow of water towards the valleys which we are exploring just now. To turn aside this flow, an earthquake would be necessary to change the mountain's centre of gravity."

"But an earthquake is always to be feared at these times," observed Gideon Spilett.

"Always," replied the engineer, "especially when the subterranean forces begin to awake, as they risk meeting with some obstruction, after a long rest. Thus, my dear Spilett, an irruption would be a serious thing for us, and it would be better that the volcano should not have the slightest desire to wake up. But we could not prevent it, could we? At any rate, even if it should occur, I do not think Prospect Heights would be seriously threatened. Between them and the mountain, the ground is considerably depressed, and if the lava should ever take a course towards the lake, it would be cast on the downs and the neighbouring parts of Shark Gulf."

"We have not yet seen any smoke at the top of the mountain, to indicate an approaching irruption," said Gideon Spilett.

"No," answered Harding, "not a vapour escapes from the crater, for it was only yesterday that I attentively surveyed the summit. But it is probable that at the lower part of the chimney, time may have accumulated rocks, cinders, hardened lava, and that this valve of which I spoke, may at any time become overcharged. But at the first serious effort, every obstacle will disappear, and you may be certain, my dear Spilett, that neither the island, which is the boiler, nor the volcano, which is the chimney, will burst under the pressure of gas. Nevertheless, I repeat, it would be better that there should not be an irruption."

"And yet we are not mistaken," remarked the reporter. "Mutterings can be distinctly heard in the very bowels of the volcano!"

"You are right," said the engineer, again listening attentively. "There can be no doubt of it. A commotion is going on there, of which we can neither estimate the importance nor the ultimate result."

Cyrus Harding and Spilett, on coming out, rejoined their companions, to whom they made known the state of affairs.

"Very well!" cried Pencroft, "the volcano wants to play his pranks! Let him try, if he likes! He will find his master!"

"Who?" asked Neb.

"Our good genius, Neb, our good genius, who will shut his mouth for him, if he so much as pretends to open it!"

As may be seen, the sailor's confidence in the tutelary deity of his island was absolute, and, certainly, the occult power, manifested until now in so many inexplicable ways, appeared to be unlimited; but also it knew how to escape the colonists' most minute researches, for, in spite of all their efforts, in spite of the more than zeal—the obstinacy—with which they carried on their exploration, the retreat of the mysterious being could not be discovered.

From the 19th to the 25th of February the circle of investigation was extended to all the northern region of Lincoln Island, whose most secret nooks were explored. The colonists even went the length of tapping every rock. The search was extended to the extreme verge of the mountain. It was explored thus to the very summit of the truncated cone terminating the first row of rocks, then to the upper ridge of the enormous hat, at the bottom of which opened the crater.

They did more; they visited the gulf, now extinct, but in whose depths the rumbling could be distinctly heard. However, no sign of smoke or vapour, no heating of the rock, indicated an approaching irruption. But neither there, nor in any other part of Mount Franklin, did the colonists find any traces of him of whom they were in search.

Their investigations were then directed to the downs. They carefully examined the high lava-cliffs of Shark Gulf from the base to the crest, although it was extremely difficult to reach even the level of the gulf. No one!—nothing!

Indeed, in these two words was summed up so much fatigue uselessly expended, so much energy producing no results, that somewhat of anger mingled with the discomfiture of Cyrus Harding and his companions.

It was now time to think of returning, for these researches could not be prolonged indefinitely. The colonists were certainly right in believing that the mysterious being did not reside on the surface of the island, and the wildest fancies haunted their excited imaginations. Pencroft and Neb, particularly, were not contented with the mystery, but allowed their imaginations to wander into the domain of the supernatural.

On the 25th of February the colonists re-entered Granite House, and by means of the double cord, carried by an arrow to the threshold of the door, they re-established communication between their habitation and the ground.

A month later they commemorated, on the 25th of March, the third anniversary of their arrival on Lincoln Island.

Chapter XIV

THREE YEARS HAVE PASSED—THE NEW VESSEL—WHAT IS AGREED ON—PROSPERITY OF THE COLONY—THE DOCKYARD— COLD OF THE SOUTHERN HEMISPHERE—WASHING LINEN— MOUNT FRANKLIN

THREE YEARS HAD PASSED AWAY SINCE THE ESCAPE OF THE PRISONERS FROM RICHMOND, and how often during those three years had they spoken of their country, always present in their thoughts!

They had no doubt that the civil war was at an end, and to them it appeared impossible that the just cause of the North had not triumphed. But what had been the incidents of this terrible war? How much blood had it not cost? How many of their friends must have fallen in the struggle? They often spoke of these things, without as yet being able to foresee the day when they would be permitted once more to see their country. To return thither, were it but for a few days, to renew the social link with the inhabited world, to establish a communication between their native land and their island, then to pass the longest, perhaps the best, portion of their existence in this colony, founded by them, and which would then be dependent on their country, was this a dream impossible to realise?

There were only two ways of accomplishing it—either a ship must appear off Lincoln Island, or the colonists must themselves build a vessel strong enough to sail to the nearest land.

"Unless," said Pencroft, "our good genius himself provides us with the means of returning to our country."

And, really, had anyone told Pencroft and Neb that a ship of 300 tons was waiting for them in Shark Gulf or at Port Balloon, they would not even have made a gesture of surprise. In their state of mind nothing appeared improbable.

But Cyrus Harding, less confident, advised them to confine themselves to fact, and more especially so with regard to the building of a vessel—a really urgent work, since it was for the purpose of depositing, as soon as possible, at Tabor Island a document indicating Ayrton's new residence.

As the *Bonadventure* no longer existed, six months at least would be required for the construction of a new vessel. Now winter was approaching, and the voyage would not be made before the following spring.

"We have time to get everything ready for the fine season," remarked the engineer, who was consulting with Pencroft about these matters. "I think, therefore, my friend, that since we have to rebuild our vessel it will be best to give her larger dimensions. The arrival of the Scotch yacht at Tabor Island is very uncertain. It may even be that, having arrived several months ago, she has again sailed after having vainly searched for some trace of Ayrton. Will it not then be best to build a ship which, if necessary, could take us either to the Polynesian Archipelago or to New Zealand? What do you think?"

"I think, captain," answered the sailor; "I think that you are as capable of building a large vessel as a small one. Neither the wood nor the tools are wanting. It is only a question of time."

"And how many months would be required to build a vessel of from 250 to 300 tons?" asked Harding.

"Seven or eight months at least," replied Pencroft. "But it must not be forgotten that winter is drawing near, and that in severe frost wood is difficult to work. We must calculate on several weeks' delay, and if our vessel is ready by next November we may think ourselves very lucky."

"Well," replied Cyrus Harding, "that will be exactly the most favourable time for undertaking a voyage of any importance, either to Tabor Island or to a more distant land."

"So it will, captain," answered the sailor. "Make out your plans then; the workmen are ready, and I imagine that Ayrton can lend us a good helping hand."

The colonists, having been consulted, approved the engineer's plan, and it was, indeed, the best thing to be done. It is true that the construction of a ship of from two to three hundred tons would be great labour, but the colonists had confidence in themselves, justified by their previous success.

Cyrus Harding then busied himself in drawing the plan of the vessel and making the model. During this time his companions employed themselves in felling and carting trees to furnish the ribs, timbers, and planks. The forest of the Far West supplied the best oaks and elms. They took advantage of the opening already made on their last excursion to form a practicable road, which they named the Far West Road, and the trees were carried to the Chimneys, where the dockyard was established. As to the road in question, the choice of trees had rendered its direction somewhat capricious, but that at the same time facilitated the access to a large part of the Serpentine Peninsula.

It was important that the trees should be quickly felled and cut up, for they could not be used while yet green, and some time was necessary to allow them to get seasoned. The carpenters, therefore, worked vigorously during the month of April, which was troubled only by a few equinoctial gales of some violence. Master Jup aided them dexterously, either by climbing to the top of a tree to fasten the ropes or by lending his stout shoulders to carry the lopped trunks.

All this timber was piled up under a large shed, built near the Chimneys, and there awaited the time for use.

The month of April was tolerably fine, as October often is in the northern zone. At the same time other work was actively continued, and soon all trace of devastation disappeared from the plateau of Prospect Heights. The mill was rebuilt, and new buildings rose in the poultry-yard. It had appeared necessary to enlarge their dimensions, for the feathered population had increased considerably. The stable now contained five onagers, four of which were well broken, and allowed themselves to be either driven or ridden, and a little colt. The colony now possessed a plow, to which the onagers were yoked like regular Yorkshire or Kentucky oxen. The colonists divided their work, and their arms never tired. Then who could have enjoyed better health than these workers, and what good humour enlivened the evenings in Granite House as they formed a thousand plans for the future!

As a matter of course Ayrton shared the common lot in every respect, and there was no longer any talk of his going to live at the corral. Nevertheless he was still sad and reserved, and joined more in the work than in the pleasures of his companions. But he was a valuable workman at need—strong, skilful, ingenious, intelligent. He was esteemed and loved by all, and he could not be ignorant of it.

In the meanwhile the corral was not abandoned. Every other day one of the settlers, driving the cart or mounted on an onager, went to look after the flock of musmons and goats and bring back the supply of milk required by Neb. These excursions at the same time afforded opportunities for hunting. Therefore Herbert and Gideon Spilett, with Top in front, traversed more often than their companions the road to the corral, and with the capital guns which they carried, capybaras, agouties, kangaroos, and wild pigs for large game, ducks, tétras, grouse, jacamars, and snipe for small, were never wanting in the house. The produce of the warren, of the oyster-bed, several turtles which were taken, excellent salmon which came up the Mercy, vegetables from the plateau, wild fruit from the forest, were riches upon riches, and Neb, the head cook, could scarcely by himself store them away.

The telegraphic wire between the corral and Granite House had of course been repaired, and it was worked whenever one or other of the settlers was at the corral and found it necessary to spend the night there. Besides, the island was safe now and no attacks were to be feared, at any rate from men.

However, that which had happened might happen again. A descent of pirates, or even of escaped convicts, was always to be feared. It was possible that companions or accomplices of Bob Harvey had been in the secret of his plans, and might be tempted to imitate him. The colonists, therefore, were careful to observe the sea around the island, and everyday their telescope swept the horizon enclosed by Union and Washington Bays. When they went to the corral they examined the sea to the west with no less attention, and by climbing the spur their gaze extended over a large section of the western horizon.

Nothing suspicious was discerned, but still it was necessary for them to be on their guard.

The engineer one evening imparted to his friends a plan which he had conceived for fortifying the corral. It appeared prudent to him to heighten the palisade and to flank it with a sort of block-house, which, if necessary, the settlers could hold against the enemy. Granite House might, by its very position, be considered impregnable; therefore the corral with its buildings, its stores, and the animals it contained, would always be the object of pirates, whoever they were, who might land on the island, and should the colonists be obliged to shut themselves up there they ought also to be able to defend themselves without any disadvantage. This was a project which might be left for consideration, and they were, besides, obliged to put off its execution until the next spring.

About the 15th of May the keel of the new vessel lay along the dockyard, and soon the stern and stern post, mortised at each of its extremities, rose almost perpendicularly. The keel, of good oak, measured 110 feet in length, this allowing a width of five-and-twenty feet to the midship beam. But this was all the carpenters could do before the arrival of the frosts and bad weather. During the following week they fixed the first of the stern timbers, but were then obliged to suspend work.

During the last days of the month the weather was extremely bad. The wind blew from the east, sometimes with the violence of a tempest. The engineer was somewhat uneasy on account of the dockyard sheds—which besides, he could not have established in any other place near to Granite House—for the islet only imperfectly sheltered the shore from the fury of the open sea, and in great storms the waves beat against the very foot of the granite cliff.

But, very fortunately, these fears were not realised. The wind shifted to the south-east, and there the beach of Granite House was completely covered by Flotsam Point.

Pencroft and Ayrton, the most zealous workmen at the new vessel, pursued their labour as long as they could. They were not men to mind the wind tearing at their hair, nor the rain wetting them to the skin, and a blow from a hammer is worth just as much in bad as in fine weather. But when a severe frost succeeded this wet period, the wood, its fibres acquiring the hardness of iron, became extremely difficult to work, and about the 10th of June, ship-building was obliged to be entirely discontinued.

Cyrus Harding and his companions had not omitted to observe how severe was the temperature during the winters of Lincoln Island. The cold was comparable to that experienced in the States of New England, situated at almost the same distance from the equator. In the northern hemisphere, or at any rate in the part occupied by British America and the north of the United States, this phenomenon is explained by the flat conformation of the territories bordering on the pole, and on which there is no intumescence of the soil to oppose any obstacle to the north winds; here, in Lincoln Island, this explanation would not suffice.

"It has even been observed," remarked Harding one day to his companions, "that in equal latitudes the islands and coast regions are less tried by the cold than inland countries. I have often heard it asserted that the winters of Lombardy, for example, are not less rigourous than those of Scotland, which results from the sea restoring during the winter the heat which it received during the summer. Islands are, therefore, in a better situation for benefiting by this restitution."

"But then, Captain Harding," asked Herbert, "why does Lincoln Island appear to escape the common law?"

"That is difficult to explain," answered the engineer. "However, I should be disposed to conjecture that this peculiarity results from the situation of the island in the southern hemisphere, which, as you know, my boy, is colder than the northern hemisphere."

"Yes," said Herbert, "and icebergs are met with in lower latitudes in the south than in the north of the Pacific."

"That is true," remarked Pencroft, "and when I have been serving on board whalers I have seen icebergs off Cape Horn."

"The severe cold experienced in Lincoln Island," said Gideon Spilett, "may then perhaps be explained by the presence of floes or icebergs comparatively near to Lincoln Island."

"Your opinion is very admissible indeed, my dear Spilett," answered Cyrus Harding, "and it is evidently to the proximity of icebergs that we owe our rigourous winters. I would draw your attention also to an entirely physical cause, which renders the southern colder than the northern hemisphere. In fact, since the sun is nearer to this hemisphere during the summer, it is necessarily more distant during the winter. This explains then the excess of temperature in the two seasons, for, if we find the winters very cold in Lincoln Island, we must not forget that the summers here, on the contrary, are very hot."

"But why, if you please, captain," asked Pencroft, knitting his brows, "why should our hemisphere, as you say, be so badly divided? It isn't just, that!"

"Friend Pencroft," answered the engineer, laughing, "whether just or not, we must submit to it, and here lies the reason for this peculiarity. The earth does not describe a circle around the sun, but an ellipse, as it must by the laws of rational mechanics. Now, the earth occupies one of the centres of the ellipse, and consequently, at the time of its transfer, it is further from the sun, that is to say, at its apogee, and at another time nearer, that is to say, at its perigee. Now it happens that it is during the winter of the southern countries that it is at its most distant point from the sun, and consequently, in a situation for those regions to feel the greatest cold. Nothing can be done to prevent that, and men, Pencroft, however learned they may be, can never change anything of the cosmographical order established by God Himself."

"And yet," added Pencroft, persisting, "the world is very learned. What a big book, captain, might be made with all that is known!"

"And what a much bigger book still with all that is not known!" answered Harding.

At last, for one reason or another, the month of June brought the cold with its accustomed intensity, and the settlers were often confined to Granite House. Ah! how wearisome this imprisonment was to them, and more particularly to Gideon Spilett.

"Look here," said he to Neb one day, "I would give you by notarial deed all the estates which will come to me someday, if you were a good-enough fellow to go, no matter where, and subscribe to some newspaper for me! Decidedly the thing that is most essential to my happiness is the knowing every morning what has happened the day before in other places than this!"

Neb began to laugh.

" 'Pon my word," he replied, "the only thing I think about is my daily work!"

The truth was that indoors as well as out there was no want of work.

The colony of Lincoln Island was now at its highest point of prosperity, achieved by three years of continued hard work. The destruction of the brig had been a new source of riches. Without speaking of the complete rig which would serve for the vessel now on the stocks, utensils and tools of all sorts, weapons and ammunition, clothes and instruments, were now piled in the store-rooms of Granite House. It had not even been necessary to resort again to the manufacture of the coarse felt materials. Though the colonists had suffered from cold during their first winter, the bad season might now come without their having any reason to dread its severity. Linen was plentiful also, and besides, they kept it with extreme care. From chloride of sodium, which is nothing else than sea-salt, Cyrus Harding easily extracted the soda and chlorine. The soda, which it was easy to change into carbonate of soda, and the chlorine, of which he made chloride of lime, were employed for various domestic purposes, and especially in bleaching linen. Besides, they did not wash more than four times a year, as was done by families in the olden times, and it may be added, that Pencroft and Gideon Spilett, while waiting for the postman to bring him his newspaper, distinguished themselves as washermen.

So passed the winter months, June, July, and August. They were severe, and the average observations of the thermometer did not give more than eight degrees of Fahrenheit. It was therefore lower in temperature than the preceding winter. But then, what splendid fires blazed continually on the hearths of Granite House, the smoke marking the granite wall with long, zebra-like streaks! Fuel was not spared, as it grew naturally a few steps from them. Besides, the chips of the wood destined for the construction of the ship enabled them to economise the coal, which required more trouble to transport.

Men and animals were all well. Master Jup was a little chilly, it must be confessed. This was perhaps his only weakness, and it was necessary to make him a well-wadded dressing-gown. But what a servant he was, clever, zealous, indefatigable, not indiscreet, not talkative, and he might have been with reason proposed as a model for all his biped brothers in the Old and New World!

"As for that," said Pencroft, "when one has four hands at one's service, of course one's work ought to be done so much the better!"

And indeed the intelligent creature did it well.

During the seven months which had passed since the last researches made round the mountain, and during the month of September, which brought back fine weather, nothing was heard of the genius of the island. His power was not manifested in any way. It is true that it would have been inutile, for no incident occurred to put the colonists to any painful trial.

Cyrus Harding even observed that if by chance the communication between the unknown and the tenants of Granite House had ever been established through the granite, and if Top's instinct had as it were felt it, there was no further sign of it during this period. The dog's growling had entirely ceased, as well as the uneasiness of the orang. The two friends—for they were so—no longer prowled round the opening of the inner well, nor did they bark or whine in that singular way which from the first the engineer had noticed. But could he be sure that this was all that was to be said about this enigma, and that he should never arrive at a solution? Could he be certain that some conjuncture would not occur which would bring the mysterious personage on the scene? Who could tell what the future might have in reserve?

At last the winter was ended, but an event, the consequences of which might be serious, occurred in the first days of the returning spring.

On the 7th of September, Cyrus Harding, having observed the crater, saw smoke curling round the summit of the mountain, its first vapours rising in the air.

Chapter XV

THE AWAKENING OF THE VOLCANO—THE FINE SEASON—
CONTINUATION OF WORK—THE EVENING OF THE 15TH OF
OCTOBER—A TELEGRAM—A QUESTION—AN ANSWER—
DEPARTURE FOR THE CORRAL—THE NOTICE—THE ADDITIONAL
WIRE—THE BASALT COAST—AT HIGH TIDE—AT LOW TIDE—
THE CAVERN—A DAZZLING LIGHT

THE COLONISTS, WARNED BY THE ENGINEER, LEFT THEIR WORK AND GAZED IN SILENCE at the summit of Mount Franklin.

The volcano had awoke, and the vapour had penetrated the mineral layer heaped at the bottom of the crater. But would the subterranean fires provoke any violent irruption? This was an event which could not be foreseen. However, even while admitting the possibility of an irruption, it was not probable that the whole of Lincoln Island would suffer from it. The flow of volcanic matter is not always disastrous, and the island had already undergone this trial, as was shown by the streams of lava hardened on the northern slopes of the mountain. Besides, from the shape of the crater—the opening broken in the upper edge—the matter would be thrown to the side opposite the fertile regions of the island.

However, the past did not necessarily answer for the future. Often, at the summit of volcanoes, the old craters close and new ones open. This had occurred in the two hemispheres—at Etna, Popocatepetl, at Orizaba—and on the eve of an irruption there is everything to be feared. In fact, an earthquake—a phenomenon which often accompanies volcanic irruptions—is enough to change the interior arrangement of a mountain, and to open new outlets for the burning lava.

Cyrus Harding explained these things to his companions, and, without exaggerating the state of things, he told them all the pros and cons. After all they could not prevent it. It did not appear likely that Granite House would be threatened unless the ground was shaken by an earthquake. But the corral would be in great danger should a new crater open in the southern side of Mount Franklin.

From that day the smoke never disappeared from the top of the mountain, and it could even be perceived that it increased in height and thickness, without any flame mingling in its heavy volumes. The phenomenon was still concentrated in the lower part of the central crater.

However, with the fine days work had been continued. The building of the vessel was hastened as much as possible, and, by means of the waterfall on the shore, Cyrus Harding managed to establish an hydraulic saw-mill, which rapidly cut up the trunks of trees into planks and joists. The mechanism of this apparatus was as simple as those used in the rustic saw-mills of Norway. A first horizontal movement to move the piece of wood, a second vertical movement to move the saw—this was all that was wanted; and the engineer succeeded by means of a wheel, two cylinders, and pulleys properly arranged. Towards the end of the month of September the skeleton of the vessel, which was to be rigged as a schooner, lay in the dockyard. The ribs were almost entirely completed, and, all the timbers having been sustained by a provisional band, the shape of the vessel could already be seen. This schooner, sharp in the bows, very slender in the after-part, would evidently be suitable for a long voyage, if wanted; but laying the planking would still take a considerable time. Very fortunately, the iron-work of the pirate brig had been saved after the explosion. From the planks and injured ribs Pencroft and Ayrton had extracted the bolts and a large quantity of copper nails. It was so much work saved for the smiths, but the carpenters had much to do.

Ship-building was interrupted for a week for the harvest, the haymaking, and the gathering in of the different crops on the plateau. This work finished, every moment was devoted to finishing the schooner. When night came the workmen were really quite exhausted. So as not to lose any time they had changed the hours for their meals; they dined at twelve o'clock, and only had their supper when daylight failed them. They then ascended to Granite House, when they were always ready to go to bed.

Sometimes, however, when the conversation bore on some interesting subject the hour for sleep was delayed for a time. The colonists then spoke of the future, and talked willingly of the changes which a voyage in the schooner to inhabited lands would make in their situation. But always, in the midst of these plans, prevailed the thought of a subsequent return to Lincoln Island. Never would they abandon this colony, founded with so much labour and with such success, and to which a communication with America would afford a fresh impetus. Pencroft and Neb especially hoped to end their days there.

"Herbert," said the sailor, "you will never abandon Lincoln Island?"

"Never, Pencroft, and especially if you make up your mind to stay there."

"That was made up long ago, my boy," answered Pencroft. "I shall expect you. You will bring me your wife and children, and I shall make jolly chaps of your youngsters!"

"That's agreed," replied Herbert, laughing and blushing at the same time.

"And you, Captain Harding," resumed Pencroft enthusiastically, "you will be still the governor of the island! Ah, how many inhabitants could it support? Ten thousand at least!"

They talked in this way, allowing Pencroft to run on, and at last the reporter actually started a newspaper—the *New Lincoln Herald!*

So is man's heart. The desire to perform a work which will endure, which will survive him, is the origin of his superiority over all other living creatures here below. It is this which has established his dominion, and this it is which justifies it, over all the world.

After that, who knows if Jup and Top had not themselves their little dream of the future.

Ayrton silently said to himself that he would like to see Lord Glenarvan again and show himself to all restored.

One evening, on the 15th of October, the conversation was prolonged later than usual. It was nine o'clock. Already, long badly concealed yawns gave warning of the hour of rest, and Pencroft was proceeding towards his bed, when the electric bell, placed in the dining-room, suddenly rang.

All were there, Cyrus Harding, Gideon Spilett, Herbert, Ayrton, Pencroft, Neb. Therefore none of the colonists were at the corral.

Cyrus Harding rose. His companions stared at each other, scarcely believing their ears.

"What does that mean?" cried Neb. "Was it the devil who rang it?"

No one answered.

"The weather is stormy," observed Herbert. "Might not its influence of electricity—"

Herbert did not finish his phrase. The engineer, towards whom all eyes were turned, shook his head negatively.

"We must wait," said Gideon Spilett. "If it is a signal, whoever it may be who has made it, he will renew it."

"But who do you think it is?" cried Neb.

"Who?" answered Pencroft, "but he—"

The sailor's sentence was cut short by a new tinkle of the bell.

Harding went to the apparatus, and sent this question to the corral:—

"What do you want?"

A few moments later the needle, moving on the alphabetic dial, gave this reply to the tenants of Granite House:—

"Come to the corral immediately."

"At last!" exclaimed Harding.

Yes! At last! The mystery was about to be unveiled. The colonists' fatigue had disappeared before the tremendous interest which was about to urge them to the corral, and all wish for rest had ceased. Without having uttered a word, in a few moments they had left Granite House, and were standing on the beach. Jup and Top alone were left behind. They could do without them.

The night was black. The new moon had disappeared at the same time as the sun. As Herbert had observed great stormy clouds formed a lowering and heavy vault, preventing any star rays. A few lightning flashes, reflections from a distant storm, illuminated the horizon.

It was possible that a few hours later the thunder would roll over the island itself. The night was very threatening.

But however deep the darkness was, it would not prevent them from finding the familiar road to the corral.

They ascended the left bank of the Mercy, reached the plateau, passed the bridge over Creek Glycerine, and advanced through the forest.

They walked at a good pace, a prey to the liveliest emotions. There was no doubt but that they were now going to learn the long-searched-for answer to the enigma, the name of that mysterious being, so deeply concerned in their life, so generous in his influence, so powerful in his action! Must not this stranger have indeed mingled with their existence, have known the smallest details, have heard all that was said in Granite House, to have been able always to act in the very nick of time?

Everyone, wrapped up in his own reflections, pressed forward. Under the arch of trees the darkness was such that even the edge of the road could not be seen. Not a sound in the forest. Both animals and birds, influenced by the heaviness of the atmosphere, remained motionless and silent. Not a breath disturbed the leaves. The footsteps of the colonists alone resounded on the hardened ground.

During the first quarter of an hour the silence was only interrupted by this remark from Pencroft:—

"We ought to have brought a torch."

And by this reply from the engineer:—

"We shall find one at the corral."

Harding and his companions had left Granite House at twelve minutes past nine. At forty-seven minutes past nine they had traversed three out of the five miles which separated the mouth of the Mercy from the corral.

At that moment sheets of lightning spread over the island and illumined the dark trees. The flashes dazzled and almost blinded them. Evidently the storm would not be long in bursting forth.

The flashes gradually became brighter and more rapid. Distant thunder growled in the sky. The atmosphere was stifling.

The colonists proceeded as if they were urged onwards by some irresistible force.

At ten o'clock a vivid flash showed them the palisade, and as they reached the gate the storm burst forth with tremendous fury.

In a minute the corral was crossed, and Harding stood before the hut.

Probably the house was occupied by the stranger, since it was from thence that the telegram had been sent. However, no light shone through the window.

The engineer knocked at the door.

No answer.

Cyrus Harding opened the door, and the settlers entered the room, which was perfectly dark. A light was struck by Neb, and in a few moments the lantern was lighted and the light thrown into every corner of the room.

There was no one there. Everything was in the state in which it had been left.

"Have we been deceived by an illusion?" murmured Cyrus Harding.

No! that was not possible! The telegram had clearly said—

"Come to the corral immediately."

They approached the table specially devoted to the use of the wire. Everything was in order—the pile on the box containing it, as well as all the apparatus.

"Who came here the last time?" asked the engineer.

"I did, captain," answered Ayrton.

"And that was—"

"Four days ago."

"Ah! a note!" cried Herbert, pointing to a paper lying on the table.

On this paper were written these words in English:—

"Follow the new wire."

"Forward!" cried Harding, who understood that the despatch had not been sent from the corral, but from the mysterious retreat, communicating directly with Granite House by means of a supplementary wire joined to the old one.

Neb took the lighted lantern, and all left the corral. The storm then burst forth with tremendous violence. The interval between each lightning-flash and each thunderclap diminished rapidly. The summit of the volcano, with its plume of vapour, could be seen by occasional flashes.

There was no telegraphic communication in any part of the corral between the house and the palisade; but the engineer, running straight to the first post, saw by the light of a flash a new wire hanging from the isolator to the ground.

"There it is!" said he.

This wire lay along the ground, and was surrounded with an isolating substance like a submarine cable, so as to assure the free transmission of the current. It appeared to pass through the wood and the southern spurs of the mountain, and consequently it ran towards the west.

"Follow it!" said Cyrus Harding.

And the settlers immediately pressed forward, guided by the wire.

The thunder continued to roar with such violence that not a word could be heard. However, there was no occasion for speaking, but to get forward as fast as possible.

Cyrus Harding and his companions then climbed the spur rising between the corral valley and that of Falls River, which they crossed at its narrowest part. The wire, sometimes stretched over the lower branches of the trees, sometimes lying on the ground, guided them surely. The engineer had supposed that the wire would perhaps stop at the bottom of the valley, and that the stranger's retreat would be there.

Nothing of the sort. They were obliged to ascend the south-western spur, and redescend on that arid plateau terminated by the strangely-wild basalt cliff. From time to time one of the colonists stooped down and felt for the wire with his hands; but there was now no doubt that the wire was running directly towards the sea. There, to a certainty, in the depths of those rocks, was the dwelling so long sought for in vain.

The sky was literally on fire. Flash succeeded flash. Several struck the summit of the volcano in the midst of the thick smoke. It appeared there as if the mountain was vomiting flame. At a few minutes to eleven the colonists arrived on the high cliff overlooking the ocean to the west. The wind had risen. The surf roared 500 feet below.

Harding calculated that they had gone a mile and a half from the corral.

At this point the wire entered among the rocks, following the steep side of a narrow ravine. The settlers followed it at the risk of occasioning a fall of the slightly-balanced rocks, and being dashed into the sea. The descent was extremely perilous, but they did not think of the danger; they were no longer masters of themselves, and an irresistible attraction drew them towards this mysterious place as the magnet draws iron.

Thus they almost unconsciously descended this ravine, which even in broad daylight would have been considered impracticable.

The stones rolled and sparkled like fiery balls when they crossed through the gleams of light. Harding was first—Ayrton last. On they went, step by step. Now they slid over the slippery rock; then they struggled to their feet and scrambled on.

At last the wire touched the rocks on the beach. The colonists had reached the bottom of the basalt cliff.

There appeared a narrow ridge, running horizontally and parallel with the sea. The settlers followed the wire along it. They had not gone a hundred paces when the ridge by a moderate incline sloped down to the level of the sea.

The engineer seized the wire and found that it disappeared beneath the waves.

His companions were stupefied.

A cry of disappointment, almost a cry of despair, escaped them! Must they then plunge beneath the water and seek there for some submarine cavern? In their excited state they would not have hesitated to do it.

The engineer stopped them.

He led his companions to a hollow in the rocks, and there—

"We must wait," said he. "The tide is high. At low water the way will be open."

"But what can make you think—" asked Pencroft.

"He would not have called us if the means had been wanting to enable us to reach him!"

Cyrus Harding spoke in a tone of such thorough conviction that no objection was raised. His remark, besides, was logical. It was quite possible that an opening, practicable at low water, though hidden now by the high tide, opened at the foot of the cliff.

There was some time to wait. The colonists remained silently crouching in a deep hollow. Rain now began to fall in torrents. The thunder was re-echoed among the rocks with a grand sonorousness.

The colonists' emotion was great. A thousand strange and extraordinary ideas crossed their brains, and they expected some grand and superhuman apparition, which alone could come up to the notion they had formed of the mysterious genius of the island.

At midnight, Harding carrying the lantern, descended to the beach to reconnoitre.

The engineer was not mistaken. The beginning of an immense excavation could be seen under the water. There the wire, bending at a right angle, entered the yawning gulf.

Cyrus Harding returned to his companions, and said simply—

"In an hour the opening will be practicable."

"It is there, then?" said Pencroft.

"Did you doubt it?" returned Harding.

"But this cavern must be filled with water to a certain height," observed Herbert.

"Either the cavern will be completely dry," replied Harding, "and in that case we can traverse it on foot, or it will not be dry, and some means of transport will be put at our disposal."

An hour passed. All climbed down through the rain to the level of the sea. There was now eight feet of the opening above the water. It was like the arch of a bridge, under which rushed the foaming water.

Leaning forward, the engineer saw a black object floating on the water. He drew it towards him. It was a boat, moored to some interior projection of the cave. This boat was iron-plated. Two oars lay at the bottom.

"Jump in!" said Harding.

In a moment the settlers were in the boat. Neb and Ayrton took the oars, Pencroft the rudder. Cyrus Harding in the bows, with the lantern, lighted the way.

The elliptical roof, under which the boat at first passed, suddenly rose; but the darkness was too deep, and the light of the lantern too slight, for either the extent, length, height, or depth of the cave to be ascertained. Solemn silence reigned in this basaltic cavern. Not a sound could penetrate into it, even the thunder peals could not pierce its thick sides.

Such immense caves exist in various parts of the world, natural crypts dating from the geological epoch of the globe. Some are filled by the sea; others contain entire lakes in their sides. Such is Fingal's Cave, in the island of Staffa, one of the Hebrides; such are the caves of Morgat, in the bay of Douarucuez, in Brittany, the caves of Bonifacior, in Corsica, those of Lyse-Fiord, in Norway; such are the immense Mammoth caverns in Kentucky, 500 feet in height, and more than twenty miles in length! In many parts of the globe, nature has excavated these caverns, and preserved them for the admiration of man.

Did the cavern which the settlers were now exploring extend to the centre of the island? For a quarter of an hour the boat had been advancing, making detours, indicated to Pencroft by the engineer in short sentences, when all at once—

"More to the right!" he commanded.

The boat, altering its course, came up alongside the right wall. The engineer wished to see if the wire still ran along the side.

The wire was there fastened to the rock.

"Forward!" said Harding.

And the two oars, plunging into the dark waters, urged the boat onwards.

On they went for another quarter of an hour, and a distance of half-a-mile must have been cleared from the mouth of the cave, when Harding's voice was again heard.

"Stop!" said he.

The boat stopped, and the colonists perceived a bright light illuminating the vast cavern, so deeply excavated in the bowels of the island, of which nothing had ever led them to suspect the existence.

At a height of a hundred feet rose the vaulted roof, supported on basalt shafts. Irregular arches, strange mouldings, appeared on the columns erected by nature in thousands from the first epochs of the formation of the globe. The basalt pillars, fitted one into the other, measured from forty to fifty feet in height, and the water, calm in spite of the tumult outside, washed their base. The brilliant focus of light, pointed out by the engineer, touched every point of rock, and flooded the walls with light.

By reflection the water reproduced the brilliant sparkles, so that the boat appeared to be floating between two glittering zones.

They could not be mistaken in the nature of the irradiation thrown from the centre light, whose clear rays broke all the angles, all the projections of the cavern. This light proceeded from an electric source, and its white colour betrayed its origin. It was the sun of this cave, and it filled it entirely.

At a sign from Cyrus Harding the oars again plunged into the water, causing a regular shower of gems, and the boat was urged forward towards the light, which was now not more than half a cable-length distant.

At this place the breadth of the sheet of water measured nearly 350 feet, and beyond the dazzling centre could be seen an enormous basaltic wall, blocking up any issue on that side. The cavern widened here considerably, the sea forming a little lake. But the roof, the side walls, the end cliff, all the prisms, all the peaks, were flooded with the electric fluid, so that the brilliancy belonged to them, and as if the light issued from them.

In the centre of the lake a long cigar-shaped object floated on the surface of the water, silent, motionless. The brilliancy which issued from it escaped from its sides as from two kilns heated to a white heat. This apparatus, similar in shape to an enormous whale, was about 250 feet long, and rose about ten or twelve above the water.

The boat slowly approached it. Cyrus Harding stood up in the bows. He gazed, a prey to violent excitement. Then, all at once, seizing the reporter's arm—

"It is he! It can only be he!" he cried, "he!—"

Then, falling back on the seat, he murmured a name which Gideon Spilett alone could hear.

The reporter evidently knew this name, for it had a wonderful effect upon him, and he answered in a hoarse voice—

"He! an outlawed man!"

"He!" said Harding.

At the engineer's command the boat approached this singular floating apparatus. The boat touched the left side, from which escaped a ray of light through a thick glass.

Harding and his companions mounted on the platform. An open hatchway was there. All darted down the opening.

At the bottom of the ladder was a deck, lighted by electricity. At the end of this deck was a door, which Harding opened.

A richly-ornamented room, quickly traversed by the colonists, was joined to a library, over which a luminous ceiling shed a flood of light.

At the end of the library a large door, also shut, was opened by the engineer.

An immense saloon—a sort of museum, in which were heaped up, with all the treasures of the mineral world, works of art, marvels of industry—appeared before the eyes of the colonists, who almost thought themselves suddenly transported into a land of enchantment.

Stretched on a rich sofa they saw a man, who did not appear to notice their presence.

Then Harding raised his voice, and to the extreme surprise of his companions, he uttered these words—

"Captain Nemo, you asked for us! We are here."

Chapter XVI

CAPTAIN NEMO—HIS FIRST WORDS—THE HISTORY OF THE RECLUSE—HIS ADVENTURES—HIS SENTIMENTS—HIS COMRADES—SUBMARINE LIFE—ALONE—THE LAST REFUGE OF THE NAUTILUS IN LINCOLN ISLAND—THE MYSTERIOUS GENIUS OF THE ISLAND

A T THESE WORDS THE RECLINING FIGURE ROSE, AND THE ELECTRIC LIGHT FELL UPON his countenance; a magnificent head, the forehead high, the glance commanding, beard white, hair abundant and falling over the shoulders.

His hand rested upon the cushion of the divan from which he had just risen. He appeared perfectly calm. It was evident that his strength had been gradually undermined by illness, but his voice seemed yet powerful, as he said in English, and in a tone which evinced extreme surprise—

"Sir, I have no name."

"Nevertheless, I know you!" replied Cyrus Harding.

Captain Nemo fixed his penetrating gaze upon the engineer, as though he were about to annihilate him.

Then, falling back amid the pillows of the divan—

"After all, what matters now?" he murmured; "I am dying!"

Cyrus Harding drew near the captain, and Gideon Spilett took his hand—it was of a feverish heat. Ayrton, Pencroft, Herbert, and Neb stood respectfully apart in an angle of the magnificent saloon, whose atmosphere was saturated with the electric fluid.

Meanwhile Captain Nemo withdrew his hand, and motioned the engineer and the reporter to be seated.

All regarded him with profound emotion. Before them they beheld that being whom they had styled the "genius of the island," the powerful protector whose intervention, in so many circumstances, had been so efficacious, the benefactor to whom they owed such a debt of gratitude! Their eyes beheld a man only, and a man at the point of death, where Pencroft and Neb had expected to find an almost supernatural being!

But how happened it that Cyrus Harding had recognised Captain Nemo? Why had the latter so suddenly risen on hearing this name uttered, a name which he had believed known to none?—

The captain had resumed his position on the divan, and leaning on his arm, he regarded the engineer, seated near him.

"You know the name I formerly bore, sir?" he asked.

"I do," answered Cyrus Harding, "and also that of this wonderful submarine vessel—"

"The *Nautilus?*" said the captain, with a faint smile.

"The *Nautilus.*"

"But do you—do you know who I am?"

"I do."

"It is nevertheless many years since I have held any communication with the inhabited world; three long years have I passed in the depth of the sea, the only place where I have found liberty! Who then can have betrayed my secret?"

"A man who was bound to you by no tie, Captain Nemo, and who, consequently, cannot be accused of treachery."

"The Frenchman who was cast on board my vessel by chance sixteen years since?"

"The same."

"He and his two companions did not then perish in the maëlstrom, in the midst of which the *Nautilus* was struggling?"

"They escaped, and a book has appeared under the title of *Twenty Thousand Leagues Under the Sea,* which contains your history."

"The history of a few months only of my life!" interrupted the captain impetuously.

"It is true," answered Cyrus Harding, "but a few months of that strange life have sufficed to make you known—"

"As a great criminal, doubtless!" said Captain Nemo, a haughty smile curling his lips. "Yes, a rebel, perhaps an outlaw against humanity!"

The engineer was silent.

"Well, sir?"

"It is not for me to judge you, Captain Nemo," answered Cyrus Harding, "at any rate as regards your past life. I am, with the rest of the world, ignorant of the motives which induced you to adopt this strange mode of existence, and I cannot judge of effects without knowing their causes; but what I *do* know is, that a beneficent hand has constantly protected us since our arrival on Lincoln Island, that we all owe our lives to a good, generous, and powerful being, and that this being so powerful, good, and generous, Captain Nemo, is yourself!"

"It is I," answered the captain simply.

The engineer and the reporter rose. Their companions had drawn near, and the gratitude with which their hearts were charged was about to express itself in their gestures and words.

Captain Nemo stopped them by a sign, and in a voice which betrayed more emotion than he doubtless intended to show.

"Wait till you have heard all," he said.*

And the captain, in a few concise sentences, ran over the events of his life.

His narrative was short, yet he was obliged to summon up his whole remaining energy to arrive at the end. He was evidently contending against extreme weakness. Several times Cyrus Harding entreated him to repose for a while, but he shook his head as a man to whom the morrow may never come, and when the reporter offered his assistance—

"It is useless," he said; "my hours are numbered."

Captain Nemo was an Indian, the Prince Dakkar, son of a rajah of the then inde-

---

* The history of Captain Nemo has, in fact, been published under the title of *Twenty Thousand Leagues Under the Sea.* Here, therefore, will apply the observation already made as to the adventures of Ayrton with regard to the discrepancy of dates. Readers should therefore refer to the note already published on this point.

pendent territory of Bundelkund. His father sent him, when ten years of age, to Europe, in order that he might receive an education in all respects complete, and in the hopes that by his talents and knowledge he might one day take a leading part in raising his long degraded and heathen country to a level with the nations of Europe.

From the age of ten years to that of thirty Prince Dakkar, endowed by Nature with her richest gifts of intellect, accumulated knowledge of every kind, and in science, literature, and art his researches were extensive and profound.

He travelled over the whole of Europe. His rank and fortune caused him to be everywhere sought after; but the pleasures of the world had for him no attractions. Though young and possessed of every personal advantage, he was ever grave—sombre even—devoured by an unquenchable thirst for knowledge, and cherishing in the recesses of his heart the hope that he might become a great and powerful ruler of a free and enlightened people.

Still, for long the love of science triumphed over all other feelings. He became an artist deeply impressed by the marvels of art, a philosopher to whom no one of the higher sciences was unknown, a statesman versed in the policy of European courts. To the eyes of those who observed him superficially he might have passed for one of those cosmopolitans, curious of knowledge, but disdaining action; one of those opulent travellers, haughty and cynical, who move incessantly from place to place, and are of no country.

This artist, this philosopher, this man was, however, still cherishing the hope instilled into him from his earliest days.

Prince Dakkar returned to Bundelkund in the year 1849. He married a noble Indian lady, who was imbued with an ambition not less ardent than that by which he was inspired. Two children were born to them, whom they tenderly loved. But domestic happiness did not prevent him from seeking to carry out the object at which he aimed. He waited an opportunity. At length, as he vainly fancied, it presented itself.

Instigated by princes equally ambitious and less sagacious and more unscrupulous than he was, the people of India were persuaded that they might successfully rise against their English rulers, who had brought them out of a state of anarchy and constant warfare and misery, and had established peace and prosperity in their country. Their ignorance and gross superstition made them the facile tools of their designing chiefs.

In 1857 the great Sepoy revolt broke out. Prince Dakkar, under the belief that he should thereby have the opportunity of attaining the object of his long-cherished ambition, was easily drawn into it. He forthwith devoted his talents and wealth to the service of this cause. He aided it in person; he fought in the front ranks; he risked his life equally with the humblest of the wretched and misguided fanatics; he was ten times wounded in twenty engagements, seeking death but finding it not, when at length the sanguinary rebels were utterly defeated, and the atrocious mutiny was brought to an end.

Never before had the British power in India been exposed to such danger, and if, as they had hoped, the Sepoys had received assistance from without, the influence and supremacy in Asia of the United Kingdom would have been a thing of the past.

The name of Prince Dakkar was at that time well known. He had fought openly and without concealment. A price was set upon his head, but he managed to escape from his pursuers.

Civilisation never recedes; the law of necessity ever forces it onwards. The Sepoys were vanquished, and the land of the rajahs of old fell again under the rule of England.

Prince Dakkar, unable to find that death he courted, returned to the mountain fastnesses of Bundelkund. There, alone in the world, overcome by disappointment at the destruction of all his vain hopes, a prey to profound disgust for all human beings, filled with hatred of the civilised world, he realised the wreck of his fortune, assembled some score of his most faithful companions, and one day disappeared, leaving no trace behind.

Where, then, did he seek that liberty denied him upon the inhabited earth? Under the waves, in the depths of the ocean, where none could follow.

The warrior became the man of science. Upon a deserted island of the Pacific he established his dockyard, and there a submarine vessel was constructed from his designs. By methods which will at some future day be revealed he had rendered subservient the illimitable forces of electricity, which, extracted from inexhaustible sources, was employed for all the requirements of his floating equipage, as a moving, lighting, and heating agent. The sea, with its countless treasures, its myriads of fish, its numberless wrecks, its enormous mammalia, and not only all that nature supplied, but also all that man had lost in its depths, sufficed for every want of the prince and his crew—and thus was his most ardent desire accomplished, never again to hold communication with the earth. He named his submarine vessel the *Nautilus*, called himself simply Captain Nemo, and disappeared beneath the seas.

During many years this strange being visited every ocean, from pole to pole. Outcast of the inhabited earth in these unknown worlds he gathered incalculable treasures. The millions lost in the Bay of Vigo, in 1702, by the galleons of Spain, furnished him with a mine of inexhaustible riches which he devoted always, anonymously, in favour of those nations who fought for the independence of their country.*

For long, however, he had held no communication with his fellow-creatures, when, during the night of the 6th of November, 1866, three men were cast on board his vessel. They were a French professor, his servant, and a Canadian fisherman. These three men had been hurled overboard by a collision which had taken place between the *Nautilus* and the United States' frigate *Abraham Lincoln,* which had chased her.

Captain Nemo learned from this professor that the *Nautilus,* taken now for a gigantic mammal of the whale species, now for a submarine vessel carrying a crew of pirates, was sought for in every sea.

He might have returned these three men to the ocean, from whence chance had brought them in contact with his mysterious existence. Instead of doing this he kept them prisoners, and during seven months they were enabled to behold all the wonders of a voyage of twenty thousand leagues under the sea.

One day, the 22d of June, 1867, these three men, who knew nothing of the past history of Captain Nemo, succeeded in escaping in one of the *Nautilus*'s boats. But as at this time the *Nautilus* was drawn into the vortex of the maëlstrom, off the coast of Norway, the captain naturally believed that the fugitives, engulfed in that frightful whirlpool, found their death at the bottom of the abyss. He was unaware that the Frenchman and his two companions had been miraculously cast on shore, that the fishermen of the Lofoten Islands had rendered them assistance, and that the professor, on his return to France, had published that work in which seven months of the strange and eventful navigation of the *Nautilus* were narrated and exposed to the curiosity of the public.

* This refers to the insurrection of the Candiotes, who were, in fact, largely assisted by Captain Nemo.

For a long time after this, Captain Nemo continued to live thus, traversing every sea. But one by one his companions died, and found their last resting-place in their cemetery of coral, in the bed of the Pacific. At last Captain Nemo remained the solitary survivor of all those who had taken refuge with him in the depths of the ocean.

He was now sixty years of age. Although alone, he succeeded in navigating the *Nautilus* towards one of those submarine caverns which had sometimes served him as a harbour.

One of these ports was hollowed beneath Lincoln Island, and at this moment furnished an asylum to the *Nautilus*.

The captain had now remained there six years, navigating the ocean no longer, but awaiting death, and that moment when he should rejoin his former companions, when by chance he observed the descent of the balloon which carried the prisoners of the Confederates. Clad in his diving dress he was walking beneath the water at a few cable-lengths from the shore of the island, when the engineer had been thrown into the sea. Moved by a feeling of compassion the captain saved Cyrus Harding.

His first impulse was to fly from the vicinity of the five castaways; but his harbor of refuge was closed, for in consequence of an elevation of the basalt, produced by the influence of volcanic action, he could no longer pass through the entrance of the vault. Though there was sufficient depth of water to allow a light craft to pass the bar, there was not enough for the *Nautilus*, whose draught of water was considerable.

Captain Nemo was compelled, therefore, to remain. He observed these men thrown without resources upon a desert island, but had no wish to be himself discovered by them. By degrees he became interested in their efforts when he saw them honest, energetic, and bound to each other by the ties of friendship. As if despite his wishes, he penetrated all the secrets of their existence. By means of the diving dress he could easily reach the well in the interior of Granite House, and climbing by the projections of rock to its upper orifice he heard the colonists as they recounted the past, and studied the present and future. He learned from them the tremendous conflict of America with America itself, for the abolition of slavery. Yes, these men were worthy to reconcile Captain Nemo with that humanity which they represented so nobly in the island.

Captain Nemo had saved Cyrus Harding. It was he also who had brought back the dog to the Chimneys, who rescued Top from the waters of the lake, who caused to fall at Flotsam Point the case containing so many things useful to the colonists, who conveyed the canoe back into the stream of the Mercy, who cast the cord from the top of Granite House at the time of the attack by the baboons, who made known the presence of Ayrton upon Tabor Island, by means of the document enclosed in the bottle, who caused the explosion of the brig by the shock of a torpedo placed at the bottom of the canal, who saved Herbert from certain death by bringing the sulphate of quinine; and finally, it was he who had killed the convicts with the electric balls, of which he possessed the secret, and which he employed in the chase of submarine creatures. Thus were explained so many apparently supernatural occurrences, and which all proved the generosity and power of the captain.

Nevertheless, this noble misanthrope longed to benefit his *protégés* still further. There yet remained much useful advice to give them, and, his heart being softened by the approach of death, he invited, as we are aware, the colonists of Granite House to visit the *Nautilus*, by means of a wire which connected it with the corral. Possibly he would not have done this had he been aware that Cyrus Harding was sufficiently acquainted with his history to address him by the name of Nemo.

The captain concluded the narrative of his life. Cyrus Harding then spoke; he recalled all the incidents which had exercised so beneficent an influence upon the colony, and in the names of his companions and himself thanked the generous being to whom they owed so much.

But Captain Nemo paid little attention; his mind appeared to be absorbed by one idea, and without taking the proffered hand of the engineer—

"Now, sir," said he, "now that you know my history, your judgment!"

In saying this, the captain evidently alluded to an important incident witnessed by the three strangers thrown on board his vessel, and which the French professor had related in his work, causing a profound and terrible sensation. Some days previous to the flight of the professor and his two companions, the *Nautilus,* being chased by a frigate in the north of the Atlantic, had hurled herself as a ram upon this frigate, and sunk her without mercy.

Cyrus Harding understood the captain's allusion, and was silent.

"It was an enemy's frigate," exclaimed Captain Nemo, transformed for an instant into the Prince Dakkar, "an enemy's frigate! It was she who attacked me—I was in a narrow and shallow bay—the frigate barred my way—and I sank her!"

A few moments of silence ensued; then the captain demanded—

"What think you of my life, gentlemen?"

Cyrus Harding extended his hand to the *ci-devant* prince and replied gravely, "Sir, your error was in supposing that the past can be resuscitated, and in contending against inevitable progress. It is one of those errors which some admire, others blame; which God alone can judge. He who is mistaken in an action which he sincerely believes to be right may be an enemy, but retains our esteem. Your error is one that we may admire, and your name has nothing to fear from the judgment of history, which does not condemn heroic folly, but its results."

The old man's breast swelled with emotion, and raising his hand to Heaven—

"Was I wrong, or in the right?" he murmured.

Cyrus Harding replied, "All great actions return to God, from whom they are derived. Captain Nemo, we, whom you have succored, shall ever mourn your loss."

Herbert, who had drawn near the captain, fell on his knees and kissed his hand.

A tear glistened in the eyes of the dying man. "My child," he said, "may God bless you!"

Chapter XVII

LAST MOMENTS OF CAPTAIN NEMO—WISHES OF THE DYING
MAN—A PARTING GIFT TO HIS FRIENDS OF A DAY—CAPTAIN
NEMO'S COFFIN—ADVICE TO THE COLONISTS—THE SUPREME
MOMENT—AT THE BOTTOM OF THE SEA

DAY HAD RETURNED. NO RAY OF LIGHT PENETRATED INTO THE PROFUNDITY OF THE cavern. It being high-water, the entrance was closed by the sea. But the artificial light, which escaped in long streams from the skylights of the *Nautilus* was as vivid as before, and the sheet of water shone around the floating vessel.

An extreme exhaustion now overcame Captain Nemo, who had fallen back upon the divan. It was useless to contemplate removing him to Granite House, for he had expressed his wish to remain in the midst of those marvels of the *Nautilus* which millions could not have purchased, and to wait there for that death which was swiftly approaching.

During a long interval of prostration, which rendered him almost unconscious, Cyrus Harding and Gideon Spilett attentively observed the condition of the dying man. It was apparent that his strength was gradually diminishing. That frame, once so robust, was now but the fragile tenement of a departing soul. All of life was concentrated in the heart and head.

The engineer and reporter consulted in whispers. Was it possible to render any aid to the dying man? Might his life, if not saved, be prolonged for some days? He himself had said that no remedy could avail, and he awaited with tranquillity that death which had for him no terrors.

"We can do nothing," said Gideon Spilett.

"But of what is he dying?" asked Pencroft.

"Life is simply fading out," replied the reporter.

"Nevertheless," said the sailor, "if we move him into the open air, and the light of the sun, he might perhaps recover."

"No, Pencroft," answered the engineer, "it is useless to attempt it. Besides, Captain Nemo would never consent to leave his vessel. He has lived for a dozen years on board the *Nautilus,* and on board the *Nautilus* he desires to die."

Without doubt Captain Nemo heard Cyrus Harding's reply, for he raised himself slightly, and in a voice more feeble, but always intelligible—

"You are right, sir," he said. "I shall die here—it is my wish; and therefore I have a request to make of you."

Cyrus Harding and his companions had drawn near the divan, and now arranged the cushions in such a manner as to better support the dying man.

They saw his eyes wander over all the marvels of this saloon, lighted by the electric rays which fell from the arabesques of the luminous ceiling. He surveyed, one after the other, the pictures hanging from the splendid tapestries of the partitions, the *chef-d'oeuvres* of the Italian, Flemish, French, and Spanish masters; the statues of marble and bronze on their pedestals; the magnificent organ, leaning against the after-partition; the aquarium, in which bloomed the most wonderful productions of the sea—marine plants, zoophytes, chaplets of pearls of inestimable value; and, finally, his eyes rested on this device, inscribed over the pediment of the museum—the motto of the *Nautilus*—

Mobilis in mobile.

His glance seemed to rest fondly for the last time on these masterpieces of art and of nature, to which he had limited his horizon during a sojourn of so many years in the abysses of the seas.

Cyrus Harding respected the captain's silence, and waited till he should speak.

After some minutes, during which, doubtless, he passed in review his whole life, Captain Nemo turned to the colonists and said—

"You consider yourselves, gentlemen, under some obligations to me?"

"Captain, believe us that we would give our lives to prolong yours."

"Promise, then," continued Captain Nemo, "to carry out my last wishes, and I shall be repaid for all I have done for you."

"We promise," said Cyrus Harding.

And by this promise he bound both himself and his companions.

"Gentlemen," resumed the captain, "to-morrow I shall be dead."

Herbert was about to utter an exclamation, but a sign from the captain arrested him.

"To-morrow I shall die, and I desire no other tomb than the *Nautilus*. It is my grave! All my friends repose in the depths of the ocean; their resting-place shall be mine."

These words were received with profound silence.

"Pay attention to my wishes," he continued. "The *Nautilus* is imprisoned in this grotto, the entrance of which is blocked up; but, although egress is impossible, the vessel may at least sink in the abyss, and there bury my remains."

The colonists listened reverently to the words of the dying man.

"To-morrow, after my death, Mr. Harding," continued the captain, "yourself and companions will leave the *Nautilus*, for all the treasures it contains must perish with me. One token alone will remain with you of Prince Dakkar, with whose history you are now acquainted. That coffer yonder contains diamonds of the value of many millions, most of them mementoes of the time when, husband and father, I thought happiness possible for me, and a collection of pearls gathered by my friends and myself in the depths of the ocean. Of this treasure, at a future day, you may make good use. In the hands of such men as yourself and your comrades, Captain Harding, money will never be a source of danger. From on high I shall still participate in your enterprises, and I fear not but that they will prosper."

After a few moments' repose, necessitated by his extreme weakness, Captain Nemo continued—

"To-morrow you will take the coffer, you will leave the saloon, of which you will close the door; then you will ascend on to the deck of the *Nautilus*, and you will lower the mainhatch so as entirely to close the vessel."

"It shall be done, captain," answered Cyrus Harding.

"Good. You will then embark in the canoe which brought you hither; but, before leaving the *Nautilus*, go to the stern and there open two large stopcocks which you will find upon the water-line. The water will penetrate into the reservoirs, and the *Nautilus* will gradually sink beneath the water to repose at the bottom of the abyss."

And comprehending a gesture of Cyrus Harding, the captain added—

"Fear nothing! You will but bury a corpse!"

Neither Cyrus Harding nor his companions ventured to offer any observation to Captain Nemo. He had expressed his last wishes, and they had nothing to do but to conform to them.

"I have your promise, gentlemen?" added Captain Nemo.

"You have, captain," replied the engineer.

The captain thanked the colonists by a sign, and requested them to leave him for some hours. Gideon Spilett wished to remain near him, in the event of a crisis coming on, but the dying man refused, saying, "I shall live until to-morrow, sir."

All left the saloon, passed through the library and the dining-room, and arrived forward, in the machine-room where the electrical apparatus was established, which supplied not only heat and light, but the mechanical power of the *Nautilus*.

The *Nautilus* was a masterpiece, containing masterpieces within itself and the engineer was struck with astonishment.

The colonists mounted the platform, which rose seven or eight feet above the water. There they beheld a thick glass lenticular covering, which protected a kind of large eye, from which flashed forth light. Behind this eye was apparently a cabin containing the wheels of the rudder, and in which was stationed the helmsman, when he navigated the *Nautilus* over the bed of the ocean, which the electric rays would evidently light up to a considerable distance.

Cyrus Harding and his companions remained for a time silent, for they were vividly impressed by what they had just seen and heard, and their hearts were deeply touched by the thought that he whose arm had so often aided them, the protector whom they had known but a few hours, was at the point of death.

Whatever might be the judgment pronounced by posterity upon the events of this, so to speak, extra-human existence, the character of Prince Dakkar would ever remain as one of those whose memory time can never efface.

"What a man!" said Pencroft. "Is it possible that he can have lived at the bottom of the sea? And it seems to me that perhaps he has not found peace there any more than elsewhere!"

"The *Nautilus*," observed Ayrton, "might have enabled us to leave Lincoln Island and reach some inhabited country."

"Good Heavens!" exclaimed Pencroft, "I for one would never risk myself in such a craft. To sail on the seas, good; but under the seas, never!"

"I believe, Pencroft," answered the reporter, "that the navigation of a submarine vessel such as the *Nautilus* ought to be very easy, and that we should soon become accustomed to it. There would be no storms, no lee-shore to fear. At some feet beneath the surface the waters of the ocean are as calm as those of a lake."

"That may be," replied the sailor, "but I prefer a gale of wind on board a well-found craft. A vessel is built to sail on the sea, and not beneath it."

"My friends," said the engineer, "it is useless, at any rate as regards the *Nautilus*, to discuss the question of submarine vessels. The *Nautilus* is not ours, and we have not the right to dispose of it. Moreover, we could in no case avail ourselves of it. Independently of the fact that it would be impossible to get it out of this cavern, whose entrance is now closed by the uprising of the basaltic rocks, Captain Nemo's wish is that it shall be buried with him. His wish is our law, and we will fulfil it."

After a somewhat prolonged conversation, Cyrus Harding and his companions again descended to the interior of the *Nautilus*. There they took some refreshment and returned to the saloon.

Captain Nemo had somewhat rallied from the prostration which had overcome him, and his eyes shone with their wonted fire. A faint smile even curled his lips.

The colonists drew around him.

"Gentlemen," said the captain, "you are brave and honest men. You have devoted yourselves to the common weal. Often have I observed your conduct. I have esteemed you—I esteem you still! Your hand, Mr. Harding."

Cyrus Harding gave his hand to the captain, who clasped it affectionately.

"It is well!" he murmured.

He resumed—

"But enough of myself. I have to speak concerning yourselves, and this Lincoln Island, upon which you have taken refuge. You now desire to leave it?"

"To return, captain!" answered Pencroft quickly.

"To return, Pencroft?" said the captain, with a smile. "I know, it is true, your love for this island. You have helped to make it what it now is, and it seems to you a paradise!"

"Our project, captain," interposed Cyrus Harding, "is to annex it to the United States, and to establish for our shipping a port so fortunately situated in this part of the Pacific."

"Your thoughts are with your country, gentlemen," continued the captain; "your toils are for her prosperity and glory. You are right. One's native land!—there should one live! there die! And I! I die far from all I loved!"

"You have some last wish to transmit," said the engineer with emotion, "some souvenir to send to those friends you have left in the mountains of India?"

"No, Captain Harding; no friends remain to me! I am the last of my race, and to all whom I have known I have long been as are the dead.—But to return to yourselves. Solitude, isolation, are painful things, and beyond human endurance. I die of having thought it possible to live alone! You should, therefore, dare all in the attempt to leave Lincoln Island, and see once more the land of your birth. I am aware that those wretches have destroyed the vessel you have built."

"We propose to construct a vessel," said Gideon Spilett, "sufficiently large to convey us to the nearest land; but if we should succeed, sooner or later we shall return to Lincoln Island. We are attached to it by too many recollections ever to forget it."

"It is here that we have known Captain Nemo," said Cyrus Harding.

"It is here only that we can make our home!" added Herbert.

"And here shall I sleep the sleep of eternity, if—" replied the captain.

He paused for a moment, and, instead of completing the sentence, said simply—

"Mr. Harding, I wish to speak with you—alone!"

The engineer's companions, respecting the wish of the dying man, retired.

Cyrus Harding remained but a few minutes alone with Captain Nemo, and soon recalled his companions; but he said nothing to them of the private matters which the dying man had confided to him.

Gideon Spilett now watched the captain with extreme care. It was evident that he was no longer sustained by his moral energy, which had lost the power of reaction against his physical weakness.

The day closed without change. The colonists did not quit the *Nautilus* for a moment. Night arrived, although it was impossible to distinguish it from day in the cavern.

Captain Nemo suffered no pain, but he was visibly sinking. His noble features, paled by the approach of death, were perfectly calm. Inaudible words escaped at intervals from his lips, bearing upon various incidents of his chequered career. Life was evidently ebbing slowly and his extremities were already cold.

Once or twice more he spoke to the colonists who stood around him, and smiled on them with that last smile which continues after death.

At length, shortly after midnight, Captain Nemo by a supreme effort succeeded in folding his arms across his breast, as if wishing in that attitude to compose himself for death.

By one o'clock his glance alone showed signs of life. A dying light gleamed in those eyes once so brilliant. Then, murmuring the words, "God and my country!" he quietly expired.

Cyrus Harding, bending low, closed the eyes of him who had once been the Prince Dakkar, and was now not even Captain Nemo.

Herbert and Pencroft sobbed aloud. Tears fell from Ayrton's eyes. Neb was on his knees by the reporter's side, motionless as a statue.

Then Cyrus Harding, extending his hand over the forehead of the dead, said solemnly—

"May his soul be with God! Let us pray!"

Some hours later the colonists fulfilled the promise made to the captain by carrying out his dying wishes.

Cyrus Harding and his companions quitted the *Nautilus*, taking with them the only memento left them by their benefactor, the coffer which contained wealth amounting to millions.

The marvellous saloon, still flooded with light, had been carefully closed. The iron door leading on deck was then securely fastened in such a manner as to prevent even a drop of water from penetrating to the interior of the *Nautilus*.

The colonists then descended into the canoe, which was moored to the side of the submarine vessel.

The canoe was now brought around to the stern. There, at the water-line, were two large stopcocks, communicating with the reservoirs employed in the submersion of the vessel.

The stopcocks were opened, the reservoirs filled, and the *Nautilus*, slowly sinking, disappeared beneath the surface of the lake.

But the colonists were yet able to follow its descent through the waves. The powerful light it gave forth lighted up the translucent water, while the cavern became gradually obscure. At length this vast effusion of electric light faded away, and soon after the *Nautilus*, now the tomb of Captain Nemo, reposed in its ocean bed.

Chapter XVIII

REFLECTIONS OF THE COLONISTS—THEIR LABOURS OF
RECONSTRUCTION RESUMED—THE 1ST OF JANUARY, 1869—A
CLOUD OVER THE SUMMIT OF THE VOLCANO—FIRST WARNINGS OF
AN IRRUPTION—AYRTON AND CYRUS HARDING AT THE CORRAL—
EXPLORATION OF THE DAKKAR GROTTO—WHAT CAPTAIN NEMO
HAD CONFIDED TO THE ENGINEER

AT BREAK OF DAY THE COLONISTS REGAINED IN SILENCE THE ENTRANCE OF THE CAVern, to which they gave the name of "Dakkar Grotto," in memory of Captain Nemo. It was now low-water, and they passed without difficulty under the arcade, washed on the right by the sea.

The canoe was left here, carefully protected from the waves. As an excess of precaution, Pencroft, Neb, and Ayrton drew it upon a little beach which bordered one of the sides of the grotto, in a spot where it could run no risk of harm.

The storm had ceased during the night. The last low mutterings of the thunder died away in the west. Rain fell no longer, but the sky was yet obscured by clouds. On the whole, this month of October, the first of the southern spring, was not ushered in by satisfactory tokens, and the wind had a tendency to shift from one point of the compass to another, which rendered it impossible to count upon settled weather.

Cyrus Harding and his companions, on leaving Dakkar Grotto, had taken the road to the corral. On their way Neb and Herbert were careful to preserve the wire which had been laid down by the captain between the corral and the grotto, and which might at a future time be of service.

The colonists spoke but little on the road. The various incidents of the night of the 15th of October had left a profound impression on their minds. The unknown being whose influence had so effectually protected them, the man whom their imagination had endowed with supernatural powers, Captain Nemo, was no more. His *Nautilus* and he were buried in the depths of the abyss. To each one of them their existence seemed even more isolated than before. They had been accustomed to count upon the intervention of that power which existed no longer, and Gideon Spilett, and even Cyrus Harding, could not escape this impression. Thus they maintained a profound silence during their journey to the corral.

Towards nine in the morning the colonists arrived at Granite House.

It had been agreed that the construction of the vessel should be actively pushed forward, and Cyrus Harding more than ever devoted his time and labour to this object. It was impossible to divine what future lay before them. Evidently the advantage to the colonists would be great of having at their disposal a substantial vessel, capable of keeping the sea even in heavy weather, and large enough to attempt, in case of need, a voyage of some duration. Even if, when their vessel should be completed, the colonists should not resolve to leave Lincoln Island as yet, in order to gain either one of the Polynesian Archipelagoes of the Pacific or the shores of New Zealand, they might at least, sooner or later, proceed to

Tabor Island, to leave there the notice relating to Ayrton. This was a precaution rendered indispensable by the possibility of the Scotch yacht reappearing in those seas, and it was of the highest importance that nothing should be neglected on this point.

The works were then resumed. Cyrus Harding, Pencroft, and Ayrton, assisted by Neb, Gideon Spilett, and Herbert, except when unavoidably called off by other necessary occupations, worked without cessation. It was important that the new vessel should be ready in five months—that is to say, by the beginning of March—if they wished to visit Tabor Island before the equinoctial gales rendered the voyage impracticable. Therefore the carpenters lost not a moment. Moreover, it was unnecessary to manufacture rigging, that of the *Speedy* having been saved entire, so that the hull only of the vessel needed to be constructed.

The end of the year 1868 found them occupied by these important labors, to the exclusion of almost all others. At the expiration of two months and a half the ribs had been set up and the first planks adjusted. It was already evident that the plans made by Cyrus Harding were admirable, and that the vessel would behave well at sea.

Pencroft brought to the task a devouring energy, and scrupled not to grumble when one or the other abandoned the carpenter's axe for the gun of the hunter. It was nevertheless necessary to keep up the stores of Granite House, in view of the approaching winter. But this did not satisfy Pencroft. The brave, honest sailor was not content when the workmen were not at the dockyard. When this happened he grumbled vigourously, and, by way of venting his feelings, did the work of six men.

The weather was very unfavourable during the whole of the summer season. For some days the heat was overpowering, and the atmosphere, saturated with electricity, was only cleared by violent storms. It was rarely that the distant growling of the thunder could not be heard, like a low but incessant murmur, such as is produced in the equatorial regions of the globe.

The 1st of January, 1869, was signalised by a storm of extreme violence, and the thunder burst several times over the island. Large trees were struck by the electric fluid and shattered, and among others one of those gigantic micocouliers which shaded the poultry-yard at the southern extremity of the lake. Had this meteor any relation to the phenomena going on in the bowels of the earth? Was there any connection between the commotion of the atmosphere and that of the interior of the earth? Cyrus Harding was inclined to think that such was the case, for the development of these storms was attended by the renewal of volcanic symptoms.

It was on the 3d of January that Herbert, having ascended at daybreak to the plateau of Prospect Heights to harness one of the onagers, perceived an enormous hat-shaped cloud rolling from the summit of the volcano.

Herbert immediately apprised the colonists, who at once joined him in watching the summit of Mount Franklin.

"Ah!" exclaimed Pencroft, "those are not vapours this time! It seems to me that the giant is not content with breathing; he must smoke!"

This figure of speech employed by the sailor exactly expressed the changes going on at the mouth of the volcano. Already for three months had the crater emitted vapours more or less dense, but which were as yet produced only by an internal ebullition of mineral substances. But now the vapours were replaced by a thick smoke, rising in the form of a greyish column, more than three hundred feet in width at its base, and which spread like an immense mushroom to a height of from seven to eight hundred feet above the summit of the mountain.

"The fire is in the chimney," observed Gideon Spilett.

"And we can't put it out!" replied Herbert.

"The volcano ought to be swept," observed Neb, who spoke as if perfectly serious.

"Well said, Neb!" cried Pencroft, with a shout of laughter; "and you'll undertake the job, no doubt?"

Cyrus Harding attentively observed the dense smoke emitted by Mount Franklin, and even listened, as if expecting to hear some distant muttering. Then, turning towards his companions, from whom he had gone somewhat apart, he said—

"The truth is, my friends, we must not conceal from ourselves that an important change is going forward. The volcanic substances are no longer in a state of ebullition, they have caught fire, and we are undoubtedly menaced by an approaching irruption."

"Well, captain," said Pencroft, "we shall witness the irruption; and if it is a good one, we'll applaud it. I don't see that we need concern ourselves further about the matter."

"It may be so," replied Cyrus Harding, "for the ancient track of the lava is still open; and thanks to this, the crater has hitherto overflowed towards the north. And yet—"

"And yet, as we can derive no advantage from an irruption, it might be better it should not take place," said the reporter.

"Who knows?" answered the sailor. "Perhaps there may be some valuable substance in this volcano, which it will spout forth, and which we may turn to good account!"

Cyrus Harding shook his head with the air of a man who augured no good from the phenomenon whose development had been so sudden. He did not regard so lightly as Pencroft the results of an irruption. If the lava, in consequence of the position of the crater, did not directly menace the wooded and cultivated parts of the island, other complications might present themselves. In fact, irruptions are not unfrequently accompanied by earthquakes; and an island of the nature of Lincoln Island, formed of substances so varied, basalt on one side, granite on the other, lava on the north, rich soil on the south, substances which consequently could not be firmly attached to each other, would be exposed to the risk of disintegration. Although, therefore, the spreading of the volcanic matter might not constitute a serious danger, any movement of the terrestrial structure which should shake the island might entail the gravest consequences.

"It seems to me," said Ayrton, who had reclined so as to place his ear to the ground, "it seems to me that I can hear a dull, rumbling sound, like that of a wagon loaded with bars of iron."

The colonists listened with the greatest attention, and were convinced that Ayrton was not mistaken. The rumbling was mingled with a subterranean roar, which formed a sort of *rinforzando*, and died slowly away, as if some violent storm had passed through the profundities of the globe. But no explosion, properly so termed, could be heard. It might therefore be concluded that the vapours and smoke found a free passage through the central shaft; and that the safety-valve being sufficiently large, no convulsion would be produced, no explosion was to be apprehended.

"Well, then!" said Pencroft, "are we not going back to work? Let Mount Franklin smoke, groan, bellow, or spout forth fire and flame as much as it pleases, that is no reason why we should be idle! Come, Ayrton, Neb, Herbert, Captain Harding, Mr. Spilett, every one of us must turn to at our work to-day! We are going to place the keelson, and a dozen pair of hands would not be too many. Before two months I want our new *Bonadventure*— for we shall keep the old name, shall we not?—to float on the waters of Port Balloon! Therefore there is not an hour to lose!"

All the colonists, their services thus requisitioned by Pencroft, descended to the dock-yard, and proceeded to place the keelson, a thick mass of wood which forms the lower portion of a ship and unites firmly the timbers of the hull. It was an arduous undertaking, in which all took part.

They continued their labours during the whole of this day, the 3d of January, without thinking further of the volcano, which could not, besides, be seen from the shore of Granite House. But once or twice, large shadows, veiling the sun, which described its diurnal arc through an extremely clear sky, indicated that a thick cloud of smoke passed between its disc and the island. The wind, blowing on the shore, carried all these vapours to the westward. Cyrus Harding and Gideon Spilett remarked these sombre appearances, and from time to time discussed the evident progress of the volcanic phenomena, but their work went on without interruption. It was, besides, of the first importance from every point of view, that the vessel should be finished with the least possible delay. In presence of the eventualities which might arise, the safety of the colonists would be to a great extent secured by their ship. Who could tell that it might not prove someday their only refuge?

In the evening, after supper, Cyrus Harding, Gideon Spilett, and Herbert again ascended the plateau of Prospect Heights. It was already dark, and the obscurity would permit them to ascertain if flames or incandescent matter thrown up by the volcano were mingled with the vapour and smoke accumulated at the mouth of the crater.

"The crater is on fire!" said Herbert, who, more active than his companions, first reached the plateau.

Mount Franklin, distant about six miles, now appeared like a gigantic torch, around the summit of which turned fuliginous flames. So much smoke, and possibly scoriae and cinders were mingled with them, that their light gleamed but faintly amid the gloom of the night. But a kind of lurid brilliancy spread over the island, against which stood out confusedly the wooded masses of the heights. Immense whirlwinds of vapour obscured the sky, through which glimmered a few stars.

"The change is rapid!" said the engineer.

"That is not surprising," answered the reporter. "The reawakening of the volcano already dates back some time. You may remember, Cyrus, that the first vapours appeared about the time we searched the sides of the mountain to discover Captain Nemo's retreat. It was, if I mistake not, about the 15th of October."

"Yes," replied Herbert, "two months and a half ago!"

"The subterranean fires have therefore been smouldering for ten weeks," resumed Gideon Spilett, "and it is not to be wondered at that they now break out with such violence!"

"Do not you feel a certain vibration of the soil?" asked Cyrus Harding.

"Yes," replied Gideon Spilett, "but there is a great difference between that and an earthquake."

"I do not affirm that we are menaced with an earthquake," answered Cyrus Harding, "may God preserve us from that! No; these vibrations are due to the effervescence of the central fire. The crust of the earth is simply the shell of a boiler, and you know that such a shell, under the pressure of steam, vibrates like a sonorous plate. It is this effect which is being produced at this moment."

"What magnificent flames!" exclaimed Herbert.

At this instant a kind of bouquet of flames shot forth from the crater, the brilliancy of which was visible even through the vapours. Thousands of luminous sheets and barbed tongues of fire were cast in various directions. Some, extending beyond the dome of smoke, dissipated it, leaving behind an incandescent powder. This was accompanied by successive explosions, resembling the discharge of a battery of mitrailleuses.

Cyrus Harding, the reporter, and Herbert, after spending an hour on the plateau of Prospect Heights, again descended to the beach, and returned to Granite House. The engineer was thoughtful and preoccupied, so much so, indeed, that Gideon Spilett enquired if he apprehended any immediate danger, of which the irruption might directly or indirectly be the cause.

"Yes, and no," answered Cyrus Harding.

"Nevertheless," continued the reporter, "would not the greatest misfortune which could happen to us be an earthquake which would overturn the island? Now, I do not suppose that this is to be feared, since the vapours and lava have found a free outlet."

"True," replied Cyrus Harding, "and I do not fear an earthquake in the sense in which the term is commonly applied to convulsions of the soil provoked by the expansion of subterranean gases. But other causes may produce great disasters."

"How so, my dear Cyrus?"

"I am not certain. I must consider. I must visit the mountain. In a few days I shall learn more on this point."

Gideon Spilett said no more, and soon, in spite of the explosions of the volcano, whose intensity increased, and which were repeated by the echoes of the island, the inhabitants of Granite House were sleeping soundly.

Three days passed by—the 4th, 5th, and 6th of January. The construction of the vessel was diligently continued, and without offering further explanations the engineer pushed forward the work with all his energy. Mount Franklin was now hooded by a sombre cloud of sinister aspect, and, amid the flames, vomiting forth incandescent rocks, some of which fell back into the crater itself. This caused Pencroft, who would only look at the matter in the light of a joke, to exclaim—

"Ah! the giant is playing at cup and ball; he is a conjurer."

In fact, the substances thrown up fell back again into the abyss, and it did not seem that the lava, though swollen by the internal pressure, had yet risen to the orifice of the crater. At any rate, the opening on the north-east, which was partly visible, poured out no torrent upon the northern slope of the mountain.

Nevertheless, however pressing was the construction of the vessel, other duties demanded the presence of the colonists on various portions of the island. Before everything it was necessary to go to the corral, where the flocks of musmons and goats were enclosed, and replenish the provision of forage for those animals. It was accordingly arranged that Ayrton should proceed thither the next day, the 7th of January; and as he was sufficient for the task, to which he was accustomed, Pencroft and the rest were somewhat surprised on hearing the engineer say to Ayrton—

"As you are going to-morrow to the corral I will accompany you."

"But, Captain Harding," exclaimed the sailor, "our working days will not be many, and if you go also we shall be two pair of hands short!"

"We shall return to-morrow," replied Cyrus Harding, "but it is necessary that I should go to the corral. I must learn how the irruption is progressing."

"The irruption! always the irruption!" answered Pencroft, with an air of discontent. "An important thing, truly, this irruption! I trouble myself very little about it."

Whatever might be the sailor's opinion, the expedition projected by the engineer was settled for the next day. Herbert wished to accompany Cyrus Harding, but he would not vex Pencroft by his absence.

The next day, at dawn, Cyrus Harding and Ayrton, mounting the cart drawn by two onagers, took the road to the corral and set off at a round trot.

Above the forest were passing large clouds, to which the crater of Mount Franklin incessantly added fuliginous matter. These clouds, which rolled heavily in the air, were evidently composed of heterogeneous substances. It was not alone from the volcano that they derived their strange opacity and weight. Scoriae, in a state of dust, like powdered pumice-stone, and greyish ashes as small as the finest feculae, were held in suspension in the midst of their thick folds. These ashes are so fine that they have been observed in the air for whole months. After the irruption of 1783 in Iceland for upwards of a year the atmosphere was thus charged with volcanic dust through which the rays of the sun were only with difficulty discernible.

But more often this pulverised matter falls, and this happened on the present occasion. Cyrus Harding and Ayrton had scarcely reached the corral when a sort of black snow like fine gunpowder fell, and instantly changed the appearance of the soil. Trees, meadows, all disappeared beneath a covering several inches in depth. But, very fortunately, the wind blew from the north-east, and the greater part of the cloud dissolved itself over the sea.

"This is very singular, Captain Harding," said Ayrton.

"It is very serious," replied the engineer. "This powdered pumice-stone, all this mineral dust, proves how grave is the convulsion going forward in the lower depths of the volcano."

"But can nothing be done?"

"Nothing, except to note the progress of the phenomenon. Do you, therefore, Ayrton, occupy yourself with the necessary work at the corral. In the meantime I will ascend just beyond the source of Red Creek and examine the condition of the mountain upon its northern aspect. Then—"

"Well, Captain Harding?"

"Then we will pay a visit to Dakkar Grotto. I wish to inspect it. At any rate I will come back for you in two hours."

Ayrton then proceeded to enter the corral, and, while waiting the engineer's return, busied himself with the musmons and goats, which seemed to feel a certain uneasiness in presence of these first signs of an irruption.

Meanwhile Cyrus Harding ascended the crest of the eastern spur, passed Red Creek, and arrived at the spot where he and his companions had discovered a sulphurous spring at the time of their first exploration.

How changed was everything! Instead of a single column of smoke he counted thirteen, forced through the soil as if violently propelled by some piston. It was evident that the crust of the earth was subjected in this part of the globe to a frightful pressure. The atmosphere was saturated with gases and carbonic acid, mingled with aqueous vapours. Cyrus Harding felt the volcanic tufa with which the plain was strewn, and which was but pulverised cinders hardened into solid blocks by time, tremble beneath him, but he could discover no traces of fresh lava.

The engineer became more assured of this when he observed all the northern part of Mount Franklin. Pillars of smoke and flame escaped from the crater; a hail of scoriae fell on the ground; but no current of lava burst from the mouth of the volcano, which proved that the volcanic matter had not yet attained the level of the superior orifice of the central shaft.

"But I would prefer that it were so," said Cyrus Harding to himself. "At any rate, I should then know that the lava had followed its accustomed track. Who can say that it may not take a new course? But the danger does not consist in that! Captain Nemo foresaw it clearly! No, the danger does not lie there!"

Cyrus Harding advanced towards the enormous causeway whose prolongation enclosed the narrow Shark Gulf. He could now sufficiently examine on this side the ancient channels of the lava. There was no doubt in his mind that the most recent irruption had occurred at a far-distant epoch.

He then returned by the same way, listening attentively to the subterranean mutterings which rolled like long-continued thunder, interrupted by deafening explosions. At nine in the morning he reached the corral.

Ayrton awaited him.

"The animals are cared for, Captain Harding," said Ayrton.

"Good, Ayrton."

"They seem uneasy, Captain Harding."

"Yes, instinct speaks through them, and instinct is never deceived."

"Are you ready?"

"Take a lamp, Ayrton," answered the engineer; "we will start at once."

Ayrton did as desired. The onagers, unharnessed, roamed in the corral. The gate was secured on the outside, and Cyrus Harding, preceding Ayrton, took the narrow path which led westward to the shore.

The soil they walked upon was choked with the pulverised matter fallen from the cloud. No quadruped appeared in the woods. Even the birds had fled. Sometimes a passing breeze raised the covering of ashes, and the two colonists, enveloped in a whirlwind of dust, lost sight of each other. They were then careful to cover their eyes and mouths with handkerchiefs, for they ran the risk of being blinded and suffocated.

It was impossible for Cyrus Harding and Ayrton, with these impediments, to make rapid progress. Moreover, the atmosphere was close, as if the oxygen had been partly burned up, and had become unfit for respiration. At every hundred paces they were obliged to stop to take breath. It was therefore past ten o'clock when the engineer and his companion reached the crest of the enormous mass of rocks of basalt and porphyry which composed the north-west coast of the island.

Ayrton and Cyrus Harding commenced the descent of this abrupt declivity, following almost step for step the difficult path which, during that stormy night, had led them to Dakkar Grotto. In open day the descent was less perilous, and, besides, the bed of ashes which covered the polished surface of the rock enabled them to make their footing more secure.

The ridge at the end of the shore, about forty feet in height, was soon reached. Cyrus Harding recollected that this elevation gradually sloped towards the level of the sea. Although the tide was at present low, no beach could he seen, and the waves, thickened by the volcanic dust, beat upon the basaltic rocks.

Cyrus Harding and Ayrton found without difficulty the entrance to Dakkar Grotto, and paused for a moment at the last rock before it.

"The iron boat should be there," said the engineer.

"It is here, Captain Harding," replied Ayrton, drawing towards him the fragile craft, which was protected by the arch of the vault.

"On board, Ayrton!"

The two colonists stepped into the boat. A slight undulation of the waves carried it farther under the low arch of the crypt, and there Ayrton, with the aid of flint and steel, lighted the lamp. He then took the oars, and the lamp having been placed in the bow of the boat, so that its rays fell before them, Cyrus Harding took the helm and steered through the shades of the grotto.

The *Nautilus* was there no longer to illuminate the cavern with its electric light. Possibly it might not yet be extinguished, but no ray escaped from the depths of the abyss in which reposed all that was mortal of Captain Nemo.

The light afforded by the lamp, although feeble, nevertheless enabled the engineer to advance slowly, following the wall of the cavern. A death-like silence reigned under the vaulted roof, or at least in the anterior portion, for soon Cyrus Harding distinctly heard the rumbling which proceeded from the bowels of the mountain.

"That comes from the volcano," he said.

Besides these sounds, the presence of chemical combinations was soon betrayed by their powerful odour, and the engineer and his companion were almost suffocated by sulphurous vapours.

"This is what Captain Nemo feared," murmured Cyrus Harding, changing countenance. "We must go to the end, notwithstanding."

"Forward!" replied Ayrton, bending to his oars and directing the boat towards the head of the cavern.

Twenty-five minutes after entering the mouth of the grotto the boat reached the extreme end.

Cyrus Harding then, standing up, cast the light of the lamp upon the walls of the cavern which separated it from the central shaft of the volcano. What was the thickness of this wall? It might be ten feet or a hundred feet—it was impossible to say. But the subterranean sounds were too perceptible to allow of the supposition that it was of any great thickness.

The engineer, after having explored the wall at a certain height horizontally, fastened the lamp to the end of an oar, and again surveyed the basaltic wall at a greater elevation.

There, through scarcely visible clefts and joinings, escaped a pungent vapour, which infected the atmosphere of the cavern. The wall was broken by large cracks, some of which extended to within two or three feet of the water's edge.

Cyrus Harding thought for a brief space. Then he said in a low voice—

"Yes! the captain was right! The danger lies there, and a terrible danger!"

Ayrton said not a word, but, upon a sign from Cyrus Harding, resumed the oars, and half-an-hour later the engineer and he reached the entrance of Dakkar Grotto.

Chapter XIX

CYRUS HARDING GIVES AN ACCOUNT OF HIS EXPLORATION—THE CONSTRUCTION OF THE SHIP PUSHED FORWARD—A LAST VISIT TO THE CORRAL—THE BATTLE BETWEEN FIRE AND WATER—ALL THAT REMAINS OF THE ISLAND—IT IS DECIDED TO LAUNCH THE VESSEL—THE NIGHT OF THE 8TH OF MARCH

THE NEXT DAY, THE 8TH DAY OF JANUARY, AFTER A DAY AND NIGHT PASSED AT THE COR- ral, where they left all in order, Cyrus Harding and Ayrton arrived at Granite House.

The engineer immediately called his companions together, and informed them of the imminent danger which threatened Lincoln Island, and from which no human power could deliver them.

"My friends," he said, and his voice betrayed the depth of his emotion, "our island is not among those which will endure while this earth endures. It is doomed to more or less speedy destruction, the cause of which it bears within itself, and from which nothing can save it."

The colonists looked at each other, then at the engineer. They did not clearly comprehend him.

"Explain yourself, Cyrus!" said Gideon Spilett.

"I will do so," replied Cyrus Harding, "or rather I will simply afford you the explanation which, during our few minutes of private conversation, was given me by Captain Nemo."

"Captain Nemo!" exclaimed the colonists.

"Yes, and it was the last service he desired to render us before his death!"

"The last service!" exclaimed Pencroft, "the last service! You will see that though he is dead he will render us others yet!"

"But what did the captain say?" enquired the reporter.

"I will tell you, my friends," said the engineer. "Lincoln Island does not resemble the other islands of the Pacific, and a fact of which Captain Nemo has made me cognisant must sooner or later bring about the subversion of its foundation."

"Nonsense! Lincoln Island, it can't be!" cried Pencroft, who, in spite of the respect he felt for Cyrus Harding, could not prevent a gesture of incredulity.

"Listen, Pencroft," resumed the engineer, "I will tell you what Captain Nemo communicated to me, and which I myself confirmed yesterday, during the exploration of Dakkar Grotto. This cavern stretches under the island as far as the volcano, and is only separated from its central shaft by the wall which terminates it. Now, this wall is seamed with fissures and clefts which already allow the sulphurous gases generated in the interior of the volcano to escape."

"Well?" said Pencroft, his brow suddenly contracting.

"Well, then, I saw that these fissures widen under the internal pressure from within, that the wall of basalt is gradually giving way, and that after a longer or shorter period it will afford a passage to the waters of the lake which fill the cavern."

"Good!" replied Pencroft, with an attempt at pleasantry. "The sea will extinguish the _____, and there will be an end of the matter!"

"_____" said Cyrus Harding, "should a day arrive when the sea, rushing through the ing lava, Lincoln Island will that day ___ central shaft into the interior of the island to the boiling island of Sicily were the Mediterranean to precipitate itself into Mount Etna."

The colonists made no answer to these significant words of the engineer. They now understood the danger by which they were menaced.

It may be added that Cyrus Harding had in no way exaggerated the danger to be apprehended. Many persons have formed an idea that it would be possible to extinguish volcanoes, which are almost always situated on the shores of a sea or lake, by opening a passage for the admission of the water. But they are not aware that this would be to incur the risk of blowing up a portion of the globe, like a boiler whose steam is suddenly expanded by intense heat. The water, rushing into a cavity whose temperature might be estimated at thousands of degrees, would be converted into steam with a sudden energy which no enclosure could resist.

It was not therefore doubtful that the island, menaced by a frightful and approaching convulsion, would endure only so long as the wall of Dakkar Grotto itself should endure. It was not even a question of months, nor of weeks, but of days; it might be of hours.

The first sentiment which the colonists felt was that of profound sorrow. They thought not so much of the peril which menaced themselves personally, but of the destruction of the island which had sheltered them, which they had cultivated, which they loved so well, and had hoped to render so flourishing. So much effort ineffectually expended, so much labour lost.

Pencroft could not prevent a large tear from rolling down his cheek, nor did he attempt to conceal it.

Some further conversation now took place. The chances yet in favour of the colonists were discussed; but finally it was agreed that there was not an hour to be lost, that the building and fitting of the vessel should be pushed forward with their utmost energy, and that this was the sole chance of safety for the inhabitants of Lincoln Island.

All hands, therefore, set to work on the vessel. What could it avail to sow, to reap, to hunt, to increase the stores of Granite House? The contents of the store-house and outbuildings contained more than sufficient to provide the ship for a voyage, however long might be its duration. But it was imperative that the ship should be ready to receive them before the inevitable catastrophe should arrive.

Their labours were now carried on with feverish ardour. By the 23d of January the vessel was half-decked over. Up to this time no change had taken place on the summit of the volcano. Vapor and smoke mingled with flames and incandescent stones were thrown up from the crater. But during the night of the 23d, in consequence of the lava attaining the level of the first stratum of the volcano, the hat-shaped cone which formed over the latter disappeared. A frightful sound was heard. The colonists at first thought the island was rent asunder, and rushed out of Granite House.

This occurred about two o'clock in the morning.

The sky appeared on fire. The superior cone, a mass of rock a thousand feet in height, and weighing thousands of millions of pounds, had been thrown down upon the island, making it tremble to its foundation. Fortunately, this cone inclined to the so in- and had fallen upon the plain of sand and tufa stretching between them. The aperture of the crater being thus enlarged projected red-hot. At the same tense that by the simple effect of reflection the at— time a torrent of lava, bursting from the new summit, poured out in long cascades, like water escaping from a vase too full, and a thousand tongues of fire crept over the sides of the volcano.

"The corral! the corral!" exclaimed Ayrton.

It was, in fact, towards the corral that the lava was rushing as the new crater faced the east, and consequently the fertile portions of the island, the springs of Red Creek and Ja-camar Wood, were menaced with instant destruction.

At Ayrton's cry the colonists rushed to the onagers' stables. The cart was at once har-nessed. All were possessed by the same thought—to hasten to the corral and set at liberty the animals it enclosed.

Before three in the morning they arrived at the corral. The cries of the terrified mus-mons and goats indicated the alarm which possessed them. Already a torrent of burning matter and liquefied minerals fell from the side of the mountain upon the meadows as far as the side of the palisade. The gate was burst open by Ayrton, and the animals, bewildered with terror, fled in all directions.

An hour afterwards the boiling lava filled the corral, converting into vapour the water of the little rivulet which ran through it, burning up the house like dry grass, and leaving not even a post of the palisade to mark the spot where the corral once stood.

To contend against this disaster would have been folly—nay, madness. In presence of Nature's grand convulsions man is powerless.

It was now daylight—the 24th of January. Cyrus Harding and his companions, before returning to Granite House, desired to ascertain the probable direction this inundation of lava was about to take. The soil sloped gradually from Mount Franklin to the east coast, and it was to be feared that, in spite of the thick Jacamar Wood, the torrent would reach the plateau of Prospect Heights.

"The lake will cover us," said Gideon Spilett.

"I hope so!" was Cyrus Harding's only reply.

The colonists were desirous of reaching the plain upon which the superior cone of Mount Franklin had fallen, but the lava arrested their progress. It had followed, on one side, the valley of Red Creek, and on the other that of Falls River, evaporating those water-courses in its passage. There was no possibility of crossing the torrent of lava; on the contrary, the colonists were obliged to retreat before it. The volcano, without its crown, was no longer recognisable, terminated as it was by a sort of flat table which re-placed the ancient crater. From two openings in its southern and eastern sides an unceasing flow of lava poured forth, thus forming two distinct streams. Above the new crater a cloud of smoke and ashes, mingled with those of the atmosphere, massed over the island. Loud peals of thunder broke, and could scarcely be distinguished from the rumblings of the mountain, whose mouth vomited forth ignited rocks, which, hurled to more than a thousand feet, burst in the air like shells. Flashes of lightning rivaled in intensity the volcano's irruption.

Towards seven in the morning the position was no longer tenable by the colonists, who accordingly took shelter in the borders of Jacamar Wood. Not only did the projectiles begin to rain around them, but the lava, overflowing the bed of Red Creek, threatened to cut off the road to the corral. The nearest rows of trees caught fire, and their sap, suddenly transformed into vapour, caused them to explode with loud reports, while others, less moist, remained unhurt in the midst of the inundation.

The colonists had again taken the road to the corral. They proceeded but slowly, frequently looking back; but, in consequence of the inclination of the soil, the lava gained rapidly in the east, and as its lower waves became solidified others, at boiling heat, covered them immediately.

Meanwhile, the principal stream of Red Creek valley became more and more menacing. All this portion of the forest was on fire, and enormous wreaths of smoke rolled over the trees, whose trunks were already consumed by the lava.

The colonists halted near the lake, about half-a-mile from the mouth of Red Creek. A question of life or death was now to be decided.

Cyrus Harding, accustomed to the consideration of important crises, and aware that he was addressing men capable of hearing the truth, whatever it might be, then said—

"Either the lake will arrest the progress of the lava, and a part of the island will be preserved from utter destruction, or the stream will overrun the forests of the Far West, and not a tree or plant will remain on the surface of the soil. We shall have no prospect but that of starvation upon these barren rocks—a death which will probably be anticipated by the explosion of the island."

"In that case," replied Pencroft, folding his arms and stamping his foot, "what's the use of working any longer on the vessel?"

"Pencroft," answered Cyrus Harding, "we must do our duty to the last!"

At this instant the river of lava, after having broken a passage through the noble trees it devoured in its course, reached the borders of the lake. At this point there was an elevation of the soil which, had it been greater, might have sufficed to arrest the torrent.

"To work!" cried Cyrus Harding.

The engineer's thought was at once understood. It might be possible to dam, as it were, the torrent, and thus compel it to pour itself into the lake.

The colonists hastened to the dockyard. They returned with shovels, picks, axes, and by means of banking the earth with the aid of fallen trees they succeeded in a few hours in raising an embankment three feet high and some hundreds of paces in length. It seemed to them, when they had finished, as if they had scarcely been working more than a few minutes.

It was not a moment too soon. The liquefied substances soon after reached the bottom of the barrier. The stream of lava swelled like a river about to overflow its banks, and threatened to demolish the sole obstacle which could prevent it from overrunning the whole Far West. But the dam held firm, and after a moment of terrible suspense the torrent precipitated itself into Grant Lake from a height of twenty feet.

The colonists, without moving or uttering a word, breathlessly regarded this strife of the two elements.

What a spectacle was this conflict between water and fire! What pen could describe the marvellous horror of this scene—what pencil could depict it? The water hissed as it evaporated by contact with the boiling lava. The vapour whirled in the air to an immeasurable height, as if the valves of an immense boiler had been suddenly opened. But, however considerable might be the volume of water contained in the lake, it must eventually be absorbed, because it was not replenished, while the stream of lava, fed from an inexhaustible source, rolled on without ceasing new waves of incandescent matter.

The first waves of lava which fell in the lake immediately solidified and accumulated so as speedily to emerge from it. Upon their surface fell other waves, which in their turn became stone, but a step nearer the centre of the lake. In this manner was formed a pier which threatened to gradually fill up the lake, which could not overflow, the water displaced by the lava being evaporated. The hissing of the water rent the air with a deafening sound, and the vapour, blown by the wind, fell in rain upon the sea. The pier became longer and longer, and the blocks of lava piled themselves one on another. Where formerly stretched the calm waters of the lake now appeared an enormous mass of smoking rocks, as if an upheaving of the soil had formed immense shoals. Imagine the waters of the lake aroused by a hurricane, then suddenly solidified by an intense frost, and some conception may be formed of the aspect of the lake three hours after the irruption of this irresistible torrent of lava.

This time water would be vanquished by fire.

Nevertheless it was a fortunate circumstance for the colonists that the effusion of lava should have been in the direction of Lake Grant. They had before them some days' respite. The plateau of Prospect Heights, Granite House, and the dockyard were for the moment preserved. And these few days it was necessary to employ them in planking, carefully calking the vessel, and launching her. The colonists would then take refuge on board the vessel, content to rig her after she should be afloat on the waters. With the danger of an explosion which threatened to destroy the island there could be no security on shore. The walls of Granite House, once so sure a retreat, might at any moment fall in upon them.

During the six following days, from the 25th to the 30th of January, the colonists accomplished as much of the construction of their vessel as twenty men could have done. They hardly allowed themselves a moment's repose, and the glare of the flames which shot from the crater enabled them to work night and day. The flow of lava continued, but perhaps less abundantly. This was fortunate, for Lake Grant was almost entirely choked up, and if more lava should accumulate it would inevitably spread over the plateau of Prospect Heights, and thence upon the beach.

But if the island was thus partially protected on this side, it was not so with the western part.

In fact, the second stream of lava, which had followed the valley of Falls River, a valley of great extent, the land on both sides of the creek being flat, met with no obstacle. The burning liquid had then spread through the forest of the Far West. At this period of the year, when the trees were dried up by a tropical heat, the forest caught fire instantaneously, in such a manner that the conflagration extended itself both by the trunks of the trees and by their higher branches, whose interlacement favoured its progress. It even appeared that the current of flame spread more rapidly among the summits of the trees than the current of lava at their bases.

Thus it happened that the wild animals, jaguars, wild boars, capybaras, koalas, and game of every kind, mad with terror, had fled to the banks of the Mercy and to the Tadorn Marsh, beyond the road to Port Balloon. But the colonists were too much occupied with their task to pay any attention to even the most formidable of these animals. They had abandoned Granite House, and would not even take shelter at the Chimneys, but encamped under a tent, near the mouth of the Mercy.

Each day Cyrus Harding and Gideon Spilett ascended the plateau of Prospect Heights. Sometimes Herbert accompanied them, but never Pencroft, who could not bear to look upon the prospect of the island now so utterly devastated.

It was, in truth, a heartrending spectacle. All the wooded part of the island was now completely bare. One single clump of green trees raised their heads at the extremity of Serpentine Peninsula. Here and there were a few grotesque blackened and branchless stumps. The side of the devastated forest was even more barren than Tadorn Marsh. The irruption of lava had been complete. Where formerly sprang up that charming verdure, the soil was now nothing but a savage mass of volcanic tufa. In the valleys of the Falls and Mercy rivers no drop of water now flowed towards the sea, and should Lake Grant be entirely dried up, the colonists would have no means of quenching their thirst. But, fortunately the lava had spared the southern corner of the lake, containing all that remained of the drinking water of the island. Towards the north-west stood out the rugged and well-defined outlines of the sides of the volcano, like a gigantic claw hovering over the island. What a sad and fearful sight, and how painful to the colonists, who, from a fertile domain covered with forests, irrigated by water-courses, and enriched by the produce of their toils, found themselves, as it were, transported to a desolate rock, upon which, but for their reserves of provisions, they could not even gather the means of subsistence!

"It is enough to break one's heart!" said Gideon Spilett, one day.

"Yes, Spilett," answered the engineer. "May God grant us the time to complete this vessel, now our sole refuge!"

"Do not you think, Cyrus, that the violence of the irruption has somewhat lessened? The volcano still vomits forth lava, but somewhat less abundantly, if I mistake not."

"It matters little," answered Cyrus Harding. "The fire is still burning in the interior of the mountain, and the sea may break in at any moment. We are in the condition of passengers whose ship is devoured by a conflagration which they cannot extinguish, and who know that sooner or later the flames must reach the powder-magazine. To work, Spilett, to work, and let us not lose an hour!"

During eight days more, that is to say until the 7th of February, the lava continued to flow, but the irruption was confined within the previous limits. Cyrus Harding feared above all lest the liquefied matter should overflow the shore, for in that event the dockyard could not escape. Moreover, about this time the colonists felt in the frame of the island vibrations which alarmed them to the highest degree.

It was the 20th of February. Yet another month must elapse before the vessel would be ready for sea. Would the island hold together till then? The intention of Pencroft and

Cyrus Harding was to launch the vessel as soon as the hull should be complete. The deck, the upperworks, the interior woodwork, and the rigging might be finished afterwards, but the essential point was that the colonists should have an assured refuge away from the island. Perhaps it might be even better to conduct the vessel to Port Balloon, that is to say, as far as possible from the centre of irruption, for at the mouth of the Mercy, between the islet and the wall of granite, it would run the risk of being crushed in the event of any convulsion. All the exertions of the voyagers were therefore concentrated upon the completion of the hull.

Thus the 3d of March arrived, and they might calculate upon launching the vessel in ten days.

Hope revived in the hearts of the colonists, who had, in this fourth year of their sojourn on Lincoln Island, suffered so many trials. Even Pencroft lost in some measure the sombre taciturnity occasioned by the devastation and ruin of his domain. His hopes, it is true, were concentrated upon his vessel.

"We shall finish it," he said to the engineer, "we shall finish it, captain, and it is time, for the season is advancing and the equinox will soon be here. Well, if necessary, we must put in to Tabor Island to spend the winter. But think of Tabor Island after Lincoln Island. Ah, how unfortunate! Who could have believed it possible?"

"Let us get on," was the engineer's invariable reply.

And they worked away without losing a moment.

"Master," asked Neb, a few days later, "do you think all this could have happened if Captain Nemo had been still alive?"

"Certainly, Neb," answered Cyrus Harding.

"I, for one, don't believe it!" whispered Pencroft to Neb.

"Nor I!" answered Neb seriously.

During the first week of March appearances again became menacing. Thousands of threads like glass, formed of fluid lava, fell like rain upon the island. The crater was again boiling with lava which overflowed the back of the volcano. The torrent flowed along the surface of the hardened tufa, and destroyed the few meager skeletons of trees which had withstood the first irruption. The stream, flowing this time towards the south-west shore of Lake Grant, stretched beyond Creek Glycerine, and invaded the plateau of Prospect Heights. This last blow to the work of the colonists was terrible. The mill, the buildings of the inner court, the stables, were all destroyed. The affrighted poultry fled in all directions. Top and Jup showed signs of the greatest alarm, as if their instinct warned them of an impending catastrophe. A large number of the animals of the island had perished in the first irruption. Those which survived found no refuge but Tadorn Marsh, save a few to which the plateau of Prospect Heights afforded an asylum. But even this last retreat was now closed to them, and the lava-torrent, flowing over the edge of the granite wall, began to pour down upon the beach its cataracts of fire. The sublime horror of this spectacle passed all description. During the night it could only be compared to a Niagara of molten fluid, with its incandescent vapours above and its boiling masses below.

The colonists were driven to their last entrenchment, and although the upper seams of the vessel were not yet calked, they decided to launch her at once.

Pencroft and Ayrton therefore set about the necessary preparations for the launch, which was to take place the morning of the next day, the 9th of March.

But during the night of the 8th an enormous column of vapour escaping from the crater rose with frightful explosions to a height of more than three thousand feet. The wall of Dakkar Grotto had evidently given way under the pressure of gases, and the sea, rushing through the central shaft into the igneous gulf, was at once converted into vapour. But the crater could not afford a sufficient outlet for this vapour. An explosion, which might have been heard at a distance of a hundred miles, shook the air. Fragments of mountains fell into the Pacific, and, in a few minutes, the ocean rolled over the spot where Lincoln Island once stood.

Chapter XX

An Isolated Rock in the Pacific—The Last Refuge of the Colonists of Lincoln Island—Death Their Only Prospect—Unexpected Succor—Why and How It Arrives—A Last Kindness—An Island on Terra Firma—The Tomb of Captain Prince Dakkar Nemo

An isolated rock, thirty feet in length, twenty in breadth, scarcely ten from the water's edge, such was the only solid point which the waves of the Pacific had not engulfed.

It was all that remained of the structure of Granite House! The wall had fallen head-long and been then shattered to fragments, and a few of the rocks of the large room were piled one above another to form this point. All around had disappeared in the abyss; the inferior cone of Mount Franklin, rent asunder by the explosion; the lava jaws of Shark Gulf, the plateau of Prospect Heights, Safety Islet, the granite rocks of Port Balloon, the basalts of Dakkar Grotto, the long Serpentine Peninsula, so distant nevertheless from the centre of the irruption. All that could now be seen of Lincoln Island was the narrow rock which now served as a refuge to the six colonists and their dog Top.

The animals had also perished in the catastrophe; the birds, as well as those representing the fauna of the island—all either crushed or drowned, and the unfortunate Jup himself had, alas! found his death in some crevice of the soil.

If Cyrus Harding, Gideon Spilett, Herbert, Pencroft, Neb, and Ayrton had survived, it was because, assembled under their tent, they had been hurled into the sea at the instant when the fragments of the island rained down on every side.

When they reached the surface they could only perceive, at half a cable-length, this mass of rocks, towards which they swam and on which they found footing.

On this barren rock they had now existed for nine days. A few provisions taken from the magazine of Granite House before the catastrophe, a little fresh water from the rain which had fallen in a hollow of the rock, was all that the unfortunate colonists possessed. Their last hope, the vessel, had been shattered to pieces. They had no means of quitting the reef; no fire, nor any means of obtaining it. It seemed that they must inevitably perish.

This day, the 18th of March, there remained only provisions for two days, although they limited their consumption to the bare necessaries of life. All their science and intelligence could avail them nothing in their present position. They were in the hand of God.

Cyrus Harding was calm, Gideon Spilett more nervous, and Pencroft, a prey to sullen anger, walked to and fro on the rock. Herbert did not for a moment quit the engineer's side, as if demanding from him that assistance he had no power to give. Neb and Ayrton were resigned to their fate.

"Ah, what a misfortune! what a misfortune!" often repeated Pencroft. "If we had but a walnut-shell to take us to Tabor Island! But we have nothing, nothing!"

"Captain Nemo did right to die," said Neb.

During the five ensuing days Cyrus Harding and his unfortunate companions husbanded their provisions with the most extreme care, eating only what would prevent them from dying of starvation. Their weakness was extreme. Herbert and Neb began to show symptoms of delirium.

Under these circumstances was it possible for them to retain even the shadow of a hope? No! What was their sole remaining chance? That a vessel should appear in sight of the rock? But they knew only too well from experience that no ships ever visited this part of the Pacific. Could they calculate that, by a truly providential coincidence, the Scotch yacht would arrive precisely at this time in search of Ayrton at Tabor Island? It was scarcely probable; and, besides, supposing she should come there, as the colonists had not been able to deposit a notice pointing out Ayrton's change of abode, the commander of the yacht, after having explored Tabor Island without results, would again set sail and return to lower latitudes.

No! no hope of being saved could be retained, and a horrible death, death from hunger and thirst, awaited them upon this rock.

Already they were stretched on the rock, inanimate, and no longer conscious of what passed around them. Ayrton alone, by a supreme effort, from time to time raised his head, and cast a despairing glance over the desert ocean.

But on the morning of the 24th of March Ayrton's arms were extended towards a point in the horizon; he raised himself, at first on his knees, then upright, and his hand seemed to make a signal.

A sail was in sight off the rock. She was evidently not without an object. The reef was the mark for which she was making in a direct line, under all steam, and the unfortunate colonists might have made her out some hours before if they had had the strength to watch the horizon.

"The *Duncan!*" murmured Ayrton—and fell back without sign of life.

*   *   *   *   *

When Cyrus Harding and his companions recovered consciousness, thanks to the attention lavished upon them, they found themselves in the cabin of a steamer, without being able to comprehend how they had escaped death.

A word from Ayrton explained everything.

"The *Duncan!*" he murmured.

"The *Duncan!*" exclaimed Cyrus Harding. And raising his hand to Heaven, he said, "Oh! Almighty God! mercifully hast Thou preserved us!"

It was, in fact, the *Duncan*, Lord Glenarvan's yacht, now commanded by Robert, son of Captain Grant, who had been despatched to Tabor Island to find Ayrton, and bring him back to his native land after twelve years of expiation.

The colonists were not only saved, but already on the way to their native country.

"Captain Grant," asked Cyrus Harding, "who can have suggested to you the idea, after having left Tabor Island, where you did not find Ayrton, of coming a hundred miles farther north-east?"

"Captain Harding," replied Robert Grant, "it was in order to find, not only Ayrton, but yourself and your companions."

"My companions and myself?"

"Doubtless, at Lincoln Island."

"At Lincoln Island!" exclaimed in a breath Gideon Spilett, Herbert, Neb, and Pencroft, in the highest degree astonished.

"How could you be aware of the existence of Lincoln Island?" enquired Cyrus Harding, "it is not even named in the charts."

"I knew of it from a document left by you on Tabor Island," answered Robert Grant.

"A document?" cried Gideon Spilett.

"Without doubt, and here it is," answered Robert Grant, producing a paper which indicated the longitude and latitude of Lincoln Island, "the present residence of Ayrton and five American colonists."

"It is Captain Nemo!" cried Cyrus Harding, after having read the notice, and recognised that the handwriting was similar to that of the paper found at the corral.

"Ah!" said Pencroft, "it was then he who took our *Bonadventure* and hazarded himself alone to go to Tabor Island!"

"In order to leave this notice," added Herbert.

"I was then right in saying," exclaimed the sailor, "that even after his death the captain would render us a last service."

"My friends," said Cyrus Harding, in a voice of the profoundest emotion, "may the God of mercy have had pity on the soul of Captain Nemo, our benefactor."

The colonists uncovered themselves at these last words of Cyrus Harding, and murmured the name of Captain Nemo.

Then Ayrton, approaching the engineer, said simply, "Where should this coffer be deposited?"

It was the coffer which Ayrton had saved at the risk of his life, at the very instant that the island had been engulfed, and which he now faithfully handed to the engineer.

"Ayrton! Ayrton!" said Cyrus Harding, deeply touched. Then, addressing Robert Grant, "Sir," he added, "you left behind you a criminal; you find in his place a man who has become honest by penitence, and whose hand I am proud to clasp in mine."

Robert Grant was now made acquainted with the strange history of Captain Nemo and the colonists of Lincoln Island. Then, observations being taken of what remained of this shoal, which must henceforward figure on the charts of the Pacific, the order was given to make all sail.

A few weeks afterwards the colonists landed in America, and found their country once more at peace after the terrible conflict in which right and justice had triumphed.

Of the treasures contained in the coffer left by Captain Nemo to the colonists of Lincoln Island, the larger portion was employed in the purchase of a vast territory in the State of Iowa. One pearl alone, the finest, was reserved from the treasure and sent to Lady Glenarvan in the name of the castaways restored to their country by the *Duncan*.

There, upon this domain, the colonists invited to labour, that is to say, to wealth and happiness, all those to whom they had hoped to offer the hospitality of Lincoln Island. There was founded a vast colony to which they gave the name of that island sunk beneath the waters of the Pacific. A river there was called the Mercy, a mountain took the name of Mount Franklin, a small lake was named Lake Grant, and the forests became the forests of the Far West. It might have been an island on *terra firma*.

There, under the intelligent hands of the engineer and his companions, everything prospered. Not one of the former colonists of Lincoln Island was absent, for they had sworn to live always together. Neb was with his master; Ayrton was there ready to sacrifice himself for all; Pencroft was more a farmer than he had ever been a sailor; Herbert, who completed his studies under the superintendence of Cyrus Harding, and Gideon Spilett, who founded the *New Lincoln Herald*, the best-informed journal in the world.

There Cyrus Harding and his companions received at intervals visits from Lord and Lady Glenarvan, Captain John Mangles and his wife, the sister of Robert Grant, Robert Grant himself, Major McNab, and all those who had taken part in the history both of Captain Grant and Captain Nemo.

There, to conclude, all were happy, united in the present as they had been in the past; but never could they forget that island upon which they had arrived poor and friendless, that island which, during four years had supplied all their wants, and of which there remained but a fragment of granite washed by the waves of the Pacific, the tomb of him who had borne the name of Captain Nemo.

ABOUT THE AUTHOR

J ULES VERNE (1828-1905) WAS BORN ON FEBRUARY 8, 1828, IN NANTES, A SEAPORT TOWN IN France that shaped his early interest in travel and adventure. He moved to Paris in 1847, where he briefly studied law and worked as a stockbroker before he turned to writing for the stage. His first published novel, *Five Weeks in a Balloon* (1863), was a colorful adventure about a team of explorers who travel to Africa by a hot air balloon. The novel was very successful, and it inaugurated a relationship between Verne and the publisher, Jules Hetzel, that would last for most of their lives. Verne contracted with Hetzel to write three novels per year for serialization in one of the publisher's magazines, and the novels he wrote, known collectively as the *Voyages extraordinaires*, were boldly imaginative tales of adventure and daring laced with speculations on developing trends in science and technology. Some, including *A Journey to the Center of the Earth* (1864), *From the Earth to the Moon* (1865) and its sequel *Round the Moon* (1876), and *Twenty Thousand Leagues Under the Sea* (1869-1870) are recognized today as early landmarks of science fiction. Verne's works were immensely popular not only in France but in England and America where they were translated some years after. The publication of serial installments of *Around the World in Eighty Days* in 1872 proved so popular that most of Verne's works thereafter were published in English simultaneous with the French edition. At the time of his death in 1905, Verne had completed more than sixty novels.